GREATEST WORKS OF
JAMES JOYCE

CLASSICS

Reprint 2023

FiNGERPRINT! CLASSiCS

An imprint of Prakash Books India Pvt. Ltd

113/A, Darya Ganj,
New Delhi-110 002
Email: info@prakashbooks.com/sales@prakashbooks.com

facebook www.facebook.com/fingerprintpublishing
twitter www.twitter.com/FingerprintP
www.fingerprintpublishing.com

ISBN: 978 93 5440 573 0

Processed & printed in India

"The time had come for him to set out on his journey westward. Yes, the newspapers were right: snow was general all over Ireland. It was falling on every part of the dark central plain, on the treeless hills, falling softly upon the Bog of Allen and, farther westward, softly falling into the dark mutinous Shannon waves. It was falling, too, upon every part of the lonely churchyard on the hill where Michael Furey lay buried. It lay thickly drifted on the crooked crosses and headstones, on the spears of the little gate, on the barren thorns. His soul swooned slowly as he heard the snow falling faintly through the universe and faintly falling, like the descent of their last end, upon all the living and the dead."

— Dubliners

B orn in Dublin, Ireland, to a well-meaning but financially inept father and a solemn, pious mother, James Joyce (1882-1941) went to the Clongowes Wood College, and then to Belvedere College, where he excelled as an actor and a writer. In 1898, he enrolled at the University College Dublin. In 1900, his first publication, an essay on Ibsen's play, appeared in the *Fortnightly Review*.

In 1902, he left for Paris but returned to Ireland upon his mother's death in 1903. In 1904, he made his first attempt at a novel, *Stephen Hero*, and also attempted to publish *A Portrait of the Artist*, an essay-story dealing with aesthetics, only to have it rejected. In the summer of the same year, he met Nora Barnacle, a chambermaid from Galway, and left Dublin with her. They stayed in Zurich before settling in Trieste for ten years, where he taught English. His short stories written during these years made up the collection *Dubliners*, which was published in 1914.

At the outset of the First World War, Joyce moved to Zurich, where he wrote *Exiles*, reworked on the early chapters of *Ulysses*, and published *A Portrait of the Artist as a Young Man* in a serial form. It appeared in twenty-five instalments in *The Egoist*. It was published in the United States in 1916 by an American publishing house, and by *The Egoist Press* in Britain in 1917. Almost a complete rewrite of the abandoned *Stephen Hero*, it is heavily autobiographical incorporating the techniques of stream of consciousness and interior monologue.

Joyce went to Paris in 1920 at an invitation from Ezra Pound and ended up living there for the next twenty years. *Ulysses* was published here in 1922. It narrates a day's events in the life of Stephen Dedalus, Leopold Bloom, and Molly Bloom, as they go about their business revealing their attitudes, sentiments, political inclinations, and their varied views about humanity. Joyce, with his dramatic intensity, draws a parallel between his characters and the characters of Homer's *Odyssey*. A remarkable modernist novel, it has survived various controversies and criticisms.

In March 1923, Joyce started working on *Finnegans Wake*, the first segment of which appeared in Ford Madox Ford's *Transatlantic Review* in 1924. The final version of the novel was published in 1939.

Joyce published a number of poetry books a well. *Chamber Music* (1907), his first full-length collection, consisted of thirty-six short lyrics. After this publication, he was included in the *Imagist Anthology*, edited by Ezra Pound. *Gas From A Burner* (1912), *Pomes Penyeach* (1927), and *Ecce Puer* (1932), include his other publications.

Joyce and his family moved to southern France, a year after *Finnegan Wake*'s publication and eventually ended back in Zurich. He died in 1941 at the age of fifty-nine.

One of the most revered writers of the twentieth century, Joyce was noted for his experimental use of language in his works. His extensive use of interior monologue, his use of a complex network of symbolic parallels drawn from mythology, history, and literature, his unique language of invented words, puns, and allusions, all form a part of his technical innovations in the art of the novel.

About this Edition

The name of James Joyce is known to all, even to those who do not delve into the world of literature. His works are read and studied even today, a century after they were published, and have garnered praise from readers and critics alike. They are so unique in the portrayal of the angst of the modern man, his struggles, his doubts on his own existence in the world, and this is relayed in the fascinating form of the stream of consciousness. Undoubtedly, Joyce's contribution to modernist literature is unparalleled.

In this beautiful hardbound edition, with gilded edges and beautiful endpapers, are two works which are considered Joyce's masterstrokes: *Ulysses* and *A Portrait of the Artist as a Young Man*.

About this Edition

Contents

Ulysses

Part

I

1

Stately, plump Buck Mulligan came from the stairhead, bearing a bowl of lather on which a mirror and a razor lay crossed. A yellow dressinggown, ungirdled, was sustained gently behind him on the mild morning air. He held the bowl aloft and intoned:

—Introibo ad altare Dei.

Halted, he peered down the dark winding stairs and called out coarsely:

—Come up, Kinch! Come up, you fearful jesuit!

Solemnly he came forward and mounted the round gunrest. He faced about and blessed gravely thrice the tower, the surrounding land and the awaking mountains. Then, catching sight of Stephen Dedalus, he bent towards him and made rapid crosses in the air, gurgling in his throat and shaking his head. Stephen Dedalus, displeased and sleepy, leaned his arms on the top of the staircase and looked coldly at the shaking gurgling face that blessed him, equine in its length, and at the light untonsured hair, grained and hued like pale oak.

Buck Mulligan peeped an instant under the mirror and then covered the bowl smartly.

—Back to barracks! he said sternly.

He added in a preacher's tone:

—For this, O dearly beloved, is the genuine Christine: body and soul and blood and ouns. Slow music, please. Shut your eyes, gents. One moment. A little trouble about those white corpuscles. Silence, all.

He peered sideways up and gave a long slow whistle of call, then paused awhile in rapt attention, his even white teeth glistening here and there with gold points. Chrysostomos. Two strong shrill whistles answered through the calm.

—Thanks, old chap, he cried briskly. That will do nicely. Switch off the current, will you?

He skipped off the gunrest and looked gravely at his watcher, gathering about his legs the loose folds of his gown. The plump shadowed face and sullen oval jowl recalled a prelate, patron of arts in the middle ages. A pleasant smile broke quietly over his lips.

—The mockery of it! he said gaily. Your absurd name, an ancient Greek!

He pointed his finger in friendly jest and went over to the parapet, laughing to himself. Stephen Dedalus stepped up, followed him wearily halfway and sat down on the edge of the gunrest, watching him still as he propped his mirror on the parapet, dipped the brush in the bowl and lathered cheeks and neck.

Buck Mulligan's gay voice went on.

—My name is absurd too: Malachi Mulligan, two dactyls. But it has a Hellenic ring, hasn't it? Tripping and sunny like the buck himself. We must go to Athens. Will you come if I can get the aunt to fork out twenty quid?

He laid the brush aside and, laughing with delight, cried:

—Will he come? The jejune jesuit!

Ceasing, he began to shave with care.

—Tell me, Mulligan, Stephen said quietly.

—Yes, my love?

—How long is Haines going to stay in this tower?

Buck Mulligan showed a shaven cheek over his right shoulder.

—God, isn't he dreadful? he said frankly. A ponderous Saxon. He thinks you're not a gentleman. God, these bloody English! Bursting with money and indigestion. Because he comes from Oxford. You know, Dedalus, you have the real Oxford manner. He can't make you out. O, my name for you is the best: Kinch, the knife-blade.

He shaved warily over his chin.

—He was raving all night about a black panther, Stephen said. Where is his guncase?

—A woful lunatic! Mulligan said. Were you in a funk?

—I was, Stephen said with energy and growing fear. Out here in the dark with a man I don't know raving and moaning to himself about shooting a black panther. You saved men from drowning. I'm not a hero, however. If he stays on here I am off.

Buck Mulligan frowned at the lather on his razorblade. He hopped down from his perch and began to search his trouser pockets hastily.

—Scutter! he cried thickly.

He came over to the gunrest and, thrusting a hand into Stephen's upper pocket, said:

—Lend us a loan of your noserag to wipe my razor.

Stephen suffered him to pull out and hold up on show by its corner a dirty crumpled handkerchief. Buck Mulligan wiped the razorblade neatly. Then, gazing over the handkerchief, he said:

—The bard's noserag! A new art colour for our Irish poets: snotgreen. You can almost taste it, can't you?

He mounted to the parapet again and gazed out over Dublin bay, his fair oakpale hair stirring slightly.

—God! he said quietly. Isn't the sea what Algy calls it: a great sweet mother? The snotgreen sea. The scrotumtightening sea. *Epi oinopa ponton.* Ah, Dedalus, the Greeks! I must teach you. You must read them in the original. *Thalatta! Thalatta!* She is our great sweet mother. Come and look.

Stephen stood up and went over to the parapet. Leaning on it he looked down on the water and on the mailboat clearing the harbour mouth of Kingstown.

—Our mighty mother! Buck Mulligan said.

He turned abruptly his grey searching eyes from the sea to Stephen's face.

—The aunt thinks you killed your mother, he said. That's why she won't let me have anything to do with you.

—Someone killed her, Stephen said gloomily.

—You could have knelt down, damn it, Kinch, when your dying mother asked you, Buck Mulligan said. I'm hyperborean as much as you. But to think of your mother begging you with her last breath to kneel down and pray for her. And you refused. There is something sinister in you . . .

He broke off and lathered again lightly his farther cheek. A tolerant smile curled his lips.

—But a lovely mummer! he murmured to himself. Kinch, the loveliest mummer of them all!

He shaved evenly and with care, in silence, seriously.

Stephen, an elbow rested on the jagged granite, leaned his palm against his brow and gazed at the fraying edge of his shiny black coat-sleeve. Pain, that was not yet the pain of love, fretted his heart. Silently, in a dream she had come to him after her death, her wasted body within its loose brown graveclothes giving off an odour of wax

17

and rosewood, her breath, that had bent upon him, mute, reproachful, a faint odour of wetted ashes. Across the threadbare cuffedge he saw the sea hailed as a great sweet mother by the wellfed voice beside him. The ring of bay and skyline held a dull green mass of liquid. A bowl of white china had stood beside her deathbed holding the green sluggish bile which she had torn up from her rotting liver by fits of loud groaning vomiting.

Buck Mulligan wiped again his razorblade.

—Ah, poor dogsbody! he said in a kind voice. I must give you a shirt and a few noserags. How are the secondhand breeks?

—They fit well enough, Stephen answered.

Buck Mulligan attacked the hollow beneath his underlip.

—The mockery of it, he said contentedly. Secondleg they should be. God knows what poxy bowsy left them off. I have a lovely pair with a hair stripe, grey. You'll look spiffing in them. I'm not joking, Kinch. You look damn well when you're dressed.

—Thanks, Stephen said. I can't wear them if they are grey.

—He can't wear them, Buck Mulligan told his face in the mirror. Etiquette is etiquette. He kills his mother but he can't wear grey trousers.

He folded his razor neatly and with stroking palps of fingers felt the smooth skin.

Stephen turned his gaze from the sea and to the plump face with its smokeblue mobile eyes.

—That fellow I was with in the Ship last night, said Buck Mulligan, says you have g. p. i. He's up in Dottyville with Connolly Norman. General paralysis of the insane!

He swept the mirror a half circle in the air to flash the tidings abroad in sunlight now radiant on the sea. His curling shaven lips laughed and the edges of his white glittering teeth. Laughter seized all his strong wellknit trunk.

—Look at yourself, he said, you dreadful bard!

Stephen bent forward and peered at the mirror held out to him, cleft by a crooked crack. Hair on end. As he and others see me. Who chose this face for me? This dogsbody to rid of vermin. It asks me too.

—I pinched it out of the skivvy's room, Buck Mulligan said. It does her all right. The aunt always keeps plain-looking servants for Malachi. Lead him not into temptation. And her name is Ursula.

Laughing again, he brought the mirror away from Stephen's peering eyes.

—The rage of Caliban at not seeing his face in a mirror, he said. If Wilde were only alive to see you!

Drawing back and pointing, Stephen said with bitterness:

—It is a symbol of Irish art. The cracked lookingglass of a servant.

Buck Mulligan suddenly linked his arm in Stephen's and walked with him round the tower, his razor and mirror clacking in the pocket where he had thrust them.

—It's not fair to tease you like that, Kinch, is it? he said kindly. God knows you have more spirit than any of them.

Parried again. He fears the lancet of my art as I fear that of his. The cold steel pen.

—Cracked lookingglass of a servant! Tell that to the oxy chap downstairs and touch him for a guinea. He's stinking with money and thinks you're not a gentleman. His old fellow made his tin by selling jalap to Zulus or some bloody swindle or other. God, Kinch, if you and I could only work together we might do something for the island. Hellenise it.

Cranly's arm. His arm.

—And to think of your having to beg from these swine. I'm the only one that knows what you are. Why don't you trust me more? What have you up your nose against me? Is it Haines? If he makes any noise here I'll bring down Seymour and we'll give him a ragging worse than they gave Clive Kempthorpe.

Young shouts of moneyed voices in Clive Kempthorpe's rooms. Palefaces: they hold their ribs with laughter, one clasping another. O, I shall expire! Break the news to her gently, Aubrey! I shall die! With slit ribbons of his shirt whipping the air he hops and hobbles round the table, with trousers down at heels, chased by Ades of Magdalen with the tailor's shears. A scared calf's face gilded with marmalade. I don't want to be debagged! Don't you play the giddy ox with me!

Shouts from the open window startling evening in the quadrangle. A deaf gardener, aproned, masked with Matthew Arnold's face, pushes his mower on the sombre lawn watching narrowly the dancing motes of grasshalms.

To ourselves . . . new paganism . . . omphalos.

—Let him stay, Stephen said. There's nothing wrong with him except at night.

—Then what is it? Buck Mulligan asked impatiently. Cough it up. I'm quite frank with you. What have you against me now?

They halted, looking towards the blunt cape of Bray Head that lay on the water like the snout of a sleeping whale. Stephen freed his arm quietly.

—Do you wish me to tell you? he asked.

—Yes, what is it? Buck Mulligan answered. I don't remember anything.

He looked in Stephen's face as he spoke. A light wind passed his brow, fanning softly his fair uncombed hair and stirring silver points of anxiety in his eyes.

Stephen, depressed by his own voice, said:

—Do you remember the first day I went to your house after my mother's death?

Buck Mulligan frowned quickly and said:

—What? Where? I can't remember anything. I remember only ideas and sensations. Why? What happened in the name of God?

—You were making tea, Stephen said, and went across the landing to get more hot water. Your mother and some visitor came out of the drawing room. She asked you who was in your room.

—Yes? Buck Mulligan said. What did I say? I forget.

—You said, Stephen answered, *O, it's only Dedalus whose mother is beastly dead.*

A flush which made him seem younger and more engaging rose to Buck Mulligan's cheek.

—Did I say that? he asked. Well? What harm is that?

He shook his constraint from him nervously.

—And what is death, he asked, your mother's or yours or my own? You saw only your mother die. I see them pop off every day in the Mater and Richmond and cut up into tripes in the dissecting room. It's a beastly thing and nothing else. It simply doesn't matter. You wouldn't kneel down to pray for your mother on her deathbed when she asked you. Why? Because you have the cursed jesuit strain in you, only it's injected the wrong way. To me it's all a mockery and beastly. Her cerebral lobes are not functioning. She calls the doctor Sir Peter Teazle and picks buttercups off the quilt. Humour her till it's over. You crossed her last wish in death and yet you sulk with me because I don't whinge like some hired mute from Lalouette's. Absurd! I suppose I did say it. I didn't mean to offend the memory of your mother.

He had spoken himself into boldness. Stephen, shielding the gaping wounds which the words had left in his heart, said very coldly:

—I am not thinking of the offence to my mother.

—Of what then? Buck Mulligan asked.

—Of the offence to me, Stephen answered.

Buck Mulligan swung round on his heel.

—O, an impossible person! he exclaimed.

He walked off quickly round the parapet. Stephen stood at his post, gazing over the calm sea towards the headland. Sea and headland now grew dim. Pulses were beating in his eyes, veiling their sight, and he felt the fever of his cheeks.

A voice within the tower called loudly:

—Are you up there, Mulligan?

—I'm coming, Buck Mulligan answered.

He turned towards Stephen and said:

—Look at the sea. What does it care about offences? Chuck Loyola, Kinch, and come on down. The Sassenach wants his morning rashers.

His head halted again for a moment at the top of the staircase, level with the roof:

—Don't mope over it all day, he said. I'm inconsequent. Give up the moody brooding.

His head vanished but the drone of his descending voice boomed out of the stairhead:

> *And no more turn aside and brood*
> *Upon love's bitter mystery*
> *For Fergus rules the brazen cars.*

Woodshadows floated silently by through the morning peace from the stairhead seaward where he gazed. Inshore and farther out the mirror of water whitened, spurned by lightshod hurrying feet. White breast of the dim sea. The twining stresses, two by two. A hand plucking the harpstrings, merging their twining chords. Wavewhite wedded words shimmering on the dim tide.

A cloud began to cover the sun slowly, wholly, shadowing the bay in deeper green. It lay beneath him, a bowl of bitter waters. Fergus' song: I sang it alone in the house, holding down the long dark chords. Her door was open: she wanted to hear my music. Silent with awe and pity I went to her bedside. She was crying in her wretched bed. For those words, Stephen: love's bitter mystery.

Where now?

Her secrets: old feather fans, tasselled dancecards, powdered with musk, a gaud of amber beads in her locked drawer. A birdcage hung in the sunny window of her house when she was a girl. She heard old Royce sing in the pantomime of Turko the Terrible and laughed with others when he sang:

> *I am the boy*
> *That can enjoy*
> *Invisibility.*

Phantasmal mirth, folded away: muskperfumed.

And no more turn aside and brood.

Folded away in the memory of nature with her toys. Memories beset his brooding brain. Her glass of water from the kitchen tap when she had approached the sacrament. A cored apple, filled with brown sugar, roasting for her at the hob on a dark autumn evening. Her shapely fingernails reddened by the blood of squashed lice from the children's shirts.

In a dream, silently, she had come to him, her wasted body within its loose graveclothes giving off an odour of wax and rosewood, her breath, bent over him with mute secret words, a faint odour of wetted ashes.

Her glazing eyes, staring out of death, to shake and bend my soul. On me alone. The ghostcandle to light her agony. Ghostly light on the tortured face. Her hoarse loud breath rattling in horror, while all prayed on their knees. Her eyes on me to strike me down. *Liliata rutilantium te confessorum turma circumdet: iubilantium te virginum chorus excipiat.*

Ghoul! Chewer of corpses!

No, mother! Let me be and let me live.

—Kinch ahoy!

Buck Mulligan's voice sang from within the tower. It came nearer up the staircase, calling again. Stephen, still trembling at his soul's cry, heard warm running sunlight and in the air behind him friendly words.

—Dedalus, come down, like a good mosey. Breakfast is ready. Haines is apologising for waking us last night. It's all right.

—I'm coming, Stephen said, turning.

—Do, for Jesus' sake, Buck Mulligan said. For my sake and for all our sakes.

His head disappeared and reappeared.

—I told him your symbol of Irish art. He says it's very clever. Touch him for a quid, will you? A guinea, I mean.

—I get paid this morning, Stephen said.

—The school kip? Buck Mulligan said. How much? Four quid? Lend us one.

—If you want it, Stephen said.

—Four shining sovereigns, Buck Mulligan cried with delight. We'll have a glorious drunk to astonish the druidy druids. Four omnipotent sovereigns.

He flung up his hands and tramped down the stone stairs, singing out of tune with a Cockney accent:

> *O, won't we have a merry time,*
> *Drinking whisky, beer and wine!*
> *On coronation,*
> *Coronation day!*
> *O, won't we have a merry time*
> *On coronation day!*

Warm sunshine merrying over the sea. The nickel shavingbowl shone, forgotten, on the parapet. Why should I bring it down? Or leave it there all day, forgotten friendship?

He went over to it, held it in his hands awhile, feeling its coolness, smelling the clammy slaver of the lather in which the brush was stuck. So I carried the boat of incense then at Clongowes. I am another now and yet the same. A servant too. A server of a servant.

In the gloomy domed livingroom of the tower Buck Mulligan's gowned form moved briskly to and fro about the hearth, hiding and revealing its yellow glow. Two shafts of soft daylight fell across the flagged floor from the high barbacans: and at the meeting of their rays a cloud of coalsmoke and fumes of fried grease floated, turning.

—We'll be choked, Buck Mulligan said. Haines, open that door, will you?

Stephen laid the shavingbowl on the locker. A tall figure rose from the hammock where it had been sitting, went to the doorway and pulled open the inner doors.

—Have you the key? a voice asked.

—Dedalus has it, Buck Mulligan said. Janey Mack, I'm choked!

He howled, without looking up from the fire:

—Kinch!

—It's in the lock, Stephen said, coming forward.

The key scraped round harshly twice and, when the heavy door had been set ajar, welcome light and bright air entered. Haines stood at the doorway, looking out. Stephen haled his upended valise to the table and sat down to wait. Buck Mulligan tossed the fry on to the dish beside him. Then he carried the dish and a large teapot over to the table, set them down heavily and sighed with relief.

—I'm melting, he said, as the candle remarked when . . . But, hush! Not a word more on that subject! Kinch, wake up! Bread, butter, honey. Haines, come in. The grub is ready. Bless us, O Lord, and these thy gifts. Where's the sugar? O, jay, there's no milk.

Stephen fetched the loaf and the pot of honey and the buttercooler from the locker. Buck Mulligan sat down in a sudden pet.

—What sort of a kip is this? he said. I told her to come after eight.

—We can drink it black, Stephen said thirstily. There's a lemon in the locker.

—O, damn you and your Paris fads! Buck Mulligan said. I want Sandycove milk.

Haines came in from the doorway and said quietly:

—That woman is coming up with the milk.

—The blessings of God on you! Buck Mulligan cried, jumping up from his chair. Sit down. Pour out the tea there. The sugar is in the bag. Here, I can't go fumbling at the damned eggs.

He hacked through the fry on the dish and slapped it out on three plates, saying:

—*In nomine Patris et Filii et Spiritus Sancti.*

Haines sat down to pour out the tea.

—I'm giving you two lumps each, he said. But, I say, Mulligan, you do make strong tea, don't you?

Buck Mulligan, hewing thick slices from the loaf, said in an old woman's wheedling voice:

24

—When I makes tea I makes tea, as old mother Grogan said. And when I makes water I makes water.

—By Jove, it is tea, Haines said.

Buck Mulligan went on hewing and wheedling:

—*So I do, Mrs Cahill,* says she. *Begob, ma'am,* says Mrs Cahill, *God send you don't make them in the one pot.*

He lunged towards his messmates in turn a thick slice of bread, impaled on his knife.

—That's folk, he said very earnestly, for your book, Haines. Five lines of text and ten pages of notes about the folk and the fishgods of Dundrum. Printed by the weird sisters in the year of the big wind.

He turned to Stephen and asked in a fine puzzled voice, lifting his brows:

—Can you recall, brother, is mother Grogan's tea and water pot spoken of in the Mabinogion or is it in the Upanishads?

—I doubt it, said Stephen gravely.

—Do you now? Buck Mulligan said in the same tone. Your reasons, pray?

—I fancy, Stephen said as he ate, it did not exist in or out of the Mabinogion. Mother Grogan was, one imagines, a kinswoman of Mary Ann.

Buck Mulligan's face smiled with delight.

—Charming! he said in a finical sweet voice, showing his white teeth and blinking his eyes pleasantly. Do you think she was? Quite charming!

Then, suddenly overclouding all his features, he growled in a hoarsened rasping voice as he hewed again vigorously at the loaf:

> —*For old Mary Ann*
> *She doesn't care a damn.*
> *But, hising up her petticoats . . .*

He crammed his mouth with fry and munched and droned.

The doorway was darkened by an entering form.

—The milk, sir!

—Come in, ma'am, Mulligan said. Kinch, get the jug.

An old woman came forward and stood by Stephen's elbow.

—That's a lovely morning, sir, she said. Glory be to God.

—To whom? Mulligan said, glancing at her. Ah, to be sure!

Stephen reached back and took the milkjug from the locker.

—The islanders, Mulligan said to Haines casually, speak frequently of the collector of prepuces.

—How much, sir? asked the old woman.

—A quart, Stephen said.

He watched her pour into the measure and thence into the jug rich white milk, not hers. Old shrunken paps. She poured again a measureful and a tilly. Old and secret she had entered from a morning world, maybe a messenger. She praised the goodness of the milk, pouring it out. Crouching by a patient cow at daybreak in the lush field, a witch on her toadstool, her wrinkled fingers quick at the squirting dugs. They lowed about her whom they knew, dewsilky cattle. Silk of the kine and poor old woman, names given her in old times. A wandering crone, lowly form of an immortal serving her conqueror and her gay betrayer, their common cuckquean, a messenger from the secret morning. To serve or to upbraid, whether he could not tell: but scorned to beg her favour.

—It is indeed, ma'am, Buck Mulligan said, pouring milk into their cups.

—Taste it, sir, she said.

He drank at her bidding.

—If we could live on good food like that, he said to her somewhat loudly, we wouldn't have the country full of rotten teeth and rotten guts. Living in a bogswamp, eating cheap food and the streets paved with dust, horsedung and consumptives' spits.

—Are you a medical student, sir? the old woman asked.

—I am, ma'am, Buck Mulligan answered.

—Look at that now, she said.

Stephen listened in scornful silence. She bows her old head to a voice that speaks to her loudly, her bonesetter, her medicineman: me she slights. To the voice that will shrive and oil for the grave all there is of her but her woman's unclean loins, of man's flesh made not in God's likeness, the serpent's prey. And to the loud voice that now bids her be silent with wondering unsteady eyes.

—Do you understand what he says? Stephen asked her.

—Is it French you are talking, sir? the old woman said to Haines.

Haines spoke to her again a longer speech, confidently.

—Irish, Buck Mulligan said. Is there Gaelic on you?

—I thought it was Irish, she said, by the sound of it. Are you from the west, sir?

—I am an Englishman, Haines answered.

—He's English, Buck Mulligan said, and he thinks we ought to speak Irish in Ireland.

—Sure we ought to, the old woman said, and I'm ashamed I don't speak the language myself. I'm told it's a grand language by them that knows.

—Grand is no name for it, said Buck Mulligan. Wonderful entirely. Fill us out some more tea, Kinch. Would you like a cup, ma'am?

—No, thank you, sir, the old woman said, slipping the ring of the milkcan on her forearm and about to go.

Haines said to her:

—Have you your bill? We had better pay her, Mulligan, hadn't we?

Stephen filled again the three cups.

—Bill, sir? she said, halting. Well, it's seven mornings a pint at twopence is seven twos is a shilling and twopence over and these three mornings a quart at fourpence is three quarts is a shilling. That's a shilling and one and two is two and two, sir.

Buck Mulligan sighed and, having filled his mouth with a crust thickly buttered on both sides, stretched forth his legs and began to search his trouser pockets.

—Pay up and look pleasant, Haines said to him, smiling.

Stephen filled a third cup, a spoonful of tea colouring faintly the thick rich milk. Buck Mulligan brought up a florin, twisted it round in his fingers and cried:

—A miracle!

He passed it along the table towards the old woman, saying:

—Ask nothing more of me, sweet. All I can give you I give.

Stephen laid the coin in her uneager hand.

—We'll owe twopence, he said.

—Time enough, sir, she said, taking the coin. Time enough. Good morning, sir.

She curtseyed and went out, followed by Buck Mulligan's tender chant:

—*Heart of my heart, were it more,*
More would be laid at your feet.

He turned to Stephen and said:

—Seriously, Dedalus. I'm stony. Hurry out to your school kip and bring us back some money. Today the bards must drink and junket. Ireland expects that every man this day will do his duty.

—That reminds me, Haines said, rising, that I have to visit your national library today.

—Our swim first, Buck Mulligan said.

He turned to Stephen and asked blandly:

—Is this the day for your monthly wash, Kinch?

Then he said to Haines:

—The unclean bard makes a point of washing once a month.

—All Ireland is washed by the gulfstream, Stephen said as he let honey trickle over a slice of the loaf.

Haines from the corner where he was knotting easily a scarf about the loose collar of his tennis shirt spoke:

—I intend to make a collection of your sayings if you will let me. Speaking to me. They wash and tub and scrub. Agenbite of inwit. Conscience. Yet here's a spot.

—That one about the cracked lookingglass of a servant being the symbol of Irish art is deuced good.

Buck Mulligan kicked Stephen's foot under the table and said with warmth of tone:

—Wait till you hear him on Hamlet, Haines.

—Well, I mean it, Haines said, still speaking to Stephen. I was just thinking of it when that poor old creature came in.

—Would I make any money by it? Stephen asked.

Haines laughed and, as he took his soft grey hat from the holdfast of the hammock, said:

—I don't know, I'm sure.

He strolled out to the doorway. Buck Mulligan bent across to Stephen and said with coarse vigour:

—You put your hoof in it now. What did you say that for?

—Well? Stephen said. The problem is to get money. From whom? From the milkwoman or from him. It's a toss up, I think.

—I blow him out about you, Buck Mulligan said, and then you come along with your lousy leer and your gloomy jesuit jibes.

—I see little hope, Stephen said, from her or from him.

Buck Mulligan sighed tragically and laid his hand on Stephen's arm.

—From me, Kinch, he said.

In a suddenly changed tone he added:

—To tell you the God's truth I think you're right. Damn all else they are good for. Why don't you play them as I do? To hell with them all. Let us get out of the kip.

He stood up, gravely ungirdled and disrobed himself of his gown, saying resignedly:

—Mulligan is stripped of his garments.

He emptied his pockets on to the table.

—There's your snotrag, he said.

And putting on his stiff collar and rebellious tie he spoke to them, chiding them, and to his dangling watchchain. His hands plunged and rummaged in his trunk while he called for a clean handkerchief. God, we'll simply have to dress the character. I want puce gloves and green boots. Contradiction. Do I contradict myself? Very well then, I contradict myself. Mercurial Malachi. A limp black missile flew out of his talking hands.

—And there's your Latin quarter hat, he said.

Stephen picked it up and put it on. Haines called to them from the doorway:

—Are you coming, you fellows?

—I'm ready, Buck Mulligan answered, going towards the door. Come out, Kinch. You have eaten all we left, I suppose. Resigned he passed out with grave words and gait, saying, wellnigh with sorrow:

—And going forth he met Butterly.

Stephen, taking his ashplant from its leaningplace, followed them out and, as they went down the ladder, pulled to the slow iron door and locked it. He put the huge key in his inner pocket.

At the foot of the ladder Buck Mulligan asked:

—Did you bring the key?

—I have it, Stephen said, preceding them.

He walked on. Behind him he heard Buck Mulligan club with his heavy bathtowel the leader shoots of ferns or grasses.

—Down, sir! How dare you, sir!

Haines asked:

—Do you pay rent for this tower?

—Twelve quid, Buck Mulligan said.

—To the secretary of state for war, Stephen added over his shoulder.

They halted while Haines surveyed the tower and said at last:

—Rather bleak in wintertime, I should say. Martello you call it?

—Billy Pitt had them built, Buck Mulligan said, when the French were on the sea. But ours is the *omphalos*.

—What is your idea of Hamlet? Haines asked Stephen.

—No, no, Buck Mulligan shouted in pain. I'm not equal to Thomas Aquinas and the fiftyfive reasons he has made out to prop it up. Wait till I have a few pints in me first.

He turned to Stephen, saying, as he pulled down neatly the peaks of his primrose waistcoat:

—You couldn't manage it under three pints, Kinch, could you?

—It has waited so long, Stephen said listlessly, it can wait longer.

—You pique my curiosity, Haines said amiably. Is it some paradox?

—Pooh! Buck Mulligan said. We have grown out of Wilde and paradoxes. It's quite simple. He proves by algebra that Hamlet's grandson is Shakespeare's grandfather and that he himself is the ghost of his own father.

—What? Haines said, beginning to point at Stephen. He himself?

Buck Mulligan slung his towel stolewise round his neck and, bending in loose laughter, said to Stephen's ear:

—O, shade of Kinch the elder! Japhet in search of a father!

—We're always tired in the morning, Stephen said to Haines. And it is rather long to tell.

Buck Mulligan, walking forward again, raised his hands.

—The sacred pint alone can unbind the tongue of Dedalus, he said.

—I mean to say, Haines explained to Stephen as they followed, this tower and these cliffs here remind me somehow of Elsinore. *That beetles o'er his base into the sea,* isn't it?

Buck Mulligan turned suddenly for an instant towards Stephen but did not speak. In the bright silent instant Stephen saw his own image in cheap dusty mourning between their gay attires.

—It's a wonderful tale, Haines said, bringing them to halt again.

Eyes, pale as the sea the wind had freshened, paler, firm and prudent. The seas' ruler, he gazed southward over the bay, empty save for the smokeplume of the mailboat vague on the bright skyline and a sail tacking by the Muglins.

—I read a theological interpretation of it somewhere, he said bemused. The Father and the Son idea. The Son striving to be atoned with the Father.

Buck Mulligan at once put on a blithe broadly smiling face. He looked at them, his wellshaped mouth open happily, his eyes, from which he had suddenly withdrawn all shrewd sense, blinking with mad gaiety. He moved a doll's head to and fro, the brims of his Panama hat quivering, and began to chant in a quiet happy foolish voice:

—I'm the queerest young fellow that ever you heard.
My mother's a jew, my father's a bird.
With Joseph the joiner I cannot agree.
So here's to disciples and Calvary.

He held up a forefinger of warning.

—If anyone thinks that I amn't divine
He'll get no free drinks when I'm making the wine
But have to drink water and wish it were plain
That I make when the wine becomes water again.

He tugged swiftly at Stephen's ashplant in farewell and, running forward to a brow of the cliff, fluttered his hands at his sides like fins or wings of one about to rise in the air, and chanted:

—Goodbye, now, goodbye! Write down all I said
And tell Tom, Dick and Harry I rose from the dead.
What's bred in the bone cannot fail me to fly
And Olivet's breezy . . . Goodbye, now, goodbye!

He capered before them down towards the fortyfoot hole, fluttering his winglike hands, leaping nimbly, Mercury's hat quivering in the fresh wind that bore back to them his brief birdsweet cries.

Haines, who had been laughing guardedly, walked on beside Stephen and said:

—We oughtn't to laugh, I suppose. He's rather blasphemous. I'm not a believer myself, that is to say. Still his gaiety takes the harm out of it somehow, doesn't it? What did he call it? Joseph the Joiner?

—The ballad of joking Jesus, Stephen answered.

—O, Haines said, you have heard it before?

—Three times a day, after meals, Stephen said drily.

—You're not a believer, are you? Haines asked. I mean, a believer in the narrow sense of the word. Creation from nothing and miracles and a personal God.

—There's only one sense of the word, it seems to me, Stephen said.

Haines stopped to take out a smooth silver case in which twinkled a green stone. He sprang it open with his thumb and offered it.

—Thank you, Stephen said, taking a cigarette.

Haines helped himself and snapped the case to. He put it back in his sidepocket and took from his waistcoatpocket a nickel tinderbox, sprang it open too, and, having lit his cigarette, held the flaming spunk towards Stephen in the shell of his hands.

—Yes, of course, he said, as they went on again. Either you believe or you don't, isn't it? Personally I couldn't stomach that idea of a personal God. You don't stand for that, I suppose?

—You behold in me, Stephen said with grim displeasure, a horrible example of free thought.

He walked on, waiting to be spoken to, trailing his ashplant by his side. Its ferrule followed lightly on the path, squealing at his heels. My familiar, after me, calling, Steeeeeeeeeeephen! A wavering line along the path. They will walk on it tonight, coming here in the dark. He wants that key. It is mine. I paid the rent. Now I eat his salt bread. Give him the key too. All. He will ask for it. That was in his eyes.

—After all, Haines began . . .

Stephen turned and saw that the cold gaze which had measured him was not all unkind.

—After all, I should think you are able to free yourself. You are your own master, it seems to me.

—I am a servant of two masters, Stephen said, an English and an Italian.

—Italian? Haines said.

A crazy queen, old and jealous. Kneel down before me.

—And a third, Stephen said, there is who wants me for odd jobs.

—Italian? Haines said again. What do you mean?

—The imperial British state, Stephen answered, his colour rising, and the holy Roman catholic and apostolic church.

Haines detached from his underlip some fibres of tobacco before he spoke.

—I can quite understand that, he said calmly. An Irishman must think like that, I daresay. We feel in England that we have treated you rather unfairly. It seems history is to blame.

The proud potent titles clanged over Stephen's memory the triumph of their brazen bells: *et unam sanctam catholicam et apostolicam ecclesiam:* the slow growth and change of rite and dogma like his own rare thoughts, a chemistry of stars. Symbol of the apostles in the mass for pope Marcellus, the voices blended, singing alone loud in affirmation: and behind their chant the vigilant angel of the church militant disarmed and menaced her heresiarchs. A horde of heresies fleeing with mitres awry: Photius and the brood of mockers of whom Mulligan was one, and Arius, warring his life long upon the consubstantiality of the Son with the Father, and Valentine, spurning Christ's terrene body, and the subtle African heresiarch Sabellius who held that the Father was Himself His own Son. Words Mulligan had spoken a moment since in mockery to the stranger. Idle mockery. The void awaits surely all them that weave the wind: a menace, a disarming and a worsting from those embattled angels of the church, Michael's host, who defend her ever in the hour of conflict with their lances and their shields.

Hear, hear! Prolonged applause. *Zut! Nom de Dieu!*

—Of course I'm a Britisher, Haines's voice said, and I feel as one. I don't want to see my country fall into the hands of German jews either. That's our national problem, I'm afraid, just now.

Two men stood at the verge of the cliff, watching: businessman, boatman.

—She's making for Bullock harbour.

The boatman nodded towards the north of the bay with some disdain.

—There's five fathoms out there, he said. It'll be swept up that way when the tide comes in about one. It's nine days today.

The man that was drowned. A sail veering about the blank bay waiting for a swollen bundle to bob up, roll over to the sun a puffy face, saltwhite. Here I am.

They followed the winding path down to the creek. Buck Mulligan stood on a stone, in shirtsleeves, his unclipped tie rippling over his shoulder. A young man clinging to a spur of rock near him, moved slowly frogwise his green legs in the deep jelly of the water.

—Is the brother with you, Malachi?

—Down in Westmeath. With the Bannons.

—Still there? I got a card from Bannon. Says he found a sweet young thing down there. Photo girl he calls her.

—Snapshot, eh? Brief exposure.

Buck Mulligan sat down to unlace his boots. An elderly man shot up near the spur of rock a blowing red face. He scrambled up by the stones, water glistening on his pate and on its garland of grey hair, water rilling over his chest and paunch and spilling jets out of his black sagging loincloth.

Buck Mulligan made way for him to scramble past and, glancing at Haines and Stephen, crossed himself piously with his thumbnail at brow and lips and breastbone.

—Seymour's back in town, the young man said, grasping again his spur of rock. Chucked medicine and going in for the army.

—Ah, go to God! Buck Mulligan said.

—Going over next week to stew. You know that red Carlisle girl, Lily?

—Yes.

—Spooning with him last night on the pier. The father is rotto with money.

—Is she up the pole?

—Better ask Seymour that.

—Seymour a bleeding officer! Buck Mulligan said.

He nodded to himself as he drew off his trousers and stood up, saying tritely:

—Redheaded women buck like goats.

He broke off in alarm, feeling his side under his flapping shirt.

—My twelfth rib is gone, he cried. I'm the *Übermensch*. Toothless Kinch and I, the supermen.

He struggled out of his shirt and flung it behind him to where his clothes lay.

—Are you going in here, Malachi?

—Yes. Make room in the bed.

The young man shoved himself backward through the water and reached the middle of the creek in two long clean strokes. Haines sat down on a stone, smoking.

—Are you not coming in? Buck Mulligan asked.

—Later on, Haines said. Not on my breakfast.

Stephen turned away.

—I'm going, Mulligan, he said.

—Give us that key, Kinch, Buck Mulligan said, to keep my chemise flat.

Stephen handed him the key. Buck Mulligan laid it across his heaped clothes.

—And twopence, he said, for a pint. Throw it there.

Stephen threw two pennies on the soft heap. Dressing, undressing. Buck Mulligan erect, with joined hands before him, said solemnly:

—He who stealeth from the poor lendeth to the Lord. Thus spake Zarathustra.

His plump body plunged.

—We'll see you again, Haines said, turning as Stephen walked up the path and smiling at wild Irish.

Horn of a bull, hoof of a horse, smile of a Saxon.

—The Ship, Buck Mulligan cried. Half twelve.

—Good, Stephen said.

He walked along the upwardcurving path.

Liliata rutilantium.
Turma circumdet.
Iubilantium te virginum.

The priest's grey nimbus in a niche where he dressed discreetly. I will not sleep here tonight. Home also I cannot go.

A voice, sweettoned and sustained, called to him from the sea. Turning the curve he waved his hand. It called again. A sleek brown head, a seal's, far out on the water, round.

Usurper.

2

Y ou, Cochrane, what city sent for him?
—Tarentum, sir.
—Very good. Well?
—There was a battle, sir.
—Very good. Where?
The boy's blank face asked the blank window.

Fabled by the daughters of memory. And yet it was in some way if not as memory fabled it. A phrase, then, of impatience, thud of Blake's wings of excess. I hear the ruin of all space, shattered glass and toppling masonry, and time one livid final flame. What's left us then?

—I forget the place, sir. 279 B. C.

—Asculum, Stephen said, glancing at the name and date in the gorescarred book.

—Yes, sir. And he said: *Another victory like that and we are done for.*

That phrase the world had remembered. A dull ease of the mind. From a hill above a corpsestrewn plain a general speaking to his officers, leaned upon his spear. Any general to any officers. They lend ear.

—You, Armstrong, Stephen said. What was the end of Pyrrhus?

—End of Pyrrhus, sir?

—I know, sir. Ask me, sir, Comyn said.

—Wait. You, Armstrong. Do you know anything about Pyrrhus?

A bag of figrolls lay snugly in Armstrong's satchel. He curled them between his palms at whiles and swallowed them softly. Crumbs adhered to the tissue of his lips. A sweetened boy's breath. Welloff people, proud that their eldest son was in the navy. Vico Road, Dalkey.

—Pyrrhus, sir? Pyrrhus, a pier.

All laughed. Mirthless high malicious laughter. Armstrong looked round at his classmates, silly glee in profile. In a moment they will laugh more loudly, aware of my lack of rule and of the fees their papas pay.

—Tell me now, Stephen said, poking the boy's shoulder with the book, what is a pier.

—A pier, sir, Armstrong said. A thing out in the water. A kind of a bridge. Kingstown pier, sir.

Some laughed again: mirthless but with meaning. Two in the back bench whispered. Yes. They knew: had never learned nor ever been innocent. All. With envy he watched their faces: Edith, Ethel, Gerty, Lily. Their likes: their breaths, too, sweetened with tea and jam, their bracelets tittering in the struggle.

—Kingstown pier, Stephen said. Yes, a disappointed bridge.

The words troubled their gaze.

—How, sir? Comyn asked. A bridge is across a river.

For Haines's chapbook. No-one here to hear. Tonight deftly amid wild drink and talk, to pierce the polished mail of his mind. What then? A jester at the court of his master, indulged and disesteemed, winning a clement master's praise. Why had they chosen all that part? Not wholly for the smooth caress. For them too history was a tale like any other too often heard, their land a pawnshop.

Had Pyrrhus not fallen by a beldam's hand in Argos or Julius Caesar not been knifed to death. They are not to be thought away. Time has branded them and fettered they are lodged in the room of the infinite possibilities they have ousted. But can those have been possible seeing that they never were? Or was that only possible which came to pass? Weave, weaver of the wind.

—Tell us a story, sir.

—O, do, sir. A ghoststory.

—Where do you begin in this? Stephen asked, opening another book.

—*Weep no more,* Comyn said.

—Go on then, Talbot.

—And the story, sir?

—After, Stephen said. Go on, Talbot.

A swarthy boy opened a book and propped it nimbly under the breastwork of his satchel. He recited jerks of verse with odd glances at the text:

—Weep no more, woful shepherds, weep no more
For Lycidas, your sorrow, is not dead,
Sunk though he be beneath the watery floor . . .

It must be a movement then, an actuality of the possible as possible. Aristotle's phrase formed itself within the gabbled verses and floated out into the studious silence of the library of Saint Genevieve where he had read, sheltered from the sin of Paris, night by night. By his elbow a delicate Siamese conned a handbook of strategy. Fed and feeding brains about me: under glowlamps, impaled, with faintly beating feelers: and in my mind's darkness a sloth of the underworld, reluctant, shy of brightness, shifting her dragon scaly folds. Thought is the thought of thought. Tranquil brightness. The soul is in a manner all that is: the soul is the form of forms. Tranquility sudden, vast, candescent: form of forms.

Talbot repeated:

—Through the dear might of Him that walked the waves,
Through the dear might . . .

—Turn over, Stephen said quietly. I don't see anything.

—What, sir? Talbot asked simply, bending forward.

His hand turned the page over. He leaned back and went on again, having just remembered. Of him that walked the waves. Here also over these craven hearts his shadow lies and on the scoffer's heart and lips and on mine. It lies upon their eager faces who offered him a coin of the tribute. To Caesar what is Caesar's, to God what is God's. A long look from dark eyes, a riddling sentence to be woven and woven on the church's looms. Ay.

Riddle me, riddle me, randy ro.
My father gave me seeds to sow.

Talbot slid his closed book into his satchel.

—Have I heard all? Stephen asked.

—Yes, sir. Hockey at ten, sir.

—Half day, sir. Thursday.

—Who can answer a riddle? Stephen asked.

They bundled their books away, pencils clacking, pages rustling.

Crowding together they strapped and buckled their satchels, all gabbling gaily:

—A riddle, sir? Ask me, sir.

—O, ask me, sir.

—A hard one, sir.

—This is the riddle, Stephen said:

> *The cock crew,*
> *The sky was blue:*
> *The bells in heaven*
> *Were striking eleven.*
> *'Tis time for this poor soul*
> *To go to heaven.*

—What is that?

—What, sir?

—Again, sir. We didn't hear.

Their eyes grew bigger as the lines were repeated. After a silence Cochrane said:

—What is it, sir? We give it up.

Stephen, his throat itching, answered:

—The fox burying his grandmother under a hollybush.

He stood up and gave a shout of nervous laughter to which their cries echoed dismay.

A stick struck the door and a voice in the corridor called:

—Hockey!

They broke asunder, sidling out of their benches, leaping them. Quickly they were gone and from the lumberroom came the rattle of sticks and clamour of their boots and tongues.

Sargent who alone had lingered came forward slowly, showing an open copybook. His tangled hair and scraggy neck gave witness of unreadiness and through his misty glasses weak eyes looked up pleading. On his cheek, dull and bloodless, a soft stain of ink lay, dateshaped, recent and damp as a snail's bed.

He held out his copybook. The word *Sums* was written on the headline. Beneath were sloping figures and at the foot a crooked signature with blind loops and a blot. Cyril Sargent: his name and seal.

—Mr Deasy told me to write them out all again, he said, and show them to you, sir.

Stephen touched the edges of the book. Futility.

—Do you understand how to do them now? he asked.

—Numbers eleven to fifteen, Sargent answered. Mr Deasy said I was to copy them off the board, sir.

—Can you do them yourself? Stephen asked.

—No, sir.

Ugly and futile: lean neck and tangled hair and a stain of ink, a snail's bed. Yet someone had loved him, borne him in her arms and in her heart. But for her the race of the world would have trampled him underfoot, a squashed boneless snail. She had loved his weak watery blood drained from her own. Was that then real? The only true thing in life? His mother's prostrate body the fiery Columbanus in holy zeal bestrode. She was no more: the trembling skeleton of a twig burnt in the fire, an odour of rosewood and wetted ashes. She had saved him from being trampled underfoot and had gone, scarcely having been. A poor soul gone to heaven: and on a heath beneath winking stars a fox, red reek of rapine in his fur, with merciless bright eyes scraped in the earth, listened, scraped up the earth, listened, scraped and scraped.

Sitting at his side Stephen solved out the problem. He proves by algebra that Shakespeare's ghost is Hamlet's grandfather. Sargent peered askance through his slanted glasses. Hockeysticks rattled in the lumberroom: the hollow knock of a ball and calls from the field.

Across the page the symbols moved in grave morrice, in the mummery of their letters, wearing quaint caps of squares and cubes. Give hands, traverse, bow to partner: so: imps of fancy of the Moors. Gone too from the world, Averroes and Moses Maimonides, dark men in mien and movement, flashing in their mocking mirrors the obscure soul of the world, a darkness shining in brightness which brightness could not comprehend.

—Do you understand now? Can you work the second for yourself?

—Yes, sir.

In long shaky strokes Sargent copied the data. Waiting always for a word of help his hand moved faithfully the unsteady symbols, a faint hue of shame flickering behind his dull skin. *Amor matris:* subjective and objective genitive. With her weak blood and wheysour milk she had fed him and hid from sight of others his swaddling bands.

Like him was I, these sloping shoulders, this gracelessness. My childhood bends beside me. Too far for me to lay a hand there once or lightly. Mine is far and his secret as our eyes. Secrets, silent, stony sit in the dark palaces of both our hearts: secrets weary of their tyranny: tyrants, willing to be dethroned.

The sum was done.

—It is very simple, Stephen said as he stood up.

—Yes, sir. Thanks, Sargent answered.

He dried the page with a sheet of thin blottingpaper and carried his copybook back to his bench.

—You had better get your stick and go out to the others, Stephen said as he followed towards the door the boy's graceless form.

—Yes, sir.

In the corridor his name was heard, called from the playfield.

—Sargent!

—Run on, Stephen said. Mr Deasy is calling you.

He stood in the porch and watched the laggard hurry towards the scrappy field where sharp voices were in strife. They were sorted in teams and Mr Deasy came away stepping over wisps of grass with gaitered feet. When he had reached the schoolhouse voices again contending called to him. He turned his angry white moustache.

—What is it now? he cried continually without listening.

—Cochrane and Halliday are on the same side, sir, Stephen said.

—Will you wait in my study for a moment, Mr Deasy said, till I restore order here.

And as he stepped fussily back across the field his old man's voice cried sternly:

—What is the matter? What is it now?

Their sharp voices cried about him on all sides: their many forms closed round him, the garish sunshine bleaching the honey of his illdyed head.

Stale smoky air hung in the study with the smell of drab abraded leather of its chairs. As on the first day he bargained with me here. As it was in the beginning, is now. On the sideboard the tray of Stuart coins, base treasure of a bog: and ever shall be. And snug in their spooncase of purple plush, faded, the twelve apostles having preached to all the gentiles: world without end.

A hasty step over the stone porch and in the corridor. Blowing out his rare moustache Mr Deasy halted at the table.

—First, our little financial settlement, he said.

He brought out of his coat a pocketbook bound by a leather thong. It slapped open and he took from it two notes, one of joined halves, and laid them carefully on the table.

—Two, he said, strapping and stowing his pocketbook away.

And now his strongroom for the gold. Stephen's embarrassed hand moved over the shells heaped in the cold stone mortar: whelks and money cowries and leopard shells: and this, whorled as an emir's turban, and this, the scallop of saint James. An old pilgrim's hoard, dead treasure, hollow shells.

A sovereign fell, bright and new, on the soft pile of the tablecloth.

—Three, Mr Deasy said, turning his little savingsbox about in his hand. These are handy things to have. See. This is for sovereigns. This is for shillings. Sixpences, halfcrowns. And here crowns. See.

He shot from it two crowns and two shillings.

—Three twelve, he said. I think you'll find that's right.

—Thank you, sir, Stephen said, gathering the money together with shy haste and putting it all in a pocket of his trousers.

—No thanks at all, Mr Deasy said. You have earned it.

Stephen's hand, free again, went back to the hollow shells. Symbols too of beauty and of power. A lump in my pocket: symbols soiled by greed and misery.

—Don't carry it like that, Mr Deasy said. You'll pull it out somewhere and lose it. You just buy one of these machines. You'll find them very handy.

Answer something.

—Mine would be often empty, Stephen said.

The same room and hour, the same wisdom: and I the same. Three times now. Three nooses round me here. Well? I can break them in this instant if I will.

—Because you don't save, Mr Deasy said, pointing his finger. You don't know yet what money is. Money is power. When you have lived as long as I have. I know, I know. If youth but knew. But what does Shakespeare say? *Put but money in thy purse.*

—Iago, Stephen murmured.

He lifted his gaze from the idle shells to the old man's stare.

—He knew what money was, Mr Deasy said. He made money. A poet, yes, but an Englishman too. Do you know what is the pride of the English? Do you know what is the proudest word you will ever hear from an Englishman's mouth?

The seas' ruler. His seacold eyes looked on the empty bay: it seems history is to blame: on me and on my words, unhating.

—That on his empire, Stephen said, the sun never sets.

—Ba! Mr Deasy cried. That's not English. A French Celt said that. He tapped his savingsbox against his thumbnail.

—I will tell you, he said solemnly, what is his proudest boast. *I paid my way.*

Good man, good man.

—*I paid my way. I never borrowed a shilling in my life.* Can you feel that? *I owe nothing.* Can you?

Mulligan, nine pounds, three pairs of socks, one pair brogues, ties. Curran, ten guineas. McCann, one guinea. Fred Ryan, two shillings. Temple, two lunches. Russell, one guinea, Cousins, ten shillings, Bob Reynolds, half a guinea, Koehler, three guineas, Mrs MacKernan, five weeks' board. The lump I have is useless.

—For the moment, no, Stephen answered.

Mr Deasy laughed with rich delight, putting back his savingsbox.

—I knew you couldn't, he said joyously. But one day you must feel it. We are a generous people but we must also be just.

—I fear those big words, Stephen said, which make us so unhappy.

Mr Deasy stared sternly for some moments over the mantelpiece at the shapely bulk of a man in tartan fillibegs: Albert Edward, Prince of Wales.

—You think me an old fogey and an old tory, his thoughtful voice said. I saw three generations since O'Connell's time. I remember the famine in '46. Do you know that the orange lodges agitated for repeal of the union twenty years before O'Connell did or before the prelates of your communion denounced him as a demagogue? You fenians forget some things.

Glorious, pious and immortal memory. The lodge of Diamond in Armagh the splendid behung with corpses of papishes. Hoarse, masked and armed, the planters' covenant. The black north and true blue bible. Croppies lie down.

Stephen sketched a brief gesture.

—I have rebel blood in me too, Mr Deasy said. On the spindle side. But I am descended from sir John Blackwood who voted for the union. We are all Irish, all kings' sons.

—Alas, Stephen said.

—*Per vias rectas*, Mr Deasy said firmly, was his motto. He voted for it and put on his topboots to ride to Dublin from the Ards of Down to do so.

> Lal the ral the ra
> The rocky road to Dublin.

A gruff squire on horseback with shiny topboots. Soft day, sir John! Soft day, your honour! . . . Day! . . . Day! . . . Two topboots jog dangling on to Dublin. Lal the ral the ra. Lal the ral the raddy.

—That reminds me, Mr Deasy said. You can do me a favour, Mr Dedalus, with some of your literary friends. I have a letter here for the press. Sit down a moment. I have just to copy the end.

He went to the desk near the window, pulled in his chair twice and read off some words from the sheet on the drum of his typewriter.

—Sit down. Excuse me, he said over his shoulder, *the dictates of common sense.* Just a moment.

He peered from under his shaggy brows at the manuscript by his elbow and, muttering, began to prod the stiff buttons of the keyboard slowly, sometimes blowing as he screwed up the drum to erase an error.

Stephen seated himself noiselessly before the princely presence. Framed around the walls images of vanished horses stood in homage, their meek heads poised in air: lord Hastings' *Repulse*, the duke of Westminster's *Shotover*, the duke of Beaufort's *Ceylon, prix de Paris*, 1866. Elfin riders sat them, watchful of a sign. He saw their speeds, backing king's colours, and shouted with the shouts of vanished crowds.

—Full stop, Mr Deasy bade his keys. *But prompt ventilation of this allimportant question . . .*

Where Cranly led me to get rich quick, hunting his winners among the mudsplashed brakes, amid the bawls of bookies on their pitches and reek of the canteen, over the motley slush. Even money *Fair Rebel.* Ten to one the field. Dicers and thimbleriggers we hurried by after the hoofs, the vying caps and jackets and past the meatfaced woman, a butcher's dame, nuzzling thirstily her clove of orange.

Shouts rang shrill from the boys' playfield and a whirring whistle.

Again: a goal. I am among them, among their battling bodies in a medley, the joust of life. You mean that knockkneed mother's darling who seems to be slightly crawsick? Jousts. Time shocked rebounds, shock by shock. Jousts, slush and uproar of battles, the frozen deathspew of the slain, a shout of spearspikes baited with men's bloodied guts.

—Now then, Mr Deasy said, rising.

He came to the table, pinning together his sheets. Stephen stood up.

—I have put the matter into a nutshell, Mr Deasy said. It's about the foot and mouth disease. Just look through it. There can be no two opinions on the matter.

May I trespass on your valuable space. That doctrine of *laissez faire* which so often in our history. Our cattle trade. The way of all our old industries. Liverpool ring which jockeyed the Galway harbour scheme. European conflagration. Grain supplies through the narrow waters of the channel. The pluterperfect imperturbability of the department of agriculture. Pardoned a classical allusion. Cassandra. By a woman who was no better than she should be. To come to the point at issue.

—I don't mince words, do I? Mr Deasy asked as Stephen read on.

Foot and mouth disease. Known as Koch's preparation. Serum and virus. Percentage of salted horses. Rinderpest. Emperor's horses at Mürzsteg, lower Austria. Veterinary surgeons. Mr Henry Blackwood Price. Courteous offer a fair trial. Dictates of common sense. Allimportant question. In every sense of the word take the bull by the horns. Thanking you for the hospitality of your columns.

—I want that to be printed and read, Mr Deasy said. You will see at the next outbreak they will put an embargo on Irish cattle. And it can be cured. It is cured. My cousin, Blackwood Price, writes to me it is regularly treated and cured in Austria by cattledoctors there. They offer to come over here. I am trying to work up influence with the department. Now I'm going to try publicity. I am surrounded by difficulties, by . . . intrigues by . . . backstairs influence by . . .

He raised his forefinger and beat the air oldly before his voice spoke.

—Mark my words, Mr Dedalus, he said. England is in the hands of the jews. In all the highest places: her finance, her press. And they are the signs of a nation's decay. Wherever they gather they eat up the nation's vital strength. I have seen it coming these years. As sure as we are standing here the jew merchants are already at their work of destruction. Old England is dying.

46

He stepped swiftly off, his eyes coming to blue life as they passed a broad sunbeam. He faced about and back again.

—Dying, he said again, if not dead by now.

The harlot's cry from street to street
Shall weave old England's windingsheet.

His eyes open wide in vision stared sternly across the sunbeam in which he halted.

—A merchant, Stephen said, is one who buys cheap and sells dear, jew or gentile, is he not?

—They sinned against the light, Mr Deasy said gravely. And you can see the darkness in their eyes. And that is why they are wanderers on the earth to this day.

On the steps of the Paris stock exchange the goldskinned men quoting prices on their gemmed fingers. Gabble of geese. They swarmed loud, uncouth about the temple, their heads thickplotting under maladroit silk hats. Not theirs: these clothes, this speech, these gestures. Their full slow eyes belied the words, the gestures eager and unoffending, but knew the rancours massed about them and knew their zeal was vain. Vain patience to heap and hoard. Time surely would scatter all. A hoard heaped by the roadside: plundered and passing on. Their eyes knew their years of wandering and, patient, knew the dishonours of their flesh.

—Who has not? Stephen said.

—What do you mean? Mr Deasy asked.

He came forward a pace and stood by the table. His underjaw fell sideways open uncertainly. Is this old wisdom? He waits to hear from me.

—History, Stephen said, is a nightmare from which I am trying to awake.

From the playfield the boys raised a shout. A whirring whistle: goal. What if that nightmare gave you a back kick?

—The ways of the Creator are not our ways, Mr Deasy said. All human history moves towards one great goal, the manifestation of God.

Stephen jerked his thumb towards the window, saying:

—That is God.

Hooray! Ay! Whrrwhee!

—What? Mr Deasy asked.

—A shout in the street, Stephen answered, shrugging his shoulders.

Mr Deasy looked down and held for a while the wings of his nose tweaked between his fingers. Looking up again he set them free.

—I am happier than you are, he said. We have committed many errors and many sins. A woman brought sin into the world. For a woman who was no better than she should be, Helen, the runaway wife of Menelaus, ten years the Greeks made war on Troy. A faithless wife first brought the strangers to our shore here, MacMurrough's wife and her leman, O'Rourke, prince of Breffni. A woman too brought Parnell low. Many errors, many failures but not the one sin. I am a struggler now at the end of my days. But I will fight for the right till the end.

For Ulster will fight
And Ulster will be right.

Stephen raised the sheets in his hand.

—Well, sir, he began.

—I foresee, Mr Deasy said, that you will not remain here very long at this work. You were not born to be a teacher, I think. Perhaps I am wrong.

—A learner rather, Stephen said.

And here what will you learn more?

Mr Deasy shook his head.

—Who knows? he said. To learn one must be humble. But life is the great teacher.

Stephen rustled the sheets again.

—As regards these, he began.

—Yes, Mr Deasy said. You have two copies there. If you can have them published at once.

Telegraph. Irish Homestead.

—I will try, Stephen said, and let you know tomorrow. I know two editors slightly.

—That will do, Mr Deasy said briskly. I wrote last night to Mr Field, M. P. There is a meeting of the cattletraders' association today at the City Arms hotel. I asked him to lay my letter before the meeting. You see if you can get it into your two papers. What are they?

—*The Evening Telegraph* . . .

—That will do, Mr Deasy said. There is no time to lose. Now I have to answer that letter from my cousin.

—Good morning, sir, Stephen said, putting the sheets in his pocket. Thank you.

—Not at all, Mr Deasy said as he searched the papers on his desk. I like to break a lance with you, old as I am.

—Good morning, sir, Stephen said again, bowing to his bent back.

He went out by the open porch and down the gravel path under the trees, hearing the cries of voices and crack of sticks from the playfield. The lions couchant on the pillars as he passed out through the gate: toothless terrors. Still I will help him in his fight. Mulligan will dub me a new name: the bullockbefriending bard.

—Mr Dedalus!

Running after me. No more letters, I hope.

—Just one moment.

—Yes, sir, Stephen said, turning back at the gate.

Mr Deasy halted, breathing hard and swallowing his breath.

—I just wanted to say, he said. Ireland, they say, has the honour of being the only country which never persecuted the jews. Do you know that? No. And do you know why?

He frowned sternly on the bright air.

—Why, sir? Stephen asked, beginning to smile.

—Because she never let them in, Mr Deasy said solemnly.

A coughball of laughter leaped from his throat dragging after it a rattling chain of phlegm. He turned back quickly, coughing, laughing, his lifted arms waving to the air.

—She never let them in, he cried again through his laughter as he stamped on gaitered feet over the gravel of the path. That's why.

On his wise shoulders through the checkerwork of leaves the sun flung spangles, dancing coins.

3

Ineluctable modality of the visible: at least that if no more, thought through my eyes. Signatures of all things I am here to read, seaspawn and seawrack, the nearing tide, that rusty boot. Snotgreen, bluesilver, rust: coloured signs. Limits of the diaphane. But he adds: in bodies. Then he was aware of them bodies before of them coloured. How? By knocking his sconce against them, sure. Go easy. Bald he was and a millionaire, *maestro di color che sanno.* Limit of the diaphane in. Why in? Diaphane, adiaphane. If you can put your five fingers through it it is a gate, if not a door. Shut your eyes and see.

Stephen closed his eyes to hear his boots crush crackling wrack and shells. You are walking through it howsomever. I am, a stride at a time. A very short space of time through very short times of space. Five, six: the *nacheinander.* Exactly: and that is the ineluctable modality of the audible. Open your eyes. No. Jesus! If I fell over a cliff that beetles o'er his base, fell through the *nebeneinander* ineluctably! I am getting on nicely in the dark. My ash sword hangs at my side. Tap with it: they do. My two feet in his boots are at the ends of his legs, *nebeneinander.* Sounds solid: made by the mallet of *Los Demiurgos.* Am I walking into eternity along Sandymount strand? Crush, crack, crick, crick. Wild sea money. Dominie Deasy kens them a'.

> *Won't you come to Sandymount,*
> *Madeline the mare?*

Rhythm begins, you see. I hear. A catalectic tetrametre of iambs marching. No, agallop: *deline the mare.*

Open your eyes now. I will. One moment. Has all vanished since? If I open and am for ever in the black adiaphane. *Basta!* I will see if I can see.

See now. There all the time without you: and ever shall be, world without end.

They came down the steps from Leahy's terrace prudently, *Frauenzimmer*: and down the shelving shore flabbily, their splayed feet sinking in the silted sand. Like me, like Algy, coming down to our mighty mother. Number one swung lourdily her midwife's bag, the other's gamp poked in the beach. From the liberties, out for the day. Mrs Florence MacCabe, relict of the late Patk MacCabe, deeply lamented, of Bride Street. One of her sisterhood lugged me squealing into life. Creation from nothing. What has she in the bag? A misbirth with a trailing navelcord, hushed in ruddy wool. The cords of all link back, strandentwining cable of all flesh. That is why mystic monks. Will you be as gods? Gaze in your *omphalos*. Hello. Kinch here. Put me on to Edenville. Aleph, alpha: nought, nought, one.

Spouse and helpmate of Adam Kadmon: Heva, naked Eve. She had no navel. Gaze. Belly without blemish, bulging big, a buckler of taut vellum, no, whiteheaped corn, orient and immortal, standing from everlasting to everlasting. Womb of sin.

Wombed in sin darkness I was too, made not begotten. By them, the man with my voice and my eyes and a ghostwoman with ashes on her breath. They clasped and sundered, did the coupler's will. From before the ages He willed me and now may not will me away or ever. A *lex eternal* stays about Him. Is that then the divine substance wherein Father and Son are consubstantial? Where is poor dear Arius to try conclusions? Warring his life long upon the contransmagnificandjewbangtantiality. Illstarred heresiarch! In a Greek watercloset he breathed his last: *euthanasia*. With beaded mitre and with crozier, stalled upon his throne, widower of a widowed see, with upstiffed *omophorion*, with clotted hinderparts.

Airs romped round him, nipping and eager airs. They are coming, waves. The whitemaned seahorses, champing, brightwindbridled, the steeds of Mananaan.

I mustn't forget his letter for the press. And after? The Ship, half twelve. By the way go easy with that money like a good young imbecile. Yes, I must.

His pace slackened. Here. Am I going to aunt Sara's or not? My consubstantial father's voice. Did you see anything of your artist brother Stephen lately? No? Sure he's not down in Strasburg terrace with his aunt Sally? Couldn't he fly a bit higher than that, eh? And and

and and tell us, Stephen, how is uncle Si? O, weeping God, the things I married into! De boys up in de hayloft. The drunken little costdrawer and his brother, the cornet player. Highly respectable gondoliers! And skeweyed Walter sirring his father, no less! Sir. Yes, sir. No, sir. Jesus wept: and no wonder, by Christ!

I pull the wheezy bell of their shuttered cottage: and wait. They take me for a dun, peer out from a coign of vantage.

—It's Stephen, sir.

—Let him in. Let Stephen in.

A bolt drawn back and Walter welcomes me.

—We thought you were someone else.

In his broad bed nuncle Richie, pillowed and blanketed, extends over the hillock of his knees a sturdy forearm. Cleanchested. He has washed the upper moiety.

—Morrow, nephew.

He lays aside the lapboard whereon he drafts his bills of costs for the eyes of master Goff and master Shapland Tandy, filing consents and common searches and a writ of *Duces Tecum*. A bogoak frame over his bald head: Wilde's *Requiescat*. The drone of his misleading whistle brings Walter back.

—Yes, sir?

—Malt for Richie and Stephen, tell mother. Where is she?

—Bathing Crissie, sir.

Papa's little bedpal. Lump of love.

—No, uncle Richie . . .

—Call me Richie. Damn your lithia water. It lowers. Whusky!

—Uncle Richie, really . . .

—Sit down or by the law Harry I'll knock you down.

Walter squints vainly for a chair.

—He has nothing to sit down on, sir.

—He has nowhere to put it, you mug. Bring in our chippendale chair. Would you like a bite of something? None of your damned lawdeedaw airs here. The rich of a rasher fried with a herring? Sure? So much the better. We have nothing in the house but backache pills.

All'erta!

He drones bars of Ferrando's *aria di sortita*. The grandest number, Stephen, in the whole opera. Listen.

His tuneful whistle sounds again, finely shaded, with rushes of the air, his fists bigdrumming on his padded knees.

This wind is sweeter.

Houses of decay, mine, his and all. You told the Clongowes gentry you had an uncle a judge and an uncle a general in the army. Come out of them, Stephen. Beauty is not there. Nor in the stagnant bay of Marsh's library where you read the fading prophecies of Joachim Abbas. For whom? The hundredheaded rabble of the cathedral close. A hater of his kind ran from them to the wood of madness, his mane foaming in the moon, his eyeballs stars. Houyhnhnm, horsenostrilled. The oval equine faces, Temple, Buck Mulligan, Foxy Campbell, Lantern jaws. Abbas father, furious dean, what offence laid fire to their brains? Paff! *Descende, calve, ut ne nimium decalveris.* A garland of grey hair on his comminated head see him me clambering down to the footpace (*descende!*), clutching a monstrance, basiliskeyed. Get down, bald poll! A choir gives back menace and echo, assisting about the altar's horns, the snorted Latin of jackpriests moving burly in their albs, tonsured and oiled and gelded, fat with the fat of kidneys of wheat.

And at the same instant perhaps a priest round the corner is elevating it. Dringdring! And two streets off another locking it into a pyx. Dringadring! And in a ladychapel another taking housel all to his own cheek. Dringdring! Down, up, forward, back. Dan Occam thought of that, invincible doctor. A misty English morning the imp hypostasis tickled his brain. Bringing his host down and kneeling he heard twine with his second bell the first bell in the transept (he is lifting his) and, rising, heard (now I am lifting) their two bells (he is kneeling) twang in diphthong.

Cousin Stephen, you will never be a saint. Isle of saints. You were awfully holy, weren't you? You prayed to the Blessed Virgin that you might not have a red nose. You prayed to the devil in Serpentine avenue that the fubsy widow in front might lift her clothes still more from the wet street. *O si, certo!* Sell your soul for that, do, dyed rags pinned round a squaw. More tell me, more still! On the top of the Howth tram alone crying to the rain: *Naked women! Naked women!* What about that, eh?

What about what? What else were they invented for?

Reading two pages apiece of seven books every night, eh? I was young. You bowed to yourself in the mirror, stepping forward to applause earnestly, striking face. Hurray for the Goddamned idiot! Hray! No-one saw: tell no-one. Books you were going to write with letters for titles. Have you read his F? O yes, but I prefer Q. Yes, but W is wonderful. O yes, W. Remember your epiphanies written on green oval leaves, deeply deep, copies to be sent if you died to all the great libraries of the world, including Alexandria? Someone was to read them there after a few thousand years, a mahamanvantara. Pico della Mirandola like. Ay, very like a whale. When one reads these strange pages of one long gone one feels that one is at one with one who once . . .

The grainy sand had gone from under his feet. His boots trod again a damp crackling mast, razorshells, squeaking pebbles, that on the unnumbered pebbles beats, wood sieved by the shipworm, lost Armada. Unwholesome sandflats waited to suck his treading soles, breathing upward sewage breath, a pocket of seaweed smouldered in seafire under a midden of man's ashes. He coasted them, walking warily. A porterbottle stood up, stogged to its waist, in the cakey sand dough. A sentinel: isle of dreadful thirst. Broken hoops on the shore; at the land a maze of dark cunning nets; farther away chalkscrawled backdoors and on the higher beach a dryingline with two crucified shirts. Ringsend: wigwams of brown steersmen and master mariners. Human shells.

He halted. I have passed the way to aunt Sara's. Am I not going there? Seems not. No-one about. He turned northeast and crossed the firmer sand towards the Pigeonhouse.

—*Qui vous a mis dans cette fichue position?*

—*C'est le pigeon, Joseph.*

Patrice, home on furlough, lapped warm milk with me in the bar MacMahon. Son of the wild goose, Kevin Egan of Paris. My father's a bird, he lapped the sweet *lait chaud* with pink young tongue, plump bunny's face. Lap, *lapin*. He hopes to win in the *gros lots*. About the nature of women he read in Michelet. But he must send me *La Vie de Jésus* by M. Léo Taxil. Lent it to his friend.

—*C'est tordant, vous savez. Moi, je suis socialiste. Je ne crois pas en l'existence de Dieu. Faut pas le dire à mon père.*

—*Il croit?*

—*Mon père, oui.*

Schluss. He laps.

My Latin quarter hat. God, we simply must dress the character. I want puce gloves. You were a student, weren't you? Of what in the other devil's name? Paysayenn. P. C. N., you know: *physiques, chimiques et naturelles.* Aha. Eating your groatsworth of *mou en civet*, fleshpots of Egypt, elbowed by belching cabmen. Just say in the most natural tone: when I was in Paris; *boul' Mich'*, I used to. Yes, used to carry punched tickets to prove an alibi if they arrested you for murder somewhere. Justice. On the night of the seventeenth of February 1904 the prisoner was seen by two witnesses. Other fellow did it: other me. Hat, tie, overcoat, nose. *Lui, c'est moi.* You seem to have enjoyed yourself.

Proudly walking. Whom were you trying to walk like? Forget: a dispossessed. With mother's money order, eight shillings, the banging door of the post office slammed in your face by the usher. Hunger toothache. *Encore deux minutes.* Look clock. Must get. *Fermé.* Hired dog! Shoot him to bloody bits with a bang shotgun, bits man spattered walls all brass buttons. Bits all khrrrrklak in place clack back. Not hurt? O, that's all right. Shake hands. See what I meant, see? O, that's all right. Shake a shake. O, that's all only all right.

You were going to do wonders, what? Missionary to Europe after fiery Columbanus. Fiacre and Scotus on their creepystools in heaven spilt from their pintpots, loudlatinlaughing: *Euge! Euge!* Pretending to speak broken English as you dragged your valise, porter threepence, across the slimy pier at Newhaven. *Comment?* Rich booty you brought back; *Le Tutu,* five tattered numbers of *Pantalon Blanc et Culotte Rouge*; a blue French telegram, curiosity to show:

—Mother dying come home father.

The aunt thinks you killed your mother. That's why she won't.

> Then here's a health to Mulligan's aunt
> And I'll tell you the reason why.
> She always kept things decent in
> The Hannigan famileye.

His feet marched in sudden proud rhythm over the sand furrows, along by the boulders of the south wall. He stared at them proudly, piled stone mammoth skulls. Gold light on sea, on sand, on boulders. The sun is there, the slender trees, the lemon houses.

Paris rawly waking, crude sunlight on her lemon streets. Moist pith of farls of bread, the froggreen wormwood, her matin incense, court the air. Belluomo rises from the bed of his wife's lover's wife, the kerchiefed housewife is astir, a saucer of acetic acid in her hand. In Rodot's Yvonne and Madeleine newmake their tumbled beauties, shattering with gold teeth *chaussons* of pastry, their mouths yellowed with the *pus* of *flan bréton.* Faces of Paris men go by, their wellpleased pleasers, curled conquistadores.

Noon slumbers. Kevin Egan rolls gunpowder cigarettes through fingers smeared with printer's ink, sipping his green fairy as Patrice his white. About us gobblers fork spiced beans down their gullets. *Un demi sétier!* A jet of coffee steam from the burnished caldron. She serves me at his beck. *Il est irlandais. Hollandais? Non fromage. Deux irlandais, nous, Irlande, vous savez ah, oui!* She thought you wanted a cheese *hollandais.* Your postprandial, do you know that word? Postprandial. There was a fellow I knew once in Barcelona, queer fellow, used to call it his postprandial. Well: *slainte!* Around the slabbed tables the tangle of wined breaths and grumbling gorges. His breath hangs over our saucestained plates, the green fairy's fang thrusting between his lips. Of Ireland, the Dalcassians, of hopes, conspiracies, of Arthur Griffith now, A E, pimander, good shepherd of men. To yoke me as his yokefellow, our crimes our common cause. You're your father's son. I know the voice. His fustian shirt, sanguineflowered, trembles its Spanish tassels at his secrets. M. Drumont, famous journalist, Drumont, know what he called queen Victoria? Old hag with the yellow teeth. *Vieille ogresse* with the *dents jaunes.* Maud Gonne, beautiful woman, *La Patrie,* M. Millevoye, Félix Faure, know how he died? Licentious men. The froeken, *bonne à tout faire,* who rubs male nakedness in the bath at Upsala. *Moi faire,* she said, *Tous les messieurs.* Not this *Monsieur,* I said. Most licentious custom. Bath a most private thing. I wouldn't let my brother, not even my own brother, most lascivious thing. Green eyes, I see you. Fang, I feel. Lascivious people.

The blue fuse burns deadly between hands and burns clear. Loose tobacco shreds catch fire: a flame and acrid smoke light our corner. Raw facebones under his peep of day boy's hat. How the head centre got away, authentic version. Got up as a young bride, man, veil, orangeblossoms, drove out the road to Malahide. Did, faith. Of lost leaders, the betrayed, wild escapes. Disguises, clutched at, gone, not here.

Spurned lover. I was a strapping young gossoon at that time, I tell you. I'll show you my likeness one day. I was, faith. Lover, for her love he prowled with colonel Richard Burke, tanist of his sept, under the walls of Clerkenwell and, crouching, saw a flame of vengeance hurl them upward in the fog. Shattered glass and toppling masonry. In gay Paree he hides, Egan of Paris, unsought by any save by me. Making his day's stations, the dingy printingcase, his three taverns, the Montmartre lair he sleeps short night in, rue de la Goutte-d'Or, damascened with flyblown faces of the gone. Loveless, landless, wifeless. She is quite nicey comfy without her outcast man, madame in rue Gît-le-Cœur, canary and two buck lodgers. Peachy cheeks, a zebra skirt, frisky as a young thing's. Spurned and undespairing. Tell Pat you saw me, won't you? I wanted to get poor Pat a job one time. *Mon fils*, soldier of France. I taught him to sing *The boys of Kilkenny are stout roaring blades*. Know that old lay? I taught Patrice that. Old Kilkenny: saint Canice, Strongbow's castle on the Nore. Goes like this. O, O. He takes me, Napper Tandy, by the hand.

> *O, O the boys of*
> *Kilkenny . . .*

Weak wasting hand on mine. They have forgotten Kevin Egan, not he them. Remembering thee, O Sion.

He had come nearer the edge of the sea and wet sand slapped his boots. The new air greeted him, harping in wild nerves, wind of wild air of seeds of brightness. Here, I am not walking out to the Kish lightship, am I? He stood suddenly, his feet beginning to sink slowly in the quaking soil. Turn back.

Turning, he scanned the shore south, his feet sinking again slowly in new sockets. The cold domed room of the tower waits. Through the barbacans the shafts of light are moving ever, slowly ever as my feet are sinking, creeping duskward over the dial floor. Blue dusk, nightfall, deep blue night. In the darkness of the dome they wait, their pushedback chairs, my obelisk valise, around a board of abandoned platters. Who to clear it? He has the key. I will not sleep there when this night comes. A shut door of a silent tower, entombing their blind bodies, the panthersahib and his pointer. Call: no answer. He lifted his feet up from the suck and turned back by the mole of boulders. Take all, keep all. My soul walks with me, form of forms. So in the moon's midwatches I pace the path above the rocks, in sable silvered, hearing Elsinore's tempting flood.

The flood is following me. I can watch it flow past from here. Get back then by the Poolbeg road to the strand there. He climbed over the sedge and eely oarweeds and sat on a stool of rock, resting his ashplant in a grike.

A bloated carcass of a dog lay lolled on bladderwrack. Before him the gunwale of a boat, sunk in sand. *Un coche ensablé* Louis Veuillot called Gautier's prose. These heavy sands are language tide and wind have silted here. And these, the stoneheaps of dead builders, a warren of weasel rats. Hide gold there. Try it. You have some. Sands and stones. Heavy of the past. Sir Lout's toys. Mind you don't get one bang on the ear. I'm the bloody well gigant rolls all them bloody well boulders, bones for my steppingstones. Feefawfum. I zmellz de bloodz odz an Iridzman.

A point, live dog, grew into sight running across the sweep of sand. Lord, is he going to attack me? Respect his liberty. You will not be master of others or their slave. I have my stick. Sit tight. From farther away, walking shoreward across from the crested tide, figures, two. The two maries. They have tucked it safe mong the bulrushes. Peekaboo. I see you. No, the dog. He is running back to them. Who?

Galleys of the Lochlanns ran here to beach, in quest of prey, their bloodbeaked prows riding low on a molten pewter surf. Dane vikings, torcs of tomahawks aglitter on their breasts when Malachi wore the collar of gold. A school of turlehide whales stranded in hot noon, spouting, hobbling in the shallows. Then from the starving cagework city a horde of jerkined dwarfs, my people, with flayers' knives, running, scaling, hacking in green blubbery whalemeat. Famine, plague and slaughters. Their blood is in me, their lusts my waves. I moved among them on the frozen Liffey, that I, a changeling, among the spluttering resin fires. I spoke to no-one: none to me.

The dog's bark ran towards him, stopped, ran back. Dog of my enemy. I just simply stood pale, silent, bayed about. *Terribilia meditans.* A primrose doublet, fortune's knave, smiled on my fear. For that are you pining, the bark of their applause? Pretenders: live their lives. The Bruce's brother, Thomas Fitzgerald, silken knight, Perkin Warbeck, York's false scion, in breeches of silk of whiterose ivory, wonder of a day, and Lambert Simnel, with a tail of nans and sutlers, a scullion crowned. All kings' sons. Paradise of pretenders then and now. He saved men from drowning and you shake at a cur's yelping. But the courtiers who mocked Guido in Or san Michele were in their own house. House of ... We don't want any of your medieval abstrusiosities. Would you do what he did? A boat would be near, a lifebuoy. *Natürlich,* put there for you. Would you or would you not? The man that was drowned nine days ago off Maiden's rock. They are waiting for him now. The truth, spit it out. I would want to. I would try. I am not a strong swimmer. Water cold soft. When I put my face into it in the basin at Clongowes. Can't see! Who's behind me? Out quickly,

quickly! Do you see the tide flowing quickly in on all sides, sheeting the lows of sand quickly, shellcocoacoloured? If I had land under my feet. I want his life still to be his, mine to be mine. A drowning man. His human eyes scream to me out of horror of his death. I . . . With him together down . . . I could not save her. Waters: bitter death: lost.

A woman and a man. I see her skirties. Pinned up, I bet.

Their dog ambled about a bank of dwindling sand, trotting, sniffing on all sides. Looking for something lost in a past life. Suddenly he made off like a bounding hare, ears flung back, chasing the shadow of a lowskimming gull. The man's shrieked whistle struck his limp ears. He turned, bounded back, came nearer, trotted on twinkling shanks. On a field tenney a buck, trippant, proper, unattired. At the lacefringe of the tide he halted with stiff forehoofs, seawardpointed ears. His snout lifted barked at the wavenoise, herds of seamorse. They serpented towards his feet, curling, unfurling many crests, every ninth, breaking, plashing, from far, from farther out, waves and waves.

Cocklepickers. They waded a little way in the water and, stooping, soused their bags and, lifting them again, waded out. The dog yelped running to them, reared up and pawed them, dropping on all fours, again reared up at them with mute bearish fawning. Unheeded he kept by them as they came towards the drier sand, a rag of wolf's tongue redpanting from his jaws. His speckled body ambled ahead of them and then loped off at a calf's gallop. The carcass lay on his path. He stopped, sniffed, stalked round it, brother, nosing closer, went round it, sniffling rapidly like a dog all over the dead dog's bedraggled fell. Dogskull, dogsniff, eyes on the ground, moves to one great goal. Ah, poor dogsbody! Here lies poor dogsbody's body.

—Tatters! Out of that, you mongrel!

The cry brought him skulking back to his master and a blunt bootless kick sent him unscathed across a spit of sand, crouched in flight. He slunk back in a curve. 't see me. Along by the edge of the mole he lolloped, dawdled, sm____ ____ ___d from under a cocked hindleg pissed against it. He trotted fo____ ___d, lifting again his hindleg, pissed quick short at an unsmelt rock. ___ simple pleasures of the poor. His hindpaws then scattered the sand: ____ his forepaws dabbled and delved. Something he buried there, his g___ ___other. He rooted in the sand, dabbling, delving and stopped to lis____ ___ the air, scraped up the sand again with a fury of his claws, soo____ ___ing, a pard, a panther, got in spousebreach, vulturing the dead.

After he woke me last night same dream or was it? Wait. Open hallway. Street of harlots. Remember. Haroun al Raschid. I am almosting it. That man led me, spoke. I was not afraid. The melon he had he held against my face. Smiled: creamfruit smell. That was the rule, said. In. Come. Red carpet spread. You will see who.

Shouldering their bags they trudged, the red Egyptians. His blued feet out of turnedup trousers slapped the clammy sand, a dull brick muffler strangling his unshaven neck. With woman steps she followed: the ruffian and his strolling mort. Spoils slung at her back. Loose sand and shellgrit crusted her bare feet. About her windraw face hair trailed. Behind her lord, his helpmate, bing awast to Romeville. When night hides her body's flaws calling under her brown shawl from an archway where dogs have mired. Her fancyman is treating two Royal Dublins in O'Loughlin's of Blackpitts. Buss her, wap in rogues' rum lingo, for, O, my dimber wapping dell! A shefiend's whiteness under her rancid rags. Fumbally's lane that night: the tanyard smells.

> *White thy fambles, red thy gan*
> *And thy quarrons dainty is.*
> *Couch a hogshead with me then.*
> *In the darkmans clip and kiss.*

Morose delectation Aquinas tunbelly calls this, *frate porcospino.* Unfallen Adam rode and not rutted. Call away let him: *thy quarrons dainty is.* Language no whit worse than his. Monkwords, marybeads jabber on their girdles: roguewords, tough nuggets patter in their pockets.

Passing now.

A side eye at my Hamlet hat. If I were suddenly naked here as I sit? I am not. Across the sands of all the world, followed by the sun's flaming sword, to the west, trekking to evening lands. She trudges, schlepps, trains, drags, trascines her load. A tide westering, moondrawn, in her wake. Tides, myriadislanded, within her, blood not mine, *oinopa ponton,* a winedark sea. Behold the handmaid of the moon. In sleep the wet sign calls her hour, bids her rise. Bridebed, childbed, bed of death, ghostcandled. *Omnis caro ad te veniet.* He comes, pale vampire, through storm his eyes, his bat sails bloodying the sea, mouth to her mouth's kiss.

Here. Put a pin in that chap, will you? My tablets. Mouth to her kiss. No. Must be two of 'em. Glue 'em well. Mouth to her mouth's kiss.

His lips lipped and mouthed fleshless lips of air: mouth to her moomb. Oomb, allwombing tomb. His mouth moulded issuing breath, unspeeched: ooeeehah: roar of cataractic planets, globed, blazing, roaring wayawayawayawayaway. Paper. The banknotes, blast them. Old Deasy's letter. Here. Thanking you for the hospitality tear the blank end off. Turning his back to the sun he bent over far to a table of rock and scribbled words. That's twice I forgot to take slips from the library counter.

His shadow lay over the rocks as he bent, ending. Why not endless till the farthest star? Darkly they are there behind this light, darkness shining in the brightness, delta of Cassiopeia, worlds. Me sits there with his augur's rod of ash, in borrowed sandals, by day beside a livid sea, unbeheld, in violet night walking beneath a reign of uncouth stars. I throw this ended shadow from me, manshape ineluctable, call it back. Endless, would it be mine, form of my form? Who watches me here? Who ever anywhere will read these written words? Signs on a white field. Somewhere to someone in your flutiest voice. The good bishop of Cloyne took the veil of the temple out of his shovel hat: veil of space with coloured emblems hatched on its field. Hold hard. Coloured on a flat: yes, that's right. Flat I see, then think distance, near, far, flat I see, east, back. Ah, see now! Falls back suddenly, frozen in stereoscope. Click does the trick. You find my words dark. Darkness is in our souls do you not think? Flutier. Our souls, shamewounded by our sins, cling to us yet more, a woman to her lover clinging, the more the more.

She trusts me, her hand gentle, the longlashed eyes. Now where the blue hell am I bringing her beyond the veil? Into the ineluctable modality of the ineluctable visuality. She, she, she. What she? The virgin at Hodges Figgis' window on Monday looking in for one of the alphabet books you were going to write. Keen glance you gave her. Wrist through the braided jesse of her sunshade. She lives in Leeson park with a grief and kickshaws, a lady of letters. Talk that to someone else, Stevie: a pickmeup. Bet she wears those curse of God stays suspenders and yellow stockings, darned with lumpy wool. Talk about apple dumplings, *piuttosto*. Where are your wits?

Touch me. Soft eyes. Soft soft soft hand. I am lonely here. O, touch me soon, now. What is that word known to all men? I am quiet here alone. Sad too. Touch, touch me.

He lay back at full stretch over the sharp rocks, cramming the scribbled note and pencil into a pocket, his hat tilted down on his eyes. That is Kevin Egan's movement I made, nodding for his nap, sabbath sleep. *Et vidit Deus. Et erant valde bona.* Alo! *Bonjour.* Welcome as the flowers in May. Under its leaf he watched through peacocktwittering lashes the southing sun. I am caught in this burning scene. Pan's hour, the faunal noon. Among gumheavy serpentplants, milkoozing fruits, where on the tawny waters leaves lie wide. Pain is far.

And no more turn aside and brood.

His gaze brooded on his broadtoed boots, a buck's castoffs, *nebeneinander.* He counted the creases of rucked leather wherein another's foot had nested warm. The foot that beat the ground in tripudium, foot I dislove. But you were delighted when Esther Osvalt's shoe went on you: girl I knew in Paris. *Tiens, quel petit pied!* Staunch friend, a brother soul: Wilde's love that dare not speak its name. His arm: Cranly's arm. He now will leave me. And the blame? As I am. As I am. All or not at all.

In long lassoes from the Cock lake the water flowed full, covering greengoldenly lagoons of sand, rising, flowing. My ashplant will float away. I shall wait. No, they will pass on, passing, chafing against the low rocks, swirling, passing. Better get this job over quick. Listen: a fourworded wavespeech: seesoo, hrss, rsseeiss, ooos. Vehement breath of waters amid seasnakes, rearing horses, rocks. In cups of rocks it slops: flop, slop, slap: bounded in barrels. And, spent, its speech ceases. It flows purling, widely flowing, floating foampool, flower unfurling.

Under the upswelling tide he saw the writhing weeds lift languidly and sway reluctant arms, hising up their petticoats, in whispering water swaying and upturning coy silver fronds. Day by day: night by night: lifted, flooded and let fall. Lord, they are weary; and, whispered to, they sigh. Saint Ambrose heard it, sigh of leaves and waves, waiting, awaiting the fullness of their times, *diebus ac noctibus iniurias patiens ingemiscit.* To no end gathered; vainly then released, forth flowing, wending back: loom of the moon. Weary too in sight of lovers, lascivious men, a naked woman shining in her courts, she draws a toil of waters.

Five fathoms out there. Full fathom five thy father lies. At one, he said. Found drowned. High water at Dublin bar. Driving before it a loose drift of rubble, fanshoals of fishes, silly shells. A corpse rising saltwhite from the undertow, bobbing a pace a pace a porpoise landward. There he is. Hook it quick. Pull. Sunk though he be beneath the watery floor. We have him. Easy now.

Bag of corpsegas sopping in foul brine. A quiver of minnows, fat of a spongy titbit, flash through the slits of his buttoned trouserfly. God becomes man becomes fish becomes barnacle goose becomes featherbed mountain. Dead breaths I living breathe, tread dead dust, devour a urinous offal from all dead. Hauled stark over the gunwale he breathes upward the stench of his green grave, his leprous nosehole snoring to the sun.

A seachange this, brown eyes saltblue. Seadeath, mildest of all deaths known to man. Old Father Ocean. *Prix de Paris*: beware of imitations. Just you give it a fair trial. We enjoyed ourselves immensely.

Come. I thirst. Clouding over. No black clouds anywhere, are there? Thunderstorm. Allbright he falls, proud lightning of the intellect, *Lucifer, dico, qui nescit occasum*. No. My cockle hat and staff and his my sandal shoon. Where? To evening lands. Evening will find itself.

He took the hilt of his ashplant, lunging with it softly, dallying still. Yes, evening will find itself in me, without me. All days make their end. By the way next when is it Tuesday will be the longest day. Of all the glad new year, mother, the rum tum tiddledy tum. Lawn Tennyson, gentleman poet. *Già*. For the old hag with the yellow teeth. And Monsieur Drumont, gentleman journalist. *Già*. My teeth are very bad. Why, I wonder. Feel. That one is going too. Shells. Ought I go to a dentist, I wonder, with that money? That one. This. Toothless Kinch, the superman. Why is that, I wonder, or does it mean something perhaps?

My handkerchief. He threw it. I remember. Did I not take it up?

His hand groped vainly in his pockets. No, I didn't. Better buy one.

He laid the dry snot picked from his nostril on a ledge of rock, carefully. For the rest let look who will.

Behind. Perhaps there is someone.

He turned his face over a shoulder, rere regardant. Moving through the air high spars of a threemaster, her sails brailed up on the crosstrees, homing, upstream, silently moving, a silent ship.

Part

II

Part

II

4

M r Leopold Bloom ate with relish the inner organs
of beasts and fowls. He liked thick giblet soup,
nutty gizzards, a stuffed roast heart, liver slices
fried with crustcrumbs, fried hencods' roes. Most of all he
liked grilled mutton kidneys which gave to his palate a fine
tang of faintly scented urine.

Kidneys were in his mind as he moved about the
kitchen softly, righting her breakfast things on the humpy
tray. Gelid light and air were in the kitchen but out of doors
gentle summer morning everywhere. Made him feel a bit
peckish.

The coals were reddening.

Another slice of bread and butter: three, four: right. She
didn't like her plate full. Right. He turned from the tray,
lifted the kettle off the hob and set it sideways on the fire. It
sat there, dull and squat, its spout stuck out. Cup of tea soon.
Good. Mouth dry. The cat walked stiffly round a leg of the
table with tail on high.

—Mkgnao!

—O, there you are, Mr Bloom said, turning from the
fire.

The cat mewed in answer and stalked again stiffly round
a leg of the table, mewing. Just how she stalks over my
writingtable. Prr. Scratch my head. Prr.

Mr Bloom watched curiously, kindly the lithe black
form. Clean to see: the gloss of her sleek hide, the white
button under the butt of her tail, the green flashing eyes. He
bent down to her, his hands on his knees.

—Milk for the pussens, he said.

—Mrkgnao! the cat cried.

They call them stupid. They understand what we say
better than we understand them. She understands all she
wants to. Vindictive too. Cruel. Her nature. Curious mice

never squeal. Seem to like it. Wonder what I look like to her. Height of a tower? No, she can jump me.

—Afraid of the chickens she is, he said mockingly. Afraid of the chookchooks. I never saw such a stupid pussens as the pussens.

Cruel. Her nature. Curious mice never squeal. Seem to like it.

—Mrkrgnao! the cat said loudly.

She blinked up out of her avid shameclosing eyes, mewing plaintively and long, showing him her milkwhite teeth. He watched the dark eyeslits narrowing with greed till her eyes were green stones. Then he went to the dresser, took the jug Hanlon's milkman had just filled for him, poured warmbubbled milk on a saucer and set it slowly on the floor.

—Gurrhr! she cried, running to lap.

He watched the bristles shining wirily in the weak light as she tipped three times and licked lightly. Wonder is it true if you clip them they can't mouse after. Why? They shine in the dark, perhaps, the tips. Or kind of feelers in the dark, perhaps.

He listened to her licking lap. Ham and eggs, no. No good eggs with this drouth. Want pure fresh water. Thursday: not a good day either for a mutton kidney at Buckley's. Fried with butter, a shake of pepper. Better a pork kidney at Dlugacz's. While the kettle is boiling. She lapped slower, then licking the saucer clean. Why are their tongues so rough? To lap better, all porous holes. Nothing she can eat? He glanced round him. No.

On quietly creaky boots he went up the staircase to the hall, paused by the bedroom door. She might like something tasty. Thin bread and butter she likes in the morning. Still perhaps: once in a way.

He said softly in the bare hall:

—I'm going round the corner. Be back in a minute.

And when he had heard his voice say it he added:

—You don't want anything for breakfast?

A sleepy soft grunt answered:

—Mn.

No. She didn't want anything. He heard then a warm heavy sigh, softer, as she turned over and the loose brass quoits of the bedstead jingled. Must get those settled really. Pity. All the way from Gibraltar. Forgotten any little Spanish she knew. Wonder what her father gave for it. Old style. Ah yes! of course. Bought it at the governor's auction. Got a short knock. Hard as nails at a bargain, old Tweedy. Yes, sir.

At Plevna that was. I rose from the ranks, sir, and I'm proud of it. Still he had brains enough to make that corner in stamps. Now that was farseeing.

His hand took his hat from the peg over his initialled heavy overcoat and his lost property office secondhand waterproof. Stamps: stickyback pictures. Daresay lots of officers are in the swim too. Course they do. The sweated legend in the crown of his hat told him mutely: Plasto's high grade ha. He peeped quickly inside the leather headband. White slip of paper. Quite safe.

On the doorstep he felt in his hip pocket for the latchkey. Not there. In the trousers I left off. Must get it. Potato I have. Creaky wardrobe. No use disturbing her. She turned over sleepily that time. He pulled the halldoor to after him very quietly, more, till the footleaf dropped gently over the threshold, a limp lid. Looked shut. All right till I come back anyhow.

He crossed to the bright side, avoiding the loose cellarflap of number seventyfive. The sun was nearing the steeple of George's church. Be a warm day I fancy. Specially in these black clothes feel it more. Black conducts, reflects, (refracts is it?), the heat. But I couldn't go in that light suit. Make a picnic of it. His eyelids sank quietly often as he walked in happy warmth. Boland's breadvan delivering with trays our daily but she prefers yesterday's loaves turnovers crisp crowns hot. Makes you feel young. Somewhere in the east: early morning: set off at dawn. Travel round in front of the sun, steal a day's march on him. Keep it up for ever never grow a day older technically. Walk along a strand, strange land, come to a city gate, sentry there, old ranker too, old Tweedy's big moustaches, leaning on a long kind of a spear. Wander through awned streets. Turbaned faces going by. Dark caves of carpet shops, big man, Turko the terrible, seated crosslegged, smoking a coiled pipe. Cries of sellers in the streets. Drink water scented with fennel, sherbet. Dander along all day. Might meet a robber or two. Well, meet him. Getting on to sundown. The shadows of the mosques among the pillars: priest with a scroll rolled up. A shiver of the trees, signal, the evening wind. I pass on. Fading gold sky. A mother watches me from her doorway. She calls her children home in their dark language. High wall: beyond strings twanged. Night sky, moon, violet, colour of Molly's new garters. Strings. Listen. A girl playing one of those instruments what do you call them: dulcimers. I pass.

Probably not a bit like it really. Kind of stuff you read: in the track of the sun. Sunburst on the titlepage. He smiled, pleasing himself. What Arthur Griffith said about the headpiece over the *Freeman* leader: a homerule sun rising up in the northwest from the laneway behind the bank of Ireland. He prolonged his pleased smile. Ikey touch that: homerule sun rising up in the northwest.

He approached Larry O'Rourke's. From the cellar grating floated up the flabby gush of porter. Through the open doorway the bar squirted out whiffs of ginger, teadust, biscuitmush. Good house, however: just the end of the city traffic. For instance M'Auley's down there: n. g. as position. Of course if they ran a tramline along the North Circular from the cattlemarket to the quays value would go up like a shot.

Baldhead over the blind. Cute old codger. No use canvassing him for an ad. Still he knows his own business best. There he is, sure enough, my bold Larry, leaning against the sugarbin in his shirtsleeves watching the aproned curate swab up with mop and bucket. Simon Dedalus takes him off to a tee with his eyes screwed up. Do you know what I'm going to tell you? What's that, Mr O'Rourke? Do you know what? The Russians, they'd only be an eight o'clock breakfast for the Japanese.

Stop and say a word: about the funeral perhaps. Sad thing about poor Dignam, Mr O'Rourke.

Turning into Dorset street he said freshly in greeting through the doorway:

—Good day, Mr O'Rourke.

—Good day to you.

—Lovely weather, sir.

—'Tis all that.

Where do they get the money? Coming up redheaded curates from the county Leitrim, rinsing empties and old man in the cellar. Then, lo and behold, they blossom out as Adam Findlaters or Dan Tallons. Then think of the competition. General thirst. Good puzzle would be cross Dublin without passing a pub. Save it they can't. Off the drunks perhaps. Put down three and carry five. What is that, a bob here and there, dribs and drabs. On the wholesale orders perhaps. Doing a double shuffle with the town travellers. Square it you with the boss and we'll split the job, see?

How much would that tot to off the porter in the month? Say

ten barrels of stuff. Say he got ten per cent off. O more. Fifteen. He passed Saint Joseph's National school. Brats' clamour. Windows open. Fresh air helps memory. Or a lilt. Ahbeesee defeegee kelomen opeecue rustyouvee doubleyou. Boys are they? Yes. Inishturk. Inishark. Inishboffin. At their joggerfry. Mine. Slieve Bloom.

He halted before Dlugacz's window, staring at the hanks of sausages, polonies, black and white. Fifteen multiplied by. The figures whitened in his mind, unsolved: displeased, he let them fade. The shiny links, packed with forcemeat, fed his gaze and he breathed in tranquilly the lukewarm breath of cooked spicy pigs' blood.

A kidney oozed bloodgouts on the willowpatterned dish: the last. He stood by the nextdoor girl at the counter. Would she buy it too, calling the items from a slip in her hand? Chapped: washing soda. And a pound and a half of Denny's sausages. His eyes rested on her vigorous hips. Woods his name is. Wonder what he does. Wife is oldish. New blood. No followers allowed. Strong pair of arms. Whacking a carpet on the clothesline. She does whack it, by George. The way her crooked skirt swings at each whack.

The ferreteyed porkbutcher folded the sausages he had snipped off with blotchy fingers, sausagepink. Sound meat there: like a stallfed heifer.

He took a page up from the pile of cut sheets: the model farm at Kinnereth on the lakeshore of Tiberias. Can become ideal winter sanatorium. Moses Montefiore. I thought he was. Farmhouse, wall round it, blurred cattle cropping. He held the page from him: interesting: read it nearer, the title, the blurred cropping cattle, the page rustling. A young white heifer. Those mornings in the cattlemarket, the beasts lowing in their pens, branded sheep, flop and fall of dung, the breeders in hobnailed boots trudging through the litter, slapping a palm on a ripemeated hindquarter, there's a prime one, unpeeled switches in their hands. He held the page aslant patiently, bending his senses and his will, his soft subject gaze at rest. The crooked skirt swinging, whack by whack by whack.

The porkbutcher snapped two sheets from the pile, wrapped up her prime sausages and made a red grimace.

—Now, my miss, he said.

She tendered a coin, smiling boldly, holding her thick wrist out.

—Thank you, my miss. And one shilling threepence change. For you, please?

Mr Bloom pointed quickly. To catch up and walk behind her if she went slowly, behind her moving hams. Pleasant to see first thing in the morning. Hurry up, damn it. Make hay while the sun shines. She stood outside the shop in sunlight and sauntered lazily to the right. He sighed down his nose: they never understand. Sodachapped hands. Crusted toenails too. Brown scapulars in tatters, defending her both ways. The sting of disregard glowed to weak pleasure within his breast. For another: a constable off duty cuddling her in Eccles' Lane. They like them sizeable. Prime sausage. O please, Mr Policeman, I'm lost in the wood.

—Threepence, please.

His hand accepted the moist tender gland and slid it into a sidepocket. Then it fetched up three coins from his trousers' pocket and laid them on the rubber prickles. They lay, were read quickly and quickly slid, disc by disc, into the till.

—Thank you, sir. Another time.

A speck of eager fire from foxeyes thanked him. He withdrew his gaze after an instant. No: better not: another time.

—Good morning, he said, moving away.

—Good morning, sir.

No sign. Gone. What matter?

He walked back along Dorset street, reading gravely. Agendath Netaim: planters' company. To purchase waste sandy tracts from Turkish government and plant with eucalyptus trees. Excellent for shade, fuel and construction. Orangegroves and immense melonfields north of Jaffa. You pay eighty marks and they plant a dunam of land for you with olives, oranges, almonds or citrons. Olives cheaper: oranges need artificial irrigation. Every year you get a sending of the crop. Your name entered for life as owner in the book of the union. Can pay ten down and the balance in yearly instalments. Bleibtreustrasse 34, Berlin, W. 15.

Nothing doing. Still an idea behind it.

He looked at the cattle, blurred in silver heat. Silverpowdered olivetrees. Quiet long days: pruning, ripening. Olives are packed in jars, eh? I have a few left from Andrews. Molly spitting them out. Knows the taste of them now. Oranges in tissue paper packed in crates. Citrons too. Wonder is poor Citron still in Saint Kevin's parade. And Mastiansky with the old cither. Pleasant evenings we had then. Molly in Citron's basketchair. Nice to hold, cool waxen fruit, hold in the hand, lift it to the nostrils and smell the perfume. Like that, heavy, sweet, wild perfume. Always the same, year after year. They fetched high prices too, Moisel told me. Arbutus place: Pleasants street: pleasant old times. Must be without a flaw, he said. Coming all that way: Spain, Gibraltar, Mediterranean, the Levant. Crates lined up on the quayside at Jaffa, chap ticking them off in a book, navvies handling them barefoot in soiled dungarees. There's whatdoyoucallhim out of. How do you? Doesn't see. Chap you know just to salute bit of a bore. His back is like that Norwegian captain's. Wonder if I'll meet him today. Watering cart. To provoke the rain. On earth as it is in heaven.

A cloud began to cover the sun slowly, wholly. Grey. Far.

No, not like that. A barren land, bare waste. Vulcanic lake, the dead sea: no fish, weedless, sunk deep in the earth. No wind could lift those waves, grey metal, poisonous foggy waters. Brimstone they called it raining down: the cities of the plain: Sodom, Gomorrah, Edom. All dead names. A dead sea in a dead land, grey and old. Old now. It bore the oldest, the first race. A bent hag crossed from Cassidy's, clutching a naggin bottle by the neck. The oldest people. Wandered far away over all the earth, captivity to captivity, multiplying, dying, being born everywhere. It lay there now. Now it could bear no more. Dead: an old woman's: the grey sunken cunt of the world.

Desolation.

Grey horror seared his flesh. Folding the page into his pocket he turned into Eccles street, hurrying homeward. Cold oils slid along his veins, chilling his blood: age crusting him with a salt cloak. Well, I am here now. Yes, I am here now. Morning mouth bad images. Got up wrong side of the bed. Must begin again those Sandow's exercises. On the hands down. Blotchy brown brick houses. Number eighty still unlet. Why is that? Valuation is only twentyeight. Towers, Battersby, North, MacArthur: parlour windows plastered with bills. Plasters on a sore eye. To smell the gentle smoke of tea, fume of the pan, sizzling butter. Be near her ample bedwarmed flesh. Yes, yes.

Quick warm sunlight came running from Berkeley road, swiftly, in slim sandals, along the brightening footpath. Runs, she runs to meet me, a girl with gold hair on the wind.

Two letters and a card lay on the hallfloor. He stooped and gathered them. Mrs Marion Bloom. His quickened heart slowed at once. Bold hand. Mrs Marion.

—Poldy!

Entering the bedroom he halfclosed his eyes and walked through warm yellow twilight towards her tousled head.

—Who are the letters for?

He looked at them. Mullingar. Milly.

—A letter for me from Milly, he said carefully, and a card to you. And a letter for you.

He laid her card and letter on the twill bedspread near the curve of her knees.

—Do you want the blind up?

Letting the blind up by gentle tugs halfway his backward eye saw her glance at the letter and tuck it under her pillow.

—That do? he asked, turning.

She was reading the card, propped on her elbow.

—She got the things, she said.

He waited till she had laid the card aside and curled herself back slowly with a snug sigh.

—Hurry up with that tea, she said. I'm parched.

—The kettle is boiling, he said.

But he delayed to clear the chair: her striped petticoat, tossed soiled linen: and lifted all in an armful on to the foot of the bed.

As he went down the kitchen stairs she called:

—Poldy!

—What?

—Scald the teapot.

On the boil sure enough: a plume of steam from the spout. He scalded and rinsed out the teapot and put in four full spoons of tea, tilting the kettle then to let the water flow in. Having set it to draw he took off the kettle, crushed the pan flat on the live coals and watched the lump of butter slide and melt. While he unwrapped the kidney the cat mewed hungrily against him. Give her too much meat she won't mouse. Say they won't eat pork. Kosher. Here. He let the bloodsmeared paper fall to her and dropped the kidney amid the sizzling butter sauce. Pepper. He sprinkled it through his fingers ringwise from the chipped eggcup.

Then he slit open his letter, glancing down the page and over. Thanks: new tam: Mr Coghlan: lough Owel picnic: young student: Blazes Boylan's seaside girls.

The tea was drawn. He filled his own moustachecup, sham crown

Derby, smiling. Silly Milly's birthday gift. Only five she was then. No, wait: four. I gave her the amberoid necklace she broke. Putting pieces of folded brown paper in the letterbox for her. He smiled, pouring.

> *O, Milly Bloom, you are my darling.*
> *You are my lookingglass from night to morning.*
> *I'd rather have you without a farthing*
> *Than Katey Keogh with her ass and garden.*

Poor old professor Goodwin. Dreadful old case. Still he was a courteous old chap. Oldfashioned way he used to bow Molly off the platform. And the little mirror in his silk hat. The night Milly brought it into the parlour. O, look what I found in professor Goodwin's hat! All we laughed. Sex breaking out even then. Pert little piece she was.

He prodded a fork into the kidney and slapped it over: then fitted the teapot on the tray. Its hump bumped as he took it up. Everything on it? Bread and butter, four, sugar, spoon, her cream. Yes. He carried it upstairs, his thumb hooked in the teapot handle.

Nudging the door open with his knee he carried the tray in and set it on the chair by the bedhead.

—What a time you were! she said.

She set the brasses jingling as she raised herself briskly, an elbow on the pillow. He looked calmly down on her bulk and between her large soft bubs, sloping within her nightdress like a shegoat's udder. The warmth of her couched body rose on the air, mingling with the fragrance of the tea she poured.

A strip of torn envelope peeped from under the dimpled pillow. In the act of going he stayed to straighten the bedspread.

—Who was the letter from? he asked.

Bold hand. Marion.

—O, Boylan, she said. He's bringing the programme.

—What are you singing?

—*Là ci darem* with J. C. Doyle, she said, and *Love's Old Sweet Song.*

Her full lips, drinking, smiled. Rather stale smell that incense leaves next day. Like foul flowerwater.

—Would you like the window open a little?

She doubled a slice of bread into her mouth, asking:

—What time is the funeral?

—Eleven, I think, he answered. I didn't see the paper.

75

Following the pointing of her finger he took up a leg of her soiled drawers from the bed. No? Then, a twisted grey garter looped round a stocking: rumpled, shiny sole.

—No: that book.

Other stocking. Her petticoat.

—It must have fell down, she said.

He felt here and there. *Voglio e non vorrei.* Wonder if she pronounces that right: *voglio.* Not in the bed. Must have slid down. He stooped and lifted the valance. The book, fallen, sprawled against the bulge of the orangekeyed chamberpot.

—Show here, she said. I put a mark in it. There's a word I wanted to ask you.

She swallowed a draught of tea from her cup held by nothandle and, having wiped her fingertips smartly on the blanket, began to search the text with the hairpin till she reached the word.

—Met him what? he asked.

—Here, she said. What does that mean?

He leaned downward and read near her polished thumbnail.

—Metempsychosis?

—Yes. Who's he when he's at home?

—Metempsychosis, he said, frowning. It's Greek: from the Greek. That means the transmigration of souls.

—O, rocks! she said. Tell us in plain words.

He smiled, glancing askance at her mocking eyes. The same young eyes. The first night after the charades. Dolphin's Barn. He turned over the smudged pages. *Ruby: the Pride of the Ring.* Hello. Illustration. Fierce Italian with carriagewhip. Must be Ruby pride of the on the floor naked. Sheet kindly lent. *The monster Maffei desisted and flung his victim from him with an oath.* Cruelty behind it all. Doped animals. Trapeze at Hengler's. Had to look the other way. Mob gaping. Break your neck and we'll break our sides. Families of them. Bone them young so they metamspychosis. That we live after death. Our souls. That a man's soul after he dies. Dignam's soul . . .

—Did you finish it? he asked.

—Yes, she said. There's nothing smutty in it. Is she in love with the first fellow all the time?

—Never read it. Do you want another?

—Yes. Get another of Paul de Kock's. Nice name he has.

She poured more tea into her cup, watching it flow sideways.

Must get that Capel street library book renewed or they'll write to Kearney, my guarantor. Reincarnation: that's the word.

—Some people believe, he said, that we go on living in another body after death, that we lived before. They call it reincarnation. That we all lived before on the earth thousands of years ago or some other planet. They say we have forgotten it. Some say they remember their past lives.

The sluggish cream wound curdling spirals through her tea. Better remind her of the word: metempsychosis. An example would be better. An example?

The *Bath of the Nymph* over the bed. Given away with the Easter number of *Photo Bits*: Splendid masterpiece in art colours. Tea before you put milk in. Not unlike her with her hair down: slimmer. Three and six I gave for the frame. She said it would look nice over the bed. Naked nymphs: Greece: and for instance all the people that lived then.

He turned the pages back.

—Metempsychosis, he said, is what the ancient Greeks called it. They used to believe you could be changed into an animal or a tree, for instance. What they called nymphs, for example.

Her spoon ceased to stir up the sugar. She gazed straight before her, inhaling through her arched nostrils.

—There's a smell of burn, she said. Did you leave anything on the fire?

—The kidney! he cried suddenly.

He fitted the book roughly into his inner pocket and, stubbing his toes against the broken commode, hurried out towards the smell, stepping hastily down the stairs with a flurried stork's legs. Pungent smoke shot up in an angry jet from a side of the pan. By prodding a prong of the fork under the kidney he detached it and turned it turtle on its back. Only a little burnt. He tossed it off the pan on to a plate and let the scanty brown gravy trickle over it.

Cup of tea now. He sat down, cut and buttered a slice of the loaf. He shore away the burnt flesh and flung it to the cat. Then he put a forkful into his mouth, chewing with discernment the toothsome pliant meat. Done to a turn. A mouthful of tea. Then he cut away dies of bread, sopped one in the gravy and put it in his mouth. What was that about some young student and a picnic? He creased out the letter at his side, reading it slowly as he chewed, sopping another die of bread in the gravy and raising it to his mouth.

Dearest Papli

Thanks ever so much for the lovely birthday present. It suits me splendid. Everyone says I am quite the belle in my new tam. I got mummy's lovely box of creams and am writing. They are lovely. I am getting on swimming in the photo business now. Mr Coghlan took one of me and Mrs Will send when developed. We did great biz yesterday. Fair day and all the beef to the heels were in. We are going to lough Owel on Monday with a few friends to make a scrap picnic. Give my love to mummy and to yourself a big kiss and thanks. I hear them at the piano downstairs. There is to be a concert in the Greville Arms on Saturday. There is a young student comes here some evenings named Bannon his cousins or something are big swells and he sings Boylan's (I was on the pop of writing Blazes Boylan's) song about those seaside girls. Tell him silly Milly sends my best respects. I must now close with fondest love

Your fond daughter

Milly

P. S. Excuse bad writing am in hurry. Byby.

M.

Fifteen yesterday. Curious, fifteenth of the month too. Her first birthday away from home. Separation. Remember the summer morning she was born, running to knock up Mrs Thornton in Denzille street. Jolly old woman. Lot of babies she must have helped into the world. She knew from the first poor little Rudy wouldn't live. Well, God is good, sir. She knew at once. He would be eleven now if he had lived.

His vacant face stared pityingly at the postscript. Excuse bad writing. Hurry. Piano downstairs. Coming out of her shell. Row with her in the XL Café about the bracelet. Wouldn't eat her cakes or speak or look. Saucebox. He sopped other dies of bread in the gravy and ate piece after piece of kidney. Twelve and six a week. Not much. Still, she might do worse. Music hall stage. Young student. He drank a draught of cooler tea to wash down his meal. Then he read the letter again: twice.

O, well: she knows how to mind herself. But if not? No, nothing has happened. Of course it might. Wait in any case till it does. A wild piece of goods. Her slim legs running up the staircase. Destiny. Ripening now. Vain: very.

He smiled with troubled affection at the kitchen window. Day I caught her in the street pinching her cheeks to make them red. Anemic a little. Was given milk too long. On the *Erin's King* that day round the Kish. Damned old tub pitching about. Not a bit funky. Her pale blue scarf loose in the wind with her hair.

> *All dimpled cheeks and curls,*
> *Your head it simply swirls.*

Seaside girls. Torn envelope. Hands stuck in his trousers' pockets, jarvey off for the day, singing. Friend of the family. Swurls, he says. Pier with lamps, summer evening, band.

> *Those girls, those girls,*
> *Those lovely seaside girls.*

Milly too. Young kisses: the first. Far away now past. Mrs Marion. Reading, lying back now, counting the strands of her hair, smiling, braiding.

A soft qualm, regret, flowed down his backbone, increasing. Will happen, yes. Prevent. Useless: can't move. Girl's sweet light lips. Will happen too. He felt the flowing qualm spread over him. Useless to move now. Lips kissed, kissing, kissed. Full gluey woman's lips.

Better where she is down there: away. Occupy her. Wanted a dog to pass the time. Might take a trip down there. August bank holiday, only two and six return. Six weeks off, however. Might work a press pass. Or through M'Coy.

The cat, having cleaned all her fur, returned to the meatstained paper, nosed at it and stalked to the door. She looked back at him, mewing. Wants to go out. Wait before a door sometime it will open. Let her wait. Has the fidgets. Electric. Thunder in the air. Was washing at her ear with her back to the fire too.

He felt heavy, full: then a gentle loosening of his bowels. He stood up, undoing the waistband of his trousers. The cat mewed to him.

—Miaow! he said in answer. Wait till I'm ready.

Heaviness: hot day coming. Too much trouble to fag up the stairs to the landing.

A paper. He liked to read at stool. Hope no ape comes knocking just as I'm.

In the table drawer he found an old number of *Titbits*. He folded it under his armpit, went to the door and opened it. The cat went up in soft bounds. Ah, wanted to go upstairs, curl up in a ball on the bed.

Listening, he heard her voice:

—Come, come, pussy. Come.

He went out through the backdoor into the garden: stood to listen towards the next garden. No sound. Perhaps hanging clothes out to dry. The maid was in the garden. Fine morning.

He bent down to regard a lean file of spearmint growing by the wall. Make a summerhouse here. Scarlet runners. Virginia creepers. Want to manure the whole place over, scabby soil. A coat of liver of sulphur. All soil like that without dung. Household slops. Loam, what is this that is? The hens in the next garden: their droppings are very good top dressing. Best of all though are the cattle, especially when they are fed on those oilcakes. Mulch of dung. Best thing to clean ladies' kid gloves. Dirty cleans. Ashes too. Reclaim the whole place. Grow peas in that corner there. Lettuce. Always have fresh greens then. Still gardens have their drawbacks. That bee or bluebottle here Whitmonday.

He walked on. Where is my hat, by the way? Must have put it back on the peg. Or hanging up on the floor. Funny I don't remember that. Hallstand too full. Four umbrellas, her raincloak. Picking up the letters. Drago's shopbell ringing. Queer I was just thinking that moment. Brown brillantined hair over his collar. Just had a wash and brushup. Wonder have I time for a bath this morning. Tara street. Chap in the paybox there got away James Stephens, they say. O'Brien.

Deep voice that fellow Dlugacz has. Agendath what is it? Now, my miss. Enthusiast.

He kicked open the crazy door of the jakes. Better be careful not to get these trousers dirty for the funeral. He went in, bowing his head under the low lintel. Leaving the door ajar, amid the stench of mouldy limewash and stale cobwebs he undid his braces. Before sitting down he peered through a chink up at the nextdoor windows. The king was in his countinghouse. Nobody.

Asquat on the cuckstool he folded out his paper, turning its pages over on his bared knees. Something new and easy. No great hurry. Keep it a bit. Our prize titbit: *Matcham's Masterstroke.* Written by Mr Philip Beaufoy, Playgoers' Club, London. Payment at the rate of one guinea a column has been made to the writer. Three and a half. Three pounds three. Three pounds, thirteen and six.

Quietly he read, restraining himself, the first column and, yielding but resisting, began the second. Midway, his last resistance yielding, he allowed his bowels to ease themselves quietly as he read, reading still patiently that slight constipation of yesterday quite gone. Hope it's not too big bring on piles again. No, just right. So. Ah! Costive. One tabloid of cascara sagrada. Life might be so. It did not move or touch him but it was something quick and neat. Print anything now. Silly season. He read on, seated calm above his own rising smell. Neat certainly. *Matcham often thinks of the masterstroke by which he won the laughing witch who now.* Begins and ends morally. *Hand in hand.* Smart. He glanced back through what he had read and, while feeling his water flow quietly, he envied kindly Mr Beaufoy who had written it and received payment of three pounds, thirteen and six.

Might manage a sketch. By Mr and Mrs L. M. Bloom. Invent a story for some proverb. Which? Time I used to try jotting down on my cuff what she said dressing. Dislike dressing together. Nicked myself shaving. Biting her nether lip, hooking the placket of her skirt. Timing her. 9.15. Did Roberts pay you yet? 9.20. What had Gretta Conroy on? 9.23. What possessed me to buy this comb? 9.24. I'm swelled after that cabbage. A speck of dust on the patent leather of her boot.

Rubbing smartly in turn each welt against her stockinged calf. Morning after the bazaar dance when May's band played Ponchielli's dance of the hours. Explain that: morning hours, noon, then evening coming on, then night hours. Washing her teeth. That was the first night. Her head dancing. Her fansticks clicking. Is that Boylan well off? He has money. Why? I noticed he had a good rich smell off his breath dancing. No use humming then. Allude to it. Strange kind of music that last night. The mirror was in shadow. She rubbed her handglass briskly on her woollen vest against her full wagging bub. Peering into it. Lines in her eyes. It wouldn't pan out somehow.

Evening hours, girls in grey gauze. Night hours then: black with daggers and eyemasks. Poetical idea: pink, then golden, then grey, then black. Still, true to life also. Day: then the night.

He tore away half the prize story sharply and wiped himself with it. Then he girded up his trousers, braced and buttoned himself. He pulled back the jerky shaky door of the jakes and came forth from the gloom into the air.

In the bright light, lightened and cooled in limb, he eyed carefully his black trousers: the ends, the knees, the houghs of the knees. What time is the funeral? Better find out in the paper.

A creak and a dark whirr in the air high up. The bells of George's church. They tolled the hour: loud dark iron.

> *Heigho! Heigho!*
> *Heigho! Heigho!*
> *Heigho! Heigho!*

Quarter to. There again: the overtone following through the air. A third.

Poor Dignam!

5

By lorries along sir John Rogerson's quay Mr Bloom walked soberly, past Windmill lane, Leask's the linseed crusher, the postal telegraph office. Could have given that address too. And past the sailors' home. He turned from the morning noises of the quayside and walked through Lime street. By Brady's cottages a boy for the skins lolled, his bucket of offal linked, smoking a chewed fagbutt. A smaller girl with scars of eczema on her forehead eyed him, listlessly holding her battered caskhoop. Tell him if he smokes he won't grow. O let him! His life isn't such a bed of roses. Waiting outside pubs to bring da home. Come home to ma, da. Slack hour: won't be many there. He crossed Townsend street, passed the frowning face of Bethel. El, yes: house of: Aleph, Beth. And past Nichols' the undertaker. At eleven it is. Time enough. Daresay Corny Kelleher bagged the job for O'Neill's. Singing with his eyes shut. Corny. Met her once in the park. In the dark. What a lark. Police tout. Her name and address she then told with my tooraloom tooraloom tay. O, surely he bagged it. Bury him cheap in a whatyoumaycall. With my tooraloom, tooraloom, tooraloom, tooraloom.

In Westland row he halted before the window of the Belfast and Oriental Tea Company and read the legends of leadpapered packets: choice blend, finest quality, family tea. Rather warm. Tea. Must get some from Tom Kernan. Couldn't ask him at a funeral, though. While his eyes still read blandly he took off his hat quietly inhaling his hairoil and sent his right hand with slow grace over his brow and hair. Very warm morning. Under their dropped lids his eyes found the tiny bow of the leather headband inside his high grade ha. Just there. His right hand came down into the bowl of his hat. His fingers found quickly a card behind the headband and transferred it to his waistcoat pocket.

So warm. His right hand once more more slowly went over his brow and hair. Then he put on his hat again, relieved: and read again: choice blend, made of the finest Ceylon brands. The far east. Lovely spot it must be: the garden of the world, big lazy leaves to float about on, cactuses, flowery meads, snaky lianas they call them. Wonder is it like that. Those Cinghalese lobbing about in the sun in *dolce far niente*, not doing a hand's turn all day. Sleep six months out of twelve. Too hot to quarrel. Influence of the climate. Lethargy. Flowers of idleness. The air feeds most. Azotes. Hothouse in Botanic gardens. Sensitive plants. Waterlilies. Petals too tired to. Sleeping sickness in the air. Walk on roseleaves. Imagine trying to eat tripe and cowheel. Where was the chap I saw in that picture somewhere? Ah yes, in the dead sea floating on his back, reading a book with a parasol open. Couldn't sink if you tried: so thick with salt. Because the weight of the water, no, the weight of the body in the water is equal to the weight of the what? Or is it the volume is equal to the weight? It's a law something like that. Vance in High school cracking his fingerjoints, teaching. The college curriculum. Cracking curriculum. What is weight really when you say the weight? Thirtytwo feet per second per second. Law of falling bodies: per second per second. They all fall to the ground. The earth. It's the force of gravity of the earth is the weight.

He turned away and sauntered across the road. How did she walk with her sausages? Like that something. As he walked he took the folded *Freeman* from his sidepocket, unfolded it, rolled it lengthwise in a baton and tapped it at each sauntering step against his trouserleg. Careless air: just drop in to see. Per second per second. Per second for every second it means. From the curbstone he darted a keen glance through the door of the postoffice. Too late box. Post here. No-one. In.

He handed the card through the brass grill.

—Are there any letters for me? he asked.

While the postmistress searched a pigeonhole he gazed at the recruiting poster with soldiers of all arms on parade: and held the tip of his baton against his nostrils, smelling freshprinted rag paper. No answer probably. Went too far last time.

The postmistress handed him back through the grill his card with a letter. He thanked her and glanced rapidly at the typed envelope.

Henry Flower Esq,
c/o P. O. Westland Row,
City.

Answered anyhow. He slipped card and letter into his sidepocket, reviewing again the soldiers on parade. Where's old Tweedy's regiment? Castoff soldier. There: bearskin cap and hackle plume. No, he's a grenadier. Pointed cuffs. There he is: royal Dublin fusiliers. Redcoats. Too showy. That must be why the women go after them. Uniform. Easier to enlist and drill. Maud Gonne's letter about taking them off O'Connell street at night: disgrace to our Irish capital. Griffith's paper is on the same tack now: an army rotten with venereal disease: overseas or halfseasover empire. Half baked they look: hypnotised like. Eyes front. Mark time. Table: able. Bed: ed. The King's own. Never see him dressed up as a fireman or a bobby. A mason, yes.

He strolled out of the postoffice and turned to the right. Talk: as if that would mend matters. His hand went into his pocket and a forefinger felt its way under the flap of the envelope, ripping it open in jerks. Women will pay a lot of heed, I don't think. His fingers drew forth the letter the letter and crumpled the envelope in his pocket. Something pinned on: photo perhaps. Hair? No.

M'Coy. Get rid of him quickly. Take me out of my way. Hate company when you.

—Hello, Bloom. Where are you off to?

—Hello, M'Coy. Nowhere in particular.

—How's the body?

—Fine. How are you?

—Just keeping alive, M'Coy said.

His eyes on the black tie and clothes he asked with low respect:

—Is there any . . . no trouble I hope? I see you're . . .

—O, no, Mr Bloom said. Poor Dignam, you know. The funeral is today.

—To be sure, poor fellow. So it is. What time?

A photo it isn't. A badge maybe.

—E . . .eleven, Mr Bloom answered.

—I must try to get out there, M'Coy said. Eleven, is it? I only heard it last night. Who was telling me? Holohan. You know Hoppy?

—I know.

Mr Bloom gazed across the road at the outsider drawn up before the door of the Grosvenor. The porter hoisted the valise up on the well. She stood still, waiting, while the man, husband, brother, like her, searched his pockets for change. Stylish kind of coat with that roll collar, warm for a day like this, looks like blanketcloth. Careless stand of her with her hands in those patch pockets. Like that haughty creature at the polo match. Women all for caste till you touch the spot. Handsome is and handsome does. Reserved about to yield. The honourable Mrs and Brutus is an honourable man. Possess her once take the starch out of her.

—I was with Bob Doran, he's on one of his periodical bends, and what do you call him Bantam Lyons. Just down there in Conway's we were.

Doran Lyons in Conway's. She raised a gloved hand to her hair. In came Hoppy. Having a wet. Drawing back his head and gazing far from beneath his vailed eyelids he saw the bright fawn skin shine in the glare, the braided drums. Clearly I can see today. Moisture about gives long sight perhaps. Talking of one thing or another. Lady's hand. Which side will she get up?

—And he said: *Sad thing about our poor friend Paddy! What Paddy?* I said. *Poor little Paddy Dignam*, he said.

Off to the country: Broadstone probably. High brown boots with laces dangling. Wellturned foot. What is he foostering over that change for? Sees me looking. Eye out for other fellow always. Good fallback. Two strings to her bow.

—*Why?* I said. *What's wrong with him?* I said.

Proud: rich: silk stockings.

—Yes, Mr Bloom said.

He moved a little to the side of M'Coy's talking head. Getting up in a minute.

—*What's wrong with him?* He said. *He's dead*, he said. And, faith, he filled up. *Is it Paddy Dignam?* I said. I couldn't believe it when I heard it. I was with him no later than Friday last or Thursday was it in the Arch. *Yes*, he said. *He's gone. He died on Monday, poor fellow.*

Watch! Watch! Silk flash rich stockings white. Watch!

A heavy tramcar honking its gong slewed between.

Lost it. Curse your noisy pugnose. Feels locked out of it. Paradise and the peri. Always happening like that. The very moment. Girl in

Eustace street hallway Monday was it settling her garter. Her friend covering the display of. *Esprit de corps*. Well, what are you gaping at?

—Yes, yes, Mr Bloom said after a dull sigh. Another gone.

—One of the best, M'Coy said.

The tram passed. They drove off towards the Loop Line bridge, her rich gloved hand on the steel grip. Flicker, flicker: the laceflare of her hat in the sun: flicker, flick.

—Wife well, I suppose? M'Coy's changed voice said.

—O, yes, Mr Bloom said. Tiptop, thanks.

He unrolled the newspaper baton idly and read idly:

> *What is home without*
> *Plumtree's Potted Meat?*
> *Incomplete.*
> *With it an abode of bliss.*

—My missus has just got an engagement. At least it's not settled yet.

Valise tack again. By the way no harm. I'm off that, thanks.

Mr Bloom turned his largelidded eyes with unhasty friendliness.

—My wife too, he said. She's going to sing at a swagger affair in the Ulster Hall, Belfast, on the twentyfifth.

—That so? M'Coy said. Glad to hear that, old man. Who's getting it up?

Mrs Marion Bloom. Not up yet. Queen was in her bedroom eating bread and. No book. Blackened court cards laid along her thigh by sevens. Dark lady and fair man. Letter. Cat furry black ball. Torn strip of envelope.

> *Love's*
> *Old*
> *Sweet*
> *Song*
> *Comes lo-ove's old . . .*

—It's a kind of a tour, don't you see, Mr Bloom said thoughtfully. *Sweeeet song.* There's a committee formed. Part shares and part profits.

M'Coy nodded, picking at his moustache stubble.

—O, well, he said. That's good news.

He moved to go.

—Well, glad to see you looking fit, he said. Meet you knocking around.

—Yes, Mr Bloom said.

—Tell you what, M'Coy said. You might put down my name at the funeral, will you? I'd like to go but I mightn't be able, you see. There's a drowning case at Sandycove may turn up and then the coroner and myself would have to go down if the body is found. You just shove in my name if I'm not there, will you?

—I'll do that, Mr Bloom said, moving to get off. That'll be all right.

—Right, M'Coy said brightly. Thanks, old man. I'd go if I possibly could. Well, tolloll. Just C. P. M'Coy will do.

—That will be done, Mr Bloom answered firmly.

Didn't catch me napping that wheeze. The quick touch. Soft mark. I'd like my job. Valise I have a particular fancy for. Leather. Capped corners, rivetted edges, double action lever lock. Bob Cowley lent him his for the Wicklow regatta concert last year and never heard tidings of it from that good day to this.

Mr Bloom, strolling towards Brunswick street, smiled. My missus has just got an. Reedy freckled soprano. Cheeseparing nose. Nice enough in its way: for a little ballad. No guts in it. You and me, don't you know: in the same boat. Softsoaping. Give you the needle that would. Can't he hear the difference? Think he's that way inclined a bit. Against my grain somehow. Thought that Belfast would fetch him. I hope that smallpox up there doesn't get worse. Suppose she wouldn't let herself be vaccinated again. Your wife and my wife.

Wonder is he pimping after me?

Mr Bloom stood at the corner, his eyes wandering over the multicoloured hoardings. Cantrell and Cochrane's Ginger Ale (Aromatic). Clery's Summer Sale. No, he's going on straight. Hello. *Leah* tonight. Mrs Bandmann Palmer. Like to see her again in that. *Hamlet* she played last night. Male impersonator. Perhaps he was a woman. Why Ophelia committed suicide. Poor papa! How he used to talk of Kate Bateman in that. Outside the Adelphi in London waited all the afternoon to get in. Year before I was born that was: sixtyfive. And Ristori in Vienna. What is this the right name is? By Mosenthal it is. Rachel, is it? No. The scene he was always talking about where the old blind Abraham recognises the voice and puts his fingers on his face.

—Nathan's voice! His son's voice! I hear the voice of Nathan who left his father to die of grief and misery in my arms, who left the house of his father and left the God of his father.

Every word is so deep, Leopold.

Poor papa! Poor man! I'm glad I didn't go into the room to look at his face. That day! O, dear! O, dear! Ffoo! Well, perhaps it was best for him.

Mr Bloom went round the corner and passed the drooping nags of the hazard. No use thinking of it any more. Nosebag time. Wish I hadn't met that M'Coy fellow.

He came nearer and heard a crunching of gilded oats, the gently champing teeth. Their full buck eyes regarded him as he went by, amid the sweet oaten reek of horsepiss. Their Eldorado. Poor jugginses! Damn all they know or care about anything with their long noses stuck in nosebags. Too full for words. Still they get their feed all right and their doss. Gelded too: a stump of black guttapercha wagging limp between their haunches. Might be happy all the same that way. Good poor brutes they look. Still their neigh can be very irritating.

He drew the letter from his pocket and folded it into the newspaper he carried. Might just walk into her here. The lane is safer.

He passed the cabman's shelter. Curious the life of drifting cabbies. All weathers, all places, time or setdown, no will of their own. *Voglio e non.* Like to give them an odd cigarette. Sociable. Shout a few flying syllables as they pass. He hummed:

> *Là ci darem la mano*
> *La la lala la la.*

He turned into Cumberland street and, going on some paces, halted in the lee of the station wall. No-one. Meade's timberyard. Piled balks. Ruins and tenements. With careful tread he passed over a hopscotch court with its forgotten pickeystone. Not a sinner. Near the timberyard a squatted child at marbles, alone, shooting the taw with a cunnythumb. A wise tabby, a blinking sphinx, watched from her warm sill. Pity to disturb them. Mohammed cut a piece out of his mantle not to wake her. Open it. And once I played marbles when I went to that old dame's school. She liked mignonette. Mrs Ellis's. And Mr? He opened the letter within the newspaper.

A flower. I think it's a. A yellow flower with flattened petals. Not annoyed then? What does she say?

Dear Henry

I got your last letter to me and thank you very much for it. I am sorry you did not like my last letter. Why did you enclose the stamps? I am awfully angry with you. I do wish I could punish you for that. I called you naughty boy because I do not like that other world. Please tell me what is the real meaning of that word? Are you not happy in your home you poor little naughty boy? I do wish I could do something for you. Please tell me what you think of poor me. I often think of the beautiful name you have. Dear Henry, when will we meet? I think of you so often you have no idea. I have never felt myself so much drawn to a man as you. I feel so bad about. Please write me a long letter and tell me more. Remember if you do not I will punish you. So now you know what I will do to you, you naughty boy, if you do not wrote. O how I long to meet you. Henry dear, do not deny my request before my patience are exhausted. Then I will tell you all. Goodbye now, naughty darling, I have such a bad headache. today. and write *by return* to your longing

Martha

P. S. Do tell me what kind of perfume does your wife use. I want to know.

He tore the flower gravely from its pinhold smelt its almost no smell and placed it in his heart pocket. Language of flowers. They like it because no-one can hear. Or a poison bouquet to strike him down. Then walking slowly forward he read the letter again, murmuring here and there a word. Angry tulips with you darling manflower punish your cactus if you don't please poor forgetmenot how I long violets to dear roses when we soon anemone meet all naughty nightstalk wife Martha's perfume. Having read it all he took it from the newspaper and put it back in his sidepocket.

Weak joy opened his lips. Changed since the first letter. Wonder did she wrote it herself. Doing the indignant: a girl of good family like me, respectable character. Could meet one Sunday after the rosary. Thank you: not having any. Usual love scrimmage. Then running round corners. Bad as a row with Molly. Cigar has a cooling effect. Narcotic. Go further next time. Naughty boy: punish: afraid of words, of course. Brutal, why not? Try it anyhow. A bit at a time.

Fingering still the letter in his pocket he drew the pin out of it. Common pin, eh? He threw it on the road. Out of her clothes somewhere: pinned together. Queer the number of pins they always have. No roses without thorns.

Flat Dublin voices bawled in his head. Those two sluts that night in the Coombe, linked together in the rain.

> *O, Mairy lost the pin of her drawers.*
> *She didn't know what to do*
> *To keep it up,*
> *To keep it up.*

It? Them. Such a bad headache. Has her roses probably. Or sitting all day typing. Eyefocus bad for stomach nerves. What perfume does your wife use. Now could you make out a thing like that?

To keep it up.

Martha, Mary. I saw that picture somewhere I forget now old master or faked for money. He is sitting in their house, talking. Mysterious. Also the two sluts in the Coombe would listen.

To keep it up.

Nice kind of evening feeling. No more wandering about. Just loll there: quiet dusk: let everything rip. Forget. Tell about places you have been, strange customs. The other one, jar on her head, was getting the supper: fruit, olives, lovely cool water out of a well, stonecold like the hole in the wall at Ashtown. Must carry a paper goblet next time I go to the trottingmatches. She listens with big dark soft eyes. Tell her: more and more: all. Then a sigh: silence. Long long long rest.

Going under the railway arch he took out the envelope, tore it swiftly in shreds and scattered them towards the road. The shreds fluttered away, sank in the dank air: a white flutter, then all sank.

Henry Flower. You could tear up a cheque for a hundred pounds in the same way. Simple bit of paper. Lord Iveagh once cashed a sevenfigure cheque for a million in the bank of Ireland. Shows you the money to be made out of porter. Still the other brother lord Ardilaun has to change his shirt four times a day, they say. Skin breeds lice or vermin. A million pounds, wait a moment. Twopence a pint, fourpence a quart, eightpence a gallon of porter, no, one and fourpence a gallon of porter. One and four into twenty: fifteen about. Yes, exactly. Fifteen millions of barrels of porter.

What am I saying barrels? Gallons. About a million barrels all the same.

An incoming train clanked heavily above his head, coach after coach. Barrels bumped in his head: dull porter slopped and churned inside. The bungholes sprang open and a huge dull flood leaked out, flowing together, winding through mudflats all over the level land, a lazy pooling swirl of liquor bearing along wideleaved flowers of its froth.

He had reached the open backdoor of All Hallows. Stepping into the porch he doffed his hat, took the card from his pocket and tucked it again behind the leather headband. Damn it. I might have tried to work M'Coy for a pass to Mullingar.

Same notice on the door. Sermon by the very reverend John Conmee S. J. on saint Peter Claver S. J. and the African Mission. Prayers for the conversion of Gladstone they had too when he was almost unconscious. The protestants are the same. Convert Dr William J. Walsh D.D. to the true religion. Save China's millions. Wonder how they explain it to the heathen Chinee. Prefer an ounce of opium. Celestials. Rank heresy for them. Buddha their god lying on his side in the museum. Taking it easy with hand under his cheek. Josssticks burning. Not like Ecce Homo. Crown of thorns and cross. Clever idea Saint Patrick the shamrock. Chopsticks? Conmee: Martin Cunningham knows him: distinguishedlooking. Sorry I didn't work him about getting Molly into the choir instead of that Father Farley who looked a fool but wasn't. They're taught that. He's not going out in bluey specs with the sweat rolling off him to baptise blacks, is he? The glasses would take their fancy, flashing. Like to see them sitting round in a ring with blub lips, entranced, listening. Still life. Lap it up like milk, I suppose.

The cold smell of sacred stone called him. He trod the worn steps, pushed the swingdoor and entered softly by the rere.

Something going on: some sodality. Pity so empty. Nice discreet place to be next some girl. Who is my neighbour? Jammed by the hour to slow music. That woman at midnight mass. Seventh heaven. Women knelt in the benches with crimson halters round their necks, heads bowed. A batch knelt at the altarrails. The priest went along

94

by them, murmuring, holding the thing in his hands. He stopped at each, took out a communion, shook a drop or two (are they in water?) off it and put it neatly into her mouth. Her hat and head sank. Then the next one. Her hat sank at once. Then the next one: a small old woman. The priest bent down to put it into her mouth, murmuring all the time. Latin. The next one. Shut your eyes and open your mouth. What? *Corpus:* body. Corpse. Good idea the Latin. Stupefies them first. Hospice for the dying. They don't seem to chew it: only swallow it down. Rum idea: eating bits of a corpse. Why the cannibals cotton to it.

He stood aside watching their blind masks pass down the aisle, one by one, and seek their places. He approached a bench and seated himself in its corner, nursing his hat and newspaper. These pots we have to wear. We ought to have hats modelled on our heads. They were about him here and there, with heads still bowed in their crimson halters, waiting for it to melt in their stomachs. Something like those mazzoth: it's that sort of bread: unleavened shewbread. Look at them. Now I bet it makes them feel happy. Lollipop. It does. Yes, bread of angels it's called. There's a big idea behind it, kind of kingdom of God is within you feel. First communicants. Hokypoky penny a lump. Then feel all like one family party, same in the theatre, all in the same swim. They do. I'm sure of that. Not so lonely. In our confraternity. Then come out a bit spreeish. Let off steam. Thing is if you really believe in it. Lourdes cure, waters of oblivion, and the Knock apparition, statues bleeding. Old fellow asleep near that confessionbox. Hence those snores. Blind faith. Safe in the arms of kingdom come. Lulls all pain. Wake this time next year.

He saw the priest stow the communion cup away, well in, and kneel an instant before it, showing a large grey bootsole from under the lace affair he had on. Suppose he lost the pin of his. He wouldn't know what to do to. Bald spot behind. Letters on his back: I. N. R. I? No: I. H. S. Molly told me one time I asked her. I have sinned: or no: I have suffered, it is. And the other one? Iron nails ran in.

Meet one Sunday after the rosary. Do not deny my request. Turn up with a veil and black bag. Dusk and the light behind her. She might be here with a ribbon round her neck and do the other thing all the same on the sly. Their character. That fellow that turned queen's evidence on the invincibles he used to receive the, Carey was his name, the communion every morning. This very church. Peter Carey, yes. No, Peter Claver I am thinking of. Denis Carey. And just imagine that. Wife and six children at home. And plotting that murder all the time. Those crawthumpers, now that's a good name for them, there's always something shiftylooking about them. They're not straight men of business either. O, no, she's not here: the flower: no, no. By the way, did I tear up that envelope? Yes: under the bridge.

The priest was rinsing out the chalice: then he tossed off the dregs smartly. Wine. Makes it more aristocratic than for example if he drank what they are used to Guinness's porter or some temperance beverage Wheatley's Dublin hop bitters or Cantrell and Cochrane's ginger ale (aromatic). Doesn't give them any of it: shew wine: only the other. Cold comfort. Pious fraud but quite right: otherwise they'd have one old booser worse than another coming along, cadging for a drink. Queer the whole atmosphere of the. Quite right. Perfectly right that is.

Mr Bloom looked back towards the choir. Not going to be any music. Pity. Who has the organ here I wonder? Old Glynn he knew how to make that instrument talk, the *vibrato*: fifty pounds a year they say he had in Gardiner street. Molly was in fine voice that day, the *Stabat Mater* of Rossini. Father Bernard Vaughan's sermon first. Christ or Pilate? Christ, but don't keep us all night over it. Music they wanted. Footdrill stopped. Could hear a pin drop. I told her to pitch her voice against that corner. I could feel the thrill in the air, the full, the people looking up:

Quis est homo.

Some of that old sacred music splendid. Mercadante: seven last words. Mozart's twelfth mass: *Gloria* in that. Those old popes keen on music, on art and statues and pictures of all kinds. Palestrina for example too. They had a gay old time while it lasted. Healthy too, chanting, regular hours, then brew liqueurs. Benedictine. Green Chartreuse. Still, having eunuchs in their choir that was coming it a bit thick. What kind of voice is it? Must be curious to hear after their own strong basses. Connoisseurs. Suppose they wouldn't feel anything after. Kind of a placid. No worry. Fall into flesh, don't they? Gluttons, tall, long legs. Who knows? Eunuch. One way out of it.

He saw the priest bend down and kiss the altar and then face about and bless all the people. All crossed themselves and stood up. Mr Bloom glanced about him and then stood up, looking over the risen hats. Stand up at the gospel of course. Then all settled down on their knees again and he sat back quietly in his bench. The priest came down from the altar, holding the thing out from him, and he and the massboy answered each other in Latin. Then the priest knelt down and began to read off a card:

—O God, our refuge and our strength . . .

Mr Bloom put his face forward to catch the words. English. Throw them the bone. I remember slightly. How long since your last mass? Glorious and immaculate virgin. Joseph, her spouse. Peter and Paul. More interesting if you understood what it was all about. Wonderful organisation certainly, goes like clockwork. Confession. Everyone wants to. Then I will tell you all. Penance. Punish me, please. Great weapon in their hands. More than doctor or solicitor. Woman dying to. And I schschschschschsch. And did you chachachachacha? And why did you? Look down at her ring to find an excuse. Whispering gallery walls have ears. Husband learn to his surprise. God's little joke. Then out she comes. Repentance skindeep. Lovely shame. Pray at an altar. Hail Mary and Holy Mary. Flowers, incense, candles melting. Hide her blushes. Salvation army blatant imitation. Reformed prostitute will address the meeting. How I found the Lord. Squareheaded chaps those must be in Rome: they work the whole show. And don't they rake in the money too? Bequests also: to the P.P. for the time being in his absolute discretion. Masses for the repose of my soul to be said publicly with open doors. Monasteries and convents. The priest in that Fermanagh will case in the witnessbox. No browbeating him. He had his answer pat for everything. Liberty and exaltation of our holy mother the church. The doctors of the church: they mapped out the whole theology of it.

The priest prayed:

—Blessed Michael, archangel, defend us in the hour of conflict. Be our safeguard against the wickedness and snares of the devil (may God restrain him, we humbly pray!): and do thou, O prince of the heavenly host, by the power of God thrust Satan down to hell and with him those other wicked spirits who wander through the world for the ruin of souls.

The priest and the massboy stood up and walked off. All over. The women remained behind: thanksgiving.

Better be shoving along. Brother Buzz. Come around with the plate perhaps. Pay your Easter duty.

He stood up. Hello. Were those two buttons of my waistcoat open all the time? Women enjoy it. Never tell you. But we. Excuse, miss, there's a (whh!) just a (whh!) fluff. Or their skirt behind, placket unhooked. Glimpses of the moon. Annoyed if you don't. Why didn't you tell me before. Still like you better untidy. Good job it wasn't farther south. He passed, discreetly buttoning, down the aisle and out through the main door into the light. He stood a moment unseeing by the cold black marble bowl while before him and behind two worshippers dipped furtive hands in the low tide of holy water. Trams: a car of Prescott's dyeworks: a widow in her weeds. Notice because I'm in mourning myself. He covered himself. How goes the time? Quarter past. Time enough yet. Better get that lotion made up. Where is this? Ah yes, the last time. Sweny's in Lincoln place. Chemists rarely move. Their green and gold beaconjars too heavy to stir. Hamilton Long's, founded in the year of the flood. Huguenot churchyard near there. Visit some day.

He walked southward along Westland row. But the recipe is in the other trousers. O, and I forgot that latchkey too. Bore this funeral affair. O well, poor fellow, it's not his fault. When was it I got it made up last? Wait. I changed a sovereign I remember. First of the month it must have been or the second. O, he can look it up in the prescriptions book.

The chemist turned back page after page. Sandy shrivelled smell he seems to have. Shrunken skull. And old. Quest for the philosopher's stone. The alchemists. Drugs age you after mental excitement. Lethargy then. Why? Reaction. A lifetime in a night. Gradually changes your character. Living all the day among herbs, ointments, disinfectants. All his alabaster lilypots. Mortar and pestle. Aq. Dist. Fol. Laur. Te Virid. Smell almost cure you like the dentist's doorbell. Doctor Whack. He ought to physic himself a bit. Electuary or emulsion. The first fellow that picked an herb to cure himself had a bit of pluck. Simples. Want to be careful. Enough stuff here to chloroform you. Test: turns blue litmus paper red. Chloroform. Overdose of laudanum. Sleeping draughts. Lovephiltres. Paragoric poppysyrup bad for cough. Clogs the pores or the phlegm. Poisons the only cures. Remedy where you least expect it. Clever of nature.

—About a fortnight ago, sir?

—Yes, Mr Bloom said.

He waited by the counter, inhaling slowly the keen reek of drugs, the dusty dry smell of sponges and loofahs. Lot of time taken up telling your aches and pains.

—Sweet almond oil and tincture of benzoin, Mr Bloom said, and then orangeflower water . . .

It certainly did make her skin so delicate white like wax.

—And white wax also, he said.

Brings out the darkness of her eyes. Looking at me, the sheet up to her eyes, Spanish, smelling herself, when I was fixing the links in my cuffs. Those homely recipes are often the best: strawberries for the teeth: nettles and rainwater: oatmeal they say steeped in buttermilk. Skinfood. One of the old queen's sons, duke of Albany was it? had only one skin. Leopold, yes. Three we have. Warts, bunions and pimples to make it worse. But you want a perfume too. What perfume does your? *Peau d'Espagne.* That orangeflower water is so fresh. Nice smell these soaps have. Pure curd soap. Time to get a bath round the corner. Hammam. Turkish. Massage. Dirt gets rolled up in your navel. Nicer if a nice girl did it. Also I think I. Yes I. Do it in the bath. Curious longing I. Water to water. Combine business with pleasure. Pity no time for massage. Feel fresh then all the day. Funeral be rather glum.

—Yes, sir, the chemist said. That was two and nine. Have you brought a bottle?

—No, Mr Bloom said. Make it up, please. I'll call later in the day and I'll take one of these soaps. How much are they?

—Fourpence, sir.

Mr Bloom raised a cake to his nostrils. Sweet lemony wax.

—I'll take this one, he said. That makes three and a penny.

—Yes, sir, the chemist said. You can pay all together, sir, when you come back.

—Good, Mr Bloom said.

He strolled out of the shop, the newspaper baton under his armpit, the coolwrapped soap in his left hand.

At his armpit Bantam Lyons' voice and hand said:

—Hello, Bloom. What's the best news? Is that today's? Show us a minute.

Shaved off his moustache again, by Jove! Long cold upper lip. To look younger. He does look balmy. Younger than I am.

Bantam Lyons's yellow blacknailed fingers unrolled the baton. Wants a wash too. Take off the rough dirt. Good morning, have you used Pears' soap? Dandruff on his shoulders. Scalp wants oiling.

—I want to see about that French horse that's running today, Bantam Lyons said. Where the bugger is it?

He rustled the pleated pages, jerking his chin on his high collar. Barber's itch. Tight collar he'll lose his hair. Better leave him the paper and get shut of him.

—You can keep it, Mr Bloom said.

—Ascot. Gold cup. Wait, Bantam Lyons muttered. Half a mo. Maximum the second.

—I was just going to throw it away, Mr Bloom said.

Bantam Lyons raised his eyes suddenly and leered weakly.

—What's that? his sharp voice said.

—I say you can keep it, Mr Bloom answered. I was going to throw it away that moment.

Bantam Lyons doubted an instant, leering: then thrust the outspread sheets back on Mr Bloom's arms.

—I'll risk it, he said. Here, thanks.

He sped off towards Conway's corner. God speed scut.

Mr Bloom folded the sheets again to a neat square and lodged the soap in it, smiling. Silly lips of that chap. Betting. Regular hotbed of it lately. Messenger boys stealing to put on sixpence. Raffle for large tender turkey. Your Christmas dinner for threepence. Jack Fleming embezzling to gamble then smuggled off to America. Keeps a hotel now. They never come back. Fleshpots of Egypt.

He walked cheerfully towards the mosque of the baths. Remind you of a mosque, redbaked bricks, the minarets. College sports today I see. He eyed the horseshoe poster over the gate of college park: cyclist doubled up like a cod in a pot. Damn bad ad. Now if they had made it round like a wheel. Then the spokes: sports, sports, sports: and the hub big: college. Something to catch the eye.

There's Hornblower standing at the porter's lodge. Keep him on hands: might take a turn in there on the nod. How do you do, Mr Hornblower? How do you do, sir?

Heavenly weather really. If life was always like that. Cricket weather. Sit around under sunshades. Over after over. Out. They can't play it here. Duck for six wickets. Still Captain Culler broke a window in the Kildare street club with a slog to square leg. Donnybrook fair more in their line. And the skulls we were acracking when M'Carthy took the floor. Heatwave. Won't last. Always passing, the stream of life, which in the stream of life we trace is dearer than them all.

Enjoy a bath now: clean trough of water, cool enamel, the gentle tepid stream. This is my body.

He foresaw his pale body reclined in it at full, naked, in a womb of warmth, oiled by scented melting soap, softly laved. He saw his trunk and limbs riprippled over and sustained, buoyed lightly upward, lemonyellow: his navel, bud of flesh: and saw the dark tangled curls of his bush floating, floating hair of the stream around the limp father of thousands, a languid floating flower.

6

Martin Cunningham, first, poked his silkhatted head into the creaking carriage and, entering deftly, seated himself. Mr Power stepped in after him, curving his height with care.

—Come on, Simon.

—After you, Mr Bloom said.

Mr Dedalus covered himself quickly and got in, saying:

—Yes, yes.

—Are we all here now? Martin Cunningham asked. Come along, Bloom.

Mr Bloom entered and sat in the vacant place. He pulled the door to after him and slammed it twice till it shut tight. He passed an arm through the armstrap and looked seriously from the open carriage window at the lowered blinds of the avenue. One dragged aside: an old woman peeping. Nose whiteflattened against the pane. Thanking her stars she was passed over. Extraordinary the interest they take in a corpse. Glad to see us go we give them such trouble coming. Job seems to suit them. Huggermugger in corners. Slop about in slipperslappers for fear he'd wake. Then getting it ready. Laying it out. Molly and Mrs Fleming making the bed. Pull it more to your side. Our windingsheet. Never know who will touch you dead. Wash and shampoo. I believe they clip the nails and the hair. Keep a bit in an envelope. Grows all the same after. Unclean job.

All waited. Nothing was said. Stowing in the wreaths probably. I am sitting on something hard. Ah, that soap: in my hip pocket. Better shift it out of that. Wait for an opportunity.

All waited. Then wheels were heard from in front, turning: then nearer: then horses' hoofs. A jolt. Their carriage began to move, creaking and swaying. Other hoofs and creaking wheels started behind. The blinds of the avenue passed and number nine with its craped knocker, door ajar. At walking pace.

They waited still, their knees jogging, till they had turned and were passing along the tramtracks. Tritonville road. Quicker. The wheels rattled rolling over the cobbled causeway and the crazy glasses shook rattling in the doorframes.

—What way is he taking us? Mr Power asked through both windows.

—Irishtown, Martin Cunningham said. Ringsend. Brunswick street.

Mr Dedalus nodded, looking out.

—That's a fine old custom, he said. I am glad to see it has not died out.

All watched awhile through their windows caps and hats lifted by passers. Respect. The carriage swerved from the tramtrack to the smoother road past Watery lane. Mr Bloom at gaze saw a lithe young man, clad in mourning, a wide hat.

—There's a friend of yours gone by, Dedalus, he said.

—Who is that?

—Your son and heir.

—Where is he? Mr Dedalus said, stretching over across.

The carriage, passing the open drains and mounds of rippedup roadway before the tenement houses, lurched round the corner and, swerving back to the tramtrack, rolled on noisily with chattering wheels. Mr Dedalus fell back, saying:

—Was that Mulligan cad with him? His *fidus Achates*!

—No, Mr Bloom said. He was alone.

—Down with his aunt Sally, I suppose, Mr Dedalus said, the Goulding faction, the drunken little costdrawer and Crissie, papa's little lump of dung, the wise child that knows her own father.

Mr Bloom smiled joylessly on Ringsend road. Wallace Bros: the bottleworks: Dodder bridge.

Richie Goulding and the legal bag. Goulding, Collis and Ward he calls the firm. His jokes are getting a bit damp. Great card he was. Waltzing in Stamer street with Ignatius Gallaher on a Sunday morning, the landlady's two hats pinned on his head. Out on the rampage all night. Beginning to tell on him now: that backache of his, I fear. Wife ironing his back. Thinks he'll cure it with pills. All breadcrumbs they are. About six hundred per cent profit.

—He's in with a lowdown crowd, Mr Dedalus snarled. That Mulligan is a contaminated bloody doubledyed ruffian by all accounts. His name stinks all over Dublin. But with the help of God and His blessed mother I'll make it my business to write a letter one of those days to his mother or his aunt or whatever she is that will open her eye as wide as a gate. I'll tickle his catastrophe, believe you me.

He cried above the clatter of the wheels:

—I won't have her bastard of a nephew ruin my son. A counterjumper's son. Selling tapes in my cousin, Peter Paul M'Swiney's. Not likely.

He ceased. Mr Bloom glanced from his angry moustache to Mr Power's mild face and Martin Cunningham's eyes and beard, gravely shaking. Noisy selfwilled man. Full of his son. He is right. Something to hand on. If little Rudy had lived. See him grow up. Hear his voice in the house. Walking beside Molly in an Eton suit. My son. Me in his eyes. Strange feeling it would be. From me. Just a chance. Must have been that morning in Raymond terrace she was at the window watching the two dogs at it by the wall of the cease to do evil. And the sergeant grinning up. She had that cream gown on with the rip she never stitched. Give us a touch, Poldy. God, I'm dying for it. How life begins.

Got big then. Had to refuse the Greystones concert. My son inside her. I could have helped him on in life. I could. Make him independent. Learn German too.

—Are we late? Mr Power asked.

—Ten minutes, Martin Cunningham said, looking at his watch.

Molly. Milly. Same thing watered down. Her tomboy oaths. O jumping Jupiter! Ye gods and little fishes! Still, she's a dear girl. Soon be a woman. Mullingar. Dearest Papli. Young student. Yes, yes: a woman too. Life, life.

The carriage heeled over and back, their four trunks swaying.

—Corny might have given us a more commodious yoke, Mr Power said.

—He might, Mr Dedalus said, if he hadn't that squint troubling him. Do you follow me?

He closed his left eye. Martin Cunningham began to brush away crustcrumbs from under his thighs.

—What is this, he said, in the name of God? Crumbs?

—Someone seems to have been making a picnic party here lately, Mr Power said.

All raised their thighs and eyed with disfavour the mildewed buttonless leather of the seats. Mr Dedalus, twisting his nose, frowned downward and said:

—Unless I'm greatly mistaken. What do you think, Martin?

—It struck me too, Martin Cunningham said.

Mr Bloom set his thigh down. Glad I took that bath. Feel my feet quite clean. But I wish Mrs Fleming had darned these socks better.

Mr Dedalus sighed resignedly.

—After all, he said, it's the most natural thing in the world.

—Did Tom Kernan turn up? Martin Cunningham asked, twirling the peak of his beard gently.

—Yes, Mr Bloom answered. He's behind with Ned Lambert and Hynes.

—And Corny Kelleher himself? Mr Power asked.

—At the cemetery, Martin Cunningham said.

—I met M'Coy this morning, Mr Bloom said. He said he'd try to come.

The carriage halted short.

—What's wrong?

—We're stopped.

—Where are we?

Mr Bloom put his head out of the window.

—The grand canal, he said.

Gasworks. Whooping cough they say it cures. Good job Milly never got it. Poor children! Doubles them up black and blue in convulsions. Shame really. Got off lightly with illnesses compared. Only measles. Flaxseed tea. Scarlatina, influenza epidemics. Canvassing for death. Don't miss this chance. Dogs' home over there. Poor old Athos! Be good to Athos, Leopold, is my last wish. Thy will be done. We obey them in the grave. A dying scrawl. He took it to heart, pined away. Quiet brute. Old men's dogs usually are.

A raindrop spat on his hat. He drew back and saw an instant of shower spray dots over the grey flags. Apart. Curious. Like through a colander. I thought it would. My boots were creaking I remember now.

—The weather is changing, he said quietly.

—A pity it did not keep up fine, Martin Cunningham said.

—Wanted for the country, Mr Power said. There's the sun again coming out.

Mr Dedalus, peering through his glasses towards the veiled sun, hurled a mute curse at the sky.

—It's as uncertain as a child's bottom, he said.

—We're off again.

The carriage turned again its stiff wheels and their trunks swayed gently. Martin Cunningham twirled more quickly the peak of his beard.

—Tom Kernan was immense last night, he said. And Paddy Leonard taking him off to his face.

—O, draw him out, Martin, Mr Power said eagerly. Wait till you hear him, Simon, on Ben Dollard's singing of *The Croppy Boy*.

—Immense, Martin Cunningham said pompously. *His singing of that simple ballad, Martin, is the most trenchant rendering I ever heard in the whole course of my experience.*

—Trenchant, Mr Power said laughing. He's dead nuts on that. And the retrospective arrangement.

—Did you read Dan Dawson's speech? Martin Cunningham asked.

—I did not then, Mr Dedalus said. Where is it?

—In the paper this morning.

Mr Bloom took the paper from his inside pocket. That book I must change for her.

—No, no, Mr Dedalus said quickly. Later on please.

Mr Bloom's glance travelled down the edge of the paper, scanning the deaths: Callan, Coleman, Dignam, Fawcett, Lowry, Naumann, Peake, what Peake is that? is it the chap was in Crosbie and Alleyne's? no, Sexton, Urbright. Inked characters fast fading on the frayed breaking paper. Thanks to the Little Flower. Sadly missed. To the inexpressible grief of his. Aged 88 after a long and tedious illness. Month's mind: Quinlan. On whose soul Sweet Jesus have mercy.

> *It is now a month since dear Henry fled*
> *To his home up above in the sky*
> *While his family weeps and mourns his loss*
> *Hoping some day to meet him on high.*

I tore up the envelope? Yes. Where did I put her letter after I read it in the bath? He patted his waistcoatpocket. There all right. Dear Henry fled. Before my patience are exhausted.

National school. Meade's yard. The hazard. Only two there now. Nodding. Full as a tick. Too much bone in their skulls. The other trotting round with a fare. An hour ago I was passing there. The jarvies raised their hats.

A pointsman's back straightened itself upright suddenly against a tramway standard by Mr Bloom's window. Couldn't they invent something automatic so that the wheel itself much handier? Well but that fellow would lose his job then? Well but then another fellow would get a job making the new invention?

Antient concert rooms. Nothing on there. A man in a buff suit with a crape armlet. Not much grief there. Quarter mourning. People in law perhaps.

They went past the bleak pulpit of saint Mark's, under the railway bridge, past the Queen's theatre: in silence. Hoardings: Eugene Stratton, Mrs Bandmann Palmer. Could I go to see *Leah* tonight, I wonder. I said I. Or the *Lily of Killarney*? Elster Grimes Opera Company. Big powerful change. Wet bright bills for next week. *Fun on the Bristol.* Martin Cunningham could work a pass for the Gaiety. Have to stand a drink or two. As broad as it's long.

He's coming in the afternoon. Her songs.

Plasto's. Sir Philip Crampton's memorial fountain bust. Who was he?

—How do you do? Martin Cunningham said, raising his palm to his brow in salute.

—He doesn't see us, Mr Power said. Yes, he does. How do you do?

—Who? Mr Dedalus asked.

—Blazes Boylan, Mr Power said. There he is airing his quiff.

Just that moment I was thinking.

Mr Dedalus bent across to salute. From the door of the Red Bank the white disc of a straw hat flashed reply: spruce figure: passed.

Mr Bloom reviewed the nails of his left hand, then those of his right hand. The nails, yes. Is there anything more in him that they she sees? Fascination. Worst man in Dublin. That keeps him alive. They sometimes feel what a person is. Instinct. But a type like that. My nails. I am just looking at them: well pared. And after: thinking alone. Body getting a bit softy. I would notice that: from remembering. What causes that? I suppose the skin can't contract quickly enough when the flesh falls off. But the shape is there. The shape is there still. Shoulders. Hips. Plump. Night of the dance dressing. Shift stuck between the cheeks behind.

He clasped his hands between his knees and, satisfied, sent his vacant glance over their faces.

Mr Power asked:

—How is the concert tour getting on, Bloom?

—O, very well, Mr Bloom said. I hear great accounts of it. It's a good idea, you see . . .

—Are you going yourself?

—Well no, Mr Bloom said. In point of fact I have to go down to the county Clare on some private business. You see the idea is to tour the chief towns. What you lose on one you can make up on the other.

—Quite so, Martin Cunningham said. Mary Anderson is up there now.

Have you good artists?

—Louis Werner is touring her, Mr Bloom said. O yes, we'll have all topnobbers. J. C. Doyle and John MacCormack I hope and. The best, in fact.

—And *Madame*, Mr Power said smiling. Last but not least.

Mr Bloom unclasped his hands in a gesture of soft politeness and clasped them. Smith O'Brien. Someone has laid a bunch of flowers there. Woman. Must be his deathday. For many happy returns. The carriage wheeling by Farrell's statue united noiselessly their unresisting knees.

Oot: a dullgarbed old man from the curbstone tendered his wares, his mouth opening: oot.

—Four bootlaces for a penny.

Wonder why he was struck off the rolls. Had his office in Hume street. Same house as Molly's namesake, Tweedy, crown solicitor for Waterford. Has that silk hat ever since. Relics of old decency. Mourning too. Terrible comedown, poor wretch! Kicked about like snuff at a wake. O'Callaghan on his last legs.

And *Madame*. Twenty past eleven. Up. Mrs Fleming is in to clean. Doing her hair, humming: *voglio e non vorrei*. No: *vorrei e non*. Looking at the tips of her hairs to see if they are split. *Mi trema un poco il*. Beautiful on that *tre* her voice is: weeping tone. A thrush. A throstle. There is a word throstle that expresses that.

His eyes passed lightly over Mr Power's goodlooking face. Greyish over the ears. *Madame*: smiling. I smiled back. A smile goes a long way. Only politeness perhaps. Nice fellow. Who knows is that true about the woman he keeps? Not pleasant for the wife. Yet they say, who was it told me, there is no carnal. You would imagine that would get played out pretty quick. Yes, it was Crofton met him one evening bringing her a pound of rumpsteak. What is this she was? Barmaid in Jury's. Or the Moira, was it?

They passed under the hugecloaked Liberator's form.

Martin Cunningham nudged Mr Power.

—Of the tribe of Reuben, he said.

A tall blackbearded figure, bent on a stick, stumping round the corner of Elvery's Elephant house, showed them a curved hand open on his spine.

—In all his pristine beauty, Mr Power said.

Mr Dedalus looked after the stumping figure and said mildly:

—The devil break the hasp of your back!

Mr Power, collapsing in laughter, shaded his face from the window as the carriage passed Gray's statue.

—We have all been there, Martin Cunningham said broadly.

His eyes met Mr Bloom's eyes. He caressed his beard, adding:

—Well, nearly all of us.

Mr Bloom began to speak with sudden eagerness to his companions' faces.

—That's an awfully good one that's going the rounds about Reuben J and the son.

—About the boatman? Mr Power asked.

—Yes. Isn't it awfully good?

—What is that? Mr Dedalus asked. I didn't hear it.

—There was a girl in the case, Mr Bloom began, and he determined to send him to the Isle of Man out of harm's way but when they were both . . .

—What? Mr Dedalus asked. That confirmed bloody hobbledehoy is it?

—Yes, Mr Bloom said. They were both on the way to the boat and he tried to drown . . .

—Drown Barabbas! Mr Dedalus cried. I wish to Christ he did!

Mr Power sent a long laugh down his shaded nostrils.

—No, Mr Bloom said, the son himself . . .

Martin Cunningham thwarted his speech rudely:

—Reuben J and the son were piking it down the quay next the river on their way to the Isle of Man boat and the young chiseller suddenly got loose and over the wall with him into the Liffey.

—For God's sake! Mr Dedalus exclaimed in fright. Is he dead?

—Dead! Martin Cunningham cried. Not he! A boatman got a pole and fished him out by the slack of the breeches and he was landed up to the father on the quay more dead than alive. Half the town was there.

—Yes, Mr Bloom said. But the funny part is . . .

—And Reuben J, Martin Cunningham said, gave the boatman a florin for saving his son's life.

A stifled sigh came from under Mr Power's hand.

—O, he did, Martin Cunningham affirmed. Like a hero. A silver florin.

—Isn't it awfully good? Mr Bloom said eagerly.

—One and eightpence too much, Mr Dedalus said drily.

Mr Power's choked laugh burst quietly in the carriage.

Nelson's pillar.

—Eight plums a penny! Eight for a penny!

—We had better look a little serious, Martin Cunningham said.

Mr Dedalus sighed.

—Ah then indeed, he said, poor little Paddy wouldn't grudge us a laugh. Many a good one he told himself.

—The Lord forgive me! Mr Power said, wiping his wet eyes with his fingers. Poor Paddy! I little thought a week ago when I saw him last and he was in his usual health that I'd be driving after him like this. He's gone from us.

—As decent a little man as ever wore a hat, Mr Dedalus said. He went very suddenly.

—Breakdown, Martin Cunningham said. Heart.

He tapped his chest sadly.

Blazing face: redhot. Too much John Barleycorn. Cure for a red nose. Drink like the devil till it turns adelite. A lot of money he spent colouring it.

Mr Power gazed at the passing houses with rueful apprehension.

—He had a sudden death, poor fellow, he said.

—The best death, Mr Bloom said.

Their wide open eyes looked at him.

—No suffering, he said. A moment and all is over. Like dying in sleep.

No-one spoke.

Dead side of the street this. Dull business by day, land agents, temperance hotel, Falconer's railway guide, civil service college, Gill's, catholic club, the industrious blind. Why? Some reason. Sun or wind. At night too. Chummies and slaveys. Under the patronage of the late Father Mathew. Foundation stone for Parnell. Breakdown. Heart.

White horses with white frontlet plumes came round the Rotunda corner, galloping. A tiny coffin flashed by. In a hurry to bury. A mourning coach. Unmarried. Black for the married. Piebald for bachelors. Dun for a nun.

—Sad, Martin Cunningham said. A child.

A dwarf's face, mauve and wrinkled like little Rudy's was. Dwarf's body, weak as putty, in a whitelined deal box. Burial friendly society pays. Penny a week for a sod of turf. Our. Little. Beggar. Baby. Meant nothing. Mistake of nature. If it's healthy it's from the mother. If not from the man. Better luck next time.

—Poor little thing, Mr Dedalus said. It's well out of it.

The carriage climbed more slowly the hill of Rutland square. Rattle his bones. Over the stones. Only a pauper. Nobody owns.

—In the midst of life, Martin Cunningham said.

—But the worst of all, Mr Power said, is the man who takes his own life.

Martin Cunningham drew out his watch briskly, coughed and put it back.

—The greatest disgrace to have in the family, Mr Power added.

—Temporary insanity, of course, Martin Cunningham said decisively. We must take a charitable view of it.

—They say a man who does it is a coward, Mr Dedalus said.

—It is not for us to judge, Martin Cunningham said.

Mr Bloom, about to speak, closed his lips again. Martin Cunningham's large eyes. Looking away now. Sympathetic human man he is. Intelligent. Like Shakespeare's face. Always a good word to say. They have no mercy on that here or infanticide. Refuse christian burial. They used to drive a stake of wood through his heart in the grave. As if it wasn't broken already. Yet sometimes they repent too late. Found in the riverbed clutching rushes. He looked at me. And that awful drunkard of a wife of his. Setting up house for her time after

112

time and then pawning the furniture on him every Saturday almost. Leading him the life of the damned. Wear the heart out of a stone, that. Monday morning. Start afresh. Shoulder to the wheel. Lord, she must have looked a sight that night Dedalus told me he was in there. Drunk about the place and capering with Martin's umbrella.

And they call me the jewel of Asia,
Of Asia,
The geisha.

He looked away from me. He knows. Rattle his bones.

That afternoon of the inquest. The redlabelled bottle on the table. The room in the hotel with hunting pictures. Stuffy it was. Sunlight through the slats of the Venetian blind. The coroner's sunlit ears, big and hairy. Boots giving evidence. Thought he was asleep first. Then saw like yellow streaks on his face. Had slipped down to the foot of the bed. Verdict: overdose. Death by misadventure. The letter. For my son Leopold.

No more pain. Wake no more. Nobody owns.

The carriage rattled swiftly along Blessington street. Over the stones.

—We are going the pace, I think, Martin Cunningham said.

—God grant he doesn't upset us on the road, Mr Power said.

—I hope not, Martin Cunningham said. That will be a great race tomorrow in Germany. The Gordon Bennett.

—Yes, by Jove, Mr Dedalus said. That will be worth seeing, faith.

As they turned into Berkeley street a streetorgan near the Basin sent over and after them a rollicking rattling song of the halls. Has anybody here seen Kelly? Kay ee double ell wy. Dead March from *Saul.* He's as bad as old Antonio. He left me on my ownio. Pirouette! The *Mater Misericordiae.* Eccles street. My house down there. Big place. Ward for incurables there. Very encouraging. Our Lady's Hospice for the dying. Deadhouse handy underneath. Where old Mrs Riordan died. They look terrible the women. Her feeding cup and rubbing her mouth with the spoon. Then the screen round her bed for her to die. Nice young student that was dressed that bite the bee gave me. He's gone over to the lying-in hospital they told me. From one extreme to the other.

The carriage galloped round a corner: stopped.

—What's wrong now?

A divided drove of branded cattle passed the windows, lowing, slouching by on padded hoofs, whisking their tails slowly on their clotted bony croups. Outside them and through them ran raddled sheep bleating their fear.

—Emigrants, Mr Power said.

—Huuuh! the drover's voice cried, his switch sounding on their flanks. Huuuh! out of that!

Thursday, of course. Tomorrow is killing day. Springers. Cuffe sold them about twentyseven quid each. For Liverpool probably. Roastbeef for old England. They buy up all the juicy ones. And then the fifth quarter lost: all that raw stuff, hide, hair, horns. Comes to a big thing in a year. Dead meat trade. Byproducts of the slaughterhouses for tanneries, soap, margarine. Wonder if that dodge works now getting dicky meat off the train at Clonsilla.

The carriage moved on through the drove.

—I can't make out why the corporation doesn't run a tramline from the parkgate to the quays, Mr Bloom said. All those animals could be taken in trucks down to the boats.

—Instead of blocking up the thoroughfare, Martin Cunningham said. Quite right. They ought to.

—Yes, Mr Bloom said, and another thing I often thought, is to have municipal funeral trams like they have in Milan, you know. Run the line out to the cemetery gates and have special trams, hearse and carriage and all. Don't you see what I mean?

—O, that be damned for a story, Mr Dedalus said. Pullman car and saloon dining room.

—A poor lookout for Corny, Mr Power added.

—Why? Mr Bloom asked, turning to Mr Dedalus. Wouldn't it be more decent than galloping two abreast?

—Well, there's something in that, Mr Dedalus granted.

—And, Martin Cunningham said, we wouldn't have scenes like that when the hearse capsized round Dunphy's and upset the coffin on to the road.

—That was terrible, Mr Power's shocked face said, and the corpse fell about the road. Terrible!

—First round Dunphy's, Mr Dedalus said, nodding. Gordon Bennett cup.

—Praises be to God! Martin Cunningham said piously.

Bom! Upset. A coffin bumped out on to the road. Burst open. Paddy Dignam shot out and rolling over stiff in the dust in a brown habit too large for him. Red face: grey now. Mouth fallen open. Asking what's up now. Quite right to close it. Looks horrid open. Then the insides decompose quickly. Much better to close up all the orifices. Yes, also. With wax. The sphincter loose. Seal up all.

—Dunphy's, Mr Power announced as the carriage turned right.

Dunphy's corner. Mourning coaches drawn up, drowning their grief. A pause by the wayside. Tiptop position for a pub. Expect we'll pull up here on the way back to drink his health. Pass round the consolation. Elixir of life.

But suppose now it did happen. Would he bleed if a nail say cut him in the knocking about? He would and he wouldn't, I suppose. Depends on where. The circulation stops. Still some might ooze out of an artery. It would be better to bury them in red: a dark red.

In silence they drove along Phibsborough road. An empty hearse trotted by, coming from the cemetery: looks relieved.

Crossguns bridge: the royal canal.

Water rushed roaring through the sluices. A man stood on his dropping barge, between clamps of turf. On the towpath by the lock a slacktethered horse. Aboard of the *Bugabu*.

Their eyes watched him. On the slow weedy waterway he had floated on his raft coastward over Ireland drawn by a haulage rope past beds of reeds, over slime, mudchoked bottles, carrion dogs. Athlone, Mullingar, Moyvalley, I could make a walking tour to see Milly by the canal. Or cycle down. Hire some old crock, safety. Wren had one the other day at the auction but a lady's. Developing waterways. James M'Cann's hobby to row me o'er the ferry. Cheaper transit. By easy stages. Houseboats. Camping out. Also hearses. To heaven by water. Perhaps I will without writing. Come as a surprise, Leixlip, Clonsilla. Dropping down lock by lock to Dublin. With turf from the midland bogs. Salute. He lifted his brown straw hat, saluting Paddy Dignam.

They drove on past Brian Boroimhe house. Near it now.

—I wonder how is our friend Fogarty getting on, Mr Power said.

—Better ask Tom Kernan, Mr Dedalus said.

—How is that? Martin Cunningham said. Left him weeping, I suppose?

—Though lost to sight, Mr Dedalus said, to memory dear.

The carriage steered left for Finglas road.

The stonecutter's yard on the right. Last lap. Crowded on the spit of land silent shapes appeared, white, sorrowful, holding out calm hands, knelt in grief, pointing. Fragments of shapes, hewn. In white silence: appealing. The best obtainable. Thos. H. Dennany, monumental builder and sculptor.

Passed.

On the curbstone before Jimmy Geary, the sexton's, an old tramp sat, grumbling, emptying the dirt and stones out of his huge dustbrown yawning boot. After life's journey.

Gloomy gardens then went by: one by one: gloomy houses.

Mr Power pointed.

—That is where Childs was murdered, he said. The last house.

—So it is, Mr Dedalus said. A gruesome case. Seymour Bushe got him off. Murdered his brother. Or so they said.

—The crown had no evidence, Mr Power said.

—Only circumstantial, Martin Cunningham added. That's the maxim of the law. Better for ninetynine guilty to escape than for one innocent person to be wrongfully condemned.

They looked. Murderer's ground. It passed darkly. Shuttered, tenantless, unweeded garden. Whole place gone to hell. Wrongfully condemned. Murder. The murderer's image in the eye of the murdered. They love reading about it. Man's head found in a garden. Her clothing consisted of. How she met her death. Recent outrage. The weapon used. Murderer is still at large. Clues. A shoelace. The body to be exhumed. Murder will out.

Cramped in this carriage. She mightn't like me to come that way without letting her know. Must be careful about women. Catch them once with their pants down. Never forgive you after. Fifteen.

The high railings of Prospect rippled past their gaze. Dark poplars, rare white forms. Forms more frequent, white shapes thronged amid the trees, white forms and fragments streaming by mutely, sustaining vain gestures on the air.

The felly harshed against the curbstone: stopped. Martin Cunningham put out his arm and, wrenching back the handle, shoved the door open with his knee. He stepped out. Mr Power and Mr Dedalus followed.

Change that soap now. Mr Bloom's hand unbuttoned his hip pocket swiftly and transferred the paperstuck soap to his inner handkerchief pocket. He stepped out of the carriage, replacing the newspaper his other hand still held.

Paltry funeral: coach and three carriages. It's all the same. Pallbearers, gold reins, requiem mass, firing a volley. Pomp of death. Beyond the hind carriage a hawker stood by his barrow of cakes and fruit. Simnel cakes those are, stuck together: cakes for the dead. Dogbiscuits. Who ate them? Mourners coming out.

He followed his companions. Mr Kernan and Ned Lambert followed, Hynes walking after them. Corny Kelleher stood by the opened hearse and took out the two wreaths. He handed one to the boy.

Where is that child's funeral disappeared to?

A team of horses passed from Finglas with toiling plodding tread, dragging through the funereal silence a creaking waggon on which lay a granite block. The waggoner marching at their head saluted.

Coffin now. Got here before us, dead as he is. Horse looking round at it with his plume skeowways. Dull eye: collar tight on his neck, pressing on a bloodvessel or something. Do they know what they cart out here every day? Must be twenty or thirty funerals every day. Then Mount Jerome for the protestants. Funerals all over the world everywhere every minute. Shovelling them under by the cartload doublequick. Thousands every hour. Too many in the world.

Mourners came out through the gates: woman and a girl. Leanjawed harpy, hard woman at a bargain, her bonnet awry. Girl's face stained with dirt and tears, holding the woman's arm, looking up at her for a sign to cry. Fish's face, bloodless and livid.

The mutes shouldered the coffin and bore it in through the gates. So much dead weight. Felt heavier myself stepping out of that bath. First the stiff: then the friends of the stiff. Corny Kelleher and the boy followed with their wreaths. Who is that beside them? Ah, the brother-in-law.

All walked after.

Martin Cunningham whispered:

—I was in mortal agony with you talking of suicide before Bloom.

—What? Mr Power whispered. How so?

—His father poisoned himself, Martin Cunningham whispered. Had the Queen's hotel in Ennis. You heard him say he was going to Clare. Anniversary.

—O God! Mr Power whispered. First I heard of it. Poisoned himself?

He glanced behind him to where a face with dark thinking eyes followed towards the cardinal's mausoleum. Speaking.

—Was he insured? Mr Bloom asked.

—I believe so, Mr Kernan answered. But the policy was heavily mortgaged. Martin is trying to get the youngster into Artane.

—How many children did he leave?

—Five. Ned Lambert says he'll try to get one of the girls into Todd's.

—A sad case, Mr Bloom said gently. Five young children.

—A great blow to the poor wife, Mr Kernan added.

—Indeed yes, Mr Bloom agreed.

Has the laugh at him now.

He looked down at the boots he had blacked and polished. She had outlived him. Lost her husband. More dead for her than for me. One must outlive the other. Wise men say. There are more women than men in the world. Condole with her. Your terrible loss. I hope you'll soon follow him. For Hindu widows only. She would marry another. Him? No. Yet who knows after. Widowhood not the thing since the old queen died. Drawn on a guncarriage. Victoria and Albert. Frogmore memorial mourning. But in the end she put a few violets in her bonnet. Vain in her heart of hearts. All for a shadow. Consort not even a king. Her son was the substance. Something new to hope for not like the past she wanted back, waiting. It never comes. One must go first: alone, under the ground: and lie no more in her warm bed.

—How are you, Simon? Ned Lambert said softly, clasping hands. Haven't seen you for a month of Sundays.

—Never better. How are all in Cork's own town?

—I was down there for the Cork park races on Easter Monday, Ned Lambert said. Same old six and eightpence. Stopped with Dick Tivy.

—And how is Dick, the solid man?

—Nothing between himself and heaven, Ned Lambert answered.

—By the holy Paul! Mr Dedalus said in subdued wonder. Dick Tivy bald?

—Martin is going to get up a whip for the youngsters, Ned Lambert said, pointing ahead. A few bob a skull. Just to keep them going till the insurance is cleared up.

—Yes, yes, Mr Dedalus said dubiously. Is that the eldest boy in front?

—Yes, Ned Lambert said, with the wife's brother. John Henry Menton is behind. He put down his name for a quid.

—I'll engage he did, Mr Dedalus said. I often told poor Paddy he ought to mind that job. John Henry is not the worst in the world.

—How did he lose it? Ned Lambert asked. Liquor, what?

—Many a good man's fault, Mr Dedalus said with a sigh.

They halted about the door of the mortuary chapel. Mr Bloom stood behind the boy with the wreath looking down at his sleek combed hair and at the slender furrowed neck inside his brandnew collar. Poor boy! Was he there when the father? Both unconscious. Lighten up at the last moment and recognise for the last time. All he might have done. I owe three shillings to O'Grady. Would he understand? The mutes bore the coffin into the chapel. Which end is his head?

After a moment he followed the others in, blinking in the screened light. The coffin lay on its bier before the chancel, four tall yellow candles at its corners. Always in front of us. Corny Kelleher, laying a wreath at each fore corner, beckoned to the boy to kneel. The mourners knelt here and there in prayingdesks. Mr Bloom stood behind near the font and, when all had knelt, dropped carefully his unfolded newspaper from his pocket and knelt his right knee upon it. He fitted his black hat gently on his left knee and, holding its brim, bent over piously.

A server bearing a brass bucket with something in it came out through a door. The whitesmocked priest came after him, tidying his stole with one hand, balancing with the other a little book against his toad's belly. Who'll read the book? I, said the rook.

They halted by the bier and the priest began to read out of his book with a fluent croak.

Father Coffey. I knew his name was like a coffin. *Domine-namine.* Bully about the muzzle he looks. Bosses the show. Muscular christian. Woe betide anyone that looks crooked at him: priest. Thou art Peter. Burst sideways like a sheep in clover Dedalus says he will. With a belly on him like a poisoned pup. Most amusing expressions that man finds. Hhhn: burst sideways.

—*Non intres in judicium cum servo tuo, Domine.*

Makes them feel more important to be prayed over in Latin. Requiem mass. Crape weepers. Blackedged notepaper. Your name on the altarlist. Chilly place this. Want to feed well, sitting in there all the morning in the gloom kicking his heels waiting for the next please. Eyes of a toad too. What swells him up that way? Molly gets swelled after cabbage. Air of the place maybe. Looks full up of bad gas. Must be an infernal lot of bad gas round the place. Butchers, for instance: they get like raw beefsteaks. Who was telling me? Mervyn Browne. Down in the vaults of saint Werburgh's lovely old organ hundred and fifty they have to bore a hole in the coffins sometimes to let out the bad gas and burn it. Out it rushes: blue. One whiff of that and you're a goner.

My kneecap is hurting me. Ow. That's better.

The priest took a stick with a knob at the end of it out of the boy's bucket and shook it over the coffin. Then he walked to the other end and shook it again. Then he came back and put it back in the bucket. As you were before you rested. It's all written down: he has to do it.

—*Et ne nos inducas in tentationem.*

The server piped the answers in the treble. I often thought it would be better to have boy servants. Up to fifteen or so. After that, of course . . .

Holy water that was, I expect. Shaking sleep out of it. He must be fed up with that job, shaking that thing over all the corpses they trot up. What harm if he could see what he was shaking it over. Every mortal day a fresh batch: middleaged men, old women, children, women dead in childbirth, men with beards, baldheaded businessmen, consumptive girls with little sparrows' breasts. All the year round he prayed the same thing over them all and shook water on top of them: sleep. On Dignam now.

—*In paradisum.*

Said he was going to paradise or is in paradise. Says that over everybody. Tiresome kind of a job. But he has to say something.

The priest closed his book and went off, followed by the server. Corny Kelleher opened the sidedoors and the gravediggers came in, hoisted the coffin again, carried it out and shoved it on their cart. Corny Kelleher gave one wreath to the boy and one to the brother-in-law. All followed them out of the sidedoors into the mild grey air. Mr Bloom came last folding his paper again into his pocket. He gazed gravely at the ground till the coffincart wheeled off to the left. The metal wheels ground the gravel with a sharp grating cry and the pack of blunt boots followed the trundled barrow along a lane of sepulchres.

The ree the ra the ree the ra the roo. Lord, I mustn't lilt here.

—The O'Connell circle, Mr Dedalus said about him.

Mr Power's soft eyes went up to the apex of the lofty cone.

—He's at rest, he said, in the middle of his people, old Dan O'. But his heart is buried in Rome. How many broken hearts are buried here, Simon!

—Her grave is over there, Jack, Mr Dedalus said. I'll soon be stretched beside her. Let Him take me whenever He likes.

Breaking down, he began to weep to himself quietly, stumbling a little in his walk. Mr Power took his arm.

—She's better where she is, he said kindly.

—I suppose so, Mr Dedalus said with a weak gasp. I suppose she is in heaven if there is a heaven.

Corny Kelleher stepped aside from his rank and allowed the mourners to plod by.

—Sad occasions, Mr Kernan began politely.

Mr Bloom closed his eyes and sadly twice bowed his head.

—The others are putting on their hats, Mr Kernan said. I suppose we can do so too. We are the last. This cemetery is a treacherous place.

They covered their heads.

—The reverend gentleman read the service too quickly, don't you think? Mr Kernan said with reproof.

Mr Bloom nodded gravely looking in the quick bloodshot eyes. Secret eyes, secret searching. Mason, I think: not sure. Beside him again. We are the last. In the same boat. Hope he'll say something else.

Mr Kernan added:

—The service of the Irish church used in Mount Jerome is simpler, more impressive I must say.

Mr Bloom gave prudent assent. The language of course was another thing.

Mr Kernan said with solemnity:

—*I am the resurrection and the life.* That touches a man's inmost heart.

—It does, Mr Bloom said.

Your heart perhaps but what price the fellow in the six feet by two with his toes to the daisies? No touching that. Seat of the affections. Broken heart. A pump after all, pumping thousands of gallons of blood every day. One fine day it gets bunged up: and there you are. Lots of them lying around here: lungs, hearts, livers. Old rusty pumps: damn the thing else. The resurrection and the life. Once you are dead you are dead. That last day idea. Knocking them all up out of their graves. Come forth, Lazarus! And he came fifth and lost the job. Get up! Last day! Then every fellow mousing around for his liver and his lights and the rest of his traps. Find damn all of himself that morning. Pennyweight of powder in a skull. Twelve grammes one pennyweight. Troy measure.

Corny Kelleher fell into step at their side.

—Everything went off A1, he said. What?

He looked on them from his drawling eye. Policeman's shoulders. With your tooraloom tooraloom.

—As it should be, Mr Kernan said.

—What? Eh? Corny Kelleher said.

Mr Kernan assured him.

—Who is that chap behind with Tom Kernan? John Henry Menton asked. I know his face.

Ned Lambert glanced back.

—Bloom, he said, Madame Marion Tweedy that was, is, I mean, the soprano. She's his wife.

—O, to be sure, John Henry Menton said. I haven't seen her for some time. She was a finelooking woman. I danced with her, wait, fifteen seventeen golden years ago, at Mat Dillon's in Roundtown. And a good armful she was.

He looked behind through the others.

—What is he? he asked. What does he do? Wasn't he in the stationery line? I fell foul of him one evening, I remember, at bowls.

Ned Lambert smiled.

—Yes, he was, he said, in Wisdom Hely's. A traveller for blottingpaper.

—In God's name, John Henry Menton said, what did she marry a coon like that for? She had plenty of game in her then.

—Has still, Ned Lambert said. He does some canvassing for ads.

John Henry Menton's large eyes stared ahead.

The barrow turned into a side lane. A portly man, ambushed among the grasses, raised his hat in homage. The gravediggers touched their caps.

—John O'Connell, Mr Power said pleased. He never forgets a friend.

Mr O'Connell shook all their hands in silence. Mr Dedalus said:

—I am come to pay you another visit.

—My dear Simon, the caretaker answered in a low voice. I don't want your custom at all.

Saluting Ned Lambert and John Henry Menton he walked on at Martin Cunningham's side puzzling two long keys at his back.

—Did you hear that one, he asked them, about Mulcahy from the Coombe?

—I did not, Martin Cunningham said.

They bent their silk hats in concert and Hynes inclined his ear. The caretaker hung his thumbs in the loops of his gold watch chain and spoke in a discreet tone to their vacant smiles.

—They tell the story, he said, that two drunks came out here one foggy evening to look for the grave of a friend of theirs. They asked for Mulcahy from the Coombe and were told where he was buried. After traipsing about in the fog they found the grave sure enough. One of the drunks spelt out the name: Terence Mulcahy. The other drunk was blinking up at a statue of Our Saviour the widow had got put up.

The caretaker blinked up at one of the sepulchres they passed. He resumed:

—And, after blinking up at the sacred figure, *Not a bloody bit like the man*, says he. *That's not Mulcahy*, says he, *whoever done it.*

Rewarded by smiles he fell back and spoke with Corny Kelleher, accepting the dockets given him, turning them over and scanning them as he walked.

—That's all done with a purpose, Martin Cunningham explained to Hynes.

—I know, Hynes said. I know that.

—To cheer a fellow up, Martin Cunningham said. It's pure goodheartedness: damn the thing else.

Mr Bloom admired the caretaker's prosperous bulk. All want to be on good terms with him. Decent fellow, John O'Connell, real good sort. Keys: like Keyes's ad: no fear of anyone getting out. No passout checks. *Habeas corpus.* I must see about that ad after the funeral. Did I write Ballsbridge on the envelope I took to cover when she disturbed me writing to Martha? Hope it's not chucked in the dead letter office. Be the better of a shave. Grey sprouting beard. That's the first sign when the hairs come out grey. And temper getting cross. Silver threads among the grey. Fancy being his wife. Wonder he had the gumption to propose to any girl. Come out and live in the graveyard. Dangle that before her. It might thrill her first. Courting death. Shades of night hovering here with all the dead stretched about. The shadows of the tombs when churchyards yawn and Daniel O'Connell must be a descendant I suppose who is this used to say he was a queer breedy man great catholic all the same like a big giant in the dark. Will o' the wisp. Gas of graves. Want to keep her mind off it to conceive at all. Women especially are so touchy. Tell her a ghost story in bed to make her sleep. Have you ever seen a ghost? Well, I have. It was a pitchdark night. The clock was on the stroke of twelve. Still they'd kiss all right if properly keyed up. Whores in Turkish graveyards. Learn anything if taken young. You might pick up a young widow here. Men like that. Love among the tombstones. Romeo. Spice of pleasure. In the midst of death we are in life. Both ends meet. Tantalising for the poor dead. Smell of grilled beefsteaks to the starving. Gnawing their vitals. Desire to grig people. Molly wanting to do it at the window. Eight children he has anyway.

He has seen a fair share go under in his time, lying around him field after field. Holy fields. More room if they buried them standing. Sitting or kneeling you couldn't. Standing? His head might come up some day above ground in a landslip with his hand pointing. All honeycombed the ground must be: oblong cells. And very neat he keeps it too: trim grass and edgings. His garden Major Gamble calls Mount Jerome. Well, so it is. Ought to be flowers of sleep. Chinese cemeteries with giant poppies growing produce the best opium Mastiansky told me. The Botanic Gardens are just over there. It's the blood sinking in the earth gives new life. Same idea those jews they said killed the christian boy. Every man his price. Well preserved fat corpse, gentleman, epicure, invaluable for fruit garden. A bargain. By carcass of William Wilkinson, auditor and accountant, lately deceased, three pounds thirteen and six. With thanks.

I daresay the soil would be quite fat with corpse manure, bones, flesh, nails. Charnelhouses. Dreadful. Turning green and pink decomposing. Rot quick in damp earth. The lean old ones tougher. Then a kind of a tallowy kind of a cheesy. Then begin to get black, black treacle oozing out of them. Then dried up. Deathmoths. Of course the cells or whatever they are go on living. Changing about. Live for ever practically. Nothing to feed on feed on themselves.

But they must breed a devil of a lot of maggots. Soil must be simply swirling with them. Your head it simply swurls. Those pretty little seaside gurls. He looks cheerful enough over it. Gives him a sense of power seeing all the others go under first. Wonder how he looks at life. Cracking his jokes too: warms the cockles of his heart. The one about the bulletin. Spurgeon went to heaven 4 a.m. this morning. 11 p.m. (closing time). Not arrived yet. Peter. The dead themselves the men anyhow would like to hear an odd joke or the women to know what's in fashion. A juicy pear or ladies' punch, hot, strong and sweet. Keep out the damp. You must laugh sometimes so better do it that way. Gravediggers in *Hamlet*. Shows the profound knowledge of the human heart. Daren't joke about the dead for two years at least. *De mortuis nil nisi prius.* Go out of mourning first. Hard to imagine his funeral. Seems a sort of a joke. Read your own obituary notice they say you live longer. Gives you second wind. New lease of life.

—How many have you for tomorrow? the caretaker asked.

—Two, Corny Kelleher said. Half ten and eleven.

The caretaker put the papers in his pocket. The barrow had ceased to trundle. The mourners split and moved to each side of the hole, stepping with care round the graves. The gravediggers bore the coffin and set its nose on the brink, looping the bands round it.

Burying him. We come to bury Cæsar. His ides of March or June. He doesn't know who is here nor care. Now who is that lankylooking galoot over there in the macintosh? Now who is he I'd like to know? Now I'd give a trifle to know who he is. Always someone turns up you never dreamt of. A fellow could live on his lonesome all his life. Yes, he could. Still he'd have to get someone to sod him after he died though he could dig his own grave. We all do. Only man buries. No, ants too. First thing strikes anybody. Bury the dead. Say Robinson Crusoe was true to life. Well then Friday buried him. Every Friday buries a Thursday if you come to look at it.

> O, poor Robinson Crusoe!
> How could you possibly do so?

Poor Dignam! His last lie on the earth in his box. When you think of them all it does seem a waste of wood. All gnawed through. They could invent a handsome bier with a kind of panel sliding, let it down that way. Ay but they might object to be buried out of another fellow's. They're so particular. Lay me in my native earth. Bit of clay from the holy land. Only a mother and deadborn child ever buried in the one coffin. I see what it means. I see. To protect him as long as possible even in the earth. The Irishman's house is his coffin. Embalming in catacombs, mummies the same idea.

Mr Bloom stood far back, his hat in his hand, counting the bared heads. Twelve. I'm thirteen. No. The chap in the macintosh is thirteen. Death's number. Where the deuce did he pop out of? He wasn't in the chapel, that I'll swear. Silly superstition that about thirteen.

Nice soft tweed Ned Lambert has in that suit. Tinge of purple. I had one like that when we lived in Lombard street west. Dressy fellow he was once. Used to change three suits in the day. Must get that grey suit of mine turned by Mesias. Hello. It's dyed. His wife I forgot he's not married or his landlady ought to have picked out those threads for him.

The coffin dived out of sight, eased down by the men straddled on the gravetrestles. They struggled up and out: and all uncovered. Twenty.

Pause.

If we were all suddenly somebody else.

Far away a donkey brayed. Rain. No such ass. Never see a dead one, they say. Shame of death. They hide. Also poor papa went away.

Gentle sweet air blew round the bared heads in a whisper. Whisper. The boy by the gravehead held his wreath with both hands staring quietly in the black open space. Mr Bloom moved behind the portly kindly caretaker. Wellcut frockcoat. Weighing them up perhaps to see which will go next. Well, it is a long rest. Feel no more. It's the moment you feel. Must be damned unpleasant. Can't believe it at first. Mistake must be: someone else. Try the house opposite. Wait, I wanted to. I haven't yet. Then darkened deathchamber. Light they want. Whispering around you. Would you like to see a priest? Then rambling and wandering. Delirium all you hid all your life. The death struggle. His sleep is not natural. Press his lower eyelid. Watching is his nose pointed is his jaw sinking are the soles of his feet yellow. Pull the pillow away and finish it off on the floor since he's doomed. Devil in that picture of sinner's death showing him a woman. Dying to embrace her in his shirt. Last act of *Lucia. Shall I nevermore behold thee?* Bam! He expires. Gone at last. People talk about you a bit: forget you. Don't forget to pray for him. Remember him in your prayers. Even Parnell. Ivy day dying out. Then they follow: dropping into a hole, one after the other.

We are praying now for the repose of his soul. Hoping you're well and not in hell. Nice change of air. Out of the fryingpan of life into the fire of purgatory.

Does he ever think of the hole waiting for himself? They say you do when you shiver in the sun. Someone walking over it. Callboy's warning. Near you. Mine over there towards Finglas, the plot I bought. Mamma, poor mamma, and little Rudy.

The gravediggers took up their spades and flung heavy clods of clay in on the coffin. Mr Bloom turned away his face. And if he was alive all the time? Whew! By jingo, that would be awful! No, no: he is dead, of course. Of course he is dead. Monday he died. They ought to have some law to pierce the heart and make sure or an electric clock or a telephone in the coffin and some kind of a canvas airhole. Flag of distress. Three days. Rather long to keep them in summer. Just as well to get shut of them as soon as you are sure there's no.

The clay fell softer. Begin to be forgotten. Out of sight, out of mind.

The caretaker moved away a few paces and put on his hat. Had enough of it. The mourners took heart of grace, one by one, covering themselves without show. Mr Bloom put on his hat and saw the portly figure make its way deftly through the maze of graves. Quietly, sure of his ground, he traversed the dismal fields.

Hynes jotting down something in his notebook. Ah, the names. But he knows them all. No: coming to me.

—I am just taking the names, Hynes said below his breath. What is your christian name? I'm not sure.

—L, Mr Bloom said. Leopold. And you might put down M'Coy's name too. He asked me to.

—Charley, Hynes said writing. I know. He was on the *Freeman* once.

So he was before he got the job in the morgue under Louis Byrne. Good idea a postmortem for doctors. Find out what they imagine they know. He died of a Tuesday. Got the run. Levanted with the cash of a few ads. Charley, you're my darling. That was why he asked me to. O well, does no harm. I saw to that, M'Coy. Thanks, old chap: much obliged. Leave him under an obligation: costs nothing.

—And tell us, Hynes said, do you know that fellow in the, fellow was over there in the . . .

He looked around.

—Macintosh. Yes, I saw him, Mr Bloom said. Where is he now?

—M'Intosh, Hynes said scribbling. I don't know who he is. Is that his name?

He moved away, looking about him.

—No, Mr Bloom began, turning and stopping. I say, Hynes! Didn't hear. What? Where has he disappeared to? Not a sign. Well of all the. Has anybody here seen? Kay ee double ell. Become invisible. Good Lord, what became of him?

A seventh gravedigger came beside Mr Bloom to take up an idle spade.

—O, excuse me!

He stepped aside nimbly.

Clay, brown, damp, began to be seen in the hole. It rose. Nearly over. A mound of damp clods rose more, rose, and the gravediggers rested their spades. All uncovered again for a few instants. The boy propped his wreath against a corner: the brother-in-law his on a lump. The gravediggers put on their caps and carried their earthy spades towards the barrow. Then knocked the blades lightly on the turf: clean. One bent to pluck from the haft a long tuft of grass. One, leaving his mates, walked slowly on with shouldered weapon, its blade blueglancing. Silently at the gravehead another coiled the coffinband. His navelcord. The brother-in-law, turning away, placed something in his free hand. Thanks in silence. Sorry, sir: trouble. Headshake. I know that. For yourselves just.

The mourners moved away slowly without aim, by devious paths, staying at whiles to read a name on a tomb.

—Let us go round by the chief's grave, Hynes said. We have time.

—Let us, Mr Power said.

They turned to the right, following their slow thoughts. With awe Mr Power's blank voice spoke:

—Some say he is not in that grave at all. That the coffin was filled with stones. That one day he will come again.

Hynes shook his head.

—Parnell will never come again, he said. He's there, all that was mortal of him. Peace to his ashes.

Mr Bloom walked unheeded along his grove by saddened angels, crosses, broken pillars, family vaults, stone hopes praying with upcast eyes, old Ireland's hearts and hands. More sensible to spend the money on some charity for the living. Pray for the repose of the soul of.

Does anybody really? Plant him and have done with him. Like down a coalshoot. Then lump them together to save time. All souls' day. Twentyseventh I'll be at his grave. Ten shillings for the gardener. He keeps it free of weeds. Old man himself. Bent down double with his shears clipping. Near death's door. Who passed away. Who departed this life. As if they did it of their own accord. Got the shove, all of them. Who kicked the bucket. More interesting if they told you what they were. So and So, wheelwright. I travelled for cork lino. I paid five shillings in the pound. Or a woman's with her saucepan. I cooked good Irish stew. Eulogy in a country churchyard it ought to be that poem of whose is it Wordsworth or Thomas Campbell. Entered into rest the protestants put it. Old Dr Murren's. The great physician called him home. Well it's God's acre for them. Nice country residence. Newly plastered and painted. Ideal spot to have a quiet smoke and read the *Church Times*. Marriage ads they never try to beautify. Rusty wreaths hung on knobs, garlands of bronzefoil. Better value that for the money. Still, the flowers are more poetical. The other gets rather tiresome, never withering. Expresses nothing. Immortelles.

A bird sat tamely perched on a poplar branch. Like stuffed. Like the wedding present alderman Hooper gave us. Hoo! Not a budge out of him. Knows there are no catapults to let fly at him. Dead animal even sadder. Silly-Milly burying the little dead bird in the kitchen matchbox, a daisychain and bits of broken chainies on the grave.

The Sacred Heart that is: showing it. Heart on his sleeve. Ought to be sideways and red it should be painted like a real heart. Ireland was dedicated to it or whatever that. Seems anything but pleased. Why this infliction? Would birds come then and peck like the boy with the basket of fruit but he said no because they ought to have been afraid of the boy. Apollo that was.

How many! All these here once walked round Dublin. Faithful departed. As you are now so once were we.

Besides how could you remember everybody? Eyes, walk, voice. Well, the voice, yes: gramophone. Have a gramophone in every grave or keep it in the house. After dinner on a Sunday. Put on poor old greatgrandfather. Kraahraark! Hellohellohello amawfullyglad kraark awfullygladaseeagain hellohello amawf krpthsth. Remind you of the voice like the photograph reminds you of the face. Otherwise you couldn't remember the face after fifteen years, say. For instance who? For instance some fellow that died when I was in Wisdom Hely's.

Rtststr! A rattle of pebbles. Wait. Stop!

He looked down intently into a stone crypt. Some animal. Wait. There he goes.

An obese grey rat toddled along the side of the crypt, moving the pebbles. An old stager: greatgrandfather: he knows the ropes. The grey alive crushed itself in under the plinth, wriggled itself in under it. Good hidingplace for treasure.

Who lives there? Are laid the remains of Robert Emery. Robert Emmet was buried here by torchlight, wasn't he? Making his rounds.

Tail gone now.

One of those chaps would make short work of a fellow. Pick the bones clean no matter who it was. Ordinary meat for them. A corpse is meat gone bad. Well and what's cheese? Corpse of milk. I read in that *Voyages in China* that the Chinese say a white man smells like a corpse. Cremation better. Priests dead against it. Devilling for the other firm. Wholesale burners and Dutch oven dealers. Time of the plague. Quicklime feverpits to eat them. Lethal chamber. Ashes to ashes. Or bury at sea. Where is that Parsee tower of silence? Eaten by birds. Earth, fire, water. Drowning they say is the pleasantest. See your whole life in a flash. But being brought back to life no. Can't bury in the air however. Out of a flying machine. Wonder does the news go about whenever a fresh one is let down. Underground communication. We learned that from them. Wouldn't be surprised. Regular square feed for them. Flies come before he's well dead. Got wind of Dignam. They wouldn't care about the smell of it. Saltwhite crumbling mush of corpse: smell, taste like raw white turnips.

The gates glimmered in front: still open. Back to the world again. Enough of this place. Brings you a bit nearer every time. Last time I was here was Mrs Sinico's funeral. Poor papa too. The love that kills. And even scraping up the earth at night with a lantern like that case I read of to get at fresh buried females or even putrefied with running gravesores. Give you the creeps after a bit. I will appear to you after death. You will see my ghost after death. My ghost will haunt you after death. There is another world after death named hell. I do not like that other world she wrote. No more do I. Plenty to see and hear and feel yet. Feel live warm beings near you. Let them sleep in their maggoty beds. They are not going to get me this innings. Warm beds: warm fullblooded life.

Martin Cunningham emerged from a sidepath, talking gravely.

Solicitor, I think. I know his face. Menton, John Henry, solicitor, commissioner for oaths and affidavits. Dignam used to be in his office. Mat Dillon's long ago. Jolly Mat. Convivial evenings. Cold fowl, cigars, the Tantalus glasses. Heart of gold really. Yes, Menton. Got his rag out that evening on the bowlinggreen because I sailed inside him. Pure fluke of mine: the bias. Why he took such a rooted dislike to me. Hate at first sight. Molly and Floey Dillon linked under the lilactree, laughing. Fellow always like that, mortified if women are by.

Got a dinge in the side of his hat. Carriage probably.

—Excuse me, sir, Mr Bloom said beside them.

They stopped.

—Your hat is a little crushed, Mr Bloom said pointing.

John Henry Menton stared at him for an instant without moving.

—There, Martin Cunningham helped, pointing also.

John Henry Menton took off his hat, bulged out the dinge and smoothed the nap with care on his coatsleeve. He clapped the hat on his head again.

—It's all right now, Martin Cunningham said.

John Henry Menton jerked his head down in acknowledgment.

—Thank you, he said shortly.

They walked on towards the gates. Mr Bloom, chapfallen, drew behind a few paces so as not to overhear. Martin laying down the law. Martin could wind a sappyhead like that round his little finger, without his seeing it.

Oyster eyes. Never mind. Be sorry after perhaps when it dawns on him. Get the pull over him that way.

Thank you. How grand we are this morning!

7

In The Heart Of
The Hibernian Metropolis

Before Nelson's pillar trams slowed, shunted, changed trolley, started for Blackrock, Kingstown and Dalkey, Clonskea, Rathgar and Terenure, Palmerston Park and upper Rathmines, Sandymount Green, Rathmines, Ringsend and Sandymount Tower, Harold's Cross. The hoarse Dublin United Tramway Company's timekeeper bawled them off:

—Rathgar and Terenure!

—Come on, Sandymount Green!

Right and left parallel clanging ringing a doubledecker and a singledeck moved from their railheads, swerved to the down line, glided parallel.

—Start, Palmerston Park!

The Wearer Of The Crown

Under the porch of the general post office shoeblacks called and polished. Parked in North Prince's street His Majesty's vermilion mailcars, bearing on their sides the royal initials, E. R., received loudly flung sacks of letters, postcards, lettercards, parcels, insured and paid, for local, provincial, British and overseas delivery.

Gentlemen Of The Press

Grossbooted draymen rolled barrels dullthudding out of Prince's stores and bumped them up on the brewery float. On the brewery float bumped dullthudding barrels rolled by grossbooted draymen out of Prince's stores.

—There it is, Red Murray said. Alexander Keyes.

—Just cut it out, will you? Mr Bloom said, and I'll take it round to the *Telegraph* office.

The door of Ruttledge's office creaked again. Davy Stephens, minute in a large capecoat, a small felt hat crowning his ringlets, passed out with a roll of papers under his cape, a king's courier.

Red Murray's long shears sliced out the advertisement from the newspaper in four clean strokes. Scissors and paste.

—I'll go through the printing works, Mr Bloom said, taking the cut square.

—Of course, if he wants a par, Red Murray said earnestly, a pen behind his ear, we can do him one.

—Right, Mr Bloom said with a nod. I'll rub that in.
We.

WILLIAM BRAYDEN,
ESQUIRE, OF OAKLANDS, SANDYMOUNT

Red Murray touched Mr Bloom's arm with the shears and whispered:

—Brayden.

Mr Bloom turned and saw the liveried porter raise his lettered cap as a stately figure entered between the newsboards of the *Weekly Freeman and National Press* and the *Freeman's Journal and National Press.* Dullthudding Guinness's barrels. It passed statelily up the staircase, steered by an umbrella, a solemn beardframed face. The broadcloth back ascended each step: back. All his brains are in the nape of his neck, Simon Dedalus says. Welts of flesh behind on him. Fat folds of neck, fat, neck, fat, neck.

—Don't you think his face is like Our Saviour? Red Murray whispered.

The door of Ruttledge's office whispered: ee: cree. They always build one door opposite another for the wind to. Way in. Way out.

Our Saviour: beardframed oval face: talking in the dusk. Mary, Martha. Steered by an umbrella sword to the footlights: Mario the tenor.

—Or like Mario, Mr Bloom said.

—Yes, Red Murray agreed. But Mario was said to be the picture of Our Saviour.

Jesusmario with rougy cheeks, doublet and spindle legs. Hand on his heart. In *Martha*.

> *Co-ome thou lost one,*
> *Co-ome thou dear one!*

THE CROZIER AND THE PEN

—His grace phoned down twice this morning, Red Murray said gravely.

They watched the knees, legs, boots vanish. Neck.

A telegram boy stepped in nimbly, threw an envelope on the counter and stepped off posthaste with a word:

—*Freeman!*

Mr Bloom said slowly:

—Well, he is one of our saviours also.

A meek smile accompanied him as he lifted the counterflap, as he passed in through a sidedoor and along the warm dark stairs and passage, along the now reverberating boards. But will he save the circulation? Thumping. Thumping.

He pushed in the glass swingdoor and entered, stepping over strewn packing paper. Through a lane of clanking drums he made his way towards Nannetti's reading closet.

WITH UNFEIGNED REGRET IT IS WE ANNOUNCE THE DISSOLUTION OF A MOST RESPECTED DUBLIN BURGESS

Hynes here too: account of the funeral probably. Thumping. Thump. This morning the remains of the late Mr Patrick Dignam. Machines. Smash a man to atoms if they got him caught. Rule the world today. His machineries are pegging away too. Like these, got out of hand: fermenting. Working away, tearing away. And that old grey rat tearing to get in.

HOW A GREAT DAILY ORGAN IS TURNED OUT

Mr Bloom halted behind the foreman's spare body, admiring a glossy crown.

Strange he never saw his real country. Ireland my country. Member for College green. He boomed that workaday worker tack for all it was worth. It's the ads and side features sell a weekly, not the stale news in the official gazette. Queen Anne is dead. Published by authority in the year one thousand and. Demesne situate in the townland of Rosenallis, barony of Tinnahinch. To all whom it may concern schedule pursuant to statute showing return of number of mules and jennets exported from Ballina. Nature notes. Cartoons. Phil Blake's weekly Pat and Bull story. Uncle Toby's page for tiny tots. Country bumpkin's queries. Dear Mr Editor, what is a good cure for flatulence? I'd like that part. Learn a lot teaching others. The personal note. M. A. P. Mainly all pictures. Shapely bathers on golden strand. World's biggest balloon. Double marriage of sisters celebrated. Two bridegrooms laughing heartily at each other. Cuprani too, printer. More Irish than the Irish.

The machines clanked in threefour time. Thump, thump, thump. Now if he got paralysed there and no-one knew how to stop them they'd clank on and on the same, print it over and over and up and back. Monkeydoodle the whole thing. Want a cool head.

—Well, get it into the evening edition, councillor, Hynes said.

Soon be calling him my lord mayor. Long John is backing him, they say.

The foreman, without answering, scribbled press on a corner of the sheet and made a sign to a typesetter. He handed the sheet silently over the dirty glass screen.

—Right: thanks, Hynes said moving off.

Mr Bloom stood in his way.

—If you want to draw the cashier is just going to lunch, he said, pointing backward with his thumb.

—Did you? Hynes asked.

—Mm, Mr Bloom said. Look sharp and you'll catch him.

—Thanks, old man, Hynes said. I'll tap him too.

He hurried on eagerly towards the *Freeman's Journal*.

Three bob I lent him in Meagher's. Three weeks. Third hint.

WE SEE THE CANVASSER AT WORK

Mr Bloom laid his cutting on Mr Nannetti's desk.

—Excuse me, councillor, he said. This ad, you see. Keyes, you remember?

136

Mr Nannetti considered the cutting awhile and nodded.

—He wants it in for July, Mr Bloom said.

The foreman moved his pencil towards it.

—But wait, Mr Bloom said. He wants it changed. Keyes, you see. He wants two keys at the top.

Hell of a racket they make. He doesn't hear it. Nannan. Iron nerves. Maybe he understands what I.

The foreman turned round to hear patiently and, lifting an elbow, began to scratch slowly in the armpit of his alpaca jacket.

—Like that, Mr Bloom said, crossing his forefingers at the top. Let him take that in first.

Mr Bloom, glancing sideways up from the cross he had made, saw the foreman's sallow face, think he has a touch of jaundice, and beyond the obedient reels feeding in huge webs of paper. Clank it. Clank it. Miles of it unreeled. What becomes of it after? O, wrap up meat, parcels: various uses, thousand and one things.

Slipping his words deftly into the pauses of the clanking he drew swiftly on the scarred woodwork.

House Of Key(E)S

—Like that, see. Two crossed keys here. A circle. Then here the name. Alexander Keyes, tea, wine and spirit merchant. So on.

Better not teach him his own business.

—You know yourself, councillor, just what he wants. Then round the top in leaded: the house of keys. You see? Do you think that's a good idea?

The foreman moved his scratching hand to his lower ribs and scratched there quietly.

—The idea, Mr Bloom said, is the house of keys. You know, councillor, the Manx parliament. Innuendo of home rule. Tourists, you know, from the isle of Man. Catches the eye, you see. Can you do that?

I could ask him perhaps about how to pronounce that *voglio*. But then if he didn't know only make it awkward for him. Better not.

—We can do that, the foreman said. Have you the design?

—I can get it, Mr Bloom said. It was in a Kilkenny paper. He has a house there too. I'll just run out and ask him. Well, you can do that and just a little par calling attention. You know the usual. Highclass licensed premises. Longfelt want. So on.

The foreman thought for an instant.

—We can do that, he said. Let him give us a three months' renewal.

A typesetter brought him a limp galleypage. He began to check it silently. Mr Bloom stood by, hearing the loud throbs of cranks, watching the silent typesetters at their cases.

ORTHOGRAPHICAL

Want to be sure of his spelling. Proof fever. Martin Cunningham forgot to give us his spellingbee conundrum this morning. It is amusing to view the unpar one ar alleled embarra two ars is it? double ess ment of a harassed pedlar while gauging au the symmetry with a y of a peeled pear under a cemetery wall. Silly, isn't it? Cemetery put in of course on account of the symmetry.

I should have said when he clapped on his topper. Thank you. I ought to have said something about an old hat or something. No. I could have said. Looks as good as new now. See his phiz then.

Sllt. The nethermost deck of the first machine jogged forward its flyboard with sllt the first batch of quirefolded papers. Sllt. Almost human the way it sllt to call attention. Doing its level best to speak. That door too sllt creaking, asking to be shut. Everything speaks in its own way. Sllt.

NOTED CHURCHMAN
AN OCCASIONAL CONTRIBUTOR

The foreman handed back the galleypage suddenly, saying:

—Wait. Where's the archbishop's letter? It's to be repeated in the *Telegraph*. Where's what's his name?

He looked about him round his loud unanswering machines.

—Monks, sir? a voice asked from the castingbox.

—Ay. Where's Monks?

—Monks!

Mr Bloom took up his cutting. Time to get out.

—Then I'll get the design, Mr Nannetti, he said, and you'll give it a good place I know.

—Monks!

—Yes, sir.

138

Three months' renewal. Want to get some wind off my chest first. Try it anyhow. Rub in August: good idea: horseshow month. Ballsbridge. Tourists over for the show.

A DAYFATHER

He walked on through the caseroom passing an old man, bowed, spectacled, aproned. Old Monks, the dayfather. Queer lot of stuff he must have put through his hands in his time: obituary notices, pubs' ads, speeches, divorce suits, found drowned. Nearing the end of his tether now. Sober serious man with a bit in the savingsbank I'd say. Wife a good cook and washer. Daughter working the machine in the parlour. Plain Jane, no damn nonsense.

AND IT WAS THE FEAST OF THE PASSOVER

He stayed in his walk to watch a typesetter neatly distributing type. Reads it backwards first. Quickly he does it. Must require some practice that. mangiD kcirtaP. Poor papa with his hagadah book, reading backwards with his finger to me. Pessach. Next year in Jerusalem. Dear, O dear! All that long business about that brought us out of the land of Egypt and into the house of bondage *alleluia.* *Shema Israel Adonai Elohenu.* No, that's the other. Then the twelve brothers, Jacob's sons. And then the lamb and the cat and the dog and the stick and the water and the butcher. And then the angel of death kills the butcher and he kills the ox and the dog kills the cat. Sounds a bit silly till you come to look into it well. Justice it means but it's everybody eating everyone else. That's what life is after all. How quickly he does that job. Practice makes perfect. Seems to see with his fingers.

Mr Bloom passed on out of the clanking noises through the gallery on to the landing. Now am I going to tram it out all the way and then catch him out perhaps. Better phone him up first. Number? Yes. Same as Citron's house. Twentyeight. Twentyeight double four.

ONLY ONCE MORE THAT SOAP

He went down the house staircase. Who the deuce scrawled all over those walls with matches? Looks as if they did it for a bet. Heavy greasy smell there always is in those works. Lukewarm glue in Thom's next door when I was there.

He took out his handkerchief to dab his nose. Citronlemon? Ah, the soap I put there. Lose it out of that pocket. Putting back his handkerchief he took out the soap and stowed it away, buttoned, into the hip pocket of his trousers.

What perfume does your wife use? I could go home still: tram: something I forgot. Just to see: before: dressing. No. Here. No.

A sudden screech of laughter came from the *Evening Telegraph* office. Know who that is. What's up? Pop in a minute to phone. Ned Lambert it is.

He entered softly.

ERIN, GREEN GEM OF THE SILVER SEA

—The ghost walks, professor MacHugh murmured softly, biscuitfully to the dusty windowpane.

Mr Dedalus, staring from the empty fireplace at Ned Lambert's quizzing face, asked of it sourly:

—Agonising Christ, wouldn't it give you a heartburn on your arse?

Ned Lambert, seated on the table, read on:

—*Or again, note the meanderings of some purling rill as it babbles on its way, tho' quarrelling with the stony obstacles, to the tumbling waters of Neptune's blue domain, mid mossy banks, fanned by gentlest zephyrs, played on by the glorious sunlight or 'neath the shadows cast o'er its pensive bosom by the overarching leafage of the giants of the forest.* What about that, Simon? he asked over the fringe of his newspaper. How's that for high?

—Changing his drink, Mr Dedalus said.

Ned Lambert, laughing, struck the newspaper on his knees, repeating:

—*The pensive bosom and the overarsing leafage.* O boys! O boys!

—And Xenophon looked upon Marathon, Mr Dedalus said, looking again on the fireplace and to the window, and Marathon looked on the sea.

—That will do, professor MacHugh cried from the window. I don't want to hear any more of the stuff.

He ate off the crescent of water biscuit he had been nibbling and, hungered, made ready to nibble the biscuit in his other hand.

High falutin stuff. Bladderbags. Ned Lambert is taking a day off I see. Rather upsets a man's day, a funeral does. He has influence they say. Old Chatterton, the vicechancellor, is his granduncle or his greatgranduncle. Close on ninety they say. Subleader for his death written this long time perhaps. Living to spite them. Might go first himself. Johnny, make room for your uncle. The right honourable Hedges Eyre Chatterton. Daresay he writes him an odd shaky cheque or two on gale days. Windfall when he kicks out. Alleluia.

—Just another spasm, Ned Lambert said.

—What is it? Mr Bloom asked.

—A recently discovered fragment of Cicero, professor MacHugh answered with pomp of tone. *Our lovely land.*

SHORT BUT TO THE POINT

—Whose land? Mr Bloom said simply.

—Most pertinent question, the professor said between his chews. With an accent on the whose.

—Dan Dawson's land Mr Dedalus said.

—Is it his speech last night? Mr Bloom asked.

Ned Lambert nodded.

—But listen to this, he said.

The doorknob hit Mr Bloom in the small of the back as the door was pushed in.

—Excuse me, J. J. O'Molloy said, entering.

Mr Bloom moved nimbly aside.

—I beg yours, he said.

—Good day, Jack.

—Come in. Come in.

—Good day.

—How are you, Dedalus?

—Well. And yourself?

J. J. O'Molloy shook his head.

SAD

Cleverest fellow at the junior bar he used to be. Decline, poor chap. That hectic flush spells finis for a man. Touch and go with him. What's in the wind, I wonder. Money worry.

—*Or again if we but climb the serried mountain peaks.*

—You're looking extra.

—Is the editor to be seen? J. J. O'Molloy asked, looking towards the inner door.

—Very much so, professor MacHugh said. To be seen and heard. He's in his sanctum with Lenehan.

J. J. O'Molloy strolled to the sloping desk and began to turn back the pink pages of the file.

Practice dwindling. A mighthavebeen. Losing heart. Gambling. Debts of honour. Reaping the whirlwind. Used to get good retainers from D. and T. Fitzgerald. Their wigs to show the grey matter. Brains on their sleeve like the statue in Glasnevin. Believe he does some literary work for the *Express* with Gabriel Conroy. Wellread fellow. Myles Crawford began on the *Independent.* Funny the way those newspaper men veer about when they get wind of a new opening. Weathercocks. Hot and cold in the same breath. Wouldn't know which to believe. One story good till you hear the next. Go for one another baldheaded in the papers and then all blows over. Hail fellow well met the next moment.

—Ah, listen to this for God' sake, Ned Lambert pleaded. *Or again if we but climb the serried mountain peaks . . .*

—Bombast! the professor broke in testily. Enough of the inflated windbag!

—*Peaks,* Ned Lambert went on, *towering high on high, to bathe our souls, as it were . . .*

—Bathe his lips, Mr Dedalus said. Blessed and eternal God! Yes? Is he taking anything for it?

—*As 'twere, in the peerless panorama of Ireland's portfolio, unmatched, despite their wellpraised prototypes in other vaunted prize regions, for very beauty, of bosky grove and undulating plain and luscious pastureland of vernal green, steeped in the transcendent translucent glow of our mild mysterious Irish twilight . . .*

HIS NATIVE DORIC

—The moon, professor MacHugh said. He forgot Hamlet.

—*That mantles the vista far and wide and wait till the glowing orb of the moon shine forth to irradiate her silver effulgence . . .*

—O! Mr Dedalus cried, giving vent to a hopeless groan. Shite and onions! That'll do, Ned. Life is too short.

He took off his silk hat and, blowing out impatiently his bushy moustache, welshcombed his hair with raking fingers.

Ned Lambert tossed the newspaper aside, chuckling with delight. An instant after a hoarse bark of laughter burst over professor MacHugh's unshaven blackspectacled face.

—Doughy Daw! he cried.

WHAT WETHERUP SAID

All very fine to jeer at it now in cold print but it goes down like hot cake that stuff. He was in the bakery line too, wasn't he? Why they call him Doughy Daw. Feathered his nest well anyhow. Daughter engaged to that chap in the inland revenue office with the motor. Hooked that nicely. Entertainments. Open house. Big blowout. Wetherup always said that. Get a grip of them by the stomach.

The inner door was opened violently and a scarlet beaked face, crested by a comb of feathery hair, thrust itself in. The bold blue eyes stared about them and the harsh voice asked:

—What is it?

—And here comes the sham squire himself! professor MacHugh said grandly.

—Getonouthat, you bloody old pedagogue! the editor said in recognition.

—Come, Ned, Mr Dedalus said, putting on his hat. I must get a drink after that.

—Drink! the editor cried. No drinks served before mass.

—Quite right too, Mr Dedalus said, going out. Come on, Ned.

Ned Lambert sidled down from the table. The editor's blue eyes roved towards Mr Bloom's face, shadowed by a smile.

—Will you join us, Myles? Ned Lambert asked.

MEMORABLE BATTLES RECALLED

—North Cork militia! the editor cried, striding to the mantelpiece. We won every time! North Cork and Spanish officers!

—Where was that, Myles? Ned Lambert asked with a reflective glance at his toecaps.

—In Ohio! the editor shouted.

—So it was, begad, Ned Lambert agreed.

Passing out he whispered to J. J. O'Molloy:

—Incipient jigs. Sad case.

—Ohio! the editor crowed in high treble from his uplifted scarlet face. My Ohio!

—A perfect cretic! the professor said. Long, short and long.

O, HARP EOLIAN!

He took a reel of dental floss from his waistcoat pocket and, breaking off a piece, twanged it smartly between two and two of his resonant unwashed teeth.

—Bingbang, bangbang.

Mr Bloom, seeing the coast clear, made for the inner door.

—Just a moment, Mr Crawford, he said. I just want to phone about an ad.

He went in.

—What about that leader this evening? professor MacHugh asked, coming to the editor and laying a firm hand on his shoulder.

—That'll be all right, Myles Crawford said more calmly. Never you fret. Hello, Jack. That's all right.

—Good day, Myles, J. J. O'Molloy said, letting the pages he held slip limply back on the file. Is that Canada swindle case on today?

The telephone whirred inside.

—Twentyeight . . . No, twenty . . . Double four . . . Yes.

SPOT THE WINNER

Lenehan came out of the inner office with *Sport's* tissues.

—Who wants a dead cert for the Gold cup? he asked. Sceptre with O. Madden up.

He tossed the tissues on to the table.

Screams of newsboys barefoot in the hall rushed near and the door was flung open.

—Hush, Lenehan said. I hear feetstoops.

Professor MacHugh strode across the room and seized the cringing urchin by the collar as the others scampered out of the hall and down the steps. The tissues rustled up in the draught, floated softly in the air blue scrawls and under the table came to earth.

—It wasn't me, sir. It was the big fellow shoved me, sir.

—Throw him out and shut the door, the editor said. There's a hurricane blowing.

Lenehan began to paw the tissues up from the floor, grunting as he stooped twice.

—Waiting for the racing special, sir, the newsboy said. It was Pat Farrell shoved me, sir.

He pointed to two faces peering in round the doorframe.

—Him, sir.

—Out of this with you, professor MacHugh said gruffly.

He hustled the boy out and banged the door to.

J. J. O'Molloy turned the files cracklingly over, murmuring, seeking:

—Continued on page six, column four.

—Yes, *Evening Telegraph* here, Mr Bloom phoned from the inner office. Is the boss . . .? Yes, *Telegraph* . . . To where? Aha! Which auction rooms? . . . Aha! I see . . . Right. I'll catch him.

A COLLISION ENSUES

The bell whirred again as he rang off. He came in quickly and bumped against Lenehan who was struggling up with the second tissue.

—*Pardon, monsieur*, Lenehan said, clutching him for an instant and making a grimace.

—My fault, Mr Bloom said, suffering his grip. Are you hurt? I'm in a hurry.

—Knee, Lenehan said.

He made a comic face and whined, rubbing his knee:

—The accumulation of the *anno Domini*.

—Sorry, Mr Bloom said.

He went to the door and, holding it ajar, paused. J. J. O'Molloy slapped the heavy pages over. The noise of two shrill voices, a mouthorgan, echoed in the bare hallway from the newsboys squatted on the doorsteps:

—*We are the boys of Wexford*
Who fought with heart and hand.

EXIT BLOOM

—I'm just running round to Bachelor's walk, Mr Bloom said, about this ad of Keyes's. Want to fix it up. They tell me he's round there in Dillon's.

He looked indecisively for a moment at their faces. The editor who, leaning against the mantelshelf, had propped his head on his hand, suddenly stretched forth an arm amply.

—Begone! he said. The world is before you.

—Back in no time, Mr Bloom said, hurrying out.

J. J. O'Molloy took the tissues from Lenehan's hand and read them, blowing them apart gently, without comment.

—He'll get that advertisement, the professor said, staring through his blackrimmed spectacles over the crossblind. Look at the young scamps after him.

—Show. Where? Lenehan cried, running to the window.

A STREET CORTÈGE

Both smiled over the crossblind at the file of capering newsboys in Mr Bloom's wake, the last zigzagging white on the breeze a mocking kite, a tail of white bowknots.

—Look at the young guttersnipe behind him hue and cry, Lenehan said, and you'll kick. O, my rib risible! Taking off his flat spaugs and the walk. Small nines. Steal upon larks.

He began to mazurka in swift caricature across the floor on sliding feet past the fireplace to J. J. O'Molloy who placed the tissues in his receiving hands.

—What's that? Myles Crawford said with a start. Where are the other two gone?

—Who? the professor said, turning. They're gone round to the Oval for a drink. Paddy Hooper is there with Jack Hall. Came over last night.

—Come on then, Myles Crawford said. Where's my hat?

He walked jerkily into the office behind, parting the vent of his jacket, jingling his keys in his back pocket. They jingled then in the air and against the wood as he locked his desk drawer.

—He's pretty well on, professor MacHugh said in a low voice.

—Seems to be, J. J. O'Molloy said, taking out a cigarettecase in murmuring meditation, but it is not always as it seems. Who has the most matches?

THE CALUMET OF PEACE

He offered a cigarette to the professor and took one himself. Lenehan promptly struck a match for them and lit their cigarettes in turn. J. J. O'Molloy opened his case again and offered it.

—*Thanky vous*, Lenehan said, helping himself.

The editor came from the inner office, a straw hat awry on his brow. He declaimed in song, pointing sternly at professor MacHugh:

> *'Twas rank and fame that tempted thee,*
> *'Twas empire charmed thy heart.*

The professor grinned, locking his long lips.

—Eh? You bloody old Roman empire? Myles Crawford said.

He took a cigarette from the open case. Lenehan, lighting it for him with quick grace, said:

—Silence for my brandnew riddle!

—*Imperium romanum*, J. J. O'Molloy said gently. It sounds nobler than British or Brixton. The word reminds one somehow of fat in the fire.

Myles Crawford blew his first puff violently towards the ceiling.

—That's it, he said. We are the fat. You and I are the fat in the fire. We haven't got the chance of a snowball in hell.

The Grandeur That Was Rome

—Wait a moment, professor MacHugh said, raising two quiet claws. We mustn't be led away by words, by sounds of words. We think of Rome, imperial, imperious, imperative.

He extended elocutionary arms from frayed stained shirtcuffs, pausing:

—What was their civilisation? Vast, I allow: but vile. Cloacae: sewers. The Jews in the wilderness and on the mountaintop said: *It is meet to be here. Let us build an altar to Jehovah.* The Roman, like the Englishman who follows in his footsteps, brought to every new shore on which he set his foot (on our shore he never set it) only his cloacal obsession. He gazed about him in his toga and he said: *It is meet to be here. Let us construct a watercloset.*

—Which they accordingly did do, Lenehan said. Our old ancient ancestors, as we read in the first chapter of Guinness's, were partial to the running stream.

—They were nature's gentlemen, J. J. O'Molloy murmured. But we have also Roman law.

—And Pontius Pilate is its prophet, professor MacHugh responded.

—Do you know that story about chief baron Palles? J. J. O'Molloy asked. It was at the royal university dinner. Everything was going swimmingly . . .

—First my riddle, Lenehan said. Are you ready?

Mr O'Madden Burke, tall in copious grey of Donegal tweed, came in from the hallway. Stephen Dedalus, behind him, uncovered as he entered.

—*Entrez, mes enfants!* Lenehan cried.

—I escort a suppliant, Mr O'Madden Burke said melodiously. Youth led by Experience visits Notoriety.

—How do you do? the editor said, holding out a hand. Come in. Your governor is just gone.

? ? ?

Lenehan said to all:

—Silence! What opera resembles a railway line? Reflect, ponder, excogitate, reply.

Stephen handed over the typed sheets, pointing to the title and signature.

—Who? the editor asked.

Bit torn off.

—Mr Garrett Deasy, Stephen said.

—That old pelters, the editor said. Who tore it? Was he short taken?

On swift sail flaming
From storm and south
He comes, pale vampire,
Mouth to my mouth.

—Good day, Stephen, the professor said, coming to peer over their shoulders. Foot and mouth? Are you turned . . .?

Bullockbefriending bard.

SHINDY IN WELLKNOWN RESTAURANT

—Good day, sir, Stephen answered blushing. The letter is not mine. Mr Garrett Deasy asked me to . . .

—O, I know him, Myles Crawford said, and I knew his wife too. The bloodiest old tartar God ever made. By Jesus, she had the foot and mouth disease and no mistake! The night she threw the soup in the waiter's face in the Star and Garter. Oho!

A woman brought sin into the world. For Helen, the runaway wife of Menelaus, ten years the Greeks. O'Rourke, prince of Breffni.

—Is he a widower? Stephen asked.

—Ay, a grass one, Myles Crawford said, his eye running down the typescript. Emperor's horses. Habsburg. An Irishman saved his life on the ramparts of Vienna. Don't you forget! Maximilian Karl O'Donnell, graf von Tirconnell in Ireland. Sent his heir over to make the king an Austrian fieldmarshal now. Going to be trouble there one day. Wild geese. O yes, every time. Don't you forget that!

—The moot point is did he forget it, J. J. O'Molloy said quietly, turning a horseshoe paperweight. Saving princes is a thank you job.

Professor MacHugh turned on him.

—And if not? he said.

—I'll tell you how it was, Myles Crawford began. A Hungarian it was one day . . .

LOST CAUSES
NOBLE MARQUESS MENTIONED

—We were always loyal to lost causes, the professor said. Success for us is the death of the intellect and of the imagination. We were never loyal to the successful. We serve them. I teach the blatant Latin language. I speak the tongue of a race the acme of whose mentality is the maxim: time is money. Material domination. *Dominus!* Lord! Where is the spirituality? Lord Jesus? Lord Salisbury? A sofa in a westend club. But the Greek!

KYRIE ELEISON!

A smile of light brightened his darkrimmed eyes, lengthened his long lips.

—The Greek! he said again. *Kyrios!* Shining word! The vowels the Semite and the Saxon know not. *Kyrie!* The radiance of the intellect. I ought to profess Greek, the language of the mind. *Kyrie eleison!* The closetmaker and the cloacamaker will never be lords of our spirit. We are liege subjects of the catholic chivalry of Europe that foundered at Trafalgar and of the empire of the spirit, not an *imperium,* that went under with the Athenian fleets at Aegospotami. Yes, yes. They went under. Pyrrhus, misled by an oracle, made a last attempt to retrieve the fortunes of Greece. Loyal to a lost cause.

He strode away from them towards the window.

—They went forth to battle, Mr O'Madden Burke said greyly, but they always fell.

—Boohoo! Lenehan wept with a little noise. Owing to a brick received in the latter half of the *matinée.* Poor, poor, poor Pyrrhus!

He whispered then near Stephen's ear:

LENEHAN'S LIMERICK

There's a ponderous pundit MacHugh
Who wears goggles of ebony hue.
As he mostly sees double
To wear them why trouble?
I can't see the Joe Miller. Can you?

In mourning for Sallust, Mulligan says. Whose mother is beastly dead.

Myles Crawford crammed the sheets into a sidepocket.

—That'll be all right, he said. I'll read the rest after. That'll be all right.

Lenehan extended his hands in protest.

—But my riddle! he said. What opera is like a railway line?

—Opera? Mr O'Madden Burke's sphinx face reriddled.

Lenehan announced gladly:

—*The Rose of Castile.* See the wheeze? Rows of cast steel. Gee!

He poked Mr O'Madden Burke mildly in the spleen. Mr O'Madden Burke fell back with grace on his umbrella, feigning a gasp.

—Help! he sighed. I feel a strong weakness.

Lenehan, rising to tiptoe, fanned his face rapidly with the rustling tissues.

The professor, returning by way of the files, swept his hand across Stephen's and Mr O'Madden Burke's loose ties.

—Paris, past and present, he said. You look like communards.

—Like fellows who had blown up the Bastile, J. J. O'Molloy said in quiet mockery. Or was it you shot the lord lieutenant of Finland between you? You look as though you had done the deed. General Bobrikoff.

OMNIUM GATHERUM

—We were only thinking about it, Stephen said.

—All the talents, Myles Crawford said. Law, the classics . . .

—The turf, Lenehan put in.

—Literature, the press.

—If Bloom were here, the professor said. The gentle art of advertisement.

—And Madam Bloom, Mr O'Madden Burke added. The vocal muse. Dublin's prime favourite.

Lenehan gave a loud cough.

—Ahem! he said very softly. O, for a fresh of breath air! I caught a cold in the park. The gate was open.

"YOU CAN DO IT!"

The editor laid a nervous hand on Stephen's shoulder.

—I want you to write something for me, he said. Something with a bite in it. You can do it. I see it in your face. *In the lexicon of youth* . . .

See it in your face. See it in your eye. Lazy idle little schemer.

—Foot and mouth disease! the editor cried in scornful invective. Great nationalist meeting in Borris-in-Ossory. All balls! Bulldosing the public! Give them something with a bite in it. Put us all into it, damn its soul. Father, Son and Holy Ghost and Jakes M'Carthy.

—We can all supply mental pabulum, Mr O'Madden Burke said.

Stephen raised his eyes to the bold unheeding stare.

—He wants you for the pressgang, J. J. O'Molloy said.

The Great Gallaher

—You can do it, Myles Crawford repeated, clenching his hand in emphasis. Wait a minute. We'll paralyse Europe as Ignatius Gallaher used to say when he was on the shaughraun, doing billiardmarking in the Clarence. Gallaher, that was a pressman for you. That was a pen. You know how he made his mark? I'll tell you. That was the smartest piece of journalism ever known. That was in eightyone, sixth of May, time of the invincibles, murder in the Phoenix park, before you were born, I suppose. I'll show you.

He pushed past them to the files.

—Look at here, he said turning. The *New York World* cabled for a special. Remember that time?

Professor MacHugh nodded.

—*New York World*, the editor said, excitedly pushing back his straw hat. Where it took place. Tim Kelly, or Kavanagh I mean. Joe Brady and the rest of them. Where Skin-the-Goat drove the car. Whole route, see?

—Skin-the-Goat, Mr O'Madden Burke said. Fitzharris. He has that cabman's shelter, they say, down there at Butt bridge. Holohan told me. You know Holohan?

—Hop and carry one, is it? Myles Crawford said.

—And poor Gumley is down there too, so he told me, minding stones for the corporation. A night watchman.

Stephen turned in surprise.

—Gumley? he said. You don't say so? A friend of my father's, is it?

—Never mind Gumley, Myles Crawford cried angrily. Let Gumley mind the stones, see they don't run away. Look at here. What did Ignatius Gallaher do? I'll tell you. Inspiration of genius. Cabled right away. Have you *Weekly Freeman* of 17 March? Right. Have you got that?

He flung back pages of the files and stuck his finger on a point.

—Take page four, advertisement for Bransome's coffee, let us say. Have you got that? Right.

The telephone whirred.

A DISTANT VOICE

—I'll answer it, the professor said, going.

—B is parkgate. Good.

His finger leaped and struck point after point, vibrating.

—T is viceregal lodge. C is where murder took place. K is Knockmaroon gate.

The loose flesh of his neck shook like a cock's wattles. An illstarched dicky jutted up and with a rude gesture he thrust it back into his waistcoat.

—Hello? *Evening Telegraph* here . . . Hello? . . . Who's there? . . . Yes . . . Yes . . . Yes.

—F to P is the route Skin-the-Goat drove the car for an alibi, Inchicore, Roundtown, Windy Arbour, Palmerston Park, Ranelagh. F. A. B. P. Got that? X is Davy's publichouse in upper Leeson street.

The professor came to the inner door.

—Bloom is at the telephone, he said.

—Tell him go to hell, the editor said promptly. X is Davy's publichouse, see?

CLEVER, VERY

—Clever, Lenehan said. Very.

—Gave it to them on a hot plate, Myles Crawford said, the whole bloody history.

Nightmare from which you will never awake.

—I saw it, the editor said proudly. I was present. Dick Adams, the besthearted bloody Corkman the Lord ever put the breath of life in, and myself.

Lenehan bowed to a shape of air, announcing:

—Madam, I'm Adam. And Able was I ere I saw Elba.

—History! Myles Crawford cried. The Old Woman of Prince's street was there first. There was weeping and gnashing of teeth over that. Out of an advertisement. Gregor Grey made the design for it. That gave him the leg up. Then Paddy Hooper worked Tay Pay who took him on to the *Star.* Now he's got in with Blumenfeld. That's press. That's talent. Pyatt! He was all their daddies!

—The father of scare journalism, Lenehan confirmed, and the brother-in-law of Chris Callinan.

—Hello? . . . Are you there? . . . Yes, he's here still. Come across yourself.

—Where do you find a pressman like that now, eh? the editor cried.

He flung the pages down.

—Clamn dever, Lenehan said to Mr O'Madden Burke.

—Very smart, Mr O'Madden Burke said.

Professor MacHugh came from the inner office.

—Talking about the invincibles, he said, did you see that some hawkers were up before the recorder . . .

—O yes, J. J. O'Molloy said eagerly. Lady Dudley was walking home through the park to see all the trees that were blown down by that cyclone last year and thought she'd buy a view of Dublin. And it turned out to be a commemoration postcard of Joe Brady or Number One or Skin-the-Goat. Right outside the viceregal lodge, imagine!

—They're only in the hook and eye department, Myles Crawford said. Psha! Press and the bar! Where have you a man now at the bar like those fellows, like Whiteside, like Isaac Butt, like silvertongued O'Hagan. Eh? Ah, bloody nonsense. Psha! Only in the halfpenny place.

His mouth continued to twitch unspeaking in nervous curls of disdain.

Would anyone wish that mouth for her kiss? How do you know? Why did you write it then?

RHYMES AND REASONS

Mouth, south. Is the mouth south someway? Or the south a mouth? Must be some. South, pout, out, shout, drouth. Rhymes: two men dressed the same, looking the same, two by two.

> . . . . *la tua pace*
> . . . . *che parlar ti piace*
> *Mentre che il vento, come fa, si tace.*

He saw them three by three, approaching girls, in green, in rose, in russet, entwining, *per l'aer perso*, in mauve, in purple, *quella pacifica oriafiamma*, gold of oriflamme, *di rimirar fè più ardenti*. But I old men, penitent, leadenfooted, underdarkneath the night: mouth south: tomb womb.

—Speak up for yourself, Mr O'Madden Burke said.

SUFFICIENT FOR THE DAY . . .

J. J. O'Molloy, smiling palely, took up the gage.

—My dear Myles, he said, flinging his cigarette aside, you put a false construction on my words. I hold no brief, as at present advised, for the third profession *qua* profession but your Cork legs are running away with you. Why not bring in Henry Grattan and Flood and Demosthenes and Edmund Burke? Ignatius Gallaher we all know and his Chapelizod boss, Harmsworth of the farthing press, and his American cousin of the Bowery guttersheet not to mention *Paddy Kelly's Budget, Pue's Occurrences* and our watchful friend *The Skibbereen Eagle*. Why bring in a master of forensic eloquence like Whiteside? Sufficient for the day is the newspaper thereof.

LINKS WITH BYGONE DAYS OF YORE

—Grattan and Flood wrote for this very paper, the editor cried in his face. Irish volunteers. Where are you now? Established 1763. Dr Lucas. Who have you now like John Philpot Curran? Psha!

—Well, J. J. O'Molloy said, Bushe K.C., for example.

—Bushe? the editor said. Well, yes: Bushe, yes. He has a strain of it in his blood. Kendal Bushe or I mean Seymour Bushe.

—He would have been on the bench long ago, the professor said, only for . . . But no matter.

J. J. O'Molloy turned to Stephen and said quietly and slowly:

—One of the most polished periods I think I ever listened to in my life fell from the lips of Seymour Bushe. It was in that case of fratricide, the Childs murder case. Bushe defended him.

And in the porches of mine ear did pour.

By the way how did he find that out? He died in his sleep. Or the other story, beast with two backs?

—What was that? the professor asked.

—He spoke on the law of evidence, J. J. O'Molloy said, of Roman justice as contrasted with the earlier Mosaic code, the *lex talionis*. And he cited the Moses of Michelangelo in the vatican.

—Ha.

—A few wellchosen words, Lenehan prefaced. Silence!

Pause. J. J. O'Molloy took out his cigarettecase.

False lull. Something quite ordinary.

Messenger took out his matchbox thoughtfully and lit his cigar.

I have often thought since on looking back over that strange time that it was that small act, trivial in itself, that striking of that match, that determined the whole aftercourse of both our lives.

A POLISHED PERIOD

J. J. O'Molloy resumed, moulding his words:

—He said of it: *that stony effigy in frozen music, horned and terrible, of the human form divine, that eternal symbol of wisdom and of prophecy which, if aught that the imagination or the hand of sculptor has wrought in marble of soultransfigured and of soultransfiguring deserves to live, deserves to live.*

His slim hand with a wave graced echo and fall.

—Fine! Myles Crawford said at once.

—The divine afflatus, Mr O'Madden Burke said.

—You like it? J. J. O'Molloy asked Stephen.

Stephen, his blood wooed by grace of language and gesture, blushed. He took a cigarette from the case. J. J. O'Molloy offered his case to Myles Crawford. Lenehan lit their cigarettes as before and took his trophy, saying:

—Muchibus thankibus.

A MAN OF HIGH MORALE

—Professor Magennis was speaking to me about you, J. J. O'Molloy said to Stephen. What do you think really of that hermetic crowd, the opal hush poets: A. E. the mastermystic? That Blavatsky woman started it. She was a nice old bag of tricks. A. E. has been telling some yankee interviewer that you came to him in the small hours of the morning to ask him about planes of consciousness.

Magennis thinks you must have been pulling A. E.'s leg. He is a man of the very highest morale, Magennis.

Speaking about me. What did he say? What did he say? What did he say about me? Don't ask.

—No, thanks, professor MacHugh said, waving the cigarettecase aside. Wait a moment. Let me say one thing. The finest display of oratory I ever heard was a speech made by John F Taylor at the college historical society. Mr Justice Fitzgibbon, the present lord justice of appeal, had spoken and the paper under debate was an essay (new for those days), advocating the revival of the Irish tongue.

He turned towards Myles Crawford and said:

—You know Gerald Fitzgibbon. Then you can imagine the style of his discourse.

—He is sitting with Tim Healy, J. J. O'Molloy said, rumour has it, on the Trinity college estates commission.

—He is sitting with a sweet thing, Myles Crawford said, in a child's frock. Go on. Well?

—It was the speech, mark you, the professor said, of a finished orator, full of courteous haughtiness and pouring in chastened diction I will not say the vials of his wrath but pouring the proud man's contumely upon the new movement. It was then a new movement. We were weak, therefore worthless.

He closed his long thin lips an instant but, eager to be on, raised an outspanned hand to his spectacles and, with trembling thumb and ringfinger touching lightly the black rims, steadied them to a new focus.

IMPROMPTU

In ferial tone he addressed J. J. O'Molloy:

—Taylor had come there, you must know, from a sickbed. That he had prepared his speech I do not believe for there was not even one shorthandwriter in the hall. His dark lean face had a growth of shaggy beard round it. He wore a loose white silk neckcloth and altogether he looked (though he was not) a dying man.

His gaze turned at once but slowly from J. J. O'Molloy's towards Stephen's face and then bent at once to the ground, seeking. His unglazed linen collar appeared behind his bent head, soiled by his withering hair. Still seeking, he said:

—When Fitzgibbon's speech had ended John F Taylor rose to reply. Briefly, as well as I can bring them to mind, his words were these.

He raised his head firmly. His eyes bethought themselves once more. Witless shellfish swam in the gross lenses to and fro, seeking outlet.

He began:

—*Mr Chairman, ladies and gentlemen: Great was my admiration in listening to the remarks addressed to the youth of Ireland a moment since by my learned friend. It seemed to me that I had been transported into a country far away from this country, into an age remote from this age, that I stood in ancient Egypt and that I was listening to the speech of some highpriest of that land addressed to the youthful Moses.*

His listeners held their cigarettes poised to hear, their smokes ascending in frail stalks that flowered with his speech. *And let our crooked smokes.* Noble words coming. Look out. Could you try your hand at it yourself?

—*And it seemed to me that I heard the voice of that Egyptian highpriest raised in a tone of like haughtiness and like pride. I heard his words and their meaning was revealed to me.*

FROM THE FATHERS

It was revealed to me that those things are good which yet are corrupted which neither if they were supremely good nor unless they were good could be corrupted. Ah, curse you! That's saint Augustine.

—*Why will you jews not accept our culture, our religion and our language? You are a tribe of nomad herdsmen: we are a mighty people. You have no cities nor no wealth: our cities are hives of humanity and our galleys, trireme and quadrireme, laden with all manner merchandise furrow the waters of the known globe. You have but emerged from primitive conditions: we have a literature, a priesthood, an agelong history and a polity.*

Nile.

Child, man, effigy.

By the Nilebank the babemaries kneel, cradle of bulrushes: a man supple in combat: stonehorned, stonebearded, heart of stone.

—*You pray to a local and obscure idol: our temples, majestic and mysterious, are the abodes of Isis and Osiris, of Horus and Ammon Ra. Yours serfdom, awe and humbleness: ours thunder and the seas. Israel is weak and few are her children:*

158

Egypt is an host and terrible are her arms. Vagrants and daylabourers are you called: the world trembles at our name.

A dumb belch of hunger cleft his speech. He lifted his voice above it boldly:

—*But, ladies and gentlemen, had the youthful Moses listened to and accepted that view of life, had he bowed his head and bowed his will and bowed his spirit before that arrogant admonition he would never have brought the chosen people out of their house of bondage, nor followed the pillar of the cloud by day. He would never have spoken with the Eternal amid lightnings on Sinai's mountaintop nor ever have come down with the light of inspiration shining in his countenance and bearing in his arms the tables of the law, graven in the language of the outlaw.*

He ceased and looked at them, enjoying a silence.

OMINOUS—FOR HIM!

J. J. O'Molloy said not without regret:

—And yet he died without having entered the land of promise.

—A sudden—at—the—moment—though—from—lingering —illness—often—previously—expectorated—demise, Lenehan added. And with a great future behind him.

The troop of bare feet was heard rushing along the hallway and pattering up the staircase.

—That is oratory, the professor said uncontradicted.

Gone with the wind. Hosts at Mullaghmast and Tara of the kings. Miles of ears of porches. The tribune's words, howled and scattered to the four winds. A people sheltered within his voice. Dead noise. Akasic records of all that ever anywhere wherever was. Love and laud him: me no more.

I have money.

—Gentlemen, Stephen said. As the next motion on the agenda paper may I suggest that the house do now adjourn?

—You take my breath away. It is not perchance a French compliment? Mr O'Madden Burke asked. 'Tis the hour, methinks, when the winejug, metaphorically speaking, is most grateful in Ye ancient hostelry.

—That it be and hereby is resolutely resolved. All that are in favour say ay, Lenehan announced. The contrary no. I declare it carried. To which particular boosing shed . . .? My casting vote is: Mooney's!

He led the way, admonishing:

—We will sternly refuse to partake of strong waters, will we not? Yes, we will not. By no manner of means.

Mr O'Madden Burke, following close, said with an ally's lunge of his umbrella:

—Lay on, Macduff!

—Chip of the old block! the editor cried, clapping Stephen on the shoulder. Let us go. Where are those blasted keys?

He fumbled in his pocket pulling out the crushed typesheets.

—Foot and mouth. I know. That'll be all right. That'll go in. Where are they? That's all right.

He thrust the sheets back and went into the inner office.

Let Us Hope

J. J. O'Molloy, about to follow him in, said quietly to Stephen:

—I hope you will live to see it published. Myles, one moment.

He went into the inner office, closing the door behind him.

—Come along, Stephen, the professor said. That is fine, isn't it? It has the prophetic vision. *Fuit Ilium!* The sack of windy Troy. Kingdoms of this world. The masters of the Mediterranean are fellaheen today.

The first newsboy came pattering down the stairs at their heels and rushed out into the street, yelling:

—Racing special!

Dublin. I have much, much to learn.

They turned to the left along Abbey street.

—I have a vision too, Stephen said.

—Yes? the professor said, skipping to get into step. Crawford will follow.

Another newsboy shot past them, yelling as he ran:

—Racing special!

Dear Dirty Dublin

Dubliners.

—Two Dublin vestals, Stephen said, elderly and pious, have lived fifty and fiftythree years in Fumbally's lane.

—Where is that? the professor asked.

—Off Blackpitts, Stephen said.

Damp night reeking of hungry dough. Against the wall. Face glistering tallow under her fustian shawl. Frantic hearts. Akasic records. Quicker, darlint!

On now. Dare it. Let there be life.

—They want to see the views of Dublin from the top of Nelson's pillar. They save up three and tenpence in a red tin letterbox moneybox. They shake out the threepenny bits and sixpences and coax out the pennies with the blade of a knife. Two and three in silver and one and seven in coppers. They put on their bonnets and best clothes and take their umbrellas for fear it may come on to rain.

—Wise virgins, professor MacHugh said.

LIFE ON THE RAW

—They buy one and fourpenceworth of brawn and four slices of panloaf at the north city dining rooms in Marlborough street from Miss Kate Collins, proprietress . . . They purchase four and twenty ripe plums from a girl at the foot of Nelson's pillar to take off the thirst of the brawn. They give two threepenny bits to the gentleman at the turnstile and begin to waddle slowly up the winding staircase, grunting, encouraging each other, afraid of the dark, panting, one asking the other have you the brawn, praising God and the Blessed Virgin, threatening to come down, peeping at the airslits. Glory be to God. They had no idea it was that high.

Their names are Anne Kearns and Florence MacCabe. Anne Kearns has the lumbago for which she rubs on Lourdes water, given her by a lady who got a bottleful from a passionist father. Florence MacCabe takes a crubeen and a bottle of double X for supper every Saturday.

—Antithesis, the professor said nodding twice. Vestal virgins. I can see them. What's keeping our friend?

He turned.

A bevy of scampering newsboys rushed down the steps, scattering in all directions, yelling, their white papers fluttering. Hard after them Myles Crawford appeared on the steps, his hat aureoling his scarlet face, talking with J. J. O'Molloy.

—Come along, the professor cried, waving his arm.

He set off again to walk by Stephen's side.

—Yes, he said. I see them.

Mr Bloom, breathless, caught in a whirl of wild newsboys near the offices of the *Irish Catholic* and *Dublin Penny Journal*, called:

—Mr Crawford! A moment!

—*Telegraph*! Racing special!

—What is it? Myles Crawford said, falling back a pace.

A newsboy cried in Mr Bloom's face:

—Terrible tragedy in Rathmines! A child bit by a bellows!

INTERVIEW WITH THE EDITOR

—Just this ad, Mr Bloom said, pushing through towards the steps, puffing, and taking the cutting from his pocket. I spoke with Mr Keyes just now. He'll give a renewal for two months, he says. After he'll see. But he wants a par to call attention in the *Telegraph* too, the Saturday pink. And he wants it copied if it's not too late I told councillor Nannetti from the *Kilkenny People*. I can have access to it in the national library. House of keys, don't you see? His name is Keyes. It's a play on the name. But he practically promised he'd give the renewal. But he wants just a little puff. What will I tell him, Mr Crawford?

K. M. A.

—Will you tell him he can kiss my arse? Myles Crawford said throwing out his arm for emphasis. Tell him that straight from the stable.

A bit nervy. Look out for squalls. All off for a drink. Arm in arm. Lenehan's yachting cap on the cadge beyond. Usual blarney. Wonder is that young Dedalus the moving spirit. Has a good pair of boots on him today. Last time I saw him he had his heels on view. Been walking in muck somewhere. Careless chap. What was he doing in Irishtown?

—Well, Mr Bloom said, his eyes returning, if I can get the design I suppose it's worth a short par. He'd give the ad, I think. I'll tell him . . .

K. M. R. I. A.

—He can kiss my royal Irish arse, Myles Crawford cried loudly over his shoulder. Any time he likes, tell him.

While Mr Bloom stood weighing the point and about to smile he strode on jerkily.

RAISING THE WIND

—*Nulla bona*, Jack, he said, raising his hand to his chin. I'm up to here. I've been through the hoop myself. I was looking for a fellow to back a bill for me no later than last week. Sorry, Jack. You must take the will for the deed. With a heart and a half if I could raise the wind anyhow.

J. J. O'Molloy pulled a long face and walked on silently. They caught up on the others and walked abreast.

—When they have eaten the brawn and the bread and wiped their twenty fingers in the paper the bread was wrapped in they go nearer to the railings.

—Something for you, the professor explained to Myles Crawford. Two old Dublin women on the top of Nelson's pillar.

SOME COLUMN!—
THAT'S WHAT WADDLER ONE SAID

—That's new, Myles Crawford said. That's copy. Out for the waxies' Dargle. Two old trickies, what?

—But they are afraid the pillar will fall, Stephen went on. They see the roofs and argue about where the different churches are: Rathmines' blue dome, Adam and Eve's, saint Laurence O'Toole's. But it makes them giddy to look so they pull up their skirts . . .

THOSE SLIGHTLY RAMBUNCTIOUS FEMALES

—Easy all, Myles Crawford said. No poetic licence. We're in the archdiocese here.

—And settle down on their striped petticoats, peering up at the statue of the onehandled adulterer.

—Onehandled adulterer! the professor cried. I like that. I see the idea. I see what you mean.

DAMES DONATE DUBLIN'S CITS SPEEDPILLS
VELOCITOUS AEROLITHS, BELIEF

—It gives them a crick in their necks, Stephen said, and they are too tired to look up or down or to speak. They put the bag of plums between them and eat the plums out of it, one after another, wiping off with their handkerchiefs the plumjuice that dribbles out of their mouths and spitting the plumstones slowly out between the railings.

He gave a sudden loud young laugh as a close. Lenehan and Mr O'Madden Burke, hearing, turned, beckoned and led on across towards Mooney's.

—Finished? Myles Crawford said. So long as they do no worse.

SOPHIST WALLOPS HAUGHTY HELEN
SQUARE ON PROBOSCIS. SPARTANS GNASH MOLARS.
ITHACANS VOW PEN IS CHAMP.

—You remind me of Antisthenes, the professor said, a disciple of Gorgias, the sophist. It is said of him that none could tell if he were bitterer against others or against himself. He was the son of a noble and a bondwoman. And he wrote a book in which he took away the palm of beauty from Argive Helen and handed it to poor Penelope.

Poor Penelope. Penelope Rich.

They made ready to cross O'Connell street.

HELLO THERE, CENTRAL!

At various points along the eight lines tramcars with motionless trolleys stood in their tracks, bound for or from Rathmines, Rathfarnham, Blackrock, Kingstown and Dalkey, Sandymount Green, Ringsend and Sandymount Tower, Donnybrook, Palmerston Park and Upper Rathmines, all still, becalmed in short circuit. Hackney cars, cabs, delivery waggons, mailvans, private broughams, aerated mineral water floats with rattling crates of bottles, rattled, rolled, horsedrawn, rapidly.

WHAT?—AND LIKEWISE—WHERE?

—But what do you call it? Myles Crawford asked. Where did they get the plums?

VIRGILIAN, SAYS PEDAGOGUE.
SOPHOMORE PLUMPS FOR OLD MAN MOSES.

—Call it, wait, the professor said, opening his long lips wide to reflect. Call it, let me see. Call it: *deus nobis hæc otia fecit.*

—No, Stephen said. I call it *A Pisgah Sight of Palestine* or *The Parable of The Plums.*

—I see, the professor said.

He laughed richly.

—I see, he said again with new pleasure. Moses and the promised land. We gave him that idea, he added to J. J. O'Molloy.

HORATIO IS CYNOSURE THIS FAIR JUNE DAY

J. J. O'Molloy sent a weary sidelong glance towards the statue and held his peace.

—I see, the professor said.

He halted on sir John Gray's pavement island and peered aloft at Nelson through the meshes of his wry smile.

DIMINISHED DIGITS PROVE TOO TITILLATING FOR
FRISKY FRUMPS. ANNE WIMBLES, FLO WANGLES—
YET CAN YOU BLAME THEM?

—Onehandled adulterer, he said smiling grimly. That tickles me, I must say.

—Tickled the old ones too, Myles Crawford said, if the God Almighty's truth was known.

8

Pineapple rock, lemon platt, butter scotch. A sugarsticky girl shovelling scoopfuls of creams for a christian brother. Some school treat. Bad for their tummies. Lozenge and comfit manufacturer to His Majesty the King. God. Save. Our. Sitting on his throne sucking red jujubes white.

A sombre Y. M. C. A. young man, watchful among the warm sweet fumes of Graham Lemon's, placed a throwaway in a hand of Mr Bloom.

Heart to heart talks.

Bloo . . . Me? No.

Blood of the Lamb.

His slow feet walked him riverward, reading. Are you saved? All are washed in the blood of the lamb. God wants blood victim. Birth, hymen, martyr, war, foundation of a building, sacrifice, kidney burntoffering, druids' altars. Elijah is coming. Dr John Alexander Dowie restorer of the church in Zion is coming.

Is coming! Is coming!! Is coming!!!
All heartily welcome.

Paying game. Torry and Alexander last year. Polygamy. His wife will put the stopper on that. Where was that ad some Birmingham firm the luminous crucifix. Our Saviour. Wake up in the dead of night and see him on the wall, hanging. Pepper's ghost idea. Iron Nails Ran In.

Phosphorus it must be done with. If you leave a bit of codfish for instance. I could see the bluey silver over it. Night I went down to the pantry in the kitchen. Don't like all the smells in it waiting to rush out. What was it she wanted? The Malaga raisins. Thinking of Spain. Before Rudy was born. The phosphorescence, that bluey greeny. Very good for the brain.

From Butler's monument house corner he glanced along Bachelor's walk. Dedalus' daughter there still outside Dillon's auctionrooms. Must be selling off some old furniture. Knew her eyes at once from the father. Lobbing about waiting for him. Home always breaks up when the mother goes. Fifteen children he had. Birth every year almost. That's in their theology or the priest won't give the poor woman the confession, the absolution. Increase and multiply. Did you ever hear such an idea? Eat you out of house and home. No families themselves to feed. Living on the fat of the land. Their butteries and larders. I'd like to see them do the black fast Yom Kippur. Crossbuns. One meal and a collation for fear he'd collapse on the altar. A housekeeper of one of those fellows if you could pick it out of her. Never pick it out of her. Like getting £. s. d. out of him. Does himself well. No guests. All for number one. Watching his water. Bring your own bread and butter. His reverence: mum's the word.

Good Lord, that poor child's dress is in flitters. Underfed she looks too. Potatoes and marge, marge and potatoes. It's after they feel it. Proof of the pudding. Undermines the constitution.

As he set foot on O'Connell bridge a puffball of smoke plumed up from the parapet. Brewery barge with export stout. England. Sea air sours it, I heard. Be interesting some day get a pass through Hancock to see the brewery. Regular world in itself. Vats of porter wonderful. Rats get in too. Drink themselves bloated as big as a collie floating. Dead drunk on the porter. Drink till they puke again like christians. Imagine drinking that! Rats: vats. Well, of course, if we knew all the things.

Looking down he saw flapping strongly, wheeling between the gaunt quay walls, gulls. Rough weather outside. If I threw myself down? Reuben J's son must have swallowed a good bellyful of that sewage. One and eightpence too much. Hhhhm. It's the droll way he comes out with the things. Knows how to tell a story too.

They wheeled lower. Looking for grub. Wait.

He threw down among them a crumpled paper ball. Elijah thirtytwo feet per sec is com. Not a bit. The ball bobbed unheeded on the wake of swells, floated under by the bridgepiers. Not such damn fools. Also the day I threw that stale cake out of the Erin's King picked it up in the wake fifty yards astern. Live by their wits. They wheeled, flapping.

The hungry famished gull
Flaps o'er the waters dull.

That is how poets write, the similar sounds. But then Shakespeare has no rhymes: blank verse. The flow of the language it is. The thoughts. Solemn.

Hamlet, I am thy father's spirit
Doomed for a certain time to walk the earth.

—Two apples a penny! Two for a penny!

His gaze passed over the glazed apples serried on her stand. Australians they must be this time of year. Shiny peels: polishes them up with a rag or a handkerchief.

Wait. Those poor birds.

He halted again and bought from the old applewoman two Banbury cakes for a penny and broke the brittle paste and threw its fragments down into the Liffey. See that? The gulls swooped silently, two, then all from their heights, pouncing on prey. Gone. Every morsel.

Aware of their greed and cunning he shook the powdery crumb from his hands. They never expected that. Manna. Live on fish, fishy flesh they have, all seabirds, gulls, seagoose. Swans from Anna Liffey swim down here sometimes to preen themselves. No accounting for tastes. Wonder what kind is swanmeat. Robinson Crusoe had to live on them.

They wheeled flapping weakly. I'm not going to throw any more. Penny quite enough. Lot of thanks I get. Not even a caw. They spread foot and mouth disease too. If you cram a turkey say on chestnutmeal it tastes like that. Eat pig like pig. But then why is it that saltwater fish are not salty? How is that?

His eyes sought answer from the river and saw a rowboat rock at anchor on the treacly swells lazily its plastered board.

Kino's
11/-
Trousers

Good idea that. Wonder if he pays rent to the corporation. How can you own water really? It's always flowing in a stream, never the same, which in the stream of life we trace. Because life is a stream.

All kinds of places are good for ads. That quack doctor for the clap used to be stuck up in all the greenhouses. Never see it now. Strictly confidential. Dr Hy Franks. Didn't cost him a red like Maginni the dancing master self advertisement. Got fellows to stick them up or stick them up himself for that matter on the q. t. running in to loosen a button. Fly by night. Just the place too. POST NO BILLS. POST 110 PILLS. Some chap with a dose burning him.

If he . . .?

O!

Eh?

No . . . No.

No, no. I don't believe it. He wouldn't surely?

No, no.

Mr Bloom moved forward, raising his troubled eyes. Think no more about that. After one. Timeball on the ballast office is down. Dunsink time. Fascinating little book that is of sir Robert Ball's. Parallax. I never exactly understood. There's a priest. Could ask him. Par it's Greek: parallel, parallax. Met him pike hoses she called it till I told her about the transmigration. O rocks!

Mr Bloom smiled O rocks at two windows of the ballast office. She's right after all. Only big words for ordinary things on account of the sound. She's not exactly witty. Can be rude too. Blurt out what I was thinking. Still, I don't know. She used to say Ben Dollard had a base barreltone voice. He has legs like barrels and you'd think he was singing into a barrel. Now, isn't that wit. They used to call him big Ben. Not half as witty as calling him base barreltone. Appetite like an albatross. Get outside of a baron of beef. Powerful man he was at stowing away number one Bass. Barrel of Bass. See? It all works out.

A procession of whitesmocked sandwichmen marched slowly towards him along the gutter, scarlet sashes across their boards. Bargains. Like that priest they are this morning: we have sinned: we have suffered. He read the scarlet letters on their five tall white hats: H. E. L. Y. S. Wisdom Hely's. Y lagging behind drew a chunk of bread from under his foreboard, crammed it into his mouth and munched as he walked. Our staple food. Three bob a day, walking along the gutters, street after street. Just keep skin and bone together, bread and skilly. They are not Boyl: no, M'Glade's men. Doesn't bring in any business either. I suggested to him about a transparent showcart with two smart girls sitting inside writing letters, copybooks, envelopes, blottingpaper. I bet that would have caught on. Smart girls writing something catch the eye at once. Everyone dying to know what she's writing. Get twenty of them round you if you stare at nothing. Have a finger in the pie. Women too. Curiosity. Pillar of salt. Wouldn't have it of course because he didn't think of it himself first. Or the inkbottle I suggested with a false stain of black celluloid. His ideas for ads like Plumtree's potted under the obituaries, cold meat department. You can't lick 'em. What? Our envelopes. Hello, Jones, where are you going? Can't stop, Robinson, I am hastening to purchase the only reliable inkeraser *Kansell,* sold by Hely's Ltd, 85 Dame street. Well out of that ruck I am. Devil of a job it was collecting accounts of those convents. Tranquilla convent. That was a nice nun there, really sweet face. Wimple suited her small head. Sister? Sister? I am sure she was crossed in love by her eyes. Very hard to bargain with that sort of a woman. I disturbed her at her devotions that morning. But glad to communicate with the outside world. Our great day, she said. Feast of Our Lady of Mount Carmel. Sweet name too: caramel. She knew I, I think she knew by the way she. If she had married she would have changed. I suppose they really were short of money. Fried everything in the best butter all the same. No lard for them. My heart's broke eating dripping. They like buttering themselves in and out. Molly tasting it, her veil up. Sister? Pat Claffey, the pawnbroker's daughter. It was a nun they say invented barbed wire.

He crossed Westmoreland street when apostrophe S had plodded by. Rover cycleshop. Those races are on today. How long ago is that? Year Phil Gilligan died. We were in Lombard street west. Wait: was in Thom's. Got the job in Wisdom Hely's year we married. Six years. Ten years ago: ninetyfour he died yes that's right the big fire at Arnott's. Val Dillon was lord mayor. The Glencree dinner. Alderman Robert O'Reilly emptying the port into his soup before the flag fell. Bobbob lapping it for the inner alderman. Couldn't hear what the band played. For what we have already received may the Lord make us. Milly was a kiddy then. Molly had that elephantgrey dress with the braided frogs. Mantailored with selfcovered buttons. She didn't like it because I sprained my ankle first day she wore choir picnic at the Sugarloaf. As if that. Old Goodwin's tall hat done up with some sticky stuff. Flies' picnic too. Never put a dress on her back like it. Fitted her like a glove, shoulders and hips. Just beginning to plump it out well. Rabbitpie we had that day. People looking after her.

Happy. Happier then. Snug little room that was with the red wallpaper. Dockrell's, one and ninepence a dozen. Milly's tubbing night. American soap I bought: elderflower. Cosy smell of her bathwater. Funny she looked soaped all over. Shapely too. Now photography. Poor papa's daguerreotype atelier he told me of. Hereditary taste.

He walked along the curbstone.

Stream of life. What was the name of that priestylooking chap was always squinting in when he passed? Weak eyes, woman. Stopped in Citron's saint Kevin's parade. Pen something. Pendennis? My memory is getting. Pen . . .? Of course it's years ago. Noise of the trams probably. Well, if he couldn't remember the dayfather's name that he sees every day.

Bartell d'Arcy was the tenor, just coming out then. Seeing her home after practice. Conceited fellow with his waxedup moustache. Gave her that song *Winds that blow from the south.*

Windy night that was I went to fetch her there was that lodge meeting on about those lottery tickets after Goodwin's concert in the supperroom or oakroom of the Mansion house. He and I behind. Sheet of her music blew out of my hand against the High school railings. Lucky it didn't. Thing like that spoils the effect of a night for her. Professor Goodwin linking her in front. Shaky on his pins, poor old sot. His farewell concerts. Positively last appearance on any stage. May be for months and may be for never. Remember her laughing at the wind, her blizzard collar up. Corner of Harcourt road remember that gust. Brrfoo! Blew up all her skirts and her boa nearly smothered old Goodwin. She did get flushed in the wind. Remember when we got home raking up the fire and frying up those pieces of lap of mutton for her supper with the Chutney sauce she liked. And the mulled rum. Could see her in the bedroom from the hearth unclamping the busk of her stays: white.

Swish and soft flop her stays made on the bed. Always warm from her. Always liked to let her self out. Sitting there after till near two taking out her hairpins. Milly tucked up in beddyhouse. Happy. Happy. That was the night . . .

—O, Mr Bloom, how do you do?

—O, how do you do, Mrs Breen?

—No use complaining. How is Molly those times? Haven't seen her for ages.

—In the pink, Mr Bloom said gaily. Milly has a position down in Mullingar, you know.

—Go away! Isn't that grand for her?

—Yes. In a photographer's there. Getting on like a house on fire. How are all your charges?

—All on the baker's list, Mrs Breen said.

How many has she? No other in sight.

—You're in black, I see. You have no . . .

—No, Mr Bloom said. I have just come from a funeral.

Going to crop up all day, I foresee. Who's dead, when and what did he die of? Turn up like a bad penny.

—O, dear me, Mrs Breen said. I hope it wasn't any near relation.

May as well get her sympathy.

—Dignam, Mr Bloom said. An old friend of mine. He died quite suddenly, poor fellow. Heart trouble, I believe. Funeral was this morning.

> *Your funeral's tomorrow*
> *While you're coming through the rye.*
> *Diddlediddle dumdum*
> *Diddlediddle . . .*

—Sad to lose the old friends, Mrs Breen's womaneyes said melancholily.

Now that's quite enough about that. Just: quietly: husband.

—And your lord and master?

Mrs Breen turned up her two large eyes. Hasn't lost them anyhow.

—O, don't be talking! she said. He's a caution to rattlesnakes. He's in there now with his lawbooks finding out the law of libel. He has me heartscalded. Wait till I show you.

Hot mockturtle vapour and steam of newbaked jampuffs rolypoly poured out from Harrison's. The heavy noonreek tickled the top of Mr Bloom's gullet. Want to make good pastry, butter, best flour, Demerara sugar, or they'd taste it with the hot tea. Or is it from her? A barefoot arab stood over the grating, breathing in the fumes. Deaden the gnaw of hunger that way. Pleasure or pain is it? Penny dinner. Knife and fork chained to the table.

Opening her handbag, chipped leather. Hatpin: ought to have a guard on those things. Stick it in a chap's eye in the tram. Rummaging.

Open. Money. Please take one. Devils if they lose sixpence. Raise Cain. Husband barging. Where's the ten shillings I gave you on Monday? Are you feeding your little brother's family? Soiled handkerchief: medicinebottle. Pastille that was fell. What is she? . . .

—There must be a new moon out, she said. He's always bad then. Do you know what he did last night?

Her hand ceased to rummage. Her eyes fixed themselves on him, wide in alarm, yet smiling.

—What? Mr Bloom asked.

Let her speak. Look straight in her eyes. I believe you. Trust me.

—Woke me up in the night, she said. Dream he had, a nightmare. Indiges.

—Said the ace of spades was walking up the stairs.

—The ace of spades! Mr Bloom said.

She took a folded postcard from her handbag.

—Read that, she said. He got it this morning.

—What is it? Mr Bloom asked, taking the card. U.P.?

—U.P.: up, she said. Someone taking a rise out of him. It's a great shame for them whoever he is.

—Indeed it is, Mr Bloom said.

She took back the card, sighing.

—And now he's going round to Mr Menton's office. He's going to take an action for ten thousand pounds, he says.

She folded the card into her untidy bag and snapped the catch.

Same blue serge dress she had two years ago, the nap bleaching. Seen its best days. Wispish hair over her ears. And that dowdy toque: three old grapes to take the harm out of it. Shabby genteel. She used to be a tasty dresser. Lines round her mouth. Only a year or so older than Molly.

See the eye that woman gave her, passing. Cruel. The unfair sex.

He looked still at her, holding back behind his look his discontent. Pungent mockturtle oxtail mulligatawny. I'm hungry too. Flakes of pastry on the gusset of her dress: daub of sugary flour stuck to her cheek. Rhubarb tart with liberal fillings, rich fruit interior. Josie Powell that was. In Luke Doyle's long ago. Dolphin's Barn, the charades. U.P.: up.

Change the subject.

—Do you ever see anything of Mrs Beaufoy? Mr Bloom asked.

—Mina Purefoy? she said.

Philip Beaufoy I was thinking. Playgoers' Club. Matcham often thinks of the masterstroke. Did I pull the chain? Yes. The last act.

—Yes.

—I just called to ask on the way in is she over it. She's in the lying-in hospital in Holles street. Dr Horne got her in. She's three days bad now.

—O, Mr Bloom said. I'm sorry to hear that.

—Yes, Mrs Breen said. And a houseful of kids at home. It's a very stiff birth, the nurse told me.

—O, Mr Bloom said.

His heavy pitying gaze absorbed her news. His tongue clacked in compassion. Dth! Dth!

—I'm sorry to hear that, he said. Poor thing! Three days! That's terrible for her.

Mrs Breen nodded.

—She was taken bad on the Tuesday . . .

Mr Bloom touched her funnybone gently, warning her:

—Mind! Let this man pass.

A bony form strode along the curbstone from the river staring with a rapt gaze into the sunlight through a heavystringed glass. Tight as a skullpiece a tiny hat gripped his head. From his arm a folded dustcoat, a stick and an umbrella dangled to his stride.

—Watch him, Mr Bloom said. He always walks outside the lampposts. Watch!

—Who is he if it's a fair question? Mrs Breen asked. Is he dotty?

—His name is Cashel Boyle O'Connor Fitzmaurice Tisdall Farrell, Mr Bloom said smiling. Watch!

—He has enough of them, she said. Denis will be like that one of these days.

She broke off suddenly.

—There he is, she said. I must go after him. Goodbye. Remember me to Molly, won't you?

—I will, Mr Bloom said.

He watched her dodge through passers towards the shopfronts. Denis Breen in skimpy frockcoat and blue canvas shoes shuffled out of Harrison's hugging two heavy tomes to his ribs. Blown in from the bay. Like old times. He suffered her to overtake him without surprise and thrust his dull grey beard towards her, his loose jaw wagging as he spoke earnestly.

Meshuggah. Off his chump.

Mr Bloom walked on again easily, seeing ahead of him in sunlight the tight skullpiece, the dangling stickumbrelladustcoat. Going the two days. Watch him! Out he goes again. One way of getting on in the world. And that other old mosey lunatic in those duds. Hard time she must have with him.

U.P.: up. I'll take my oath that's Alf Bergan or Richie Goulding. Wrote it for a lark in the Scotch house I bet anything. Round to Menton's office. His oyster eyes staring at the postcard. Be a feast for the gods.

He passed the *Irish Times*. There might be other answers lying there. Like to answer them all. Good system for criminals. Code. At their lunch now. Clerk with the glasses there doesn't know me. O, leave them there to simmer. Enough bother wading through fortyfour of them. Wanted, smart lady typist to aid gentleman in literary work. I called you naughty darling because I do not like that other world. Please tell me what is the meaning. Please tell me what perfume does your wife. Tell me who made the world. The way they spring those questions on you. And the other one Lizzie Twigg. My literary efforts have had the good fortune to meet with the approval of the eminent poet A. E. (Mr Geo. Russell). No time to do her hair drinking sloppy tea with a book of poetry.

Best paper by long chalks for a small ad. Got the provinces now. Cook and general, exc. cuisine, housemaid kept. Wanted live man for spirit counter. Resp. girl (R. C.) wishes to hear of post in fruit or pork shop. James Carlisle made that. Six and a half per cent dividend. Made a big deal on Coates's shares. Ca' canny. Cunning old Scotch hunks. All the toady news. Our gracious and popular vicereine. Bought the *Irish Field* now. Lady Mountcashel has quite recovered after her confinement and rode out with the Ward Union staghounds at the enlargement yesterday at Rathoath. Uneatable fox. Pothunters too. Fear injects juices make it tender enough for them. Riding astride. Sit her horse like a man. Weightcarrying huntress. No sidesaddle or pillion for her, not for Joe. First to the meet and in at the death. Strong as a brood mare some of those horsey women. Swagger around livery stables. Toss off a glass of brandy neat while you'd say knife. That one at the Grosvenor this morning. Up with her on the car: wishswish. Stonewall or fivebarred gate put her mount to it. Think that pugnosed driver did it out of spite. Who is this she was like? O yes! Mrs Miriam Dandrade that sold me her old wraps and black underclothes in the Shelbourne hotel. Divorced Spanish American. Didn't take a feather out of her my handling them. As if I was her clotheshorse. Saw her in the viceregal party when Stubbs the park ranger got me in with Whelan of the *Express*. Scavenging what the quality left. High tea. Mayonnaise I poured on the plums thinking it was custard. Her ears ought to have tingled for a few weeks after. Want to be a bull for her. Born courtesan. No nursery work for her, thanks.

Poor Mrs Purefoy! Methodist husband. Method in his madness. Saffron bun and milk and soda lunch in the educational dairy. Y. M. C. A. Eating with a stopwatch, thirtytwo chews to the minute. And still his muttonchop whiskers grew. Supposed to be well connected. Theodore's cousin in Dublin Castle. One tony relative in every family. Hardy annuals he presents her with. Saw him out at the Three Jolly Topers marching along bareheaded and his eldest boy carrying one in a marketnet. The squallers. Poor thing! Then having to give the breast year after year all hours of the night. Selfish those t.t's are. Dog in the manger. Only one lump of sugar in my tea, if you please.

He stood at Fleet street crossing. Luncheon interval. A sixpenny at Rowe's? Must look up that ad in the national library. An eightpenny in the Burton. Better. On my way.

He walked on past Bolton's Westmoreland house. Tea. Tea. Tea. I forgot to tap Tom Kernan.

Sss. Dth, dth, dth! Three days imagine groaning on a bed with a vinegared handkerchief round her forehead, her belly swollen out. Phew! Dreadful simply! Child's head too big: forceps. Doubled up inside her trying to butt its way out blindly, groping for the way out. Kill me that would. Lucky Molly got over hers lightly. They ought to invent something to stop that. Life with hard labour. Twilight sleep idea: queen Victoria was given that. Nine she had. A good layer. Old woman that lived in a shoe she had so many children. Suppose he was consumptive. Time someone thought about it instead of gassing about the what was it the pensive bosom of the silver effulgence. Flapdoodle to feed fools on. They could easily have big establishments whole thing quite painless out of all the taxes give every child born five quid at compound interest up to twentyone five per cent is a hundred shillings and five tiresome pounds multiply by twenty decimal system encourage people to put by money save hundred and ten and a bit twentyone years want to work it out on paper come to a tidy sum more than you think.

Not stillborn of course. They are not even registered. Trouble for nothing.

Funny sight two of them together, their bellies out. Molly and Mrs Moisel. Mothers' meeting. Phthisis retires for the time being, then returns. How flat they look all of a sudden after. Peaceful eyes. Weight off their mind. Old Mrs Thornton was a jolly old soul. All my babies, she said. The spoon of pap in her mouth before she fed them. O, that's nyumnyum. Got her hand crushed by old Tom Wall's son. His first bow to the public. Head like a prize pumpkin. Snuffy Dr Murren. People knocking them up at all hours. For God' sake, doctor. Wife in her throes. Then keep them waiting months for their fee. To attendance on your wife. No gratitude in people. Humane doctors, most of them.

Before the huge high door of the Irish house of parliament a flock of pigeons flew. Their little frolic after meals. Who will we do it on? I pick the fellow in black. Here goes. Here's good luck. Must be thrilling from the air. Apjohn, myself and Owen Goldberg up in the trees near Goose green playing the monkeys. Mackerel they called me.

A squad of constables debouched from College street, marching in Indian file. Goosestep. Foodheated faces, sweating helmets, patting their truncheons. After their feed with a good load of fat soup under their belts. Policeman's lot is oft a happy one. They split up in groups and scattered, saluting, towards their beats. Let out to graze. Best moment to attack one in pudding time. A punch in his dinner. A squad of others, marching irregularly, rounded Trinity railings making for the station. Bound for their troughs. Prepare to receive cavalry. Prepare to receive soup.

He crossed under Tommy Moore's roguish finger. They did right to put him up over a urinal: meeting of the waters. Ought to be places for women. Running into cakeshops. Settle my hat straight. *There is not in this wide world a vallee.* Great song of Julia Morkan's. Kept her voice up to the very last. Pupil of Michael Balfe's, wasn't she?

He gazed after the last broad tunic. Nasty customers to tackle. Jack Power could a tale unfold: father a G man. If a fellow gave them trouble being lagged they let him have it hot and heavy in the bridewell. Can't blame them after all with the job they have especially the young hornies. That horsepoliceman the day Joe Chamberlain was given his degree in Trinity he got a run for his money. My word he did! His horse's hoofs clattering after us down Abbey street. Lucky I had the presence of mind to dive into Manning's or I was souped. He did come a wallop, by George. Must have cracked his skull on the cobblestones. I oughtn't to have got myself swept along with those medicals. And the Trinity jibs in their mortarboards. Looking for trouble. Still I got to know that young Dixon who dressed that sting for me in the Mater and now he's in Holles street where Mrs Purefoy. Wheels within wheels. Police whistle in my ears still. All skedaddled. Why he fixed on me. Give me in charge. Right here it began.

—Up the Boers!

—Three cheers for De Wet!

—We'll hang Joe Chamberlain on a sourapple tree.

Silly billies: mob of young cubs yelling their guts out. Vinegar hill. The Butter exchange band. Few years' time half of them magistrates and civil servants. War comes on: into the army helterskelter: same fellows used to. Whether on the scaffold high.

Never know who you're talking to. Corny Kelleher he has Harvey Duff in his eye. Like that Peter or Denis or James Carey that blew the gaff on the invincibles. Member of the corporation too. Egging raw youths on to get in the know all the time drawing secret service pay from the castle. Drop him like a hot potato. Why those plainclothes men are always courting slaveys. Easily twig a man used to uniform. Squarepushing up against a backdoor. Maul her a bit. Then the next thing on the menu. And who is the gentleman does be visiting there? Was the young master saying anything? Peeping Tom through the keyhole. Decoy duck. Hotblooded young student fooling round her fat arms ironing.

—Are those yours, Mary?

—I don't wear such things . . . Stop or I'll tell the missus on you. Out half the night.

—There are great times coming, Mary. Wait till you see.

—Ah, gelong with your great times coming.

Barmaids too. Tobacco shopgirls.

James Stephens' idea was the best. He knew them. Circles of ten so that a fellow couldn't round on more than his own ring. Sinn Fein. Back out you get the knife. Hidden hand. Stay in. The firing squad. Turnkey's daughter got him out of Richmond, off from Lusk. Putting up in the Buckingham Palace hotel under their very noses. Garibaldi.

You must have a certain fascination: Parnell. Arthur Griffith is a squareheaded fellow but he has no go in him for the mob. Or gas about our lovely land. Gammon and spinach. Dublin Bakery Company's tearoom. Debating societies. That republicanism is the best form of government. That the language question should take precedence of the economic question. Have your daughters inveigling them to your house. Stuff them up with meat and drink. Michaelmas goose. Here's a good lump of thyme seasoning under the apron for you. Have another quart of goosegrease before it gets too cold. Halffed enthusiasts. Penny roll and a walk with the band. No grace for the carver. The thought that the other chap pays best sauce in the world. Make themselves thoroughly at home. Show us over those apricots, meaning peaches. The not far distant day. Homerule sun rising up in the northwest.

His smile faded as he walked, a heavy cloud hiding the sun slowly, shadowing Trinity's surly front. Trams passed one another, ingoing, outgoing, clanging. Useless words. Things go on same, day after day: squads of police marching out, back: trams in, out. Those two loonies mooching about. Dignam carted off. Mina Purefoy swollen belly on a bed groaning to have a child tugged out of her. One born every second somewhere. Other dying every second. Since I fed the birds five minutes. Three hundred kicked the bucket. Other three hundred born, washing the blood off, all are washed in the blood of the lamb, bawling maaaaaa.

Cityful passing away, other cityful coming, passing away too: other coming on, passing on. Houses, lines of houses, streets, miles of pavements, piledup bricks, stones. Changing hands. This owner, that. Landlord never dies they say. Other steps into his shoes when he gets his notice to quit. They buy the place up with gold and still they have all the gold. Swindle in it somewhere. Piled up in cities, worn away age after age. Pyramids in sand. Built on bread and onions. Slaves Chinese wall. Babylon. Big stones left. Round towers. Rest rubble, sprawling suburbs, jerrybuilt. Kerwan's mushroom houses built of breeze. Shelter, for the night.

No-one is anything.

This is the very worst hour of the day. Vitality. Dull, gloomy: hate this hour. Feel as if I had been eaten and spewed.

Provost's house. The reverend Dr Salmon: tinned salmon. Well tinned in there. Like a mortuary chapel. Wouldn't live in it if they paid me. Hope they have liver and bacon today. Nature abhors a vacuum.

The sun freed itself slowly and lit glints of light among the silverware opposite in Walter Sexton's window by which John Howard Parnell passed, unseeing.

There he is: the brother. Image of him. Haunting face. Now that's a coincidence. Course hundreds of times you think of a person and don't meet him. Like a man walking in his sleep. No-one knows him. Must be a corporation meeting today. They say he never put on the city marshal's uniform since he got the job. Charley Kavanagh used to come out on his high horse, cocked hat, puffed, powdered and shaved. Look at the woebegone walk of him. Eaten a bad egg. Poached eyes on ghost. I have a pain. Great man's brother: his brother's brother. He'd look nice on the city charger. Drop into the D. B. C. probably for his coffee, play chess there. His brother used men as pawns. Let them all go to pot. Afraid to pass a remark on him. Freeze them up with that eye of his. That's the fascination: the name. All a bit touched. Mad Fanny and his other sister Mrs Dickinson driving about with scarlet harness. Bolt upright like surgeon M'Ardle. Still David Sheehy beat him for south Meath. Apply for the Chiltern Hundreds and retire into public life. The patriot's banquet. Eating orangepeels in the park. Simon Dedalus said when they put him in parliament that Parnell would come back from the grave and lead him out of the House of Commons by the arm.

—Of the twoheaded octopus, one of whose heads is the head upon which the ends of the world have forgotten to come while the other speaks with a Scotch accent. The tentacles . . .

They passed from behind Mr Bloom along the curbstone. Beard and bicycle. Young woman.

And there he is too. Now that's really a coincidence: second time. Coming events cast their shadows before. With the approval of the eminent poet, Mr Geo. Russell. That might be Lizzie Twigg with him. A. E.: what does that mean? Initials perhaps. Albert Edward, Arthur Edmund, Alphonsus Eb Ed El Esquire. What was he saying? The ends of the world with a Scotch accent. Tentacles: octopus. Something occult: symbolism. Holding forth. She's taking it all in. Not saying a word. To aid gentleman in literary work.

His eyes followed the high figure in homespun, beard and bicycle, a listening woman at his side. Coming from the vegetarian. Only weggebobbles and fruit. Don't eat a beefsteak. If you do the eyes of that cow will pursue you through all eternity. They say it's healthier.

Wind and watery though. Tried it. Keep you on the run all day. Bad as a bloater. Dreams all night. Why do they call that thing they gave me nutsteak? Nutarians. Fruitarians. To give you the idea you are eating rumpsteak. Absurd. Salty too. They cook in soda. Keep you sitting by the tap all night.

Her stockings are loose over her ankles. I detest that: so tasteless. Those literary etherial people they are all. Dreamy, cloudy, symbolistic. Esthetes they are. I wouldn't be surprised if it was that kind of food you see produces the like waves of the brain the poetical. For example one of those policemen sweating Irish stew into their shirts you couldn't squeeze a line of poetry out of him. Don't know what poetry is even. Must be in a certain mood.

> *The dreamy cloudy gull*
> *Waves o'er the waters dull.*

He crossed at Nassau street corner and stood before the window of Yeates and Son, pricing the fieldglasses. Or will I drop into old Harris's and have a chat with young Sinclair? Wellmannered fellow. Probably at his lunch. Must get those old glasses of mine set right. Goerz lenses six guineas. Germans making their way everywhere. Sell on easy terms to capture trade. Undercutting. Might chance on a pair in the railway lost property office. Astonishing the things people leave behind them in trains and cloakrooms. What do they be thinking about? Women too. Incredible. Last year travelling to Ennis had to pick up that farmer's daughter's bag and hand it to her at Limerick junction. Unclaimed money too. There's a little watch up there on the roof of the bank to test those glasses by.

His lids came down on the lower rims of his irides. Can't see it. If you imagine it's there you can almost see it. Can't see it.

He faced about and, standing between the awnings, held out his right hand at arm's length towards the sun. Wanted to try that often. Yes: completely. The tip of his little finger blotted out the sun's disk. Must be the focus where the rays cross. If I had black glasses. Interesting. There was a lot of talk about those sunspots when we were in Lombard street west. Looking up from the back garden. Terrific explosions they are. There will be a total eclipse this year: autumn some time.

Now that I come to think of it that ball falls at Greenwich time. It's the clock is worked by an electric wire from Dunsink. Must go out there some first Saturday of the month. If I could get an introduction to professor Joly or learn up something about his family. That would do to: man always feels complimented. Flattery where least expected. Nobleman proud to be descended from some king's mistress. His foremother. Lay it on with a trowel. Cap in hand goes through the land. Not go in and blurt out what you know you're not to: what's parallax? Show this gentleman the door.

Ah.

His hand fell to his side again.

Never know anything about it. Waste of time. Gasballs spinning about, crossing each other, passing. Same old dingdong always. Gas: then solid: then world: then cold: then dead shell drifting around, frozen rock, like that pineapple rock. The moon. Must be a new moon out, she said. I believe there is.

He went on by la Maison Claire.

Wait. The full moon was the night we were Sunday fortnight exactly there is a new moon. Walking down by the Tolka. Not bad for a Fairview moon. She was humming. The young May moon she's beaming, love. He other side of her. Elbow, arm. He. Glowworm's la-amp is gleaming, love. Touch. Fingers. Asking. Answer. Yes.

Stop. Stop. If it was it was. Must.

Mr Bloom, quickbreathing, slowlier walking passed Adam court.

With a keep quiet relief his eyes took note this is the street here middle of the day of Bob Doran's bottle shoulders. On his annual bend, M'Coy said. They drink in order to say or do something or *cherchez la femme*. Up in the Coombe with chummies and streetwalkers and then the rest of the year sober as a judge.

Yes. Thought so. Sloping into the Empire. Gone. Plain soda would do him good. Where Pat Kinsella had his Harp theatre before Whitbred ran the Queen's. Broth of a boy. Dion Boucicault business with his harvestmoon face in a poky bonnet. Three Purty Maids from School. How time flies, eh? Showing long red pantaloons under his skirts. Drinkers, drinking, laughed spluttering, their drink against their breath. More power, Pat. Coarse red: fun for drunkards: guffaw and smoke. Take off that white hat. His parboiled eyes. Where is he now? Beggar somewhere. The harp that once did starve us all.

I was happier then. Or was that I? Or am I now I? Twentyeight I was. She twentythree. When we left Lombard street west something changed. Could never like it again after Rudy. Can't bring back time. Like holding water in your hand. Would you go back to then? Just beginning then. Would you? Are you not happy in your home you poor little naughty boy? Wants to sew on buttons for me. I must answer. Write it in the library.

Grafton street gay with housed awnings lured his senses. Muslin prints, silkdames and dowagers, jingle of harnesses, hoofthuds lowringing in the baking causeway. Thick feet that woman has in the white stockings. Hope the rain mucks them up on her. Countrybred chawbacon. All the beef to the heels were in. Always gives a woman clumsy feet. Molly looks out of plumb.

He passed, dallying, the windows of Brown Thomas, silk mercers. Cascades of ribbons. Flimsy China silks. A tilted urn poured from its mouth a flood of bloodhued poplin: lustrous blood. The huguenots brought that here. *La causa è santa!* Tara tara. Great chorus that. Taree tara. Must be washed in rainwater. Meyerbeer. Tara: bom bom bom.

Pincushions. I'm a long time threatening to buy one. Sticking them all over the place. Needles in window curtains.

He bared slightly his left forearm. Scrape: nearly gone. Not today anyhow. Must go back for that lotion. For her birthday perhaps. Junejulyaugseptember eighth. Nearly three months off. Then she mightn't like it. Women won't pick up pins. Say it cuts lo.

Gleaming silks, petticoats on slim brass rails, rays of flat silk stockings.

Useless to go back. Had to be. Tell me all.

High voices. Sunwarm silk. Jingling harnesses. All for a woman, home and houses, silkwebs, silver, rich fruits spicy from Jaffa. Agendath Netaim. Wealth of the world.

A warm human plumpness settled down on his brain. His brain yielded. Perfume of embraces all him assailed. With hungered flesh obscurely, he mutely craved to adore.

Duke street. Here we are. Must eat. The Burton. Feel better then.

He turned Combridge's corner, still pursued. Jingling, hoofthuds. Perfumed bodies, warm, full. All kissed, yielded: in deep summer fields, tangled pressed grass, in trickling hallways of tenements, along sofas, creaking beds.

—Jack, love!
—Darling!
—Kiss me, Reggy!

—My boy!

—Love!

His heart astir he pushed in the door of the Burton restaurant. Stink gripped his trembling breath: pungent meatjuice, slush of greens. See the animals feed.

Men, men, men.

Perched on high stools by the bar, hats shoved back, at the tables calling for more bread no charge, swilling, wolfing gobfuls of sloppy food, their eyes bulging, wiping wetted moustaches. A pallid suetfaced young man polished his tumbler knife fork and spoon with his napkin. New set of microbes. A man with an infant's saucestained napkin tucked round him shovelled gurgling soup down his gullet. A man spitting back on his plate: halfmasticated gristle: gums: no teeth to chewchewchew it. Chump chop from the grill. Bolting to get it over. Sad booser's eyes. Bitten off more than he can chew. Am I like that? See ourselves as others see us. Hungry man is an angry man. Working tooth and jaw. Don't! O! A bone! That last pagan king of Ireland Cormac in the schoolpoem choked himself at Sletty southward of the Boyne. Wonder what he was eating. Something galoptious. Saint Patrick converted him to Christianity. Couldn't swallow it all however.

—Roast beef and cabbage.

—One stew.

Smells of men. Spat-on sawdust, sweetish warmish cigarettesmoke, reek of plug, spilt beer, men's beery piss, the stale of ferment.

His gorge rose.

Couldn't eat a morsel here. Fellow sharpening knife and fork to eat all before him, old chap picking his tootles. Slight spasm, full, chewing the cud. Before and after. Grace after meals. Look on this picture then on that. Scoffing up stewgravy with sopping sippets of bread. Lick it off the plate, man! Get out of this.

He gazed round the stooled and tabled eaters, tightening the wings of his nose.

—Two stouts here.

—One corned and cabbage.

That fellow ramming a knifeful of cabbage down as if his life depended on it. Good stroke. Give me the fidgets to look. Safer to eat from his three hands. Tear it limb from limb. Second nature to him. Born with a silver knife in his mouth. That's witty, I think. Or no. Silver means born rich. Born with a knife. But then the allusion is lost.

An illgirt server gathered sticky clattering plates. Rock, the head bailiff, standing at the bar blew the foamy crown from his tankard. Well up: it splashed yellow near his boot. A diner, knife and fork upright, elbows on table, ready for a second helping stared towards the foodlift across his stained square of newspaper. Other chap telling him something with his mouth full. Sympathetic listener. Table talk. I munched hum un thu Unchster Bunk un Munchday. Ha? Did you, faith?

Mr Bloom raised two fingers doubtfully to his lips. His eyes said:

—Not here. Don't see him.

Out. I hate dirty eaters.

He backed towards the door. Get a light snack in Davy Byrne's. Stopgap. Keep me going. Had a good breakfast.

—Roast and mashed here.

—Pint of stout.

Every fellow for his own, tooth and nail. Gulp. Grub. Gulp. Gobstuff.

He came out into clearer air and turned back towards Grafton street. Eat or be eaten. Kill! Kill!

Suppose that communal kitchen years to come perhaps. All trotting down with porringers and tommycans to be filled. Devour contents in the street. John Howard Parnell example the provost of Trinity every mother's son don't talk of your provosts and provost of Trinity women and children cabmen priests parsons fieldmarshals archbishops. From Ailesbury road, Clyde road, artisans' dwellings, north Dublin union, lord mayor in his gingerbread coach, old queen in a bathchair. My plate's empty. After you with our incorporated drinkingcup. Like sir Philip Crampton's fountain. Rub off the microbes with your handkerchief. Next chap rubs on a new batch with his. Father O'Flynn would make hares of them all. Have rows all the same. All for number one. Children fighting for the scrapings of the pot. Want a souppot as big as the Phoenix park. Harpooning flitches and hindquarters out of it. Hate people all round you. City Arms hotel *table d'hôte* she called it. Soup, joint and sweet. Never know whose thoughts you're chewing. Then who'd wash up all the plates and forks? Might be all feeding on tabloids that time. Teeth getting worse and worse.

After all there's a lot in that vegetarian fine flavour of things from the earth garlic of course it stinks after Italian organgrinders crisp of onions mushrooms truffles. Pain to the animal too. Pluck and draw fowl. Wretched brutes there at the cattlemarket waiting for the poleaxe to split their skulls open. Moo. Poor trembling calves. Meh. Staggering bob. Bubble and squeak. Butchers' buckets wobbly lights. Give us that brisket off the hook. Plup. Raw head and bloody bones. Flayed glasseyed sheep hung from their haunches, sheepsnouts bloodypapered snivelling nosejam on sawdust. Top and lashers going out. Don't maul them pieces, young one.

Hot fresh blood they prescribe for decline. Blood always needed. Insidious. Lick it up smokinghot, thick sugary. Famished ghosts.

Ah, I'm hungry.

He entered Davy Byrne's. Moral pub. He doesn't chat. Stands a drink now and then. But in leapyear once in four. Cashed a cheque for me once.

What will I take now? He drew his watch. Let me see now. Shandygaff?

—Hello, Bloom, Nosey Flynn said from his nook.

—Hello, Flynn.

—How's things?

—Tiptop . . . Let me see. I'll take a glass of burgundy and . . . let me see.

Sardines on the shelves. Almost taste them by looking. Sandwich? Ham and his descendants musterred and bred there. Potted meats. What is home without Plumtree's potted meat? Incomplete. What a stupid ad! Under the obituary notices they stuck it. All up a plumtree. Dignam's potted meat. Cannibals would with lemon and rice. White missionary too salty. Like pickled pork. Expect the chief consumes the parts of honour. Ought to be tough from exercise. His wives in a row to watch the effect. *There was a right royal old nigger. Who ate or something the somethings of the reverend Mr MacTrigger.* With it an abode of bliss. Lord knows what concoction. Cauls mouldy tripes windpipes faked and minced up. Puzzle find the meat. Kosher. No meat and milk together. Hygiene that was what they call now. Yom Kippur fast spring cleaning of inside. Peace and war depend on some fellow's digestion. Religions. Christmas turkeys and geese. Slaughter of innocents. Eat drink and be merry. Then casual wards full after. Heads bandaged. Cheese digests all but itself. Mity cheese.

—Have you a cheese sandwich?

—Yes, sir.

Like a few olives too if they had them. Italian I prefer. Good glass of burgundy take away that. Lubricate. A nice salad, cool as a cucumber, Tom Kernan can dress. Puts gusto into it. Pure olive oil. Milly served me that cutlet with a sprig of parsley. Take one Spanish onion. God made food, the devil the cooks. Devilled crab.

—Wife well?

—Quite well, thanks . . . A cheese sandwich, then. Gorgonzola, have you?

—Yes, sir.

Nosey Flynn sipped his grog.

—Doing any singing those times?

Look at his mouth. Could whistle in his own ear. Flap ears to match. Music. Knows as much about it as my coachman. Still better tell him. Does no harm. Free ad.

—She's engaged for a big tour end of this month. You may have heard perhaps.

—No. O, that's the style. Who's getting it up?

The curate served.

—How much is that?

—Seven d., sir . . . Thank you, sir.

Mr Bloom cut his sandwich into slender strips. *Mr MacTrigger.* Easier than the dreamy creamy stuff. *His five hundred wives. Had the time of their lives.*

—Mustard, sir?

—Thank you.

He studded under each lifted strip yellow blobs. *Their lives.* I have it. *It grew bigger and bigger and bigger.*

—Getting it up? he said. Well, it's like a company idea, you see. Part shares and part profits.

—Ay, now I remember, Nosey Flynn said, putting his hand in his pocket to scratch his groin. Who is this was telling me? Isn't Blazes Boylan mixed up in it?

A warm shock of air heat of mustard hanched on Mr Bloom's heart. He raised his eyes and met the stare of a bilious clock. Two. Pub clock five minutes fast. Time going on. Hands moving. Two. Not yet.

His midriff yearned then upward, sank within him, yearned more longly, longingly.

Wine.

He smellsipped the cordial juice and, bidding his throat strongly to speed it, set his wineglass delicately down.

—Yes, he said. He's the organiser in point of fact.

No fear: no brains.

Nosey Flynn snuffled and scratched. Flea having a good square meal.

—He had a good slice of luck, Jack Mooney was telling me, over that boxingmatch Myler Keogh won again that soldier in the Portobello barracks. By God, he had the little kipper down in the county Carlow he was telling me . . .

Hope that dewdrop doesn't come down into his glass. No, snuffled it up.

—For near a month, man, before it came off. Sucking duck eggs by God till further orders. Keep him off the boose, see? O, by God, Blazes is a hairy chap.

Davy Byrne came forward from the hindbar in tuckstitched shirtsleeves, cleaning his lips with two wipes of his napkin. Herring's blush. Whose smile upon each feature plays with such and such replete. Too much fat on the parsnips.

—And here's himself and pepper on him, Nosey Flynn said. Can you give us a good one for the Gold cup?

—I'm off that, Mr Flynn, Davy Byrne answered. I never put anything on a horse.

—You're right there, Nosey Flynn said.

Mr Bloom ate his strips of sandwich, fresh clean bread, with relish of disgust pungent mustard, the feety savour of green cheese. Sips of his wine soothed his palate. Not logwood that. Tastes fuller this weather with the chill off.

Nice quiet bar. Nice piece of wood in that counter. Nicely planed. Like the way it curves there.

—I wouldn't do anything at all in that line, Davy Byrne said. It ruined many a man, the same horses.

Vintners' sweepstake. Licensed for the sale of beer, wine and spirits for consumption on the premises. Heads I win tails you lose.

—True for you, Nosey Flynn said. Unless you're in the know. There's no straight sport going now. Lenehan gets some good ones. He's giving Sceptre today. Zinfandel's the favourite, Lord Howard de Walden's, won at Epsom. Morny Cannon is riding him. I could have got seven to one against Saint Amant a fortnight before.

—That so? Davy Byrne said . . .

He went towards the window and, taking up the pettycash book, scanned its pages.

—I could, faith, Nosey Flynn said, snuffling. That was a rare bit of horseflesh. Saint Frusquin was her sire. She won in a thunderstorm, Rothschild's filly, with wadding in her ears. Blue jacket and yellow cap. Bad luck to big Ben Dollard and his John O'Gaunt. He put me off it. Ay.

He drank resignedly from his tumbler, running his fingers down the flutes.

—Ay, he said, sighing.

Mr Bloom, champing, standing, looked upon his sigh. Nosey numbskull. Will I tell him that horse Lenehan? He knows already. Better let him forget. Go and lose more. Fool and his money. Dewdrop coming down again. Cold nose he'd have kissing a woman. Still they might like. Prickly beards they like. Dogs' cold noses. Old Mrs Riordan with the rumbling stomach's Skye terrier in the City Arms hotel. Molly fondling him in her lap. O, the big doggy-bowwowsywowsy!

Wine soaked and softened rolled pith of bread mustard a moment mawkish cheese. Nice wine it is. Taste it better because I'm not thirsty. Bath of course does that. Just a bite or two. Then about six o'clock I can. Six. Six. Time will be gone then. She . . .

Mild fire of wine kindled his veins. I wanted that badly. Felt so off colour. His eyes unhungrily saw shelves of tins: sardines, gaudy lobsters' claws. All the odd things people pick up for food. Out of shells, periwinkles with a pin, off trees, snails out of the ground the French eat, out of the sea with bait on a hook. Silly fish learn nothing in a thousand years. If you didn't know risky putting anything into your mouth. Poisonous berries. Johnny Magories. Roundness you think good. Gaudy colour warns you off. One fellow told another and so on. Try it on the dog first. Led on by the smell or the look. Tempting fruit. Ice cones. Cream. Instinct. Orangegroves for instance. Need artificial irrigation. Bleibtreustrasse. Yes but what about oysters. Unsightly like a clot of phlegm. Filthy shells. Devil to open them too. Who found them out? Garbage, sewage they feed on. Fizz and Red bank oysters. Effect on the sexual. Aphrodis. He was in the Red Bank this morning. Was he oysters old fish at table perhaps he young flesh in bed no June has no ar no oysters. But there are people like things high. Tainted game. Jugged hare. First catch your hare. Chinese eating eggs fifty years old, blue and green again. Dinner of thirty courses. Each dish harmless might mix inside. Idea for a poison mystery. That archduke Leopold was it no yes or was it Otto one of those Habsburgs? Or who was it used to eat the scruff off his own head? Cheapest lunch in town. Of course aristocrats, then the others copy to be in the fashion. Milly too rock oil and flour. Raw pastry I like myself. Half the catch of oysters they throw back in the sea to keep up the price. Cheap no-one would buy. Caviare. Do the grand. Hock in green glasses. Swell blowout. Lady this. Powdered bosom pearls. The *élite. Crème de la crème.* They want special dishes to pretend they're. Hermit with a platter of pulse keep down the stings of the flesh. Know me come eat with me. Royal sturgeon high sheriff, Coffey, the butcher, right to venisons of the forest from his ex. Send him back the half of a cow. Spread I saw down in the Master of the Rolls' kitchen area. Whitehatted *chef* like a rabbi. Combustible duck. Curly cabbage *à la duchesse de Parme.* Just as well to write it on the bill of fare so you can know what you've eaten. Too many drugs spoil the broth. I know it myself. Dosing it with Edwards' desiccated soup. Geese stuffed silly for them. Lobsters boiled alive. Do ptake some ptarmigan. Wouldn't mind being a waiter in a swell hotel. Tips, evening dress, halfnaked ladies. May I tempt you to a little more filleted lemon sole, miss Dubedat? Yes, do bedad. And she did bedad. Huguenot name I expect that. A miss Dubedat lived in Killiney, I remember. *Du de la* is French. Still it's the same fish perhaps old Micky Hanlon of Moore street ripped the guts out of making money hand over fist finger in fishes' gills can't write his name on a cheque think he was painting the landscape with his mouth twisted. Moooikill A Aitcha Ha ignorant as a kish of brogues, worth fifty thousand pounds.

Stuck on the pane two flies buzzed, stuck.

Glowing wine on his palate lingered swallowed. Crushing in the winepress grapes of Burgundy. Sun's heat it is. Seems to a secret touch telling me memory. Touched his sense moistened remembered. Hidden under wild ferns on Howth below us bay sleeping: sky. No sound. The sky. The bay purple by the Lion's head. Green by Drumleck. Yellowgreen towards Sutton. Fields of undersea, the lines faint brown in grass, buried cities. Pillowed on my coat she had her hair, earwigs in the heather scrub my hand under her nape, you'll toss me all. O wonder! Coolsoft with ointments her hand touched me, caressed: her eyes upon me did not turn away. Ravished over

her I lay, full lips full open, kissed her mouth. Yum. Softly she gave
me in my mouth the seedcake warm and chewed. Mawkish pulp her
mouth had mumbled sweetsour of her spittle. Joy: I ate it: joy. Young
life, her lips that gave me pouting. Soft warm sticky gumjelly lips.
Flowers her eyes were, take me, willing eyes. Pebbles fell. She lay still.
A goat. No-one. High on Ben Howth rhododendrons a nannygoat
walking surefooted, dropping currants. Screened under ferns she
laughed warmfolded. Wildly I lay on her, kissed her: eyes, her lips, her
stretched neck beating, woman's breasts full in her blouse of nun's
veiling, fat nipples upright. Hot I tongued her. She kissed me. I was
kissed. All yielding she tossed my hair. Kissed, she kissed me.

Me. And me now.

Stuck, the flies buzzed.

His downcast eyes followed the silent veining of the oaken slab.
Beauty: it curves: curves are beauty. Shapely goddesses, Venus, Juno:
curves the world admires. Can see them library museum standing in
the round hall, naked goddesses. Aids to digestion. They don't care
what man looks. All to see. Never speaking. I mean to say to fellows
like Flynn. Suppose she did Pygmalion and Galatea what would she
say first? Mortal! Put you in your proper place. Quaffing nectar at
mess with gods golden dishes, all ambrosial. Not like a tanner lunch
we have, boiled mutton, carrots and turnips, bottle of Allsop. Nectar
imagine it drinking electricity: gods' food. Lovely forms of women
sculped Junonian. Immortal lovely. And we stuffing food in one hole
and out behind: food, chyle, blood, dung, earth, food: have to feed it
like stoking an engine. They have no. Never looked. I'll look today.
Keeper won't see. Bend down let something fall see if she.

Dribbling a quiet message from his bladder came to go to do not
to do there to do. A man and ready he drained his glass to the lees and
walked, to men too they gave themselves, manly conscious, lay with
men lovers, a youth enjoyed her, to the yard.

When the sound of his boots had ceased Davy Byrne said from
his book:

—What is this he is? Isn't he in the insurance line?

—He's out of that long ago, Nosey Flynn said. He does canvassing
for the *Freeman*.

—I know him well to see, Davy Byrne said. Is he in trouble?

—Trouble? Nosey Flynn said. Not that I heard of. Why?

—I noticed he was in mourning.

—Was he? Nosey Flynn said. So he was, faith. I asked him how was all at home. You're right, by God. So he was.

—I never broach the subject, Davy Byrne said humanely, if I see a gentleman is in trouble that way. It only brings it up fresh in their minds.

—It's not the wife anyhow, Nosey Flynn said. I met him the day before yesterday and he coming out of that Irish farm dairy John Wyse Nolan's wife has in Henry street with a jar of cream in his hand taking it home to his better half. She's well nourished, I tell you. Plovers on toast.

—And is he doing for the *Freeman?* Davy Byrne said.

Nosey Flynn pursed his lips.

—He doesn't buy cream on the ads he picks up. You can make bacon of that.

—How so? Davy Byrne asked, coming from his book.

Nosey Flynn made swift passes in the air with juggling fingers. He winked.

—He's in the craft, he said.

—Do you tell me so? Davy Byrne said.

—Very much so, Nosey Flynn said. Ancient free and accepted order. He's an excellent brother. Light, life and love, by God. They give him a leg up. I was told that by a—well, I won't say who.

—Is that a fact?

—O, it's a fine order, Nosey Flynn said. They stick to you when you're down. I know a fellow was trying to get into it. But they're as close as damn it. By God they did right to keep the women out of it.

Davy Byrne smiledyawnednodded all in one:

—Iiiiiichaaaaaaach!

—There was one woman, Nosey Flynn said, hid herself in a clock to find out what they do be doing. But be damned but they smelt her out and swore her in on the spot a master mason. That was one of the saint Legers of Doneraile.

Davy Byrne, sated after his yawn, said with tearwashed eyes:

—And is that a fact? Decent quiet man he is. I often saw him in here and I never once saw him—you know, over the line.

—God Almighty couldn't make him drunk, Nosey Flynn said firmly. Slips off when the fun gets too hot. Didn't you see him look at his watch? Ah, you weren't there. If you ask him to have a drink first thing he does he outs with the watch to see what he ought to imbibe. Declare to God he does.

—There are some like that, Davy Byrne said. He's a safe man, I'd say.

—He's not too bad, Nosey Flynn said, snuffling it up. He's been known to put his hand down too to help a fellow. Give the devil his due. O, Bloom has his good points. But there's one thing he'll never do.

His hand scrawled a dry pen signature beside his grog.

—I know, Davy Byrne said.

—Nothing in black and white, Nosey Flynn said.

Paddy Leonard and Bantam Lyons came in. Tom Rochford followed frowning, a plaining hand on his claret waistcoat.

—Day, Mr Byrne.

—Day, gentlemen.

They paused at the counter.

—Who's standing? Paddy Leonard asked.

—I'm sitting anyhow, Nosey Flynn answered.

—Well, what'll it be? Paddy Leonard asked.

—I'll take a stone ginger, Bantam Lyons said.

—How much? Paddy Leonard cried. Since when, for God' sake? What's yours, Tom?

—How is the main drainage? Nosey Flynn asked, sipping.

For answer Tom Rochford pressed his hand to his breastbone and hiccupped.

—Would I trouble you for a glass of fresh water, Mr Byrne? he said.

—Certainly, sir.

Paddy Leonard eyed his alemates.

—Lord love a duck, he said. Look at what I'm standing drinks to! Cold water and gingerpop! Two fellows that would suck whisky off a sore leg. He has some bloody horse up his sleeve for the Gold cup. A dead snip.

—Zinfandel is it? Nosey Flynn asked.

Tom Rochford spilt powder from a twisted paper into the water set before him.

—That cursed dyspepsia, he said before drinking.

—Breadsoda is very good, Davy Byrne said.

Tom Rochford nodded and drank.

—Is it Zinfandel?

—Say nothing! Bantam Lyons winked. I'm going to plunge five bob on my own.

—Tell us if you're worth your salt and be damned to you, Paddy Leonard said. Who gave it to you?

Mr Bloom on his way out raised three fingers in greeting.

—So long! Nosey Flynn said.

The others turned.

—That's the man now that gave it to me, Bantam Lyons whispered.

—Prrwht! Paddy Leonard said with scorn. Mr Byrne, sir, we'll take two of your small Jamesons after that and a . . .

—Stone ginger, Davy Byrne added civilly.

—Ay, Paddy Leonard said. A suckingbottle for the baby.

Mr Bloom walked towards Dawson street, his tongue brushing his teeth smooth. Something green it would have to be: spinach, say. Then with those Röntgen rays searchlight you could.

At Duke lane a ravenous terrier choked up a sick knuckly cud on the cobblestones and lapped it with new zest. Surfeit. Returned with thanks having fully digested the contents. First sweet then savoury. Mr Bloom coasted warily. Ruminants. His second course. Their upper jaw they move. Wonder if Tom Rochford will do anything with that invention of his? Wasting time explaining it to Flynn's mouth. Lean people long mouths. Ought to be a hall or a place where inventors could go in and invent free. Course then you'd have all the cranks pestering.

He hummed, prolonging in solemn echo the closes of the bars:

> Don Giovanni, a cenar teco
> M'invitasti.

Feel better. Burgundy. Good pick me up. Who distilled first? Some chap in the blues. Dutch courage. That *Kilkenny People* in the national library now I must.

Bare clean closestools waiting in the window of William Miller, plumber, turned back his thoughts. They could: and watch it all the way down, swallow a pin sometimes come out of the ribs years after, tour round the body changing biliary duct spleen squirting liver gastric juice coils of intestines like pipes. But the poor buffer would have to stand all the time with his insides entrails on show. Science.

—*A cenar teco*.

What does that *teco* mean? Tonight perhaps.

> *Don Giovanni, thou hast me invited*
> *To come to supper tonight,*
> *The rum the rumdum.*

Doesn't go properly.

Keyes: two months if I get Nannetti to. That'll be two pounds ten about two pounds eight. Three Hynes owes me. Two eleven. Prescott's dyeworks van over there. If I get Billy Prescott's ad: two fifteen. Five guineas about. On the pig's back.

Could buy one of those silk petticoats for Molly, colour of her new garters.

Today. Today. Not think.

Tour the south then. What about English wateringplaces? Brighton, Margate. Piers by moonlight. Her voice floating out. Those lovely seaside girls. Against John Long's a drowsing loafer lounged in heavy thought, gnawing a crusted knuckle. Handy man wants job. Small wages. Will eat anything.

Mr Bloom turned at Gray's confectioner's window of unbought tarts and passed the reverend Thomas Connellan's bookstore. *Why I left the church of Rome? Birds' Nest.* Women run him. They say they used to give pauper children soup to change to protestants in the time of the potato blight. Society over the way papa went to for the conversion of poor jews. Same bait. Why we left the church of Rome.

A blind stripling stood tapping the curbstone with his slender cane. No tram in sight. Wants to cross.

—Do you want to cross? Mr Bloom asked.

The blind stripling did not answer. His wallface frowned weakly. He moved his head uncertainly.

—You're in Dawson street, Mr Bloom said. Molesworth street is opposite. Do you want to cross? There's nothing in the way.

The cane moved out trembling to the left. Mr Bloom's eye followed its line and saw again the dyeworks' van drawn up before Drago's. Where I saw his brillantined hair just when I was. Horse drooping. Driver in John Long's. Slaking his drouth.

—There's a van there, Mr Bloom said, but it's not moving. I'll see you across. Do you want to go to Molesworth street?

—Yes, the stripling answered. South Frederick street.

—Come, Mr Bloom said.

He touched the thin elbow gently: then took the limp seeing hand to guide it forward.

Say something to him. Better not do the condescending. They mistrust what you tell them. Pass a common remark.

—The rain kept off.

No answer.

Stains on his coat. Slobbers his food, I suppose. Tastes all different for him. Have to be spoonfed first. Like a child's hand, his hand. Like Milly's was. Sensitive. Sizing me up I daresay from my hand. Wonder if he has a name. Van. Keep his cane clear of the horse's legs: tired drudge get his doze. That's right. Clear. Behind a bull: in front of a horse.

—Thanks, sir.

Knows I'm a man. Voice.

—Right now? First turn to the left.

The blind stripling tapped the curbstone and went on his way, drawing his cane back, feeling again.

Mr Bloom walked behind the eyeless feet, a flatcut suit of herringbone tweed. Poor young fellow! How on earth did he know that van was there? Must have felt it. See things in their forehead perhaps: kind of sense of volume. Weight or size of it, something blacker than the dark. Wonder would he feel it if something was removed. Feel a gap. Queer idea of Dublin he must have, tapping his way round by the stones. Could he walk in a beeline if he hadn't that cane? Bloodless pious face like a fellow going in to be a priest.

Penrose! That was that chap's name.

Look at all the things they can learn to do. Read with their fingers. Tune pianos. Or we are surprised they have any brains. Why we think a deformed person or a hunchback clever if he says something we might say. Of course the other senses are more. Embroider. Plait baskets. People ought to help. Workbasket I could buy for Molly's birthday. Hates sewing. Might take an objection. Dark men they call them.

Sense of smell must be stronger too. Smells on all sides, bunched together. Each street different smell. Each person too. Then the spring, the summer: smells. Tastes? They say you can't taste wines with your eyes shut or a cold in the head. Also smoke in the dark they say get no pleasure.

And with a woman, for instance. More shameless not seeing. That girl passing the Stewart institution, head in the air. Look at me. I have them all on. Must be strange not to see her. Kind of a form in his mind's eye. The voice, temperatures: when he touches her with his fingers must almost see the lines, the curves. His hands on her hair, for instance. Say it was black, for instance. Good. We call it black. Then passing over her white skin. Different feel perhaps. Feeling of white.

Postoffice. Must answer. Fag today. Send her a postal order two shillings, half a crown. Accept my little present. Stationer's just here too. Wait. Think over it.

With a gentle finger he felt ever so slowly the hair combed back above his ears. Again. Fibres of fine fine straw. Then gently his finger felt the skin of his right cheek. Downy hair there too. Not smooth enough. The belly is the smoothest. No-one about. There he goes into Frederick street. Perhaps to Levenston's dancing academy piano. Might be settling my braces.

Walking by Doran's publichouse he slid his hand between his waistcoat and trousers and, pulling aside his shirt gently, felt a slack fold of his belly. But I know it's whitey yellow. Want to try in the dark to see.

He withdrew his hand and pulled his dress to.

Poor fellow! Quite a boy. Terrible. Really terrible. What dreams would he have, not seeing? Life a dream for him. Where is the justice being born that way? All those women and children excursion beanfeast burned and drowned in New York. Holocaust. Karma they call that transmigration for sins you did in a past life the reincarnation met him pike hoses. Dear, dear, dear. Pity, of course: but somehow you can't cotton on to them someway.

Sir Frederick Falkiner going into the freemasons' hall. Solemn as Troy. After his good lunch in Earlsfort terrace. Old legal cronies cracking a magnum. Tales of the bench and assizes and annals of the bluecoat school. I sentenced him to ten years. I suppose he'd turn up his nose at that stuff I drank. Vintage wine for them, the year marked on a dusty bottle. Has his own ideas of justice in the recorder's court. Wellmeaning old man. Police chargesheets crammed with cases get their percentage manufacturing crime. Sends them to the rightabout. The devil on moneylenders. Gave Reuben J a great strawcalling. Now he's really what they call a dirty jew. Power those judges have. Crusty old topers in wigs. Bear with a sore paw. And may the Lord have mercy on your soul.

Hello, placard. Mirus bazaar. His Excellency the lord lieutenant. Sixteenth. Today it is. In aid of funds for Mercer's hospital. *The Messiah* was first given for that. Yes. Handel. What about going out there: Ballsbridge. Drop in on Keyes. No use sticking to him like a leech. Wear out my welcome. Sure to know someone on the gate.

Mr Bloom came to Kildare street. First I must. Library.

Straw hat in sunlight. Tan shoes. Turnedup trousers. It is. It is.

His heart quopped softly. To the right. Museum. Goddesses. He swerved to the right.

Is it? Almost certain. Won't look. Wine in my face. Why did I? Too heady. Yes, it is. The walk. Not see. Get on.

Making for the museum gate with long windy steps he lifted his eyes. Handsome building. Sir Thomas Deane designed. Not following me?

Didn't see me perhaps. Light in his eyes.

The flutter of his breath came forth in short sighs. Quick. Cold statues: quiet there. Safe in a minute.

No. Didn't see me. After two. Just at the gate.

My heart!

His eyes beating looked steadfastly at cream curves of stone. Sir Thomas Deane was the Greek architecture.

Look for something I.

His hasty hand went quick into a pocket, took out, read unfolded Agendath Netaim. Where did I?

Busy looking.

He thrust back quick Agendath.

Afternoon she said.

I am looking for that. Yes, that. Try all pockets. Handker. *Freeman.* Where did I? Ah, yes. Trousers. Potato. Purse. Where?

Hurry. Walk quietly. Moment more. My heart.

His hand looking for the where did I put found in his hip pocket soap lotion have to call tepid paper stuck. Ah soap there I yes. Gate.

Safe!

9

Urbane, to comfort them, the quaker librarian purred:
—And we have, have we not, those priceless pages
of *Wilhelm Meister.* A great poet on a great brother
poet. A hesitating soul taking arms against a sea of troubles,
torn by conflicting doubts, as one sees in real life.

He came a step a sinkapace forward on neatsleather
creaking and a step backward a sinkapace on the solemn floor.

A noiseless attendant setting open the door but slightly
made him a noiseless beck.

—Directly, said he, creaking to go, albeit lingering. The
beautiful ineffectual dreamer who comes to grief against
hard facts. One always feels that Goethe's judgments are so
true. True in the larger analysis.

Twicreakingly analysis he corantoed off. Bald, most
zealous by the door he gave his large ear all to the attendant's
words: heard them: and was gone.

Two left.

—Monsieur de la Palice, Stephen sneered, was alive
fifteen minutes before his death.

—Have you found those six brave medicals, John
Eglinton asked with elder's gall, to write *Paradise Lost* at your
dictation? *The Sorrows of Satan* he calls it.

Smile. Smile Cranly's smile.

> *First he tickled her*
> *Then he patted her*
> *Then he passed the female catheter*
> *For he was a medical*
> *Jolly old medi . . .*

—I feel you would need one more for *Hamlet.* Seven is
dear to the mystic mind. The shining seven W. B. calls them.

Glittereyed his rufous skull close to his greencapped desklamp sought the face bearded amid darkgreener shadow, an ollav, holyeyed. He laughed low: a sizar's laugh of Trinity: unanswered.

> *Orchestral Satan, weeping many a rood*
> *Tears such as angels weep.*
> *Ed egli avea del cul fatto trombetta.*

He holds my follies hostage.

Cranly's eleven true Wicklowmen to free their sireland. Gaptoothed Kathleen, her four beautiful green fields, the stranger in her house. And one more to hail him: *ave, rabbi*: the Tinahely twelve. In the shadow of the glen he cooees for them. My soul's youth I gave him, night by night. God speed. Good hunting.

Mulligan has my telegram.

Folly. Persist.

—Our young Irish bards, John Eglinton censured, have yet to create a figure which the world will set beside Saxon Shakespeare's Hamlet though I admire him, as old Ben did, on this side idolatry.

—All these questions are purely academic, Russell oracled out of his shadow. I mean, whether Hamlet is Shakespeare or James I or Essex. Clergymen's discussions of the historicity of Jesus. Art has to reveal to us ideas, formless spiritual essences. The supreme question about a work of art is out of how deep a life does it spring. The painting of Gustave Moreau is the painting of ideas. The deepest poetry of Shelley, the words of Hamlet bring our minds into contact with the eternal wisdom, Plato's world of ideas. All the rest is the speculation of schoolboys for schoolboys.

A. E. has been telling some yankee interviewer. Wall, tarnation strike me!

—The schoolmen were schoolboys first, Stephen said superpolitely. Aristotle was once Plato's schoolboy.

—And has remained so, one should hope, John Eglinton sedately said. One can see him, a model schoolboy with his diploma under his arm.

He laughed again at the now smiling bearded face.

Formless spiritual. Father, Word and Holy Breath. Allfather, the heavenly man. Hiesos Kristos, magician of the beautiful, the Logos who suffers in us at every moment. This verily is that. I am the fire upon the altar. I am the sacrificial butter.

Dunlop, Judge, the noblest Roman of them all, A. E., Arval, the Name Ineffable, in heaven hight: K. H., their master, whose identity is no secret to adepts. Brothers of the great white lodge always watching to see if they can help. The Christ with the bridesister, moisture of light, born of an ensouled virgin, repentant sophia, departed to the plane of buddhi. The life esoteric is not for ordinary person. O. P. must work off bad karma first. Mrs Cooper Oakley once glimpsed our very illustrious sister H. P. B.'s elemental.

O, fie! Out on't! *Pfuiteufel!* You naughtn't to look, missus, so you naughtn't when a lady's ashowing of her elemental.

Mr Best entered, tall, young, mild, light. He bore in his hand with grace a notebook, new, large, clean, bright.

—That model schoolboy, Stephen said, would find Hamlet's musings about the afterlife of his princely soul, the improbable, insignificant and undramatic monologue, as shallow as Plato's.

John Eglinton, frowning, said, waxing wroth:

—Upon my word it makes my blood boil to hear anyone compare Aristotle with Plato.

—Which of the two, Stephen asked, would have banished me from his commonwealth?

Unsheathe your dagger definitions. Horseness is the whatness of allhorse. Streams of tendency and eons they worship. God: noise in the street: very peripatetic. Space: what you damn well have to see. Through spaces smaller than red globules of man's blood they creepycrawl after Blake's buttocks into eternity of which this vegetable world is but a shadow. Hold to the now, the here, through which all future plunges to the past.

Mr Best came forward, amiable, towards his colleague.

—Haines is gone, he said.

—Is he?

—I was showing him Jubainville's book. He's quite enthusiastic, don't you know, about Hyde's *Lovesongs of Connacht*. I couldn't bring him in to hear the discussion. He's gone to Gill's to buy it.

Bound thee forth, my booklet, quick
To greet the callous public.

Writ, I ween, 'twas not my wish
In lean unlovely English.

—The peatsmoke is going to his head, John Eglinton opined. We feel in England. Penitent thief. Gone. I smoked his baccy. Green twinkling stone. An emerald set in the ring of the sea.

—People do not know how dangerous lovesongs can be, the auric egg of Russell warned occultly. The movements which work revolutions in the world are born out of the dreams and visions in a peasant's heart on the hillside. For them the earth is not an exploitable ground but the living mother. The rarefied air of the academy and the arena produce the sixshilling novel, the musichall song. France produces the finest flower of corruption in Mallarmé but the desirable life is revealed only to the poor of heart, the life of Homer's Phæacians.

From these words Mr Best turned an unoffending face to Stephen.

—Mallarmé, don't you know, he said, has written those wonderful prose poems Stephen MacKenna used to read to me in Paris. The one about *Hamlet*. He says: *il se promène, lisant au livre de lui-même,* don't you know, *reading the book of himself.* He describes *Hamlet* given in a French town, don't you know, a provincial town. They advertised it.

His free hand graciously wrote tiny signs in air.

Hamlet
ou
Le Distrait
Pièce de Shakespeare

He repeated to John Eglinton's newgathered frown:

—*Pièce de Shakespeare,* don't you know. It's so French. The French point of view. *Hamlet ou . . .*

—The absentminded beggar, Stephen ended.

John Eglinton laughed.

—Yes, I suppose it would be, he said. Excellent people, no doubt, but distressingly shortsighted in some matters.

Sumptuous and stagnant exaggeration of murder.

—A deathsman of the soul Robert Greene called him, Stephen said. Not for nothing was he a butcher's son, wielding the sledded poleaxe and spitting in his palms. Nine lives are taken off for his father's one. Our Father who art in purgatory. Khaki Hamlets don't hesitate to shoot. The bloodboltered shambles in act five is a forecast of the concentration camp sung by Mr Swinburne.

Cranly, I his mute orderly, following battles from afar.

> *Whelps and dams of murderous foes whom none*
> *But we had spared . . .*

Between the Saxon smile and yankee yawp. The devil and the deep sea.

—He will have it that *Hamlet* is a ghoststory, John Eglinton said for Mr Best's behoof. Like the fat boy in Pickwick he wants to make our flesh creep.

> *List! List! O List!*

My flesh hears him: creeping, hears.

> *If thou didst ever . . .*

—What is a ghost? Stephen said with tingling energy. One who has faded into impalpability through death, through absence, through change of manners. Elizabethan London lay as far from Stratford as corrupt Paris lies from virgin Dublin. Who is the ghost from *limbo patrum*, returning to the world that has forgotten him? Who is King Hamlet?

John Eglinton shifted his spare body, leaning back to judge.

Lifted.

—It is this hour of a day in mid June, Stephen said, begging with a swift glance their hearing. The flag is up on the playhouse by the bankside. The bear Sackerson growls in the pit near it, Paris garden. Canvasclimbers who sailed with Drake chew their sausages among the groundlings.

Local colour. Work in all you know. Make them accomplices.

—Shakespeare has left the huguenot's house in Silver street and walks by the swanmews along the riverbank. But he does not stay to feed the pen chivying her game of cygnets towards the rushes. The swan of Avon has other thoughts.

Composition of place. Ignatius Loyola, make haste to help me!

—The play begins. A player comes on under the shadow, made up in the castoff mail of a court buck, a wellset man with a bass voice. It is the ghost, the king, a king and no king, and the player is Shakespeare who has studied *Hamlet* all the years of his life which were not vanity in order to play the part of the spectre. He speaks the words to Burbage, the young player who stands before him beyond the rack of cerecloth, calling him by a name:

Hamlet, I am thy father's spirit,

bidding him list. To a son he speaks, the son of his soul, the prince, young Hamlet and to the son of his body, Hamnet Shakespeare, who has died in Stratford that his namesake may live for ever.

—Is it possible that that player Shakespeare, a ghost by absence, and in the vesture of buried Denmark, a ghost by death, speaking his own words to his own son's name (had Hamnet Shakespeare lived he would have been prince Hamlet's twin), is it possible, I want to know, or probable that he did not draw or foresee the logical conclusion of those premises: you are the dispossessed son: I am the murdered father: your mother is the guilty queen, Ann Shakespeare, born Hathaway?

—But this prying into the family life of a great man, Russell began impatiently.

Art thou there, truepenny?

—Interesting only to the parish clerk. I mean, we have the plays. I mean when we read the poetry of *King Lear* what is it to us how the poet lived? As for living our servants can do that for us, Villiers de l'Isle has said. Peeping and prying into greenroom gossip of the day, the poet's drinking, the poet's debts. We have *King Lear*: and it is immortal.

Mr Best's face, appealed to, agreed.

Flow over them with your waves and with your waters, Mananaan,
Mananaan MacLir . . .

How now, sirrah, that pound he lent you when you were hungry?
Marry, I wanted it.
Take thou this noble.
Go to! You spent most of it in Georgina Johnson's bed, clergyman's daughter. Agenbite of inwit.

Do you intend to pay it back?

O, yes.

When? Now?

Well . . . No.

When, then?

I paid my way. I paid my way.

Steady on. He's from beyant Boyne water. The northeast corner. You owe it.

Wait. Five months. Molecules all change. I am other I now. Other I got pound.

Buzz. Buzz.

But I, entelechy, form of forms, am I by memory because under everchanging forms.

I that sinned and prayed and fasted.

A child Conmee saved from pandies.

I, I and I. I.

A. E. I. O. U.

—Do you mean to fly in the face of the tradition of three centuries? John Eglinton's carping voice asked. Her ghost at least has been laid for ever. She died, for literature at least, before she was born.

—She died, Stephen retorted, sixtyseven years after she was born. She saw him into and out of the world. She took his first embraces. She bore his children and she laid pennies on his eyes to keep his eyelids closed when he lay on his deathbed.

Mother's deathbed. Candle. The sheeted mirror. Who brought me into this world lies there, bronzelidded, under few cheap flowers. *Liliata rutilantium.*

I wept alone.

John Eglinton looked in the tangled glowworm of his lamp.

—The world believes that Shakespeare made a mistake, he said, and got out of it as quickly and as best he could.

—Bosh! Stephen said rudely. A man of genius makes no mistakes. His errors are volitional and are the portals of discovery.

Portals of discovery opened to let in the quaker librarian, softcreakfooted, bald, eared and assiduous.

—A shrew, John Eglinton said shrewdly, is not a useful portal of discovery, one should imagine. What useful discovery did Socrates learn from Xanthippe?

—Dialectic, Stephen answered: and from his mother how to bring thoughts into the world. What he learnt from his other wife Myrto (*absit nomen!*), Socratididion's Epipsychidion, no man, not a woman, will ever know. But neither the midwife's lore nor the caudlelectures saved him from the archons of Sinn Fein and their naggin of hemlock.

—But Ann Hathaway? Mr Best's quiet voice said forgetfully. Yes, we seem to be forgetting her as Shakespeare himself forgot her.

His look went from brooder's beard to carper's skull, to remind, to chide them not unkindly, then to the baldpink lollard costard, guiltless though maligned.

—He had a good groatsworth of wit, Stephen said, and no truant memory. He carried a memory in his wallet as he trudged to Romeville whistling *The girl I left behind me.* If the earthquake did not time it we should know where to place poor Wat, sitting in his form, the cry of hounds, the studded bridle and her blue windows. That memory, *Venus and Adonis,* lay in the bedchamber of every light-of-love in London. Is Katharine the shrew illfavoured? Hortensio calls her young and beautiful. Do you think the writer of *Antony and Cleopatra,* a passionate pilgrim, had his eyes in the back of his head that he chose the ugliest doxy in all Warwickshire to lie withal? Good: he left her and gained the world of men. But his boywomen are the women of a boy. Their life, thought, speech are lent them by males. He chose badly? He was chosen, it seems to me. If others have their will Ann hath a way. By cock, she was to blame. She put the comether on him, sweet and twentysix. The greyeyed goddess who bends over the boy Adonis, stooping to conquer, as prologue to the swelling act, is a boldfaced Stratford wench who tumbles in a cornfield a lover younger than herself.

And my turn? When?

Come!

—Ryefield, Mr Best said brightly, gladly, raising his new book, gladly, brightly.

He murmured then with blond delight for all:

> *Between the acres of the rye*
> *These pretty countryfolk would lie.*

Paris: the wellpleased pleaser.

A tall figure in bearded homespun rose from shadow and unveiled its cooperative watch.

—I am afraid I am due at the *Homestead*.

Whither away? Exploitable ground.

—Are you going? John Eglinton's active eyebrows asked. Shall we see you at Moore's tonight? Piper is coming.

—Piper! Mr Best piped. Is Piper back?

Peter Piper pecked a peck of pick of peck of pickled pepper.

—I don't know if I can. Thursday. We have our meeting. If I can get away in time.

Yogibogeybox in Dawson chambers. *Isis Unveiled*. Their Pali book we tried to pawn. Crosslegged under an umbrel umbershoot he thrones an Aztec logos, functioning on astral levels, their oversoul, mahamahatma. The faithful hermetists await the light, ripe for chelaship, ringroundabout him. Louis H. Victory. T. Caulfield Irwin. Lotus ladies tend them i'the eyes, their pineal glands aglow. Filled with his god, he thrones, Buddh under plantain. Gulfer of souls, engulfer. Hesouls, shesouls, shoals of souls. Engulfed with wailing creecries, whirled, whirling, they bewail.

> *In quintessential triviality*
> *For years in this fleshcase a shesoul dwelt.*

—They say we are to have a literary surprise, the quaker librarian said, friendly and earnest. Mr Russell, rumour has it, is gathering together a sheaf of our younger poets' verses. We are all looking forward anxiously.

Anxiously he glanced in the cone of lamplight where three faces, lighted, shone.

See this. Remember.

Stephen looked down on a wide headless caubeen, hung on his ashplanthandle over his knee. My casque and sword. Touch lightly with two index fingers. Aristotle's experiment. One or two? Necessity is that in virtue of which it is impossible that one can be otherwise. Argal, one hat is one hat.

Listen.

Young Colum and Starkey. George Roberts is doing the commercial part. Longworth will give it a good puff in the *Express*. O, will he? I liked Colum's *Drover*. Yes, I think he has that queer thing genius. Do you think he has genius really? Yeats admired his line: *As in wild earth a Grecian vase*. Did he? I hope you'll be able to come tonight. Malachi Mulligan is coming too. Moore asked him to bring Haines. Did you hear Miss Mitchell's joke about Moore and Martyn? That Moore is Martyn's wild oats? Awfully clever, isn't it? They remind one of Don Quixote and Sancho Panza. Our national epic has yet to be written, Dr Sigerson says. Moore is the man for it. A knight of the rueful countenance here in Dublin. With a saffron kilt? O'Neill Russell? O, yes, he must speak the grand old tongue. And his Dulcinea? James Stephens is doing some clever sketches. We are becoming important, it seems.

Cordelia. *Cordoglio.* Lir's loneliest daughter.

Nookshotten. Now your best French polish.

—Thank you very much, Mr Russell, Stephen said, rising. If you will be so kind as to give the letter to Mr Norman . . .

—O, yes. If he considers it important it will go in. We have so much correspondence.

—I understand, Stephen said. Thanks.

God ild you. The pigs' paper. Bullockbefriending.

Synge has promised me an article for *Dana* too. Are we going to be read? I feel we are. The Gaelic league wants something in Irish. I hope you will come round tonight. Bring Starkey.

Stephen sat down.

The quaker librarian came from the leavetakers. Blushing, his mask said:

—Mr Dedalus, your views are most illuminating.

He creaked to and fro, tiptoing up nearer heaven by the altitude of a chopine, and, covered by the noise of outgoing, said low:

—Is it your view, then, that she was not faithful to the poet?

Alarmed face asks me. Why did he come? Courtesy or an inward light?

—Where there is a reconciliation, Stephen said, there must have been first a sundering.

—Yes.

Christfox in leather trews, hiding, a runaway in blighted treeforks, from hue and cry. Knowing no vixen, walking lonely in the chase. Women he won to him, tender people, a whore of Babylon, ladies of justices, bully tapsters' wives. Fox and geese. And in New Place a slack dishonoured body that once was comely, once as sweet, as fresh as cinnamon, now her leaves falling, all, bare, frighted of the narrow grave and unforgiven.

—Yes. So you think . . .

The door closed behind the outgoer.

Rest suddenly possessed the discreet vaulted cell, rest of warm and brooding air.

A vestal's lamp.

Here he ponders things that were not: what Cæsar would have lived to do had he believed the soothsayer: what might have been: possibilities of the possible as possible: things not known: what name Achilles bore when he lived among women.

Coffined thoughts around me, in mummycases, embalmed in spice of words. Thoth, god of libraries, a birdgod, moonycrowned. And I heard the voice of that Egyptian highpriest. *In painted chambers loaded with tilebooks.*

They are still. Once quick in the brains of men. Still: but an itch of death is in them, to tell me in my ear a maudlin tale, urge me to wreak their will.

—Certainly, John Eglinton mused, of all great men he is the most enigmatic. We know nothing but that he lived and suffered. Not even so much. Others abide our question. A shadow hangs over all the rest.

—But *Hamlet* is so personal, isn't it? Mr Best pleaded. I mean, a kind of private paper, don't you know, of his private life. I mean, I don't care a button, don't you know, who is killed or who is guilty . . .

He rested an innocent book on the edge of the desk, smiling his defiance. His private papers in the original. *Ta an bad ar an tir. Taim in mo shagart.* Put beurla on it, littlejohn.

Quoth littlejohn Eglinton:

—I was prepared for paradoxes from what Malachi Mulligan told us but I may as well warn you that if you want to shake my belief that Shakespeare is Hamlet you have a stern task before you.

Bear with me.

Stephen withstood the bane of miscreant eyes glinting stern under wrinkled brows. A basilisk. *E quando vede l'uomo l'attosca.* Messer Brunetto, I thank thee for the word.

—As we, or mother Dana, weave and unweave our bodies, Stephen said, from day to day, their molecules shuttled to and fro, so does the artist weave and unweave his image. And as the mole on my right breast is where it was when I was born, though all my body has been woven of new stuff time after time, so through the ghost of the unquiet father the image of the unliving son looks forth. In the intense instant of imagination, when the mind, Shelley says, is a fading coal, that which I was is that which I am and that which in possibility I may come to be. So in the future, the sister of the past, I may see myself as I sit here now but by reflection from that which then I shall be.

Drummond of Hawthornden helped you at that stile.

—Yes, Mr Best said youngly. I feel Hamlet quite young. The bitterness might be from the father but the passages with Ophelia are surely from the son.

Has the wrong sow by the lug. He is in my father. I am in his son.

—That mole is the last to go, Stephen said, laughing.

John Eglinton made a nothing pleasing mow.

—If that were the birthmark of genius, he said, genius would be a drug in the market. The plays of Shakespeare's later years which Renan admired so much breathe another spirit.

—The spirit of reconciliation, the quaker librarian breathed.

—There can be no reconciliation, Stephen said, if there has not been a sundering.

Said that.

—If you want to know what are the events which cast their shadow over the hell of time of *King Lear, Othello, Hamlet, Troilus and Cressida,* look to see when and how the shadow lifts. What softens the heart of a man, shipwrecked in storms dire, Tried, like another Ulysses, Pericles, prince of Tyre?

Head, redconecapped, buffeted, brineblinded.

—A child, a girl, placed in his arms, Marina.

—The leaning of sophists towards the bypaths of apocrypha is a constant quantity, John Eglinton detected. The highroads are dreary but they lead to the town.

Good Bacon: gone musty. Shakespeare Bacon's wild oats. Cypherjugglers going the highroads. Seekers on the great quest. What town, good masters? Mummed in names: A. E., eon: Magee, John Eglinton. East of the sun, west of the moon: *Tir na n-og.* Booted the twain and staved.

How many miles to Dublin?
Three score and ten, sir.
Will we be there by candlelight?

—Mr Brandes accepts it, Stephen said, as the first play of the closing period.

—Does he? What does Mr Sidney Lee, or Mr Simon Lazarus as some aver his name is, say of it?

—Marina, Stephen said, a child of storm, Miranda, a wonder, Perdita, that which was lost. What was lost is given back to him: his daughter's child. *My dearest wife*, Pericles says, *was like this maid*. Will any man love the daughter if he has not loved the mother?

—The art of being a grandfather, Mr Best gan murmur. *L'art d'être grand* . . .

—Will he not see reborn in her, with the memory of his own youth added, another image?

Do you know what you are talking about? Love, yes. Word known to all men. *Amor vero aliquid alicui bonum vult unde et ea quae concupiscimus* . . .

—His own image to a man with that queer thing genius is the standard of all experience, material and moral. Such an appeal will touch him. The images of other males of his blood will repel him. He will see in them grotesque attempts of nature to foretell or to repeat himself.

The benign forehead of the quaker librarian enkindled rosily with hope.

—I hope Mr Dedalus will work out his theory for the enlightenment of the public. And we ought to mention another Irish commentator, Mr George Bernard Shaw. Nor should we forget Mr Frank Harris. His articles on Shakespeare in the *Saturday Review* were surely brilliant. Oddly enough he too draws for us an unhappy relation with the dark lady of the sonnets. The favoured rival is William Herbert, earl of Pembroke. I own that if the poet must be rejected such a rejection would seem more in harmony with—what shall I say?—our notions of what ought not to have been.

Felicitously he ceased and held a meek head among them, auk's egg, prize of their fray.

He thous and thees her with grave husbandwords. Dost love, Miriam? Dost love thy man?

—That may be too, Stephen said. There's a saying of Goethe's which Mr Magee likes to quote. Beware of what you wish for in youth because you will get it in middle life. Why does he send to one who is a *buonaroba*, a bay where all men ride, a maid of honour with a scandalous girlhood, a lordling to woo for him? He was himself a lord of language and had made himself a coistrel gentleman and he had written *Romeo and Juliet.* Why? Belief in himself has been untimely killed. He was overborne in a cornfield first (ryefield, I should say) and he will never be a victor in his own eyes after nor play victoriously the game of laugh and lie down. Assumed dongiovannism will not save him. No later undoing will undo the first undoing. The tusk of the boar has wounded him there where love lies ableeding. If the shrew is worsted yet there remains to her woman's invisible weapon. There is, I feel in the words, some goad of the flesh driving him into a new passion, a darker shadow of the first, darkening even his own understanding of himself. A like fate awaits him and the two rages commingle in a whirlpool.

They list. And in the porches of their ears I pour.

—The soul has been before stricken mortally, a poison poured in the porch of a sleeping ear. But those who are done to death in sleep cannot know the manner of their quell unless their Creator endow their souls with that knowledge in the life to come. The poisoning and the beast with two backs that urged it King Hamlet's ghost could not know of were he not endowed with knowledge by his creator. That is why the speech (his lean unlovely English) is always turned elsewhere, backward. Ravisher and ravished, what he would but would not, go with him from Lucrece's bluecircled ivory globes to Imogen's breast, bare, with its mole cinquespotted. He goes back, weary of the creation he has piled up to hide him from himself, an old dog licking an old sore. But, because loss is his gain, he passes on towards eternity in undiminished personality, untaught by the wisdom he has written or by the laws he has revealed. His beaver is up. He is a ghost, a shadow now, the wind by Elsinore's rocks or what you will, the sea's voice, a voice heard only in the heart of him who is the substance of his shadow, the son consubstantial with the father.

—Amen! was responded from the doorway.

Hast thou found me, O mine enemy?

Entr'acte.

A ribald face, sullen as a dean's, Buck Mulligan came forward, then blithe in motley, towards the greeting of their smiles. My telegram.

—You were speaking of the gaseous vertebrate, if I mistake not? he asked of Stephen.

Primrosevested he greeted gaily with his doffed Panama as with a bauble.

They make him welcome. *Was Du verlachst wirst Du noch dienen.*

Brood of mockers: Photius, pseudomalachi, Johann Most.

He Who Himself begot middler the Holy Ghost and Himself sent Himself, Agenbuyer, between Himself and others, Who, put upon by His fiends, stripped and whipped, was nailed like bat to barndoor, starved on crosstree, Who let Him bury, stood up, harrowed hell, fared into heaven and there these nineteen hundred years sitteth on the right hand of His Own Self but yet shall come in the latter day to doom the quick and dead when all the quick shall be dead already.

Glo—o—ri—a in ex—cel—sis De—o.

He lifts his hands. Veils fall. O, flowers! Bells with bells with bells aquiring.

—Yes, indeed, the quaker librarian said. A most instructive discussion. Mr Mulligan, I'll be bound, has his theory too of the play and of Shakespeare. All sides of life should be represented.

He smiled on all sides equally.

Buck Mulligan thought, puzzled:

—Shakespeare? he said. I seem to know the name.

A flying sunny smile rayed in his loose features.

—To be sure, he said, remembering brightly. The chap that writes like Synge.

Mr Best turned to him.

—Haines missed you, he said. Did you meet him? He'll see you after at the D. B. C. He's gone to Gill's to buy Hyde's *Lovesongs of Connacht.*

—I came through the museum, Buck Mulligan said. Was he here?

—The bard's fellowcountrymen, John Eglinton answered, are rather tired perhaps of our brilliancies of theorising. I hear that an actress played Hamlet for the fourhundredandeighth time last night in Dublin. Vining held that the prince was a woman. Has no-one made him out to be an Irishman? Judge Barton, I believe, is searching for some clues. He swears (His Highness not His Lordship) by saint Patrick.

—The most brilliant of all is that story of Wilde's, Mr Best said, lifting his brilliant notebook. That *Portrait of Mr W. H.* where he proves that the sonnets were written by a Willie Hughes, a man all hues.

—For Willie Hughes, is it not? the quaker librarian asked.

Or Hughie Wills? Mr William Himself. W. H.: who am I?

—I mean, for Willie Hughes, Mr Best said, amending his gloss easily. Of course it's all paradox, don't you know, Hughes and hews and hues, the colour, but it's so typical the way he works it out. It's the very essence of Wilde, don't you know. The light touch.

His glance touched their faces lightly as he smiled, a blond ephebe. Tame essence of Wilde.

You're darned witty. Three drams of usquebaugh you drank with Dan Deasy's ducats.

How much did I spend? O, a few shillings.

For a plump of pressmen. Humour wet and dry.

Wit. You would give your five wits for youth's proud livery he pranks in. Lineaments of gratified desire.

There be many mo. Take her for me. In pairing time. Jove, a cool ruttime send them. Yea, turtledove her.

Eve. Naked wheatbellied sin. A snake coils her, fang in's kiss.

—Do you think it is only a paradox? the quaker librarian was asking. The mocker is never taken seriously when he is most serious.

They talked seriously of mocker's seriousness.

Buck Mulligan's again heavy face eyed Stephen awhile. Then, his head wagging, he came near, drew a folded telegram from his pocket. His mobile lips read, smiling with new delight.

—Telegram! he said. Wonderful inspiration! Telegram! A papal bull!

He sat on a corner of the unlit desk, reading aloud joyfully:

—*The sentimentalist is he who would enjoy without incurring the immense debtorship for a thing done.* Signed: Dedalus. Where did you launch it from? The kips? No. College Green. Have you drunk the four quid? The aunt is going to call on your unsubstantial father. Telegram! Malachi Mulligan, The Ship, lower Abbey street. O, you peerless mummer! O, you priestified Kinchite!

Joyfully he thrust message and envelope into a pocket but keened in a querulous brogue:

—It's what I'm telling you, mister honey, it's queer and sick we were, Haines and myself, the time himself brought it in. 'Twas murmur we did for a gallus potion would rouse a friar, I'm thinking, and he limp with leching. And we one hour and two hours and three hours in Connery's sitting civil waiting for pints apiece.

He wailed:

—And we to be there, mavrone, and you to be unbeknownst sending us your conglomerations the way we to have our tongues out a yard long like the drouthy clerics do be fainting for a pussful.

Stephen laughed.

Quickly, warningfully Buck Mulligan bent down.

—The tramper Synge is looking for you, he said, to murder you. He heard you pissed on his halldoor in Glasthule. He's out in pampooties to murder you.

—Me! Stephen exclaimed. That was your contribution to literature.

Buck Mulligan gleefully bent back, laughing to the dark eavesdropping ceiling.

—Murder you! he laughed.

Harsh gargoyle face that warred against me over our mess of hash of lights in rue Saint-André-des-Arts. In words of words for words, palabras. Oisin with Patrick. Faunman he met in Clamart woods, brandishing a winebottle. *C'est vendredi saint!* Murthering Irish. His image, wandering, he met. I mine. I met a fool i' the forest.

—Mr Lyster, an attendant said from the door ajar.

—. . . in which everyone can find his own. So Mr Justice Madden in his *Diary of Master William Silence* has found the hunting terms . . . Yes? What is it?

—There's a gentleman here, sir, the attendant said, coming forward and offering a card. From the *Freeman*. He wants to see the files of the *Kilkenny People* for last year.

—Certainly, certainly, certainly. Is the gentleman? . . .

He took the eager card, glanced, not saw, laid down unglanced, looked, asked, creaked, asked:

—Is he? . . . O, there!

Brisk in a galliard he was off, out. In the daylit corridor he talked with voluble pains of zeal, in duty bound, most fair, most kind, most honest broadbrim.

—This gentleman? *Freeman's Journal? Kilkenny People?* To be sure. Good day, sir. *Kilkenny* . . . We have certainly . . .

A patient silhouette waited, listening.

—All the leading provincial . . . *Northern Whig, Cork Examiner, Enniscorthy Guardian,* 1903 . . . Will you please? . . . Evans, conduct this gentleman . . . If you just follow the atten . . . Or, please allow me . . . This way . . . Please, sir . . .

Voluble, dutiful, he led the way to all the provincial papers, a bowing dark figure following his hasty heels.

The door closed.

—The sheeny! Buck Mulligan cried.

He jumped up and snatched the card.

—What's his name? Ikey Moses? Bloom.

He rattled on:

—Jehovah, collector of prepuces, is no more. I found him over in the museum where I went to hail the foamborn Aphrodite. The Greek mouth that has never been twisted in prayer. Every day we must do homage to her. *Life of life, thy lips enkindle.*

Suddenly he turned to Stephen:

—He knows you. He knows your old fellow. O, I fear me, he is Greeker than the Greeks. His pale Galilean eyes were upon her mesial groove. Venus Kallipyge. O, the thunder of those loins! *The god pursuing the maiden hid.*

—We want to hear more, John Eglinton decided with Mr Best's approval. We begin to be interested in Mrs S. Till now we had thought of her, if at all, as a patient Griselda, a Penelope stayathome.

—Antisthenes, pupil of Gorgias, Stephen said, took the palm of beauty from Kyrios Menelaus' brooddam, Argive Helen, the wooden mare of Troy in whom a score of heroes slept, and handed it to poor Penelope. Twenty years he lived in London and, during part of that time, he drew a salary equal to that of the lord chancellor of Ireland. His life was rich. His art, more than the art of feudalism as Walt Whitman called it, is the art of surfeit. Hot herringpies, green mugs of sack, honeysauces, sugar of roses, marchpane, gooseberried pigeons, ringocandies. Sir Walter Raleigh, when they arrested him, had half a million francs on his back including a pair of fancy stays. The gombeen woman Eliza Tudor had underlinen enough to vie with her of Sheba. Twenty years he dallied there between conjugial love and its chaste delights and scortatory love and its foul pleasures. You know

Manningham's story of the burgher's wife who bade Dick Burbage to her bed after she had seen him in *Richard III* and how Shakespeare, overhearing, without more ado about nothing, took the cow by the horns and, when Burbage came knocking at the gate, answered from the capon's blankets: *William the conqueror came before Richard III*. And the gay lakin, mistress Fitton, mount and cry O, and his dainty birdsnies, lady Penelope Rich, a clean quality woman is suited for a player, and the punks of the bankside, a penny a time.

Cours la Reine. *Encore vingt sous. Nous ferons de petites cochonneries. Minette? Tu veux?*

—The height of fine society. And sir William Davenant of Oxford's mother with her cup of canary for any cockcanary.

Buck Mulligan, his pious eyes upturned, prayed:

—Blessed Margaret Mary Anycock!

—And Harry of six wives' daughter. And other lady friends from neighbour seats as Lawn Tennyson, gentleman poet, sings. But all those twenty years what do you suppose poor Penelope in Stratford was doing behind the diamond panes?

Do and do. Thing done. In a rosery of Fetter lane of Gerard, herbalist, he walks, greyedauburn. An azured harebell like her veins. Lids of Juno's eyes, violets. He walks. One life is all. One body. Do. But do. Afar, in a reek of lust and squalor, hands are laid on whiteness.

Buck Mulligan rapped John Eglinton's desk sharply.

—Whom do you suspect? he challenged.

—Say that he is the spurned lover in the sonnets. Once spurned twice spurned. But the court wanton spurned him for a lord, his dearmylove.

Love that dare not speak its name.

—As an Englishman, you mean, John sturdy Eglinton put in, he loved a lord.

Old wall where sudden lizards flash. At Charenton I watched them.

—It seems so, Stephen said, when he wants to do for him, and for all other and singular uneared wombs, the holy office an ostler does for the stallion. Maybe, like Socrates, he had a midwife to mother as he had a shrew to wife. But she, the giglot wanton, did not break a bedvow. Two deeds are rank in that ghost's mind: a broken vow and the dullbrained yokel on whom her favour has declined, deceased husband's brother. Sweet Ann, I take it, was hot in the blood. Once a wooer, twice a wooer.

Stephen turned boldly in his chair.

—The burden of proof is with you not with me, he said frowning. If you deny that in the fifth scene of *Hamlet* he has branded her with infamy tell me why there is no mention of her during the thirtyfour years between the day she married him and the day she buried him. All those women saw their men down and under: Mary, her goodman John, Ann, her poor dear Willun, when he went and died on her, raging that he was the first to go, Joan, her four brothers, Judith, her husband and all her sons, Susan, her husband too, while Susan's daughter, Elizabeth, to use granddaddy's words, wed her second, having killed her first.

O, yes, mention there is. In the years when he was living richly in royal London to pay a debt she had to borrow forty shillings from her father's shepherd. Explain you then. Explain the swansong too wherein he has commended her to posterity.

He faced their silence.

To whom thus Eglinton:
    You mean the will.
But that has been explained, I believe, by jurists.
She was entitled to her widow's dower
At common law. His legal knowledge was great
Our judges tell us.
    Him Satan fleers,
Mocker:
    And therefore he left out her name
From the first draft but he did not leave out
The presents for his granddaughter, for his daughters,
For his sister, for his old cronies in Stratford
And in London. And therefore when he was urged,
As I believe, to name her
He left her his
Secondbest
Bed.
    Punkt.

Leftherhis
Secondbest

Leftherhis
Bestabed
Secabest
Leftabed.

Woa!

—Pretty countryfolk had few chattels then, John Eglinton observed, as they have still if our peasant plays are true to type.

—He was a rich country gentleman, Stephen said, with a coat of arms and landed estate at Stratford and a house in Ireland yard, a capitalist shareholder, a bill promoter, a tithefarmer. Why did he not leave her his best bed if he wished her to snore away the rest of her nights in peace?

—It is clear that there were two beds, a best and a secondbest, Mr Secondbest Best said finely.

—*Separatio a mensa et a thalamo*, bettered Buck Mulligan and was smiled on.

—Antiquity mentions famous beds, Second Eglinton puckered, bedsmiling. Let me think.

—Antiquity mentions that Stagyrite schoolurchin and bald heathen sage, Stephen said, who when dying in exile frees and endows his slaves, pays tribute to his elders, wills to be laid in earth near the bones of his dead wife and bids his friends be kind to an old mistress (don't forget Nell Gwynn Herpyllis) and let her live in his villa.

—Do you mean he died so? Mr Best asked with slight concern. I mean . . .

—He died dead drunk, Buck Mulligan capped. A quart of ale is a dish for a king. O, I must tell you what Dowden said!

—What? asked Besteglinton.

William Shakespeare and company, limited. The people's William. For terms apply: E. Dowden, Highfield house . . .

—Lovely! Buck Mulligan suspired amorously. I asked him what he thought of the charge of pederasty brought against the bard. He lifted his hands and said: *All we can say is that life ran very high in those days*. Lovely!

Catamite.

—The sense of beauty leads us astray, said beautifulinsadness Best to ugling Eglinton.

Steadfast John replied severe:

—The doctor can tell us what those words mean. You cannot eat your cake and have it.

Sayest thou so? Will they wrest from us, from me, the palm of beauty?

—And the sense of property, Stephen said. He drew Shylock out of his own long pocket. The son of a maltjobber and moneylender he was himself a cornjobber and moneylender, with ten tods of corn hoarded in the famine riots. His borrowers are no doubt those divers of worship mentioned by Chettle Falstaff who reported his uprightness of dealing. He sued a fellowplayer for the price of a few bags of malt and exacted his pound of flesh in interest for every money lent. How else could Aubrey's ostler and callboy get rich quick? All events brought grist to his mill. Shylock chimes with the jewbaiting that followed the hanging and quartering of the queen's leech Lopez, his jew's heart being plucked forth while the sheeny was yet alive: *Hamlet* and *Macbeth* with the coming to the throne of a Scotch philosophaster with a turn for witchroasting. The lost armada is his jeer in *Love's Labour Lost*. His pageants, the histories, sail fullbellied on a tide of Mafeking enthusiasm. Warwickshire jesuits are tried and we have a porter's theory of equivocation. The *Sea Venture* comes home from Bermudas and the play Renan admired is written with Patsy Caliban, our American cousin. The sugared sonnets follow Sidney's. As for fay Elizabeth, otherwise carrotty Bess, the gross virgin who inspired *The Merry Wives of Windsor*, let some meinherr from Almany grope his life long for deephid meanings in the depths of the buckbasket.

I think you're getting on very nicely. Just mix up a mixture of theolologicophilolological. *Mingo, minxi, mictum, mingere.*

—Prove that he was a jew, John Eglinton dared, expectantly. Your dean of studies holds he was a holy Roman.

Sufflaminandus sum.

—He was made in Germany, Stephen replied, as the champion French polisher of Italian scandals.

—A myriadminded man, Mr Best reminded. Coleridge called him myriadminded.

Amplius. In societate humana hoc est maxime necessarium ut sit amicitia inter multos.

—Saint Thomas, Stephen began . . .

—*Ora pro nobis*, Monk Mulligan groaned, sinking to a chair.

There he keened a wailing rune.

—*Pogue mahone! Acushla machree!* Ibs destroyed we are from this day! Ibs destroyed we are surely!

All smiled their smiles.

—Saint Thomas, Stephen smiling said, whose gorbellied works I enjoy reading in the original, writing of incest from a standpoint different from that of the new Viennese school Mr Magee spoke of, likens it in his wise and curious way to an avarice of the emotions. He means that the love so given to one near in blood is covetously withheld from some stranger who, it may be, hungers for it. Jews, whom christians tax with avarice, are of all races the most given to intermarriage. Accusations are made in anger. The christian laws which built up the hoards of the jews (for whom, as for the lollards, storm was shelter) bound their affections too with hoops of steel. Whether these be sins or virtues old Nobodaddy will tell us at doomsday leet. But a man who holds so tightly to what he calls his rights over what he calls his debts will hold tightly also to what he calls his rights over her whom he calls his wife. No sir smile neighbour shall covet his ox or his wife or his manservant or his maidservant or his jackass.

—Or his jennyass, Buck Mulligan antiphoned.

—Gentle Will is being roughly handled, gentle Mr Best said gently.

—Which will? gagged sweetly Buck Mulligan. We are getting mixed.

—The will to live, John Eglinton philosophised, for poor Ann, Will's widow, is the will to die.

—*Requiescat!* Stephen prayed.

> *What of all the will to do?*
> *It has vanished long ago . . .*

—She lies laid out in stark stiffness in that secondbest bed, the mobled queen, even though you prove that a bed in those days was as rare as a motorcar is now and that its carvings were the wonder of seven parishes. In old age she takes up with gospellers (one stayed with her at New Place and drank a quart of sack the town council paid for but in which bed he slept it skills not to ask) and heard she had a soul. She read or had read to her his chapbooks preferring them to the *Merry Wives* and, loosing her nightly waters on the jordan, she thought over *Hooks and Eyes for Believers' Breeches* and *The most Spiritual Snuffbox to*

Make the Most Devout Souls Sneeze. Venus has twisted her lips in prayer. Agenbite of inwit: remorse of conscience. It is an age of exhausted whoredom groping for its god.

—History shows that to be true, *inquit Eglintonus Chronolologos.* The ages succeed one another. But we have it on high authority that a man's worst enemies shall be those of his own house and family. I feel that Russell is right. What do we care for his wife or father? I should say that only family poets have family lives. Falstaff was not a family man. I feel that the fat knight is his supreme creation.

Lean, he lay back. Shy, deny thy kindred, the unco guid. Shy, supping with the godless, he sneaks the cup. A sire in Ultonian Antrim bade it him. Visits him here on quarter days. Mr Magee, sir, there's a gentleman to see you. Me? Says he's your father, sir. Give me my Wordsworth. Enter Magee Mor Matthew, a rugged rough rugheaded kern, in strossers with a buttoned codpiece, his nether stocks bemired with clauber of ten forests, a wand of wilding in his hand.

Your own? He knows your old fellow. The widower.

Hurrying to her squalid deathlair from gay Paris on the quayside I touched his hand. The voice, new warmth, speaking. Dr Bob Kenny is attending her. The eyes that wish me well. But do not know me.

—A father, Stephen said, battling against hopelessness, is a necessary evil. He wrote the play in the months that followed his father's death. If you hold that he, a greying man with two marriageable daughters, with thirtyfive years of life, *nel mezzo del cammin di nostra vita,* with fifty of experience, is the beardless undergraduate from Wittenberg then you must hold that his seventyyear old mother is the lustful queen. No. The corpse of John Shakespeare does not walk the night. From hour to hour it rots and rots. He rests, disarmed of fatherhood, having devised that mystical estate upon his son. Boccaccio's Calandrino was the first and last man who felt himself with child. Fatherhood, in the sense of conscious begetting, is unknown to man. It is a mystical estate, an apostolic succession, from only begetter to only begotten. On that mystery and not on the madonna which the cunning Italian intellect flung to the mob of Europe the church is founded and founded irremovably because founded, like the world, macro and microcosm, upon the void. Upon incertitude, upon unlikelihood. *Amor matris,* subjective and objective genitive, may be the only true thing in life. Paternity may be a legal fiction. Who is the father of any son that any son should love him or he any son?

What the hell are you driving at?

I know. Shut up. Blast you. I have reasons.

Amplius. Adhuc. Iterum. Postea.

Are you condemned to do this?

—They are sundered by a bodily shame so steadfast that the criminal annals of the world, stained with all other incests and bestialities, hardly record its breach. Sons with mothers, sires with daughters, lesbic sisters, loves that dare not speak their name, nephews with grandmothers, jailbirds with keyholes, queens with prize bulls. The son unborn mars beauty: born, he brings pain, divides affection, increases care. He is a new male: his growth is his father's decline, his youth his father's envy, his friend his father's enemy.

In rue Monsieur-le-Prince I thought it.

—What links them in nature? An instant of blind rut.

Am I a father? If I were?

Shrunken uncertain hand.

—Sabellius, the African, subtlest heresiarch of all the beasts of the field, held that the Father was Himself His Own Son. The bulldog of Aquin, with whom no word shall be impossible, refutes him. Well: if the father who has not a son be not a father can the son who has not a father be a son? When Rutlandbaconsouthamptonshakespeare or another poet of the same name in the comedy of errors wrote *Hamlet* he was not the father of his own son merely but, being no more a son, he was and felt himself the father of all his race, the father of his own grandfather, the father of his unborn grandson who, by the same token, never was born, for nature, as Mr Magee understands her, abhors perfection.

Eglintoneyes, quick with pleasure, looked up shybrightly. Gladly glancing, a merry puritan, through the twisted eglantine.

Flatter. Rarely. But flatter.

—Himself his own father, Sonmulligan told himself. Wait. I am big with child. I have an unborn child in my brain. Pallas Athena! A play! The play's the thing! Let me parturiate!

He clasped his paunchbrow with both birthaiding hands.

—As for his family, Stephen said, his mother's name lives in the forest of Arden. Her death brought from him the scene with Volumnia in *Coriolanus*. His boyson's death is the deathscene of young Arthur in *King John*. Hamlet, the black prince, is Hamnet Shakespeare. Who the girls in *The Tempest*, in *Pericles*, in *Winter's Tale* are we know.

Who Cleopatra, fleshpot of Egypt, and Cressid and Venus are we may guess. But there is another member of his family who is recorded.

—The plot thickens, John Eglinton said.

The quaker librarian, quaking, tiptoed in, quake, his mask, quake, with haste, quake, quack.

Door closed. Cell. Day.

They list. Three. They.

I you he they.

Come, mess.

STEPHEN: He had three brothers, Gilbert, Edmund, Richard. Gilbert in his old age told some cavaliers he got a pass for nowt from Maister Gatherer one time mass he did and he seen his brud Maister Wull the playwriter up in Lunnon in a wrastling play wud a man on's back. The playhouse sausage filled Gilbert's soul. He is nowhere: but an Edmund and a Richard are recorded in the works of sweet William.

MAGEEGLINJOHN: Names! What's in a name?

BEST: That is my name, Richard, don't you know. I hope you are going to say a good word for Richard, don't you know, for my sake. (*Laughter*)

BUCKMULLIGAN: (*Piano, diminuendo*)

> *Then outspoke medical Dick*
> *To his comrade medical Davy . . .*

STEPHEN: In his trinity of black Wills, the villain shakebags, Iago, Richard Crookback, Edmund in *King Lear*, two bear the wicked uncles' names. Nay, that last play was written or being written while his brother Edmund lay dying in Southwark.

BEST: I hope Edmund is going to catch it. I don't want Richard, my name . . .

(*Laughter*)

QUAKERLYSTER: (*A tempo*) But he that filches from me my good name . . .

STEPHEN: (*Stringendo*) He has hidden his own name, a fair name, William, in the plays, a super here, a clown there, as a painter of old Italy set his face in a dark corner of his canvas. He has revealed it in the sonnets where there is Will in overplus. Like John o'Gaunt his name is dear to him, as dear as the coat and crest he toadied for, on a bend sable a spear or steeled argent, honorificabilitudinitatibus, dearer than his glory of greatest shakescene in the country. What's in a name? That is what we ask ourselves in childhood when we write the name that we are told is ours. A star, a daystar, a firedrake, rose at his birth. It shone by day in the heavens alone, brighter than Venus in the night, and by night it shone over delta in Cassiopeia, the recumbent constellation which is the signature of his initial among the stars. His eyes watched it, lowlying on the horizon, eastward of the bear, as he walked by the slumberous summer fields at midnight returning from Shottery and from her arms.

Both satisfied. I too.

Don't tell them he was nine years old when it was quenched.

And from her arms.

Wait to be wooed and won. Ay, meacock. Who will woo you?

Read the skies. *Autontimorumenos. Bous Stephanoumenos.* Where's your configuration? Stephen, Stephen, cut the bread even. S. D.: *sua donna. Già: di lui. Gelindo risolve di non amare* S. D.

—What is that, Mr Dedalus? the quaker librarian asked. Was it a celestial phenomenon?

—A star by night, Stephen said. A pillar of the cloud by day.

What more's to speak?

Stephen looked on his hat, his stick, his boots.

Stephanos, my crown. My sword. His boots are spoiling the shape of my feet. Buy a pair. Holes in my socks. Handkerchief too.

—You make good use of the name, John Eglinton allowed. Your own name is strange enough. I suppose it explains your fantastical humour.

Me, Magee and Mulligan.

Fabulous artificer. The hawklike man. You flew. Whereto? Newhaven-Dieppe, steerage passenger. Paris and back. Lapwing. Icarus. *Pater, ait.* Seabedabbled, fallen, weltering. Lapwing you are. Lapwing be.

Mr Best eagerquietly lifted his book to say:

—That's very interesting because that brother motive, don't you know, we find also in the old Irish myths. Just what you say. The three brothers Shakespeare. In Grimm too, don't you know, the fairytales. The third brother that always marries the sleeping beauty and wins the best prize.

Best of Best brothers. Good, better, best.

The quaker librarian springhalted near.

—I should like to know, he said, which brother you . . . I understand you to suggest there was misconduct with one of the brothers . . . But perhaps I am anticipating?

He caught himself in the act: looked at all: refrained.

An attendant from the doorway called:

—Mr Lyster! Father Dineen wants . . .

—O, Father Dineen! Directly.

Swiftly rectly creaking rectly rectly he was rectly gone.

John Eglinton touched the foil.

—Come, he said. Let us hear what you have to say of Richard and Edmund. You kept them for the last, didn't you?

—In asking you to remember those two noble kinsmen nuncle Richie and nuncle Edmund, Stephen answered, I feel I am asking too much perhaps. A brother is as easily forgotten as an umbrella.

Lapwing.

Where is your brother? Apothecaries' hall. My whetstone. Him, then Cranly, Mulligan: now these. Speech, speech. But act. Act speech. They mock to try you. Act. Be acted on.

Lapwing.

I am tired of my voice, the voice of Esau. My kingdom for a drink. On.

—You will say those names were already in the chronicles from which he took the stuff of his plays. Why did he take them rather than others? Richard, a whoreson crookback, misbegotten, makes love to a widowed Ann (what's in a name?), woos and wins her, a whoreson merry widow. Richard the conqueror, third brother, came after William the conquered. The other four acts of that play hang limply from that first. Of all his kings Richard is the only king unshielded by Shakespeare's reverence, the angel of the world. Why is the underplot of *King Lear* in which Edmund figures lifted out of Sidney's *Arcadia* and spatchcocked on to a Celtic legend older than history?

—That was Will's way, John Eglinton defended. We should not now combine a Norse saga with an excerpt from a novel by George Meredith. *Que voulez-vous?* Moore would say. He puts Bohemia on the seacoast and makes Ulysses quote Aristotle.

—Why? Stephen answered himself. Because the theme of the false or the usurping or the adulterous brother or all three in one is to Shakespeare, what the poor are not, always with him. The note of banishment, banishment from the heart, banishment from home, sounds uninterruptedly from *The Two Gentlemen of Verona* onward till Prospero breaks his staff, buries it certain fathoms in the earth and drowns his book. It doubles itself in the middle of his life, reflects itself in another, repeats itself, protasis, epitasis, catastasis, catastrophe. It repeats itself again when he is near the grave, when his married daughter Susan, chip of the old block, is accused of adultery. But it was the original sin that darkened his understanding, weakened his will and left in him a strong inclination to evil. The words are those of my lords bishops of Maynooth. An original sin and, like original sin, committed by another in whose sin he too has sinned. It is between the lines of his last written words, it is petrified on his tombstone under which her four bones are not to be laid. Age has not withered it. Beauty and peace have not done it away. It is in infinite variety everywhere in the world he has created, in *Much Ado about Nothing*, twice in *As you like It*, in *The Tempest*, in *Hamlet*, in *Measure for Measure*—and in all the other plays which I have not read.

He laughed to free his mind from his mind's bondage.

Judge Eglinton summed up.

—The truth is midway, he affirmed. He is the ghost and the prince. He is all in all.

—He is, Stephen said. The boy of act one is the mature man of act five. All in all. In *Cymbeline*, in *Othello* he is bawd and cuckold. He acts and is acted on. Lover of an ideal or a perversion, like José he kills the real Carmen. His unremitting intellect is the hornmad Iago ceaselessly willing that the moor in him shall suffer.

—Cuckoo! Cuckoo! Cuck Mulligan clucked lewdly. O word of fear!

Dark dome received, reverbed.

—And what a character is Iago! undaunted John Eglinton exclaimed. When all is said Dumas *fils* (or is it Dumas *père?*) is right. After God Shakespeare has created most.

—Man delights him not nor woman neither, Stephen said. He returns after a life of absence to that spot of earth where he was born, where he has always been, man and boy, a silent witness and there, his journey of life ended, he plants his mulberrytree in the earth. Then dies. The motion is ended. Gravediggers bury Hamlet *père* and Hamlet *fils*. A king and a prince at last in death, with incidental music. And, what though murdered and betrayed, bewept by all frail tender hearts for, Dane or Dubliner, sorrow for the dead is the only husband from whom they refuse to be divorced. If you like the epilogue look long on it: prosperous Prospero, the good man rewarded, Lizzie, grandpa's lump of love, and nuncle Richie, the bad man taken off by poetic justice to the place where the bad niggers go. Strong curtain. He found in the world without as actual what was in his world within as possible. Maeterlinck says: *If Socrates leave his house today he will find the sage seated on his doorstep. If Judas go forth tonight it is to Judas his steps will tend.* Every life is many days, day after day. We walk through ourselves, meeting robbers, ghosts, giants, old men, young men, wives, widows, brothers-in-love, but always meeting ourselves. The playwright who wrote the folio of this world and wrote it badly (He gave us light first and the sun two days later), the lord of things as they are whom the most Roman of catholics call *dio boia*, hangman god, is doubtless all in all in all of us, ostler and butcher, and would be bawd and cuckold too but that in the economy of heaven, foretold by Hamlet, there are no more marriages, glorified man, an androgynous angel, being a wife unto himself.

—*Eureka!* Buck Mulligan cried. *Eureka!*

Suddenly happied he jumped up and reached in a stride John Eglinton's desk.

—May I? he said. The Lord has spoken to Malachi.

He began to scribble on a slip of paper.

Take some slips from the counter going out.

—Those who are married, Mr Best, douce herald, said, all save one, shall live. The rest shall keep as they are.

He laughed, unmarried, at Eglinton Johannes, of arts a bachelor.

Unwed, unfancied, ware of wiles, they fingerponder nightly each his variorum edition of *The Taming of the Shrew.*

—You are a delusion, said roundly John Eglinton to Stephen. You have brought us all this way to show us a French triangle. Do you believe your own theory?

—No, Stephen said promptly.

—Are you going to write it? Mr Best asked. You ought to make it a dialogue, don't you know, like the Platonic dialogues Wilde wrote.

John Eclecticon doubly smiled.

—Well, in that case, he said, I don't see why you should expect payment for it since you don't believe it yourself. Dowden believes there is some mystery in *Hamlet* but will say no more. Herr Bleibtreu, the man Piper met in Berlin, who is working up that Rutland theory, believes that the secret is hidden in the Stratford monument. He is going to visit the present duke, Piper says, and prove to him that his ancestor wrote the plays. It will come as a surprise to his grace. But he believes his theory.

I believe, O Lord, help my unbelief. That is, help me to believe or help me to unbelieve? Who helps to believe? *Egomen.* Who to unbelieve? Other chap.

—You are the only contributor to *Dana* who asks for pieces of silver. Then I don't know about the next number. Fred Ryan wants space for an article on economics.

Fraidrine. Two pieces of silver he lent me. Tide you over. Economics.

—For a guinea, Stephen said, you can publish this interview.

Buck Mulligan stood up from his laughing scribbling, laughing: and then gravely said, honeying malice:

—I called upon the bard Kinch at his summer residence in upper Mecklenburgh street and found him deep in the study of the *Summa contra Gentiles* in the company of two gonorrheal ladies, Fresh Nelly and Rosalie, the coalquay whore.

He broke away.

—Come, Kinch. Come, wandering Ængus of the birds.

Come, Kinch. You have eaten all we left. Ay. I will serve you your orts and offals.

Stephen rose.

Life is many days. This will end.

—We shall see you tonight, John Eglinton said. *Notre ami* Moore says Malachi Mulligan must be there.

Buck Mulligan flaunted his slip and panama.

—Monsieur Moore, he said, lecturer on French letters to the youth of Ireland. I'll be there. Come, Kinch, the bards must drink. Can you walk straight?

Laughing, he . . .

Swill till eleven. Irish nights entertainment.

Lubber . . .

Stephen followed a lubber . . .

One day in the national library we had a discussion. Shakes. After. His lub back: I followed. I gall his kibe.

Stephen, greeting, then all amort, followed a lubber jester, a wellkempt head, newbarbered, out of the vaulted cell into a shattering daylight of no thought.

What have I learned? Of them? Of me?

Walk like Haines now.

The constant readers' room. In the readers' book Cashel Boyle O'Connor Fitzmaurice Tisdall Farrell parafes his polysyllables. Item: was Hamlet mad? The quaker's pate godlily with a priesteen in booktalk.

—O please do, sir . . . I shall be most pleased . . .

Amused Buck Mulligan mused in pleasant murmur with himself, selfnodding:

—A pleased bottom.

The turnstile.

Is that? . . . Blueribboned hat . . . Idly writing . . . What? Looked? . . .

The curving balustrade: smoothsliding Mincius.

Puck Mulligan, panamahelmeted, went step by step, iambing, trolling:

> *John Eglinton, my jo, John,*
> *Why won't you wed a wife?*

He spluttered to the air:

—O, the chinless Chinaman! Chin Chon Eg Lin Ton. We went over to their playbox, Haines and I, the plumbers' hall. Our players are creating a new art for Europe like the Greeks or M. Maeterlinck. Abbey Theatre! I smell the pubic sweat of monks.

He spat blank.

Forgot: any more than he forgot the whipping lousy Lucy gave him. And left the *femme de trente ans*. And why no other children born? And his first child a girl?

Afterwit. Go back.

The dour recluse still there (he has his cake) and the douce youngling, minion of pleasure, Phedo's toyable fair hair.

Eh . . . I just eh . . . wanted . . . I forgot . . . he . . .

—Longworth and M'Curdy Atkinson were there . . .

Puck Mulligan footed featly, trilling:

> *I hardly hear the purlieu cry*
> *Or a Tommy talk as I pass one by*

Before my thoughts begin to run
On F. M'Curdy Atkinson,
The same that had the wooden leg
And that filibustering filibeg
That never dared to slake his drouth,
Magee that had the chinless mouth.
Being afraid to marry on earth
They masturbated for all they were worth.

Jest on. Know thyself.

Halted, below me, a quizzer looks at me. I halt.

—Mournful mummer, Buck Mulligan moaned. Synge has left off wearing black to be like nature. Only crows, priests and English coal are black.

A laugh tripped over his lips.

—Longworth is awfully sick, he said, after what you wrote about that old hake Gregory. O you inquisitional drunken jewjesuit! She gets you a job on the paper and then you go and slate her drivel to Jaysus. Couldn't you do the Yeats touch?

He went on and down, mopping, chanting with waving graceful arms:

—The most beautiful book that has come out of our country in my time. One thinks of Homer.

He stopped at the stairfoot.

—I have conceived a play for the mummers, he said solemnly. The pillared Moorish hall, shadows entwined. Gone the nine men's morrice with caps of indices.

In sweetly varying voices Buck Mulligan read his tablet:

Everyman His Own Wife
or
A Honeymoon in the Hand
(a national immorality in three orgasms)
by
Ballocky Mulligan.

He turned a happy patch's smirk to Stephen, saying:

—The disguise, I fear, is thin. But listen.

He read, *marcato:*

—Characters:

TODY TOSTOFF (*a ruined Pole*)
CRAB (*a bushranger*)
MEDICAL DICK
    and   } (*two birds with one stone*)
MEDICAL DAVY
MOTHER GROGAN (*a watercarrier*)
FRESH NELLY
    and
ROSALIE (*the coalquay whore*).

He laughed, lolling a to and fro head, walking on, followed by Stephen: and mirthfully he told the shadows, souls of men:

—O, the night in the Camden hall when the daughters of Erin had to lift their skirts to step over you as you lay in your mulberrycoloured, multicoloured, multitudinous vomit!

—The most innocent son of Erin, Stephen said, for whom they ever lifted them.

About to pass through the doorway, feeling one behind, he stood aside.

Part. The moment is now. Where then? If Socrates leave his house today, if Judas go forth tonight. Why? That lies in space which I in time must come to, ineluctably.

My will: his will that fronts me. Seas between.

A man passed out between them, bowing, greeting.

—Good day again, Buck Mulligan said.

The portico.

Here I watched the birds for augury. Ængus of the birds. They go, they come. Last night I flew. Easily flew. Men wondered. Street of harlots after. A creamfruit melon he held to me. In. You will see.

—The wandering jew, Buck Mulligan whispered with clown's awe. Did you see his eye? He looked upon you to lust after you. I fear thee, ancient mariner. O, Kinch, thou art in peril. Get thee a breechpad.

Manner of Oxenford.

Day. Wheelbarrow sun over arch of bridge.

A dark back went before them, step of a pard, down, out by the gateway, under portcullis barbs.

234

They followed.

Offend me still. Speak on.

Kind air defined the coigns of houses in Kildare street. No birds. Frail from the housetops two plumes of smoke ascended, pluming, and in a flaw of softness softly were blown.

Cease to strive. Peace of the druid priests of Cymbeline: hierophantic: from wide earth an altar.

Laud we the gods
And let our crooked smokes climb to their nostrils
From our bless'd altars.

10

The superior, the very reverend John Conmee S. J. reset his smooth watch in his interior pocket as he came down the presbytery steps. Five to three. Just nice time to walk to Artane. What was that boy's name again? Dignam. Yes. *Vere dignum et iustum est.* Brother Swan was the person to see. Mr Cunningham's letter. Yes. Oblige him, if possible. Good practical catholic: useful at mission time.

A onelegged sailor, swinging himself onward by lazy jerks of his crutches, growled some notes. He jerked short before the convent of the sisters of charity and held out a peaked cap for alms towards the very reverend John Conmee S. J. Father Conmee blessed him in the sun for his purse held, he knew, one silver crown.

Father Conmee crossed to Mountjoy square. He thought, but not for long, of soldiers and sailors, whose legs had been shot off by cannonballs, ending their days in some pauper ward, and of cardinal Wolsey's words: *If I had served my God as I have served my king He would not have abandoned me in my old days.* He walked by the treeshade of sunnywinking leaves: and towards him came the wife of Mr David Sheehy M. P.

—Very well, indeed, father. And you, father?

Father Conmee was wonderfully well indeed. He would go to Buxton probably for the waters. And her boys, were they getting on well at Belvedere? Was that so? Father Conmee was very glad indeed to hear that. And Mr Sheehy himself? Still in London. The house was still sitting, to be sure it was. Beautiful weather it was, delightful indeed. Yes, it was very probable that Father Bernard Vaughan would come again to preach. O, yes: a very great success. A wonderful man really.

Father Conmee was very glad to see the wife of Mr David Sheehy M. P. looking so well and he begged to be remembered to Mr David Sheehy M. P. Yes, he would certainly call.

—Good afternoon, Mrs Sheehy.

Father Conmee doffed his silk hat and smiled, as he took leave, at the jet beads of her mantilla inkshining in the sun. And smiled yet again, in going. He had cleaned his teeth, he knew, with arecanut paste.

Father Conmee walked and, walking, smiled for he thought on Father Bernard Vaughan's droll eyes and cockney voice.

—Pilate! Wy don't you old back that owlin mob?

A zealous man, however. Really he was. And really did great good in his way. Beyond a doubt. He loved Ireland, he said, and he loved the Irish. Of good family too would one think it? Welsh, were they not?

O, lest he forget. That letter to father provincial.

Father Conmee stopped three little schoolboys at the corner of Mountjoy square. Yes: they were from Belvedere. The little house. Aha. And were they good boys at school? O. That was very good now. And what was his name? Jack Sohan. And his name? Ger. Gallaher. And the other little man? His name was Brunny Lynam. O, that was a very nice name to have.

Father Conmee gave a letter from his breast to Master Brunny Lynam and pointed to the red pillarbox at the corner of Fitzgibbon street.

—But mind you don't post yourself into the box, little man, he said.

The boys sixeyed Father Conmee and laughed:

—O, sir.

—Well, let me see if you can post a letter, Father Conmee said.

Master Brunny Lynam ran across the road and put Father Conmee's letter to father provincial into the mouth of the bright red letterbox. Father Conmee smiled and nodded and smiled and walked along Mountjoy square east.

Mr Denis J Maginni, professor of dancing &c, in silk hat, slate frockcoat with silk facings, white kerchief tie, tight lavender trousers, canary gloves and pointed patent boots, walking with grave deportment most respectfully took the curbstone as he passed lady Maxwell at the corner of Dignam's court.

Was that not Mrs M'Guinness?

Mrs M'Guinness, stately, silverhaired, bowed to Father Conmee from the farther footpath along which she sailed. And Father Conmee smiled and saluted. How did she do?

A fine carriage she had. Like Mary, queen of Scots, something. And to think that she was a pawnbroker! Well, now! Such a . . . what should he say? . . . such a queenly mien.

Father Conmee walked down Great Charles street and glanced at the shutup free church on his left. The reverend T. R. Greene B. A. will (D. V.) speak. The incumbent they called him. He felt it incumbent on him to say a few words. But one should be charitable. Invincible ignorance. They acted according to their lights.

Father Conmee turned the corner and walked along the North Circular road. It was a wonder that there was not a tramline in such an important thoroughfare. Surely, there ought to be.

A band of satchelled schoolboys crossed from Richmond street. All raised untidy caps. Father Conmee greeted them more than once benignly. Christian brother boys.

Father Conmee smelt incense on his right hand as he walked. Saint Joseph's church, Portland row. For aged and virtuous females. Father Conmee raised his hat to the Blessed Sacrament. Virtuous: but occasionally they were also badtempered.

Near Aldborough house Father Conmee thought of that spendthrift nobleman. And now it was an office or something.

Father Conmee began to walk along the North Strand road and was saluted by Mr William Gallagher who stood in the doorway of his shop. Father Conmee saluted Mr William Gallagher and perceived the odours that came from baconflitches and ample cools of butter. He passed Grogan's the Tobacconist against which newsboards leaned and told of a dreadful catastrophe in New York. In America those things were continually happening. Unfortunate people to die like that, unprepared. Still, an act of perfect contrition.

Father Conmee went by Daniel Bergin's publichouse against the window of which two unlabouring men lounged. They saluted him and were saluted.

Father Conmee passed H. J. O'Neill's funeral establishment where Corny Kelleher totted figures in the daybook while he chewed a blade of hay. A constable on his beat saluted Father Conmee and Father Conmee saluted the constable. In Youkstetter's, the porkbutcher's, Father Conmee observed pig's puddings, white and black and red, lie neatly curled in tubes.

Moored under the trees of Charleville Mall Father Conmee saw a turfbarge, a towhorse with pendent head, a bargeman with a hat of dirty straw seated amidships, smoking and staring at a branch of poplar above him. It was idyllic: and Father Conmee reflected on the providence of the Creator who had made turf to be in bogs whence men might dig it out and bring it to town and hamlet to make fires in the houses of poor people.

On Newcomen bridge the very reverend John Conmee S. J. of saint Francis Xavier's church, upper Gardiner street, stepped on to an outward bound tram.

Off an inward bound tram stepped the reverend Nicholas Dudley C. C. of saint Agatha's church, north William street, on to Newcomen bridge.

At Newcomen bridge Father Conmee stepped into an outward bound tram for he disliked to traverse on foot the dingy way past Mud Island.

Father Conmee sat in a corner of the tramcar, a blue ticket tucked with care in the eye of one plump kid glove, while four shillings, a sixpence and five pennies chuted from his other plump glovepalm into his purse. Passing the ivy church he reflected that the ticket inspector usually made his visit when one had carelessly thrown away the ticket. The solemnity of the occupants of the car seemed to Father Conmee excessive for a journey so short and cheap. Father Conmee liked cheerful decorum.

It was a peaceful day. The gentleman with the glasses opposite Father Conmee had finished explaining and looked down. His wife, Father Conmee supposed. A tiny yawn opened the mouth of the wife of the gentleman with the glasses. She raised her small gloved fist, yawned ever so gently, tiptapping her small gloved fist on her opening mouth and smiled tinily, sweetly.

Father Conmee perceived her perfume in the car. He perceived also that the awkward man at the other side of her was sitting on the edge of the seat.

Father Conmee at the altarrails placed the host with difficulty in the mouth of the awkward old man who had the shaky head.

At Annesley bridge the tram halted and, when it was about to go, an old woman rose suddenly from her place to alight. The conductor pulled the bellstrap to stay the car for her. She passed out with her basket and a marketnet: and Father Conmee saw the conductor help her and net and basket down: and Father Conmee thought that, as she had nearly passed the end of the penny fare, she was one of those good souls who had always to be told twice *bless you, my child,* that they have been absolved, *pray for me.* But they had so many worries in life, so many cares, poor creatures.

From the hoardings Mr Eugene Stratton grimaced with thick niggerlips at Father Conmee.

Father Conmee thought of the souls of black and brown and yellow men and of his sermon on saint Peter Claver S. J. and the African mission and of the propagation of the faith and of the millions of black and brown and yellow souls that had not received the baptism of water when their last hour came like a thief in the night. That book by the Belgian jesuit, *Le Nombre des Élus,* seemed to Father Conmee a reasonable plea. Those were millions of human souls created by God in His Own likeness to whom the faith had not (D. V.) been brought. But they were God's souls, created by God. It seemed to Father Conmee a pity that they should all be lost, a waste, if one might say.

At the Howth road stop Father Conmee alighted, was saluted by the conductor and saluted in his turn.

The Malahide road was quiet. It pleased Father Conmee, road and name. The joybells were ringing in gay Malahide. Lord Talbot de Malahide, immediate hereditary lord admiral of Malahide and the seas adjoining. Then came the call to arms and she was maid, wife and widow in one day. Those were old worldish days, loyal times in joyous townlands, old times in the barony.

Father Conmee, walking, thought of his little book *Old Times in the Barony* and of the book that might be written about jesuit houses and of Mary Rochfort, daughter of lord Molesworth, first countess of Belvedere.

A listless lady, no more young, walked alone the shore of lough Ennel, Mary, first countess of Belvedere, listlessly walking in the evening, not startled when an otter plunged. Who could know the truth? Not the jealous lord Belvedere and not her confessor if she had not committed adultery fully, *eiaculatio seminis inter vas naturale mulieris,* with her husband's brother? She would half confess if she had not all sinned as women did. Only God knew and she and he, her husband's brother.

Father Conmee thought of that tyrannous incontinence, needed however for man's race on earth, and of the ways of God which were not our ways.

Don John Conmee walked and moved in times of yore. He was humane and honoured there. He bore in mind secrets confessed and he smiled at smiling noble faces in a beeswaxed drawing room, ceiled with full fruit clusters. And the hands of a bride and of a bridegroom, noble to noble, were impalmed by Don John Conmee.

It was a charming day.

The lychgate of a field showed Father Conmee breadths of cabbages, curtseying to him with ample underleaves. The sky showed him a flock of small white clouds going slowly down the wind. *Moutonner,* the French said. A just and homely word.

Father Conmee, reading his office, watched a flock of muttoning clouds over Rathcoffey. His thinsocked ankles were tickled by the stubble of Clongowes field. He walked there, reading in the evening, and heard the cries of the boys' lines at their play, young cries in the quiet evening. He was their rector: his reign was mild.

Father Conmee drew off his gloves and took his rededged breviary out. An ivory bookmark told him the page.

Nones. He should have read that before lunch. But lady Maxwell had come.

Father Conmee read in secret *Pater* and *Ave* and crossed his breast. *Deus in adiutorium.*

He walked calmly and read mutely the nones, walking and reading till he came to Res in *Beati immaculati: Principium verborum tuorum veritas: in eternum omnia iudicia iustitiæ tuæ.*

A flushed young man came from a gap of a hedge and after him came a young woman with wild nodding daisies in her hand. The young man raised his cap abruptly: the young woman abruptly bent and with slow care detached from her light skirt a clinging twig.

Father Conmee blessed both gravely and turned a thin page of his breviary. *Sin: Principes persecuti sunt me gratis: et a verbis tuis formidavit cor meum.*

***

Corny Kelleher closed his long daybook and glanced with his drooping eye at a pine coffinlid sentried in a corner. He pulled himself erect, went to it and, spinning it on its axle, viewed its shape and brass furnishings. Chewing his blade of hay he laid the coffinlid by and came to the doorway. There he tilted his hatbrim to give shade to his eyes and leaned against the doorcase, looking idly out.

Father John Conmee stepped into the Dollymount tram on Newcomen bridge.

Corny Kelleher locked his largefooted boots and gazed, his hat downtilted, chewing his blade of hay.

Constable 57C, on his beat, stood to pass the time of day.

—That's a fine day, Mr Kelleher.

—Ay, Corny Kelleher said.

—It's very close, the constable said.

Corny Kelleher sped a silent jet of hayjuice arching from his mouth while a generous white arm from a window in Eccles street flung forth a coin.

—What's the best news? he asked.

—I seen that particular party last evening, the constable said with bated breath.

***

A onelegged sailor crutched himself round MacConnell's corner, skirting Rabaiotti's icecream car, and jerked himself up Eccles street. Towards Larry O'Rourke, in shirtsleeves in his doorway, he growled unamiably:

—*For England* . . .

He swung himself violently forward past Katey and Boody Dedalus, halted and growled:

—*home and beauty.*

J. J. O'Molloy's white careworn face was told that Mr Lambert was in the warehouse with a visitor.

A stout lady stopped, took a copper coin from her purse and dropped it into the cap held out to her. The sailor grumbled thanks, glanced sourly at the unheeding windows, sank his head and swung himself forward four strides.

He halted and growled angrily:

—*For England* . . .

Two barefoot urchins, sucking long liquorice laces, halted near him, gaping at his stump with their yellowslobbered mouths.

He swung himself forward in vigorous jerks, halted, lifted his head towards a window and bayed deeply:

—home and beauty.

The gay sweet chirping whistling within went on a bar or two, ceased. The blind of the window was drawn aside. A card *Unfurnished Apartments* slipped from the sash and fell. A plump bare generous arm shone, was seen, held forth from a white petticoatbodice and taut shiftstraps. A woman's hand flung forth a coin over the area railings. It fell on the path.

One of the urchins ran to it, picked it up and dropped it into the minstrel's cap, saying:

—There, sir.

***

Katey and Boody Dedalus shoved in the door of the close-steaming kitchen.

—Did you put in the books? Boody asked.

Maggy at the range rammed down a greyish mass beneath bubbling suds twice with her potstick and wiped her brow.

—They wouldn't give anything on them, she said.

Father Conmee walked through Clongowes fields, his thinsocked ankles tickled by stubble.

—Where did you try? Boody asked.

—M'Guinness's.

Boody stamped her foot and threw her satchel on the table.

—Bad cess to her big face! she cried.

Katey went to the range and peered with squinting eyes.

—What's in the pot? she asked.

—Shirts, Maggy said.

Boody cried angrily:

—Crickey, is there nothing for us to eat?

Katey, lifting the kettlelid in a pad of her stained skirt, asked:

—And what's in this?

A heavy fume gushed in answer.

—Peasoup, Maggy said.

—Where did you get it? Katey asked.

—Sister Mary Patrick, Maggy said.

The lacquey rang his bell.

—Barang!

Boody sat down at the table and said hungrily:

—Give us it here.

Maggy poured yellow thick soup from the kettle into a bowl.

Katey, sitting opposite Boody, said quietly, as her fingertip lifted to her mouth random crumbs:

—A good job we have that much. Where's Dilly?

—Gone to meet father, Maggy said.

Boody, breaking big chunks of bread into the yellow soup, added:

—Our father who art not in heaven.

Maggy, pouring yellow soup in Katey's bowl, exclaimed:

—Boody! For shame!

A skiff, a crumpled throwaway, Elijah is coming, rode lightly down the Liffey, under Loopline bridge, shooting the rapids where water chafed around the bridgepiers, sailing eastward past hulls and anchorchains, between the Customhouse old dock and George's quay.

***

The blond girl in Thornton's bedded the wicker basket with rustling fibre. Blazes Boylan handed her the bottle swathed in pink tissue paper and a small jar.

—Put these in first, will you? he said.

—Yes, sir, the blond girl said. And the fruit on top.

—That'll do, game ball, Blazes Boylan said.

She bestowed fat pears neatly, head by tail, and among them ripe shamefaced peaches.

Blazes Boylan walked here and there in new tan shoes about the fruitsmelling shop, lifting fruits, young juicy crinkled and plump red tomatoes, sniffing smells.

H. E. L. Y.'s filed before him, tallwhitehatted, past Tangier lane, plodding towards their goal.

He turned suddenly from a chip of strawberries, drew a gold watch from his fob and held it at its chain's length.

—Can you send them by tram? Now?

A darkbacked figure under Merchants' arch scanned books on the hawker's cart.

—Certainly, sir. Is it in the city?

—O, yes, Blazes Boylan said. Ten minutes.

The blond girl handed him a docket and pencil.

—Will you write the address, sir?

Blazes Boylan at the counter wrote and pushed the docket to her.

—Send it at once, will you? he said. It's for an invalid.

—Yes, sir. I will, sir.

Blazes Boylan rattled merry money in his trousers' pocket.

—What's the damage? he asked.

The blond girl's slim fingers reckoned the fruits.

Blazes Boylan looked into the cut of her blouse. A young pullet. He took a red carnation from the tall stemglass.

—This for me? he asked gallantly.

The blond girl glanced sideways at him, got up regardless, with his tie a bit crooked, blushing.

—Yes, sir, she said.

Bending archly she reckoned again fat pears and blushing peaches.

Blazes Boylan looked in her blouse with more favour, the stalk of the red flower between his smiling teeth.

—May I say a word to your telephone, missy? he asked roguishly.

***

—*Ma!* Almidano Artifoni said.

He gazed over Stephen's shoulder at Goldsmith's knobby poll.

Two carfuls of tourists passed slowly, their women sitting fore, gripping the handrests. Palefaces. Men's arms frankly round their stunted forms. They looked from Trinity to the blind columned porch of the bank of Ireland where pigeons roocoocooed.

—*Anch'io ho avuto di queste idee*, Almidano Artifoni said, *quand' ero giovine come Lei. Eppoi mi sono convinto che il mondo è una bestia. È peccato. Perchè la sua voce . . . sarebbe un cespite di rendita, via. Invece, Lei si sacrifica.*

—*Sacrifizio incruento,* Stephen said smiling, swaying his ashplant in slow swingswong from its midpoint, lightly.

—*Speriamo,* the round mustachioed face said pleasantly. *Ma, dia retta a me. Ci rifletta.*

By the stern stone hand of Grattan, bidding halt, an Inchicore tram unloaded straggling Highland soldiers of a band.

—*Ci rifletterò,* Stephen said, glancing down the solid trouserleg.

—*Ma, sul serio, eh?* Almidano Artifoni said.

His heavy hand took Stephen's firmly. Human eyes. They gazed curiously an instant and turned quickly towards a Dalkey tram.

—*Eccolo,* Almidano Artifoni said in friendly haste. *Venga a trovarmi e ci pensi. Addio, caro.*

—*Arrivederla, maestro,* Stephen said, raising his hat when his hand was freed. *E grazie.*

—*Di che?* Almidano Artifoni said. *Scusi, eh? Tante belle cose!*

Almidano Artifoni, holding up a baton of rolled music as a signal, trotted on stout trousers after the Dalkey tram. In vain he trotted, signalling in vain among the rout of barekneed gillies smuggling implements of music through Trinity gates.

***

Miss Dunne hid the Capel street library copy of *The Woman in White* far back in her drawer and rolled a sheet of gaudy notepaper into her typewriter.

Too much mystery business in it. Is he in love with that one, Marion? Change it and get another by Mary Cecil Haye.

The disk shot down the groove, wobbled a while, ceased and ogled them: six.

Miss Dunne clicked on the keyboard:

—16 June 1904.

Five tallwhitehatted sandwichmen between Monypeny's corner and the slab where Wolfe Tone's statue was not, eeled themselves turning H. E. L. Y.'s and plodded back as they had come.

Then she stared at the large poster of Marie Kendall, charming soubrette, and, listlessly lolling, scribbled on the jotter sixteens and capital esses. Mustard hair and dauby cheeks. She's not nicelooking, is she? The way she's holding up her bit of a skirt. Wonder will that fellow be at the band tonight. If I could get that dressmaker to make a concertina skirt like Susy Nagle's. They kick out grand. Shannon and all the boatclub swells never took his eyes off her. Hope to goodness he won't keep me here till seven.

The telephone rang rudely by her ear.

—Hello. Yes, sir. No, sir. Yes, sir. I'll ring them up after five. Only those two, sir, for Belfast and Liverpool. All right, sir. Then I can go after six if you're not back. A quarter after. Yes, sir. Twentyseven and six. I'll tell him. Yes: one, seven, six.

She scribbled three figures on an envelope.

—Mr Boylan! Hello! That gentleman from *Sport* was in looking for you. Mr Lenehan, yes. He said he'll be in the Ormond at four. No, sir. Yes, sir. I'll ring them up after five.

***

Two pink faces turned in the flare of the tiny torch.

—Who's that? Ned Lambert asked. Is that Crotty?

—Ringabella and Crosshaven, a voice replied groping for foothold.

—Hello, Jack, is that yourself? Ned Lambert said, raising in salute his pliant lath among the flickering arches. Come on. Mind your steps there.

The vesta in the clergyman's uplifted hand consumed itself in a long soft flame and was let fall. At their feet its red speck died: and mouldy air closed round them.

—How interesting! a refined accent said in the gloom.

—Yes, sir, Ned Lambert said heartily. We are standing in the historic council chamber of saint Mary's abbey where silken Thomas proclaimed himself a rebel in 1534. This is the most historic spot in all Dublin. O'Madden Burke is going to write something about it one of these days. The old bank of Ireland was over the way till the time of the union and the original jews' temple was here too before they built their synagogue over in Adelaide road. You were never here before, Jack, were you?

—No, Ned.

—He rode down through Dame walk, the refined accent said, if my memory serves me. The mansion of the Kildares was in Thomas court.

—That's right, Ned Lambert said. That's quite right, sir.

—If you will be so kind then, the clergyman said, the next time to allow me perhaps . . .

—Certainly, Ned Lambert said. Bring the camera whenever you like. I'll get those bags cleared away from the windows. You can take it from here or from here.

In the still faint light he moved about, tapping with his lath the piled seedbags and points of vantage on the floor.

From a long face a beard and gaze hung on a chessboard.

—I'm deeply obliged, Mr Lambert, the clergyman said. I won't trespass on your valuable time . . .

—You're welcome, sir, Ned Lambert said. Drop in whenever you like. Next week, say. Can you see?

—Yes, yes. Good afternoon, Mr Lambert. Very pleased to have met you.

—Pleasure is mine, sir, Ned Lambert answered.

He followed his guest to the outlet and then whirled his lath away among the pillars. With J. J. O'Molloy he came forth slowly into Mary's abbey where draymen were loading floats with sacks of carob and palmnut meal, O'Connor, Wexford.

He stood to read the card in his hand.

—The reverend Hugh C. Love, Rathcoffey. Present address: Saint Michael's, Sallins. Nice young chap he is. He's writing a book about the Fitzgeralds he told me. He's well up in history, faith.

The young woman with slow care detached from her light skirt a clinging twig.

—I thought you were at a new gunpowder plot, J. J. O'Molloy said.

Ned Lambert cracked his fingers in the air.

—God! he cried. I forgot to tell him that one about the earl of Kildare after he set fire to Cashel cathedral. You know that one? *I'm bloody sorry I did it,* says he, *but I declare to God I thought the archbishop was inside.* He mightn't like it, though. What? God, I'll tell him anyhow. That was the great earl, the Fitzgerald Mor. Hot members they were all of them, the Geraldines.

The horses he passed started nervously under their slack harness. He slapped a piebald haunch quivering near him and cried:

—Woa, sonny!

He turned to J. J. O'Molloy and asked:

—Well, Jack. What is it? What's the trouble? Wait awhile. Hold hard.

With gaping mouth and head far back he stood still and, after an instant, sneezed loudly.

—Chow! he said. Blast you!

—The dust from those sacks, J. J. O'Molloy said politely.

—No, Ned Lambert gasped, I caught a . . . cold night before . . . blast your soul . . . night before last . . . and there was a hell of a lot of draught . . .

He held his handkerchief ready for the coming . . .

—I was . . . Glasnevin this morning . . . poor little . . . what do you call him . . . Chow! . . . Mother of Moses!

***

Tom Rochford took the top disk from the pile he clasped against his claret waistcoat.

—See? he said. Say it's turn six. In here, see. Turn Now On.

He slid it into the left slot for them. It shot down the groove, wobbled a while, ceased, ogling them: six.

Lawyers of the past, haughty, pleading, beheld pass from the consolidated taxing office to Nisi Prius court Richie Goulding carrying the costbag of Goulding, Collis and Ward and heard rustling from the admiralty division of king's bench to the court of appeal an elderly female with false teeth smiling incredulously and a black silk skirt of great amplitude.

—See? he said. See now the last one I put in is over here: Turns Over. The impact. Leverage, see?

He showed them the rising column of disks on the right.

—Smart idea, Nosey Flynn said, snuffling. So a fellow coming in late can see what turn is on and what turns are over.

—See? Tom Rochford said.

He slid in a disk for himself: and watched it shoot, wobble, ogle, stop: four. Turn Now On.

—I'll see him now in the Ormond, Lenehan said, and sound him. One good turn deserves another.

—Do, Tom Rochford said. Tell him I'm Boylan with impatience.

—Goodnight, M'Coy said abruptly. When you two begin . . .

Nosey Flynn stooped towards the lever, snuffling at it.

—But how does it work here, Tommy? he asked.

—Tooraloo, Lenehan said. See you later.

He followed M'Coy out across the tiny square of Crampton court.

—He's a hero, he said simply.

—I know, M'Coy said. The drain, you mean.

—Drain? Lenehan said. It was down a manhole.

They passed Dan Lowry's musichall where Marie Kendall, charming soubrette, smiled on them from a poster a dauby smile.

Going down the path of Sycamore street beside the Empire musichall Lenehan showed M'Coy how the whole thing was. One of those manholes like a bloody gaspipe and there was the poor devil stuck down in it, half choked with sewer gas. Down went Tom Rochford anyhow, booky's vest and all, with the rope round him. And be damned but he got the rope round the poor devil and the two were hauled up.

—The act of a hero, he said.

At the Dolphin they halted to allow the ambulance car to gallop past them for Jervis street.

—This way, he said, walking to the right. I want to pop into Lynam's to see Sceptre's starting price. What's the time by your gold watch and chain?

M'Coy peered into Marcus Tertius Moses' sombre office, then at O'Neill's clock.

—After three, he said. Who's riding her?

—O. Madden, Lenehan said. And a game filly she is.

While he waited in Temple bar M'Coy dodged a banana peel with gentle pushes of his toe from the path to the gutter. Fellow might damn easy get a nasty fall there coming along tight in the dark.

The gates of the drive opened wide to give egress to the viceregal cavalcade.

—Even money, Lenehan said returning. I knocked against Bantam Lyons in there going to back a bloody horse someone gave him that hasn't an earthly. Through here.

They went up the steps and under Merchants' arch. A darkbacked figure scanned books on the hawker's cart.

—There he is, Lenehan said.

—Wonder what he's buying, M'Coy said, glancing behind.

—*Leopoldo or the Bloom is on the Rye,* Lenehan said.

—He's dead nuts on sales, M'Coy said. I was with him one day and he bought a book from an old one in Liffey street for two bob. There were fine plates in it worth double the money, the stars and the moon and comets with long tails. Astronomy it was about.

Lenehan laughed.

—I'll tell you a damn good one about comets' tails, he said. Come over in the sun.

They crossed to the metal bridge and went along Wellington quay by the riverwall.

Master Patrick Aloysius Dignam came out of Mangan's, late Fehrenbach's, carrying a pound and a half of porksteaks.

—There was a long spread out at Glencree reformatory, Lenehan said eagerly. The annual dinner, you know. Boiled shirt affair. The lord mayor was there, Val Dillon it was, and sir Charles Cameron and Dan Dawson spoke and there was music. Bartell d'Arcy sang and Benjamin Dollard . . .

—I know, M'Coy broke in. My missus sang there once.

—Did she? Lenehan said.

A card *Unfurnished Apartments* reappeared on the windowsash of number 7 Eccles street.

He checked his tale a moment but broke out in a wheezy laugh.

—But wait till I tell you, he said. Delahunt of Camden street had the catering and yours truly was chief bottlewasher. Bloom and the wife were there. Lashings of stuff we put up: port wine and sherry and curacao to which we did ample justice. Fast and furious it was. After liquids came solids. Cold joints galore and mince pies . . .

—I know, M'Coy said. The year the missus was there . . .

Lenehan linked his arm warmly.

—But wait till I tell you, he said. We had a midnight lunch too after all the jollification and when we sallied forth it was blue o'clock the morning after the night before. Coming home it was a gorgeous winter's night on the Featherbed Mountain. Bloom and Chris Callinan were on one side of the car and I was with the wife on the other. We started singing glees and duets: *Lo, the early beam of morning.* She was well primed with a good load of Delahunt's port under her bellyband. Every jolt the bloody car gave I had her bumping up against me. Hell's delights! She has a fine pair, God bless her. Like that.

He held his caved hands a cubit from him, frowning:

—I was tucking the rug under her and settling her boa all the time. Know what I mean?

His hands moulded ample curves of air. He shut his eyes tight in delight, his body shrinking, and blew a sweet chirp from his lips.

—The lad stood to attention anyhow, he said with a sigh. She's a gamey mare and no mistake. Bloom was pointing out all the stars and the comets in the heavens to Chris Callinan and the jarvey: the great bear and Hercules and the dragon, and the whole jingbang lot. But, by God, I was lost, so to speak, in the milky way. He knows them all, faith. At last she spotted a weeny weeshy one miles away. *And what star is that, Poldy?* says she. By God, she had Bloom cornered. *That one, is it?* says Chris Callinan, *sure that's only what you might call a pinprick.* By God, he wasn't far wide of the mark.

Lenehan stopped and leaned on the riverwall, panting with soft laughter.

—I'm weak, he gasped.

M'Coy's white face smiled about it at instants and grew grave. Lenehan walked on again. He lifted his yachtingcap and scratched his hindhead rapidly. He glanced sideways in the sunlight at M'Coy.

—He's a cultured allroundman, Bloom is, he said seriously. He's not one of your common or garden . . . you know . . . There's a touch of the artist about old Bloom.

***

Mr Bloom turned over idly pages of *The Awful Disclosures of Maria Monk*, then of Aristotle's *Masterpiece*. Crooked botched print. Plates: infants cuddled in a ball in bloodred wombs like livers of slaughtered cows. Lots of them like that at this moment all over the world. All butting with their skulls to get out of it. Child born every minute somewhere. Mrs Purefoy.

He laid both books aside and glanced at the third: *Tales of the Ghetto* by Leopold von Sacher Masoch.

—That I had, he said, pushing it by.

The shopman let two volumes fall on the counter.

—Them are two good ones, he said.

Onions of his breath came across the counter out of his ruined mouth. He bent to make a bundle of the other books, hugged them against his unbuttoned waistcoat and bore them off behind the dingy curtain.

On O'Connell bridge many persons observed the grave deportment and gay apparel of Mr Denis J Maginni, professor of dancing &c.

Mr Bloom, alone, looked at the titles. *Fair Tyrants* by James Lovebirch. Know the kind that is. Had it? Yes.

He opened it. Thought so.

A woman's voice behind the dingy curtain. Listen: the man.

No: she wouldn't like that much. Got her it once.

He read the other title: *Sweets of Sin*. More in her line. Let us see.

He read where his finger opened.

—*All the dollarbills her husband gave her were spent in the stores on wondrous gowns and costliest frillies. For him! For Raoul!*

Yes. This. Here. Try.

—*Her mouth glued on his in a luscious voluptuous kiss while his hands felt for the opulent curves inside her déshabillé.*

Yes. Take this. The end.

—*You are late, he spoke hoarsely, eying her with a suspicious glare. The beautiful woman threw off her sabletrimmed wrap, displaying her queenly shoulders and heaving embonpoint. An imperceptible smile played round her perfect lips as she turned to him calmly.*

Mr Bloom read again: *The beautiful woman.*

Warmth showered gently over him, cowing his flesh. Flesh yielded amply amid rumpled clothes: whites of eyes swooning up. His nostrils arched themselves for prey. Melting breast ointments (*for him! For Raoul!*). Armpits' oniony sweat. Fishgluey slime (*her heaving embonpoint!*). Feel! Press! Crished! Sulphur dung of lions!

Young! Young!

An elderly female, no more young, left the building of the courts of chancery, king's bench, exchequer and common pleas, having heard in the lord chancellor's court the case in lunacy of Potterton, in the admiralty division the summons, exparte motion, of the owners of the Lady Cairns versus the owners of the barque Mona, in the court of appeal reservation of judgment in the case of Harvey versus the Ocean Accident and Guarantee Corporation.

Phlegmy coughs shook the air of the bookshop, bulging out the dingy curtains. The shopman's uncombed grey head came out and his unshaven reddened face, coughing. He raked his throat rudely, puked phlegm on the floor. He put his boot on what he had spat, wiping his sole along it, and bent, showing a rawskinned crown, scantily haired.

Mr Bloom beheld it.

Mastering his troubled breath, he said:

—I'll take this one.

The shopman lifted eyes bleared with old rheum.

—*Sweets of Sin,* he said, tapping on it. That's a good one.

***

The lacquey by the door of Dillon's auctionrooms shook his handbell twice again and viewed himself in the chalked mirror of the cabinet.

Dilly Dedalus, loitering by the curbstone, heard the beats of the bell, the cries of the auctioneer within. Four and nine. Those lovely curtains. Five shillings. Cosy curtains. Selling new at two guineas. Any advance on five shillings? Going for five shillings.

The lacquey lifted his handbell and shook it:

—Barang!

Bang of the lastlap bell spurred the halfmile wheelmen to their sprint. J. A. Jackson, W. E. Wylie, A. Munro and H. T. Gahan, their stretched necks wagging, negotiated the curve by the College library.

Mr Dedalus, tugging a long moustache, came round from Williams's row. He halted near his daughter.

—It's time for you, she said.

—Stand up straight for the love of the lord Jesus, Mr Dedalus said. Are you trying to imitate your uncle John, the cornetplayer, head upon shoulder? Melancholy God!

Dilly shrugged her shoulders. Mr Dedalus placed his hands on them and held them back.

—Stand up straight, girl, he said. You'll get curvature of the spine. Do you know what you look like?

He let his head sink suddenly down and forward, hunching his shoulders and dropping his underjaw.

—Give it up, father, Dilly said. All the people are looking at you.

Mr Dedalus drew himself upright and tugged again at his moustache.

—Did you get any money? Dilly asked.

—Where would I get money? Mr Dedalus said. There is no-one in Dublin would lend me fourpence.

—You got some, Dilly said, looking in his eyes.

—How do you know that? Mr Dedalus asked, his tongue in his cheek.

Mr Kernan, pleased with the order he had booked, walked boldly along James's street.

—I know you did, Dilly answered. Were you in the Scotch house now?

—I was not, then, Mr Dedalus said, smiling. Was it the little nuns taught you to be so saucy? Here.

He handed her a shilling.

—See if you can do anything with that, he said.

—I suppose you got five, Dilly said. Give me more than that.

—Wait awhile, Mr Dedalus said threateningly. You're like the rest of them, are you? An insolent pack of little bitches since your poor mother died. But wait awhile. You'll all get a short shrift and a long day from me. Low blackguardism! I'm going to get rid of you. Wouldn't care if I was stretched out stiff. He's dead. The man upstairs is dead.

He left her and walked on. Dilly followed quickly and pulled his coat.

—Well, what is it? he said, stopping.

The lacquey rang his bell behind their backs.

—Barang!

—Curse your bloody blatant soul, Mr Dedalus cried, turning on him.

The lacquey, aware of comment, shook the lolling clapper of his bell but feebly:

—Bang!

Mr Dedalus stared at him.

—Watch him, he said. It's instructive. I wonder will he allow us to talk.

—You got more than that, father, Dilly said.

—I'm going to show you a little trick, Mr Dedalus said. I'll leave you all where Jesus left the jews. Look, there's all I have. I got two shillings from Jack Power and I spent twopence for a shave for the funeral.

He drew forth a handful of copper coins, nervously.

—Can't you look for some money somewhere? Dilly said.

Mr Dedalus thought and nodded.

—I will, he said gravely. I looked all along the gutter in O'Connell street. I'll try this one now.

—You're very funny, Dilly said, grinning.

—Here, Mr Dedalus said, handing her two pennies. Get a glass of milk for yourself and a bun or a something. I'll be home shortly.

He put the other coins in his pocket and started to walk on.

The viceregal cavalcade passed, greeted by obsequious policemen, out of Parkgate.

—I'm sure you have another shilling, Dilly said.

The lacquey banged loudly.

Mr Dedalus amid the din walked off, murmuring to himself with a pursing mincing mouth gently:

—The little nuns! Nice little things! O, sure they wouldn't do anything! O, sure they wouldn't really! Is it little sister Monica!

***

From the sundial towards James's gate walked Mr Kernan, pleased with the order he had booked for Pulbrook Robertson, boldly along James's street, past Shackleton's offices. Got round him all right. How do you do, Mr Crimmins? First rate, sir. I was afraid you might be up in your other establishment in Pimlico. How are things going? Just keeping alive. Lovely weather we're having. Yes, indeed. Good for the country. Those farmers are always grumbling. I'll just take a thimbleful of your best gin, Mr Crimmins. A small gin, sir. Yes, sir. Terrible affair that *General Slocum* explosion. Terrible, terrible! A thousand casualties. And heartrending scenes. Men trampling down women and children. Most brutal thing. What do they say was the cause? Spontaneous combustion. Most scandalous revelation. Not a single lifeboat would float and the firehose all burst. What I can't understand is how the inspectors ever allowed a boat like that . . . Now, you're talking straight, Mr Crimmins. You know why? Palm oil. Is that a fact? Without a doubt. Well now, look at that. And America they say is the land of the free. I thought we were bad here.

I smiled at him. *America,* I said quietly, just like that. *What is it? The sweepings of every country including our own. Isn't that true?* That's a fact.

Graft, my dear sir. Well, of course, where there's money going there's always someone to pick it up.

Saw him looking at my frockcoat. Dress does it. Nothing like a dressy appearance. Bowls them over.

—Hello, Simon, Father Cowley said. How are things?

—Hello, Bob, old man, Mr Dedalus answered, stopping.

Mr Kernan halted and preened himself before the sloping mirror of Peter Kennedy, hairdresser. Stylish coat, beyond a doubt. Scott of Dawson street. Well worth the half sovereign I gave Neary for it. Never built under three guineas. Fits me down to the ground. Some Kildare street club toff had it probably. John Mulligan, the manager of the Hibernian bank, gave me a very sharp eye yesterday on Carlisle bridge as if he remembered me.

Aham! Must dress the character for those fellows. Knight of the road. Gentleman. And now, Mr Crimmins, may we have the honour of your custom again, sir. The cup that cheers but not inebriates, as the old saying has it.

North wall and sir John Rogerson's quay, with hulls and anchorchains, sailing westward, sailed by a skiff, a crumpled throwaway, rocked on the ferrywash, Elijah is coming.

Mr Kernan glanced in farewell at his image. High colour, of course. Grizzled moustache. Returned Indian officer. Bravely he bore his stumpy body forward on spatted feet, squaring his shoulders. Is that Ned Lambert's brother over the way, Sam? What? Yes. He's as like it as damn it. No. The windscreen of that motorcar in the sun there. Just a flash like that. Damn like him.

Aham! Hot spirit of juniper juice warmed his vitals and his breath. Good drop of gin, that was. His frocktails winked in bright sunshine to his fat strut.

Down there Emmet was hanged, drawn and quartered. Greasy black rope. Dogs licking the blood off the street when the lord lieutenant's wife drove by in her noddy.

Bad times those were. Well, well. Over and done with. Great topers too. Fourbottle men.

Let me see. Is he buried in saint Michan's? Or no, there was a midnight burial in Glasnevin. Corpse brought in through a secret door in the wall. Dignam is there now. Went out in a puff. Well, well. Better turn down here. Make a detour.

Mr Kernan turned and walked down the slope of Watling street by the corner of Guinness's visitors' waitingroom. Outside the Dublin Distillers Company's stores an outside car without fare or jarvey stood, the reins knotted to the wheel. Damn dangerous thing. Some Tipperary bosthoon endangering the lives of the citizens. Runaway horse.

Denis Breen with his tomes, weary of having waited an hour in John Henry Menton's office, led his wife over O'Connell bridge, bound for the office of Messrs Collis and Ward.

Mr Kernan approached Island street.

Times of the troubles. Must ask Ned Lambert to lend me those reminiscences of sir Jonah Barrington. When you look back on it all now in a kind of retrospective arrangement. Gaming at Daly's. No cardsharping then. One of those fellows got his hand nailed to the table by a dagger. Somewhere here lord Edward Fitzgerald escaped from major Sirr. Stables behind Moira house.

Damn good gin that was.

Fine dashing young nobleman. Good stock, of course. That ruffian, that sham squire, with his violet gloves gave him away. Course they were on the wrong side. They rose in dark and evil days. Fine poem that is: Ingram. They were gentlemen. Ben Dollard does sing that ballad touchingly. Masterly rendition.

At the siege of Ross did my father fall.

A cavalcade in easy trot along Pembroke quay passed, outriders leaping, leaping in their, in their saddles. Frockcoats. Cream sunshades.

Mr Kernan hurried forward, blowing pursily.

His Excellency! Too bad! Just missed that by a hair. Damn it! What a pity!

***

Stephen Dedalus watched through the webbed window the lapidary's fingers prove a timedulled chain. Dust webbed the window and the showtrays. Dust darkened the toiling fingers with their vulture nails. Dust slept on dull coils of bronze and silver, lozenges of cinnabar, on rubies, leprous and winedark stones.

Born all in the dark wormy earth, cold specks of fire, evil, lights shining in the darkness. Where fallen archangels flung the stars of their brows. Muddy swinesnouts, hands, root and root, gripe and wrest them.

She dances in a foul gloom where gum burns with garlic. A sailorman, rustbearded, sips from a beaker rum and eyes her. A long and seafed silent rut. She dances, capers, wagging her sowish haunches and her hips, on her gross belly flapping a ruby egg.

Old Russell with a smeared shammy rag burnished again his gem, turned it and held it at the point of his Moses' beard. Grandfather ape gloating on a stolen hoard.

And you who wrest old images from the burial earth? The brainsick words of sophists: Antisthenes. A lore of drugs. Orient and immortal wheat standing from everlasting to everlasting.

Two old women fresh from their whiff of the briny trudged through Irishtown along London bridge road, one with a sanded tired umbrella, one with a midwife's bag in which eleven cockles rolled.

The whirr of flapping leathern bands and hum of dynamos from the powerhouse urged Stephen to be on. Beingless beings. Stop! Throb always without you and the throb always within. Your heart

259

you sing of. I between them. Where? Between two roaring worlds where they swirl, I. Shatter them, one and both. But stun myself too in the blow. Shatter me you who can. Bawd and butcher were the words. I say! Not yet awhile. A look around.

Yes, quite true. Very large and wonderful and keeps famous time. You say right, sir. A Monday morning, 'twas so, indeed.

Stephen went down Bedford row, the handle of the ash clacking against his shoulderblade. In Clohissey's window a faded 1860 print of Heenan boxing Sayers held his eye. Staring backers with square hats stood round the roped prizering. The heavyweights in tight loincloths proposed gently each to other his bulbous fists. And they are throbbing: heroes' hearts.

He turned and halted by the slanted bookcart.

—Twopence each, the huckster said. Four for sixpence.

Tattered pages. *The Irish Beekeeper. Life and Miracles of the Curé of Ars. Pocket Guide to Killarney.*

I might find here one of my pawned schoolprizes. *Stephano Dedalo, alumno optimo, palmam ferenti.*

Father Conmee, having read his little hours, walked through the hamlet of Donnycarney, murmuring vespers.

Binding too good probably. What is this? Eighth and ninth book of Moses. Secret of all secrets. Seal of King David. Thumbed pages: read and read. Who has passed here before me? How to soften chapped hands. Recipe for white wine vinegar. How to win a woman's love. For me this. Say the following talisman three times with hands folded:

—*Se el yilo nebrakada femininum! Amor me solo! Sanktus! Amen.*

Who wrote this? Charms and invocations of the most blessed abbot Peter Salanka to all true believers divulged. As good as any other abbot's charms, as mumbling Joachim's. Down, baldynoddle, or we'll wool your wool.

—What are you doing here, Stephen?

Dilly's high shoulders and shabby dress.

Shut the book quick. Don't let see.

—What are you doing? Stephen said.

A Stuart face of nonesuch Charles, lank locks falling at its sides. It glowed as she crouched feeding the fire with broken boots. I told her of Paris. Late lieabed under a quilt of old overcoats, fingering a pinchbeck bracelet, Dan Kelly's token. *Nebrakada femininum.*

—What have you there? Stephen asked.

—I bought it from the other cart for a penny, Dilly said, laughing nervously. Is it any good?

My eyes they say she has. Do others see me so? Quick, far and daring. Shadow of my mind.

He took the coverless book from her hand. Chardenal's French primer.

—What did you buy that for? he asked. To learn French?

She nodded, reddening and closing tight her lips.

Show no surprise. Quite natural.

—Here, Stephen said. It's all right. Mind Maggy doesn't pawn it on you. I suppose all my books are gone.

—Some, Dilly said. We had to.

She is drowning. Agenbite. Save her. Agenbite. All against us. She will drown me with her, eyes and hair. Lank coils of seaweed hair around me, my heart, my soul. Salt green death.

We.

Agenbite of inwit. Inwit's agenbite.

Misery! Misery!

***

—Hello, Simon, Father Cowley said. How are things?

—Hello, Bob, old man, Mr Dedalus answered, stopping.

They clasped hands loudly outside Reddy and Daughter's. Father Cowley brushed his moustache often downward with a scooping hand.

—What's the best news? Mr Dedalus said.

—Why then not much, Father Cowley said. I'm barricaded up, Simon, with two men prowling around the house trying to effect an entrance.

—Jolly, Mr Dedalus said. Who is it?

—O, Father Cowley said. A certain gombeen man of our acquaintance.

—With a broken back, is it? Mr Dedalus asked.

—The same, Simon, Father Cowley answered. Reuben of that ilk. I'm just waiting for Ben Dollard. He's going to say a word to long John to get him to take those two men off. All I want is a little time.

He looked with vague hope up and down the quay, a big apple bulging in his neck.

—I know, Mr Dedalus said, nodding. Poor old bockedy Ben! He's always doing a good turn for someone. Hold hard!

He put on his glasses and gazed towards the metal bridge an instant.

—There he is, by God, he said, arse and pockets.

Ben Dollard's loose blue cutaway and square hat above large slops crossed the quay in full gait from the metal bridge. He came towards them at an amble, scratching actively behind his coattails.

As he came near Mr Dedalus greeted:

—Hold that fellow with the bad trousers.

—Hold him now, Ben Dollard said.

Mr Dedalus eyed with cold wandering scorn various points of Ben Dollard's figure. Then, turning to Father Cowley with a nod, he muttered sneeringly:

—That's a pretty garment, isn't it, for a summer's day?

—Why, God eternally curse your soul, Ben Dollard growled furiously, I threw out more clothes in my time than you ever saw.

He stood beside them beaming, on them first and on his roomy clothes from points of which Mr Dedalus flicked fluff, saying:

—They were made for a man in his health, Ben, anyhow.

—Bad luck to the jewman that made them, Ben Dollard said. Thanks be to God he's not paid yet.

—And how is that *basso profondo*, Benjamin? Father Cowley asked.

Cashel Boyle O'Connor Fitzmaurice Tisdall Farrell, murmuring, glassyeyed, strode past the Kildare street club.

Ben Dollard frowned and, making suddenly a chanter's mouth, gave forth a deep note.

—Aw! he said.

—That's the style, Mr Dedalus said, nodding to its drone.

—What about that? Ben Dollard said. Not too dusty? What?

He turned to both.

—That'll do, Father Cowley said, nodding also.

The reverend Hugh C. Love walked from the old chapterhouse of saint Mary's abbey past James and Charles Kennedy's, rectifiers, attended by Geraldines tall and personable, towards the Tholsel beyond the ford of hurdles.

Ben Dollard with a heavy list towards the shopfronts led them forward, his joyful fingers in the air.

—Come along with me to the subsheriff's office, he said. I want to show you the new beauty Rock has for a bailiff. He's a cross between Lobengula and Lynchehaun. He's well worth seeing, mind you. Come along. I saw John Henry Menton casually in the Bodega just now and it will cost me a fall if I don't . . . Wait awhile . . . We're on the right lay, Bob, believe you me.

—For a few days tell him, Father Cowley said anxiously.

Ben Dollard halted and stared, his loud orifice open, a dangling button of his coat wagging brightbacked from its thread as he wiped away the heavy shraums that clogged his eyes to hear aright.

—What few days? he boomed. Hasn't your landlord distrained for rent?

—He has, Father Cowley said.

—Then our friend's writ is not worth the paper it's printed on, Ben Dollard said. The landlord has the prior claim. I gave him all the particulars. 29 Windsor avenue. Love is the name?

—That's right, Father Cowley said. The reverend Mr Love. He's a minister in the country somewhere. But are you sure of that?

—You can tell Barabbas from me, Ben Dollard said, that he can put that writ where Jacko put the nuts.

He led Father Cowley boldly forward, linked to his bulk.

—Filberts I believe they were, Mr Dedalus said, as he dropped his glasses on his coatfront, following them.

***

—The youngster will be all right, Martin Cunningham said, as they passed out of the Castleyard gate.

The policeman touched his forehead.

—God bless you, Martin Cunningham said, cheerily.

He signed to the waiting jarvey who chucked at the reins and set on towards Lord Edward street.

Bronze by gold, Miss Kennedy's head by Miss Douce's head, appeared above the crossblind of the Ormond hotel.

—Yes, Martin Cunningham said, fingering his beard. I wrote to Father Conmee and laid the whole case before him.

—You could try our friend, Mr Power suggested backward.

—Boyd? Martin Cunningham said shortly. Touch me not.

John Wyse Nolan, lagging behind, reading the list, came after them quickly down Cork hill.

On the steps of the City hall Councillor Nannetti, descending, hailed Alderman Cowley and Councillor Abraham Lyon ascending.

The castle car wheeled empty into upper Exchange street.

—Look here, Martin, John Wyse Nolan said, overtaking them at the *Mail* office. I see Bloom put his name down for five shillings.

—Quite right, Martin Cunningham said, taking the list. And put down the five shillings too.

—Without a second word either, Mr Power said.

—Strange but true, Martin Cunningham added.

John Wyse Nolan opened wide eyes.

—I'll say there is much kindness in the jew, he quoted, elegantly.

They went down Parliament street.

—There's Jimmy Henry, Mr Power said, just heading for Kavanagh's.

—Righto, Martin Cunningham said. Here goes.

Outside *la Maison Claire* Blazes Boylan waylaid Jack Mooney's brother-in-law, humpy, tight, making for the liberties.

John Wyse Nolan fell back with Mr Power, while Martin Cunningham took the elbow of a dapper little man in a shower of hail suit, who walked uncertainly, with hasty steps past Micky Anderson's watches.

—The assistant town clerk's corns are giving him some trouble, John Wyse Nolan told Mr Power.

They followed round the corner towards James Kavanagh's winerooms. The empty castle car fronted them at rest in Essex gate. Martin Cunningham, speaking always, showed often the list at which Jimmy Henry did not glance.

—And long John Fanning is here too, John Wyse Nolan said, as large as life.

The tall form of long John Fanning filled the doorway where he stood.

—Good day, Mr Subsheriff, Martin Cunningham said, as all halted and greeted.

Long John Fanning made no way for them. He removed his large Henry Clay decisively and his large fierce eyes scowled intelligently over all their faces.

—Are the conscript fathers pursuing their peaceful deliberations? he said with rich acrid utterance to the assistant town clerk.

Hell open to christians they were having, Jimmy Henry said

pettishly, about their damned Irish language. Where was the marshal, he wanted to know, to keep order in the council chamber. And old Barlow the macebearer laid up with asthma, no mace on the table, nothing in order, no quorum even, and Hutchinson, the lord mayor, in Llandudno and little Lorcan Sherlock doing *locum tenens* for him. Damned Irish language, language of our forefathers.

Long John Fanning blew a plume of smoke from his lips.

Martin Cunningham spoke by turns, twirling the peak of his beard, to the assistant town clerk and the subsheriff, while John Wyse Nolan held his peace.

—What Dignam was that? long John Fanning asked.

Jimmy Henry made a grimace and lifted his left foot.

—O, my corns! he said plaintively. Come upstairs for goodness' sake till I sit down somewhere. Uff! Ooo! Mind!

Testily he made room for himself beside long John Fanning's flank and passed in and up the stairs.

—Come on up, Martin Cunningham said to the subsheriff. I don't think you knew him or perhaps you did, though.

With John Wyse Nolan Mr Power followed them in.

—Decent little soul he was, Mr Power said to the stalwart back of long John Fanning ascending towards long John Fanning in the mirror.

—Rather lowsized. Dignam of Menton's office that was, Martin Cunningham said.

Long John Fanning could not remember him.

Clatter of horsehoofs sounded from the air.

—What's that? Martin Cunningham said.

All turned where they stood. John Wyse Nolan came down again. From the cool shadow of the doorway he saw the horses pass Parliament street, harness and glossy pasterns in sunlight shimmering. Gaily they went past before his cool unfriendly eyes, not quickly. In saddles of the leaders, leaping leaders, rode outriders.

—What was it? Martin Cunningham asked, as they went on up the staircase.

—The lord lieutenantgeneral and general governor of Ireland, John Wyse Nolan answered from the stairfoot.

***

As they trod across the thick carpet Buck Mulligan whispered behind his Panama to Haines:

—Parnell's brother. There in the corner.

They chose a small table near the window, opposite a longfaced man whose beard and gaze hung intently down on a chessboard.

—Is that he? Haines asked, twisting round in his seat.

—Yes, Mulligan said. That's John Howard, his brother, our city marshal.

John Howard Parnell translated a white bishop quietly and his grey claw went up again to his forehead whereat it rested. An instant after, under its screen, his eyes looked quickly, ghostbright, at his foe and fell once more upon a working corner.

—I'll take a *mélange,* Haines said to the waitress.

—Two *mélanges,* Buck Mulligan said. And bring us some scones and butter and some cakes as well.

When she had gone he said, laughing:

—We call it D. B. C. because they have damn bad cakes. O, but you missed Dedalus on *Hamlet.*

Haines opened his newbought book.

—I'm sorry, he said. Shakespeare is the happy huntingground of all minds that have lost their balance.

The onelegged sailor growled at the area of 14 Nelson street:

—*England expects* . . .

Buck Mulligan's primrose waistcoat shook gaily to his laughter.

—You should see him, he said, when his body loses its balance. Wandering Ængus I call him.

—I am sure he has an *idée fixe,* Haines said, pinching his chin thoughtfully with thumb and forefinger. Now I am speculating what it would be likely to be. Such persons always have.

Buck Mulligan bent across the table gravely.

—They drove his wits astray, he said, by visions of hell. He will never capture the Attic note. The note of Swinburne, of all poets, the white death and the ruddy birth. That is his tragedy. He can never be a poet. The joy of creation . . .

—Eternal punishment, Haines said, nodding curtly. I see. I tackled him this morning on belief. There was something on his mind, I saw. It's rather interesting because professor Pokorny of Vienna makes an interesting point out of that.

Buck Mulligan's watchful eyes saw the waitress come. He helped her to unload her tray.

—He can find no trace of hell in ancient Irish myth, Haines said, amid the cheerful cups. The moral idea seems lacking, the sense of destiny, of retribution. Rather strange he should have just that fixed idea. Does he write anything for your movement?

He sank two lumps of sugar deftly longwise through the whipped cream. Buck Mulligan slit a steaming scone in two and plastered butter over its smoking pith. He bit off a soft piece hungrily.

—Ten years, he said, chewing and laughing. He is going to write something in ten years.

—Seems a long way off, Haines said, thoughtfully lifting his spoon. Still, I shouldn't wonder if he did after all.

He tasted a spoonful from the creamy cone of his cup.

—This is real Irish cream I take it, he said with forbearance. I don't want to be imposed on.

Elijah, skiff, light crumpled throwaway, sailed eastward by flanks of ships and trawlers, amid an archipelago of corks, beyond new Wapping street past Benson's ferry, and by the threemasted schooner *Rosevean* from Bridgwater with bricks.

***

Almidano Artifoni walked past Holles street, past Sewell's yard. Behind him Cashel Boyle O'Connor Fitzmaurice Tisdall Farrell, with stickumbrelladustcoat dangling, shunned the lamp before Mr Law Smith's house and, crossing, walked along Merrion square. Distantly behind him a blind stripling tapped his way by the wall of College park.

Cashel Boyle O'Connor Fitzmaurice Tisdall Farrell walked as far as Mr Lewis Werner's cheerful windows, then turned and strode back along Merrion square, his stickumbrelladustcoat dangling.

At the corner of Wilde's house he halted, frowned at Elijah's name announced on the Metropolitan hall, frowned at the distant pleasance of duke's lawn. His eyeglass flashed frowning in the sun. With ratsteeth bared he muttered:

—*Coactus volui.*

He strode on for Clare street, grinding his fierce word.

As he strode past Mr Bloom's dental windows the sway of his dustcoat brushed rudely from its angle a slender tapping cane and swept onwards, having buffeted a thewless body. The blind stripling turned his sickly face after the striding form.

—God's curse on you, he said sourly, whoever you are! You're blinder nor I am, you bitch's bastard!

***

Opposite Ruggy O'Donohoe's Master Patrick Aloysius Dignam, pawing the pound and a half of Mangan's, late Fehrenbach's, porksteaks he had been sent for, went along warm Wicklow street dawdling. It was too blooming dull sitting in the parlour with Mrs Stoer and Mrs Quigley and Mrs MacDowell and the blind down and they all at their sniffles and sipping sups of the superior tawny sherry uncle Barney brought from Tunney's. And they eating crumbs of the cottage fruitcake, jawing the whole blooming time and sighing.

After Wicklow lane the window of Madame Doyle, courtdress milliner, stopped him. He stood looking in at the two puckers stripped to their pelts and putting up their props. From the sidemirrors two mourning Masters Dignam gaped silently. Myler Keogh, Dublin's pet lamb, will meet sergeantmajor Bennett, the Portobello bruiser, for a purse of fifty sovereigns. Gob, that'd be a good pucking match to see. Myler Keogh, that's the chap sparring out to him with the green sash. Two bar entrance, soldiers half price. I could easy do a bunk on ma. Master Dignam on his left turned as he turned. That's me in mourning. When is it? May the twentysecond. Sure, the blooming thing is all over. He turned to the right and on his right Master Dignam turned, his cap awry, his collar sticking up. Buttoning it down, his chin lifted, he saw the image of Marie Kendall, charming soubrette, beside the two puckers. One of them mots that do be in the packets of fags Stoer smokes that his old fellow welted hell out of him for one time he found out.

Master Dignam got his collar down and dawdled on. The best pucker going for strength was Fitzsimons. One puck in the wind from that fellow would knock you into the middle of next week, man. But the best pucker for science was Jem Corbet before Fitzsimons knocked the stuffings out of him, dodging and all.

In Grafton street Master Dignam saw a red flower in a toff's mouth and a swell pair of kicks on him and he listening to what the drunk was telling him and grinning all the time.

No Sandymount tram.

Master Dignam walked along Nassau street, shifted the porksteaks to his other hand. His collar sprang up again and he tugged it down. The blooming stud was too small for the buttonhole of the shirt, blooming end to it. He met schoolboys with satchels. I'm not going tomorrow either, stay away till Monday. He met other schoolboys. Do they notice I'm in mourning? Uncle Barney said he'd get it into the paper tonight. Then they'll all see it in the paper and read my name printed and pa's name.

His face got all grey instead of being red like it was and there was a fly walking over it up to his eye. The scrunch that was when they were screwing the screws into the coffin: and the bumps when they were bringing it downstairs.

Pa was inside it and ma crying in the parlour and uncle Barney telling the men how to get it round the bend. A big coffin it was, and high and heavylooking. How was that? The last night pa was boosed he was standing on the landing there bawling out for his boots to go out to Tunney's for to boose more and he looked butty and short in his shirt. Never see him again. Death, that is. Pa is dead. My father is dead. He told me to be a good son to ma. I couldn't hear the other things he said but I saw his tongue and his teeth trying to say it better. Poor pa. That was Mr Dignam, my father. I hope he's in purgatory now because he went to confession to Father Conroy on Saturday night.

***

William Humble, earl of Dudley, and lady Dudley, accompanied by lieutenantcolonel Heseltine, drove out after luncheon from the viceregal lodge. In the following carriage were the honourable Mrs Paget, Miss de Courcy and the honourable Gerald Ward A. D. C. in attendance.

The cavalcade passed out by the lower gate of Phoenix park saluted by obsequious policemen and proceeded past Kingsbridge along the northern quays. The viceroy was most cordially greeted on his way through the metropolis. At Bloody bridge Mr Thomas Kernan beyond the river greeted him vainly from afar. Between Queen's and Whitworth bridges lord Dudley's viceregal carriages passed and were unsaluted by Mr Dudley White, B. L., M. A., who stood on Arran quay outside Mrs M. E. White's, the pawnbroker's, at the corner of Arran street west stroking his nose with his forefinger, undecided whether he should arrive at Phibsborough more quickly by a triple change of tram or by hailing a car or on foot through Smithfield, Constitution hill and Broadstone terminus. In the porch of Four Courts Richie Goulding with the costbag of Goulding, Collis and Ward saw him with surprise. Past Richmond bridge at the doorstep of the office of Reuben J Dodd, solicitor, agent for the Patriotic Insurance Company, an elderly female about to enter changed her plan and retracing her steps by King's windows smiled credulously on the representative of His Majesty. From its sluice in Wood quay wall under Tom Devan's office Poddle river hung out in fealty a tongue of liquid sewage. Above the crossblind of the Ormond hotel, gold by bronze, Miss Kennedy's head by Miss Douce's head watched and admired. On Ormond quay Mr Simon Dedalus, steering his way from the greenhouse for the subsheriff's office, stood still in midstreet and brought his hat low. His Excellency graciously returned Mr Dedalus' greeting. From Cahill's corner the reverend Hugh C. Love, M. A., made obeisance unperceived, mindful of lords deputies whose hands benignant had held of yore rich advowsons. On Grattan bridge Lenehan and M'Coy, taking leave of each other, watched the carriages go by. Passing by Roger Greene's office and Dollard's big red printinghouse Gerty MacDowell, carrying the Catesby's cork lino letters for her father who was laid up, knew by the style it was the lord and lady lieutenant but she couldn't see what Her Excellency had on because the tram and Spring's big yellow furniture van had to stop in front of her on account of its being the lord lieutenant. Beyond Lundy Foot's from the shaded door of Kavanagh's winerooms John Wyse Nolan smiled with unseen coldness towards the lord lieutenantgeneral and general governor of Ireland. The Right Honourable William Humble, earl of Dudley, G. C. V. O., passed Micky Anderson's all times ticking watches and Henry and James's wax smartsuited freshcheeked models, the gentleman Henry, *dernier cri* James. Over against Dame gate Tom Rochford and Nosey Flynn watched the approach of the cavalcade. Tom Rochford, seeing the eyes of lady Dudley fixed on him, took his thumbs quickly out of the pockets of his claret waistcoat and doffed his cap to her. A charming *soubrette,* great Marie Kendall, with dauby cheeks and lifted skirt smiled daubily from her poster upon William Humble, earl of Dudley, and upon lieutenantcolonel H. G. Heseltine, and also upon the honourable Gerald Ward A. D. C. From the window of the D. B. C. Buck Mulligan gaily, and Haines gravely, gazed down on the viceregal equipage over the shoulders of eager guests, whose mass of forms darkened the chessboard whereon John Howard Parnell looked intently. In Fownes's street Dilly Dedalus, straining her sight upward from Chardenal's first French primer, saw sunshades spanned and wheelspokes spinning in the glare. John Henry Menton, filling the doorway of Commercial Buildings, stared from winebig oyster eyes, holding a fat gold hunter watch not looked at in his fat left hand not feeling it. Where the foreleg of King Billy's horse pawed the air Mrs Breen plucked her hastening husband back from under the hoofs of the outriders. She shouted in his ear the tidings. Understanding, he shifted his tomes to his left breast and saluted the second carriage. The honourable Gerald Ward A. D. C., agreeably surprised, made haste to reply. At Ponsonby's corner a jaded white flagon H. halted and four tallhatted white flagons halted behind him, E. L. Y.'s, while outriders pranced past and carriages. Opposite Pigott's music warerooms Mr Denis J Maginni, professor of dancing &c, gaily apparelled, gravely walked, outpassed by a viceroy and unobserved. By the provost's wall came jauntily Blazes Boylan, stepping in tan shoes and socks with skyblue clocks to the refrain of *My girl's a Yorkshire girl.*

Blazes Boylan presented to the leaders' skyblue frontlets and high action a skyblue tie, a widebrimmed straw hat at a rakish angle and a suit of indigo serge. His hands in his jacket pockets forgot to salute but he offered to the three ladies the bold admiration of his eyes and the red flower between his lips. As they drove along Nassau street His Excellency drew the attention of his bowing consort to the programme of music which was being discoursed in College park. Unseen brazen highland laddies blared and drumthumped after the *cortège*:

> But though she's a factory lass
> And wears no fancy clothes.
> Baraabum.
> Yet I've a sort of a

271

Yorkshire relish for
My little Yorkshire rose.
Baraabum.

Thither of the wall the quartermile flat handicappers, M. C. Green, H. Shrift, T. M. Patey, C. Scaife, J. B. Jeffs, G. N. Morphy, F. Stevenson, C. Adderly and W. C. Huggard, started in pursuit. Striding past Finn's hotel Cashel Boyle O'Connor Fitzmaurice Tisdall Farrell stared through a fierce eyeglass across the carriages at the head of Mr M. E. Solomons in the window of the Austro-Hungarian viceconsulate. Deep in Leinster street by Trinity's postern a loyal king's man, Hornblower, touched his tallyho cap. As the glossy horses pranced by Merrion square Master Patrick Aloysius Dignam, waiting, saw salutes being given to the gent with the topper and raised also his new black cap with fingers greased by porksteak paper. His collar too sprang up. The viceroy, on his way to inaugurate the Mirus bazaar in aid of funds for Mercer's hospital, drove with his following towards Lower Mount street. He passed a blind stripling opposite Broadbent's. In Lower Mount street a pedestrian in a brown macintosh, eating dry bread, passed swiftly and unscathed across the viceroy's path. At the Royal Canal bridge, from his hoarding, Mr Eugene Stratton, his blub lips agrin, bade all comers welcome to Pembroke township. At Haddington road corner two sanded women halted themselves, an umbrella and a bag in which eleven cockles rolled to view with wonder the lord mayor and lady mayoress without his golden chain. On Northumberland and Lansdowne roads His Excellency acknowledged punctually salutes from rare male walkers, the salute of two small schoolboys at the garden gate of the house said to have been admired by the late queen when visiting the Irish capital with her husband, the prince consort, in 1849 and the salute of Almidano Artifoni's sturdy trousers swallowed by a closing door.

11

B ronze by gold heard the hoofirons, steelyringing.
   Imperthnthn thnthnthn.
   Chips, picking chips off rocky thumbnail, chips.
Horrid! And gold flushed more.
A husky fifenote blew.
Blew. Blue bloom is on the.
Goldpinnacled hair.
A jumping rose on satiny breast of satin, rose of Castile.
Trilling, trilling: Idolores.
Peep! Who's in the . . . peepofgold?
Tink cried to bronze in pity.
And a call, pure, long and throbbing. Longindying call.
Decoy. Soft word. But look: the bright stars fade. Notes
chirruping answer.
O rose! Castile. The morn is breaking.
Jingle jingle jaunted jingling.
Coin rang. Clock clacked.
Avowal. *Sonnez*. I could. Rebound of garter. Not leave
thee. Smack. *La cloche!* Thigh smack. Avowal. Warm.
Sweetheart, goodbye!
Jingle. Bloo.
Boomed crashing chords. When love absorbs. War! War!
The tympanum.
A sail! A veil awave upon the waves.
Lost. Throstle fluted. All is lost now.
Horn. Hawhorn.
When first he saw. Alas!
Full tup. Full throb.
Warbling. Ah, lure! Alluring.
Martha! Come!
Clapclap. Clipclap. Clappyclap.
Goodgod henev erheard inall.
Deaf bald Pat brought pad knife took up.

A moonlit nightcall: far, far.

I feel so sad. P. S. So lonely blooming.

Listen!

The spiked and winding cold seahorn. Have you the? Each, and for other, plash and silent roar.

Pearls: when she. Liszt's rhapsodies. Hissss.

You don't?

Did not: no, no: believe: Lidlyd. With a cock with a carra.

Black. Deepsounding. Do, Ben, do.

Wait while you wait. Hee hee. Wait while you hee.

But wait!

Low in dark middle earth. Embedded ore.

Naminedamine. Preacher is he:

All gone. All fallen.

Tiny, her tremulous fernfoils of maidenhair.

Amen! He gnashed in fury.

Fro. To, fro. A baton cool protruding.

Bronzelydia by Minagold.

By bronze, by gold, in oceangreen of shadow. Bloom. Old Bloom.

One rapped, one tapped, with a carra, with a cock.

Pray for him! Pray, good people!

His gouty fingers nakkering.

Big Benaben. Big Benben.

Last rose Castile of summer left bloom I feel so sad alone.

Pwee! Little wind piped wee.

True men. Lid Ker Cow De and Doll. Ay, ay. Like you men. Will lift your tschink with tschunk.

Fff! Oo!

Where bronze from anear? Where gold from afar? Where hoofs?

Rrrpr. Kraa. Kraandl.

Then not till then. My eppripfftaph. Be pfrwritt.

Done.

Begin!

Bronze by gold, Miss Douce's head by Miss Kennedy's head, over the crossblind of the Ormond bar heard the viceregal hoofs go by, ringing steel.

—Is that her? asked miss Kennedy.

Miss Douce said yes, sitting with his ex, pearl grey and *eau de Nil.*

—Exquisite contrast, miss Kennedy said.

When all agog miss Douce said eagerly:

—Look at the fellow in the tall silk.

—Who? Where? gold asked more eagerly.

—In the second carriage, miss Douce's wet lips said, laughing in the sun.

He's looking. Mind till I see.

She darted, bronze, to the backmost corner, flattening her face against the pane in a halo of hurried breath.

Her wet lips tittered:

—He's killed looking back.

She laughed:

—O wept! Aren't men frightful idiots?

With sadness.

Miss Kennedy sauntered sadly from bright light, twining a loose hair behind an ear. Sauntering sadly, gold no more, she twisted twined a hair. Sadly she twined in sauntering gold hair behind a curving ear.

—It's them has the fine times, sadly then she said.

A man.

Bloowho went by by Moulang's pipes bearing in his breast the sweets of sin, by Wine's antiques, in memory bearing sweet sinful words, by Carroll's dusky battered plate, for Raoul.

The boots to them, them in the bar, them barmaids came. For them unheeding him he banged on the counter his tray of chattering china. And

—There's your teas, he said.

Miss Kennedy with manners transposed the teatray down to an upturned lithia crate, safe from eyes, low.

—What is it? loud boots unmannerly asked.

—Find out, miss Douce retorted, leaving her spyingpoint.

—Your *beau*, is it?

A haughty bronze replied:

—I'll complain to Mrs de Massey on you if I hear any more of your impertinent insolence.

—Imperthnthn thnthnthn, bootssnout sniffed rudely, as he retreated as she threatened as he had come.

Bloom.

On her flower frowning miss Douce said:

—Most aggravating that young brat is. If he doesn't conduct himself I'll wring his ear for him a yard long.

Ladylike in exquisite contrast.

—Take no notice, miss Kennedy rejoined.

She poured in a teacup tea, then back in the teapot tea. They cowered under their reef of counter, waiting on footstools, crates upturned, waiting for their teas to draw. They pawed their blouses, both of black satin, two and nine a yard, waiting for their teas to draw, and two and seven.

Yes, bronze from anear, by gold from afar, heard steel from anear, hoofs ring from afar, and heard steelhoofs ringhoof ringsteel.

—Am I awfully sunburnt?

Miss bronze unbloused her neck.

—No, said miss Kennedy. It gets brown after. Did you try the borax with the cherry laurel water?

Miss Douce halfstood to see her skin askance in the barmirror gildedlettered where hock and claret glasses shimmered and in their midst a shell.

—And leave it to my hands, she said.

—Try it with the glycerine, miss Kennedy advised.

Bidding her neck and hands adieu miss Douce

—Those things only bring out a rash, replied, reseated. I asked that old fogey in Boyd's for something for my skin.

Miss Kennedy, pouring now a fulldrawn tea, grimaced and prayed:

—O, don't remind me of him for mercy' sake!

—But wait till I tell you, miss Douce entreated.

Sweet tea miss Kennedy having poured with milk plugged both two ears with little fingers.

—No, don't, she cried.

—I won't listen, she cried.

But Bloom?

Miss Douce grunted in snuffy fogey's tone:

—For your what? says he.

Miss Kennedy unplugged her ears to hear, to speak: but said, but prayed again:

—Don't let me think of him or I'll expire. The hideous old wretch! That night in the Antient Concert Rooms.

She sipped distastefully her brew, hot tea, a sip, sipped, sweet tea.

—Here he was, miss Douce said, cocking her bronze head three quarters, ruffling her nosewings. Hufa! Hufa!

Shrill shriek of laughter sprang from miss Kennedy's throat. Miss Douce huffed and snorted down her nostrils that quivered imperthnthn like a snout in quest.

—O! shrieking, miss Kennedy cried. Will you ever forget his goggle eye?

Miss Douce chimed in in deep bronze laughter, shouting:

—And your other eye!

Bloowhose dark eye read Aaron Figatner's name. Why do I always think Figather? Gathering figs, I think. And Prosper Loré's huguenot name. By Bassi's blessed virgins Bloom's dark eyes went by. Bluerobed, white under, come to me. God they believe she is: or goddess. Those today. I could not see. That fellow spoke. A student. After with Dedalus' son. He might be Mulligan. All comely virgins. That brings those rakes of fellows in: her white.

By went his eyes. The sweets of sin. Sweet are the sweets.

Of sin.

In a giggling peal young goldbronze voices blended, Douce with Kennedy your other eye. They threw young heads back, bronze gigglegold, to let freefly their laughter, screaming, your other, signals to each other, high piercing notes.

Ah, panting, sighing, sighing, ah, fordone, their mirth died down.

Miss Kennedy lipped her cup again, raised, drank a sip and giggle-giggled. Miss Douce, bending over the teatray, ruffled again her nose and rolled droll fattened eyes. Again Kennygiggles, stooping, her fair pinnacles of hair, stooping, her tortoise napecomb showed, spluttered out of her mouth her tea, choking in tea and laughter, coughing with choking, crying:

—O greasy eyes! Imagine being married to a man like that! she cried. With his bit of beard!

Douce gave full vent to a splendid yell, a full yell of full woman, delight, joy, indignation.

—Married to the greasy nose! she yelled.

Shrill, with deep laughter, after, gold after bronze, they urged each each to peal after peal, ringing in changes, bronzegold, goldbronze, shrilldeep, to laughter after laughter. And then laughed more. Greasy I knows. Exhausted, breathless, their shaken heads they laid, braided and pinnacled by glossycombed, against the counterledge. All flushed (O!), panting, sweating (O!), all breathless.

Married to Bloom, to greaseabloom.

—O saints above! miss Douce said, sighed above her jumping rose. I wished I hadn't laughed so much. I feel all wet.

—O, miss Douce! miss Kennedy protested. You horrid thing!

And flushed yet more (you horrid!), more goldenly.

By Cantwell's offices roved Greaseabloom, by Ceppi's virgins, bright of their oils. Nannetti's father hawked those things about, wheedling at doors as I. Religion pays. Must see him for that par. Eat first. I want. Not yet. At four, she said. Time ever passing. Clockhands turning. On. Where eat? The Clarence, Dolphin. On. For Raoul. Eat. If I net five guineas with those ads. The violet silk petticoats. Not yet. The sweets of sin.

Flushed less, still less, goldenly paled.

Into their bar strolled Mr Dedalus. Chips, picking chips off one of his rocky thumbnails. Chips. He strolled.

—O, welcome back, miss Douce.

He held her hand. Enjoyed her holidays?

—Tiptop.

He hoped she had nice weather in Rostrevor.

—Gorgeous, she said. Look at the holy show I am. Lying out on the strand all day.

Bronze whiteness.

—That was exceedingly naughty of you, Mr Dedalus told her and pressed her hand indulgently. Tempting poor simple males.

Miss Douce of satin douced her arm away.

—O go away! she said. You're very simple, I don't think.

He was.

—Well now I am, he mused. I looked so simple in the cradle they christened me simple Simon.

—You must have been a doaty, miss Douce made answer. And what did the doctor order today?

—Well now, he mused, whatever you say yourself. I think I'll trouble you for some fresh water and a half glass of whisky.

Jingle.

—With the greatest alacrity, miss Douce agreed.

With grace of alacrity towards the mirror gilt Cantrell and Cochrane's she turned herself. With grace she tapped a measure of gold whisky from her crystal keg. Forth from the skirt of his coat Mr Dedalus brought pouch and pipe. Alacrity she served. He blew through the flue two husky fifenotes.

—By Jove, he mused, I often wanted to see the Mourne mountains. Must be a great tonic in the air down there. But a long threatening comes at last, they say. Yes. Yes.

Yes. He fingered shreds of hair, her maidenhair, her mermaid's, into the bowl. Chips. Shreds. Musing. Mute.

None nought said nothing. Yes.

Gaily miss Douce polished a tumbler, trilling:

—O, Idolores, queen of the eastern seas!

—Was Mr Lidwell in today?

In came Lenehan. Round him peered Lenehan. Mr Bloom reached Essex bridge. Yes, Mr Bloom crossed bridge of Yessex. To Martha I must write. Buy paper. Daly's. Girl there civil. Bloom. Old Bloom. Blue bloom is on the rye.

—He was in at lunchtime, miss Douce said.

Lenehan came forward.

—Was Mr Boylan looking for me?

He asked. She answered:

—Miss Kennedy, was Mr Boylan in while I was upstairs?

She asked. Miss voice of Kennedy answered, a second teacup poised, her gaze upon a page:

—No. He was not.

Miss gaze of Kennedy, heard, not seen, read on. Lenehan round the sandwichbell wound his round body round.

—Peep! Who's in the corner?

No glance of Kennedy rewarding him he yet made overtures. To mind her stops. To read only the black ones: round o and crooked ess.

Jingle jaunty jingle.

Girlgold she read and did not glance. Take no notice. She took no notice while he read by rote a solfa fable for her, plappering flatly:

—Ah fox met ah stork. Said thee fox too thee stork: Will you put your bill down inn my troath and pull upp ah bone?

He droned in vain. Miss Douce turned to her tea aside.

He sighed aside:

—Ah me! O my!

He greeted Mr Dedalus and got a nod.

—Greetings from the famous son of a famous father.

—Who may he be? Mr Dedalus asked.

Lenehan opened most genial arms. Who?

—Who may he be? he asked. Can you ask? Stephen, the youthful bard.

Dry.

Mr Dedalus, famous father, laid by his dry filled pipe.

—I see, he said. I didn't recognise him for the moment. I hear he is keeping very select company. Have you seen him lately?

He had.

—I quaffed the nectarbowl with him this very day, said Lenehan. In Mooney's *en ville* and in Mooney's *sur mer*. He had received the rhino for the labour of his muse.

He smiled at bronze's teabathed lips, at listening lips and eyes:

—The *élite* of Erin hung upon his lips. The ponderous pundit, Hugh MacHugh, Dublin's most brilliant scribe and editor and that minstrel boy of the wild wet west who is known by the euphonious appellation of the O'Madden Burke.

After an interval Mr Dedalus raised his grog and

—That must have been highly diverting, said he. I see.

He see. He drank. With faraway mourning mountain eye. Set down his glass.

He looked towards the saloon door.

—I see you have moved the piano.

—The tuner was in today, miss Douce replied, tuning it for the smoking concert and I never heard such an exquisite player.

—Is that a fact?

—Didn't he, miss Kennedy? The real classical, you know. And blind too, poor fellow. Not twenty I'm sure he was.

—Is that a fact? Mr Dedalus said.

He drank and strayed away.

—So sad to look at his face, miss Douce condoled.

God's curse on bitch's bastard.

Tink to her pity cried a diner's bell. To the door of the bar and dining room came bald Pat, came bothered Pat, came Pat, waiter of Ormond. Lager for diner. Lager without alacrity she served.

With patience Lenehan waited for Boylan with impatience, for jinglejaunty blazes boy.

Upholding the lid he (who?) gazed in the coffin (coffin?) at the oblique triple (piano!) wires. He pressed (the same who pressed indulgently her hand), soft pedalling, a triple of keys to see the thicknesses of felt advancing, to hear the muffled hammerfall in action.

Two sheets cream vellum paper one reserve two envelopes when I was in Wisdom Hely's wise Bloom in Daly's Henry Flower bought. Are you not happy in your home? Flower to console me and a pin cuts lo. Means something, language of flow. Was it a daisy? Innocence that is. Respectable girl meet after mass. Thanks awfully muchly. Wise Bloom eyed on the door a poster, a swaying mermaid smoking mid nice waves. Smoke mermaids, coolest whiff of all. Hair streaming: lovelorn. For some man. For Raoul. He eyed and saw afar on Essex bridge a gay hat riding on a jaunting car. It is. Again. Third time. Coincidence.

Jingling on supple rubbers it jaunted from the bridge to Ormond quay. Follow. Risk it. Go quick. At four. Near now. Out.

—Twopence, sir, the shopgirl dared to say.

—Aha . . . I was forgetting . . . Excuse . . .

—And four.

At four she. Winsomely she on Bloohimwhom smiled. Bloo smi qui go. Ternoon. Think you're the only pebble on the beach? Does that to all.

For men.

In drowsy silence gold bent on her page.

From the saloon a call came, long in dying. That was a tuningfork the tuner had that he forgot that he now struck. A call again. That he now poised that it now throbbed. You hear? It throbbed, pure, purer, softly and softlier, its buzzing prongs. Longer in dying call.

Pat paid for diner's popcorked bottle: and over tumbler, tray and popcorked bottle ere he went he whispered, bald and bothered, with miss Douce.

—*The bright stars fade* . . .

A voiceless song sang from within, singing:

—*. . . the morn is breaking.*

A duodene of birdnotes chirruped bright treble answer under sensitive hands. Brightly the keys, all twinkling, linked, all harpsichording, called to a voice to sing the strain of dewy morn, of youth, of love's leavetaking, life's, love's morn.

—*The dewdrops pearl* . . .

Lenehan's lips over the counter lisped a low whistle of decoy.

—But look this way, he said, rose of Castile.

Jingle jaunted by the curb and stopped.

She rose and closed her reading, rose of Castile: fretted, forlorn, dreamily rose.

—Did she fall or was she pushed? he asked her.

She answered, slighting:

—Ask no questions and you'll hear no lies.

Like lady, ladylike.

Blazes Boylan's smart tan shoes creaked on the barfloor where he strode. Yes, gold from anear by bronze from afar. Lenehan heard and knew and hailed him:

—See the conquering hero comes.

Between the car and window, warily walking, went Bloom, unconquered hero. See me he might. The seat he sat on: warm. Black wary hecat walked towards Richie Goulding's legal bag, lifted aloft, saluting.

—*And I from thee . . .*

—I heard you were round, said Blazes Boylan.

He touched to fair miss Kennedy a rim of his slanted straw. She smiled on him. But sister bronze outsmiled her, preening for him her richer hair, a bosom and a rose.

Smart Boylan bespoke potions.

—What's your cry? Glass of bitter? Glass of bitter, please, and a sloegin for me. Wire in yet?

Not yet. At four she. Who said four?

Cowley's red lugs and bulging apple in the door of the sheriff's office.

Avoid. Goulding a chance. What is he doing in the Ormond? Car waiting. Wait.

Hello. Where off to? Something to eat? I too was just. In here. What, Ormond? Best value in Dublin. Is that so? Dining room. Sit tight there. See, not be seen. I think I'll join you. Come on. Richie led on. Bloom followed bag. Dinner fit for a prince.

Miss Douce reached high to take a flagon, stretching her satin arm, her bust, that all but burst, so high.

—O! O! jerked Lenehan, gasping at each stretch. O!

But easily she seized her prey and led it low in triumph.

—Why don't you grow? asked Blazes Boylan.

Shebronze, dealing from her oblique jar thick syrupy liquor for his lips, looked as it flowed (flower in his coat: who gave him?), and syrupped with her voice:

—Fine goods in small parcels.

That is to say she. Neatly she poured slowsyrupy sloe.

—Here's fortune, Blazes said.

He pitched a broad coin down. Coin rang.

—Hold on, said Lenehan, till I . . .

—Fortune, he wished, lifting his bubbled ale.

—Sceptre will win in a canter, he said.

—I plunged a bit, said Boylan winking and drinking. Not on my own, you know. Fancy of a friend of mine.

Lenehan still drank and grinned at his tilted ale and at miss Douce's lips that all but hummed, not shut, the oceansong her lips had trilled. Idolores. The eastern seas.

Clock whirred. Miss Kennedy passed their way (flower, wonder who gave), bearing away teatray. Clock clacked.

Miss Douce took Boylan's coin, struck boldly the cashregister. It clanged. Clock clacked. Fair one of Egypt teased and sorted in the till and hummed and handed coins in change. Look to the west. A clack. For me.

—What time is that? asked Blazes Boylan. Four?

O'clock.

Lenehan, small eyes ahunger on her humming, bust ahumming, tugged Blazes Boylan's elbowsleeve.

—Let's hear the time, he said.

The bag of Goulding, Collis, Ward led Bloom by ryebloom flowered tables. Aimless he chose with agitated aim, bald Pat attending, a table near the door. Be near. At four. Has he forgotten? Perhaps a trick. Not come: whet appetite. I couldn't do. Wait, wait. Pat, waiter, waited.

Sparkling bronze azure eyed Blazure's skyblue bow and eyes.

—Go on, pressed Lenehan. There's no-one. He never heard.

—. . . to Flora's lips did hie.

High, a high note pealed in the treble clear.

Bronzedouce communing with her rose that sank and rose sought Blazes Boylan's flower and eyes.

—Please, please.

He pleaded over returning phrases of avowal.

—I could not leave thee . . .

—Afterwits, miss Douce promised coyly.

—No, now, urged Lenehan. Sonnez la cloche! O do! There's no-one.

She looked. Quick. Miss Kenn out of earshot. Sudden bent. Two kindling faces watched her bend.

Quavering the chords strayed from the air, found it again, lost chord, and lost and found it, faltering.

—Go on! Do! *Sonnez!*

Bending, she nipped a peak of skirt above her knee. Delayed. Taunted them still, bending, suspending, with wilful eyes.

—*Sonnez!*

Smack. She set free sudden in rebound her nipped elastic garter smackwarm against her smackable a woman's warmhosed thigh.

—*La cloche!* cried gleeful Lenehan. Trained by owner. No sawdust there.

She smilesmirked supercilious (wept! aren't men?), but, lightward gliding, mild she smiled on Boylan.

—You're the essence of vulgarity, she in gliding said.

Boylan, eyed, eyed. Tossed to fat lips his chalice, drank off his chalice tiny, sucking the last fat violet syrupy drops. His spellbound eyes went after, after her gliding head as it went down the bar by mirrors, gilded arch for ginger ale, hock and claret glasses shimmering, a spiky shell, where it concerted, mirrored, bronze with sunnier bronze.

Yes, bronze from anearby.

—. . .*Sweetheart, goodbye!*

—I'm off, said Boylan with impatience.

He slid his chalice brisk away, grasped his change.

—Wait a shake, begged Lenehan, drinking quickly. I wanted to tell you. Tom Rochford . . .

—Come on to blazes, said Blazes Boylan, going.

Lenehan gulped to go.

—Got the horn or what? he said. Wait. I'm coming.

He followed the hasty creaking shoes but stood by nimbly by the threshold, saluting forms, a bulky with a slender.

—How do you do, Mr Dollard?

—Eh? How do? How do? Ben Dollard's vague bass answered, turning an instant from Father Cowley's woe. He won't give you any trouble, Bob. Alf Bergan will speak to the long fellow. We'll put a barleystraw in that Judas Iscariot's ear this time.

Sighing Mr Dedalus came through the saloon, a finger soothing an eyelid.

—Hoho, we will, Ben Dollard yodled jollily. Come on, Simon. Give us a ditty. We heard the piano.

Bald Pat, bothered waiter, waited for drink orders. Power for

286

Richie. And Bloom? Let me see. Not make him walk twice. His corns. Four now. How warm this black is. Course nerves a bit. Refracts (is it?) heat. Let me see. Cider. Yes, bottle of cider.

—What's that? Mr Dedalus said. I was only vamping, man.

—Come on, come on, Ben Dollard called. Begone dull care. Come, Bob.

He ambled Dollard, bulky slops, before them (hold that fellow with the: hold him now) into the saloon. He plumped him Dollard on the stool. His gouty paws plumped chords. Plumped, stopped abrupt.

Bald Pat in the doorway met tealess gold returning. Bothered, he wanted Power and cider. Bronze by the window, watched, bronze from afar.

Jingle a tinkle jaunted.

Bloom heard a jing, a little sound. He's off. Light sob of breath Bloom sighed on the silent bluehued flowers. Jingling. He's gone. Jingle. Hear.

—Love and War, Ben, Mr Dedalus said. God be with old times.

Miss Douce's brave eyes, unregarded, turned from the crossblind, smitten by sunlight. Gone. Pensive (who knows?), smitten (the smiting light), she lowered the dropblind with a sliding cord. She drew down pensive (why did he go so quick when I?) about her bronze, over the bar where bald stood by sister gold, inexquisite contrast, contrast inexquisite nonexquisite, slow cool dim seagreen sliding depth of shadow, *eau de Nil.*

—Poor old Goodwin was the pianist that night, Father Cowley reminded them. There was a slight difference of opinion between himself and the Collard grand.

There was.

—A symposium all his own, Mr Dedalus said. The devil wouldn't stop him. He was a crotchety old fellow in the primary stage of drink.

—God, do you remember? Ben bulky Dollard said, turning from the punished keyboard. And by Japers I had no wedding garment.

They laughed all three. He had no wed. All trio laughed. No wedding garment.

—Our friend Bloom turned in handy that night, Mr Dedalus said. Where's my pipe, by the way?

He wandered back to the bar to the lost chord pipe. Bald Pat carried two diners' drinks, Richie and Poldy. And Father Cowley laughed again.

—I saved the situation, Ben, I think.

—You did, averred Ben Dollard. I remember those tight trousers too. That was a brilliant idea, Bob.

Father Cowley blushed to his brilliant purply lobes. He saved the situa. Tight trou. Brilliant ide.

—I knew he was on the rocks, he said. The wife was playing the piano in the coffee palace on Saturdays for a very trifling consideration and who was it gave me the wheeze she was doing the other business? Do you remember? We had to search all Holles street to find them till the chap in Keogh's gave us the number. Remember?

Ben remembered, his broad visage wondering.

—By God, she had some luxurious operacloaks and things there.

Mr Dedalus wandered back, pipe in hand.

—Merrion square style. Balldresses, by God, and court dresses. He wouldn't take any money either. What? Any God's quantity of cocked hats and boleros and trunkhose. What?

—Ay, ay, Mr Dedalus nodded. Mrs Marion Bloom has left off clothes of all descriptions.

Jingle jaunted down the quays. Blazes sprawled on bounding tyres.

Liver and bacon. Steak and kidney pie. Right, sir. Right, Pat.

Mrs Marion. Met him pike hoses. Smell of burn. Of Paul de Kock. Nice name he.

—What's this her name was? A buxom lassy. Marion . . .

—Tweedy.

—Yes. Is she alive?

—And kicking.

—She was a daughter of . . .

—Daughter of the regiment.

—Yes, begad. I remember the old drummajor.

Mr Dedalus struck, whizzed, lit, puffed savoury puff after

—Irish? I don't know, faith. Is she, Simon?

Puff after stiff, a puff, strong, savoury, crackling.

—Buccinator muscle is . . . What? . . . Bit rusty . . . O, she is . . . My Irish Molly, O.

He puffed a pungent plumy blast.

—From the rock of Gibraltar . . . all the way.

They pined in depth of ocean shadow, gold by the beerpull, bronze by maraschino, thoughtful all two. Mina Kennedy, 4 Lismore terrace, Drumcondra with Idolores, a queen, Dolores, silent.

Pat served, uncovered dishes. Leopold cut liver slices. As said before he ate with relish the inner organs, nutty gizzards, fried cods' roes while Richie Goulding, Collis, Ward ate steak and kidney, steak then kidney, bite by bite of pie he ate Bloom ate they ate.

Bloom with Goulding, married in silence, ate. Dinners fit for princes.

By Bachelor's walk jogjaunty jingled Blazes Boylan, bachelor, in sun in heat, mare's glossy rump atrot, with flick of whip, on bounding tyres: sprawled, warmseated, Boylan impatience, ardentbold. Horn. Have you the? Horn. Have you the? Haw haw horn.

Over their voices Dollard bassooned attack, booming over bombarding chords:

—*When love absorbs my ardent soul* . . .

Roll of Bensoulbenjamin rolled to the quivery loveshivery roofpanes.

—War! War! cried Father Cowley. You're the warrior.

—So I am, Ben Warrior laughed. I was thinking of your landlord. Love or money.

He stopped. He wagged huge beard, huge face over his blunder huge.

—Sure, you'd burst the tympanum of her ear, man, Mr Dedalus said through smoke aroma, with an organ like yours.

In bearded abundant laughter Dollard shook upon the keyboard. He would.

—Not to mention another membrane, Father Cowley added. Half time, Ben. *Amoroso ma non troppo.* Let me there.

Miss Kennedy served two gentlemen with tankards of cool stout. She passed a remark. It was indeed, first gentleman said, beautiful weather. They drank cool stout. Did she know where the lord lieutenant was going? And heard steelhoofs ringhoof ring. No, she couldn't say. But it would be in the paper. O, she need not trouble. No trouble. She waved about her outspread *Independent,* searching, the lord lieutenant, her pinnacles of hair slowmoving, lord lieuten. Too much trouble, first gentleman said. O, not in the least. Way he looked that. Lord lieutenant. Gold by bronze heard iron steel.

—. . . . . *my ardent soul*
I care not foror the morrow.

In liver gravy Bloom mashed mashed potatoes. Love and War someone is. Ben Dollard's famous. Night he ran round to us to borrow a dress suit for that concert. Trousers tight as a drum on him. Musical porkers. Molly did laugh when he went out. Threw herself back across the bed, screaming, kicking. With all his belongings on show. O saints above, I'm drenched! O, the women in the front row! O, I never laughed so many! Well, of course that's what gives him the base barreltone. For instance eunuchs. Wonder who's playing. Nice touch. Must be Cowley. Musical. Knows whatever note you play. Bad breath he has, poor chap. Stopped.

Miss Douce, engaging, Lydia Douce, bowed to suave solicitor, George Lidwell, gentleman, entering. Good afternoon. She gave her moist (a lady's) hand to his firm clasp. Afternoon. Yes, she was back. To the old dingdong again.

—Your friends are inside, Mr Lidwell.

George Lidwell, suave, solicited, held a lydiahand.

Bloom ate liv as said before. Clean here at least. That chap in the Burton, gummy with gristle. No-one here: Goulding and I. Clean tables, flowers, mitres of napkins. Pat to and fro. Bald Pat. Nothing to do. Best value in Dub.

Piano again. Cowley it is. Way he sits in to it, like one together, mutual understanding. Tiresome shapers scraping fiddles, eye on the bowend, sawing the cello, remind you of toothache. Her high long snore. Night we were in the box. Trombone under blowing like a grampus, between the acts, other brass chap unscrewing, emptying spittle. Conductor's legs too, bagstrousers, jiggedy jiggedy. Do right to hide them.

Jiggedy jingle jaunty jaunty.

Only the harp. Lovely. Gold glowering light. Girl touched it. Poop of a lovely. Gravy's rather good fit for a. Golden ship. Erin. The harp that once or twice. Cool hands. Ben Howth, the rhododendrons. We are their harps. I. He. Old. Young.

—Ah, I couldn't, man, Mr Dedalus said, shy, listless.

Strongly.

—Go on, blast you! Ben Dollard growled. Get it out in bits.

—*M'appari,* Simon, Father Cowley said.

Down stage he strode some paces, grave, tall in affliction, his long arms outheld. Hoarsely the apple of his throat hoarsed softly. Softly he sang to a dusty seascape there: *A Last Farewell.* A headland, a ship, a sail upon the billows. Farewell. A lovely girl, her veil awave upon the wind upon the headland, wind around her.

Cowley sang:

—*M'appari tutt'amor:*
Il mio sguardo l'incontr . . .

She waved, unhearing Cowley, her veil, to one departing, dear one, to wind, love, speeding sail, return.

—Go on, Simon.

—Ah, sure, my dancing days are done, Ben . . . Well . . .

Mr Dedalus laid his pipe to rest beside the tuningfork and, sitting, touched the obedient keys.

—No, Simon, Father Cowley turned. Play it in the original. One flat.

The keys, obedient, rose higher, told, faltered, confessed, confused.

Up stage strode Father Cowley.

—Here, Simon, I'll accompany you, he said. Get up.

By Graham Lemon's pineapple rock, by Elvery's elephant jingly jogged.

Steak, kidney, liver, mashed, at meat fit for princes sat princes Bloom and Goulding. Princes at meat they raised and drank, Power and cider.

Most beautiful tenor air ever written, Richie said: *Sonnambula*. He heard Joe Maas sing that one night. Ah, what M'Guckin! Yes. In his way. Choirboy style. Maas was the boy. Massboy. A lyrical tenor if you like. Never forget it. Never.

Tenderly Bloom over liverless bacon saw the tightened features strain. Backache he. Bright's bright eye. Next item on the programme. Paying the piper. Pills, pounded bread, worth a guinea a box. Stave it off awhile. Sings too: *Down among the dead men*. Appropriate. Kidney pie. Sweets to the. Not making much hand of it. Best value in. Characteristic of him. Power. Particular about his drink. Flaw in the glass, fresh Vartry water. Fecking matches from counters to save. Then squander a sovereign in dribs and drabs. And when he's wanted not a farthing. Screwed refusing to pay his fare. Curious types.

Never would Richie forget that night. As long as he lived: never. In the gods of the old Royal with little Peake. And when the first note.

Speech paused on Richie's lips.

Coming out with a whopper now. Rhapsodies about damn all. Believes his own lies. Does really. Wonderful liar. But want a good memory.

—Which air is that? asked Leopold Bloom.

—*All is lost now.*

Richie cocked his lips apout. A low incipient note sweet banshee murmured: all. A thrush. A throstle. His breath, birdsweet, good teeth he's proud of, fluted with plaintive woe. Is lost. Rich sound. Two notes in one there. Blackbird I heard in the hawthorn valley. Taking my motives he twined and turned them. All most too new call is lost in all. Echo. How sweet the answer. How is that done? All lost now. Mournful he whistled. Fall, surrender, lost.

Bloom bent leopold ear, turning a fringe of doyley down under the vase. Order. Yes, I remember. Lovely air. In sleep she went to him. Innocence in the moon. Brave. Don't know their danger. Still hold her back. Call name. Touch water. Jingle jaunty. Too late. She longed to go. That's why. Woman. As easy stop the sea. Yes: all is lost.

—A beautiful air, said Bloom lost Leopold. I know it well.

Never in all his life had Richie Goulding.

He knows it well too. Or he feels. Still harping on his daughter. Wise child that knows her father, Dedalus said. Me?

Bloom askance over liverless saw. Face of the all is lost. Rollicking Richie once. Jokes old stale now. Wagging his ear. Napkinring in his eye. Now begging letters he sends his son with. Crosseyed Walter sir I did sir. Wouldn't trouble only I was expecting some money. Apologise.

Piano again. Sounds better than last time I heard. Tuned probably. Stopped again.

Dollard and Cowley still urged the lingering singer out with it.

—With it, Simon.

—It, Simon.

—Ladies and gentlemen, I am most deeply obliged by your kind solicitations.

—It, Simon.

—I have no money but if you will lend me your attention I shall endeavour to sing to you of a heart bowed down.

By the sandwichbell in screening shadow Lydia, her bronze and rose, a lady's grace, gave and withheld: as in cool glaucous *eau de Nil* Mina to tankards two her pinnacles of gold.

The harping chords of prelude closed. A chord, longdrawn, expectant, drew a voice away.

—*When first I saw that form endearing . . .*

Richie turned.

292

—Si Dedalus' voice, he said.

Braintipped, cheek touched with flame, they listened feeling that flow endearing flow over skin limbs human heart soul spine. Bloom signed to Pat, bald Pat is a waiter hard of hearing, to set ajar the door of the bar. The door of the bar. So. That will do. Pat, waiter, waited, waiting to hear, for he was hard of hear by the door.

—*Sorrow from me seemed to depart.*

Through the hush of air a voice sang to them, low, not rain, not leaves in murmur, like no voice of strings or reeds or whatdoyoucallthem dulcimers touching their still ears with words, still hearts of their each his remembered lives. Good, good to hear: sorrow from them each seemed to from both depart when first they heard. When first they saw, lost Richie Poldy, mercy of beauty, heard from a person wouldn't expect it in the least, her first merciful lovesoft oftloved word.

Love that is singing: love's old sweet song. Bloom unwound slowly the elastic band of his packet. Love's old sweet *sonnez la* gold. Bloom wound a skein round four forkfingers, stretched it, relaxed, and wound it round his troubled double, fourfold, in octave, gyved them fast.

—*Full of hope and all delighted* . . .

Tenors get women by the score. Increase their flow. Throw flower at his feet. When will we meet? My head it simply. Jingle all delighted. He can't sing for tall hats. Your head it simply swirls. Perfumed for him. What perfume does your wife? I want to know. Jing. Stop. Knock. Last look at mirror always before she answers the door. The hall. There? How do you? I do well. There? What? Or? Phial of cachous, kissing comfits, in her satchel. Yes? Hands felt for the opulent.

Alas the voice rose, sighing, changed: loud, full, shining, proud.

—*But alas, 'twas idle dreaming* . . .

Glorious tone he has still. Cork air softer also their brogue. Silly man! Could have made oceans of money. Singing wrong words. Wore out his wife: now sings. But hard to tell. Only the two themselves. If he doesn't break down. Keep a trot for the avenue. His hands and feet sing too. Drink. Nerves overstrung. Must be abstemious to sing. Jenny Lind soup: stock, sage, raw eggs, half pint of cream. For creamy dreamy.

Tenderness it welled: slow, swelling, full it throbbed. That's the chat. Ha, give! Take! Throb, a throb, a pulsing proud erect.

Words? Music? No: it's what's behind.

Bloom looped, unlooped, noded, disnoded.

Bloom. Flood of warm jamjam lickitup secretness flowed to flow in music out, in desire, dark to lick flow invading. Tipping her tepping her tapping her topping her. Tup. Pores to dilate dilating. Tup. The joy the feel the warm the. Tup. To pour o'er sluices pouring gushes. Flood, gush, flow, joygush, tupthrob. Now! Language of love.

—. . .*ray of hope is . . .*

Beaming. Lydia for Lidwell squeak scarcely hear so ladylike the muse unsqueaked a ray of hopk.

Martha it is. Coincidence. Just going to write. Lionel's song. Lovely name you have. Can't write. Accept my little pres. Play on her heartstrings pursestrings too. She's a. I called you naughty boy. Still the name: Martha. How strange! Today.

The voice of Lionel returned, weaker but unwearied. It sang again to Richie Poldy Lydia Lidwell also sang to Pat open mouth ear waiting to wait. How first he saw that form endearing, how sorrow seemed to part, how look, form, word charmed him Gould Lidwell, won Pat Bloom's heart.

Wish I could see his face, though. Explain better. Why the barber in Drago's always looked my face when I spoke his face in the glass. Still hear it better here than in the bar though farther.

—*Each graceful look . . .*

First night when first I saw her at Mat Dillon's in Terenure. Yellow, black lace she wore. Musical chairs. We two the last. Fate. After her. Fate. Round and round slow. Quick round. We two. All looked. Halt. Down she sat. All ousted looked. Lips laughing. Yellow knees.

—*Charmed my eye . . .*

Singing. *Waiting* she sang. I turned her music. Full voice of perfume of what perfume does your lilactrees. Bosom I saw, both full, throat warbling. First I saw. She thanked me. Why did she me? Fate. Spanishy eyes. Under a peartree alone patio this hour in old Madrid one side in shadow Dolores shedolores. At me. Luring. Ah, alluring.

—*Martha! Ah, Martha!*

Quitting all languor Lionel cried in grief, in cry of passion dominant to love to return with deepening yet with rising chords of harmony. In cry of lionel loneliness that she should know, must martha feel. For only her he waited. Where? Here there try there here all try where. Somewhere.

—*Co-ome, thou lost one!*

294

Co-ome, thou dear one!

Alone. One love. One hope. One comfort me. Martha, chestnote, return!

—*Come!*

It soared, a bird, it held its flight, a swift pure cry, soar silver orb it leaped serene, speeding, sustained, to come, don't spin it out too long long breath he breath long life, soaring high, high resplendent, aflame, crowned, high in the effulgence symbolistic, high, of the etherial bosom, high, of the high vast irradiation everywhere all soaring all around about the all, the endlessnessnessness . . .

—*To me!*

Siopold!

Consumed.

Come. Well sung. All clapped. She ought to. Come. To me, to him, to her, you too, me, us.

—Bravo! Clapclap. Good man, Simon. Clappyclapclap. Encore! Clapclipclap clap. Sound as a bell. Bravo, Simon! Clapclopclap. Encore, enclap, said, cried, clapped all, Ben Dollard, Lydia Douce, George Lidwell, Pat, Mina Kennedy, two gentlemen with two tankards, Cowley, first gent with tank and bronze Miss Douce and gold Miss Mina.

Blazes Boylan's smart tan shoes creaked on the barfloor, said before. Jingle by monuments of sir John Gray, Horatio onehandled Nelson, reverend father Theobald Mathew, jaunted, as said before just now. Atrot, in heat, heatseated. *Cloche. Sonnez la. Cloche. Sonnez la.* Slower the mare went up the hill by the Rotunda, Rutland square. Too slow for Boylan, blazes Boylan, impatience Boylan, joggled the mare.

An afterclang of Cowley's chords closed, died on the air made richer.

And Richie Goulding drank his Power and Leopold Bloom his cider drank, Lidwell his Guinness, second gentleman said they would partake of two more tankards if she did not mind. Miss Kennedy smirked, disserving, coral lips, at first, at second. She did not mind.

—Seven days in jail, Ben Dollard said, on bread and water. Then you'd sing, Simon, like a garden thrush.

Lionel Simon, singer, laughed. Father Bob Cowley played. Mina Kennedy served. Second gentleman paid. Tom Kernan strutted in. Lydia, admired, admired. But Bloom sang dumb.

Admiring.

Richie, admiring, descanted on that man's glorious voice. He remembered one night long ago. Never forget that night. Si sang *'Twas rank and fame*: in Ned Lambert's 'twas. Good God he never heard in all his life a note like that he never did *then false one we had better part* so clear so God he never heard *since love lives not* a clinking voice lives not ask Lambert he can tell you too.

Goulding, a flush struggling in his pale, told Mr Bloom, face of the night, Si in Ned Lambert's, Dedalus house, sang *'Twas rank and fame*.

He, Mr Bloom, listened while he, Richie Goulding, told him, Mr Bloom, of the night he, Richie, heard him, Si Dedalus, sing *'Twas rank and fame* in his, Ned Lambert's, house.

Brothers-in-law: relations. We never speak as we pass by. Rift in the lute I think. Treats him with scorn. See. He admires him all the more. The night Si sang. The human voice, two tiny silky chords, wonderful, more than all others.

That voice was a lamentation. Calmer now. It's in the silence after you feel you hear. Vibrations. Now silent air.

Bloom ungyved his crisscrossed hands and with slack fingers plucked the slender catgut thong. He drew and plucked. It buzz, it twanged. While Goulding talked of Barraclough's voice production, while Tom Kernan, harking back in a retrospective sort of arrangement talked to listening Father Cowley, who played a voluntary, who nodded as he played. While big Ben Dollard talked with Simon Dedalus, lighting, who nodded as he smoked, who smoked.

Thou lost one. All songs on that theme. Yet more Bloom stretched his string. Cruel it seems. Let people get fond of each other: lure them on. Then tear asunder. Death. Explos. Knock on the head. Outtohelloutofthat. Human life. Dignam. Ugh, that rat's tail wriggling! Five bob I gave. *Corpus paradisum*. Corncrake croaker: belly like a poisoned pup. Gone. They sing. Forgotten. I too. And one day she with. Leave her: get tired. Suffer then. Snivel. Big spanishy eyes goggling at nothing. Her wavy heavy hair uncombed.

Yet too much happy bores. He stretched more, more. Are you not happy in your? Twang. It snapped.

Jingle into Dorset street.

Miss Douce withdrew her satiny arm, reproachful, pleased.

—Don't make half so free, said she, till we are better acquainted.

George Lidwell told her really and truly: but she did not believe.

First gentleman told Mina that was so. She asked him was that so. And second tankard told her so. That that was so.

Miss Douce, miss Lydia, did not believe: miss Kennedy, Mina, did not believe: George Lidwell, no: miss Dou did not: the first, the first: gent with the tank: believe, no, no: did not, miss Kenn: Lidlydiawell: the tank.

Better write it here. Quills in the postoffice chewed and twisted.

Bald Pat at a sign drew nigh. A pen and ink. He went. A pad. He went. A pad to blot. He heard, deaf Pat.

—Yes, Mr Bloom said, teasing the curling catgut line. It certainly is. Few lines will do. My present. All that Italian florid music is. Who is this wrote? Know the name you know better. Take out sheet notepaper, envelope: unconcerned. It's so characteristic.

—Grandest number in the whole opera, Goulding said.

—It is, Bloom said.

Numbers it is. All music when you come to think. Two multiplied by two divided by half is twice one. Vibrations: chords those are. One plus two plus six is seven. Do anything you like with figures juggling. Always find out this equal to that. Symmetry under a cemetery wall. He doesn't see my mourning. Callous: all for his own gut. Musemathematics. And you think you're listening to the etherial. But suppose you said it like: Martha, seven times nine minus x is thirtyfive thousand. Fall quite flat. It's on account of the sounds it is.

Instance he's playing now. Improvising. Might be what you like, till you hear the words. Want to listen sharp. Hard. Begin all right: then hear chords a bit off: feel lost a bit. In and out of sacks, over barrels, through wirefences, obstacle race. Time makes the tune. Question of mood you're in. Still always nice to hear. Except scales up and down, girls learning. Two together nextdoor neighbours. Ought to invent dummy pianos for that. *Blumenlied* I bought for her. The name. Playing it slow, a girl, night I came home, the girl. Door of the stables near Cecilia street. Milly no taste. Queer because we both, I mean.

Bald deaf Pat brought quite flat pad ink. Pat set with ink pen quite flat pad. Pat took plate dish knife fork. Pat went.

It was the only language Mr Dedalus said to Ben. He heard them as a boy in Ringabella, Crosshaven, Ringabella, singing their barcaroles. Queenstown harbour full of Italian ships. Walking, you know, Ben, in the moonlight with those earthquake hats. Blending their voices. God, such music, Ben. Heard as a boy. Cross Ringabella haven mooncarole.

Sour pipe removed he held a shield of hand beside his lips that cooed a moonlight nightcall, clear from anear, a call from afar, replying.

Down the edge of his *Freeman* baton ranged Bloom's, your other eye, scanning for where did I see that. Callan, Coleman, Dignam Patrick. Heigho! Heigho! Fawcett. Aha! Just I was looking . . .

Hope he's not looking, cute as a rat. He held unfurled his *Freeman*. Can't see now. Remember write Greek ees. Bloom dipped, Bloo mur: dear sir. Dear Henry wrote: dear Mady. Got your lett and flow. Hell did I put? Some pock or oth. It is utterl imposs. Underline *imposs*. To write today.

Bore this. Bored Bloom tambourined gently with I am just reflecting fingers on flat pad Pat brought.

On. Know what I mean. No, change that ee. Accep my poor litt pres enclos. Ask her no answ. Hold on. Five Dig. Two about here. Penny the gulls. Elijah is com. Seven Davy Byrne's. Is eight about. Say half a crown. My poor little pres: p. o. two and six. Write me a long. Do you despise? Jingle, have you the? So excited. Why do you call me naught? You naughty too? O, Mairy lost the string of her. Bye for today. Yes, yes, will tell you. Want to. To keep it up. Call me that other. Other world she wrote. My patience are exhaust. To keep it up. You must believe. Believe. The tank. It. Is. True.

Folly am I writing? Husbands don't. That's marriage does, their wives. Because I'm away from. Suppose. But how? She must. Keep young. If she found out. Card in my high grade ha. No, not tell all. Useless pain. If they don't see. Woman. Sauce for the gander.

A hackney car, number three hundred and twentyfour, driver Barton James of number one Harmony avenue, Donnybrook, on which sat a fare, a young gentleman, stylishly dressed in an indigoblue serge suit made by George Robert Mesias, tailor and cutter, of number five Eden quay, and wearing a straw hat very dressy, bought of John Plasto of number one Great Brunswick street, hatter. Eh? This is the jingle that joggled and jingled. By Dlugacz' porkshop bright tubes of Agendath trotted a gallantbuttocked mare.

—Answering an ad? keen Richie's eyes asked Bloom.

—Yes, Mr Bloom said. Town traveller. Nothing doing, I expect.

Bloom mur: best references. But Henry wrote: it will excite me. You know how. In haste. Henry. Greek ee. Better add postscript. What is he playing now? Improvising. Intermezzo. P. S. The rum tum tum. How will you pun? You punish me? Crooked skirt swinging, whack by. Tell me I want to. Know. O. Course if I didn't I wouldn't ask. La la la ree. Trails off there sad in minor. Why minor sad? Sign H. They like sad tail at end. P. P. S. La la la ree. I feel so sad today. La ree. So lonely. Dee.

He blotted quick on pad of Pat. Envel. Address. Just copy out of paper. Murmured: Messrs Callan, Coleman and Co, limited. Henry wrote:

Miss Martha Clifford
c/o P. O.
Dolphin's Barn Lane
Dublin.

Blot over the other so he can't read. There. Right. Idea prize titbit. Something detective read off blottingpad. Payment at the rate of guinea per col. Matcham often thinks the laughing witch. Poor Mrs Purefoy. U.p.: up.

Too poetical that about the sad. Music did that. Music hath charms. Shakespeare said. Quotations every day in the year. To be or not to be. Wisdom while you wait.

In Gerard's rosery of Fetter lane he walks, greyedauburn. One life is all. One body. Do. But do.

Done anyhow. Postal order, stamp. Postoffice lower down. Walk now. Enough. Barney Kiernan's I promised to meet them. Dislike that job. House of mourning. Walk. Pat! Doesn't hear. Deaf beetle he is.

Car near there now. Talk. Talk. Pat! Doesn't. Settling those napkins. Lot of ground he must cover in the day. Paint face behind on him then he'd be two. Wish they'd sing more. Keep my mind off.

Bald Pat who is bothered mitred the napkins. Pat is a waiter hard of his hearing. Pat is a waiter who waits while you wait. Hee hee hee hee. He waits while you wait. Hee hee. A waiter is he. Hee hee hee hee. He waits while you wait. While you wait if you wait he will wait while you wait. Hee hee hee hee. Hoh. Wait while you wait.

Douce now. Douce Lydia. Bronze and rose.

She had a gorgeous, simply gorgeous, time. And look at the lovely shell she brought.

To the end of the bar to him she bore lightly the spiked and winding seahorn that he, George Lidwell, solicitor, might hear.

—Listen! she bade him.

Under Tom Kernan's ginhot words the accompanist wove music slow. Authentic fact. How Walter Bapty lost his voice. Well, sir, the husband took him by the throat. *Scoundrel,* said he, *You'll sing no more lovesongs.* He did, faith, sir Tom. Bob Cowley wove. Tenors get wom. Cowley lay back.

Ah, now he heard, she holding it to his ear. Hear! He heard. Wonderful. She held it to her own. And through the sifted light pale gold in contrast glided. To hear.

Tap.

Bloom through the bardoor saw a shell held at their ears. He heard more faintly that that they heard, each for herself alone, then each for other, hearing the plash of waves, loudly, a silent roar.

Bronze by a weary gold, anear, afar, they listened.

Her ear too is a shell, the peeping lobe there. Been to the seaside. Lovely seaside girls. Skin tanned raw. Should have put on coldcream first make it brown. Buttered toast. O and that lotion mustn't forget. Fever near her mouth. Your head it simply. Hair braided over: shell with seaweed. Why do they hide their ears with seaweed hair? And Turks the mouth, why? Her eyes over the sheet. Yashmak. Find the way in. A cave. No admittance except on business.

The sea they think they hear. Singing. A roar. The blood it is. Souse in the ear sometimes. Well, it's a sea. Corpuscle islands.

Wonderful really. So distinct. Again. George Lidwell held its murmur, hearing: then laid it by, gently.

—What are the wild waves saying? he asked her, smiled.

Charming, seasmiling and unanswering Lydia on Lidwell smiled.

Tap.

By Larry O'Rourke's, by Larry, bold Larry O', Boylan swayed and Boylan turned.

From the forsaken shell miss Mina glided to her tankards waiting. No, she was not so lonely archly miss Douce's head let Mr Lidwell know. Walks in the moonlight by the sea. No, not alone. With whom? She nobly answered: with a gentleman friend.

Bob Cowley's twinkling fingers in the treble played again. The landlord has the prior. A little time. Long John. Big Ben. Lightly he played a light bright tinkling measure for tripping ladies, arch and smiling, and for their gallants, gentlemen friends. One: one, one, one, one, one: two, one, three, four.

Sea, wind, leaves, thunder, waters, cows lowing, the cattlemarket, cocks, hens don't crow, snakes hissss. There's music everywhere. Ruttledge's door: ee creaking. No, that's noise. Minuet of *Don Giovanni* he's playing now. Court dresses of all descriptions in castle chambers dancing. Misery. Peasants outside. Green starving faces eating dockleaves. Nice that is. Look: look, look, look, look, look: you look at us.

That's joyful I can feel. Never have written it. Why? My joy is other joy. But both are joys. Yes, joy it must be. Mere fact of music shows you are. Often thought she was in the dumps till she began to lilt. Then know.

M'Coy valise. My wife and your wife. Squealing cat. Like tearing silk. Tongue when she talks like the clapper of a bellows. They can't manage men's intervals. Gap in their voices too. Fill me. I'm warm, dark, open. Molly in *quis est homo*: Mercadante. My ear against the wall to hear. Want a woman who can deliver the goods.

Jog jig jogged stopped. Dandy tan shoe of dandy Boylan socks skyblue clocks came light to earth.

O, look we are so! Chamber music. Could make a kind of pun on that. It is a kind of music I often thought when she. Acoustics that is. Tinkling. Empty vessels make most noise. Because the acoustics, the resonance changes according as the weight of the water is equal to the law of falling water. Like those rhapsodies of Liszt's, Hungarian, gipsyeyed. Pearls. Drops. Rain. Diddleiddle addleaddle ooddleooddle. Hissss. Now. Maybe now. Before.

One rapped on a door, one tapped with a knock, did he knock Paul de Kock with a loud proud knocker with a cock carracarracarra cock. Cockcock.

Tap.

—*Qui sdegno,* Ben, said Father Cowley.

—No, Ben, Tom Kernan interfered. *The Croppy Boy.* Our native Doric.

—Ay do, Ben, Mr Dedalus said. Good men and true.

—Do, do, they begged in one.

I'll go. Here, Pat, return. Come. He came, he came, he did not stay. To me. How much?

—What key? Six sharps?

—F sharp major, Ben Dollard said.

Bob Cowley's outstretched talons griped the black deepsounding chords.

Must go prince Bloom told Richie prince. No, Richie said. Yes, must. Got money somewhere. He's on for a razzle backache spree. Much? He seehears lipspeech. One and nine. Penny for yourself. Here. Give him twopence tip. Deaf, bothered. But perhaps he has wife and family waiting, waiting Patty come home. Hee hee hee hee. Deaf wait while they wait.

But wait. But hear. Chords dark. Lugugugubrious. Low. In a cave of the dark middle earth. Embedded ore. Lumpmusic.

The voice of dark age, of unlove, earth's fatigue made grave approach and painful, come from afar, from hoary mountains, called on good men and true. The priest he sought. With him would he speak a word.

Tap.

Ben Dollard's voice. Base barreltone. Doing his level best to say it. Croak of vast manless moonless womoonless marsh. Other comedown. Big ships' chandler's business he did once. Remember: rosiny ropes, ships' lanterns. Failed to the tune of ten thousand pounds. Now in the Iveagh home. Cubicle number so and so. Number one Bass did that for him.

The priest's at home. A false priest's servant bade him welcome. Step in. The holy father. With bows a traitor servant. Curlycues of chords.

Ruin them. Wreck their lives. Then build them cubicles to end their days in. Hushaby. Lullaby. Die, dog. Little dog, die.

The voice of warning, solemn warning, told them the youth had entered a lonely hall, told them how solemn fell his footsteps there, told them the gloomy chamber, the vested priest sitting to shrive.

Decent soul. Bit addled now. Thinks he'll win in *Answers*, poets' picture puzzle. We hand you crisp five pound note. Bird sitting hatching in a nest. Lay of the last minstrel he thought it was. See blank tee what domestic animal? Tee dash ar most courageous mariner. Good voice he has still. No eunuch yet with all his belongings.

Listen. Bloom listened. Richie Goulding listened. And by the door deaf Pat, bald Pat, tipped Pat, listened.

The chords harped slower.

The voice of penance and of grief came slow, embellished, tremulous. Ben's contrite beard confessed. *in nomine Domini*, in God's name he knelt. He beat his hand upon his breast, confessing: *mea culpa*.

Latin again. That holds them like birdlime. Priest with the communion corpus for those women. Chap in the mortuary, coffin or coffey, *corpusnomine*. Wonder where that rat is by now. Scrape.

Tap.

They listened. Tankards and miss Kennedy. George Lidwell, eyelid well expressive, fullbusted satin. Kernan. Si.

The sighing voice of sorrow sang. His sins. Since Easter he had cursed three times. You bitch's bast. And once at masstime he had gone to play. Once by the churchyard he had passed and for his mother's rest he had not prayed. A boy. A croppy boy.

Bronze, listening, by the beerpull gazed far away. Soulfully. Doesn't half know I'm. Molly great dab at seeing anyone looking.

Bronze gazed far sideways. Mirror there. Is that best side of her face? They always know. Knock at the door. Last tip to titivate.

Cockcarracarra.

What do they think when they hear music? Way to catch rattlesnakes. Night Michael Gunn gave us the box. Tuning up. Shah of Persia liked that best. Remind him of home sweet home. Wiped his nose in curtain too. Custom his country perhaps. That's music too. Not as bad as it sounds. Tootling. Brasses braying asses through uptrunks. Doublebasses helpless, gashes in their sides. Woodwinds mooing cows. Semigrand open crocodile music hath jaws. Woodwind like Goodwin's name.

She looked fine. Her crocus dress she wore lowcut, belongings on show. Clove her breath was always in theatre when she bent to ask a question. Told her what Spinoza says in that book of poor papa's. Hypnotised, listening. Eyes like that. She bent. Chap in dresscircle staring down into her with his operaglass for all he was worth. Beauty of music you must hear twice. Nature woman half a look. God made the country man the tune. Met him pike hoses. Philosophy. O rocks!

All gone. All fallen. At the siege of Ross his father, at Gorey all his brothers fell. To Wexford, we are the boys of Wexford, he would. Last of his name and race.

I too. Last of my race. Milly young student. Well, my fault perhaps. No son. Rudy. Too late now. Or if not? If not? If still?

He bore no hate.

Hate. Love. Those are names. Rudy. Soon I am old.

Big Ben his voice unfolded. Great voice Richie Goulding said, a flush struggling in his pale, to Bloom soon old. But when was young?

Ireland comes now. My country above the king. She listens. Who fears to speak of nineteen four? Time to be shoving. Looked enough.

—*Bless me, father,* Dollard the croppy cried. *Bless me and let me go.*

Tap.

Bloom looked, unblessed to go. Got up to kill: on eighteen bob a week. Fellows shell out the dibs. Want to keep your weathereye open. Those girls, those lovely. By the sad sea waves. Chorusgirl's romance. Letters read out for breach of promise. From Chickabiddy's own Mumpsypum. Laughter in court. Henry. I never signed it. The lovely name you.

Low sank the music, air and words. Then hastened. The false priest rustling soldier from his cassock. A yeoman captain. They know it all by heart. The thrill they itch for. Yeoman cap.

Tap. Tap.

Thrilled she listened, bending in sympathy to hear.

Blank face. Virgin should say: or fingered only. Write something on it: page. If not what becomes of them? Decline, despair. Keeps them young. Even admire themselves. See. Play on her. Lip blow. Body of white woman, a flute alive. Blow gentle. Loud. Three holes, all women. Goddess I didn't see. They want it. Not too much polite. That's why he gets them. Gold in your pocket, brass in your face. Say something. Make her hear. With look to look. Songs without words. Molly, that hurdygurdy boy. She knew he meant the monkey was sick. Or because so like the Spanish. Understand animals too that way. Solomon did. Gift of nature.

Ventriloquise. My lips closed. Think in my stom. What?

Will? You? I. Want. You. To.

With hoarse rude fury the yeoman cursed, swelling in apoplectic bitch's bastard. A good thought, boy, to come. One hour's your time to live, your last.

Tap. Tap.

Thrill now. Pity they feel. To wipe away a tear for martyrs that want to, dying to, die. For all things dying, for all things born. Poor Mrs Purefoy. Hope she's over. Because their wombs.

A liquid of womb of woman eyeball gazed under a fence of lashes, calmly, hearing. See real beauty of the eye when she not speaks. On yonder river. At each slow satiny heaving bosom's wave (her heaving embon) red rose rose slowly sank red rose. Heartbeats: her breath: breath that is life. And all the tiny tiny fernfoils trembled of maidenhair.

But look. The bright stars fade. O rose! Castile. The morn. Ha. Lidwell. For him then not for. Infatuated. I like that? See her from here though. Popped corks, splashes of beerfroth, stacks of empties.

On the smooth jutting beerpull laid Lydia hand, lightly, plumply, leave it to my hands. All lost in pity for croppy. Fro, to: to, fro: over the polished knob (she knows his eyes, my eyes, her eyes) her thumb and finger passed in pity: passed, reposed and, gently touching, then slid so smoothly, slowly down, a cool firm white enamel baton protruding through their sliding ring.

With a cock with a carra.

Tap. Tap. Tap.

I hold this house. Amen. He gnashed in fury. Traitors swing.

The chords consented. Very sad thing. But had to be.

Get out before the end. Thanks, that was heavenly. Where's my hat. Pass by her. Can leave that *Freeman*. Letter I have. Suppose she were the? No. Walk, walk, walk. Like Cashel Boylo Connoro Coylo Tisdall Maurice Tisntdall Farrell. Waaaaaaalk.

Well, I must be. Are you off? Yrfmstbyes. Blmstup. O'er ryehigh blue. Ow. Bloom stood up. Soap feeling rather sticky behind. Must have sweated: music. That lotion, remember. Well, so long. High grade. Card inside. Yes.

By deaf Pat in the doorway straining ear Bloom passed.

At Geneva barrack that young man died. At Passage was his body laid. Dolor! O, he dolores! The voice of the mournful chanter called to dolorous prayer.

By rose, by satiny bosom, by the fondling hand, by slops, by empties, by popped corks, greeting in going, past eyes and maidenhair, bronze and faint gold in deepseashadow, went Bloom, soft Bloom, I feel so lonely Bloom.

Tap. Tap. Tap.

Pray for him, prayed the bass of Dollard. You who hear in peace. Breathe a prayer, drop a tear, good men, good people. He was the croppy boy.

Scaring eavesdropping boots croppy bootsboy Bloom in the Ormond hallway heard the growls and roars of bravo, fat backslapping, their boots all treading, boots not the boots the boy. General chorus off for a swill to wash it down. Glad I avoided.

—Come on, Ben, Simon Dedalus cried. By God, you're as good as ever you were.

—Better, said Tomgin Kernan. Most trenchant rendition of that ballad, upon my soul and honour it is.

—Lablache, said Father Cowley.

Ben Dollard bulkily cachuchad towards the bar, mightily praisefed and all big roseate, on heavyfooted feet, his gouty fingers nakkering castagnettes in the air.

Big Benaben Dollard. Big Benben. Big Benben.

Rrr.

And deepmoved all, Simon trumping compassion from foghorn nose, all laughing they brought him forth, Ben Dollard, in right good cheer.

—You're looking rubicund, George Lidwell said.

Miss Douce composed her rose to wait.

—Ben machree, said Mr Dedalus, clapping Ben's fat back shoulderblade. Fit as a fiddle only he has a lot of adipose tissue concealed about his person.

Rrrrrrrsss.

—Fat of death, Simon, Ben Dollard growled.

Richie rift in the lute alone sat: Goulding, Collis, Ward. Uncertainly he waited. Unpaid Pat too.

Tap. Tap. Tap. Tap.

Miss Mina Kennedy brought near her lips to ear of tankard one.

—Mr Dollard, they murmured low.

—Dollard, murmured tankard.

Tank one believed: miss Kenn when she: that doll he was: she doll: the tank.

He murmured that he knew the name. The name was familiar to him, that is to say. That was to say he had heard the name of. Dollard, was it? Dollard, yes.

Yes, her lips said more loudly, Mr Dollard. He sang that song lovely, murmured Mina. Mr Dollard. And *The last rose of summer* was a lovely song. Mina loved that song. Tankard loved the song that Mina.

'Tis the last rose of summer dollard left bloom felt wind wound round inside.

Gassy thing that cider: binding too. Wait. Postoffice near Reuben J's one and eightpence too. Get shut of it. Dodge round by Greek street. Wish I hadn't promised to meet. Freer in air. Music. Gets on your nerves. Beerpull. Her hand that rocks the cradle rules the. Ben Howth. That rules the world.

Far. Far. Far. Far.

Tap. Tap. Tap. Tap.

Up the quay went Lionelleopold, naughty Henry with letter for Mady, with sweets of sin with frillies for Raoul with met him pike hoses went Poldy on.

Tap blind walked tapping by the tap the curbstone tapping, tap by tap.

Cowley, he stuns himself with it: kind of drunkenness. Better give way only half way the way of a man with a maid. Instance enthusiasts. All ears. Not lose a demisemiquaver. Eyes shut. Head nodding in time. Dotty. You daren't budge. Thinking strictly prohibited. Always talking shop. Fiddlefaddle about notes.

All a kind of attempt to talk. Unpleasant when it stops because you never know exac. Organ in Gardiner street. Old Glynn fifty quid a year. Queer up there in the cockloft, alone, with stops and locks and keys. Seated all day at the organ. Maunder on for hours, talking to himself or the other fellow blowing the bellows. Growl angry, then shriek cursing (want to have wadding or something in his no don't she cried), then all of a soft sudden wee little wee little pipy wind.

Pwee! A wee little wind piped eeee. In Bloom's little wee.

—Was he? Mr Dedalus said, returning with fetched pipe. I was with him this morning at poor little Paddy Dignam's . . .

—Ay, the Lord have mercy on him.

—By the bye there's a tuningfork in there on the . . .

Tap. Tap. Tap. Tap.

—The wife has a fine voice. Or had. What? Lidwell asked.

—O, that must be the tuner, Lydia said to Simonlionel first I saw, forgot it when he was here.

Blind he was she told George Lidwell second I saw. And played so exquisitely, treat to hear. Exquisite contrast: bronzelid, minagold.

—Shout! Ben Dollard shouted, pouring. Sing out!

—'lldo! cried Father Cowley.

Rrrrrr.

I feel I want . . .

Tap. Tap. Tap. Tap. Tap

—Very, Mr Dedalus said, staring hard at a headless sardine.

Under the sandwichbell lay on a bier of bread one last, one lonely, last sardine of summer. Bloom alone.

—Very, he stared. The lower register, for choice.

Tap. Tap. Tap. Tap. Tap. Tap. Tap. Tap.

Bloom went by Barry's. Wish I could. Wait. That wonderworker if I had. Twentyfour solicitors in that one house. Counted them. Litigation. Love one another. Piles of parchment. Messrs Pick and Pocket have power of attorney. Goulding, Collis, Ward.

But for example the chap that wallops the big drum. His vocation: Mickey Rooney's band. Wonder how it first struck him. Sitting at home after pig's cheek and cabbage nursing it in the armchair. Rehearsing his band part. Pom. Pompedy. Jolly for the wife. Asses' skins. Welt them through life, then wallop after death. Pom. Wallop. Seems to be what you call yashmak or I mean kismet. Fate.

Tap. Tap. A stripling, blind, with a tapping cane came taptaptapping by Daly's window where a mermaid hair all streaming (but he couldn't see) blew whiffs of a mermaid (blind couldn't), mermaid, coolest whiff of all.

Instruments. A blade of grass, shell of her hands, then blow. Even comb and tissuepaper you can knock a tune out of. Molly in her shift in Lombard street west, hair down. I suppose each kind of trade made its own, don't you see? Hunter with a horn. Haw. Have you the? *Cloche. Sonnez la.* Shepherd his pipe. Pwee little wee. Policeman a whistle. Locks and keys! Sweep! Four o'clock's all's well! Sleep! All is lost now. Drum? Pompedy. Wait. I know. Towncrier, bumbailiff. Long John. Waken the dead. Pom. Dignam. Poor little *nominedomine*. Pom. It is music. I mean of course it's all pom pom pom very much what they call *da capo*. Still you can hear. As we march, we march along, march along. Pom.

I must really. Fff. Now if I did that at a banquet. Just a question of custom shah of Persia. Breathe a prayer, drop a tear. All the same he must have been a bit of a natural not to see it was a yeoman cap. Muffled up. Wonder who was that chap at the grave in the brown macin. O, the whore of the lane!

A frowsy whore with black straw sailor hat askew came glazily in the day along the quay towards Mr Bloom. When first he saw that form endearing? Yes, it is. I feel so lonely. Wet night in the lane. Horn. Who had the? Heehaw shesaw. Off her beat here. What is she? Hope she. Psst! Any chance of your wash. Knew Molly. Had me decked. Stout lady does be with you in the brown costume. Put you off your stroke, that. Appointment we made knowing we'd never, well hardly ever. Too dear too near to home sweet home. Sees me, does she? Looks a fright in the day. Face like dip. Damn her. O, well, she has to live like the rest. Look in here.

In Lionel Marks's antique saleshop window haughty Henry Lionel Leopold dear Henry Flower earnestly Mr Leopold Bloom envisaged battered candlesticks melodeon oozing maggoty blowbags. Bargain: six bob. Might learn to play. Cheap. Let her pass. Course everything is dear if you don't want it. That's what good salesman is. Make you buy what he wants to sell. Chap sold me the Swedish razor he shaved me with. Wanted to charge me for the edge he gave it. She's passing now. Six bob.

Must be the cider or perhaps the burgund.

Near bronze from anear near gold from afar they chinked their clinking glasses all, brighteyed and gallant, before bronze Lydia's tempting last rose of summer, rose of Castile. First Lid, De, Cow, Ker, Doll, a fifth: Lidwell, Si Dedalus, Bob Cowley, Kernan and big Ben Dollard.

Tap. A youth entered a lonely Ormond hall.

Bloom viewed a gallant pictured hero in Lionel Marks's window. Robert Emmet's last words. Seven last words. Of Meyerbeer that is.

—True men like you men.

—Ay, ay, Ben.

—Will lift your glass with us.

They lifted.

Tschink. Tschunk.

Tip. An unseeing stripling stood in the door. He saw not bronze. He saw not gold. Nor Ben nor Bob nor Tom nor Si nor George nor tanks nor Richie nor Pat. Hee hee hee hee. He did not see.

Seabloom, greaseabloom viewed last words. Softly. *When my country takes her place among.*

Prrprr.

Must be the bur.

Fff! Oo. Rrpr.

Nations of the earth. No-one behind. She's passed. *Then and not till then.* Tram kran kran kran. Good oppor. Coming. Krandlkrankran. I'm sure it's the burgund. Yes. One, two. *Let my epitaph be.* Kraaaaaa. *Written. I have.*

Pprrpffrrppffff.

Done.

12

I was just passing the time of day with old Troy of the D.
M. P. at the corner of Arbour hill there and be damned
but a bloody sweep came along and he near drove his
gear into my eye. I turned around to let him have the weight
of my tongue when who should I see dodging along Stony
Batter only Joe Hynes.

—Lo, Joe, says I. How are you blowing? Did you see
that bloody chimneysweep near shove my eye out with his
brush?

—Soot's luck, says Joe. Who's the old ballocks you were
talking to?

—Old Troy, says I, was in the force. I'm on two
minds not to give that fellow in charge for obstructing the
thoroughfare with his brooms and ladders.

—What are you doing round those parts? says Joe.

—Devil a much, says I. There's a bloody big foxy thief
beyond by the garrison church at the corner of Chicken
lane—old Troy was just giving me a wrinkle about him—
lifted any God's quantity of tea and sugar to pay three bob
a week said he had a farm in the county Down off a hop-
of-my-thumb by the name of Moses Herzog over there near
Heytesbury street.

—Circumcised? says Joe.

—Ay, says I. A bit off the top. An old plumber named
Geraghty. I'm hanging on to his taw now for the past
fortnight and I can't get a penny out of him.

—That the lay you're on now? says Joe.

—Ay, says I. How are the mighty fallen! Collector of
bad and doubtful debts. But that's the most notorious bloody
robber you'd meet in a day's walk and the face on him all
pockmarks would hold a shower of rain. *Tell him,* says he, *I
dare him,* says he, *and I doubledare him to send you round here again
or if he does,* says he, *I'll have him summonsed up before the court, so*

I will, for trading without a licence. And he after stuffing himself till he's fit to burst. Jesus, I had to laugh at the little jewy getting his shirt out. *He drink me my teas. He eat me my sugars. Because he no pay me my moneys?*

For nonperishable goods bought of Moses Herzog, of 13 Saint Kevin's parade in the city of Dublin, Wood quay ward, merchant, hereinafter called the vendor, and sold and delivered to Michael E. Geraghty, esquire, of 29 Arbour hill in the city of Dublin, Arran quay ward, gentleman, hereinafter called the purchaser, videlicet, five pounds avoirdupois of first choice tea at three shillings and no pence per pound avoirdupois and three stone avoirdupois of sugar, crushed crystal, at threepence per pound avoirdupois, the said purchaser debtor to the said vendor of one pound five shillings and sixpence sterling for value received which amount shall be paid by said purchaser to said vendor in weekly instalments every seven calendar days of three shillings and no pence sterling: and the said nonperishable goods shall not be pawned or pledged or sold or otherwise alienated by the said purchaser but shall be and remain and be held to be the sole and exclusive property of the said vendor to be disposed of at his good will and pleasure until the said amount shall have been duly paid by the said purchaser to the said vendor in the manner herein set forth as this day hereby agreed between the said vendor, his heirs, successors, trustees and assigns of the one part and the said purchaser, his heirs, successors, trustees and assigns of the other part.

—Are you a strict t. t.? says Joe.

—Not taking anything between drinks, says I.

—What about paying our respects to our friend? says Joe.

—Who? says I. Sure, he's out in John of God's off his head, poor man.

—Drinking his own stuff? says Joe.

—Ay, says I. Whisky and water on the brain.

—Come around to Barney Kiernan's, says Joe. I want to see the citizen.

—Barney mavourneen's be it, says I. Anything strange or wonderful, Joe?

—Not a word, says Joe. I was up at that meeting in the City Arms.

—What was that, Joe? says I.

—Cattle traders, says Joe, about the foot and mouth disease. I want to give the citizen the hard word about it.

So we went around by the Linenhall barracks and the back of the courthouse talking of one thing or another. Decent fellow Joe when he has it but sure like that he never has it. Jesus, I couldn't get over that bloody foxy Geraghty, the daylight robber. For trading without a licence, says he.

In Inisfail the fair there lies a land, the land of holy Michan. There rises a watchtower beheld of men afar. There sleep the mighty dead as in life they slept, warriors and princes of high renown. A pleasant land it is in sooth of murmuring waters, fishful streams where sport the gurnard, the plaice, the roach, the halibut, the gibbed haddock, the grilse, the dab, the brill, the flounder, the pollock, the mixed coarse fish generally and other denizens of the aqueous kingdom too numerous to be enumerated. In the mild breezes of the west and of the east the lofty trees wave in different directions their firstclass foliage, the wafty sycamore, the Lebanonian cedar, the exalted planetree, the eugenic eucalyptus and other ornaments of the arboreal world with which that region is thoroughly well supplied. Lovely maidens sit in close proximity to the roots of the lovely trees singing the most lovely songs while they play with all kinds of lovely objects as for example golden ingots, silvery fishes, crans of herrings, drafts of eels, codlings, creels of fingerlings, purple seagems and playful insects. And heroes voyage from afar to woo them, from Eblana to Slievemargy, the peerless princes of unfettered Munster and of Connacht the just and of smooth sleek Leinster and of Cruachan's land and of Armagh the splendid and of the noble district of Boyle, princes, the sons of kings.

And there rises a shining palace whose crystal glittering roof is seen by mariners who traverse the extensive sea in barks built expressly for that purpose, and thither come all herds and fatlings and firstfruits of that land for O'Connell Fitzsimon takes toll of them, a chieftain descended from chieftains. Thither the extremely large wains bring foison of the fields, flaskets of cauliflowers, floats of spinach, pineapple chunks, Rangoon beans, strikes of tomatoes, drums of figs, drills of Swedes, spherical potatoes and tallies of iridescent kale, York and Savoy, and trays of onions, pearls of the earth, and punnets of mushrooms and custard marrows and fat vetches and bere and rape and red green yellow brown russet sweet big bitter ripe pomellated apples and chips of strawberries and sieves of gooseberries, pulpy and pelurious, and strawberries fit for princes and raspberries from their canes.

—I dare him, says he, and I doubledare him. Come out here, Geraghty, you notorious bloody hill and dale robber!

And by that way wend the herds innumerable of bellwethers and flushed ewes and shearling rams and lambs and stubble geese and medium steers and roaring mares and polled calves and longwools and storesheep and Cuffe's prime springers and culls and sowpigs and baconhogs and the various different varieties of highly distinguished swine and Angus heifers and polly bulllocks of immaculate pedigree together with prime premiated milchcows and beeves: and there is ever heard a trampling, cackling, roaring, lowing, bleating, bellowing, rumbling, grunting, champing, chewing, of sheep and pigs and heavyhooved kine from pasturelands of Lusk and Rush and Carrickmines and from the streamy vales of Thomond, from the M'Gillicuddy's reeks the inaccessible and lordly Shannon the unfathomable, and from the gentle declivities of the place of the race of Kiar, their udders distended with superabundance of milk and butts of butter and rennets of cheese and farmer's firkins and targets of lamb and crannocks of corn and oblong eggs in great hundreds, various in size, the agate with this dun.

So we turned into Barney Kiernan's and there, sure enough, was the citizen up in the corner having a great confab with himself and that bloody mangy mongrel, Garryowen, and he waiting for what the sky would drop in the way of drink.

—There he is, says I, in his gloryhole, with his cruiskeen lawn and his load of papers, working for the cause.

The bloody mongrel let a grouse out of him would give you the creeps. Be a corporal work of mercy if someone would take the life of that bloody dog. I'm told for a fact he ate a good part of the breeches off a constabulary man in Santry that came round one time with a blue paper about a licence.

—Stand and deliver, says he.

—That's all right, citizen, says Joe. Friends here.

—Pass, friends, says he.

Then he rubs his hand in his eye and says he:

—What's your opinion of the times?

Doing the rapparee and Rory of the hill. But, begob, Joe was equal to the occasion.

—I think the markets are on a rise, says he, sliding his hand down his fork.

So begob the citizen claps his paw on his knee and he says:
—Foreign wars is the cause of it.
And says Joe, sticking his thumb in his pocket:
—It's the Russians wish to tyrannise.
—Arrah, give over your bloody codding, Joe, says I. I've a thirst
on me I wouldn't sell for half a crown.
—Give it a name, citizen, says Joe.
—Wine of the country, says he.
—What's yours? says Joe.
—Ditto MacAnaspey, says I.
—Three pints, Terry, says Joe. And how's the old heart, citizen?
says he.
—Never better, a chara, says he. What Garry? Are we going to
win? Eh?
And with that he took the bloody old towser by the scruff of the
neck and, by Jesus, he near throttled him.
The figure seated on a large boulder at the foot of a round tower
was that of a broadshouldered deepchested stronglimbed frankeyed
redhaired freelyfreckled shaggybearded widemouthed largenosed
longheaded deepvoiced barekneed brawnyhanded hairylegged
ruddyfaced sinewyarmed hero. From shoulder to shoulder he measured
several ells and his rocklike mountainous knees were covered, as was
likewise the rest of his body wherever visible, with a strong growth
of tawny prickly hair in hue and toughness similar to the mountain
gorse (Ulex Europeus). The widewinged nostrils, from which bristles of
the same tawny hue projected, were of such capaciousness that within
their cavernous obscurity the fieldlark might easily have lodged her
nest. The eyes in which a tear and a smile strove ever for the mastery
were of the dimensions of a goodsized cauliflower. A powerful
current of warm breath issued at regular intervals from the profound
cavity of his mouth while in rhythmic resonance the loud strong hale
reverberations of his formidable heart thundered rumblingly causing
the ground, the summit of the lofty tower and the still loftier walls of
the cave to vibrate and tremble.
He wore a long unsleeved garment of recently flayed oxhide
reaching to the knees in a loose kilt and this was bound about his
middle by a girdle of plaited straw and rushes. Beneath this he wore
trews of deerskin, roughly stitched with gut. His nether extremities
were encased in high Balbriggan buskins dyed in lichen purple, the feet

being shod with brogues of salted cowhide laced with the windpipe of the same beast. From his girdle hung a row of seastones which jangled at every movement of his portentous frame and on these were graven with rude yet striking art the tribal images of many Irish heroes and heroines of antiquity, Cuchulin, Conn of hundred battles, Niall of nine hostages, Brian of Kincora, the ardri Malachi, Art MacMurragh, Shane O'Neill, Father John Murphy, Owen Roe, Patrick Sarsfield, Red Hugh O'Donnell, Red Jim MacDermott, Soggarth Eoghan O'Growney, Michael Dwyer, Francy Higgins, Henry Joy M'Cracken, Goliath, Horace Wheatley, Thomas Conneff, Peg Woffington, the Village Blacksmith, Captain Moonlight, Captain Boycott, Dante Alighieri, Christopher Columbus, S. Fursa, S. Brendan, Marshal MacMahon, Charlemagne, Theobald Wolfe Tone, the Mother of the Maccabees, the Last of the Mohicans, the Rose of Castile, the Man for Galway, The Man that Broke the Bank at Monte Carlo, The Man in the Gap, The Woman Who Didn't, Benjamin Franklin, Napoleon Bonaparte, John L. Sullivan, Cleopatra, Savourneen Deelish, Julius Caesar, Paracelsus, sir Thomas Lipton, William Tell, Michelangelo Hayes, Muhammad, the Bride of Lammermoor, Peter the Hermit, Peter the Packer, Dark Rosaleen, Patrick W. Shakespeare, Brian Confucius, Murtagh Gutenberg, Patricio Velasquez, Captain Nemo, Tristan and Isolde, the first Prince of Wales, Thomas Cook and Son, the Bold Soldier Boy, Arrah na Pogue, Dick Turpin, Ludwig Beethoven, the Colleen Bawn, Waddler Healy, Angus the Culdee, Dolly Mount, Sidney Parade, Ben Howth, Valentine Greatrakes, Adam and Eve, Arthur Wellesley, Boss Croker, Herodotus, Jack the Giantkiller, Gautama Buddha, Lady Godiva, The Lily of Killarney, Balor of the Evil Eye, the Queen of Sheba, Acky Nagle, Joe Nagle, Alessandro Volta, Jeremiah O'Donovan Rossa, Don Philip O'Sullivan Beare. A couched spear of acuminated granite rested by him while at his feet reposed a savage animal of the canine tribe whose stertorous gasps announced that he was sunk in uneasy slumber, a supposition confirmed by hoarse growls and spasmodic movements which his master repressed from time to time by tranquilising blows of a mighty cudgel rudely fashioned out of paleolithic stone.

So anyhow Terry brought the three pints Joe was standing and begob the sight nearly left my eyes when I saw him land out a quid. O, as true as I'm telling you. A goodlooking sovereign.

—And there's more where that came from, says he.

—Were you robbing the poorbox, Joe? says I.

—Sweat of my brow, says Joe. 'Twas the prudent member gave me the wheeze.

—I saw him before I met you, says I, sloping around by Pill lane and Greek street with his cod's eye counting up all the guts of the fish.

Who comes through Michan's land, bedight in sable armour? O'Bloom, the son of Rory: it is he. Impervious to fear is Rory's son: he of the prudent soul.

—For the old woman of Prince's street, says the citizen, the subsidised organ. The pledgebound party on the floor of the house. And look at this blasted rag, says he. Look at this, says he. *The Irish Independent,* if you please, founded by Parnell to be the workingman's friend. Listen to the births and deaths in the *Irish all for Ireland Independent,* and I'll thank you and the marriages.

And he starts reading them out:

—Gordon, Barnfield crescent, Exeter; Redmayne of Iffley, Saint Anne's on Sea: the wife of William T Redmayne of a son. How's that, eh? Wright and Flint, Vincent and Gillett to Rotha Marion daughter of Rosa and the late George Alfred Gillett, 179 Clapham road, Stockwell, Playwood and Ridsdale at Saint Jude's, Kensington by the very reverend Dr Forrest, dean of Worcester. Eh? Deaths. Bristow, at Whitehall lane, London: Carr, Stoke Newington, of gastritis and heart disease: Cockburn, at the Moat house, Chepstow . . .

—I know that fellow, says Joe, from bitter experience.

—Cockburn. Dimsey, wife of David Dimsey, late of the admiralty: Miller, Tottenham, aged eightyfive: Welsh, June 12, at 35 Canning street, Liverpool, Isabella Helen. How's that for a national press, eh, my brown son! How's that for Martin Murphy, the Bantry jobber?

—Ah, well, says Joe, handing round the boose. Thanks be to God they had the start of us. Drink that, citizen.

—I will, says he, honourable person.

—Health, Joe, says I. And all down the form.

Ah! Ow! Don't be talking! I was blue mouldy for the want of that pint. Declare to God I could hear it hit the pit of my stomach with a click.

And lo, as they quaffed their cup of joy, a godlike messenger came swiftly in, radiant as the eye of heaven, a comely youth and behind him there passed an elder of noble gait and countenance, bearing the sacred scrolls of law and with him his lady wife a dame of peerless lineage, fairest of her race.

Little Alf Bergan popped in round the door and hid behind Barney's snug, squeezed up with the laughing. And who was sitting up there in the corner that I hadn't seen snoring drunk blind to the world only Bob Doran. I didn't know what was up and Alf kept making signs out of the door. And begob what was it only that bloody old pantaloon Denis Breen in his bathslippers with two bloody big books tucked under his oxter and the wife hotfoot after him, unfortunate wretched woman, trotting like a poodle. I thought Alf would split.

—Look at him, says he. Breen. He's traipsing all round Dublin with a postcard someone sent him with U.P.: up on it to take a li . . .

And he doubled up.

—Take a what? says I.

—Libel action, says he, for ten thousand pounds.

—O hell! says I.

The bloody mongrel began to growl that'd put the fear of God in you seeing something was up but the citizen gave him a kick in the ribs.

—*Bi i dho husht,* says he.

—Who? says Joe.

—Breen, says Alf. He was in John Henry Menton's and then he went round to Collis and Ward's and then Tom Rochford met him and sent him round to the subsheriff's for a lark. O God, I've a pain laughing. U. P.: up. The long fellow gave him an eye as good as a process and now the bloody old lunatic is gone round to Green street to look for a G man.

—When is long John going to hang that fellow in Mountjoy? says Joe.

—Bergan, says Bob Doran, waking up. Is that Alf Bergan?

—Yes, says Alf. Hanging? Wait till I show you. Here, Terry, give us a pony. That bloody old fool! Ten thousand pounds. You should have seen long John's eye. U.P. . . .

And he started laughing.

—Who are you laughing at? says Bob Doran. Is that Bergan?

—Hurry up, Terry boy, says Alf.

Terence O'Ryan heard him and straightway brought him a crystal cup full of the foamy ebon ale which the noble twin brothers Bungiveagh and Bungardilaun brew ever in their divine alevats, cunning as the sons of deathless Leda. For they garner the succulent berries of the hop and mass and sift and bruise and brew them and they mix therewith sour juices and bring the must to the sacred fire and cease not night or day from their toil, those cunning brothers, lords of the vat.

Then did you, chivalrous Terence, hand forth, as to the manner born, that nectarous beverage and you offered the crystal cup to him that thirsted, the soul of chivalry, in beauty akin to the immortals.

But he, the young chief of the O'Bergan's, could ill brook to be outdone in generous deeds but gave therefor with gracious gesture a testoon of costliest bronze. Thereon embossed in excellent smithwork was seen the image of a queen of regal port, scion of the house of Brunswick, Victoria her name, Her Most Excellent Majesty, by grace of God of the United Kingdom of Great Britain and Ireland and of the British dominions beyond the sea, queen, defender of the faith, Empress of India, even she, who bore rule, a victress over many peoples, the wellbeloved, for they knew and loved her from the rising of the sun to the going down thereof, the pale, the dark, the ruddy and the ethiop.

—What's that bloody freemason doing, says the citizen, prowling up and down outside?

—What's that? says Joe.

—Here you are, says Alf, chucking out the rhino. Talking about hanging, I'll show you something you never saw. Hangmen's letters. Look at here.

So he took a bundle of wisps of letters and envelopes out of his pocket.

—Are you codding? says I.

—Honest injun, says Alf. Read them.

So Joe took up the letters.

—Who are you laughing at? says Bob Doran.

So I saw there was going to be a bit of a dust. Bob's a queer chap when the porter's up in him so says I just to make talk:

—How's Willy Murray those times, Alf?

—I don't know, says Alf. I saw him just now in Capel street with Paddy Dignam. Only I was running after that . . .

—You what? says Joe, throwing down the letters. With who?

—With Dignam, says Alf.

—Is it Paddy? says Joe.

—Yes, says Alf. Why?

—Don't you know he's dead? says Joe.

—Paddy Dignam dead! says Alf.

—Ay, says Joe.

—Sure I'm after seeing him not five minutes ago, says Alf, as plain as a pikestaff.

—Who's dead? says Bob Doran.

—You saw his ghost then, says Joe, God between us and harm.

—What? says Alf. Good Christ, only five . . . What? . . . And Willy Murray with him, the two of them there near whatdoyoucallhim's . . . What? Dignam dead?

—What about Dignam? says Bob Doran. Who's talking about . . .?

—Dead! says Alf. He's no more dead than you are.

—Maybe so, says Joe. They took the liberty of burying him this morning anyhow.

—Paddy? says Alf.

—Ay, says Joe. He paid the debt of nature, God be merciful to him.

—Good Christ! says Alf.

Begob he was what you might call flabbergasted.

In the darkness spirit hands were felt to flutter and when prayer by tantras had been directed to the proper quarter a faint but increasing luminosity of ruby light became gradually visible, the apparition of the etheric double being particularly lifelike owing to the discharge of jivic rays from the crown of the head and face. Communication was effected through the pituitary body and also by means of the orangefiery and scarlet rays emanating from the sacral region and solar plexus. Questioned by his earthname as to his whereabouts in the heavenworld he stated that he was now on the path of prālāyā or return but was still submitted to trial at the hands of certain bloodthirsty entities on the lower astral levels. In reply to a question as to his first sensations in the great divide beyond he stated that previously he had seen as in a glass darkly but that those who had passed over had summit possibilities of atmic development opened up to them. Interrogated as to whether life there resembled our experience in the flesh he stated that he had heard from more favoured beings now in the spirit that their abodes were equipped with every modern home comfort such as tālāfānā, ālāvātār, hātākāldā, wātāklāsāt and that the highest adepts were steeped in waves of volupcy of the very purest nature. Having requested a quart of buttermilk this was brought and evidently afforded relief. Asked if he had any message for the living he exhorted all who were still at the wrong side of Māyā to acknowledge the true path for it was reported in devanic circles that Mars and Jupiter were out for mischief on the eastern angle where the ram has power. It was then queried whether there were any special desires on the part of the defunct and the reply was: *We greet you, friends of earth, who are still in the body. Mind C. K. doesn't pile it on.* It was ascertained that the reference was to Mr Cornelius Kelleher, manager of Messrs H. J. O'Neill's popular funeral establishment, a personal friend of the defunct, who had been responsible for the carrying out of the interment arrangements. Before departing he requested that it should be told to his dear son Patsy that the other boot which he had been looking for was at present under the commode in the return room and that the pair should be sent to Cullen's to be soled only as the heels were still good. He stated that this had greatly perturbed his peace of mind in the other region and earnestly requested that his desire should be made known.

Assurances were given that the matter would be attended to and it was intimated that this had given satisfaction.

He is gone from mortal haunts: O'Dignam, sun of our morning. Fleet was his foot on the bracken: Patrick of the beamy brow. Wail, Banba, with your wind: and wail, O ocean, with your whirlwind.

—There he is again, says the citizen, staring out.

—Who? says I.

—Bloom, says he. He's on point duty up and down there for the last ten minutes.

And, begob, I saw his physog do a peep in and then slidder off again.

Little Alf was knocked bawways. Faith, he was.

—Good Christ! says he. I could have sworn it was him.

And says Bob Doran, with the hat on the back of his poll, lowest blackguard in Dublin when he's under the influence:

—Who said Christ is good?

—I beg your parsnips, says Alf.

—Is that a good Christ, says Bob Doran, to take away poor little Willy Dignam?

—Ah, well, says Alf, trying to pass it off. He's over all his troubles.

But Bob Doran shouts out of him.

—He's a bloody ruffian, I say, to take away poor little Willy Dignam.

Terry came down and tipped him the wink to keep quiet, that they didn't want that kind of talk in a respectable licensed premises. And Bob Doran starts doing the weeps about Paddy Dignam, true as you're there.

—The finest man, says he, snivelling, the finest purest character. The tear is bloody near your eye. Talking through his bloody hat. Fitter for him go home to the little sleepwalking bitch he married, Mooney, the bumbailiff's daughter, mother kept a kip in Hardwicke street, that used to be stravaging about the landings Bantam Lyons told me that was stopping there at two in the morning without a stitch on her, exposing her person, open to all comers, fair field and no favour.

—The noblest, the truest, says he. And he's gone, poor little Willy, poor little Paddy Dignam.

And mournful and with a heavy heart he bewept the extinction of that beam of heaven.

Old Garryowen started growling again at Bloom that was skeezing round the door.

—Come in, come on, he won't eat you, says the citizen.

So Bloom slopes in with his cod's eye on the dog and he asks Terry was Martin Cunningham there.

—O, Christ M'Keown, says Joe, reading one of the letters. Listen to this, will you?

And he starts reading out one.

> 7 Hunter Street,
> Liverpool.

To the High Sheriff of Dublin,
> *Dublin.*

Honoured sir i beg to offer my services in the abovementioned painful case i hanged Joe Gann in Bootle jail on the 12 of Febuary 1900 and i hanged . . .

—Show us, Joe, says I.

—. . . *private Arthur Chace for fowl murder of Jessie Tilsit in Pentonville prison and i was assistant when . . .*

—Jesus, says I.

—. . . *Billington executed the awful murderer Toad Smith . . .*

The citizen made a grab at the letter.

—Hold hard, says Joe, *i have a special nack of putting the noose once in he can't get out hoping to be favoured i remain, honoured sir, my terms is five ginnees.*

H. Rumbold,
Master Barber.

—And a barbarous bloody barbarian he is too, says the citizen.

—And the dirty scrawl of the wretch, says Joe. Here, says he, take them to hell out of my sight, Alf. Hello, Bloom, says he, what will you have?

So they started arguing about the point, Bloom saying he wouldn't and he couldn't and excuse him no offence and all to that and then he said well he'd just take a cigar. Gob, he's a prudent member and no mistake.

—Give us one of your prime stinkers, Terry, says Joe.

And Alf was telling us there was one chap sent in a mourning card with a black border round it.

—They're all barbers, says he, from the black country that would hang their own fathers for five quid down and travelling expenses.

And he was telling us there's two fellows waiting below to pull his heels down when he gets the drop and choke him properly and then they chop up the rope after and sell the bits for a few bob a skull.

In the dark land they bide, the vengeful knights of the razor. Their deadly coil they grasp: yea, and therein they lead to Erebus whatsoever wight hath done a deed of blood for I will on nowise suffer it even so saith the Lord.

So they started talking about capital punishment and of course Bloom comes out with the why and the wherefore and all the codology of the business and the old dog smelling him all the time I'm told those jewies does have a sort of a queer odour coming off them for dogs about I don't know what all deterrent effect and so forth and so on.

—There's one thing it hasn't a deterrent effect on, says Alf.

—What's that? says Joe.

—The poor bugger's tool that's being hanged, says Alf.

—That so? says Joe.

—God's truth, says Alf. I heard that from the head warder that was in Kilmainham when they hanged Joe Brady, the invincible. He

323

told me when they cut him down after the drop it was standing up in their faces like a poker.

—Ruling passion strong in death, says Joe, as someone said.

—That can be explained by science, says Bloom. It's only a natural phenomenon, don't you see, because on account of the . . .

And then he starts with his jawbreakers about phenomenon and science and this phenomenon and the other phenomenon.

The distinguished scientist Herr Professor Luitpold Blumenduft tendered medical evidence to the effect that the instantaneous fracture of the cervical vertebrae and consequent scission of the spinal cord would, according to the best approved tradition of medical science, be calculated to inevitably produce in the human subject a violent ganglionic stimulus of the nerve centres of the genital apparatus, thereby causing the elastic pores of the *corpora cavernosa* to rapidly dilate in such a way as to instantaneously facilitate the flow of blood to that part of the human anatomy known as the penis or male organ resulting in the phenomenon which has been denominated by the faculty a morbid upwards and outwards philoprogenitive erection *in articulo mortis per diminutionem capitis.*

So of course the citizen was only waiting for the wink of the word and he starts gassing out of him about the invincibles and the old guard and the men of sixtyseven and who fears to speak of ninetyeight and Joe with him about all the fellows that were hanged, drawn and transported for the cause by drumhead courtmartial and a new Ireland and new this, that and the other. Talking about new Ireland he ought to go and get a new dog so he ought. Mangy ravenous brute sniffing and sneezing all round the place and scratching his scabs. And round he goes to Bob Doran that was standing Alf a half one sucking up for what he could get. So of course Bob Doran starts doing the bloody fool with him:

—Give us the paw! Give the paw, doggy! Good old doggy! Give the paw here! Give us the paw!

Arrah, bloody end to the paw he'd paw and Alf trying to keep him from tumbling off the bloody stool atop of the bloody old dog and he talking all kinds of drivel about training by kindness and thoroughbred dog and intelligent dog: give you the bloody pip. Then he starts scraping a few bits of old biscuit out of the bottom of a Jacobs' tin he told Terry to bring. Gob, he golloped it down like old boots and his tongue hanging out of him a yard long for more. Near ate the tin and all, hungry bloody mongrel.

And the citizen and Bloom having an argument about the point, the brothers Sheares and Wolfe Tone beyond on Arbour Hill and Robert Emmet and die for your country, the Tommy Moore touch about Sara Curran and she's far from the land. And Bloom, of course, with his knockmedown cigar putting on swank with his lardy face. Phenomenon! The fat heap he married is a nice old phenomenon with a back on her like a ballalley. Time they were stopping up in the *City Arms* pisser Burke told me there was an old one there with a cracked loodheramaun of a nephew and Bloom trying to get the soft side of her doing the mollycoddle playing bézique to come in for a bit of the wampum in her will and not eating meat of a Friday because the old one was always thumping her craw and taking the lout out for a walk. And one time he led him the rounds of Dublin and, by the holy farmer, he never cried crack till he brought him home as drunk as a boiled owl and he said he did it to teach him the evils of alcohol and by herrings, if the three women didn't near roast him, it's a queer story, the old one, Bloom's wife and Mrs O'Dowd that kept the hotel. Jesus, I had to laugh at pisser Burke taking them off chewing the fat. And Bloom with his *but don't you see?* and *but on the other hand.* And sure, more be token, the lout I'm told was in Power's after, the blender's, round in Cope street going home footless in a cab five times in the week after drinking his way through all the samples in the bloody establishment. Phenomenon!

—The memory of the dead, says the citizen taking up his pintglass and glaring at Bloom.

—Ay, ay, says Joe.

—You don't grasp my point, says Bloom. What I mean is . . .

—*Sinn Fein!* says the citizen. *Sinn Fein amhain!* The friends we love are by our side and the foes we hate before us.

The last farewell was affecting in the extreme. From the belfries far and near the funereal deathbell tolled unceasingly while all around the gloomy precincts rolled the ominous warning of a hundred muffled drums punctuated by the hollow booming of pieces of ordnance. The deafening claps of thunder and the dazzling flashes of lightning which lit up the ghastly scene testified that the artillery of heaven had lent its supernatural pomp to the already gruesome spectacle. A torrential rain poured down from the floodgates of the angry heavens upon the bared heads of the assembled multitude which numbered at the lowest computation five hundred thousand persons. A posse of Dublin

Metropolitan police superintended by the Chief Commissioner in person maintained order in the vast throng for whom the York street brass and reed band whiled away the intervening time by admirably rendering on their blackdraped instruments the matchless melody endeared to us from the cradle by Speranza's plaintive muse. Special quick excursion trains and upholstered charabancs had been provided for the comfort of our country cousins of whom there were large contingents. Considerable amusement was caused by the favourite Dublin streetsingers L-n-h-n and M-ll-g-n who sang *The Night before Larry was stretched* in their usual mirth-provoking fashion. Our two inimitable drolls did a roaring trade with their broadsheets among lovers of the comedy element and nobody who has a corner in his heart for real Irish fun without vulgarity will grudge them their hardearned pennies. The children of the Male and Female Foundling Hospital who thronged the windows overlooking the scene were delighted with this unexpected addition to the day's entertainment and a word of praise is due to the Little Sisters of the Poor for their excellent idea of affording the poor fatherless and motherless children a genuinely instructive treat. The viceregal houseparty which included many wellknown ladies was chaperoned by Their Excellencies to the most favourable positions on the grandstand while the picturesque foreign delegation known as the Friends of the Emerald Isle was accommodated on a tribune directly opposite. The delegation, present in full force, consisted of Commendatore Bacibaci Beninobenone (the semiparalysed *doyen* of the party who had to be assisted to his seat by the aid of a powerful steam crane), Monsieur Pierrepaul Petitépatant, the Grandjoker Vladinmire Pokethankertscheff, the Archjoker Leopold Rudolph von Schwanzenbad-Hodenthaler, Countess Marha Virága Kisászony Putrápesthi, Hiram Y. Bomboost, Count Athanatos Karamelopulos, Ali Baba Backsheesh Rahat Lokum Effendi, Señor Hidalgo Caballero Don Pecadillo y Palabras y Paternoster de la Malora de la Malaria, Hokopoko Harakiri, Hi Hung Chang, Olaf Kobberkeddelsen, Mynheer Trik van Trumps, Pan Poleaxe Paddyrisky, Goosepond Prhklstr Kratchinabritchisitch, Borus Hupinkoff, Herr Hurhausdirektorpresident Hans Chuechli-Steuerli, Nationalgymnasiummuseumsanatoriumandsuspensoriums ordinaryprivatdocentgeneralhistoryspecialprofessordoctor Kriegfried Ueberallgemein. All the delegates without exception expressed themselves in the strongest possible heterogeneous terms concerning the nameless barbarity which they had been called upon to witness. An animated altercation (in which all took part) ensued among the F. O. T. E. I. as to whether the eighth or the ninth of March was the correct date of the birth of Ireland's patron saint. In the course of the argument cannonballs, scimitars, boomerangs, blunderbusses, stinkpots, meatchoppers, umbrellas, catapults, knuckledusters, sandbags, lumps of pig iron were resorted to and blows were freely exchanged. The baby policeman, Constable MacFadden, summoned by special courier from Booterstown, quickly restored order and with lightning promptitude proposed the seventeenth of the month as a solution equally honourable for both contending parties. The readywitted ninefooter's suggestion at once appealed to all and was unanimously accepted. Constable MacFadden was heartily congratulated by all the F. O. T. E. I., several of whom were bleeding profusely. Commendatore Beninobenone having been extricated from underneath the presidential armchair, it was explained by his legal adviser Avvocato Pagamimi that the various articles secreted in his thirtytwo pockets had been abstracted by him during the affray from the pockets of his junior colleagues in the hope of bringing them to their senses. The objects (which included several hundred ladies' and gentlemen's gold and silver watches) were promptly restored to their rightful owners and general harmony reigned supreme.

Quietly, unassumingly Rumbold stepped on to the scaffold in faultless morning dress and wearing his favourite flower, the *Gladiolus Cruentus*. He announced his presence by that gentle Rumboldian cough which so many have tried (unsuccessfully) to imitate—short, painstaking yet withal so characteristic of the man. The arrival of the world-renowned headsman was greeted by a roar of acclamation from the huge concourse, the viceregal ladies waving their handkerchiefs in their excitement while the even more excitable foreign delegates cheered vociferously in a medley of cries, *hoch, banzai, eljen, zivio, chinchin, polla kronia, hiphip, vive, Allah*, amid which the ringing *evviva* of the delegate of the land of song (a high double F recalling those piercingly lovely notes with which the eunuch Catalani beglamoured our greatgreatgrandmothers) was easily distinguishable. It was exactly seventeen o'clock. The signal for prayer was then promptly given by megaphone and in an instant all heads were bared, the commendatore's patriarchal sombrero, which has been in the possession of his family since the revolution of Rienzi, being removed by his medical adviser in attendance, Dr Pippi. The learned prelate who administered the last comforts of holy religion to the hero martyr when about to pay the death penalty knelt in a most christian spirit in a pool of rainwater, his cassock above his hoary head, and offered up to the throne of grace fervent prayers of supplication. Hard by the block stood the grim figure of the executioner, his visage being concealed in a tengallon pot with two circular perforated apertures through which his eyes glowered furiously. As he awaited the fatal signal he tested the edge of his horrible weapon by honing it upon his brawny forearm or decapitated in rapid succession a flock of sheep which had been provided by the admirers of his fell but necessary office. On a handsome mahogany table near him were neatly arranged the quartering knife, the various finely tempered disembowelling appliances (specially supplied by the worldfamous firm of cutlers, Messrs John Round and Sons, Sheffield), a terra cotta saucepan for the reception of the duodenum, colon, blind intestine and appendix etc when successfully extracted and two commodious milkjugs destined to receive the most precious blood of the most precious victim. The housesteward of the amalgamated cats' and dogs' home was in attendance to convey these vessels when replenished to that beneficent institution. Quite an excellent repast consisting of rashers and eggs, fried steak and onions, done to a nicety, delicious hot breakfast rolls and invigorating tea had been considerately provided by the authorities for the consumption of the central figure of the tragedy who was in capital spirits when prepared for death and evinced the keenest interest in the proceedings from beginning to end but he, with an abnegation rare in these our times, rose nobly to the occasion and expressed the dying wish (immediately acceded to) that the meal should be divided in aliquot parts among the members of the sick and indigent roomkeepers' association as a token of his regard and esteem. The *nec* and *non plus ultra* of emotion were reached when the blushing bride elect burst her way through the serried ranks of the bystanders and flung herself upon the muscular bosom of him who was about to be launched into eternity for her sake. The hero folded her willowy form in a loving embrace murmuring fondly *Sheila, my own.* Encouraged by this use of her christian name she kissed passionately all the various suitable areas of his person which the decencies of prison garb permitted her ardour to reach. She swore to him as they mingled the salt streams of their tears that she would ever cherish his memory, that she would never forget her hero boy who went to his death with a song on his lips as if he were but going to a hurling match in Clonturk park. She brought back to his recollection the happy days of blissful childhood together on the banks of Anna Liffey when they had indulged in the innocent pastimes of the young and, oblivious of the dreadful present, they both laughed heartily, all the spectators, including the venerable pastor, joining in the general merriment. That monster audience simply rocked with delight. But anon they were overcome with grief and clasped their hands for the last time. A fresh torrent of tears burst from their lachrymal ducts and the vast concourse of people, touched to the inmost core, broke into heartrending sobs, not the least affected being the aged prebendary himself. Big strong men, officers of the peace and genial giants of the royal Irish constabulary, were making frank use of their handkerchiefs and it is safe to say that there was not a dry eye in that record assemblage. A most romantic incident occurred when a handsome young Oxford graduate, noted for his chivalry towards the fair sex, stepped forward and, presenting his visiting card, bankbook and genealogical tree, solicited the hand of the hapless young lady, requesting her to name the day, and was accepted on the spot. Every lady in the audience was presented with a tasteful souvenir of the occasion in the shape of a skull and crossbones brooch, a timely and generous act which evoked a fresh outburst of emotion: and when the gallant young Oxonian (the bearer, by the way, of one of the most timehonoured names in Albion's history) placed on the finger of his blushing *fiancée* an expensive engagement ring with emeralds set in the form of a fourleaved shamrock the excitement knew no bounds. Nay, even the stern provostmarshal, lieutenantcolonel Tomkin-Maxwell ffrenchmullan Tomlinson, who presided on the sad occasion, he who had blown a considerable number of sepoys from the cannonmouth without flinching, could not now restrain his natural emotion. With his mailed gauntlet he brushed away a furtive tear and was overheard, by those privileged burghers who happened to be in his immediate *entourage*, to murmur to himself in a faltering undertone:

—God blimey if she aint a clinker, that there bleeding tart. Blimey it makes me kind of bleeding cry, straight, it does, when I sees her cause I thinks of my old mashtub what's waiting for me down Limehouse way.

So then the citizen begins talking about the Irish language and the corporation meeting and all to that and the shoneens that can't speak their own language and Joe chipping in because he stuck someone for a quid and Bloom putting in his old goo with his twopenny stump that he cadged off of Joe and talking about the Gaelic league and the antitreating league and drink, the curse of Ireland. Antitreating is about the size of it. Gob, he'd let you pour all manner of drink down his throat till the Lord would call him before you'd ever see the froth of his pint. And one night I went in with a fellow into one of their musical evenings, song and dance about she could get up on a truss of hay she could my Maureen Lay and there was a fellow with a Ballyhooly blue ribbon badge spiffing out of him in Irish and a lot of colleen bawns going about with temperance beverages and selling medals and oranges and lemonade and a few old dry buns, gob, flahoolagh entertainment, don't be talking. Ireland sober is Ireland free. And then an old fellow starts blowing into his bagpipes and all the gougers shuffling their feet to the tune the old cow died of. And one or two sky pilots having an eye around that there was no goings on with the females, hitting below the belt.

So howandever, as I was saying, the old dog seeing the tin was empty starts mousing around by Joe and me. I'd train him by kindness, so I would, if he was my dog. Give him a rousing fine kick now and again where it wouldn't blind him.

—Afraid he'll bite you? says the citizen, jeering.

—No, says I. But he might take my leg for a lamppost.

So he calls the old dog over.

—What's on you, Garry? says he.

Then he starts hauling and mauling and talking to him in Irish and the old towser growling, letting on to answer, like a duet in the opera. Such growling you never heard as they let off between them. Someone that has nothing better to do ought to write a letter *pro bono publico* to the papers about the muzzling order for a dog the like of that. Growling and grousing and his eye all bloodshot from the drouth is in it and the hydrophobia dropping out of his jaws.

All those who are interested in the spread of human culture among the lower animals (and their name is legion) should make a point of not missing the really marvellous exhibition of cynanthropy given by the famous old Irish red setter wolfdog formerly known by the *sobriquet* of Garryowen and recently rechristened by his large circle of friends and acquaintances Owen Garry. The exhibition, which is the result of years of training by kindness and a carefully thoughtout dietary system, comprises, among other achievements, the recitation of verse. Our greatest living phonetic expert (wild horses shall not drag it from us!) has left no stone unturned in his efforts to delucidate and compare the verse recited and has found it bears a *striking* resemblance (the italics are ours) to the ranns of ancient Celtic bards. We are not speaking so much of those delightful lovesongs with which the writer who conceals his identity under the graceful pseudonym of the Little Sweet Branch has familiarised the bookloving world but rather (as a contributor D. O. C. points out in an interesting communication published by an evening contemporary) of the harsher and more personal note which is found in the satirical effusions of the famous Raftery and of Donal MacConsidine to say nothing of a more modern lyrist at present very much in the public eye. We subjoin a specimen which has been rendered into English by an eminent scholar whose name for the moment we are not at liberty to disclose though we believe that our readers will find the topical allusion rather more than an indication. The metrical system of the canine original, which recalls the intricate alliterative and isosyllabic rules of the Welsh englyn, is infinitely more complicated but we believe our readers will agree that the spirit has been well caught. Perhaps it should be added that the effect is greatly increased if Owen's verse be spoken somewhat slowly and indistinctly in a tone suggestive of suppressed rancour.

> *The curse of my curses*
> *Seven days every day*
> *And seven dry Thursdays*
> *On you, Barney Kiernan,*
> *Has no sup of water*
> *To cool my courage,*
> *And my guts red roaring*
> *After Lowry's lights.*

So he told Terry to bring some water for the dog and, gob, you could hear him lapping it up a mile off. And Joe asked him would he have another.

—I will, says he, *a chara*, to show there's no ill feeling.

Gob, he's not as green as he's cabbagelooking. Arsing around from one pub to another, leaving it to your own honour, with old

Giltrap's dog and getting fed up by the ratepayers and corporators. Entertainment for man and beast. And says Joe:

—Could you make a hole in another pint?

—Could a swim duck? says I.

—Same again, Terry, says Joe. Are you sure you won't have anything in the way of liquid refreshment? says he.

—Thank you, no, says Bloom. As a matter of fact I just wanted to meet Martin Cunningham, don't you see, about this insurance of poor Dignam's. Martin asked me to go to the house. You see, he, Dignam, I mean, didn't serve any notice of the assignment on the company at the time and nominally under the act the mortgagee can't recover on the policy.

—Holy Wars, says Joe, laughing, that's a good one if old Shylock is landed. So the wife comes out top dog, what?

—Well, that's a point, says Bloom, for the wife's admirers.

—Whose admirers? says Joe.

—The wife's advisers, I mean, says Bloom.

Then he starts all confused mucking it up about mortgagor under the act like the lord chancellor giving it out on the bench and for the benefit of the wife and that a trust is created but on the other hand that Dignam owed Bridgeman the money and if now the wife or the widow contested the mortgagee's right till he near had the head of me addled with his mortgagor under the act. He was bloody safe he wasn't run in himself under the act that time as a rogue and vagabond only he had a friend in court. Selling bazaar tickets or what do you call it royal Hungarian privileged lottery. True as you're there. O, commend me to an israelite! Royal and privileged Hungarian robbery.

So Bob Doran comes lurching around asking Bloom to tell Mrs Dignam he was sorry for her trouble and he was very sorry about the funeral and to tell her that he said and everyone who knew him said that there was never a truer, a finer than poor little Willy that's dead to tell her. Choking with bloody foolery. And shaking Bloom's hand doing the tragic to tell her that. Shake hands, brother. You're a rogue and I'm another.

—Let me, said he, so far presume upon our acquaintance which, however slight it may appear if judged by the standard of mere time, is founded, as I hope and believe, on a sentiment of mutual esteem as to request of you this favour. But, should I have overstepped the limits of reserve let the sincerity of my feelings be the excuse for my boldness.

—No, rejoined the other, I appreciate to the full the motives which actuate your conduct and I shall discharge the office you entrust to me consoled by the reflection that, though the errand be one of sorrow, this proof of your confidence sweetens in some measure the bitterness of the cup.

—Then suffer me to take your hand, said he. The goodness of your heart, I feel sure, will dictate to you better than my inadequate words the expressions which are most suitable to convey an emotion whose poignancy, were I to give vent to my feelings, would deprive me even of speech.

And off with him and out trying to walk straight. Boosed at five o'clock. Night he was near being lagged only Paddy Leonard knew the bobby, 14A. Blind to the world up in a shebeen in Bride street after closing time, fornicating with two shawls and a bully on guard, drinking porter out of teacups. And calling himself a Frenchy for the shawls, Joseph Manuo, and talking against the Catholic religion, and he serving mass in Adam and Eve's when he was young with his eyes shut, who wrote the new testament, and the old testament, and hugging and smugging. And the two shawls killed with the laughing, picking his pockets, the bloody fool and he spilling the porter all over the bed and the two shawls screeching laughing at one another. *How is your testament? Have you got an old testament?* Only Paddy was passing there, I tell you what. Then see him of a Sunday with his little concubine of a wife, and she wagging her tail up the aisle of the chapel with her patent boots on her, no less, and her violets, nice as pie, doing the little lady. Jack Mooney's sister. And the old prostitute of a mother procuring rooms to street couples. Gob, Jack made him toe the line. Told him if he didn't patch up the pot, Jesus, he'd kick the shite out of him.

So Terry brought the three pints.

—Here, says Joe, doing the honours. Here, citizen.

—*Slan leat*, says he.

—Fortune, Joe, says I. Good health, citizen.

Gob, he had his mouth half way down the tumbler already. Want a small fortune to keep him in drinks.

—Who is the long fellow running for the mayoralty, Alf? says Joe.

—Friend of yours, says Alf.

—Nannan? says Joe. The mimber?

—I won't mention any names, says Alf.

—I thought so, says Joe. I saw him up at that meeting now with William Field, M. P., the cattle traders.

—Hairy Iopas, says the citizen, that exploded volcano, the darling of all countries and the idol of his own.

So Joe starts telling the citizen about the foot and mouth disease and the cattle traders and taking action in the matter and the citizen sending them all to the rightabout and Bloom coming out with his sheepdip for the scab and a hoose drench for coughing calves and the guaranteed remedy for timber tongue. Because he was up one time in a knacker's yard. Walking about with his book and pencil here's my head and my heels are coming till Joe Cuffe gave him the order of the boot for giving lip to a grazier. Mister Knowall. Teach your grandmother how to milk ducks. Pisser Burke was telling me in the hotel the wife used to be in rivers of tears some times with Mrs O'Dowd crying her eyes out with her eight inches of fat all over her. Couldn't loosen her farting strings but old cod's eye was waltzing around her showing her how to do it. What's your programme today? Ay. Humane methods. Because the poor animals suffer and experts say and the best known remedy that doesn't cause pain to the animal and on the sore spot administer gently. Gob, he'd have a soft hand under a hen.

Ga Ga Gara. Klook Klook Klook. Black Liz is our hen. She lays eggs for us. When she lays her egg she is so glad. Gara. Klook Klook Klook. Then comes good uncle Leo. He puts his hand under black Liz and takes her fresh egg. Ga ga ga ga Gara. Klook Klook Klook.

—Anyhow, says Joe, Field and Nannetti are going over tonight to London to ask about it on the floor of the house of commons.

—Are you sure, says Bloom, the councillor is going? I wanted to see him, as it happens.

—Well, he's going off by the mailboat, says Joe, tonight.

—That's too bad, says Bloom. I wanted particularly. Perhaps only Mr Field is going. I couldn't phone. No. You're sure?

—Nannan's going too, says Joe. The league told him to ask a question tomorrow about the commissioner of police forbidding Irish games in the park. What do you think of that, citizen? *The Sluagh na h-Eireann.*

Mr Cowe Conacre (Multifarnham. Nat.): Arising out of the question of my honourable friend, the member for Shillelagh, may I ask the right honourable gentleman whether the government has issued orders that these animals shall be slaughtered though no medical evidence is forthcoming as to their pathological condition?

Mr Allfours (Tamoshant. Con.): Honourable members are already in possession of the evidence produced before a committee of the whole house. I feel I cannot usefully add anything to that. The answer to the honourable member's question is in the affirmative.

Mr Orelli O'Reilly (Montenotte. Nat.): Have similar orders been issued for the slaughter of human animals who dare to play Irish games in the Phoenix park?

Mr Allfours: The answer is in the negative.

Mr Cowe Conacre: Has the right honourable gentleman's famous Mitchelstown telegram inspired the policy of gentlemen on the Treasury bench? (O! O!)

Mr Allfours: I must have notice of that question.

Mr Staylewit (Buncombe. Ind.): Don't hesitate to shoot.

(Ironical opposition cheers.)

The speaker: Order! Order!

(The house rises. Cheers.)

—There's the man, says Joe, that made the Gaelic sports revival. There he is sitting there. The man that got away James Stephens. The champion of all Ireland at putting the sixteen pound shot. What was your best throw, citizen?

—*Na bacleis*, says the citizen, letting on to be modest. There was a time I was as good as the next fellow anyhow.

—Put it there, citizen, says Joe. You were and a bloody sight better.

—Is that really a fact? says Alf.

—Yes, says Bloom. That's well known. Did you not know that?

So off they started about Irish sports and shoneen games the like of lawn tennis and about hurley and putting the stone and racy of the soil and building up a nation once again and all to that. And of course Bloom had to have his say too about if a fellow had a rower's heart violent exercise was bad. I declare to my antimacassar if you took up a straw from the bloody floor and if you said to Bloom: *Look at, Bloom. Do you see that straw? That's a straw.* Declare to my aunt he'd talk about it for an hour so he would and talk steady.

A most interesting discussion took place in the ancient hall of *Brian O'Ciarnain's* in *Sraid na Bretaine Bheag*, under the auspices of *Sluagh na h-Eireann*, on the revival of ancient Gaelic sports and the importance of physical culture, as understood in ancient Greece and ancient Rome and ancient Ireland, for the development of the race. The venerable president of the noble order was in the chair and the attendance was of large dimensions. After an instructive discourse by the chairman, a magnificent oration eloquently and forcibly expressed, a most interesting and instructive discussion of the usual high standard of excellence ensued as to the desirability of the revivability of the ancient games and sports of our ancient Panceltic forefathers. The wellknown and highly respected worker in the cause of our old tongue, Mr Joseph M'Carthy Hynes, made an eloquent appeal for the resuscitation of the ancient Gaelic sports and pastimes, practised morning and evening by Finn MacCool, as calculated to revive the best traditions of manly strength and prowess handed down to us from ancient ages. L. Bloom, who met with a mixed reception of applause and hisses, having espoused the negative the vocalist chairman brought the discussion to a close, in response to repeated requests and hearty plaudits from all parts of a bumper house, by a remarkably noteworthy rendering of the immortal Thomas Osborne Davis' evergreen verses (happily too familiar to need recalling here) *A nation once again* in the execution of which the veteran patriot champion may be said without fear of contradiction to have fairly excelled himself. The Irish Caruso-Garibaldi was in superlative form and his stentorian notes were heard to the greatest advantage in the timehonoured anthem sung as only our citizen can sing it. His superb highclass vocalism, which by its superquality greatly enhanced his already international reputation, was vociferously applauded by the large audience among which were to be noticed many prominent members of the clergy as well as representatives of the press and the bar and the other learned professions. The proceedings then terminated.

Amongst the clergy present were the very rev. William Delany, S. J., L. L. D.; the rt rev. Gerald Molloy, D. D.; the rev. P. J. Kavanagh, C. S. Sp.; the rev. T. Waters, C. C.; the rev. John M. Ivers, P. P.; the rev. P. J. Cleary, O. S. F.; the rev. L. J. Hickey, O. P.; the very rev. Fr. Nicholas, O. S. F. C.; the very rev. B. Gorman, O. D. C.; the rev. T. Maher, S. J.; the very rev. James Murphy, S. J.; the rev. John Lavery, V. F.; the very rev. William Doherty, D. D.; the rev. Peter Fagan, O. M.; the rev. T. Brangan, O. S. A.; the rev. J. Flavin, C. C.; the rev. M. A. Hackett, C. C.; the rev. W. Hurley, C. C.; the rt rev. Mgr M'Manus, V. G.; the rev. B. R. Slattery, O. M. I.; the very rev. M. D. Scally, P. P.; the rev. F. T.

Purcell, O. P.; the very rev. Timothy canon Gorman, P. P.; the rev. J. Flanagan, C. C. The laity included P. Fay, T. Quirke, etc., etc.

—Talking about violent exercise, says Alf, were you at that Keogh-Bennett match?

—No, says Joe.

—I heard So and So made a cool hundred quid over it, says Alf.

—Who? Blazes? says Joe.

And says Bloom:

—What I meant about tennis, for example, is the agility and training the eye.

—Ay, Blazes, says Alf. He let out that Myler was on the beer to run up the odds and he swatting all the time.

—We know him, says the citizen. The traitor's son. We know what put English gold in his pocket.

—True for you, says Joe.

And Bloom cuts in again about lawn tennis and the circulation of the blood, asking Alf:

—Now, don't you think, Bergan?

—Myler dusted the floor with him, says Alf. Heenan and Sayers was only a bloody fool to it. Handed him the father and mother of a beating. See the little kipper not up to his navel and the big fellow swiping. God, he gave him one last puck in the wind, Queensberry rules and all, made him puke what he never ate.

It was a historic and a hefty battle when Myler and Percy were scheduled to don the gloves for the purse of fifty sovereigns. Handicapped as he was by lack of poundage, Dublin's pet lamb made up for it by superlative skill in ringcraft. The final bout of fireworks was a gruelling for both champions. The welterweight sergeantmajor had tapped some lively claret in the previous mixup during which Keogh had been receivergeneral of rights and lefts, the artilleryman putting in some neat work on the pet's nose, and Myler came on looking groggy. The soldier got to business, leading off with a powerful left jab to which the Irish gladiator retaliated by shooting out a stiff one flush to the point of Bennett's jaw. The redcoat ducked but the Dubliner lifted him with a left hook, the body punch being a fine one. The men came to handigrips. Myler quickly became busy and got his man under, the bout ending with the bulkier man on the ropes, Myler punishing him. The Englishman, whose right eye was nearly closed, took his corner where he was liberally drenched with water and when the bell went came on gamey and brimful of pluck, confident of knocking out the fistic Eblanite in jigtime. It was a fight to a finish and the best man for it. The two fought like tigers and excitement ran fever high. The referee twice cautioned Pucking Percy for holding but the pet was tricky and his footwork a treat to watch. After a brisk exchange of courtesies during which a smart upper cut of the military man brought blood freely from his opponent's mouth the lamb suddenly waded in all over his man and landed a terrific left to Battling Bennett's stomach, flooring him flat. It was a knockout clean and clever. Amid tense expectation the Portobello bruiser was being counted out when Bennett's second Ole Pfotts Wettstein threw in the towel and the Santry boy was declared victor to the frenzied cheers of the public who broke through the ringropes and fairly mobbed him with delight.

—He knows which side his bread is buttered, says Alf. I hear he's running a concert tour now up in the north.

—He is, says Joe. Isn't he?

—Who? says Bloom. Ah, yes. That's quite true. Yes, a kind of summer tour, you see. Just a holiday.

—Mrs Bloom is the bright particular star, isn't she? says Joe.

—My wife? says Bloom. She's singing, yes. I think it will be a success too.

He's an excellent man to organise. Excellent.

Hoho begob says I to myself says I. That explains the milk in the cocoanut and absence of hair on the animal's chest. Blazes doing the tootle on the flute. Concert tour. Dirty Dan the dodger's son off Island bridge that sold the same horses twice over to the government to fight the Boers. Old Whatwhat. I called about the poor and water rate, Mr Boylan. You what? The water rate, Mr Boylan. You whatwhat? That's the bucko that'll organise her, take my tip. 'Twixt me and you Caddareesh.

Pride of Calpe's rocky mount, the ravenhaired daughter of Tweedy. There grew she to peerless beauty where loquat and almond scent the air. The gardens of Alameda knew her step: the garths of olives knew and bowed. The chaste spouse of Leopold is she: Marion of the bountiful bosoms.

And lo, there entered one of the clan of the O'Molloy's, a comely hero of white face yet withal somewhat ruddy, his majesty's counsel learned in the law, and with him the prince and heir of the noble line of Lambert.

—Hello, Ned.

—Hello, Alf.
—Hello, Jack.
—Hello, Joe.
—God save you, says the citizen.
—Save you kindly, says J. J. What'll it be, Ned?
—Half one, says Ned.
So J. J. ordered the drinks.
—Were you round at the court? says Joe.
—Yes, says J. J. He'll square that, Ned, says he.
—Hope so, says Ned.

Now what were those two at? J. J. getting him off the grand jury list and the other give him a leg over the stile. With his name in Stubbs's. Playing cards, hobnobbing with flash toffs with a swank glass in their eye, adrinking fizz and he half smothered in writs and garnishee orders. Pawning his gold watch in Cummins of Francis street where no-one would know him in the private office when I was there with Pisser releasing his boots out of the pop. What's your name, sir? Dunne, says he. Ay, and done says I. Gob, he'll come home by weeping cross one of those days, I'm thinking.

—Did you see that bloody lunatic Breen round there? says Alf. U.P.: up.
—Yes, says J. J. Looking for a private detective.
—Ay, says Ned. And he wanted right go wrong to address the court only Corny Kelleher got round him telling him to get the handwriting examined first.
—Ten thousand pounds, says Alf, laughing. God, I'd give anything to hear him before a judge and jury.
—Was it you did it, Alf? says Joe. The truth, the whole truth and nothing but the truth, so help you Jimmy Johnson.
—Me? says Alf. Don't cast your nasturtiums on my character.
—Whatever statement you make, says Joe, will be taken down in evidence against you.
—Of course an action would lie, says J. J. It implies that he is not *compos mentis*. U.P.: up.
—*Compos* your eye! says Alf, laughing. Do you know that he's balmy? Look at his head. Do you know that some mornings he has to get his hat on with a shoehorn.
—Yes, says J. J., but the truth of a libel is no defence to an indictment for publishing it in the eyes of the law.

—Ha ha, Alf, says Joe.

—Still, says Bloom, on account of the poor woman, I mean his wife.

—Pity about her, says the citizen. Or any other woman marries a half and half.

—How half and half? says Bloom. Do you mean he . . .

—Half and half I mean, says the citizen. A fellow that's neither fish nor flesh.

—Nor good red herring, says Joe.

—That what's I mean, says the citizen. A pishogue, if you know what that is.

Begob I saw there was trouble coming. And Bloom explaining he meant on account of it being cruel for the wife having to go round after the old stuttering fool. Cruelty to animals so it is to let that bloody povertystricken Breen out on grass with his beard out tripping him, bringing down the rain. And she with her nose cockahoop after she married him because a cousin of his old fellow's was pewopener to the pope. Picture of him on the wall with his Smashall Sweeney's moustaches, the signior Brini from Summerhill, the eyetallyano, papal Zouave to the Holy Father, has left the quay and gone to Moss street. And who was he, tell us? A nobody, two pair back and passages, at seven shillings a week, and he covered with all kinds of breastplates bidding defiance to the world.

—And moreover, says J. J., a postcard is publication. It was held to be sufficient evidence of malice in the testcase Sadgrove v. Hole. In my opinion an action might lie.

Six and eightpence, please. Who wants your opinion? Let us drink our pints in peace. Gob, we won't be let even do that much itself.

—Well, good health, Jack, says Ned.

—Good health, Ned, says J. J.

—There he is again, says Joe.

—Where? says Alf.

And begob there he was passing the door with his books under his oxter and the wife beside him and Corny Kelleher with his wall eye looking in as they went past, talking to him like a father, trying to sell him a secondhand coffin.

—How did that Canada swindle case go off? says Joe.

—Remanded, says J. J.

One of the bottlenosed fraternity it was went by the name of James Wought alias Saphiro alias Spark and Spiro, put an ad in the papers saying he'd give a passage to Canada for twenty bob. What? Do you see any green in the white of my eye? Course it was a bloody barney. What? Swindled them all, skivvies and badhachs from the county Meath, ay, and his own kidney too. J. J. was telling us there was an ancient Hebrew Zaretsky or something weeping in the witnessbox with his hat on him, swearing by the holy Moses he was stuck for two quid.

—Who tried the case? says Joe.

—Recorder, says Ned.

—Poor old sir Frederick, says Alf, you can cod him up to the two eyes.

—Heart as big as a lion, says Ned. Tell him a tale of woe about arrears of rent and a sick wife and a squad of kids and, faith, he'll dissolve in tears on the bench.

—Ay, says Alf. Reuben J was bloody lucky he didn't clap him in the dock the other day for suing poor little Gumley that's minding stones, for the corporation there near Butt bridge.

And he starts taking off the old recorder letting on to cry:

—A most scandalous thing! This poor hardworking man! How many children? Ten, did you say?

—Yes, your worship. And my wife has the typhoid.

—And the wife with typhoid fever! Scandalous! Leave the court immediately, sir. No, sir, I'll make no order for payment. How dare you, sir, come up before me and ask me to make an order! A poor hardworking industrious man! I dismiss the case.

And whereas on the sixteenth day of the month of the oxeyed goddess and in the third week after the feastday of the Holy and Undivided Trinity, the daughter of the skies, the virgin moon being then in her first quarter, it came to pass that those learned judges repaired them to the halls of law. There master Courtenay, sitting in his own chamber, gave his rede and master Justice Andrews, sitting without a jury in the probate court, weighed well and pondered the claim of the first chargeant upon the property in the matter of the will propounded and final testamentary disposition *in re* the real and personal estate of the late lamented Jacob Halliday, vintner, deceased, versus Livingstone, an infant, of unsound mind, and another. And to the solemn court of Green street there came sir Frederick the Falconer. And he sat him there about the hour of five o'clock to administer the law of the brehons at the commission for all that and those parts to be holden in and for the county of the city of Dublin. And there sat with him the high sinhedrim of the twelve tribes of Iar, for every tribe one man, of the tribe of Patrick and of the tribe of Hugh and of the tribe of Owen and of the tribe of Conn and of the tribe of Oscar and of the tribe of Fergus and of the tribe of Finn and of the tribe of Dermot and of the tribe of Cormac and of the tribe of Kevin and of the tribe of Caolte and of the tribe of Ossian, there being in all twelve good men and true. And he conjured them by Him who died on rood that they should well and truly try and true deliverance make in the issue joined between their sovereign lord the king and the prisoner at the bar and true verdict give according to the evidence so help them God and kiss the book. And they rose in their seats, those twelve of Iar, and they swore by the name of Him Who is from everlasting that they would do His rightwiseness. And straightway the minions of the law led forth from their donjon keep one whom the sleuthhounds of justice had apprehended in consequence of information received. And they shackled him hand and foot and would take of him ne bail ne mainprise but preferred a charge against him for he was a malefactor.

—Those are nice things, says the citizen, coming over here to Ireland filling the country with bugs.

So Bloom lets on he heard nothing and he starts talking with Joe, telling him he needn't trouble about that little matter till the first but if he would just say a word to Mr Crawford. And so Joe swore high and holy by this and by that he'd do the devil and all.

—Because, you see, says Bloom, for an advertisement you must have repetition. That's the whole secret.

—Rely on me, says Joe.

—Swindling the peasants, says the citizen, and the poor of Ireland. We want no more strangers in our house.

—O, I'm sure that will be all right, Hynes, says Bloom. It's just that Keyes, you see.

—Consider that done, says Joe.

—Very kind of you, says Bloom.

—The strangers, says the citizen. Our own fault. We let them come in. We brought them in. The adulteress and her paramour brought the Saxon robbers here.

—Decree *nisi,* says J. J.

And Bloom letting on to be awfully deeply interested in nothing, a spider's web in the corner behind the barrel, and the citizen scowling after him and the old dog at his feet looking up to know who to bite and when.

—A dishonoured wife, says the citizen, that's what's the cause of all our misfortunes.

—And here she is, says Alf, that was giggling over the *Police Gazette* with Terry on the counter, in all her warpaint.

—Give us a squint at her, says I.

And what was it only one of the smutty yankee pictures Terry borrows off of Corny Kelleher. Secrets for enlarging your private parts. Misconduct of society belle. Norman W. Tupper, wealthy Chicago contractor, finds pretty but faithless wife in lap of officer Taylor. Belle in her bloomers misconducting herself, and her fancyman feeling for her tickles and Norman W. Tupper bouncing in with his peashooter just in time to be late after she doing the trick of the loop with officer Taylor.

—O jakers, Jenny, says Joe, how short your shirt is!

—There's hair, Joe, says I. Get a queer old tailend of corned beef off of that one, what?

So anyhow in came John Wyse Nolan and Lenehan with him with a face on him as long as a late breakfast.

—Well, says the citizen, what's the latest from the scene of action? What did those tinkers in the city hall at their caucus meeting decide about the Irish language?

O'Nolan, clad in shining armour, low bending made obeisance to the puissant and high and mighty chief of all Erin and did him to wit of that which had befallen, how that the grave elders of the most obedient city, second of the realm, had met them in the tholsel, and there, after due prayers to the gods who dwell in ether supernal, had taken solemn counsel whereby they might, if so be it might be, bring once more into honour among mortal men the winged speech of the seadivided Gael.

—It's on the march, says the citizen. To hell with the bloody brutal Sassenachs and their *patois*.

So J. J. puts in a word, doing the toff about one story was good till you heard another and blinking facts and the Nelson policy, putting your blind eye to the telescope and drawing up a bill of attainder to impeach a nation, and Bloom trying to back him up moderation and botheration and their colonies and their civilisation.

—Their syphilisation, you mean, says the citizen. To hell with them! The curse of a goodfornothing God light sideways on the bloody thicklugged sons of whores' gets! No music and no art and no literature worthy of the name. Any civilisation they have they stole from us. Tonguetied sons of bastards' ghosts.

—The European family, says J. J. . . . .

—They're not European, says the citizen. I was in Europe with Kevin Egan of Paris. You wouldn't see a trace of them or their language anywhere in Europe except in a *cabinet d'aisance.*

And says John Wyse:

—Full many a flower is born to blush unseen.

And says Lenehan that knows a bit of the lingo:

—*Conspuez les Anglais! Perfide Albion!*

He said and then lifted he in his rude great brawny strengthy hands the medher of dark strong foamy ale and, uttering his tribal slogan *Lamh Dearg Abu,* he drank to the undoing of his foes, a race of mighty valorous heroes, rulers of the waves, who sit on thrones of alabaster silent as the deathless gods.

—What's up with you, says I to Lenehan. You look like a fellow that had lost a bob and found a tanner.

—Gold cup, says he.

—Who won, Mr Lenehan? says Terry.

—*Throwaway,* says he, at twenty to one. A rank outsider. And the rest nowhere.

—And Bass's mare? says Terry.

—Still running, says he. We're all in a cart. Boylan plunged two quid on my tip *Sceptre* for himself and a lady friend.

—I had half a crown myself, says Terry, on *Zinfandel* that Mr Flynn gave me. Lord Howard de Walden's.

—Twenty to one, says Lenehan. Such is life in an outhouse. *Throwaway,* says he. Takes the biscuit, and talking about bunions. Frailty, thy name is *Sceptre.*

So he went over to the biscuit tin Bob Doran left to see if there was anything he could lift on the nod, the old cur after him backing his luck with his mangy snout up. Old Mother Hubbard went to the cupboard.

—Not there, my child, says he.

—Keep your pecker up, says Joe. She'd have won the money only for the other dog.

And J. J. and the citizen arguing about law and history with Bloom sticking in an odd word.

—Some people, says Bloom, can see the mote in others' eyes but they can't see the beam in their own.

—*Raimeis*, says the citizen. There's no-one as blind as the fellow that won't see, if you know what that means. Where are our missing twenty millions of Irish should be here today instead of four, our lost tribes? And our potteries and textiles, the finest in the whole world! And our wool that was sold in Rome in the time of Juvenal and our flax and our damask from the looms of Antrim and our Limerick lace, our tanneries and our white flint glass down there by Ballybough and our Huguenot poplin that we have since Jacquard de Lyon and our woven silk and our Foxford tweeds and ivory raised point from the Carmelite convent in New Ross, nothing like it in the whole wide world. Where are the Greek merchants that came through the pillars of Hercules, the Gibraltar now grabbed by the foe of mankind, with gold and Tyrian purple to sell in Wexford at the fair of Carmen? Read Tacitus and Ptolemy, even Giraldus Cambrensis. Wine, peltries, Connemara marble, silver from Tipperary, second to none, our farfamed horses even today, the Irish hobbies, with king Philip of Spain offering to pay customs duties for the right to fish in our waters. What do the yellowjohns of Anglia owe us for our ruined trade and our ruined hearths? And the beds of the Barrow and Shannon they won't deepen with millions of acres of marsh and bog to make us all die of consumption?

—As treeless as Portugal we'll be soon, says John Wyse, or Heligoland with its one tree if something is not done to reafforest the land. Larches, firs, all the trees of the conifer family are going fast. I was reading a report of lord Castletown's . . .

—Save them, says the citizen, the giant ash of Galway and the chieftain elm of Kildare with a fortyfoot bole and an acre of foliage. Save the trees of Ireland for the future men of Ireland on the fair hills of Eire, O.

—Europe has its eyes on you, says Lenehan.

The fashionable international world attended *en masse* this afternoon at the wedding of the chevalier Jean Wyse de Neaulan, grand high chief ranger of the Irish National Foresters, with Miss Fir Conifer of Pine Valley. Lady Sylvester Elmshade, Mrs Barbara Lovebirch, Mrs Poll Ash, Mrs Holly Hazeleyes, Miss Daphne Bays, Miss Dorothy

Canebrake, Mrs Clyde Twelvetrees, Mrs Rowan Greene, Mrs Helen Vinegadding, Miss Virginia Creeper, Miss Gladys Beech, Miss Olive Garth, Miss Blanche Maple, Mrs Maud Mahogany, Miss Myra Myrtle, Miss Priscilla Elderflower, Miss Bee Honeysuckle, Miss Grace Poplar, Miss O Mimosa San, Miss Rachel Cedarfrond, the Misses Lilian and Viola Lilac, Miss Timidity Aspenall, Mrs Kitty Dewey-Mosse, Miss May Hawthorne, Mrs Gloriana Palme, Mrs Liana Forrest, Mrs Arabella Blackwood and Mrs Norma Holyoake of Oakholme Regis graced the ceremony by their presence. The bride who was given away by her father, the of the Glands, looked exquisitely charming in a creation carried out in green mercerised silk, moulded on an underslip of gloaming grey, sashed with a yoke of broad emerald and finished with a triple flounce of darkerhued fringe, the scheme being relieved by bretelles and hip insertions of acorn bronze. The maids of honour, Miss Larch Conifer and Miss Spruce Conifer, sisters of the bride, wore very becoming costumes in the same tone, a dainty *motif* of plume rose being worked into the pleats in a pinstripe and repeated capriciously in the jadegreen toques in the form of heron feathers of paletinted coral. Senhor Enrique Flor presided at the organ with his wellknown ability and, in addition to the prescribed numbers of the nuptial mass, played a new and striking arrangement of *Woodman, spare that tree* at the conclusion of the service. On leaving the church of Saint Fiacre *in Horto* after the papal blessing the happy pair were subjected to a playful crossfire of hazelnuts, beechmast, bayleaves, catkins of willow, ivytod, hollyberries, mistletoe sprigs and quicken shoots. Mr and Mrs Wyse Conifer Neaulan will spend a quiet honeymoon in the Black Forest.

—And our eyes are on Europe, says the citizen. We had our trade with Spain and the French and with the Flemings before those mongrels were pupped, Spanish ale in Galway, the winebark on the winedark waterway.

—And will again, says Joe.

—And with the help of the holy mother of God we will again, says the citizen, clapping his thigh. Our harbours that are empty will be full again, Queenstown, Kinsale, Galway, Blacksod Bay, Ventry in the kingdom of Kerry, Killybegs, the third largest harbour in the wide world with a fleet of masts of the Galway Lynches and the Cavan O'Reillys and the O'Kennedys of Dublin when the earl of Desmond could make a treaty with the emperor Charles the Fifth himself. And will again, says he, when the first Irish battleship is seen breasting the waves with our own flag to the fore, none of your Henry Tudor's harps, no, the oldest flag afloat, the flag of the province of Desmond and Thomond, three crowns on a blue field, the three sons of Milesius.

And he took the last swig out of the pint. Moya. All wind and piss like a tanyard cat. Cows in Connacht have long horns. As much as his bloody life is worth to go down and address his tall talk to the assembled multitude in Shanagolden where he daren't show his nose with the Molly Maguires looking for him to let daylight through him for grabbing the holding of an evicted tenant.

—Hear, hear to that, says John Wyse. What will you have?

—An imperial yeomanry, says Lenehan, to celebrate the occasion.

—Half one, Terry, says John Wyse, and a hands up. Terry! Are you asleep?

—Yes, sir, says Terry. Small whisky and bottle of Allsop. Right, sir.

Hanging over the bloody paper with Alf looking for spicy bits instead of attending to the general public. Picture of a butting match, trying to crack their bloody skulls, one chap going for the other with his head down like a bull at a gate. And another one: *Black Beast Burned in Omaha, Ga.* A lot of Deadwood Dicks in slouch hats and they firing at a Sambo strung up in a tree with his tongue out and a bonfire under him. Gob, they ought to drown him in the sea after and electrocute and crucify him to make sure of their job.

—But what about the fighting navy, says Ned, that keeps our foes at bay?

—I'll tell you what about it, says the citizen. Hell upon earth it is. Read the revelations that's going on in the papers about flogging on the training ships at Portsmouth. A fellow writes that calls himself *Disgusted One.*

So he starts telling us about corporal punishment and about the crew of tars and officers and rearadmirals drawn up in cocked hats and the parson with his protestant bible to witness punishment and a young lad brought out, howling for his ma, and they tie him down on the buttend of a gun.

—A rump and dozen, says the citizen, was what that old ruffian sir John Beresford called it but the modern God's Englishman calls it caning on the breech.

And says John Wyse:

—'Tis a custom more honoured in the breach than in the observance.

Then he was telling us the master at arms comes along with a long cane and he draws out and he flogs the bloody backside off of the poor lad till he yells meila murder.

—That's your glorious British navy, says the citizen, that bosses the earth. The fellows that never will be slaves, with the only hereditary chamber on the face of God's earth and their land in the hands of a dozen gamehogs and cottonball barons. That's the great empire they boast about of drudges and whipped serfs.

—On which the sun never rises, says Joe.

—And the tragedy of it is, says the citizen, they believe it. The unfortunate yahoos believe it.

They believe in rod, the scourger almighty, creator of hell upon earth, and in Jacky Tar, the son of a gun, who was conceived of unholy boast, born of the fighting navy, suffered under rump and dozen, was scarified, flayed and curried, yelled like bloody hell, the third day he arose again from the bed, steered into haven, sitteth on his beamend till further orders whence he shall come to drudge for a living and be paid.

—But, says Bloom, isn't discipline the same everywhere. I mean wouldn't it be the same here if you put force against force?

Didn't I tell you? As true as I'm drinking this porter if he was at his last gasp he'd try to downface you that dying was living.

—We'll put force against force, says the citizen. We have our greater Ireland beyond the sea. They were driven out of house and home in the black 47. Their mudcabins and their shielings by the roadside were laid low by the batteringram and the *Times* rubbed its hands and told the whitelivered Saxons there would soon be as few Irish in Ireland as redskins in America. Even the Grand Turk sent us his piastres. But the Sassenach tried to starve the nation at home while the land was full of crops that the British hyenas bought and sold in Rio de Janeiro. Ay, they drove out the peasants in hordes. Twenty thousand of them died in the coffinships. But those that came to the land of the free remember the land of bondage. And they will come again and with a vengeance, no cravens, the sons of Granuaile, the champions of Kathleen ni Houlihan.

—Perfectly true, says Bloom. But my point was . . .

—We are a long time waiting for that day, citizen, says Ned. Since the poor old woman told us that the French were on the sea and landed at Killala.

—Ay, says John Wyse. We fought for the royal Stuarts that reneged us against the Williamites and they betrayed us. Remember Limerick and the broken treatystone. We gave our best blood to France and Spain, the wild geese. Fontenoy, eh? And Sarsfield and O'Donnell, duke of Tetuan in Spain, and Ulysses Browne of Camus that was fieldmarshal to Maria Teresa. But what did we ever get for it?

—The French! says the citizen. Set of dancing masters! Do you know what it is? They were never worth a roasted fart to Ireland. Aren't they trying to make an *Entente cordiale* now at Tay Pay's dinnerparty with perfidious Albion? Firebrands of Europe and they always were.

—*Conspuez les Français*, says Lenehan, nobbling his beer.

—And as for the Prooshians and the Hanoverians, says Joe, haven't we had enough of those sausageeating bastards on the throne from George the elector down to the German lad and the flatulent old bitch that's dead?

Jesus, I had to laugh at the way he came out with that about the old one with the winkers on her, blind drunk in her royal palace every night of God, old Vic, with her jorum of mountain dew and her coachman carting her up body and bones to roll into bed and she pulling him by the whiskers and singing him old bits of songs about *Ehren on the Rhine* and come where the boose is cheaper.

—Well, says J. J. We have Edward the peacemaker now.

—Tell that to a fool, says the citizen. There's a bloody sight more pox than pax about that boyo. Edward Guelph-Wettin!

—And what do you think, says Joe, of the holy boys, the priests and bishops of Ireland doing up his room in Maynooth in His Satanic Majesty's racing colours and sticking up pictures of all the horses his jockeys rode. The earl of Dublin, no less.

—They ought to have stuck up all the women he rode himself, says little Alf.

And says J. J.:

—Considerations of space influenced their lordships' decision.

—Will you try another, citizen? says Joe.

—Yes, sir, says he. I will.

—You? says Joe.

—Beholden to you, Joe, says I. May your shadow never grow less.

—Repeat that dose, says Joe.

Bloom was talking and talking with John Wyse and he quite excited with his dunducketymudcoloured mug on him and his old plumeyes rolling about.

—Persecution, says he, all the history of the world is full of it. Perpetuating national hatred among nations.

—But do you know what a nation means? says John Wyse.

—Yes, says Bloom.

—What is it? says John Wyse.

—A nation? says Bloom. A nation is the same people living in the same place.

—By God, then, says Ned, laughing, if that's so I'm a nation for I'm living in the same place for the past five years.

So of course everyone had the laugh at Bloom and says he, trying to muck out of it:

—Or also living in different places.

—That covers my case, says Joe.

—What is your nation if I may ask? says the citizen.

—Ireland, says Bloom. I was born here. Ireland.

The citizen said nothing only cleared the spit out of his gullet and, gob, he spat a Red bank oyster out of him right in the corner.

—After you with the push, Joe, says he, taking out his handkerchief to swab himself dry.

—Here you are, citizen, says Joe. Take that in your right hand and repeat after me the following words.

The muchtreasured and intricately embroidered ancient Irish facecloth attributed to Solomon of Droma and Manus Tomaltach og MacDonogh, authors of the Book of Ballymote, was then carefully produced and called forth prolonged admiration. No need to dwell on the legendary beauty of the cornerpieces, the acme of art, wherein one can distinctly discern each of the four evangelists in turn presenting to each of the four masters his evangelical symbol, a bogoak sceptre, a North American puma (a far nobler king of beasts than the British article, be it said in passing), a Kerry calf and a golden eagle from Carrantuohill. The scenes depicted on the emunctory field, showing our ancient duns and raths and cromlechs and grianauns and seats of learning and maledictive stones, are as wonderfully beautiful and the pigments as delicate as when the Sligo illuminators gave free rein to their artistic fantasy long long ago in the time of the Barmecides. Glendalough, the lovely lakes of Killarney, the ruins of Clonmacnois,

Cong Abbey, Glen Inagh and the Twelve Pins, Ireland's Eye, the Green Hills of Tallaght, Croagh Patrick, the brewery of Messrs Arthur Guinness, Son and Company (Limited), Lough Neagh's banks, the vale of Ovoca, Isolde's tower, the Mapas obelisk, Sir Patrick Dun's hospital, Cape Clear, the glen of Aherlow, Lynch's castle, the Scotch house, Rathdown Union Workhouse at Loughlinstown, Tullamore jail, Castleconnel rapids, Kilballymacshonakill, the cross at Monasterboice, Jury's Hotel, S. Patrick's Purgatory, the Salmon Leap, Maynooth college refectory, Curley's hole, the three birthplaces of the first duke of Wellington, the rock of Cashel, the bog of Allen, the Henry Street Warehouse, Fingal's Cave—all these moving scenes are still there for us today rendered more beautiful still by the waters of sorrow which have passed over them and by the rich incrustations of time.

—Show us over the drink, says I. Which is which?

—That's mine, says Joe, as the devil said to the dead policeman.

—And I belong to a race too, says Bloom, that is hated and persecuted. Also now. This very moment. This very instant.

Gob, he near burnt his fingers with the butt of his old cigar.

—Robbed, says he. Plundered. Insulted. Persecuted. Taking what belongs to us by right. At this very moment, says he, putting up his fist, sold by auction in Morocco like slaves or cattle.

—Are you talking about the new Jerusalem? says the citizen.

—I'm talking about injustice, says Bloom.

—Right, says John Wyse. Stand up to it then with force like men.

That's an almanac picture for you. Mark for a softnosed bullet. Old lardyface standing up to the business end of a gun. Gob, he'd adorn a sweepingbrush, so he would, if he only had a nurse's apron on him. And then he collapses all of a sudden, twisting around all the opposite, as limp as a wet rag.

—But it's no use, says he. Force, hatred, history, all that. That's not life for men and women, insult and hatred. And everybody knows that it's the very opposite of that that is really life.

—What? says Alf.

—Love, says Bloom. I mean the opposite of hatred. I must go now, says he to John Wyse. Just round to the court a moment to see if Martin is there. If he comes just say I'll be back in a second. Just a moment.

Who's hindering you? And off he pops like greased lightning.

—A new apostle to the gentiles, says the citizen. Universal love.

—Well, says John Wyse. Isn't that what we're told. Love your neighbour.

—That chap? says the citizen. Beggar my neighbour is his motto. Love, moya! He's a nice pattern of a Romeo and Juliet.

Love loves to love love. Nurse loves the new chemist. Constable 14A loves Mary Kelly. Gerty MacDowell loves the boy that has the bicycle. M. B. loves a fair gentleman. Li Chi Han lovey up kissy Cha Pu Chow. Jumbo, the elephant, loves Alice, the elephant. Old Mr Verschoyle with the ear trumpet loves old Mrs Verschoyle with the turnedin eye. The man in the brown macintosh loves a lady who is dead. His Majesty the King loves Her Majesty the Queen. Mrs Norman W. Tupper loves officer Taylor. You love a certain person. And this person loves that other person because everybody loves somebody but God loves everybody.

—Well, Joe, says I, your very good health and song. More power, citizen.

—Hurrah, there, says Joe.

—The blessing of God and Mary and Patrick on you, says the citizen.

And he ups with his pint to wet his whistle.

—We know those canters, says he, preaching and picking your pocket. What about sanctimonious Cromwell and his ironsides that put the women and children of Drogheda to the sword with the bible text *God is love* pasted round the mouth of his cannon? The bible! Did you read that skit in the *United Irishman* today about that Zulu chief that's visiting England?

—What's that? says Joe.

So the citizen takes up one of his paraphernalia papers and he starts reading out:

—A delegation of the chief cotton magnates of Manchester was presented yesterday to His Majesty the Alaki of Abeakuta by Gold Stick in Waiting, Lord Walkup of Walkup on Eggs, to tender to His Majesty the heartfelt thanks of British traders for the facilities afforded them in his dominions. The delegation partook of luncheon at the conclusion of which the dusky potentate, in the course of a happy speech, freely translated by the British chaplain, the reverend Ananias Praisegod Barebones, tendered his best thanks to Massa Walkup and emphasised the cordial relations existing between Abeakuta and the British empire, stating that he treasured as one of his dearest possessions an illuminated bible, the volume of the word of God and the secret of England's greatness, graciously presented to him by the white chief woman, the great squaw Victoria, with a personal dedication from the august hand of the Royal Donor. The Alaki then drank a lovingcup of firstshot usquebaugh to the toast *Black and White* from the skull of his immediate predecessor in the dynasty Kakachakachak, surnamed Forty Warts, after which he visited the chief factory of Cottonopolis and signed his mark in the visitors' book, subsequently executing a charming old Abeakutic wardance, in the course of which he swallowed several knives and forks, amid hilarious applause from the girl hands.

—Widow woman, says Ned. I wouldn't doubt her. Wonder did he put that bible to the same use as I would.

—Same only more so, says Lenehan. And thereafter in that fruitful land the broadleaved mango flourished exceedingly.

—Is that by Griffith? says John Wyse.

—No, says the citizen. It's not signed Shanganagh. It's only initialled: P.

—And a very good initial too, says Joe.

—That's how it's worked, says the citizen. Trade follows the flag.

—Well, says J. J., if they're any worse than those Belgians in the Congo Free State they must be bad. Did you read that report by a man what's this his name is?

—Casement, says the citizen. He's an Irishman.

—Yes, that's the man, says J. J. Raping the women and girls and flogging the natives on the belly to squeeze all the red rubber they can out of them.

—I know where he's gone, says Lenehan, cracking his fingers.

—Who? says I.

—Bloom, says he. The courthouse is a blind. He had a few bob on *Throwaway* and he's gone to gather in the shekels.

—Is it that whiteeyed kaffir? says the citizen, that never backed a horse in anger in his life?

—That's where he's gone, says Lenehan. I met Bantam Lyons going to back that horse only I put him off it and he told me Bloom gave him the tip. Bet you what you like he has a hundred shillings to five on. He's the only man in Dublin has it. A dark horse.

—He's a bloody dark horse himself, says Joe.

—Mind, Joe, says I. Show us the entrance out.

—There you are, says Terry.

Goodbye Ireland I'm going to Gort. So I just went round the back of the yard to pumpship and begob (hundred shillings to five) while I was letting off my (*Throwaway* twenty to) letting off my load gob says I to myself I knew he was uneasy in his (two pints off of Joe and one in Slattery's off) in his mind to get off the mark to (hundred shillings is five quid) and when they were in the (dark horse) pisser Burke was telling me card party and letting on the child was sick (gob, must have done about a gallon) flabbyarse of a wife speaking down the tube *she's better* or *she's* (ow!) all a plan so he could vamoose with the pool if he won or (Jesus, full up I was) trading without a licence (ow!) Ireland my nation says he (hoik! phthook!) never be up to those bloody (there's the last of it) Jerusalem (ah!) cuckoos.

So anyhow when I got back they were at it dingdong, John Wyse saying it was Bloom gave the ideas for Sinn Fein to Griffith to put in his paper all kinds of jerrymandering, packed juries and swindling the taxes off of the government and appointing consuls all over the world to walk about selling Irish industries. Robbing Peter to pay Paul. Gob, that puts the bloody kybosh on it if old sloppy eyes is mucking up the show. Give us a bloody chance. God save Ireland from the likes of that bloody mouseabout. Mr Bloom with his argol bargol. And his old fellow before him perpetrating frauds, old Methusalem Bloom, the robbing bagman, that poisoned himself with the prussic acid after he swamping the country with his baubles and his penny diamonds. Loans by post on easy terms. Any amount of money advanced on note of hand. Distance no object. No security. Gob, he's like Lanty MacHale's goat that'd go a piece of the road with every one.

—Well, it's a fact, says John Wyse. And there's the man now that'll tell you all about it, Martin Cunningham.

Sure enough the castle car drove up with Martin on it and Jack Power with him and a fellow named Crofter or Crofton, pensioner out of the collector general's, an orangeman Blackburn does have on the registration and he drawing his pay or Crawford gallivanting around the country at the king's expense.

Our travellers reached the rustic hostelry and alighted from their palfreys.

—Ho, varlet! cried he, who by his mien seemed the leader of the party. Saucy knave! To us!

So saying he knocked loudly with his swordhilt upon the open lattice.

Mine host came forth at the summons, girding him with his tabard.

—Give you good den, my masters, said he with an obsequious bow.

—Bestir thyself, sirrah! cried he who had knocked. Look to our steeds. And for ourselves give us of your best for ifaith we need it.

—Lackaday, good masters, said the host, my poor house has but a bare larder. I know not what to offer your lordships.

—How now, fellow? cried the second of the party, a man of pleasant countenance, So servest thou the king's messengers, master Taptun?

An instantaneous change overspread the landlord's visage.

—Cry you mercy, gentlemen, he said humbly. An you be the king's messengers (God shield His Majesty!) you shall not want for aught. The king's friends (God bless His Majesty!) shall not go afasting in my house I warrant me.

—Then about! cried the traveller who had not spoken, a lusty trencherman by his aspect. Hast aught to give us?

Mine host bowed again as he made answer:

—What say you, good masters, to a squab pigeon pasty, some collops of venison, a saddle of veal, widgeon with crisp hog's bacon, a boar's head with pistachios, a bason of jolly custard, a medlar tansy and a flagon of old Rhenish?

—Gadzooks! cried the last speaker. That likes me well. Pistachios!

—Aha! cried he of the pleasant countenance. A poor house and a bare larder, quotha! 'Tis a merry rogue.

So in comes Martin asking where was Bloom.

—Where is he? says Lenehan. Defrauding widows and orphans.

—Isn't that a fact, says John Wyse, what I was telling the citizen about Bloom and the Sinn Fein?

—That's so, says Martin. Or so they allege.

—Who made those allegations? says Alf.

—I, says Joe. I'm the alligator.

—And after all, says John Wyse, why can't a jew love his country like the next fellow?

—Why not? says J. J., when he's quite sure which country it is.

—Is he a jew or a gentile or a holy Roman or a swaddler or what the hell is he? says Ned. Or who is he? No offence, Crofton.

—Who is Junius? says J. J.

—We don't want him, says Crofter the Orangeman or presbyterian.

—He's a perverted jew, says Martin, from a place in Hungary and it was he drew up all the plans according to the Hungarian system. We know that in the castle.

—Isn't he a cousin of Bloom the dentist? says Jack Power.

—Not at all, says Martin. Only namesakes. His name was Virag, the father's name that poisoned himself. He changed it by deedpoll, the father did.

—That's the new Messiah for Ireland! says the citizen. Island of saints and sages!

—Well, they're still waiting for their redeemer, says Martin. For that matter so are we.

—Yes, says J. J., and every male that's born they think it may be their Messiah. And every jew is in a tall state of excitement, I believe, till he knows if he's a father or a mother.

—Expecting every moment will be his next, says Lenehan.

—O, by God, says Ned, you should have seen Bloom before that son of his that died was born. I met him one day in the south city markets buying a tin of Neave's food six weeks before the wife was delivered.

—*En ventre sa mère*, says J. J.

—Do you call that a man? says the citizen.

—I wonder did he ever put it out of sight, says Joe.

—Well, there were two children born anyhow, says Jack Power.

—And who does he suspect? says the citizen.

Gob, there's many a true word spoken in jest. One of those mixed middlings he is. Lying up in the hotel Pisser was telling me once a month with headache like a totty with her courses. Do you know what I'm telling you? It'd be an act of God to take a hold of a fellow the like of that and throw him in the bloody sea. Justifiable homicide, so it would. Then sloping off with his five quid without putting up a pint of stuff like a man. Give us your blessing. Not as much as would blind your eye.

—Charity to the neighbour, says Martin. But where is he? We can't wait.

—A wolf in sheep's clothing, says the citizen. That's what he is. Virag from Hungary! Ahasuerus I call him. Cursed by God.

—Have you time for a brief libation, Martin? says Ned.

—Only one, says Martin. We must be quick. J. J. and S.

—You, Jack? Crofton? Three half ones, Terry.

—Saint Patrick would want to land again at Ballykinlar and convert us, says the citizen, after allowing things like that to contaminate our shores.

—Well, says Martin, rapping for his glass. God bless all here is my prayer.

—Amen, says the citizen.

—And I'm sure He will, says Joe.

And at the sound of the sacring bell, headed by a crucifer with acolytes, thurifers, boatbearers, readers, ostiarii, deacons and subdeacons, the blessed company drew nigh of mitred abbots and priors and guardians and monks and friars: the monks of Benedict of Spoleto, Carthusians and Camaldolesi, Cistercians and Olivetans, Oratorians and Vallombrosans, and the friars of Augustine, Brigittines, Premonstratensians, Servi, Trinitarians, and the children of Peter Nolasco: and therewith from Carmel mount the children of Elijah prophet led by Albert bishop and by Teresa of Avila, calced and other: and friars, brown and grey, sons of poor Francis, capuchins, cordeliers, minimes and observants and the daughters of Clara: and the sons of Dominic, the friars preachers, and the sons of Vincent: and the monks of S. Wolstan: and Ignatius his children: and the confraternity of the christian brothers led by the reverend brother Edmund Ignatius Rice. And after came all saints and martyrs, virgins and confessors: S. Cyr and S. Isidore Arator and S. James the Less and S. Phocas of Sinope and S. Julian Hospitator and S. Felix de Cantalice and S. Simon Stylites and S. Stephen Protomartyr and S. John of God and S. Ferreol and S. Leugarde and S. Theodotus and S. Vulmar and S. Richard and S. Vincent de Paul and S. Martin of Todi and S. Martin of Tours and S. Alfred and S. Joseph and S. Denis and S. Cornelius and S. Leopold and S. Bernard and S. Terence and S. Edward and S. Owen Caniculus and S. Anonymous and S. Eponymous and S. Pseudonymous and S. Homonymous and S. Paronymous and S. Synonymous and S. Laurence O'Toole and S. James of Dingle and Compostella and S. Columcille and S. Columba and S. Celestine and S. Colman and S. Kevin and S. Brendan and S. Frigidian and S. Senan and S. Fachtna and S. Columbanus and S. Gall and S. Fursey and S. Fintan and S. Fiacre and S. John Nepomuc and S. Thomas Aquinas and S. Ives of Brittany and S. Michan and S. Herman-Joseph and the three patrons of holy youth S. Aloysius

Gonzaga and S. Stanislaus Kostka and S. John Berchmans and the saints Gervasius, Servasius and Bonifacius and S. Bride and S. Kieran and S. Canice of Kilkenny and S. Jarlath of Tuam and S. Finbarr and S. Pappin of Ballymun and Brother Aloysius Pacificus and Brother Louis Bellicosus and the saints Rose of Lima and of Viterbo and S. Martha of Bethany and S. Mary of Egypt and S. Lucy and S. Brigid and S. Attracta and S. Dympna and S. Ita and S. Marion Calpensis and the Blessed Sister Teresa of the Child Jesus and S. Barbara and S. Scholastica and S. Ursula with eleven thousand virgins. And all came with nimbi and aureoles and gloriae, bearing palms and harps and swords and olive crowns, in robes whereon were woven the blessed symbols of their efficacies, inkhorns, arrows, loaves, cruses, fetters, axes, trees, bridges, babes in a bathtub, shells, wallets, shears, keys, dragons, lilies, buckshot, beards, hogs, lamps, bellows, beehives, soupladles, stars, snakes, anvils, boxes of vaseline, bells, crutches, forceps, stags' horns, watertight boots, hawks, millstones, eyes on a dish, wax candles, aspergills, unicorns. And as they wended their way by Nelson's Pillar, Henry street, Mary street, Capel street, Little Britain street chanting the introit in *Epiphania Domini* which beginneth *Surge, illuminare* and thereafter most sweetly the gradual *Omnes* which saith *de Saba venient* they did divers wonders such as casting out devils, raising the dead to life, multiplying fishes, healing the halt and the blind, discovering various articles which had been mislaid, interpreting and fulfilling the scriptures, blessing and prophesying. And last, beneath a canopy of cloth of gold came the reverend Father O'Flynn attended by Malachi and Patrick. And when the good fathers had reached the appointed place, the house of Bernard Kiernan and Co, limited, 8, 9 and 10 little Britain street, wholesale grocers, wine and brandy shippers, licensed for the sale of beer, wine and spirits for consumption on the premises, the celebrant blessed the house and censed the mullioned windows and the groynes and the vaults and the arrises and the capitals and the pediments and the cornices and the engrailed arches and the spires and the cupolas and sprinkled the lintels thereof with blessed water and prayed that God might bless that house as he had blessed the house of Abraham and Isaac and Jacob and make the angels of His light to inhabit therein. And entering he blessed the viands and the beverages and the company of all the blessed answered his prayers.

—*Adiutorium nostrum in nomine Domini.*

—*Qui fecit cœlum et terram.*

—*Dominus vobiscum.*

—*Et cum spiritu tuo.*

And he laid his hands upon that he blessed and gave thanks and he prayed and they all with him prayed:

—*Deus, cuius verbo sanctificantur omnia, benedictionem tuam effunde super creaturas istas: et praesta ut quisquis eis secundum legem et voluntatem Tuam cum gratiarum actione usus fuerit per invocationem sanctissimi nominis Tui corporis sanitatem et animæ tutelam Te auctore percipiat per Christum Dominum nostrum.*

—And so say all of us, says Jack.

—Thousand a year, Lambert, says Crofton or Crawford.

—Right, says Ned, taking up his John Jameson. And butter for fish.

I was just looking around to see who the happy thought would strike when be damned but in he comes again letting on to be in a hell of a hurry.

—I was just round at the courthouse, says he, looking for you. I hope I'm not . . .

—No, says Martin, we're ready.

Courthouse my eye and your pockets hanging down with gold and silver. Mean bloody scut. Stand us a drink itself. Devil a sweet fear! There's a jew for you! All for number one. Cute as a shithouse rat. Hundred to five.

—Don't tell anyone, says the citizen.

—Beg your pardon, says he.

—Come on boys, says Martin, seeing it was looking blue. Come along now.

—Don't tell anyone, says the citizen, letting a bawl out of him. It's a secret.

And the bloody dog woke up and let a growl.

—Bye bye all, says Martin.

And he got them out as quick as he could, Jack Power and Crofton or whatever you call him and him in the middle of them letting on to be all at sea and up with them on the bloody jaunting car.

—Off with you, says Martin to the jarvey.

The milkwhite dolphin tossed his mane and, rising in the golden poop the helmsman spread the bellying sail upon the wind and stood off forward with all sail set, the spinnaker to larboard. A many comely nymphs drew nigh to starboard and to larboard and, clinging to the sides of the noble bark, they linked their shining forms as doth the cunning wheelwright when he fashions about the heart of his wheel the equidistant rays whereof each one is sister to another and he binds them all with an outer ring and giveth speed to the feet of men whenas they ride to a hosting or contend for the smile of ladies fair. Even so did they come and set them, those willing nymphs, the undying sisters. And they laughed, sporting in a circle of their foam: and the bark clave the waves.

But begob I was just lowering the heel of the pint when I saw the citizen getting up to waddle to the door, puffing and blowing with the dropsy, and he cursing the curse of Cromwell on him, bell, book and candle in Irish, spitting and spatting out of him and Joe and little Alf round him like a leprechaun trying to peacify him.

—Let me alone, says he.

And begob he got as far as the door and they holding him and he bawls out of him:

—Three cheers for Israel!

Arrah, sit down on the parliamentary side of your arse for Christ' sake and don't be making a public exhibition of yourself. Jesus, there's always some bloody clown or other kicking up a bloody murder about bloody nothing. Gob, it'd turn the porter sour in your guts, so it would.

And all the ragamuffins and sluts of the nation round the door and Martin telling the jarvey to drive ahead and the citizen bawling and Alf and Joe at him to whisht and he on his high horse about the jews and the loafers calling for a speech and Jack Power trying to get him to sit down on the car and hold his bloody jaw and a loafer with a patch over his eye starts singing *If the man in the moon was a jew, jew, jew* and a slut shouts out of her:

—Eh, mister! Your fly is open, mister!

And says he:

—Mendelssohn was a jew and Karl Marx and Mercadante and Spinoza. And the Saviour was a jew and his father was a jew. Your God.

—He had no father, says Martin. That'll do now. Drive ahead.

—Whose God? says the citizen.

—Well, his uncle was a jew, says he. Your God was a jew. Christ was a jew like me.

Gob, the citizen made a plunge back into the shop.

—By Jesus, says he, I'll brain that bloody jewman for using the holy name. By Jesus, I'll crucify him so I will. Give us that biscuitbox here.

—Stop! Stop! says Joe.

A large and appreciative gathering of friends and acquaintances from the metropolis and greater Dublin assembled in their thousands to bid farewell to Nagyaságos uram Lipóti Virag, late of Messrs Alexander Thom's, printers to His Majesty, on the occasion of his departure for the distant clime of Százharminczbrojúgulyás-Dugulás (Meadow of Murmuring Waters). The ceremony which went off with great *éclat* was characterised by the most affecting cordiality. An illuminated scroll of ancient Irish vellum, the work of Irish artists, was presented to the distinguished phenomenologist on behalf of a large section of the community and was accompanied by the gift of a silver casket, tastefully executed in the style of ancient Celtic ornament, a work which reflects every credit on the makers, Messrs Jacob *agus* Jacob. The departing guest was the recipient of a hearty ovation, many of those who were present being visibly moved when the select orchestra of Irish pipes struck up the wellknown strains of *Come Back to Erin*, followed immediately by *Rakóczsy's March*. Tarbarrels and bonfires were lighted along the coastline of the four seas on the summits of the Hill of Howth, Three Rock Mountain, Sugarloaf, Bray Head, the mountains of Mourne, the Galtees, the Ox and Donegal and Sperrin peaks, the Nagles and the Bograghs, the Connemara hills, the reeks of M'Gillicuddy, Slieve Aughty, Slieve Bernagh and Slieve Bloom. Amid cheers that rent the welkin, responded to by answering cheers from a big muster of henchmen on the distant Cambrian and Caledonian hills, the mastodontic pleasureship slowly moved away saluted by a final floral tribute from the representatives of the fair sex who were present in large numbers while, as it proceeded down the river, escorted by a flotilla of barges, the flags of the Ballast office and Custom House were dipped in salute as were also those of the electrical power station at the Pigeonhouse and the Poolbeg Light. *Visszontlátásra, kedvés barátom! Visszontlátásra!* Gone but not forgotten.

Gob, the devil wouldn't stop him till he got hold of the bloody tin anyhow and out with him and little Alf hanging on to his elbow and he shouting like a stuck pig, as good as any bloody play in the Queen's royal theatre:

—Where is he till I murder him?

And Ned and J. J. paralysed with the laughing.

—Bloody wars, says I, I'll be in for the last gospel.

But as luck would have it the jarvey got the nag's head round the other way and off with him.

—Hold on, citizen, says Joe. Stop!

Begob he drew his hand and made a swipe and let fly. Mercy of God the sun was in his eyes or he'd have left him for dead. Gob, he near sent it into the county Longford. The bloody nag took fright and the old mongrel after the car like bloody hell and all the populace shouting and laughing and the old tinbox clattering along the street.

The catastrophe was terrific and instantaneous in its effect. The observatory of Dunsink registered in all eleven shocks, all of the fifth grade of Mercalli's scale, and there is no record extant of a similar seismic disturbance in our island since the earthquake of 1534, the year of the rebellion of Silken Thomas. The epicentre appears to have been that part of the metropolis which constitutes the Inn's Quay ward and parish of Saint Michan covering a surface of fortyone acres, two roods and one square pole or perch. All the lordly residences in the vicinity of the palace of justice were demolished and that noble edifice itself, in which at the time of the catastrophe important legal debates were in progress, is literally a mass of ruins beneath which it is to be feared all the occupants have been buried alive. From the reports of eyewitnesses it transpires that the seismic waves were accompanied by a violent atmospheric perturbation of cyclonic character. An article of headgear since ascertained to belong to the much respected clerk of the crown and peace Mr George Fottrell and a silk umbrella with gold handle with the engraved initials, crest, coat of arms and house number of the erudite and worshipful chairman of quarter sessions sir Frederick Falkiner, recorder of Dublin, have been discovered by search parties in remote parts of the island respectively, the former on the third basaltic ridge of the giant's causeway, the latter embedded to the extent of one foot three inches in the sandy beach of Holeopen bay near the old head of Kinsale. Other eyewitnesses depose that they observed an incandescent object of enormous proportions hurtling through the atmosphere at a terrifying velocity in a trajectory directed southwest by west. Messages of condolence and sympathy are being hourly received from all parts of the different continents and the sovereign pontiff has been graciously pleased to decree that a special *missa pro defunctis* shall be celebrated simultaneously by the ordinaries of each and every cathedral church of all the episcopal dioceses subject to the spiritual authority of the Holy See in suffrage of the souls of those faithful departed who have been so unexpectedly called away from our midst. The work of salvage, removal of *débris,* human remains etc has been entrusted to Messrs Michael Meade and Son, 159 Great Brunswick street, and Messrs T. and C. Martin, 77, 78, 79 and 80 North Wall, assisted by the men and officers of the Duke of Cornwall's light infantry under the general supervision of H. R. H., rear admiral, the right honourable sir Hercules Hannibal Habeas Corpus Anderson, K. G., K. P., K. T., P. C., K. C. B., M. P., J. P., M. B., D. S. O., S. O. D., M. F. H., M. R. I. A., B. L., Mus. Doc., P. L. G., F. T. C. D., F. R. U. I., F. R. C. P. I. and F. R. C. S. I.

You never saw the like of it in all your born puff. Gob, if he got that lottery ticket on the side of his poll he'd remember the gold cup, he would so, but begob the citizen would have been lagged for assault and battery and Joe for aiding and abetting. The jarvey saved his life by furious driving as sure as God made Moses. What? O, Jesus, he did. And he let a volley of oaths after him.

—Did I kill him, says he, or what?

And he shouting to the bloody dog:

—After him, Garry! After him, boy!

And the last we saw was the bloody car rounding the corner and old sheepsface on it gesticulating and the bloody mongrel after it with his lugs back for all he was bloody well worth to tear him limb from limb. Hundred to five! Jesus, he took the value of it out of him, I promise you.

When, lo, there came about them all a great brightness and they beheld the chariot wherein He stood ascend to heaven. And they beheld Him in the chariot, clothed upon in the glory of the brightness, having raiment as of the sun, fair as the moon and terrible that for awe they durst not look upon Him. And there came a voice out of heaven, calling: *Elijah! Elijah!* And He answered with a main cry: *Abba! Adonai!* And they beheld Him even Him, ben Bloom Elijah, amid clouds of angels ascend to the glory of the brightness at an angle of fortyfive degrees over Donohoe's in Little Green street like a shot off a shovel.

13

The summer evening had begun to fold the world in its mysterious embrace. Far away in the west the sun was setting and the last glow of all too fleeting day lingered lovingly on sea and strand, on the proud promontory of dear old Howth guarding as ever the waters of the bay, on the weedgrown rocks along Sandymount shore and, last but not least, on the quiet church whence there streamed forth at times upon the stillness the voice of prayer to her who is in her pure radiance a beacon ever to the stormtossed heart of man, Mary, star of the sea.

The three girl friends were seated on the rocks, enjoying the evening scene and the air which was fresh but not too chilly. Many a time and oft were they wont to come there to that favourite nook to have a cosy chat beside the sparkling waves and discuss matters feminine, Cissy Caffrey and Edy Boardman with the baby in the pushcar and Tommy and Jacky Caffrey, two little curlyheaded boys, dressed in sailor suits with caps to match and the name H. M. S. *Belleisle* printed on both. For Tommy and Jacky Caffrey were twins, scarce four years old and very noisy and spoiled twins sometimes but for all that darling little fellows with bright merry faces and endearing ways about them. They were dabbling in the sand with their spades and buckets, building castles as children do, or playing with their big coloured ball, happy as the day was long. And Edy Boardman was rocking the chubby baby to and fro in the pushcar while that young gentleman fairly chuckled with delight. He was but eleven months and nine days old and, though still a tiny toddler, was just beginning to lisp his first babyish words. Cissy Caffrey bent over to him to tease his fat little plucks and the dainty dimple in his chin.

—Now, baby, Cissy Caffrey said. Say out big, big. I want a drink of water.

And baby prattled after her:

—A jink a jink a jawbo.

Cissy Caffrey cuddled the wee chap for she was awfully fond of children, so patient with little sufferers and Tommy Caffrey could never be got to take his castor oil unless it was Cissy Caffrey that held his nose and promised him the scatty heel of the loaf or brown bread with golden syrup on. What a persuasive power that girl had! But to be sure baby Boardman was as good as gold, a perfect little dote in his new fancy bib. None of your spoilt beauties, Flora MacFlimsy sort, was Cissy Caffrey. A truerhearted lass never drew the breath of life, always with a laugh in her gipsylike eyes and a frolicsome word on her cherryripe red lips, a girl lovable in the extreme. And Edy Boardman laughed too at the quaint language of little brother.

But just then there was a slight altercation between Master Tommy and Master Jacky. Boys will be boys and our two twins were no exception to this golden rule. The apple of discord was a certain castle of sand which Master Jacky had built and Master Tommy would have it right go wrong that it was to be architecturally improved by a frontdoor like the Martello tower had. But if Master Tommy was headstrong Master Jacky was selfwilled too and, true to the maxim that every little Irishman's house is his castle, he fell upon his hated rival and to such purpose that the wouldbe assailant came to grief and (alas to relate!) the coveted castle too. Needless to say the cries of discomfited Master Tommy drew the attention of the girl friends.

—Come here, Tommy, his sister called imperatively. At once! And you, Jacky, for shame to throw poor Tommy in the dirty sand. Wait till I catch you for that.

His eyes misty with unshed tears Master Tommy came at her call for their big sister's word was law with the twins. And in a sad plight he was too after his misadventure. His little man-o'-war top and unmentionables were full of sand but Cissy was a past mistress in the art of smoothing over life's tiny troubles and very quickly not one speck of sand was to be seen on his smart little suit. Still the blue eyes were glistening with hot tears that would well up so she kissed away the hurtness and shook her hand at Master Jacky the culprit and said if she was near him she wouldn't be far from him, her eyes dancing in admonition.

—Nasty bold Jacky! she cried.

She put an arm round the little mariner and coaxed winningly:

—What's your name? Butter and cream?

—Tell us who is your sweetheart, spoke Edy Boardman. Is Cissy your sweetheart?

—Nao, tearful Tommy said.

—Is Edy Boardman your sweetheart? Cissy queried.

—Nao, Tommy said.

—I know, Edy Boardman said none too amiably with an arch glance from her shortsighted eyes. I know who is Tommy's sweetheart. Gerty is Tommy's sweetheart.

—Nao, Tommy said on the verge of tears.

Cissy's quick motherwit guessed what was amiss and she whispered to Edy Boardman to take him there behind the pushcar where the gentleman couldn't see and to mind he didn't wet his new tan shoes.

But who was Gerty?

Gerty MacDowell who was seated near her companions, lost in thought, gazing far away into the distance was, in very truth, as fair a specimen of winsome Irish girlhood as one could wish to see. She was pronounced beautiful by all who knew her though, as folks often said, she was more a Giltrap than a MacDowell. Her figure was slight and graceful, inclining even to fragility but those iron jelloids she had been taking of late had done her a world of good much better than the Widow Welch's female pills and she was much better of those discharges she used to get and that tired feeling. The waxen pallor of her face was almost spiritual in its ivorylike purity though her rosebud mouth was a genuine Cupid's bow, Greekly perfect. Her hands were of finely veined alabaster with tapering fingers and as white as lemonjuice and queen of ointments could make them though it was not true that she used to wear kid gloves in bed or take a milk footbath either. Bertha Supple told that once to Edy Boardman, a deliberate lie, when she was black out at daggers drawn with Gerty (the girl chums had of course their little tiffs from time to time like the rest of mortals) and she told her not to let on whatever she did that it was her that told her or she'd never speak to her again. No. Honour where honour is due. There was an innate refinement, a languid queenly *hauteur* about Gerty which was unmistakably evidenced in her delicate hands and higharched instep. Had kind fate but willed her to be born a gentlewoman of high degree in her own right and had she only received the benefit of a good education Gerty MacDowell might easily have held her own beside any lady in the land and have seen herself exquisitely gowned with jewels on her brow and patrician suitors at her feet vying with one another to pay their devoirs to her. Mayhap it was this, the love that might have been, that lent to her softlyfeatured face at whiles a look, tense with suppressed meaning, that imparted a strange yearning tendency to the beautiful eyes, a charm few could resist. Why have women such eyes of witchery? Gerty's were of the bluest Irish blue, set off by lustrous lashes and dark expressive brows. Time was when those brows were not so silkily seductive. It was Madame Vera Verity, directress of the Woman Beautiful page of the Princess Novelette, who had first advised her to try eyebrowleine which gave that haunting expression to the eyes, so becoming in leaders of fashion, and she had never regretted it. Then there was blushing scientifically cured and how to be tall increase your height and you have a beautiful face but your nose? That would suit Mrs Dignam because she had a button one. But Gerty's crowning glory was her wealth of wonderful hair. It was dark brown with a natural wave in it. She had cut it that very morning on account of the new moon and it nestled about her pretty head in a profusion of luxuriant clusters and pared her nails too, Thursday for wealth. And just now at Edy's words as a telltale flush, delicate as the faintest rosebloom, crept into her cheeks she looked so lovely in her sweet girlish shyness that of a surety God's fair land of Ireland did not hold her equal.

For an instant she was silent with rather sad downcast eyes. She was about to retort but something checked the words on her tongue. Inclination prompted her to speak out: dignity told her to be silent. The pretty lips pouted awhile but then she glanced up and broke out into a joyous little laugh which had in it all the freshness of a young May morning. She knew right well, no-one better, what made squinty Edy say that because of him cooling in his attentions when it was simply a lovers' quarrel. As per usual somebody's nose was out of joint about the boy that had the bicycle off the London bridge road always riding up and down in front of her window. Only now his father kept him in in the evenings studying hard to get an exhibition in the intermediate that was on and he was going to go to Trinity college to study for a doctor when he left the high school like his brother W. E. Wylie who was racing in the bicycle races in Trinity college university. Little recked he perhaps for what she felt, that dull aching void in her heart sometimes, piercing to the core. Yet he was young and perchance he might learn to love her in time. They were protestants in his family and of course Gerty knew Who came first and after Him the Blessed Virgin and then Saint Joseph. But he was undeniably handsome with an exquisite nose and he was what he looked, every inch a gentleman, the shape of his head too at the back without his cap on that she would know anywhere something off the common and the way he turned the bicycle at the lamp with his hands off the bars and also the nice perfume of those good cigarettes and besides they were both of a size too he and she and that was why Edy Boardman thought she was so frightfully clever because he didn't go and ride up and down in front of her bit of a garden.

Gerty was dressed simply but with the instinctive taste of a votary of Dame Fashion for she felt that there was just a might that he might be out. A neat blouse of electric blue selftinted by dolly dyes (because it was expected in the *Lady's Pictorial* that electric blue would be worn) with a smart vee opening down to the division and kerchief pocket (in which she always kept a piece of cottonwool scented with her favourite perfume because the handkerchief spoiled the sit) and a navy threequarter skirt cut to the stride showed off her slim graceful figure to perfection. She wore a coquettish little love of a hat of wideleaved nigger straw contrast trimmed with an underbrim of eggblue chenille and at the side a butterfly bow of silk to tone. All Tuesday week afternoon she was hunting to match that chenille but at last she found what she wanted at Clery's summer sales, the very it, slightly shopsoiled but you would never notice, seven fingers two and a penny. She did it up all by herself and what joy was hers when she tried it on then, smiling at the lovely reflection which the mirror gave back to her! And when she put it on the waterjug to keep the shape she knew that that would take the shine out of some people she knew. Her shoes were the newest thing in footwear (Edy Boardman prided herself that she was very *petite* but she never had a foot like Gerty MacDowell, a five, and never would ash, oak or elm) with patent toecaps and just one smart buckle over her higharched instep. Her wellturned ankle displayed its perfect proportions beneath her skirt and just the proper amount and no more of her shapely limbs encased in finespun hose with highspliced heels and wide garter tops. As for undies they were Gerty's chief care and who that knows the fluttering hopes and fears of sweet seventeen (though Gerty would never see seventeen again) can find it in his heart to blame her? She had four dinky sets with awfully pretty stitchery, three garments and nighties extra, and each set slotted with different coloured ribbons, rosepink, pale blue, mauve and peagreen, and she aired them herself and blued them when they came home from the wash and ironed them and she had a brickbat to keep the iron on because she wouldn't trust those washerwomen as far as she'd see them scorching the things. She was wearing the blue for luck, hoping against hope, her own colour and lucky too for a bride to have a bit of blue somewhere on her because the green she wore that day week brought grief because his father brought him in to study for the intermediate exhibition and because she thought perhaps he might be out because when she was dressing that morning she nearly slipped up the old pair on her inside out and that was for luck and lovers' meeting if you put those things on inside out or if they got untied that he was thinking about you so long as it wasn't of a Friday.

And yet and yet! That strained look on her face! A gnawing sorrow is there all the time. Her very soul is in her eyes and she would give worlds to be in the privacy of her own familiar chamber where, giving way to tears, she could have a good cry and relieve her pentup feelings though not too much because she knew how to cry nicely before the mirror. You are lovely, Gerty, it said. The paly light of evening falls upon a face infinitely sad and wistful. Gerty MacDowell yearns in vain. Yes, she had known from the very first that her daydream of a marriage has been arranged and the weddingbells ringing for Mrs Reggy Wylie T. C. D. (because the one who married the elder brother would be Mrs Wylie) and in the fashionable intelligence Mrs Gertrude Wylie was wearing a sumptuous confection of grey trimmed with expensive blue fox was not to be. He was too young to understand. He would not believe in love, a woman's birthright. The night of the party long ago in Stoer's (he was still in short trousers) when they were alone and he stole an arm round her waist she went white to the very lips. He called her little one in a strangely husky voice and snatched a half kiss (the first!) but it was only the end of her nose and then he hastened from the room with a remark about refreshments. Impetuous fellow! Strength of character had never been Reggy Wylie's strong point and he who would woo and win Gerty MacDowell must be a man among men. But waiting, always waiting to be asked and it was leap year too and would soon be over. No prince charming is her beau ideal to lay a rare and wondrous love at her feet but rather a manly man with a strong quiet face who had not found his ideal, perhaps his hair slightly flecked with grey, and who would understand, take her in his sheltering arms, strain her to him in all the strength of his deep passionate nature and comfort her with a long long kiss. It would be like heaven. For such a one she yearns this balmy summer eve. With all the heart of her she longs to be his only, his affianced bride for riches for poor, in sickness in health, till death us two part, from this to this day forward.

And while Edy Boardman was with little Tommy behind the pushcar she was just thinking would the day ever come when she could call herself his little wife to be. Then they could talk about her till they went blue in the face, Bertha Supple too, and Edy, little spitfire, because she would be twentytwo in November. She would care for him with creature comforts too for Gerty was womanly wise and knew that a mere man liked that feeling of hominess. Her griddlecakes done to a goldenbrown hue and queen Ann's pudding of delightful creaminess had won golden opinions from all because she had a lucky hand also for lighting a fire, dredge in the fine selfraising flour and always stir in the same direction, then cream the milk and sugar and whisk well the white of eggs though she didn't like the eating part when there were any people that made her shy and often she wondered why you couldn't eat something poetical like violets or roses and they would have a beautifully appointed drawing room with pictures and engravings and the photograph of grandpapa Giltrap's lovely dog Garryowen that almost talked it was so human and chintz covers for the chairs and that silver toastrack in Clery's summer jumble sales like they have in rich houses. He would be tall with broad shoulders (she had always admired tall men for a husband) with glistening white teeth under his carefully trimmed sweeping moustache and they would go on the continent for their honeymoon (three wonderful weeks!) and then, when they settled down in a nice snug and cosy little homely house, every morning they would both have brekky, simple but perfectly served, for their own two selves and before he went out to business he would give his dear little wifey a good hearty hug and gaze for a moment deep down into her eyes.

Edy Boardman asked Tommy Caffrey was he done and he said yes so then she buttoned up his little knickerbockers for him and told him to run off and play with Jacky and to be good now and not to fight. But Tommy said he wanted the ball and Edy told him no that baby was playing with the ball and if he took it there'd be wigs on the green but Tommy said it was his ball and he wanted his ball and he pranced on the ground, if you please. The temper of him! O, he was a man already was little Tommy Caffrey since he was out of pinnies. Edy told him no, no and to be off now with him and she told Cissy Caffrey not to give in to him.

—You're not my sister, naughty Tommy said. It's my ball.

But Cissy Caffrey told baby Boardman to look up, look up high at her finger and she snatched the ball quickly and threw it along the sand and Tommy after it in full career, having won the day.

—Anything for a quiet life, laughed Ciss.

And she tickled tiny tot's two cheeks to make him forget and played here's the lord mayor, here's his two horses, here's his gingerbread carriage and here he walks in, chinchopper, chinchopper, chinchopper chin. But Edy got as cross as two sticks about him getting his own way like that from everyone always petting him.

—I'd like to give him something, she said, so I would, where I won't say.

—On the beeoteetom, laughed Cissy merrily.

Gerty MacDowell bent down her head and crimsoned at the idea of Cissy saying an unladylike thing like that out loud she'd be ashamed of her life to say, flushing a deep rosy red, and Edy Boardman said she was sure the gentleman opposite heard what she said. But not a pin cared Ciss.

—Let him! she said with a pert toss of her head and a piquant tilt of her nose. Give it to him too on the same place as quick as I'd look at him.

Madcap Ciss with her golliwog curls. You had to laugh at her sometimes. For instance when she asked you would you have some more Chinese tea and jaspberry ram and when she drew the jugs too and the men's faces on her nails with red ink make you split your sides or when she wanted to go where you know she said she wanted to run and pay a visit to the Miss White. That was just like Cissycums. O, and will you ever forget her the evening she dressed up in her father's suit and hat and the burned cork moustache and walked down Tritonville road, smoking a cigarette. There was none to come up to her for fun. But she was sincerity itself, one of the bravest and truest hearts heaven ever made, not one of your twofaced things, too sweet to be wholesome.

And then there came out upon the air the sound of voices and the pealing anthem of the organ. It was the men's temperance retreat conducted by the missioner, the reverend John Hughes S. J., rosary, sermon and benediction of the Most Blessed Sacrament. They were there gathered together without distinction of social class (and a most edifying spectacle it was to see) in that simple fane beside the waves, after the storms of this weary world, kneeling before the feet of the immaculate, reciting the litany of Our Lady of Loreto, beseeching her to intercede for them, the old familiar words, holy Mary, holy virgin of virgins. How sad to poor Gerty's ears! Had her father only avoided the clutches of the demon drink, by taking the pledge or those powders the drink habit cured in Pearson's Weekly, she might now be rolling in her carriage, second to none. Over and over had she told herself that as she mused by the dying embers in a brown study without the lamp because she hated two lights or oftentimes gazing out of the window dreamily by the hour at the rain falling on the rusty bucket, thinking. But that vile decoction which has ruined so many hearths and homes had cast its shadow over her childhood days. Nay, she had even witnessed in the home circle deeds of violence caused by intemperance and had seen her own father, a prey to the fumes of intoxication, forget himself completely for if there was one thing of all things that Gerty knew it was that the man who lifts his hand to a woman save in the way of kindness, deserves to be branded as the lowest of the low.

And still the voices sang in supplication to the Virgin most powerful, Virgin most merciful. And Gerty, rapt in thought, scarce saw or heard her companions or the twins at their boyish gambols or the gentleman off Sandymount green that Cissy Caffrey called the man that was so like himself passing along the strand taking a short walk. You never saw him any way screwed but still and for all that she would not like him for a father because he was too old or something or on account of his face (it was a palpable case of Doctor Fell) or his carbuncly nose with the pimples on it and his sandy moustache a bit white under his nose. Poor father! With all his faults she loved him still when he sang *Tell me, Mary, how to woo thee* or *My love and cottage near Rochelle* and they had stewed cockles and lettuce with Lazenby's salad dressing for supper and when he sang *The moon hath raised* with Mr Dignam that died suddenly and was buried, God have mercy on him, from a stroke. Her mother's birthday that was and Charley was home on his holidays and Tom and Mr Dignam and Mrs and Patsy and Freddy Dignam and they were to have had a group taken. No-one would have thought the end was so near. Now he was laid to rest. And her mother said to him to let that be a warning to him for the rest of his days and he couldn't even go to the funeral on account of the gout and she had to go into town to bring him the letters and samples from his office about Catesby's cork lino, artistic, standard designs, fit for a palace, gives tiptop wear and always bright and cheery in the home.

A sterling good daughter was Gerty just like a second mother in the house, a ministering angel too with a little heart worth its weight in gold. And when her mother had those raging splitting headaches who was it rubbed the menthol cone on her forehead but Gerty though she didn't like her mother's taking pinches of snuff and that was the only single thing they ever had words about, taking snuff. Everyone thought the world of her for her gentle ways. It was Gerty who turned off the gas at the main every night and it was Gerty who tacked up on the wall of that place where she never forgot every fortnight the chlorate of lime Mr Tunney the grocer's christmas almanac, the picture of halcyon days where a young gentleman in the costume they used to wear then with a threecornered hat was offering a bunch of flowers to his ladylove with oldtime chivalry through her lattice window. You could see there was a story behind it. The colours were done something lovely. She was in a soft clinging white in a studied attitude and the gentleman was in chocolate and he looked a thorough aristocrat. She often looked at them dreamily when she went there for a certain purpose and felt her own arms that were white and soft just like hers with the sleeves back and thought about those times because she had found out in Walker's pronouncing dictionary that belonged to grandpapa Giltrap about the halcyon days what they meant.

The twins were now playing in the most approved brotherly fashion till at last Master Jacky who was really as bold as brass there was no getting behind that deliberately kicked the ball as hard as ever he could down towards the seaweedy rocks. Needless to say poor Tommy was not slow to voice his dismay but luckily the gentleman in black who was sitting there by himself came gallantly to the rescue and intercepted the ball. Our two champions claimed their plaything with lusty cries and to avoid trouble Cissy Caffrey called to the gentleman to throw it to her please. The gentleman aimed the ball once or twice and then threw it up the strand towards Cissy Caffrey but it rolled down the slope and stopped right under Gerty's skirt near the little pool by the rock. The twins clamoured again for it and Cissy told her to kick it away and let them fight for it so Gerty drew back her foot but she wished their stupid ball hadn't come rolling down to her and she gave a kick but she missed and Edy and Cissy laughed.

—If you fail try again, Edy Boardman said.

Gerty smiled assent and bit her lip. A delicate pink crept into her pretty cheek but she was determined to let them see so she just lifted her skirt a little but just enough and took good aim and gave the ball a jolly good kick and it went ever so far and the two twins after it down towards the shingle. Pure jealousy of course it was nothing else to draw attention on account of the gentleman opposite looking. She felt the warm flush, a danger signal always with Gerty MacDowell, surging and flaming into her cheeks. Till then they had only exchanged glances of the most casual but now under the brim of her new hat she ventured a look at him and the face that met her gaze there in the twilight, wan and strangely drawn, seemed to her the saddest she had ever seen.

Through the open window of the church the fragrant incense was wafted and with it the fragrant names of her who was conceived without stain of original sin, spiritual vessel, pray for us, honourable vessel, pray for us, vessel of singular devotion, pray for us, mystical rose. And careworn hearts were there and toilers for their daily bread and many who had erred and wandered, their eyes wet with contrition but for all that bright with hope for the reverend father Father Hughes had told them what the great saint Bernard said in his famous prayer of Mary, the most pious Virgin's intercessory power that it was not recorded in any age that those who implored her powerful protection were ever abandoned by her.

The twins were now playing again right merrily for the troubles of childhood are but as fleeting summer showers. Cissy Caffrey played with baby Boardman till he crowed with glee, clapping baby hands in air. Peep she cried behind the hood of the pushcar and Edy asked where was Cissy gone and then Cissy popped up her head and cried ah! and, my word, didn't the little chap enjoy that! And then she told him to say papa.

—Say papa, baby. Say pa pa pa pa pa pa pa.

And baby did his level best to say it for he was very intelligent for eleven months everyone said and big for his age and the picture of health, a perfect little bunch of love, and he would certainly turn out to be something great, they said.

—Haja ja ja haja.

Cissy wiped his little mouth with the dribbling bib and wanted him to sit up properly and say pa pa pa but when she undid the strap she cried out, holy saint Denis, that he was possing wet and to double the half blanket the other way under him. Of course his infant majesty was most obstreperous at such toilet formalities and he let everyone know it:

—Habaa baaaahabaaa baaaa.

And two great big lovely big tears coursing down his cheeks. It was all no use soothering him with no, nono, baby, no and telling him about the geegee and where was the puffpuff but Ciss, always readywitted, gave him in his mouth the teat of the suckingbottle and the young heathen was quickly appeased.

Gerty wished to goodness they would take their squalling baby home out of that and not get on her nerves, no hour to be out, and the little brats of twins. She gazed out towards the distant sea. It was like the paintings that man used to do on the pavement with all the coloured chalks and such a pity too leaving them there to be all blotted out, the evening and the clouds coming out and the Bailey light on Howth and to hear the music like that and the perfume of those incense they burned in the church like a kind of waft. And while she gazed her heart went pitapat. Yes, it was her he was looking at, and there was meaning in his look. His eyes burned into her as though they would search her through and through, read her very soul. Wonderful eyes they were, superbly expressive, but could you trust them? People were so queer. She could see at once by his dark eyes and his pale intellectual face that he was a foreigner, the image of the photo she had of Martin Harvey, the matinee idol, only for the moustache which she preferred because she wasn't stagestruck like Winny Rippingham that wanted they two to always dress the same on account of a play but she could not see whether he had an aquiline nose or a slightly *retroussé* from where he was sitting. He was in deep mourning, she could see that, and the story of a haunting sorrow was written on his face. She would have given worlds to know what it was. He was looking up so intently, so still, and he saw her kick the ball and perhaps he could see the bright steel buckles of her shoes if she swung them like that thoughtfully with the toes down. She was glad that something told her to put on the transparent stockings thinking Reggy Wylie might be out but that was far away. Here was that of which she had so often dreamed. It was he who mattered and there was joy on her face because she wanted him because she felt instinctively that he was like no-one else. The very heart of the girlwoman went out to him, her dreamhusband, because she knew on the instant it was him. If he had suffered, more sinned against than sinning, or even, even, if he had been himself a sinner, a wicked man, she cared not. Even if he was a protestant or methodist she could convert him easily if he truly loved her. There were wounds that wanted healing with heartbalm. She was a womanly woman not like other flighty girls unfeminine he had known, those cyclists showing off what they hadn't got and she just yearned to know all, to forgive all if she could make him fall in love with her, make him forget the memory of the past. Then mayhap he would embrace her gently, like a real man, crushing her soft body to him, and love her, his ownest girlie, for herself alone.

Refuge of sinners. Comfortress of the afflicted. *Ora pro nobis*. Well has it been said that whosoever prays to her with faith and constancy can never be lost or cast away: and fitly is she too a haven of refuge for the afflicted because of the seven dolours which transpierced her own heart. Gerty could picture the whole scene in the church, the stained glass windows lighted up, the candles, the flowers and the blue banners of the blessed Virgin's sodality and Father Conroy was helping Canon O'Hanlon at the altar, carrying things in and out with his eyes cast down. He looked almost a saint and his confessionbox was so quiet and clean and dark and his hands were just like white wax and if ever she became a Dominican nun in their white habit perhaps he might come to the convent for the novena of Saint Dominic. He told her that time when she told him about that in confession, crimsoning up to the roots of her hair for fear he could see, not to be troubled because that was only the voice of nature and we were all subject to nature's laws, he said, in this life and that that was no sin because that came from the nature of woman instituted by God, he said, and that Our Blessed Lady herself said to the archangel Gabriel be it done unto me according to Thy Word. He was so kind and holy and often and often she thought and thought could she work a ruched teacosy with embroidered floral design for him as a present or a clock but they had a clock she noticed on the mantelpiece white and gold with a canarybird that came out of a little house to tell the time the day she went there about the flowers for the forty hours' adoration because it was hard to know what sort of a present to give or perhaps an album of illuminated views of Dublin or some place.

The exasperating little brats of twins began to quarrel again and Jacky threw the ball out towards the sea and they both ran after it. Little monkeys common as ditchwater. Someone ought to take them and give them a good hiding for themselves to keep them in their places, the both of them. And Cissy and Edy shouted after them to come back because they were afraid the tide might come in on them and be drowned.

—Jacky! Tommy!

Not they! What a great notion they had! So Cissy said it was the very last time she'd ever bring them out. She jumped up and called them and she ran down the slope past him, tossing her hair behind her which had a good enough colour if there had been more of it but with all the thingamerry she was always rubbing into it she couldn't get it to grow long because it wasn't natural so she could just go and throw her hat at it. She ran with long gandery strides it was a wonder she didn't rip up her skirt at the side that was too tight on her because there was a lot of the tomboy about Cissy Caffrey and she was a forward piece whenever she thought she had a good opportunity to show off and just because she was a good runner she ran like that so that he could see all the end of her petticoat running and her skinny shanks up as far as possible. It would have served her just right if she had tripped up over something accidentally on purpose with her high crooked French heels on her to make her look tall and got a fine tumble. *Tableau!* That would have been a very charming exposé for a gentleman like that to witness.

Queen of angels, queen of patriarchs, queen of prophets, of all saints, they prayed, queen of the most holy rosary and then Father Conroy handed the thurible to Canon O'Hanlon and he put in the incense and censed the Blessed Sacrament and Cissy Caffrey caught the two twins and she was itching to give them a ringing good clip on the ear but she didn't because she thought he might be watching but she never made a bigger mistake in all her life because Gerty could see without looking that he never took his eyes off of her and then Canon O'Hanlon handed the thurible back to Father Conroy and knelt down looking up at the Blessed Sacrament and the choir began to sing the *Tantum ergo* and she just swung her foot in and out in time as the music rose and fell to the *Tantumer gosa cramen tum*. Three and eleven she paid for those stockings in Sparrow's of George's street on the Tuesday, no the Monday before Easter and there wasn't a brack on them and that was what he was looking at, transparent, and not at her insignificant ones that had neither shape nor form (the cheek of her!) because he had eyes in his head to see the difference for himself.

Cissy came up along the strand with the two twins and their ball with her hat anyhow on her to one side after her run and she did look a streel tugging the two kids along with the flimsy blouse she bought only a fortnight before like a rag on her back and a bit of her petticoat hanging like a caricature. Gerty just took off her hat for a moment to settle her hair and a prettier, a daintier head of nutbrown tresses was never seen on a girl's shoulders—a radiant little vision, in sooth, almost maddening in its sweetness. You would have to travel many a long mile before you found a head of hair the like of that. She could almost see the swift answering flash of admiration in his eyes that set her tingling in every nerve. She put on her hat so that she could see from underneath the brim and swung her buckled shoe faster for her breath caught as she caught the expression in his eyes. He was eying her as a snake eyes its prey. Her woman's instinct told her that she had raised the devil in him and at the thought a burning scarlet swept from throat to brow till the lovely colour of her face became a glorious rose.

Edy Boardman was noticing it too because she was squinting at Gerty, half smiling, with her specs like an old maid, pretending to nurse the baby. Irritable little gnat she was and always would be and that was why no-one could get on with her poking her nose into what was no concern of hers. And she said to Gerty:

—A penny for your thoughts.

—What? replied Gerty with a smile reinforced by the whitest of teeth. I was only wondering was it late.

Because she wished to goodness they'd take the snottynosed twins and their babby home to the mischief out of that so that was why she just gave a gentle hint about its being late. And when Cissy came up Edy asked her the time and Miss Cissy, as glib as you like, said it was half past kissing time, time to kiss again. But Edy wanted to know because they were told to be in early.

—Wait, said Cissy, I'll run ask my uncle Peter over there what's the time by his conundrum.

So over she went and when he saw her coming she could see him take his hand out of his pocket, getting nervous, and beginning to play with his watchchain, looking up at the church. Passionate nature though he was Gerty could see that he had enormous control over himself. One moment he had been there, fascinated by a loveliness that made him gaze, and the next moment it was the quiet gravefaced gentleman, selfcontrol expressed in every line of his distinguishedlooking figure.

Cissy said to excuse her would he mind please telling her what was the right time and Gerty could see him taking out his watch, listening to it and looking up and clearing his throat and he said he was very sorry his watch was stopped but he thought it must be after eight because the sun was set. His voice had a cultured ring in it and though he spoke in measured accents there was a suspicion of a quiver in the mellow tones. Cissy said thanks and came back with her tongue out and said uncle said his waterworks were out of order.

Then they sang the second verse of the *Tantum ergo* and Canon O'Hanlon got up again and censed the Blessed Sacrament and knelt down and he told Father Conroy that one of the candles was just going to set fire to the flowers and Father Conroy got up and settled it all right and she could see the gentleman winding his watch and listening to the works and she swung her leg more in and out in time. It was getting darker but he could see and he was looking all the time that he was winding the watch or whatever he was doing to it and then he put it back and put his hands back into his pockets. She felt a kind of a sensation rushing all over her and she knew by the feel of her scalp and that irritation against her stays that that thing must be coming on because the last time too was when she clipped her hair on account of the moon. His dark eyes fixed themselves on her again drinking in her every contour, literally worshipping at her shrine. If ever there was undisguised admiration in a man's passionate gaze it was there plain to be seen on that man's face. It is for you, Gertrude MacDowell, and you know it.

Edy began to get ready to go and it was high time for her and Gerty noticed that that little hint she gave had had the desired effect because it was a long way along the strand to where there was the place to push up the pushcar and Cissy took off the twins' caps and tidied their hair to make herself attractive of course and Canon O'Hanlon stood up with his cope poking up at his neck and Father

Conroy handed him the card to read off and he read out *Panem de coelo praestitisti eis* and Edy and Cissy were talking about the time all the time and asking her but Gerty could pay them back in their own coin and she just answered with scathing politeness when Edy asked her was she heartbroken about her best boy throwing her over. Gerty winced sharply. A brief cold blaze shone from her eyes that spoke volumes of scorn immeasurable. It hurt—O yes, it cut deep because Edy had her own quiet way of saying things like that she knew would wound like the confounded little cat she was. Gerty's lips parted swiftly to frame the word but she fought back the sob that rose to her throat, so slim, so flawless, so beautifully mouldcd it seemed one an artist might have dreamed of. She had loved him better than he knew. Lighthearted deceiver and fickle like all his sex he would never understand what he had meant to her and for an instant there was in the blue eyes a quick stinging of tears. Their eyes were probing her mercilessly but with a brave effort she sparkled back in sympathy as she glanced at her new conquest for them to see.

—O, responded Gerty, quick as lightning, laughing, and the proud head flashed up. I can throw my cap at who I like because it's leap year.

Her words rang out crystalclear, more musical than the cooing of the ringdove, but they cut the silence icily. There was that in her young voice that told that she was not a one to be lightly trifled with. As for Mr Reggy with his swank and his bit of money she could just chuck him aside as if he was so much filth and never again would she cast as much as a second thought on him and tear his silly postcard into a dozen pieces. And if ever after he dared to presume she could give him one look of measured scorn that would make him shrivel up on the spot. Miss puny little Edy's countenance fell to no slight extent and Gerty could see by her looking as black as thunder that she was simply in a towering rage though she hid it, the little kinnatt, because that shaft had struck home for her petty jealousy and they both knew that she was something aloof, apart, in another sphere, that she was not of them and never would be and there was somebody else too that knew it and saw it so they could put that in their pipe and smoke it.

Edy straightened up baby Boardman to get ready to go and Cissy tucked in the ball and the spades and buckets and it was high time too because the sandman was on his way for Master Boardman junior. And Cissy told him too that billy winks was coming and that baby was to go deedaw and baby looked just too ducky, laughing up out of his gleeful eyes, and Cissy poked him like that out of fun in his wee fat tummy and baby, without as much as by your leave, sent up his compliments to all and sundry on to his brandnew dribbling bib.

—O my! Puddeny pie! protested Ciss. He has his bib destroyed.

The slight *contretemps* claimed her attention but in two twos she set that little matter to rights.

Gerty stifled a smothered exclamation and gave a nervous cough and Edy asked what and she was just going to tell her to catch it while it was flying but she was ever ladylike in her deportment so she simply passed it off with consummate tact by saying that that was the benediction because just then the bell rang out from the steeple over the quiet seashore because Canon O'Hanlon was up on the altar with the veil that Father Conroy put round his shoulders giving the benediction with the Blessed Sacrament in his hands.

How moving the scene there in the gathering twilight, the last glimpse of Erin, the touching chime of those evening bells and at the same time a bat flew forth from the ivied belfry through the dusk, hither, thither, with a tiny lost cry. And she could see far away the lights of the lighthouses so picturesque she would have loved to do with a box of paints because it was easier than to make a man and soon the lamplighter would be going his rounds past the presbyterian church grounds and along by shady Tritonville avenue where the couples walked and lighting the lamp near her window where Reggy Wylie used to turn his freewheel like she read in that book *The Lamplighter* by Miss Cummins, author of *Mabel Vaughan* and other tales. For Gerty had her dreams that no-one knew of. She loved to read poetry and when she got a keepsake from Bertha Supple of that lovely confession album with the coralpink cover to write her thoughts in she laid it in the drawer of her toilettable which, though it did not err on the side of luxury, was scrupulously neat and clean. It was there she kept her girlish treasure trove, the tortoiseshell combs, her child of Mary badge, the whiterose scent, the eyebrowleine, her alabaster pouncetbox and the ribbons to change when her things came home from the wash and there were some beautiful thoughts written in it in violet ink that she bought in Hely's of Dame Street for she felt that she too could write poetry if she could only express herself like that poem that appealed to her so deeply that she had copied out of the newspaper she found one evening round the potherbs. *Art thou real, my ideal?* it was called by Louis J Walsh, Magherafelt, and after there was something about *twilight, wilt thou ever?* and ofttimes the beauty of poetry, so sad in its transient loveliness, had misted her eyes with silent tears for she felt that the years were slipping by for her, one by one, and but for that one shortcoming she knew she need fear no competition and that was an accident coming down Dalkey hill and she always tried to conceal it. But it must end, she felt. If she saw that magic lure in his eyes there would be no holding back for her. Love laughs at locksmiths. She would make the great sacrifice. Her every effort would be to share his thoughts. Dearer than the whole world would she be to him and gild his days with happiness. There was the allimportant question and she was dying to know was he a married man or a widower who had lost his wife or some tragedy like the nobleman with the foreign name from the land of song had to have her put into a madhouse, cruel only to be kind. But even if— what then? Would it make a very great difference? From everything in the least indelicate her finebred nature instinctively recoiled. She loathed that sort of person, the fallen women off the accommodation walk beside the Dodder that went with the soldiers and coarse men with no respect for a girl's honour, degrading the sex and being taken up to the police station. No, no: not that. They would be just good friends like a big brother and sister without all that other in spite of the conventions of Society with a big ess. Perhaps it was an old flame he was in mourning for from the days beyond recall. She thought she understood. She would try to understand him because men were so different. The old love was waiting, waiting with little white hands stretched out, with blue appealing eyes. Heart of mine! She would follow, her dream of love, the dictates of her heart that told her he was her all in all, the only man in all the world for her for love was the master guide. Nothing else mattered. Come what might she would be wild, untrammelled, free.

Canon O'Hanlon put the Blessed Sacrament back into the tabernacle and genuflected and the choir sang *Laudate Dominum omnes gentes* and then he locked the tabernacle door because the benediction was over and Father Conroy handed him his hat to put on and crosscat Edy asked wasn't she coming but Jacky Caffrey called out:

—O, look, Cissy!

And they all looked was it sheet lightning but Tommy saw it too over the trees beside the church, blue and then green and purple.

—It's fireworks, Cissy Caffrey said.

And they all ran down the strand to see over the houses and the church, helterskelter, Edy with the pushcar with baby Boardman in it and Cissy holding Tommy and Jacky by the hand so they wouldn't fall running.

—Come on, Gerty, Cissy called. It's the bazaar fireworks.

But Gerty was adamant. She had no intention of being at their beck and call. If they could run like rossies she could sit so she said she could see from where she was. The eyes that were fastened upon her set her pulses tingling. She looked at him a moment, meeting his glance, and a light broke in upon her. Whitehot passion was in that face, passion silent as the grave, and it had made her his. At last they were left alone without the others to pry and pass remarks and she knew he could be trusted to the death, steadfast, a sterling man, a man of inflexible honour to his fingertips. His hands and face were working and a tremour went over her. She leaned back far to look up where the fireworks were and she caught her knee in her hands so as not to fall back looking up and there was no-one to see only him and her when she revealed all her graceful beautifully shaped legs like that, supply soft and delicately rounded, and she seemed to hear the panting of his heart, his hoarse breathing, because she knew too about the passion of men like that, hotblooded, because Bertha Supple told her once in dead secret and made her swear she'd never about the gentleman lodger that was staying with them out of the Congested Districts Board that had pictures cut out of papers of those skirtdancers and highkickers and she said he used to do something not very nice that you could imagine sometimes in the bed. But this was altogether different from a thing like that because there was all the difference because she could almost feel him draw her face to his and the first quick hot touch of his handsome lips. Besides there was absolution so long as you didn't do the other thing before being married and there ought to be women priests that would understand without your telling out and Cissy Caffrey too sometimes had that dreamy kind of dreamy look in her eyes so that she too, my dear, and Winny Rippingham so mad about actors' photographs and besides it was on account of that other thing coming on the way it did.

And Jacky Caffrey shouted to look, there was another and she leaned back and the garters were blue to match on account of the transparent and they all saw it and they all shouted to look, look, there it was and she leaned back ever so far to see the fireworks and something queer was flying through the air, a soft thing, to and fro, dark. And she saw a long Roman candle going up over the trees, up, up, and, in the tense hush, they were all breathless with excitement as it went higher and higher and she had to lean back more and more to look up after it, high, high, almost out of sight, and her face was suffused with a divine, an entrancing blush from straining back and he could see her other things too, nainsook knickers, the fabric that caresses the skin, better than those other pettiwidth, the green, four and eleven, on account of being white and she let him and she saw that he saw and then it went so high it went out of sight a moment and she was trembling in every limb from being bent so far back that he had a full view high up above her knee where no-one ever not even on the swing or wading and she wasn't ashamed and he wasn't either to look in that immodest way like that because he couldn't resist the sight of the wondrous revealment half offered like those skirtdancers behaving so immodest before gentlemen looking and he kept on looking, looking. She would fain have cried to him chokingly, held out her snowy slender arms to him to come, to feel his lips laid on her white brow, the cry of a young girl's love, a little strangled cry, wrung from her, that cry that has rung through the ages. And then a rocket sprang and bang shot blind blank and O! then the Roman candle burst and it was like a sigh of O! and everyone cried O! O! in raptures and it gushed out of it a stream of rain gold hair threads and they shed and ah! they were all greeny dewy stars falling with golden, O so lovely, O, soft, sweet, soft!

Then all melted away dewily in the grey air: all was silent. Ah! She glanced at him as she bent forward quickly, a pathetic little glance of piteous protest, of shy reproach under which he coloured like a girl. He was leaning back against the rock behind. Leopold Bloom (for it is he) stands silent, with bowed head before those young guileless eyes. What a brute he had been! At it again? A fair unsullied soul had called to him and, wretch that he was, how had he answered? An utter cad he had been! He of all men! But there was an infinite store of mercy in those eyes, for him too a word of pardon even though he had erred and sinned and wandered. Should a girl tell? No, a thousand times no. That was their secret, only theirs, alone in the hiding twilight and there was none to know or tell save the little bat that flew so softly through the evening to and fro and little bats don't tell.

Cissy Caffrey whistled, imitating the boys in the football field to show what a great person she was: and then she cried:

—Gerty! Gerty! We're going. Come on. We can see from farther up.

Gerty had an idea, one of love's little ruses. She slipped a hand into her kerchief pocket and took out the wadding and waved in reply of course without letting him and then slipped it back. Wonder if he's too far to. She rose. Was it goodbye? No. She had to go but they would meet again, there, and she would dream of that till then, tomorrow, of her dream of yester eve. She drew herself up to her full height. Their souls met in a last lingering glance and the eyes that reached her heart, full of a strange shining, hung enraptured on her sweet flowerlike face. She half smiled at him wanly, a sweet forgiving smile, a smile that verged on tears, and then they parted.

Slowly, without looking back she went down the uneven strand to Cissy, to Edy to Jacky and Tommy Caffrey, to little baby Boardman. It was darker now and there were stones and bits of wood on the strand and slippy seaweed. She walked with a certain quiet dignity characteristic of her but with care and very slowly because—because Gerty MacDowell was . . .

Tight boots? No. She's lame! O!

Mr Bloom watched her as she limped away. Poor girl! That's why she's left on the shelf and the others did a sprint. Thought something was wrong by the cut of her jib. Jilted beauty. A defect is ten times worse in a woman. But makes them polite. Glad I didn't know it when she was on show. Hot little devil all the same. I wouldn't mind. Curiosity like a nun or a negress or a girl with glasses. That squinty one is delicate. Near her monthlies, I expect, makes them feel ticklish. I have such a bad headache today. Where did I put the letter? Yes, all right. All kinds of crazy longings. Licking pennies. Girl in Tranquilla convent that nun told me liked to smell rock oil. Virgins go mad in the end I suppose. Sister? How many women in Dublin have it today? Martha, she. Something in the air. That's the moon. But then why don't all women menstruate at the same time with the same moon, I mean? Depends on the time they were born I suppose. Or all start scratch then get out of step. Sometimes Molly and Milly together. Anyhow I got the best of that. Damned glad I didn't do it in the bath this morning over her silly I will punish you letter. Made up for that tramdriver this morning. That gouger M'Coy stopping me to say nothing. And his wife engagement in the country valise, voice like a pickaxe. Thankful for small mercies. Cheap too. Yours for the asking. Because they want it themselves. Their natural craving. Shoals of them every evening poured out of offices. Reserve better. Don't want it they throw it at you. Catch 'em alive, O. Pity they can't see themselves. A dream of wellfilled hose. Where was that? Ah, yes. Mutoscope pictures in Capel street: for men only. Peeping Tom. Willy's hat and what the girls did with it. Do they snapshot those girls or is it all a fake? *Lingerie* does it. Felt for the curves inside her *déshabillé*. Excites them also when they're. I'm all clean come and dirty me. And they like dressing one another for the sacrifice. Milly delighted with Molly's new blouse. At first. Put them all on to take them all off. Molly. Why I bought her the violet garters. Us too: the tie he wore, his lovely socks and turnedup trousers. He wore a pair of gaiters the night that first we met. His lovely shirt was shining beneath his what? of jet. Say a woman loses a charm with every pin she takes out. Pinned together. O, Mairy lost the pin of her. Dressed up to the nines for somebody. Fashion part of their charm. Just changes when you're on the track of the secret. Except the east: Mary, Martha: now as then. No reasonable offer refused. She wasn't in a hurry either. Always off to a fellow when they are. They never forget an appointment. Out on spec probably. They believe in chance because like themselves. And the others inclined to give her an odd dig. Girl friends at school, arms round each other's necks or with ten fingers locked, kissing and whispering secrets about nothing in the convent garden. Nuns with whitewashed faces, cool coifs and their rosaries going up and down, vindictive too for what they can't get. Barbed wire. Be sure now and write to me. And I'll write to you. Now won't you? Molly and Josie Powell. Till Mr Right comes along, then meet once in a blue moon. *Tableau!* O, look who it is for the love of God! How are you at all? What have you been doing with yourself? Kiss and delighted to, kiss, to see you. Picking holes in each other's appearance. You're looking splendid. Sister souls. Showing their teeth at one another. How many have you left? Wouldn't lend each other a pinch of salt.

Ah!

Devils they are when that's coming on them. Dark devilish appearance. Molly often told me feel things a ton weight. Scratch the sole of my foot. O that way! O, that's exquisite! Feel it myself too. Good to rest once in a way. Wonder if it's bad to go with them then.

Safe in one way. Turns milk, makes fiddlestrings snap. Something about withering plants I read in a garden. Besides they say if the flower withers she wears she's a flirt. All are. Daresay she felt I. When you feel like that you often meet what you feel. Liked me or what? Dress they look at. Always know a fellow courting: collars and cuffs. Well cocks and lions do the same and stags. Same time might prefer a tie undone or something. Trousers? Suppose I when I was? No. Gently does it. Dislike rough and tumble. Kiss in the dark and never tell. Saw something in me. Wonder what. Sooner have me as I am than some poet chap with bearsgrease plastery hair, lovelock over his dexter optic. To aid gentleman in literary. Ought to attend to my appearance my age. Didn't let her see me in profile. Still, you never know. Pretty girls and ugly men marrying. Beauty and the beast. Besides I can't be so if Molly. Took off her hat to show her hair. Wide brim. Bought to hide her face, meeting someone might know her, bend down or carry a bunch of flowers to smell. Hair strong in rut. Ten bob I got for Molly's combings when we were on the rocks in Holles street. Why not? Suppose he gave her money. Why not? All a prejudice. She's worth ten, fifteen, more, a pound. What? I think so. All that for nothing. Bold hand: Mrs Marion. Did I forget to write address on that letter like the postcard I sent to Flynn? And the day I went to Drimmie's without a necktie. Wrangle with Molly it was put me off. No, I remember. Richie Goulding: he's another. Weighs on his mind. Funny my watch stopped at half past four. Dust. Shark liver oil they use to clean. Could do it myself. Save. Was that just when he, she?

O, he did. Into her. She did. Done.

Ah!

Mr Bloom with careful hand recomposed his wet shirt. O Lord, that little limping devil. Begins to feel cold and clammy. Aftereffect not pleasant. Still you have to get rid of it someway. They don't care. Complimented perhaps. Go home to nicey bread and milky and say night prayers with the kiddies. Well, aren't they? See her as she is spoil all. Must have the stage setting, the rouge, costume, position, music. The name too. *Amours* of actresses. Nell Gwynn, Mrs Bracegirdle, Maud Branscombe. Curtain up. Moonlight silver effulgence. Maiden discovered with pensive bosom. Little sweetheart come and kiss me. Still, I feel. The strength it gives a man. That's the secret of it. Good job I let off there behind the wall coming out of Dignam's. Cider that was. Otherwise I couldn't have. Makes you want to sing after. *Lacaus esant taratara.* Suppose I spoke to her. What about? Bad plan however if you don't know how to end the conversation. Ask them a question they ask you another. Good idea if you're stuck. Gain time. But then you're in a cart. Wonderful of course if you say: good evening, and you see she's on for it: good evening. O but the dark evening in the Appian way I nearly spoke to Mrs Clinch O thinking she was. Whew! Girl in Meath street that night. All the dirty things I made her say. All wrong of course. My arks she called it. It's so hard to find one who. Aho! If you don't answer when they solicit must be horrible for them till they harden. And kissed my hand when I gave her the extra two shillings. Parrots. Press the button and the bird will squeak. Wish she hadn't called me sir. O, her mouth in the dark! And you a married man with a single girl! That's what they enjoy. Taking a man from another woman. Or even hear of it. Different with me. Glad to get away from other chap's wife. Eating off his cold plate. Chap in the Burton today spitting back gumchewed gristle. French letter still in my pocketbook. Cause of half the trouble. But might happen sometime, I don't think. Come in, all is prepared. I dreamt. What? Worst is beginning. How they change the venue when it's not what they like. Ask you do you like mushrooms because she once knew a gentleman who. Or ask you what someone was going to say when he changed his mind and stopped. Yet if I went the whole hog, say: I want to, something like that. Because I did. She too. Offend her. Then make it up. Pretend to want something awfully, then cry off for her sake. Flatters them. She must have been thinking of someone else all the time. What harm? Must since she came to the use of reason, he, he and he. First kiss does the trick. The propitious moment. Something inside them goes pop. Mushy like, tell by their eye, on the sly. First thoughts are best. Remember that till their dying day. Molly, lieutenant Mulvey that kissed her under the Moorish wall beside the gardens. Fifteen she told me. But her breasts were developed. Fell asleep then. After Glencree dinner that was when we drove home. Featherbed mountain. Gnashing her teeth in sleep. Lord mayor had his eye on her too. Val Dillon. Apoplectic.

There she is with them down there for the fireworks. My fireworks. Up like a rocket, down like a stick. And the children, twins they must be, waiting for something to happen. Want to be grownups. Dressing in mother's clothes. Time enough, understand all the ways of the world. And the dark one with the mop head and the nigger mouth. I knew she could whistle. Mouth made for that. Like Molly. Why that highclass whore in Jammet's wore her veil only to her nose. Would you mind, please, telling me the right time? I'll tell you the right time up a dark lane. Say prunes and prisms forty times every morning, cure for fat lips. Caressing the little boy too. Onlookers see most of the game. Of course they understand birds, animals, babies. In their line.

Didn't look back when she was going down the strand. Wouldn't give that satisfaction. Those girls, those girls, those lovely seaside girls. Fine eyes she had, clear. It's the white of the eye brings that out not so much the pupil. Did she know what I? Course. Like a cat sitting beyond a dog's jump. Women never meet one like that Wilkins in the high school drawing a picture of Venus with all his belongings on show. Call that innocence? Poor idiot! His wife has her work cut out for her. Never see them sit on a bench marked *Wet Paint*. Eyes all over them. Look under the bed for what's not there. Longing to get the fright of their lives. Sharp as needles they are. When I said to Molly the man at the corner of Cuffe street was goodlooking, thought she might like, twigged at once he had a false arm. Had, too. Where do they get that? Typist going up Roger Greene's stairs two at a time to show her understandings. Handed down from father to, mother to daughter, I mean. Bred in the bone. Milly for example drying her handkerchief on the mirror to save the ironing. Best place for an ad to catch a woman's eye on a mirror. And when I sent her for Molly's Paisley shawl to Prescott's by the way that ad I must, carrying home the change in her stocking! Clever little minx. I never told her. Neat way she carries parcels too. Attract men, small thing like that. Holding up her hand, shaking it, to let the blood flow back when it was red. Who did you learn that from? Nobody. Something the nurse taught me. O, don't they know! Three years old she was in front of Molly's dressingtable, just before we left Lombard street west. Me have a nice pace. Mullingar. Who knows? Ways of the world. Young student. Straight on her pins anyway not like the other. Still she was game. Lord, I am wet. Devil you are. Swell of her calf. Transparent stockings, stretched to breaking point. Not like that frump today. A. E. Rumpled stockings. Or the one in Grafton street. White. Wow! Beef to the heel.

A monkey puzzle rocket burst, spluttering in darting crackles. Zrads and zrads, zrads, zrads. And Cissy and Tommy and Jacky ran out to see and Edy after with the pushcar and then Gerty beyond the curve of the rocks. Will she? Watch! Watch! See! Looked round. She smelt an onion. Darling, I saw, your. I saw all.

Lord!

Did me good all the same. Off colour after Kiernan's, Dignam's. For this relief much thanks. In *Hamlet,* that is. Lord! It was all things combined. Excitement. When she leaned back, felt an ache at the butt of my tongue. Your head it simply swirls. He's right. Might have made a worse fool of myself however. Instead of talking about nothing. Then I will tell you all. Still it was a kind of language between us. It couldn't be? No, Gerty they called her. Might be false name however like my name and the address Dolphin's barn a blind.

Her maiden name was Jemina Brown
And she lived with her mother in Irishtown.

Place made me think of that I suppose. All tarred with the same brush. Wiping pens in their stockings. But the ball rolled down to her as if it understood. Every bullet has its billet. Course I never could throw anything straight at school. Crooked as a ram's horn. Sad however because it lasts only a few years till they settle down to potwalloping and papa's pants will soon fit Willy and fuller's earth for the baby when they hold him out to do ah ah. No soft job. Saves them. Keeps them out of harm's way. Nature. Washing child, washing corpse. Dignam. Children's hands always round them. Cocoanut skulls, monkeys, not even closed at first, sour milk in their swaddles and tainted curds. Oughtn't to have given that child an empty teat to suck. Fill it up with wind. Mrs Beaufoy, Purefoy. Must call to the hospital. Wonder is nurse Callan there still. She used to look over some nights when Molly was in the Coffee Palace. That young doctor O'Hare I noticed her brushing his coat. And Mrs Breen and Mrs Dignam once like that too, marriageable. Worst of all at night Mrs Duggan told me in the City Arms. Husband rolling in drunk, stink of pub off him like a polecat. Have that in your nose in the dark, whiff of stale boose. Then ask in the morning: was I drunk last night? Bad policy however to fault the husband. Chickens come home to roost. They stick by one another like glue. Maybe the women's fault also. That's where Molly can knock spots off them. It's the blood of the south. Moorish. Also the form, the figure. Hands felt for the opulent. Just compare for instance those others. Wife locked up at home, skeleton in the cupboard. Allow me to introduce my. Then they trot you out some kind of a nondescript, wouldn't know what to call her. Always see a fellow's weak point in his wife. Still there's destiny in it, falling in love. Have their own secrets between them. Chaps that would go to the dogs if some woman didn't take them in hand. Then little chits of girls, height of a shilling in coppers, with little hubbies. As God made them he matched them. Sometimes children turn out well enough. Twice nought makes one. Or old rich chap of seventy and blushing bride. Marry in May and repent in December. This wet is very unpleasant. Stuck. Well the foreskin is not back. Better detach.

Ow!

Other hand a sixfooter with a wifey up to his watchpocket. Long and the short of it. Big he and little she. Very strange about my watch. Wristwatches are always going wrong. Wonder is there any magnetic influence between the person because that was about the time he. Yes, I suppose, at once. Cat's away, the mice will play. I remember looking in Pill lane. Also that now is magnetism. Back of everything magnetism. Earth for instance pulling this and being pulled. That causes movement. And time, well that's the time the movement takes. Then if one thing stopped the whole ghesabo would stop bit by bit. Because it's all arranged. Magnetic needle tells you what's going on in the sun, the stars. Little piece of steel iron. When you hold out the fork. Come. Come. Tip. Woman and man that is. Fork and steel. Molly, he. Dress up and look and suggest and let you see and see more and defy you if you're a man to see that and, like a sneeze coming, legs, look, look and if you have any guts in you. Tip. Have to let fly.

Wonder how is she feeling in that region. Shame all put on before third person. More put out about a hole in her stocking. Molly, her underjaw stuck out, head back, about the farmer in the ridingboots and spurs at the horse show. And when the painters were in Lombard street west. Fine voice that fellow had. How Giuglini began. Smell that I did. Like flowers. It was too. Violets. Came from the turpentine probably in the paint. Make their own use of everything. Same time doing it scraped her slipper on the floor so they wouldn't hear. But lots of them can't kick the beam, I think. Keep that thing up for hours. Kind of a general all round over me and half down my back.

Wait. Hm. Hm. Yes. That's her perfume. Why she waved her hand. I leave you this to think of me when I'm far away on the pillow.

What is it? Heliotrope? No. Hyacinth? Hm. Roses, I think. She'd like scent of that kind. Sweet and cheap: soon sour. Why Molly likes opoponax. Suits her, with a little jessamine mixed. Her high notes and her low notes. At the dance night she met him, dance of the hours. Heat brought it out. She was wearing her black and it had the perfume of the time before. Good conductor, is it? Or bad? Light too. Suppose there's some connection. For instance if you go into a cellar where it's dark. Mysterious thing too. Why did I smell it only now? Took its time in coming like herself, slow but sure. Suppose it's ever so many millions of tiny grains blown across. Yes, it is. Because those spice islands, Cinghalese this morning, smell them leagues off. Tell you what it is. It's like a fine fine veil or web they have all over the skin, fine like what do you call it gossamer, and they're always spinning it out of them, fine as anything, like rainbow colours without knowing it. Clings to everything she takes off. Vamp of her stockings. Warm shoe. Stays. Drawers: little kick, taking them off. Byby till next time. Also the cat likes to sniff in her shift on the bed. Know her smell in a thousand. Bathwater too. Reminds me of strawberries and cream. Wonder where it is really. There or the armpits or under the neck. Because you get it out of all holes and corners. Hyacinth perfume made of oil of ether or something. Muskrat. Bag under their tails. One grain pour off odour for years. Dogs at each other behind. Good evening. Evening. How do you sniff? Hm. Hm. Very well, thank you. Animals go by that. Yes now, look at it that way. We're the same. Some women, instance, warn you off when they have their period. Come near. Then get a hogo you could hang your hat on. Like what? Potted herrings gone stale or. Boof! Please keep off the grass.

Perhaps they get a man smell off us. What though? Cigary gloves long John had on his desk the other day. Breath? What you eat and drink gives that. No. Mansmell, I mean. Must be connected with that because priests that are supposed to be are different. Women buzz round it like flies round treacle. Railed off the altar get on to it at any cost. The tree of forbidden priest. O, father, will you? Let me be the first to. That diffuses itself all through the body, permeates. Source of life. And it's extremely curious the smell. Celery sauce. Let me.

Mr Bloom inserted his nose. Hm. Into the. Hm. Opening of his waistcoat. Almonds or. No. Lemons it is. Ah no, that's the soap.

O by the by that lotion. I knew there was something on my mind. Never went back and the soap not paid. Dislike carrying bottles like that hag this morning. Hynes might have paid me that three shillings. I could mention Meagher's just to remind him. Still if he works that paragraph. Two and nine. Bad opinion of me he'll have. Call tomorrow. How much do I owe you? Three and nine? Two and nine, sir. Ah. Might stop him giving credit another time. Lose your customers that way. Pubs do. Fellows run up a bill on the slate and then slinking around the back streets into somewhere else.

Here's this nobleman passed before. Blown in from the bay. Just went as far as turn back. Always at home at dinnertime. Looks mangled out: had a good tuck in. Enjoying nature now. Grace after meals. After supper walk a mile. Sure he has a small bank balance somewhere, government sit. Walk after him now make him awkward like those newsboys me today. Still you learn something. See ourselves as others see us. So long as women don't mock what matter? That's the way to find out. Ask yourself who is he now. *The Mystery Man on the Beach*, prize titbit story by Mr Leopold Bloom. Payment at the rate of one guinea per column. And that fellow today at the graveside in the brown macintosh. Corns on his kismet however. Healthy perhaps absorb all the. Whistle brings rain they say. Must be some somewhere. Salt in the Ormond damp. The body feels the atmosphere. Old Betty's joints are on the rack. Mother Shipton's prophecy that is about ships around they fly in the twinkling. No. Signs of rain it is. The royal reader. And distant hills seem coming nigh.

Howth. Bailey light. Two, four, six, eight, nine. See. Has to change or they might think it a house. Wreckers. Grace Darling. People afraid of the dark. Also glowworms, cyclists: lightingup time. Jewels diamonds flash better. Women. Light is a kind of reassuring. Not going to hurt you. Better now of course than long ago. Country roads. Run you through the small guts for nothing. Still two types there are you bob against. Scowl or smile. Pardon! Not at all. Best time to spray plants too in the shade after the sun. Some light still. Red rays are longest. Roygbiv Vance taught us: red, orange, yellow, green, blue, indigo, violet. A star I see. Venus? Can't tell yet. Two. When three it's night. Were those nightclouds there all the time? Looks like a phantom ship. No. Wait. Trees are they? An optical illusion. Mirage. Land of the setting sun this. Homerule sun setting in the southeast. My native land, goodnight.

Dew falling. Bad for you, dear, to sit on that stone. Brings on white fluxions. Never have little baby then less he was big strong fight his way up through. Might get piles myself. Sticks too like a summer cold, sore on the mouth. Cut with grass or paper worst. Friction of the position. Like to be that rock she sat on. O sweet little, you don't know how nice you looked. I begin to like them at that age. Green apples. Grab at all that offer. Suppose it's the only time we cross legs, seated. Also the library today: those girl graduates. Happy chairs under them. But it's the evening influence. They feel all that. Open like flowers, know their hours, sunflowers, Jerusalem artichokes, in ballrooms, chandeliers, avenues under the lamps. Nightstock in Mat Dillon's garden where I kissed her shoulder. Wish I had a full length oilpainting of her then. June that was too I wooed. The year returns. History repeats itself. Ye crags and peaks I'm with you once again. Life, love, voyage round your own little world. And now? Sad about her lame of course but must be on your guard not to feel too much pity. They take advantage.

All quiet on Howth now. The distant hills seem. Where we. The rhododendrons. I am a fool perhaps. He gets the plums, and I the plumstones. Where I come in. All that old hill has seen. Names change: that's all. Lovers: yum yum.

Tired I feel now. Will I get up? O wait. Drained all the manhood out of me, little wretch. She kissed me. Never again. My youth. Only once it comes. Or hers. Take the train there tomorrow. No. Returning not the same. Like kids your second visit to a house. The new I want. Nothing new under the sun. Care of P. O. Dolphin's Barn. Are you not happy in your? Naughty darling. At Dolphin's barn charades in Luke Doyle's house. Mat Dillon and his bevy of daughters: Tiny, Atty, Floey, Maimy, Louy, Hetty. Molly too. Eightyseven that was. Year before we. And the old major, partial to his drop of spirits. Curious she an only child, I an only child. So it returns. Think you're escaping and run into yourself. Longest way round is the shortest way home. And just when he and she. Circus horse walking in a ring. Rip van Winkle we played. Rip: tear in Henny Doyle's overcoat. Van: breadvan delivering. Winkle: cockles and periwinkles. Then I did Rip van Winkle coming back. She leaned on the sideboard watching. Moorish eyes. Twenty years asleep in Sleepy Hollow. All changed. Forgotten. The young are old. His gun rusty from the dew.

Ba. What is that flying about? Swallow? Bat probably. Thinks I'm a tree, so blind. Have birds no smell? Metempsychosis. They believed you could be changed into a tree from grief. Weeping willow. Ba.

There he goes. Funny little beggar. Wonder where he lives. Belfry up there. Very likely. Hanging by his heels in the odour of sanctity. Bell scared him out, I suppose. Mass seems to be over. Could hear them all at it. Pray for us. And pray for us. And pray for us. Good idea the repetition. Same thing with ads. Buy from us. And buy from us. Yes, there's the light in the priest's house. Their frugal meal. Remember about the mistake in the valuation when I was in Thom's. Twentyeight it is. Two houses they have. Gabriel Conroy's brother is curate. Ba. Again. Wonder why they come out at night like mice. They're a mixed breed. Birds are like hopping mice. What frightens them, light or noise? Better sit still. All instinct like the bird in drouth got water out of the end of a jar by throwing in pebbles. Like a little man in a cloak he is with tiny hands. Weeny bones. Almost see them shimmering, kind of a bluey white. Colours depend on the light you see. Stare the sun for example like the eagle then look at a shoe see a blotch blob yellowish. Wants to stamp his trademark on everything. Instance, that cat this morning on the staircase. Colour of brown turf. Say you never see them with three colours. Not true. That half tabbywhite tortoiseshell in the *City Arms* with the letter 'em on her forehead. Body fifty different colours. Howth a while ago amethyst. Glass flashing. That's how that wise man what's his name with the burning glass. Then the heather goes on fire. It can't be tourists' matches. What? Perhaps the sticks dry rub together in the wind and light. Or broken bottles in the furze act as a burning glass in the sun. Archimedes. I have it! My memory's not so bad.

Ba. Who knows what they're always flying for. Insects? That bee last week got into the room playing with his shadow on the ceiling. Might be the one bit me, come back to see. Birds too. Never find out. Or what they say. Like our small talk. And says she and says he. Nerve they have to fly over the ocean and back. Lots must be killed in storms, telegraph wires. Dreadful life sailors have too. Big brutes of oceangoing steamers floundering along in the dark, lowing out like seacows. *Faugh a ballagh!* Out of that, bloody curse to you! Others in vessels, bit of a handkerchief sail, pitched about like snuff at a wake when the stormy winds do blow. Married too. Sometimes away for years at the ends of the earth somewhere. No ends really because it's round. Wife in every port they say. She has a good job if she minds it till Johnny comes marching home again. If ever he does. Smelling the tail end of ports. How can they like the sea? Yet they do. The anchor's weighed. Off he sails with a scapular or a medal on him for luck. Well. And the tephilim no what's this they call it poor papa's father had on his door to touch. That brought us out of the land of Egypt and into the house of bondage. Something in all those superstitions because when you go out never know what dangers. Hanging on to a plank or astride of a beam for grim life, lifebelt round him, gulping salt water, and that's the last of his nibs till the sharks catch hold of him. Do fish ever get seasick?

Then you have a beautiful calm without a cloud, smooth sea, placid, crew and cargo in smithereens, Davy Jones' locker, moon looking down so peaceful. Not my fault, old cockalorum.

A last lonely candle wandered up the sky from Mirus bazaar in search of funds for Mercer's hospital and broke, drooping, and shed a cluster of violet but one white stars. They floated, fell: they faded. The shepherd's hour: the hour of folding: hour of tryst. From house to house, giving his everwelcome double knock, went the nine o'clock postman, the glowworm's lamp at his belt gleaming here and there through the laurel hedges. And among the five young trees a hoisted lintstock lit the lamp at Leahy's terrace. By screens of lighted windows, by equal gardens a shrill voice went crying, wailing: *Evening Telegraph, stop press edition! Result of the Gold Cup races!* and from the door of Dignam's house a boy ran out and called. Twittering the bat flew here, flew there. Far out over the sands the coming surf crept, grey. Howth settled for slumber, tired of long days, of yumyum rhododendrons (he was old) and felt gladly the night breeze lift, ruffle his fell of ferns. He lay but opened a red eye unsleeping, deep and slowly breathing, slumberous but awake. And far on Kish bank the anchored lightship twinkled, winked at Mr Bloom.

Life those chaps out there must have, stuck in the same spot. Irish Lights board. Penance for their sins. Coastguards too. Rocket and breeches buoy and lifeboat. Day we went out for the pleasure cruise in the Erin's King, throwing them the sack of old papers. Bears in the zoo. Filthy trip. Drunkards out to shake up their livers. Puking overboard to feed the herrings. Nausea. And the women, fear of God in their faces. Milly, no sign of funk. Her blue scarf loose, laughing. Don't know what death is at that age. And then their stomachs clean. But being lost they fear. When we hid behind the tree at Crumlin. I didn't want to. Mamma! Mamma! Babes in the wood. Frightening them with masks too. Throwing them up in the air to catch them.

I'll murder you. Is it only half fun? Or children playing battle. Whole earnest. How can people aim guns at each other. Sometimes they go off. Poor kids! Only troubles wildfire and nettlerash. Calomel purge I got her for that. After getting better asleep with Molly. Very same teeth she has. What do they love? Another themselves? But the morning she chased her with the umbrella. Perhaps so as not to hurt. I felt her pulse. Ticking. Little hand it was: now big. Dearest Papli. All that the hand says when you touch. Loved to count my waistcoat buttons. Her first stays I remember. Made me laugh to see. Little paps to begin with. Left one is more sensitive, I think. Mine too. Nearer the heart? Padding themselves out if fat is in fashion. Her growing pains at night, calling, wakening me. Frightened she was when her nature came on her first. Poor child! Strange moment for the mother too. Brings back her girlhood. Gibraltar. Looking from Buena Vista. O'Hara's tower. The seabirds screaming. Old Barbary ape that gobbled all his family. Sundown, gunfire for the men to cross the lines. Looking out over the sea she told me. Evening like this, but clear, no clouds. I always thought I'd marry a lord or a rich gentleman coming with a private yacht. *Buenas noches, señorita. El hombre ama la muchacha hermosa.* Why me? Because you were so foreign from the others.

Better not stick here all night like a limpet. This weather makes you dull. Must be getting on for nine by the light. Go home. Too late for *Leah, Lily of Killarney.* No. Might be still up. Call to the hospital to see. Hope she's over. Long day I've had. Martha, the bath, funeral, house of Keyes, museum with those goddesses, Dedalus' song. Then that bawler in Barney Kiernan's. Got my own back there. Drunken ranters what I said about his God made him wince. Mistake to hit back. Or? No. Ought to go home and laugh at themselves. Always want to be swilling in company. Afraid to be alone like a child of two. Suppose he hit me. Look at it other way round. Not so bad then. Perhaps not to hurt he meant. Three cheers for Israel. Three cheers for the sister-in-law he hawked about, three fangs in her mouth. Same style of beauty. Particularly nice old party for a cup of tea. The sister of the wife of the wild man of Borneo has just come to town. Imagine that in the early morning at close range. Everyone to his taste as Morris said when he kissed the cow. But Dignam's put the boots on it. Houses of mourning so depressing because you never know. Anyhow she wants the money. Must call to those Scottish Widows as I promised. Strange name. Takes it for granted we're going to pop off first. That widow on Monday was it outside Cramer's that looked at me. Buried the poor husband but progressing favourably on the premium. Her widow's mite. Well? What do you expect her to do? Must wheedle her way along. Widower I hate to see. Looks so forlorn. Poor man O'Connor wife and five children poisoned by mussels here. The sewage. Hopeless. Some good matronly woman in a porkpie hat to mother him. Take him in tow, platter face and a large apron. Ladies' grey flannelette bloomers, three shillings a pair, astonishing bargain. Plain and loved, loved for ever, they say. Ugly: no woman thinks she is. Love, lie and be handsome for tomorrow we die. See him sometimes walking about trying to find out who played the trick. U. P.: up. Fate that is. He, not me. Also a shop often noticed. Curse seems to dog it. Dreamt last night? Wait. Something confused. She had red slippers on. Turkish. Wore the breeches. Suppose she does? Would I like her in pyjamas? Damned hard to answer. Nannetti's gone. Mailboat. Near Holyhead by now. Must nail that ad of Keyes's. Work Hynes and Crawford. Petticoats for Molly. She has something to put in them. What's that? Might be money.

Mr Bloom stooped and turned over a piece of paper on the strand. He brought it near his eyes and peered. Letter? No. Can't read. Better go. Better. I'm tired to move. Page of an old copybook. All those holes and pebbles. Who could count them? Never know what you find. Bottle with story of a treasure in it, thrown from a wreck. Parcels post. Children always want to throw things in the sea. Trust? Bread cast on the waters. What's this? Bit of stick.

O! Exhausted that female has me. Not so young now. Will she come here tomorrow? Wait for her somewhere for ever. Must come back. Murderers do. Will I?

Mr Bloom with his stick gently vexed the thick sand at his foot. Write a message for her. Might remain. What?

I.

Some flatfoot tramp on it in the morning. Useless. Washed away. Tide comes here. Saw a pool near her foot. Bend, see my face there, dark mirror, breathe on it, stirs. All these rocks with lines and scars and letters. O, those transparent! Besides they don't know. What is the meaning of that other world. I called you naughty boy because I do not like.

AM. Λ.

No room. Let it go.

Mr Bloom effaced the letters with his slow boot. Hopeless thing sand. Nothing grows in it. All fades. No fear of big vessels coming up here. Except Guinness's barges. Round the Kish in eighty days. Done half by design.

He flung his wooden pen away. The stick fell in silted sand, stuck. Now if you were trying to do that for a week on end you couldn't. Chance. We'll never meet again. But it was lovely. Goodbye, dear. Thanks. Made me feel so young.

Short snooze now if I had. Must be near nine. Liverpool boat long gone. Not even the smoke. And she can do the other. Did too. And Belfast. I won't go. Race there, race back to Ennis. Let him. Just close my eyes a moment. Won't sleep, though. Half dream. It never comes the same. Bat again. No harm in him. Just a few.

O sweety all your little girlwhite up I saw dirty bracegirdle made me do love sticky we two naughty Grace darling she him half past the bed met him pike hoses frillies for Raoul de perfume your wife black hair heave under embon *señorita* young eyes Mulvey plump bubs me breadvan Winkle red slippers she rusty sleep wander years of dreams return tail end Agendath swoony lovey showed me her next year in drawers return next in her next her next.

A bat flew. Here. There. Here. Far in the grey a bell chimed. Mr Bloom with open mouth, his left boot sanded sideways, leaned, breathed. Just for a few

Cuckoo
Cuckoo
Cuckoo.

The clock on the mantelpiece in the priest's house cooed where Canon O'Hanlon and Father Conroy and the reverend John Hughes S. J. were taking tea and sodabread and butter and fried mutton chops with catsup and talking about

Cuckoo
Cuckoo
Cuckoo.

Because it was a little canarybird that came out of its little house to tell the time that Gerty MacDowell noticed the time she was there because she was as quick as anything about a thing like that, was Gerty MacDowell, and she noticed at once that that foreign gentleman that was sitting on the rocks looking was

Cuckoo
Cuckoo
Cuckoo.

14

Deshil Holles Eamus. Deshil Holles Eamus. Deshil Holles Eamus.

Send us bright one, light one, Horhorn, quickening and wombfruit. Send us bright one, light one, Horhorn, quickening and wombfruit. Send us bright one, light one, Horhorn, quickening and wombfruit.

Hoopsa boyaboy hoopsa! Hoopsa boyaboy hoopsa! Hoopsa boyaboy hoopsa!

Universally that person's acumen is esteemed very little perceptive concerning whatsoever matters are being held as most profitably by mortals with sapience endowed to be studied who is ignorant of that which the most in doctrine erudite and certainly by reason of that in them high mind's ornament deserving of veneration constantly maintain when by general consent they affirm that other circumstances being equal by no exterior splendour is the prosperity of a nation more efficaciously asserted than by the measure of how far forward may have progressed the tribute of its solicitude for that proliferent continuance which of evils the original if it be absent when fortunately present constitutes the certain sign of omnipollent nature's incorrupted benefaction. For who is there who anything of some significance has apprehended but is conscious that that exterior splendour may be the surface of a downwardtending lutulent reality or on the contrary anyone so is there unilluminated as not to perceive that as no nature's boon can contend against the bounty of increase so it behoves every most just citizen to become the exhortator and admonisher of his semblables and to tremble lest what had in the past been by the nation excellently commenced might be in the future not with similar excellence accomplished if an inverecund habit shall have gradually traduced the honourable by ancestors transmitted customs to that thither of profundity that that one was audacious excessively who would have the hardihood to rise affirming that no more odious offence can for anyone be than to oblivious neglect to consign that evangel simultaneously command and promise which on all mortals with prophecy of abundance or with diminution's menace that exalted of reiteratedly procreating function ever irrevocably enjoined?

It is not why therefore we shall wonder if, as the best historians relate, among the Celts, who nothing that was not in its nature admirable admired, the art of medicine shall have been highly honoured. Not to speak of hostels, leperyards, sweating chambers, plaguegraves, their greatest doctors, the O'Shiels, the O'Hickeys, the O'Lees, have sedulously set down the divers methods by which the sick and the relapsed found again health whether the malady had been the trembling withering or loose boyconnell flux. Certainly in every public work which in it anything of gravity contains preparation should be with importance commensurate and therefore a plan was by them adopted (whether by having preconsidered or as the maturation of experience it is difficult in being said which the discrepant opinions of subsequent inquirers are not up to the present congrued to render manifest) whereby maternity was so far from all accident possibility removed that whatever care the patient in that allhardest of woman hour chiefly required and not solely for the copiously opulent but also for her who not being sufficiently moneyed scarcely and often not even scarcely could subsist valiantly and for an inconsiderable emolument was provided.

To her nothing already then and thenceforward was anyway able to be molestful for this chiefly felt all citizens except with proliferent mothers prosperity at all not to can be and as they had received eternity gods mortals generation to befit them her beholding, when the case was so hoving itself, parturient in vehicle thereward carrying desire immense among all one another was impelling on of her to be received into that domicile. O thing of prudent nation not merely in being seen but also even in being related worthy of being praised that they her by anticipation went seeing mother, that she by them suddenly to be about to be cherished had been begun she felt!

Before born bliss babe had. Within womb won he worship. Whatever in that one case done commodiously done was. A couch by midwives attended with wholesome food reposeful, cleanest swaddles as though forthbringing were now done and by wise foresight set: but to this no less of what drugs there is need and surgical implements which are pertaining to her case not omitting aspect of all very distracting spectacles in various latitudes by our terrestrial orb offered together with images, divine and human, the cogitation of which by sejunct females is to tumescence conducive or eases issue in the high sunbright wellbuilt fair home of mothers when, ostensibly far gone and reproductitive, it is come by her thereto to lie in, her term up.

Some man that wayfaring was stood by housedoor at night's oncoming. Of Israel's folk was that man that on earth wandering far had fared. Stark ruth of man his errand that him lone led till that house.

Of that house A. Horne is lord. Seventy beds keeps he there teeming mothers are wont that they lie for to thole and bring forth bairns hale so God's angel to Mary quoth. Watchers tway there walk, white sisters in ward sleepless. Smarts they still, sickness soothing: in twelve moons thrice an hundred. Truest bedthanes they twain are, for Horne holding wariest ward.

In ward wary the watcher hearing come that man mildhearted eft rising with swire ywimpled to him her gate wide undid. Lo, levin leaping lightens in eyeblink Ireland's westward welkin. Full she drad that God the Wreaker all mankind would fordo with water for his evil sins. Christ's rood made she on breastbone and him drew that he would rathe infare under her thatch. That man her will wotting worthful went in Horne's house.

Loth to irk in Horne's hall hat holding the seeker stood. On her stow he ere was living with dear wife and lovesome daughter that then over land and seafloor nine years had long outwandered. Once her in townhithe meeting he to her bow had not doffed. Her to forgive now he craved with good ground of her allowed that that of him swiftseen face, hers, so young then had looked. Light swift her eyes kindled, bloom of blushes his word winning.

As her eyes then ongot his weeds swart therefor sorrow she feared. Glad after she was that ere adread was. Her he asked if O'Hare Doctor tidings sent from far coast and she with grameful sigh him answered that O'Hare Doctor in heaven was. Sad was the man that word to hear that him so heavied in bowels ruthful. All she there told him, ruing death for friend so young, algate sore unwilling God's rightwiseness to withsay. She said that he had a fair sweet death through God His goodness with masspriest to be shriven, holy housel and sick men's oil to his limbs. The man then right earnest asked the nun of which death the dead man was died and the nun answered him and said that he was died in Mona Island through bellycrab three year agone come Childermas and she prayed to God the Allruthful to have his dear soul in his undeathliness. He heard her sad words, in held hat sad staring. So stood they there both awhile in wanhope sorrowing one with other.

Therefore, everyman, look to that last end that is thy death and the dust that gripeth on every man that is born of woman for as he came naked forth from his mother's womb so naked shall he wend him at the last for to go as he came.

The man that was come in to the house then spoke to the nursingwoman and he asked her how it fared with the woman that lay there in childbed. The nursingwoman answered him and said that that woman was in throes now full three days and that it would be a hard birth unneth to bear but that now in a little it would be. She said thereto that she had seen many births of women but never was none so hard as was that woman's birth. Then she set it all forth to him for because she knew the man that time was had lived nigh that house. The man hearkened to her words for he felt with wonder women's woe in the travail that they have of motherhood and he wondered to look on her face that was a fair face for any man to see but yet was she left after long years a handmaid. Nine twelve bloodflows chiding her childless.

And whiles they spake the door of the castle was opened and there nighed them a mickle noise as of many that sat there at meat. And there came against the place as they stood a young learningknight yclept Dixon. And the traveller Leopold was couth to him sithen it had happed that they had had ado each with other in the house of misericord where this learningknight lay by cause the traveller Leopold came there to be healed for he was sore wounded in his breast by a spear wherewith a horrible and dreadful dragon was smitten him for which he did do make a salve of volatile salt and chrism as much as he might suffice. And he said now that he should go in to that castle for to make merry with them that were there. And the traveller Leopold said that he should go otherwhither for he was a man of cautels and a subtile. Also the lady was of his avis and repreved the learningknight though she trowed well that the traveller had said thing that was false for his subtility. But the learningknight would not hear say nay nor do her mandement ne have him in aught contrarious to his list and he said how it was a marvellous castle. And the traveller Leopold went into the castle for to rest him for a space being sore of limb after many marches environing in divers lands and sometime venery.

And in the castle was set a board that was of the birchwood of Finlandy and it was upheld by four dwarfmen of that country but they durst not move more for enchantment. And on this board were frightful swords and knives that are made in a great cavern by swinking demons out of white flames that they fix then in the horns of buffalos and stags that there abound marvellously. And there were vessels that are wrought by magic of Mahound out of seasand and the air by a warlock with his breath that he blases in to them like to bubbles. And full fair cheer and rich was on the board that no wight could devise a fuller ne richer. And there was a vat of silver that was moved by craft to open in the which lay strange fishes withouten heads though misbelieving men nie that this be possible thing without they see it natheless they are so. And these fishes lie in an oily water brought there from Portugal land because of the fatness that therein is like to the juices of the olivepress. And also it was a marvel to see in that castle how by magic they make a compost out of fecund wheatkidneys out of Chaldee that by aid of certain angry spirits that they do in to it swells up wondrously like to a vast mountain. And they teach the serpents there to entwine themselves up on long sticks out of the ground and of the scales of these serpents they brew out a brewage like to mead.

And the learning knight let pour for childe Leopold a draught and halp thereto the while all they that were there drank every each. And childe Leopold did up his beaver for to pleasure him and took apertly somewhat in amity for he never drank no manner of mead which he then put by and anon full privily he voided the more part in his neighbour glass and his neighbour nist not of this wile. And he sat down in that castle with them for to rest him there awhile. Thanked be Almighty God.

This meanwhile this good sister stood by the door and begged them at the reverence of Jesu our alther liege Lord to leave their wassailing for there was above one quick with child, a gentle dame, whose time hied fast. Sir Leopold heard on the upfloor cry on high and he wondered what cry that it was whether of child or woman and I marvel, said he, that it be not come or now. Meseems it dureth overlong. And he was ware and saw a franklin that hight Lenehan on that side the table that was older than any of the tother and for that they both were knights virtuous in the one emprise and eke by cause that he was elder he spoke to him full gently. But, said he, or it be long too she will bring forth by God His bounty and have joy of her childing for she hath waited marvellous long. And the franklin that had drunken said, Expecting each moment to be her next. Also he took the cup that stood tofore him for him needed never none asking nor desiring of him to drink and, Now drink, said he, fully delectably, and he quaffed as far as he might to their both's health for he was a passing good man of his lustiness. And sir Leopold that was the goodliest guest that ever sat in scholars' hall and that was the meekest man and the kindest that ever laid husbandly hand under hen and that was the very truest knight of the world one that ever did minion service to lady gentle pledged him courtly in the cup. Woman's woe with wonder pondering.

Now let us speak of that fellowship that was there to the intent to be drunken an they might. There was a sort of scholars along either side the board, that is to wit, Dixon yclept junior of saint Mary Merciable's with other his fellows Lynch and Madden, scholars of medicine, and the franklin that hight Lenehan and one from Alba Longa, one Crotthers, and young Stephen that had mien of a frere that was at head of the board and Costello that men clepen Punch Costello all long of a mastery of him erewhile gested (and of all them, reserved young Stephen, he was the most drunken that demanded still of more mead) and beside the meek sir Leopold. But on young Malachi they waited for that he promised to have come and such as intended to no goodness said how he had broke his avow. And sir Leopold sat with them for he bore fast friendship to sir Simon and to this his son young Stephen and for that his languor becalmed him there after longest wanderings insomuch as they feasted him for that time in the honourablest manner. Ruth red him, love led on with will to wander, loth to leave.

For they were right witty scholars. And he heard their aresouns each gen other as touching birth and righteousness, young Madden maintaining that put such case it were hard the wife to die (for so it had fallen out a matter of some year agone with a woman of Eblana in Horne's house that now was trespassed out of this world and the self night next before her death all leeches and pothecaries had taken

counsel of her case). And they said farther she should live because
in the beginning, they said, the woman should bring forth in pain
and wherefore they that were of this imagination affirmed how young
Madden had said truth for he had conscience to let her die. And
not few and of these was young Lynch were in doubt that the world
was now right evil governed as it was never other howbeit the mean
people believed it otherwise but the law nor his judges did provide no
remedy. A redress God grant. This was scant said but all cried with
one acclaim nay, by our Virgin Mother, the wife should live and the
babe to die. In colour whereof they waxed hot upon that head what
with argument and what for their drinking but the franklin Lenehan
was prompt each when to pour them ale so that at the least way mirth
might not lack. Then young Madden showed all the whole affair and
said how that she was dead and how for holy religion sake by rede of
palmer and bedesman and for a vow he had made to Saint Ultan of
Arbraccan her goodman husband would not let her death whereby
they were all wondrous grieved. To whom young Stephen had these
words following: Murmur, sirs, is eke oft among lay folk. Both babe
and parent now glorify their Maker, the one in limbo gloom, the other
in purgefire. But, gramercy, what of those Godpossibled souls that
we nightly impossibilise, which is the sin against the Holy Ghost,
Very God, Lord and Giver of Life? For, sirs, he said, our lust is
brief. We are means to those small creatures within us and nature
has other ends than we. Then said Dixon junior to Punch Costello
wist he what ends. But he had overmuch drunken and the best word
he could have of him was that he would ever dishonest a woman
whoso she were or wife or maid or leman if it so fortuned him to be
delivered of his spleen of lustihead. Whereat Crotthers of Alba Longa
sang young Malachi's praise of that beast the unicorn how once in the
millennium he cometh by his horn, the other all this while, pricked
forward with their jibes wherewith they did malice him, witnessing
all and several by saint Foutinus his engines that he was able to do
any manner of thing that lay in man to do. Thereat laughed they all
right jocundly only young Stephen and sir Leopold which never durst
laugh too open by reason of a strange humour which he would not
bewray and also for that he rued for her that bare whoso she might
be or wheresoever. Then spake young Stephen orgulous of mother
Church that would cast him out of her bosom, of law of canons, of
Lilith, patron of abortions, of bigness wrought by wind of seeds of

brightness or by potency of vampires mouth to mouth or, as Virgilius saith, by the influence of the occident or by the reek of moonflower or an she lie with a woman which her man has but lain with, *effectu secuto*, or peradventure in her bath according to the opinions of Averroes and Moses Maimonides. He said also how at the end of the second month a human soul was infused and how in all our holy mother foldeth ever souls for God's greater glory whereas that earthly mother which was but a dam to bear beastly should die by canon for so saith he that holdeth the fisherman's seal, even that blessed Peter on which rock was holy church for all ages founded. All they bachelors then asked of sir Leopold would he in like case so jeopard her person as risk life to save life. A wariness of mind he would answer as fitted all and, laying hand to jaw, he said dissembling, as his wont was, that as it was informed him, who had ever loved the art of physic as might a layman, and agreeing also with his experience of so seldomseen an accident it was good for that mother Church belike at one blow had birth and death pence and in such sort deliverly he scaped their questions. That is truth, pardy, said Dixon, and, or I err, a pregnant word. Which hearing young Stephen was a marvellous glad man and he averred that he who stealeth from the poor lendeth to the Lord for he was of a wild manner when he was drunken and that he was now in that taking it appeared eftsoons.

But sir Leopold was passing grave maugre his word by cause he still had pity of the terrorcausing shrieking of shrill women in their labour and as he was minded of his good lady Marion that had borne him an only manchild which on his eleventh day on live had died and no man of art could save so dark is destiny. And she was wondrous stricken of heart for that evil hap and for his burial did him on a fair corselet of lamb's wool, the flower of the flock, lest he might perish utterly and lie akeled (for it was then about the midst of the winter) and now sir Leopold that had of his body no manchild for an heir looked upon him his friend's son and was shut up in sorrow for his forepassed happiness and as sad as he was that him failed a son of such gentle courage (for all accounted him of real parts) so grieved he also in no less measure for young Stephen for that he lived riotously with those wastrels and murdered his goods with whores.

About that present time young Stephen filled all cups that stood empty so as there remained but little mo if the prudenter had not shadowed their approach from him that still plied it very busily who, praying for the intentions of the sovereign pontiff, he gave them for a pledge the vicar of Christ which also as he said is vicar of Bray. Now drink we, quod he, of this mazer and quaff ye this mead which is not indeed parcel of my body but my soul's bodiment. Leave ye fraction of bread to them that live by bread alone. Be not afeard neither for any want for this will comfort more than the other will dismay. See ye here. And he showed them glistering coins of the tribute and goldsmith notes the worth of two pound nineteen shilling that he had, he said, for a song which he writ. They all admired to see the foresaid riches in such dearth of money as was herebefore. His words were then these as followeth: Know all men, he said, time's ruins build eternity's mansions. What means this? Desire's wind blasts the thorntree but after it becomes from a bramblebush to be a rose upon the rood of time. Mark me now. In woman's womb word is made flesh but in the spirit of the maker all flesh that passes becomes the word that shall not pass away. This is the postcreation. *Omnis caro ad te veniet.* No question but her name is puissant who aventried the dear corse of our Agenbuyer, Healer and Herd, our mighty mother and mother most venerable and Bernardus saith aptly that She hath an *omnipotentiam deiparae supplicem,* that is to wit, an almightiness of petition because she is the second Eve and she won us, saith Augustine too, whereas that other, our grandam, which we are linked up with by successive anastomosis of navelcords sold us all, seed, breed and generation, for a penny pippin. But here is the matter now. Or she knew him, that second I say, and was but creature of her creature, *vergine madre, figlia di tuo figlio,* or she knew him not and then stands she in the one denial or ignorancy with Peter Piscator who lives in the house that Jack built and with Joseph the joiner patron of the happy demise of all unhappy marriages, *parceque M. Léo Taxil nous a dit que qui l'avait mise dans cette fichue position c'était le sacré pigeon, ventre de Dieu! Entweder* transubstantiality *oder* consubstantiality but in no case subsubstantiality. And all cried out upon it for a very scurvy word. A pregnancy without joy, he said, a birth without pangs, a body without blemish, a belly without bigness. Let the lewd with faith and fervour worship. With will will we withstand, withsay.

Hereupon Punch Costello dinged with his fist upon the board and would sing a bawdy catch *Staboo Stabella* about a wench that was put in pod of a jolly swashbuckler in Almany which he did straightways now attack: *The first three months she was not well, Staboo,* when here nurse

Quigley from the door angerly bid them hist ye should shame you nor was it not meet as she remembered them being her mind was to have all orderly against lord Andrew came for because she was jealous that no gasteful turmoil might shorten the honour of her guard. It was an ancient and a sad matron of a sedate look and christian walking, in habit dun beseeming her megrims and wrinkled visage, nor did her hortative want of it effect for incontinently Punch Costello was of them all embraided and they reclaimed the churl with civil rudeness some and shaked him with menace of blandishments others whiles they all chode with him, a murrain seize the dolt, what a devil he would be at, thou chuff, thou puny, thou got in peasestraw, thou losel, thou chitterling, thou spawn of a rebel, thou dykedropt, thou abortion thou, to shut up his drunken drool out of that like a curse of God ape, the good sir Leopold that had for his cognisance the flower of quiet, margerain gentle, advising also the time's occasion as most sacred and most worthy to be most sacred. In Horne's house rest should reign.

To be short this passage was scarce by when Master Dixon of Mary in Eccles, goodly grinning, asked young Stephen what was the reason why he had not cided to take friar's vows and he answered him obedience in the womb, chastity in the tomb but involuntary poverty all his days. Master Lenehan at this made return that he had heard of those nefarious deeds and how, as he heard hereof counted, he had besmirched the lily virtue of a confiding female which was corruption of minors and they all intershowed it too, waxing merry and toasting to his fathership. But he said very entirely it was clean contrary to their suppose for he was the eternal son and ever virgin. Thereat mirth grew in them the more and they rehearsed to him his curious rite of wedlock for the disrobing and deflowering of spouses, as the priests use in Madagascar island, she to be in guise of white and saffron, her groom in white and grain, with burning of nard and tapers, on a bridebed while clerks sung kyries and the anthem *Ut novetur sexus omnis corporis mysterium* till she was there unmaided. He gave them then a much admirable hymen minim by those delicate poets Master John Fletcher and Master Francis Beaumont that is in their *Maid's Tragedy* that was writ for a like twining of lovers: *To bed, to bed* was the burden of it to be played with accompanable concent upon the virginals. An exquisite dulcet epithalame of most mollificative suadency for juveniles amatory whom the odoriferous flambeaus of the paranymphs have escorted to the quadrupedal proscenium of connubial communion.

Well met they were, said Master Dixon, joyed, but, harkee, young sir, better were they named Beau Mount and Lecher for, by my troth, of such a mingling much might come. Young Stephen said indeed to his best remembrance they had but the one doxy between them and she of the stews to make shift with in delights amorous for life ran very high in those days and the custom of the country approved with it. Greater love than this, he said, no man hath that a man lay down his wife for his friend. Go thou and do likewise. Thus, or words to that effect, saith Zarathustra, sometime regius professor of French letters to the university of Oxtail nor breathed there ever that man to whom mankind was more beholden. Bring a stranger within thy tower it will go hard but thou wilt have the secondbest bed. *Orate, fratres, pro memetipso.* And all the people shall say, Amen. Remember, Erin, thy generations and thy days of old, how thou settedst little by me and by my word and broughtedst in a stranger to my gates to commit fornication in my sight and to wax fat and kick like Jeshurum. Therefore hast thou sinned against my light and hast made me, thy lord, to be the slave of servants. Return, return, Clan Milly: forget me not, O Milesian. Why hast thou done this abomination before me that thou didst spurn me for a merchant of jalaps and didst deny me to the Roman and to the Indian of dark speech with whom thy daughters did lie luxuriously? Look forth now, my people, upon the land of behest, even from Horeb and from Nebo and from Pisgah and from the Horns of Hatten unto a land flowing with milk and money. But thou hast suckled me with a bitter milk: my moon and my sun thou hast quenched for ever. And thou hast left me alone for ever in the dark ways of my bitterness: and with a kiss of ashes hast thou kissed my mouth. This tenebrosity of the interior, he proceeded to say, hath not been illumined by the wit of the septuagint nor so much as mentioned for the Orient from on high which brake hell's gates visited a darkness that was foraneous. Assuefaction minorates atrocities (as Tully saith of his darling Stoics) and Hamlet his father showeth the prince no blister of combustion. The adiaphane in the noon of life is an Egypt's plague which in the nights of prenativity and postmortemity is their most proper *ubi* and *quomodo.* And as the ends and ultimates of all things accord in some mean and measure with their inceptions and originals, that same multiplicit concordance which leads forth growth from birth accomplishing by a retrogressive metamorphosis that minishing and ablation towards the final which is agreeable unto nature so is it with our subsolar being. The aged sisters draw us into life: we wail, batten, sport, clip, clasp, sunder, dwindle, die: over us dead they bend. First, saved from waters of old Nile, among bulrushes, a bed of fasciated wattles: at last the cavity of a mountain, an occulted sepulchre amid the conclamation of the hillcat and the ossifrage. And as no man knows the ubicity of his tumulus nor to what processes we shall thereby be ushered nor whether to Tophet or to Edenville in the like way is all hidden when we would backward see from what region of remoteness the whatness of our whoness hath fetched his whenceness.

Thereto Punch Costello roared out mainly *Etienne chanson* but he loudly bid them, lo, wisdom hath built herself a house, this vast majestic longstablished vault, the crystal palace of the Creator, all in applepie order, a penny for him who finds the pea.

> *Behold the mansion reared by dedal Jack*
> *See the malt stored in many a refluent sack,*
> *In the proud cirque of Jackjohn's bivouac.*

A black crack of noise in the street here, alack, bawled back. Loud on left Thor thundered: in anger awful the hammerhurler. Came now the storm that hist his heart. And Master Lynch bade him have a care to flout and witwanton as the god self was angered for his hellprate and paganry. And he that had erst challenged to be so doughty waxed wan as they might all mark and shrank together and his pitch that was before so haught uplift was now of a sudden quite plucked down and his heart shook within the cage of his breast as he tasted the rumour of that storm. Then did some mock and some jeer and Punch Costello fell hard again to his yale which Master Lenehan vowed he would do after and he was indeed but a word and a blow on any the least colour. But the braggart boaster cried that an old Nobodaddy was in his cups it was muchwhat indifferent and he would not lag behind his lead. But this was only to dye his desperation as cowed he crouched in Horne's hall. He drank indeed at one draught to pluck up a heart of any grace for it thundered long rumblingly over all the heavens so that Master Madden, being godly certain whiles, knocked him on his ribs upon that crack of doom and Master Bloom, at the braggart's side, spoke to him calming words to slumber his great fear, advertising how it was no other thing but a hubbub noise that he heard, the discharge of fluid from the thunderhead, look you, having taken place, and all of the order of a natural phenomenon.

But was young Boasthard's fear vanquished by Calmer's words? No, for he had in his bosom a spike named Bitterness which could not by words be done away. And was he then neither calm like the one nor godly like the other? He was neither as much as he would have liked to be either. But could he not have endeavoured to have found again as in his youth the bottle Holiness that then he lived withal? Indeed no for Grace was not there to find that bottle. Heard he then in that clap the voice of the god Bringforth or, what Calmer said, a hubbub of Phenomenon? Heard? Why, he could not but hear unless he had plugged him up the tube Understanding (which he had not done). For through that tube he saw that he was in the land of Phenomenon where he must for a certain one day die as he was like the rest too a passing show. And would he not accept to die like the rest and pass away? By no means would he though he must nor would he make more shows according as men do with wives which Phenomenon has commanded them to do by the book Law. Then wotted he nought of that other land which is called Believe-on-Me, that is the land of promise which behoves to the king Delightful and shall be for ever where there is no death and no birth neither wiving nor mothering at which all shall come as many as believe on it? Yes, Pious had told him of that land and Chaste had pointed him to the way but the reason was that in the way he fell in with a certain whore of an eyepleasing exterior whose name, she said, is Bird-in-the-Hand and she beguiled him wrongways from the true path by her flatteries that she said to him as, Ho, you pretty man, turn aside hither and I will show you a brave place, and she lay at him so flatteringly that she had him in her grot which is named Two-in-the-Bush or, by some learned, Carnal Concupiscence.

This was it what all that company that sat there at commons in Manse of Mothers the most lusted after and if they met with this whore Bird-in-the-Hand (which was within all foul plagues, monsters and a wicked devil) they would strain the last but they would make at her and know her. For regarding Believe-on-Me they said it was nought else but notion and they could conceive no thought of it for, first, Two-in-the-Bush whither she ticed them was the very goodliest grot and in it were four pillows on which were four tickets with these words printed on them, Pickaback and Topsyturvy and Shameface and Cheek by Jowl and, second, for that foul plague Allpox and the monsters they cared not for them for Preservative had given them a stout shield of oxengut and, third, that they might take no hurt neither from Offspring that was that wicked devil by virtue of this same shield which was named Killchild. So were they all in their blind fancy, Mr Cavil and Mr Sometimes Godly, Mr Ape Swillale, Mr False Franklin, Mr Dainty Dixon, Young Boasthard and Mr Cautious Calmer. Wherein, O wretched company, were ye all deceived for that was the voice of the god that was in a very grievous rage that he would presently lift his arm up and spill their souls for their abuses and their spillings done by them contrariwise to his word which forth to bring brenningly biddeth.

So Thursday sixteenth June Patk. Dignam laid in clay of an apoplexy and after hard drought, please God, rained, a bargeman coming in by water a fifty mile or thereabout with turf saying the seed won't sprout, fields athirst, very sadcoloured and stunk mightily, the quags and tofts too. Hard to breathe and all the young quicks clean consumed without sprinkle this long while back as no man remembered to be without. The rosy buds all gone brown and spread out blobs and on the hills nought but dry flag and faggots that would catch at first fire. All the world saying, for aught they knew, the big wind of last February a year that did havoc the land so pitifully a small thing beside this barrenness. But by and by, as said, this evening after sundown, the wind sitting in the west, biggish swollen clouds to be seen as the night increased and the weatherwise poring up at them and some sheet lightnings at first and after, past ten of the clock, one great stroke with a long thunder and in a brace of shakes all scamper pellmell within door for the smoking shower, the men making shelter for their straws with a clout or kerchief, womenfolk skipping off with kirtles catched up soon as the pour came. In Ely place, Baggot street, Duke's lawn, thence through Merrion green up to Holles street a swash of water flowing that was before bonedry and not one chair or coach or fiacre seen about but no more crack after that first. Over against the Rt. Hon. Mr Justice Fitzgibbon's door (that is to sit with Mr Healy the lawyer upon the college lands) Mal. Mulligan a gentleman's gentleman that had but come from Mr Moore's the writer's (that was a papish but is now, folk say, a good Williamite) chanced against Alec. Bannon in a cut bob (which are now in with dance cloaks of Kendal green) that was new got to town from Mullingar with the stage where his coz and Mal M's brother will stay a month yet till Saint Swithin and asks what in the earth he does there, he bound home and he to Andrew Horne's being stayed for to crush a cup of wine, so he said, but would tell him of a skittish heifer, big of her age and beef to the heel, and all this while poured with rain and so both together on to Horne's. There Leop. Bloom of Crawford's journal sitting snug with a covey of wags, likely brangling fellows, Dixon jun., scholar of my lady of Mercy's, Vin. Lynch, a Scots fellow, Will. Madden, T. Lenehan, very sad about a racer he fancied and Stephen D. Leop. Bloom there for a languor he had but was now better, he having dreamed tonight a strange fancy of his dame Mrs Moll with red slippers on in a pair of Turkey trunks which is thought by those in ken to be for a change and Mistress Purefoy there, that got in through pleading her belly, and now on the stools, poor body, two days past her term, the midwives sore put to it and can't deliver, she queasy for a bowl of riceslop that is a shrewd drier up of the insides and her breath very heavy more than good and should be a bullyboy from the knocks, they say, but God give her soon issue. 'Tis her ninth chick to live, I hear, and Lady day bit off her last chick's nails that was then a twelvemonth and with other three all breastfed that died written out in a fair hand in the king's bible. Her hub fifty odd and a methodist but takes the sacrament and is to be seen any fair sabbath with a pair of his boys off Bullock harbour dapping on the sound with a heavybraked reel or in a punt he has trailing for flounder and pollock and catches a fine bag, I hear. In sum an infinite great fall of rain and all refreshed and will much increase the harvest yet those in ken say after wind and water fire shall come for a prognostication of Malachi's almanac (and I hear that Mr Russell has done a prophetical charm of the same gist out of the Hindustanish for his farmer's gazette) to have three things in all but this a mere fetch without bottom of reason for old crones and bairns yet sometimes they are found in the right guess with their queerities no telling how.

With this came up Lenehan to the feet of the table to say how the letter was in that night's gazette and he made a show to find it about him (for he swore with an oath that he had been at pains about it) but on Stephen's persuasion he gave over the search and was bidden to sit near by which he did mighty brisk. He was a kind of sport gentleman that went for a merryandrew or honest pickle and what belonged of women, horseflesh or hot scandal he had it pat. To tell the truth he was mean in fortunes and for the most part hankered about the coffeehouses and low taverns with crimps, ostlers, bookies, Paul's men, runners, flatcaps, waistcoateers, ladies of the bagnio and other rogues of the game or with a chanceable catchpole or a tipstaff often at nights till broad day of whom he picked up between his sackpossets much loose gossip. He took his ordinary at a boilingcook's and if he had but gotten into him a mess of broken victuals or a platter of tripes with a bare tester in his purse he could always bring himself off with his tongue, some randy quip he had from a punk or whatnot that every mother's son of them would burst their sides. The other, Costello that is, hearing this talk asked was it poetry or a tale. Faith, no, he says, Frank (that was his name), 'tis all about Kerry cows that are to be butchered along of the plague. But they can go hang, says he with a wink, for me with their bully beef, a pox on it. There's as good fish in this tin as ever came out of it and very friendly he offered to take of some salty sprats that stood by which he had eyed wishly in the meantime and found the place which was indeed the chief design of his embassy as he was sharpset. *Mort aux vaches*, says Frank then in the French language that had been indentured to a brandyshipper that has a winelodge in Bordeaux and he spoke French like a gentleman too. From a child this Frank had been a donought that his father, a headborough, who could ill keep him to school to learn his letters and the use of the globes, matriculated at the university to study the mechanics but he took the bit between his teeth like a raw colt and was more familiar with the justiciary and the parish beadle than with his volumes. One time he would be a playactor, then a sutler or a welsher, then nought would keep him from the bearpit and the cocking main, then he was for the ocean sea or to hoof it on the roads with the romany folk, kidnapping a squire's heir by favour of moonlight or fecking maids' linen or choking chicken behind a hedge. He had been off as many times as a cat has lives and back again with naked pockets as many more to his father the headborough who shed a pint of tears as often as he saw him. What, says Mr Leopold with his hands across, that was earnest to know the drift of it, will they slaughter all? I protest I saw them but this day morning going to the Liverpool boats, says he. I can scarce believe 'tis so bad, says he. And he had experience of the like brood beasts and of springers, greasy hoggets and wether wool, having been some years before actuary for Mr Joseph Cuffe, a worthy salesmaster that drove his trade for live stock and meadow auctions hard by Mr Gavin Low's yard in Prussia street. I question with you there, says he. More like 'tis the hoose or the timber tongue. Mr Stephen, a little moved but very handsomely told him no such matter and that he had dispatches from the emperor's chief tailtickler thanking him for the hospitality, that was sending over Doctor Rinderpest, the bestquoted cowcatcher in all Muscovy, with a bolus or two of physic to take the bull by the horns. Come, come, says Mr Vincent, plain dealing. He'll find himself on the horns of a dilemma if he meddles with a bull that's Irish, says he. Irish by name and irish by nature, says Mr Stephen, and he sent the ale purling about, an Irish bull in an English chinashop. I conceive you, says Mr Dixon. It is that same bull that was sent to our island by farmer Nicholas, the bravest cattlebreeder of them all, with an emerald ring in his nose. True for you, says Mr Vincent cross the table, and a bullseye into the bargain, says he, and a plumper and a portlier bull, says he, never shit on shamrock. He had horns galore, a coat of cloth of gold and a sweet smoky breath coming out of his nostrils so that the women of our island, leaving doughballs and rollingpins, followed after him hanging his bulliness in daisychains. What for that, says Mr Dixon, but before he came over farmer Nicholas that was a eunuch had him properly gelded by a college of doctors who were no better off than himself. So be off now, says he, and do all my cousin german the lord Harry tells you and take a farmer's blessing, and with that he slapped his posteriors very soundly. But the slap and the blessing stood him friend, says Mr Vincent, for to make up he taught him a trick worth two of the other so that maid, wife, abbess and widow to this day affirm that they would rather any time of the month whisper in his ear in the dark of a cowhouse or get a lick on the nape from his long holy tongue than lie with the finest strapping young ravisher in the four fields of all Ireland. Another then put in his word: And they dressed him, says he, in a point shift and petticoat with a tippet and girdle and ruffles on his wrists and clipped his forelock and rubbed him all over with spermacetic oil and built stables for him at every turn of the road with a gold manger in each full of the best hay in the market so that he could doss and dung to his heart's content. By this time the father of the faithful (for so they called him) was grown so heavy that he could scarce walk to pasture. To remedy which our cozening dames and damsels brought him his fodder in their apronlaps and as soon as his belly was full he would rear up on his hind quarters to show their ladyships a mystery and roar and bellow out of him in bulls' language and they all after him. Ay, says another, and so pampered was he that he would suffer nought to grow in all the land but green grass for himself (for that was the only colour to his mind) and there was a board put up on a hillock in the middle of the island with a printed notice, saying: By the Lord Harry, Green is the grass that grows on the ground. And, says Mr Dixon, if ever he got scent of a cattleraider in Roscommon or the wilds of Connemara or a husbandman in Sligo that was sowing as much as a handful of mustard or a bag of rapeseed out he'd run amok over half the countryside rooting up with his horns whatever was planted and all by lord Harry's orders. There was bad blood between them at first, says Mr Vincent, and the lord Harry called farmer Nicholas all the old Nicks in the world and an old whoremaster that kept seven trulls in his house and I'll meddle in his matters, says he. I'll make that animal smell hell, says he, with the help of that good pizzle my father left me. But one evening, says Mr Dixon, when the lord Harry was cleaning his royal pelt to go to dinner after winning a boatrace (he had spade oars for himself but the first rule of the course was that the others were to row with pitchforks) he discovered in himself a wonderful likeness to a bull and on picking up a blackthumbed chapbook that he kept in the pantry he found sure enough that he was a lefthanded descendant of the famous champion bull of the Romans, *Bos Bovum*, which is good bog Latin for boss of the show. After that, says Mr Vincent, the lord Harry put his head into a cow's drinkingtrough in the presence of all his courtiers and pulling it out again told them all his new name. Then, with the water running off him, he got into an old smock and skirt that had belonged to his grandmother and bought a grammar of the bulls' language to study but he could never learn a word of it except the first personal pronoun which he copied out big and got off by heart and if ever he went out for a walk he filled his pockets with chalk to write it upon what took his fancy, the side of a rock or a teahouse table or a bale of cotton or a corkfloat. In short, he and the bull of Ireland were soon as fast friends as an arse and a shirt. They were, says Mr Stephen, and the end was that the men of the island seeing no help was toward, as the ungrate women were all of one mind, made a wherry raft, loaded themselves and their bundles of chattels on shipboard, set all masts erect, manned the yards, sprang their luff, heaved to, spread three sheets in the wind, put her head between wind and water, weighed anchor, ported her helm, ran up the jolly Roger, gave three times three, let the bullgine run, pushed off in their bumboat and put to sea to recover the main of America. Which was the occasion, says Mr Vincent, of the composing by a boatswain of that rollicking chanty:

> —*Pope Peter's but a pissabed.*
> *A man's a man for a' that.*

Our worthy acquaintance Mr Malachi Mulligan now appeared in the doorway as the students were finishing their apologue accompanied with a friend whom he had just rencountered, a young gentleman, his name Alec Bannon, who had late come to town, it being his intention to buy a colour or a cornetcy in the fencibles and list for the wars. Mr Mulligan was civil enough to express some relish of it all the more as it jumped with a project of his own for the cure of the very evil that had been touched on. Whereat he handed round to the company a set of pasteboard cards which he had had printed that day at Mr Quinnell's bearing a legend printed in fair italics: *Mr Malachi Mulligan. Fertiliser and Incubator. Lambay Island.* His project, as he went on to expound, was to withdraw from the round of idle pleasures such as form the chief business of sir Fopling Popinjay and sir Milksop Quidnunc in town and to devote himself to the noblest task for which our bodily organism has been framed. Well, let us hear of it, good my friend, said Mr Dixon. I make no doubt it smacks of wenching. Come, be seated, both. 'Tis as cheap sitting as standing. Mr Mulligan accepted of the invitation and, expatiating upon his design, told his hearers that he had been led into this thought by a consideration of the causes of sterility, both the inhibitory and the prohibitory, whether the inhibition in its turn were due to conjugal vexations or to a parsimony of the balance as well as whether the prohibition proceeded from defects congenital or from proclivities acquired. It grieved him plaguily, he said, to see the nuptial couch defrauded of its dearest pledges: and to reflect upon so many agreeable females with rich jointures, a prey to the vilest bonzes, who hide their flambeau under a bushel in an uncongenial cloister or lose their womanly bloom in the embraces of some unaccountable muskin when they might multiply the inlets of happiness, sacrificing the inestimable jewel of their sex when a hundred pretty fellows were at hand to caress, this, he assured them, made his heart weep. To curb this inconvenient (which he concluded due to a suppression of latent heat), having advised with certain counsellors of worth and inspected into this matter, he had resolved to purchase in fee simple for ever the freehold of Lambay island from its holder, lord Talbot de Malahide, a Tory gentleman of note much in favour with our ascendancy party. He proposed to set up there a national fertilising farm to be named *Omphalos* with an obelisk hewn and erected after the fashion of Egypt and to offer his dutiful yeoman services for the fecundation of any female of what grade of life soever who should there direct to him with the desire of fulfilling the functions of her natural. Money was no object, he said, nor would he take a penny for his pains. The poorest kitchenwench no less than the opulent lady of fashion, if so be their constructions and their tempers were warm persuaders for their petitions, would find in him their man. For his nutriment he shewed how he would feed himself exclusively upon a diet of savoury tubercles and fish and coneys there, the flesh of these latter prolific rodents being highly recommended for his purpose, both broiled and stewed with a blade of mace and a pod or two of capsicum chillies. After this homily which he delivered with much warmth of asseveration Mr Mulligan in a trice put off from his hat a kerchief with which he had shielded it. They both, it seems, had been overtaken by the rain and for all their mending their pace had taken water, as might be observed by Mr Mulligan's smallclothes of a hodden grey which was now somewhat piebald. His project meanwhile was very favourably entertained by his auditors and won hearty eulogies from all though Mr Dixon of Mary's excepted to it, asking with a finicking air did he purpose also to carry coals to Newcastle. Mr Mulligan however made court to the scholarly by an apt quotation from the classics which, as it dwelt upon his memory, seemed to him a sound and tasteful support of his contention: *Talis ac tanta depravatio hujus seculi, O quirites, ut matresfamiliarum nostrae lascivas cujuslibet semiviri libici titillationes testibus ponderosis atque excelsis erectionibus centurionum Romanorum magnopere anteponunt,* while for those of ruder wit he drove home his point by analogies of the animal kingdom more suitable to their stomach, the buck and doe of the forest glade, the farmyard drake and duck.

Valuing himself not a little upon his elegance, being indeed a proper man of person, this talkative now applied himself to his dress with animadversions of some heat upon the sudden whimsy of the atmospherics while the company lavished their encomiums upon the project he had advanced. The young gentleman, his friend, overjoyed as he was at a passage that had late befallen him, could not forbear to tell it his nearest neighbour. Mr Mulligan, now perceiving the table, asked for whom were those loaves and fishes and, seeing the stranger, he made him a civil bow and said, Pray, sir, was you in need of any professional assistance we could give? Who, upon his offer, thanked him very heartily, though preserving his proper distance, and replied that he was come there about a lady, now an inmate of Horne's house, that was in an interesting condition, poor body, from woman's woe (and here he fetched a deep sigh) to know if her happiness had yet taken place. Mr Dixon, to turn the table, took on to ask of Mr Mulligan himself whether his incipient ventripotence, upon which he rallied him, betokened an ovoblastic gestation in the prostatic utricle or male womb or was due, as with the noted physician, Mr Austin Meldon, to a wolf in the stomach. For answer Mr Mulligan, in a gale of laughter at his smalls, smote himself bravely below the diaphragm, exclaiming with an admirable droll mimic of Mother Grogan (the most excellent creature of her sex though 'tis pity she's a trollop): There's a belly that never bore a bastard. This was so happy a conceit that it renewed the storm of mirth and threw the whole room into the most violent agitations of delight. The spry rattle had run on in the same vein of mimicry but for some larum in the antechamber.

Here the listener who was none other than the Scotch student, a little fume of a fellow, blond as tow, congratulated in the liveliest fashion with the young gentleman and, interrupting the narrative at a salient point, having desired his visavis with a polite beck to have the obligingness to pass him a flagon of cordial waters at the same time by a questioning poise of the head (a whole century of polite breeding had not achieved so nice a gesture) to which was united an equivalent but contrary balance of the bottle asked the narrator as plainly as was ever done in words if he might treat him with a cup of it. *Mais bien sûr*, noble stranger, said he cheerily, *et mille compliments*. That you may and very opportunely. There wanted nothing but this cup to crown my felicity. But, gracious heaven, was I left with but a crust in my wallet and a cupful of water from the well, my God, I would accept of them and find it in my heart to kneel down upon the ground and give thanks to the powers above for the happiness vouchsafed me by the Giver of good things. With these words he approached the goblet to his lips, took a complacent draught of the cordial, slicked his hair and, opening his bosom, out popped a locket that hung from a silk riband, that very picture which he had cherished ever since her hand had wrote therein. Gazing upon those features with a world of tenderness, Ah, Monsieur, he said, had you but beheld her as I did with these eyes at that affecting instant with her dainty tucker and her new coquette cap (a gift for her feastday as she told me prettily) in such an artless disorder, of so melting a tenderness, 'pon my conscience, even you, Monsieur, had been impelled by generous nature to deliver yourself wholly into the hands of such an enemy or to quit the field for ever. I declare, I was never so touched in all my life. God, I thank thee, as the Author of my days! Thrice happy will he be whom so amiable a creature will bless with her favours. A sigh of affection gave eloquence to these words and, having replaced the locket in his bosom, he wiped his eye and sighed again. Beneficent Disseminator of blessings to all Thy creatures, how great and universal must be that sweetest of Thy tyrannies which can hold in thrall the free and the bond, the simple swain and the polished coxcomb, the lover in the heyday of reckless passion and the husband of maturer years. But indeed, sir, I wander from the point. How mingled and imperfect are all our sublunary joys. Maledicity! he exclaimed in anguish. Would to God that foresight had but remembered me to take my cloak along! I could weep to think of it. Then, though it had poured seven showers, we were neither of us a penny the worse. But beshrew me, he cried, clapping hand to his forehead, tomorrow will be a new day and, thousand thunders, I know of a *marchand de capotes*, Monsieur Poyntz, from whom I can have for a *livre* as snug a cloak of the French fashion as ever kept a lady from wetting. Tut, tut! cries Le Fécondateur, tripping in, my friend Monsieur Moore, that most accomplished traveller (I have just cracked a half bottle *avec lui* in a circle of the best wits of the town), is my authority that in Cape Horn, *ventre biche*, they have a rain that will wet through any, even the stoutest cloak. A drenching of that violence, he tells me, *sans blague*, has sent more than one luckless fellow in good earnest posthaste to another world. Pooh! A *livre*! cries Monsieur Lynch. The clumsy things are dear at a sou. One umbrella, were it no bigger than a fairy mushroom, is worth ten such stopgaps. No woman of any wit would wear one. My dear Kitty told me today that she would dance in a deluge before ever she would starve in such an ark of salvation for, as she reminded me (blushing piquantly and whispering in my ear though there was none to snap her words but giddy butterflies), dame Nature, by the divine blessing, has implanted it in our hearts and it has become a household word that *il y a deux choses* for which the innocence of our original garb, in other circumstances a breach of the proprieties, is the fittest, nay, the only garment. The first, said she (and here my pretty philosopher, as I handed her to her tilbury, to fix my attention, gently tipped with her tongue the outer chamber of my ear), the first is a bath . . . But at this point a bell tinkling in the hall cut short a discourse which promised so bravely for the enrichment of our store of knowledge.

Amid the general vacant hilarity of the assembly a bell rang and, while all were conjecturing what might be the cause, Miss Callan entered and, having spoken a few words in a low tone to young Mr Dixon, retired with a profound bow to the company. The presence even for a moment among a party of debauchees of a woman endued with every quality of modesty and not less severe than beautiful refrained the humourous sallies even of the most licentious but her departure was the signal for an outbreak of ribaldry. Strike me silly, said Costello, a low fellow who was fuddled. A monstrous fine bit of cowflesh! I'll be sworn she has rendezvoused you. What, you dog? Have you a way with them? Gad's bud, immensely so, said Mr Lynch. The bedside manner it is that they use in the Mater hospice. Demme, does not Doctor O'Gargle chuck the nuns there under the chin. As I look to be saved I had it from my Kitty who has been wardmaid there any time these seven months. Lawksamercy, doctor, cried the young blood in the primrose vest, feigning a womanish simper and with immodest squirmings of his body, how you do tease a body! Drat the man! Bless me, I'm all of a wibbly wobbly. Why, you're as bad as dear little Father Cantekissem, that you are! May this pot of four half choke me, cried Costello, if she aint in the family way. I knows a lady what's got a white swelling quick as I claps eyes on her. The young surgeon, however, rose and begged the company to excuse his retreat as the nurse had just then informed him that he was needed in the ward. Merciful providence had been pleased to put a period to the sufferings of the lady who was *enceinte* which she had borne with a laudable fortitude and she had given birth to a bouncing boy. I want patience, said he, with those who, without wit to enliven or learning to instruct, revile an ennobling profession which, saving the reverence due to the Deity, is the greatest power for happiness upon the earth. I am positive when I say that if need were I could produce a cloud of witnesses to the excellence of her noble exercitations which, so far from being a byword, should be a glorious incentive in the human breast. I cannot away with them. What? Malign such an one, the amiable Miss Callan, who is the lustre of her own sex and the astonishment of ours? And at an instant the most momentous that can befall a puny child of clay? Perish the thought! I shudder to think of the future of a race where the seeds of such malice have been sown and where no right reverence is rendered to mother and maid in house of Horne. Having delivered himself of this rebuke he saluted those present on the by and repaired to the door. A murmur of approval arose from all and some were for ejecting the low soaker without more ado, a design which would have been effected nor would he have received more than his bare deserts had he not abridged his transgression by affirming with a horrid imprecation (for he swore a round hand) that he was as good a son of the true fold as ever drew breath. Stap my vitals, said he, them was always the sentiments of honest Frank Costello which I was bred up most particular to honour thy father and thy mother that had the best hand to a rolypoly or a hasty pudding as you ever see what I always looks back on with a loving heart.

To revert to Mr Bloom who, after his first entry, had been conscious of some impudent mocks which he however had borne with as being the fruits of that age upon which it is commonly charged that it knows not pity. The young sparks, it is true, were as full of extravagancies as overgrown children: the words of their tumultuary discussions were difficultly understood and not often nice: their testiness and outrageous *mots* were such that his intellects resiled from: nor were they scrupulously sensible of the proprieties though their fund of strong animal spirits spoke in their behalf. But the word of Mr Costello was an unwelcome language for him for he nauseated the wretch that seemed to him a cropeared creature of a misshapen gibbosity, born out of wedlock and thrust like a crookback toothed and feet first into the world, which the dint of the surgeon's pliers in his skull lent indeed a colour to, so as to put him in thought of that missing link of creation's chain desiderated by the late ingenious Mr Darwin. It was now for more than the middle span of our allotted years that he had passed through the thousand vicissitudes of existence and, being of a wary ascendancy and self a man of rare forecast, he had enjoined his heart to repress all motions of a rising choler and, by intercepting them with the readiest precaution, foster within his breast that plenitude of sufferance which base minds jeer at, rash judgers scorn and all find tolerable and but tolerable. To those who create themselves wits at the cost of feminine delicacy (a habit of mind which he never did hold with) to them he would concede neither to bear the name nor to herit the tradition of a proper breeding: while for such that, having lost all forbearance, can lose no more, there remained the sharp antidote of experience to cause their insolency to beat a precipitate and inglorious retreat. Not but what he could feel with mettlesome youth which, caring nought for the mows of dotards or the gruntlings of the severe, is ever (as the chaste fancy of the Holy Writer expresses it) for eating of the tree forbid it yet not so far forth as to pretermit humanity upon any condition soever towards a gentlewoman when she was about her lawful occasions. To conclude, while from the sister's words he had reckoned upon a speedy delivery he was, however, it must be owned, not a little alleviated by the intelligence that the issue so auspicated after an ordeal of such duress now testified once more to the mercy as well as to the bounty of the Supreme Being.

Accordingly he broke his mind to his neighbour, saying that, to express his notion of the thing, his opinion (who ought not perchance to express one) was that one must have a cold constitution and a frigid genius not to be rejoiced by this freshest news of the fruition of her confinement since she had been in such pain through no fault of hers. The dressy young blade said it was her husband's that put her in that expectation or at least it ought to be unless she were another Ephesian matron. I must acquaint you, said Mr Crotthers, clapping on the table so as to evoke a resonant comment of emphasis, old Glory Allelujurum was round again today, an elderly man with dundrearies, preferring through his nose a request to have word of Wilhelmina, my life, as he calls her. I bade him hold himself in readiness for that the event would burst anon. 'Slife, I'll be round with you. I cannot but extol the virile potency of the old bucko that could still knock another child out of her. All fell to praising of it, each after his own fashion, though the same young blade held with his former view that another than her conjugial had been the man in the gap, a clerk in orders, a linkboy (virtuous) or an itinerant vendor of articles needed in every household. Singular, communed the guest with himself, the wonderfully unequal faculty of metempsychosis possessed by them, that the puerperal dormitory and the dissecting theatre should be the seminaries of such frivolity, that the mere acquisition of academic titles should suffice to transform in a pinch of time these votaries of levity into exemplary practitioners of an art which most men anywise eminent have esteemed the noblest. But, he further added, it is mayhap to relieve the pentup feelings that in common oppress them for I have more than once observed that birds of a feather laugh together.

But with what fitness, let it be asked of the noble lord, his patron, has this alien, whom the concession of a gracious prince has admitted to civic rights, constituted himself the lord paramount of our internal polity? Where is now that gratitude which loyalty should have counselled? During the recent war whenever the enemy had a temporary advantage with his granados did this traitor to his kind not seize that moment to discharge his piece against the empire of which he is a tenant at will while he trembled for the security of his four per cents? Has he forgotten this as he forgets all benefits received? Or is it that from being a deluder of others he has become at last his own dupe as he is, if report belie him not, his own and his only enjoyer? Far be it from candour to violate the bedchamber of a respectable lady, the daughter of a gallant major, or to cast the most distant reflections upon her virtue but if he challenges attention there (as it was indeed highly his interest not to have done) then be it so. Unhappy woman, she has been too long and too persistently denied her legitimate prerogative to listen to his objurgations with any other feeling than the derision of the desperate. He says this, a censor of morals, a very pelican in his piety, who did not scruple, oblivious of the ties of nature, to attempt illicit intercourse with a female domestic drawn from the lowest strata of society! Nay, had the hussy's scouringbrush not been her tutelary angel, it had gone with her as hard as with Hagar, the Egyptian! In the question of the grazing lands his peevish asperity is notorious and in Mr Cuffe's hearing brought upon him from an indignant rancher a scathing retort couched in terms as straightforward as they were bucolic. It ill becomes him to preach that gospel. Has he not nearer home a seedfield that lies fallow for the want of the ploughshare? A habit reprehensible at puberty is second nature and an opprobrium in middle life. If he must dispense his balm of Gilead in nostrums and apothegms of dubious taste to restore to health a generation of unfledged profligates let his practice consist better with the doctrines that now engross him. His marital breast is the repository of secrets which decorum is reluctant to adduce. The lewd suggestions of some faded beauty may console him for a consort neglected and debauched but this new exponent of morals and healer of ills is at his best an exotic tree which, when rooted in its native orient, throve and flourished and was abundant in balm but, transplanted to a clime more temperate, its roots have lost their quondam vigour while the stuff that comes away from it is stagnant, acid and inoperative.

The news was imparted with a circumspection recalling the ceremonial usage of the Sublime Porte by the second female infirmarian to the junior medical officer in residence, who in his turn announced to the delegation that an heir had been born. When he had betaken himself to the women's apartment to assist at the prescribed ceremony of the afterbirth in the presence of the secretary of state for domestic affairs and the members of the privy council, silent in unanimous exhaustion and approbation the delegates, chafing under the length and solemnity of their vigil and hoping that the joyful occurrence would palliate a licence which the simultaneous absence of abigail and obstetrician rendered the easier, broke out at once into a strife of tongues. In vain the voice of Mr Canvasser Bloom was heard endeavouring to urge, to mollify, to refrain. The moment was too propitious for the display of that discursiveness which seemed the only bond of union among tempers so divergent. Every phase of the situation was successively eviscerated: the prenatal repugnance of uterine brothers, the Caesarean section, posthumity with respect to the father and, that rarer form, with respect to the mother, the fratricidal case known as the Childs Murder and rendered memorable by the impassioned plea of Mr Advocate Bushe which secured the acquittal of the wrongfully accused, the rights of primogeniture and king's bounty touching twins and triplets, miscarriages and infanticides, simulated or dissimulated, the acardiac *foetus in foetu* and aprosopia due to a congestion, the agnathia of certain chinless Chinamen (cited by Mr Candidate Mulligan) in consequence of defective reunion of the maxillary knobs along the medial line so that (as he said) one ear could hear what the other spoke, the benefits of anaesthesia or twilight sleep, the prolongation of labour pains in advanced gravidancy by reason of pressure on the vein, the premature relentment of the amniotic fluid (as exemplified in the actual case) with consequent peril of sepsis to the matrix, artificial insemination by means of syringes, involution of the womb consequent upon the menopause, the problem of the perpetration of the species in the case of females impregnated by delinquent rape, that distressing manner of delivery called by the Brandenburghers *Sturzgeburt,* the recorded instances of multiseminal, twikindled and monstrous births conceived during the catamenic period or of consanguineous parents—in a word all the cases of human nativity which Aristotle has classified in his masterpiece with chromolithographic illustrations. The gravest problems of obstetrics and forensic medicine were examined with as much animation as the most popular beliefs on the state of pregnancy such as the forbidding to a gravid woman to step over a countrystile lest, by her movement, the navelcord should strangle her creature and the injunction upon her in the event of a yearning, ardently and ineffectually entertained, to place her hand against that part of her person which long usage has consecrated as the seat of castigation. The abnormalities of harelip, breastmole, supernumerary digits, negro's inkle, strawberry mark and portwine stain were alleged by one as a *prima facie* and natural hypothetical explanation of those swineheaded (the case of Madame Grissel Steevens was not forgotten) or doghaired infants occasionally born. The hypothesis of a plasmic memory, advanced by the Caledonian envoy and worthy of the metaphysical traditions of the land he stood for, envisaged in such cases an arrest of embryonic development at some stage antecedent to the human. An outlandish delegate sustained against both these views, with such heat as almost carried conviction, the theory of copulation between women and the males of brutes, his authority being his own avouchment in support of fables such as that of the Minotaur which the genius of the elegant Latin poet has handed down to us in the pages of his Metamorphoses. The impression made by his words was immediate but shortlived. It was effaced as easily as it had been evoked by an allocution from Mr Candidate Mulligan in that vein of pleasantry which none better than he knew how to affect, postulating as the supremest object of desire a nice clean old man. Contemporaneously, a heated argument having arisen between Mr Delegate Madden and Mr Candidate Lynch regarding the juridical and theological dilemma created in the event of one Siamese twin predeceasing the other, the difficulty by mutual consent was referred to Mr Canvasser Bloom for instant submittal to Mr Coadjutor Deacon Dedalus. Hitherto silent, whether the better to show by preternatural gravity that curious dignity of the garb with which he was invested or in obedience to an inward voice, he delivered briefly and, as some thought, perfunctorily the ecclesiastical ordinance forbidding man to put asunder what God has joined.

But Malachias' tale began to freeze them with horror. He conjured up the scene before them. The secret panel beside the chimney slid back and in the recess appeared . . . Haines! Which of us did not feel his flesh creep! He had a portfolio full of Celtic literature in one hand, in the other a phial marked *Poison*. Surprise, horror, loathing were depicted on all faces while he eyed them with a ghostly grin. I anticipated some such reception, he began with an eldritch laugh, for which, it seems, history is to blame. Yes, it is true. I am the murderer of Samuel Childs. And how I am punished! The inferno has no terrors for me. This is the appearance is on me. Tare and ages, what way would I be resting at all, he muttered thickly, and I tramping Dublin this while back with my share of songs and himself after me the like of a soulth or a bullawurrus? My hell, and Ireland's, is in this life. It is what I tried to obliterate my crime. Distractions, rookshooting, the Erse language (he recited some), laudanum (he raised the phial to his lips), camping out. In vain! His spectre stalks me. Dope is my only hope . . . Ah! Destruction! The black panther! With a cry he suddenly vanished and the panel slid back. An instant later his head appeared in the door opposite and said: Meet me at Westland Row station at ten past eleven. He was gone. Tears gushed from the eyes of the dissipated host. The seer raised his hand to heaven, murmuring: The vendetta of Mananaun! The sage repeated: *Lex talionis*. The sentimentalist is he who would enjoy without incurring the immense debtorship for a thing done. Malachias, overcome by emotion, ceased. The mystery was unveiled. Haines was the third brother. His real name was Childs. The black panther was himself the ghost of his own father. He drank drugs to obliterate. For this relief much thanks. The lonely house by the graveyard is uninhabited. No soul will live there. The spider pitches her web in the solitude. The nocturnal rat peers from his hole. A curse is on it. It is haunted. Murderer's ground.

What is the age of the soul of man? As she hath the virtue of the chameleon to change her hue at every new approach, to be gay with the merry and mournful with the downcast, so too is her age changeable as her mood. No longer is Leopold, as he sits there, ruminating, chewing the cud of reminiscence, that staid agent of publicity and holder of a modest substance in the funds. A score of years are blown away. He is young Leopold. There, as in a retrospective arrangement, a mirror within a mirror (hey, presto!), he beholdeth himself. That young figure of then is seen, precociously manly, walking on a nipping morning from the old house in Clanbrassil street to the high school, his booksatchel on him bandolierwise, and in it a goodly hunk of wheaten loaf, a mother's thought. Or it is the same figure, a year or so gone over, in his first hard hat (ah, that was a day!), already on the road, a fullfledged traveller for the family firm, equipped with an orderbook, a scented handkerchief (not for show only), his case of bright trinketware (alas! a thing now of the past!) and a quiverful of compliant smiles for this or that halfwon housewife reckoning it out upon her fingertips or for a budding virgin, shyly acknowledging (but the heart? tell me!) his studied baisemoins. The scent, the smile, but, more than these, the dark eyes and oleaginous address, brought home at duskfall many a commission to the head of the firm, seated with Jacob's pipe after like labours in the paternal ingle (a meal of noodles, you may be sure, is aheating), reading through round horned spectacles some paper from the Europe of a month before. But hey, presto, the mirror is breathed on and the young knighterrant recedes, shrivels, dwindles to a tiny speck within the mist. Now he is himself paternal and these about him might be his sons. Who can say? The wise father knows his own child. He thinks of a drizzling night in Hatch street, hard by the bonded stores there, the first. Together (she is a poor waif, a child of shame, yours and mine and of all for a bare shilling and her luckpenny), together they hear the heavy tread of the watch as two raincaped shadows pass the new royal university. Bridie! Bridie Kelly! He will never forget the name, ever remember the night: first night, the bridenight. They are entwined in nethermost darkness, the willer with the willed, and in an instant (*fiat!*) light shall flood the world. Did heart leap to heart? Nay, fair reader. In a breath 'twas done but—hold! Back! It must not be! In terror the poor girl flees away through the murk. She is the bride of darkness, a daughter of night. She dare not bear the sunnygolden babe of day. No, Leopold. Name and memory solace thee not. That youthful illusion of thy strength was taken from thee—and in vain. No son of thy loins is by thee. There is none now to be for Leopold, what Leopold was for Rudolph.

The voices blend and fuse in clouded silence: silence that is the infinite of space: and swiftly, silently the soul is wafted over regions of cycles of generations that have lived. A region where grey twilight ever descends, never falls on wide sagegreen pasturefields, shedding her dusk, scattering a perennial dew of stars. She follows her mother with ungainly steps, a mare leading her fillyfoal. Twilight phantoms are they, yet moulded in prophetic grace of structure, slim shapely haunches, a supple tendonous neck, the meek apprehensive skull. They fade, sad phantoms: all is gone. Agendath is a waste land, a home of screechowls and the sandblind upupa. Netaim, the golden, is no more. And on the highway of the clouds they come, muttering thunder of rebellion, the ghosts of beasts. Huuh! Hark! Huuh! Parallax stalks behind and goads them, the lancinating lightnings of whose brow are scorpions. Elk and yak, the bulls of Bashan and of Babylon, mammoth and mastodon, they come trooping to the sunken sea, *Lacus Mortis.* Ominous revengeful zodiacal host! They moan, passing upon the clouds, horned and capricorned, the trumpeted with the tusked, the lionmaned, the giantantlered, snouter and crawler, rodent, ruminant and pachyderm, all their moving moaning multitude, murderers of the sun.

Onward to the dead sea they tramp to drink, unslaked and with horrible gulpings, the salt somnolent inexhaustible flood. And the equine portent grows again, magnified in the deserted heavens, nay to heaven's own magnitude, till it looms, vast, over the house of Virgo. And lo, wonder of metempsychosis, it is she, the everlasting bride, harbinger of the daystar, the bride, ever virgin. It is she, Martha, thou lost one, Millicent, the young, the dear, the radiant. How serene does she now arise, a queen among the Pleiades, in the penultimate antelucan hour, shod in sandals of bright gold, coifed with a veil of what do you call it gossamer. It floats, it flows about her starborn flesh and loose it streams, emerald, sapphire, mauve and heliotrope, sustained on currents of the cold interstellar wind, winding, coiling, simply swirling, writhing in the skies a mysterious writing till, after a myriad metamorphoses of symbol, it blazes, Alpha, a ruby and triangled sign upon the forehead of Taurus.

Francis was reminding Stephen of years before when they had been at school together in Conmee's time. He asked about Glaucon, Alcibiades, Pisistratus. Where were they now? Neither knew. You have spoken of the past and its phantoms, Stephen said. Why think of them? If I call them into life across the waters of Lethe will not the poor ghosts troop to my call? Who supposes it? I, Bous Stephanoumenos, bullockbefriending bard, am lord and giver of their life. He encircled his gadding hair with a coronal of vineleaves, smiling at Vincent. That answer and those leaves, Vincent said to him, will adorn you more fitly when something more, and greatly more, than a capful of light odes can call your genius father. All who wish you well hope this for you. All desire to see you bring forth the work you meditate, to acclaim you Stephaneforos. I heartily wish you may not fail them. O no, Vincent Lenehan said, laying a hand on the shoulder near him. Have no fear. He could not leave his mother an orphan. The young man's face grew dark. All could see how hard it was for him to be reminded of his promise and of his recent loss. He would have withdrawn from the feast had not the noise of voices allayed the smart. Madden had lost five drachmas on Sceptre for a whim of the rider's name: Lenehan as much more. He told them of the race. The flag fell and, huuh! off, scamper, the mare ran out freshly with O. Madden up. She was leading the field. All hearts were beating. Even Phyllis could not contain herself. She waved her scarf and cried: Huzzah! Sceptre wins! But in the straight on the run home when all were in close order the dark horse Throwaway drew level, reached, outstripped her. All was lost now. Phyllis was silent: her eyes were sad anemones. Juno, she cried, I am undone. But her lover consoled her and brought her a bright casket of gold in which lay some oval sugarplums which she partook. A tear fell: one only. A whacking fine whip, said Lenehan, is W. Lane. Four winners yesterday and three today. What rider is like him? Mount him on the camel or the boisterous buffalo the victory in a hack canter is still his. But let us bear it as was the ancient wont. Mercy on the luckless! Poor Sceptre! he said with a light sigh. She is not the filly that she was. Never, by this hand, shall we behold such another. By gad, sir, a queen of them. Do you remember her, Vincent? I wish you could have seen my queen today, Vincent said. How young she was and radiant (Lalage were scarce fair beside her) in her yellow shoes and frock of muslin, I do not know the right name of it. The chestnuts that shaded us were in bloom: the air drooped with their persuasive odour and with pollen floating by us. In the sunny patches one might easily have cooked on a stone a batch of those buns with Corinth fruit in them that Periplipomenes sells in his booth near the bridge. But she had nought for her teeth but the arm with which I held her and in that she nibbled mischievously when I pressed too close. A week ago she lay ill, four days on the couch, but today she was free, blithe, mocked at peril. She is more taking then. Her posies too! Mad romp that she is, she had pulled her fill as we reclined together. And in your ear, my friend, you will not think who met us as we left the field. Conmee himself! He was walking by the hedge, reading, I think a brevier book with, I doubt not, a witty letter in it from Glycera or Chloe to keep the page. The sweet creature turned all colours in her confusion, feigning to reprove a slight disorder in her dress: a slip of underwood clung there for the very trees adore her. When Conmee had passed she glanced at her lovely echo in that little mirror she carries. But he had been kind. In going by he had blessed us. The gods too are ever kind, Lenehan said. If I had poor luck with Bass's mare perhaps this draught of his may serve me more propensely. He was laying his hand upon a winejar: Malachi saw it and withheld his act, pointing to the stranger and to the scarlet label. Warily, Malachi whispered, preserve a druid silence. His soul is far away. It is as painful perhaps to be awakened from a vision as to be born. Any object, intensely regarded, may be a gate of access to the incorruptible eon of the gods. Do you not think it, Stephen? Theosophos told me so, Stephen answered, whom in a previous existence Egyptian priests initiated into the mysteries of karmic law. The lords of the moon, Theosophos told me, an orangefiery shipload from planet Alpha of the lunar chain would not assume the etheric doubles and these were therefore incarnated by the rubycoloured egos from the second constellation.

However, as a matter of fact though, the preposterous surmise about him being in some description of a doldrums or other or mesmerised which was entirely due to a misconception of the shallowest character, was not the case at all. The individual whose visual organs while the above was going on were at this juncture commencing to exhibit symptoms of animation was as astute if not astuter than any man living and anybody that conjectured the contrary would have found themselves pretty speedily in the wrong shop. During the past four minutes or thereabouts he had been staring hard at a certain amount of number one Bass bottled by Messrs Bass and Co at Burton-on-Trent which happened to be situated amongst a lot of others right opposite to where he was and which was certainly calculated to attract anyone's remark on account of its scarlet appearance. He was simply and solely, as it subsequently transpired for reasons best known to himself, which put quite an altogether different complexion on the proceedings, after the moment before's observations about boyhood days and the turf, recollecting two or three private transactions of his own which the other two were as mutually innocent of as the babe unborn. Eventually, however, both their eyes met and as soon as it began to dawn on him that the other was endeavouring to help himself to the thing he involuntarily determined to help him himself and so he accordingly took hold of the neck of the mediumsized glass recipient which contained the fluid sought after and made a capacious hole in it by pouring a lot of it out with, also at the same time, however, a considerable degree of attentiveness in order not to upset any of the beer that was in it about the place.

The debate which ensued was in its scope and progress an epitome of the course of life. Neither place nor council was lacking in dignity. The debaters were the keenest in the land, the theme they were engaged on the loftiest and most vital. The high hall of Horne's house had never beheld an assembly so representative and so varied nor had the old rafters of that establishment ever listened to a language so encyclopaedic. A gallant scene in truth it made. Crotthers was there at the foot of the table in his striking Highland garb, his face glowing from the briny airs of the Mull of Galloway. There too, opposite to him, was Lynch whose countenance bore already the stigmata of early depravity and premature wisdom. Next the Scotchman was the place assigned to Costello, the eccentric, while at his side was seated in stolid repose the squat form of Madden. The chair of the resident indeed stood vacant before the hearth but on either flank of it the figure of Bannon in explorer's kit of tweed shorts and salted cowhide brogues contrasted sharply with the primrose elegance and townbred manners of Malachi Roland St John Mulligan. Lastly at the head of the board was the young poet who found a refuge from his labours of pedagogy and metaphysical inquisition in the convivial atmosphere of Socratic discussion, while to right and left of him were accommodated the flippant prognosticator, fresh from the hippodrome, and that vigilant wanderer, soiled by the dust of travel and combat and stained by the mire of an indelible dishonour, but from whose steadfast and constant heart no lure or peril or threat or degradation could ever efface the image of that voluptuous loveliness which the inspired pencil of Lafayette has limned for ages yet to come.

It had better be stated here and now at the outset that the perverted transcendentalism to which Mr S. Dedalus' (Div. Scep.) contentions would appear to prove him pretty badly addicted runs directly counter to accepted scientific methods. Science, it cannot be too often repeated, deals with tangible phenomena. The man of science like the man in the street has to face hardheaded facts that cannot be blinked and explain them as best he can. There may be, it is true, some questions which science cannot answer—at present—such as the first problem submitted by Mr L. Bloom (Pubb. Canv.) regarding the future determination of sex. Must we accept the view of Empedocles of Trinacria that the right ovary (the postmenstrual period, assert others) is responsible for the birth of males or are the too long neglected spermatozoa or nemasperms the differentiating factors or is it, as most embryologists incline to opine, such as Culpepper, Spallanzani, Blumenbach, Lusk, Hertwig, Leopold and Valenti, a mixture of both? This would be tantamount to a cooperation (one of nature's favourite devices) between the *nisus formativus* of the nemasperm on the one hand and on the other a happily chosen position, *succubitus felix*, of the passive element. The other problem raised by the same inquirer is scarcely less vital: infant mortality. It is interesting because, as he pertinently remarks, we are all born in the same way but we all die in different ways. Mr M. Mulligan (Hyg. et Eug. Doc.) blames the sanitary conditions in which our greylunged citizens contract adenoids, pulmonary complaints etc. by inhaling the bacteria which lurk in dust. These factors, he alleged, and the revolting spectacles offered by our streets, hideous publicity posters, religious ministers of all denominations, mutilated soldiers and sailors, exposed scorbutic cardrivers, the suspended carcases of dead animals, paranoic bachelors and unfructified duennas—these, he said, were accountable for any and every fallingoff in the calibre of the race. Kalipedia, he prophesied, would soon be generally adopted and all the graces of life, genuinely good music, agreeable literature, light philosophy, instructive pictures, plastercast reproductions of the classical statues such as Venus and Apollo, artistic coloured photographs of prize babies, all these little attentions would enable ladies who were in a particular condition to pass the intervening months in a most enjoyable manner. Mr J. Crotthers (Disc. Bacc.) attributes some of these demises to abdominal trauma in the case of women workers subjected to heavy labours in the workshop and to marital discipline in the home but by far the vast majority to neglect, private or official, culminating in the exposure of newborn infants, the practice of criminal abortion or in the atrocious crime of infanticide. Although the former (we are thinking of neglect) is undoubtedly only too true the case he cites of nurses forgetting to count the sponges in the peritoneal cavity is too rare to be normative. In fact when one comes to look into it the wonder is that so many pregnancies and deliveries go off so well as they do, all things considered and in spite of our human shortcomings which often baulk nature in her intentions. An ingenious suggestion is that thrown out by Mr V. Lynch (Bacc. Arith.) that both natality and mortality, as well as all other phenomena of evolution, tidal movements, lunar phases, blood temperatures, diseases in general, everything, in fine, in nature's vast workshop from the extinction of some remote sun to the blossoming of one of the countless flowers which beautify our public parks is subject to a law of numeration as yet unascertained. Still the plain straightforward question why a child of normally healthy parents and seemingly a healthy child and properly looked after succumbs unaccountably in early childhood (though other children of the same marriage do not) must certainly, in the poet's words, give us pause. Nature, we may rest assured, has her own good and cogent reasons for whatever she does and in all probability such deaths are due to some law of anticipation by which organisms in which morbous germs have taken up their residence (modern science has conclusively shown that only the plasmic substance can be said to be immortal) tend to disappear at an increasingly earlier stage of development, an arrangement which, though productive of pain to some of our feelings (notably the maternal), is nevertheless, some of us think, in the long run beneficial to the race in general in securing thereby the survival of the fittest. Mr S. Dedalus' (Div. Scep.) remark (or should it be called an interruption?) that an omnivorous being which can masticate, deglute, digest and apparently pass through the ordinary channel with pluterperfect imperturbability such multifarious aliments as cancrenous females emaciated by parturition, corpulent professional gentlemen, not to speak of jaundiced politicians and chlorotic nuns, might possibly find gastric relief in an innocent collation of staggering bob, reveals as nought else could and in a very unsavoury light the tendency above alluded to. For the enlightenment of those who are not so intimately acquainted with the minutiae of the municipal abattoir as this morbidminded esthete and embryo philosopher who for all his overweening bumptiousness in things scientific can scarcely distinguish an acid from an alkali prides himself on being, it should perhaps be stated that staggering bob in the vile parlance of our lowerclass licensed victuallers signifies the cookable and eatable flesh

of a calf newly dropped from its mother. In a recent public controversy
with Mr L. Bloom (Pubb. Canv.) which took place in the commons'
hall of the National Maternity Hospital, 29, 30 and 31 Holles street,
of which, as is well known, Dr A. Horne (Lic. in Midw., F. K. Q. C.
P. I.) is the able and popular master, he is reported by eyewitnesses
as having stated that once a woman has let the cat into the bag (an
esthete's allusion, presumably, to one of the most complicated and
marvellous of all nature's processes—the act of sexual congress) she
must let it out again or give it life, as he phrased it, to save her own.
At the risk of her own, was the telling rejoinder of his interlocutor,
none the less effective for the moderate and measured tone in which
it was delivered.

Meanwhile the skill and patience of the physician had brought
about a happy *accouchement*. It had been a weary weary while both for
patient and doctor. All that surgical skill could do was done and the
brave woman had manfully helped. She had. She had fought the good
fight and now she was very very happy. Those who have passed on,
who have gone before, are happy too as they gaze down and smile
upon the touching scene. Reverently look at her as she reclines there
with the motherlight in her eyes, that longing hunger for baby fingers
(a pretty sight it is to see), in the first bloom of her new motherhood,
breathing a silent prayer of thanksgiving to One above, the Universal
Husband. And as her loving eyes behold her babe she wishes only one
blessing more, to have her dear Doady there with her to share her
joy, to lay in his arms that mite of God's clay, the fruit of their lawful
embraces. He is older now (you and I may whisper it) and a trifle
stooped in the shoulders yet in the whirligig of years a grave dignity
has come to the conscientious second accountant of the Ulster bank,
College Green branch. O Doady, loved one of old, faithful lifemate
now, it may never be again, that faroff time of the roses! With the old
shake of her pretty head she recalls those days. God! How beautiful
now across the mist of years! But their children are grouped in her
imagination about the bedside, hers and his, Charley, Mary Alice,
Frederick Albert (if he had lived), Mamy, Budgy (Victoria Frances),
Tom, Violet Constance Louisa, darling little Bobsy (called after our
famous hero of the South African war, lord Bobs of Waterford and
Candahar) and now this last pledge of their union, a Purefoy if ever
there was one, with the true Purefoy nose. Young hopeful will be
christened Mortimer Edward after the influential third cousin of Mr

Purefoy in the Treasury Remembrancer's office, Dublin Castle. And so time wags on: but father Cronion has dealt lightly here. No, let no sigh break from that bosom, dear gentle Mina. And Doady, knock the ashes from your pipe, the seasoned briar you still fancy when the curfew rings for you (may it be the distant day!) and dout the light whereby you read in the Sacred Book for the oil too has run low, and so with a tranquil heart to bed, to rest. He knows and will call in His own good time. You too have fought the good fight and played loyally your man's part. Sir, to you my hand. Well done, thou good and faithful servant!

There are sins or (let us call them as the world calls them) evil memories which are hidden away by man in the darkest places of the heart but they abide there and wait. He may suffer their memory to grow dim, let them be as though they had not been and all but persuade himself that they were not or at least were otherwise. Yet a chance word will call them forth suddenly and they will rise up to confront him in the most various circumstances, a vision or a dream, or while timbrel and harp soothe his senses or amid the cool silver tranquility of the evening or at the feast, at midnight, when he is now filled with wine. Not to insult over him will the vision come as over one that lies under her wrath, not for vengeance to cut him off from the living but shrouded in the piteous vesture of the past, silent, remote, reproachful.

The stranger still regarded on the face before him a slow recession of that false calm there, imposed, as it seemed, by habit or some studied trick, upon words so embittered as to accuse in their speaker an unhealthiness, a *flair,* for the cruder things of life. A scene disengages itself in the observer's memory, evoked, it would seem, by a word of so natural a homeliness as if those days were really present there (as some thought) with their immediate pleasures. A shaven space of lawn one soft May evening, the wellremembered grove of lilacs at Roundtown, purple and white, fragrant slender spectators of the game but with much real interest in the pellets as they run slowly forward over the sward or collide and stop, one by its fellow, with a brief alert shock. And yonder about that grey urn where the water moves at times in thoughtful irrigation you saw another as fragrant sisterhood, Floey, Atty, Tiny and their darker friend with I know not what of arresting in her pose then, Our Lady of the Cherries, a comely brace of them pendent from an ear, bringing out the foreign warmth of the skin so daintily against the cool ardent fruit. A lad of four or five in linseywoolsey (blossomtime but there will be cheer in the kindly hearth when ere long the bowls are gathered and hutched) is standing on the urn secured by that circle of girlish fond hands. He frowns a little just as this young man does now with a perhaps too conscious enjoyment of the danger but must needs glance at whiles towards where his mother watches from the *piazzetta* giving upon the flowerclose with a faint shadow of remoteness or of reproach (*alles Vergängliche*) in her glad look.

Mark this farther and remember. The end comes suddenly. Enter that antechamber of birth where the studious are assembled and note their faces. Nothing, as it seems, there of rash or violent. Quietude of custody, rather, befitting their station in that house, the vigilant watch of shepherds and of angels about a crib in Bethlehem of Juda long ago. But as before the lightning the serried stormclouds, heavy with preponderant excess of moisture, in swollen masses turgidly distended, compass earth and sky in one vast slumber, impending above parched field and drowsy oxen and blighted growth of shrub and verdure till in an instant a flash rives their centres and with the reverberation of the thunder the cloudburst pours its torrent, so and not otherwise was the transformation, violent and instantaneous, upon the utterance of the word.

Burke's! outflings my lord Stephen, giving the cry, and a tag and bobtail of all them after, cockerel, jackanapes, welsher, pilldoctor, punctual Bloom at heels with a universal grabbing at headgear, ashplants, bilbos, Panama hats and scabbards, Zermatt alpenstocks and what not. A dedale of lusty youth, noble every student there. Nurse Callan taken aback in the hallway cannot stay them nor smiling surgeon coming downstairs with news of placentation ended, a full pound if a milligramme. They hark him on. The door! It is open? Ha! They are out, tumultuously, off for a minute's race, all bravely legging it, Burke's of Denzille and Holles their ulterior goal. Dixon follows giving them sharp language but raps out an oath, he too, and on. Bloom stays with nurse a thought to send a kind word to happy mother and nurseling up there. Doctor Diet and Doctor Quiet. Looks she too not other now? Ward of watching in Horne's house has told its tale in that washedout pallor. Then all being gone, a glance of motherwit helping, he whispers close in going: Madam, when comes the storkbird for thee?

The air without is impregnated with raindew moisture, life essence celestial, glistening on Dublin stone there under starshiny *coelum.* God's air, the Allfather's air, scintillant circumambient cessile air. Breathe it deep into thee. By heaven, Theodore Purefoy, thou hast done a doughty deed and no botch! Thou art, I vow, the remarkablest progenitor barring none in this chaffering allincluding most farraginous chronicle. Astounding! In her lay a Godframed Godgiven preformed possibility which thou hast fructified with thy modicum of man's work. Cleave to her! Serve! Toil on, labour like a very bandog and let scholarment and all Malthusiasts go hang. Thou art all their daddies, Theodore. Art drooping under thy load, bemoiled with butcher's bills at home and ingots (not thine!) in the countinghouse? Head up! For every newbegotten thou shalt gather thy homer of ripe wheat. See, thy fleece is drenched. Dost envy Darby Dullman there with his Joan? A canting jay and a rheumeyed curdog is all their progeny. Pshaw, I tell thee! He is a mule, a dead gasteropod, without vim or stamina, not worth a cracked kreutzer. Copulation without population! No, say I! Herod's slaughter of the innocents were the truer name. Vegetables, forsooth, and sterile cohabitation! Give her beefsteaks, red, raw, bleeding! She is a hoary pandemonium of ills, enlarged glands, mumps, quinsy, bunions, hayfever, bedsores, ringworm, floating kidney, Derbyshire neck, warts, bilious attacks, gallstones, cold feet, varicose veins. A truce to threnes and trentals and jeremies and all such congenital defunctive music! Twenty years of it, regret them not. With thee it was not as with many that will and would and wait and never—do. Thou sawest thy America, thy lifetask, and didst charge to cover like the transpontine bison. How saith Zarathustra? *Deine Kuh Trübsal melkest Du. Nun Trinkst Du die süsse Milch des Euters.* See! it displodes for thee in abundance. Drink, man, an udderful! Mother's milk, Purefoy, the milk of human kin, milk too of those burgeoning stars overhead rutilant in thin rainvapour, punch milk, such as those rioters will quaff in their guzzling den, milk of madness, the honeymilk of Canaan's land. Thy cow's dug was tough, what? Ay, but her milk is hot and sweet and fattening. No dollop this but thick rich bonnyclaber. To her, old patriarch! Pap! *Per deam Partulam et Pertundam nunc est bibendum!*

All off for a buster, armstrong, hollering down the street. Bonafides. Where you slep las nigh? Timothy of the battered naggin. Like ole Billyo. Any brollies or gumboots in the fambly? Where the

Henry Nevil's sawbones and ole clo? Sorra one o' me knows. Hurrah there, Dix! Forward to the ribbon counter. Where's Punch? All serene. Jay, look at the drunken minister coming out of the maternity hospal! *Benedicat vos omnipotens Deus, Pater et Filius.* A make, mister. The Denzille lane boys. Hell, blast ye! Scoot. Righto, Isaacs, shove 'em out of the bleeding limelight. Yous join uz, dear sir? No hentrusion in life. Lou heap good man. Allee samee dis bunch. *En avant, mes enfants!* Fire away number one on the gun. Burke's! Burke's! Thence they advanced five parasangs. Slattery's mounted foot. Where's that bleeding awfur? Parson Steve, apostates' creed! No, no, Mulligan! Abaft there! Shove ahead. Keep a watch on the clock. Chuckingout time. Mullee! What's on you? *Ma mère m'a mariée.* British Beatitudes! *Retamplatan digidi boumboum.* Ayes have it. To be printed and bound at the Druiddrum press by two designing females. Calf covers of pissedon green. Last word in art shades. Most beautiful book come out of Ireland my time. *Silentium!* Get a spurt on. Tention. Proceed to nearest canteen and there annex liquor stores. March! Tramp, tramp, tramp, the boys are (attitudes!) parching. Beer, beef, business, bibles, bulldogs battleships, buggery and bishops. Whether on the scaffold high. Beer, beef, trample the bibles. When for Irelandear. Trample the trampellers. Thunderation! Keep the durned millingtary step. We fall. Bishops boosebox. Halt! Heave to. Rugger. Scrum in. No touch kicking. Wow, my tootsies! You hurt? Most amazingly sorry!

Query. Who's astanding this here do? Proud possessor of damnall. Declare misery. Bet to the ropes. Me nantee saltee. Not a red at me this week gone. Yours? Mead of our fathers for the *Übermensch.* Dittoh. Five number ones. You, sir? Ginger cordial. Chase me, the cabby's caudle. Stimulate the caloric. Winding of his ticker. Stopped short never to go again when the old. Absinthe for me, savvy? *Caramba!* Have an eggnog or a prairie oyster. Enemy? Avuncular's got my timepiece. Ten to. Obligated awful. Don't mention it. Got a pectoral trauma, eh, Dix? Pos fact. Got bet be a boomblebee whenever he wus settin sleepin in hes bit garten. Digs up near the Mater. Buckled he is. Know his dona? Yup, sartin I do. Full of a dure. See her in her dishybilly. Peels off a credit. Lovey lovekin. None of your lean kine, not much. Pull down the blind, love. Two Ardilauns. Same here. Look slippery. If you fall don't wait to get up. Five, seven, nine. Fine! Got a prime pair of mincepies, no kid. And her take me to rests and her anker of rum. Must be seen to be believed. Your starving eyes and allbeplastered neck you stole my heart, O gluepot. Sir? Spud again the rheumatiz? All poppycock, you'll scuse me saying. For the hoi polloi. I vear thee beest a gert vool. Well, doc? Back fro Lapland? Your corporosity sagaciating O K? How's the squaws and papooses? Womanbody after going on the straw? Stand and deliver. Password. There's hair. Ours the white death and the ruddy birth. Hi! Spit in your own eye, boss! Mummer's wire. Cribbed out of Meredith. Jesified, orchidised, polycimical jesuit! Aunty mine's writing Pa Kinch. Baddybad Stephen lead astray goodygood Malachi.

Hurroo! Collar the leather, youngun. Roun wi the nappy. Here, Jock braw Hielentman's your barleybree. Lang may your lum reek and your kailpot boil! My tipple. *Merci.* Here's to us. How's that? Leg before wicket. Don't stain my brandnew sitinems. Give's a shake of peppe, you there. Catch aholt. Caraway seed to carry away. Twig? Shrieks of silence. Every cove to his gentry mort. Venus Pandemos. *Les petites femmes.* Bold bad girl from the town of Mullingar. Tell her I was axing at her. Hauding Sara by the wame. On the road to Malahide. Me? If she who seduced me had left but the name. What do you want for ninepence? Machree, macruiskeen. Smutty Moll for a mattress jig. And a pull all together. *Ex!*

Waiting, guvnor? Most deciduously. Bet your boots on. Stunned like, seeing as how no shiners is acoming. Underconstumble? He've got the chink *ad lib.* Seed near free poun on un a spell ago a said war hisn. Us come right in on your invite, see? Up to you, matey. Out with the oof. Two bar and a wing. You larn that go off of they there Frenchy bilks? Won't wash here for nuts nohow. Lil chile velly solly. Ise de cutest colour coon down our side. Gawds teruth, Chawley. We are nae fou. We're nae tha fou. Au reservoir, Mossoo. Tanks you.

'Tis, sure. What say? In the speakeasy. Tight. I shee you, shir. Bantam, two days teetee. Bowsing nowt but claretwine. Garn! Have a glint, do. Gum, I'm jiggered. And been to barber he have. Too full for words. With a railway bloke. How come you so? Opera he'd like? Rose of Castile. Rows of cast. Police! Some H2O for a gent fainted. Look at Bantam's flowers. Gemini. He's going to holler. The colleen bawn. My colleen bawn. O, cheese it! Shut his blurry Dutch oven with a firm hand. Had the winner today till I tipped him a dead cert. The ruffin cly the nab of Stephen Hand as give me the jady coppaleen. He strike a telegramboy paddock wire big bug Bass to the depot. Shove him a joey and grahamise. Mare on form hot order. Guinea to a goosegog.

Tell a cram, that. Gospeltrue. Criminal diversion? I think that yes. Sure thing. Land him in chokeechokee if the harman beck copped the game. Madden back Madden's a maddening back. O lust our refuge and our strength. Decamping. Must you go? Off to mammy. Stand by. Hide my blushes someone. All in if he spots me. Come ahome, our Bantam. Horryvar, mong vioo. Dinna forget the cowslips for hersel. Cornfide. Wha gev ye thon colt? Pal to pal. Jannock. Of John Thomas, her spouse. No fake, old man Leo. S'elp me, honest injun. Shiver my timbers if I had. There's a great big holy friar. Vyfor you no me tell? Vel, I ses, if that aint a sheeny nachez, vel, I vil get misha mishinnah. Through yerd our lord, Amen.

You move a motion? Steve boy, you're going it some. More bluggy drunkables? Will immensely splendiferous stander permit one stooder of most extreme poverty and one largesize grandacious thirst to terminate one expensive inaugurated libation? Give's a breather. Landlord, landlord, have you good wine, staboo? Hoots, mon, a wee drap to pree. Cut and come again. Right. Boniface! Absinthe the lot. *Nos omnes biberimus viridum toxicum diabolus capiat posterioria nostria.* Closingtime, gents. Eh? Rome boose for the Bloom toff. I hear you say onions? Bloo? Cadges ads. Photo's papli, by all that's gorgeous. Play low, pardner. Slide. *Bonsoir la compagnie.* And snares of the poxfiend. Where's the buck and Namby Amby? Skunked? Leg bail. Aweel, ye maun e'en gang yer gates. Checkmate. King to tower. Kind Kristyann wil yu help yung man hoose frend tuk bungellow kee tu find plais whear tu lay crown of his hed 2 night. Crickey, I'm about sprung. Tarnally dog gone my shins if this beent the bestest puttiest longbreak yet. Item, curate, couple of cookies for this child. Cot's plood and prandypalls, none! Not a pite of sheeses? Thrust syphilis down to hell and with him those other licensed spirits. Time, gents! Who wander through the world. Health all! *À la vôtre!*

Golly, whatten tunket's yon guy in the mackintosh? Dusty Rhodes. Peep at his wearables. By mighty! What's he got? Jubilee mutton. Bovril, by James. Wants it real bad. D'ye ken bare socks? Seedy cuss in the Richmond? Rawthere! Thought he had a deposit of lead in his penis. Trumpery insanity. Bartle the Bread we calls him. That, sir, was once a prosperous cit. Man all tattered and torn that married a maiden all forlorn. Slung her hook, she did. Here see lost love. Walking Mackintosh of lonely canyon. Tuck and turn in. Schedule time. Nix for the hornies. Pardon? Seen him today at a runefal? Chum o' yourn passed in his checks? Ludamassy! Pore piccaninnies! Thou'll no be telling me thot, Pold veg! Did ums blubble bigsplash crytears cos fren Padney was took off in black bag? Of all de darkies Massa Pat was verra best. I never see the like since I was born. *Tiens, tiens*, but it is well sad, that, my faith, yes. O, get, rev on a gradient one in nine. Live axle drives are souped. Lay you two to one Jenatzy licks him ruddy well hollow. Jappies? High angle fire, inyah! Sunk by war specials. Be worse for him, says he, nor any Rooshian. Time all. There's eleven of them. Get ye gone. Forward, woozy wobblers! Night. Night. May Allah the Excellent One your soul this night ever tremendously conserve.

Your attention! We're nae tha fou. The Leith police dismisseth us. The least tholice. Ware hawks for the chap puking. Unwell in his abominable regions. Yooka. Night. Mona, my true love. Yook. Mona, my own love. Ook.

Hark! Shut your obstropolos. Pflaap! Pflaap! Blaze on. There she goes. Brigade! Bout ship. Mount street way. Cut up! Pflaap! Tally ho. You not come? Run, skelter, race. Pflaaaap!

Lynch! Hey? Sign on long o' me. Denzille lane this way. Change here for Bawdyhouse. We two, she said, will seek the kips where shady Mary is. Righto, any old time. *Laetabuntur in cubilibus suis.* You coming long? Whisper, who the sooty hell's the johnny in the black duds? Hush! Sinned against the light and even now that day is at hand when he shall come to judge the world by fire. Pflaap! *Ut implerentur scripturae.* Strike up a ballad. Then outspake medical Dick to his comrade medical Davy. Christicle, who's this excrement yellow gospeller on the Merrion hall? Elijah is coming! Washed in the blood of the Lamb. Come on you winefizzling, ginsizzling, booseguzzling existences! Come on, you dog-gone, bullnecked, beetlebrowed, hogjowled, peanutbrained, weaseleyed fourflushers, false alarms and excess baggage! Come on, you triple extract of infamy! Alexander J Christ Dowie, that's my name, that's yanked to glory most half this planet from Frisco beach to Vladivostok. The Deity aint no nickel dime bumshow. I put it to you that He's on the square and a corking fine business proposition. He's the grandest thing yet and don't you forget it. Shout salvation in King Jesus. You'll need to rise precious early, you sinner there, if you want to diddle the Almighty God. Pflaaaap! Not half. He's got a coughmixture with a punch in it for you, my friend, in his back pocket. Just you try it on.

15

(*T*he Mabbot street entrance of nighttown, before which stretches an uncobbled tramsiding set with skeleton tracks, red and green will-o'-the-wisps and danger signals. Rows of grimy houses with gaping doors. Rare lamps with faint rainbow fans. Round Rabaiotti's halted ice gondola stunted men and women squabble. They grab wafers between which are wedged lumps of coral and copper snow. Sucking, they scatter slowly. Children. The swancomb of the gondola, highreared, forges on through the murk, white and blue under a lighthouse. Whistles call and answer.*)

THE CALLS: Wait, my love, and I'll be with you.

THE ANSWERS: Round behind the stable.

(*A deafmute idiot with goggle eyes, his shapeless mouth dribbling, jerks past, shaken in Saint Vitus' dance. A chain of children's hands imprisons him.*)

THE CHILDREN: Kithogue! Salute!

THE IDIOT: (*Lifts a palsied left arm and gurgles.*) Grhahute!

THE CHILDREN: Where's the great light?

THE IDIOT: (*Gobbling.*) Ghaghahest.

(*They release him. He jerks on. A pigmy woman swings on a rope slung between two railings, counting. A form sprawled against a dustbin and muffled by its arm and hat snores, groans, grinding growling teeth, and snores again. On a step a gnome totting among a rubbishtip crouches to shoulder a sack of rags and bones. A crone standing by with a smoky oillamp rams her last bottle in the maw of his sack. He heaves his booty, tugs askew his peaked cap and hobbles off mutely. The crone makes back for her lair, swaying her lamp. A bandy child, asquat on the doorstep with a paper shuttlecock, crawls sidling after her in spurts, clutches her skirt, scrambles up. A drunken navvy grips with both hands the railings of an area, lurching heavily. At a corner two night watch in shouldercapes, their hands upon their staffholsters, loom tall. A plate crashes: a woman screams: a child wails. Oaths of a man roar, mutter, cease. Figures wander, lurk, peer from warrens. In a room lit by a candle stuck in a bottleneck a slut*) *combs out the tatts from the hair of a scrofulous child. Cissy Caffrey's voice, still young, sings shrill from a lane.)*

CISSY CAFFREY:

> I gave it to Molly
> Because she was jolly,
> The leg of the duck,
> The leg of the duck.

(Private Carr and Private Compton, swaggersticks tight in their oxters, as they march unsteadily rightaboutface and burst together from their mouths a volleyed fart. Laughter of men from the lane. A hoarse virago retorts.)

THE VIRAGO: Signs on you, hairy arse. More power the Cavan girl.

CISSY CAFFREY: More luck to me. Cavan, Cootehill and Belturbet. *(She sings.)*

> I gave it to Nelly
> To stick in her belly,
> The leg of the duck,
> The leg of the duck.

(Private Carr and Private Compton turn and counterretort, their tunics bloodbright in a lampglow, black sockets of caps on their blond cropped polls. Stephen Dedalus and Lynch pass through the crowd close to the redcoats.)

PRIVATE COMPTON: *(Jerks his finger.)* Way for the parson.

PRIVATE CARR: *(Turns and calls.)* What ho, parson!

CISSY CAFFREY: *(Her voice soaring higher.)*

> She has it, she got it,
> Wherever she put it,
> The leg of the duck.

(Stephen, flourishing the ashplant in his left hand, chants with joy the introit for paschal time. Lynch, his jockeycap low on his brow, attends him, a sneer of discontent wrinkling his face.)

STEPHEN: *Vidi aquam egredientem de templo a latere dextro. Alleluia.*

(The famished snaggletusks of an elderly bawd protrude from a doorway.)

THE BAWD: *(Her voice whispering huskily.)* Sst! Come here till I tell you. Maidenhead inside. Sst!

450

STEPHEN: (*Altius aliquantulum.*) *Et omnes ad quos pervenit aqua ista.*

THE BAWD: (*Spits in their trail her jet of venom.*) Trinity medicals. Fallopian tube. All prick and no pence.

(*Edy Boardman, sniffling, crouched with Bertha Supple, draws her shawl across her nostrils.*)

EDY BOARDMAN: (*Bickering.*) And says the one: I seen you up Faithful place with your squarepusher, the greaser off the railway, in his cometobed hat. Did you, says I. That's not for you to say, says I. You never seen me in the mantrap with a married highlander, says I. The likes of her! Stag that one is! Stubborn as a mule! And her walking with two fellows the one time, Kilbride, the enginedriver, and lancecorporal Oliphant.

STEPHEN: (*Triumphaliter.*) *Salvi facti sunt.*

(*He flourishes his ashplant, shivering the lamp image, shattering light over the world. A liver and white spaniel on the prowl slinks after him, growling. Lynch scares it with a kick.*)

LYNCH: So that?

STEPHEN: (*Looks behind.*) So that gesture, not music not odour, would be a universal language, the gift of tongues rendering visible not the lay sense but the first entelechy, the structural rhythm.

LYNCH: Pornosophical philotheology. Metaphysics in Mecklenburgh street!

STEPHEN: We have shrewridden Shakespeare and henpecked Socrates. Even the allwisest Stagyrite was bitted, bridled and mounted by a light of love.

LYNCH: Ba!

STEPHEN: Anyway, who wants two gestures to illustrate a loaf and a jug? This movement illustrates the loaf and jug of bread or wine in Omar. Hold my stick.

LYNCH: Damn your yellow stick. Where are we going?

STEPHEN: Lecherous lynx, to *la belle dame sans merci,* Georgina Johnson, *ad deam qui laetificat iuventutem meam.*

(*Stephen thrusts the ashplant on him and slowly holds out his hands, his head going back till both hands are a span from his breast, down turned, in planes intersecting, the fingers about to part, the left being higher.*)

LYNCH: Which is the jug of bread? It skills not. That or the customhouse. Illustrate thou. Here take your crutch and walk.

(*They pass. Tommy Caffrey scrambles to a gaslamp and, clasping, climbs in spasms. From the top spur he slides down. Jacky Caffrey clasps to climb. The*) *navvy lurches against the lamp. The twins scuttle off in the dark. The navvy, swaying, presses a forefinger against a wing of his nose and ejects from the farther nostril a long liquid jet of snot. Shouldering the lamp he staggers away through the crowd with his flaring cresset.*

Snakes of river fog creep slowly. From drains, clefts, cesspools, middens arise on all sides stagnant fumes. A glow leaps in the south beyond the seaward reaches of the river. The navvy, staggering forward, cleaves the crowd and lurches towards the tramsiding. On the farther side under the railway bridge Bloom appears, flushed, panting, cramming bread and chocolate into a sidepocket. From Gillen's hairdresser's window a composite portrait shows him gallant Nelson's image. A concave mirror at the side presents to him lovelorn longlost lugubru Booloohoom. Grave Gladstone sees him level, Bloom for Bloom. He passes, struck by the stare of truculent Wellington, but in the convex mirror grin unstruck the bonham eyes and fatchuck cheekchops of Jollypoldy the rixdix doldy.

At Antonio Rabaiotti's door Bloom halts, sweated under the bright arclamp. He disappears. In a moment he reappears and hurries on.)

BLOOM: Fish and taters. N. g. Ah!

(He disappears into Olhausen's, the porkbutcher's, under the downcoming rollshutter. A few moments later he emerges from under the shutter, puffing Poldy, blowing Bloohoom. In each hand he holds a parcel, one containing a lukewarm pig's crubeen, the other a cold sheep's trotter, sprinkled with wholepepper. He gasps, standing upright. Then bending to one side he presses a parcel against his ribs and groans.)

BLOOM: Stitch in my side. Why did I run?

(He takes breath with care and goes forward slowly towards the lampset siding. The glow leaps again.)

BLOOM: What is that? A flasher? Searchlight.

(He stands at Cormack's corner, watching.)

BLOOM: *Aurora borealis* or a steel foundry? Ah, the brigade, of course. South side anyhow. Big blaze. Might be his house. Beggar's bush. We're safe. *(He hums cheerfully.)* London's burning, London's burning! On fire, on fire! *(He catches sight of the navvy lurching through the crowd at the farther side of Talbot street.)* I'll miss him. Run. Quick. Better cross here.

(He darts to cross the road. Urchins shout.)

THE URCHINS: Mind out, mister!

(Two cyclists, with lighted paper lanterns aswing, swim by him, grazing him, their bells rattling.)

THE BELLS: Haltyaltyaltyall.

BLOOM: (*Halts erect, stung by a spasm.*) Ow!

(*He looks round, darts forward suddenly. Through rising fog a dragon sandstrewer, travelling at caution, slews heavily down upon him, its huge red headlight winking, its trolley hissing on the wire. The motorman bangs his footgong.*)

THE GONG: Bang Bang Bla Bak Blud Bugg Bloo.

(*The brake cracks violently. Bloom, raising a policeman's whitegloved hand, blunders stifflegged out of the track. The motorman, thrown forward, pugnosed, on the guidewheel, yells as he slides past over chains and keys.*)

THE MOTORMAN: Hey, shitbreeches, are you doing the hat trick?

(*Bloom trickleaps to the curbstone and halts again. He brushes a mudflake from his cheek with a parcelled hand.*)

BLOOM: No thoroughfare. Close shave that but cured the stitch. Must take up Sandow's exercises again. On the hands down. Insure against street accident too. The Providential. (*He feels his trouser pocket.*) Poor mamma's panacea. Heel easily catch in track or bootlace in a cog. Day the wheel of the black Maria peeled off my shoe at Leonard's corner. Third time is the charm. Shoe trick. Insolent driver. I ought to report him. Tension makes them nervous. Might be the fellow balked me this morning with that horsey woman. Same style of beauty. Quick of him all the same. The stiff walk. True word spoken in jest. That awful cramp in Lad lane. Something poisonous I ate. Emblem of luck. Why? Probably lost cattle. Mark of the beast. (*He closes his eyes an instant.*) Bit light in the head. Monthly or effect of the other. Brainfogfag. That tired feeling. Too much for me now. Ow!

(*A sinister figure leans on plaited legs against O'Beirne's wall, a visage unknown, injected with dark mercury. From under a wideleaved sombrero the figure regards him with evil eye.*)

BLOOM: *Buenas noches, señorita Blanca, que calle es esta?*

THE FIGURE: (*Impassive, raises a signal arm.*) Password. *Sraid Mabbot.*

BLOOM: Haha. *Merci.* Esperanto. *Slan leath.* (*He mutters.*) Gaelic league spy, sent by that fireeater.

(*He steps forward. A sackshouldered ragman bars his path. He steps left, ragsackman left.*)

BLOOM: I beg.

(*He leaps right, sackragman right.*)

BLOOM: I beg.

(*He swerves, sidles, stepaside, slips past and on.*)

BLOOM: Keep to the right, right, right. If there is a signpost planted by the Touring Club at Stepaside who procured that public boon? I who lost my way and contributed to the columns of the *Irish Cyclist* the letter headed *In darkest Stepaside*. Keep, keep, keep to the right. Rags and bones at midnight. A fence more likely. First place murderer makes for. Wash off his sins of the world.

(*Jacky Caffrey, hunted by Tommy Caffrey, runs full tilt against Bloom.*)

BLOOM: O.

(*Shocked, on weak hams, he halts. Tommy and Jacky vanish there, there. Bloom pats with parcelled hands watch, fobpocket, bookpocket, pursepoke, sweets of sin, potato soap.*)

BLOOM: Beware of pickpockets. Old thieves' dodge. Collide. Then snatch your purse.

(*The retriever approaches sniffing, nose to the ground. A sprawled form sneezes. A stooped bearded figure appears garbed in the long caftan of an elder in Zion and a smokingcap with magenta tassels. Horned spectacles hang down at the wings of the nose. Yellow poison streaks are on the drawn face.*)

RUDOLPH: Second halfcrown waste money today. I told you not go with drunken goy ever. So you catch no money.

BLOOM: (*Hides the crubeen and trotter behind his back and, crestfallen, feels warm and cold feetmeat.*) Ja, ich weiss, papachi.

RUDOLPH: What you making down this place? Have you no soul? (*With feeble vulture talons he feels the silent face of Bloom.*) Are you not my son Leopold, the grandson of Leopold? Are you not my dear son Leopold who left the house of his father and left the god of his fathers Abraham and Jacob?

BLOOM: (*With precaution.*) I suppose so, father. Mosenthal. All that's left of him.

RUDOLPH: (*Severely.*) One night they bring you home drunk as dog after spend your good money. What you call them running chaps?

BLOOM: (*In youth's smart blue Oxford suit with white vestslips, narrowshouldered, in brown Alpine hat, wearing gent's sterling silver waterbury keyless watch and double curb Albert with seal attached, one side of him coated with stiffening mud.*) Harriers, father. Only that once.

RUDOLPH: Once! Mud head to foot. Cut your hand open. Lockjaw. They make you kaputt, Leopoldleben. You watch them chaps.

BLOOM: (*Weakly.*) They challenged me to a sprint. It was muddy. I slipped.

RUDOLPH: (*With contempt.*) Goim nachez! Nice spectacles for your poor mother!

BLOOM: Mamma!

ELLEN BLOOM: (*In pantomime dame's stringed mobcap, widow Twankey's crinoline and bustle, blouse with muttonleg sleeves buttoned behind, grey mittens and cameo brooch, her plaited hair in a crispine net, appears over the staircase banisters, a slanted candlestick in her hand, and cries out in shrill alarm.*) O blessed Redeemer, what have they done to him! My smelling salts! (*She hauls up a reef of skirt and ransacks the pouch of her striped blay petticoat. A phial, an Agnus Dei, a shrivelled potato and a celluloid doll fall out.*) Sacred Heart of Mary, where were you at all at all?

(*Bloom, mumbling, his eyes downcast, begins to bestow his parcels in his filled pockets but desists, muttering.*)

A VOICE: (*Sharply.*) Poldy!

BLOOM: Who? (*He ducks and wards off a blow clumsily.*) At your service.

(*He looks up. Beside her mirage of datepalms a handsome woman in Turkish costume stands before him. Opulent curves fill out her scarlet trousers and jacket, slashed with gold. A wide yellow cummerbund girdles her. A white yashmak, violet in the night, covers her face, leaving free only her large dark eyes and raven hair.*)

BLOOM: Molly!

MARION: Welly? Mrs Marion from this out, my dear man, when you speak to me. (*Satirically.*) Has poor little hubby cold feet waiting so long?

BLOOM: (*Shifts from foot to foot.*) No, no. Not the least little bit.

(*He breathes in deep agitation, swallowing gulps of air, questions, hopes, crubeens for her supper, things to tell her, excuse, desire, spellbound. A coin gleams on her forehead. On her feet are jewelled toerings. Her ankles are linked by a slender fetterchain. Beside her a camel, hooded with a turreting turban, waits. A silk ladder of innumerable rungs climbs to his bobbing howdah. He ambles near with disgruntled hindquarters. Fiercely she slaps his haunch, her goldcurb wristbangles angriling, scolding him in Moorish.*)

MARION: Nebrakada! Femininum!

(*The camel, lifting a foreleg, plucks from a tree a large mango fruit, offers it to his mistress, blinking, in his cloven hoof, then droops his head and, grunting, with uplifted neck, fumbles to kneel. Bloom stoops his back for leapfrog.*)

BLOOM: I can give you . . . I mean as your business menagerer . . . Mrs Marion . . . if you . . .

MARION: So you notice some change? (*Her hands passing slowly over her trinketed stomacher, a slow friendly mockery in her eyes.*) O Poldy, Poldy, you are a poor old stick in the mud! Go and see life. See the wide world.

BLOOM: I was just going back for that lotion whitewax, orangeflower water. Shop closes early on Thursday. But the first thing in the morning. (*He pats divers pockets.*) This moving kidney. Ah!

(*He points to the south, then to the east. A cake of new clean lemon soap arises, diffusing light and perfume.*)

THE SOAP:

> We're a capital couple are Bloom and I.
> He brightens the earth. I polish the sky.

(*The freckled face of Sweny, the druggist, appears in the disc of the soapsun.*)

SWENY: Three and a penny, please.

BLOOM: Yes. For my wife. Mrs Marion. Special recipe.

MARION: (*Softly.*) Poldy!

BLOOM: Yes, ma'am?

MARION: *Ti trema un poco il cuore?*

(*In disdain she saunters away, plump as a pampered pouter pigeon, humming the duet from* Don Giovanni.)

BLOOM: Are you sure about that *Voglio*? I mean the pronunciati . . .

(*He follows, followed by the sniffing terrier. The elderly bawd seizes his sleeve, the bristles of her chinmole glittering.*)

THE BAWD: Ten shillings a maidenhead. Fresh thing was never touched. Fifteen. There's no-one in it only her old father that's dead drunk.

(*She points. In the gap of her dark den furtive, rainbedraggled, Bridie Kelly stands.*)

BRIDIE: Hatch street. Any good in your mind?

(*With a squeak she flaps her bat shawl and runs. A burly rough pursues with booted strides. He stumbles on the steps, recovers, plunges into gloom. Weak squeaks of laughter are heard, weaker.*)

THE BAWD: (*Her wolfeyes shining.*) He's getting his pleasure. You won't get a virgin in the flash houses. Ten shillings. Don't be all night before the polis in plain clothes sees us. Sixtyseven is a bitch.

(*Leering, Gerty Macdowell limps forward. She draws from behind, ogling, and shows coyly her bloodied clout.*)

GERTY: With all my worldly goods I thee and thou. (*She murmurs.*) You did that. I hate you.

BLOOM: I? When? You're dreaming. I never saw you.

THE BAWD: Leave the gentleman alone, you cheat. Writing the

gentleman false letters. Streetwalking and soliciting. Better for your mother take the strap to you at the bedpost, hussy like you.

GERTY: (*To Bloom.*) When you saw all the secrets of my bottom drawer. (*She paws his sleeve, slobbering.*) Dirty married man! I love you for doing that to me.

(*She glides away crookedly. Mrs Breen in man's frieze overcoat with loose bellows pockets, stands in the causeway, her roguish eyes wideopen, smiling in all her herbivorous buckteeth.*)

MRS BREEN: Mr . . .

BLOOM: (*Coughs gravely.*) Madam, when we last had this pleasure by letter dated the sixteenth instant . . .

MRS BREEN: Mr Bloom! You down here in the haunts of sin! I caught you nicely! Scamp!

BLOOM: (*Hurriedly.*) Not so loud my name. Whatever do you think of me? Don't give me away. Walls have ears. How do you do? It's ages since I. You're looking splendid. Absolutely it. Seasonable weather we are having this time of year. Black refracts heat. Short cut home here. Interesting quarter. Rescue of fallen women. Magdalen asylum. I am the secretary . . .

MRS BREEN: (*Holds up a finger.*) Now, don't tell a big fib! I know somebody won't like that. O just wait till I see Molly! (*Slily.*) Account for yourself this very sminute or woe betide you!

BLOOM: (*Looks behind.*) She often said she'd like to visit. Slumming. The exotic, you see. Negro servants in livery too if she had money. Othello black brute. Eugene Stratton. Even the bones and cornerman at the Livermore christies. Bohee brothers. Sweep for that matter.

(*Tom and Sam Bohee, coloured coons in white duck suits, scarlet socks, upstarched Sambo chokers and large scarlet asters in their buttonholes, leap out. Each has his banjo slung. Their paler smaller negroid hands jingle the twingtwang wires. Flashing white Kaffir eyes and tusks they rattle through a breakdown in clumsy clogs, twinging, singing, back to back, toe heel, heel toe, with smackfatclacking nigger lips.*)

TOM AND SAM:

> There's someone in the house with Dina
> There's someone in the house, I know,
> There's someone in the house with Dina
> Playing on the old banjo.

(*They whisk black masks from raw babby faces: then, chuckling, chortling, trumming, twanging, they diddle diddle cakewalk dance away.*)

BLOOM: (*With a sour tenderish smile.*) A little frivol, shall we, if you are so inclined? Would you like me perhaps to embrace you just for a fraction of a second?

MRS BREEN: (*Screams gaily.*) O, you ruck! You ought to see yourself!

BLOOM: For old sake' sake. I only meant a square party, a mixed marriage mingling of our different little conjugials. You know I had a soft corner for you. (*Gloomily.*) 'Twas I sent you that valentine of the dear gazelle.

MRS BREEN: Glory Alice, you do look a holy show! Killing simply. (*She puts out her hand inquisitively.*) What are you hiding behind your back? Tell us, there's a dear.

BLOOM: (*Seizes her wrist with his free hand.*) Josie Powell that was, prettiest deb in Dublin. How time flies by! Do you remember, harking back in a retrospective arrangement, Old Christmas night, Georgina Simpson's housewarming while they were playing the Irving Bishop game, finding the pin blindfold and thoughtreading? Subject, what is in this snuffbox?

MRS BREEN: You were the lion of the night with your seriocomic recitation and you looked the part. You were always a favourite with the ladies.

BLOOM: (*Squire of dames, in dinner jacket with wateredsilk facings, blue masonic badge in his buttonhole, black bow and mother-of-pearl studs, a prismatic champagne glass tilted in his hand.*) Ladies and gentlemen, I give you Ireland, home and beauty.

MRS BREEN: The dear dead days beyond recall. Love's old sweet song.

BLOOM: (*Meaningfully dropping his voice.*) I confess I'm teapot with curiosity to find out whether some person's something is a little teapot at present.

MRS BREEN: (*Gushingly.*) Tremendously teapot! London's teapot and I'm simply teapot all over me! (*She rubs sides with him.*) After the parlour mystery games and the crackers from the tree we sat on the staircase ottoman. Under the mistletoe. Two is company.

BLOOM: (*Wearing a purple Napoleon hat with an amber halfmoon, his fingers and thumb passing slowly down to her soft moist meaty palm which she surrenders gently.*) The witching hour of night. I took the splinter out of this hand, carefully, slowly. (*Tenderly, as he slips on her finger a ruby ring.*) Là ci darem la mano.

MRS BREEN: (*In a onepiece evening frock executed in moonlight blue, a tinsel sylph's diadem on her brow with her dancecard fallen beside her moonblue satin slipper, curves her palm softly, breathing quickly.*) *Voglio e non.* You're hot! You're scalding! The left hand nearest the heart.

BLOOM: When you made your present choice they said it was beauty and the beast. I can never forgive you for that. (*His clenched fist at his brow.*) Think what it means. All you meant to me then. (*Hoarsely.*) Woman, it's breaking me!

(*Denis Breen, whitetallhatted, with Wisdom Hely's sandwichboards, shuffles past them in carpet slippers, his dull beard thrust out, muttering to right and left. Little Alf Bergan, cloaked in the pall of the ace of spades, dogs him to left and right, doubled in laughter.*)

ALF BERGAN: (*Points jeering at the sandwichboards.*) U. P.: Up.

MRS BREEN: (*To Bloom.*) High jinks below stairs. (*She gives him the glad eye.*) Why didn't you kiss the spot to make it well? You wanted to.

BLOOM: (*Shocked.*) Molly's best friend! Could you?

MRS BREEN: (*Her pulpy tongue between her lips, offers a pigeon kiss.*) Hnhn. The answer is a lemon. Have you a little present for me there?

BLOOM: (*Offhandedly.*) Kosher. A snack for supper. The home without potted meat is incomplete. I was at *Leah*, Mrs Bandmann Palmer. Trenchant exponent of Shakespeare. Unfortunately threw away the programme. Rattling good place round there for pigs' feet. Feel.

(*Richie Goulding, three ladies' hats pinned on his head, appears weighted to one side by the black legal bag of Collis and Ward on which a skull and crossbones are painted in white limewash. He opens it and shows it full of polonies, kippered herrings, Findon haddies and tightpacked pills.*)

RICHIE: Best value in Dub.

(*Bald Pat, bothered beetle, stands on the curbstone, folding his napkin, waiting to wait.*)

PAT: (*Advances with a tilted dish of spillspilling gravy.*) Steak and kidney. Bottle of lager. Hee hee hee. Wait till I wait.

RICHIE: Goodgod. Inev erate inall . . .

(*With hanging head he marches doggedly forward. The navvy, lurching by, gores him with his flaming pronghorn.*)

RICHIE: (*With a cry of pain, his hand to his back.*) Ah! Bright's! Lights!

BLOOM: (*Points to the navvy.*) A spy. Don't attract attention. I hate stupid crowds. I am not on pleasure bent. I am in a grave predicament.

MRS BREEN: Humbugging and deluthering as per usual with your cock and bull story.

BLOOM: I want to tell you a little secret about how I came to be here. But you must never tell. Not even Molly. I have a most particular reason.

MRS BREEN: (*All agog.*) O, not for worlds.

BLOOM: Let's walk on. Shall us?

MRS BREEN: Let's.

(*The bawd makes an unheeded sign. Bloom walks on with Mrs Breen. The terrier follows, whining piteously, wagging his tail.*)

THE BAWD: Jewman's melt!

BLOOM: (*In an oatmeal sporting suit, a sprig of woodbine in the lapel, tony buff shirt, shepherd's plaid Saint Andrew's cross scarftie, white spats, fawn dustcoat on his arm, tawny red brogues, fieldglasses in bandolier and a grey billycock hat.*) Do you remember a long long time, years and years ago, just after Milly, Marionette we called her, was weaned when we all went together to Fairyhouse races, was it?

MRS BREEN: (*In smart Saxe tailormade, white velours hat and spider veil.*) Leopardstown.

BLOOM: I mean, Leopardstown. And Molly won seven shillings on a three year old named Nevertell and coming home along by Foxrock in that old fiveseater shanderadan of a waggonette you were in your heyday then and you had on that new hat of white velours with a surround of molefur that Mrs Hayes advised you to buy because it was marked down to nineteen and eleven, a bit of wire and an old rag of velveteen, and I'll lay you what you like she did it on purpose . . .

MRS BREEN: She did, of course, the cat! Don't tell me! Nice adviser!

BLOOM: Because it didn't suit you one quarter as well as the other ducky little tammy toque with the bird of paradise wing in it that I admired on you and you honestly looked just too fetching in it though it was a pity to kill it, you cruel naughty creature, little mite of a thing with a heart the size of a fullstop.

MRS BREEN: (*Squeezes his arm, simpers.*) Naughty cruel I was!

BLOOM: (*Low, secretly, ever more rapidly.*) And Molly was eating a sandwich of spiced beef out of Mrs Joe Gallaher's lunch basket. Frankly, though she had her advisers or admirers, I never cared much for her style. She was . . .

MRS BREEN: Too . . .

BLOOM: Yes. And Molly was laughing because Rogers and Maggot O'Reilly were mimicking a cock as we passed a farmhouse and Marcus Tertius Moses, the tea merchant, drove past us in a gig with his daughter, Dancer Moses was her name, and the poodle in her lap bridled up and you asked me if I ever heard or read or knew or came across . . .

MRS BREEN: (*Eagerly.*) Yes, yes, yes, yes, yes, yes, yes.

(*She fades from his side. Followed by the whining dog he walks on towards hellsgates. In an archway a standing woman, bent forward, her feet apart, pisses cowily. Outside a shuttered pub a bunch of loiterers listen to a tale which their brokensnouted gaffer rasps out with raucous humour. An armless pair of them flop wrestling, growling, in maimed sodden playfight.*)

THE GAFFER: (*Crouches, his voice twisted in his snout.*) And when Cairns came down from the scaffolding in Beaver street what was he after doing it into only into the bucket of porter that was there waiting on the shavings for Derwan's plasterers.

THE LOITERERS: (*Guffaw with cleft palates.*) O jays!

(*Their paintspeckled hats wag. Spattered with size and lime of their lodges they frisk limblessly about him.*)

BLOOM: Coincidence too. They think it funny. Anything but that. Broad daylight. Trying to walk. Lucky no woman.

THE LOITERERS: Jays, that's a good one. Glauber salts. O jays, into the men's porter.

(*Bloom passes. Cheap whores, singly, coupled, shawled, dishevelled, call from lanes, doors, corners.*)

THE WHORES:

> Are you going far, queer fellow?
> How's your middle leg?
> Got a match on you?
> Eh, come here till I stiffen it for you.

(*He plodges through their sump towards the lighted street beyond. From a bulge of window curtains a gramophone rears a battered brazen trunk. In the shadow a shebeenkeeper haggles with the navvy and the two redcoats.*)

THE NAVVY: (*Belching.*) Where's the bloody house?

THE SHEBEENKEEPER: Purdon street. Shilling a bottle of stout. Respectable woman.

THE NAVVY: (*Gripping the two redcoats, staggers forward with them.*) Come on, you British army!

PRIVATE CARR: (*Behind his back.*) He aint half balmy.

PRIVATE COMPTON: (*Laughs.*) What ho!

PRIVATE CARR: (*To the navvy.*) Portobello barracks canteen. You ask for Carr. Just Carr.

THE NAVVY: (*Shouts.*)

We are the boys. Of Wexford.

PRIVATE COMPTON: Say! What price the sergeantmajor?

PRIVATE CARR: Bennett? He's my pal. I love old Bennett.

THE NAVVY: (*Shouts.*)

The galling chain.
And free our native land.

(*He staggers forward, dragging them with him. Bloom stops, at fault. The dog approaches, his tongue outlolling, panting.*)

BLOOM: Wildgoose chase this. Disorderly houses. Lord knows where they are gone. Drunks cover distance double quick. Nice mixup. Scene at Westland row. Then jump in first class with third ticket. Then too far. Train with engine behind. Might have taken me to Malahide or a siding for the night or collision. Second drink does it. Once is a dose. What am I following him for? Still, he's the best of that lot. If I hadn't heard about Mrs Beaufoy Purefoy I wouldn't have gone and wouldn't have met. Kismet. He'll lose that cash. Relieving office here. Good biz for cheapjacks, organs. What do ye lack? Soon got, soon gone. Might have lost my life too with that mangongwheeltracktrolleyglarejuggernaut only for presence of mind. Can't always save you, though. If I had passed Truelock's window that day two minutes later would have been shot. Absence of body. Still if bullet only went through my coat get damages for shock, five hundred pounds. What was he? Kildare street club toff. God help his gamekeeper.

(*He gazes ahead, reading on the wall a scrawled chalk legend* Wet Dream *and a phallic design.*) Odd! Molly drawing on the frosted carriagepane at Kingstown. What's that like? (*Gaudy dollwomen loll in the lighted doorways, in window embrasures, smoking birdseye cigarettes. The odour of the sicksweet weed floats towards him in slow round ovalling wreaths.*)

THE WREATHS: Sweet are the sweets. Sweets of sin.

BLOOM: My spine's a bit limp. Go or turn? And this food? Eat it and get all pigsticky. Absurd I am. Waste of money. One and eightpence too much.(*The retriever drives a cold snivelling muzzle against his hand, wagging his tail.*) Strange how they take to me. Even that brute today. Better speak to him first. Like women they like *rencontres.* Stinks like a polecat. *Chacun son goût.* He might be mad. Dogdays. Uncertain in his movements. Good fellow! Fido! Good fellow! Garryowen! (*The wolfdog sprawls on his back, wriggling obscenely with begging paws, his long black tongue lolling out.*) Influence of his surroundings. Give and have done with it. Provided nobody. (*Calling encouraging words he shambles back with a furtive poacher's tread, dogged by the setter into a dark stalestunk corner. He unrolls one parcel and goes to dump the crubeen softly but holds back and feels the trotter.*) Sizeable for threepence. But then I have it in my left hand. Calls for more effort. Why? Smaller from want of use. O, let it slide. Two and six.

(*With regret he lets the unrolled crubeen and trotter slide. The mastiff mauls the bundle clumsily and gluts himself with growling greed, crunching the bones. Two raincaped watch approach, silent, vigilant. They murmur together.*)

THE WATCH: Bloom. Of Bloom. For Bloom. Bloom.

(*Each lays hand on Bloom's shoulder.*)

FIRST WATCH: Caught in the act. Commit no nuisance.

BLOOM: (*Stammers.*) I am doing good to others.

(*A covey of gulls, storm petrels, rises hungrily from Liffey slime with Banbury cakes in their beaks.*)

THE GULLS: Kaw kave kankury kake.

BLOOM: The friend of man. Trained by kindness.

(*He points. Bob Doran, toppling from a high barstool, sways over the munching spaniel.*)

BOB DORAN: Towser. Give us the paw. Give the paw.

(*The bulldog growls, his scruff standing, a gobbet of pig's knuckle between his molars through which rabid scumspittle dribbles. Bob Doran falls silently into an area.*)

SECOND WATCH: Prevention of cruelty to animals.

BLOOM: (*Enthusiastically.*) A noble work! I scolded that tramdriver on Harold's cross bridge for illusing the poor horse with his harness scab. Bad French I got for my pains. Of course it was frosty and the last tram. All tales of circus life are highly demoralising.

(*Signor Maffei, passionpale, in liontamer's costume with diamond studs in his shirtfront, steps forward, holding a circus paperhoop, a curling carriagewhip and a revolver with which he covers the gorging boarhound.*)

SIGNOR MAFFEI: (*With a sinister smile.*) Ladies and gentlemen, my educated greyhound. It was I broke in the bucking broncho Ajax with my patent spiked saddle for carnivores. Lash under the belly with a knotted thong. Block tackle and a strangling pulley will bring your lion to heel, no matter how fractious, even *Leo ferox* there, the Libyan maneater. A redhot crowbar and some liniment rubbing on the burning part produced Fritz of Amsterdam, the thinking hyena. (*He glares.*) I possess the Indian sign. The glint of my eye does it with these breastsparklers. (*With a bewitching smile.*) I now introduce Mademoiselle Ruby, the pride of the ring.

FIRST WATCH: Come. Name and address.

BLOOM: I have forgotten for the moment. Ah, yes! (*He takes off his high grade hat, saluting.*) Dr Bloom, Leopold, dental surgeon. You have heard of von Blum Pasha. Umpteen millions. *Donnerwetter!* Owns half Austria. Egypt. Cousin.

FIRST WATCH: Proof.

(*A card falls from inside the leather headband of Bloom's hat.*)

BLOOM: (*In red fez, cadi's dress coat with broad green sash, wearing a false badge of the Legion of Honour, picks up the card hastily and offers it.*) Allow me. My club is the Junior Army and Navy. Solicitors: Messrs John Henry Menton, 27 Bachelor's Walk.

FIRST WATCH: (*Reads.*) Henry Flower. No fixed abode. Unlawfully watching and besetting.

SECOND WATCH: An alibi. You are cautioned.

BLOOM: (*Produces from his heartpocket a crumpled yellow flower.*) This is the flower in question. It was given me by a man I don't know his name. (*Plausibly.*) You know that old joke, rose of Castile. Bloom. The change of name. Virag. (*He murmurs privately and confidentially.*) We are engaged you see, sergeant. Lady in the case. Love entanglement. (*He shoulders the second watch gently.*) Dash it all. It's a way we gallants have in the navy. Uniform that does it. (*He turns gravely to the first watch.*) Still, of course, you do get your Waterloo sometimes. Drop in some evening and have a glass of old Burgundy. (*To the second watch gaily.*) I'll introduce you, inspector. She's game. Do it in the shake of a lamb's tail.

(*A dark mercurialised face appears, leading a veiled figure.*)

THE DARK MERCURY: The Castle is looking for him. He was drummed out of the army.

MARTHA: (*Thickveiled, a crimson halter round her neck, a copy of the* Irish Times *in her hand, in tone of reproach, pointing.*) Henry! Leopold! Lionel, thou lost one! Clear my name.

FIRST WATCH: (*Sternly.*) Come to the station.

BLOOM: (*Scared, hats himself, steps back, then, plucking at his heart and lifting his right forearm on the square, he gives the sign and dueguard of fellowcraft.*) No, no, worshipful master, light of love. Mistaken identity. The Lyons mail. Lesurques and Dubosc. You remember the Childs fratricide case. We medical men. By striking him dead with a hatchet. I am wrongfully accused. Better one guilty escape than ninetynine wrongfully condemned.

MARTHA: (*Sobbing behind her veil.*) Breach of promise. My real name is Peggy Griffin. He wrote to me that he was miserable. I'll tell my brother, the Bective rugger fullback, on you, heartless flirt.

BLOOM: (*Behind his hand.*) She's drunk. The woman is inebriated. (*He murmurs vaguely the pass of Ephraim.*) Shitbroleeth.

SECOND WATCH: (*Tears in his eyes, to Bloom.*) You ought to be thoroughly well ashamed of yourself.

BLOOM: Gentlemen of the jury, let me explain. A pure mare's nest. I am a man misunderstood. I am being made a scapegoat of. I am a respectable married man, without a stain on my character. I live in Eccles street. My wife, I am the daughter of a most distinguished commander, a gallant upstanding gentleman, what do you call him, Majorgeneral Brian Tweedy, one of Britain's fighting men who helped to win our battles. Got his majority for the heroic defence of Rorke's Drift.

FIRST WATCH: Regiment.

BLOOM: (*Turns to the gallery.*) The royal Dublins, boys, the salt of the earth, known the world over. I think I see some old comrades in arms up there among you. The R. D. F., with our own Metropolitan police, guardians of our homes, the pluckiest lads and the finest body of men, as physique, in the service of our sovereign.

A VOICE: Turncoat! Up the Boers! Who booed Joe Chamberlain?

BLOOM: (*His hand on the shoulder of the first watch.*) My old dad too was a J. P. I'm as staunch a Britisher as you are, sir. I fought with the colours for king and country in the absentminded war under general Gough in the park and was disabled at Spion Kop and Bloemfontein, was mentioned in dispatches. I did all a white man could. (*With quiet feeling.*) Jim Bludso. Hold her nozzle again the bank.

FIRST WATCH: Profession or trade.

BLOOM: Well, I follow a literary occupation, author-journalist. In fact we are just bringing out a collection of prize stories of which I am the inventor, something that is an entirely new departure. I am connected with the British and Irish press. If you ring up . . .

(*Myles Crawford strides out jerkily, a quill between his teeth. His scarlet beak blazes within the aureole of his straw hat. He dangles a hank of Spanish onions in one hand and holds with the other hand a telephone receiver nozzle to his ear.*)

MYLES CRAWFORD: (*His cock's wattles wagging.*) Hello, seventyseven eightfour. Hello. *Freeman's Urinal* and *Weekly Arsewipe* here. Paralyse Europe. You which? Bluebags? Who writes? Is it Bloom?

(*Mr Philip Beaufoy, palefaced, stands in the witnessbox, in accurate morning dress, outbreast pocket with peak of handkerchief showing, creased lavender trousers and patent boots. He carries a large portfolio labelled* Matcham's Masterstrokes.)

BEAUFOY: (*Drawls.*) No, you aren't. Not by a long shot if I know it. I don't see it, that's all. No born gentleman, no-one with the most rudimentary promptings of a gentleman would stoop to such particularly loathsome conduct. One of those, my lord. A plagiarist. A soapy sneak masquerading as a literateur. It's perfectly obvious that with the most inherent baseness he has cribbed some of my bestselling copy, really gorgeous stuff, a perfect gem, the love passages in which are beneath suspicion. The Beaufoy books of love and great possessions, with which your lordship is doubtless familiar, are a household word throughout the kingdom.

BLOOM: (*Murmurs with hangdog meekness glum.*) That bit about the laughing witch hand in hand I take exception to, if I may . . .

BEAUFOY: (*His lip upcurled, smiles superciliously on the court.*) You funny ass, you! You're too beastly awfully weird for words! I don't think you need over excessively disincommodate yourself in that regard. My literary agent Mr J. B. Pinker is in attendance. I presume, my lord, we shall receive the usual witnesses' fees, shan't we? We are considerably out of pocket over this bally pressman johnny, this jackdaw of Rheims, who has not even been to a university.

BLOOM: (*Indistinctly.*) University of life. Bad art.

BEAUFOY: (*Shouts.*) It's a damnably foul lie, showing the moral rottenness of the man! (*He extends his portfolio.*) We have here damning evidence, the *corpus delicti*, my lord, a specimen of my maturer work disfigured by the hallmark of the beast.

A VOICE FROM THE GALLERY:

Moses, Moses, king of the jews,
Wiped his arse in the Daily News.

BLOOM: (*Bravely.*) Overdrawn.

BEAUFOY: You low cad! You ought to be ducked in the horsepond, you rotter! (*To the court.*) Why, look at the man's private life! Leading a quadruple existence! Street angel and house devil. Not fit to be mentioned in mixed society! The archconspirator of the age!

BLOOM: (*To the court.*) And he, a bachelor, how . . .

FIRST WATCH: The King versus Bloom. Call the woman Driscoll.

THE CRIER: Mary Driscoll, scullerymaid!

(*Mary Driscoll, a slipshod servant girl, approaches. She has a bucket on the crook of her arm and a scouringbrush in her hand.*)

SECOND WATCH: Another! Are you of the unfortunate class?

MARY DRISCOLL: (*Indignantly.*) I'm not a bad one. I bear a respectable character and was four months in my last place. I was in a situation, six pounds a year and my chances with Fridays out and I had to leave owing to his carryings on.

FIRST WATCH: What do you tax him with?

MARY DRISCOLL: He made a certain suggestion but I thought more of myself as poor as I am.

BLOOM: (*In housejacket of ripplecloth, flannel trousers, heelless slippers, unshaven, his hair rumpled: softly.*) I treated you white. I gave you mementos, smart emerald garters far above your station. Incautiously I took your part when you were accused of pilfering. There's a medium in all things. Play cricket.

MARY DRISCOLL: (*Excitedly.*) As God is looking down on me this night if ever I laid a hand to them oylsters!

FIRST WATCH: The offence complained of? Did something happen?

MARY DRISCOLL: He surprised me in the rere of the premises, Your honour, when the missus was out shopping one morning with a request for a safety pin. He held me and I was discoloured in four places as a result. And he interfered twict with my clothing.

BLOOM: She counterassaulted.

MARY DRISCOLL: (*Scornfully.*) I had more respect for the scouringbrush, so I had. I remonstrated with him, Your lord, and he remarked: keep it quiet.

(*General laughter.*)

GEORGE FOTTRELL: (*Clerk of the crown and peace, resonantly.*) Order in court! The accused will now make a bogus statement.

(*Bloom, pleading not guilty and holding a fullblown waterlily, begins a long unintelligible speech. They would hear what counsel had to say in his stirring address to the grand jury. He was down and out but, though branded as a black sheep, if he might say so, he meant to reform, to retrieve the memory of the past in a purely sisterly way and return to nature as a purely domestic animal. A sevenmonths' child, he had been carefully brought up and nurtured by an aged bedridden parent. There might have been lapses of an erring father but he wanted to turn over a new leaf and now, when at long last in sight of the whipping post, to lead a homely life in the evening of his days, permeated by the affectionate surroundings of the heaving bosom of the family. An acclimatised Britisher, he had seen that summer eve from the footplate of an engine cab of the Loop line railway company while the rain refrained from falling glimpses, as it were, through the windows of loveful households in Dublin city and urban district of scenes truly rural of happiness of the better land with Dockrell's wallpaper at one and ninepence a dozen, innocent Britishborn bairns lisping prayers to the Sacred Infant, youthful scholars grappling with their pensums or model young ladies playing on the pianoforte or anon all with fervour reciting the family rosary round the crackling Yulelog while in the boreens and green lanes the colleens with their swains strolled what times the strains of the organtoned melodeon Britannia metalbound with four acting stops and twelvefold bellows, a sacrifice, greatest bargain ever . . .*)

(*Renewed laughter. He mumbles incoherently. Reporters complain that they cannot hear.*)

LONGHAND AND SHORTHAND: (*Without looking up from their notebooks.*) Loosen his boots.

PROFESSOR MACHUGH: (*From the presstable, coughs and calls.*) Cough it up, man. Get it out in bits.

(*The crossexamination proceeds* re *Bloom and the bucket. A large bucket. Bloom himself. Bowel trouble. In Beaver street. Gripe, yes. Quite bad. A plasterer's bucket. By walking stifflegged. Suffered untold misery. Deadly agony. About noon. Love or burgundy. Yes, some spinach. Crucial moment. He did not look in the bucket. Nobody. Rather a mess. Not completely. A* Titbits *back number.*)

(*Uproar and catcalls. Bloom in a torn frockcoat stained with whitewash, dinged silk hat sideways on his head, a strip of stickingplaster across his nose, talks inaudibly.*)

J. J. O'MOLLOY: (*In barrister's grey wig and stuffgown, speaking with a voice of pained protest.*) This is no place for indecent levity at the expense of an erring mortal disguised in liquor. We are not in a beargarden nor at an Oxford rag nor is this a travesty of justice. My client is an infant, a poor foreign immigrant who started scratch as a stowaway and is now trying to turn an honest penny. The trumped up misdemeanour was due to a momentary aberration of heredity, brought on by hallucination, such familiarities as the alleged guilty occurrence being quite permitted in my client's native place, the land of the Pharaoh. *Prima facie,* I put it to you that there was no attempt at carnally knowing. Intimacy did not occur and the offence complained of by Driscoll, that her virtue was solicited, was not repeated. I would deal in especial with atavism. There have been cases of shipwreck and somnambulism in my client's family. If the accused could speak he could a tale unfold—one of the strangest that have ever been narrated between the covers of a book. He himself, my lord, is a physical wreck from cobbler's weak chest. His submission is that he is of Mongolian extraction and irresponsible for his actions. Not all there, in fact.

BLOOM: (*Barefoot, pigeonbreasted, in lascar's vest and trousers, apologetic toes turned in, opens his tiny mole's eyes and looks about him dazedly, passing a slow hand across his forehead. Then he hitches his belt sailor fashion and with a shrug of oriental obeisance salutes the court, pointing one thumb heavenward.*) Him makee velly muchee fine night. (*He begins to lilt simply.*)

> Li li poo lil chile
> Blingee pigfoot evly night
> Payee two shilly . . .

(*He is howled down.*)
J. J. O'MOLLOY: (*Hotly to the populace.*) This is a lonehand fight. By Hades, I will not have any client of mine gagged and badgered in this fashion by a pack of curs and laughing hyenas. The Mosaic code has superseded the law of the jungle. I say it and I say it emphatically, without wishing for one moment to defeat the ends of justice, accused was not accessory before the act and prosecutrix has not been tampered with. The young person was treated by defendant as if she were his very own daughter. (*Bloom takes J. J. O'Molloy's hand and raises it to his lips.*) I shall call rebutting evidence to prove up to the hilt that the hidden hand is again at its old game. When in doubt persecute Bloom. My client, an innately bashful man, would be the last man in the world to do anything ungentlemanly which injured modesty could object to or cast a stone at a girl who took the wrong turning when some dastard, responsible for her condition, had worked his own sweet will on her. He wants to go straight. I regard him as the whitest man I

know. He is down on his luck at present owing to the mortgaging of his extensive property at Agendath Netaim in faraway Asia Minor, slides of which will now be shown. (*To Bloom.*) I suggest that you will do the handsome thing.

BLOOM: A penny in the pound.

(*The image of the lake of Kinnereth with blurred cattle cropping in silver haze is projected on the wall. Moses Dlugacz, ferreteyed albino, in blue dungarees, stands up in the gallery, holding in each hand an orange citron and a pork kidney.*)

DLUGACZ: (*Hoarsely.*) Bleibtreustrasse, Berlin, W. 13.

(*J. J. O'Molloy steps on to a low plinth and holds the lapel of his coat with solemnity. His face lengthens, grows pale and bearded, with sunken eyes, the blotches of phthisis and hectic cheekbones of John F. Taylor. He applies his handkerchief to his mouth and scrutinises the galloping tide of rosepink blood.*)

J. J. O'MOLLOY: (*Almost voicelessly.*) Excuse me. I am suffering from a severe chill, have recently come from a sickbed. A few wellchosen words. (*He assumes the avine head, foxy moustache and proboscidal eloquence of Seymour Bushe.*) When the angel's book comes to be opened if aught that the pensive bosom has inaugurated of soultransfigured and of soultransfiguring deserves to live I say accord the prisoner at the bar the sacred benefit of the doubt.

(*A paper with something written on it is handed into court.*)

BLOOM: (*In court dress.*) Can give best references. Messrs Callan, Coleman. Mr Wisdom Hely J. P. My old chief Joe Cuffe. Mr V. B. Dillon, ex lord mayor of Dublin. I have moved in the charmed circle of the highest . . . Queens of Dublin society. (*Carelessly.*) I was just chatting this afternoon at the viceregal lodge to my old pals, sir Robert and lady Ball, astronomer royal, at the levee. Sir Bob, I said . . .

MRS YELVERTON BARRY: (*In lowcorsaged opal balldress and elbowlength ivory gloves, wearing a sabletrimmed brickquilted dolman, a comb of brilliants and panache of osprey in her hair.*) Arrest him, constable. He wrote me an anonymous letter in prentice backhand when my husband was in the North Riding of Tipperary on the Munster circuit, signed James Lovebirch. He said that he had seen from the gods my peerless globes as I sat in a box of the *Theatre Royal* at a command performance of *La Cigale*. I deeply inflamed him, he said. He made improper overtures to me to misconduct myself at half past four p.m. on the following Thursday, Dunsink time. He offered to send me through the post a work of fiction by Monsieur Paul de Kock, entitled *The Girl with the Three Pairs of Stays.*

MRS BELLINGHAM: (*In cap and seal coney mantle, wrapped up to the nose, steps out of her brougham and scans through tortoiseshell quizzing-glasses which she takes from inside her huge opossum muff.*) Also to me. Yes, I believe it is the same objectionable person. Because he closed my carriage door outside sir Thornley Stoker's one sleety day during the cold snap of February ninetythree when even the grid of the wastepipe and the ballstop in my bath cistern were frozen. Subsequently he enclosed a bloom of edelweiss culled on the heights, as he said, in my honour. I had it examined by a botanical expert and elicited the information that it was a blossom of the homegrown potato plant purloined from a forcingcase of the model farm.

MRS YELVERTON BARRY: Shame on him!

(*A crowd of sluts and ragamuffins surges forward.*)

THE SLUTS AND RAGAMUFFINS: (*Screaming.*) Stop thief! Hurrah there, Bluebeard! Three cheers for Ikey Mo!

SECOND WATCH: (*Produces handcuffs.*) Here are the darbies.

MRS BELLINGHAM: He addressed me in several handwritings with fulsome compliments as a Venus in furs and alleged profound pity for my frostbound coachman Palmer while in the same breath he expressed himself as envious of his earflaps and fleecy sheepskins and of his fortunate proximity to my person, when standing behind my chair wearing my livery and the armourial bearings of the Bellingham escutcheon garnished sable, a buck's head couped or. He lauded almost extravagantly my nether extremities, my swelling calves in silk hose drawn up to the limit, and eulogised glowingly my other hidden treasures in priceless lace which, he said, he could conjure up. He urged me (Stating that he felt it his mission in life to urge me.) to defile the marriage bed, to commit adultery at the earliest possible opportunity.

THE HONOURABLE MRS MERVYN TALBOYS: (*In amazon costume, hard hat, jackboots cockspurred, vermilion waistcoat, fawn musketeer gauntlets with braided drums, long train held up and hunting crop with which she strikes her welt constantly.*) Also me. Because he saw me on the polo ground of the Phoenix park at the match All Ireland versus the Rest of Ireland. My eyes, I know, shone divinely as I watched Captain Slogger Dennehy of the Inniskillings win the final chukkar on his darling cob *Centaur.* This plebeian Don Juan observed me from behind a hackney car and sent me in double envelopes an obscene photograph, such as are sold after dark on Paris boulevards, insulting to any lady. I have it still.

It represents a partially nude señorita, frail and lovely (his wife, as he solemnly assured me, taken by him from nature), practising illicit intercourse with a muscular torero, evidently a blackguard. He urged me to do likewise, to misbehave, to sin with officers of the garrison. He implored me to soil his letter in an unspeakable manner, to chastise him as he richly deserves, to bestride and ride him, to give him a most vicious horsewhipping.

MRS BELLINGHAM: Me too.

MRS YELVERTON BARRY: Me too.

(*Several highly respectable Dublin ladies hold up improper letters received from Bloom.*)

THE HONOURABLE MRS MERVYN TALBOYS: (*Stamps her jingling spurs in a sudden paroxysm of fury.*) I will, by the God above me. I'll scourge the pigeonlivered cur as long as I can stand over him. I'll flay him alive.

BLOOM: (*His eyes closing, quails expectantly.*) Here? (*He squirms.*) Again! (*He pants cringing.*) I love the danger.

THE HONOURABLE MRS MERVYN TALBOYS: Very much so! I'll make it hot for you. I'll make you dance Jack Latten for that.

MRS BELLINGHAM: Tan his breech well, the upstart! Write the stars and stripes on it!

MRS YELVERTON BARRY: Disgraceful! There's no excuse for him! A married man!

BLOOM: All these people. I meant only the spanking idea. A warm tingling glow without effusion. Refined birching to stimulate the circulation.

THE HONOURABLE MRS MERVYN TALBOYS: (*Laughs derisively.*) O, did you, my fine fellow? Well, by the living God, you'll get the surprise of your life now, believe me, the most unmerciful hiding a man ever bargained for. You have lashed the dormant tigress in my nature into fury.

MRS BELLINGHAM: (*Shakes her muff and quizzing-glasses vindictively.*) Make him smart, Hanna dear. Give him ginger. Thrash the mongrel within an inch of his life. The cat-o'-nine-tails. Geld him. Vivisect him.

BLOOM: (*Shuddering, shrinking, joins his hands: with hangdog mien.*) O cold! O shivery! It was your ambrosial beauty. Forget, forgive. Kismet. Let me off this once. (*He offers the other cheek.*)

MRS YELVERTON BARRY: (*Severely.*) Don't do so on any account, Mrs Talboys! He should be soundly trounced!

THE HONOURABLE MRS MERVYN TALBOYS: (*Unbuttoning her gauntlet violently.*) I'll do no such thing. Pigdog and always was ever since he was pupped! To dare address me! I'll flog him black and blue in the public streets. I'll dig my spurs in him up to the rowel. He is a wellknown cuckold. (*She swishes her huntingcrop savagely in the air.*) Take down his trousers without loss of time. Come here, sir! Quick! Ready?

BLOOM: (*Trembling, beginning to obey.*) The weather has been so warm.

(*Davy Stephens, ringletted, passes with a bevy of barefoot newsboys.*)

DAVY STEPHENS: *Messenger of the Sacred Heart* and *Evening Telegraph* with Saint Patrick's Day supplement. Containing the new addresses of all the cuckolds in Dublin.

(*The very reverend Canon O'Hanlon in cloth of gold cope elevates and exposes a marble timepiece. Before him Father Conroy and the reverend John Hughes S. J. bend low.*)

THE TIMEPIECE: (*Unportalling.*)

> Cuckoo.
> Cuckoo.
> Cuckoo.

(*The brass quoits of a bed are heard to jingle.*)

THE QUOITS: Jigjag. Jigajiga. Jigjag.

(*A panel of fog rolls back rapidly, revealing rapidly in the jurybox the faces of Martin Cunningham, foreman, silkhatted, Jack Power, Simon Dedalus, Tom Kernan, Ned Lambert, John Henry Menton, Myles Crawford, Lenehan, Paddy Leonard, Nosey Flynn, M'Coy and the featureless face of a Nameless One.*)

THE NAMELESS ONE: Bareback riding. Weight for age. Gob, he organised her.

THE JURORS: (*All their heads turned to his voice.*) Really?

THE NAMELESS ONE: (*Snarls.*) Arse over tip. Hundred shillings to five.

THE JURORS: (*All their heads lowered in assent.*) Most of us thought as much.

FIRST WATCH: He is a marked man. Another girl's plait cut. Wanted: Jack the Ripper. A thousand pounds reward.

SECOND WATCH: (*Awed, whispers.*) And in black. A mormon. Anarchist.

THE CRIER: (*Loudly.*) Whereas Leopold Bloom of no fixed abode is a wellknown dynamitard, forger, bigamist, bawd and cuckold and a public nuisance to the citizens of Dublin and whereas at this commission of assizes the most honourable . . .

(*His Honour, sir Frederick Falkiner, recorder of Dublin, in judicial garb of grey stone rises from the bench, stonebearded. He bears in his arms an umbrella sceptre. From his forehead arise starkly the Mosaic ramshorns.*)

THE RECORDER: I will put an end to this white slave traffic and rid Dublin of this odious pest. Scandalous! (*He dons the black cap.*) Let him be taken, Mr Subsheriff, from the dock where he now stands and detained in custody in Mountjoy prison during His Majesty's pleasure and there be hanged by the neck until he is dead and therein fail not at your peril or may the Lord have mercy on your soul. Remove him. (*A black skullcap descends upon his head.*)

(*The subsheriff Long John Fanning appears, smoking a pungent Henry Clay.*)

LONG JOHN FANNING: (*Scowls and calls with rich rolling utterance.*) Who'll hang Judas Iscariot?

(*H. Rumbold, master barber, in a bloodcoloured jerkin and tanner's apron, a rope coiled over his shoulder, mounts the block. A life preserver and a nailstudded bludgeon are stuck in his belt. He rubs grimly his grappling hands, knobbed with knuckledusters.*)

RUMBOLD: (*To the recorder with sinister familiarity.*) Hanging Harry, your Majesty, the Mersey terror. Five guineas a jugular. Neck or nothing.

(*The bells of George's church toll slowly, loud dark iron.*)

THE BELLS: Heigho! Heigho!

BLOOM: (*Desperately.*) Wait. Stop. Gulls. Good heart. I saw. Innocence. Girl in the monkeyhouse. Zoo. Lewd chimpanzee. (*Breathlessly.*) Pelvic basin. Her artless blush unmanned me. (*Overcome with emotion.*) I left the precincts. (He turns to a figure in the crowd, appealing.) Hynes, may I speak to you? You know me. That three shillings you can keep. If you want a little more . . .

HYNES: (*Coldly.*) You are a perfect stranger.

SECOND WATCH: (*Points to the corner.*) The bomb is here.

FIRST WATCH: Infernal machine with a time fuse.

BLOOM: No, no. Pig's feet. I was at a funeral.

FIRST WATCH: (*Draws his truncheon.*) Liar!

(*The beagle lifts his snout, showing the grey scorbutic face of Paddy Dignam. He has gnawed all. He exhales a putrid carcasefed breath. He grows to human size and shape. His dachshund coat becomes a brown mortuary habit. His green eye flashes bloodshot. Half of one ear, all the nose and both thumbs are ghouleaten.*)

PADDY DIGNAM: (*In a hollow voice.*) It is true. It was my funeral. Doctor Finucane pronounced life extinct when I succumbed to the disease from natural causes.

(*He lifts his mutilated ashen face moonwards and bays lugubriously.*)

BLOOM: (*In triumph.*) You hear?

PADDY DIGNAM: Bloom, I am Paddy Dignam's spirit. List, list, O list!

BLOOM: The voice is the voice of Esau.

SECOND WATCH: (*Blesses himself.*) How is that possible?

FIRST WATCH: It is not in the penny catechism.

PADDY DIGNAM: By metempsychosis. Spooks.

A VOICE: O rocks.

PADDY DIGNAM: (*Earnestly.*) Once I was in the employ of Mr J. H. Menton, solicitor, commissioner for oaths and affidavits, of 27 Bachelor's Walk. Now I am defunct, the wall of the heart hypertrophied. Hard lines. The poor wife was awfully cut up. How is she bearing it? Keep her off that bottle of sherry. (*He looks round him.*) A lamp. I must satisfy an animal need. That buttermilk didn't agree with me.

(*The portly figure of John O'Connell, caretaker, stands forth, holding a bunch of keys tied with crape. Beside him stands Father Coffey, chaplain, toadbellied, wrynecked, in a surplice and bandanna nightcap, holding sleepily a staff of twisted poppies.*)

FATHER COFFEY: (*Yawns, then chants with a hoarse croak.*) Namine. Jacobs. Vobiscuits. Amen.

JOHN O'CONNELL: (*Foghorns stormily through his megaphone.*) Dignam, Patrick T, deceased.

PADDY DIGNAM: (*With pricked up ears, winces.*) Overtones. (*He wriggles forward and places an ear to the ground.*) My master's voice!

JOHN O'CONNELL: Burial docket letter number U. P. eightyfive thousand. Field seventeen. House of Keys. Plot, one hundred and one.

(*Paddy Dignam listens with visible effort, thinking, his tail stiffpointed, his ears cocked.*)

PADDY DIGNAM: Pray for the repose of his soul.

(*He worms down through a coalhole, his brown habit trailing its tether over rattling pebbles. After him toddles an obese grandfather rat on fungus turtle paws under a grey carapace. Dignam's voice, muffled, is heard baying under ground:* Dignam's dead and gone below. *Tom Rochford, robinredbreasted, in cap and breeches, jumps from his twocolumned machine.*)

Tom Rochford: (*A hand to his breastbone, bows.*) Reuben J. A florin I find him. (*He fixes the manhole with a resolute stare.*) My turn now on. Follow me up to Carlow.

(*He executes a daredevil salmon leap in the air and is engulfed in the coalhole. Two discs on the columns wobble, eyes of nought. All recedes. Bloom plodges forward again through the sump. Kisses chirp amid the rifts of fog. A piano sounds. He stands before a lighted house, listening. The kisses, winging from their bowers, fly about him, twittering, warbling, cooing.*)

The Kisses: (*Warbling.*) Leo! (*Twittering.*) Icky licky micky sticky for Leo! (*Cooing.*) Coo coocoo! Yummyyum, Womwom! (*Warbling.*) Big comebig! Pirouette! Leopopold! (*Twittering.*) Leeolee! (*Warbling.*) O Leo!

(*They rustle, flutter upon his garments, alight, bright giddy flecks, silvery sequins.*)

Bloom: A man's touch. Sad music. Church music. Perhaps here.

(*Zoe Higgins, a young whore in a sapphire slip, closed with three bronze buckles, a slim black velvet fillet round her throat, nods, trips down the steps and accosts him.*)

Zoe: Are you looking for someone? He's inside with his friend.

Bloom: Is this Mrs Mack's?

Zoe: No, eightyone. Mrs Cohen's. You might go farther and fare worse. Mother Slipperslapper. (*Familiarly.*) She's on the job herself tonight with the vet her tipster that gives her all the winners and pays for her son in Oxford. Working overtime but her luck's turned today. (*Suspiciously.*) You're not his father, are you?

Bloom: Not I!

Zoe: You both in black. Has little mousey any tickles tonight?

(*His skin, alert, feels her fingertips approach. A hand glides over his left thigh.*)

Zoe: How's the nuts?

Bloom: Off side. Curiously they are on the right. Heavier, I suppose. One in a million my tailor, Mesias, says.

Zoe: (*In sudden alarm.*) You've a hard chancre.

Bloom: Not likely.

Zoe: I feel it.

(*Her hand slides into his left trouser pocket and brings out a hard black shrivelled potato. She regards it and Bloom with dumb moist lips.*)

Bloom: A talisman. Heirloom.

Zoe: For Zoe? For keeps? For being so nice, eh?

(*She puts the potato greedily into a pocket then links his arm, cuddling him with supple warmth. He smiles uneasily. Slowly, note by note, oriental music is played. He gazes in the tawny crystal of her eyes, ringed with kohol. His smile softens.)*

ZOE: You'll know me the next time.

BLOOM: (*Forlornly.*) I never loved a dear gazelle but it was sure to . . .

(Gazelles are leaping, feeding on the mountains. Near are lakes. Round their shores file shadows black of cedargroves. Aroma rises, a strong hairgrowth of resin. It burns, the orient, a sky of sapphire, cleft by the bronze flight of eagles. Under it lies the womancity, nude, white, still, cool, in luxury. A fountain murmurs among damask roses. Mammoth roses murmur of scarlet winegrapes. A wine of shame, lust, blood exudes, strangely murmuring.)

ZOE: (*Murmuring singsong with the music, her odalisk lips lusciously smeared with salve of swinefat and rosewater.*) Schorach ani wenowach, benoith Hierushaloim.

BLOOM: (*Fascinated.*) I thought you were of good stock by your accent.

ZOE: And you know what thought did?

(She bites his ear gently with little goldstopped teeth, sending on him a cloying breath of stale garlic. The roses draw apart, disclose a sepulchre of the gold of kings and their mouldering bones.)

BLOOM: (*Draws back, mechanically caressing her right bub with a flat awkward hand.*) Are you a Dublin girl?

ZOE: (*Catches a stray hair deftly and twists it to her coil.*) No bloody fear. I'm English. Have you a swaggerroot?

Bloom: (*As before.*) Rarely smoke, dear. Cigar now and then. Childish device. (*Lewdly*) The mouth can be better engaged than with a cylinder of rank weed.

ZOE: Go on. Make a stump speech out of it.

BLOOM: (*In workman's corduroy overalls, black gansy with red floating tie and apache cap.*) Mankind is incorrigible. Sir Walter Ralegh brought from the new world that potato and that weed, the one a killer of pestilence by absorption, the other a poisoner of the ear, eye, heart, memory, will, understanding, all. That is to say he brought the poison a hundred years before another person whose name I forget brought the food. Suicide. Lies. All our habits. Why, look at our public life!

(Midnight chimes from distant steeples.)

THE CHIMES: Turn again, Leopold! Lord mayor of Dublin!

BLOOM: (*In alderman's gown and chain.*) Electors of Arran Quay, Inns Quay, Rotunda, Mountjoy and North Dock, better run a tramline, I say, from the cattlemarket to the river. That's the music of the future. That's my programme. *Cui bono?* But our bucaneering Vanderdeckens in their phantom ship of finance . . .

AN ELECTOR: Three times three for our future chief magistrate!

(*The aurora borealis of the torchlight procession leaps.*)

THE TORCHBEARERS: Hooray!

(*Several wellknown burgesses, city magnates and freemen of the city shake hands with Bloom and congratulate him. Timothy Harrington, late thrice Lord Mayor of Dublin, imposing in mayoral scarlet, gold chain and white silk tie, confers with councillor Lorcan Sherlock, locum tenens. They nod vigorously in agreement.*)

LATE LORD MAYOR HARRINGTON: (*In scarlet robe with mace, gold mayoral chain and large white silk scarf.*) That alderman sir Leo Bloom's speech be printed at the expense of the ratepayers. That the house in which he was born be ornamented with a commemorative tablet and that the thoroughfare hitherto known as Cow Parlour off Cork street be henceforth designated Boulevard Bloom.

COUNCILLOR LORCAN SHERLOCK: Carried unanimously.

BLOOM: (*Impassionedly.*) These flying Dutchmen or lying Dutchmen as they recline in their upholstered poop, casting dice, what reck they? Machines is their cry, their chimera, their panacea. Laboursaving apparatuses, supplanters, bugbears, manufactured monsters for mutual murder, hideous hobgoblins produced by a horde of capitalistic lusts upon our prostituted labour. The poor man starves while they are grassing their royal mountain stags or shooting peasants and phartridges in their purblind pomp of pelf and power. But their reign is rover for rever and ever and ev . . .

(*Prolonged applause. Venetian masts, maypoles and festal arches spring up. A streamer bearing the legends* Cead Mile Failte *and* Mah Ttob Melek Israel *spans the street. All the windows are thronged with sightseers, chiefly ladies. Along the route the regiments of the Royal Dublin Fusiliers, the King's own Scottish Borderers, the Cameron Highlanders and the Welsh Fusiliers, standing to attention, keep back the crowd. Boys from High school are perched on the lampposts, telegraph poles, windowsills, cornices, gutters, chimneypots, railings, rainspouts, whistling and cheering. The pillar of the cloud appears. A fife and drum band is heard in the distance playing the Kol Nidre. The beaters approach with imperial eagles hoisted, trailing banners and waving oriental palms. The chryselephantine papal standard rises high, surrounded by pennons of the civic flag. The van of the procession appears headed by John Howard Parnell,*) *city marshal, in a chessboard tabard, the Athlone Poursuivant and Ulster King of Arms. They are followed by the Right Honourable Joseph Hutchinson, lord mayor of Dublin, his lordship the lord mayor of Cork, their worships the mayors of Limerick, Galway, Sligo and Waterford, twentyeight Irish representative peers, sirdars, grandees and maharajahs bearing the cloth of estate, the Dublin Metropolitan Fire Brigade, the chapter of the saints of finance in their plutocratic order of precedence, the bishop of Down and Connor, His Eminence Michael cardinal Logue, archbishop of Armagh, primate of all Ireland, His Grace, the most reverend Dr William Alexander, archbishop of Armagh, primate of all Ireland, the chief rabbi, the presbyterian moderator, the heads of the baptist, anabaptist, methodist and Moravian chapels and the honorary secretary of the society of friends. After them march the guilds and trades and trainbands with flying colours: coopers, bird fanciers, millwrights, newspaper canvassers, law scriveners, masseurs, vintners, trussmakers, chimneysweeps, lard refiners, tabinet and poplin weavers, farriers, Italian warehousemen, church decorators, bootjack manufacturers, undertakers, silk mercers, lapidaries, salesmasters, corkcutters, assessors of fire losses, dyers and cleaners, export bottlers, fellmongers, ticketwriters, heraldic seal engravers, horse repository hands, bullion brokers, cricket and archery outfitters, riddlemakers, egg and potato factors, hosiers and glovers, plumbing contractors. After them march gentlemen of the bedchamber, Black Rod, Deputy Garter, Gold Stick, the master of horse, the lord great chamberlain, the earl marshal, the high constable carrying the sword of state, saint Stephen's iron crown, the chalice and bible. Four buglers on foot blow a sennet. Beefeaters reply, winding clarions of welcome. Under an arch of triumph Bloom appears, bareheaded, in a crimson velvet mantle trimmed with ermine, bearing Saint Edward's staff, the orb and sceptre with the dove, the curtana. He is seated on a milkwhite horse with long flowing crimson tail, richly caparisoned, with golden headstall. Wild excitement. The ladies from their balconies throw down rosepetals. The air is perfumed with essences. The men cheer. Bloom's boys run amid the bystanders with branches of hawthorn and wrenbushes.)*

BLOOM'S BOYS:

The wren, the wren,
The king of all birds,
Saint Stephen's his day
Was caught in the furze.

A BLACKSMITH: (*Murmurs.*) For the honour of God! And is that Bloom? He scarcely looks thirtyone.

A PAVIOR AND FLAGGER: That's the famous Bloom now, the world's greatest reformer. Hats off!

(*All uncover their heads. Women whisper eagerly.*)

A MILLIONAIRESS: (*Richly.*) Isn't he simply wonderful?

A NOBLEWOMAN: (*Nobly.*) All that man has seen!

A FEMINIST: (*Masculinely.*) And done!

A BELLHANGER: A classic face! He has the forehead of a thinker.

(*Bloom's weather. A sunburst appears in the northwest.*)

THE BISHOP OF DOWN AND CONNOR: I here present your undoubted emperor-president and king-chairman, the most serene and potent and very puissant ruler of this realm. God save Leopold the First!

ALL: God save Leopold the First!

BLOOM: (*In dalmatic and purple mantle, to the bishop of Down and Connor, with dignity.*) Thanks, somewhat eminent sir.

WILLIAM, ARCHBISHOP OF ARMAGH: (*In purple stock and shovel hat.*) Will you to your power cause law and mercy to be executed in all your judgments in Ireland and territories thereunto belonging?

BLOOM: (*Placing his right hand on his testicles, swears.*) So may the Creator deal with me. All this I promise to do.

MICHAEL, ARCHBISHOP OF ARMAGH: (*Pours a cruse of hairoil over Bloom's head.*) *Gaudium magnum annuntio vobis. Habemus carneficem.* Leopold, Patrick, Andrew, David, George, be thou anointed!

(*Bloom assumes a mantle of cloth of gold and puts on a ruby ring. He ascends and stands on the stone of destiny. The representative peers put on at the same time their twentyeight crowns. Joybells ring in Christ church, Saint Patrick's, George's and gay Malahide. Mirus bazaar fireworks go up from all sides with symbolical phallopyrotechnic designs. The peers do homage, one by one, approaching and genuflecting.*)

THE PEERS: I do become your liege man of life and limb to earthly worship.

(*Bloom holds up his right hand on which sparkles the Koh-i-Noor diamond. His palfrey neighs. Immediate silence. Wireless intercontinental and interplanetary transmitters are set for reception of message.*)

BLOOM: My subjects! We hereby nominate our faithful charger Copula Felix hereditary Grand Vizier and announce that we have this day repudiated our former spouse and have bestowed our royal hand upon the princess Selene, the splendour of night.

(*The former morganatic spouse of Bloom is hastily removed in the Black*

Maria. The princess Selene, in moonblue robes, a silver crescent on her head, descends from a Sedan chair, borne by two giants. An outburst of cheering.)

JOHN HOWARD PARNELL: *(Raises the royal standard.)* Illustrious Bloom! Successor to my famous brother!

BLOOM: *(Embraces John Howard Parnell.)* We thank you from our heart, John, for this right royal welcome to green Erin, the promised land of our common ancestors.

(The freedom of the city is presented to him embodied in a charter. The keys of Dublin, crossed on a crimson cushion, are given to him. He shows all that he is wearing green socks.)

TOM KERNAN: You deserve it, your honour.

BLOOM: On this day twenty years ago we overcame the hereditary enemy at Ladysmith. Our howitzers and camel swivel guns played on his lines with telling effect. Half a league onward! They charge! All is lost now! Do we yield? No! We drive them headlong! Lo! We charge! Deploying to the left our light horse swept across the heights of Plevna and, uttering their warcry *Bonafide Sabaoth*, sabred the Saracen gunners to a man.

THE CHAPEL OF FREEMAN TYPESETTERS: Hear! Hear!

JOHN WYSE NOLAN: There's the man that got away James Stephens.

A BLUECOAT SCHOOLBOY: Bravo!

AN OLD RESIDENT: You're a credit to your country, sir, that's what you are.

AN APPLEWOMAN: He's a man like Ireland wants.

BLOOM: My beloved subjects, a new era is about to dawn. I, Bloom, tell you verily it is even now at hand. Yea, on the word of a Bloom, ye shall ere long enter into the golden city which is to be, the new Bloomusalem in the Nova Hibernia of the future.

(Thirtytwo workmen, wearing rosettes, from all the counties of Ireland, under the guidance of Derwan the builder, construct the new Bloomusalem. It is a colossal edifice with crystal roof, built in the shape of a huge pork kidney, containing forty thousand rooms. In the course of its extension several buildings and monuments are demolished. Government offices are temporarily transferred to railway sheds. Numerous houses are razed to the ground. The inhabitants are lodged in barrels and boxes, all marked in red with the letters: L. B. Several paupers fall from a ladder. A part of the walls of Dublin, crowded with loyal sightseers, collapses.)

THE SIGHTSEERS: *(Dying.) Morituri te salutant. (They die.)*

(A man in a brown macintosh springs up through a trapdoor. He points an elongated finger at Bloom.)

THE MAN IN THE MACINTOSH: Don't you believe a word he says. That man is Leopold M'Intosh, the notorious fireraiser. His real name is Higgins.

BLOOM: Shoot him! Dog of a christian! So much for M'Intosh!

(*A cannonshot. The man in the macintosh disappears. Bloom with his sceptre strikes down poppies. The instantaneous deaths of many powerful enemies, graziers, members of parliament, members of standing committees, are reported. Bloom's bodyguard distribute Maundy money, commemoration medals, loaves and fishes, temperance badges, expensive Henry Clay cigars, free cowbones for soup, rubber preservatives in sealed envelopes tied with gold thread, butter scotch, pineapple rock,* billets doux *in the form of cocked hats, readymade suits, porringers of toad in the hole, bottles of Jeyes' Fluid, purchase stamps, 40 days' indulgences, spurious coins, dairyfed pork sausages, theatre passes, season tickets available for all tramlines, coupons of the royal and privileged Hungarian lottery, penny dinner counters, cheap reprints of the World's Twelve Worst Books: Froggy And Fritz (politic), Care of the Baby (infantilic), 50 Meals for 7/6 (culinic), Was Jesus a Sun Myth? (historic), Expel that Pain (medic), Infant's Compendium of the Universe (cosmic), Let's All Chortle (hilaric), Canvasser's Vade Mecum (journalic), Loveletters of Mother Assistant (erotic), Who's Who in Space (astric), Songs that Reached Our Heart (melodic), Pennywise's Way to Wealth (parsimonic). A general rush and scramble. Women press forward to touch the hem of Bloom's robe. The lady Gwendolen Dubedat bursts through the throng, leaps on his horse and kisses him on both cheeks amid great acclamation. A magnesium flashlight photograph is taken. Babes and sucklings are held up.*)

THE WOMEN: Little father! Little father!

THE BABES AND SUCKLINGS:

> Clap clap hands till Poldy comes home,
> Cakes in his pocket for Leo alone.

(*Bloom, bending down, pokes Baby Boardman gently in the stomach.*)

BABY BOARDMAN: (*Hiccups, curdled milk flowing from his mouth.*) Hajajaja.

BLOOM: (*Shaking hands with a blind stripling.*) My more than Brother! (*Placing his arms round the shoulders of an old couple.*) Dear old friends! (*He plays pussy fourcorners with ragged boys and girls.*) Peep! Bopeep! (*He wheels twins in a perambulator.*) Ticktacktwo wouldyousetashoe? (*He performs juggler's tricks, draws red, orange, yellow, green, blue, indigo and violet silk handkerchiefs from his mouth.*) Roygbiv. 32 feet per second. (*He consoles a widow.*) Absence makes the heart grow younger. (*He dances the Highland fling with grotesque antics.*) Leg it, ye devils! (*He kisses the bedsores of a palsied veteran.*) Honourable wounds! (*He trips up a fat policeman.*) U. p: up. U. p: up. (*He whispers in the ear of a blushing waitress and laughs kindly.*) Ah, naughty, naughty! (*He eats a raw turnip offered him by Maurice Butterly, farmer.*) Fine! Splendid! (*He refuses to accept three shillings offered him by Joseph Hynes, journalist.*) My dear fellow, not at all! (*He gives his coat to a beggar.*) Please accept. (*He takes part in a stomach race with elderly male and female cripples.*) Come on, boys! Wriggle it, girls!

THE CITIZEN: (*Choked with emotion, brushes aside a tear in his emerald muffler.*) May the good God bless him!

(*The rams' horns sound for silence. The standard of Zion is hoisted.*)

BLOOM: (*Uncloaks impressively, revealing obesity, unrolls a paper and reads solemnly.*) Aleph Beth Ghimel Daleth Hagadah Tephilim Kosher Yom Kippur Hanukah Roschaschana Beni Brith Bar Mitzvah Mazzoth Askenazim Meshuggah Talith.

(*An official translation is read by Jimmy Henry, assistant town clerk.*)

JIMMY HENRY: The Court of Conscience is now open. His Most Catholic Majesty will now administer open air justice. Free medical and legal advice, solution of doubles and other problems. All cordially invited. Given at this our loyal city of Dublin in the year 1 of the Paradisiacal Era.

PADDY LEONARD: What am I to do about my rates and taxes?

BLOOM: Pay them, my friend.

PADDY LEONARD: Thank you.

NOSEY FLYNN: Can I raise a mortgage on my fire insurance?

BLOOM: (*Obdurately.*) Sirs, take notice that by the law of torts you are bound over in your own recognisances for six months in the sum of five pounds.

J. J. O'MOLLOY: A Daniel did I say? Nay! A Peter O'Brien!

NOSEY FLYNN: Where do I draw the five pounds?

PISSER BURKE: For bladder trouble?

BLOOM:

Acid. nit. hydrochlor. dil., 20 minims
Tinct. nux vom., 5 minims
Extr. taraxel. lig., 30 minims.
Aq. dis. ter in die.

CHRIS CALLINAN: What is the parallax of the subsolar ecliptic of Aldebaran?

BLOOM: Pleased to hear from you, Chris. K. II.

JOE HYNES: Why aren't you in uniform?

BLOOM: When my progenitor of sainted memory wore the uniform of the Austrian despot in a dank prison where was yours?

BEN DOLLARD: Pansies?

BLOOM: Embellish (beautify) suburban gardens.

BEN DOLLARD: When twins arrive?

BLOOM: Father (pater, dad) starts thinking.

LARRY O'ROURKE: An eight day licence for my new premises. You remember me, sir Leo, when you were in number seven. I'm sending around a dozen of stout for the missus.

BLOOM: (*Coldly.*) You have the advantage of me. Lady Bloom accepts no presents.

CROFTON: This is indeed a festivity.

BLOOM: (*Solemnly.*) You call it a festivity. I call it a sacrament.

ALEXANDER KEYES: When will we have our own house of keys?

BLOOM: I stand for the reform of municipal morals and the plain ten commandments. New worlds for old. Union of all, jew, moslem and gentile. Three acres and a cow for all children of nature. Saloon motor hearses. Compulsory manual labour for all. All parks open to the public day and night. Electric dishscrubbers. Tuberculosis, lunacy, war and mendicancy must now cease. General amnesty, weekly carnival with masked licence, bonuses for all, esperanto the universal language with universal brotherhood. No more patriotism of barspongers and dropsical impostors. Free money, free rent, free love and a free lay church in a free lay state.

O'MADDEN BURKE: Free fox in a free henroost.

DAVY BYRNE: (*Yawning.*) Iiiiiiiiiaaaaaaach!

BLOOM: Mixed races and mixed marriage.

LENEHAN: What about mixed bathing?

(*Bloom explains to those near him his schemes for social regeneration. All agree with him. The keeper of the Kildare street museum appears, dragging a lorry on which are the shaking statues of several naked goddesses, Venus Callipyge, Venus Pandemos, Venus Metempsychosis, and plaster figures, also naked, representing the new nine muses, Commerce, Operatic Music, Amor, Publicity, Manufacture, Liberty of Speech, Plural Voting, Gastronomy, Private Hygiene, Seaside Concert Entertainments, Painless Obstetrics and Astronomy for the People.*)

FATHER FARLEY: He is an episcopalian, an agnostic, an anythingarian seeking to overthrow our holy faith.

MRS RIORDAN: (*Tears up her will.*) I'm disappointed in you! You bad man!

MOTHER GROGAN: (*Removes her boot to throw it at Bloom.*) You beast! You abominable person!

NOSEY FLYNN: Give us a tune, Bloom. One of the old sweet songs.

BLOOM: (*With rollicking humour.*)

> I vowed that I never would leave her,
> She turned out a cruel deceiver.
> With my tooraloom tooraloom tooraloom tooraloom.

HOPPY HOLOHAN: Good old Bloom! There's nobody like him after all.

PADDY LEONARD: Stage Irishman!

BLOOM: What railway opera is like a tramline in Gibraltar? The Rows of Casteele.

(*Laughter.*)

LENEHAN: Plagiarist! Down with Bloom!

THE VEILED SIBYL: (*Enthusiastically.*) I'm a Bloomite and I glory in it. I believe in him in spite of all. I'd give my life for him, the funniest man on earth.

BLOOM: (*Winks at the bystanders.*) I bet she's a bonny lassie.

THEODORE PUREFOY: (*In fishingcap and oilskin jacket.*) He employs a mechanical device to frustrate the sacred ends of nature.

THE VEILED SIBYL: (*Stabs herself.*) My hero god! (*She dies.*)

(*Many most attractive and enthusiastic women also commit suicide by stabbing, drowning, drinking prussic acid, aconite, arsenic, opening their veins, refusing food, casting themselves under steamrollers, from the top of Nelson's Pillar, into the great vat of Guinness's brewery, asphyxiating themselves by placing their heads in gasovens, hanging themselves in stylish garters, leaping from windows of different storeys.*)

ALEXANDER J DOWIE: (*Violently.*) Fellowchristians and anti-Bloomites, the man called Bloom is from the roots of hell, a disgrace to christian men. A fiendish libertine from his earliest years this stinking goat of Mendes gave precocious signs of infantile debauchery, recalling the cities of the plain, with a dissolute granddam. This vile hypocrite, bronzed with infamy, is the white bull mentioned in the

Apocalypse. A worshipper of the Scarlet Woman, intrigue is the very breath of his nostrils. The stake faggots and the caldron of boiling oil are for him. Caliban!

THE MOB: Lynch him! Roast him! He's as bad as Parnell was. Mr Fox!

(*Mother Grogan throws her boot at Bloom. Several shopkeepers from upper and lower Dorset street throw objects of little or no commercial value, hambones, condensed milk tins, unsaleable cabbage, stale bread, sheep's tails, odd pieces of fat.*)

BLOOM: (*Excitedly.*) This is midsummer madness, some ghastly joke again. By heaven, I am guiltless as the unsunned snow! It was my brother Henry. He is my double. He lives in number 2 Dolphin's Barn. Slander, the viper, has wrongfully accused me. Fellowcountrymen, *sgenl inn ban bata coisde gan capall*. I call on my old friend, Dr Malachi Mulligan, sex specialist, to give medical testimony on my behalf.

DR MULLIGAN: (*In motor jerkin, green motorgoggles on his brow.*) Dr Bloom is bisexually abnormal. He has recently escaped from Dr Eustace's private asylum for demented gentlemen. Born out of bedlock hereditary epilepsy is present, the consequence of unbridled lust. Traces of elephantiasis have been discovered among his ascendants. There are marked symptoms of chronic exhibitionism. Ambidexterity is also latent. He is prematurely bald from selfabuse, perversely idealistic in consequence, a reformed rake, and has metal teeth. In consequence of a family complex he has temporarily lost his memory and I believe him to be more sinned against than sinning. I have made a pervaginal examination and, after application of the acid test to 5427 anal, axillary, pectoral and pubic hairs, I declare him to be *virgo intacta*.

(*Bloom holds his high grade hat over his genital organs.*)

DR MADDEN: Hypsospadia is also marked. In the interest of coming generations I suggest that the parts affected should be preserved in spirits of wine in the national teratological museum.

DR CROTTHERS: I have examined the patient's urine. It is albuminoid. Salivation is insufficient, the patellar reflex intermittent.

DR PUNCH COSTELLO: The *fetor judaicus* is most perceptible.

DR DIXON: (*Reads a bill of health.*) Professor Bloom is a finished example of the new womanly man. His moral nature is simple and lovable. Many have found him a dear man, a dear person. He is a rather quaint fellow on the whole, coy though not feebleminded in the medical sense. He has written a really beautiful letter, a poem in itself, to the court missionary of the Reformed Priests' Protection Society which clears up everything. He is practically a total abstainer and I can affirm that he sleeps on a straw litter and eats the most Spartan food, cold dried grocer's peas. He wears a hairshirt of pure Irish manufacture winter and summer and scourges himself every Saturday. He was, I understand, at one time a firstclass misdemeanant in Glencree reformatory. Another report states that he was a very posthumous child. I appeal for clemency in the name of the most sacred word our vocal organs have ever been called upon to speak. He is about to have a baby.

(*General commotion and compassion. Women faint. A wealthy American makes a street collection for Bloom. Gold and silver coins, blank cheques, banknotes, jewels, treasury bonds, maturing bills of exchange, I. O. U's, wedding rings, watchchains, lockets, necklaces and bracelets are rapidly collected.*)

BLOOM: O, I so want to be a mother.

MRS THORNTON: (*In nursetender's gown.*) Embrace me tight, dear. You'll be soon over it. Tight, dear.

(*Bloom embraces her tightly and bears eight male yellow and white children. They appear on a redcarpeted staircase adorned with expensive plants. All the octuplets are handsome, with valuable metallic faces, wellmade, respectably dressed and wellconducted, speaking five modern languages fluently and interested in various arts and sciences. Each has his name printed in legible letters on his shirtfront: Nasodoro, Goldfinger, Chrysostomos, Maindorée, Silversmile, Silberselber, Vifargent, Panargyros. They are immediately appointed to positions of high public trust in several different countries as managing directors of banks, traffic managers of railways, chairmen of limited liability companies, vicechairmen of hotel syndicates.*)

A VOICE: Bloom, are you the Messiah ben Joseph or ben David?

BLOOM: (*Darkly.*) You have said it.

BROTHER BUZZ: Then perform a miracle like Father Charles.

BANTAM LYONS: Prophesy who will win the Saint Leger.

(*Bloom walks on a net, covers his left eye with his left ear, passes through several walls, climbs Nelson's Pillar, hangs from the top ledge by his eyelids, eats twelve dozen oysters (shells included), heals several sufferers from king's evil, contracts his face so as to resemble many historical personages, Lord Beaconsfield, Lord Byron, Wat Tyler, Moses of Egypt, Moses Maimonides, Moses Mendelssohn, Henry Irving, Rip van Winkle, Kossuth, Jean Jacques Rousseau, Baron Leopold*)

Rothschild, Robinson Crusoe, Sherlock Holmes, Pasteur, turns each foot simultaneously in different directions, bids the tide turn back, eclipses the sun by extending his little finger.)

BRINI, PAPAL NUNCIO: (*In papal zouave's uniform, steel cuirasses as breastplate, armplates, thighplates, legplates, large profane moustaches and brown paper mitre.*) Leopoldi autem generatio. Moses begat Noah and Noah begat Eunuch and Eunuch begat O'Halloran and O'Halloran begat Guggenheim and Guggenheim begat Agendath and Agendath begat Netaim and Netaim begat Le Hirsch and Le Hirsch begat Jesurum and Jesurum begat MacKay and MacKay begat Ostrolopsky and Ostrolopsky begat Smerdoz and Smerdoz begat Weiss and Weiss begat Schwarz and Schwarz begat Adrianopoli and Adrianopoli begat Aranjuez and Aranjuez begat Lewy Lawson and Lewy Lawson begat Ichabudonosor and Ichabudonosor begat O'Donnell Magnus and O'Donnell Magnus begat Christbaum and Christbaum begat ben Maimun and ben Maimun begat Dusty Rhodes and Dusty Rhodes begat Benamor and Benamor begat Jones-Smith and Jones-Smith begat Savorgnanovich and Savorgnanovich begat Jasperstone and Jasperstone begat Vingtetunieme and Vingtetunieme begat Szombathely and Szombathely begat Virag and Virag begat Bloom *et vocabitur nomen eius Emmanuel.*

A DEADHAND: (*Writes on the wall.*) Bloom is a cod.

CRAB: (*In bushranger's kit.*) What did you do in the cattlecreep behind Kilbarrack?

A FEMALE INFANT: (*Shakes a rattle.*) And under Ballybough bridge?

A HOLLYBUSH: And in the devil's glen?

BLOOM: (*Blushes furiously all over from frons to nates, three tears falling from his left eye.*) Spare my past.

THE IRISH EVICTED TENANTS: (*In bodycoats, kneebreeches, with Donnybrook fair shillelaghs.*) Sjambok him!

(*Bloom with asses' ears seats himself in the pillory with crossed arms, his feet protruding. He whistles* Don Giovanni, a cenar teco. *Artane orphans, joining hands, caper round him. Girls of the Prison Gate Mission, joining hands, caper round in the opposite direction.*)

THE ARTANE ORPHANS:

You hig, you hog, you dirty dog!
You think the ladies love you!

THE PRISON GATE GIRLS:

> If you see Kay
> Tell him he may
> See you in tea
> Tell him from me.

HORNBLOWER: (*In ephod and huntingcap, announces.*) And he shall carry the sins of the people to Azazel, the spirit which is in the wilderness, and to Lilith, the nighthag. And they shall stone him and defile him, yea, all from Agendath Netaim and from Mizraim, the land of Ham.

(*All the people cast soft pantomime stones at Bloom. Many bonafide travellers and ownerless dogs come near him and defile him. Mastiansky and Citron approach in gaberdines, wearing long earlocks. They wag their beards at Bloom.*)

MASTIANSKY AND CITRON: Belial! Laemlein of Istria, the false Messiah! Abulafia! Recant!

(*George R Mesias, Bloom's tailor, appears, a tailor's goose under his arm, presenting a bill.*)

MESIAS: To alteration one pair trousers eleven shillings.

BLOOM: (*Rubs his hands cheerfully.*) Just like old times. Poor Bloom!

(*Reuben J Dodd, blackbearded Iscariot, bad shepherd, bearing on his shoulders the drowned corpse of his son, approaches the pillory.*)

REUBEN J: (*Whispers hoarsely.*) The squeak is out. A split is gone for the flatties. Nip the first rattler.

THE FIRE BRIGADE: Pflaap!

BROTHER BUZZ: (*Invests Bloom in a yellow habit with embroidery of painted flames and high pointed hat. He places a bag of gunpowder round his neck and hands him over to the civil power, saying.*) Forgive him his trespasses.

(*Lieutenant Myers of the Dublin Fire Brigade by general request sets fire to Bloom. Lamentations.*)

THE CITIZEN: Thank heaven!

BLOOM: (*In a seamless garment marked* I. H. S. *stands upright amid phoenix flames.*) Weep not for me, O daughters of Erin.

(*He exhibits to Dublin reporters traces of burning. The daughters of Erin, in black garments, with large prayerbooks and long lighted candles in their hands, kneel down and pray.*)

THE DAUGHTERS OF ERIN:

Kidney of Bloom, pray for us
Flower of the Bath, pray for us
Mentor of Menton, pray for us
Canvasser for the Freeman, pray for us
Charitable Mason, pray for us
Wandering Soap, pray for us
Sweets of Sin, pray for us
Music without Words, pray for us
Reprover of the Citizen, pray for us
Friend of all Frillies, pray for us
Midwife Most Merciful, pray for us
Potato Preservative against Plague and Pestilence, pray for us.

(*A choir of six hundred voices, conducted by Vincent O'Brien, sings the chorus from Handel's Messiah* Alleluia for the Lord God Omnipotent reigneth, *accompanied on the organ by Joseph Glynn. Bloom becomes mute, shrunken, carbonised.*)

ZOE: Talk away till you're black in the face.

BLOOM: (*In caubeen with clay pipe stuck in the band, dusty brogues, an emigrant's red handkerchief bundle in his hand, leading a black bogoak pig by a sugaun, with a smile in his eye.*) Let me be going now, woman of the house, for by all the goats in Connemara I'm after having the father and mother of a bating. (*With a tear in his eye.*) All insanity. Patriotism, sorrow for the dead, music, future of the race. To be or not to be. Life's dream is o'er. End it peacefully. They can live on. (*He gazes far away mournfully.*) I am ruined. A few pastilles of aconite. The blinds drawn. A letter. Then lie back to rest. (*He breathes softly.*) No more. I have lived. Fare. Farewell.

ZOE: (*Stiffly, her finger in her neckfillet.*) Honest? Till the next time. (*She sneers.*) Suppose you got up the wrong side of the bed or came too quick with your best girl. O, I can read your thoughts!

BLOOM: (*Bitterly.*) Man and woman, love, what is it? A cork and bottle. I'm sick of it. Let everything rip.

ZOE: (*In sudden sulks.*) I hate a rotter that's insincere. Give a bleeding whore a chance.

BLOOM: (*Repentantly.*) I am very disagreeable. You are a necessary evil. Where are you from? London?

ZOE: (*Glibly.*) Hog's Norton where the pigs plays the organs. I'm Yorkshire born. (*She holds his hand which is feeling for her nipple.*) I say, Tommy Tittlemouse. Stop that and begin worse. Have you cash for a short time? Ten shillings?

BLOOM: (*Smiles, nods slowly.*) More, houri, more.

ZOE: And more's mother? (*She pats him offhandedly with velvet paws.*) Are you coming into the musicroom to see our new pianola? Come and I'll peel off.

BLOOM: (*Feeling his occiput dubiously with the unparalleled embarrassment of a harassed pedlar gauging the symmetry of her peeled pears.*) Somebody would be dreadfully jealous if she knew. The greeneyed monster. (*Earnestly.*) You know how difficult it is. I needn't tell you.

ZOE: (*Flattered.*) What the eye can't see the heart can't grieve for. (*She pats him.*) Come.

BLOOM: Laughing witch! The hand that rocks the cradle.

ZOE: Babby!

BLOOM: (*In babylinen and pelisse, bigheaded, with a caul of dark hair, fixes big eyes on her fluid slip and counts its bronze buckles with a chubby finger, his moist tongue lolling and lisping.*) One two tlee: tlee tlwo tlone.

THE BUCKLES: Love me. Love me not. Love me.

ZOE: Silent means consent. (*With little parted talons she captures his hand, her forefinger giving to his palm the passtouch of secret monitor, luring him to doom.*) Hot hands cold gizzard.

(*He hesitates amid scents, music, temptations. She leads him towards the steps, drawing him by the odour of her armpits, the vice of her painted eyes, the rustle of her slip in whose sinuous folds lurks the lion reek of all the male brutes that have possessed her.*)

THE MALE BRUTES: (*Exhaling sulphur of rut and dung and ramping in their loosebox, faintly roaring, their drugged heads swaying to and fro.*) Good!

(*Zoe and Bloom reach the doorway where two sister whores are seated. They examine him curiously from under their pencilled brows and smile to his hasty bow. He trips awkwardly.*)

ZOE: (*Her lucky hand instantly saving him.*) Hoopsa! Don't fall upstairs.

BLOOM: The just man falls seven times. (*He stands aside at the threshold.*) After you is good manners.

ZOE: Ladies first, gentlemen after.

(*She crosses the threshold. He hesitates. She turns and, holding out her hands, draws him over. He hops. On the antlered rack of the hall hang a man's*) *hat and waterproof. Bloom uncovers himself but, seeing them, frowns, then smiles, preoccupied. A door on the return landing is flung open. A man in purple shirt and grey trousers, brownsocked, passes with an ape's gait, his bald head and goatee beard upheld, hugging a full waterjugjar, his twotailed black braces dangling at heels. Averting his face quickly Bloom bends to examine on the halltable the spaniel eyes of a running fox: then, his lifted head sniffing, follows Zoe into the musicroom. A shade of mauve tissuepaper dims the light of the chandelier. Round and round a moth flies, colliding, escaping. The floor is covered with an oilcloth mosaic of jade and azure and cinnabar rhomboids. Footmarks are stamped over it in all senses, heel to heel, heel to hollow, toe to toe, feet locked, a morris of shuffling feet without body phantoms, all in a scrimmage higgledypiggledy. The walls are tapestried with a paper of yewfronds and clear glades. In the grate is spread a screen of peacock feathers. Lynch squats crosslegged on the hearthrug of matted hair, his cap back to the front. With a wand he beats time slowly. Kitty Ricketts, a bony pallid whore in navy costume, doeskin gloves rolled back from a coral wristlet, a chain purse in her hand, sits perched on the edge of the table swinging her leg and glancing at herself in the gilt mirror over the mantelpiece. A tag of her corsetlace hangs slightly below her jacket. Lynch indicates mockingly the couple at the piano.)*

KITTY: *(Coughs behind her hand.)* She's a bit imbecillic. *(She signs with a waggling forefinger.)* Blemblem. *(Lynch lifts up her skirt and white petticoat with the wand. She settles them down quickly.)* Respect yourself. *(She hiccups, then bends quickly her sailor hat under which her hair glows, red with henna.)* O, excuse!

ZOE: More limelight, Charley. *(She goes to the chandelier and turns the gas full cock.)*

KITTY: *(Peers at the gasjet.)* What ails it tonight?

LYNCH: *(Deeply.)* Enter a ghost and hobgoblins.

ZOE: Clap on the back for Zoe.

(The wand in Lynch's hand flashes: a brass poker. Stephen stands at the pianola on which sprawl his hat and ashplant. With two fingers he repeats once more the series of empty fifths. Florry Talbot, a blond feeble goosefat whore in a tatterdemalion gown of mildewed strawberry, lolls spreadeagle in the sofacorner, her limp forearm pendent over the bolster, listening. A heavy stye droops over her sleepy eyelid.)

KITTY: *(Hiccups again with a kick of her horsed foot.)* O, excuse!

ZOE: *(Promptly.)* Your boy's thinking of you. Tie a knot on your shift.

(Kitty Ricketts bends her head. Her boa uncoils, slides, glides over her shoulder, back, arm, chair to the ground. Lynch lifts the curled catterpillar on his

wand. She snakes her neck, nestling. Stephen glances behind at the squatted figure with its cap back to the front.)

STEPHEN: As a matter of fact it is of no importance whether Benedetto Marcello found it or made it. The rite is the poet's rest. It may be an old hymn to Demeter or also illustrate *Cœla enarrant gloriam Domini.* It is susceptible of nodes or modes as far apart as hyperphrygian and mixolydian and of texts so divergent as priests haihooping round David's that is Circe's or what am I saying Ceres' altar and David's tip from the stable to his chief bassoonist about the alrightness of his almightiness. *Mais nom de nom,* that is another pair of trousers. *Jetez la gourme. Faut que jeunesse se passe.* (*He stops, points at Lynch's cap, smiles, laughs.*) Which side is your knowledge bump?

THE CAP: (*With saturnine spleen.*) Bah! It is because it is. Woman's reason. Jewgreek is greekjew. Extremes meet. Death is the highest form of life. Bah!

STEPHEN: You remember fairly accurately all my errors, boasts, mistakes. How long shall I continue to close my eyes to disloyalty? Whetstone!

THE CAP: Bah!

STEPHEN: Here's another for you. (*He frowns.*) The reason is because the fundamental and the dominant are separated by the greatest possible interval which . . .

THE CAP: Which? Finish. You can't.

STEPHEN: (*With an effort.*) Interval which. Is the greatest possible ellipse. Consistent with. The ultimate return. The octave. Which.

THE CAP: Which?

(*Outside the gramophone begins to blare* The Holy City.)

STEPHEN: (*Abruptly.*) What went forth to the ends of the world to traverse not itself, God, the sun, Shakespeare, a commercial traveller, having itself traversed in reality itself becomes that self. Wait a moment. Wait a second. Damn that fellow's noise in the street. Self which it itself was ineluctably preconditioned to become. *Ecco!*

LYNCH: (*With a mocking whinny of laughter grins at Bloom and Zoe Higgins.*) What a learned speech, eh?

ZOE: (*Briskly.*) God help your head, he knows more than you have forgotten.

(*With obese stupidity Florry Talbot regards Stephen.*)

FLORRY: They say the last day is coming this summer.

KITTY: No!

ZOE: (*Explodes in laughter.*) Great unjust God!

FLORRY: (*Offended.*) Well, it was in the papers about Antichrist. O, my foot's tickling.

(*Ragged barefoot newsboys, jogging a wagtail kite, patter past, yelling.*)

THE NEWSBOYS: Stop press edition. Result of the rockinghorse races. Sea serpent in the royal canal. Safe arrival of Antichrist.

(*Stephen turns and sees Bloom.*)

STEPHEN: A time, times and half a time.

(*Reuben J Antichrist, wandering jew, a clutching hand open on his spine, stumps forward. Across his loins is slung a pilgrim's wallet from which protrude promissory notes and dishonoured bills. Aloft over his shoulder he bears a long boatpole from the hook of which the sodden huddled mass of his only son, saved from Liffey waters, hangs from the slack of its breeches. A hobgoblin in the image of Punch Costello, hipshot, crookbacked, hydrocephalic, prognathic with receding forehead and Ally Sloper nose, tumbles in somersaults through the gathering darkness.*)

ALL: What?

THE HOBGOBLIN: (*His jaws chattering, capers to and fro, goggling his eyes, squeaking, kangaroohopping with outstretched clutching arms, then all at once thrusts his lipless face through the fork of his thighs.*) Il vient! C'est moi! L'homme qui rit! L'homme primigène! (*He whirls round and round with dervish howls.*) Sieurs et dames, faites vos jeux! (*He crouches juggling. Tiny roulette planets fly from his hands.*) Les jeux sont faits! (*The planets rush together, uttering crepitant cracks.*) Rien va plus! (*The planets, buoyant balloons, sail swollen up and away. He springs off into vacuum.*)

FLORRY: (*Sinking into torpor, crossing herself secretly.*) The end of the world!

(*A female tepid effluvium leaks out from her. Nebulous obscurity occupies space. Through the drifting fog without the gramophone blares over coughs and feetshuffling.*)

THE GRAMOPHONE: Jerusalem!

Open your gates and sing

Hosanna . . .

(*A rocket rushes up the sky and bursts. A white star falls from it, proclaiming the consummation of all things and second coming of Elijah. Along an infinite invisible tightrope taut from zenith to nadir the End of the World, a twoheaded octopus in gillie's kilts, busby and tartan filibegs, whirls through the murk, head over heels, in the form of the Three Legs of Man.*)

THE END OF THE WORLD: (*With a Scotch accent.*) Wha'll dance the keel row, the keel row, the keel row?

(Over the possing drift and choking breathcoughs, Elijah's voice, harsh as a corncrake's, jars on high. Perspiring in a loose lawn surplice with funnel sleeves he is seen, vergerfaced, above a rostrum about which the banner of old glory is draped. He thumps the parapet.)

ELIJAH: No yapping, if you please, in this booth. Jake Crane, Creole Sue, Dove Campbell, Abe Kirschner, do your coughing with your mouths shut. Say, I am operating all this trunk line. Boys, do it now. God's time is 12.25. Tell mother you'll be there. Rush your order and you play a slick ace. Join on right here. Book through to eternity junction, the nonstop run. Just one word more. Are you a god or a doggone clod? If the second advent came to Coney Island are we ready? Florry Christ, Stephen Christ, Zoe Christ, Bloom Christ, Kitty Christ, Lynch Christ, it's up to you to sense that cosmic force. Have we cold feet about the cosmos? No. Be on the side of the angels. Be a prism. You have that something within, the higher self. You can rub shoulders with a Jesus, a Gautama, an Ingersoll. Are you all in this vibration? I say you are. You once nobble that, congregation, and a buck joyride to heaven becomes a back number. You got me? It's a lifebrightener, sure. The hottest stuff ever was. It's the whole pie with jam in. It's just the cutest snappiest line out. It is immense, supersumptuous. It restores. It vibrates. I know and I am some vibrator. Joking apart and, getting down to bedrock, A. J. Christ Dowie and the harmonial philosophy, have you got that? O. K. Seventyseven west sixtyninth street. Got me? That's it. You call me up by sunphone any old time. Bumboosers, save your stamps. *(He shouts.)* Now then our glory song. All join heartily in the singing. Encore! *(He sings.)* Jeru . . .

THE GRAMOPHONE: *(Drowning his voice.)* Whorusalaminyourhighhohhhh . . . *(The disc rasps gratingly against the needle.)*

THE THREE WHORES: *(Covering their ears, squawk.)* Ahhkkk!

ELIJAH: *(In rolledup shirtsleeves, black in the face, shouts at the top of his voice, his arms uplifted.)* Big Brother up there, Mr President, you hear what I done just been saying to you. Certainly, I sort of believe strong in you, Mr President. I certainly am thinking now Miss Higgins and Miss Ricketts got religion way inside them. Certainly seems to me I don't never see no wusser scared female than the way you been, Miss Florry, just now as I done seed you. Mr President, you come long and help me save our sisters dear. *(He winks at his audience.)* Our Mr President, he twig the whole lot and he aint saying nothing.

KITTY-KATE: I forgot myself. In a weak moment I erred and did what I did on Constitution hill. I was confirmed by the bishop and enrolled in the brown scapular. My mother's sister married a Montmorency. It was a working plumber was my ruination when I was pure.

ZOE-FANNY: I let him larrup it into me for the fun of it.

FLORRY-TERESA: It was in consequence of a portwine beverage on top of Hennessy's three star. I was guilty with Whelan when he slipped into the bed.

STEPHEN: In the beginning was the word, in the end the world without end. Blessed be the eight beatitudes.

(*The beatitudes, Dixon, Madden, Crotthers, Costello, Lenehan, Bannon, Mulligan and Lynch in white surgical students' gowns, four abreast, goosestepping, tramp fast past in noisy marching.*)

THE BEATITUDES: (*Incoherently.*) Beer beef battledog buybull businum barnum buggerum bishop.

LYSTER: (*In quakergrey kneebreeches and broadbrimmed hat, says discreetly.*) He is our friend. I need not mention names. Seek thou the light.

(*He corantos by. Best enters in hairdresser's attire, shinily laundered, his locks in curlpapers. He leads John Eglinton who wears a mandarin's kimono of Nankeen yellow, lizardlettered, and a high pagoda hat.*)

BEST: (*Smiling, lifts the hat and displays a shaven poll from the crown of which bristles a pigtail toupee tied with an orange topknot.*) I was just beautifying him, don't you know. A thing of beauty, don't you know, Yeats says, or I mean, Keats says.

JOHN EGLINTON: (*Produces a greencapped dark lantern and flashes it towards a corner: with carping accent.*) Esthetics and cosmetics are for the boudoir. I am out for truth. Plain truth for a plain man. Tanderagee wants the facts and means to get them.

(*In the cone of the searchlight behind the coalscuttle, ollave, holyeyed, the bearded figure of Mananaun MacLir broods, chin on knees. He rises slowly. A cold seawind blows from his druid mouth. About his head writhe eels and elvers. He is encrusted with weeds and shells. His right hand holds a bicycle pump. His left hand grasps a huge crayfish by its two talons.*)

MANANAUN MACLIR: (*With a voice of waves.*) Aum! Hek! Wal! Ak! Lub! Mor! Ma! White yoghin of the gods. Occult pimander of Hermes Trismegistos. (*With a voice of whistling seawind.*) Punarjanam patsypunjaub! I won't have my leg pulled. It has been said by one: beware the left, the cult of Shakti. (*With a cry of stormbirds.*) Shakti

496

Shiva, darkhidden Father! (*He smites with his bicycle pump the crayfish in his left hand. On its cooperative dial glow the twelve signs of the zodiac. He wails with the vehemence of the ocean.*) Aum! Baum! Pyjaum! I am the light of the homestead! I am the dreamery creamery butter.

(*A skeleton judashand strangles the light. The green light wanes to mauve. The gasjet wails whistling.*)

THE GASJET: Pooah! Pfuiiiiiii!

(*Zoe runs to the chandelier and, crooking her leg, adjusts the mantle.*)

ZOE: Who has a fag as I'm here?

LYNCH: (*Tossing a cigarette on to the table.*) Here.

ZOE: (*Her head perched aside in mock pride.*) Is that the way to hand the *pot* to a lady? (*She stretches up to light the cigarette over the flame, twirling it slowly, showing the brown tufts of her armpits. Lynch with his poker lifts boldly a side of her slip. Bare from her garters up her flesh appears under the sapphire a nixie's green. She puffs calmly at her cigarette.*) Can you see the beautyspot of my behind?

LYNCH: I'm not looking

ZOE: (*Makes sheep's eyes.*) No? You wouldn't do a less thing. Would you suck a lemon?

(*Squinting in mock shame she glances with sidelong meaning at Bloom, then twists round towards him, pulling her slip free of the poker. Blue fluid again flows over her flesh. Bloom stands, smiling desirously, twirling his thumbs. Kitty Ricketts licks her middle finger with her spittle and, gazing in the mirror, smooths both eyebrows. Lipoti Virag, basilicogrammate, chutes rapidly down through the chimneyflue and struts two steps to the left on gawky pink stilts. He is sausaged into several overcoats and wears a brown macintosh under which he holds a roll of parchment. In his left eye flashes the monocle of Cashel Boyle O'Connor Fitzmaurice Tisdall Farrell. On his head is perched an Egyptian pshent. Two quills project over his ears.*)

VIRAG: (*Heels together, bows.*) My name is Virag Lipoti, of Szombathely. (*He coughs thoughtfully, drily.*) Promiscuous nakedness is much in evidence hereabouts, eh? Inadvertently her backview revealed the fact that she is not wearing those rather intimate garments of which you are a particular devotee. The injection mark on the thigh I hope you perceived? Good.

BLOOM: Granpapachi. But . . .

VIRAG: Number two on the other hand, she of the cherry rouge and coiffeuse white, whose hair owes not a little to our tribal elixir of gopherwood, is in walking costume and tightly staysed by her sit,

I should opine. Backbone in front, so to say. Correct me but I always understood that the act so performed by skittish humans with glimpses of lingerie appealed to you in virtue of its exhibitionististicicity. In a word. Hippogriff. Am I right?

BLOOM: She is rather lean.

VIRAG: (*Not unpleasantly.*) Absolutely! Well observed and those pannier pockets of the skirt and slightly pegtop effect are devised to suggest bunchiness of hip. A new purchase at some monster sale for which a gull has been mulcted. Meretricious finery to deceive the eye. Observe the attention to details of dustspecks. Never put on you tomorrow what you can wear today. Parallax! (*With a nervous twitch of his head.*) Did you hear my brain go snap? Pollysyllabax!

BLOOM: (*An elbow resting in a hand, a forefinger against his cheek.*) She seems sad.

VIRAG: (*Cynically, his weasel teeth bared yellow, draws down his left eye with a finger and barks hoarsely.*) Hoax! Beware of the flapper and bogus mournful. Lily of the alley. All possess bachelor's button discovered by Rualdus Columbus. Tumble her. Columble her. Chameleon. (*More genially.*) Well then, permit me to draw your attention to item number three. There is plenty of her visible to the naked eye. Observe the mass of oxygenated vegetable matter on her skull. What ho, she bumps! The ugly duckling of the party, longcasted and deep in keel.

BLOOM: (*Regretfully.*) When you come out without your gun.

VIRAG: We can do you all brands, mild, medium and strong. Pay your money, take your choice. How happy could you be with either . . .

BLOOM: With . . .?

VIRAG: (*His tongue upcurling.*) Lyum! Look. Her beam is broad. She is coated with quite a considerable layer of fat. Obviously mammal in weight of bosom you remark that she has in front well to the fore two protuberances of very respectable dimensions, inclined to fall in the noonday soupplate, while on her rere lower down are two additional protuberances, suggestive of potent rectum and tumescent for palpation, which leave nothing to be desired save compactness. Such fleshy parts are the product of careful nurture. When coopfattened their livers reach an elephantine size. Pellets of new bread with fennygreek and gumbenjamin swamped down by potions of green tea endow them during their brief existence with natural pincushions of quite colossal blubber. That suits your book, eh? Fleshhotpots of

Egypt to hanker after. Wallow in it. Lycopodium. (*His throat twitches.*) Slapbang! There he goes again.

BLOOM: The stye I dislike.

VIRAG: (*Arches his eyebrows.*) Contact with a goldring, they say. *Argumentum ad feminam*, as we said in old Rome and ancient Greece in the consulship of Diplodocus and Ichthyosauros. For the rest Eve's sovereign remedy. Not for sale. Hire only. Huguenot. (*He twitches.*) It is a funny sound. (*He coughs encouragingly.*) But possibly it is only a wart. I presume you shall have remembered what I will have taught you on that head? Wheatenmeal with honey and nutmeg.

BLOOM: (*Reflecting.*) Wheatenmeal with lycopodium and syllabax. This searching ordeal. It has been an unusually fatiguing day, a chapter of accidents. Wait. I mean, wartsblood spreads warts, you said . . .

VIRAG: (*Severely, his nose hardhumped, his side eye winking.*) Stop twirling your thumbs and have a good old thunk. See, you have forgotten. Exercise your mnemotechnic. *La causa è santa*. Tara. Tara. (*Aside.*) He will surely remember.

BLOOM: Rosemary also did I understand you to say or willpower over parasitic tissues. Then nay no I have an inkling. The touch of a deadhand cures. Mnemo?

VIRAG: (*Excitedly.*) I say so. I say so. E'en so. Technic. (*He taps his parchmentroll energetically.*) This book tells you how to act with all descriptive particulars. Consult index for agitated fear of aconite, melancholy of muriatic, priapic pulsatilla. Virag is going to talk about amputation. Our old friend caustic. They must be starved. Snip off with horsehair under the denned neck. But, to change the venue to the Bulgar and the Basque, have you made up your mind whether you like or dislike women in male habiliments? (*With a dry snigger.*) You intended to devote an entire year to the study of the religious problem and the summer months of 1886 to square the circle and win that million. Pomegranate! From the sublime to the ridiculous is but a step. Pyjamas, let us say? Or stockingette gussetted knickers, closed? Or, put we the case, those complicated combinations, camiknickers? (*He crows derisively.*) Keekeereekee!

(*Bloom surveys uncertainly the three whores then gazes at the veiled mauve light, hearing the everflying moth.*)

BLOOM: I wanted then to have now concluded. Nightdress was never. Hence this. But tomorrow is a new day will be. Past was is today. What now is will then morrow as now was be past yester.

VIRAG: (*Prompts in a pig's whisper.*) Insects of the day spend their brief existence in reiterated coition, lured by the smell of the inferiorly pulchritudinous female possessing extendified pudendal nerve in dorsal region. Pretty Poll! (*His yellow parrotbeak gabbles nasally.*) They had a proverb in the Carpathians in or about the year five thousand five hundred and fifty of our era. One tablespoonful of honey will attract friend Bruin more than half a dozen barrels of first choice malt vinegar. Bear's buzz bothers bees. But of this apart. At another time we may resume. We were very pleased, we others. (*He coughs and, bending his brow, rubs his nose thoughtfully with a scooping hand.*) You shall find that these night insects follow the light. An illusion for remember their complex unadjustable eye. For all these knotty points see the seventeenth book of my Fundamentals of Sexology or the Love Passion which Doctor L. B. says is the book sensation of the year. Some, to example, there are again whose movements are automatic. Perceive. That is his appropriate sun. Nightbird nightsun nighttown. Chase me, Charley! (*He blows into Bloom's ear.*) Buzz!

BLOOM: Bee or bluebottle too other day butting shadow on wall dazed self then me wandered dazed down shirt good job I . . .

VIRAG: (*His face impassive, laughs in a rich feminine key.*) Splendid! Spanish fly in his fly or mustard plaster on his dibble. (*He gobbles gluttonously with turkey wattles.*) Bubbly jock! Bubbly jock! Where are we? Open Sesame! Cometh forth! (*He unrolls his parchment rapidly and reads, his glowworm's nose running backwards over the letters which he claws.*) Stay, good friend. I bring thee thy answer. Redbank oysters will shortly be upon us. I'm the best o'cook. Those succulent bivalves may help us and the truffles of Perigord, tubers dislodged through mister omnivorous porker, were unsurpassed in cases of nervous debility or viragitis. Though they stink yet they sting. (*He wags his head with cackling raillery.*) Jocular. With my eyeglass in my ocular. (*He sneezes.*) Amen!

BLOOM: (*Absently.*) Ocularly woman's bivalve case is worse. Always open sesame. The cloven sex. Why they fear vermin, creeping things. Yet Eve and the serpent contradicts. Not a historical fact. Obvious analogy to my idea. Serpents too are gluttons for woman's milk. Wind their way through miles of omnivorous forest to sucksucculent her breast dry. Like those bubblyjocular Roman matrons one reads of in Elephantuliasis.

VIRAG: (*His mouth projected in hard wrinkles, eyes stonily forlornly closed, psalms in outlandish monotone.*) That the cows with their those distended udders that they have been the the known . . .

BLOOM: I am going to scream. I beg your pardon. Ah? So. (*He repeats.*) Spontaneously to seek out the saurian's lair in order to entrust their teats to his avid suction. Ant milks aphis. (*Profoundly.*) Instinct rules the world. In life. In death.

VIRAG: (*Head askew, arches his back and hunched wingshoulders, peers at the moth out of blear bulged eyes, points a horning claw and cries.*) Who's moth moth? Who's dear Gerald? Dear Ger, that you? O dear, he is Gerald. O, I much fear he shall be most badly burned. Will some pleashe pershon not now impediment so catastrophics mit agitation of firstclass tablenumpkin? (*He mews.*) Puss puss puss puss! (*He sighs, draws back and stares sideways down with dropping underjaw.*) Well, well. He doth rest anon. (*He snaps his jaws suddenly on the air.*)

THE MOTH:

> I'm a tiny tiny thing
> Ever flying in the spring
> Round and round a ringaring.
> Long ago I was a king
> Now I do this kind of thing
> On the wing, on the wing!
> Bing!

(*He rushes against the mauve shade, flapping noisily.*) Pretty pretty pretty pretty pretty pretty petticoats.

(*From left upper entrance with two gliding steps Henry Flower comes forward to left front centre. He wears a dark mantle and drooping plumed sombrero. He carries a silverstringed inlaid dulcimer and a longstemmed bamboo Jacob's pipe, its clay bowl fashioned as a female head. He wears dark velvet hose and silverbuckled pumps. He has the romantic Saviour's face with flowing locks, thin beard and moustache. His spindlelegs and sparrow feet are those of the tenor Mario, prince of Candia. He settles down his goffered ruffs and moistens his lips with a passage of his amorous tongue.*)

HENRY: (*In a low dulcet voice, touching the strings of his guitar.*) There is a flower that bloometh.

(*Virag truculent, his jowl set, stares at the lamp. Grave Bloom regards Zoe's neck. Henry gallant turns with pendant dewlap to the piano.*)

STEPHEN: (*To himself.*) Play with your eyes shut. Imitate pa. Filling my belly with husks of swine. Too much of this. I will arise and go to my. Expect this is the. Steve, thou art in a parlous way. Must visit old Deasy or telegraph. Our interview of this morning has left on me a deep impression. Though our ages. Will write fully tomorrow. I'm partially drunk, by the way. (*He touches the keys again.*) Minor chord comes now. Yes. Not much however.

(*Almidano Artifoni holds out a batonroll of music with vigorous moustachework.*)

ARTIFONI: *Ci rifletta. Lei rovina tutto.*

FLORRY: Sing us something. Love's old sweet song.

STEPHEN: No voice. I am a most finished artist. Lynch, did I show you the letter about the lute?

FLORRY: (*Smirking.*) The bird that can sing and won't sing.

(*The Siamese twins, Philip Drunk and Philip Sober, two Oxford dons with lawnmowers, appear in the window embrasure. Both are masked with Matthew Arnold's face.*)

PHILIP SOBER: Take a fool's advice. All is not well. Work it out with the buttend of a pencil, like a good young idiot. Three pounds twelve you got, two notes, one sovereign, two crowns, if youth but knew. Mooney's en ville, Mooney's sur mer, the Moira, Larchet's, Holles street hospital, Burke's. Eh? I am watching you.

PHILIP DRUNK: (*Impatiently.*) Ah, bosh, man. Go to hell! I paid my way. If I could only find out about octaves. Reduplication of personality. Who was it told me his name? (*His lawnmower begins to purr.*) Aha, yes. *Zoe mou sas agapo.* Have a notion I was here before. When was it not Atkinson his card I have somewhere. Mac Somebody. Unmack I have it. He told me about, hold on, Swinburne, was it, no?

FLORRY: And the song?

STEPHEN: Spirit is willing but the flesh is weak.

FLORRY: Are you out of Maynooth? You're like someone I knew once.

STEPHEN: Out of it now. (*To himself.*) Clever.

PHILIP DRUNK AND PHILIP SOBER: (*Their lawnmowers purring with a rigadoon of grasshalms.*) Clever ever. Out of it out of it. By the bye have you the book, the thing, the ashplant? Yes, there it, yes. Cleverever outofitnow. Keep in condition. Do like us.

ZOE: There was a priest down here two nights ago to do his bit of business with his coat buttoned up. You needn't try to hide, I says to him. I know you've a Roman collar.

VIRAG: Perfectly logical from his standpoint. Fall of man. (*Harshly, his pupils waxing.*) To hell with the pope! Nothing new under the sun. I am the Virag who disclosed the Sex Secrets of Monks and Maidens. Why I left the church of Rome. Read the Priest, the Woman and the Confessional. Penrose. Flipperty Jippert. (*He wriggles.*) Woman, undoing with sweet pudor her belt of rushrope, offers her allmoist yoni to man's lingam. Short time after man presents woman with pieces of jungle meat. Woman shows joy and covers herself with featherskins. Man loves her yoni fiercely with big lingam, the stiff one. (*He cries.*) *Coactus volui.* Then giddy woman will run about. Strong man grapses woman's wrist. Woman squeals, bites, spucks. Man, now fierce angry, strikes woman's fat yadgana. (*He chases his tail.*) Piffpaff! Popo! (*He stops, sneezes.*) Pchp! (*He worries his butt.*) Prrrrrht!

LYNCH: I hope you gave the good father a penance. Nine glorias for shooting a bishop.

ZOE: (*Spouts walrus smoke through her nostrils.*) He couldn't get a connection. Only, you know, sensation. A dry rush.

BLOOM: Poor man!

ZOE: (*Lightly.*) Only for what happened him.

BLOOM: How?

VIRAG: (*A diabolic rictus of black luminosity contracting his visage, cranes his scraggy neck forward. He lifts a mooncalf nozzle and howls.*) *Verfluchte Goim!* He had a father, forty fathers. He never existed. Pig God! He had two left feet. He was Judas Iacchia, a Libyan eunuch, the pope's bastard. (*He leans out on tortured forepaws, elbows bent rigid, his eye agonising in his flat skullneck and yelps over the mute world.*) A son of a whore. Apocalypse.

KITTY: And Mary Shortall that was in the lock with the pox she got from Jimmy Pidgeon in the blue caps had a child off him that couldn't swallow and was smothered with the convulsions in the mattress and we all subscribed for the funeral.

PHILIP DRUNK: (*Gravely.*) *Qui vous a mis dans cette fichue position, Philippe?*

PHILIP SOBER: (*Gaily.*) *C'était le sacré pigeon, Philippe.*

(*Kitty unpins her hat and sets it down calmly, patting her henna hair. And a prettier, a daintier head of winsome curls was never seen on a whore's shoulders. Lynch puts on her hat. She whips it off.*)

LYNCH: (*Laughs.*) And to such delights has Metchnikoff inoculated anthropoid apes.

FLORRY: (*Nods.*) Locomotor ataxy.

ZOE: (*Gaily.*) O, my dictionary.

LYNCH: Three wise virgins.

VIRAG: (*Agueshaken, profuse yellow spawn foaming over his bony epileptic lips.*) She sold lovephiltres, whitewax, orangeflower. Panther, the Roman centurion, polluted her with his genitories. (*He sticks out a flickering phosphorescent scorpion tongue, his hand on his fork.*) Messiah! He burst her tympanum. (*With gibbering baboon's cries he jerks his hips in the cynical spasm.*) Hik! Hek! Hak! Hok! Huk! Kok! Kuk!

(*Ben Jumbo Dollard, rubicund, musclebound, hairynostrilled, hugebearded, cabbageeared, shaggychested, shockmaned, fatpapped, stands forth, his loins and genitals tightened into a pair of black bathing bagslops.*)

BEN DOLLARD: (*Nakkering castanet bones in his huge padded paws, yodels jovially in base barreltone.*) When love absorbs my ardent soul.

(*The virgins Nurse Callan and Nurse Quigley burst through the ringkeepers and the ropes and mob him with open arms.*)

THE VIRGINS: (*Gushingly.*) Big Ben! Ben my Chree!

A VOICE: Hold that fellow with the bad breeches.

BEN DOLLARD: (*Smites his thigh in abundant laughter.*) Hold him now.

HENRY: (*Caressing on his breast a severed female head, murmurs.*) Thine heart, mine love. (*He plucks his lutestrings.*) When first I saw . . .

VIRAG: (*Sloughing his skins, his multitudinous plumage moulting.*) Rats! (*He yawns, showing a coalblack throat, and closes his jaws by an upward push of his parchmentroll.*) After having said which I took my departure. Farewell. Fare thee well. *Dreck!*

(*Henry Flower combs his moustache and beard rapidly with a pocketcomb and gives a cow's lick to his hair. Steered by his rapier, he glides to the door, his wild harp slung behind him. Virag reaches the door in two ungainly stilthops, his tail cocked, and deftly claps sideways on the wall a pusyellow flybill, butting it with his head.*)

THE FLYBILL: K. 11. Post No Bills. Strictly confidential. Dr Hy Franks.

HENRY: All is lost now.

(*Virag unscrews his head in a trice and holds it under his arm.*)

VIRAG'S HEAD: Quack!

(*Exeunt severally.*)

STEPHEN: (*Over his shoulder to Zoe.*) You would have preferred the fighting parson who founded the protestant error. But beware Antisthenes, the dog sage, and the last end of Arius Heresiarchus. The agony in the closet.

LYNCH: All one and the same God to her.

STEPHEN: (*Devoutly.*) And sovereign Lord of all things.
FLORRY: (*To Stephen.*) I'm sure you're a spoiled priest. Or a monk.
LYNCH: He is. A cardinal's son.
STEPHEN: Cardinal sin. Monks of the screw.

(*His Eminence Simon Stephen Cardinal Dedalus, Primate of all Ireland, appears in the doorway, dressed in red soutane, sandals and socks. Seven dwarf simian acolytes, also in red, cardinal sins, uphold his train, peeping under it. He wears a battered silk hat sideways on his head. His thumbs are stuck in his armpits and his palms outspread. Round his neck hangs a rosary of corks ending on his breast in a corkscrew cross. Releasing his thumbs, he invokes grace from on high with large wave gestures and proclaims with bloated pomp:*)

THE CARDINAL:

> Conservio lies captured
> He lies in the lowest dungeon
> With manacles and chains around his limbs
> Weighing upwards of three tons.

(*He looks at all for a moment, his right eye closed tight, his left cheek puffed out. Then, unable to repress his merriment, he rocks to and fro, arms akimbo, and sings with broad rollicking humour:*)

> O, the poor little fellow
> Hihihihihis legs they were yellow
> He was plump, fat and heavy and brisk as a snake
> But some bloody savage
> To graize his white cabbage
> He murdered Nell Flaherty's duckloving drake.

(*A multitude of midges swarms white over his robe. He scratches himself with crossed arms at his ribs, grimacing, and exclaims:*)

I'm suffering the agony of the damned. By the hoky fiddle, thanks be to Jesus those funny little chaps are not unanimous. If they were they'd walk me off the face of the bloody globe.

(*His head aslant he blesses curtly with fore and middle fingers, imparts the Easter kiss and doubleshuffles off comically, swaying his hat from side to side, shrinking quickly to the size of his trainbearers. The dwarf acolytes, giggling, peeping, nudging, ogling, Easterkissing, zigzag behind him. His voice is heard mellow from afar, merciful male, melodious:*)

a widower, was a regular barometer from it. He believed in animal heat. A skin of tabby lined his winter waistcoat. Near the end, remembering king David and the Sunamite, he shared his bed with Athos, faithful after death. A dog's spittle as you probably . . . (*He winces.*) Ah!

RICHIE GOULDING: (*Bagweighted, passes the door.*) Mocking is catch. Best value in Dub. Fit for a prince's. Liver and kidney.

THE FAN: (*Tapping.*) All things end. Be mine. Now.

BLOOM: (*Undecided.*) All now? I should not have parted with my talisman. Rain, exposure at dewfall on the searocks, a peccadillo at my time of life. Every phenomenon has a natural cause.

THE FAN: (*Points downwards slowly.*) You may.

BLOOM: (*Looks downwards and perceives her unfastened bootlace.*) We are observed.

THE FAN: (*Points downwards quickly.*) You must.

BLOOM: (*With desire, with reluctance.*) I can make a true black knot. Learned when I served my time and worked the mail order line for Kellett's. Experienced hand. Every knot says a lot. Let me. In courtesy. I knelt once before today. Ah!

(*Bella raises her gown slightly and, steadying her pose, lifts to the edge of a chair a plump buskined hoof and a full pastern, silksocked. Bloom, stifflegged, aging, bends over her hoof and with gentle fingers draws out and in her laces.*)

BLOOM: (*Murmurs lovingly.*) To be a shoefitter in Manfield's was my love's young dream, the darling joys of sweet buttonhooking, to lace up crisscrossed to kneelength the dressy kid footwear satinlined, so incredibly impossibly small, of Clyde Road ladies. Even their wax model Raymonde I visited daily to admire her cobweb hose and stick of rhubarb toe, as worn in Paris.

The Hoof: Smell my hot goathide. Feel my royal weight.

BLOOM: (*Crosslacing.*) Too tight?

THE HOOF: If you bungle, Handy Andy, I'll kick your football for you.

BLOOM: Not to lace the wrong eyelet as I did the night of the bazaar dance. Bad luck. Hook in wrong tache of her . . . person you mentioned. That night she met . . . Now!

(*He knots the lace. Bella places her foot on the floor. Bloom raises his head. Her heavy face, her eyes strike him in midbrow. His eyes grow dull, darker and pouched, his nose thickens.*)

BLOOM: (*Mumbles.*) Awaiting your further orders we remain, gentlemen, . . .

BELLO: (*With a hard basilisk stare, in a baritone voice.*) Hound of dishonour!

BLOOM: (*Infatuated.*) Empress!

BELLO: (*His heavy cheekchops sagging.*) Adorer of the adulterous rump!

BLOOM: (*Plaintively.*) Hugeness!

BELLO: Dungdevourer!

BLOOM: (*With sinews semiflexed.*) Magmagnificence!

BELLO: Down! (*He taps her on the shoulder with his fan.*) Incline feet forward! Slide left foot one pace back! You will fall. You are falling. On the hands down!

BLOOM: (*Her eyes upturned in the sign of admiration, closing, yaps.*) Truffles!

(*With a piercing epileptic cry she sinks on all fours, grunting, snuffling, rooting at his feet: then lies, shamming dead, with eyes shut tight, trembling eyelids, bowed upon the ground in the attitude of most excellent master.*)

BELLO: (*With bobbed hair, purple gills, fat moustache rings round his shaven mouth, in mountaineer's puttees, green silverbuttoned coat, sport skirt and alpine hat with moorcock's feather, his hands stuck deep in his breeches pockets, places his heel on her neck and grinds it in.*) Footstool! Feel my entire weight. Bow, bondslave, before the throne of your despot's glorious heels so glistening in their proud erectness.

BLOOM: (*Enthralled, bleats.*) I promise never to disobey.

BELLO: (*Laughs loudly.*) Holy smoke! You little know what's in store for you. I'm the Tartar to settle your little lot and break you in! I'll bet Kentucky cocktails all round I shame it out of you, old son. Cheek me, I dare you. If you do tremble in anticipation of heel discipline to be inflicted in gym costume.

(*Bloom creeps under the sofa and peers out through the fringe.*)

ZOE: (*Widening her slip to screen her.*) She's not here.

BLOOM: (*Closing her eyes.*) She's not here.

FLORRY: (*Hiding her with her gown.*) She didn't mean it, Mr Bello. She'll be good, sir.

KITTY: Don't be too hard on her, Mr Bello. Sure you won't, ma'amsir.

BELLO: (*Coaxingly.*) Come, ducky dear, I want a word with you, darling, just to administer correction. Just a little heart to heart talk, sweety. (*Bloom puts out her timid head.*) There's a good girly now. (*Bello grabs her hair violently and drags her forward.*) I only want to correct you for your own good on a soft safe spot. How's that tender behind? O, ever so gently, pet. Begin to get ready.

BLOOM: (*Fainting.*) Don't tear my . . .

BELLO: (*Savagely.*) The nosering, the pliers, the bastinado, the hanging hook, the knout I'll make you kiss while the flutes play like the Nubian slave of old. You're in for it this time! I'll make you remember me for the balance of your natural life. (*His forehead veins swollen, his face congested.*) I shall sit on your ottoman saddleback every morning after my thumping good breakfast of Matterson's fat hamrashers and a bottle of Guinness's porter. (*He belches.*) And suck my thumping good Stock Exchange cigar while I read the *Licensed Victualler's Gazette*. Very possibly I shall have you slaughtered and skewered in my stables and enjoy a slice of you with crisp crackling from the baking tin basted and baked like sucking pig with rice and lemon or currant sauce. It will hurt you. (*He twists her arm. Bloom squeals, turning turtle.*)

BLOOM: Don't be cruel, nurse! Don't!

BELLO: (*Twisting.*) Another!

BLOOM: (*Screams.*) O, it's hell itself! Every nerve in my body aches like mad!

BELLO: (*Shouts.*) Good, by the rumping jumping general! That's the best bit of news I heard these six weeks. Here, don't keep me waiting, damn you! (*He slaps her face.*)

BLOOM: (*Whimpers.*) You're after hitting me. I'll tell . . .

BELLO: Hold him down, girls, till I squat on him.

ZOE: Yes. Walk on him! I will.

FLORRY: I will. Don't be greedy.

KITTY: No, me. Lend him to me.

(*The brothel cook, Mrs Keogh, wrinkled, greybearded, in a greasy bib, men's grey and green socks and brogues, floursmeared, a rollingpin stuck with raw pastry in her bare red arm and hand, appears at the door.*)

MRS KEOGH: (*Ferociously.*) Can I help? (*They hold and pinion Bloom.*)

BELLO: (*Squats with a grunt on Bloom's upturned face, puffing cigarsmoke, nursing a fat leg.*) I see Keating Clay is elected chairman of the Richmond asylum and by the by Guinness's preference shares are at sixteen three quarters. Curse me for a fool that didn't buy that lot Craig and Gardner told me about. Just my infernal luck, curse it. And that Goddamned outsider *Throwaway* at twenty to one. (*He quenches his cigar angrily on Bloom's ear.*) Where's that Goddamned cursed ashtray?

BLOOM: (*Goaded, buttocksmothered.*) O! O! Monsters! Cruel one!

BELLO: Ask for that every ten minutes. Beg. Pray for it as you never prayed before. (*He thrusts out a figged fist and foul cigar.*) Here, kiss that. Both. Kiss. (*He throws a leg astride and, pressing with horseman's knees, calls in a hard voice.*) Gee up! A cockhorse to Banbury cross. I'll ride him for the Eclipse stakes. (*He bends sideways and squeezes his mount's testicles roughly, shouting.*) Ho! Off we pop! I'll nurse you in proper fashion. (*He horserides cockhorse, leaping in the, in the saddle.*) The lady goes a pace a pace and the coachman goes a trot a trot and the gentleman goes a gallop a gallop a gallop a gallop.

FLORRY: (*Pulls at Bello.*) Let me on him now. You had enough. I asked before you.

ZOE: (*Pulling at Florry.*) Me. Me. Are you not finished with him yet, suckeress?

BLOOM: (*Stifling.*) Can't.

BELLO: Well, I'm not. Wait. (*He holds in his breath.*) Curse it. Here. This bung's about burst. (*He uncorks himself behind: then, contorting his features, farts loudly.*) Take that! (*He recorks himself.*) Yes, by Jingo, sixteen three quarters.

BLOOM: (*A sweat breaking out over him.*) Not man. (*He sniffs.*) Woman.

BELLO: (*Stands up.*) No more blow hot and cold. What you longed for has come to pass. Henceforth you are unmanned and mine in earnest, a thing under the yoke. Now for your punishment frock. You will shed your male garments, you understand, Ruby Cohen? and don the shot silk luxuriously rustling over head and shoulders. And quickly too!

BLOOM: (*Shrinks.*) Silk, mistress said! O crinkly! scrapy! Must I tiptouch it with my nails?

BELLO: (*Points to his whores.*) As they are now so will you be, wigged, singed, perfumesprayed, ricepowdered, with smoothshaven armpits. Tape measurements will be taken next your skin. You will be laced with cruel force into vicelike corsets of soft dove coutille with whalebone busk to the diamondtrimmed pelvis, the absolute outside edge, while your figure, plumper than when at large, will be restrained in nettight frocks, pretty two ounce petticoats and fringes and things stamped, of course, with my houseflag, creations of lovely lingerie for Alice and nice scent for Alice. Alice will feel the pullpull. Martha and Mary will be a little chilly at first in such delicate thighcasing but the frilly flimsiness of lace round your bare knees will remind you . . .

Bloom: (*A charming soubrette with dauby cheeks, mustard hair and large male hands and nose, leering mouth.*) I tried her things on only twice, a small prank, in Holles street. When we were hard up I washed them to save the laundry bill. My own shirts I turned. It was the purest thrift.

BELLO: (*Jeers.*) Little jobs that make mother pleased, eh? And showed off coquettishly in your domino at the mirror behind closedrawn blinds your unskirted thighs and hegoat's udders in various poses of surrender, eh? Ho! ho! I have to laugh! That secondhand black operatop shift and short trunkleg naughties all split up the stitches at her last rape that Mrs Miriam Dandrade sold you from the Shelbourne hotel, eh?

BLOOM: Miriam. Black. Demimondaine.

BELLO: (*Guffaws.*) Christ Almighty it's too tickling, this! You were a nicelooking Miriam when you clipped off your backgate hairs and lay swooning in the thing across the bed as Mrs Dandrade about to be violated by lieutenant Smythe-Smythe, Mr Philip Augustus Blockwell M. P., signor Laci Daremo, the robust tenor, blueeyed Bert, the liftboy, Henri Fleury of Gordon Bennett fame, Sheridan, the quadroon Croesus, the varsity wetbob eight from old Trinity, Ponto, her splendid Newfoundland and Bobs, dowager duchess of Manorhamilton. (*He guffaws again.*) Christ, wouldn't it make a Siamese cat laugh?

BLOOM: (*Her hands and features working.*) It was Gerald converted me to be a true corsetlover when I was female impersonator in the High School play *Vice Versa*. It was dear Gerald. He got that kink, fascinated by sister's stays. Now dearest Gerald uses pinky greasepaint and gilds his eyelids. Cult of the beautiful.

BELLO: (*With wicked glee.*) Beautiful! Give us a breather! When you took your seat with womanish care, lifting your billowy flounces, on the smoothworn throne.

BLOOM: Science. To compare the various joys we each enjoy. (*Earnestly.*) And really it's better the position . . . because often I used to wet . . .

BELLO: (*Sternly.*) No insubordination! The sawdust is there in the corner for you. I gave you strict instructions, didn't I? Do it standing, sir! I'll teach you to behave like a jinkleman! If I catch a trace on your swaddles. Aha! By the ass of the Dorans you'll find I'm a martinet. The sins of your past are rising against you. Many. Hundreds.

THE SINS OF THE PAST: (*In a medley of voices.*) He went through a form of clandestine marriage with at least one woman in the shadow of the Black church. Unspeakable messages he telephoned mentally to

Miss Dunn at an address in D'Olier street while he presented himself indecently to the instrument in the callbox. By word and deed he frankly encouraged a nocturnal strumpet to deposit fecal and other matter in an unsanitary outhouse attached to empty premises. In five public conveniences he wrote pencilled messages offering his nuptial partner to all strongmembered males. And by the offensively smelling vitriol works did he not pass night after night by loving courting couples to see if and what and how much he could see? Did he not lie in bed, the gross boar, gloating over a nauseous fragment of wellused toilet paper presented to him by a nasty harlot, stimulated by gingerbread and a postal order?

BELLO: (*Whistles loudly.*) Say! What was the most revolting piece of obscenity in all your career of crime? Go the whole hog. Puke it out! Be candid for once.

(*Mute inhuman faces throng forward, leering, vanishing, gibbering, Booloohoom. Poldy Kock, Bootlaces a penny, Cassidy's hag, blind stripling, Larry Rhinoceros, the girl, the woman, the whore, the other, the . . .*)

BLOOM: Don't ask me! Our mutual faith. Pleasants street. I only thought the half of the . . . I swear on my sacred oath . . .

BELLO: (*Peremptorily.*) Answer. Repugnant wretch! I insist on knowing. Tell me something to amuse me, smut or a bloody good ghoststory or a line of poetry, quick, quick, quick! Where? How? What time? With how many? I give you just three seconds. One! Two! Thr . . .

BLOOM: (*Docile, gurgles.*) I rererepugnosed in rererere-pugnant . . .

BELLO: (*Imperiously.*) O, get out, you skunk! Hold your tongue! Speak when you're spoken to.

BLOOM: (*Bows.*) Master! Mistress! Mantamer!

(*He lifts his arms. His bangle bracelets fall.*)

BELLO: (*Satirically.*) By day you will souse and bat our smelling underclothes also when we ladies are unwell, and swab out our latrines with dress pinned up and a dishclout tied to your tail. Won't that be nice? (*He places a ruby ring on her finger.*) And there now! With this ring I thee own. Say, thank you, mistress.

BLOOM: Thank you, mistress.

BELLO: You will make the beds, get my tub ready, empty the pisspots in the different rooms, including old Mrs Keogh's the cook's, a sandy one. Ay, and rinse the seven of them well, mind, or lap it up like champagne. Drink me piping hot. Hop! You will dance attendance

MILLY: My! It's Papli! But, O Papli, how old you've grown!

BELLO: Changed, eh? Our whatnot, our writingtable where we never wrote, aunt Hegarty's armchair, our classic reprints of old masters. A man and his menfriends are living there in clover. The *Cuckoos' Rest!* Why not? How many women had you, eh, following them up dark streets, flatfoot, exciting them by your smothered grunts, what, you male prostitute? Blameless dames with parcels of groceries. Turn about. Sauce for the goose, my gander O.

BLOOM: They . . . I . . .

BELLO: (*Cuttingly.*) Their heelmarks will stamp the Brusselette carpet you bought at Wren's auction. In their horseplay with Moll the romp to find the buck flea in her breeches they will deface the little statue you carried home in the rain for art for art's sake. They will violate the secrets of your bottom drawer. Pages will be torn from your handbook of astronomy to make them pipespills. And they will spit in your ten shilling brass fender from Hampton Leedom's.

BLOOM: Ten and six. The act of low scoundrels. Let me go. I will return. I will prove . . .

A VOICE: Swear!

(*Bloom clenches his fists and crawls forward, a bowieknife between his teeth.*)

BELLO: As a paying guest or a kept man? Too late. You have made your secondbest bed and others must lie in it. Your epitaph is written. You are down and out and don't you forget it, old bean.

Bloom: Justice! All Ireland versus one! Has nobody . . . ? (*He bites his thumb.*)

BELLO: Die and be damned to you if you have any sense of decency or grace about you. I can give you a rare old wine that'll send you skipping to hell and back. Sign a will and leave us any coin you have! If you have none see you damn well get it, steal it, rob it! We'll bury you in our shrubbery jakes where you'll be dead and dirty with old Cuck Cohen, my stepnephew I married, the bloody old gouty procurator and sodomite with a crick in his neck, and my other ten or eleven husbands, whatever the buggers' names were, suffocated in the one cesspool. (*He explodes in a loud phlegmy laugh.*) We'll manure you, Mr Flower! (*He pipes scoffingly.*) Byby, Poldy! Byby, Papli!

BLOOM: (*Clasps his head.*) My willpower! Memory! I have sinned! I have suff . . .

(*He weeps tearlessly.*)

BELLO: (*Sneers.*) Crybaby! Crocodile tears!

516

(*Bloom, broken, closely veiled for the sacrifice, sobs, his face to the earth. The passing bell is heard. Darkshawled figures of the circumcised, in sackcloth and ashes, stand by the wailing wall. M. Shulomowitz, Joseph Goldwater, Moses Herzog, Harris Rosenberg, M. Moisel, J. Citron, Minnie Watchman, P. Mastiansky, The Reverend Leopold Abramovitz, Chazen. With swaying arms they wail in pneuma over the recreant Bloom.*)

THE CIRCUMCISED: (*In dark guttural chant as they cast dead sea fruit upon him, no flowers.*) Shema Israel Adonai Elohenu Adonai Echad.

VOICES: (*Sighing.*) So he's gone. Ah yes. Yes, indeed. Bloom? Never heard of him. No? Queer kind of chap. There's the widow. That so? Ah, yes.

(*From the suttee pyre the flame of gum camphire ascends. The pall of incense smoke screens and disperses. Out of her oakframe a nymph with hair unbound, lightly clad in teabrown artcolours, descends from her grotto and passing under interlacing yews stands over Bloom.*)

THE YEWS: (*Their leaves whispering.*) Sister. Our sister. Ssh!

THE NYMPH: (*Softly.*) Mortal! (*Kindly.*) Nay, dost not weepest!

BLOOM: (*Crawls jellily forward under the boughs, streaked by sunlight, with dignity.*) This position. I felt it was expected of me. Force of habit.

THE NYMPH: Mortal! You found me in evil company, highkickers, coster picnicmakers, pugilists, popular generals, immoral panto boys in fleshtights and the nifty shimmy dancers, La Aurora and Karini, musical act, the hit of the century. I was hidden in cheap pink paper that smelt of rock oil. I was surrounded by the stale smut of clubmen, stories to disturb callow youth, ads for transparencies, truedup dice and bustpads, proprietary articles and why wear a truss with testimonial from ruptured gentleman. Useful hints to the married.

BLOOM: (*Lifts a turtle head towards her lap.*) We have met before. On another star.

THE NYMPH: (*Sadly.*) Rubber goods. Neverrip brand as supplied to the aristocracy. Corsets for men. I cure fits or money refunded. Unsolicited testimonials for Professor Waldmann's wonderful chest exuber. My bust developed four inches in three weeks, reports Mrs Gus Rublin with photo.

BLOOM: You mean *Photo Bits*?

THE NYMPH: I do. You bore me away, framed me in oak and tinsel, set me above your marriage couch. Unseen, one summer eve, you kissed me in four places. And with loving pencil you shaded my eyes, my bosom and my shame.

BLOOM: (*Humbly kisses her long hair.*) Your classic curves, beautiful immortal, I was glad to look on you, to praise you, a thing of beauty, almost to pray.

THE NYMPH: During dark nights I heard your praise.

BLOOM: (*Quickly.*) Yes, yes. You mean that I . . . Sleep reveals the worst side of everyone, children perhaps excepted. I know I fell out of bed or rather was pushed. Steel wine is said to cure snoring. For the rest there is that English invention, pamphlet of which I received some days ago, incorrectly addressed. It claims to afford a noiseless, inoffensive vent. (*He sighs.*) 'Twas ever thus. Frailty, thy name is marriage.

THE NYMPH: (*Her fingers in her ears.*) And words. They are not in my dictionary.

BLOOM: You understood them?

THE YEWS: Ssh!

THE NYMPH: (*Covers her face with her hands.*) What have I not seen in that chamber? What must my eyes look down on?

BLOOM: (*Apologetically.*) I know. Soiled personal linen, wrong side up with care. The quoits are loose. From Gibraltar by long sea long ago.

THE NYMPH: (*Bends her head.*) Worse, worse!

BLOOM: (*Reflects precautiously.*) That antiquated commode. It wasn't her weight. She scaled just eleven stone nine. She put on nine pounds after weaning. It was a crack and want of glue. Eh? And that absurd orangekeyed utensil which has only one handle.

(*The sound of a waterfall is heard in bright cascade.*)

THE WATERFALL:

Poulaphouca Poulaphouca
Poulaphouca Poulaphouca.

THE YEWS: (*Mingling their boughs.*) Listen. Whisper. She is right, our sister. We grew by Poulaphouca waterfall. We gave shade on languorous summer days.

JOHN WYSE NOLAN: (*In the background, in Irish National Forester's uniform, doffs his plumed hat.*) Prosper! Give shade on languorous days, trees of Ireland!

THE YEWS: (*Murmuring.*) Who came to Poulaphouca with the High School excursion? Who left his nutquesting classmates to seek our shade?

BLOOM: (*Scared.*) High School of Poula? Mnemo? Not in full possession of faculties. Concussion. Run over by tram.

THE ECHO: Sham!

BLOOM: (*Pigeonbreasted, bottleshouldered, padded, in nondescript juvenile grey and black striped suit, too small for him, white tennis shoes, bordered stockings with turnover tops and a red schoolcap with badge.*) I was in my teens, a growing boy. A little then sufficed, a jolting car, the mingling odours of the ladies' cloakroom and lavatory, the throng penned tight on the old Royal stairs (for they love crushes, instinct of the herd, and the dark sexsmelling theatre unbridles vice), even a pricelist of their hosiery. And then the heat. There were sunspots that summer. End of school. And tipsycake. Halcyon days.

(*Halcyon days, high school boys in blue and white football jerseys and shorts, Master Donald Turnbull, Master Abraham Chatterton, Master Owen Goldberg, Master Jack Meredith, Master Percy Apjohn, stand in a clearing of the trees and shout to Master Leopold Bloom.*)

THE HALCYON DAYS: Mackerel! Live us again. Hurray! (*They cheer.*)

BLOOM: (*Hobbledehoy, warmgloved, mammamufflered, starred with spent snowballs, struggles to rise.*) Again! I feel sixteen! What a lark! Let's ring all the bells in Montague street. (*He cheers feebly.*) Hurray for the High School!

THE ECHO: Fool!

THE YEWS: (*Rustling.*) She is right, our sister. Whisper. (*Whispered kisses are heard in all the wood. Faces of hamadryads peep out from the boles and among the leaves and break, blossoming into bloom.*) Who profaned our silent shade?

THE NYMPH: (*Coyly, through parting fingers.*) There? In the open air?

THE YEWS: (*Sweeping downward.*) Sister, yes. And on our virgin sward.

THE WATERFALL:

Poulaphouca Poulaphouca
Phoucaphouca Phoucaphouca.

THE NYMPH: (*With wide fingers.*) O, infamy!

BLOOM: I was precocious. Youth. The fauna. I sacrificed to the god of the forest. The flowers that bloom in the spring. It was pairing time. Capillary attraction is a natural phenomenon. Lotty Clarke, flaxenhaired, I saw at her night toilette through illclosed curtains with poor papa's operaglasses: The wanton ate grass wildly. She rolled downhill at Rialto bridge to tempt me with her flow of animal spirits. She climbed their crooked tree and I . . . A saint couldn't resist it. The demon possessed me. Besides, who saw?

(*Staggering Bob, a whitepolled calf, thrusts a ruminating head with humid nostrils through the foliage.*)

STAGGERING BOB: (*Large teardrops rolling from his prominent eyes, snivels.*) Me. Me see.

BLOOM: Simply satisfying a need I . . . (*With pathos.*) No girl would when I went girling. Too ugly. They wouldn't play . . .

(*High on Ben Howth through rhododendrons a nannygoat passes, plumpuddered, buttytailed, dropping currants.*)

THE NANNYGOAT: (*Bleats.*) Megeggaggegg! Nannannanny!

BLOOM: (*Hatless, flushed, covered with burrs of thistledown and gorsespine.*) Regularly engaged. Circumstances alter cases. (*He gazes intently downwards on the water.*) Thirtytwo head over heels per second. Press nightmare. Giddy Elijah. Fall from cliff. Sad end of government printer's clerk. (*Through silversilent summer air the dummy of Bloom, rolled in a mummy, rolls roteatingly from the Lion's Head cliff into the purple waiting waters.*)

THE DUMMYMUMMY: Bbbbblllllblblblblobschbg!

(*Far out in the bay between Bailey and Kish lights the* Erin's King *sails, sending a broadening plume of coalsmoke from her funnel towards the land.*)

COUNCILLOR NANNETTI: (*Alone on deck, in dark alpaca, yellowkitefaced, his hand in his waistcoat opening, declaims.*) When my country takes her place among the nations of the earth, then, and not till then, let my epitaph be written. I have . . .

BLOOM: Done. Prff!

THE NYMPH: (*Loftily.*) We immortals, as you saw today, have not such a place and no hair there either. We are stonecold and pure. We eat electric light. (*She arches her body in lascivious crispation, placing her forefinger in her mouth.*) Spoke to me. Heard from behind. How then could you . . .?

BLOOM: (*Pawing the heather abjectly.*) O, I have been a perfect pig. Enemas too I have administered. One third of a pint of quassia to which add a tablespoonful of rocksalt. Up the fundament. With Hamilton Long's syringe, the ladies' friend.

THE NYMPH: In my presence. The powderpuff. (*She blushes and makes a knee.*) And the rest!

BLOOM: (*Dejected.*) Yes. *Peccavi!* I have paid homage on that living altar where the back changes name. (*With sudden fervour.*) For why should the dainty scented jewelled hand, the hand that rules . . .?

(*Figures wind serpenting in slow woodland pattern around the treestems, cooeeing.*)

THE VOICE OF KITTY: (*In the thicket.*) Show us one of them cushions.

THE VOICE OF FLORRY: Here.

(*A grouse wings clumsily through the underwood.*)

THE VOICE OF LYNCH: (*In the thicket.*) Whew! Piping hot!

THE VOICE OF ZOE: (*From the thicket.*) Came from a hot place.

THE VOICE OF VIRAG: (*A birdchief, bluestreaked and feathered in war panoply with his assegai, striding through a crackling canebrake over beechmast and acorns.*) Hot! Hot! Ware Sitting Bull!

BLOOM: It overpowers me. The warm impress of her warm form. Even to sit where a woman has sat, especially with divaricated thighs, as though to grant the last favours, most especially with previously well uplifted white sateen coatpans. So womanly, full. It fills me full.

THE WATERFALL:

Phillaphulla Poulaphouca
Poulaphouca Poulaphouca.

THE YEWS: Ssh! Sister, speak!

THE NYMPH: (*Eyeless, in nun's white habit, coif and hugewinged wimple, softly, with remote eyes.*) Tranquilla convent. Sister Agatha. Mount Carmel. The apparitions of Knock and Lourdes. No more desire. (*She reclines her head, sighing.*) Only the ethereal. Where dreamy creamy gull waves o'er the waters dull.

(*Bloom half rises. His back trouserbutton snaps.*)

THE BUTTON: Bip!

(*Two sluts of the Coombe dance rainily by, shawled, yelling flatly.*)

THE SLUTS:

O, Leopold lost the pin of his drawers
He didn't know what to do,
To keep it up,
To keep it up.

(*Bella goes to the table to count the money while Stephen talks to himself in monosyllables. Zoe bends over the table. Kitty leans over Zoe's neck. Lynch gets up, rights his cap and, clasping Kitty's waist, adds his head to the group.*)

FLORRY: (*Strives heavily to rise.*) Ow! My foot's asleep. (*She limps over to the table. Bloom approaches.*)

BELLA, ZOE, KITTY, LYNCH, BLOOM: (*Chattering and squabbling.*) The gentleman . . . ten shillings . . . paying for the three . . . allow me a moment . . . this gentleman pays separate . . . who's touching it? . . . ow! . . . mind who you're pinching . . . are you staying the night or a short time? . . . who did? . . . you're a liar, excuse me . . . the gentleman paid down like a gentleman . . . drink . . . it's long after eleven.

STEPHEN: (*At the pianola, making a gesture of abhorrence.*) No bottles! What, eleven? A riddle!

ZOE: (*Lifting up her pettigown and folding a half sovereign into the top of her stocking.*) Hard earned on the flat of my back.

LYNCH: (*Lifting Kitty from the table.*) Come!

KITTY: Wait. (*She clutches the two crowns.*)

FLORRY: And me?

LYNCH: Hoopla! (*He lifts her, carries her and bumps her down on the sofa.*)

STEPHEN:

> The fox crew, the cocks flew,
> The bells in heaven
> Were striking eleven.
> 'Tis time for her poor soul
> To get out of heaven.

BLOOM: (*Quietly lays a half sovereign on the table between Bella and Florry.*) So. Allow me. (*He takes up the poundnote.*) Three times ten. We're square.

BELLA: (*Admiringly.*) You're such a slyboots, old cocky. I could kiss you.

ZOE: (*Points.*) Him? Deep as a drawwell. (*Lynch bends Kitty back over the sofa and kisses her. Bloom goes with the poundnote to Stephen.*)

BLOOM: This is yours.

STEPHEN: How is that? *Le distrait* or absentminded beggar. (*He fumbles again in his pocket and draws out a handful of coins. An object falls.*) That fell.

BLOOM: (*Stooping, picks up and hands a box of matches.*) This.

STEPHEN: Lucifer. Thanks.

BLOOM: (*Quietly.*) You had better hand over that cash to me to take care of. Why pay more?

STEPHEN: (*Hands him all his coins.*) Be just before you are generous.

BLOOM: I will but is it wise? (*He counts.*) One, seven, eleven, and five. Six. Eleven. I don't answer for what you may have lost.

STEPHEN: Why striking eleven? Proparoxyton. Moment before the next Lessing says. Thirsty fox. (*He laughs loudly.*) Burying his grandmother. Probably he killed her.

BLOOM: That is one pound six and eleven. One pound seven, say.

STEPHEN: Doesn't matter a rambling damn.

BLOOM: No, but . . .

STEPHEN: (*Comes to the table.*) Cigarette, please. (*Lynch tosses a cigarette from the sofa to the table.*) And so Georgina Johnson is dead and married. (*A cigarette appears on the table. Stephen looks at it.*) Wonder. Parlour magic. Married. Hm. (*He strikes a match and proceeds to light the cigarette with enigmatic melancholy.*)

LYNCH: (*Watching him.*) You would have a better chance of lighting it if you held the match nearer.

STEPHEN: (*Brings the match near his eye.*) Lynx eye. Must get glasses. Broke them yesterday. Sixteen years ago. Distance. The eye sees all flat. (*He draws the match away. It goes out.*) Brain thinks. Near: far. Ineluctable modality of the visible. (*He frowns mysteriously.*) Hm. Sphinx. The beast that has two backs at midnight. Married.

ZOE: It was a commercial traveller married her and took her away with him.

FLORRY: (*Nods.*) Mr Lambe from London.

STEPHEN: Lamb of London, who takest away the sins of our world.

LYNCH: (*Embracing Kitty on the sofa, chants deeply.*) *Dona nobis pacem.*

(*The cigarette slips from Stephen's fingers. Bloom picks it up and throws it in the grate.*)

BLOOM: Don't smoke. You ought to eat. Cursed dog I met. (*To Zoe.*) You have nothing?

ZOE: Is he hungry?

STEPHEN: (*Extends his hand to her smiling and chants to the air of the bloodoath in the* Dusk of the Gods.*)

Hangende Hunger,
Fragende Frau,
Macht uns alle kaputt.

ZOE: (*Tragically.*) Hamlet, I am thy father's gimlet! (*She takes his hand.*) Blue eyes beauty I'll read your hand. (*She points to his forehead.*) No wit, no wrinkles. (*She counts.*) Two, three, Mars, that's courage. (*Stephen shakes his head.*) No kid.

LYNCH: Sheet lightning courage. The youth who could not shiver and shake. (*To Zoe.*) Who taught you palmistry?

ZOE: (*Turns.*) Ask my ballocks that I haven't got. (*To Stephen.*) I see it in your face. The eye, like that. (*She frowns with lowered head.*)

LYNCH: (*Laughing, slaps Kitty behind twice.*) Like that. Pandybat.

(*Twice loudly a pandybat cracks, the coffin of the pianola flies open, the bald little round jack-in-the-box head of Father Dolan springs up.*)

FATHER DOLAN: Any boy want flogging? Broke his glasses? Lazy idle little schemer. See it in your eye.

(*Mild, benign, rectorial, reproving, the head of Don John Conmee rises from the pianola coffin.*)

DON JOHN CONMEE: Now, Father Dolan! Now. I'm sure that Stephen is a very good little boy!

ZOE: (*Examining Stephen's palm.*) Woman's hand.

STEPHEN: (*Murmurs.*) Continue. Lie. Hold me. Caress. I never could read His handwriting except His criminal thumbprint on the haddock.

ZOE: What day were you born?

STEPHEN: Thursday. Today.

ZOE: Thursday's child has far to go. (*She traces lines on his hand.*) Line of fate. Influential friends.

FLORRY: (*Pointing.*) Imagination.

ZOE: Mount of the moon. You'll meet with a . . . (*She peers at his hands abruptly.*) I won't tell you what's not good for you. Or do you want to know?

BLOOM: (*Detaches her fingers and offers his palm.*) More harm than good. Here. Read mine.

BELLA: Show. (*She turns up Bloom's hand.*) I thought so. Knobby knuckles for the women.

ZOE: (*Peering at Bloom's palm.*) Gridiron. Travels beyond the sea and marry money.

BLOOM: Wrong.

ZOE: (*Quickly.*) O, I see. Short little finger. Henpecked husband. That wrong?

(*Black Liz, a huge rooster hatching in a chalked circle, rises, stretches her wings and clucks.*)

BLACK LIZ: Gara. Klook. Klook. Klook.

(*She sidles from her newlaid egg and waddles off.*)

BLOOM: (*Points to his hand.*) That weal there is an accident. Fell and cut it twentytwo years ago. I was sixteen.

ZOE: I see, says the blind man. Tell us news.

STEPHEN: See? Moves to one great goal. I am twentytwo. Sixteen years ago he was twentytwo too. Sixteen years ago I twentytwo tumbled. Twentytwo years ago he sixteen fell off his hobbyhorse. (*He winces.*) Hurt my hand somewhere. Must see a dentist. Money?

(*Zoe whispers to Florry. They giggle. Bloom releases his hand and writes idly on the table in backhand, pencilling slow curves.*)

FLORRY: What?

(*A hackneycar, number three hundred and twentyfour, with a gallantbuttocked mare, driven by James Barton, Harmony Avenue, Donnybrook, trots past. Blazes Boylan and Lenehan sprawl swaying on the sideseats. The Ormond boots crouches behind on the axle. Sadly over the crossblind Lydia Douce and Mina Kennedy gaze.*)

THE BOOTS: (*Jogging, mocks them with thumb and wriggling wormfingers.*) Haw haw have you the horn?

(*Bronze by gold they whisper.*)

ZOE: (*To Florry.*) Whisper.

(*They whisper again.*)

(*Over the well of the car Blazes Boylan leans, his boater straw set sideways, a red flower in his mouth. Lenehan in yachtsman's cap and white shoes officiously detaches a long hair from Blazes Boylan's coat shoulder.*)

LENEHAN: Ho! What do I here behold? Were you brushing the cobwebs off a few quims?

BOYLAN: (*Sated, smiles.*) Plucking a turkey.

LENEHAN: A good night's work.

BOYLAN: (*Holding up four thick bluntungulated fingers, winks.*) Blazes Kate! Up to sample or your money back. (*He holds out a forefinger.*) Smell that.

LENEHAN: (*Smells gleefully.*) Ah! Lobster and mayonnaise. Ah!

ZOE AND FLORRY: (*Laugh together.*) Ha ha ha ha.

BOYLAN: (*Jumps surely from the car and calls loudly for all to hear.*) Hello, Bloom! Mrs Bloom dressed yet?

BLOOM: (*In flunkey's prune plush coat and kneebreeches, buff stockings and powdered wig.*) I'm afraid not, sir. The last articles . . .

BOYLAN: (*Tosses him sixpence.*) Here, to buy yourself a gin and splash. (*He hangs his hat smartly on a peg of Bloom's antlered head.*) Show me in. I have a little private business with your wife, you understand?

BLOOM: Thank you, sir. Yes, sir. Madam Tweedy is in her bath, sir.

MARION: He ought to feel himself highly honoured. (*She plops splashing out of the water.*) Raoul darling, come and dry me. I'm in my pelt. Only my new hat and a carriage sponge.

BOYLAN: (*A merry twinkle in his eye.*) Topping!

BELLA: What? What is it?

(*Zoe whispers to her.*)

MARION: Let him look, the pishogue! Pimp! And scourge himself! I'll write to a powerful prostitute or Bartholomona, the bearded woman, to raise weals out on him an inch thick and make him bring me back a signed and stamped receipt.

BOYLAN: (*Clasps himself.*) Here, I can't hold this little lot much longer. (*He strides off on stiff cavalry legs.*)

BELLA: (*Laughing.*) Ho ho ho ho.

BOYLAN: (*To Bloom, over his shoulder.*) You can apply your eye to the keyhole and play with yourself while I just go through her a few times.

BLOOM: Thank you, sir. I will, sir. May I bring two men chums to witness the deed and take a snapshot? (*He holds out an ointment jar.*) Vaseline, sir? Orangeflower . . .? Lukewarm water . . .?

KITTY: (*From the sofa.*) Tell us, Florry. Tell us. What . . .

(*Florry whispers to her. Whispering lovewords murmur, liplapping loudly, poppysmic plopslop.*)

MINA KENNEDY: (*Her eyes upturned.*) O, it must be like the scent of geraniums and lovely peaches! O, he simply idolises every bit of her! Stuck together! Covered with kisses!

LYDIA DOUCE: (*Her mouth opening.*) Yumyum. O, he's carrying her round the room doing it! Ride a cockhorse. You could hear them in Paris and New York. Like mouthfuls of strawberries and cream.

KITTY: (*Laughing.*) Hee hee hee.

BOYLAN'S VOICE: (*Sweetly, hoarsely, in the pit of his stomach.*) Ah! Godblazeqrukbrukarchkrasht!

MARION'S VOICE: (*Hoarsely, sweetly, rising to her throat.*) O! Weeshwashtkissinapooisthnapoohuck?

BLOOM: (*His eyes wildly dilated, clasps himself.*) Show! Hide! Show! Plough her! More! Shoot!

BELLA, ZOE, FLORRY, KITTY: Ho ho! Ha ha! Hee hee!

LYNCH: (*Points.*) The mirror up to nature. (*He laughs.*) Hu hu hu hu hu!

(*Stephen and Bloom gaze in the mirror. The face of William Shakespeare, beardless, appears there, rigid in facial paralysis, crowned by the reflection of the reindeer antlered hatrack in the hall.*)

SHAKESPEARE: (*In dignified ventriloquy.*) 'Tis the loud laugh bespeaks the vacant mind. (*To Bloom.*) Thou thoughtest as how thou wastest invisible. Gaze. (*He crows with a black capon's laugh.*) Iagogo! How my Oldfellow chokit his Thursdaymornun. Iagogogo!

BLOOM: (*Smiles yellowly at the three whores.*) When will I hear the joke?

ZOE: Before you're twice married and once a widower.

BLOOM: Lapses are condoned. Even the great Napoleon when measurements were taken next the skin after his death . . .

(*Mrs Dignam, widow woman, her snubnose and cheeks flushed with deathtalk, tears and Tunney's tawny sherry, hurries by in her weeds, her bonnet awry, rouging and powdering her cheeks, lips and nose, a pen chivvying her brood of cygnets. Beneath her skirt appear her late husband's everyday trousers and turnedup boots, large eights. She holds a Scottish widow's insurance policy and a large marquee umbrella under which her brood run with her, Patsy hopping on one shod foot, his collar loose, a hank of porksteaks dangling, Freddy whimpering, Susy with a crying cod's mouth, Alice struggling with the baby. She cuffs them on, her streamers flaunting aloft.*)

FREDDY: Ah, ma, you're dragging me along!

SUSY: Mamma, the beeftea is fizzing over!

SHAKESPEARE: (*With paralytic rage.*) Weda seca whokilla farst.

(*The face of Martin Cunningham, bearded, refeatures Shakespeare's beardless face. The marquee umbrella sways drunkenly, the children run aside. Under the umbrella appears Mrs Cunningham in Merry Widow hat and kimono gown. She glides sidling and bowing, twirling japanesily.*)

MRS CUNNINGHAM: (*Sings.*)

And they call me the jewel of Asia!

MARTIN CUNNINGHAM: (*Gazes on her, impassive.*) Immense! Most bloody awful demirep!

STEPHEN: *Et exaltabuntur cornua iusti.* Queens lay with prize bulls. Remember Pasiphae for whose lust my grandoldgrossfather made the first confessionbox. Forget not Madam Grissel Steevens nor the suine scions of the house of Lambert. And Noah was drunk with wine. And his ark was open.

BELLA: None of that here. Come to the wrong shop.

LYNCH: Let him alone. He's back from Paris.

ZOE: (*Runs to stephen and links him.*) O go on! Give us some parleyvoo.

(*Stephen claps hat on head and leaps over to the fireplace where he stands with shrugged shoulders, finny hands outspread, a painted smile on his face.*)

LYNCH: (*Pommelling on the sofa.*) Rmm Rmm Rmm Rrrrrrmmmmm.

STEPHEN: (*Gabbles with marionette jerks.*) Thousand places of entertainment to expense your evenings with lovely ladies saling gloves and other things perhaps hers heart beerchops perfect fashionable house very eccentric where lots cocottes beautiful dressed much about princesses like are dancing cancan and walking there parisian clowneries extra foolish for bachelors foreigns the same if talking a poor english how much smart they are on things love and sensations voluptuous. Misters very selects for is pleasure must to visit heaven and hell show with mortuary candles and they tears silver which occur every night. Perfectly shocking terrific of religion's things mockery seen in universal world. All chic womans which arrive full of modesty then disrobe and squeal loud to see vampire man debauch nun very fresh young with *dessous troublants.* (*He clacks his tongue loudly.*) Ho, là là! Ce pif qu'il a!

LYNCH: *Vive le vampire!*

THE WHORES: Bravo! Parleyvoo!

STEPHEN: (*Grimacing with head back, laughs loudly, clapping himself.*) Great success of laughing. Angels much prostitutes like and holy apostles big damn ruffians. *Demimondaines* nicely handsome sparkling of diamonds very amiable costumed. Or do you are fond better what belongs they moderns pleasure turpitude of old mans? (*He points about him with grotesque gestures which Lynch and the whores reply to.*) Caoutchouc statue woman reversible or lifesize tompeeptom of virgins nudities very lesbic the kiss five ten times. Enter, gentleman, to see in mirror every positions trapezes all that machine there besides also if desire act awfully bestial butcher's boy pollutes in warm veal liver or omlet on the belly *pièce de Shakespeare.*

BELLA: (*Clapping her belly sinks back on the sofa, with a shout of laughter.*) An omelette on the . . . Ho! ho! ho! ho! . . . Omelette on the . . .

STEPHEN: (*Mincingly.*) I love you, sir darling. Speak you englishman tongue for *double entente cordiale.* O yes, *mon loup.* How much cost? Waterloo. Watercloset. (*He ceases suddenly and holds up a forefinger.*)

BELLA: (*Laughing.*) Omelette . . .

THE WHORES: (*Laughing.*) Encore! Encore!

STEPHEN: Mark me. I dreamt of a watermelon.

ZOE: Go abroad and love a foreign lady.

LYNCH: Across the world for a wife.

FLORRY: Dreams goes by contraries.

STEPHEN: (*Extends his arms.*) It was here. Street of harlots. In Serpentine avenue Beelzebub showed me her, a fubsy widow. Where's the red carpet spread?

BLOOM: (*Approaching Stephen.*) Look . . .

STEPHEN: No, I flew. My foes beneath me. And ever shall be. World without end. (*He cries.*) *Pater!* Free!

BLOOM: I say, look . . .

STEPHEN: Break my spirit, will he? O *merde alors!* (*He cries, his vulture talons sharpened.*) Hola! Hillyho!

(*Simon Dedalus' voice hilloes in answer, somewhat sleepy but ready.*)

SIMON: That's all right. (*He swoops uncertainly through the air, wheeling, uttering cries of heartening, on strong ponderous buzzard wings.*) Ho, boy! Are you going to win? Hoop! Pschatt! Stable with those halfcastes. Wouldn't let them within the bawl of an ass. Head up! Keep our flag flying! An eagle gules volant in a field argent displayed. Ulster king at arms! Haihoop! (*He makes the beagle's call, giving tongue.*) Bulbul! Burblblburblbl! Hai, boy!

(*The fronds and spaces of the wallpaper file rapidly across country. A stout fox, drawn from covert, brush pointed, having buried his grandmother, runs swift for the open, brighteyed, seeking badger earth, under the leaves. The pack of staghounds follows, nose to the ground, sniffing their quarry, beaglebaying, burblbrbling to be blooded. Ward Union huntsmen and huntswomen live with them, hot for a kill. From Six Mile Point, Flathouse, Nine Mile Stone follow the footpeople with knotty sticks, hayforks, salmongaffs, lassos, flockmasters with stockwhips, bearbaiters with tomtoms, toreadors with bullswords, grey negroes waving torches. The crowd bawls of dicers, crown and anchor players, thimbleriggers, broadsmen. Crows and touts, hoarse bookies in high wizard hats clamour deafeningly.*)

THE CROWD:

> Card of the races. Racing card!
> Ten to one the field!
> Tommy on the clay here! Tommy on the clay!
> Ten to one bar one! Ten to one bar one!
> Try your luck on Spinning Jenny!
> Ten to one bar one!
> Sell the monkey, boys! Sell the monkey!
> I'll give ten to one!
> Ten to one bar one!

(*A dark horse, riderless, bolts like a phantom past the winningpost, his mane moonfoaming, his eyeballs stars. The field follows, a bunch of bucking mounts. Skeleton horses, Sceptre, Maximum the Second, Zinfandel, the Duke of Westminster's Shotover, Repulse, the Duke of Beaufort's Ceylon, prix de Paris. Dwarfs ride them, rustyarmoured, leaping, leaping in their, in their saddles. Last in a drizzle of rain on a brokenwinded isabelle nag, Cock of the North, the favourite, honey cap, green jacket, orange sleeves, Garrett Deasy up, gripping the reins, a hockeystick at the ready. His nag on spavined whitegaitered feet jogs along the rocky road.*)

THE ORANGE LODGES: (*Jeering.*) Get down and push, mister. Last lap! You'll be home the night!

GARRETT DEASY: (*Bolt upright, his nailscraped face plastered with postagestamps, brandishes his hockeystick, his blue eyes flashing in the prism of the chandelier as his mount lopes by at schooling gallop.*)

Per vias rectas!

(*A yoke of buckets leopards all over him and his rearing nag a torrent of mutton broth with dancing coins of carrots, barley, onions, turnips, potatoes.*)

THE GREEN LODGES: Soft day, sir John! Soft day, your honour!

(*Private Carr, Private Compton and Cissy Caffrey pass beneath the windows, singing in discord.*)

STEPHEN: Hark! Our friend noise in the street.

ZOE: (*Holds up her hand.*) Stop!

PRIVATE CARR, PRIVATE COMPTON AND CISSY CAFFREY:

> Yet I've a sort of a
> Yorkshire relish for . . .

ZOE: That's me. (*She claps her hands.*) Dance! Dance! (*She runs to the pianola.*) Who has twopence?

BLOOM: Who'll . . .?

LYNCH: (*Handing her coins.*) Here.

STEPHEN: (*Cracking his fingers impatiently.*) Quick! Quick! Where's my augur's rod? (*He runs to the piano and takes his ashplant, beating his foot in tripudium.*)

ZOE: (*Turns the drumhandle.*) There.

(*She drops two pennies in the slot. Gold, pink and violet lights start forth. The drum turns purring in low hesitation waltz. Professor Goodwin, in a bowknotted periwig, in court dress, wearing a stained inverness cape, bent in two from incredible age, totters across the room, his hands fluttering. He sits tinily on the pianostool and lifts and beats handless sticks of arms on the keyboard, nodding with damsel's grace, his bowknot bobbing.*)

ZOE: (*Twirls round herself, heeltapping.*) Dance. Anybody here for there? Who'll dance? Clear the table.

(*The pianola with changing lights plays in waltz time the prelude of* My Girl's a Yorkshire Girl. *Stephen throws his ashplant on the table and seizes Zoe round the waist. Florry and Bella push the table towards the fireplace. Stephen, arming Zoe with exaggerated grace, begins to waltz her round the room. Bloom stands aside. Her sleeve falling from gracing arms, reveals a white fleshflower of vaccination. Between the curtains Professor Maginni inserts a leg on the toepoint of which spins a silk hat. With a deft kick he sends it spinning to his crown and jauntyhatted skates in. He wears a slate frockcoat with claret silk lapels, a gorget of cream tulle, a green lowcut waistcoat, stock collar with white kerchief, tight lavender trousers, patent pumps and canary gloves. In his buttonhole is an immense dahlia. He twirls in reversed directions a clouded cane, then wedges it tight in his oxter. He places a hand lightly on his breastbone, bows, and fondles his flower and buttons.*)

MAGINNI: The poetry of motion, art of calisthenics. No connection with Madam Legget Byrne's or Levenston's. Fancy dress balls arranged. Deportment. The Katty Lanner step. So. Watch me! My terpsichorean abilities. (*He minuets forward three paces on tripping bee's feet.*) Tout le monde en avant! Révérence! Tout le monde en place!

(*The prelude ceases. Professor Goodwin, beating vague arms shrivels, sinks, his live cape falling about the stool. The air in firmer waltz time sounds. Stephen and Zoe circle freely. The lights change, glow, fade gold rosy violet.*)

THE PIANOLA:

> Two young fellows were talking about their girls,
> girls, girls,
> Sweethearts they'd left behind . . .

(From a corner the morning hours run out, goldhaired, slimsandalled, in girlish blue, waspwaisted, with innocent hands. Nimbly they dance, twirling their skipping ropes. The hours of noon follow in amber gold. Laughing, linked, high haircombs flashing, they catch the sun in mocking mirrors, lifting their arms.)

MAGINNI: *(Clipclaps glovesilent hands.) Carré! Avant deux!* Breathe evenly! *Balance!*

(The morning and noon hours waltz in their places, turning, advancing to each other, shaping their curves, bowing visavis. Cavaliers behind them arch and suspend their arms, with hands descending to, touching, rising from their shoulders.)

HOURS: You may touch my.

CAVALIERS: May I touch your?

HOURS: O, but lightly!

CAVALIERS: O, so lightly!

THE PIANOLA:

> My little shy little lass has a waist.

(Zoe and Stephen turn boldly with looser swing. The twilight hours advance from long landshadows, dispersed, lagging, languideyed, their cheeks delicate with cipria and false faint bloom. They are in grey gauze with dark bat sleeves that flutter in the land breeze.)

MAGINNI: *Avant huit! Traversé! Salut! Cours de mains! Croisé!*

(The night hours, one by one, steal to the last place. Morning, noon and twilight hours retreat before them. They are masked, with daggered hair and bracelets of dull bells. Weary they curchycurchy under veils.)

THE BRACELETS: Heigho! Heigho!

ZOE: *(Twirling, her hand to her brow.)* O!

MAGINNI: *Les tiroirs! Chaîne de dames! La corbeille! Dos à dos!*

(Arabesquing wearily they weave a pattern on the floor, weaving, unweaving, curtseying, twirling, simply swirling.)

ZOE: I'm giddy!

(She frees herself, droops on a chair. Stephen seizes Florry and turns with her.)

MAGINNI: *Boulangère! Les ronds! Les ponts! Chevaux de bois! Escargots!*

(*Twining, receding, with interchanging hands the night hours link each each with arching arms in a mosaic of movements. Stephen and Florry turn cumbrously.*)

MAGINNI: *Dansez avec vos dames! Changez de dames! Donnez le petit bouquet à votre dame! Remerciez!*

THE PIANOLA:

> Best, best of all,
> Baraabum!

KITTY: (*Jumps up.*) O, they played that on the hobbyhorses at the *Mirus* bazaar!

(*She runs to Stephen. He leaves Florry brusquely and seizes Kitty. A screaming bittern's harsh high whistle shrieks. Groangrousegurgling Toft's cumbersome whirligig turns slowly the room right roundabout the room.*)

THE PIANOLA:

> My girl's a Yorkshire girl.

ZOE:

> Yorkshire through and through. Come on all!

(*She seizes Florry and waltzes her.*)

STEPHEN: *Pas seul!*

(*He wheels Kitty into Lynch's arms, snatches up his ashplant from the table and takes the floor. All wheel whirl waltz twirl. Bloombella Kittylynch Florryzoe jujuby women. Stephen with hat ashplant frogsplits in middle highkicks with skykicking mouth shut hand clasp part under thigh. With clang tinkle boomhammer tallyho hornblower blue green yellow flashes Toft's cumbersome turns with hobbyhorse riders from gilded snakes dangled, bowels fandango leaping spurn soil foot and fall again.*)

THE PIANOLA:

> Though she's a factory lass
> And wears no fancy clothes.

(*Closeclutched swift swifter with glareblareflare scudding they scootlootshoot lumbering by. Baraabum!*)

TUTTI: Encore! Bis! Bravo! Encore!

SIMON: Think of your mother's people!

STEPHEN: Dance of death.

(*Bang fresh barang bang of lacquey's bell, horse, nag, steer, piglings, Conmee on Christass, lame crutch and leg sailor in cockboat armfolded ropepulling hitching stamp hornpipe through and through. Baraabum! On nags hogs bellhorses Gadarene swine Corny in coffin. Steel shark stone onehandled Nelson two trickies Frauenzimmer plumstained from pram falling bawling. Gum he's a champion. Fuseblue peer from barrel rev. evensong Love on hackney jaunt Blazes blind coddoubled bicyclers Dilly with snowcake no fancy clothes. Then in last switchback lumbering up and down bump mashtub sort of viceroy and reine relish for tublumber bumpshire rose. Baraabum!*)

(*The couples fall aside. Stephen whirls giddily. Room whirls back. Eyes closed he totters. Red rails fly spacewards. Stars all around suns turn roundabout. Bright midges dance on walls. He stops dead.*)

STEPHEN: Ho!

(*Stephen's mother, emaciated, rises stark through the floor, in leper grey with a wreath of faded orangeblossoms and a torn bridal veil, her face worn and noseless, green with gravemould. Her hair is scant and lank. She fixes her bluecircled hollow eyesockets on Stephen and opens her toothless mouth uttering a silent word. A choir of virgins and confessors sing voicelessly.*)

THE CHOIR:

Liliata rutilantium te confessorum . . .
Iubilantium te virginum . . .

(*From the top of a tower Buck Mulligan, in particoloured jester's dress of puce and yellow and clown's cap with curling bell, stands gaping at her, a smoking buttered split scone in his hand.*)

BUCK MULLIGAN: She's beastly dead. The pity of it! Mulligan meets the afflicted mother. (*He upturns his eyes.*) Mercurial Malachi!

THE MOTHER: (*With the subtle smile of death's madness.*) I was once the beautiful May Goulding. I am dead.

STEPHEN: (*Horrorstruck.*) Lemur, who are you? No. What bogeyman's trick is this?

BUCK MULLIGAN: (*Shakes his curling capbell.*) The mockery of it! Kinch dogsbody killed her bitchbody. She kicked the bucket. (*Tears of molten butter fall from his eyes on to the scone.*) Our great sweet mother! *Epi oinopa ponton.*

536

THE MOTHER: (*Comes nearer, breathing upon him softly her breath of wetted ashes.*) All must go through it, Stephen. More women than men in the world. You too. Time will come.

STEPHEN: (*Choking with fright, remorse and horror.*) They say I killed you, mother. He offended your memory. Cancer did it, not I. Destiny.

THE MOTHER: (*A green rill of bile trickling from a side of her mouth.*) You sang that song to me. *Love's bitter mystery.*

STEPHEN: (*Eagerly.*) Tell me the word, mother, if you know now. The word known to all men.

THE MOTHER: Who saved you the night you jumped into the train at Dalkey with Paddy Lee? Who had pity for you when you were sad among the strangers? Prayer is allpowerful. Prayer for the suffering souls in the Ursuline manual and forty days' indulgence. Repent, Stephen.

STEPHEN: The ghoul! Hyena!

THE MOTHER: I pray for you in my other world. Get Dilly to make you that boiled rice every night after your brainwork. Years and years I loved you, O, my son, my firstborn, when you lay in my womb.

ZOE: (*Fanning herself with the grate fan.*) I'm melting!

FLORRY: (*Points to Stephen.*) Look! He's white.

BLOOM: (*Goes to the window to open it more.*) Giddy.

THE MOTHER: (*With smouldering eyes.*) Repent! O, the fire of hell!

STEPHEN: (*Panting.*) His noncorrosive sublimate! The corpsechewer! Raw head and bloody bones.

THE MOTHER: (*Her face drawing near and nearer, sending out an ashen breath.*) Beware! (*She raises her blackened withered right arm slowly towards Stephen's breast with outstretched finger.*) Beware God's hand! (*A green crab with malignant red eyes sticks deep its grinning claws in Stephen's heart.*)

STEPHEN: (*Strangled with rage.*) Shite! (*His features grow drawn grey and old.*)

BLOOM: (*At the window.*) What?

STEPHEN: *Ah non, par exemple!* The intellectual imagination! With me all or not at all. *Non serviam!*

FLORRY: Give him some cold water. Wait. (*She rushes out.*)

THE MOTHER: (*Wrings her hands slowly, moaning desperately.*) O Sacred Heart of Jesus, have mercy on him! Save him from hell, O Divine Sacred Heart!

STEPHEN: No! No! No! Break my spirit, all of you, if you can! I'll bring you all to heel!

THE MOTHER: (*In the agony of her deathrattle.*) Have mercy on Stephen, Lord, for my sake! Inexpressible was my anguish when expiring with love, grief and agony on Mount Calvary.

STEPHEN: *Nothung!*

(*He lifts his ashplant high with both hands and smashes the chandelier. Time's livid final flame leaps and, in the following darkness, ruin of all space, shattered glass and toppling masonry.*)

THE GASJET: Pwfungg!

BLOOM: Stop!

LYNCH: (*Rushes forward and seizes Stephen's hand.*) Here! Hold on! Don't run amok!

BELLA: Police!

(*Stephen, abandoning his ashplant, his head and arms thrown back stark, beats the ground and flies from the room, past the whores at the door.*)

BELLA: (*Screams.*) After him!

(*The two whores rush to the halldoor. Lynch and Kitty and Zoe stampede from the room. They talk excitedly. Bloom follows, returns.*)

THE WHORES: (*Jammed in the doorway, pointing.*) Down there.

ZOE: (*Pointing.*) There. There's something up.

BELLA: Who pays for the lamp? (*She seizes Bloom's coattail.*) Here, you were with him. The lamp's broken.

BLOOM: (*Rushes to the hall, rushes back.*) What lamp, woman?

A WHORE: He tore his coat.

BELLA: (*Her eyes hard with anger and cupidity, points.*) Who's to pay for that? Ten shillings. You're a witness.

BLOOM: (*Snatches up Stephen's ashplant.*) Me? Ten shillings? Haven't you lifted enough off him? Didn't he . . .?

BELLA: (*Loudly.*) Here, none of your tall talk. This isn't a brothel. A ten shilling house.

BLOOM: (*His head under the lamp, pulls the chain. Pulling, the gasjet lights up a crushed mauve purple shade. He raises the ashplant.*) Only the chimney's broken. Here is all he . . .

BELLA: (*Shrinks back and screams.*) Jesus! Don't!

BLOOM: (*Warding off a blow.*) To show you how he hit the paper. There's not sixpenceworth of damage done. Ten shillings!

FLORRY: (*With a glass of water, enters.*) Where is he?

BELLA: Do you want me to call the police?

BLOOM: O, I know. Bulldog on the premises. But he's a Trinity student. Patrons of your establishment. Gentlemen that pay the rent. (*He makes a masonic sign.*) Know what I mean? Nephew of the vicechancellor. You don't want a scandal.

BELLA: (*Angrily.*) Trinity. Coming down here ragging after the boatraces and paying nothing. Are you my commander here or? Where is he? I'll charge him! Disgrace him, I will! (*She shouts.*) Zoe! Zoe!

BLOOM: (*Urgently.*) And if it were your own son in Oxford? (*Warningly.*) I know.

BELLA: (*Almost speechless.*) Who are. Incog!

ZOE: (*In the doorway.*) There's a row on.

BLOOM: What? Where? (*He throws a shilling on the table and starts.*) That's for the chimney. Where? I need mountain air.

(*He hurries out through the hall. The whores point. Florry follows, spilling water from her tilted tumbler. On the doorstep all the whores clustered talk volubly, pointing to the right where the fog has cleared off. From the left arrives a jingling hackney car. It slows to in front of the house. Bloom at the halldoor perceives Corny Kelleher who is about to dismount from the car with two silent lechers. He averts his face. Bella from within the hall urges on her whores. They blow ickylickysticky yumyum kisses. Corny Kelleher replies with a ghastly lewd smile. The silent lechers turn to pay the jarvey. Zoe and Kitty still point right. Bloom, parting them swiftly, draws his caliph's hood and poncho and hurries down the steps with sideways face. Incog Haroun al Raschid he flits behind the silent lechers and hastens on by the railings with fleet step of a pard strewing the drag behind him, torn envelopes drenched in aniseed. The ashplant marks his stride. A pack of bloodhounds, led by Hornblower of Trinity brandishing a dogwhip in tallyho cap and an old pair of grey trousers, follows from far, picking up the scent, nearer, baying, panting, at fault, breaking away, throwing their tongues, biting his heels, leaping at his tail. He walks, runs, zigzags, gallops, lugs laid back. He is pelted with gravel, cabbagestumps, biscuitboxes, eggs, potatoes, dead codfish, woman's slipperslappers. After him freshfound the hue and cry zigzag gallops in hot pursuit of follow my leader: 65 C, 66 C, night watch, John Henry Menton, Wisdom Hely, V. B. Dillon, Councillor Nannetti, Alexander Keyes, Larry O'Rourke, Joe Cuffe, Mrs O'Dowd, Pisser Burke, The Nameless One, Mrs Riordan, The Citizen, Garryowen, Whodoyoucallhim, Strangeface, Fellowthatsolike, Sawhimbefore, Chapwithawen, Chris Callinan, sir Charles Cameron, Benjamin Dollard, Lenehan, Bartell d'Arcy, Joe Hynes, red Murray, editor Brayden, T. M. Healy, Mr Justice Fitzgibbon, John Howard Parnell, the reverend Tinned Salmon, Professor Joly, Mrs Breen, Denis Breen, Theodore Purefoy, Mina Purefoy, the Westland Row postmistress, C. P. M'Coy, friend of Lyons, Hoppy*

Holohan, maninthestreet, othermaninthestreet, Footballboots, pugnosed driver, rich protestant lady, Davy Byrne, Mrs Ellen M'Guinness, Mrs Joe Gallaher, George Lidwell, Jimmy Henry on corns, Superintendent Laracy, Father Cowley, Crofton out of the Collector-general's, Dan Dawson, dental surgeon Bloom with tweezers, Mrs Bob Doran, Mrs Kennefick, Mrs Wyse Nolan, John Wyse Nolan, handsomemarriedwomanrubbedagainstwidebehindinClonskea tram, the bookseller of Sweets of Sin, *Miss Dubedatandshedidbedad, Mesdames Gerald and Stanislaus Moran of Roebuck, the managing clerk of Drimmie's, Wetherup, colonel Hayes, Mastiansky, Citron, Penrose, Aaron Figatner, Moses Herzog, Michael E Geraghty, Inspector Troy, Mrs Galbraith, the constable off Eccles street corner, old doctor Brady with stethoscope, the mystery man on the beach, a retriever, Mrs Miriam Dandrade and all her lovers.*)

THE HUE AND CRY: (*Helterskelterpelterwelter.*) He's Bloom! Stop Bloom! Stopabloom! Stopperrobber! Hi! Hi! Stophim on the corner!

(*At the corner of Beaver street beneath the scaffolding Bloom panting stops on the fringe of the noisy quarrelling knot, a lot not knowing a jot what hi! hi! row and wrangle round the whowhat brawlaltogether.*)

STEPHEN: (*With elaborate gestures, breathing deeply and slowly.*) You are my guests. Uninvited. By virtue of the fifth of George and seventh of Edward. History to blame. Fabled by mothers of memory.

PRIVATE CARR: (*To Cissy Caffrey.*) Was he insulting you?

STEPHEN: Addressed her in vocative feminine. Probably neuter. Ungenitive.

VOICES: No, he didn't. I seen him. The girl there. He was in Mrs Cohen's. What's up? Soldier and civilian.

CISSY CAFFREY: I was in company with the soldiers and they left me to do—you know, and the young man run up behind me. But I'm faithful to the man that's treating me though I'm only a shilling whore.

STEPHEN: (*Catches sight of Lynch's and Kitty's heads.*) Hail, Sisyphus. (*He points to himself and the others.*) Poetic. Uropoetic.

VOICES: Shes faithfultheman.

CISSY CAFFREY: Yes, to go with him. And me with a soldier friend.

PRIVATE COMPTON: He doesn't half want a thick ear, the blighter. Biff him one, Harry.

PRIVATE CARR: (*To Cissy.*) Was he insulting you while me and him was having a piss?

LORD TENNYSON: (*Gentleman poet in Union Jack blazer and cricket flannels, bareheaded, flowingbearded.*) Theirs not to reason why.

PRIVATE COMPTON: Biff him, Harry.

STEPHEN: (*To Private Compton.*) I don't know your name but you are quite right. Doctor Swift says one man in armour will beat ten men in their shirts. Shirt is synechdoche. Part for the whole.

CISSY CAFFREY: (*To the crowd.*) No, I was with the privates.

STEPHEN: (*Amiably.*) Why not? The bold soldier boy. In my opinion every lady for example . . .

PRIVATE CARR: (*His cap awry, advances to Stephen.*) Say, how would it be, governor, if I was to bash in your jaw?

STEPHEN: (*Looks up to the sky.*) How? Very unpleasant. Noble art of selfpretence. Personally, I detest action. (*He waves his hand.*) Hand hurts me slightly. *Enfin ce sont vos oignons.* (*To Cissy Caffrey.*) Some trouble is on here. What is it precisely?

DOLLY GRAY: (*From her balcony waves her handkerchief, giving the sign of the heroine of Jericho.*) Rahab. Cook's son, goodbye. Safe home to Dolly. Dream of the girl you left behind and she will dream of you.

(*The soldiers turn their swimming eyes.*)

BLOOM: (*Elbowing through the crowd, plucks Stephen's sleeve vigorously.*) Come now, professor, that carman is waiting.

STEPHEN: (*Turns.*) Eh? (*He disengages himself.*) Why should I not speak to him or to any human being who walks upright upon this oblate orange? (*He points his finger.*) I'm not afraid of what I can talk to if I see his eye. Retaining the perpendicular.

(*He staggers a pace back.*)

BLOOM: (*Propping him.*) Retain your own.

STEPHEN: (*Laughs emptily.*) My centre of gravity is displaced. I have forgotten the trick. Let us sit down somewhere and discuss. Struggle for life is the law of existence but but human philirenists, notably the tsar and the king of England, have invented arbitration. (*He taps his brow.*) But in here it is I must kill the priest and the king.

BIDDY THE CLAP: Did you hear what the professor said? He's a professor out of the college.

CUNTY KATE: I did. I heard that.

BIDDY THE CLAP: He expresses himself with such marked refinement of phraseology.

CUNTY KATE: Indeed, yes. And at the same time with such apposite trenchancy.

PRIVATE CARR: (*Pulls himself free and comes forward.*) What's that you're saying about my king?

(*Edward the Seventh appears in an archway. He wears a white jersey on which an image of the Sacred Heart is stitched with the insignia of Garter and Thistle, Golden Fleece, Elephant of Denmark, Skinner's and Probyn's horse, Lincoln's Inn bencher and ancient and honourable artillery company of Massachusetts. He sucks a red jujube. He is robed as a grand elect perfect and sublime mason with trowel and apron, marked* made in Germany. *In his left hand he holds a plasterer's bucket on which is printed* Défense d'uriner. *A roar of welcome greets him.*)

EDWARD THE SEVENTH: (*Slowly, solemnly but indistinctly.*) Peace, perfect peace. For identification, bucket in my hand. Cheerio, boys. (*He turns to his subjects.*) We have come here to witness a clean straight fight and we heartily wish both men the best of good luck. Mahak makar a bak.

(*He shakes hands with Private Carr, Private Compton, Stephen, Bloom and Lynch. General applause. Edward the Seventh lifts his bucket graciously in acknowledgment.*)

PRIVATE CARR: (*To Stephen.*) Say it again.

STEPHEN: (*Nervous, friendly, pulls himself up.*) I understand your point of view though I have no king myself for the moment. This is the age of patent medicines. A discussion is difficult down here. But this is the point. You die for your country. Suppose. (*He places his arm on Private Carr's sleeve.*) Not that I wish it for you. But I say: Let my country die for me. Up to the present it has done so. I didn't want it to die. Damn death. Long live life!

EDWARD THE SEVENTH: (*Levitates over heaps of slain, in the garb and with the halo of Joking Jesus, a white jujube in his phosphorescent face.*)

My methods are new and are causing surprise.
To make the blind see I throw dust in their eyes.

STEPHEN: Kings and unicorns! (*He falls back a pace.*) Come somewhere and we'll . . . What was that girl saying? . . .

PRIVATE COMPTON: Eh, Harry, give him a kick in the knackers. Stick one into Jerry.

BLOOM: (*To the privates, softly.*) He doesn't know what he's saying. Taken a little more than is good for him. Absinthe. Greeneyed monster. I know him. He's a gentleman, a poet. It's all right.

STEPHEN: (*Nods, smiling and laughing.*) Gentleman, patriot, scholar and judge of impostors.

PRIVATE CARR: I don't give a bugger who he is.

PRIVATE COMPTON: We don't give a bugger who he is.

STEPHEN: I seem to annoy them. Green rag to a bull.

(*Kevin Egan of Paris in black Spanish tasselled shirt and peep-o'-day boy's hat signs to Stephen.*)

KEVIN EGAN: H'lo! *Bonjour!* The *vieille ogresse* with the *dents jaunes.*

(*Patrice Egan peeps from behind, his rabbitface nibbling a quince leaf.*)

PATRICE: *Socialiste!*

DON EMILE PATRIZIO FRANZ RUPERT POPE HENNESSY: (*In medieval hauberk, two wild geese volant on his helm, with noble indignation points a mailed hand against the privates.*) Werf those eykes to footboden, big grand porcos of johnyellows todos covered of gravy!

BLOOM: (*To Stephen.*) Come home. You'll get into trouble.

STEPHEN: (*Swaying.*) I don't avoid it. He provokes my intelligence.

BIDDY THE CLAP: One immediately observes that he is of patrician lineage.

THE VIRAGO: Green above the red, says he. Wolfe Tone.

THE BAWD: The red's as good as the green. And better. Up the soldiers! Up King Edward!

A ROUGH: (*Laughs.*) Ay! Hands up to De Wet.

THE CITIZEN: (*With a huge emerald muffler and shillelagh, calls.*)

> May the God above
> Send down a dove
> With teeth as sharp as razors
> To slit the throats
> Of the English dogs
> That hanged our Irish leaders.

THE CROPPY BOY: (*The ropenoose round his neck, gripes in his issuing bowels with both hands.*)

> I bear no hate to a living thing,
> But I love my country beyond the king.

RUMBOLD, DEMON BARBER: (*Accompanied by two blackmasked assistants, advances with gladstone bag which he opens.*) Ladies and gents, cleaver purchased by Mrs Pearcy to slay Mogg. Knife with which Voisin dismembered the wife of a compatriot and hid remains in a sheet in the cellar, the unfortunate female's throat being cut from ear to ear. Phial containing arsenic retrieved from body of Miss Barron which sent Seddon to the gallows.

(*He jerks the rope. The assistants leap at the victim's legs and drag him downward, grunting: the croppy boy's tongue protrudes violently.*)

THE CROPPY BOY:

Horhot ho hray hor hother's hest.

(*He gives up the ghost. A violent erection of the hanged sends gouts of sperm spouting through his deathclothes on to the cobblestones. Mrs Bellingham, Mrs Yelverton Barry and the Honourable Mrs Mervyn Talboys rush forward with their handkerchiefs to sop it up.*)

RUMBOLD: I'm near it myself. (*He undoes the noose.*) Rope which hanged the awful rebel. Ten shillings a time. As applied to Her Royal Highness. (*He plunges his head into the gaping belly of the hanged and draws out his head again clotted with coiled and smoking entrails.*) My painful duty has now been done. God save the king!

EDWARD THE SEVENTH: (*Dances slowly, solemnly, rattling his bucket, and sings with soft contentment.*)

On coronation day, on coronation day,
O, won't we have a merry time,
Drinking whisky, beer and wine!

PRIVATE CARR: Here. What are you saying about my king?

STEPHEN: (*Throws up his hands.*) O, this is too monotonous! Nothing. He wants my money and my life, though want must be his master, for some brutish empire of his. Money I haven't. (*He searches his pockets vaguely.*) Gave it to someone.

PRIVATE CARR: Who wants your bleeding money?

STEPHEN: (*Tries to move off.*) Will someone tell me where I am least likely to meet these necessary evils? *Ça se voit aussi à Paris.* Not that I . . . But, by Saint Patrick . . .!

(*The women's heads coalesce. Old Gummy Granny in sugarloaf hat appears seated on a toadstool, the deathflower of the potato blight on her breast.*)

STEPHEN: Aha! I know you, gammer! Hamlet, revenge! The old sow that eats her farrow!

OLD GUMMY GRANNY: (*Rocking to and fro.*) Ireland's sweetheart, the king of Spain's daughter, alanna. Strangers in my house, bad manners to them! (*She keens with banshee woe.*) Ochone! Ochone! Silk of the kine! (*She wails.*) You met with poor old Ireland and how does she stand?

STEPHEN: How do I stand you? The hat trick! Where's the third person of the Blessed Trinity? Soggarth Aroon? The reverend Carrion Crow.

CISSY CAFFREY: (*Shrill.*) Stop them from fighting!

A ROUGH: Our men retreated.

PRIVATE CARR: (*Tugging at his belt.*) I'll wring the neck of any fucker says a word against my fucking king.

BLOOM: (*Terrified.*) He said nothing. Not a word. A pure misunderstanding.

THE CITIZEN: *Erin go bragh!*

(*Major Tweedy and the Citizen exhibit to each other medals, decorations, trophies of war, wounds. Both salute with fierce hostility.*)

PRIVATE COMPTON: Go it, Harry. Do him one in the eye. He's a proboer.

STEPHEN: Did I? When?

BLOOM: (*To the redcoats.*) We fought for you in South Africa, Irish missile troops. Isn't that history? Royal Dublin Fusiliers. Honoured by our monarch.

THE NAVVY: (*Staggering past.*) O, yes! O God, yes! O, make the kwawr a krowawr! O! Bo!

(*Casqued halberdiers in armour thrust forward a pentice of gutted spearpoints. Major Tweedy, moustached like Turko the terrible, in bearskin cap with hackleplume and accoutrements, with epaulettes, gilt chevrons and sabretaches, his breast bright with medals, toes the line. He gives the pilgrim warrior's sign of the knights templars.*)

MAJOR TWEEDY: (*Growls gruffly.*) Rorke's Drift! Up, guards, and at them! Mahar shalal hashbaz.

PRIVATE CARR: I'll do him in.

PRIVATE COMPTON: (*Waves the crowd back.*) Fair play, here. Make a bleeding butcher's shop of the bugger.

(*Massed bands blare* Garryowen *and* God save the King.)

CISSY CAFFREY: They're going to fight. For me!

CUNTY KATE: The brave and the fair.

BIDDY THE CLAP: Methinks yon sable knight will joust it with the best.

CUNTY KATE: (*Blushing deeply.*) Nay, madam. The gules doublet and merry saint George for me!

STEPHEN:

> The harlot's cry from street to street
> Shall weave Old Ireland's windingsheet.

PRIVATE CARR: (*Loosening his belt, shouts.*) I'll wring the neck of any fucking bastard says a word against my bleeding fucking king.

BLOOM: (*Shakes Cissy Caffrey's shoulders.*) Speak, you! Are you struck dumb? You are the link between nations and generations. Speak, woman, sacred lifegiver!

CISSY CAFFREY: (*Alarmed, seizes Private Carr's sleeve.*) Amn't I with you? Amn't I your girl? Cissy's your girl. (*She cries.*) Police!

STEPHEN: (*Ecstatically, to Cissy Caffrey.*)

> White thy fambles, red thy gan
> And thy quarrons dainty is.

VOICES: Police!

DISTANT VOICES: Dublin's burning! Dublin's burning! On fire, on fire!

(*Brimstone fires spring up. Dense clouds roll past. Heavy Gatling guns boom. Pandemonium. Troops deploy. Gallop of hoofs. Artillery. Hoarse commands. Bells clang. Backers shout. Drunkards bawl. Whores screech. Foghorns hoot. Cries of valour. Shrieks of dying. Pikes clash on cuirasses. Thieves rob the slain. Birds of prey, winging from the sea, rising from marshlands, swooping from eyries, hover screaming, gannets, cormorants, vultures, goshawks, climbing woodcocks, peregrines, merlins, blackgrouse, sea eagles, gulls, albatrosses, barnacle geese. The midnight sun is darkened. The earth trembles. The dead of Dublin from Prospect and Mount Jerome in white sheepskin overcoats and black goatfell cloaks arise and appear to many. A chasm opens with a noiseless yawn. Tom Rochford, winner, in athlete's singlet and breeches, arrives at the head of the national hurdle handicap and leaps into the void. He is followed by a race of runners and leapers. In wild attitudes they spring from the brink. Their bodies plunge. Factory lasses with fancy clothes toss redhot Yorkshire baraabombs. Society ladies lift their skirts above their heads to protect themselves. Laughing witches in red cutty sarks ride through the air on broomsticks. Quakerlyster plasters blisters. It rains dragons' teeth. Armed heroes spring up from furrows. They exchange in amity the pass of knights of the red cross and fight duels with cavalry sabres: Wolfe Tone against Henry Grattan, Smith O'Brien against Daniel O'Connell, Michael Davitt against Isaac Butt,*)

Justin M'Carthy against Parnell, Arthur Griffith against John Redmond, John O'Leary against Lear O'Johnny, Lord Edward Fitzgerald against Lord Gerald Fitzedward, The O'Donoghue of the Glens against The Glens of The O'Donoghue. On an eminence, the centre of the earth, rises the fieldaltar of Saint Barbara. Black candles rise from its gospel and epistle horns. From the high barbacans of the tower two shafts of light fall on the smokepalled altarstone. On the altarstone Mrs Mina Purefoy, goddess of unreason, lies, naked, fettered, a chalice resting on her swollen belly. Father Malachi O'Flynn in a lace petticoat and reversed chasuble, his two left feet back to the front, celebrates camp mass. The Reverend Mr Hugh C Haines Love M. A. in a plain cassock and mortarboard, his head and collar back to the front, holds over the celebrant's head an open umbrella.)

FATHER MALACHI O'FLYNN: *Introibo ad altare diaboli.*

THE REVEREND MR HAINES LOVE: To the devil which hath made glad my young days.

FATHER MALACHI O'FLYNN: (*Takes from the chalice and elevates a blooddripping host.*) *Corpus meum.*

THE REVEREND MR HAINES LOVE: (*Raises high behind the celebrant's petticoat, revealing his grey bare hairy buttocks between which a carrot is stuck.*) My body.

THE VOICE OF ALL THE DAMNED: Htengier Tnetopinmo Dog Drol eht rof, Aiulella!

(*From on high the voice of Adonai calls.*)

ADONAI: Dooooooooooog!

THE VOICE OF ALL THE BLESSED: Alleluia, for the Lord God Omnipotent reigneth!

(*From on high the voice of Adonai calls.*)

ADONAI: Goooooooooood!

(*In strident discord peasants and townsmen of Orange and Green factions sing* Kick the Pope *and* Daily, daily sing to Mary.)

PRIVATE CARR: (*With ferocious articulation.*) I'll do him in, so help me fucking Christ! I'll wring the bastard fucker's bleeding blasted fucking windpipe!

(*The retriever, nosing on the fringe of the crowd, barks noisily.*)

OLD GUMMY GRANNY: (*Thrusts a dagger towards Stephen's hand.*) Remove him, acushla. At 8.35 a.m. you will be in heaven and Ireland will be free. (*She prays.*) O good God, take him!

BLOOM: (*Runs to Lynch.*) Can't you get him away?

LYNCH: He likes dialectic, the universal language. Kitty! (*To Bloom.*) Get him away, you. He won't listen to me.

(*He drags Kitty away.*)

STEPHEN: (*Points.*) *Exit Judas. Et laqueo se suspendit.*

BLOOM: (*Runs to Stephen.*) Come along with me now before worse happens. Here's your stick.

STEPHEN: Stick, no. Reason. This feast of pure reason.

CISSY CAFFREY: (*Pulling Private Carr.*) Come on, you're boosed. He insulted me but I forgive him. (*Shouting in his ear.*) I forgive him for insulting me.

BLOOM: (*Over Stephen's shoulder.*) Yes, go. You see he's incapable.

PRIVATE CARR: (*Breaks loose.*) I'll insult him.

(*He rushes towards Stephen, fist outstretched, and strikes him in the face. Stephen totters, collapses, falls, stunned. He lies prone, his face to the sky, his hat rolling to the wall. Bloom follows and picks it up.*)

MAJOR TWEEDY: (*Loudly.*) Carbine in bucket! Cease fire! Salute!

THE RETRIEVER: (*Barking furiously.*) Ute ute ute ute ute ute ute ute.

THE CROWD: Let him up! Don't strike him when he's down! Air! Who? The soldier hit him. He's a professor. Is he hurted? Don't manhandle him! He's fainted!

(*The retriever, nosing on the fringe of the crowd, barks noisily*)

A HAG: What call had the redcoat to strike the gentleman and he under the influence. Let them go and fight the Boers!

THE BAWD: Listen to who's talking! Hasn't the soldier a right to go with his girl? He gave him the coward's blow.

(*They grab at each other's hair, claw at each other and spit.*)

THE RETRIEVER: (*Barking.*) Wow wow wow.

BLOOM: (*Shoves them back, loudly.*) Get back, stand back!

PRIVATE COMPTON: (*Tugging his comrade.*) Here. Bugger off, Harry. Here's the cops! (*Two raincaped watch, tall, stand in the group.*)

FIRST WATCH: What's wrong here?

PRIVATE COMPTON: We were with this lady. And he insulted us. And assaulted my chum. (*The retriever barks.*) Who owns the bleeding tyke?

CISSY CAFFREY: (*With expectation.*) Is he bleeding!

A MAN: (*Rising from his knees.*) No. Gone off. He'll come to all right.

BLOOM: (*Glances sharply at the man.*) Leave him to me. I can easily . . .

SECOND WATCH: Who are you? Do you know him?

PRIVATE CARR: (*Lurches towards the watch.*) He insulted my lady friend.

BLOOM: (*Angrily.*) You hit him without provocation. I'm a witness. Constable, take his regimental number.

SECOND WATCH: I don't want your instructions in the discharge of my duty.

PRIVATE COMPTON: (*Pulling his comrade.*) Here, bugger off Harry. Or Bennett'll shove you in the lockup.

PRIVATE CARR: (*Staggering as he is pulled away.*) God fuck old Bennett. He's a whitearsed bugger. I don't give a shit for him.

FIRST WATCH: (*Takes out his notebook.*) What's his name?

BLOOM: (*Peering over the crowd.*) I just see a car there. If you give me a hand a second, sergeant . . .

FIRST WATCH: Name and address.

(*Corny Kelleher, weepers round his hat, a death wreath in his hand, appears among the bystanders.*)

BLOOM: (*Quickly.*) O, the very man! (*He whispers.*) Simon Dedalus' son. A bit sprung. Get those policemen to move those loafers back.

SECOND WATCH: Night, Mr Kelleher.

CORNY KELLEHER: (*To the watch, with drawling eye.*) That's all right. I know him. Won a bit on the races. Gold cup. Throwaway. (*He laughs.*) Twenty to one. Do you follow me?

FIRST WATCH: (*Turns to the crowd.*) Here, what are you all gaping at? Move on out of that.

(*The crowd disperses slowly, muttering, down the lane.*)

CORNY KELLEHER: Leave it to me, sergeant. That'll be all right. (*He laughs, shaking his head.*) We were often as bad ourselves, ay or worse. What? Eh, what?

FIRST WATCH: (*Laughs.*) I suppose so.

CORNY KELLEHER: (*Nudges the second watch.*) Come and wipe your name off the slate. (*He lilts, wagging his head.*) With my tooraloom tooraloom tooraloom tooraloom. What, eh, do you follow me?

SECOND WATCH: (*Genially.*) Ah, sure we were too.

CORNY KELLEHER: (*Winking.*) Boys will be boys. I've a car round there.

SECOND WATCH: All right, Mr Kelleher. Good night.

CORNY KELLEHER: I'll see to that.

BLOOM: (*Shakes hands with both of the watch in turn.*) Thank you very much, gentlemen. Thank you. (*He mumbles confidentially.*) We don't want any scandal, you understand. Father is a wellknown highly respected citizen. Just a little wild oats, you understand.

FIRST WATCH: O. I understand, sir.

SECOND WATCH: That's all right, sir.

FIRST WATCH: It was only in case of corporal injuries I'd have to report it at the station.

BLOOM: (*Nods rapidly.*) Naturally. Quite right. Only your bounden duty.

SECOND WATCH: It's our duty.

CORNY KELLEHER: Good night, men.

THE WATCH: (*Saluting together.*) Night, gentlemen. (*They move off with slow heavy tread.*)

BLOOM: (*Blows.*) Providential you came on the scene. You have a car? . . .

CORNY KELLEHER: (*Laughs, pointing his thumb over his right shoulder to the car brought up against the scaffolding.*) Two commercials that were standing fizz in Jammet's. Like princes, faith. One of them lost two quid on the race. Drowning his grief. And were on for a go with the jolly girls. So I landed them up on Behan's car and down to nighttown.

BLOOM: I was just going home by Gardiner street when I happened to . . .

CORNY KELLEHER: (*Laughs.*) Sure they wanted me to join in with the mots. No, by God, says I. Not for old stagers like myself and yourself. (*He laughs again and leers with lacklustre eye.*) Thanks be to God we have it in the house, what, eh, do you follow me? Hah, hah, hah!

BLOOM: (*Tries to laugh.*) He, he, he! Yes. Matter of fact I was just visiting an old friend of mine there, Virag, you don't know him (poor fellow, he's laid up for the past week) and we had a liquor together and I was just making my way home . . .

(*The horse neighs.*)

THE HORSE: Hohohohohohoh! Hohohohome!

CORNY KELLEHER: Sure it was Behan our jarvey there that told me after we left the two commercials in Mrs Cohen's and I told him to pull up and got off to see. (*He laughs.*) Sober hearsedrivers a speciality. Will I give him a lift home? Where does he hang out? Somewhere in Cabra, what?

BLOOM: No, in Sandycove, I believe, from what he let drop.

(*Stephen, prone, breathes to the stars. Corny Kelleher, asquint, drawls at the horse. Bloom, in gloom, looms down.*)

CORNY KELLEHER: (*Scratches his nape.*) Sandycove! (*He bends down and calls to Stephen.*) Eh! (*He calls again.*) Eh! He's covered with shavings anyhow. Take care they didn't lift anything off him.

BLOOM: No, no, no. I have his money and his hat here and stick.

CORNY KELLEHER: Ah, well, he'll get over it. No bones broken. Well, I'll shove along. (*He laughs.*) I've a rendezvous in the morning. Burying the dead. Safe home!

THE HORSE: (*Neighs.*) Hohohohohome.

BLOOM: Good night. I'll just wait and take him along in a few . . .

(*Corny Kelleher returns to the outside car and mounts it. The horse harness jingles.*)

CORNY KELLEHER: (*From the car, standing.*) Night.

BLOOM: Night.

(*The jarvey chucks the reins and raises his whip encouragingly. The car and horse back slowly, awkwardly, and turn. Corny Kelleher on the sideseat sways his head to and fro in sign of mirth at Bloom's plight. The jarvey joins in the mute pantomimic merriment nodding from the farther seat. Bloom shakes his head in mute mirthful reply. With thumb and palm Corny Kelleher reassures that the two bobbies will allow the sleep to continue for what else is to be done. With a slow nod Bloom conveys his gratitude as that is exactly what Stephen needs. The car jingles tooraloom round the corner of the tooraloom lane. Corny Kelleher again reassuralooms with his hand. Bloom with his hand assuralooms Corny Kelleher that he is reassuraloomtay. The tinkling hoofs and jingling harness grow fainter with their tooralooloo looloo lay. Bloom, holding in his hand Stephen's hat, festooned with shavings, and ashplant, stands irresolute. Then he bends to him and shakes him by the shoulder.*)

BLOOM: Eh! Ho! (*There is no answer; he bends again.*) Mr Dedalus! (*There is no answer.*) The name if you call. Somnambulist. (*He bends again and, hesitating, brings his mouth near the face of the prostrate form.*) Stephen! (*There is no answer. He calls again.*) Stephen!

STEPHEN: (*Groans.*) Who? Black panther. Vampire. (*He sighs and stretches himself, then murmurs thickly with prolonged vowels.*)

Who . . . drive . . . Fergus now
And pierce . . . wood's woven shade? . . .

(*He turns on his left side, sighing, doubling himself together.*)

BLOOM: Poetry. Well educated. Pity. (*He bends again and undoes the buttons of Stephen's waistcoat.*) To breathe. (*He brushes the woodshavings from

Stephen's clothes with light hand and fingers.) One pound seven. Not hurt anyhow. (*He listens.*) What?

STEPHEN: (*Murmurs.*)

. . . shadows . . . the woods
. . . white breast . . . dim sea.

(*He stretches out his arms, sighs again and curls his body. Bloom, holding the hat and ashplant, stands erect. A dog barks in the distance. Bloom tightens and loosens his grip on the ashplant. He looks down on Stephen's face and form.*)

BLOOM: (*Communes with the night.*) Face reminds me of his poor mother. In the shady wood. The deep white breast. Ferguson, I think I caught. A girl. Some girl. Best thing could happen him. (*He murmurs.*) . . . swear that I will always hail, ever conceal, never reveal, any part or parts, art or arts . . . (*He murmurs.*) . . . in the rough sands of the sea . . . a cabletow's length from the shore . . . where the tide ebbs . . . and flows . . .

(*Silent, thoughtful, alert he stands on guard, his fingers at his lips in the attitude of secret master. Against the dark wall a figure appears slowly, a fairy boy of eleven, a changeling, kidnapped, dressed in an Eton suit with glass shoes and a little bronze helmet, holding a book in his hand. He reads from right to left inaudibly, smiling, kissing the page.*)

BLOOM: (*Wonderstruck, calls inaudibly.*) Rudy!

RUDY: (*Gazes, unseeing, into Bloom's eyes and goes on reading, kissing, smiling. He has a delicate mauve face. On his suit he has diamond and ruby buttons. In his free left hand he holds a slim ivory cane with a violet bowknot. A white lambkin peeps out of his waistcoat pocket.*)

Part

III

16

Preparatory to anything else Mr Bloom brushed off the greater bulk of the shavings and handed Stephen the hat and ashplant and bucked him up generally in orthodox Samaritan fashion which he very badly needed. His (Stephen's) mind was not exactly what you would call wandering but a bit unsteady and on his expressed desire for some beverage to drink Mr Bloom in view of the hour it was and there being no pump of Vartry water available for their ablutions let alone drinking purposes hit upon an expedient by suggesting, off the reel, the propriety of the cabman's shelter, as it was called, hardly a stonesthrow away near Butt bridge where they might hit upon some drinkables in the shape of a milk and soda or a mineral. But how to get there was the rub. For the nonce he was rather nonplussed but inasmuch as the duty plainly devolved upon him to take some measures on the subject he pondered suitable ways and means during which Stephen repeatedly yawned. So far as he could see he was rather pale in the face so that it occurred to him as highly advisable to get a conveyance of some description which would answer in their then condition, both of them being e.d.ed, particularly Stephen, always assuming that there was such a thing to be found. Accordingly after a few such preliminaries as brushing, in spite of his having forgotten to take up his rather soapsuddy handkerchief after it had done yeoman service in the shaving line, they both walked together along Beaver street or, more properly, lane as far as the farrier's and the distinctly fetid atmosphere of the livery stables at the corner of Montgomery street where they made tracks to the left from thence debouching into Amiens street round by the corner of Dan Bergin's. But as he confidently anticipated there was not a sign of a Jehu plying for hire anywhere to be seen except a fourwheeler, probably engaged by some fellows inside on the spree, outside the

North Star hotel and there was no symptom of its budging a quarter of an inch when Mr Bloom, who was anything but a professional whistler, endeavoured to hail it by emitting a kind of a whistle, holding his arms arched over his head, twice.

This was a quandary but, bringing common sense to bear on it, evidently there was nothing for it but put a good face on the matter and foot it which they accordingly did. So, bevelling around by Mullett's and the Signal House which they shortly reached, they proceeded perforce in the direction of Amiens street railway terminus, Mr Bloom being handicapped by the circumstance that one of the back buttons of his trousers had, to vary the timehonoured adage, gone the way of all buttons though, entering thoroughly into the spirit of the thing, he heroically made light of the mischance. So as neither of them were particularly pressed for time, as it happened, and the temperature refreshing since it cleared up after the recent visitation of Jupiter Pluvius, they dandered along past by where the empty vehicle was waiting without a fare or a jarvey. As it so happened a Dublin United Tramways Company's sandstrewer happened to be returning and the elder man recounted to his companion *à propos* of the incident his own truly miraculous escape of some little while back. They passed the main entrance of the Great Northern railway station, the starting point for Belfast, where of course all traffic was suspended at that late hour and passing the backdoor of the morgue (a not very enticing locality, not to say gruesome to a degree, more especially at night) ultimately gained the Dock Tavern and in due course turned into Store street, famous for its C division police station. Between this point and the high at present unlit warehouses of Beresford place Stephen thought to think of Ibsen, associated with Baird's the stonecutter's in his mind somehow in Talbot place, first turning on the right, while the other who was acting as his *fidus Achates* inhaled with internal satisfaction the smell of James Rourke's city bakery, situated quite close to where they were, the very palatable odour indeed of our daily bread, of all commodities of the public the primary and most indispensable. Bread, the staff of life, earn your bread, O tell me where is fancy bread, at Rourke's the baker's it is said.

En route to his taciturn and, not to put too fine a point on it, not yet perfectly sober companion Mr Bloom who at all events was in complete possession of his faculties, never more so, in fact disgustingly sober, spoke a word of caution *re* the dangers of nighttown, women of ill fame and swell mobsmen, which, barely permissible once in a while though not as a habitual practice, was of the nature of a regular deathtrap for young fellows of his age particularly if they had acquired drinking habits under the influence of liquor unless you knew a little jiujitsu for every contingency as even a fellow on the broad of his back could administer a nasty kick if you didn't look out. Highly providential was the appearance on the scene of Corny Kelleher when Stephen was blissfully unconscious but for that man in the gap turning up at the eleventh hour the finis might have been that he might have been a candidate for the accident ward or, failing that, the bridewell and an appearance in the court next day before Mr Tobias or, he being the solicitor rather, old Wall, he meant to say, or Mahony which simply spelt ruin for a chap when it got bruited about. The reason he mentioned the fact was that a lot of those policemen, whom he cordially disliked, were admittedly unscrupulous in the service of the Crown and, as Mr Bloom put it, recalling a case or two in the A division in Clanbrassil street, prepared to swear a hole through a ten gallon pot. Never on the spot when wanted but in quiet parts of the city, Pembroke road for example, the guardians of the law were well in evidence, the obvious reason being they were paid to protect the upper classes. Another thing he commented on was equipping soldiers with firearms or sidearms of any description liable to go off at any time which was tantamount to inciting them against civilians should by any chance they fall out over anything. You frittered away your time, he very sensibly maintained, and health and also character besides which, the squandermania of the thing, fast women of the *demimonde* ran away with a lot of £. s. d. into the bargain and the greatest danger of all was who you got drunk with though, touching the much vexed question of stimulants, he relished a glass of choice old wine in season as both nourishing and bloodmaking and possessing aperient virtues (notably a good burgundy which he was a staunch believer in) still never beyond a certain point where he invariably drew the line as it simply led to trouble all round to say nothing of your being at the tender mercy of others practically. Most of all he commented adversely on the desertion of Stephen by all his pubhunting *confrères* but one, a most glaring piece of ratting on the part of his brother medicos under all the circs.

—And that one was Judas, Stephen said, who up to then had said nothing whatsoever of any kind.

Discussing these and kindred topics they made a beeline across the back of the Customhouse and passed under the Loop Line bridge where a brazier of coke burning in front of a sentrybox or something like one attracted their rather lagging footsteps. Stephen of his own accord stopped for no special reason to look at the heap of barren cobblestones and by the light emanating from the brazier he could just make out the darker figure of the corporation watchman inside the gloom of the sentrybox. He began to remember that this had happened or had been mentioned as having happened before but it cost him no small effort before he remembered that he recognised in the sentry a *quondam* friend of his father's, Gumley. To avoid a meeting he drew nearer to the pillars of the railway bridge.

—Someone saluted you, Mr Bloom said.

A figure of middle height on the prowl evidently under the arches saluted again, calling:

—*Night!*

Stephen of course started rather dizzily and stopped to return the compliment. Mr Bloom actuated by motives of inherent delicacy inasmuch as he always believed in minding his own business moved off but nevertheless remained on the *qui vive* with just a shade of anxiety though not funkyish in the least. Though unusual in the Dublin area he knew that it was not by any means unknown for desperadoes who had next to nothing to live on to be abroad waylaying and generally terrorising peaceable pedestrians by placing a pistol at their head in some secluded spot outside the city proper, famished loiterers of the Thames embankment category they might be hanging about there or simply marauders ready to decamp with whatever boodle they could in one fell swoop at a moment's notice, your money or your life, leaving you there to point a moral, gagged and garrotted.

Stephen, that is when the accosting figure came to close quarters, though he was not in an over sober state himself recognised Corley's breath redolent of rotten cornjuice. Lord John Corley some called him and his genealogy came about in this wise. He was the eldest son of inspector Corley of the G division, lately deceased, who had married a certain Katherine Brophy, the daughter of a Louth farmer. His grandfather Patrick Michael Corley of New Ross had married the widow of a publican there whose maiden name had been Katherine (also) Talbot. Rumour had it (though not proved) that she descended from the house of the lords Talbot de Malahide in whose mansion, really an unquestionably fine residence of its kind and well worth seeing, her mother or aunt or some relative, a woman, as the tale went, of extreme beauty, had enjoyed the distinction of being in service in the washkitchen. This therefore was the reason why the still comparatively young though dissolute man who now addressed Stephen was spoken of by some with facetious proclivities as Lord John Corley.

Taking Stephen on one side he had the customary doleful ditty to tell. Not as much as a farthing to purchase a night's lodgings. His friends had all deserted him. Furthermore he had a row with Lenehan and called him to Stephen a mean bloody swab with a sprinkling of a number of other uncalledfor expressions. He was out of a job and implored of Stephen to tell him where on God's earth he could get something, anything at all, to do. No, it was the daughter of the mother in the washkitchen that was fostersister to the heir of the house or else they were connected through the mother in some way, both occurrences happening at the same time if the whole thing wasn't a complete fabrication from start to finish. Anyhow he was all in.

—I wouldn't ask you only, pursued he, on my solemn oath and God knows I'm on the rocks.

—There'll be a job tomorrow or next day, Stephen told him, in a boys' school at Dalkey for a gentleman usher. Mr Garrett Deasy. Try it. You may mention my name.

—Ah, God, Corley replied, sure I couldn't teach in a school, man. I was never one of your bright ones, he added with a half laugh. I got stuck twice in the junior at the christian brothers.

—I have no place to sleep myself, Stephen informed him.

Corley at the first go-off was inclined to suspect it was something to do with Stephen being fired out of his digs for bringing in a bloody tart off the street. There was a dosshouse in Marlborough street, Mrs Maloney's, but it was only a tanner touch and full of undesirables but M'Conachie told him you got a decent enough do in the Brazen Head over in Winetavern street (which was distantly suggestive to the person addressed of friar Bacon) for a bob. He was starving too though he hadn't said a word about it.

Though this sort of thing went on every other night or very near it still Stephen's feelings got the better of him in a sense though he knew that Corley's brandnew rigmarole on a par with the others was hardly deserving of much credence. However *haud ignarus malorum miseris succurrere disco etcetera* as the Latin poet remarks especially as luck would have it he got paid his screw after every middle of the month on the sixteenth which was the date of the month as a matter of fact though a good bit of the wherewithal was demolished. But the cream of the joke was nothing would get it out of Corley's head that he was living in affluence and hadn't a thing to do but hand out the needful. Whereas. He put his hand in a pocket anyhow not with the idea of finding any food there but thinking he might lend him anything up to a bob or so in lieu so that he might endeavour at all events and get sufficient to eat but the result was in the negative for, to his chagrin, he found his cash missing. A few broken biscuits were all the result of his investigation. He tried his hardest to recollect for the moment whether he had lost as well he might have or left because in that contingency it was not a pleasant lookout, very much the reverse in fact. He was altogether too fagged out to institute a thorough search though he tried to recollect. About biscuits he dimly remembered. Who now exactly gave them he wondered or where was or did he buy. However in another pocket he came across what he surmised in the dark were pennies, erroneously however, as it turned out.

—Those are halfcrowns, man, Corley corrected him.

And so in point of fact they turned out to be. Stephen anyhow lent him one of them.

—Thanks, Corley answered, you're a gentleman. I'll pay you back one time. Who's that with you? I saw him a few times in the Bleeding Horse in Camden street with Boylan, the billsticker. You might put in a good word for us to get me taken on there. I'd carry a sandwichboard only the girl in the office told me they're full up for the next three weeks, man. God, you've to book ahead, man, you'd think it was for the Carl Rosa. I don't give a shite anyway so long as I get a job, even as a crossing sweeper.

Subsequently being not quite so down in the mouth after the two and six he got he informed Stephen about a fellow by the name of Bags Comisky that he said Stephen knew well out of Fullam's, the shipchandler's, bookkeeper there that used to be often round in Nagle's back with O'Mara and a little chap with a stutter the name of Tighe. Anyhow he was lagged the night before last and fined ten bob for a drunk and disorderly and refusing to go with the constable.

Mr Bloom in the meanwhile kept dodging about in the vicinity of the cobblestones near the brazier of coke in front of the corporation watchman's sentrybox who evidently a glutton for work, it struck him, was having a quiet forty winks for all intents and purposes on his own private account while Dublin slept. He threw an odd eye at the same time now and then at Stephen's anything but immaculately attired interlocutor as if he had seen that nobleman somewhere or other though where he was not in a position to truthfully state nor had he the remotest idea when. Being a levelheaded individual who could give points to not a few in point of shrewd observation he also remarked on his very dilapidated hat and slouchy wearing apparel generally testifying to a chronic impecuniosity. Palpably he was one of his hangerson but for the matter of that it was merely a question of one preying on his nextdoor neighbour all round, in every deep, so to put it, a deeper depth and for the matter of that if the man in the street chanced to be in the dock himself penal servitude with or without the option of a fine would be a very *rara avis* altogether. In any case he had a consummate amount of cool assurance intercepting people at that hour of the night or morning. Pretty thick that was certainly.

The pair parted company and Stephen rejoined Mr Bloom who, with his practised eye, was not without perceiving that he had succumbed to the blandiloquence of the other parasite. Alluding to the encounter he said, laughingly, Stephen, that is:

—He is down on his luck. He asked me to ask you to ask somebody named Boylan, a billsticker, to give him a job as a sandwichman.

At this intelligence, in which he seemingly evinced little interest, Mr Bloom gazed abstractedly for the space of a half a second or so in the direction of a bucketdredger, rejoicing in the farfamed name of Eblana, moored alongside Customhouse quay and quite possibly out of repair, whereupon he observed evasively:

—Everybody gets their own ration of luck, they say. Now you mention it his face was familiar to me. But, leaving that for the moment, how much did you part with, he queried, if I am not too inquisitive?

—Half a crown, Stephen responded. I daresay he needs it to sleep somewhere.

—Needs! Mr Bloom ejaculated, professing not the least surprise at the intelligence, I can quite credit the assertion and I guarantee he invariably does. Everyone according to his needs or everyone according to his deeds. But, talking about things in general, where, added he with a smile, will you sleep yourself? Walking to Sandycove is out of the question. And even supposing you did you won't get in after what occurred at Westland Row station. Simply fag out there for nothing. I don't mean to presume to dictate to you in the slightest degree but why did you leave your father's house?

—To seek misfortune, was Stephen's answer.

—I met your respected father on a recent occasion, Mr Bloom diplomatically returned, today in fact, or to be strictly accurate, on yesterday. Where does he live at present? I gathered in the course of conversation that he had moved.

—I believe he is in Dublin somewhere, Stephen answered unconcernedly. Why?

—A gifted man, Mr Bloom said of Mr Dedalus senior, in more respects than one and a born *raconteur* if ever there was one. He takes great pride, quite legitimate, out of you. You could go back perhaps, he hasarded, still thinking of the very unpleasant scene at Westland Row terminus when it was perfectly evident that the other two, Mulligan, that is, and that English tourist friend of his, who eventually euchred their third companion, were patently trying as if the whole bally station belonged to them to give Stephen the slip in the confusion, which they did.

There was no response forthcoming to the suggestion however, such as it was, Stephen's mind's eye being too busily engaged in repicturing his family hearth the last time he saw it with his sister Dilly sitting by the ingle, her hair hanging down, waiting for some weak Trinidad shell cocoa that was in the sootcoated kettle to be done so that she and he could drink it with the oatmealwater for milk after the Friday herrings they had eaten at two a penny with an egg apiece for Maggy, Boody and Katey, the cat meanwhile under the mangle devouring a mess of eggshells and charred fish heads and bones on a square of brown paper, in accordance with the third precept of the church to fast and abstain on the days commanded, it being quarter tense or if not, ember days or something like that.

—No, Mr Bloom repeated again, I wouldn't personally repose much trust in that boon companion of yours who contributes the humorous element, Dr Mulligan, as a guide, philosopher and friend if I were in your shoes. He knows which side his bread is buttered on though in all probability he never realised what it is to be without regular meals. Of course you didn't notice as much as I did. But it wouldn't occasion me the least surprise to learn that a pinch of tobacco or some narcotic was put in your drink for some ulterior object.

He understood however from all he heard that Dr Mulligan was a versatile allround man, by no means confined to medicine only, who was rapidly coming to the fore in his line and, if the report was verified, bade fair to enjoy a flourishing practice in the not too distant future as a tony medical practitioner drawing a handsome fee for his services in addition to which professional status his rescue of that man from certain drowning by artificial respiration and what they call first aid at Skerries, or Malahide was it?, was, he was bound to admit, an exceedingly plucky deed which he could not too highly praise, so that frankly he was utterly at a loss to fathom what earthly reason could be at the back of it except he put it down to sheer cussedness or jealousy, pure and simple.

—Except it simply amounts to one thing and he is what they call picking your brains, he ventured to throw out.

The guarded glance of half solicitude half curiosity augmented by friendliness which he gave at Stephen's at present morose expression of features did not throw a flood of light, none at all in fact on the problem as to whether he had let himself be badly bamboozled to judge by two or three lowspirited remarks he let drop or the other way about saw through the affair and for some reason or other best known to himself allowed matters to more or less. Grinding poverty did have that effect and he more than conjectured that, high educational abilities though he possessed, he experienced no little difficulty in making both ends meet.

Adjacent to the men's public urinal they perceived an icecream car round which a group of presumably Italians in heated altercation were getting rid of voluble expressions in their vivacious language in a particularly animated way, there being some little differences between the parties.

—*Puttana madonna, che ci dia i quattrini! Ho ragione? Culo rotto!*
—*Intendiamoci. Mezzo sovrano più* . . .
—*Dice lui, però!*
—*Mezzo.*
—*Farabutto! Mortacci sui!*
—*Ma ascolta! Cinque la testa più* . . .

Mr Bloom and Stephen entered the cabman's shelter, an unpretentious wooden structure, where, prior to then, he had rarely if ever been before, the former having previously whispered to the latter a few hints anent the keeper of it said to be the once famous

Skin-the-Goat Fitzharris, the invincible, though he could not vouch for the actual facts which quite possibly there was not one vestige of truth in. A few moments later saw our two noctambules safely seated in a discreet corner only to be greeted by stares from the decidedly miscellaneous collection of waifs and strays and other nondescript specimens of the genus *homo* already there engaged in eating and drinking diversified by conversation for whom they seemingly formed an object of marked curiosity.

—Now touching a cup of coffee, Mr Bloom ventured to plausibly suggest to break the ice, it occurs to me you ought to sample something in the shape of solid food, say, a roll of some description.

Accordingly his first act was with characteristic *sangfroid* to order these commodities quietly. The *hoi polloi* of jarvies or stevedores or whatever they were after a cursory examination turned their eyes apparently dissatisfied, away though one redbearded bibulous individual, portion of whose hair was greyish, a sailor probably, still stared for some appreciable time before transferring his rapt attention to the floor. Mr Bloom, availing himself of the right of free speech, he having just a bowing acquaintance with the language in dispute, though, to be sure, rather in a quandary over *voglio*, remarked to his *protégé* in an audible tone of voice *à propos* of the battle royal in the street which was still raging fast and furious:

—A beautiful language. I mean for singing purposes. Why do you not write your poetry in that language? *Bella Poetria!* It is so melodious and full. *Belladonna. Voglio.*

Stephen, who was trying his dead best to yawn if he could, suffering from lassitude generally, replied:

—To fill the ear of a cow elephant. They were haggling over money.

—Is that so? Mr Bloom asked. Of course, he subjoined pensively, at the inward reflection of there being more languages to start with than were absolutely necessary, it may be only the southern glamour that surrounds it.

The keeper of the shelter in the middle of this *tête-à-tête* put a boiling swimming cup of a choice concoction labelled coffee on the table and a rather antediluvian specimen of a bun, or so it seemed. After which he beat a retreat to his counter, Mr Bloom determining to have a good square look at him later on so as not to appear to. For which reason he encouraged Stephen to proceed with his eyes while he did the honours by surreptitiously pushing the cup of what was temporarily supposed to be called coffee gradually nearer him.

—Sounds are impostures, Stephen said after a pause of some little time, like names. Cicero, Podmore, Napoleon, Mr Goodbody. Jesus, Mr Doyle. Shakespeares were as common as Murphies. What's in a name?

—Yes, to be sure, Mr Bloom unaffectedly concurred. Of course. Our name was changed too, he added, pushing the socalled roll across.

The redbearded sailor who had his weather eye on the newcomers boarded Stephen, whom he had singled out for attention in particular, squarely by asking:

—And what might your name be?

Just in the nick of time Mr Bloom touched his companion's boot but Stephen, apparently disregarding the warm pressure from an unexpected quarter, answered:

—Dedalus.

The sailor stared at him heavily from a pair of drowsy baggy eyes, rather bunged up from excessive use of boose, preferably good old Hollands and water.

—You know Simon Dedalus? he asked at length.

—I've heard of him, Stephen said.

Mr Bloom was all at sea for a moment, seeing the others evidently eavesdropping too.

—He's Irish, the seaman bold affirmed, staring still in much the same way and nodding. All Irish.

—All too Irish, Stephen rejoined.

As for Mr Bloom he could neither make head or tail of the whole business and he was just asking himself what possible connection when the sailor of his own accord turned to the other occupants of the shelter with the remark:

—I seen him shoot two eggs off two bottles at fifty yards over his shoulder. The lefthand dead shot.

Though he was slightly hampered by an occasional stammer and his gestures being also clumsy as it was still he did his best to explain.

—Bottles out there, say. Fifty yards measured. Eggs on the bottles. Cocks his gun over his shoulder. Aims.

He turned his body half round, shut up his right eye completely. Then he screwed his features up someway sideways and glared out into the night with an unprepossessing cast of countenance.

—Pom! he then shouted once.

The entire audience waited, anticipating an additional detonation, there being still a further egg.

—Pom! he shouted twice.

Egg two evidently demolished, he nodded and winked, adding bloodthirstily:

> —*Buffalo Bill shoots to kill,*
> *Never missed nor he never will.*

A silence ensued till Mr Bloom for agreeableness' sake just felt like asking him whether it was for a marksmanship competition like the Bisley.

—Beg pardon, the sailor said.

—Long ago? Mr Bloom pursued without flinching a hairsbreadth.

—Why, the sailor replied, relaxing to a certain extent under the magic influence of diamond cut diamond, it might be a matter of ten years. He toured the wide world with Hengler's Royal Circus. I seen him do that in Stockholm.

—Curious coincidence, Mr Bloom confided to Stephen unobtrusively.

—Murphy's my name, the sailor continued. D. B. Murphy of Carrigaloe. Know where that is?

—Queenstown harbour, Stephen replied.

—That's right, the sailor said. Fort Camden and Fort Carlisle. That's where I hails from. I belongs there. That's where I hails from. My little woman's down there. She's waiting for me, I know. *For England, home and beauty.* She's my own true wife I haven't seen for seven years now, sailing about.

Mr Bloom could easily picture his advent on this scene, the homecoming to the mariner's roadside shieling after having diddled Davy Jones, a rainy night with a blind moon. Across the world for a wife. Quite a number of stories there were on that particular Alice Ben Bolt topic, Enoch Arden and Rip van Winkle and does anybody hereabouts remember Caoc O'Leary, a favourite and most trying declamation piece by the way of poor John Casey and a bit of perfect poetry in its own small way. Never about the runaway wife coming back, however much devoted to the absentee. The face at the window! Judge of his astonishment when he finally did breast the tape and the awful truth dawned upon him anent his better half, wrecked in his affections. You little expected me but I've come to stay and make a fresh start. There she sits, a grasswidow, at the selfsame fireside. Believes me dead, rocked in the cradle of the deep. And there sits uncle Chubb or Tomkin, as the case might be, the publican of the Crown and Anchor, in shirtsleeves, eating rumpsteak and onions. No chair for father. Broo! The wind! Her brandnew arrival is on her knee, *post mortem* child. With a high ro! and a randy ro! and my galloping tearing tandy, O! Bow to the inevitable. Grin and bear it. I remain with much love your brokenhearted husband W. B. Murphy.

The sailor, who scarcely seemed to be a Dublin resident, turned to one of the jarvies with the request:

—You don't happen to have such a thing as a spare chaw about you?

The jarvey addressed as it happened had not but the keeper took a die of plug from his good jacket hanging on a nail and the desired object was passed from hand to hand.

—Thank you, the sailor said.

He deposited the quid in his gob and, chewing and with some slow stammers, proceeded:

—We come up this morning eleven o'clock. The threemaster *Rosevean* from Bridgwater with bricks. I shipped to get over. Paid off this afternoon. There's my discharge. See? D. B. Murphy. A. B. S.

In confirmation of which statement he extricated from an inside pocket and handed to his neighbour a not very cleanlooking folded document.

—You must have seen a fair share of the world, the keeper remarked, leaning on the counter.

—Why, the sailor answered upon reflection upon it, I've circumnavigated a bit since I first joined on. I was in the Red Sea. I was in China and North America and South America. We was chased by pirates one voyage. I seen icebergs plenty, growlers. I was in Stockholm and the Black Sea, the Dardanelles under Captain Dalton, the best bloody man that ever scuttled a ship. I seen Russia. *Gospodi pomilyou.* That's how the Russians prays.

—You seen queer sights, don't be talking, put in a jarvey.

—Why, the sailor said, shifting his partially chewed plug. I seen queer things too, ups and downs. I seen a crocodile bite the fluke of an anchor same as I chew that quid.

He took out of his mouth the pulpy quid and, lodging it between his teeth, bit ferociously:

—Khaan! Like that. And I seen maneaters in Peru that eats corpses and the livers of horses. Look here. Here they are. A friend of mine sent me.

He fumbled out a picture postcard from his inside pocket which seemed to be in its way a species of repository and pushed it along the table. The printed matter on it stated: *Choza de Indios. Beni, Bolivia.*

All focussed their attention at the scene exhibited, a group of savage women in striped loincloths, squatted, blinking, suckling, frowning, sleeping amid a swarm of infants (there must have been quite a score of them) outside some primitive shanties of osier.

—Chews coca all day, the communicative tarpaulin added. Stomachs like breadgraters. Cuts off their diddies when they can't bear no more children.

See them sitting there stark ballocknaked eating a dead horse's liver raw.

His postcard proved a centre of attraction for Messrs the greenhorns for several minutes if not more.

—Know how to keep them off? he inquired generally.

Nobody volunteering a statement he winked, saying:

—Glass. That boggles 'em. Glass.

Mr Bloom, without evincing surprise, unostentatiously turned over the card to peruse the partially obliterated address and postmark. It ran as follows: *Tarjeta Postal, Señor A Boudin, Galeria Becche, Santiago, Chile.* There was no message evidently, as he took particular notice. Though not an implicit believer in the lurid story narrated (or the eggsniping transaction for that matter despite William Tell and the Lazarillo-Don Cesar de Bazan incident depicted in *Maritana* on which occasion the former's ball passed through the latter's hat) having detected a discrepancy between his name (assuming he was the person he represented himself to be and not sailing under false colours after having boxed the compass on the strict q.t. somewhere) and the fictitious addressee of the missive which made him nourish some suspicions of our friend's *bona fides* nevertheless it reminded him in a way of a longcherished plan he meant to one day realise some Wednesday or Saturday of travelling to London *via* long sea not to say that he had ever travelled extensively to any great extent but he was at heart a born adventurer though by a trick of fate he had consistently remained a landlubber except you call going to Holyhead which was his longest. Martin Cunningham frequently said he would work a pass through Egan but some deuced hitch or other eternally cropped up with the net result that the scheme fell through. But even suppose it did come to planking down the needful and breaking Boyd's heart it was not so dear, purse permitting, a few guineas at the outside considering the fare to Mullingar where he figured on going was five and six, there and back. The trip would benefit health on account of the bracing ozone and be in every way thoroughly pleasurable, especially for a chap whose liver was out of order, seeing the different places along the route, Plymouth, Falmouth, Southampton and so on culminating in an instructive tour of the sights of the great metropolis, the spectacle of our modern Babylon where doubtless he would see the greatest improvement, tower, abbey, wealth of Park lane to renew acquaintance with. Another thing just struck him as a by no means bad notion was he might have a gaze around on the spot to see about trying to make arrangements about a concert tour of summer music embracing the most prominent pleasure resorts, Margate with mixed bathing and firstrate hydros and spas, Eastbourne, Scarborough, Margate and so on, beautiful Bournemouth, the Channel islands and similar bijou spots, which might prove highly remunerative. Not, of course, with a hole and corner scratch company or local ladies on the job, witness Mrs C. P. M'Coy type lend me your valise and I'll post you the ticket. No, something top notch, an all star Irish caste, the Tweedy-Flower grand opera company with his own legal consort as leading lady as a sort of counterblast to the Elster Grimes and Moody-Manners, perfectly simple matter and he was quite sanguine of success, providing puffs in the local papers could be managed by some fellow with a bit of bounce who could pull the indispensable wires and thus combine business with pleasure. But who? That was the rub.

Also, without being actually positive, it struck him a great field was to be opened up in the line of opening up new routes to keep pace with the times *apropos* of the Fishguard-Rosslare route which, it was mooted, was once more on the *tapis* in the circumlocution departments with the usual quantity of red tape and dillydallying of effete fogeydom and dunderheads generally. A great opportunity there certainly was for push and enterprise to meet the travelling needs of the public at large, the average man, i.e. Brown, Robinson and Co.

It was a subject of regret and absurd as well on the face of it and no small blame to our vaunted society that the man in the street, when the system really needed toning up, for the matter of a couple of paltry pounds was debarred from seeing more of the world they lived in instead of being always and ever cooped up since my old stick-in-the-mud took me for a wife. After all, hang it, they had their eleven and more humdrum months of it and merited a radical change of *venue* after the grind of city life in the summertime for choice when dame Nature is at her spectacular best constituting nothing short of a new lease of life. There were equally excellent opportunities for vacationists in the home island, delightful sylvan spots for rejuvenation, offering a plethora of attractions as well as a bracing tonic for the system in and around Dublin and its picturesque environs even, Poulaphouca to which there was a steamtram, but also farther away from the madding crowd in Wicklow, rightly termed the garden of Ireland, an ideal neighbourhood for elderly wheelmen so long as it didn't come down, and in the wilds of Donegal where if report spoke true the *coup d'œil* was exceedingly grand though the lastnamed locality was not easily getatable so that the influx of visitors was not as yet all that it might be considering the signal benefits to be derived from it while Howth with its historic associations and otherwise, Silken Thomas, Grace O'Malley, George IV, rhododendrons several hundred feet above sealevel was a favourite haunt with all sorts and conditions of men especially in the spring when young men's fancy, though it had its own toll of deaths by falling off the cliffs by design or accidentally, usually, by the way, on their left leg, it being only about three quarters of an hour's run from the pillar. Because of course uptodate tourist travelling was as yet merely in its infancy, so to speak, and the accommodation left much to be desired. Interesting to fathom it seemed to him from a motive of curiosity, pure and simple, was whether it was the traffic that created the route or viceversa or the two sides in fact. He turned back the other side of the card, picture, and passed it along to Stephen.

—I seen a Chinese one time, related the doughty narrator, that had little pills like putty and he put them in the water and they opened and every pill was something different. One was a ship, another was a house, another was a flower. Cooks rats in your soup, he appetisingly added, the Chinese does.

Possibly perceiving an expression of dubiosity on their faces the globetrotter went on, adhering to his adventures.

—And I seen a man killed in Trieste by an Italian chap. Knife in his back. Knife like that.

Whilst speaking he produced a dangerouslooking claspknife quite in keeping with his character and held it in the striking position.

—In a knockingshop it was count of a tryon between two smugglers. Fellow hid behind a door, come up behind him. Like that. *Prepare to meet your God*, says he. Chuk! It went into his back up to the butt.

His heavy glance drowsily roaming about kind of defied their further questions even should they by any chance want to.

—That's a good bit of steel, repeated he, examining his formidable *stiletto*.

After which harrowing *dénouement* sufficient to appal the stoutest he snapped the blade to and stowed the weapon in question away as before in his chamber of horrors, otherwise pocket.

—They're great for the cold steel, somebody who was evidently quite in the dark said for the benefit of them all. That was why they thought the park murders of the invincibles was done by foreigners on account of them using knives.

At this remark passed obviously in the spirit of *where ignorance is bliss* Mr Bloom and Stephen, each in his own particular way, both instinctively exchanged meaning glances, in a religious silence of the strictly *entre nous* variety however, towards where Skin-the-Goat, *alias* the keeper, not turning a hair, was drawing spurts of liquid from his boiler affair. His inscrutable face which was really a work of art, a perfect study in itself, beggaring description, conveyed the impression that he didn't understand one jot of what was going on. Funny, very!

There ensued a somewhat lengthy pause. One man was reading in fits and starts a stained by coffee evening journal, another the card with the natives *choza de*, another the seaman's discharge. Mr Bloom, so far as he was personally concerned, was just pondering in pensive mood. He vividly recollected when the occurrence alluded to took place as well as yesterday, roughly some score of years previously in the days of the land troubles, when it took the civilised world by storm, figuratively speaking, early in the eighties, eightyone to be correct, when he was just turned fifteen.

—Ay, boss, the sailor broke in. Give us back them papers.

The request being complied with he clawed them up with a scrape.

—Have you seen the rock of Gibraltar? Mr Bloom inquired.

The sailor grimaced, chewing, in a way that might be read as yes, ay or no.

—Ah, you've touched there too, Mr Bloom said, Europa point, thinking he had, in the hope that the rover might possibly by some reminiscences but he failed to do so, simply letting spirt a jet of spew into the sawdust, and shook his head with a sort of lazy scorn.

—What year would that be about? Mr B interrogated. Can you recall the boats?

Our *soi-disant* sailor munched heavily awhile hungrily before answering:

—I'm tired of all them rocks in the sea, he said, and boats and ships. Salt junk all the time.

Tired seemingly, he ceased. His questioner perceiving that he was not likely to get a great deal of change out of such a wily old customer, fell to woolgathering on the enormous dimensions of the water about the globe, suffice it to say that, as a casual glance at the map revealed, it covered fully three fourths of it and he fully realised accordingly what it meant to rule the waves. On more than one occasion, a dozen at the lowest, near the North Bull at Dollymount he had remarked a superannuated old salt, evidently derelict, seated habitually near the not particularly redolent sea on the wall, staring quite obliviously at it and it at him, dreaming of fresh woods and pastures new as someone somewhere sings. And it left him wondering why. Possibly he had tried to find out the secret for himself, floundering up and down the antipodes and all that sort of thing and over and under, well, not exactly under, tempting the fates. And the odds were twenty to nil there was really no secret about it at all. Nevertheless, without going into the *minutiae* of the business, the eloquent fact remained that the sea was there in all its glory and in the natural course of things somebody or other had to sail on it and fly in the face of providence though it merely went to show how people usually contrived to load that sort of onus on to the other fellow like the hell idea and the lottery and insurance which were run on identically the same lines so that for that very reason if no other lifeboat Sunday was a highly laudable institution to which the public at large, no matter where living inland or seaside, as the case might be, having it brought home to them like that should extend its gratitude also to the harbourmasters and coastguard service who had to man the rigging and push off and out amid the elements whatever the season when duty called *Ireland expects that every man* and so on and sometimes had a terrible time of it in the wintertime not forgetting the Irish lights, Kish and others, liable to capsize at any moment, rounding which he once with his daughter had experienced some remarkably choppy, not to say stormy, weather.

—There was a fellow sailed with me in the *Rover*, the old seadog, himself a rover, proceeded, went ashore and took up a soft job as gentleman's valet at six quid a month. Them are his trousers I've on me and he gave me an oilskin and that jackknife. I'm game for that job, shaving and brushup. I hate roaming about. There's my son now, Danny, run off to sea and his mother got him took in a draper's in Cork where he could be drawing easy money.

—What age is he? queried one hearer who, by the way, seen from the side, bore a distant resemblance to Henry Campbell, the townclerk, away from the carking cares of office, unwashed of course and in a seedy getup and a strong suspicion of nosepaint about the nasal appendage.

—Why, the sailor answered with a slow puzzled utterance, my son, Danny? He'd be about eighteen now, way I figure it.

The Skibbereen father hereupon tore open his grey or unclean anyhow shirt with his two hands and scratched away at his chest on which was to be seen an image tattooed in blue Chinese ink intended to represent an anchor.

—There was lice in that bunk in Bridgwater, he remarked, sure as nuts. I must get a wash tomorrow or next day. It's them black lads I objects to. I hate those buggers. Suck your blood dry, they does.

Seeing they were all looking at his chest he accommodatingly dragged his shirt more open so that on top of the timehonoured symbol of the mariner's hope and rest they had a full view of the figure 16 and a young man's sideface looking frowningly rather.

—Tattoo, the exhibitor explained. That was done when we were lying becalmed off Odessa in the Black Sea under Captain Dalton. Fellow, the name of Antonio, done that. There he is himself, a Greek.

—Did it hurt much doing it? one asked the sailor.

That worthy, however, was busily engaged in collecting round the. Someway in his. Squeezing or.

—See here, he said, showing Antonio. There he is cursing the mate. And there he is now, he added, the same fellow, pulling the skin with his fingers, some special knack evidently, and he laughing at a yarn.

And in point of fact the young man named Antonio's livid face did actually look like forced smiling and the curious effect excited the unreserved admiration of everybody including Skin-the-Goat, who this time stretched over.

—Ay, ay, sighed the sailor, looking down on his manly chest. He's gone too. Ate by sharks after. Ay, ay.

He let go of the skin so that the profile resumed the normal expression of before.

—Neat bit of work, one longshoreman said.

—And what's the number for? loafer number two queried.

—Eaten alive? a third asked the sailor.

—Ay, ay, sighed again the latter personage, more cheerily this time with some sort of a half smile for a brief duration only in the direction of the questioner about the number. Ate. A Greek he was.

And then he added with rather gallowsbird humour considering his alleged end:

—*As bad as old Antonio,*
For he left me on my ownio.

The face of a streetwalker glazed and haggard under a black straw hat peered askew round the door of the shelter palpably reconnoitring on her own with the object of bringing more grist to her mill. Mr Bloom, scarcely knowing which way to look, turned away on the moment flusterfied but outwardly calm, and, picking up from the table the pink sheet of the Abbey street organ which the jarvey, if such he was, had laid aside, he picked it up and looked at the pink of the paper though why pink. His reason for so doing was he recognised on the moment round the door the same face he had caught a fleeting glimpse of that afternoon on Ormond quay, the partially idiotic female, namely, of the lane who knew the lady in the brown costume does be with you (Mrs Bloom) and begged the chance of his washing. Also why washing which seemed rather vague than not? Your washing. Still candour compelled him to admit he had washed his wife's undergarments when soiled in Holles street and women would and did too a man's similar garments initialled with Bewley and Draper's marking ink (hers were, that is) if they really loved him, that is to say, love me, love my dirty shirt. Still just then, being on tenterhooks, he desired the female's room more than her company so it came as a genuine relief when the keeper made her a rude sign to take herself off. Round the side of the *Evening Telegraph* he just caught a fleeting glimpse of her face round the side of the door with a kind of demented glassy grin showing that she was not exactly all there, viewing with evident amusement the group of gazers round skipper Murphy's nautical chest and then there was no more of her.

—The gunboat, the keeper said.

—It beats me, Mr Bloom confided to Stephen, medically I am speaking, how a wretched creature like that from the Lock hospital reeking with disease can be barefaced enough to solicit or how any man in his sober senses, if he values his health in the least. Unfortunate creature! Of course I suppose some man is ultimately responsible for her condition. Still no matter what the cause is from . . .

Stephen had not noticed her and shrugged his shoulders, merely remarking:

—In this country people sell much more than she ever had and do a roaring trade. Fear not them that sell the body but have not power to buy the soul. She is a bad merchant. She buys dear and sells cheap.

The elder man, though not by any manner of means an old maid or a prude, said it was nothing short of a crying scandal that ought to be put a stop to *instanter* to say that women of that stamp (quite apart from any oldmaidish squeamishness on the subject), a necessary evil, were not licensed and medically inspected by the proper authorities, a thing, he could truthfully state, he, as a *paterfamilias*, was a stalwart advocate of from the very first start. Whoever embarked on a policy of the sort, he said, and ventilated the matter thoroughly would confer a lasting boon on everybody concerned.

—You as a good catholic, he observed, talking of body and soul, believe in the soul. Or do you mean the intelligence, the brainpower as such, as distinct from any outside object, the table, let us say, that cup. I believe in that myself because it has been explained by competent men as the convolutions of the grey matter. Otherwise we would never have such inventions as X rays, for instance. Do you?

Thus cornered, Stephen had to make a superhuman effort of memory to try and concentrate and remember before he could say:

—They tell me on the best authority it is a simple substance and therefore incorruptible. It would be immortal, I understand, but for the possibility of its annihilation by its First Cause Who, from all I can hear, is quite capable of adding that to the number of His other practical jokes, *corruptio per se* and *corruptio per accidens* both being excluded by court etiquette.

Mr Bloom thoroughly acquiesced in the general gist of this though the mystical finesse involved was a bit out of his sublunary depth still he felt bound to enter a demurrer on the head of simple, promptly rejoining:

—Simple? I shouldn't think that is the proper word. Of course, I grant you, to concede a point, you do knock across a simple soul once in a blue moon. But what I am anxious to arrive at is it is one thing for instance to invent those rays Röntgen did or the telescope like Edison, though I believe it was before his time Galileo was the man, I mean, and the same applies to the laws, for example, of a farreaching natural phenomenon such as electricity but it's a horse of quite another colour to say you believe in the existence of a supernatural God.

—O that, Stephen expostulated, has been proved conclusively by several of the bestknown passages in Holy Writ, apart from circumstantial evidence.

On this knotty point however the views of the pair, poles apart as they were both in schooling and everything else with the marked difference in their respective ages, clashed.

—Has been? the more experienced of the two objected, sticking to his original point with a smile of unbelief. I'm not so sure about that. That's a matter for everyman's opinion and, without dragging in the sectarian side of the business, I beg to differ with you *in toto* there. My belief is, to tell you the candid truth, that those bits were genuine forgeries all of them put in by monks most probably or it's the big question of our national poet over again, who precisely wrote them like *Hamlet* and Bacon, as, you who know your Shakespeare infinitely better than I, of course I needn't tell you. Can't you drink that coffee, by the way? Let me stir it. And take a piece of that bun. It's like one of our skipper's bricks disguised. Still no-one can give what he hasn't got. Try a bit.

—Couldn't, Stephen contrived to get out, his mental organs for the moment refusing to dictate further.

Faultfinding being a proverbially bad hat Mr Bloom thought well to stir or try to the clotted sugar from the bottom and reflected with something approaching acrimony on the Coffee Palace and its temperance (and lucrative) work. To be sure it was a legitimate object and beyond yea or nay did a world of good, shelters such as the present one they were in run on teetotal lines for vagrants at night, concerts, dramatic evenings and useful lectures (admittance free) by qualified men for the lower orders. On the other hand he had a distinct and painful recollection they paid his wife, Madam Marion Tweedy who had been prominently associated with it at one time, a very modest remuneration indeed for her pianoplaying. The idea, he was strongly inclined to believe, was to do good and net a profit, there being no competition to speak of. Sulphate of copper poison SO4 or something in some dried peas he remembered reading of in a cheap eatinghouse somewhere but he couldn›t remember when it was or where. Anyhow inspection, medical inspection, of all eatables seemed to him more than ever necessary which possibly accounted for the vogue of Dr Tibble›s Vi-Cocoa on account of the medical analysis involved.

—Have a shot at it now, he ventured to say of the coffee after being stirred.

Thus prevailed on to at any rate taste it Stephen lifted the heavy mug from the brown puddle it clopped out of when taken up by the handle and took a sip of the offending beverage.

—Still it's solid food, his good genius urged, I'm a stickler for solid food, his one and only reason being not gormandising in the least but regular meals as the *sine qua non* for any kind of proper work, mental or manual. You ought to eat more solid food. You would feel a different man.

—Liquids I can eat, Stephen said. But O, oblige me by taking away that knife. I can't look at the point of it. It reminds me of Roman history.

Mr Bloom promptly did as suggested and removed the incriminated article, a blunt hornhandled ordinary knife with nothing particularly Roman or antique about it to the lay eye, observing that the point was the least conspicuous point about it.

—Our mutual friend's stories are like himself, Mr Bloom *apropos* of knives remarked to his *confidante sotto voce*. Do you think they are genuine? He could spin those yarns for hours on end all night long and lie like old boots. Look at him.

Yet still though his eyes were thick with sleep and sea air life was full of a host of things and coincidences of a terrible nature and it was quite within the bounds of possibility that it was not an entire fabrication though at first blush there was not much inherent probability in all the spoof he got off his chest being strictly accurate gospel.

He had been meantime taking stock of the individual in front of him and Sherlockholmesing him up ever since he clapped eyes on him. Though a wellpreserved man of no little stamina, if a trifle prone to baldness, there was something spurious in the cut of his jib that suggested a jail delivery and it required no violent stretch of imagination to associate such a weirdlooking specimen with the oakum and treadmill fraternity. He might even have done for his man supposing it was his own case he told, as people often did about others, namely, that he killed him himself and had served his four or five goodlooking years in durance vile to say nothing of the Antonio personage (no relation to the dramatic personage of identical name who sprang from the pen of our national poet) who expiated his crimes in the melodramatic manner above described. On the other hand he might be only bluffing, a pardonable weakness because meeting unmistakable mugs, Dublin residents, like those jarvies waiting news from abroad would tempt any ancient mariner who sailed the ocean seas to draw the long bow about the schooner *Hesperus* and etcetera. And when all was said and done the lies a fellow told about himself couldn't probably hold a proverbial candle to the wholesale whoppers other fellows coined about him.

—Mind you, I'm not saying that it's all a pure invention, he resumed. Analogous scenes are occasionally, if not often, met with. Giants, though that is rather a far cry, you see once in a way, Marcella the midget queen. In those waxworks in Henry street I myself saw some Aztecs, as they are called, sitting bowlegged, they couldn't straighten their legs if you paid them because the muscles here, you see, he proceeded, indicating on his companion the brief outline of the sinews or whatever you like to call them behind the right knee, were utterly powerless from sitting that way so long cramped up, being adored as gods. There's an example again of simple souls.

However reverting to friend Sinbad and his horrifying adventures (who reminded him a bit of Ludwig, *alias* Ledwidge, when he occupied the boards of the Gaiety when Michael Gunn was identified with the management in the *Flying Dutchman*, a stupendous success, and his host of admirers came in large numbers, everyone simply flocking to hear him though ships of any sort, phantom or the reverse, on the stage usually fell a bit flat as also did trains) there was nothing intrinsically incompatible about it, he conceded. On the contrary that stab in the back touch was quite in keeping with those italianos though candidly he was none the less free to admit those icecreamers and friers in the fish way not to mention the chip potato variety and so forth over in little Italy there near the Coombe were sober thrifty hardworking fellows except perhaps a bit too given to pothunting the harmless necessary animal of the feline persuasion of others at night so as to have a good old succulent tuckin with garlic *de rigueur* off him or her next day on the quiet and, he added, on the cheap.

—Spaniards, for instance, he continued, passionate temperaments like that, impetuous as Old Nick, are given to taking the law into their own hands and give you your quietus doublequick with those poignards they carry in the abdomen. It comes from the great heat, climate generally. My wife is, so to speak, Spanish, half that is. Point of fact she could actually claim Spanish nationality if she wanted, having been born in (technically) Spain, i.e. Gibraltar. She has the Spanish type. Quite dark, regular brunette, black. I for one certainly believe climate accounts for character. That's why I asked you if you wrote your poetry in Italian.

—The temperaments at the door, Stephen interposed with, were very passionate about ten shillings. *Roberto ruba roba sua.*

—Quite so, Mr Bloom dittoed.

—Then, Stephen said staring and rambling on to himself or some unknown listener somewhere, we have the impetuosity of Dante and the isosceles triangle miss Portinari he fell in love with and Leonardo and san Tommaso Mastino.

—It's in the blood, Mr Bloom acceded at once. All are washed in the blood of the sun. Coincidence I just happened to be in the Kildare street museum today, shortly prior to our meeting if I can so call it, and I was just looking at those antique statues there. The splendid proportions of hips, bosom. You simply don't knock against those kind of women here. An exception here and there. Handsome yes, pretty in a way you find but what I'm talking about is the female form. Besides they have so little taste in dress, most of them, which greatly enhances a woman's natural beauty, no matter what you say. Rumpled stockings, it may be, possibly is, a foible of mine but still it's a thing I simply hate to see.

Interest, however, was starting to flag somewhat all round and then the others got on to talking about accidents at sea, ships lost in a fog, collisions with icebergs, all that sort of thing. Shipahoy of course had his own say to say. He had doubled the cape a few odd times and weathered a monsoon, a kind of wind, in the China seas and through all those perils of the deep there was one thing, he declared, stood to him or words to that effect, a pious medal he had that saved him.

So then after that they drifted on to the wreck off Daunt's rock, wreck of that illfated Norwegian barque nobody could think of her name for the moment till the jarvey who had really quite a look of Henry Campbell remembered it *Palme* on Booterstown strand. That was the talk of the town that year (Albert William Quill wrote a fine piece of original verse of distinctive merit on the topic for the Irish *Times*), breakers running over her and crowds and crowds on the shore in commotion petrified with horror. Then someone said something about the case of the s. s. *Lady Cairns* of Swansea run into by the *Mona* which was on an opposite tack in rather muggyish weather and lost with all hands on deck. No aid was given. Her master, the *Mona's*, said he was afraid his collision bulkhead would give way. She had no water, it appears, in her hold.

At this stage an incident happened. It having become necessary for him to unfurl a reef the sailor vacated his seat.

—Let me cross your bows mate, he said to his neighbour who was just gently dropping off into a peaceful doze.

He made tracks heavily, slowly with a dumpy sort of a gait to the door, stepped heavily down the one step there was out of the shelter and bore due left. While he was in the act of getting his bearings Mr Bloom who noticed when he stood up that he had two flasks of presumably ship's rum sticking one out of each pocket for the private consumption of his burning interior, saw him produce a bottle and uncork it or unscrew and, applying its nozzle to his lips, take a good old delectable swig out of it with a gurgling noise. The irrepressible Bloom, who also had a shrewd suspicion that the old stager went out on a manœuvre after the counterattraction in the shape of a female who however had disappeared to all intents and purposes, could by straining just perceive him, when duly refreshed by his rum puncheon exploit, gaping up at the piers and girders of the Loop line rather out of his depth as of course it was all radically altered since his last visit and greatly improved. Some person or persons invisible directed him to the male urinal erected by the cleansing committee all over the place for the purpose but after a brief space of time during which silence reigned supreme the sailor, evidently giving it a wide berth, eased himself closer at hand, the noise of his bilgewater some little time subsequently splashing on the ground where it apparently awoke a horse of the cabrank. A hoof scooped anyway for new foothold after sleep and harness jingled. Slightly disturbed in his sentrybox by the brazier of live coke the watcher of the corporation stones who, though now broken down and fast breaking up, was none other in stern reality than the Gumley aforesaid, now practically on the parish rates, given the temporary job by Pat Tobin in all human probability from dictates of humanity knowing him before shifted about and shuffled in his box before composing his limbs again in to the arms of Morpheus, a truly amazing piece of hard lines in its most virulent form on a fellow most respectably connected and familiarised with decent home comforts all his life who came in for a cool £ 100 a year at one time which of course the doublebarrelled ass proceeded to make general ducks and drakes of. And there he was at the end of his tether after having often painted the town tolerably pink without a beggarly stiver. He drank needless to be told and it pointed only once more a moral when he might quite easily be in a large way of business if—a big if, however—he had contrived to cure himself of his particular partiality.

All meantime were loudly lamenting the falling off in Irish shipping, coastwise and foreign as well, which was all part and parcel of the same thing. A Palgrave Murphy boat was put off the ways at Alexandra basin, the only launch that year. Right enough the harbours were there only no ships ever called.

There were wrecks and wreckers, the keeper said, who was evidently *au fait*.

What he wanted to ascertain was why that ship ran bang against the only rock in Galway bay when the Galway harbour scheme was mooted by a Mr Worthington or some name like that, eh? Ask the then captain, he advised them, how much palmoil the British government gave him for that day's work, Captain John Lever of the Lever Line.

—Am I right, skipper? he queried of the sailor, now returning after his private potation and the rest of his exertions.

That worthy picking up the scent of the fagend of the song or words growled in wouldbe music but with great vim some kind of chanty or other in seconds or thirds. Mr Bloom's sharp ears heard him then expectorate the plug probably (which it was), so that he must have lodged it for the time being in his fist while he did the drinking and making water jobs and found it a bit sour after the liquid fire in question. Anyhow in he rolled after his successful libation— *cum*—potation, introducing an atmosphere of drink into the *soirée*, boisterously trolling, like a veritable son of a seacook:

> —*The biscuits was as hard as brass*
> *And the beef as salt as Lot's wife's arse.*
> *O, Johnny Lever!*
> *Johnny Lever, O!*

After which effusion the redoubtable specimen duly arrived on the scene and regaining his seat he sank rather than sat heavily on the form provided. Skin-the-Goat, assuming he was he, evidently with an axe to grind, was airing his grievances in a forcible-feeble philippic anent the natural resources of Ireland or something of that sort which he described in his lengthy dissertation as the richest country bar none on the face of God's earth, far and away superior to England, with coal in large quantities, six million pounds worth of pork exported every year, ten millions between butter and eggs and all the riches drained out of it by England levying taxes on the poor people that paid through the nose always and gobbling up the best meat in the market and a lot more surplus steam in the same vein. Their conversation accordingly became general and all agreed that that was a fact. You could grow any mortal thing in Irish soil, he stated, and there was that Colonel Everard down there in Navan growing tobacco. Where would you find anywhere the like of Irish bacon? But a day of reckoning, he stated *crescendo* with no uncertain voice, thoroughly monopolising all the conversation, was in store for mighty England, despite her power of pelf on account of her crimes. There would be a fall and the greatest fall in history. The Germans and the Japs were going to have their little lookin, he affirmed. The Boers were the beginning of the end. Brummagem England was toppling already and her downfall would be Ireland, her Achilles heel, which he explained to them about the vulnerable point of Achilles, the Greek hero, a point his auditors at once seized as he completely gripped their attention by showing the tendon referred to on his boot. His advice to every Irishman was: stay in the land of your birth and work for Ireland and live for Ireland. Ireland, Parnell said, could not spare a single one of her sons.

Silence all round marked the termination of his *finale*. The impervious navigator heard these lurid tidings, undismayed.

—Take a bit of doing, boss, retaliated that rough diamond palpably a bit peeved in response to the foregoing truism.

To which cold douche referring to downfall and so on the keeper concurred but nevertheless held to his main view.

—Who's the best troops in the army? the grizzled old veteran irately interrogated. And the best jumpers and racers? And the best admirals and generals we've got? Tell me that.

—The Irish, for choice, retorted the cabby like Campbell, facial blemishes apart.

—That's right, the old tarpaulin corroborated. The Irish catholic peasant. He's the backbone of our empire. You know Jem Mullins?

While allowing him his individual opinions as everyman the keeper added he cared nothing for any empire, ours or his, and considered no Irishman worthy of his salt that served it. Then they began to have a few irascible words when it waxed hotter, both, needless to say, appealing to the listeners who followed the passage of arms with interest so long as they didn't indulge in recriminations and come to blows.

From inside information extending over a series of years Mr Bloom was rather inclined to poohpooh the suggestion as egregious balderdash for, pending that consummation devoutly to be or not to be wished for, he was fully cognisant of the fact that their neighbours across the channel, unless they were much bigger fools than he took them for, rather concealed their strength than the opposite. It was quite on a par with the quixotic idea in certain quarters that in a hundred million years the coal seam of the sister island would be played out and if, as time went on, that turned out to be how the cat jumped all he could personally say on the matter was that as a host of contingencies, equally relevant to the issue, might occur ere then it was highly advisable in the interim to try to make the most of both countries even though poles apart. Another little interesting point, the amours of whores and chummies, to put it in common parlance, reminded him Irish soldiers had as often fought for England as against her, more so, in fact. And now, why? So the scene between the pair of them, the licensee of the place rumoured to be or have been

Fitzharris, the famous invincible, and the other, obviously bogus, reminded him forcibly as being on all fours with the confidence trick, supposing, that is, it was prearranged as the lookeron, a student of the human soul if anything, the others seeing least of the game. And as for the lessee or keeper, who probably wasn't the other person at all, he (Bloom) couldn't help feeling and most properly it was better to give people like that the goby unless you were a blithering idiot altogether and refuse to have anything to do with them as a golden rule in private life and their felonsetting, there always being the offchance of a Dannyman coming forward and turning queen's evidence or king's now like Denis or Peter Carey, an idea he utterly repudiated. Quite apart from that he disliked those careers of wrongdoing and crime on principle. Yet, though such criminal propensities had never been an inmate of his bosom in any shape or form, he certainly did feel and no denying it (while inwardly remaining what he was) a certain kind of admiration for a man who had actually brandished a knife, cold steel, with the courage of his political convictions (though, personally, he would never be a party to any such thing), off the same bat as those love vendettas of the south, have her or swing for her, when the husband frequently, after some words passed between the two concerning her relations with the other lucky mortal (he having had the pair watched), inflicted fatal injuries on his adored one as a result of an alternative postnuptial *liaison* by plunging his knife into her, until it just struck him that Fitz, nicknamed Skin-the-Goat, merely drove the car for the actual perpetrators of the outrage and so was not, if he was reliably informed, actually party to the ambush which, in point of fact, was the plea some legal luminary saved his skin on. In any case that was very ancient history by now and as for our friend, the pseudo Skin-the-etcetera, he had transparently outlived his welcome. He ought to have either died naturally or on the scaffold high. Like actresses, always farewell positively last performance then come up smiling again. Generous to a fault of course, temperamental, no economising or any idea of the sort, always snapping at the bone for the shadow. So similarly he had a very shrewd suspicion that Mr Johnny Lever got rid of some £. s. d. in the course of his perambulations round the docks in the congenial atmosphere of the *Old Ireland* tavern, come back to Erin and so on. Then as for the other he had heard not so long before the same identical lingo as he told Stephen how he simply but effectually silenced the offender.

—He took umbrage at something or other, that muchinjured but on the whole eventempered person declared, I let slip. He called me a jew and in a heated fashion offensively. So I without deviating from plain facts in the least told him his God, I mean Christ, was a jew too and all his family like me though in reality I'm not. That was one for him. A soft answer turns away wrath. He hadn't a word to say for himself as everyone saw. Am I not right?

He turned a long you are wrong gaze on Stephen of timorous dark pride at the soft impeachment with a glance also of entreaty for he seemed to glean in a kind of a way that it wasn't all exactly.

—*Ex quibus*, Stephen mumbled in a noncommittal accent, their two or four eyes conversing, *Christus* or Bloom his name is or after all any other, *secundum carnem*.

—Of course, Mr Bloom proceeded to stipulate, you must look at both sides of the question. It is hard to lay down any hard and fast rules as to right and wrong but room for improvement all round there certainly is though every country, they say, our own distressful included, has the government it deserves. But with a little goodwill all round. It's all very fine to boast of mutual superiority but what about mutual equality. I resent violence and intolerance in any shape or form. It never reaches anything or stops anything. A revolution must come on the due instalments plan. It's a patent absurdity on the face of it to hate people because they live round the corner and speak another vernacular, in the next house so to speak.

—Memorable bloody bridge battle and seven minutes' war, Stephen assented, between Skinner's alley and Ormond market.

Yes, Mr Bloom thoroughly agreed, entirely endorsing the remark, that was overwhelmingly right. And the whole world was full of that sort of thing.

—You just took the words out of my mouth, he said. A hocuspocus of conflicting evidence that candidly you couldn't remotely . . .

All those wretched quarrels, in his humble opinion, stirring up bad blood, from some bump of combativeness or gland of some kind, erroneously supposed to be about a punctilio of honour and a flag, were very largely a question of the money question which was at the back of everything, greed and jealousy, people never knowing when to stop.

—They accuse, remarked he audibly. He turned away from the others, who probably . . . and spoke nearer to, so as the others . . . in case they . . .

—Jews, he softly imparted in an aside in Stephen's ear, are accused of ruining. Not a vestige of truth in it, I can safely say. History, would you be surprised to learn, proves up to the hilt Spain decayed when the inquisition hounded the jews out and England prospered when Cromwell, an uncommonly able ruffian who in other respects has much to answer for, imported them. Why? Because they are imbued with the proper spirit. They are practical and are proved to be so. I don't want to indulge in any because you know the standard works on the subject and then orthodox as you are. But in the economic, not touching religion, domain the priest spells poverty. Spain again, you saw in the war, compared with goahead America. Turks. It's in the dogma. Because if they didn't believe they'd go straight to heaven when they die they'd try to live better, at least so I think. That's the juggle on which the p.p.'s raise the wind on false pretences. I'm, he resumed with dramatic force, as good an Irishman as that rude person I told you about at the outset and I want to see everyone, concluded he, all creeds and classes *pro rata* having a comfortable tidysized income, in no niggard fashion either, something in the neighbourhood of £ 300 per annum. That's the vital issue at stake and it's feasible and would be provocative of friendlier intercourse between man and man. At least that's my idea for what it's worth. I call that patriotism. *Ubi patria*, as we learned a smattering of in our classical days in *Alma Mater, vita bene*. Where you can live well, the sense is, if you work.

Over his untastable apology for a cup of coffee, listening to this synopsis of things in general, Stephen stared at nothing in particular. He could hear, of course, all kinds of words changing colour like those crabs about Ringsend in the morning burrowing quickly into all colours of different sorts of the same sand where they had a home somewhere beneath or seemed to. Then he looked up and saw the eyes that said or didn't say the words the voice he heard said, if you work.

—Count me out, he managed to remark, meaning work.

The eyes were surprised at this observation because as he, the person who owned them pro tem. observed or rather his voice speaking did, all must work, have to, together.

—I mean, of course, the other hastened to affirm, work in the widest possible sense. Also literary labour not merely for the kudos of the thing. Writing for the newspapers which is the readiest channel nowadays. That's work too. Important work. After all, from the little I know of you, after all the money expended on your education you are entitled to recoup yourself and command your price. You have every bit as much right to live by your pen in pursuit of your philosophy as the peasant has. What? You both belong to Ireland, the brain and the brawn. Each is equally important.

—You suspect, Stephen retorted with a sort of a half laugh, that I may be important because I belong to the *faubourg Saint Patrice* called Ireland for short.

—I would go a step farther, Mr Bloom insinuated.

—But I suspect, Stephen interrupted, that Ireland must be important because it belongs to me.

—What belongs, queried Mr Bloom bending, fancying he was perhaps under some misapprehension. Excuse me. Unfortunately, I didn't catch the latter portion. What was it you . . .?

Stephen, patently crosstempered, repeated and shoved aside his mug of coffee or whatever you like to call it none too politely, adding:

—We can't change the country. Let us change the subject.

At this pertinent suggestion Mr Bloom, to change the subject, looked down but in a quandary, as he couldn't tell exactly what construction to put on belongs to which sounded rather a far cry. The rebuke of some kind was clearer than the other part. Needless to say the fumes of his recent orgy spoke then with some asperity in a curious bitter way foreign to his sober state. Probably the homelife to which Mr B attached the utmost importance had not been all that was needful or he hadn't been familiarised with the right sort of people. With a touch of fear for the young man beside him whom he furtively scrutinised with an air of some consternation remembering he had just come back from Paris, the eyes more especially reminding him forcibly of father and sister, failing to throw much light on the subject, however, he brought to mind instances of cultured fellows that promised so brilliantly nipped in the bud of premature decay and nobody to blame but themselves. For instance there was the case of O'Callaghan, for one, the halfcrazy faddist, respectably connected though of inadequate means, with his mad vagaries among whose other gay doings when rotto and making himself a nuisance to everybody all round he was in the habit of ostentatiously sporting in public a suit of brown paper (a fact). And then the usual *dénouement* after the fun had gone on fast and furious he got landed into hot water and had to be spirited away by a few friends, after a strong hint to a blind horse from John Mallon of Lower Castle Yard, so as not to be made amenable under section two of the criminal law amendment act, certain names of those subpœnaed being handed in but not divulged for reasons which will occur to anyone with a pick of brains. Briefly, putting two and two together, six sixteen which he pointedly turned a deaf ear to, Antonio and so forth, jockeys and esthetes and the tattoo which was all the go in the seventies or thereabouts even in the house of lords because early in life the occupant of the throne, then heir apparent, the other members of the upper ten and other high personages simply following in the footsteps of the head of the state, he reflected about the errors of notorieties and crowned heads running counter to morality such as the Cornwall case a number of years before under their veneer in a way scarcely intended by nature, a thing good Mrs Grundy, as the law stands, was terribly down on though not for the reason they thought they were probably whatever it was except women chiefly who were always fiddling more or less at one another it being largely a matter of dress and all the rest of it. Ladies who like distinctive underclothing should, and every welltailored man must, trying to make the gap wider between them by innuendo and give more of a genuine filip to acts of impropriety between the two, she unbuttoned his and then he untied her, mind the pin, whereas savages in the cannibal islands, say, at ninety degrees in the shade not caring a continental. However, reverting to the original, there were on the other hand others who had forced their way to the top from the lowest rung by the aid of their bootstraps. Sheer force of natural genius, that. With brains, sir.

For which and further reasons he felt it was his interest and duty even to wait on and profit by the unlookedfor occasion though why he could not exactly tell being as it was already several shillings to the bad having in fact let himself in for it. Still to cultivate the acquaintance of someone of no uncommon calibre who could provide food for reflection would amply repay any small. Intellectual stimulation, as such, was, he felt, from time to time a firstrate tonic for the mind. Added to which was the coincidence of meeting, discussion, dance, row, old salt of the here today and gone tomorrow type, night loafers, the whole galaxy of events, all went to make up a miniature cameo of the world we live in especially as the lives of the submerged tenth, viz. coalminers, divers, scavengers etc., were very much under the microscope lately. To improve the shining hour he wondered whether

he might meet with anything approaching the same luck as Mr Philip
Beaufoy if taken down in writing suppose he were to pen something
out of the common groove (as he fully intended doing) at the rate of
one guinea per column. *My Experiences*, let us say, *in a Cabman's Shelter.*

The pink edition extra sporting of the *Telegraph* tell a graphic lie
lay, as luck would have it, beside his elbow and as he was just puzzling
again, far from satisfied, over a country belonging to him and the
preceding rebus the vessel came from Bridgwater and the postcard
was addressed A. Boudin find the captain's age, his eyes went aimlessly
over the respective captions which came under his special province the
allembracing give us this day our daily press. First he got a bit of a start
but it turned out to be only something about somebody named H. du
Boyes, agent for typewriters or something like that. Great battle, Tokio.
Lovemaking in Irish, £ 200 damages. Gordon Bennett. Emigration
Swindle. Letter from His Grace. William †. Ascot meeting, the Gold
Cup. Victory of outsider *Throwaway* recalls Derby of '92 when Capt.
Marshall's dark horse *Sir Hugo* captured the blue ribband at long odds.
New York disaster. Thousand lives lost. Foot and Mouth. Funeral of
the late Mr Patrick Dignam.

So to change the subject he read about Dignam R. I. P. which,
he reflected, was anything but a gay sendoff. Or a change of address
anyway.

—*This morning* (Hynes put it in of course) *the remains of the late Mr
Patrick Dignam were removed from his residence, no 9 Newbridge Avenue,
Sandymount, for interment in Glasnevin. The deceased gentleman was a most
popular and genial personality in city life and his demise after a brief illness
came as a great shock to citizens of all classes by whom he is deeply regretted.
The obsequies, at which many friends of the deceased were present, were carried
out* (certainly Hynes wrote it with a nudge from Corny) *by Messrs
H. J. O'Neill and Son, 164 North Strand Road. The mourners included:
Patk. Dignam (son), Bernard Corrigan (brother-in-law), Jno. Henry Menton,
solr, Martin Cunningham, John Power, eatondph 1/8 ador dorador douradora*
(must be where he called Monks the dayfather about Keyes's ad)
*Thomas Kernan, Simon Dedalus, Stephen Dedalus B. A., Edw. J. Lambert,
Cornelius T. Kelleher, Joseph M'C Hynes, L. Boom, CP M'Coy,—M'Intosh
and several others.*

Nettled not a little by L. *Boom* (as it incorrectly stated) and the line
of bitched type but tickled to death simultaneously by C. P. M'Coy
and Stephen Dedalus B. A. who were conspicuous, needless to say,

by their total absence (to say nothing of M'Intosh) L. Boom pointed it out to his companion B. A. engaged in stifling another yawn, half nervousness, not forgetting the usual crop of nonsensical howlers of misprints.

—Is that first epistle to the Hebrews, he asked as soon as his bottom jaw would let him, in? Text: open thy mouth and put thy foot in it.

—It is. Really, Mr Bloom said (though first he fancied he alluded to the archbishop till he added about foot and mouth with which there could be no possible connection) overjoyed to set his mind at rest and a bit flabbergasted at Myles Crawford's after all managing to. There.

While the other was reading it on page two Boom (to give him for the nonce his new misnomer) whiled away a few odd leisure moments in fits and starts with the account of the third event at Ascot on page three, his side. Value 1000 sovs with 3000 sovs in specie added. For entire colts and fillies. Mr F. Alexander's *Throwaway*, b. h. by *Rightaway-Thrale*, 5 yrs, 9 st 4 lbs (W. Lane) 1. Lord Howard de Walden's *Zinfandel* (M. Cannon) 2. Mr W. Bass's *Sceptre* 3. Betting 5 to 4 on *Zinfandel*, 20 to 1 *Throwaway* (off). *Sceptre* a shade heavier. It was anybody's race then the rank outsider drew to the fore, got long lead, beating Lord Howard de Walden's chestnut colt and Mr W. Bass's bay filly Sceptre on a 2 1/2 mile course. Winner trained by Braime so that Lenehan's version of the business was all pure buncombe. Secured the verdict cleverly by a length. 1000 sovs with 3000 in specie. Also ran: J de Bremond's (French horse Bantam Lyons was anxiously inquiring after not in yet but expected any minute) *Maximum II*. Different ways of bringing off a coup. Lovemaking damages. Though that halfbaked Lyons ran off at a tangent in his impetuosity to get left. Of course gambling eminently lent itself to that sort of thing though as the event turned out the poor fool hadn't much reason to congratulate himself on his pick, the forlorn hope. Guesswork it reduced itself to eventually.

—There was every indication they would arrive at that, he, Bloom, said.

—Who? the other, whose hand by the way was hurt, said.

One morning you would open the paper, the cabman affirmed, and read: *Return of Parnell*. He bet them what they liked. A Dublin fusilier was in that shelter one night and said he saw him in South Africa. Pride it was killed him. He ought to have done away with himself or lain low for a time after committee room no 15 until he was his old self again with no-one to point a finger at him. Then they would all to a man have gone down on their marrowbones to him to come back when he had recovered his senses. Dead he wasn't. Simply absconded somewhere. The coffin they brought over was full of stones. He changed his name to De Wet, the Boer general. He made a mistake to fight the priests. And so forth and so on.

All the same Bloom (properly so dubbed) was rather surprised at their memories for in nine cases out of ten it was a case of tarbarrels and not singly but in their thousands and then complete oblivion because it was twenty odd years. Highly unlikely of course there was even a shadow of truth in the stones and, even supposing, he thought a return highly inadvisable, all things considered. Something evidently riled them in his death. Either he petered out too tamely of acute pneumonia just when his various different political arrangements were nearing completion or whether it transpired he owed his death to his having neglected to change his boots and clothes after a wetting when a cold resulted and failing to consult a specialist he being confined to his room till he eventually died of it amid widespread regret before a fortnight was at an end or quite possibly they were distressed to find the job was taken out of their hands. Of course nobody being acquainted with his movements even before there was absolutely no clue as to his whereabouts which were decidedly of the *Alice, where art thou* order even prior to his starting to go under several aliases such as Fox and Stewart so the remark which emanated from friend cabby might be within the bounds of possibility. Naturally then it would prey on his mind as a born leader of men which undoubtedly he was and a commanding figure, a sixfooter or at any rate five feet ten or eleven in his stockinged feet, whereas Messrs So and So who, though they weren't even a patch on the former man, ruled the roost after their redeeming features were very few and far between. It certainly pointed a moral, the idol with feet of clay, and then seventytwo of his trusty henchmen rounding on him with mutual mudslinging. And the identical same with murderers. You had to come back. That haunting sense kind of drew you. To show the understudy in the title *rôle* how to. He saw him once on the auspicious occasion when they broke up the type in the *Insuppressible* or was it *United Ireland*, a privilege he keenly appreciated, and, in point of fact, handed him his silk hat when it was knocked off and he said *Thank you*, excited as he undoubtedly was under his frigid exterior notwithstanding the little misadventure mentioned between the cup and the lip: what's bred in the bone. Still as regards return. You were a lucky dog if they didn't set the terrier at you directly you got back. Then a lot of shillyshally usually followed, Tom for and Dick and Harry against. And then, number one, you came up against the man in possession and had to produce your credentials like the claimant in the Tichborne case, Roger Charles Tichborne, *Bella* was the boat's name to the best of his recollection he, the heir, went down in as the evidence went to show and there was a tattoo mark too in Indian ink, lord Bellew was it, as he might very easily have picked up the details from some pal on board ship and then, when got up to tally with the description given, introduce himself with: *Excuse me, my name is So and So* or some such commonplace remark. A more prudent course, as Bloom said to the not over effusive, in fact like the distinguished personage under discussion beside him, would have been to sound the lie of the land first.

—That bitch, that English whore, did for him, the shebeen proprietor commented. She put the first nail in his coffin.

—Fine lump of a woman all the same, the *soi-disant* townclerk Henry Campbell remarked, and plenty of her. She loosened many a man's thighs. I seen her picture in a barber's. The husband was a captain or an officer.

—Ay, Skin-the-Goat amusingly added, he was and a cottonball one.

This gratuitous contribution of a humorous character occasioned a fair amount of laughter among his *entourage*. As regards Bloom he, without the faintest suspicion of a smile, merely gazed in the direction of the door and reflected upon the historic story which had aroused extraordinary interest at the time when the facts, to make matters worse, were made public with the usual affectionate letters that passed between them full of sweet nothings. First it was strictly Platonic till nature intervened and an attachment sprang up between them till bit by bit matters came to a climax and the matter became the talk of the town till the staggering blow came as a welcome intelligence to not a few evildisposed, however, who were resolved upon encompassing his downfall though the thing was public property all along though not to anything like the sensational extent that it subsequently blossomed into. Since their names were coupled, though, since he was her declared favourite, where was the particular necessity to proclaim it to the rank and file from the housetops, the fact, namely, that he had shared her bedroom which came out in the witnessbox on oath when a thrill went through the packed court literally electrifying everybody in the shape of witnesses swearing to having witnessed him on such and such a particular date in the act of scrambling out of an upstairs apartment with the assistance of a ladder in night apparel, having gained admittance in the same fashion, a fact the weeklies, addicted to the lubric a little, simply coined shoals of money out of. Whereas the simple fact of the case was it was simply a case of the husband not being up to the scratch, with nothing in common between them beyond the name, and then a real man arriving on the scene, strong to the verge of weakness, falling a victim to her siren charms and forgetting home ties, the usual sequel, to bask in the loved one's smiles. The eternal question of the life connubial, needless to say, cropped up. Can real love, supposing there happens to be another chap in the case, exist between married folk? Poser. Though it was no concern of theirs absolutely if he regarded her with affection, carried away by a wave of folly. A magnificent specimen of manhood he was truly augmented obviously by gifts of a high order, as compared with the other military supernumerary that is (who was just the usual everyday *farewell, my gallant captain* kind of an individual in the light dragoons, the 18th hussars to be accurate) and inflammable doubtless (the fallen leader, that is, not the other) in his own peculiar way which she of course, woman, quickly perceived as highly likely to carve his way to fame which he almost bid fair to do till the priests and ministers of the gospel as a whole, his erstwhile staunch adherents, and his beloved evicted tenants for whom he had done yeoman service in the rural parts of the country by taking up the cudgels on their behalf in a way that exceeded their most sanguine expectations, very effectually cooked his matrimonial goose, thereby heaping coals of fire on his head much in the same way as the fabled ass›s kick. Looking back now in a retrospective kind of arrangement all seemed a kind of dream. And then coming back was the worst thing you ever did because it went without saying you would feel out of place as things always moved with the times. Why, as he reflected, Irishtown strand, a locality he had not been in for quite a number of years looked different somehow since, as it happened, he went to reside on the north side. North or south, however, it was just the wellknown case of hot passion, pure and simple, upsetting the applecart with a vengeance and just bore out the very thing he was saying as she also was Spanish or half so, types that wouldn't do things by halves, passionate abandon of the south, casting every shred of decency to the winds.

—Just bears out what I was saying, he, with glowing bosom said to Stephen, about blood and the sun. And, if I don't greatly mistake she was Spanish too.

—The king of Spain's daughter, Stephen answered, adding something or other rather muddled about farewell and adieu to you Spanish onions and the first land called the Deadman and from Ramhead to Scilly was so and so many.

—Was she? Bloom ejaculated, surprised though not astonished by any means, I never heard that rumour before. Possible, especially there, it was as she lived there. So, Spain.

Carefully avoiding a book in his pocket *Sweets of,* which reminded him by the by of that Capel street library book out of date, he took out his pocketbook and, turning over the various contents it contained rapidly finally he.

—Do you consider, by the by, he said, thoughtfully selecting a faded photo which he laid on the table, that a Spanish type?

Stephen, obviously addressed, looked down on the photo showing a large sized lady with her fleshy charms on evidence in an open fashion as she was in the full bloom of womanhood in evening dress cut ostentatiously low for the occasion to give a liberal display of bosom, with more than vision of breasts, her full lips parted and some perfect teeth, standing near, ostensibly with gravity, a piano on the rest of which was *In Old Madrid,* a ballad, pretty in its way, which was then all the vogue. Her (the lady's) eyes, dark, large, looked at Stephen, about to smile about something to be admired, Lafayette of Westmoreland street, Dublin's premier photographic artist, being responsible for the esthetic execution.

—Mrs Bloom, my wife the *prima donna* Madam Marion Tweedy, Bloom indicated. Taken a few years since. In or about ninety six. Very like her then.

Beside the young man he looked also at the photo of the lady now his legal wife who, he intimated, was the accomplished daughter of Major Brian Tweedy and displayed at an early age remarkable proficiency as a singer having even made her bow to the public when her years numbered barely sweet sixteen. As for the face it was a speaking likeness in expression but it did not do justice to her figure which came in for a lot of notice usually and which did not come out to the best advantage in that getup. She could without difficulty, he said, have posed for the ensemble, not to dwell on certain opulent curves of the. He dwelt, being a bit of an artist in his spare time, on the female form in general developmentally because, as it so happened, no later than that afternoon he had seen those Grecian statues, perfectly developed as works of art, in the National Museum. Marble could give the original, shoulders, back, all the symmetry, all the rest. Yes, puritanisme, it does though, Saint Joseph's sovereign thievery alors (Bandez!) Figne toi trop. Whereas no photo could because it simply wasn't art in a word.

The spirit moving him he would much have liked to follow Jack Tar's good example and leave the likeness there for a very few minutes to speak for itself on the plea he so that the other could drink in the beauty for himself, her stage presence being, frankly, a treat in itself which the camera could not at all do justice to. But it was scarcely professional etiquette so. Though it was a warm pleasant sort of a night now yet wonderfully cool for the season considering, for sunshine after storm. And he did feel a kind of need there and then to follow suit like a kind of inward voice and satisfy a possible need by moving a motion. Nevertheless he sat tight just viewing the slightly soiled photo creased by opulent curves, none the worse for wear however, and looked away thoughtfully with the intention of not further increasing the other's possible embarrassment while gauging her symmetry of heaving *embonpoint*. In fact the slight soiling was only an added charm like the case of linen slightly soiled, good as new, much better in fact with the starch out. Suppose she was gone when he? I looked for the lamp which she told me came into his mind but merely as a passing fancy of his because he then recollected the morning littered bed etcetera and the book about Ruby with met him pike hoses (*sic*) in it which must have fell down sufficiently appropriately beside the domestic chamberpot with apologies to Lindley Murray.

The vicinity of the young man he certainly relished, educated, *distingué* and impulsive into the bargain, far and away the pick of the bunch though you wouldn't think he had it in him yet you would. Besides he said the picture was handsome which, say what you like, it was though at the moment she was distinctly stouter. And why not? An awful lot of makebelieve went on about that sort of thing involving a lifelong slur with the usual splash page of gutterpress about the same old matrimonial tangle alleging misconduct with professional golfer or the newest stage favourite instead of being honest and aboveboard about the whole business. How they were fated to meet and an attachment sprang up between the two so that their names were coupled in the public eye was told in court with letters containing the habitual mushy and compromising expressions leaving no loophole to show that they openly cohabited two or three times a week at some wellknown seaside hotel and relations, when the thing ran its normal course, became in due course intimate. Then the decree *nisi* and the King's proctor tries to show cause why and, he failing to quash it, *nisi* was made absolute. But as for that the two misdemeanants, wrapped up as they largely were in one another, could safely afford to ignore it as they very largely did till the matter was put in the hands of a solicitor who filed a petition for the party wronged in due course. He, Bloom, enjoyed the distinction of being close to Erin's uncrowned king in the flesh when the thing occurred on the historic *fracas* when the fallen leader's, who notoriously stuck to his guns to the last drop even when clothed in the mantle of adultery, (leader's) trusty henchmen to the number of ten or a dozen or possibly even more than that penetrated into the printing works of the *Insuppressible* or no it was *United Ireland* (a by no means by the by appropriate appellative) and broke up the typecases with hammers or something like that all on account of some scurrilous effusions from the facile pens of the O'Brienite scribes at the usual mudslinging occupation reflecting on the erstwhile tribune's private morals. Though palpably a radically altered man he was still a commanding figure though carelessly garbed as usual with that look of settled purpose which went a long way with the shillyshallyers till they discovered to their vast discomfiture that their idol had feet of clay after placing him upon a pedestal which she, however, was the first to perceive. As those were particularly hot times in the general hullaballoo Bloom sustained a minor injury from a nasty prod of some chap's elbow in the crowd that of course congregated lodging some place about the pit of the stomach, fortunately not of a grave character. His hat (Parnell's) a silk one was inadvertently knocked off and, as a matter of strict history, Bloom was the man who picked it up in the crush after witnessing the occurrence meaning to return it to him (and return it to him he did with the utmost celerity) who panting and hatless and whose thoughts were miles away from his hat at the time all the same being a gentleman born with a stake in the country he, as a matter of fact, having gone into it more for the kudos of the thing than anything else, what's bred in the bone instilled into him in infancy at his mother's knee in the shape of knowing what good form was came out at once because he turned round to the donor and thanked him with perfect *aplomb*, saying: *Thank you, sir,* though in a very different tone of voice from the ornament of the legal profession whose headgear Bloom also set to rights earlier in the course of the day, history repeating itself with a difference, after the burial of a mutual friend when they had left him alone in his glory after the grim task of having committed his remains to the grave.

On the other hand what incensed him more inwardly was the blatant jokes of the cabman and so on who passed it all off as a jest, laughing immoderately, pretending to understand everything, the why and the wherefore, and in reality not knowing their own minds, it being a case for the two parties themselves unless it ensued that the legitimate husband happened to be a party to it owing to some anonymous letter from the usual boy Jones, who happened to come across them at the crucial moment in a loving position locked in one another's arms, drawing attention to their illicit proceedings and leading up to a domestic rumpus and the erring fair one begging forgiveness of her lord and master upon her knees and promising to sever the connection and not receive his visits any more if only the aggrieved husband would overlook the matter and let bygones be bygones with tears in her eyes though possibly with her tongue in her fair cheek at the same time as quite possibly there were several others. He personally, being of a sceptical bias, believed and didn't make the smallest bones about saying so either that man or men in the plural were always hanging around on the waiting list about a lady, even supposing she was the best wife in the world and they got on fairly well together for the sake of argument, when, neglecting her duties, she chose to be tired of wedded life and was on for a little flutter in polite debauchery to press their attentions on her with improper intent, the upshot being that her affections centred on another, the cause of many *liaisons* between still attractive married women getting on for fair and forty and younger men, no doubt as several famous cases of feminine infatuation proved up to the hilt.

It was a thousand pities a young fellow, blessed with an allowance of brains as his neighbour obviously was, should waste his valuable time with profligate women who might present him with a nice dose to last him his lifetime. In the nature of single blessedness he would one day take unto himself a wife when Miss Right came on the scene but in the interim ladies' society was a *conditio sine qua non* though he had the gravest possible doubts, not that he wanted in the smallest to pump Stephen about Miss Ferguson (who was very possibly the particular lodestar who brought him down to Irishtown so early in the morning), as to whether he would find much satisfaction basking in the boy and girl courtship idea and the company of smirking misses without a penny to their names bi or triweekly with the orthodox preliminary canter of complimentplaying and walking out leading up to fond lovers' ways and flowers and chocs. To think of him house and homeless, rooked by some landlady worse than any stepmother, was really too bad at his age. The queer suddenly things he popped out with attracted the elder man who was several years the other's senior or like his father but something substantial he certainly ought to eat even were it only an eggflip made on unadulterated maternal nutriment or, failing that, the homely Humpty Dumpty boiled.

—At what o'clock did you dine? he questioned of the slim form and tired though unwrinkled face.

—Some time yesterday, Stephen said.

—Yesterday! exclaimed Bloom till he remembered it was already tomorrow Friday. Ah, you mean it's after twelve!

—The day before yesterday, Stephen said, improving on himself.

Literally astounded at this piece of intelligence Bloom reflected. Though they didn't see eye to eye in everything a certain analogy there somehow was as if both their minds were travelling, so to speak, in the one train of thought. At his age when dabbling in politics roughly some score of years previously when he had been a *quasi* aspirant to parliamentary honours in the Buckshot Foster days he too recollected in retrospect (which was a source of keen satisfaction in itself) he had a sneaking regard for those same ultra ideas. For instance when the evicted tenants question, then at its first inception, bulked largely in people's mind though, it goes without saying, not contributing a copper or pinning his faith absolutely to its dictums, some of which wouldn't exactly hold water, he at the outset in principle at all events was in thorough sympathy with peasant possession as voicing the trend of modern opinion (a partiality, however, which, realising his mistake, he was subsequently partially cured of) and even was twitted with going a step farther than Michael Davitt in the striking views he at one time inculcated as a backtothelander, which was one reason he strongly resented the innuendo put upon him in so barefaced a fashion by our friend at the gathering of the clans in Barney Kiernan's so that he, though often considerably misunderstood and the least pugnacious of mortals, be it repeated, departed from his customary habit to give him (metaphorically) one in the gizzard though, so far as politics themselves were concerned, he was only too conscious of the casualties invariably resulting from propaganda and displays of mutual animosity and the misery and suffering it entailed as a foregone conclusion on fine young fellows, chiefly, destruction of the fittest, in a word.

Anyhow upon weighing up the pros and cons, getting on for one, as it was, it was high time to be retiring for the night. The crux was it was a bit risky to bring him home as eventualities might possibly ensue (somebody having a temper of her own sometimes) and spoil the hash altogether as on the night he misguidedly brought home a dog (breed unknown) with a lame paw (not that the cases were either identical or the reverse though he had hurt his hand too) to Ontario Terrace as he very distinctly remembered, having been there, so to speak. On the other hand it was altogether far and away too late for the Sandymount or Sandycove suggestion so that he was in some perplexity as to which of the two alternatives. Everything pointed to the fact that it behoved him to avail himself to the full of the opportunity, all things considered. His initial impression was he was a shade standoffish or not over effusive but it grew on him someway. For one thing he mightn't what you call jump at the idea, if approached, and what mostly worried him was he didn't know how to lead up to it or word it exactly, supposing he did entertain the proposal, as it would afford him very great personal pleasure if he would allow him to help to put coin in his way or some wardrobe, if found suitable. At all events he wound up by concluding, eschewing for the nonce hidebound precedent, a cup of Epps's cocoa and a shakedown for the night plus the use of a rug or two and overcoat doubled into a pillow at least he would be in safe hands and as warm as a toast on a trivet he failed to perceive any very vast amount of harm in that always with the proviso no rumpus of any sort was kicked up. A move had to be made because that merry old soul, the grasswidower in question who appeared to be glued to the spot, didn't appear in any particular hurry to wend his way home to his dearly beloved Queenstown and it was highly likely some sponger's bawdyhouse of retired beauties where age was no bar off Sheriff street lower would be the best clue to that equivocal character's whereabouts for a few days to come, alternately racking their feelings (the mermaids') with sixchamber revolver anecdotes verging on the tropical calculated to freeze the marrow of anybody's bones and mauling their largesized charms betweenwhiles with rough and tumble gusto to the accompaniment of large potations of potheen and the usual blarney about himself for as to who he in reality was let x equal my right name and address, as Mr Algebra remarks *passim*. At the same time he inwardly chuckled over his gentle repartee to the blood and ouns champion about his god being a jew. People could put up with being bitten by a wolf but what properly riled them was a bite from a sheep. The most vulnerable point too of tender Achilles. Your god was a jew. Because mostly they appeared to imagine he came from Carrick-on-Shannon or somewhereabouts in the county Sligo.

—I propose, our hero eventually suggested after mature reflection while prudently pocketing her photo, as it's rather stuffy here you just come home with me and talk things over. My diggings are quite close in the vicinity. You can't drink that stuff. Do you like cocoa? Wait. I'll just pay this lot.

The best plan clearly being to clear out, the remainder being plain sailing, he beckoned, while prudently pocketing the photo, to the keeper of the shanty who didn't seem to.

—Yes, that's the best, he assured Stephen to whom for the matter of that Brazen Head or him or anywhere else was all more or less.

All kinds of Utopian plans were flashing through his (B's) busy brain, education (the genuine article), literature, journalism, prize titbits, up to date billing, concert tours in English watering resorts packed with hydros and seaside theatres, turning money away, duets in Italian with the accent perfectly true to nature and a quantity of other things, no necessity, of course, to tell the world and his wife from the housetops about it, and a slice of luck. An opening was all was wanted. Because he more than suspected he had his father's voice to bank his hopes on which it was quite on the cards he had so it would be just as well, by the way no harm, to trail the conversation in the direction of that particular red herring just to.

The cabby read out of the paper he had got hold of that the former viceroy, earl Cadogan, had presided at the cabdrivers' association dinner in London somewhere. Silence with a yawn or two accompanied this thrilling announcement. Then the old specimen in the corner who appeared to have some spark of vitality left read out that sir Anthony MacDonnell had left Euston for the chief secretary's lodge or words to that effect. To which absorbing piece of intelligence echo answered why.

—Give us a squint at that literature, grandfather, the ancient mariner put in, manifesting some natural impatience.

—And welcome, answered the elderly party thus addressed.

The sailor lugged out from a case he had a pair of greenish goggles which he very slowly hooked over his nose and both ears.

—Are you bad in the eyes? the sympathetic personage like the townclerk queried.

—Why, answered the seafarer with the tartan beard, who seemingly was a bit of a literary cove in his own small way, staring out of seagreen portholes as you might well describe them as, I uses goggles reading. Sand in the Red Sea done that. One time I could read a book in the dark, manner of speaking. *The Arabian Nights Entertainment* was my favourite and *Red as a Rose is She*.

Thereupon he pawed the journal open and pored upon Lord only knows what, found drowned or the exploits of King Willow, Iremonger having made a hundred and something second wicket not out for Notts, during which time (completely regardless of Ire) the keeper was intensely occupied loosening an apparently new or secondhand boot which manifestly pinched him as he muttered against whoever it was sold it, all of them who were sufficiently awake enough to be picked out by their facial expressions, that is to say, either simply looking on glumly or passing a trivial remark.

To cut a long story short Bloom, grasping the situation, was the first to rise from his seat so as not to outstay their welcome having first and foremost, being as good as his word that he would foot the bill for the occasion, taken the wise precaution to unobtrusively motion to mine host as a parting shot a scarcely perceptible sign when the others were not looking to the effect that the amount due was forthcoming, making a grand total of fourpence (the amount he deposited unobtrusively in four coppers, literally the last of the Mohicans), he having previously spotted on the printed pricelist for all who ran to read opposite him in unmistakable figures, coffee 2d, confectionery do, and honestly well worth twice the money once in a way, as Wetherup used to remark.

—Come, he counselled to close the *séance*.

Seeing that the ruse worked and the coast was clear they left the shelter or shanty together and the *élite* society of oilskin and company whom nothing short of an earthquake would move out of their *dolce far niente*. Stephen, who confessed to still feeling poorly and fagged out, paused at the, for a moment, the door.

—One thing I never understood, he said to be original on the spur of the moment. Why they put tables upside down at night, I mean chairs upside down, on the tables in cafés. To which impromptu the neverfailing Bloom replied without a moment's hesitation, saying straight off:

—To sweep the floor in the morning.

So saying he skipped around, nimbly considering, frankly at the same time apologetic to get on his companion's right, a habit of his, by the bye, his right side being, in classical idiom, his tender Achilles. The night air was certainly now a treat to breathe though Stephen was a bit weak on his pins.

—It will (the air) do you good, Bloom said, meaning also the walk, in a moment. The only thing is to walk then you'll feel a different man. Come. It's not far. Lean on me.

Accordingly he passed his left arm in Stephen's right and led him on accordingly.

—Yes, Stephen said uncertainly because he thought he felt a strange kind of flesh of a different man approach him, sinewless and wobbly and all that.

Anyhow they passed the sentrybox with stones, brazier etc. where the municipal supernumerary, ex-Gumley, was still to all intents and purposes wrapped in the arms of Murphy, as the adage has it, dreaming of fresh fields and pastures new. And *apropos* of coffin of stones the analogy was not at all bad as it was in fact a stoning to death on the part of seventytwo out of eighty odd constituencies that ratted at the time of the split and chiefly the belauded peasant class, probably the selfsame evicted tenants he had put in their holdings.

So they turned on to chatting about music, a form of art for which Bloom, as a pure amateur, possessed the greatest love, as they made tracks arm in arm across Beresford place. Wagnerian music, though confessedly grand in its way, was a bit too heavy for Bloom and hard to follow at the first go-off but the music of Mercadante's *Huguenots*, Meyerbeer's *Seven Last Words on the Cross* and Mozart's *Twelfth Mass* he simply revelled in, the *Gloria* in that being, to his mind, the acme of first class music as such, literally knocking everything else into a cocked hat. He infinitely preferred the sacred music of the catholic church to anything the opposite shop could offer in that line such as those Moody and Sankey hymns or *Bid me to live and I will live thy protestant to be*. He also yielded to none in his admiration of Rossini's *Stabat Mater*, a work simply abounding in immortal numbers, in which his wife, Madam Marion Tweedy, made a hit, a veritable sensation, he might safely say, greatly adding to her other laurels and putting the others totally in the shade, in the jesuit fathers' church in upper Gardiner street, the sacred edifice being thronged to the doors to hear her with virtuosos, or *virtuosi* rather. There was the unanimous opinion that there was none to come up to her and suffice it to say in a place of worship for music of a sacred character there was a generally voiced desire for an encore. On the whole though favouring preferably light opera of the *Don Giovanni* description and *Martha*, a gem in its line, he had a *penchant*, though with only a surface knowledge, for the severe classical school such as Mendelssohn. And talking of that, taking it for granted he knew all about the old favourites, he mentioned *par excellence* Lionel's air in *Martha, M'appari*, which, curiously enough, he had heard or overheard, to be more accurate, on yesterday, a privilege he keenly appreciated, from the lips of Stephen's respected father, sung to perfection, a study of the number, in fact, which made all the others take a back seat. Stephen, in reply to a politely put query, said he didn't sing it but launched out into praises of Shakespeare's songs, at least of in or about that period, the lutenist Dowland who lived in Fetter lane near Gerard the herbalist, who *anno ludendo hausi, Doulandus*, an instrument he was contemplating purchasing from Mr Arnold Dolmetsch, whom Bloom did not quite recall though the name certainly sounded familiar, for sixtyfive guineas and Farnaby and son with their *dux* and *comes* conceits and Byrd (William) who played the virginals, he said, in the Queen's chapel or anywhere else he found them and one Tomkins who made toys or airs and John Bull.

On the roadway which they were approaching whilst still speaking beyond the swingchains a horse, dragging a sweeper, paced on the paven ground, brushing a long swathe of mire up so that with the noise Bloom was not perfectly certain whether he had caught aright the allusion to sixtyfive guineas and John Bull. He inquired if it was John Bull the political celebrity of that ilk, as it struck him, the two identical names, as a striking coincidence.

By the chains the horse slowly swerved to turn, which perceiving, Bloom, who was keeping a sharp lookout as usual, plucked the other's sleeve gently, jocosely remarking:

—Our lives are in peril tonight. Beware of the steamroller.

They thereupon stopped. Bloom looked at the head of a horse not worth anything like sixtyfive guineas, suddenly in evidence in the dark quite near so that it seemed new, a different grouping of bones and even flesh because palpably it was a fourwalker, a hipshaker, a blackbuttocker, a taildangler, a headhanger putting his hind foot foremost the while the lord of his creation sat on the perch, busy with his thoughts. But such a good poor brute he was sorry he hadn't a lump of sugar but, as he wisely reflected, you could scarcely be prepared for every emergency that might crop up. He was just a big nervous foolish noodly kind of a horse, without a second care in the world. But even a dog, he reflected, take that mongrel in Barney Kiernan's, of the same size, would be a holy horror to face. But it was no animal's fault in particular if he was built that way like the camel, ship of the desert, distilling grapes into potheen in his hump. Nine tenths of them all could be caged or trained, nothing beyond the art of man barring the bees. Whale with a harpoon hairpin, alligator tickle the small of his back and he sees the joke, chalk a circle for a rooster, tiger my eagle eye. These timely reflections anent the brutes of the field occupied his mind somewhat distracted from Stephen's words while the ship of the street was manœuvring and Stephen went on about the highly interesting old.

—What's this I was saying? Ah, yes! My wife, he intimated, plunging *in medias res*, would have the greatest of pleasure in making your acquaintance as she is passionately attached to music of any kind.

He looked sideways in a friendly fashion at the sideface of Stephen, image of his mother, which was not quite the same as the usual handsome blackguard type they unquestionably had an insatiable hankering after as he was perhaps not that way built.

Still, supposing he had his father's gift as he more than suspected, it opened up new vistas in his mind such as Lady Fingall's Irish industries, concert on the preceding Monday, and aristocracy in general.

Exquisite variations he was now describing on an air *Youth here has End* by Jans Pieter Sweelinck, a Dutchman of Amsterdam where the frows come from. Even more he liked an old German song of *Johannes*

Jeep about the clear sea and the voices of sirens, sweet murderers of men, which boggled Bloom a bit:

> *Von der Sirenen Listigkeit*
> *Tun die Poeten dichten.*

These opening bars he sang and translated *extempore*. Bloom, nodding, said he perfectly understood and begged him to go on by all means which he did.

A phenomenally beautiful tenor voice like that, the rarest of boons, which Bloom appreciated at the very first note he got out, could easily, if properly handled by some recognised authority on voice production such as Barraclough and being able to read music into the bargain, command its own price where baritones were ten a penny and procure for its fortunate possessor in the near future an *entrée* into fashionable houses in the best residential quarters of financial magnates in a large way of business and titled people where with his university degree of B. A. (a huge ad in its way) and gentlemanly bearing to all the more influence the good impression he would infallibly score a distinct success, being blessed with brains which also could be utilised for the purpose and other requisites, if his clothes were properly attended to so as to the better worm his way into their good graces as he, a youthful tyro in society's sartorial niceties, hardly understood how a little thing like that could militate against you. It was in fact only a matter of months and he could easily foresee him participating in their musical and artistic *conversazioni* during the festivities of the Christmas season, for choice, causing a slight flutter in the dovecotes of the fair sex and being made a lot of by ladies out for sensation, cases of which, as he happened to know, were on record—in fact, without giving the show away, he himself once upon a time, if he cared to, could easily have. Added to which of course would be the pecuniary emolument by no means to be sneezed at, going hand in hand with his tuition fees. Not, he parenthesised, that for the sake of filthy lucre he need necessarily embrace the lyric platform as a walk in life for any lengthy space of time. But a step in the required direction it was beyond yea or nay and both monetarily and mentally it contained no reflection on his dignity in the smallest and it often turned in uncommonly handy to be handed a cheque at a muchneeded moment when every little helped. Besides, though taste latterly had deteriorated to a degree, original music like that, different from the conventional rut, would rapidly have a great vogue as it would be a decided novelty for Dublin's musical world after the usual hackneyed run of catchy tenor solos foisted on a confiding public by Ivan St Austell and Hilton St Just and their *genus omne*. Yes, beyond a shadow of a doubt he could with all the cards in his hand and he had a capital opening to make a name for himself and win a high place in the city's esteem where he could command a stiff figure and, booking ahead, give a grand concert for the patrons of the King street house, given a backerup, if one were forthcoming to kick him upstairs, so to speak, a big *if*, however, with some impetus of the goahead sort to obviate the inevitable procrastination which often tripped up a too much fêted prince of good fellows. And it need not detract from the other by one iota as, being his own master, he would have heaps of time to practise literature in his spare moments when desirous of so doing without its clashing with his vocal career or containing anything derogatory whatsoever as it was a matter for himself alone. In fact, he had the ball at his feet and that was the very reason why the other, possessed of a remarkably sharp nose for smelling a rat of any sort, hung on to him at all.

The horse was just then. And later on at a propitious opportunity he purposed (Bloom did), without anyway prying into his private affairs on the *fools step in where angels* principle, advising him to sever his connection with a certain budding practitioner who, he noticed, was prone to disparage and even to a slight extent with some hilarious pretext when not present, deprecate him, or whatever you like to call it which in Bloom's humble opinion threw a nasty sidelight on that side of a person's character, no pun intended.

The horse having reached the end of his tether, so to speak, halted and, rearing high a proud feathering tail, added his quota by letting fall on the floor which the brush would soon brush up and polish, three smoking globes of turds. Slowly three times, one after another, from a full crupper he mired. And humanely his driver waited till he (or she) had ended, patient in his scythed car.

Side by side Bloom, profiting by the *contretemps*, with Stephen passed through the gap of the chains, divided by the upright, and, stepping over a strand of mire, went across towards Gardiner street lower, Stephen singing more boldly, but not loudly, the end of the ballad.

Und alle Schiffe brücken.

The driver never said a word, good, bad or indifferent, but merely watched the two figures, as he sat on his lowbacked car, both black, one full, one lean, walk towards the railway bridge, *to be married by Father Maher.* As they walked they at times stopped and walked again continuing their *tête à tête* (which, of course, he was utterly out of) about sirens, enemies of man's reason, mingled with a number of other topics of the same category, usurpers, historical cases of the kind while the man in the sweeper car or you might as well call it in the sleeper car who in any case couldn't possibly hear because they were too far simply sat in his seat near the end of lower Gardiner street *and looked after their lowbacked car.*

17

W hat parallel courses did Bloom and Stephen follow returning?

Starting united both at normal walking pace from Beresford place they followed in the order named Lower and Middle Gardiner streets and Mountjoy square, west: then, at reduced pace, each bearing left, Gardiner's place by an inadvertence as far as the farther corner of Temple street: then, at reduced pace with interruptions of halt, bearing right, Temple street, north, as far as Hardwicke place. Approaching, disparate, at relaxed walking pace they crossed both the circus before George's church diametrically, the chord in any circle being less than the arc which it subtends.

Of what did the duumvirate deliberate during their itinerary?

Music, literature, Ireland, Dublin, Paris, friendship, woman, prostitution, diet, the influence of gaslight or the light of arc and glowlamps on the growth of adjoining paraheliotropic trees, exposed corporation emergency dustbuckets, the Roman catholic church, ecclesiastical celibacy, the Irish nation, jesuit education, careers, the study of medicine, the past day, the maleficent influence of the presabbath, Stephen's collapse.

Did Bloom discover common factors of similarity between their respective like and unlike reactions to experience?

Both were sensitive to artistic impressions, musical in preference to plastic or pictorial. Both preferred a continental to an insular manner of life, a cisatlantic to a transatlantic place of residence. Both indurated by early domestic training and an inherited tenacity of heterodox resistance professed their disbelief in many orthodox religious, national, social and ethical doctrines. Both admitted the alternately stimulating and obtunding influence of heterosexual magnetism.

Were their views on some points divergent?

Stephen dissented openly from Bloom's views on the importance of dietary and civic selfhelp while Bloom dissented tacitly from Stephen's views on the eternal affirmation of the spirit of man in literature. Bloom assented covertly to Stephen's rectification of the anachronism involved in assigning the date of the conversion of the Irish nation to christianity from druidism by Patrick son of Calpornus, son of Potitus, son of Odyssus, sent by pope Celestine I in the year 432 in the reign of Leary to the year 260 or thereabouts in the reign of Cormac MacArt († 266 A.D.), suffocated by imperfect deglutition of aliment at Sletty and interred at Rossnaree. The collapse which Bloom ascribed to gastric inanition and certain chemical compounds of varying degrees of adulteration and alcoholic strength, accelerated by mental exertion and the velocity of rapid circular motion in a relaxing atmosphere, Stephen attributed to the reapparition of a matutinal cloud (perceived by both from two different points of observation Sandycove and Dublin) at first no bigger than a woman's hand.

Was there one point on which their views were equal and negative?

The influence of gaslight or electric light on the growth of adjoining paraheliotropic trees.

Had Bloom discussed similar subjects during nocturnal perambulations in the past?

In 1884 with Owen Goldberg and Cecil Turnbull at night on public thoroughfares between Longwood avenue and Leonard's corner and Leonard's corner and Synge street and Synge street and Bloomfield avenue. In 1885 with Percy Apjohn in the evenings, reclined against the wall between Gibraltar villa and Bloomfield house in Crumlin, barony of Uppercross. In 1886 occasionally with casual acquaintances and prospective purchasers on doorsteps, in front parlours, in third class railway carriages of suburban lines. In 1888 frequently with major Brian Tweedy and his daughter Miss Marion Tweedy, together and separately on the lounge in Matthew Dillon's house in Roundtown. Once in 1892 and once in 1893 with

Julius (Juda) Mastiansky, on both occasions in the parlour of his (Bloom's) house in Lombard street, west.

What reflection concerning the irregular sequence of dates 1884, 1885, 1886, 1888, 1892, 1893, 1904 did Bloom make before their arrival at their destination?

He reflected that the progressive extension of the field of individual development and experience was regressively accompanied by a restriction of the converse domain of interindividual relations.

As in what ways?

From inexistence to existence he came to many and was as one received: existence with existence he was with any as any with any: from existence to nonexistence gone he would be by all as none perceived.

What act did Bloom make on their arrival at their destination?

At the housesteps of the 4th of the equidifferent uneven numbers, number 7 Eccles street, he inserted his hand mechanically into the back pocket of his trousers to obtain his latchkey.

Was it there?

It was in the corresponding pocket of the trousers which he had worn on the day but one preceding.

Why was he doubly irritated?

Because he had forgotten and because he remembered that he had reminded himself twice not to forget.

What were then the alternatives before the, premeditatedly (respectively) and inadvertently, keyless couple?

To enter or not to enter. To knock or not to knock.

Bloom's decision?

A stratagem. Resting his feet on the dwarf wall, he climbed over the area railings, compressed his hat on his head, grasped two points at the lower union of rails and stiles, lowered his body gradually by its length of five feet nine inches and a half to within two feet ten inches of the area pavement and allowed his body to move freely in space by separating himself from the railings and crouching in preparation for the impact of the fall.

Did he fall?

By his body's known weight of eleven stone and four pounds in avoirdupois measure, as certified by the graduated machine for periodical selfweighing in the premises of Francis Froedman, pharmaceutical chemist of 19 Frederick street, north, on the last feast of the Ascension, to wit, the twelfth day of May of the bissextile year one thousand nine hundred and four of the christian era (jewish era five thousand six hundred and sixtyfour, mohammadan era one thousand three hundred and twentytwo), golden number 5, epact 13, solar cycle 9, dominical letters C B, Roman indiction 2, Julian period 6617, MCMIV.

Did he rise uninjured by concussion?

Regaining new stable equilibrium he rose uninjured though concussed by the impact, raised the latch of the area door by the exertion of force at its freely moving flange and by leverage of the first kind applied at its fulcrum, gained retarded access to the kitchen through the subadjacent scullery, ignited a lucifer match by friction, set free inflammable coal gas by turning on the ventcock, lit a high flame which, by regulating, he reduced to quiescent candescence and lit finally a portable candle.

What discrete succession of images did Stephen meanwhile perceive?

Reclined against the area railings he perceived through the transparent kitchen panes a man regulating a gasflame of 14 CP, a man lighting a candle of 1 CP, a man removing in turn each of his two boots, a man leaving the kitchen holding a candle.

Did the man reappear elsewhere?

After a lapse of four minutes the glimmer of his candle was discernible through the semitransparent semicircular glass fanlight over the halldoor. The halldoor turned gradually on its hinges. In the open space of the doorway the man reappeared without his hat, with his candle.

Did Stephen obey his sign?

Yes, entering softly, he helped to close and chain the door and followed softly along the hallway the man's back and listed feet and lighted candle past a lighted crevice of doorway on the left and carefully down a turning staircase of more than five steps into the kitchen of Bloom's house.

What did Bloom do?

He extinguished the candle by a sharp expiration of breath upon its flame, drew two spoonseat deal chairs to the hearthstone, one for Stephen with its back to the area window, the other for himself when necessary, knelt on one knee, composed in the grate a pyre of crosslaid resintipped sticks and various coloured papers and irregular polygons of best Abram coal at twentyone shillings a ton from the yard of Messrs Flower and M'Donald of 14 D'Olier street, kindled it at three projecting points of paper with one ignited lucifer match, thereby releasing the potential energy contained in the fuel by allowing its carbon and hydrogen elements to enter into free union with the oxygen of the air.

Of what similar apparitions did Stephen think?

Of others elsewhere in other times who, kneeling on one knee or on two, had kindled fires for him, of Brother Michael in the infirmary of the college of the Society of Jesus at Clongowes Wood, Sallins, in the county of Kildare: of his father, Simon Dedalus, in an unfurnished room of his first residence in Dublin, number thirteen Fitzgibbon street: of his godmother Miss Kate Morkan in the house of her dying sister Miss Julia Morkan at 15 Usher's Island: of his aunt Sara, wife of Richie (Richard) Goulding, in the kitchen of their lodgings at 62 Clanbrassil street: of his mother Mary, wife of Simon Dedalus, in the kitchen of number twelve North Richmond street on the morning of the feast of Saint Francis Xavier 1898: of the dean of studies, Father Butt, in the physics' theatre of university College, 16 Stephen's Green, north: of his sister Dilly (Delia) in his father's house in Cabra.

What did Stephen see on raising his gaze to the height of a yard from the fire towards the opposite wall?

Under a row of five coiled spring housebells a curvilinear rope, stretched between two holdfasts athwart across the recess beside the chimney pier, from which hung four smallsized square handkerchiefs folded unattached consecutively in adjacent rectangles and one pair of ladies' grey hose with Lisle suspender tops and feet in their habitual position clamped by three erect wooden pegs two at their outer extremities and the third at their point of junction.

What did Bloom see on the range?

On the right (smaller) hob a blue enamelled saucepan: on the left (larger) hob a black iron kettle.

What did Bloom do at the range?

He removed the saucepan to the left hob, rose and carried the iron kettle to the sink in order to tap the current by turning the faucet to let it flow.

Did it flow?

Yes. From Roundwood reservoir in county Wicklow of a cubic capacity of 2400 million gallons, percolating through a subterranean aqueduct of filter mains of single and double pipeage constructed at an initial plant cost of £ 5 per linear yard by way of the Dargle, Rathdown, Glen of the Downs and Callowhill to the 26 acre reservoir at Stillorgan, a distance of 22 statute miles, and thence, through a system of relieving tanks, by a gradient of 250 feet to the city boundary at Eustace bridge, upper Leeson street, though from prolonged summer drouth and daily supply of 12 1/2 million gallons the water had fallen below the sill of the overflow weir for which reason the borough surveyor and waterworks engineer, Mr Spencer Harty, C. E., on the instructions of the waterworks committee had prohibited the use of municipal water for purposes other than those of consumption (envisaging the possibility of recourse being had to the impotable water of the Grand and Royal canals as in 1893) particularly as the South Dublin Guardians, notwithstanding their ration of 15 gallons per day per pauper supplied through a 6 inch metre, had been convicted of a wastage of 20,000 gallons per night by a reading of their metre on the affirmation of the law agent of the corporation, Mr Ignatius Rice, solicitor, thereby acting to the detriment of another section of the public, selfsupporting taxpayers, solvent, sound.

What in water did Bloom, waterlover, drawer of water, watercarrier, returning to the range, admire?

Its universality: its democratic equality and constancy to its nature in seeking its own level: its vastness in the ocean of Mercator's projection: its unplumbed profundity in the Sundam trench of the Pacific exceeding 8000 fathoms: the restlessness of its waves and surface particles visiting in turn all points of its seaboard:

the independence of its units: the variability of states of sea: its hydrostatic quiescence in calm: its hydrokinetic turgidity in neap and spring tides: its subsidence after devastation: its sterility in the circumpolar icecaps, arctic and antarctic: its climatic and commercial significance: its preponderance of 3 to 1 over the dry land of the globe: its indisputable hegemony extending in square leagues over all the region below the subequatorial tropic of Capricorn: the multisecular stability of its primeval basin: its luteofulvous bed: its capacity to dissolve and hold in solution all soluble substances including millions of tons of the most precious metals: its slow erosions of peninsulas and islands, its persistent formation of homothetic islands, peninsulas and downwardtending promontories: its alluvial deposits: its weight and volume and density: its imperturbability in lagoons and highland tarns: its gradation of colours in the torrid and temperate and frigid zones: its vehicular ramifications in continental lakecontained streams and confluent oceanflowing rivers with their tributaries and transoceanic currents, gulfstream, north and south equatorial courses: its violence in seaquakes, waterspouts, Artesian wells, eruptions, torrents, eddies, freshets, spates, groundswells, watersheds, waterpartings, geysers, cataracts, whirlpools, maelstroms, inundations, deluges, cloudbursts: its vast circumterrestrial ahorizontal curve: its secrecy in springs and latent humidity, revealed by rhabdomantic or hygrometric instruments and exemplified by the well by the hole in the wall at Ashtown gate, saturation of air, distillation of dew: the simplicity of its composition, two constituent parts of hydrogen with one constituent part of oxygen: its healing virtues: its buoyancy in the waters of the Dead Sea: its persevering penetrativeness in runnels, gullies, inadequate dams, leaks on shipboard: its properties for cleansing, quenching thirst and fire, nourishing vegetation: its infallibility as paradigm and paragon: its metamorphoses as vapour, mist, cloud, rain, sleet, snow, hail: its strength in rigid hydrants: its variety of forms in loughs and bays and gulfs and bights and guts and lagoons and atolls and archipelagos and sounds and fjords and minches and tidal estuaries and arms of sea: its solidity in glaciers, icebergs, icefloes: its docility in working hydraulic millwheels, turbines, dynamos, electric power stations, bleachworks, tanneries, scutchmills: its utility in canals, rivers, if navigable, floating and graving docks: its potentiality derivable from harnessed tides or watercourses falling from level to level: its submarine fauna and flora (anacoustic, photophobe), numerically, if not literally, the inhabitants of the globe: its ubiquity as constituting 90 % of the human body: the noxiousness of its effluvia in lacustrine marshes, pestilential fens, faded flowerwater, stagnant pools in the waning moon.

Having set the halffilled kettle on the now burning coals, why did he return to the stillflowing tap?

To wash his soiled hands with a partially consumed tablet of Barrington's lemonflavoured soap, to which paper still adhered, (bought thirteen hours previously for fourpence and still unpaid for), in fresh cold neverchanging everchanging water and dry them, face and hands, in a long redbordered holland cloth passed over a wooden revolving roller.

What reason did Stephen give for declining Bloom's offer?

That he was hydrophobe, hating partial contact by immersion or total by submersion in cold water, (his last bath having taken place in the month of October of the preceding year), disliking the aqueous substances of glass and crystal, distrusting aquacities of thought and language.

What impeded Bloom from giving Stephen counsels of hygiene and prophylactic to which should be added suggestions concerning a preliminary wetting of the head and contraction of the muscles with rapid splashing of the face and neck and thoracic and epigastric region in case of sea or river bathing, the parts of the human anatomy most sensitive to cold being the nape, stomach and thenar or sole of foot?

The incompatibility of aquacity with the erratic originality of genius.

What additional didactic counsels did he similarly repress?

Dietary: concerning the respective percentage of protein and caloric energy in bacon, salt ling and butter, the absence of the former in the lastnamed and the abundance of the latter in the firstnamed.

Which seemed to the host to be the predominant qualities of his guest?

Confidence in himself, an equal and opposite power of abandonment and recuperation.

What concomitant phenomenon took place in the vessel of liquid by the agency of fire?

The phenomenon of ebullition. Fanned by a constant updraught of ventilation between the kitchen and the chimneyflue, ignition was communicated from the faggots of precombustible fuel to polyhedral masses of bituminous coal, containing in compressed mineral form the foliated fossilised decidua of primeval forests which had in turn derived their vegetative existence from the sun, primal source of heat (radiant), transmitted through omnipresent luminiferous diathermanous ether. Heat (convected), a mode of motion developed by such combustion, was constantly and increasingly conveyed from the source of calorification to the liquid contained in the vessel, being radiated through the uneven unpolished dark surface of the metal iron, in part reflected, in part absorbed, in part transmitted, gradually raising the temperature of the water from normal to boiling point, a rise in temperature expressible as the result of an expenditure of 72 thermal units needed to raise 1 pound of water from 50° to 212° Fahrenheit.

What announced the accomplishment of this rise in temperature?

A double falciform ejection of water vapour from under the kettlelid at both sides simultaneously.

For what personal purpose could Bloom have applied the water so boiled?

To shave himself.

What advantages attended shaving by night?

A softer beard: a softer brush if intentionally allowed to remain from shave to shave in its agglutinated lather: a softer skin if unexpectedly encountering female acquaintances in remote places at incustomary hours: quiet reflections upon the course of the day: a cleaner sensation when awaking after a fresher sleep since matutinal noises, premonitions and perturbations, a clattered milkcan, a postman's double knock, a paper read, reread while lathering, relathering the same spot, a shock, a shoot, with thought of aught he sought though fraught with nought might cause a faster rate of shaving and a nick on which incision plaster with precision cut and humected and applied adhered: which was to be done.

Why did absence of light disturb him less than presence of noise? Because of the surety of the sense of touch in his firm full masculine feminine passive active hand.

What quality did it (his hand) possess but with what counteracting influence?

The operative surgical quality but that he was reluctant to shed human blood even when the end justified the means, preferring, in their natural order, heliotherapy, psychophysicotherapeutics, osteopathic surgery.

What lay under exposure on the lower, middle and upper shelves of the kitchen dresser, opened by Bloom?

On the lower shelf five vertical breakfast plates, six horizontal breakfast saucers on which rested inverted breakfast cups, a moustachecup, uninverted, and saucer of Crown Derby, four white goldrimmed eggcups, an open shammy purse displaying coins, mostly copper, and a phial of aromatic (violet) comfits. On the middle shelf a chipped eggcup containing pepper, a drum of table salt, four conglomerated black olives in oleaginous paper, an empty pot of Plumtree's potted meat, an oval wicker basket bedded with fibre and containing one Jersey pear, a halfempty bottle of William Gilbey and Co's white invalid port, half disrobed of its swathe of coralpink tissue paper, a packet of Epps's soluble cocoa, five ounces of Anne Lynch's choice tea at 2/- per lb in a crinkled leadpaper bag, a cylindrical canister containing the best crystallised lump sugar, two onions, one, the larger, Spanish, entire, the other, smaller, Irish, bisected with augmented surface and more redolent, a jar of Irish Model Dairy's cream, a jug of brown crockery containing a naggin and a quarter of soured adulterated milk, converted by heat into water, acidulous serum and semisolidified curds, which added to the quantity subtracted for Mr Bloom's and Mrs Fleming's breakfasts, made one imperial pint, the total quantity originally delivered, two cloves, a halfpenny and a small dish containing a slice of fresh ribsteak. On the upper shelf a battery of jamjars (empty) of various sizes and proveniences.

What attracted his attention lying on the apron of the dresser? Four polygonal fragments of two lacerated scarlet betting tickets, numbered 8 87, 88 6.

What reminiscences temporarily corrugated his brow?

Reminiscences of coincidences, truth stranger than fiction, preindicative of the result of the Gold Cup flat handicap, the official and definitive result of which he had read in the *Evening Telegraph*, late pink edition, in the cabman's shelter, at Butt bridge.

Where had previous intimations of the result, effected or projected, been received by him?

In Bernard Kiernan's licensed premises 8, 9 and 10 little Britain street: in David Byrne's licensed premises, 14 Duke street: in O'Connell street lower, outside Graham Lemon's when a dark man had placed in his hand a throwaway (subsequently thrown away), advertising Elijah, restorer of the church in Zion: in Lincoln place outside the premises of F. W. Sweny and Co (Limited), dispensing chemists, when, when Frederick M. (Bantam) Lyons had rapidly and successively requested, perused and restituted the copy of the current issue of the *Freeman's Journal* and *National Press* which he had been about to throw away (subsequently thrown away), he had proceeded towards the oriental edifice of the Turkish and Warm Baths, 11 Leinster street, with the light of inspiration shining in his countenance and bearing in his arms the secret of the race, graven in the language of prediction.

What qualifying considerations allayed his perturbations?

The difficulties of interpretation since the significance of any event followed its occurrence as variably as the acoustic report followed the electrical discharge and of counterestimating against an actual loss by failure to interpret the total sum of possible losses proceeding originally from a successful interpretation.

His mood?

He had not risked, he did not expect, he had not been disappointed, he was satisfied.

What satisfied him?

To have sustained no positive loss. To have brought a positive gain to others. Light to the gentiles.

How did Bloom prepare a collation for a gentile?

He poured into two teacups two level spoonfuls, four in all, of Epps's soluble cocoa and proceeded according to the directions for use printed on the label, to each adding after sufficient time for infusion the prescribed ingredients for diffusion in the manner and in the quantity prescribed.

What supererogatory marks of special hospitality did the host show his guest?

Relinquishing his symposiarchal right to the moustache cup of imitation Crown Derby presented to him by his only daughter, Millicent (Milly), he substituted a cup identical with that of his guest and served extraordinarily to his guest and, in reduced measure, to himself the viscous cream ordinarily reserved for the breakfast of his wife Marion (Molly).

Was the guest conscious of and did he acknowledge these marks of hospitality?

His attention was directed to them by his host jocosely, and he accepted them seriously as they drank in jocoserious silence Epps's massproduct, the creature cocoa.

Were there marks of hospitality which he contemplated but suppressed, reserving them for another and for himself on future occasions to complete the act begun?

The reparation of a fissure of the length of 1 1/2 inches in the right side of his guest's jacket. A gift to his guest of one of the four lady's handkerchiefs, if and when ascertained to be in a presentable condition.

Who drank more quickly?

Bloom, having the advantage of ten seconds at the initiation and taking, from the concave surface of a spoon along the handle of which a steady flow of heat was conducted, three sips to his opponent's one, six to two, nine to three.

What cerebration accompanied his frequentative act?

Concluding by inspection but erroneously that his silent companion was engaged in mental composition he reflected on the pleasures derived from literature of instruction rather than of amusement as he himself had applied to the works of William Shakespeare more than once for the solution of difficult problems in imaginary or real life.

Had he found their solution?

In spite of careful and repeated reading of certain classical passages, aided by a glossary, he had derived imperfect conviction from the text, the answers not bearing in all points.

What lines concluded his first piece of original verse written by him, potential poet, at the age of 11 in 1877 on the occasion of the offering of three prizes of 10/-, 5/- and 2/6 respectively for competition by the *Shamrock*, a weekly newspaper?

> *An ambition to squint*
> *At my verses in print*
> *Makes me hope that for these you'll find room.*
> *If you so condescend?*
> *Then please place at the end*
> *The name of yours truly, L. Bloom.*

Did he find four separating forces between his temporary guest and him?

Name, age, race, creed.

What anagrams had he made on his name in youth?

Leopold Bloom

Ellpodbomool

Molldopeloob

Bollopedoom

Old Ollebo, M. P.

What acrostic upon the abbreviation of his first name had he (kinetic poet) sent to Miss Marion (Molly) Tweedy on the 14 February 1888?

> *Poets oft have sung in rhyme*
> *Of music sweet their praise divine.*
> *Let them hymn it nine times nine.*
> *Dearer far than song or wine.*
> *You are mine. The world is mine.*

What had prevented him from completing a topical song (music by R. G. Johnston) on the events of the past, or fixtures for the actual, years, entitled *If Brian Boru could but come back and see old Dublin now*, commissioned by Michael Gunn, lessee of the Gaiety Theatre, 46, 47, 48, 49 South King street, and to be introduced into the sixth scene, the valley of diamonds, of the second edition (30 January 1893) of the grand annual Christmas pantomime *Sinbad the Sailor* (produced by R. Shelton 26 December 1892, written by Greenleaf Whittier, scenery by George A. Jackson and Cecil Hicks, costumes by Mrs and Miss Whelan under the personal supervision of Mrs Michael Gunn, ballets by Jessie Noir, harlequinade by Thomas Otto) and sung by Nelly Bouverist, principal girl?

Firstly, oscillation between events of imperial and of local interest, the anticipated diamond jubilee of Queen Victoria (born 1820, acceded 1837) and the posticipated opening of the new municipal fish market: secondly, apprehension of opposition from extreme circles on the questions of the respective visits of Their Royal Highnesses the duke and duchess of York (real) and of His Majesty King Brian Boru (imaginary): thirdly, a conflict between professional etiquette and professional emulation concerning the recent erections of the Grand Lyric Hall on Burgh Quay and the Theatre Royal in Hawkins street: fourthly, distraction resultant from compassion for Nelly Bouverist's non-intellectual, non-political, non-topical expression of countenance and concupiscence caused by Nelly Bouverist's revelations of white articles of non-intellectual, non-political, non-topical underclothing while she (Nelly Bouverist) was in the articles: fifthly, the difficulties of the selection of appropriate music and humorous allusions from *Everybody's Book of Jokes* (1000 pages and a laugh in every one): sixthly, the rhymes, homophonous and cacophonous, associated with the names of the new lord mayor, Daniel Tallon, the new high sheriff, Thomas Pile and the new solicitorgeneral, Dunbar Plunket Barton.

What relation existed between their ages?

16 years before in 1888 when Bloom was of Stephen's present age Stephen was 6. 16 years after in 1920 when Stephen would be of Bloom's present age Bloom would be 54. In 1936 when Bloom would be 70 and Stephen 54 their ages initially in the ratio of 16 to 0 would be as 17 1/2 to 13 1/2, the proportion increasing and the disparity diminishing according as arbitrary future years were added, for if the

proportion existing in 1883 had continued immutable, conceiving that to be possible, till then 1904 when Stephen was 22 Bloom would be 374 and in 1920 when Stephen would be 38, as Bloom then was, Bloom would be 646 while in 1952 when Stephen would have attained the maximum postdiluvian age of 70 Bloom, being 1190 years alive having been born in the year 714, would have surpassed by 221 years the maximum antediluvian age, that of Methusalah, 969 years, while, if Stephen would continue to live until he would attain that age in the year 3072 A. D., Bloom would have been obliged to have been alive 83,300 years, having been obliged to have been born in the year 81,396 B. C.

What events might nullify these calculations?

The cessation of existence of both or either, the inauguration of a new era or calendar, the annihilation of the world and consequent extermination of the human species, inevitable but impredictable.

How many previous encounters proved their preexisting acquaintance?

Two. The first in the lilacgarden of Matthew Dillon's house, Medina Villa, Kimmage road, Roundtown, in 1887, in the company of Stephen's mother, Stephen being then of the age of 5 and reluctant to give his hand in salutation. The second in the coffeeroom of Breslin's hotel on a rainy Sunday in the January of 1892, in the company of Stephen's father and Stephen's granduncle, Stephen being then 5 years older.

Did Bloom accept the invitation to dinner given then by the son and afterwards seconded by the father?

Very gratefully, with grateful appreciation, with sincere appreciative gratitude, in appreciatively grateful sincerity of regret, he declined.

Did their conversation on the subject of these reminiscences reveal a third connecting link between them?

Mrs Riordan (Dante), a widow of independent means, had resided in the house of Stephen's parents from 1 September 1888 to 29 December 1891 and had also resided during the years 1892, 1893 and 1894 in the City Arms Hotel owned by Elizabeth O'Dowd of 54

Prussia street where, during parts of the years 1893 and 1894, she had been a constant informant of Bloom who resided also in the same hotel, being at that time a clerk in the employment of Joseph Cuffe of 5 Smithfield for the superintendence of sales in the adjacent Dublin Cattle market on the North Circular road.

Had he performed any special corporal work of mercy for her?

He had sometimes propelled her on warm summer evenings, an infirm widow of independent, if limited, means, in her convalescent bathchair with slow revolutions of its wheels as far as the corner of the North Circular road opposite Mr Gavin Low's place of business where she had remained for a certain time scanning through his onelensed binocular fieldglasses unrecognisable citizens on tramcars, roadster bicycles equipped with inflated pneumatic tyres, hackney carriages, tandems, private and hired landaus, dogcarts, ponytraps and brakes passing from the city to the Phœnix Park and *vice versa*.

Why could he then support that his vigil with the greater equanimity?

Because in middle youth he had often sat observing through a rondel of bossed glass of a multicoloured pane the spectacle offered with continual changes of the thoroughfare without, pedestrians, quadrupeds, velocipedes, vehicles, passing slowly, quickly, evenly, round and round and round the rim of a round and round precipitous globe.

What distinct different memories had each of her now eight years deceased?

The older, her bezique cards and counters, her Skye terrier, her supposititious wealth, her lapses of responsiveness and incipient catarrhal deafness: the younger, her lamp of colza oil before the statue of the Immaculate Conception, her green and maroon brushes for Charles Stewart Parnell and for Michael Davitt, her tissue papers.

Were there no means still remaining to him to achieve the rejuvenation which these reminiscences divulged to a younger companion rendered the more desirable?

The indoor exercises, formerly intermittently practised, subsequently abandoned, prescribed in Eugen Sandow's *Physical Strength and How to Obtain It* which, designed particularly for commercial men engaged in sedentary occupations, were to be made with mental concentration in front of a mirror so as to bring into play the various families of muscles and produce successively a pleasant rigidity, a more pleasant relaxation and the most pleasant repristination of juvenile agility.

Had any special agility been his in earlier youth?

Though ringweight lifting had been beyond his strength and the full circle gyration beyond his courage yet as a High school scholar he had excelled in his stable and protracted execution of the half lever movement on the parallel bars in consequence of his abnormally developed abdominal muscles.

Did either openly allude to their racial difference?
Neither.

What, reduced to their simplest reciprocal form, were Bloom's thoughts about Stephen's thoughts about Bloom and about Stephen's thoughts about Bloom's thoughts about Stephen?

He thought that he thought that he was a jew whereas he knew that he knew that he knew that he was not.

What, the enclosures of reticence removed, were their respective parentages?

Bloom, only born male transubstantial heir of Rudolf Virag (subsequently Rudolph Bloom) of Szombathely, Vienna, Budapest, Milan, London and Dublin and of Ellen Higgins, second daughter of Julius Higgins (born Karoly) and Fanny Higgins (born Hegarty). Stephen, eldest surviving male consubstantial heir of Simon Dedalus of Cork and Dublin and of Mary, daughter of Richard and Christina Goulding (born Grier).

Had Bloom and Stephen been baptised, and where and by whom, cleric or layman?

Bloom (three times), by the reverend Mr Gilmer Johnston M. A., alone, in the protestant church of Saint Nicholas Without, Coombe, by James O'Connor, Philip Gilligan and James Fitzpatrick, together, under a pump in the village of Swords, and by the reverend Charles Malone C. C., in the church of the Three Patrons, Rathgar. Stephen (once) by the reverend Charles Malone C. C., alone, in the church of the Three Patrons, Rathgar.

Did they find their educational careers similar?

Substituting Stephen for Bloom Stoom would have passed successively through a dame's school and the high school. Substituting Bloom for Stephen Blephen would have passed successively through the preparatory, junior, middle and senior grades of the intermediate and through the matriculation, first arts, second arts and arts degree courses of the royal university.

Why did Bloom refrain from stating that he had frequented the university of life?

Because of his fluctuating incertitude as to whether this observation had or had not been already made by him to Stephen or by Stephen to him.

What two temperaments did they individually represent?

The scientific. The artistic.

What proofs did Bloom adduce to prove that his tendency was towards applied, rather than towards pure, science?

Certain possible inventions of which he had cogitated when reclining in a state of supine repletion to aid digestion, stimulated by his appreciation of the importance of inventions now common but once revolutionary, for example, the aeronautic parachute, the reflecting telescope, the spiral corkscrew, the safety pin, the mineral water siphon, the canal lock with winch and sluice, the suction pump.

Were these inventions principally intended for an improved scheme of kindergarten?

Yes, rendering obsolete popguns, elastic airbladders, games of hazard, catapults. They comprised astronomical kaleidoscopes exhibiting the twelve constellations of the zodiac from Aries to Pisces, miniature mechanical orreries, arithmetical gelatine lozenges, geometrical to correspond with zoological biscuits, globemap playing balls, historically costumed dolls.

What also stimulated him in his cogitations?

The financial success achieved by Ephraim Marks and Charles A. James, the former by his 1d bazaar at 42 George's street, south, the latter at his 6 1/2d shop and world's fancy fair and waxwork exhibition at 30 Henry street, admission 2d, children 1d: and the infinite possibilities hitherto unexploited of the modern art of advertisement if condensed in triliteral monoideal symbols, vertically of maximum visibility (divined), horizontally of maximum legibility (deciphered) and of magnetising efficacy to arrest involuntary attention, to interest, to convince, to decide.

Such as?

K. 11. Kino's 11/- Trousers.

House of Keys. Alexander J. Keyes.

Such as not?

Look at this long candle. Calculate when it burns out and you receive gratis 1 pair of our special non-compo boots, guaranteed 1 candle power. Address: Barclay and Cook, 18 Talbot street.

Bacilikil (Insect Powder).

Veribest (Boot Blacking).

Uwantit (Combined pocket twoblade penknife with corkscrew, nailfile and pipecleaner).

Such as never?

What is home without Plumtree's Potted Meat?

Incomplete.

With it an abode of bliss.

Manufactured by George Plumtree, 23 Merchants' quay, Dublin, put up in 4 oz pots, and inserted by Councillor Joseph P. Nannetti, M. P., Rotunda Ward, 19 Hardwicke street, under the obituary notices and anniversaries of deceases. The name on the label is Plumtree. A plumtree in a meatpot, registered trade mark. Beware of imitations. Peatmot. Trumplee. Moutpat. Plamtroo.

Which example did he adduce to induce Stephen to deduce that originality, though producing its own reward, does not invariably conduce to success?

His own ideated and rejected project of an illuminated showcart, drawn by a beast of burden, in which two smartly dressed girls were to be seated engaged in writing.

What suggested scene was then constructed by Stephen?

Solitary hotel in mountain pass. Autumn. Twilight. Fire lit. In dark corner young man seated. Young woman enters. Restless.

Solitary. She sits. She goes to window. She stands. She sits. Twilight. She thinks. On solitary hotel paper she writes. She thinks. She writes. She sighs. Wheels and hoofs. She hurries out. He comes from his dark corner. He seizes solitary paper. He holds it towards fire. Twilight. He reads. Solitary.

What?

In sloping, upright and backhands: Queen's Hotel, Queen's Hotel, Queen's Hotel. Queen's Ho . . .

What suggested scene was then reconstructed by Bloom?

The Queen's Hotel, Ennis, county Clare, where Rudolph Bloom (Rudolf Virag) died on the evening of the 27 June 1886, at some hour unstated, in consequence of an overdose of monkshood (aconite) selfadministered in the form of a neuralgic liniment composed of 2 parts of aconite liniment to 1 of chloroform liniment (purchased by him at 10.20 a.m. on the morning of 27 June 1886 at the medical hall of Francis Dennehy, 17 Church street, Ennis) after having, though not in consequence of having, purchased at 3.15 p.m. on the afternoon of 27 June 1886 a new boater straw hat, extra smart (after having, though not in consequence of having, purchased at the hour and in the place aforesaid, the toxin aforesaid), at the general drapery store of James Cullen, 4 Main street, Ennis.

Did he attribute this homonymity to information or coincidence or intuition?

Coincidence.

Did he depict the scene verbally for his guest to see?

He preferred himself to see another's face and listen to another's words by which potential narration was realised and kinetic temperament relieved.

Did he see only a second coincidence in the second scene narrated to him, described by the narrator as *A Pisgah Sight of Palestine* or *The Parable of the Plums*?

It, with the preceding scene and with others unnarrated but existent by implication, to which add essays on various subjects or moral apothegms (e.g. *My Favourite Hero* or *Procrastination is the Thief of Time*) composed during schoolyears, seemed to him to contain in itself and in conjunction with the personal equation certain possibilities of financial, social, personal and sexual success, whether specially collected and selected as model pedagogic themes (of cent per cent merit) for the use of preparatory and junior grade students or contributed in printed form, following the precedent of Philip Beaufoy or Doctor Dick or Heblon's *Studies in Blue*, to a publication of certified circulation and solvency or employed verbally as intellectual stimulation for sympathetic auditors, tacitly appreciative of successful narrative and confidently augurative of successful achievement, during the increasingly longer nights gradually following the summer solstice on the day but three following, videlicet, Tuesday, 21 June (S. Aloysius Gonzaga), sunrise 3.33 a.m., sunset 8.29 p.m.

Which domestic problem as much as, if not more than, any other frequently engaged his mind?

What to do with our wives.

What had been his hypothetical singular solutions?

Parlour games (dominos, halma, tiddledywinks, spilikins, cup and ball, nap, spoil five, bezique, twentyfive, beggar my neighbour, draughts, chess or backgammon): embroidery, darning or knitting for the policeaided clothing society: musical duets, mandoline and guitar, piano and flute, guitar and piano: legal scrivenery or envelope addressing: biweekly visits to variety entertainments: commercial activity as pleasantly commanding and pleasingly obeyed mistress proprietress in a cool dairy shop or warm cigar divan: the clandestine satisfaction of erotic irritation in masculine brothels, state inspected and medically controlled: social visits, at regular infrequent prevented intervals and with regular frequent preventive superintendence, to and from female acquaintances of recognised respectability in the vicinity: courses of evening instruction specially designed to render liberal instruction agreeable.

What instances of deficient mental development in his wife inclined him in favour of the lastmentioned (ninth) solution?

In disoccupied moments she had more than once covered a sheet of paper with signs and hieroglyphics which she stated were Greek and Irish and Hebrew characters. She had interrogated constantly at varying intervals as to the correct method of writing the capital initial of the name of a city in Canada, Quebec. She understood little of political complications, internal, or balance of power, external. In calculating the addenda of bills she frequently had recourse to digital aid. After completion of laconic epistolary compositions she abandoned the implement of calligraphy in the encaustic pigment, exposed to the corrosive action of copperas, green vitriol and nutgall. Unusual polysyllables of foreign origin she interpreted phonetically or by false analogy or by both: metempsychosis (met him pike hoses), *alias* (a mendacious person mentioned in sacred scripture).

What compensated in the false balance of her intelligence for these and such deficiencies of judgment regarding persons, places and things?

The false apparent parallelism of all perpendicular arms of all balances, proved true by construction. The counterbalance of her proficiency of judgment regarding one person, proved true by experiment.

How had he attempted to remedy this state of comparative ignorance?

Variously. By leaving in a conspicuous place a certain book open at a certain page: by assuming in her, when alluding explanatorily, latent knowledge: by open ridicule in her presence of some absent other's ignorant lapse.

With what success had he attempted direct instruction?

She followed not all, a part of the whole, gave attention with interest comprehended with surprise, with care repeated, with greater difficulty remembered, forgot with ease, with misgiving rerembered, rerepeated with error.

What system had proved more effective?

Indirect suggestion implicating selfinterest.

Example?

She disliked umbrella with rain, he liked woman with umbrella, she disliked new hat with rain, he liked woman with new hat, he bought new hat with rain, she carried umbrella with new hat.

Accepting the analogy implied in his guest's parable which examples of postexilic eminence did he adduce?

Three seekers of the pure truth, Moses of Egypt, Moses Maimonides, author of *More Nebukim* (Guide of the Perplexed) and Moses Mendelssohn of such eminence that from Moses (of Egypt) to Moses (Mendelssohn) there arose none like Moses (Maimonides).

What statement was made, under correction, by Bloom concerning a fourth seeker of pure truth, by name Aristotle, mentioned, with permission, by Stephen?

That the seeker mentioned had been a pupil of a rabbinical philosopher, name uncertain.

Were other anapocryphal illustrious sons of the law and children of a selected or rejected race mentioned?

Felix Bartholdy Mendelssohn (composer), Baruch Spinoza (philosopher), Mendoza (pugilist), Ferdinand Lassalle (reformer, duellist).

What fragments of verse from the ancient Hebrew and ancient Irish languages were cited with modulations of voice and translation of texts by guest to host and by host to guest?

By Stephen: *suil, suil, suil arun, suil go siocair agus suil go cuin* (walk, walk, walk your way, walk in safety, walk with care).

By Bloom: *Kifeloch, harimon rakatejch m'baad l'zamatejch* (thy temple amid thy hair is as a slice of pomegranate).

How was a glyphic comparison of the phonic symbols of both languages made in substantiation of the oral comparison?

By juxtaposition. On the penultimate blank page of a book of inferior literary style, entitled *Sweets of Sin* (produced by Bloom and so manipulated that its front cover came in contact with the surface of the table) with a pencil (supplied by Stephen) Stephen wrote the Irish characters for gee, eh, dee, 'em, simple and modified, and Bloom in turn wrote the Hebrew characters ghimel, aleph, daleth and (in the absence of mem) a substituted qoph, explaining their arithmetical values as ordinal and cardinal numbers, videlicet 3, 1, 4, and 100.

Was the knowledge possessed by both of each of these languages, the extinct and the revived, theoretical or practical?

Theoretical, being confined to certain grammatical rules of accidence and syntax and practically excluding vocabulary.

What points of contact existed between these languages and between the peoples who spoke them?

The presence of guttural sounds, diacritic aspirations, epenthetic and servile letters in both languages: their antiquity, both having been taught on the plain of Shinar 242 years after the deluge in the seminary instituted by Fenius Farsaigh, descendant of Noah, progenitor of Israel, and ascendant of Heber and Heremon, progenitors of Ireland: their archaeological, genealogical, hagiographical, exegetical, homiletic, toponomastic, historical and religious literatures comprising the works of rabbis and culdees, Torah, Talmud (Mischna and Ghemara), Massor, Pentateuch, Book of the Dun Cow, Book of Ballymote, Garland of Howth, Book of Kells: their dispersal, persecution, survival and revival: the isolation of their synagogical and ecclesiastical rites in ghetto (S. Mary's Abbey) and masshouse (Adam and Eve's tavern): the proscription of their national costumes in penal laws and jewish dress acts: the restoration in Chanah David of Zion and the possibility of Irish political autonomy or devolution.

What anthem did Bloom chant partially in anticipation of that multiple, ethnically irreducible consummation?

Kolod balejwaw pnimah
Nefesch, jehudi, homijah.

Why was the chant arrested at the conclusion of this first distich?
In consequence of defective mnemotechnic.

How did the chanter compensate for this deficiency?
By a periphrastic version of the general text.

In what common study did their mutual reflections merge?
The increasing simplification traceable from the Egyptian epigraphic hieroglyphs to the Greek and Roman alphabets and the anticipation of modern stenography and telegraphic code in the cuneiform inscriptions (Semitic) and the virgular quinquecostate ogham writing (Celtic).

Did the guest comply with his host's request?
Doubly, by appending his signature in Irish and Roman characters.

What was Stephen's auditive sensation?

He heard in a profound ancient male unfamiliar melody the accumulation of the past.

What was Bloom's visual sensation?

He saw in a quick young male familiar form the predestination of a future.

What were Stephen's and Bloom's quasisimultaneous volitional quasisensations of concealed identities?

Visually, Stephen's: The traditional figure of hypostasis, depicted by Johannes Damascenus, Lentulus Romanus and Epiphanius Monachus as leucodermic, sesquipedalian with winedark hair.

Auditively, Bloom's: The traditional accent of the ecstasy of catastrophe.

What future careers had been possible for Bloom in the past and with what exemplars?

In the church, Roman, Anglican or Nonconformist: exemplars, the very reverend John Conmee S. J., the reverend T. Salmon, D. D., provost of Trinity college, Dr Alexander J. Dowie. At the bar, English or Irish: exemplars, Seymour Bushe, K. C., Rufus Isaacs, K. C. On the stage, modern or Shakespearean: exemplars, Charles Wyndham, high comedian, Osmond Tearle († 1901), exponent of Shakespeare.

Did the host encourage his guest to chant in a modulated voice a strange legend on an allied theme?

Reassuringly, their place, where none could hear them talk, being secluded, reassured, the decocted beverages, allowing for subsolid residual sediment of a mechanical mixture, water plus sugar plus cream plus cocoa, having been consumed.

Recite the first (major) part of this chanted legend.

Little Harry Hughes and his schoolfellows all
Went out for to play ball.
And the very first ball little Harry Hughes played
He drove it o'er the jew's garden wall.
And the very second ball little Harry Hughes played

He broke the jew's windows all.

Little Harry Hughes and his school fellows all Went out for to play ball Went out for to play ball. And the very first ball Little Harry Hughes played He drove it oer the Jews garden Wall. He Drove it oer the Jews garden wall. And the very second ball Little Harry Hughes played He broke the Jews windows all He broke the Jews windows all.

How did the son of Rudolph receive this first part?

With unmixed feeling. Smiling, a jew, he heard with pleasure and saw the unbroken kitchen window.

Recite the second part (minor) of the legend.

> *Then out there came the jew's daughter*
> *And she all dressed in green.*
> *"Come back, come back, you pretty little boy,*
> *And play your ball again."*

> *"I can't come back and I won't come back*
> *Without my schoolfellows all.*
> *For if my master he did hear*
> *He'd make it a sorry ball."*
> *She took him by the lilywhite hand*
> *And led him along the hall*
> *Until she led him to a room*
> *Where none could hear him call.*
> *She took a penknife out of her pocket*

And cut off his little head.
And now he'll play his ball no more
For he lies among the dead.

How did the father of Millicent receive this second part?

With mixed feelings. Unsmiling, he heard and saw with wonder a jew's daughter, all dressed in green.

Condense Stephen's commentary.

One of all, the least of all, is the victim predestined. Once by inadvertence twice by design he challenges his destiny. It comes when he is abandoned and challenges him reluctant and, as an apparition of hope and youth, holds him unresisting. It leads him to a strange habitation, to a secret infidel apartment, and there, implacable, immolates him, consenting.

Why was the host (victim predestined) sad?

He wished that a tale of a deed should be told of a deed not by him should by him not be told.

Why was the host (reluctant, unresisting) still?

In accordance with the law of the conservation of energy.

Why was the host (secret infidel) silent?

He weighed the possible evidences for and against ritual murder: the incitations of the hierarchy, the superstition of the populace, the propagation of rumour in continued fraction of veridicity, the envy of opulence, the influence of retaliation, the sporadic reappearance of atavistic delinquency, the mitigating circumstances of fanaticism, hypnotic suggestion and somnambulism.

From which (if any) of these mental or physical disorders was he not totally immune?

From hypnotic suggestion: once, waking, he had not recognised his sleeping apartment: more than once, waking, he had been for an indefinite time incapable of moving or uttering sounds. From somnambulism: once, sleeping, his body had risen, crouched and crawled in the direction of a heatless fire and, having attained its destination, there, curled, unheated, in night attire had lain, sleeping.

Had this latter or any cognate phenomenon declared itself in any member of his family?

Twice, in Holles street and in Ontario terrace, his daughter Millicent (Milly) at the ages of 6 and 8 years had uttered in sleep an exclamation of terror and had replied to the interrogations of two figures in night attire with a vacant mute expression.

What other infantile memories had he of her?

15 June 1889. A querulous newborn female infant crying to cause and lessen congestion. A child renamed Padney Socks she shook with shocks her moneybox: counted his three free moneypenny buttons, one, tloo, tlee: a doll, a boy, a sailor she cast away: blond, born of two dark, she had blond ancestry, remote, a violation, Herr Hauptmann Hainau, Austrian army, proximate, a hallucination, lieutenant Mulvey, British navy.

What endemic characteristics were present?

Conversely the nasal and frontal formation was derived in a direct line of lineage which, though interrupted, would continue at distant intervals to more distant intervals to its most distant intervals.

What memories had he of her adolescence?

She relegated her hoop and skippingrope to a recess. On the duke's lawn, entreated by an English visitor, she declined to permit him to make and take away her photographic image (objection not stated). On the South Circular road in the company of Elsa Potter, followed by an individual of sinister aspect, she went half way down Stamer street and turned abruptly back (reason of change not stated). On the vigil of the 15th anniversary of her birth she wrote a letter from Mullingar, county Westmeath, making a brief allusion to a local student (faculty and year not stated).

Did that first division, portending a second division, afflict him?
Less than he had imagined, more than he had hoped.

What second departure was contemporaneously perceived by him similarly, if differently?
A temporary departure of his cat.

Why similarly, why differently?
Similarly, because actuated by a secret purpose the quest of a new male (Mullingar student) or of a healing herb (valerian). Differently, because of different possible returns to the inhabitants or to the habitation.

In other respects were their differences similar?
In passivity, in economy, in the instinct of tradition, in unexpectedness.

As?
Inasmuch as leaning she sustained her blond hair for him to ribbon it for her (cf neckarching cat). Moreover, on the free surface of the lake in Stephen's green amid inverted reflections of trees her uncommented spit, describing concentric circles of waterrings, indicated by the constancy of its permanence the locus of a somnolent prostrate fish (cf mousewatching cat). Again, in order to remember the date, combatants, issue and consequences of a famous military engagement she pulled a plait of her hair (cf earwashing cat). Furthermore, silly Milly, she dreamed of having had an unspoken unremembered conversation with a horse whose name had been Joseph to whom (which) she had offered a tumblerful of lemonade which it (he) had appeared to have accepted (cf hearthdreaming cat). Hence, in passivity, in economy, in the instinct of tradition, in unexpectedness, their differences were similar.

In what way had he utilised gifts 1) an owl, 2) a clock, given as matrimonial auguries, to interest and to instruct her?
As object lessons to explain: 1) the nature and habits of oviparous animals, the possibility of aerial flight, certain abnormalities of vision, the secular process of imbalsamation: 2) the principle of the pendulum, exemplified in bob, wheelgear and regulator, the translation in terms

of human or social regulation of the various positions of clockwise moveable indicators on an unmoving dial, the exactitude of the recurrence per hour of an instant in each hour when the longer and the shorter indicator were at the same angle of inclination, *videlicet*, 5 5/11 minutes past each hour per hour in arithmetical progression.

In what manners did she reciprocate?

She remembered: on the 27th anniversary of his birth she presented to him a breakfast moustachecup of imitation Crown Derby porcelain ware. She provided: at quarter day or thereabouts if or when purchases had been made by him not for her she showed herself attentive to his necessities, anticipating his desires. She admired: a natural phenomenon having been explained by him to her she expressed the immediate desire to possess without gradual acquisition a fraction of his science, the moiety, the quarter, a thousandth part.

What proposal did Bloom, diambulist, father of Milly, somnambulist, make to Stephen, noctambulist?

To pass in repose the hours intervening between Thursday (proper) and Friday (normal) on an extemporised cubicle in the apartment immediately above the kitchen and immediately adjacent to the sleeping apartment of his host and hostess.

What various advantages would or might have resulted from a prolongation of such an extemporisation?

For the guest: security of domicile and seclusion of study. For the host: rejuvenation of intelligence, vicarious satisfaction. For the hostess: disintegration of obsession, acquisition of correct Italian pronunciation.

Why might these several provisional contingencies between a guest and a hostess not necessarily preclude or be precluded by a permanent eventuality of reconciliatory union between a schoolfellow and a jew's daughter?

Because the way to daughter led through mother, the way to mother through daughter.

To what inconsequent polysyllabic question of his host did the guest return a monosyllabic negative answer?

If he had known the late Mrs Emily Sinico, accidentally killed at Sydney Parade railway station, 14 October 1903.

What inchoate corollary statement was consequently suppressed by the host?

A statement explanatory of his absence on the occasion of the interment of Mrs Mary Dedalus (born Goulding), 26 June 1903, vigil of the anniversary of the decease of Rudolph Bloom (born Virag).

Was the proposal of asylum accepted?

Promptly, inexplicably, with amicability, gratefully it was declined.

What exchange of money took place between host and guest?

The former returned to the latter, without interest, a sum of money (£ 1. 7s. 0.), one pound seven shillings sterling, advanced by the latter to the former.

What counterproposals were alternately advanced, accepted, modified, declined, restated in other terms, reaccepted, ratified, reconfirmed?

To inaugurate a prearranged course of Italian instruction, place the residence of the instructed. To inaugurate a course of vocal instruction, place the residence of the instructress. To inaugurate a series of static, semistatic and peripatetic intellectual dialogues, places the residence of both speakers (if both speakers were resident in the same place), the *Ship* hotel and tavern, 6 Lower Abbey street (W. and E. Connery, proprietors), the National Library of Ireland, 10 Kildare street, the National Maternity Hospital, 29, 30 and 31 Holles street, a public garden, the vicinity of a place of worship, a conjunction of two or more public thoroughfares, the point of bisection of a right line drawn between their residences (if both speakers were resident in different places).

What rendered problematic for Bloom the realisation of these mutually selfexcluding propositions?

The irreparability of the past: once at a performance of Albert Hengler's circus in the Rotunda, Rutland square, Dublin, an intuitive particoloured clown in quest of paternity had penetrated from the ring to a place in the auditorium where Bloom, solitary, was seated and had publicly declared to an exhilarated audience that he (Bloom) was his (the clown's) papa. The imprevidibility of the future: once in the summer of 1898 he (Bloom) had marked a florin (2s.) with three notches on the milled edge and tendered it in payment of an account due to and received by J. and T. Davy, family grocers, 1 Charlemont Mall, Grand Canal, for circulation on the waters of civic finance, for possible, circuitous or direct, return.

Was the clown Bloom's son?
No.

Had Bloom's coin returned?
Never.

Why would a recurrent frustration the more depress him?
Because at the critical turningpoint of human existence he desired to amend many social conditions, the product of inequality and avarice and international animosity.

He believed then that human life was infinitely perfectible, eliminating these conditions?
There remained the generic conditions imposed by natural, as distinct from human law, as integral parts of the human whole: the necessity of destruction to procure alimentary sustenance: the painful character of the ultimate functions of separate existence, the agonies of birth and death: the monotonous menstruation of simian and (particularly) human females extending from the age of puberty to the menopause: inevitable accidents at sea, in mines and factories: certain very painful maladies and their resultant surgical operations, innate lunacy and congenital criminality, decimating epidemics: catastrophic cataclysms which make terror the basis of human mentality: seismic upheavals the epicentres of which are located in densely populated regions: the fact of vital growth, through convulsions of metamorphosis, from infancy through maturity to decay.

Why did he desist from speculation?
Because it was a task for a superior intelligence to substitute other more acceptable phenomena in the place of the less acceptable phenomena to be removed.

Did Stephen participate in his dejection?
He affirmed his significance as a conscious rational animal

proceeding syllogistically from the known to the unknown and a conscious rational reagent between a micro and a macrocosm ineluctably constructed upon the incertitude of the void.

Was this affirmation apprehended by Bloom?
Not verbally. Substantially.

What comforted his misapprehension?
That as a competent keyless citizen he had proceeded energetically from the unknown to the known through the incertitude of the void.

In what order of precedence, with what attendant ceremony was the exodus from the house of bondage to the wilderness of inhabitation effected?

Lighted Candle in Stick
borne by
BLOOM
Diaconal Hat on Ashplant
borne by
STEPHEN

With what intonation *secreto* of what commemorative psalm?
The 113th, *modus peregrinus: In exitu Israël de Egypto: domus Jacob de populo barbaro.*

What did each do at the door of egress?
Bloom set the candlestick on the floor. Stephen put the hat on his head.

For what creature was the door of egress a door of ingress?
For a cat.
What spectacle confronted them when they, first the host, then the guest, emerged silently, doubly dark, from obscurity by a passage from the rere of the house into the penumbra of the garden?
The heaventree of stars hung with humid nightblue fruit.

With what meditations did Bloom accompany his demonstration to his companion of various constellations?

Meditations of evolution increasingly vaster: of the moon invisible in incipient lunation, approaching perigee: of the infinite lattiginous scintillating uncondensed milky way, discernible by daylight by an observer placed at the lower end of a cylindrical vertical shaft 5000 ft deep sunk from the surface towards the centre of the earth: of Sirius (alpha in Canis Maior) 10 lightyears (57,000,000,000,000 miles) distant and in volume 900 times the dimension of our planet: of Arcturus: of the precession of equinoxes: of Orion with belt and sextuple sun theta and nebula in which 100 of our solar systems could be contained: of moribund and of nascent new stars such as Nova in 1901: of our system plunging towards the constellation of Hercules: of the parallax or parallactic drift of socalled fixed stars, in reality evermoving wanderers from immeasurably remote eons to infinitely remote futures in comparison with which the years, threescore and ten, of allotted human life formed a parenthesis of infinitesimal brevity.

Were there obverse meditations of involution increasingly less vast?

Of the eons of geological periods recorded in the stratifications of the earth: of the myriad minute entomological organic existences concealed in cavities of the earth, beneath removable stones, in hives and mounds, of microbes, germs, bacteria, bacilli, spermatozoa: of the incalculable trillions of billions of millions of imperceptible molecules contained by cohesion of molecular affinity in a single pinhead: of the universe of human serum constellated with red and white bodies, themselves universes of void space constellated with other bodies, each, in continuity, its universe of divisible component bodies of which each was again divisible in divisions of redivisible component bodies, dividends and divisors ever diminishing without actual division till, if the progress were carried far enough, nought nowhere was never reached.

Why did he not elaborate these calculations to a more precise result?

Because some years previously in 1886 when occupied with the problem of the quadrature of the circle he had learned of the existence of a number computed to a relative degree of accuracy to be of such magnitude and of so many places, e.g., the 9th power of the 9th power of 9, that, the result having been obtained, 33 closely printed volumes of 1000 pages each of innumerable quires and reams of India paper would have to be requisitioned in order to contain the complete tale of its printed integers of units, tens, hundreds, thousands, tens of thousands, hundreds of thousands, millions, tens of millions, hundreds of millions, billions, the nucleus of the nebula of every digit of every series containing succinctly the potentiality of being raised to the utmost kinetic elaboration of any power of any of its powers.

Did he find the problems of the inhabitability of the planets and their satellites by a race, given in species, and of the possible social and moral redemption of said race by a redeemer, easier of solution?

Of a different order of difficulty. Conscious that the human organism, normally capable of sustaining an atmospheric pressure of 19 tons, when elevated to a considerable altitude in the terrestrial atmosphere suffered with arithmetical progression of intensity, according as the line of demarcation between troposphere and stratosphere was approximated from nasal hemorrhage, impeded respiration and vertigo, when proposing this problem for solution, he had conjectured as a working hypothesis which could not be proved impossible that a more adaptable and differently anatomically constructed race of beings might subsist otherwise under Martian, Mercurial, Veneral, Jovian, Saturnian, Neptunian or Uranian sufficient and equivalent conditions, though an apogean humanity of beings created in varying forms with finite differences resulting similar to the whole and to one another would probably there as here remain inalterably and inalienably attached to vanities, to vanities of vanities and to all that is vanity.

And the problem of possible redemption? The minor was proved by the major.

Which various features of the constellations were in turn considered?

The various colours significant of various degrees of vitality (white, yellow, crimson, vermilion, cinnabar): their degrees of brilliancy: their magnitudes revealed up to and including the 7th: their positions: the waggoner's star: Walsingham way: the chariot of David: the annular cinctures of Saturn: the condensation of spiral nebulae into suns: the interdependent gyrations of double suns: the independent synchronous discoveries of Galileo, Simon Marius,

Piazzi, Le Verrier, Herschel, Galle: the systematisations attempted by Bode and Kepler of cubes of distances and squares of times of revolution: the almost infinite compressibility of hirsute comets and their vast elliptical egressive and reentrant orbits from perihelion to aphelion: the sidereal origin of meteoric stones: the Libyan floods on Mars about the period of the birth of the younger astroscopist: the annual recurrence of meteoric showers about the period of the feast of S. Lawrence (martyr, 10 August): the monthly recurrence known as the new moon with the old moon in her arms: the posited influence of celestial on human bodies: the appearance of a star (1st magnitude) of exceeding brilliancy dominating by night and day (a new luminous sun generated by the collision and amalgamation in incandescence of two nonluminous exsuns) about the period of the birth of William Shakespeare over delta in the recumbent neversetting constellation of Cassiopeia and of a star (2nd magnitude) of similar origin but of lesser brilliancy which had appeared in and disappeared from the constellation of the Corona Septentrionalis about the period of the birth of Leopold Bloom and of other stars of (presumably) similar origin which had (effectively or presumably) appeared in and disappeared from the constellation of Andromeda about the period of the birth of Stephen Dedalus, and in and from the constellation of Auriga some years after the birth and death of Rudolph Bloom, junior, and in and from other constellations some years before or after the birth or death of other persons: the attendant phenomena of eclipses, solar and lunar, from immersion to emersion, abatement of wind, transit of shadow, taciturnity of winged creatures, emergence of nocturnal or crepuscular animals, persistence of infernal light, obscurity of terrestrial waters, pallor of human beings.

His (Bloom's) logical conclusion, having weighed the matter and allowing for possible error?

That it was not a heaventree, not a heavengrot, not a heavenbeast, not a heavenman. That it was a Utopia, there being no known method from the known to the unknown: an infinity renderable equally finite by the suppositious apposition of one or more bodies equally of the same and of different magnitudes: a mobility of illusory forms immobilised in space, remobilised in air: a past which possibly had ceased to exist as a present before its probable spectators had entered actual present existence.

Was he more convinced of the esthetic value of the spectacle?

Indubitably in consequence of the reiterated examples of poets in the delirium of the frenzy of attachment or in the abasement of rejection invoking ardent sympathetic constellations or the frigidity of the satellite of their planet.

Did he then accept as an article of belief the theory of astrological influences upon sublunary disasters?

It seemed to him as possible of proof as of confutation and the nomenclature employed in its selenographical charts as attributable to verifiable intuition as to fallacious analogy: the lake of dreams, the sea of rains, the gulf of dews, the ocean of fecundity.

What special affinities appeared to him to exist between the moon and woman?

Her antiquity in preceding and surviving successive tellurian generations: her nocturnal predominance: her satellitic dependence: her luminary reflection: her constancy under all her phases, rising and setting by her appointed times, waxing and waning: the forced invariability of her aspect: her indeterminate response to inaffirmative interrogation: her potency over effluent and refluent waters: her power to enamour, to mortify, to invest with beauty, to render insane, to incite to and aid delinquency: the tranquil inscrutability of her visage: the terribility of her isolated dominant implacable resplendent propinquity: her omens of tempest and of calm: the stimulation of her light, her motion and her presence: the admonition of her craters, her arid seas, her silence: her splendour, when visible: her attraction, when invisible.

What visible luminous sign attracted Bloom's, who attracted Stephen's, gaze?

In the second storey (rere) of his (Bloom's) house the light of a paraffin oil lamp with oblique shade projected on a screen of roller blind supplied by Frank O'Hara, window blind, curtain pole and revolving shutter manufacturer, 16 Aungier street.

How did he elucidate the mystery of an invisible attractive person, his wife Marion (Molly) Bloom, denoted by a visible splendid sign, a lamp?

With indirect and direct verbal allusions or affirmations: with subdued affection and admiration: with description: with impediment: with suggestion.

Both then were silent?
Silent, each contemplating the other in both mirrors of the reciprocal flesh of theirhisnothis fellowfaces.

Were they indefinitely inactive?
At Stephen's suggestion, at Bloom's instigation both, first Stephen, then Bloom, in penumbra urinated, their sides contiguous, their organs of micturition reciprocally rendered invisible by manual circumposition, their gazes, first Bloom's, then Stephen's, elevated to the projected luminous and semiluminous shadow.

Similarly?
The trajectories of their, first sequent, then simultaneous, urinations were dissimilar: Bloom's longer, less irruent, in the incomplete form of the bifurcated penultimate alphabetical letter, who in his ultimate year at High School (1880) had been capable of attaining the point of greatest altitude against the whole concurrent strength of the institution, 210 scholars: Stephen's higher, more sibilant, who in the ultimate hours of the previous day had augmented by diuretic consumption an insistent vesical pressure.

What different problems presented themselves to each concerning the invisible audible collateral organ of the other?
To Bloom: the problems of irritability, tumescence, rigidity, reactivity, dimension, sanitariness, pilosity.
To Stephen: the problem of the sacerdotal integrity of Jesus circumcised (1st January, holiday of obligation to hear mass and abstain from unnecessary servile work) and the problem as to whether the divine prepuce, the carnal bridal ring of the holy Roman catholic apostolic church, conserved in Calcata, were deserving of simple hyperduly or of the fourth degree of latria accorded to the abscission of such divine excrescences as hair and toenails.

What celestial sign was by both simultaneously observed?
A star precipitated with great apparent velocity across the

firmament from Vega in the Lyre above the zenith beyond the stargroup of the Tress of Berenice towards the zodiacal sign of Leo.

How did the centripetal remainer afford egress to the centrifugal departer?

By inserting the barrel of an arruginated male key in the hole of an unstable female lock, obtaining a purchase on the bow of the key and turning its wards from right to left, withdrawing a bolt from its staple, pulling inward spasmodically an obsolescent unhinged door and revealing an aperture for free egress and free ingress.

How did they take leave, one of the other, in separation?

Standing perpendicular at the same door and on different sides of its base, the lines of their valedictory arms, meeting at any point and forming any angle less than the sum of two right angles.

What sound accompanied the union of their tangent, the disunion of their (respectively) centrifugal and centripetal hands?

The sound of the peal of the hour of the night by the chime of the bells in the church of Saint George.

What echoes of that sound were by both and each heard?
By Stephen:

Liliata rutilantium. Turma circumdet.
Iubilantium te virginum. Chorus excipiat.

By Bloom:

Heigho, heigho,
Heigho, heigho.

Where were the several members of the company which with Bloom that day at the bidding of that peal had travelled from Sandymount in the south to Glasnevin in the north?

Martin Cunningham (in bed), Jack Power (in bed), Simon Dedalus (in bed), Ned Lambert (in bed), Tom Kernan (in bed), Joe Hynes (in bed), John Henry Menton (in bed), Bernard Corrigan (in bed), Patsy Dignam (in bed), Paddy Dignam (in the grave).

Alone, what did Bloom hear?

The double reverberation of retreating feet on the heavenborn earth, the double vibration of a jew's harp in the resonant lane.

Alone, what did Bloom feel?

The cold of interstellar space, thousands of degrees below freezing point or the absolute zero of Fahrenheit, Centigrade or Réaumur: the incipient intimations of proximate dawn.

Of what did bellchime and handtouch and footstep and lonechill remind him?

Of companions now in various manners in different places defunct: Percy Apjohn (killed in action, Modder River), Philip Gilligan (phthisis, Jervis Street hospital), Matthew F. Kane (accidental drowning, Dublin Bay), Philip Moisel (pyemia, Heytesbury street), Michael Hart (phthisis, Mater Misericordiae hospital), Patrick Dignam (apoplexy, Sandymount).

What prospect of what phenomena inclined him to remain?

The disparition of three final stars, the diffusion of daybreak, the apparition of a new solar disk.

Had he ever been a spectator of those phenomena?

Once, in 1887, after a protracted performance of charades in the house of Luke Doyle, Kimmage, he had awaited with patience the apparition of the diurnal phenomenon, seated on a wall, his gaze turned in the direction of Mizrach, the east.

He remembered the initial paraphenomena?

More active air, a matutinal distant cock, ecclesiastical clocks at various points, avine music, the isolated tread of an early wayfarer, the visible diffusion of the light of an invisible luminous body, the first golden limb of the resurgent sun perceptible low on the horizon.

Did he remain?

With deep inspiration he returned, retraversing the garden, reentering the passage, reclosing the door. With brief suspiration he reassumed the candle, reascended the stairs, reapproached the door of the front room, hallfloor, and reentered.

What suddenly arrested his ingress?

The right temporal lobe of the hollow sphere of his cranium came into contact with a solid timber angle where, an infinitesimal but sensible fraction of a second later, a painful sensation was located in consequence of antecedent sensations transmitted and registered.

Describe the alterations effected in the disposition of the articles of furniture.

A sofa upholstered in prune plush had been translocated from opposite the door to the ingleside near the compactly furled Union Jack (an alteration which he had frequently intended to execute): the blue and white checker inlaid majolicatopped table had been placed opposite the door in the place vacated by the prune plush sofa: the walnut sideboard (a projecting angle of which had momentarily arrested his ingress) had been moved from its position beside the door to a more advantageous but more perilous position in front of the door: two chairs had been moved from right and left of the ingleside to the position originally occupied by the blue and white checker inlaid majolicatopped table.

Describe them.

One: a squat stuffed easychair, with stout arms extended and back slanted to the rere, which, repelled in recoil, had then upturned an irregular fringe of a rectangular rug and now displayed on its amply upholstered seat a centralised diffusing and diminishing discolouration. The other: a slender splayfoot chair of glossy cane curves, placed directly opposite the former, its frame from top to seat and from seat to base being varnished dark brown, its seat being a bright circle of white plaited rush.

What significances attached to these two chairs?

Significances of similitude, of posture, of symbolism, of circumstantial evidence, of testimonial supermanence.

What occupied the position originally occupied by the sideboard?

A vertical piano (Cadby) with exposed keyboard, its closed coffin supporting a pair of long yellow ladies' gloves and an emerald ashtray containing four consumed matches, a partly consumed cigarette and two discoloured ends of cigarettes, its musicrest supporting the music in the key of G natural for voice and piano of *Love's Old Sweet Song* (words by G. Clifton Bingham, composed by J. L. Molloy, sung by Madam Antoinette Sterling) open at the last page with the final indications *ad libitum, forte*, pedal, *animato*, sustained pedal, *ritirando*, close.

With what sensations did Bloom contemplate in rotation these objects?

With strain, elevating a candlestick: with pain, feeling on his right temple a contused tumescence: with attention, focussing his gaze on a large dull passive and a slender bright active: with solicitation, bending and downturning the upturned rugfringe: with amusement, remembering Dr Malachi Mulligan's scheme of colour containing the gradation of green: with pleasure, repeating the words and antecedent act and perceiving through various channels of internal sensibility the consequent and concomitant tepid pleasant diffusion of gradual discolouration.

His next proceeding?

From an open box on the majolicatopped table he extracted a black diminutive cone, one inch in height, placed it on its circular base on a small tin plate, placed his candlestick on the right corner of the mantelpiece, produced from his waistcoat a folded page of prospectus (illustrated) entitled Agendath Netaim, unfolded the same, examined it superficially, rolled it into a thin cylinder, ignited it in the candleflame, applied it when ignited to the apex of the cone till the latter reached the stage of rutilance, placed the cylinder in the basin of the candlestick disposing its unconsumed part in such a manner as to facilitate total combustion.

What followed this operation?

The truncated conical crater summit of the diminutive volcano emitted a vertical and serpentine fume redolent of aromatic oriental incense.

What homothetic objects, other than the candlestick, stood on the mantelpiece?

A timepiece of striated Connemara marble, stopped at the hour of 4.46 a.m. on the 21 March 1896, matrimonial gift of Matthew Dillon:

a dwarf tree of glacial arborescence under a transparent bellshade, matrimonial gift of Luke and Caroline Doyle: an embalmed owl, matrimonial gift of Alderman John Hooper.

What interchanges of looks took place between these three objects and Bloom?

In the mirror of the giltbordered pierglass the undecorated back of the dwarf tree regarded the upright back of the embalmed owl. Before the mirror the matrimonial gift of Alderman John Hooper with a clear melancholy wise bright motionless compassionate gaze regarded Bloom while Bloom with obscure tranquil profound motionless compassionated gaze regarded the matrimonial gift of Luke and Caroline Doyle.

What composite asymmetrical image in the mirror then attracted his attention?

The image of a solitary (ipsorelative) mutable (aliorelative) man.

Why solitary (ipsorelative)?

Brothers and sisters had he none.
Yet that man's father was his grandfather's son.

Why mutable (aliorelative)?

From infancy to maturity he had resembled his maternal procreatrix. From maturity to senility he would increasingly resemble his paternal procreator.

What final visual impression was communicated to him by the mirror?

The optical reflection of several inverted volumes improperly arranged and not in the order of their common letters with scintillating titles on the two bookshelves opposite.

Catalogue these books.

Thom's Dublin Post Office Directory, 1886.

Denis Florence M'Carthy's *Poetical Works* (copper beechleaf bookmark at p. 5).

Shakespeare's *Works* (dark crimson morocco, goldtooled).

The Useful Ready Reckoner (brown cloth).

The Secret History of the Court of Charles II (red cloth, tooled binding).

The Child's Guide (blue cloth).

The Beauties of Killarney (wrappers).

When We Were Boys by William O'Brien M. P. (green cloth, slightly faded, envelope bookmark at p. 217).

Thoughts from Spinoza (maroon leather).

The Story of the Heavens by Sir Robert Ball (blue cloth).

Ellis's *Three Trips to Madagascar* (brown cloth, title obliterated).

The Stark-Munro Letters by A. Conan Doyle, property of the City of Dublin Public Library, 106 Capel street, lent 21 May (Whitsun Eve) 1904, due 4 June 1904, 13 days overdue (black cloth binding, bearing white letternumber ticket).

Voyages in China by "Viator" (recovered with brown paper, red ink title).

Philosophy of the Talmud (sewn pamphlet).

Lockhart's *Life of Napoleon* (cover wanting, marginal annotations, minimising victories, aggrandising defeats of the protagonist).

Soll und Haben by Gustav Freytag (black boards, Gothic characters, cigarette coupon bookmark at p. 24).

Hozier's *History of the Russo-Turkish War* (brown cloth, 2 volumes, with gummed label, Garrison Library, Governor's Parade, Gibraltar, on verso of cover).

Laurence Bloomfield in Ireland by William Allingham (second edition, green cloth, gilt trefoil design, previous owner's name on recto of flyleaf erased).

A Handbook of Astronomy (cover, brown leather, detached, 5 plates, antique letterpress long primer, author's footnotes nonpareil, marginal clues brevier, captions small pica).

The Hidden Life of Christ (black boards).

In the Track of the Sun (yellow cloth, titlepage missing, recurrent title intestation).

Physical Strength and How to Obtain It by Eugen Sandow (red cloth).

Short but yet Plain Elements of Geometry written in French by F. Ignat. Pardies and rendered into Englifh by John Harris D. D. London, printed for R. Knaplock at the Bifhop's Head, MDCCXI, with dedicatory epiftle to his worthy friend Charles Cox, efquire, Member of Parliament for the burgh of Southwark and having ink calligraphed statement on the flyleaf certifying that the book was the property of

Michael Gallagher, dated this 10th day of May 1822 and requeſting the perſon who should find it, if the book should be loſt or go aſtray, to reſtore it to Michael Gallagher, carpenter, Dufery Gate, Enniſcorthy, county Wicklow, the fineſt place in the world.

What reflections occupied his mind during the process of reversion of the inverted volumes?

The necessity of order, a place for everything and everything in its place: the deficient appreciation of literature possessed by females: the incongruity of an apple incuneated in a tumbler and of an umbrella inclined in a closestool: the insecurity of hiding any secret document behind, beneath or between the pages of a book.

Which volume was the largest in bulk?

Hozier's *History of the Russo-Turkish War.*

What among other data did the second volume of the work in question contain?

The name of a decisive battle (forgotten), frequently remembered by a decisive officer, major Brian Cooper Tweedy (remembered).

Why, firstly and secondly, did he not consult the work in question?

Firstly, in order to exercise mnemotechnic: secondly, because after an interval of amnesia, when, seated at the central table, about to consult the work in question, he remembered by mnemotechnic the name of the military engagement, Plevna.

What caused him consolation in his sitting posture?

The candour, nudity, pose, tranquility, youth, grace, sex, counsel of a statue erect in the centre of the table, an image of Narcissus purchased by auction from P. A. Wren, 9 Bachelor's Walk.

What caused him irritation in his sitting posture?

Inhibitory pressure of collar (size 17) and waistcoat (5 buttons), two articles of clothing superfluous in the costume of mature males and inelastic to alterations of mass by expansion.

How was the irritation allayed?

He removed his collar, with contained black necktie and

collapsible stud, from his neck to a position on the left of the table. He unbuttoned successively in reversed direction waistcoat, trousers, shirt and vest along the medial line of irregular incrispated black hairs extending in triangular convergence from the pelvic basin over the circumference of the abdomen and umbilicular fossicle along the medial line of nodes to the intersection of the sixth pectoral vertebrae, thence produced both ways at right angles and terminating in circles described about two equidistant points, right and left, on the summits of the mammary prominences. He unbraced successively each of six minus one braced trouser buttons, arranged in pairs, of which one incomplete.

What involuntary actions followed?

He compressed between 2 fingers the flesh circumjacent to a cicatrice in the left infracostal region below the diaphragm resulting from a sting inflicted 2 weeks and 3 days previously (23 May 1904) by a bee. He scratched imprecisely with his right hand, though insensible of prurition, various points and surfaces of his partly exposed, wholly abluted skin. He inserted his left hand into the left lower pocket of his waistcoat and extracted and replaced a silver coin (1 shilling), placed there (presumably) on the occasion (17 October 1903) of the interment of Mrs Emily Sinico, Sydney Parade.

Compile the budget for 16 June 1904.

Debit	£.	s.	d.	Credit	£.	s.	d.
1 Pork kidney	0	0	3	Cash in hand	0	4	9
1 Copy Freeman's Journal	0	0	1	Commission recd. Freeman's Journal	1	7	6
1 Bath and Gratification	0	1	6	Loan (Stephen Dedalus)	1	7	0
Tramfare	0	0	1				
1 In Memoriam Patrick Dignam	0	5	0				
2 Banbury cakes	0	0	1				
1 Lunch	0	0	7				
1 Renewal fee for book	0	1	0				

1 Packet Notepaper and Envelopes	0	0	2
1 Dinner and Gratification	0	2	0
1 Postal Order and Stamp	0	2	8
Tramfare	0	0	1
1 Pig's Foot	0	0	4
1 Sheep's Trotter	0	0	3
1 Cake Fry's Plain Chocolate	0	0	1
1 Square Soda Bread	0	0	4
1 Coffee and Bun	0	0	4
Loan (Stephen Dedalus) refunded	1	7	0
BALANCE	0	17	5
	2	19	3

2 19 3

Did the process of divestiture continue?

Sensible of a benignant persistent ache in his footsoles he extended his foot to one side and observed the creases, protuberances and salient points caused by foot pressure in the course of walking repeatedly in several different directions, then, inclined, he disnoded the laceknots, unhooked and loosened the laces, took off each of his two boots for the second time, detached the partially moistened right sock through the fore part of which the nail of his great toe had again effracted, raised his right foot and, having unhooked a purple elastic sock suspender, took off his right sock, placed his unclothed right foot on the margin of the seat of his chair, picked at and gently lacerated the protruding part of the great toenail, raised the part lacerated to his nostrils and inhaled the odour of the quick, then, with satisfaction, threw away the lacerated ungual fragment.

Why with satisfaction?

Because the odour inhaled corresponded to other odours inhaled of other ungual fragments, picked and lacerated by Master Bloom, pupil of Mrs Ellis's juvenile school, patiently each night in the act of brief genuflection and nocturnal prayer and ambitious meditation.

In what ultimate ambition had all concurrent and consecutive ambitions now coalesced?

Not to inherit by right of primogeniture, gavelkind or borough English, or possess in perpetuity an extensive demesne of a sufficient number of acres, roods and perches, statute land measure (valuation £ 42), of grazing turbary surrounding a baronial hall with gatelodge and carriage drive nor, on the other hand, a terracehouse or semidetached villa, described as *Rus in Urbe* or *Qui si sana*, but to purchase by private treaty in fee simple a thatched bungalowshaped 2 storey dwellinghouse of southerly aspect, surmounted by vane and lightning conductor, connected with the earth, with porch covered by parasitic plants (ivy or Virginia creeper), halldoor, olive green, with smart carriage finish and neat doorbrasses, stucco front with gilt tracery at eaves and gable, rising, if possible, upon a gentle eminence with agreeable prospect from balcony with stone pillar parapet over unoccupied and unoccupyable interjacent pastures and standing in 5 or 6 acres of its own ground, at such a distance from the nearest public thoroughfare as to render its houselights visible at night above and through a quickset hornbeam hedge of topiary cutting, situate at a given point not less than 1 statute mile from the periphery of the metropolis, within a time limit of not more than 15 minutes from tram or train line (e.g., Dundrum, south, or Sutton, north, both localities equally reported by trial to resemble the terrestrial poles in being favourable climates for phthisical subjects), the premises to be held under feefarm grant, lease 999 years, the messuage to consist of 1 drawing room with baywindow (2 lancets), thermometer affixed, 1 sitting room, 4 bedrooms, 2 servants' rooms, tiled kitchen with close range and scullery, lounge hall fitted with linen wallpresses, fumed oak sectional bookcase containing the Encyclopaedia Britannica and New Century Dictionary, transverse obsolete medieval and oriental weapons, dinner gong, alabaster lamp, bowl pendant, vulcanite automatic telephone receiver with adjacent directory, handtufted Axminster carpet with cream ground and trellis border, loo table with pillar and claw legs, hearth with massive firebrasses and ormolu mantel chronometer clock, guaranteed timekeeper with cathedral chime, barometer with hygrographic chart, comfortable lounge settees and corner fitments, upholstered in ruby plush with good springing and sunk centre, three banner Japanese screen and cuspidors (club style, rich winecoloured leather, gloss renewable with a minimum of labour by use of linseed oil and vinegar) and pyramidically prismatic central chandelier lustre, bentwood perch with fingertame parrot (expurgated language), embossed mural paper at 10/- per dozen with transverse swags of carmine floral design and top crown frieze, staircase, three continuous flights at successive right angles, of varnished cleargrained oak, treads and risers, newel, balusters and handrail, with steppedup panel dado, dressed with camphorated wax: bathroom, hot and cold supply, reclining and shower: water closet on mezzanine provided with opaque singlepane oblong window, tipup seat, bracket lamp, brass tierod and brace, armrests, footstool and artistic oleograph on inner face of door: ditto, plain: servants' apartments with separate sanitary and hygienic necessaries for cook, general and betweenmaid (salary, rising by biennial unearned increments of £ 2, with comprehensive fidelity insurance, annual bonus (£ 1) and retiring allowance (based on the 65 system) after 30 years' service), pantry, buttery, larder, refrigerator, outoffices, coal and wood cellarage with winebin (still and sparkling vintages) for distinguished guests, if entertained to dinner (evening dress), carbon monoxide gas supply throughout.

What additional attractions might the grounds contain?

As addenda, a tennis and fives court, a shrubbery, a glass summerhouse with tropical palms, equipped in the best botanical manner, a rockery with waterspray, a beehive arranged on humane principles, oval flowerbeds in rectangular grassplots set with eccentric ellipses of scarlet and chrome tulips, blue scillas, crocuses, polyanthus, sweet William, sweet pea, lily of the valley (bulbs obtainable from sir James W. Mackey (Limited) wholesale and retail seed and bulb merchants and nurserymen, agents for chemical manures, 23 Sackville street, upper), an orchard, kitchen garden and vinery, protected against illegal trespassers by glasstopped mural enclosures, a lumbershed with padlock for various inventoried implements.

As?

Eeltraps, lobsterpots, fishingrods, hatchet, steelyard, grindstone, clodcrusher, swatheturner, carriagesack, telescope ladder, 10 tooth rake, washing clogs, haytedder, tumbling rake, billhook, paintpot, brush, hoe and so on.

What improvements might be subsequently introduced?

A rabbitry and fowlrun, a dovecote, a botanical conservatory, 2 hammocks (lady's and gentleman's), a sundial shaded and sheltered by laburnum or lilac trees, an exotically harmonically accorded Japanese tinkle gatebell affixed to left lateral gatepost, a capacious waterbutt, a lawnmower with side delivery and grassbox, a lawnsprinkler with hydraulic hose.

What facilities of transit were desirable?

When citybound frequent connection by train or tram from their respective intermediate station or terminal. When countrybound velocipedes, a chainless freewheel roadster cycle with side basketcar attached, or draught conveyance, a donkey with wicker trap or smart phaeton with good working solidungular cob (roan gelding, 14 h).

What might be the name of this erigible or erected residence?

Bloom Cottage. Saint Leopold's. Flowerville.

Could Bloom of 7 Eccles street foresee Bloom of Flowerville?

In loose allwool garments with Harris tweed cap, price 8/6, and useful garden boots with elastic gussets and wateringcan, planting aligned young firtrees, syringing, pruning, staking, sowing hayseed, trundling a weedladen wheelbarrow without excessive fatigue at sunset amid the scent of newmown hay, ameliorating the soil, multiplying wisdom, achieving longevity.

What syllabus of intellectual pursuits was simultaneously possible?

Snapshot photography, comparative study of religions, folklore relative to various amatory and superstitious practices, contemplation of the celestial constellations.

What lighter recreations?

Outdoor: garden and fieldwork, cycling on level macadamised causeways, ascents of moderately high hills, natation in secluded fresh water and unmolested river boating in secure wherry or light curricle with kedge anchor on reaches free from weirs and rapids (period of estivation), vespertinal perambulation or equestrian circumprocession with inspection of sterile landscape and contrastingly agreeable cottagers' fires of smoking peat turves (period of hibernation).

Indoor: discussion in tepid security of unsolved historical and criminal problems: lecture of unexpurgated exotic erotic masterpieces: house carpentry with toolbox containing hammer, awl nails, screws, tintacks, gimlet, tweezers, bullnose plane and turnscrew.

Might he become a gentleman farmer of field produce and live stock?

Not impossibly, with 1 or 2 stripper cows, 1 pike of upland hay and requisite farming implements, e.g., an end-to-end churn, a turnip pulper etc.

What would be his civic functions and social status among the county families and landed gentry?

Arranged successively in ascending powers of hierarchical order, that of gardener, groundsman, cultivator, breeder, and at the zenith of his career, resident magistrate or justice of the peace with a family crest and coat of arms and appropriate classical motto (*Semper paratus*), duly recorded in the court directory (Bloom, Leopold P., M. P., P. C., K. P., L. L. D. (*honoris causa*), Bloomville, Dundrum) and mentioned in court and fashionable intelligence (Mr and Mrs Leopold Bloom have left Kingstown for England).

What course of action did he outline for himself in such capacity?

A course that lay between undue clemency and excessive rigour: the dispensation in a heterogeneous society of arbitrary classes, incessantly rearranged in terms of greater and lesser social inequality, of unbiassed homogeneous indisputable justice, tempered with mitigants of the widest possible latitude but exactable to the uttermost farthing with confiscation of estate, real and personal, to the crown. Loyal to the highest constituted power in the land, actuated by an innate love of rectitude his aims would be the strict maintenance of public order, the repression of many abuses though not of all simultaneously (every measure of reform or retrenchment being a preliminary solution to be contained by fluxion in the final solution), the upholding of the letter of the law (common, statute and law merchant) against all traversers in covin and trespassers acting in contravention of bylaws and regulations, all resuscitators (by trespass and petty larceny of kindlings) of venville rights, obsolete by desuetude, all orotund instigators of international persecution, all perpetuators of international animosities, all menial molestors of domestic conviviality, all recalcitrant violators of domestic connubiality.

Prove that he had loved rectitude from his earliest youth.

To Master Percy Apjohn at High School in 1880 he had divulged his disbelief in the tenets of the Irish (protestant) church (to which his father Rudolf Virag (later Rudolph Bloom) had been converted from the Israelitic faith and communion in 1865 by the Society for promoting Christianity among the jews) subsequently abjured by him in favour of Roman catholicism at the epoch of and with a view to his matrimony in 1888. To Daniel Magrane and Francis Wade in 1882 during a juvenile friendship (terminated by the premature emigration of the former) he had advocated during nocturnal perambulations the political theory of colonial (e.g. Canadian) expansion and the evolutionary theories of Charles Darwin, expounded in *The Descent of Man* and *The Origin of Species*. In 1885 he had publicly expressed his adherence to the collective and national economic programme advocated by James Fintan Lalor, John Fisher Murray, John Mitchel, J. F. X. O'Brien and others, the agrarian policy of Michael Davitt, the constitutional agitation of Charles Stewart Parnell (M. P. for Cork City), the programme of peace, retrenchment and reform of William Ewart Gladstone (M. P. for Midlothian, N. B.) and, in support of his political convictions, had climbed up into a secure position amid the ramifications of a tree on Northumberland road to see the entrance (2 February 1888) into the capital of a demonstrative torchlight procession of 20,000 torchbearers, divided into 120 trade corporations, bearing 2000 torches in escort of the marquess of Ripon and (honest) John Morley.

How much and how did he propose to pay for this country residence?

As per prospectus of the Industrious Foreign Acclimatised Nationalised Friendly Stateaided Building Society (incorporated 1874), a maximum of £60 per annum, being 1/6 of an assured income, derived from giltedged securities, representing at 5% simple interest on capital of £1200 (estimate of price at 20 years' purchase), of which 1/3 to be paid on acquisition and the balance in the form of annual rent, viz. £800 plus 2 1/2% interest on the same, repayable quarterly in equal annual instalments until extinction by amortisation of loan advanced for purchase within a period of 20 years, amounting to an annual rental of £ 64, headrent included, the titledeeds to remain in possession of the lender or lenders with a saving clause envisaging forced sale, foreclosure and mutual compensation in the event of protracted failure to pay the terms assigned, otherwise the messuage to become the absolute property of the tenant occupier upon expiry of the period of years stipulated.

What rapid but insecure means to opulence might facilitate immediate purchase?

A private wireless telegraph which would transmit by dot and dash system the result of a national equine handicap (flat or steeplechase) of 1 or more miles and furlongs won by an outsider at odds of 50 to 1 at 3 hr 8 m p.m. at Ascot (Greenwich time), the message being received and available for betting purposes in Dublin at 2.59 p.m. (Dunsink time). The unexpected discovery of an object of great monetary value (precious stone, valuable adhesive or impressed postage stamps (7 schilling, mauve, imperforate, Hamburg, 1866: 4 pence, rose, blue paper, perforate, Great Britain, 1855: 1 franc, stone, official, rouletted, diagonal surcharge, Luxemburg, 1878), antique dynastical ring, unique relic) in unusual repositories or by unusual means: from the air (dropped by an eagle in flight), by fire (amid the carbonised remains of an incendiated edifice), in the sea (amid flotsam, jetsam, lagan and derelict), on earth (in the gizzard of a comestible fowl). A Spanish prisoner's donation of a distant treasure of valuables or specie or bullion lodged with a solvent banking corporation 100 years previously at 5% compound interest of the collective worth of £ 5,000,000 stg (five million pounds sterling). A contract with an inconsiderate contractee for the delivery of 32 consignments of some given commodity in consideration of cash payment on delivery per delivery at the initial rate of 1/4d to be increased constantly in the geometrical progression of 2 (1/4d, 1/2d, 1d, 2d, 4d, 8d, 1s 4d, 2s 8d to 32 terms). A prepared scheme based on a study of the laws of probability to break the bank at Monte Carlo. A solution of the secular problem of the quadrature of the circle, government premium £ 1,000,000 sterling.

Was vast wealth acquirable through industrial channels?

The reclamation of dunams of waste arenary soil, proposed in the prospectus of Agendath Netaim, Bleibtreustrasse, Berlin, W. 15, by the cultivation of orange plantations and melonfields and reafforestation. The utilisation of waste paper, fells of sewer rodents, human excrement possessing chemical properties, in view of the vast production of the first, vast number of the second and immense quantity of the third, every normal human being of average vitality and appetite producing annually, cancelling byproducts of water, a sum total of 80 lbs. (mixed animal and vegetable diet), to be multiplied by 4,386,035, the total population of Ireland according to census returns of 1901.

Were there schemes of wider scope?

A scheme to be formulated and submitted for approval to the harbour commissioners for the exploitation of white coal (hydraulic power), obtained by hydroelectric plant at peak of tide at Dublin bar or at head of water at Poulaphouca or Powerscourt or catchment basins of main streams for the economic production of 500,000 W. H. P. of electricity. A scheme to enclose the peninsular delta of the North Bull at Dollymount and erect on the space of the foreland, used for golf links and rifle ranges, an asphalted esplanade with casinos, booths, shooting galleries, hotels, boardinghouses, readingrooms, establishments for mixed bathing. A scheme for the use of dogvans and goatvans for the delivery of early morning milk. A scheme for the development of Irish tourist traffic in and around Dublin by means of petrolpropelled riverboats, plying in the fluvial fairway between Island bridge and Ringsend, charabancs, narrow gauge local railways, and pleasure steamers for coastwise navigation (10/- per person per day, guide (trilingual) included). A scheme for the repristination of passenger and goods traffics over Irish waterways, when freed from weedbeds. A scheme to connect by tramline the Cattle Market (North Circular road and Prussia street) with the quays (Sheriff street, lower, and East Wall), parallel with the Link line railway laid (in conjunction with the Great Southern and Western railway line) between the cattle park, Liffey junction, and terminus of Midland Great Western Railway 43 to 45 North Wall, in proximity to the terminal stations or Dublin branches of Great Central Railway, Midland Railway of England, City of Dublin Steam Packet Company, Lancashire and Yorkshire Railway Company, Dublin and Glasgow Steam Packet Company, Glasgow, Dublin and Londonderry Steam Packet Company (Laird line), British and Irish Steam Packet Company, Dublin and Morecambe Steamers, London and North Western Railway Company, Dublin

Port and Docks Board Landing Sheds and transit sheds of Palgrave, Murphy and Company, steamship owners, agents for steamers from Mediterranean, Spain, Portugal, France, Belgium and Holland and for Liverpool Underwriters' Association, the cost of acquired rolling stock for animal transport and of additional mileage operated by the Dublin United Tramways Company, limited, to be covered by graziers' fees.

Positing what protasis would the contraction for such several schemes become a natural and necessary apodosis?

Given a guarantee equal to the sum sought, the support, by deed of gift and transfer vouchers during donor's lifetime or by bequest after donor's painless extinction, of eminent financiers (Blum Pasha, Rothschild Guggenheim, Hirsch, Montefiore, Morgan, Rockefeller) possessing fortunes in 6 figures, amassed during a successful life, and joining capital with opportunity the thing required was done.

What eventuality would render him independent of such wealth?
The independent discovery of a goldseam of inexhaustible ore.

For what reason did he meditate on schemes so difficult of realisation?
It was one of his axioms that similar meditations or the automatic relation to himself of a narrative concerning himself or tranquil recollection of the past when practised habitually before retiring for the night alleviated fatigue and produced as a result sound repose and renovated vitality.

His justifications?
As a physicist he had learned that of the 70 years of complete human life at least 2/7ths, viz. 20 years are passed in sleep. As a philosopher he knew that at the termination of any allotted life only an infinitesimal part of any person's desires has been realised. As a physiologist he believed in the artificial placation of malignant agencies chiefly operative during somnolence.

What did he fear?
The committal of homicide or suicide during sleep by an aberration of the light of reason, the incommensurable categorical intelligence situated in the cerebral convolutions.

What were habitually his final meditations?

Of some one sole unique advertisement to cause passers to stop in wonder, a poster novelty, with all extraneous accretions excluded, reduced to its simplest and most efficient terms not exceeding the span of casual vision and congruous with the velocity of modern life.

What did the first drawer unlocked contain?

A Vere Foster's handwriting copybook, property of Milly (Millicent) Bloom, certain pages of which bore diagram drawings, marked *Papli*, which showed a large globular head with 5 hairs erect, 2 eyes in profile, the trunk full front with 3 large buttons, 1 triangular foot: 2 fading photographs of queen Alexandra of England and of Maud Branscombe, actress and professional beauty: a Yuletide card, bearing on it a pictorial representation of a parasitic plant, the legend *Mizpah*, the date Xmas 1892, the name of the senders: from Mr and Mrs M. Comerford, the versicle: *May this Yuletide bring to thee, Joy and peace and welcome glee*: a butt of red partly liquefied sealing wax, obtained from the stores department of Messrs Hely's, Ltd., 89, 90, and 91 Dame street: a box containing the remainder of a gross of gilt "J" pennibs, obtained from same department of same firm: an old sandglass which rolled containing sand which rolled: a sealed prophecy (never unsealed) written by Leopold Bloom in 1886 concerning the consequences of the passing into law of William Ewart Gladstone's Home Rule bill of 1886 (never passed into law): a bazaar ticket, No. 2004, of S. Kevin's Charity Fair, price 6d, 100 prizes: an infantile epistle, dated, small 'em monday, reading: capital pee Papli comma capital aitch How are you note of interrogation capital eye I am very well full stop new paragraph signature with flourishes capital 'em Milly no stop: a cameo brooch, property of Ellen Bloom (born Higgins), deceased: a cameo scarfpin, property of Rudolph Bloom (born Virag), deceased: 3 typewritten letters, addressee, Henry Flower, c/o. P. O. Westland Row, addresser, Martha Clifford, c/o. P. O. Dolphin's Barn: the transliterated name and address of the addresser of the 3 letters in reversed alphabetic boustrophedonic punctated quadrilinear cryptogram (vowels suppressed) N. IGS./WI. UU. OX/W. OKS. MH/Y. IM: a press cutting from an English weekly periodical *Modern Society*, subject corporal chastisement in girls' schools: a pink ribbon which had festooned an Easter egg in the year 1899: two partly uncoiled rubber preservatives with reserve pockets, purchased by post from Box 32, P. O., Charing Cross, London, W. C.: 1 pack of 1 dozen creamlaid envelopes and feintruled notepaper, watermarked, now reduced by 3: some assorted Austrian-Hungarian coins: 2 coupons of the Royal and Privileged Hungarian Lottery: a lowpower magnifying glass: 2 erotic photocards showing a) buccal coition between nude senorita (rere presentation, superior position) and nude torero (fore presentation, inferior position) b) anal violation by male religious (fully clothed, eyes abject) of female religious (partly clothed, eyes direct), purchased by post from Box 32, P. O., Charing Cross, London, W. C.: a press cutting of recipe for renovation of old tan boots: a 1d adhesive stamp, lavender, of the reign of Queen Victoria: a chart of the measurements of Leopold Bloom compiled before, during and after 2 months' consecutive use of Sandow-Whiteley's pulley exerciser (men's 15/-, athlete's 20/-) viz. chest 28 in and 29 1/2 in, biceps 9 in and 10 in, forearm 8 1/2 in and 9 in, thigh 10 in and 12 in, calf 11 in and 12 in: 1 prospectus of The Wonderworker, the world's greatest remedy for rectal complaints, direct from Wonderworker, Coventry House, South Place, London E C, addressed (erroneously) to Mrs L. Bloom with brief accompanying note commencing (erroneously): Dear Madam.

Quote the textual terms in which the prospectus claimed advantages for this thaumaturgic remedy.

It heals and soothes while you sleep, in case of trouble in breaking wind, assists nature in the most formidable way, insuring instant relief in discharge of gases, keeping parts clean and free natural action, an initial outlay of 7/6 making a new man of you and life worth living. Ladies find Wonderworker especially useful, a pleasant surprise when they note delightful result like a cool drink of fresh spring water on a sultry summer's day. Recommend it to your lady and gentlemen friends, lasts a lifetime. Insert long round end. Wonderworker.

Were there testimonials?
Numerous. From clergyman, British naval officer, wellknown author, city man, hospital nurse, lady, mother of five, absentminded beggar.

How did absentminded beggar's concluding testimonial conclude?
What a pity the government did not supply our men with

wonderworkers during the South African campaign! What a relief it would have been!

What object did Bloom add to this collection of objects?

A 4th typewritten letter received by Henry Flower (let H. F. be L. B.) from Martha Clifford (find M. C.).

What pleasant reflection accompanied this action?

The reflection that, apart from the letter in question, his magnetic face, form and address had been favourably received during the course of the preceding day by a wife (Mrs Josephine Breen, born Josie Powell), a nurse, Miss Callan (Christian name unknown), a maid, Gertrude (Gerty, family name unknown).

What possibility suggested itself?

The possibility of exercising virile power of fascination in the not immediate future after an expensive repast in a private apartment in the company of an elegant courtesan, of corporal beauty, moderately mercenary, variously instructed, a lady by origin.

What did the 2nd drawer contain?

Documents: the birth certificate of Leopold Paula Bloom: an endowment assurance policy of £ 500 in the Scottish Widows' Assurance Society, intestated Millicent (Milly) Bloom, coming into force at 25 years as with profit policy of £ 430, £ 462-10-0 and £ 500 at 60 years or death, 65 years or death and death, respectively, or with profit policy (paidup) of £ 299-10-0 together with cash payment of £ 133-10-0, at option: a bank passbook issued by the Ulster Bank, College Green branch showing statement of a/c for halfyear ending 31 December 1903, balance in depositor's favour: £ 18-14-6 (eighteen pounds, fourteen shillings and sixpence, sterling), net personalty: certificate of possession of £ 900, Canadian 4% (inscribed) government stock (free of stamp duty): dockets of the Catholic Cemeteries' (Glasnevin) Committee, relative to a graveplot purchased: a local press cutting concerning change of name by deedpoll.

Quote the textual terms of this notice.

I, Rudolph Virag, now resident at no. 52 Clanbrassil street, Dublin, formerly of Szombathely in the kingdom of Hungary, hereby give notice that I have assumed and intend henceforth upon all occasions and at all times to be known by the name of Rudolph Bloom.

What other objects relative to Rudolph Bloom (born Virag) were in the 2nd drawer?

An indistinct daguerreotype of Rudolf Virag and his father Leopold Virag executed in the year 1852 in the portrait atelier of their (respectively) 1st and 2nd cousin, Stefan Virag of Szesfehervar, Hungary. An ancient haggadah book in which a pair of hornrimmed convex spectacles inserted marked the passage of thanksgiving in the ritual prayers for Pessach (Passover): a photocard of the Queen's Hotel, Ennis, proprietor, Rudolph Bloom: an envelope addressed: *To My Dear Son Leopold.*

What fractions of phrases did the lecture of those five whole words evoke?

Tomorrow will be a week that I received . . . it is no use Leopold to be . . . with your dear mother . . . that is not more to stand . . . to her . . . all for me is out . . . be kind to Athos, Leopold . . . my dear son . . . always . . . of me . . . *das Herz* . . . *Gott* . . . *dein* . . .

What reminiscences of a human subject suffering from progressive melancholia did these objects evoke in Bloom?

An old man, widower, unkempt of hair, in bed, with head covered, sighing: an infirm dog, Athos: aconite, resorted to by increasing doses of grains and scruples as a palliative of recrudescent neuralgia: the face in death of a septuagenarian, suicide by poison.

Why did Bloom experience a sentiment of remorse?

Because in immature impatience he had treated with disrespect certain beliefs and practices.

As?

The prohibition of the use of fleshmeat and milk at one meal: the hebdomadary symposium of incoordinately abstract, perfervidly concrete mercantile coexreligionist excompatriots: the circumcision of male infants: the supernatural character of Judaic scripture: the ineffability of the tetragrammaton: the sanctity of the sabbath.

How did these beliefs and practices now appear to him?

Not more rational than they had then appeared, not less rational than other beliefs and practices now appeared.

What first reminiscence had he of Rudolph Bloom (deceased)?

Rudolph Bloom (deceased) narrated to his son Leopold Bloom (aged 6) a retrospective arrangement of migrations and settlements in and between Dublin, London, Florence, Milan, Vienna, Budapest, Szombathely with statements of satisfaction (his grandfather having seen Maria Theresia, empress of Austria, queen of Hungary), with commercial advice (having taken care of pence, the pounds having taken care of themselves). Leopold Bloom (aged 6) had accompanied these narrations by constant consultation of a geographical map of Europe (political) and by suggestions for the establishment of affiliated business premises in the various centres mentioned.

Had time equally but differently obliterated the memory of these migrations in narrator and listener?

In narrator by the access of years and in consequence of the use of narcotic toxin: in listener by the access of years and in consequence of the action of distraction upon vicarious experiences.

What idiosyncracies of the narrator were concomitant products of amnesia?

Occasionally he ate without having previously removed his hat. Occasionally he drank voraciously the juice of gooseberry fool from an inclined plate. Occasionally he removed from his lips the traces of food by means of a lacerated envelope or other accessible fragment of paper.

What two phenomena of senescence were more frequent?

The myopic digital calculation of coins, eructation consequent upon repletion.

What object offered partial consolation for these reminiscences?

The endowment policy, the bank passbook, the certificate of the possession of scrip.

Reduce Bloom by cross multiplication of reverses of fortune, from which these supports protected him, and by elimination of all positive values to a negligible negative irrational unreal quantity.

Successively, in descending helotic order: Poverty: that of the outdoor hawker of imitation jewellery, the dun for the recovery of bad and doubtful debts, the poor rate and deputy cess collector. Mendicancy: that of the fraudulent bankrupt with negligible assets paying 1/4d in the £, sandwichman, distributor of throwaways, nocturnal vagrant, insinuating sycophant, maimed sailor, blind stripling, superannuated bailiff's man, marfeast, lickplate, spoilsport, pickthank, eccentric public laughingstock seated on bench of public park under discarded perforated umbrella. Destitution: the inmate of Old Man's House (Royal Hospital), Kilmainham, the inmate of Simpson's Hospital for reduced but respectable men permanently disabled by gout or want of sight. Nadir of misery: the aged impotent disfranchised ratesupported moribund lunatic pauper.

With which attendant indignities?

The unsympathetic indifference of previously amiable females, the contempt of muscular males, the acceptance of fragments of bread, the simulated ignorance of casual acquaintances, the latration of illegitimate unlicensed vagabond dogs, the infantile discharge of decomposed vegetable missiles, worth little or nothing, nothing or less than nothing.

By what could such a situation be precluded?
By decease (change of state): by departure (change of place).

Which preferably?
The latter, by the line of least resistance.

What considerations rendered departure not entirely undesirable?
Constant cohabitation impeding mutual toleration of personal defects. The habit of independent purchase increasingly cultivated. The necessity to counteract by impermanent sojourn the permanence of arrest.

What considerations rendered departure not irrational?

The parties concerned, uniting, had increased and multiplied, which being done, offspring produced and educed to maturity, the parties, if not disunited were obliged to reunite for increase and multiplication, which was absurd, to form by reunion the original couple of uniting parties, which was impossible.

What considerations rendered departure desirable?

The attractive character of certain localities in Ireland and abroad, as represented in general geographical maps of polychrome design or in special ordnance survey charts by employment of scale numerals and hachures.

In Ireland?

The cliffs of Moher, the windy wilds of Connemara, lough Neagh with submerged petrified city, the Giant's Causeway, Fort Camden and Fort Carlisle, the Golden Vale of Tipperary, the islands of Aran, the pastures of royal Meath, Brigid's elm in Kildare, the Queen's Island shipyard in Belfast, the Salmon Leap, the lakes of Killarney.

Abroad?

Ceylon (with spicegardens supplying tea to Thomas Kernan, agent for Pulbrook, Robertson and Co, 2 Mincing Lane, London, E. C., 5 Dame street, Dublin), Jerusalem, the holy city (with mosque of Omar and gate of Damascus, goal of aspiration), the straits of Gibraltar (the unique birthplace of Marion Tweedy), the Parthenon (containing statues of nude Grecian divinities), the Wall street money market (which controlled international finance), the Plaza de Toros at La Linea, Spain (where O'Hara of the Camerons had slain the bull), Niagara (over which no human being had passed with impunity), the land of the Eskimos (eaters of soap), the forbidden country of Thibet (from which no traveller returns), the bay of Naples (to see which was to die), the Dead Sea.

Under what guidance, following what signs?

At sea, septentrional, by night the polestar, located at the point of intersection of the right line from beta to alpha in Ursa Maior produced and divided externally at omega and the hypotenuse of the rightangled triangle formed by the line alpha omega so produced and the line alpha delta of Ursa Maior. On land, meridional, a bispherical moon, revealed in imperfect varying phases of lunation through the posterior interstice of the imperfectly occluded skirt of a carnose negligent perambulating female, a pillar of the cloud by day.

What public advertisement would divulge the occultation of the departed?

£ 5 reward, lost, stolen or strayed from his residence 7 Eccles street, missing gent about 40, answering to the name of Bloom, Leopold (Poldy), height 5 ft 9 1/2 inches, full build, olive complexion, may have since grown a beard, when last seen was wearing a black suit. Above sum will be paid for information leading to his discovery.

What universal binomial denominations would be his as entity and nonentity?

Assumed by any or known to none. Everyman or Noman.

What tributes his?

Honour and gifts of strangers, the friends of Everyman. A nymph immortal, beauty, the bride of Noman.

Would the departed never nowhere nohow reappear?

Ever he would wander, selfcompelled, to the extreme limit of his cometary orbit, beyond the fixed stars and variable suns and telescopic planets, astronomical waifs and strays, to the extreme boundary of space, passing from land to land, among peoples, amid events. Somewhere imperceptibly he would hear and somehow reluctantly, suncompelled, obey the summons of recall. Whence, disappearing from the constellation of the Northern Crown he would somehow reappear reborn above delta in the constellation of Cassiopeia and after incalculable eons of peregrination return an estranged avenger, a wreaker of justice on malefactors, a dark crusader, a sleeper awakened, with financial resources (by supposition) surpassing those of Rothschild or the silver king.

What would render such return irrational?

An unsatisfactory equation between an exodus and return in time through reversible space and an exodus and return in space through irreversible time.

What play of forces, inducing inertia, rendered departure undesirable?

The lateness of the hour, rendering procrastinatory: the obscurity of the night, rendering invisible: the uncertainty of thoroughfares, rendering perilous: the necessity for repose, obviating movement: the proximity of an occupied bed, obviating research: the anticipation of warmth (human) tempered with coolness (linen), obviating desire and rendering desirable: the statue of Narcissus, sound without echo, desired desire.

What advantages were possessed by an occupied, as distinct from an unoccupied bed?

The removal of nocturnal solitude, the superior quality of human (mature female) to inhuman (hotwaterjar) calefaction, the stimulation of matutinal contact, the economy of mangling done on the premises in the case of trousers accurately folded and placed lengthwise between the spring mattress (striped) and the woollen mattress (biscuit section).

What past consecutive causes, before rising preapprehended, of accumulated fatigue did Bloom, before rising, silently recapitulate?

The preparation of breakfast (burnt offering): intestinal congestion and premeditative defecation (holy of holies): the bath (rite of John): the funeral (rite of Samuel): the advertisement of Alexander Keyes (Urim and Thummim): the unsubstantial lunch (rite of Melchisedek): the visit to museum and national library (holy place): the bookhunt along Bedford row, Merchants' Arch, Wellington Quay (Simchath Torah): the music in the Ormond Hotel (Shira Shirim): the altercation with a truculent troglodyte in Bernard Kiernan's premises (holocaust): a blank period of time including a cardrive, a visit to a house of mourning, a leavetaking (wilderness): the eroticism produced by feminine exhibitionism (rite of Onan): the prolonged delivery of Mrs Mina Purefoy (heave offering): the visit to the disorderly house of Mrs Bella Cohen, 82 Tyrone street, lower, and subsequent brawl and chance medley in Beaver street (Armageddon): nocturnal perambulation to and from the cabman's shelter, Butt Bridge (atonement).

What selfimposed enigma did Bloom about to rise in order to go so as to conclude lest he should not conclude involuntarily apprehend?

The cause of a brief sharp unforeseen heard loud lone crack emitted by the insentient material of a strainveined timber table.

What selfinvolved enigma did Bloom risen, going, gathering multicoloured multiform multitudinous garments, voluntarily apprehending, not comprehend?
Who was M'Intosh?

What selfevident enigma pondered with desultory constancy during 30 years did Bloom now, having effected natural obscurity by the extinction of artificial light, silently suddenly comprehend?
Where was Moses when the candle went out?

What imperfections in a perfect day did Bloom, walking, charged with collected articles of recently disvested male wearing apparel, silently, successively, enumerate?
A provisional failure to obtain renewal of an advertisement: to obtain a certain quantity of tea from Thomas Kernan (agent for Pulbrook, Robertson and Co, 5 Dame Street, Dublin, and 2 Mincing Lane, London E. C.): to certify the presence or absence of posterior rectal orifice in the case of Hellenic female divinities: to obtain admission (gratuitous or paid) to the performance of *Leah* by Mrs Bandmann Palmer at the Gaiety Theatre, 46, 47, 48, 49 South King street.

What impression of an absent face did Bloom, arrested, silently recall?
The face of her father, the late Major Brian Cooper Tweedy, Royal Dublin Fusiliers, of Gibraltar and Rehoboth, Dolphin's Barn.

What recurrent impressions of the same were possible by hypothesis?
Retreating, at the terminus of the Great Northern Railway, Amiens street, with constant uniform acceleration, along parallel lines meeting at infinity, if produced: along parallel lines, reproduced from infinity, with constant uniform retardation, at the terminus of the Great Northern Railway, Amiens street, returning.

What miscellaneous effects of female personal wearing apparel were perceived by him?

A pair of new inodorous halfsilk black ladies' hose, a pair of new violet garters, a pair of outsize ladies' drawers of India mull, cut on generous lines, redolent of opoponax, jessamine and Muratti's Turkish cigarettes and containing a long bright steel safety pin, folded curvilinear, a camisole of batiste with thin lace border, an accordion underskirt of blue silk moirette, all these objects being disposed irregularly on the top of a rectangular trunk, quadruple battened, having capped corners, with multicoloured labels, initialled on its fore side in white lettering B. C. T. (Brian Cooper Tweedy).

What impersonal objects were perceived?

A commode, one leg fractured, totally covered by square cretonne cutting, apple design, on which rested a lady's black straw hat. Orangekeyed ware, bought of Henry Price, basket, fancy goods, chinaware and ironmongery manufacturer, 21, 22, 23 Moore street, disposed irregularly on the washstand and floor and consisting of basin, soapdish and brushtray (on the washstand, together), pitcher and night article (on the floor, separate).

Bloom's acts?

He deposited the articles of clothing on a chair, removed his remaining articles of clothing, took from beneath the bolster at the head of the bed a folded long white nightshirt, inserted his head and arms into the proper apertures of the nightshirt, removed a pillow from the head to the foot of the bed, prepared the bedlinen accordingly and entered the bed.

How?

With circumspection, as invariably when entering an abode (his own or not his own): with solicitude, the snakespiral springs of the mattress being old, the brass quoits and pendent viper radii loose and tremulous under stress and strain: prudently, as entering a lair or ambush of lust or adders: lightly, the less to disturb: reverently, the bed of conception and of birth, of consummation of marriage and of breach of marriage, of sleep and of death.

What did his limbs, when gradually extended, encounter?

New clean bedlinen, additional odours, the presence of a human form, female, hers, the imprint of a human form, male, not his, some crumbs, some flakes of potted meat, recooked, which he removed.

If he had smiled why would he have smiled?

To reflect that each one who enters imagines himself to be the first to enter whereas he is always the last term of a preceding series even if the first term of a succeeding one, each imagining himself to be first, last, only and alone whereas he is neither first nor last nor only nor alone in a series originating in and repeated to infinity.

What preceding series?

Assuming Mulvey to be the first term of his series, Penrose, Bartell d'Arcy, professor Goodwin, Julius Mastiansky, John Henry Menton, Father Bernard Corrigan, a farmer at the Royal Dublin Society's Horse Show, Maggot O'Reilly, Matthew Dillon, Valentine Blake Dillon (Lord Mayor of Dublin), Christopher Callinan, Lenehan, an Italian organgrinder, an unknown gentleman in the Gaiety Theatre, Benjamin Dollard, Simon Dedalus, Andrew (Pisser) Burke, Joseph Cuffe, Wisdom Hely, Alderman John Hooper, Dr Francis Brady, Father Sebastian of Mount Argus, a bootblack at the General Post Office, Hugh E. (Blazes) Boylan and so each and so on to no last term.

What were his reflections concerning the last member of this series and late occupant of the bed?

Reflections on his vigour (a bounder), corporal proportion (a billsticker), commercial ability (a bester), impressionability (a boaster).

Why for the observer impressionability in addition to vigour, corporal proportion and commercial ability? Because he had observed with augmenting frequency in the preceding members of the same series the same concupiscence, inflammably transmitted, first with alarm, then with understanding, then with desire, finally with fatigue, with alternating symptoms of epicene comprehension and apprehension.

With what antagonistic sentiments were his subsequent reflections affected?

Envy, jealousy, abnegation, equanimity.

Envy?

Of a bodily and mental male organism specially adapted for the superincumbent posture of energetic human copulation and energetic piston and cylinder movement necessary for the complete satisfaction of a constant but not acute concupiscence resident in a bodily and mental female organism, passive but not obtuse.

Jealousy?

Because a nature full and volatile in its free state, was alternately the agent and reagent of attraction. Because attraction between agent(s) and reagent(s) at all instants varied, with inverse proportion of increase and decrease, with incessant circular extension and radial reentrance. Because the controlled contemplation of the fluctuation of attraction produced, if desired, a fluctuation of pleasure.

Abnegation?

In virtue of a) acquaintance initiated in September 1903 in the establishment of George Mesias, merchant tailor and outfitter, 5 Eden Quay, b) hospitality extended and received in kind, reciprocated and reappropriated in person, c) comparative youth subject to impulses of ambition and magnanimity, colleagual altruism and amorous egoism, d) extraracial attraction, intraracial inhibition, supraracial prerogative, e) an imminent provincial musical tour, common current expenses, net proceeds divided.

Equanimity?

As as natural as any and every natural act of a nature expressed or understood executed in natured nature by natural creatures in accordance with his, her and their natured natures, of dissimilar similarity. As not so calamitous as a cataclysmic annihilation of the planet in consequence of a collision with a dark sun. As less reprehensible than theft, highway robbery, cruelty to children and animals, obtaining money under false pretences, forgery, embezzlement, misappropriation of public money, betrayal of public trust, malingering, mayhem, corruption of minors, criminal libel, blackmail, contempt of court, arson, treason, felony, mutiny on the high seas, trespass, burglary, jailbreaking, practice of unnatural vice, desertion from armed forces in the field, perjury, poaching, usury, intelligence with the king's enemies, impersonation, criminal assault, manslaughter, wilful and premeditated murder. As not more abnormal than all other parallel processes of adaptation to altered conditions of existence, resulting in a reciprocal equilibrium between the bodily organism and its attendant circumstances, foods, beverages, acquired habits, indulged inclinations, significant disease. As more than inevitable, irreparable.

Why more abnegation than jealousy, less envy than equanimity?

From outrage (matrimony) to outrage (adultery) there arose nought but outrage (copulation) yet the matrimonial violator of the matrimonially violated had not been outraged by the adulterous violator of the adulterously violated.

What retribution, if any?

Assassination, never, as two wrongs did not make one right. Duel by combat, no. Divorce, not now. Exposure by mechanical artifice (automatic bed) or individual testimony (concealed ocular witnesses), not yet. Suit for damages by legal influence or simulation of assault with evidence of injuries sustained (selfinflicted), not impossibly. Hushmoney by moral influence, possibly. If any, positively, connivance, introduction of emulation (material, a prosperous rival agency of publicity: moral, a successful rival agent of intimacy), depreciation, alienation, humiliation, separation protecting the one separated from the other, protecting the separator from both.

By what reflections did he, a conscious reactor against the void of incertitude, justify to himself his sentiments?

The preordained frangibility of the hymen: the presupposed intangibility of the thing in itself: the incongruity and disproportion between the selfprolonging tension of the thing proposed to be done and the selfabbreviating relaxation of the thing done: the fallaciously inferred debility of the female: the muscularity of the male: the variations of ethical codes: the natural grammatical transition by inversion involving no alteration of sense of an aorist preterite proposition (parsed as masculine subject, monosyllabic onomatopoeic transitive verb with direct feminine object) from the active voice into its correlative aorist preterite proposition (parsed as feminine subject, auxiliary verb and quasimonosyllabic onomatopoeic past participle with complementary masculine agent) in the passive voice:

the continued product of seminators by generation: the continual production of semen by distillation: the futility of triumph or protest or vindication: the inanity of extolled virtue: the lethargy of nescient matter: the apathy of the stars.

In what final satisfaction did these antagonistic sentiments and reflections, reduced to their simplest forms, converge?

Satisfaction at the ubiquity in eastern and western terrestrial hemispheres, in all habitable lands and islands explored or unexplored (the land of the midnight sun, the islands of the blessed, the isles of Greece, the land of promise), of adipose anterior and posterior female hemispheres, redolent of milk and honey and of excretory sanguine and seminal warmth, reminiscent of secular families of curves of amplitude, insusceptible of moods of impression or of contrarieties of expression, expressive of mute immutable mature animality.

The visible signs of antesatisfaction?

An approximate erection: a solicitous adversion: a gradual elevation: a tentative revelation: a silent contemplation.

Then?

He kissed the plump mellow yellow smellow melons of her rump, on each plump melonous hemisphere, in their mellow yellow furrow, with obscure prolonged provocative melonsmellonous osculation.

The visible signs of postsatisfaction?

A silent contemplation: a tentative velation: a gradual abasement: a solicitous aversion: a proximate erection.

What followed this silent action?

Somnolent invocation, less somnolent recognition, incipient excitation, catechetical interrogation.

With what modifications did the narrator reply to this interrogation?

Negative: he omitted to mention the clandestine correspondence between Martha Clifford and Henry Flower, the public altercation at, in and in the vicinity of the licensed premises of Bernard Kiernan and Co, Limited, 8, 9 and 10 Little Britain street, the erotic provocation and response thereto caused by the exhibitionism of Gertrude (Gerty), surname unknown. Positive: he included mention of a performance by Mrs Bandmann Palmer of *Leah* at the Gaiety Theatre, 46, 47, 48, 49 South King street, an invitation to supper at Wynn's (Murphy's) Hotel, 35, 36 and 37 Lower Abbey street, a volume of peccaminous pornographical tendency entituled *Sweets of Sin*, anonymous author a gentleman of fashion, a temporary concussion caused by a falsely calculated movement in the course of a postcenal gymnastic display, the victim (since completely recovered) being Stephen Dedalus, professor and author, eldest surviving son of Simon Dedalus, of no fixed occupation, an aeronautical feat executed by him (narrator) in the presence of a witness, the professor and author aforesaid, with promptitude of decision and gymnastic flexibility.

Was the narration otherwise unaltered by modifications?
Absolutely.

Which event or person emerged as the salient point of his narration?
Stephen Dedalus, professor and author.

What limitations of activity and inhibitions of conjugal rights were perceived by listener and narrator concerning themselves during the course of this intermittent and increasingly more laconic narration?
By the listener a limitation of fertility inasmuch as marriage had been celebrated 1 calendar month after the 18th anniversary of her birth (8 September 1870), viz. 8 October, and consummated on the same date with female issue born 15 June 1889, having been anticipatorily consummated on the 10 September of the same year and complete carnal intercourse, with ejaculation of semen within the natural female organ, having last taken place 5 weeks previous, viz. 27 November 1893, to the birth on 29 December 1893 of second (and only male) issue, deceased 9 January 1894, aged 11 days, there remained a period of 10 years, 5 months and 18 days during which carnal intercourse had been incomplete, without ejaculation of semen within the natural female organ. By the narrator a limitation of activity, mental and corporal, inasmuch as complete mental intercourse between himself and the listener had not taken place since the consummation of puberty, indicated by catamenic hemorrhage, of the female issue of narrator and listener, 15 September 1903, there

remained a period of 9 months and 1 day during which, in consequence of a preestablished natural comprehension in incomprehension between the consummated females (listener and issue), complete corporal liberty of action had been circumscribed.

How?

By various reiterated feminine interrogation concerning the masculine destination whither, the place where, the time at which, the duration for which, the object with which in the case of temporary absences, projected or effected.

What moved visibly above the listener's and the narrator's invisible thoughts?

The upcast reflection of a lamp and shade, an inconstant series of concentric circles of varying gradations of light and shadow.

In what directions did listener and narrator lie?

Listener, S. E. by E.: Narrator, N. W. by W.: on the 53rd parallel of latitude, N., and 6th meridian of longitude, W.: at an angle of 45° to the terrestrial equator.

In what state of rest or motion?

At rest relatively to themselves and to each other. In motion being each and both carried westward, forward and rereward respectively, by the proper perpetual motion of the earth through everchanging tracks of neverchanging space.

In what posture?

Listener: reclined semilaterally, left, left hand under head, right leg extended in a straight line and resting on left leg, flexed, in the attitude of Gea-Tellus, fulfilled, recumbent, big with seed. Narrator: reclined laterally, left, with right and left legs flexed, the index finger and thumb of the right hand resting on the bridge of the nose, in the attitude depicted in a snapshot photograph made by Percy Apjohn, the childman weary, the manchild in the womb.

Womb? Weary?

He rests. He has travelled.

With?

Sinbad the Sailor and Tinbad the Tailor and Jinbad the Jailer and Whinbad the Whaler and Ninbad the Nailer and Finbad the Failer and Binbad the Bailer and Pinbad the Pailer and Minbad the Mailer and Hinbad the Hailer and Rinbad the Railer and Dinbad the Kailer and Vinbad the Quailer and Linbad the Yailer and Xinbad the Phthailer.

When?

Going to dark bed there was a square round Sinbad the Sailor roc's auk's egg in the night of the bed of all the auks of the rocs of Darkinbad the Brightdayler.

Where?

18

Yes because he never did a thing like that before as ask to get his breakfast in bed with a couple of eggs since the *City Arms* hotel when he used to be pretending to be laid up with a sick voice doing his highness to make himself interesting for that old faggot Mrs Riordan that he thought he had a great leg of and she never left us a farthing all for masses for herself and her soul greatest miser ever was actually afraid to lay out 4d for her methylated spirit telling me all her ailments she had too much old chat in her about politics and earthquakes and the end of the world let us have a bit of fun first God help the world if all the women were her sort down on bathingsuits and lownecks of course nobody wanted her to wear them I suppose she was pious because no man would look at her twice I hope Ill never be like her a wonder she didnt want us to cover our faces but she was a welleducated woman certainly and her gabby talk about Mr Riordan here and Mr Riordan there I suppose he was glad to get shut of her and her dog smelling my fur and always edging to get up under my petticoats especially then still I like that in him polite to old women like that and waiters and beggars too hes not proud out of nothing but not always if ever he got anything really serious the matter with him its much better for them to go into a hospital where everything is clean but I suppose Id have to dring it into him for a month yes and then wed have a hospital nurse next thing on the carpet have him staying there till they throw him out or a nun maybe like the smutty photo he has shes as much a nun as Im not yes because theyre so weak and puling when theyre sick they want a woman to get well if his nose bleeds youd think it was O tragic and that dyinglooking one off the south circular when he sprained his foot at the choir party at the sugarloaf Mountain the day I wore that dress Miss Stack bringing him flowers the worst old ones she could find at the bottom of the basket anything at all to get into a mans bedroom with her old maids voice trying to imagine he was dying on account of her to never see thy face again though he looked more like a man with his beard a bit grown in the bed father was the same besides I hate bandaging and dosing when he cut his toe with the razor paring his corns afraid hed get bloodpoisoning but if it was a thing I was sick then wed see what attention only of course the woman hides it not to give all the trouble they do yes he came somewhere Im sure by his appetite anyway love its not or hed be off his feed thinking of her so either it was one of those night women if it was down there he was really and the hotel story he made up a pack of lies to hide it planning it Hynes kept me who did I meet ah yes I met do you remember Menton and who else who let me see that big babbyface I saw him and he not long married flirting with a young girl at Pooles Myriorama and turned my back on him when he slinked out looking quite conscious what harm but he had the impudence to make up to me one time well done to him mouth almighty and his boiled eyes of all the big stupoes I ever met and thats called a solicitor only for I hate having a long wrangle in bed or else if its not that its some little bitch or other he got in with somewhere or picked up on the sly if they only knew him as well as I do yes because the day before yesterday he was scribbling something a letter when I came into the front room to show him Dignams death in the paper as if something told me and he covered it up with the blottingpaper pretending to be thinking about business so very probably that was it to somebody who thinks she has a softy in him because all men get a bit like that at his age especially getting on to forty he is now so as to wheedle any money she can out of him no fool like an old fool and then the usual kissing my bottom was to hide it not that I care two straws now who he does it with or knew before that way though Id like to find out so long as I dont have the two of them under my nose all the time like that slut that Mary we had in Ontario terrace padding out her false bottom to excite him bad enough to get the smell of those painted women off him once or twice I had a suspicion by getting him to come near me when I found the long hair on his coat without that one when I went into the kitchen pretending he was drinking water 1 woman is not enough for them it was all his fault of course ruining servants then proposing that she could eat at our table on Christmas day if you please O no thank you

not in my house stealing my potatoes and the oysters 2/6 per doz
going out to see her aunt if you please common robbery so it was but
I was sure he had something on with that one it takes me to find out
a thing like that he said you have no proof it was her proof O yes her
aunt was very fond of oysters but I told her what I thought of her
suggesting me to go out to be alone with her I wouldnt lower myself
to spy on them the garters I found in her room the Friday she was out
that was enough for me a little bit too much her face swelled up on
her with temper when I gave her her weeks notice I saw to that better
do without them altogether do out the rooms myself quicker only for
the damn cooking and throwing out the dirt I gave it to him anyhow
either she or me leaves the house I couldnt even touch him if I thought
he was with a dirty barefaced liar and sloven like that one denying it
up to my face and singing about the place in the W C too because she
knew she was too well off yes because he couldnt possibly do without
it that long so he must do it somewhere and the last time he came on
my bottom when was it the night Boylan gave my hand a great squeeze
going along by the Tolka in my hand there steals another I just pressed
the back of his like that with my thumb to squeeze back singing the
young May moon shes beaming love because he has an idea about
him and me hes not such a fool he said Im dining out and going to
the Gaiety though Im not going to give him the satisfaction in any
case God knows hes a change in a way not to be always and ever
wearing the same old hat unless I paid some nicelooking boy to do it
since I cant do it myself a young boy would like me Id confuse him a
little alone with him if we were Id let him see my garters the new ones
and make him turn red looking at him seduce him I know what boys
feel with that down on their cheek doing that frigging drawing out
the thing by the hour question and answer would you do this that and
the other with the coalman yes with a bishop yes I would because I
told him about some dean or bishop was sitting beside me in the jews
temples gardens when I was knitting that woollen thing a stranger to
Dublin what place was it and so on about the monuments and he
tired me out with statues encouraging him making him worse than he
is who is in your mind now tell me who are you thinking of who is it
tell me his name who tell me who the German Emperor is it yes
imagine Im him think of him can you feel him trying to make a
whore of me what he never will he ought to give it up now at this age
of his life simply ruination for any woman and no satisfaction in it

pretending to like it till he comes and then finish it off myself anyway and it makes your lips pale anyhow its done now once and for all with all the talk of the world about it people make its only the first time after that its just the ordinary do it and think no more about it why cant you kiss a man without going and marrying him first you sometimes love to wildly when you feel that way so nice all over you you cant help yourself I wish some man or other would take me sometime when hes there and kiss me in his arms theres nothing like a kiss long and hot down to your soul almost paralyses you then I hate that confession when I used to go to Father Corrigan he touched me father and what harm if he did where and I said on the canal bank like a fool but whereabouts on your person my child on the leg behind high up was it yes rather high up was it where you sit down yes O Lord couldnt he say bottom right out and have done with it what has that got to do with it and did you whatever way he put it I forget no father and I always think of the real father what did he want to know for when I already confessed it to God he had a nice fat hand the palm moist always I wouldnt mind feeling it neither would he Id say by the bullneck in his horsecollar I wonder did he know me in the box I could see his face he couldnt see mine of course hed never turn or let on still his eyes were red when his father died theyre lost for a woman of course must be terrible when a man cries let alone them Id like to be embraced by one in his vestments and the smell of incense off him like the pope besides theres no danger with a priest if youre married hes too careful about himself then give something to H H the pope for a penance I wonder was he satisfied with me one thing I didnt like his slapping me behind going away so familiarly in the hall though I laughed Im not a horse or an ass am I I suppose he was thinking of his fathers I wonder is he awake thinking of me or dreaming am I in it who gave him that flower he said he bought he smelt of some kind of drink not whisky or stout or perhaps the sweety kind of paste they stick their bills up with some liqueur Id like to sip those richlooking green and yellow expensive drinks those stagedoor johnnies drink with the opera hats I tasted once with my finger dipped out of that American that had the squirrel talking stamps with father he had all he could do to keep himself from falling asleep after the last time after we took the port and potted meat it had a fine salty taste yes because I felt lovely and tired myself and fell asleep as sound as a top the moment I popped straight into bed till that thunder woke

me up God be merciful to us I thought the heavens were coming
down about us to punish us when I blessed myself and said a Hail
Mary like those awful thunderbolts in Gibraltar as if the world was
coming to an end and then they come and tell you theres no God
what could you do if it was running and rushing about nothing only
make an act of contrition the candle I lit that evening in Whitefriars
street chapel for the month of May see it brought its luck though hed
scoff if he heard because he never goes to church mass or meeting he
says your soul you have no soul inside only grey matter because he
doesnt know what it is to have one yes when I lit the lamp because he
must have come 3 or 4 times with that tremendous big red brute of a
thing he has I thought the vein or whatever the dickens they call it
was going to burst though his nose is not so big after I took off all my
things with the blinds down after my hours dressing and perfuming
and combing it like iron or some kind of a thick crowbar standing all
the time he must have eaten oysters I think a few dozen he was in
great singing voice no I never in all my life felt anyone had one the
size of that to make you feel full up he must have eaten a whole sheep
after whats the idea making us like that with a big hole in the middle
of us or like a Stallion driving it up into you because thats all they
want out of you with that determined vicious look in his eye I had to
halfshut my eyes still he hasnt such a tremendous amount of spunk in
him when I made him pull out and do it on me considering how big
it is so much the better in case any of it wasnt washed out properly the
last time I let him finish it in me nice invention they made for women
for him to get all the pleasure but if someone gave them a touch of it
themselves theyd know what I went through with Milly nobody
would believe cutting her teeth too and Mina Purefoys husband give
us a swing out of your whiskers filling her up with a child or twins
once a year as regular as the clock always with a smell of children off
her the one they called budgers or something like a nigger with a
shock of hair on it Jesusjack the child is a black the last time I was
there a squad of them falling over one another and bawling you
couldnt hear your ears supposed to be healthy not satisfied till they
have us swollen out like elephants or I dont know what supposing I
risked having another not off him though still if he was married Im
sure hed have a fine strong child but I dont know Poldy has more
spunk in him yes thatd be awfully jolly I suppose it was meeting Josie
Powell and the funeral and thinking about me and Boylan set him off

well he can think what he likes now if thatll do him any good I know
they were spooning a bit when I came on the scene he was dancing
and sitting out with her the night of Georgina Simpsons housewarming
and then he wanted to ram it down my neck it was on account of not
liking to see her a wallflower that was why we had the standup row
over politics he began it not me when he said about Our Lord being
a carpenter at last he made me cry of course a woman is so sensitive
about everything I was fuming with myself after for giving in only for
I knew he was gone on me and the first socialist he said He was he
annoyed me so much I couldnt put him into a temper still he knows
a lot of mixedup things especially about the body and the inside I
often wanted to study up that myself what we have inside us in that
family physician I could always hear his voice talking when the room
was crowded and watch him after that I pretended I had a coolness
on with her over him because he used to be a bit on the jealous side
whenever he asked who are you going to and I said over to Floey and
he made me the present of Byrons poems and the three pairs of gloves
so that finished that I could quite easily get him to make it up any
time I know how Id even supposing he got in with her again and was
going out to see her somewhere Id know if he refused to eat the
onions I know plenty of ways ask him to tuck down the collar of my
blouse or touch him with my veil and gloves on going out 1 kiss then
would send them all spinning however alright well see then let him
go to her she of course would only be too delighted to pretend shes
mad in love with him that I wouldnt so much mind Id just go to her
and ask her do you love him and look her square in the eyes she
couldnt fool me but he might imagine he was and make a declaration
to her with his plabbery kind of a manner like he did to me though I
had the devils own job to get it out of him though I liked him for that
it showed he could hold in and wasnt to be got for the asking he was
on the pop of asking me too the night in the kitchen I was rolling the
potato cake theres something I want to say to you only for I put him
off letting on I was in a temper with my hands and arms full of pasty
flour in any case I let out too much the night before talking of dreams
so I didnt want to let him know more than was good for him she used
to be always embracing me Josie whenever he was there meaning him
of course glauming me over and when I said I washed up and down
as far as possible asking me and did you wash possible the women are
always egging on to that putting it on thick when hes there they know

by his sly eye blinking a bit putting on the indifferent when they come out with something the kind he is what spoils him I dont wonder in the least because he was very handsome at that time trying to look like Lord Byron I said I liked though he was too beautiful for a man and he was a little before we got engaged afterwards though she didnt like it so much the day I was in fits of laughing with the giggles I couldnt stop about all my hairpins falling out one after another with the mass of hair I had youre always in great humour she said yes because it grigged her because she knew what it meant because I used to tell her a good bit of what went on between us not all but just enough to make her mouth water but that wasnt my fault she didnt darken the door much after we were married I wonder what shes got like now after living with that dotty husband of hers she had her face beginning to look drawn and run down the last time I saw her she must have been just after a row with him because I saw on the moment she was edging to draw down a conversation about husbands and talk about him to run him down what was it she told me O yes that sometimes he used to go to bed with his muddy boots on when the maggot takes him just imagine having to get into bed with a thing like that that might murder you any moment what a man well its not the one way everyone goes mad Poldy anyhow whatever he does always wipes his feet on the mat when he comes in wet or shine and always blacks his own boots too and he always takes off his hat when he comes up in the street like then and now hes going about in his slippers to look for £ 10000 for a postcard up up O sweetheart May wouldnt a thing like that simply bore you stiff to extinction actually too stupid even to take his boots off now what could you make of a man like that Id rather die 20 times over than marry another of their sex of course hed never find another woman like me to put up with him the way I do know me come sleep with me yes and he knows that too at the bottom of his heart take that Mrs Maybrick that poisoned her husband for what I wonder in love with some other man yes it was found out on her wasnt she the downright villain to go and do a thing like that of course some men can be dreadfully aggravating drive you mad and always the worst word in the world what do they ask us to marry them for if were so bad as all that comes to yes because they cant get on without us white Arsenic she put in his tea off flypaper wasnt it I wonder why they call it that if I asked him hed say its from the Greek leave us as wise as we were before she must have been

madly in love with the other fellow to run the chance of being hanged
O she didnt care if that was her nature what could she do besides
theyre not brutes enough to go and hang a woman surely are they
     theyre all so different Boylan talking about the shape of my foot
he noticed at once even before he was introduced when I was in the
D B C with Poldy laughing and trying to listen I was waggling my foot
we both ordered 2 teas and plain bread and butter I saw him looking
with his two old maids of sisters when I stood up and asked the girl
where it was what do I care with it dropping out of me and that black
closed breeches he made me buy takes you half an hour to let them
down wetting all myself always with some brandnew fad every other
week such a long one I did I forgot my suede gloves on the seat
behind that I never got after some robber of a woman and he wanted
me to put it in the Irish times lost in the ladies lavatory D B C Dame
street finder return to Mrs Marion Bloom and I saw his eyes on my
feet going out through the turning door he was looking when I
looked back and I went there for tea 2 days after in the hope but he
wasnt now how did that excite him because I was crossing them when
we were in the other room first he meant the shoes that are too tight
to walk in my hand is nice like that if I only had a ring with the stone
for my month a nice aquamarine Ill stick him for one and a gold
bracelet I dont like my foot so much still I made him spend once with
my foot the night after Goodwins botchup of a concert so cold and
windy it was well we had that rum in the house to mull and the fire
wasnt black out when he asked to take off my stockings lying on the
hearthrug in Lombard street west and another time it was my muddy
boots hed like me to walk in all the horses dung I could find but of
course hes not natural like the rest of the world that I what did he say
I could give 9 points in 10 to Katty Lanner and beat her what does
that mean I asked him I forget what he said because the stoppress
edition just passed and the man with the curly hair in the Lucan dairy
thats so polite I think I saw his face before somewhere I noticed him
when I was tasting the butter so I took my time Bartell dArcy too
that he used to make fun of when he commenced kissing me on the
choir stairs after I sang Gounods *Ave Maria* what are we waiting for
O my heart kiss me straight on the brow and part which is my brown
part he was pretty hot for all his tinny voice too my low notes he was
always raving about if you can believe him I liked the way he used his
mouth singing then he said wasnt it terrible to do that there in a place

like that I dont see anything so terrible about it Ill tell him about that some day not now and surprise him ay and Ill take him there and show him the very place too we did it so now there you are like it or lump it he thinks nothing can happen without him knowing he hadnt an idea about my mother till we were engaged otherwise hed never have got me so cheap as he did he was 10 times worse himself anyhow begging me to give him a tiny bit cut off my drawers that was the evening coming along Kenilworth square he kissed me in the eye of my glove and I had to take it off asking me questions is it permitted to enquire the shape of my bedroom so I let him keep it as if I forgot it to think of me when I saw him slip it into his pocket of course hes mad on the subject of drawers thats plain to be seen always skeezing at those brazenfaced things on the bicycles with their skirts blowing up to their navels even when Milly and I were out with him at the open air fete that one in the cream muslin standing right against the sun so he could see every atom she had on when he saw me from behind following in the rain I saw him before he saw me however standing at the corner of the Harolds cross road with a new raincoat on him with the muffler in the Zingari colours to show off his complexion and the brown hat looking slyboots as usual what was he doing there where hed no business they can go and get whatever they like from anything at all with a skirt on it and were not to ask any questions but they want to know where were you where are you going I could feel him coming along skulking after me his eyes on my neck he had been keeping away from the house he felt it was getting too warm for him so I halfturned and stopped then he pestered me to say yes till I took off my glove slowly watching him he said my openwork sleeves were too cold for the rain anything for an excuse to put his hand anear me drawers drawers the whole blessed time till I promised to give him the pair off my doll to carry about in his waistcoat pocket *O Maria Santisima* he did look a big fool dreeping in the rain splendid set of teeth he had made me hungry to look at them and beseeched of me to lift the orange petticoat I had on with the sunray pleats that there was nobody he said hed kneel down in the wet if I didnt so persevering he would too and ruin his new raincoat you never know what freak theyd take alone with you theyre so savage for it if anyone was passing so I lifted them a bit and touched his trousers outside the way I used to Gardner after with my ring hand to keep him from doing worse where it was too public I was dying to find out was he circumcised he was shaking like a jelly all over they want to do everything too quick take all the pleasure out of it and father waiting all the time for his dinner he told me to say I left my purse in the butchers and had to go back for it what a Deceiver then he wrote me that letter with all those words in it how could he have the face to any woman after his company manners making it so awkward after when we met asking me have I offended you with my eyelids down of course he saw I wasnt he had a few brains not like that other fool Henny Doyle he was always breaking or tearing something in the charades I hate an unlucky man and if I knew what it meant of course I had to say no for form sake dont understand you I said and wasnt it natural so it is of course it used to be written up with a picture of a womans on that wall in Gibraltar with that word I couldnt find anywhere only for children seeing it too young then writing every morning a letter sometimes twice a day I liked the way he made love then he knew the way to take a woman when he sent me the 8 big poppies because mine was the 8th then I wrote the night he kissed my heart at Dolphins barn I couldnt describe it simply it makes you feel like nothing on earth but he never knew how to embrace well like Gardner I hope hell come on Monday as he said at the same time four I hate people who come at all hours answer the door you think its the vegetables then its somebody and you all undressed or the door of the filthy sloppy kitchen blows open the day old frostyface Goodwin called about the concert in Lombard street and I just after dinner all flushed and tossed with boiling old stew dont look at me professor I had to say Im a fright yes but he was a real old gent in his way it was impossible to be more respectful nobody to say youre out you have to peep out through the blind like the messengerboy today I thought it was a putoff first him sending the port and the peaches first and I was just beginning to yawn with nerves thinking he was trying to make a fool of me when I knew his tattarrattat at the door he must have been a bit late because it was 1/4 after 3 when I saw the 2 Dedalus girls coming from school I never know the time even that watch he gave me never seems to go properly Id want to get it looked after when I threw the penny to that lame sailor for England home and beauty when I was whistling there is a charming girl I love and I hadnt even put on my clean shift or powdered myself or a thing then this day week were to go to Belfast just as well he has to go to Ennis his fathers anniversary the 27th it wouldnt be pleasant if he did suppose

our rooms at the hotel were beside each other and any fooling went
on in the new bed I couldnt tell him to stop and not bother me with
him in the next room or perhaps some protestant clergyman with a
cough knocking on the wall then hed never believe the next day we
didnt do something its all very well a husband but you cant fool a
lover after me telling him we never did anything of course he didnt
believe me no its better hes going where he is besides something
always happens with him the time going to the Mallow Concert at
Maryborough ordering boiling soup for the two of us then the bell
rang out he walks down the platform with the soup splashing about
taking spoonfuls of it hadnt he the nerve and the waiter after him
making a holy show of us screeching and confusion for the engine to
start but he wouldnt pay till he finished it the two gentlemen in the
3rd class carriage said he was quite right so he was too hes so
pigheaded sometimes when he gets a thing into his head a good job
he was able to open the carriage door with his knife or theyd have
taken us on to Cork I suppose that was done out of revenge on him
O I love jaunting in a train or a car with lovely soft cushions I wonder
will he take a 1st class for me he might want to do it in the train by
tipping the guard well O I suppose therell be the usual idiots of men
gaping at us with their eyes as stupid as ever they can possibly be that
was an exceptional man that common workman that left us alone in
the carriage that day going to Howth Id like to find out something
about him 1 or 2 tunnels perhaps then you have to look out of the
window all the nicer then coming back suppose I never came back
what would they say eloped with him that gets you on on the stage
the last concert I sang at where its over a year ago when was it St
Teresas hall Clarendon St little chits of missies they have now singing
Kathleen Kearney and her like on account of father being in the army
and my singing the absentminded beggar and wearing a brooch for
Lord Roberts when I had the map of it all and Poldy not Irish enough
was it him managed it this time I wouldnt put it past him like he got
me on to sing in the *Stabat Mater* by going around saying he was
putting Lead Kindly Light to music I put him up to that till the
jesuits found out he was a freemason thumping the piano lead Thou
me on copied from some old opera yes and he was going about with
some of them Sinner Fein lately or whatever they call themselves
talking his usual trash and nonsense he says that little man he showed
me without the neck is very intelligent the coming man Griffiths is he

well he doesnt look it thats all I can say still it must have been him he knew there was a boycott I hate the mention of their politics after the war that Pretoria and Ladysmith and Bloemfontein where Gardner lieut Stanley G 8th Bn 2nd East Lancs Rgt of enteric fever he was a lovely fellow in khaki and just the right height over me Im sure he was brave too he said I was lovely the evening we kissed goodbye at the canal lock my Irish beauty he was pale with excitement about going away or wed be seen from the road he couldnt stand properly and I so hot as I never felt they could have made their peace in the beginning or old oom Paul and the rest of the other old Krugers go and fight it out between them instead of dragging on for years killing any finelooking men there were with their fever if he was even decently shot it wouldnt have been so bad I love to see a regiment pass in review the first time I saw the Spanish cavalry at La Roque it was lovely after looking across the bay from Algeciras all the lights of the rock like fireflies or those sham battles on the 15 acres the Black Watch with their kilts in time at the march past the 10th hussars the prince of Wales own or the lancers O the lancers theyre grand or the Dublins that won Tugela his father made his money over selling the horses for the cavalry well he could buy me a nice present up in Belfast after what I gave him theyve lovely linen up there or one of those nice kimono things I must buy a mothball like I had before to keep in the drawer with them it would be exciting going round with him shopping buying those things in a new city better leave this ring behind want to keep turning and turning to get it over the knuckle there or they might bell it round the town in their papers or tell the police on me but theyd think were married O let them all go and smother themselves for the fat lot I care he has plenty of money and hes not a marrying man so somebody better get it out of him if I could find out whether he likes me I looked a bit washy of course when I looked close in the handglass powdering a mirror never gives you the expression besides scrooching down on me like that all the time with his big hipbones hes heavy too with his hairy chest for this heat always having to lie down for them better for him put it into me from behind the way Mrs Mastiansky told me her husband made her like the dogs do it and stick out her tongue as far as ever she could and he so quiet and mild with his tingating cither can you ever be up to men the way it takes them lovely stuff in that blue suit he had on and stylish tie and socks with the skyblue silk things on them hes certainly welloff I know by the cut his clothes have and his heavy watch but he was like a perfect devil for a few minutes after he came back with the stoppress tearing up the tickets and swearing blazes because he lost 20 quid he said he lost over that outsider that won and half he put on for me on account of Lenehans tip cursing him to the lowest pits that sponger he was making free with me after the Glencree dinner coming back that long joult over the featherbed mountain after the lord Mayor looking at me with his dirty eyes Val Dillon that big heathen I first noticed him at dessert when I was cracking the nuts with my teeth I wished I could have picked every morsel of that chicken out of my fingers it was so tasty and browned and as tender as anything only for I didnt want to eat everything on my plate those forks and fishslicers were hallmarked silver too I wish I had some I could easily have slipped a couple into my muff when I was playing with them then always hanging out of them for money in a restaurant for the bit you put down your throat we have to be thankful for our mangy cup of tea itself as a great compliment to be noticed the way the world is divided in any case if its going to go on I want at least two other good chemises for one thing and but I dont know what kind of drawers he likes none at all I think didnt he say yes and half the girls in Gibraltar never wore them either naked as God made them that Andalusian singing her Manola she didnt make much secret of what she hadnt yes and the second pair of silkette stockings is laddered after one days wear I could have brought them back to Lewers this morning and kicked up a row and made that one change them only not to upset myself and run the risk of walking into him and ruining the whole thing and one of those kidfitting corsets Id want advertised cheap in the Gentlewoman with elastic gores on the hips he saved the one I have but thats no good what did they say they give a delightful figure line 11/6 obviating that unsightly broad appearance across the lower back to reduce flesh my belly is a bit too big Ill have to knock off the stout at dinner or am I getting too fond of it the last they sent from ORourkes was as flat as a pancake he makes his money easy Larry they call him the old mangy parcel he sent at Xmas a cottage cake and a bottle of hogwash he tried to palm off as claret that he couldnt get anyone to drink God spare his spit for fear hed die of the drouth or I must do a few breathing exercises I wonder is that antifat any good might overdo it the thin ones are not so much the fashion now garters that much I have the violet pair I wore today thats all he bought me out of the cheque he got on the first O no there was the face lotion I finished the last of yesterday that made my skin like new I told him over and over again get that made up in the same place and dont forget it God only knows whether he did after all I said to him Ill know by the bottle anyway if not I suppose Ill only have to wash in my piss like beeftea or chickensoup with some of that opoponax and violet I thought it was beginning to look coarse or old a bit the skin underneath is much finer where it peeled off there on my finger after the burn its a pity it isnt all like that and the four paltry handkerchiefs about 6/- in all sure you cant get on in this world without style all going in food and rent when I get it Ill lash it around I tell you in fine style I always want to throw a handful of tea into the pot measuring and mincing if I buy a pair of old brogues itself do you like those new shoes yes were they Ive no clothes at all the brown costume and the skirt and jacket and the one at the cleaners 3 whats that for any woman cutting up this old hat and patching up the other the men wont look at you and women try to walk on you because they know youve no man then with all the things getting dearer every day for the 4 years more I have of life up to 35 no Im what am I at all Ill be 33 in September will I what O well look at that Mrs Galbraith shes much older than me I saw her when I was out last week her beautys on the wane she was a lovely woman magnificent head of hair on her down to her waist tossing it back like that like Kitty OShea in Grantham street 1st thing I did every morning to look across see her combing it as if she loved it and was full of it pity I only got to know her the day before we left and that Mrs Langtry the jersey lily the prince of Wales was in love with I suppose hes like the first man going the roads only for the name of a king theyre all made the one way only a black mans Id like to try a beauty up to what was she 45 there was some funny story about the jealous old husband what was it at all and an oyster knife he went no he made her wear a kind of a tin thing round her and the prince of Wales yes he had the oyster knife cant be true a thing like that like some of those books he brings me the works of Master Francois Somebody supposed to be a priest about a child born out of her ear because her bumgut fell out a nice word for any priest to write and her a—e as if any fool wouldnt know what that meant I hate that pretending of all things with that old blackguards face on him anybody can see its not true and that Ruby and Fair Tyrants he brought me that twice I remember when I came to page 50 the part about where she hangs him up out of a hook with a cord flagellate sure theres nothing for a woman in that all invention made up about he drinking the champagne out of her slipper after the ball was over like the infant Jesus in the crib at Inchicore in the Blessed Virgins arms sure no woman could have a child that big taken out of her and I thought first it came out of her side because how could she go to the chamber when she wanted to and she a rich lady of course she felt honoured H R H he was in Gibraltar the year I was born I bet he found lilies there too where he planted the tree he planted more than that in his time he might have planted me too if hed come a bit sooner then I wouldnt be here as I am he ought to chuck that Freeman with the paltry few shillings he knocks out of it and go into an office or something where hed get regular pay or a bank where they could put him up on a throne to count the money all the day of course he prefers plottering about the house so you cant stir with him any side whats your programme today I wish hed even smoke a pipe like father to get the smell of a man or pretending to be mooching about for advertisements when he could have been in Mr Cuffes still only for what he did then sending me to try and patch it up I could have got him promoted there to be the manager he gave me a great mirada once or twice first he was as stiff as the mischief really and truly Mrs Bloom only I felt rotten simply with the old rubbishy dress that I lost the leads out of the tails with no cut in it but theyre coming into fashion again I bought it simply to please him I knew it was no good by the finish pity I changed my mind of going to Todd and Burns as I said and not Lees it was just like the shop itself rummage sale a lot of trash I hate those rich shops get on your nerves nothing kills me altogether only he thinks he knows a great lot about a womans dress and cooking mathering everything he can scour off the shelves into it if I went by his advices every blessed hat I put on does that suit me yes take that thats alright the one like a weddingcake standing up miles off my head he said suited me or the dishcover one coming down on my backside on pins and needles about the shopgirl in that place in Grafton street I had the misfortune to bring him into and she as insolent as ever she could be with her smirk saying Im afraid were giving you too much trouble what shes there for but I stared it out of her yes he was awfully stiff and no wonder but he changed the second time he looked Poldy pigheaded as usual like the soup but I could see him looking very hard at my chest when he stood up to open the door for me it was nice of him to show me out in any case Im extremely sorry Mrs Bloom believe me without making it too marked the first time after him being insulted and me being supposed to be his wife I just half smiled I know my chest was out that way at the door when he said Im extremely sorry and Im sure you were

yes I think he made them a bit firmer sucking them like that so long he made me thirsty titties he calls them I had to laugh yes this one anyhow stiff the nipple gets for the least thing Ill get him to keep that up and Ill take those eggs beaten up with marsala fatten them out for him what are all those veins and things curious the way its made 2 the same in case of twins theyre supposed to represent beauty placed up there like those statues in the museum one of them pretending to hide it with her hand are they so beautiful of course compared with what a man looks like with his two bags full and his other thing hanging down out of him or sticking up at you like a hatrack no wonder they hide it with a cabbageleaf that disgusting Cameron highlander behind the meat market or that other wretch with the red head behind the tree where the statue of the fish used to be when I was passing pretending he was pissing standing out for me to see it with his babyclothes up to one side the Queens own they were a nice lot its well the Surreys relieved them theyre always trying to show it to you every time nearly I passed outside the mens greenhouse near the Harcourt street station just to try some fellow or other trying to catch my eye as if it was 1 of the 7 wonders of the world O and the stink of those rotten places the night coming home with Poldy after the Comerfords party oranges and lemonade to make you feel nice and watery I went into 1 of them it was so biting cold I couldnt keep it when was that 93 the canal was frozen yes it was a few months after a pity a couple of the Camerons werent there to see me squatting in the mens place meadero I tried to draw a picture of it before I tore it up like a sausage or something I wonder theyre not afraid going about of getting a kick or a bang of something there the woman is beauty of course thats admitted when he said I could pose for a picture naked to some rich fellow in Holles street when he lost the job in Helys and I was selling the clothes and strumming in the coffee palace would I be like that bath of the nymph with my hair down yes only shes younger or Im a little like that dirty bitch in that Spanish photo he has nymphs used they go about like that I asked him about her and that word met something with hoses in it and he came out with some jawbreakers about the incarnation he never can explain a thing simply the way a body can understand then he goes and burns the bottom out of the pan all for his Kidney this one not so much theres the mark of his teeth still where he tried to bite the nipple I had to scream out arent they fearful trying to hurt you I had a great breast of milk with Milly enough for two what was the reason of that he said I could have got a pound a week as a wet nurse all swelled out the morning that delicate looking student that stopped in no 28 with the Citrons Penrose nearly caught me washing through the window only for I snapped up the towel to my face that was his studenting hurt me they used to weaning her till he got doctor Brady to give me the belladonna prescription I had to get him to suck them they were so hard he said it was sweeter and thicker than cows then he wanted to milk me into the tea well hes beyond everything I declare somebody ought to put him in the budget if I only could remember the one half of the things and write a book out of it the works of Master Poldy yes and its so much smoother the skin much an hour he was at them Im sure by the clock like some kind of a big infant I had at me they want everything in their mouth all the pleasure those men get out of a woman I can feel his mouth O Lord I must stretch myself I wished he was here or somebody to let myself go with and come again like that I feel all fire inside me or if I could dream it when he made me spend the 2nd time tickling me behind with his finger I was coming for about 5 minutes with my legs round him I had to hug him after O Lord I wanted to shout out all sorts of things fuck or shit or anything at all only not to look ugly or those lines from the strain who knows the way hed take it you want to feel your way with a man theyre not all like him thank God some of them want you to be so nice about it I noticed the contrast he does it and doesnt talk I gave my eyes that look with my hair a bit loose from the tumbling and my tongue between my lips up to him the savage brute Thursday Friday one Saturday two Sunday three O Lord I cant wait till Monday

frseeeeeeeefronnnng train somewhere whistling the strength those engines have in them like big giants and the water rolling all over and out of them all sides like the end of Loves old sweeeetsonnnng the poor men that have to be out all the night from their wives and families in those roasting engines stifling it was today Im glad I burned the half of those old Freemans and Photo Bits leaving things like that lying about hes getting very careless and threw the rest of them up in the W C I'll get him to cut them tomorrow for me instead of having them there for the next year to get a few pence for them have him asking wheres last Januarys paper and all those old overcoats I bundled out of the hall making the place hotter than it is that rain was lovely and refreshing just after my beauty sleep I thought it was going to get like Gibraltar my goodness the heat there before the levanter came on black as night and the glare of the rock standing up in it like a big giant compared with their 3 Rock mountain they think is so great with the red sentries here and there the poplars and they all whitehot and the smell of the rainwater in those tanks watching the sun all the time weltering down on you faded all that lovely frock fathers friend Mrs Stanhope sent me from the B Marche paris what a shame my dearest Doggerina she wrote on it she was very nice whats this her other name was just a p c to tell you I sent the little present have just had a jolly warm bath and feel a very clean dog now enjoyed it wogger she called him wogger wd give anything to be back in Gib and hear you sing Waiting and in old Madrid Concone is the name of those exercises he bought me one of those new some word I couldnt make out shawls amusing things but tear for the least thing still there lovely I think dont you will always think of the lovely teas we had together scrumptious currant scones and raspberry wafers I adore well now dearest Doggerina be sure and write soon kind she left out regards to your father also Captain Grove with love yrs affly Hester x x x x x she didnt look a bit married just like a girl he was years older than her wogger he was awfully fond of me when he held down the wire with his foot for me to step over at the bullfight at La Linea when that matador Gomez was given the bulls ear these clothes we have to wear whoever invented them expecting you to walk up Killiney hill then for example at that picnic all staysed up you cant do a blessed thing in them in a crowd run or jump out of the way thats why I was afraid when that other ferocious old Bull began to charge the banderilleros with the sashes and the 2 things in their hats and the brutes of men shouting bravo toro sure the women were as bad in their nice white mantillas ripping all the whole insides out of those poor horses I never heard of such a thing in all my life yes he used to break his heart at me taking off the dog barking in bell lane poor brute and it sick what became of them ever I suppose theyre dead long ago the 2 of them its like all through a mist makes you feel so old I

made the scones of course I had everything all to myself then a girl
Hester we used to compare our hair mine was thicker than hers she
showed me how to settle it at the back when I put it up and whats this
else how to make a knot on a thread with the one hand we were like
cousins what age was I then the night of the storm I slept in her bed
she had her arms round me then we were fighting in the morning with
the pillow what fun he was watching me whenever he got an
opportunity at the band on the Alameda esplanade when I was with
father and Captain Grove I looked up at the church first and then at
the windows then down and our eyes met I felt something go through
me like all needles my eyes were dancing I remember after when I
looked at myself in the glass hardly recognised myself the change he
was attractive to a girl in spite of his being a little bald intelligent
looking disappointed and gay at the same time he was like Thomas in
the shadow of Ashlydyat I had a splendid skin from the sun and the
excitement like a rose I didnt get a wink of sleep it wouldnt have been
nice on account of her but I could have stopped it in time she gave me
the Moonstone to read that was the first I read of Wilkie Collins East
Lynne I read and the shadow of Ashlydyat Mrs Henry Wood Henry
Dunbar by that other woman I lent him afterwards with Mulveys
photo in it so as he see I wasnt without and Lord Lytton Eugene
Aram Molly bawn she gave me by Mrs Hungerford on account of the
name I dont like books with a Molly in them like that one he brought
me about the one from Flanders a whore always shoplifting anything
she could cloth and stuff and yards of it this blanket is too heavy on
me thats better I havent even one decent nightdress this thing gets all
rolled under me besides him and his fooling thats better I used to be
weltering then in the heat my shift drenched with the sweat stuck in
the cheeks of my bottom on the chair when I stood up they were so
fattish and firm when I got up on the sofa cushions to see with my
clothes up and the bugs tons of them at night and the mosquito nets
I couldnt read a line Lord how long ago it seems centuries of course
they never came back and she didnt put her address right on it either
she may have noticed her wogger people were always going away and
we never I remember that day with the waves and the boats with their
high heads rocking and the smell of ship those Officers uniforms on
shore leave made me seasick he didnt say anything he was very serious
I had the high buttoned boots on and my skirt was blowing she kissed
me six or seven times didnt I cry yes I believe I did or near it my lips

were taittering when I said goodbye she had a Gorgeous wrap of some special kind of blue colour on her for the voyage made very peculiarly to one side like and it was extremely pretty it got as dull as the devil after they went I was almost planning to run away mad out of it somewhere were never easy where we are father or aunt or marriage waiting always waiting to guiiiide him toooo me waiting nor speeeed his flying feet their damn guns bursting and booming all over the shop especially the Queens birthday and throwing everything down in all directions if you didnt open the windows when general Ulysses Grant whoever he was or did supposed to be some great fellow landed off the ship and old Sprague the consul that was there from before the flood dressed up poor man and he in mourning for the son then the same old bugles for reveille in the morning and drums rolling and the unfortunate poor devils of soldiers walking about with messtins smelling the place more than the old longbearded jews in their jellibees and levites assembly and sound clear and gunfire for the men to cross the lines and the warden marching with his keys to lock the gates and the bagpipes and only captain Groves and father talking about Rorkes drift and Plevna and sir Garnet Wolseley and Gordon at Khartoum lighting their pipes for them everytime they went out drunken old devil with his grog on the windowsill catch him leaving any of it picking his nose trying to think of some other dirty story to tell up in a corner but he never forgot himself when I was there sending me out of the room on some blind excuse paying his compliments the Bushmills whisky talking of course but hed do the same to the next woman that came along I suppose he died of galloping drink ages ago the days like years not a letter from a living soul except the odd few I posted to myself with bits of paper in them so bored sometimes I could fight with my nails listening to that old Arab with the one eye and his heass of an instrument singing his heah heah aheah all my compriment on your hotchapotch of your heass as bad as now with the hands hanging off me looking out of the window if there was a nice fellow even in the opposite house that medical in Holles street the nurse was after when I put on my gloves and hat at the window to show I was going out not a notion what I meant arent they thick never understand what you say even youd want to print it up on a big poster for them not even if you shake hands twice with the left he didnt recognise me either when I half frowned at him outside Westland row chapel where does their great intelligence come in Id like to know grey matter they have it all in their tail if you ask me those country gougers up in the City Arms intelligence they had a damn sight less than the bulls and cows they were selling the meat and the coalmans bell that noisy bugger trying to swindle me with the wrong bill he took out of his hat what a pair of paws and pots and pans and kettles to mend any broken bottles for a poor man today and no visitors or post ever except his cheques or some advertisement like that wonderworker they sent him addressed dear Madam only his letter and the card from Milly this morning see she wrote a letter to him who did I get the last letter from O Mrs Dwenn now what possessed her to write from Canada after so many years to know the recipe I had for pisto madrileno Floey Dillon since she wrote to say she was married to a very rich architect if Im to believe all I hear with a villa and eight rooms her father was an awfully nice man he was near seventy always goodhumoured well now Miss Tweedy or Miss Gillespie theres the piannyer that was a solid silver coffee service he had too on the mahogany sideboard then dying so far away I hate people that have always their poor story to tell everybody has their own troubles that poor Nancy Blake died a month ago of acute neumonia well I didnt know her so well as all that she was Floeys friend more than mine poor Nancy its a bother having to answer he always tells me the wrong things and no stops to say like making a speech your sad bereavement sympathy I always make that mistake and newphew with 2 double yous in I hope hell write me a longer letter the next time if its a thing he really likes me O thanks be to the great God I got somebody to give me what I badly wanted to put some heart up into me youve no chances at all in this place like you used long ago I wish somebody would write me a loveletter his wasnt much and I told him he could write what he liked yours ever Hugh Boylan in old Madrid stuff silly women believe love is sighing I am dying still if he wrote it I suppose thered be some truth in it true or no it fills up your whole day and life always something to think about every moment and see it all round you like a new world I could write the answer in bed to let him imagine me short just a few words not those long crossed letters Atty Dillon used to write to the fellow that was something in the four courts that jilted her after out of the ladies letterwriter when I told her to say a few simple words he could twist how he liked not acting with precipat precipitancy with equal candour the greatest earthly happiness answer to a gentlemans proposal affirmatively my goodness theres nothing else its all very fine for them but as for being a woman as soon as youre old they might as well throw you out in the bottom of the ash pit.

Mulveys was the first when I was in bed that morning and Mrs Rubio brought it in with the coffee she stood there standing when I asked her to hand me and I pointing at them I couldnt think of the word a hairpin to open it with ah horquilla disobliging old thing and it staring her in the face with her switch of false hair on her and vain about her appearance ugly as she was near 80 or a 100 her face a mass of wrinkles with all her religion domineering because she never could get over the Atlantic fleet coming in half the ships of the world and the Union Jack flying with all her carabineros because 4 drunken English sailors took all the rock from them and because I didnt run into mass often enough in Santa Maria to please her with her shawl up on her except when there was a marriage on with all her miracles of the saints and her black blessed virgin with the silver dress and the sun dancing 3 times on Easter Sunday morning and when the priest was going by with the bell bringing the vatican to the dying blessing herself for his Majestad an admirer he signed it I near jumped out of my skin I wanted to pick him up when I saw him following me along the Calle Real in the shop window then he tipped me just in passing but I never thought hed write making an appointment I had it inside my petticoat bodice all day reading it up in every hole and corner while father was up at the drill instructing to find out by the handwriting or the language of stamps singing I remember shall I wear a white rose and I wanted to put on the old stupid clock to near the time he was the first man kissed me under the Moorish wall my sweetheart when a boy it never entered my head what kissing meant till he put his tongue in my mouth his mouth was sweetlike young I put my knee up to him a few times to learn the way what did I tell him I was engaged for for fun to the son of a Spanish nobleman named Don Miguel de la Flora and he believed me that I was to be married to him in 3 years time theres many a true word spoken in jest there is a flower that bloometh a few things I told him true about myself just for him to be imagining the Spanish girls he didnt like I suppose one of them wouldnt have him I got him excited he crushed all the flowers on my bosom he brought me he couldnt count the pesetas and the perragordas till I taught him Cappoquin he came from he said on the black water but it was too short then the day before he left May yes it was May when the infant king of Spain was born Im always like that in the spring Id like a new fellow every year up on the tiptop under the rockgun near OHaras tower I told him it was struck by lightning and all about the old Barbary apes they sent to Clapham without a tail careering all over the show on each others back Mrs Rubio said she was a regular old rock scorpion robbing the chickens out of Inces farm and throw stones at you if you went anear he was looking at me I had that white blouse on open in the front to encourage him as much as I could without too openly they were just beginning to be plump I said I was tired we lay over the firtree cove a wild place I suppose it must be the highest rock in existence the galleries and casemates and those frightful rocks and Saint Michaels cave with the icicles or whatever they call them hanging down and ladders all the mud plotching my boots Im sure thats the way down the monkeys go under the sea to Africa when they die the ships out far like chips that was the Malta boat passing yes the sea and the sky you could do what you liked lie there for ever he caressed them outside they love doing that its the roundness there I was leaning over him with my white ricestraw hat to take the newness out of it the left side of my face the best my blouse open for his last day transparent kind of shirt he had I could see his chest pink he wanted to touch mine with his for a moment but I wouldnt let him he was awfully put out first for fear you never know consumption or leave me with a child embarazada that old servant Ines told me that one drop even if it got into you at all after I tried with the Banana but I was afraid it might break and get lost up in me somewhere because they once took something down out of a woman that was up there for years covered with limesalts theyre all mad to get in there where they come out of youd think they could never go far enough up and then theyre done with you in a way till the next time yes because theres a wonderful feeling there so tender all the time how did we finish it off yes O yes I pulled him off into my handkerchief pretending not to be excited but I opened my legs I wouldnt let him touch me inside my petticoat because I had a skirt opening up the side I tormented the life out of him first tickling him I loved rousing that dog in the hotel rrrsssstt awokwokawok his eyes shut and a bird flying below us he was shy all the same I liked him like that moaning I made him blush a little when I got over him that way when I unbuttoned him and took his out and drew back the skin it had a kind of eye in it theyre all Buttons men down the middle on the wrong side of them Molly darling he called me what was his name Jack Joe Harry Mulvey was it yes I think a lieutenant he was rather fair he had a laughing kind of a voice so I went round to the whatyoucallit everything was whatyoucallit moustache had he he said hed come back Lord its just like yesterday to me and if I was married hed do it to me and I promised him yes faithfully Id let him block me now flying perhaps hes dead or killed or a captain or admiral its nearly 20 years if I said firtree cove he would if he came up behind me and put his hands over my eyes to guess who I might recognise him hes young still about 40 perhaps hes married some girl on the black water and is quite changed they all do they havent half the character a woman has she little knows what I did with her beloved husband before he ever dreamt of her in broad daylight too in the sight of the whole world you might say they could have put an article about it in the Chronicle I was a bit wild after when I blew out the old bag the biscuits were in from Benady Bros and exploded it Lord what a bang all the woodcocks and pigeons screaming coming back the same way that we went over middle hill round by the old guardhouse and the jews burialplace pretending to read out the Hebrew on them I wanted to fire his pistol he said he hadnt one he didnt know what to make of me with his peak cap on that he always wore crooked as often as I settled it straight H M s Calypso swinging my hat that old Bishop that spoke off the altar his long preach about womans higher functions about girls now riding the bicycle and wearing peak caps and the new woman bloomers God send him sense and me more money I suppose theyre called after him I never thought that would be my name Bloom when I used to write it in print to see how it looked on a visiting card or practising for the butcher and oblige M Bloom youre looking blooming Josie used to say after I married him well its better than Breen or Briggs does brig or those awful names with bottom in them Mrs Ramsbottom or some other kind of a bottom Mulvey I wouldnt go mad about either or suppose I divorced him Mrs Boylan my mother whoever she was might have given me a nicer name the Lord knows after the lovely one she had Lunita Laredo the fun we had running along Williss road to Europa point twisting in and out all round the other side of Jersey they were shaking and dancing about in my blouse like Millys little ones now when she runs up the stairs I loved looking down at them I was jumping up at the pepper trees and the white poplars pulling the leaves off and throwing them at him he went to India he was to write

706

the voyages those men have to make to the ends of the world and back its the least they might get a squeeze or two at a woman while they can going out to be drowned or blown up somewhere I went up Windmill hill to the flats that Sunday morning with captain Rubios that was dead spyglass like the sentry had he said hed have one or two from on board I wore that frock from the B Marche paris and the coral necklace the straits shining I could see over to Morocco almost the bay of Tangier white and the Atlas mountain with snow on it and the straits like a river so clear Harry Molly darling I was thinking of him on the sea all the time after at mass when my petticoat began to slip down at the elevation weeks and weeks I kept the handkerchief under my pillow for the smell of him there was no decent perfume to be got in that Gibraltar only that cheap peau dEspagne that faded and left a stink on you more than anything else I wanted to give him a memento he gave me that clumsy Claddagh ring for luck that I gave Gardner going to south Africa where those Boers killed him with their war and fever but they were well beaten all the same as if it brought its bad luck with it like an opal or pearl still it must have been pure 18 carrot gold because it was very heavy but what could you get in a place like that the sandfrog shower from Africa and that derelict ship that came up to the harbour Marie the Marie whatyoucallit no he hadnt a moustache that was Gardner yes I can see his face cleanshaven Frseeeeeeeeeeeeeeeeeeeefrong that train again weeping tone once in the dear deaead days beyondre call close my eyes breath my lips forward kiss sad look eyes open piano ere oer the world the mists began I hate that istsbeg comes loves sweet soooooooooooong Ill let that out full when I get in front of the footlights again Kathleen Kearney and her lot of squealers Miss This Miss That Miss Theother lot of sparrowfarts skitting around talking about politics they know as much about as my backside anything in the world to make themselves someway interesting Irish homemade beauties soldiers daughter am I ay and whose are you bootmakers and publicans I beg your pardon coach I thought you were a wheelbarrow theyd die down dead off their feet if ever they got a chance of walking down the Alameda on an officers arm like me on the bandnight my eyes flash my bust that they havent passion God help their poor head I knew more about men and life when I was 15 than theyll all know at 50 they dont know how to sing a song like that Gardner said no man could look at my mouth and teeth smiling like that and not think of it I was afraid he mightnt like my accent first he so English all father left me in spite of his stamps Ive my mothers eyes and figure anyhow he always said theyre so snotty about themselves some of those cads he wasnt a bit like that he was dead gone on my lips let them get a husband first thats fit to be looked at and a daughter like mine or see if they can excite a swell with money that can pick and choose whoever he wants like Boylan to do it 4 or 5 times locked in each others arms or the voice either I could have been a prima donna only I married him comes looooves old deep down chin back not too much make it double My Ladys Bower is too long for an encore about the moated grange at twilight and vaunted rooms yes Ill sing Winds that blow from the south that he gave after the choirstairs performance Ill change that lace on my black dress to show off my bubs and Ill yes by God Ill get that big fan mended make them burst with envy my hole is itching me always when I think of him I feel I want to I feel some wind in me better go easy not wake him have him at it again slobbering after washing every bit of myself back belly and sides if we had even a bath itself or my own room anyway I wish hed sleep in some bed by himself with his cold feet on me give us room even to let a fart God or do the least thing better yes hold them like that a bit on my side piano quietly sweeeee theres that train far away pianissimo eeeee one more song

that was a relief wherever you be let your wind go free who knows if that pork chop I took with my cup of tea after was quite good with the heat I couldnt smell anything off it Im sure that queerlooking man in the porkbutchers is a great rogue I hope that lamp is not smoking fill my nose up with smuts better than having him leaving the gas on all night I couldnt rest easy in my bed in Gibraltar even getting up to see why am I so damned nervous about that though I like it in the winter its more company O Lord it was rotten cold too that winter when I was only about ten was I yes I had the big doll with all the funny clothes dressing her up and undressing that icy wind skeeting across from those mountains the something Nevada sierra nevada standing at the fire with the little bit of a short shift I had up to heat myself I loved dancing about in it then make a race back into bed Im sure that fellow opposite used to be there the whole time watching with the lights out in the summer and I in my skin hopping around I used to love myself then stripped at the washstand dabbing and creaming only when it came to the chamber performance I put out the light too so then there were 2 of us goodbye to my sleep for this night anyhow I hope hes not going to get in with those medicals leading him astray to imagine hes young again coming in at 4 in the morning it must be if not more still he had the manners not to wake me what do they find to gabber about all night squandering money and getting drunker and drunker couldnt they drink water then he starts giving us his orders for eggs and tea and Findon haddy and hot buttered toast I suppose well have him sitting up like the king of the country pumping the wrong end of the spoon up and down in his egg wherever he learned that from and I love to hear him falling up the stairs of a morning with the cups rattling on the tray and then play with the cat she rubs up against you for her own sake I wonder has she fleas shes as bad as a woman always licking and lecking but I hate their claws I wonder do they see anything that we cant staring like that when she sits at the top of the stairs so long and listening as I wait always what a robber too that lovely fresh plaice I bought I think Ill get a bit of fish tomorrow or today is it Friday yes I will with some blancmange with black currant jam like long ago not those 2 lb pots of mixed plum and apple from the London and Newcastle Williams and Woods goes twice as far only for the bones I hate those eels cod yes Ill get a nice piece of cod Im always getting enough for 3 forgetting anyway Im sick of that everlasting butchers meat from Buckleys loin chops and leg beef and rib steak and scrag of mutton and calfs pluck the very name is enough or a picnic suppose we all gave 5/- each and or let him pay it and invite some other woman for him who Mrs Fleming and drove out to the furry glen or the strawberry beds wed have him examining all the horses toenails first like he does with the letters no not with Boylan there yes with some cold veal and ham mixed sandwiches there are little houses down at the bottom of the banks there on purpose but its as hot as blazes he says not a bank holiday anyhow I hate those ruck of Mary Ann coalboxes out for the day Whit Monday is a cursed day too no wonder that bee bit him better the seaside but Id never again in this life get into a boat with him after him at Bray telling the boatman he knew how to row if anyone asked could he ride the steeplechase for the gold cup hed say yes then it came on to get rough the old thing crookeding about and the weight all down my side telling me pull the right reins now pull the left and the tide all swamping in floods in through the bottom and his oar slipping out of the stirrup its a mercy we werent all drowned he can swim of course me no theres no danger whatsoever keep yourself calm in his flannel trousers Id like to have tattered them down off him before all the people and give him what that one calls flagellate till he was black and blue do him all the good in the world only for that longnosed chap I dont know who he is with that other beauty Burke out of the City Arms hotel was there spying around as usual on the slip always where he wasnt wanted if there was a row on youd vomit a better face there was no love lost between us thats 1 consolation I wonder what kind is that book he brought me Sweets of Sin by a gentleman of fashion some other Mr de Kock I suppose the people gave him that nickname going about with his tube from one woman to another I couldnt even change my new white shoes all ruined with the saltwater and the hat I had with that feather all blowy and tossed on me how annoying and provoking because the smell of the sea excited me of course the sardines and the bream in Catalan bay round the back of the rock they were fine all silver in the fishermens baskets old Luigi near a hundred they said came from Genoa and the tall old chap with the earrings I dont like a man you have to climb up to to get at I suppose theyre all dead and rotten long ago besides I dont like being alone in this big barracks of a place at night I suppose Ill have to put up with it I never brought a bit of salt in even when we moved in the confusion musical academy he was going to make on the first floor drawing room with a brassplate or Blooms private hotel he suggested go and ruin himself altogether the way his father did down in Ennis like all the things he told father he was going to do and me but I saw through him telling me all the lovely places we could go for the honeymoon Venice by moonlight with the gondolas and the lake of Como he had a picture cut out of some paper of and mandolines and lanterns O how nice I said whatever I liked he was going to do immediately if not sooner will you be my man will you carry my can he ought to get a leather medal with a putty rim for all the plans he invents then leaving us here all day youd never know what old beggar at the door for a crust with his long story might be a tramp and put his foot in the way to prevent me shutting it like that picture of that hardened criminal he was called in Lloyds Weekly news 20 years in jail then he comes out and murders an old woman for her money imagine his poor wife or mother or whoever she is such a face youd run miles away from I couldnt rest easy till I bolted all the doors and windows to make sure but its worse again being locked up like in a prison or a madhouse they ought to be all shot or the cat of nine tails a big brute like that that would attack a poor old woman to murder her in her bed Id cut them off him so I would not that hed be much use still better than nothing the night I was sure I heard burglars in the kitchen and he went down in his shirt with a candle and a poker as if he was looking for a mouse as white as a sheet frightened out of his wits making as much noise as he possibly could for the burglars benefit there isnt much to steal indeed the Lord knows still its the feeling especially now with Milly away such an idea for him to send the girl down there to learn to take photographs on account of his grandfather instead of sending her to Skerrys academy where shed have to learn not like me getting all at school only hed do a thing like that all the same on account of me and Boylan thats why he did it Im certain the way he plots and plans everything out I couldnt turn round with her in the place lately unless I bolted the door first gave me the fidgets coming in without knocking first when I put the chair against the door just as I was washing myself there below with the glove get on your nerves then doing the loglady all day put her in a glasscase with two at a time to look at her if he knew she broke off the hand off that little gimcrack statue with her roughness and carelessness before she left that I got that little Italian boy to mend so that you cant see the join for 2 shillings wouldnt even teem the potatoes for you of course shes right not to ruin her hands I noticed he was always talking to her lately at the table explaining things in the paper and she pretending to understand sly of course that comes from his side of the house he cant say I pretend things can he Im too honest as a matter of fact and helping her into her coat but if there was anything wrong with her its me shed tell not him I suppose he thinks Im finished out and laid on the shelf well Im not no nor anything like it well see well see now shes well on for flirting too with Tom Devans two sons imitating me whistling with those romps of Murray girls calling for her can Milly come out please shes in great demand to pick what they can out of her round in Nelson street riding Harry Devans bicycle at night its as well he sent her where she is she was just getting out of bounds wanting to go on the skatingrink and smoking their cigarettes through their nose I smelt it off her dress when I was biting off the thread of the button I sewed on to the bottom of her jacket she couldnt hide much from me I tell you only I oughtnt to have stitched it and it on her it brings a parting and the last plumpudding too split in 2 halves see it comes out no matter what they say her tongue is a bit too long for my taste your blouse is open too low she says to me the pan calling the kettle blackbottom and I had to tell her not to cock her legs up like that on show on the windowsill before all the people passing they all look at her like me when I was her age of course any old rag looks well on you then a great touchmenot too in her own way at the Only Way in the Theatre royal take your foot away out of that I hate people touching me afraid of her life Id crush her skirt with the pleats a lot of that touching must go on in theatres in the crush in the dark theyre always trying to wiggle up to you that fellow in the pit at the Gaiety for Beerbohm Tree in Trilby the last time Ill ever go there to be squashed like that for any Trilby or her barebum every two minutes tipping me there and looking away hes a bit daft I think I saw him after trying to get near two stylishdressed ladies outside Switzers window at the same little game I recognised him on the moment the face and everything but he didnt remember me yes and she didnt even want me to kiss her at the Broadstone going away well I hope shell get someone to dance attendance on her the way I did when she was down with the mumps and her glands swollen wheres this and wheres that of course she cant feel anything deep yet I never came properly till I was what 22 or so it went into the wrong place always only the usual girls nonsense and giggling that Conny Connolly writing to her in white ink on black paper sealed with sealingwax though she clapped when the curtain came down because he looked so handsome then we had Martin Harvey for breakfast dinner and supper I thought to myself afterwards it must be real love if a man gives up his life for her that way for nothing I suppose there are a few men like that left its hard to believe in it though unless it really happened to me the majority of them with not a particle of love in their natures to find two people like that nowadays full up of each other that would feel the same way as you do theyre usually a bit foolish in the head his father must have been a bit queer to go and poison himself after her still poor old man I suppose he felt lost shes always making love to my things too the few old rags I have wanting to put her hair up at 15 my powder too only ruin her skin on her shes time enough for that all her life after of course shes restless knowing shes pretty with her lips so red a pity they wont stay that way I was too but theres no use going to the fair with the thing answering me like a fishwoman when I asked to go for a half a stone of potatoes the day we met Mrs Joe Gallaher at the trottingmatches and she pretended not to see us in her trap with

Friery the solicitor we werent grand enough till I gave her 2 damn fine cracks across the ear for herself take that now for answering me like that and that for your impudence she had me that exasperated of course contradicting I was badtempered too because how was it there was a weed in the tea or I didnt sleep the night before cheese I ate was it and I told her over and over again not to leave knives crossed like that because she has nobody to command her as she said herself well if he doesnt correct her faith I will that was the last time she turned on the teartap I was just like that myself they darent order me about the place its his fault of course having the two of us slaving here instead of getting in a woman long ago am I ever going to have a proper servant again of course then shed see him coming Id have to let her know or shed revenge it arent they a nuisance that old Mrs Fleming you have to be walking round after her putting the things into her hands sneezing and farting into the pots well of course shes old she cant help it a good job I found that rotten old smelly dishcloth that got lost behind the dresser I knew there was something and opened the area window to let out the smell bringing in his friends to entertain them like the night he walked home with a dog if you please that might have been mad especially Simon Dedalus son his father such a criticiser with his glasses up with his tall hat on him at the cricket match and a great big hole in his sock one thing laughing at the other and his son that got all those prizes for whatever he won them in the intermediate imagine climbing over the railings if anybody saw him that knew us I wonder he didnt tear a big hole in his grand funeral trousers as if the one nature gave wasnt enough for anybody hawking him down into the dirty old kitchen now is he right in his head I ask pity it wasnt washing day my old pair of drawers might have been hanging up too on the line on exhibition for all hed ever care with the ironmould mark the stupid old bundle burned on them he might think was something else and she never even rendered down the fat I told her and now shes going such as she was on account of her paralysed husband getting worse theres always something wrong with them disease or they have to go under an operation or if its not that its drink and he beats her Ill have to hunt around again for someone every day I get up theres some new thing on sweet God sweet God well when Im stretched out dead in my grave I suppose Ill have some peace I want to get up a minute if Im let wait O Jesus wait yes that thing has come on me yes now wouldnt that afflict you of course all the poking and rooting and ploughing he had up in me now what am I to do Friday Saturday Sunday wouldnt that pester the soul out of a body unless he likes it some men do God knows theres always something wrong with us 5 days every 3 or 4 weeks usual monthly auction isnt it simply sickening that night it came on me like that the one and only time we were in a box that Michael Gunn gave him to see Mrs Kendal and her husband at the Gaiety something he did about insurance for him in Drimmies I was fit to be tied though I wouldnt give in with that gentleman of fashion staring down at me with his glasses and him the other side of me talking about Spinoza and his soul thats dead I suppose millions of years ago I smiled the best I could all in a swamp leaning forward as if I was interested having to sit it out then to the last tag I wont forget that wife of Scarli in a hurry supposed to be a fast play about adultery that idiot in the gallery hissing the woman adulteress he shouted I suppose he went and had a woman in the next lane running round all the back ways after to make up for it I wish he had what I had then hed boo I bet the cat itself is better off than us have we too much blood up in us or what O patience above its pouring out of me like the sea anyhow he didnt make me pregnant as big as he is I dont want to ruin the clean sheets I just put on I suppose the clean linen I wore brought it on too damn it damn it and they always want to see a stain on the bed to know youre a virgin for them all thats troubling them theyre such fools too you could be a widow or divorced 40 times over a daub of red ink would do or blackberry juice no thats too purply O Jamesy let me up out of this pooh sweets of sin whoever suggested that business for women what between clothes and cooking and children this damned old bed too jingling like the dickens I suppose they could hear us away over the other side of the park till I suggested to put the quilt on the floor with the pillow under my bottom I wonder is it nicer in the day I think it is easy I think Ill cut all this hair off me there scalding me I might look like a young girl wouldnt he get the great suckin the next time he turned up my clothes on me Id give anything to see his face wheres the chamber gone easy Ive a holy horror of its breaking under me after that old commode I wonder was I too heavy sitting on his knee I made him sit on the easychair purposely when I took off only my blouse and skirt first in the other room he was so busy where he oughtnt to be he never felt me I hope my breath was sweet after those kissing comfits easy God I remember one time I could scout it out

714

straight whistling like a man almost easy O Lord how noisy I hope
theyre bubbles on it for a wad of money from some fellow Ill have to
perfume it in the morning dont forget I bet he never saw a better pair
of thighs than that look how white they are the smoothest place is
right there between this bit here how soft like a peach easy God I
wouldnt mind being a man and get up on a lovely woman O Lord
what a row youre making like the jersey lily easy easy O how the
waters come down at Lahore

who knows is there anything the matter with my insides or have I
something growing in me getting that thing like that every week
when was it last I Whit Monday yes its only about 3 weeks I ought to
go to the doctor only it would be like before I married him when I had
that white thing coming from me and Floey made me go to that dry
old stick Dr Collins for womens diseases on Pembroke road your
vagina he called it I suppose thats how he got all the gilt mirrors and
carpets getting round those rich ones off Stephens green running up
to him for every little fiddlefaddle her vagina and her cochinchina
theyve money of course so theyre all right I wouldnt marry him not if
he was the last man in the world besides theres something queer about
their children always smelling around those filthy bitches all sides
asking me if what I did had an offensive odour what did he want me
to do but the one thing gold maybe what a question if I smathered it
all over his wrinkly old face for him with all my compriments I
suppose hed know then and could you pass it easily pass what I
thought he was talking about the rock of Gibraltar the way he put it
thats a very nice invention too by the way only I like letting myself
down after in the hole as far as I can squeeze and pull the chain then
to flush it nice cool pins and needles still theres something in it I
suppose I always used to know by Millys when she was a child whether
she had worms or not still all the same paying him for that how much
is that doctor one guinea please and asking me had I frequent
omissions where do those old fellows get all the words they have
omissions with his shortsighted eyes on me cocked sideways I wouldnt
trust him too far to give me chloroform or God knows what else still
I liked him when he sat down to write the thing out frowning so
severe his nose intelligent like that you be damned you lying strap O
anything no matter who except an idiot he was clever enough to spot
that of course that was all thinking of him and his mad crazy letters
my Precious one everything connected with your glorious Body

everything underlined that comes from it is a thing of beauty and of joy for ever something he got out of some nonsensical book that he had me always at myself 4 and 5 times a day sometimes and I said I hadnt are you sure O yes I said I am quite sure in a way that shut him up I knew what was coming next only natural weakness it was he excited me I dont know how the first night ever we met when I was living in Rehoboth terrace we stood staring at one another for about 10 minutes as if we met somewhere I suppose on account of my being jewess looking after my mother he used to amuse me the things he said with the half sloothering smile on him and all the Doyles said he was going to stand for a member of Parliament O wasnt I the born fool to believe all his blather about home rule and the land league sending me that long strool of a song out of the Huguenots to sing in French to be more classy O beau pays de la Touraine that I never even sang once explaining and rigmaroling about religion and persecution he wont let you enjoy anything naturally then might he as a great favour the very 1st opportunity he got a chance in Brighton square running into my bedroom pretending the ink got on his hands to wash it off with the Albion milk and sulphur soap I used to use and the gelatine still round it O I laughed myself sick at him that day I better not make an alnight sitting on this affair they ought to make chambers a natural size so that a woman could sit on it properly he kneels down to do it I suppose there isnt in all creation another man with the habits he has look at the way hes sleeping at the foot of the bed how can he without a hard bolster its well he doesnt kick or he might knock out all my teeth breathing with his hand on his nose like that Indian god he took me to show one wet Sunday in the museum in Kildare street all yellow in a pinafore lying on his side on his hand with his ten toes sticking out that he said was a bigger religion than the jews and Our Lords both put together all over Asia imitating him as hes always imitating everybody I suppose he used to sleep at the foot of the bed too with his big square feet up in his wifes mouth damn this stinking thing anyway wheres this those napkins are ah yes I know I hope the old press doesnt creak ah I knew it would hes sleeping hard had a good time somewhere still she must have given him great value for his money of course he has to pay for it from her O this nuisance of a thing I hope theyll have something better for us in the other world tying ourselves up God help us thats all right for tonight now the lumpy old jingly bed always reminds me of old Cohen

I suppose he scratched himself in it often enough and he thinks father bought it from Lord Napier that I used to admire when I was a little girl because I told him easy piano O I like my bed God here we are as bad as ever after 16 years how many houses were we in at all Raymond terrace and Ontario terrace and Lombard street and Holles street and he goes about whistling every time were on the run again his huguenots or the frogs march pretending to help the men with our 4 sticks of furniture and then the City Arms hotel worse and worse says Warden Daly that charming place on the landing always somebody inside praying then leaving all their stinks after them always know who was in there last every time were just getting on right something happens or he puts his big foot in it Thoms and Helys and Mr Cuffes and Drimmies either hes going to be run into prison over his old lottery tickets that was to be all our salvations or he goes and gives impudence well have him coming home with the sack soon out of the Freeman too like the rest on account of those Sinner Fein or the freemasons then well see if the little man he showed me dribbling along in the wet all by himself round by Coadys lane will give him much consolation that he says is so capable and sincerely Irish he is indeed judging by the sincerity of the trousers I saw on him wait theres Georges church bells wait 3 quarters the hour wait two oclock well thats a nice hour of the night for him to be coming home at to anybody climbing down into the area if anybody saw him Ill knock him off that little habit tomorrow first Ill look at his shirt to see or Ill see if he has that French letter still in his pocketbook I suppose he thinks I dont know deceitful men all their 20 pockets arent enough for their lies then why should we tell them even if its the truth they dont believe you then tucked up in bed like those babies in the Aristocrats Masterpiece he brought me another time as if we hadnt enough of that in real life without some old Aristocrat or whatever his name is disgusting you more with those rotten pictures children with two heads and no legs thats the kind of villainy theyre always dreaming about with not another thing in their empty heads they ought to get slow poison the half of them then tea and toast for him buttered on both sides and newlaid eggs I suppose Im nothing any more when I wouldnt let him lick me in Holles street one night man man tyrant as ever for the one thing he slept on the floor half the night naked the way the jews used when somebody dies belonged to them and wouldnt eat any breakfast or speak a word wanting to be petted so I thought I stood out enough for one time and let him he does it all wrong too thinking only of his own pleasure his tongue is too flat or I dont know what he forgets that wethen I dont Ill make him do it again if he doesnt mind himself and lock him down to sleep in the coalcellar with the blackbeetles I wonder was it her Josie off her head with my castoffs hes such a born liar too no hed never have the courage with a married woman thats why he wants me and Boylan though as for her Denis as she calls him that forlornlooking spectacle you couldnt call him a husband yes its some little bitch hes got in with even when I was with him with Milly at the College races that Hornblower with the childs bonnet on the top of his nob let us into by the back way he was throwing his sheeps eyes at those two doing skirt duty up and down I tried to wink at him first no use of course and thats the way his money goes this is the fruits of Mr Paddy Dignam yes they were all in great style at the grand funeral in the paper Boylan brought in if they saw a real officers funeral thatd be something reversed arms muffled drums the poor horse walking behind in black L Boom and Tom Kernan that drunken little barrelly man that bit his tongue off falling down the mens W C drunk in some place or other and Martin Cunningham and the two Dedaluses and Fanny MCoys husband white head of cabbage skinny thing with a turn in her eye trying to sing my songs shed want to be born all over again and her old green dress with the lowneck as she cant attract them any other way like dabbling on a rainy day I see it all now plainly and they call that friendship killing and then burying one another and they all with their wives and families at home more especially Jack Power keeping that barmaid he does of course his wife is always sick or going to be sick or just getting better of it and hes a goodlooking man still though hes getting a bit grey over the ears theyre a nice lot all of them well theyre not going to get my husband again into their clutches if I can help it making fun of him then behind his back I know well when he goes on with his idiotics because he has sense enough not to squander every penny piece he earns down their gullets and looks after his wife and family goodfornothings poor Paddy Dignam all the same Im sorry in a way for him what are his wife and 5 children going to do unless he was insured comical little teetotum always stuck up in some pub corner and her or her son waiting Bill Bailey wont you please come home her widows weeds wont improve her appearance theyre awfully becoming though if youre goodlooking what men wasnt he

yes he was at the Glencree dinner and Ben Dollard base barreltone
the night he borrowed the swallowtail to sing out of in Holles street
squeezed and squashed into them and grinning all over his big Dolly
face like a wellwhipped childs botty didnt he look a balmy ballocks
sure enough that must have been a spectacle on the stage imagine
paying 5/- in the preserved seats for that to see him trotting off in his
trowlers and Simon Dedalus too he was always turning up half
screwed singing the second verse first the old love is the new was one
of his so sweetly sang the maiden on the hawthorn bough he was
always on for flirtyfying too when I sang Maritana with him at Freddy
Mayers private opera he had a delicious glorious voice Phoebe dearest
goodbye sweetheart *sweet* heart he always sang it not like Bartell dArcy
sweet *tart* goodbye of course he had the gift of the voice so there was
no art in it all over you like a warm showerbath O Maritana wildwood
flower we sang splendidly though it was a bit too high for my register
even transposed and he was married at the time to May Goulding but
then hed say or do something to knock the good out of it hes a
widower now I wonder what sort is his son he says hes an author and
going to be a university professor of Italian and Im to take lessons
what is he driving at now showing him my photo its not good of me I
ought to have got it taken in drapery that never looks out of fashion
still I look young in it I wonder he didnt make him a present of it
altogether and me too after all why not I saw him driving down to the
Kingsbridge station with his father and mother I was in mourning
thats 11 years ago now yes hed be 11 though what was the good in
going into mourning for what was neither one thing nor the other the
first cry was enough for me I heard the deathwatch too ticking in the
wall of course he insisted hed go into mourning for the cat I suppose
hes a man now by this time he was an innocent boy then and a darling
little fellow in his lord Fauntleroy suit and curly hair like a prince on
the stage when I saw him at Mat Dillons he liked me too I remember
they all do wait by God yes wait yes hold on he was on the cards this
morning when I laid out the deck union with a young stranger neither
dark nor fair you met before I thought it meant him but hes no chicken
nor a stranger either besides my face was turned the other way what
was the 7th card after that the 10 of spades for a journey by land then
there was a letter on its way and scandals too the 3 queens and the 8
of diamonds for a rise in society yes wait it all came out and 2 red 8s
for new garments look at that and didnt I dream something too yes

there was something about poetry in it I hope he hasnt long greasy hair hanging into his eyes or standing up like a red Indian what do they go about like that for only getting themselves and their poetry laughed at I always liked poetry when I was a girl first I thought he was a poet like lord Byron and not an ounce of it in his composition I thought he was quite different I wonder is he too young hes about wait 88 I was married 88 Milly is 15 yesterday 89 what age was he then at Dillons 5 or 6 about 88 I suppose hes 20 or more Im not too old for him if hes 23 or 24 I hope hes not that stuckup university student sort no otherwise he wouldnt go sitting down in the old kitchen with him taking Eppss cocoa and talking of course he pretended to understand it all probably he told him he was out of Trinity college hes very young to be a professor I hope hes not a professor like Goodwin was he was a potent professor of John Jameson they all write about some woman in their poetry well I suppose he wont find many like me where softly sighs of love the light guitar where poetry is in the air the blue sea and the moon shining so beautifully coming back on the nightboat from Tarifa the lighthouse at Europa point the guitar that fellow played was so expressive will I ever go back there again all new faces two glancing eyes a lattice hid Ill sing that for him theyre my eyes if hes anything of a poet two eyes as darkly bright as loves own star arent those beautiful words as loves young star itll be a change the Lord knows to have an intelligent person to talk to about yourself not always listening to him and Billy Prescotts ad and Keyess ad and Tom the Devils ad then if anything goes wrong in their business we have to suffer Im sure hes very distinguished Id like to meet a man like that God not those other ruck besides hes young those fine young men I could see down in Margate strand bathingplace from the side of the rock standing up in the sun naked like a God or something and then plunging into the sea with them why arent all men like that thered be some consolation for a woman like that lovely little statue he bought I could look at him all day long curly head and his shoulders his finger up for you to listen theres real beauty and poetry for you I often felt I wanted to kiss him all over also his lovely young cock there so simple I wouldnt mind taking him in my mouth if nobody was looking as if it was asking you to suck it so clean and white he looks with his boyish face I would too in 1/2 a minute even if some of it went down what its only like gruel or the dew theres no danger besides hed be so clean compared with those pigs of men I suppose never dream of washing it from 1 years end to the other the most of them only thats what gives the women the moustaches Im sure itll be grand if I can only get in with a handsome young poet at my age Ill throw them the 1st thing in the morning till I see if the wishcard comes out or Ill try pairing the lady herself and see if he comes out Ill read and study all I can find or learn a bit off by heart if I knew who he likes so he wont think me stupid if he thinks all women are the same and I can teach him the other part Ill make him feel all over him till he half faints under me then hell write about me lover and mistress publicly too with our 2 photographs in all the papers when he becomes famous O but then what am I going to do about him though

no thats no way for him has he no manners nor no refinement nor no nothing in his nature slapping us behind like that on my bottom because I didnt call him Hugh the ignoramus that doesnt know poetry from a cabbage thats what you get for not keeping them in their proper place pulling off his shoes and trousers there on the chair before me so barefaced without even asking permission and standing out that vulgar way in the half of a shirt they wear to be admired like a priest or a butcher or those old hypocrites in the time of Julius Caesar of course hes right enough in his way to pass the time as a joke sure you might as well be in bed with what with a lion God Im sure hed have something better to say for himself an old Lion would O well I suppose its because they were so plump and tempting in my short petticoat he couldnt resist they excite myself sometimes its well for men all the amount of pleasure they get off a womans body were so round and white for them always I wished I was one myself for a change just to try with that thing they have swelling up on you so hard and at the same time so soft when you touch it my uncle John has a thing long I heard those cornerboys saying passing the comer of Marrowbone lane my aunt Mary has a thing hairy because it was dark and they knew a girl was passing it didnt make me blush why should it either its only nature and he puts his thing long into my aunt Marys hairy etcetera and turns out to be you put the handle in a sweepingbrush men again all over they can pick and choose what they please a married woman or a fast widow or a girl for their different tastes like those houses round behind Irish street no but were to be always chained up theyre not going to be chaining me up no damn fear once I start I tell you for their stupid husbands jealousy why cant we all remain friends over it instead of quarrelling her husband found it out what they did together well naturally and if he did can he undo it hes coronado anyway whatever he does and then he going to the other mad extreme about the wife in Fair Tyrants of course the man never even casts a 2nd thought on the husband or wife either its the woman he wants and he gets her what else were we given all those desires for Id like to know I cant help it if Im young still can I its a wonder Im not an old shrivelled hag before my time living with him so cold never embracing me except sometimes when hes asleep the wrong end of me not knowing I suppose who he has any man thatd kiss a womans bottom Id throw my hat at him after that hed kiss anything unnatural where we havent 1 atom of any kind of expression in us all of us the same 2 lumps of lard before ever Id do that to a man pfooh the dirty brutes the mere thought is enough I kiss the feet of you senorita theres some sense in that didnt he kiss our halldoor yes he did what a madman nobody understands his cracked ideas but me still of course a woman wants to be embraced 20 times a day almost to make her look young no matter by who so long as to be in love or loved by somebody if the fellow you want isnt there sometimes by the Lord God I was thinking would I go around by the quays there some dark evening where nobodyd know me and pick up a sailor off the sea thatd be hot on for it and not care a pin whose I was only do it off up in a gate somewhere or one of those wildlooking gipsies in Rathfarnham had their camp pitched near the Bloomfield laundry to try and steal our things if they could I only sent mine there a few times for the name model laundry sending me back over and over some old ones odd stockings that blackguardlooking fellow with the fine eyes peeling a switch attack me in the dark and ride me up against the wall without a word or a murderer anybody what they do themselves the fine gentlemen in their silk hats that K C lives up somewhere this way coming out of Hardwicke lane the night he gave us the fish supper on account of winning over the boxing match of course it was for me he gave it I knew him by his gaiters and the walk and when I turned round a minute after just to see there was a woman after coming out of it too some filthy prostitute then he goes home to his wife after that only I suppose the half of those sailors are rotten again with disease O move over your big carcass out of that for the love of Mike listen to him the winds that waft my sighs to thee so well he may sleep and sigh the great Suggester Don Poldo de la Flora if he knew how he came out on the cards this morning hed have something to sigh for a dark man in some perplexity between 2 7s too

in prison for Lord knows what he does that I dont know and Im to be
slooching around down in the kitchen to get his lordship his breakfast
while hes rolled up like a mummy will I indeed did you ever see me
running Id just like to see myself at it show them attention and they
treat you like dirt I dont care what anybody says itd be much better for
the world to be governed by the women in it you wouldnt see women
going and killing one another and slaughtering when do you ever see
women rolling around drunk like they do or gambling every penny
they have and losing it on horses yes because a woman whatever she
does she knows where to stop sure they wouldnt be in the world at all
only for us they dont know what it is to be a woman and a mother how
could they where would they all of them be if they hadnt all a mother
to look after them what I never had thats why I suppose hes running
wild now out at night away from his books and studies and not living
at home on account of the usual rowy house I suppose well its a poor
case that those that have a fine son like that theyre not satisfied and I
none was he not able to make one it wasnt my fault we came together
when I was watching the two dogs up in her behind in the middle of
the naked street that disheartened me altogether I suppose I oughtnt
to have buried him in that little woolly jacket I knitted crying as I was
but give it to some poor child but I knew well Id never have another
our 1st death too it was we were never the same since O Im not going
to think myself into the glooms about that any more I wonder why he
wouldnt stay the night I felt all the time it was somebody strange he
brought in instead of roving around the city meeting God knows who
nightwalkers and pickpockets his poor mother wouldnt like that if she
was alive ruining himself for life perhaps still its a lovely hour so silent
I used to love coming home after dances the air of the night they have
friends they can talk to weve none either he wants what he wont get or
its some woman ready to stick her knife in you I hate that in women
no wonder they treat us the way they do we are a dreadful lot of bitches
I suppose its all the troubles we have makes us so snappy Im not like
that he could easy have slept in there on the sofa in the other room I
suppose he was as shy as a boy he being so young hardly 20 of me in
the next room hed have heard me on the chamber arrah what harm
Dedalus I wonder its like those names in Gibraltar Delapaz Delagracia
they had the devils queer names there father Vilaplana of Santa Maria
that gave me the rosary Rosales y OReilly in the Calle las Siete
Revueltas and Pisimbo and Mrs Opisso in Governor street O what a

name Id go and drown myself in the first river if I had a name like her
O my and all the bits of streets Paradise ramp and Bedlam ramp and
Rodgers ramp and Crutchetts ramp and the devils gap steps well small
blame to me if I am a harumscarum I know I am a bit I declare to God
I dont feel a day older than then I wonder could I get my tongue round
any of the Spanish como esta usted muy bien gracias y usted see I
havent forgotten it all I thought I had only for the grammar a noun is
the name of any person place or thing pity I never tried to read that
novel cantankerous Mrs Rubio lent me by Valera with the questions in
it all upside down the two ways I always knew wed go away in the end
I can tell him the Spanish and he tell me the Italian then hell see Im
not so ignorant what a pity he didnt stay Im sure the poor fellow was
dead tired and wanted a good sleep badly I could have brought him in
his breakfast in bed with a bit of toast so long as I didnt do it on the
knife for bad luck or if the woman was going her rounds with the
watercress and something nice and tasty there are a few olives in the
kitchen he might like I never could bear the look of them in Abrines I
could do the criada the room looks all right since I changed it the
other way you see something was telling me all the time Id have to
introduce myself not knowing me from Adam very funny wouldnt it
Im his wife or pretend we were in Spain with him half awake without
a Gods notion where he is dos huevos estrellados senor Lord the
cracked things come into my head sometimes itd be great fun
supposing he stayed with us why not theres the room upstairs empty
and Millys bed in the back room he could do his writing and studies
at the table in there for all the scribbling he does at it and if he wants
to read in bed in the morning like me as hes making the breakfast for
1 he can make it for 2 Im sure Im not going to take in lodgers off the
street for him if he takes a gesabo of a house like this Id love to have a
long talk with an intelligent welleducated person Id have to get a nice
pair of red slippers like those Turks with the fez used to sell or yellow
and a nice semitransparent morning gown that I badly want or a
peachblossom dressing jacket like the one long ago in Walpoles only
8/6 or 18/6 Ill just give him one more chance Ill get up early in the
morning Im sick of Cohens old bed in any case I might go over to the
markets to see all the vegetables and cabbages and tomatoes and
carrots and all kinds of splendid fruits all coming in lovely and fresh
who knows whod be the 1st man Id meet theyre out looking for it in
the morning Mamy Dillon used to say they are and the night too that

was her massgoing Id love a big juicy pear now to melt in your mouth like when I used to be in the longing way then Ill throw him up his eggs and tea in the moustachecup she gave him to make his mouth bigger I suppose hed like my nice cream too I know what Ill do Ill go about rather gay not too much singing a bit now and then mi fa pietà Masetto then Ill start dressing myself to go out presto non son più forte Ill put on my best shift and drawers let him have a good eyeful out of that to make his micky stand for him Ill let him know if thats what he wanted that his wife is fucked yes and damn well fucked too up to my neck nearly not by him 5 or 6 times handrunning theres the mark of his spunk on the clean sheet I wouldnt bother to even iron it out that ought to satisfy him if you dont believe me feel my belly unless I made him stand there and put him into me Ive a mind to tell him every scrap and make him do it out in front of me serve him right its all his own fault if I am an adulteress as the thing in the gallery said O much about it if thats all the harm ever we did in this vale of tears God knows its not much doesnt everybody only they hide it I suppose thats what a woman is supposed to be there for or He wouldnt have made us the way He did so attractive to men then if he wants to kiss my bottom Ill drag open my drawers and bulge it right out in his face as large as life he can stick his tongue 7 miles up my hole as hes there my brown part then Ill tell him I want £ 1 or perhaps 30/- Ill tell him I want to buy underclothes then if he gives me that well he wont be too bad I dont want to soak it all out of him like other women do I could often have written out a fine cheque for myself and write his name on it for a couple of pounds a few times he forgot to lock it up besides he wont spend it Ill let him do it off on me behind provided he doesnt smear all my good drawers O I suppose that cant be helped Ill do the indifferent 1 or 2 questions Ill know by the answers when hes like that he cant keep a thing back I know every turn in him Ill tighten my bottom well and let out a few smutty words smellrump or lick my shit or the first mad thing comes into my head then Ill suggest about yes O wait now sonny my turn is coming Ill be quite gay and friendly over it O but I was forgetting this bloody pest of a thing pfooh you wouldnt know which to laugh or cry were such a mixture of plum and apple no Ill have to wear the old things so much the better itll be more pointed hell never know whether he did it or not there thats good enough for you any old thing at all then Ill wipe him off me just like a business his omission then Ill go out Ill have him eying up at the ceiling where is she gone now make him want me thats the only way a quarter after what an unearthly hour I suppose theyre just getting up in China now combing out their pigtails for the day well soon have the nuns ringing the angelus theyve nobody coming in to spoil their sleep except an odd priest or two for his night office or the alarmclock next door at cockshout clattering the brains out of itself let me see if I can doze off 1 2 3 4 5 what kind of flowers are those they invented like the stars the wallpaper in Lombard street was much nicer the apron he gave me was like that something only I only wore it twice better lower this lamp and try again so as I can get up early Ill go to Lambes there beside Findlaters and get them to send us some flowers to put about the place in case he brings him home tomorrow today I mean no no Fridays an unlucky day first I want to do the place up someway the dust grows in it I think while Im asleep then we can have music and cigarettes I can accompany him first I must clean the keys of the piano with milk whatll I wear shall I wear a white rose or those fairy cakes in Liptons I love the smell of a rich big shop at 7 1/2d a lb or the other ones with the cherries in them and the pinky sugar 11d a couple of lbs of those a nice plant for the middle of the table Id get that cheaper in wait wheres this I saw them not long ago I love flowers Id love to have the whole place swimming in roses God of heaven theres nothing like nature the wild mountains then the sea and the waves rushing then the beautiful country with the fields of oats and wheat and all kinds of things and all the fine cattle going about that would do your heart good to see rivers and lakes and flowers all sorts of shapes and smells and colours springing up even out of the ditches primroses and violets nature it is as for them saying theres no God I wouldnt give a snap of my two fingers for all their learning why dont they go and create something I often asked him atheists or whatever they call themselves go and wash the cobbles off themselves first then they go howling for the priest and they dying and why why because theyre afraid of hell on account of their bad conscience ah yes I know them well who was the first person in the universe before there was anybody that made it all who ah that they dont know neither do I so there you are they might as well try to stop the sun from rising tomorrow the sun shines for you he said the day we were lying among the rhododendrons on Howth head in the grey tweed suit and his straw hat the day I got him to propose to me yes first I gave him the bit of seedcake out of my mouth and it was leapyear like now yes 16 years ago my God after that long kiss I near

726

lost my breath yes he said I was a flower of the mountain yes so we are flowers all a womans body yes that was one true thing he said in his life and the sun shines for you today yes that was why I liked him because I saw he understood or felt what a woman is and I knew I could always get round him and I gave him all the pleasure I could leading him on till he asked me to say yes and I wouldnt answer first only looked out over the sea and the sky I was thinking of so many things he didnt know of Mulvey and Mr Stanhope and Hester and father and old captain Groves and the sailors playing all birds fly and I say stoop and washing up dishes they called it on the pier and the sentry in front of the governors house with the thing round his white helmet poor devil half roasted and the Spanish girls laughing in their shawls and their tall combs and the auctions in the morning the Greeks and the jews and the Arabs and the devil knows who else from all the ends of Europe and Duke street and the fowl market all clucking outside Larby Sharons and the poor donkeys slipping half asleep and the vague fellows in the cloaks asleep in the shade on the steps and the big wheels of the carts of the bulls and the old castle thousands of years old yes and those handsome Moors all in white and turbans like kings asking you to sit down in their little bit of a shop and Ronda with the old windows of the posadas 2 glancing eyes a lattice hid for her lover to kiss the iron and the wineshops half open at night and the castanets and the night we missed the boat at Algeciras the watchman going about serene with his lamp and O that awful deepdown torrent O and the sea the sea crimson sometimes like fire and the glorious sunsets and the figtrees in the Alameda gardens yes and all the queer little streets and the pink and blue and yellow houses and the rosegardens and the jessamine and geraniums and cactuses and Gibraltar as a girl where I was a Flower of the mountain yes when I put the rose in my hair like the Andalusian girls used or shall I wear a red yes and how he kissed me under the Moorish wall and I thought well as well him as another and then I asked him with my eyes to ask again yes and then he asked me would I yes to say yes my mountain flower and first I put my arms around him yes and drew him down to me so he could feel my breasts all perfume yes and his heart was going like mad and yes I said yes I will Yes.

Trieste-Zürich-Paris
1914-1921

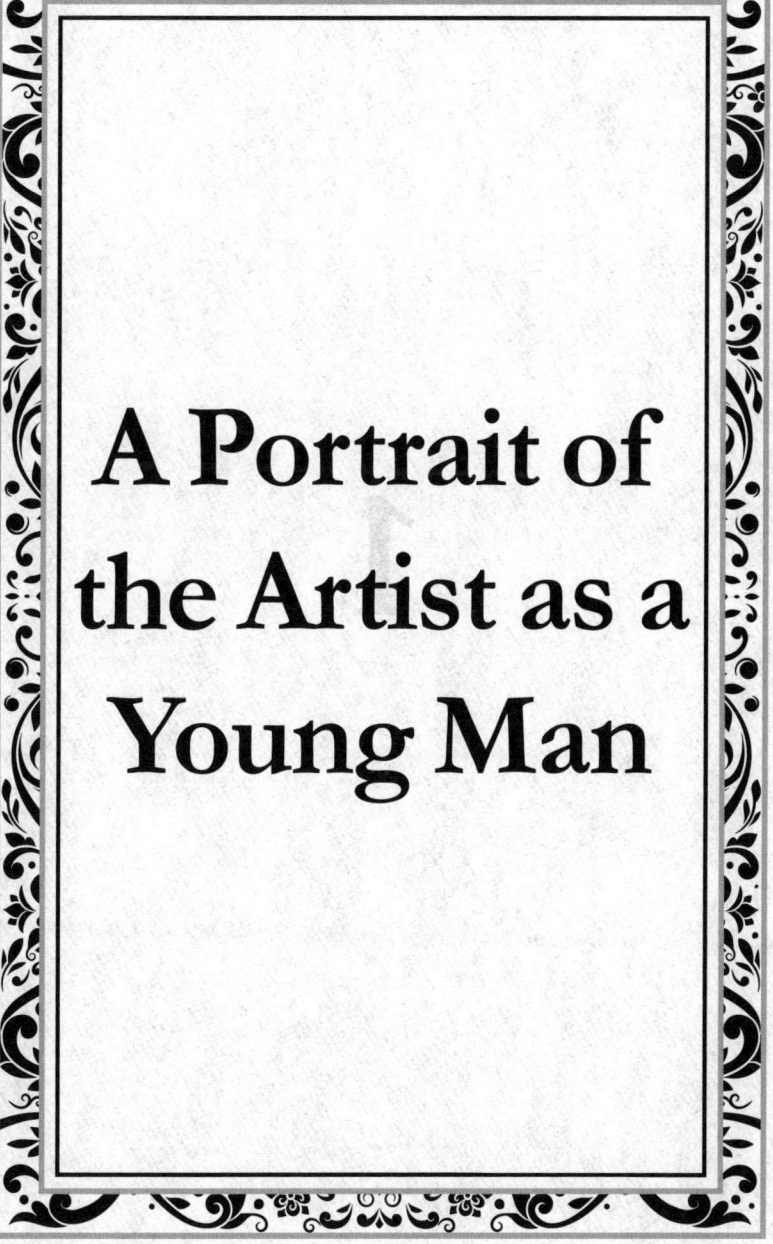

A Portrait of the Artist as a Young Man

1

Once upon a time and a very good time it was there was a moocow coming down along the road and this moocow that was coming down along the road met a nicens little boy named baby tuckoo . . .

His father told him that story: his father looked at him through a glass: he had a hairy face.

He was baby tuckoo. The moocow came down the road where Betty Byrne lived: she sold lemon platt.

> *O, the wild rose blossoms*
> *On the little green place.*

He sang that song. That was his song.

> *O, the green wothe botheth.*

When you wet the bed first it is warm then it gets cold. His mother put on the oilsheet. That had the queer smell.

His mother had a nicer smell than his father. She played on the piano the sailor's hornpipe for him to dance. He danced:

> *Tralala lala,*
> *Tralala tralaladdy,*
> *Tralala lala,*
> *Tralala lala.*

Uncle Charles and Dante clapped. They were older than his father and mother but uncle Charles was older than Dante.

Dante had two brushes in her press. The brush with the maroon velvet back was for Michael Davitt and the brush with the green velvet back was for Parnell. Dante gave him a cachou every time he brought her a piece of tissue paper.

The Vances lived in number seven. They had a different father and mother. They were Eileen's father and mother. When they were grown up he was going to marry Eileen. He hid under the table. His mother said:

—O, Stephen will apologize.

Dante said:

—O, if not, the eagles will come and pull out his eyes.—

> *Pull out his eyes,*
> *Apologize,*
> *Apologize,*
> *Pull out his eyes.*

> *Apologize,*
> *Pull out his eyes,*
> *Pull out his eyes,*
> *Apologize.*

The wide playgrounds were swarming with boys. All were shouting and the prefects urged them on with strong cries. The evening air was pale and chilly and after every charge and thud of the footballers the greasy leather orb flew like a heavy bird through the grey light. He kept on the fringe of his line, out of sight of his prefect, out of the reach of the rude feet, feigning to run now and then. He felt his body small and weak amid the throng of the players and his eyes were weak and watery. Rody Kickham was not like that: he would be captain of the third line all the fellows said.

Rody Kickham was a decent fellow but Nasty Roche was a stink. Rody Kickham had greaves in his number and a hamper in the refectory. Nasty Roche had big hands. He called the Friday pudding dog-in-the-blanket. And one day he had asked:

—What is your name?

Stephen had answered:

Stephen Dedalus.

Then Nasty Roche had said:

—What kind of a name is that?

And when Stephen had not been able to answer Nasty Roche had asked:

—What is your father?

Stephen had answered:

—A gentleman.

Then Nasty Roche had asked:

—Is he a magistrate?

He crept about from point to point on the fringe of his line, making little runs now and then. But his hands were bluish with cold. He kept his hands in the side pockets of his belted grey suit. That was a belt round his pocket. And belt was also to give a fellow a belt. One day a fellow said to Cantwell:

—I'd give you such a belt in a second.

Cantwell had answered:

—Go and fight your match. Give Cecil Thunder a belt. I'd like to see you. He'd give you a toe in the rump for yourself.

That was not a nice expression. His mother had told him not to speak with the rough boys in the college. Nice mother! The first day in the hall of the castle when she had said goodbye she had put up her veil double to her nose to kiss him: and her nose and eyes were red. But he had pretended not to see that she was going to cry. She was a nice mother but she was not so nice when she cried. And his father had given him two five-shilling pieces for pocket money. And his father had told him if he wanted anything to write home to him and, whatever he did, never to peach on a fellow. Then at the door of the castle the rector had shaken hands with his father and mother, his soutane fluttering in the breeze, and the car had driven off with his father and mother on it. They had cried to him from the car, waving their hands:

—Goodbye, Stephen, goodbye!

—Goodbye, Stephen, goodbye!

He was caught in the whirl of a scrimmage and, fearful of the flashing eyes and muddy boots, bent down to look through the legs. The fellows were struggling and groaning and their legs were rubbing and kicking and stamping. Then Jack Lawton's yellow boots dodged out the ball and all the other boots and legs ran after. He ran after them a little way and then stopped. It was useless to run on. Soon they would be going home for the holidays. After supper in the study hall he would change the number pasted up inside his desk from seventy-seven to seventy-six.

It would be better to be in the study hall than out there in the cold. The sky was pale and cold but there were lights in the castle.

He wondered from which window Hamilton Rowan had thrown his hat on the ha-ha and had there been flowerbeds at that time under the windows. One day when he had been called to the castle the butler had shown him the marks of the soldiers' slugs in the wood of the door and had given him a piece of shortbread that the community ate. It was nice and warm to see the lights in the castle. It was like something in a book. Perhaps Leicester Abbey was like that. And there were nice sentences in Doctor Cornwell's Spelling Book. They were like poetry but they were only sentences to learn the spelling from.

> *Wolsey died in Leicester Abbey*
> *Where the abbots buried him.*
> *Canker is a disease of plants,*
> *Cancer one of animals.*

It would be nice to lie on the hearthrug before the fire, leaning his head upon his hands, and think on those sentences. He shivered as if he had cold slimy water next his skin. That was mean of Wells to shoulder him into the square ditch because he would not swop his little snuff box for Wells's seasoned hacking chestnut, the conqueror of forty. How cold and slimy the water had been! A fellow had once seen a big rat jump into the scum. Mother was sitting at the fire with Dante waiting for Brigid to bring in the tea. She had her feet on the fender and her jewelly slippers were so hot and they had such a lovely warm smell! Dante knew a lot of things. She had taught him where the Mozambique Channel was and what was the longest river in America and what was the name of the highest mountain in the moon. Father Arnall knew more than Dante because he was a priest but both his father and uncle Charles said that Dante was a clever woman and a well-read woman. And when Dante made that noise after dinner and then put up her hand to her mouth: that was heartburn.

A voice cried far out on the playground:

—All in!

Then other voices cried from the lower and third lines:

—All in! All in!

The players closed around, flushed and muddy, and he went among them, glad to go in. Rody Kickham held the ball by its greasy lace. A fellow asked him to give it one last: but he walked on without even answering the fellow. Simon Moonan told him not to because the prefect was looking. The fellow turned to Simon Moonan and said:

—We all know why you speak. You are McGlade's suck.

Suck was a queer word. The fellow called Simon Moonan that name because Simon Moonan used to tie the prefect's false sleeves behind his back and the prefect used to let on to be angry. But the sound was ugly. Once he had washed his hands in the lavatory of the Wicklow Hotel and his father pulled the stopper up by the chain after and the dirty water went down through the hole in the basin. And when it had all gone down slowly the hole in the basin had made a sound like that: suck. Only louder.

To remember that and the white look of the lavatory made him feel cold and then hot. There were two cocks that you turned and water came out: cold and hot. He felt cold and then a little hot: and he could see the names printed on the cocks. That was a very queer thing.

And the air in the corridor chilled him too. It was queer and wettish. But soon the gas would be lit and in burning it made a light noise like a little song. Always the same: and when the fellows stopped talking in the playroom you could hear it.

It was the hour for sums. Father Arnall wrote a hard sum on the board and then said:

—Now then, who will win? Go ahead, York! Go ahead, Lancaster!

Stephen tried his best, but the sum was too hard and he felt confused. The little silk badge with the white rose on it that was pinned on the breast of his jacket began to flutter. He was no good at sums, but he tried his best so that York might not lose. Father Arnall's face looked very black, but he was not in a wax: he was laughing. Then Jack Lawton cracked his fingers and Father Arnall looked at his copybook and said:

—Right. Bravo Lancaster! The red rose wins. Come on now, York! Forge ahead!

Jack Lawton looked over from his side. The little silk badge with the red rose on it looked very rich because he had a blue sailor top on. Stephen felt his own face red too, thinking of all the bets about who would get first place in elements, Jack Lawton or he. Some weeks Jack Lawton got the card for first and some weeks he got the card for first. His white silk badge fluttered and fluttered as he worked at the next sum and heard Father Arnall's voice. Then all his eagerness passed away and he felt his face quite cool. He thought his face must be white because it felt so cool. He could not get out the answer for the sum but it did not matter. White roses and red roses: those were beautiful colours to think of. And the cards for first place and second place and third place were beautiful colours too: pink and cream and lavender. Lavender and cream and pink roses were beautiful to think of. Perhaps a wild rose might be like those colours and he remembered the song about the wild rose blossoms on the little green place. But you could not have a green rose. But perhaps somewhere in the world you could.

The bell rang and then the classes began to file out of the rooms and along the corridors towards the refectory. He sat looking at the two prints of butter on his plate but could not eat the damp bread. The tablecloth was damp and limp. But he drank off the hot weak tea which the clumsy scullion, girt with a white apron, poured into his cup. He wondered whether the scullion's apron was damp too or whether all white things were cold and damp. Nasty Roche and Saurin drank cocoa that their people sent them in tins. They said they could not drink the tea; that it was hogwash. Their fathers were magistrates, the fellows said.

All the boys seemed to him very strange. They had all fathers and mothers and different clothes and voices. He longed to be at home and lay his head on his mother's lap. But he could not: and so he longed for the play and study and prayers to be over and to be in bed.

He drank another cup of hot tea and Fleming said:

—What's up? Have you a pain or what's up with you?

—I don't know, Stephen said.

—Sick in your breadbasket, Fleming said, because your face looks white. It will go away.

—O yes, Stephen said.

But he was not sick there. He thought that he was sick in his heart if you could be sick in that place. Fleming was very decent to ask him. He wanted to cry. He leaned his elbows on the table and shut and opened the flaps of his ears. Then he heard the noise of the refectory every time he opened the flaps of his ears. It made a roar like a train at night. And when he closed the flaps the roar was shut off like a train going into a tunnel. That night at Dalkey the train had roared like that and then, when it went into the tunnel, the roar stopped. He closed his eyes and the train went on, roaring and then stopping; roaring again, stopping. It was nice to hear it roar and stop and then roar out of the tunnel again and then stop.

Then the higher line fellows began to come down along the matting in the middle of the refectory, Paddy Rath and Jimmy Magee and the Spaniard who was allowed to smoke cigars and the little Portuguese who wore the woolly cap. And then the lower line tables and the tables of the third line. And every single fellow had a different way of walking.

He sat in a corner of the playroom pretending to watch a game of dominoes and once or twice he was able to hear for an instant the little song of the gas. The prefect was at the door with some boys and Simon Moonan was knotting his false sleeves. He was telling them something about Tullabeg.

Then he went away from the door and Wells came over to Stephen and said:

—Tell us, Dedalus, do you kiss your mother before you go to bed?

Stephen answered:

—I do.

Wells turned to the other fellows and said:

—O, I say, here's a fellow says he kisses his mother every night before he goes to bed.

The other fellows stopped their game and turned round, laughing. Stephen blushed under their eyes and said:

—I do not.

Wells said:

—O, I say, here's a fellow says he doesn't kiss his mother before he goes to bed.

They all laughed again. Stephen tried to laugh with them. He felt his whole body hot and confused in a moment. What was the right answer to the question? He had given two and still Wells laughed. But Wells must know the right answer for he was in third of grammar. He tried to think of Wells's mother but he did not dare to raise his eyes to Wells's face. He did not like Wells's face. It was Wells who had shouldered him into the square ditch the day before because he would not swop his little snuff box for Wells's seasoned hacking chestnut, the conqueror of forty. It was a mean thing to do; all the fellows said it was. And how cold and slimy the water had been! And a fellow had once seen a big rat jump plop into the scum.

The cold slime of the ditch covered his whole body; and, when the bell rang for study and the lines filed out of the playrooms, he felt the cold air of the corridor and staircase inside his clothes. He still tried to think what was the right answer. Was it right to kiss his mother or wrong to kiss his mother? What did that mean, to kiss? You put your face up like that to say good night and then his mother put her face down. That was to kiss. His mother put her lips on his cheek; her lips were soft and they wetted his cheek; and they made a tiny little noise: kiss. Why did people do that with their two faces?

Sitting in the study hall he opened the lid of his desk and changed the number pasted up inside from seventy-seven to seventy-six. But the Christmas vacation was very far away: but one time it would come because the earth moved round always.

There was a picture of the earth on the first page of his geography: a big ball in the middle of clouds. Fleming had a box of crayons and one night during free study he had coloured the earth green and the clouds maroon. That was like the two brushes in Dante's press, the brush with the green velvet back for Parnell and the brush with the maroon velvet back for Michael Davitt. But he had not told Fleming to colour them those colours. Fleming had done it himself.

He opened the geography to study the lesson; but he could not learn the names of places in America. Still they were all different places that had different names. They were all in different countries and the countries were in continents and the continents were in the world and the world was in the universe.

He turned to the flyleaf of the geography and read what he had written there: himself, his name and where he was.

Stephen Dedalus
Class of Elements
Clongowes Wood College
Sallins
County Kildare
Ireland
Europe
The World
The Universe

That was in his writing: and Fleming one night for a cod had written on the opposite page:

Stephen Dedalus is my name,
Ireland is my nation.
Clongowes is my dwellingplace
And heaven my expectation.

He read the verses backwards but then they were not poetry. Then he read the flyleaf from the bottom to the top till he came to his own name. That was he: and he read down the page again. What was after the universe? Nothing. But was there anything round the universe to show where it stopped before the nothing place began? It could not be a wall; but there could be a thin thin line there all round everything. It was very big to think about everything and everywhere. Only God could do that. He tried to think what a big thought that must be; but he could only think of God. God was God's name just as his name was Stephen. *Dieu* was the French for God and that was God's name too; and when anyone prayed to God and said *Dieu* then God knew at once that it was a French person that was praying. But, though there were different names for God in all the different languages in the world and God understood what all the people who prayed said in their different languages, still God remained always the same God and God's real name was God.

It made him very tired to think that way. It made him feel his head very big. He turned over the flyleaf and looked wearily at the green round earth in the middle of the maroon clouds. He wondered which was right, to be for the green or for the maroon, because Dante had ripped the green velvet back off the brush that was for Parnell one day with her scissors and had told him that Parnell was a bad man. He wondered if they were arguing at home about that. That was called politics. There were two sides in it: Dante was on one side and his father and Mr Casey were on the other side but his mother and uncle Charles were on no side. Every day there was something in the paper about it.

It pained him that he did not know well what politics meant and that he did not know where the universe ended. He felt small and weak. When would he be like the fellows in poetry and rhetoric? They had big voices and big boots and they studied trigonometry.

That was very far away. First came the vacation and then the next term and then vacation again and then again another term and then again the vacation. It was like a train going in and out of tunnels and that was like the noise of the boys eating in the refectory when you opened and closed the flaps of the ears. Term, vacation; tunnel, out; noise, stop. How far away it was! It was better to go to bed to sleep. Only prayers in the chapel and then bed. He shivered and yawned. It would be lovely in bed after the sheets got a bit hot. First they were so cold to get into. He shivered to think how cold they were first. But then they got hot and then he could sleep. It was lovely to be tired. He yawned again. Night prayers and then bed: he shivered and wanted to yawn. It would be lovely in a few minutes. He felt a warm glow creeping up from the cold shivering sheets, warmer and warmer till he felt warm all over, ever so warm and yet he shivered a little and still wanted to yawn.

The bell rang for night prayers and he filed out of the study hall after the others and down the staircase and along the corridors to the chapel. The corridors were darkly lit and the chapel was darkly lit. Soon all would be dark and sleeping. There was cold night air in the chapel and the marbles were the colour the sea was at night. The sea was cold day and night: but it was colder at night. It was cold and dark under the seawall beside his father's house. But the kettle would be on the hob to make punch.

The prefect of the chapel prayed above his head and his memory knew the responses:

> *O Lord open our lips*
> *And our mouths shall announce Thy praise.*
> *Incline unto our aid, O God!*
> *O Lord make haste to help us!*

There was a cold night smell in the chapel. But it was a holy smell. It was not like the smell of the old peasants who knelt at the back of the chapel at Sunday mass. That was a smell of air and rain and turf and corduroy. But they were very holy peasants. They breathed behind him on his neck and sighed as they prayed. They lived in Clane, a fellow said: there were little cottages there and he had seen a woman standing at the half-door of a cottage with a child in her arms as the cars had come past from Sallins. It would be lovely to sleep for one night in that cottage before the fire of smoking turf, in the dark lit by the fire, in the warm dark, breathing the smell of the peasants, air and rain and turf and corduroy. But O, the road there between the trees was dark! You would be lost in the dark. It made him afraid to think of how it was.

He heard the voice of the prefect of the chapel saying the last prayers. He prayed it too against the dark outside under the trees.

Visit, we beseech Thee, O Lord, this habitation and drive away from it all the snares of the enemy. May Thy holy angels dwell herein to preserve us in peace and may Thy blessings be always upon us through Christ Our Lord. Amen.

His fingers trembled as he undressed himself in the dormitory. He told his fingers to hurry up. He had to undress and then kneel and say his own prayers and be in bed before the gas was lowered so that he might not go to hell when he died. He rolled his stockings off and put on his nightshirt quickly and knelt trembling at his bedside and repeated his prayers quickly, fearing that the gas would go down. He felt his shoulders shaking as he murmured:

God bless my father and my mother and spare them to me!
God bless my little brothers and sisters and spare them to me!
God bless Dante and Uncle Charles and spare them to me!

He blessed himself and climbed quickly into bed and, tucking the end of the nightshirt under his feet, curled himself together under the cold white sheets, shaking and trembling. But he would not go to hell when he died; and the shaking would stop. A voice bade the boys in the dormitory good night. He peered out for an instant over the coverlet and saw the yellow curtains round and before his bed that shut him off on all sides. The light was lowered quietly.

The prefect's shoes went away. Where? Down the staircase and along the corridors or to his room at the end? He saw the dark. Was it true about the black dog that walked there at night with eyes as big as carriage-lamps? They said it was the ghost of a murderer. A long shiver of fear flowed over his body. He saw the dark entrance hall of the castle. Old servants in old dress were in the ironing-room above the staircase. It was long ago. The old servants were quiet. There was a fire there, but the hall was still dark. A figure came up the staircase from the hall. He wore the white cloak of a marshal; his face was pale and strange; he held his hand pressed to his side. He looked out of strange eyes at the old servants. They looked at him and saw their master's face and cloak and knew that he had received his death-wound. But only the dark was where they looked: only dark silent air. Their master had received his death-wound on the battlefield of Prague far away over the sea. He was standing on the field; his hand was pressed to his side; his face was pale and strange and he wore the white cloak of a marshal.

O how cold and strange it was to think of that! All the dark was cold and strange. There were pale strange faces there, great eyes like carriage-lamps. They were the ghosts of murderers, the figures of marshals who had received their death-wound on battlefields far away over the sea. What did they wish to say that their faces were so strange?

Visit, we beseech Thee, O Lord, this habitation and drive away from it all . . .

Going home for the holidays! That would be lovely: the fellows had told him. Getting up on the cars in the early wintry morning outside the door of the castle. The cars were rolling on the gravel. Cheers for the rector!

Hurray! Hurray! Hurray!

The cars drove past the chapel and all caps were raised. They drove merrily along the country roads. The drivers pointed with their whips to Bodenstown. The fellows cheered. They passed the farmhouse of the Jolly Farmer. Cheer after cheer after cheer. Through Clane they drove, cheering and cheered. The peasant women stood at the half-doors, the men stood here and there. The lovely smell there was in the wintry air: the smell of Clane: rain and wintry air and turf smouldering and corduroy.

The train was full of fellows: a long long chocolate train with cream facings. The guards went to and fro opening, closing, locking, unlocking the doors. They were men in dark blue and silver; they had silvery whistles and their keys made a quick music: click, click: click, click. And the train raced on over the flat lands and past the Hill of Allen. The telegraph poles were passing, passing. The train went on and on. It knew. There were lanterns in the hall of his father's house and ropes of green branches. There were holly and ivy round the pierglass and holly and ivy, green and red, twined round the chandeliers. There were red holly and green ivy round the old portraits on the walls. Holly and ivy for him and for Christmas.

Lovely . . .

All the people. Welcome home, Stephen! Noises of welcome. His mother kissed him. Was that right? His father was a marshal now: higher than a magistrate. Welcome home, Stephen!

Noises . . .

There was a noise of curtain-rings running back along the rods, of water being splashed in the basins. There was a noise of rising and dressing and washing in the dormitory: a noise of clapping of hands as the prefect went up and down telling the fellows to look sharp. A pale sunlight showed the yellow curtains drawn back, the tossed beds. His bed was very hot and his face and body were very hot.

He got up and sat on the side of his bed. He was weak. He tried to pull on his stocking. It had a horrid rough feel. The sunlight was queer and cold.

Fleming said:

—Are you not well?

He did not know; and Fleming said:

—Get back into bed. I'll tell McGlade you're not well.

—He's sick.

—Who is?

—Tell McGlade.

—Get back into bed.

—Is he sick?

A fellow held his arms while he loosened the stocking clinging to his foot and climbed back into the hot bed.

He crouched down between the sheets, glad of their tepid glow. He heard the fellows talk among themselves about him as they dressed for mass. It was a mean thing to do, to shoulder him into the square ditch, they were saying.

Then their voices ceased; they had gone. A voice at his bed said:

—Dedalus, don't spy on us, sure you won't?

Wells's face was there. He looked at it and saw that Wells was afraid.

—I didn't mean to. Sure you won't?

His father had told him, whatever he did, never to peach on a fellow. He shook his head and answered no and felt glad. Wells said:

—I didn't mean to, honour bright. It was only for cod. I'm sorry.

The face and the voice went away. Sorry because he was afraid. Afraid that it was some disease. Canker was a disease of plants and cancer one of animals: or another different. That was a long time ago then out on the playgrounds in the evening light, creeping from point to point on the fringe of his line, a heavy bird flying low through the grey light. Leicester Abbey lit up. Wolsey died there. The abbots buried him themselves.

It was not Wells's face, it was the prefect's. He was not foxing. No, no: he was sick really. He was not foxing. And he felt the prefect's hand on his forehead; and he felt his forehead warm and damp against the prefect's cold damp hand. That was the way a rat felt, slimy and damp and cold. Every rat had two eyes to look out of. Sleek slimy coats, little little feet tucked up to jump, black slimy eyes to look out of. They could understand how to jump. But the minds of rats could not understand trigonometry. When they were dead they lay on their sides. Their coats dried then. They were only dead things.

The prefect was there again and it was his voice that was saying that he was to get up, that Father Minister had said he was to get up and dress and go to the infirmary. And while he was dressing himself as quickly as he could the prefect said:

—We must pack off to Brother Michael because we have the collywobbles!

He was very decent to say that. That was all to make him laugh. But he could not laugh because his cheeks and lips were all shivery: and then the prefect had to laugh by himself.

The prefect cried:

—Quick march! Hayfoot! Strawfoot!

They went together down the staircase and along the corridor and past the bath. As he passed the door he remembered with a vague fear the warm turf-coloured bogwater, the warm moist air, the noise of plunges, the smell of the towels, like medicine.

Brother Michael was standing at the door of the infirmary and from the door of the dark cabinet on his right came a smell like medicine. That came from the bottles on the shelves. The prefect spoke to Brother Michael and Brother Michael answered and called the prefect sir. He had reddish hair mixed with grey and a queer look.

It was queer that he would always be a brother. It was queer too that you could not call him sir because he was a brother and had a different kind of look. Was he not holy enough or why could he not catch up on the others?

There were two beds in the room and in one bed there was a fellow: and when they went in he called out:

—Hello! It's young Dedalus! What's up?

—The sky is up, Brother Michael said.

He was a fellow out of the third of grammar and, while Stephen was undressing, he asked Brother Michael to bring him a round of buttered toast.

—Ah, do! he said.

—Butter you up! said Brother Michael. You'll get your walking papers in the morning when the doctor comes.

—Will I? the fellow said. I'm not well yet.

Brother Michael repeated:

—You'll get your walking papers. I tell you.

He bent down to rake the fire. He had a long back like the long back of a tramhorse. He shook the poker gravely and nodded his head at the fellow out of third of grammar.

Then Brother Michael went away and after a while the fellow out of third of grammar turned in towards the wall and fell asleep.

That was the infirmary. He was sick then. Had they written home to tell his mother and father? But it would be quicker for one of the priests to go himself to tell them. Or he would write a letter for the priest to bring.

Dear Mother,

I am sick. I want to go home. Please come and take me home. I am in the infirmary.

Your fond son,

Stephen

How far away they were! There was cold sunlight outside the window. He wondered if he would die. You could die just the same on a sunny day. He might die before his mother came. Then he would have a dead mass in the chapel like the way the fellows had told him it was when Little had died. All the fellows would be at the mass, dressed in black, all with sad faces. Wells too would be there but no fellow would look at him. The rector would be there in a cope of black and gold and there would be tall yellow candles on the altar and round the catafalque. And they would carry the coffin out of the chapel slowly and he would be buried in the little graveyard of the community off the main avenue of limes. And Wells would be sorry then for what he had done. And the bell would toll slowly.

He could hear the tolling. He said over to himself the song that Brigid had taught him.

> *Dingdong! The castle bell!*
> *Farewell, my mother!*
> *Bury me in the old churchyard*
> *Beside my eldest brother.*
> *My coffin shall be black,*
> *Six angels at my back,*
> *Two to sing and two to pray*
> *And two to carry my soul away.*

How beautiful and sad that was! How beautiful the words were where they said *Bury me in the old churchyard!* A tremor passed over his body. How sad and how beautiful! He wanted to cry quietly but not for himself: for the words, so beautiful and sad, like music. The bell! The bell! Farewell! O farewell!

The cold sunlight was weaker and Brother Michael was standing at his bedside with a bowl of beef-tea. He was glad for his mouth was hot and dry. He could hear them playing in the playgrounds. And the day was going on in the college just as if he were there.

Then Brother Michael was going away and the fellow out of the third of grammar told him to be sure and come back and tell him all the news in the paper. He told Stephen that his name was Athy and that his father kept a lot of racehorses that were spiffing jumpers and that his father would give a good tip to Brother Michael any time he wanted it because Brother Michael was very decent and always told him the news out of the paper they got every day up in the castle. There was every kind of news in the paper: accidents, shipwrecks, sports, and politics.

—Now it is all about politics in the papers, he said. Do your people talk about that too?

—Yes, Stephen said.

—Mine too, he said.

Then he thought for a moment and said:

—You have a queer name, Dedalus, and I have a queer name too, Athy. My name is the name of a town. Your name is like Latin.

Then he asked:

—Are you good at riddles?

Stephen answered:

—Not very good.

Then he said:

—Can you answer me this one? Why is the county of Kildare like the leg of a fellow's breeches?

Stephen thought what could be the answer and then said:

—I give it up.

—Because there is a thigh in it, he said. Do you see the joke? Athy is the town in the county Kildare and a thigh is the other thigh.

—Oh, I see, Stephen said.

—That's an old riddle, he said.

After a moment he said:

—I say!

—What? asked Stephen.

—You know, he said, you can ask that riddle another way.

—Can you? said Stephen.

—The same riddle, he said. Do you know the other way to ask it?

—No, said Stephen.

—Can you not think of the other way? he said.

He looked at Stephen over the bedclothes as he spoke. Then he lay back on the pillow and said:

—There is another way but I won't tell you what it is.

Why did he not tell it? His father, who kept the racehorses, must be a magistrate too like Saurin's father and Nasty Roche's father. He thought of his own father, of how he sang songs while his mother played and of how he always gave him a shilling when he asked for sixpence and he felt sorry for him that he was not a magistrate like the other boys' fathers. Then why was he sent to that place with them? But his father had told him that he would be no stranger there because his granduncle had presented an address to the liberator there fifty years before. You could know the people of that time by their old dress. It seemed to him a solemn time: and he wondered if that was the time when the fellows in Clongowes wore blue coats with brass buttons and yellow waistcoats and caps of rabbitskin and drank beer like grown-up people and kept greyhounds of their own to course the hares with.

He looked at the window and saw that the daylight had grown weaker. There would be cloudy grey light over the playgrounds. There was no noise on the playgrounds. The class must be doing the themes or perhaps Father Arnall was reading out of the book.

It was queer that they had not given him any medicine. Perhaps Brother Michael would bring it back when he came. They said you got stinking stuff to drink when you were in the infirmary. But he felt better now than before. It would be nice getting better slowly. You could get a book then. There was a book in the library about Holland. There were lovely foreign names in it and pictures of strange looking cities and ships. It made you feel so happy.

How pale the light was at the window! But that was nice. The fire rose and fell on the wall. It was like waves. Someone had put coal on and he heard voices. They were talking. It was the noise of the waves. Or the waves were talking among themselves as they rose and fell.

He saw the sea of waves, long dark waves rising and falling, dark under the moonless night. A tiny light twinkled at the pierhead where the ship was entering: and he saw a multitude of people gathered by the waters' edge to see the ship that was entering their harbour. A tall man stood on the deck, looking out towards the flat dark land: and by the light at the pierhead he saw his face, the sorrowful face of Brother Michael.

He saw him lift his hand towards the people and heard him say in a loud voice of sorrow over the waters:

—He is dead. We saw him lying upon the catafalque.

A wail of sorrow went up from the people.

—Parnell! Parnell! He is dead!

They fell upon their knees, moaning in sorrow.

And he saw Dante in a maroon velvet dress and with a green velvet mantle hanging from her shoulders walking proudly and silently past the people who knelt by the water's edge.

***

A great fire, banked high and red, flamed in the grate and under the ivy-twined branches of the chandelier the Christmas table was spread. They had come home a little late and still dinner was not ready: but it would be ready in a jiffy his mother had said. They were waiting for the door to open and for the servants to come in, holding the big dishes covered with their heavy metal covers.

All were waiting: uncle Charles, who sat far away in the shadow of the window, Dante and Mr Casey, who sat in the easy-chairs at either side of the hearth, Stephen, seated on a chair between them, his feet resting on the toasted boss. Mr Dedalus looked at himself in the pierglass above the mantelpiece, waxed out his moustache ends and then, parting his coat-tails, stood with his back to the glowing fire: and still from time to time he withdrew a hand from his coat-tail to wax out one of his moustache ends. Mr Casey leaned his head to one side and, smiling, tapped the gland of his neck with his fingers. And Stephen smiled too for he knew now that it was not true that Mr Casey had a purse of silver in his throat. He smiled to think how the silvery noise which Mr Casey used to make had deceived him. And when he had tried to open Mr Casey's hand to see if the purse of silver was hidden there he had seen that the fingers could not be straightened out: and Mr Casey had told him that he had got those three cramped fingers making a birthday present for Queen Victoria.

Mr Casey tapped the gland of his neck and smiled at Stephen with sleepy eyes: and Mr Dedalus said to him:

—Yes. Well now, that's all right. O, we had a good walk, hadn't we, John? Yes . . . I wonder if there's any likelihood of dinner this evening. Yes . . . O, well now, we got a good breath of ozone round the Head today. Ay, bedad.

He turned to Dante and said:

—You didn't stir out at all, Mrs Riordan?

Dante frowned and said shortly:

—No.

Mr Dedalus dropped his coat-tails and went over to the sideboard. He brought forth a great stone jar of whisky from the locker and filled the decanter slowly, bending now and then to see how much he had poured in. Then replacing the jar in the locker he poured a little of the whisky into two glasses, added a little water and came back with them to the fireplace.

—A thimbleful, John, he said, just to whet your appetite.

Mr Casey took the glass, drank, and placed it near him on the mantelpiece. Then he said:

—Well, I can't help thinking of our friend Christopher manufacturing . . .

He broke into a fit of laughter and coughing and added:

—. . . manufacturing that champagne for those fellows.

Mr Dedalus laughed loudly.

—Is it Christy? he said. There's more cunning in one of those warts on his bald head than in a pack of jack foxes.

He inclined his head, closed his eyes, and, licking his lips profusely, began to speak with the voice of the hotel keeper.

—And he has such a soft mouth when he's speaking to you, don't you know. He's very moist and watery about the dewlaps, God bless him.

Mr Casey was still struggling through his fit of coughing and laughter. Stephen, seeing and hearing the hotel keeper through his father's face and voice, laughed.

Mr Dedalus put up his eyeglass and, staring down at him, said quietly and kindly:

—What are you laughing at, you little puppy, you?

The servants entered and placed the dishes on the table. Mrs Dedalus followed and the places were arranged.

—Sit over, she said.

Mr Dedalus went to the end of the table and said:

—Now, Mrs Riordan, sit over. John, sit you down, my hearty.

He looked round to where uncle Charles sat and said:

—Now then, sir, there's a bird here waiting for you.

When all had taken their seats he laid his hand on the cover and then said quickly, withdrawing it:

—Now, Stephen.

Stephen stood up in his place to say the grace before meals:

Bless us, O Lord, and these Thy gifts which through Thy bounty we are about to receive through Christ our Lord. Amen.

All blessed themselves and Mr Dedalus with a sigh of pleasure lifted from the dish the heavy cover pearled around the edge with glistening drops.

Stephen looked at the plump turkey which had lain, trussed and skewered, on the kitchen table. He knew that his father had paid a guinea for it in Dunn's of D'Olier Street and that the man had prodded it often at the breastbone to show how good it was: and he remembered the man's voice when he had said:

—Take that one, sir. That's the real Ally Daly.

Why did Mr Barrett in Clongowes call his pandybat a turkey? But Clongowes was far away: and the warm heavy smell of turkey and ham and celery rose from the plates and dishes and the great fire was banked high and red in the grate and the green ivy and red holly made you feel so happy and when dinner was ended the big plum pudding would be carried in, studded with peeled almonds and sprigs of holly, with bluish fire running around it and a little green flag flying from the top.

It was his first Christmas dinner and he thought of his little brothers and sisters who were waiting in the nursery, as he had often waited, till the pudding came. The deep low collar and the Eton jacket made him feel queer and oldish: and that morning when his mother had brought him down to the parlour, dressed for mass, his father had cried. That was because he was thinking of his own father. And uncle Charles had said so too.

Mr Dedalus covered the dish and began to eat hungrily. Then he said:

—Poor old Christy, he's nearly lopsided now with roguery.

—Simon, said Mrs Dedalus, you haven't given Mrs Riordan any sauce.

Mr Dedalus seized the sauceboat.

—Haven't I? he cried. Mrs Riordan, pity the poor blind.

Dante covered her plate with her hands and said:

—No, thanks.

Mr Dedalus turned to uncle Charles.

—How are you off, sir?

—Right as the mail, Simon.

—You, John?

—I'm all right. Go on yourself.

—Mary? Here, Stephen, here's something to make your hair curl.

He poured sauce freely over Stephen's plate and set the boat again on the table. Then he asked uncle Charles was it tender. Uncle Charles could not speak because his mouth was full; but he nodded that it was.

—That was a good answer our friend made to the canon. What? said Mr Dedalus.

—I didn't think he had that much in him, said Mr Casey.

—*I'll pay your dues, father, when you cease turning the house of god into a polling-booth.*

—A nice answer, said Dante, for any man calling himself a catholic to give to his priest.

—They have only themselves to blame, said Mr Dedalus suavely. If they took a fool's advice they would confine their attention to religion.

—It is religion, Dante said. They are doing their duty in warning the people.

—We go to the house of God, Mr Casey said, in all humility to pray to our Maker and not to hear election addresses.

—It is religion, Dante said again. They are right. They must direct their flocks.

—And preach politics from the altar, is it? asked Mr Dedalus.

—Certainly, said Dante. It is a question of public morality. A priest would not be a priest if he did not tell his flock what is right and what is wrong.

Mrs Dedalus laid down her knife and fork, saying:

—For pity sake and for pity sake let us have no political discussion on this day of all days in the year.

—Quite right, ma'am, said uncle Charles. Now, Simon, that's quite enough now. Not another word now.

—Yes, yes, said Mr Dedalus quickly.

He uncovered the dish boldly and said:

—Now then, who's for more turkey?

Nobody answered. Dante said:

—Nice language for any catholic to use!

—Mrs Riordan, I appeal to you, said Mrs Dedalus, to let the matter drop now.

Dante turned on her and said:

—And am I to sit here and listen to the pastors of my church being flouted?

—Nobody is saying a word against them, said Mr Dedalus, so long as they don't meddle in politics.

—The bishops and priests of Ireland have spoken, said Dante, and they must be obeyed.

—Let them leave politics alone, said Mr Casey, or the people may leave their church alone.

—You hear? said Dante, turning to Mrs Dedalus.

—Mr Casey! Simon! said Mrs Dedalus, let it end now.

—Too bad! Too bad! said uncle Charles.

—What? cried Mr Dedalus. Were we to desert him at the bidding of the English people?

—He was no longer worthy to lead, said Dante. He was a public sinner.

—We are all sinners and black sinners, said Mr Casey coldly.

—*Woe be to the man by whom the scandal cometh! said Mrs Riordan. It would be better for him that a millstone were tied about his neck and that he were cast into the depths of the sea rather than that he should scandalize one of these, my least little ones.* That is the language of the Holy Ghost.

—And very bad language if you ask me, said Mr Dedalus coolly.

—Simon! Simon! said uncle Charles. The boy.

—Yes, yes, said Mr Dedalus. I meant about the . . . I was thinking about the bad language of the railway porter. Well now, that's all right. Here, Stephen, show me your plate, old chap. Eat away now. Here.

He heaped up the food on Stephen's plate and served uncle Charles and Mr Casey to large pieces of turkey and splashes of sauce. Mrs Dedalus was eating little and Dante sat with her hands in her lap. She was red in the face. Mr Dedalus rooted with the carvers at the end of the dish and said:

—There's a tasty bit here we call the pope's nose. If any lady or gentleman . . .

He held a piece of fowl up on the prong of the carving fork. Nobody spoke. He put it on his own plate, saying:

—Well, you can't say but you were asked. I think I had better eat it myself because I'm not well in my health lately.

He winked at Stephen and, replacing the dish-cover, began to eat again.

There was a silence while he ate. Then he said:

—Well now, the day kept up fine after all. There were plenty of strangers down too.

Nobody spoke. He said again:

—I think there were more strangers down than last Christmas.

He looked round at the others whose faces were bent towards their plates and, receiving no reply, waited for a moment and said bitterly:

—Well, my Christmas dinner has been spoiled anyhow.

—There could be neither luck nor grace, Dante said, in a house where there is no respect for the pastors of the church.

Mr Dedalus threw his knife and fork noisily on his plate.

—Respect! he said. Is it for Billy with the lip or for the tub of guts up in Armagh? Respect!

—Princes of the church, said Mr Casey with slow scorn.

—Lord Leitrim's coachman, yes, said Mr Dedalus.

—They are the Lord's anointed, Dante said. They are an honour to their country.

—Tub of guts, said Mr Dedalus coarsely. He has a handsome face, mind you, in repose. You should see that fellow lapping up his bacon and cabbage of a cold winter's day. O Johnny!

He twisted his features into a grimace of heavy bestiality and made a lapping noise with his lips.

—Really, Simon, you should not speak that way before Stephen. It's not right.

—O, he'll remember all this when he grows up, said Dante hotly—the language he heard against God and religion and priests in his own home.

—Let him remember too, cried Mr Casey to her from across the table, the language with which the priests and the priests' pawns broke Parnell's heart and hounded him into his grave. Let him remember that too when he grows up.

—Sons of bitches! cried Mr Dedalus. When he was down they turned on him to betray him and rend him like rats in a sewer. Low-lived dogs! And they look it! By Christ, they look it!

—They behaved rightly, cried Dante. They obeyed their bishops and their priests. Honour to them!

—Well, it is perfectly dreadful to say that not even for one day in the year, said Mrs Dedalus, can we be free from these dreadful disputes!

Uncle Charles raised his hands mildly and said:

—Come now, come now, come now! Can we not have our opinions whatever they are without this bad temper and this bad language? It is too bad surely.

Mrs Dedalus spoke to Dante in a low voice but Dante said loudly:

—I will not say nothing. I will defend my church and my religion when it is insulted and spit on by renegade catholics.

Mr Casey pushed his plate rudely into the middle of the table and, resting his elbows before him, said in a hoarse voice to his host:

—Tell me, did I tell you that story about a very famous spit?

—You did not, John, said Mr Dedalus.

—Why then, said Mr Casey, it is a most instructive story. It happened not long ago in the county Wicklow where we are now.

He broke off and, turning towards Dante, said with quiet indignation:

—And I may tell you, ma'am, that I, if you mean me, am no renegade catholic. I am a catholic as my father was and his father before him and his father before him again, when we gave up our lives rather than sell our faith.

—The more shame to you now, Dante said, to speak as you do.

—The story, John, said Mr Dedalus smiling. Let us have the story anyhow.

—Catholic indeed! repeated Dante ironically. The blackest protestant in the land would not speak the language I have heard this evening.

Mr Dedalus began to sway his head to and fro, crooning like a country singer.

—I am no protestant, I tell you again, said Mr Casey, flushing.

Mr Dedalus, still crooning and swaying his head, began to sing in a grunting nasal tone:

> *O, come all you Roman catholics*
> *That never went to mass.*

He took up his knife and fork again in good humour and set to eating, saying to Mr Casey:

—Let us have the story, John. It will help us to digest.

Stephen looked with affection at Mr Casey's face which stared across the table over his joined hands. He liked to sit near him at the fire, looking up at his dark fierce face. But his dark eyes were never fierce and his slow voice was good to listen to. But why was he then against the priests? Because Dante must be right then. But he had heard his father say that she was a spoiled nun and that she had come out of the convent in the Alleghanies when her brother had got the money from the savages for the trinkets and the chainies. Perhaps that made her severe against Parnell. And she did not like him to play with Eileen because Eileen was a protestant and when she was young she knew children that used to play with protestants and the protestants used to make fun of the litany of the Blessed Virgin. *Tower of Ivory*, they used to say, *House of Gold!* How could a woman be a tower of ivory or a house of gold? Who was right then? And he remembered the evening in the infirmary in Clongowes, the dark waters, the light at the pierhead and the moan of sorrow from the people when they had heard.

Eileen had long white hands. One evening when playing tig she had put her hands over his eyes: long and white and thin and cold and soft. That was ivory: a cold white thing. That was the meaning of *Tower of Ivory*.

—The story is very short and sweet, Mr Casey said. It was one day down in Arklow, a cold bitter day, not long before the chief died. May God have mercy on him!

He closed his eyes wearily and paused. Mr Dedalus took a bone from his plate and tore some meat from it with his teeth, saying:

—Before he was killed, you mean.

Mr Casey opened his eyes, sighed and went on:

—It was down in Arklow one day. We were down there at a meeting and after the meeting was over we had to make our way to the railway station through the crowd. Such booing and baaing, man, you never heard. They called us all the names in the world. Well there was one old lady, and a drunken old harridan she was surely, that paid all her attention to me. She kept dancing along beside me in the mud bawling and screaming into my face: *Priest-Hunter! The Paris Funds! Mr Fox! Kitty O'Shea!*

—And what did you do, John? asked Mr Dedalus.

—I let her bawl away, said Mr Casey. It was a cold day and to keep up my heart I had (saving your presence, ma'am) a quid of Tullamore in my mouth and sure I couldn't say a word in any case because my mouth was full of tobacco juice.

—Well, John?

—Well. I let her bawl away, to her heart's content, *Kitty O'Shea* and the rest of it till at last she called that lady a name that I won't sully this Christmas board nor your ears, ma'am, nor my own lips by repeating.

He paused. Mr Dedalus, lifting his head from the bone, asked:

—And what did you do, John?

—Do! said Mr Casey. She stuck her ugly old face up at me when she said it and I had my mouth full of tobacco juice. I bent down to her and *Phth!* says I to her like that.

He turned aside and made the act of spitting.

—*Phth!* says I to her like that, right into her eye.

He clapped his hand to his eye and gave a hoarse scream of pain.

—*O Jesus, Mary and Joseph! says she. I'm blinded! I'm blinded and drownded!*
He stopped in a fit of coughing and laughter, repeating:
—*I'm blinded entirely.*

Mr Dedalus laughed loudly and lay back in his chair while uncle Charles swayed his head to and fro.

Dante looked terribly angry and repeated while they laughed:
—Very nice! Ha! Very nice!

It was not nice about the spit in the woman's eye. But what was the name the woman had called Kitty O'Shea that Mr Casey would not repeat? He thought of Mr Casey walking through the crowds of people and making speeches from a wagonette. That was what he had been in prison for and he remembered that one night Sergeant O'Neill had come to the house and had stood in the hall, talking in a low voice with his father and chewing nervously at the chinstrap of his cap. And that night Mr Casey had not gone to Dublin by train but a car had come to the door and he had heard his father say something about the Cabinteely road.

He was for Ireland and Parnell and so was his father: and so was Dante too for one night at the band on the esplanade she had hit a gentleman on the head with her umbrella because he had taken off his hat when the band played *God save the Queen* at the end.

Mr Dedalus gave a snort of contempt.

—Ah, John, he said. It is true for them. We are an unfortunate priest-ridden race and always were and always will be till the end of the chapter.

Uncle Charles shook his head, saying:
—A bad business! A bad business!

Mr Dedalus repeated:
—A priest-ridden Godforsaken race!

He pointed to the portrait of his grandfather on the wall to his right.

—Do you see that old chap up there, John? he said. He was a good Irishman when there was no money in the job. He was condemned to death as a whiteboy. But he had a saying about our clerical friends, that he would never let one of them put his two feet under his mahogany.

Dante broke in angrily:
—If we are a priest-ridden race we ought to be proud of it! They are the apple of God's eye. *Touch them not, says* Christ, *for they are the apple of My eye.*

—And can we not love our country then? asked Mr Casey. Are we not to follow the man that was born to lead us?

—A traitor to his country! replied Dante. A traitor, an adulterer! The priests were right to abandon him. The priests were always the true friends of Ireland.

—Were they, faith? said Mr Casey.

He threw his fist on the table and, frowning angrily, protruded one finger after another.

—Didn't the bishops of Ireland betray us in the time of the union when Bishop Lanigan presented an address of loyalty to the Marquess Cornwallis? Didn't the bishops and priests sell the aspirations of their country in 1829 in return for catholic emancipation? Didn't they denounce the fenian movement from the pulpit and in the confession box? And didn't they dishonour the ashes of Terence Bellew MacManus?

His face was glowing with anger and Stephen felt the glow rise to his own cheek as the spoken words thrilled him. Mr Dedalus uttered a guffaw of coarse scorn.

—O, by God, he cried, I forgot little old Paul Cullen! Another apple of God's eye!

Dante bent across the table and cried to Mr Casey:

—Right! Right! They were always right! God and morality and religion come first.

Mrs Dedalus, seeing her excitement, said to her:

—Mrs Riordan, don't excite yourself answering them.

—God and religion before everything! Dante cried. God and religion before the world.

Mr Casey raised his clenched fist and brought it down on the table with a crash.

—Very well then, he shouted hoarsely, if it comes to that, no God for Ireland!

—John! John! cried Mr Dedalus, seizing his guest by the coat sleeve.

Dante stared across the table, her cheeks shaking. Mr Casey struggled up from his chair and bent across the table towards her, scraping the air from before his eyes with one hand as though he were tearing aside a cobweb.

—No God for Ireland! he cried. We have had too much God In Ireland. Away with God!

—Blasphemer! Devil! screamed Dante, starting to her feet and almost spitting in his face.

Uncle Charles and Mr Dedalus pulled Mr Casey back into his chair again, talking to him from both sides reasonably. He stared before him out of his dark flaming eyes, repeating:

—Away with God, I say!

Dante shoved her chair violently aside and left the table, upsetting her napkin-ring which rolled slowly along the carpet and came to rest against the foot of an easy-chair. Mrs Dedalus rose quickly and followed her towards the door. At the door Dante turned round violently and shouted down the room, her cheeks flushed and quivering with rage:

—Devil out of hell! We won! We crushed him to death! Fiend!

The door slammed behind her.

Mr Casey, freeing his arms from his holders, suddenly bowed his head on his hands with a sob of pain.

—Poor Parnell! he cried loudly. My dead king!

He sobbed loudly and bitterly.

Stephen, raising his terror-stricken face, saw that his father's eyes were full of tears.

***

The fellows talked together in little groups.

One fellow said:

—They were caught near the Hill of Lyons.

—Who caught them?

—Mr Gleeson and the minister. They were on a car. The same fellow added:

—A fellow in the higher line told me.

Fleming asked:

—But why did they run away, tell us?

—I know why, Cecil Thunder said. Because they had fecked cash out of the rector's room.

—Who fecked it?

—Kickham's brother. And they all went shares in it.

—But that was stealing. How could they have done that?

—A fat lot you know about it, Thunder! Wells said. I know why they scut.

—Tell us why.

—I was told not to, Wells said.

—O, go on, Wells, all said. You might tell us. We won't let it out.

Stephen bent forward his head to hear. Wells looked round to see if anyone was coming. Then he said secretly:

—You know the altar wine they keep in the press in the sacristy?

—Yes.

—Well, they drank that and it was found out who did it by the smell. And that's why they ran away, if you want to know.

And the fellow who had spoken first said:

—Yes, that's what I heard too from the fellow in the higher line.

The fellows all were silent. Stephen stood among them, afraid to speak, listening. A faint sickness of awe made him feel weak. How could they have done that? He thought of the dark silent sacristy. There were dark wooden presses there where the crimped surplices lay quietly folded. It was not the chapel but still you had to speak under your breath. It was a holy place. He remembered the summer evening he had been there to be dressed as boatbearer, the evening of the Procession to the little altar in the wood. A strange and holy place. The boy that held the censer had swung it lifted by the middle chain to keep the coals lighting. That was called charcoal: and it had burned quietly as the fellow had swung it gently and had given off a weak sour smell. And then when all were vested he had stood holding out the boat to the rector and the rector had put a spoonful of incense in it and it had hissed on the red coals.

The fellows were talking together in little groups here and there on the playground. The fellows seemed to him to have grown smaller: that was because a sprinter had knocked him down the day before, a fellow out of second of grammar. He had been thrown by the fellow's machine lightly on the cinder path and his spectacles had been broken in three pieces and some of the grit of the cinders had gone into his mouth.

That was why the fellows seemed to him smaller and farther away and the goalposts so thin and far and the soft grey sky so high up. But there was no play on the football grounds for cricket was coming: and some said that Barnes would be prof and some said it would be Flowers. And all over the playgrounds they were playing rounders and bowling twisters and lobs. And from here and from there came the sounds of the cricket bats through the soft grey air. They said: pick, pack, pock, puck: little drops of water in a fountain slowly falling in the brimming bowl.

Athy, who had been silent, said quietly:

—You are all wrong.

All turned towards him eagerly.

—Why?

—Do you know?

—Who told you?

—Tell us, Athy.

Athy pointed across the playground to where Simon Moonan was walking by himself kicking a stone before him.

—Ask him, he said.

The fellows looked there and then said:

—Why him?

—Is he in it?

—Tell us, Athy. Go on. You might if you know.

Athy lowered his voice and said:

—Do you know why those fellows scut? I will tell you but you must not let on you know.

He paused for a moment and then said mysteriously:

—They were caught with Simon Moonan and Tusker Boyle in the square one night.

The fellows looked at him and asked:

—Caught?

—What doing?

Athy said:

—Smugging.

All the fellows were silent: and Athy said:

—And that's why.

Stephen looked at the faces of the fellows but they were all looking across the playground. He wanted to ask somebody about it. What did that mean about the smugging in the square? Why did the five fellows out of the higher line run away for that? It was a joke, he thought. Simon Moonan had nice clothes and one night he had shown him a ball of creamy sweets that the fellows of the football fifteen had rolled down to him along the carpet in the middle of the refectory when he was at the door. It was the night of the match against the Bective Rangers; and the ball was made just like a red and green apple only it opened and it was full of the creamy sweets. And one day Boyle had said that an elephant had two tuskers instead of two tusks and that was why he was called Tusker Boyle but some fellows called him Lady Boyle because he was always at his nails, paring them.

Eileen had long thin cool white hands too because she was a girl. They were like ivory; only soft. That was the meaning of *Tower of Ivory* but protestants could not understand it and made fun of it. One day he had stood beside her looking into the hotel grounds. A waiter was running up a trail of bunting on the flagstaff and a fox terrier was scampering to and fro on the sunny lawn. She had put her hand into his pocket where his hand was and he had felt how cool and thin and soft her hand was. She had said that pockets were funny things to have: and then all of a sudden she had broken away and had run laughing down the sloping curve of the path. Her fair hair had streamed out behind her like gold in the sun. *Tower of Ivory. House of Gold.* By thinking of things you could understand them.

But why in the square? You went there when you wanted to do something. It was all thick slabs of slate and water trickled all day out of tiny pinholes and there was a queer smell of stale water there. And behind the door of one of the closets there was a drawing in red pencil of a bearded man in a Roman dress with a brick in each hand and underneath was the name of the drawing:

Balbus was building a wall.

Some fellow had drawn it there for a cod. It had a funny face but it was very like a man with a beard. And on the wall of another closet there was written in backhand in beautiful writing:

Julius Caesar wrote The Calico Belly.

Perhaps that was why they were there because it was a place where some fellows wrote things for cod. But all the same it was queer what Athy said and the way he said it. It was not a cod because they had run away. He looked with the others across the playground and began to feel afraid.

At last Fleming said:

—And we are all to be punished for what other fellows did?

—I won't come back, see if I do, Cecil Thunder said. Three days' silence in the refectory and sending us up for six and eight every minute.

—Yes, said Wells. And old Barrett has a new way of twisting the note so that you can't open it and fold it again to see how many ferulae you are to get. I won't come back too.

—Yes, said Cecil Thunder, and the prefect of studies was in second of grammar this morning.

—Let us get up a rebellion, Fleming said. Will we?

All the fellows were silent. The air was very silent and you could hear the cricket bats but more slowly than before: pick, pock.

Wells asked:

—What is going to be done to them?

—Simon Moonan and Tusker are going to be flogged, Athy said, and the fellows in the higher line got their choice of flogging or being expelled.

—And which are they taking? asked the fellow who had spoken first.

—All are taking expulsion except Corrigan, Athy answered. He's going to be flogged by Mr Gleeson.

—I know why, Cecil Thunder said. He is right and the other fellows are wrong because a flogging wears off after a bit but a fellow that has been expelled from college is known all his life on account of it. Besides Gleeson won't flog him hard.

—It's best of his play not to, Fleming said.

—I wouldn't like to be Simon Moonan and Tusker, Cecil Thunder said. But I don't believe they will be flogged. Perhaps they will be sent up for twice nine.

—No, no, said Athy. They'll both get it on the vital spot.

Wells rubbed himself and said in a crying voice:

—Please, sir, let me off!

Athy grinned and turned up the sleeves of his jacket, saying:

It can't be helped;
It must be done.
So down with your breeches
And out with your bum.

The fellows laughed; but he felt that they were a little afraid. In the silence of the soft grey air he heard the cricket bats from here and from there: pock. That was a sound to hear but if you were hit then you would feel a pain. The pandybat made a sound too but not like that. The fellows said it was made of whalebone and leather with lead inside: and he wondered what was the pain like. There were different kinds of sounds. A long thin cane would have a high whistling sound and he wondered what was that pain like. It made him shivery to think of it and cold: and what Athy said too. But what was there to laugh at in it? It made him shivery: but that was because you always felt like a shiver when you let down your trousers. It was the same in the bath when you undressed yourself. He wondered who had to let them down, the master or the boy himself. O how could they laugh about it that way?

He looked at Athy's rolled-up sleeves and knuckly inky hands. He had rolled up his sleeves to show how Mr Gleeson would roll up his sleeves. But Mr Gleeson had round shiny cuffs and clean white wrists and fattish white hands and the nails of them were long and pointed. Perhaps he pared them too like Lady Boyle. But they were terribly long and pointed nails. So long and cruel they were, though the white fattish hands were not cruel but gentle. And though he trembled with cold and fright to think of the cruel long nails and of the high whistling sound of the cane and of the chill you felt at the end of your shirt when you undressed yourself yet he felt a feeling of queer quiet pleasure inside him to think of the white fattish hands, clean and strong and gentle. And he thought of what Cecil Thunder had said: that Mr Gleeson would not flog Corrigan hard. And Fleming had said he would not because it was best of his play not to. But that was not why

A voice from far out on the playground cried:

—All in!

And other voices cried:

—All in! All in!

During the writing lesson he sat with his arms folded, listening to the slow scraping of the pens. Mr Harford went to and fro making little signs in red pencil and sometimes sitting beside the boy to show him how to hold his pen. He had tried to spell out the headline for himself though he knew already what it was for it was the last of the book. *Zeal without prudence is like a ship adrift.* But the lines of the letters were like fine invisible threads and it was only by closing his right eye tight and staring out of the left eye that he could make out the full curves of the capital.

But Mr Harford was very decent and never got into a wax. All the other masters got into dreadful waxes. But why were they to suffer for what fellows in the higher line did? Wells had said that they had drunk some of the altar wine out of the press in the sacristy and that it had been found out who had done it by the smell. Perhaps they had stolen a monstrance to run away with and sell it somewhere. That must have been a terrible sin, to go in there quietly at night, to open the dark press and steal the flashing gold thing into which God was put on the altar in the middle of flowers and candles at benediction while the incense went up in clouds at both sides as the fellow swung the censer and Dominic Kelly sang the first part by himself in the choir. But God was not in it of course when they stole it. But still it was a strange and a great sin even to touch it. He thought of it with deep awe; a terrible and strange sin: it thrilled him to think of it in the silence when the pens scraped lightly. But to drink the altar wine out of the press and be found out by the smell was a sin too: but it was not terrible and strange. It only made you feel a little sickish on account of the smell of the wine. Because on the day when he had made his first holy communion in the chapel he had shut his eyes and opened his mouth and put out his tongue a little: and when the rector had stooped down to give him the holy communion he had smelt a faint winy smell off the rector's breath after the wine of the mass. The word was beautiful: wine. It made you think of dark purple because the grapes were dark purple that grew in Greece outside houses like white temples. But the faint smell of the rector's breath had made him feel a sick feeling on the morning of his first communion. The day of your first communion was the happiest day of your life. And once a lot of generals had asked Napoleon what was the happiest day of his life. They thought he would say the day he won some great battle or the day he was made an emperor. But he said:

—Gentlemen, the happiest day of my life was the day on which I made my first holy communion.

Father Arnall came in and the Latin lesson began and he remained still, leaning on the desk with his arms folded. Father Arnall gave out the theme-books and he said that they were scandalous and that they were all to be written out again with the corrections at once. But the worst of all was Fleming's theme because the pages were stuck together by a blot: and Father Arnall held it up by a corner and said it was an insult to any master to send him up such a theme. Then he asked Jack Lawton to decline the noun *mare* and Jack Lawton stopped at the ablative singular and could not go on with the plural.

—You should be ashamed of yourself, said Father Arnall sternly. You, the leader of the class!

Then he asked the next boy and the next and the next. Nobody knew. Father Arnall became very quiet, more and more quiet as each boy tried to answer it and could not. But his face was black-looking and his eyes were staring though his voice was so quiet. Then he asked Fleming and Fleming said that the word had no plural. Father Arnall suddenly shut the book and shouted at him:

—Kneel out there in the middle of the class. You are one of the idlest boys I ever met. Copy out your themes again the rest of you.

Fleming moved heavily out of his place and knelt between the two last benches. The other boys bent over their theme-books and began to write. A silence filled the classroom and Stephen, glancing timidly at Father Arnall's dark face, saw that it was a little red from the wax he was in.

Was that a sin for Father Arnall to be in a wax or was he allowed to get into a wax when the boys were idle because that made them study better or was he only letting on to be in a wax? It was because he was allowed, because a priest would know what a sin was and would not do it. But if he did it one time by mistake what would he do to go to confession? Perhaps he would go to confession to the minister. And if the minister did it he would go to the rector: and the rector to the provincial: and the provincial to the general of the jesuits. That was called the order: and he had heard his father say that they were all clever men. They could all have become high-up people in the world if they had not become jesuits. And he wondered what Father Arnall and Paddy Barrett would have become and what Mr McGlade and Mr Gleeson would have become if they had not become jesuits. It was hard to think what because you would have to think of them in a different way with different coloured coats and trousers and with beards and moustaches and different kinds of hats.

The door opened quietly and closed. A quick whisper ran through the class: the prefect of studies. There was an instant of dead silence and then the loud crack of a pandybat on the last desk. Stephen's heart leapt up in fear.

—Any boys want flogging here, Father Arnall? cried the prefect of studies. Any lazy idle loafers that want flogging in this class?

He came to the middle of the class and saw Fleming on his knees.

—Hoho! he cried. Who is this boy? Why is he on his knees? What is your name, boy?

—Fleming, sir.

—Hoho, Fleming! An idler of course. I can see it in your eye. Why is he on his knees, Father Arnall?

—He wrote a bad Latin theme, Father Arnall said, and he missed all the questions in grammar.

—Of course he did! cried the prefect of studies, of course he did! A born idler! I can see it in the corner of his eye.

He banged his pandybat down on the desk and cried:

—Up, Fleming! Up, my boy!

Fleming stood up slowly.

—Hold out! cried the prefect of studies.

Fleming held out his hand. The pandybat came down on it with a loud smacking sound: one, two, three, four, five, six.

—Other hand!

The pandybat came down again in six loud quick smacks.

—Kneel down! cried the prefect of studies.

Fleming knelt down, squeezing his hands under his armpits, his face contorted with pain; but Stephen knew how hard his hands were because Fleming was always rubbing rosin into them. But perhaps he was in great pain for the noise of the pandybat was terrible. Stephen's heart was beating and fluttering.

—At your work, all of you! shouted the prefect of studies. We want no lazy idle loafers here, lazy idle little schemers. At your work, I tell you. Father Dolan will be in to see you every day. Father Dolan will be in tomorrow.

He poked one of the boys in the side with his pandybat, saying:

—You, boy! When will Father Dolan be in again?

—Tomorrow, sir, said Tom Furlong's voice.

—Tomorrow and tomorrow and tomorrow, said the prefect of studies. Make up your minds for that. Every day Father Dolan. Write away. You, boy, who are you?

Stephen's heart jumped suddenly.

—Dedalus, sir.

—Why are you not writing like the others?

—I . . . my . . .

He could not speak with fright.

—Why is he not writing, Father Arnall?

—He broke his glasses, said Father Arnall, and I exempted him from work.

—Broke? What is this I hear? What is this? Your name is! said the prefect of studies.

—Dedalus, sir.

—Out here, Dedalus. Lazy little schemer. I see schemer in your face. Where did you break your glasses?

Stephen stumbled into the middle of the class, blinded by fear and haste.

—Where did you break your glasses? repeated the prefect of studies.

—The cinder-path, sir.

—Hoho! The cinder-path! cried the prefect of studies. I know that trick.

Stephen lifted his eyes in wonder and saw for a moment Father Dolan's white-grey not young face, his baldy white-grey head with fluff at the sides of it, the steel rims of his spectacles and his no-coloured eyes looking through the glasses. Why did he say he knew that trick?

—Lazy idle little loafer! cried the prefect of studies. Broke my glasses! An old schoolboy trick! Out with your hand this moment!

Stephen closed his eyes and held out in the air his trembling hand with the palm upwards. He felt the prefect of studies touch it for a moment at the fingers to straighten it and then the swish of the sleeve of the soutane as the pandybat was lifted to strike. A hot burning stinging tingling blow like the loud crack of a broken stick made his trembling hand crumple together like a leaf in the fire: and at the sound and the pain scalding tears were driven into his eyes. His whole body was shaking with fright, his arm was shaking and his crumpled burning livid hand shook like a loose leaf in the air. A cry sprang to his lips, a prayer to be let off. But though the tears scalded his eyes and his limbs quivered with pain and fright he held back the hot tears and the cry that scalded his throat.

—Other hand! shouted the prefect of studies.

Stephen drew back his maimed and quivering right arm and held out his left hand. The soutane sleeve swished again as the pandybat was lifted and a loud crashing sound and a fierce maddening tingling burning pain made his hand shrink together with the palms and fingers in a livid quivering mass. The scalding water burst forth from his eyes and, burning with shame and agony and fear, he drew back his shaking arm in terror and burst out into a whine of pain. His body shook with a palsy of fright and in shame and rage he felt the scalding cry come from his throat and the scalding tears falling out of his eyes and down his flaming cheeks.

—Kneel down, cried the prefect of studies.

Stephen knelt down quickly pressing his beaten hands to his sides. To think of them beaten and swollen with pain all in a moment made him feel so sorry for them as if they were not his own but someone else's that he felt sorry for. And as he knelt, calming the last sobs in his throat and feeling the burning tingling pain pressed into his sides, he thought of the hands which he had held out in the air with the palms up and of the firm touch of the prefect of studies when he had steadied the shaking fingers and of the beaten swollen reddened mass of palm and fingers that shook helplessly in the air.

—Get at your work, all of you, cried the prefect of studies from the door. Father Dolan will be in every day to see if any boy, any lazy idle little loafer wants flogging. Every day. Every day.

The door closed behind him.

The hushed class continued to copy out the themes. Father Arnall rose from his seat and went among them, helping the boys with gentle words and telling them the mistakes they had made. His voice was very gentle and soft. Then he returned to his seat and said to Fleming and Stephen:

—You may return to your places, you two.

Fleming and Stephen rose and, walking to their seats, sat down. Stephen, scarlet with shame, opened a book quickly with one weak hand and bent down upon it, his face close to the page.

It was unfair and cruel because the doctor had told him not to read without glasses and he had written home to his father that morning to send him a new pair. And Father Arnall had said that he need not study till the new glasses came. Then to be called a schemer before the class and to be pandied when he always got the card for first or second and was the leader of the Yorkists! How could the prefect of studies know that it was a trick? He felt the touch of the prefect's fingers as they had steadied his hand and at first he had thought he was going to shake hands with him because the fingers were soft and firm: but then in an instant he had heard the swish of the soutane sleeve and the crash. It was cruel and unfair to make him kneel in the middle of the class then: and Father Arnall had told them both that they might return to their places without making any difference between them. He listened to Father Arnall's low and gentle voice as he corrected the themes. Perhaps he was sorry now and wanted to be decent. But it was unfair and cruel. The prefect of studies was a priest but that was cruel and unfair. And his white-grey face and the no-coloured eyes behind the steel-rimmed spectacles were cruel looking because he had steadied the hand first with his firm soft fingers and that was to hit it better and louder.

—It's a stinking mean thing, that's what it is, said Fleming in the corridor as the classes were passing out in file to the refectory, to pandy a fellow for what is not his fault.

—You really broke your glasses by accident, didn't you? Nasty Roche asked.

Stephen felt his heart filled by Fleming's words and did not answer.

—Of course he did! said Fleming. I wouldn't stand it. I'd go up and tell the rector on him.

—Yes, said Cecil Thunder eagerly, and I saw him lift the pandy-bat over his shoulder and he's not allowed to do that.

—Did they hurt you much? Nasty Roche asked.

—Very much, Stephen said.

—I wouldn't stand it, Fleming repeated, from Baldyhead or any other Baldyhead. It's a stinking mean low trick, that's what it is. I'd go straight up to the rector and tell him about it after dinner.

—Yes, do. Yes, do, said Cecil Thunder.

—Yes, do. Yes, go up and tell the rector on him, Dedalus, said Nasty Roche, because he said that he'd come in tomorrow again and pandy you.

—Yes, yes. Tell the rector, all said.

And there were some fellows out of second of grammar listening and one of them said:

—The senate and the Roman people declared that Dedalus had been wrongly punished.

It was wrong; it was unfair and cruel; and, as he sat in the refectory, he suffered time after time in memory the same humiliation until he began to wonder whether it might not really be that there was something in his face which made him look like a schemer and he wished he had a little mirror to see. But there could not be; and it was unjust and cruel and unfair.

He could not eat the blackish fish fritters they got on Wednesdays in lent and one of his potatoes had the mark of the spade in it. Yes, he would do what the fellows had told him. He would go up and tell the rector that he had been wrongly punished. A thing like that had been done before by somebody in history, by some great person whose head was in the books of history. And the rector would declare that he had been wrongly punished because the senate and the Roman people always declared that the men who did that had been wrongly punished. Those were the great men whose names were in Richmal Magnall's Questions. History was all about those men and what they did and that was what Peter Parley's Tales about Greece and Rome were all about. Peter Parley himself was on the first page in a picture. There was a road over a heath with grass at the side and little bushes: and Peter Parley had a broad hat like a protestant minister and a big stick and he was walking fast along the road to Greece and Rome.

It was easy what he had to do. All he had to do was when the dinner was over and he came out in his turn to go on walking but not out to the corridor but up the staircase on the right that led to the castle. He had nothing to do but that: to turn to the right and walk fast up the staircase and in half a minute he would be in the low dark narrow corridor that led through the castle to the rector's room. And every fellow had said that it was unfair, even the fellow out of second of grammar who had said that about the senate and the Roman people.

What would happen? He heard the fellows of the higher line stand up at the top of the refectory and heard their steps as they came down the matting: Paddy Rath and Jimmy Magee and the Spaniard and the Portuguese and the fifth was big Corrigan who was going to be flogged by Mr Gleeson. That was why the prefect of studies had called him a schemer and pandied him for nothing: and, straining his weak eyes, tired with the tears, he watched big Corrigan's broad shoulders and big hanging black head passing in the file. But he had done something and besides Mr Gleeson would not flog him hard: and he remembered how big Corrigan looked in the bath. He had skin the same colour as the turf-coloured bogwater in the shallow end of the bath and when he walked along the side his feet slapped loudly on the wet tiles and at every step his thighs shook a little because he was fat.

The refectory was half empty and the fellows were still passing out in file. He could go up the staircase because there was never a priest or a prefect outside the refectory door. But he could not go. The rector would side with the prefect of studies and think it was a schoolboy trick and then the prefect of studies would come in every day the same, only it would be worse because he would be dreadfully waxy at any fellow going up to the rector about him. The fellows had told him to go but they would not go themselves. They had forgotten all about it. No, it was best to forget all about it and perhaps the prefect of studies had only said he would come in. No, it was best to hide out of the way because when you were small and young you could often escape that way.

The fellows at his table stood up. He stood up and passed out among them in the file. He had to decide. He was coming near the door. If he went on with the fellows he could never go up to the rector because he could not leave the playground for that. And if he went and was pandied all the same all the fellows would make fun and talk about young Dedalus going up to the rector to tell on the prefect of studies.

He was walking down along the matting and he saw the door before him. It was impossible: he could not. He thought of the baldy head of the prefect of studies with the cruel no-coloured eyes looking at him and he heard the voice of the prefect of studies asking him twice what his name was. Why could he not remember the name when he was told the first time? Was he not listening the first time or was it to make fun out of the name? The great men in the history had names like that and nobody made fun of them. It was his own name that he should have made fun of if he wanted to make fun. Dolan: it was like the name of a woman who washed clothes.

He had reached the door and, turning quickly up to the right, walked up the stairs and, before he could make up his mind to come back, he had entered the low dark narrow corridor that led to the castle. And as he crossed the threshold of the door of the corridor he saw, without turning his head to look, that all the fellows were looking after him as they went filing by.

He passed along the narrow dark corridor, passing little doors that were the doors of the rooms of the community. He peered in front of him and right and left through the gloom and thought that those must be portraits. It was dark and silent and his eyes were weak and tired with tears so that he could not see. But he thought they were the portraits of the saints and great men of the order who were looking down on him silently as he passed: saint Ignatius Loyola holding an open book and pointing to the words *Ad Majorem Dei Gloriam* in it; saint Francis Xavier pointing to his chest; Lorenzo Ricci with his berretta on his head like one of the prefects of the lines, the three patrons of holy youth—saint Stanislaus Kostka, saint Aloysius Gonzago, and Blessed John Berchmans, all with young faces because they died when they were young, and Father Peter Kenny sitting in a chair wrapped in a big cloak.

He came out on the landing above the entrance hall and looked about him. That was where Hamilton Rowan had passed and the marks of the soldiers' slugs were there. And it was there that the old servants had seen the ghost in the white cloak of a marshal.

An old servant was sweeping at the end of the landing. He asked him where was the rector's room and the old servant pointed to the door at the far end and looked after him as he went on to it and knocked.

There was no answer. He knocked again more loudly and his heart jumped when he heard a muffled voice say:

—Come in!

He turned the handle and opened the door and fumbled for the handle of the green baize door inside. He found it and pushed it open and went in.

He saw the rector sitting at a desk writing. There was a skull on the desk and a strange solemn smell in the room like the old leather of chairs.

His heart was beating fast on account of the solemn place he was in and the silence of the room: and he looked at the skull and at the rector's kind-looking face.

—Well, my little man, said the rector, what is it?

Stephen swallowed down the thing in his throat and said:

—I broke my glasses, sir.

The rector opened his mouth and said:

—O!

Then he smiled and said:

—Well, if we broke our glasses we must write home for a new pair.

—I wrote home, sir, said Stephen, and Father Arnall said I am not to study till they come.

—Quite right! said the rector.

Stephen swallowed down the thing again and tried to keep his legs and his voice from shaking.

—But, sir—

—Yes?

—Father Dolan came in today and pandied me because I was not writing my theme.

The rector looked at him in silence and he could feel the blood rising to his face and the tears about to rise to his eyes.

The rector said:

—Your name is Dedalus, isn't it?

—Yes, sir . . .

—And where did you break your glasses?

—On the cinder-path, sir. A fellow was coming out of the bicycle house and I fell and they got broken. I don't know the fellow's name.

The rector looked at him again in silence. Then he smiled and said:

—O, well, it was a mistake; I am sure Father Dolan did not know.

—But I told him I broke them, sir, and he pandied me.

—Did you tell him that you had written home for a new pair? the rector asked.

—No, sir.

—O well then, said the rector, Father Dolan did not understand. You can say that I excuse you from your lessons for a few days.

Stephen said quickly for fear his trembling would prevent him:

—Yes, sir, but Father Dolan said he will come in tomorrow to pandy me again for it.

—Very well, the rector said, it is a mistake and I shall speak to Father Dolan myself. Will that do now?

Stephen felt the tears wetting his eyes and murmured:

—O yes sir, thanks.

The rector held his hand across the side of the desk where the skull was and Stephen, placing his hand in it for a moment, felt a cool moist palm.

—Good day now, said the rector, withdrawing his hand and bowing.

—Good day, sir, said Stephen.

He bowed and walked quietly out of the room, closing the doors carefully and slowly.

But when he had passed the old servant on the landing and was again in the low narrow dark corridor he began to walk faster and faster. Faster and faster he hurried on through the gloom excitedly. He bumped his elbow against the door at the end and, hurrying down the staircase, walked quickly through the two corridors and out into the air.

He could hear the cries of the fellows on the playgrounds. He broke into a run and, running quicker and quicker, ran across the cinderpath and reached the third line playground, panting.

The fellows had seen him running. They closed round him in a ring, pushing one against another to hear.

—Tell us! Tell us!

—What did he say?

—Did you go in?

—What did he say?

—Tell us! Tell us!

He told them what he had said and what the rector had said and, when he had told them, all the fellows flung their caps spinning up into the air and cried:

—Hurroo!

They caught their caps and sent them up again spinning sky-high and cried again:

—Hurroo! Hurroo!

They made a cradle of their locked hands and hoisted him up among them and carried him along till he struggled to get free. And when he had escaped from them they broke away in all directions, flinging their caps again into the air and whistling as they went spinning up and crying:

—Hurroo!

And they gave three groans for Baldyhead Dolan and three cheers for Conmee and they said he was the decentest rector that was ever in Clongowes.

The cheers died away in the soft grey air. He was alone. He was happy and free; but he would not be anyway proud with Father Dolan. He would be very quiet and obedient: and he wished that he could do something kind for him to show him that he was not proud.

The air was soft and grey and mild and evening was coming. There was the smell of evening in the air, the smell of the fields in the country where they digged up turnips to peel them and eat them when they went out for a walk to Major Barton's, the smell there was in the little wood beyond the pavilion where the gallnuts were.

The fellows were practising long shies and bowling lobs and slow twisters. In the soft grey silence he could hear the bump of the balls: and from here and from there through the quiet air the sound of the cricket bats: pick, pack, pock, puck: like drops of water in a fountain falling softly in the brimming bowl.

2

U ncle Charles smoked such black twist that at last his nephew suggested to him to enjoy his morning smoke in a little outhouse at the end of the garden.

—Very good, Simon. All serene, Simon, said the old man tranquilly. Anywhere you like. The outhouse will do me nicely: it will be more salubrious.

—Damn me, said Mr Dedalus frankly, if I know how you can smoke such villainous awful tobacco. It's like gunpowder, by God.

—It's very nice, Simon, replied the old man. Very cool and mollifying.

Every morning, therefore, uncle Charles repaired to his outhouse but not before he had greased and brushed scrupulously his back hair and brushed and put on his tall hat. While he smoked the brim of his tall hat and the bowl of his pipe were just visible beyond the jambs of the outhouse door. His arbour, as he called the reeking outhouse which he shared with the cat and the garden tools, served him also as a sounding-box: and every morning he hummed contentedly one of his favourite songs: *O, twine me a bower* or *Blue eyes and golden hair* or *The Groves of Blarney* while the grey and blue coils of smoke rose slowly from his pipe and vanished in the pure air.

During the first part of the summer in Blackrock uncle Charles was Stephen's constant companion. Uncle Charles was a hale old man with a well tanned skin, rugged features and white side whiskers. On week days he did messages between the house in Carysfort Avenue and those shops in the main street of the town with which the family dealt. Stephen was glad to go with him on these errands for uncle Charles helped him very liberally to handfuls of whatever was exposed in open boxes and barrels outside the counter.

He would seize a handful of grapes and sawdust or three or four American apples and thrust them generously into his grandnephew's hand while the shopman smiled uneasily; and, on Stephen's feigning reluctance to take them, he would frown and say:

—Take them, sir. Do you hear me, sir? They're good for your bowels.

When the order list had been booked the two would go on to the park where an old friend of Stephen's father, Mike Flynn, would be found seated on a bench, waiting for them. Then would begin Stephen's run round the park. Mike Flynn would stand at the gate near the railway station, watch in hand, while Stephen ran round the track in the style Mike Flynn favoured, his head high lifted, his knees well lifted and his hands held straight down by his sides. When the morning practice was over the trainer would make his comments and sometimes illustrate them by shuffling along for a yard or so comically in an old pair of blue canvas shoes. A small ring of wonderstruck children and nursemaids would gather to watch him and linger even when he and uncle Charles had sat down again and were talking athletics and politics. Though he had heard his father say that Mike Flynn had put some of the best runners of modern times through his hands Stephen often glanced at his trainer's flabby stubble-covered face, as it bent over the long stained fingers through which he rolled his cigarette, and with pity at the mild lustreless blue eyes which would look up suddenly from the task and gaze vaguely into the blue distance while the long swollen fingers ceased their rolling and grains and fibres of tobacco fell back into the pouch.

On the way home uncle Charles would often pay a visit to the chapel and, as the font was above Stephen's reach, the old man would dip his hand and then sprinkle the water briskly about Stephen's clothes and on the floor of the porch. While he prayed he knelt on his red handkerchief and read above his breath from a thumb blackened prayer book wherein catchwords were printed at the foot of every page. Stephen knelt at his side respecting, though he did not share, his piety. He often wondered what his grand-uncle prayed for so seriously. Perhaps he prayed for the souls in purgatory or for the grace of a happy death or perhaps he prayed that God might send him back a part of the big fortune he had squandered in Cork.

On Sundays Stephen with his father and his grand-uncle took their constitutional. The old man was a nimble walker in spite of his corns and often ten or twelve miles of the road were covered. The little village of Stillorgan was the parting of the ways. Either they went to the left towards the Dublin mountains or along the Goatstown road and thence into Dundrum, coming home by Sandyford. Trudging along the road or standing in some grimy wayside public house his elders spoke constantly of the subjects nearer their hearts, of Irish politics, of Munster and of the legends of their own family, to all of which Stephen lent an avid ear. Words which he did not understand he said over and over to himself till he had learnt them by heart: and through them he had glimpses of the real world about them. The hour when he too would take part in the life of that world seemed drawing near and in secret he began to make ready for the great part which he felt awaited him the nature of which he only dimly apprehended.

His evenings were his own; and he pored over a ragged translation of *The Count of Monte Cristo*. The figure of that dark avenger stood forth in his mind for whatever he had heard or divined in childhood of the strange and terrible. At night he built up on the parlour table an image of the wonderful island cave out of transfers and paper flowers and coloured tissue paper and strips of the silver and golden paper in which chocolate is wrapped. When he had broken up this scenery, weary of its tinsel, there would come to his mind the bright picture of Marseille, of sunny trellises, and of Mercedes. Outside Blackrock, on the road that led to the mountains, stood a small whitewashed house in the garden of which grew many rosebushes: and in this house, he told himself, another Mercedes lived. Both on the outward and on the homeward journey he measured distance by this landmark: and in his imagination he lived through a long train of adventures, marvellous as those in the book itself, towards the close of which there appeared an image of himself, grown older and sadder, standing in a moonlit garden with Mercedes who had so many years before slighted his love, and with a sadly proud gesture of refusal, saying:

—Madam, I never eat muscatel grapes.

He became the ally of a boy named Aubrey Mills and founded with him a gang of adventurers in the avenue. Aubrey carried a whistle dangling from his buttonhole and a bicycle lamp attached to his belt while the others had short sticks thrust daggerwise through theirs. Stephen, who had read of Napoleon's plain style of dress, chose to remain unadorned and thereby heightened for himself the pleasure of taking counsel with his lieutenant before giving orders. The gang made forays into the gardens of old maids or went down to the castle and fought a battle on the shaggy weed-grown rocks, coming home after it weary stragglers with the stale odours of the foreshore in their nostrils and the rank oils of the seawrack upon their hands and in their hair.

Aubrey and Stephen had a common milkman and often they drove out in the milk-car to Carrickmines where the cows were at grass. While the men were milking the boys would take turns in riding the tractable mare round the field. But when autumn came the cows were driven home from the grass: and the first sight of the filthy cowyard at Stradbrook with its foul green puddles and clots of liquid dung and steaming bran troughs, sickened Stephen's heart. The cattle which had seemed so beautiful in the country on sunny days revolted him and he could not even look at the milk they yielded.

The coming of September did not trouble him this year for he was not to be sent back to Clongowes. The practice in the park came to an end when Mike Flynn went into hospital. Aubrey was at school and had only an hour or two free in the evening. The gang fell asunder and there were no more nightly forays or battles on the rocks. Stephen sometimes went round with the car which delivered the evening milk and these chilly drives blew away his memory of the filth of the cowyard and he felt no repugnance at seeing the cow hairs and hayseeds on the milkman's coat. Whenever the car drew up before a house he waited to catch a glimpse of a well scrubbed kitchen or of a softly lighted hall and to see how the servant would hold the jug and how she would close the door. He thought it should be a pleasant life enough, driving along the roads every evening to deliver milk, if he had warm gloves and a fat bag of gingernuts in his pocket to eat from. But the same foreknowledge which had sickened his heart and made his legs sag suddenly as he raced round the park, the same intuition which had made him glance with mistrust at his trainer's flabby stubble-covered face as it bent heavily over his long stained fingers, dissipated any vision of the future. In a vague way he understood that his father was in trouble and that this was the reason why he himself had not been sent back to Clongowes. For some time he had felt the slight change in his house; and those changes in what he had deemed unchangeable were so many slight shocks to his boyish conception of the world. The ambition which he felt astir at times in the darkness of his soul sought no outlet. A dusk like that of the outer world obscured his mind as he heard the mare's hoofs clattering along the tramtrack on the Rock Road and the great can swaying and rattling behind him.

He returned to Mercedes and, as he brooded upon her image, a strange unrest crept into his blood. Sometimes a fever gathered within him and led him to rove alone in the evening along the quiet avenue. The peace of the gardens and the kindly lights in the windows poured a tender influence into his restless heart. The noise of children at play annoyed him and their silly voices made him feel, even more keenly than he had felt at Clongowes, that he was different from others. He did not want to play. He wanted to meet in the real world the unsubstantial image which his soul so constantly beheld. He did not know where to seek it or how, but a premonition which led him on told him that this image would, without any overt act of his, encounter him. They would meet quietly as if they had known each other and had made their tryst, perhaps at one of the gates or in some more secret place. They would be alone, surrounded by darkness and silence: and in that moment of supreme tenderness he would be transfigured. He would fade into something impalpable under her eyes and then in a moment he would be transfigured. Weakness and timidity and inexperience would fall from him in that magic moment.

***

Two great yellow caravans had halted one morning before the door and men had come tramping into the house to dismantle it. The furniture had been hustled out through the front garden which was strewn with wisps of straw and rope ends and into the huge vans at the gate. When all had been safely stowed the vans had set off noisily down the avenue: and from the window of the railway carriage, in which he had sat with his red-eyed mother, Stephen had seen them lumbering along the Merrion Road.

The parlour fire would not draw that evening and Mr Dedalus rested the poker against the bars of the grate to attract the flame. Uncle Charles dozed in a corner of the half furnished uncarpeted room and near him the family portraits leaned against the wall. The lamp on the table shed a weak light over the boarded floor, muddied by the feet of the van-men. Stephen sat on a footstool beside his father listening to a long and incoherent monologue. He understood little or nothing of it at first but he became slowly aware that his father had enemies and that some fight was going to take place. He felt, too, that he was being enlisted for the fight, that some duty was being laid upon his shoulders. The sudden flight from the comfort and revery of Blackrock, the passage through the gloomy foggy city, the thought of the bare cheerless house in which they were now to live made his heart heavy, and again an intuition, a foreknowledge of the future came to him. He understood also why the servants had often whispered together in the hall and why his father had often stood on the hearthrug with his back to the fire, talking loudly to uncle Charles who urged him to sit down and eat his dinner.

—There's a crack of the whip left in me yet, Stephen, old chap, said Mr Dedalus, poking at the dull fire with fierce energy. We're not dead yet, sonny. No, by the Lord Jesus (God forgive me) not half dead.

Dublin was a new and complex sensation. Uncle Charles had grown so witless that he could no longer be sent out on errands and the disorder in settling in the new house left Stephen freer than he had been in Blackrock. In the beginning he contented himself with circling timidly round the neighbouring square or, at most, going half way down one of the side streets but when he had made a skeleton map of the city in his mind he followed boldly one of its central lines until he reached the customhouse. He passed unchallenged among the docks and along the quays wondering at the multitude of corks that lay bobbing on the surface of the water in a thick yellow scum, at the crowds of quay porters and the rumbling carts and the ill-dressed bearded policeman. The vastness and strangeness of the life suggested to him by the bales of merchandise stocked along the walls or swung aloft out of the holds of steamers wakened again in him the unrest which had sent him wandering in the evening from garden to garden in search of Mercedes. And amid this new bustling life he might have fancied himself in another Marseille but that he missed the bright sky and the sum-warmed trellises of the wineshops. A vague dissatisfaction grew up within him as he looked on the quays and on the river and on the lowering skies and yet he continued to wander up and down day after day as if he really sought someone that eluded him.

He went once or twice with his mother to visit their relatives: and though they passed a jovial array of shops lit up and adorned for Christmas his mood of embittered silence did not leave him. The causes of his embitterment were many, remote and near. He was angry with himself for being young and the prey of restless foolish impulses, angry also with the change of fortune which was reshaping the world about him into a vision of squalor and insincerity. Yet his anger lent nothing to the vision. He chronicled with patience what he saw, detaching himself from it and tasting its mortifying flavour in secret.

He was sitting on the backless chair in his aunt's kitchen. A lamp with a reflector hung on the japanned wall of the fireplace and by its light his aunt was reading the evening paper that lay on her knees. She looked a long time at a smiling picture that was set in it and said musingly:

—The beautiful Mabel Hunter!

A ringletted girl stood on tiptoe to peer at the picture and said softly:

—What is she in, mud?

—In a pantomime, love.

The child leaned her ringletted head against her mother's sleeve, gazing on the picture, and murmured as if fascinated:

—The beautiful Mabel Hunter!

As if fascinated, her eyes rested long upon those demurely taunting eyes and she murmured devotedly:

—Isn't she an exquisite creature?

And the boy who came in from the street, stamping crookedly under his stone of coal, heard her words. He dropped his load promptly on the floor and hurried to her side to see. He mauled the edges of the paper with his reddened and blackened hands, shouldering her aside and complaining that he could not see.

He was sitting in the narrow breakfast room high up in the old dark-windowed house. The firelight flickered on the wall and beyond the window a spectral dusk was gathering upon the river. Before the fire an old woman was busy making tea and, as she bustled at the task, she told in a low voice of what the priest and the doctor had said. She told too of certain changes they had seen in her of late and of her odd ways and sayings. He sat listening to the words and following the ways of adventure that lay open in the coals, arches and vaults and winding galleries and jagged caverns.

Suddenly he became aware of something in the doorway. A skull appeared suspended in the gloom of the doorway. A feeble creature like a monkey was there, drawn thither by the sound of voices at the fire. A whining voice came from the door asking:

—Is that Josephine?

The old bustling woman answered cheerily from the fireplace:

—No, Ellen, it's Stephen.

—O . . . O, good evening, Stephen.

He answered the greeting and saw a silly smile break over the face in the doorway.

—Do you want anything, Ellen? asked the old woman at the fire.

But she did not answer the question and said:

—I thought it was Josephine. I thought you were Josephine, Stephen.

And, repeating this several times, she fell to laughing feebly.

He was sitting in the midst of a children's party at Harold's Cross. His silent watchful manner had grown upon him and he took little part in the games. The children, wearing the spoils of their crackers, danced and romped noisily and, though he tried to share their merriment, he felt himself a gloomy figure amid the gay cocked hats and sunbonnets.

But when he had sung his song and withdrawn into a snug corner of the room he began to taste the joy of his loneliness. The mirth, which in the beginning of the evening had seemed to him false and trivial, was like a soothing air to him, passing gaily by his senses, hiding from other eyes the feverish agitation of his blood while through the circling of the dancers and amid the music and laughter her glance travelled to his corner, flattering, taunting, searching, exciting his heart.

In the hall the children who had stayed latest were putting on their things: the party was over. She had thrown a shawl about her and, as they went together towards the tram, sprays of her fresh warm breath flew gaily above her cowled head and her shoes tapped blithely on the glassy road.

It was the last tram. The lank brown horses knew it and shook their bells to the clear night in admonition. The conductor talked with the driver, both nodding often in the green light of the lamp. On the empty seats of the tram were scattered a few coloured tickets. No sound of footsteps came up or down the road. No sound broke the peace of the night save when the lank brown horses rubbed their noses together and shook their bells.

They seemed to listen, he on the upper step and she on the lower. She came up to his step many times and went down to hers again between their phrases and once or twice stood close beside him for some moments on the upper step, forgetting to go down, and then went down. His heart danced upon her movements like a cork upon a tide. He heard what her eyes said to him from beneath their cowl and knew that in some dim past, whether in life or revery, he had heard their tale before. He saw her urge her vanities, her fine dress and sash and long black stockings, and knew that he had yielded to them a thousand times. Yet a voice within him spoke above the noise of his dancing heart, asking him would he take her gift to which he had only to stretch out his hand. And he remembered the day when he and Eileen had stood looking into the hotel grounds, watching the waiters running up a trail of bunting on the flagstaff and the fox terrier scampering to and fro on the sunny lawn and how, all of a sudden, she had broken out into a peal of laughter and had run down the sloping curve of the path. Now, as then, he stood listlessly in his place, seemingly a tranquil watcher of the scene before him.

—She too wants me to catch hold of her, he thought. That's why she came with me to the tram. I could easily catch hold of her when she comes up to my step: nobody is looking. I could hold her and kiss her.

But he did neither: and, when he was sitting alone in the deserted tram, he tore his ticket into shreds and stared gloomily at the corrugated footboard.

The next day he sat at his table in the bare upper room for many hours. Before him lay a new pen, a new bottle of ink and a new emerald exercise. From force of habit he had written at the top of the first page the initial letters of the jesuit motto: A.M.D.G. On the first line of the page appeared the title of the verses he was trying to write: To E— C—. He knew it was right to begin so for he had seen similar titles in the collected poems of Lord Byron. When he had written this title and drawn an ornamental line underneath he fell into a daydream and began to draw diagrams on the cover of the book. He saw himself sitting at his table in Bray the morning after the discussion at the Christmas dinner table, trying to write a poem about Parnell on the back of one of his father's second moiety notices. But his brain had then refused to grapple with the theme and, desisting, he had covered the page with the names and addresses of certain of his classmates:

Roderick Kickham
John Lawton
Anthony MacSwiney
Simon Moonan

Now it seemed as if he would fail again but, by dint of brooding on the incident, he thought himself into confidence. During this process all those elements which he deemed common and insignificant fell out of the scene. There remained no trace of the tram itself nor of the tram-men nor of the horses: nor did he and she appear vividly. The verses told only of the night and the balmy breeze and the maiden lustre of the moon. Some undefined sorrow was hidden in the hearts of the protagonists as they stood in silence beneath the leafless trees and when the moment of farewell had come the kiss, which had been withheld by one, was given by both. After this the letters L. D. S. were written at the foot of the page, and, having hidden the book, he went into his mother's bedroom and gazed at his face for a long time in the mirror of her dressing-table.

But his long spell of leisure and liberty was drawing to its end. One evening his father came home full of news which kept his tongue busy all through dinner. Stephen had been awaiting his father's return for there had been mutton hash that day and he knew that his father would make him dip his bread in the gravy. But he did not relish the hash for the mention of Clongowes had coated his palate with a scum of disgust.

—I walked bang into him, said Mr Dedalus for the fourth time, just at the corner of the square.

—Then I suppose, said Mrs Dedalus, he will be able to arrange it. I mean about Belvedere.

—Of course he will, said Mr Dedalus. Don't I tell you he's provincial of the order now?

—I never liked the idea of sending him to the christian brothers myself, said Mrs Dedalus.

—Christian brothers be damned! said Mr Dedalus. Is it with Paddy Stink and Micky Mud? No, let him stick to the jesuits in God's name since he began with them. They'll be of service to him in after years. Those are the fellows that can get you a position.

—And they're a very rich order, aren't they, Simon?

—Rather. They live well, I tell you. You saw their table at Clongowes. Fed up, by God, like gamecocks.

Mr Dedalus pushed his plate over to Stephen and bade him finish what was on it.

—Now then, Stephen, he said, you must put your shoulder to the wheel, old chap. You've had a fine long holiday.

—O, I'm sure he'll work very hard now, said Mrs Dedalus, especially when he has Maurice with him.

—O, Holy Paul, I forgot about Maurice, said Mr Dedalus. Here, Maurice! Come here, you thick-headed ruffian! Do you know I'm going to send you to a college where they'll teach you to spell c.a.t. cat. And I'll buy you a nice little penny handkerchief to keep your nose dry. Won't that be grand fun?

Maurice grinned at his father and then at his brother. Mr Dedalus screwed his glass into his eye and stared hard at both his sons. Stephen mumbled his bread without answering his father's gaze.

—By the bye, said Mr Dedalus at length, the rector, or provincial rather, was telling me that story about you and Father Dolan. You're an impudent thief, he said.

—O, he didn't, Simon!

—Not he! said Mr Dedalus. But he gave me a great account of the whole affair. We were chatting, you know, and one word borrowed another. And, by the way, who do you think he told me will get that job in the corporation? But I'll tell you that after. Well, as I was saying, we were chatting away quite friendly and he asked me did our friend here wear glasses still, and then he told me the whole story.

—And was he annoyed, Simon?

—Annoyed? Not he! *Manly little chap!* he said.

Mr Dedalus imitated the mincing nasal tone of the provincial.

Father Dolan and I, when I told them all at dinner about it, Father Dolan and I had a great laugh over it. *You better mind yourself Father Dolan,* said I, *or young Dedalus will send you up for twice nine.* We had a famous laugh together over it. Ha! Ha! Ha!

Mr Dedalus turned to his wife and interjected in his natural voice:

—Shows you the spirit in which they take the boys there. O, a jesuit for your life, for diplomacy!

He reassumed the provincial's voice and repeated:

—*I told them all at dinner about it and Father Dolan and I and all of us we had a hearty laugh together over it. Ha! Ha! Ha!*

***

The night of the Whitsuntide play had come and Stephen from the window of the dressing-room looked out on the small grass-plot across which lines of Chinese lanterns were stretched. He watched the visitors come down the steps from the house and pass into the theatre. Stewards in evening dress, old Belvedereans, loitered in groups about the entrance to the theatre and ushered in the visitors with ceremony. Under the sudden glow of a lantern he could recognize the smiling face of a priest.

The Blessed Sacrament had been removed from the tabernacle and the first benches had been driven back so as to leave the dais of the altar and the space before it free. Against the walls stood companies of barbells and Indian clubs; the dumbbells were piled in one corner: and in the midst of countless hillocks of gymnasium shoes and sweaters and singlets in untidy brown parcels there stood the stout leather-jacketed vaulting horse waiting its turn to be carried up on the stage and set in the middle of the winning team at the end of the gymnastic display.

Stephen, though in deference to his reputation for essay writing he had been elected secretary to the gymnasium, had had no part in the first section of the programme but in the play which formed the second section he had the chief part, that of a farcical pedagogue. He had been cast for it on account of his stature and grave manners for he was now at the end of his second year at Belvedere and in number two.

A score of the younger boys in white knickers and singlets came pattering down from the stage, through the vestry and to the chapel. The vestry and chapel were peopled with eager masters and boys. The plump bald sergeant major was testing with his foot the springboard of the vaulting horse. The lean young man in a long overcoat, who was to give a special display of intricate club swinging, stood near watching with interest, his silver-coated clubs peeping out of his deep side-pockets. The hollow rattle of the wooden dumbbells was heard as another team made ready to go up on the stage: and in another moment the excited prefect was hustling the boys through the vestry like a flock of geese, flapping the wings of his soutane nervously and crying to the laggards to make haste. A little troop of Neapolitan peasants were practising their steps at the end of the chapel, some circling their arms above their heads, some swaying their baskets of paper violets and curtsying. In a dark corner of the chapel at the gospel side of the altar a stout old lady knelt amid her copious black skirts. When she stood up a pink-dressed figure, wearing a curly golden wig and an old-fashioned straw sunbonnet, with black pencilled eyebrows and cheeks delicately rouged and powdered, was discovered. A low murmur of curiosity ran round the chapel at the discovery of this girlish figure. One of the prefects, smiling and nodding his head, approached the dark corner and, having bowed to the stout old lady, said pleasantly:

—Is this a beautiful young lady or a doll that you have here, Mrs Tallon?

Then, bending down to peer at the smiling painted face under the leaf of the bonnet, he exclaimed:

—No! Upon my word I believe it's little Bertie Tallon after all!

Stephen at his post by the window heard the old lady and the priest laugh together and heard the boys' murmurs of admiration behind him as they passed forward to see the little boy who had to dance the sunbonnet dance by himself. A movement of impatience escaped him. He let the edge of the blind fall and, stepping down from the bench on which he had been standing, walked out of the chapel.

He passed out of the schoolhouse and halted under the shed that flanked the garden. From the theatre opposite came the muffled noise of the audience and sudden brazen clashes of the soldiers' band. The light spread upwards from the glass roof making the theatre seem a festive ark, anchored among the hulks of houses, her frail cables of lanterns looping her to her moorings. A side door of the theatre opened suddenly and a shaft of light flew across the grass plots. A sudden burst of music issued from the ark, the prelude of a waltz: and when the side door closed again the listener could hear the faint rhythm of the music. The sentiment of the opening bars, their languor and supple movement, evoked the incommunicable emotion which had been the cause of all his day's unrest and of his impatient movement of a moment before. His unrest issued from him like a wave of sound: and on the tide of flowing music the ark was journeying, trailing her cables of lanterns in her wake. Then a noise like dwarf artillery broke the movement. It was the clapping that greeted the entry of the dumbbell team on the stage.

At the far end of the shed near the street a speck of pink light showed in the darkness and as he walked towards it he became aware of a faint aromatic odour. Two boys were standing in the shelter of a doorway, smoking, and before he reached them he had recognised Heron by his voice.

—Here comes the noble Dedalus! cried a high throaty voice. Welcome to our trusty friend!

This welcome ended in a soft peal of mirthless laughter as Heron salaamed and then began to poke the ground with his cane.

—Here I am, said Stephen, halting and glancing from Heron to his friend.

The latter was a stranger to him but in the darkness, by the aid of the glowing cigarette tips, he could make out a pale dandyish face over which a smile was travelling slowly, a tall overcoated figure and a hard hat. Heron did not trouble himself about an introduction but said instead:

—I was just telling my friend Wallis what a lark it would be tonight if you took off the rector in the part of the schoolmaster. It would be a ripping good joke.

Heron made a poor attempt to imitate for his friend Wallis the rector's pedantic bass and then, laughing at his failure, asked Stephen to do it.

—Go on, Dedalus, he urged, you can take him off rippingly. *He that will not hear the churcha let him be to theea as the heathena and the publicana.*

The imitation was prevented by a mild expression of anger from Wallis in whose mouthpiece the cigarette had become too tightly wedged.

—Damn this blankety blank holder, he said, taking it from his mouth and smiling and frowning upon it tolerantly. It's always getting stuck like that. Do you use a holder?

—I don't smoke, answered Stephen.

—No, said Heron, Dedalus is a model youth. He doesn't smoke and he doesn't go to bazaars and he doesn't flirt and he doesn't damn anything or damn all.

Stephen shook his head and smiled in his rival's flushed and mobile face, beaked like a bird's. He had often thought it strange that Vincent Heron had a bird's face as well as a bird's name. A shock of pale hair lay on the forehead like a ruffled crest: the forehead was narrow and bony and a thin hooked nose stood out between the close-set prominent eyes which were light and inexpressive. The rivals were school friends. They sat together in class, knelt together in the chapel, talked together after beads over their lunches. As the fellows in number one were undistinguished dullards, Stephen and Heron had been during the year the virtual heads of the school. It was they who went up to the rector together to ask for a free day or to get a fellow off.

—O by the way, said Heron suddenly, I saw your governor going in.

The smile waned on Stephen's face. Any allusion made to his father by a fellow or by a master put his calm to rout in a moment. He waited in timorous silence to hear what Heron might say next. Heron, however, nudged him expressively with his elbow and said:

—You're a sly dog, Dedalus!

—Why so? said Stephen.

—You'd think butter wouldn't melt in your mouth said Heron. But I'm afraid you're a sly dog.

—Might I ask you what you are talking about? said Stephen urbanely.

—Indeed you might, answered Heron. We saw her, Wallis, didn't we? And deucedly pretty she is too. And inquisitive! *And what part does Stephen take, Mr Dedalus? And will Stephen not sing, Mr Dedalus?* Your governor was staring at her through that eyeglass of his for all he was worth so that I think the old man has found you out too. I wouldn't care a bit, by Jove. She's ripping, isn't she, Wallis?

—Not half bad, answered Wallis quietly as he placed his holder once more in a corner of his mouth.

A shaft of momentary anger flew through Stephen's mind at these indelicate allusions in the hearing of a stranger. For him there was nothing amusing in a girl's interest and regard. All day he had thought of nothing but their leave-taking on the steps of the tram at Harold's Cross, the stream of moody emotions it had made to course through him and the poem he had written about it. All day he had imagined a new meeting with her for he knew that she was to come to the play. The old restless moodiness had again filled his breast as it had done on the night of the party, but had not found an outlet in verse. The growth and knowledge of two years of boyhood stood between then and now, forbidding such an outlet: and all day the stream of gloomy tenderness within him had started forth and returned upon itself in dark courses and eddies, wearying him in the end until the pleasantry of the prefect and the painted little boy had drawn from him a movement of impatience.

—So you may as well admit, Heron went on, that we've fairly found you out this time. You can't play the saint on me any more, that's one sure five.

A soft peal of mirthless laughter escaped from his lips and, bending down as before, he struck Stephen lightly across the calf of the leg with his cane, as if in jesting reproof.

Stephen's moment of anger had already passed. He was neither flattered nor confused, but simply wished the banter to end. He scarcely resented what had seemed to him a silly indelicateness for he knew that the adventure in his mind stood in no danger from these words: and his face mirrored his rival's false smile.

—Admit! repeated Heron, striking him again with his cane across the calf of the leg.

The stroke was playful but not so lightly given as the first one had been. Stephen felt the skin tingle and glow slightly and almost painlessly; and, bowing submissively, as if to meet his companion's jesting mood, began to recite the *Confiteor*. The episode ended well, for both Heron and Wallis laughed indulgently at the irreverence.

The confession came only from Stephen's lips and, while they spoke the words, a sudden memory had carried him to another scene called up, as if by magic, at the moment when he had noted the faint cruel dimples at the corners of Heron's smiling lips and had felt the familiar stroke of the cane against his calf and had heard the familiar word of admonition:

—Admit.

It was towards the close of his first term in the college when he was in number six. His sensitive nature was still smarting under the lashes of an undivined and squalid way of life. His soul was still disquieted and cast down by the dull phenomenon of Dublin. He had emerged from a two years' spell of revery to find himself in the midst of a new scene, every event and figure of which affected him intimately, disheartened him or allured and, whether alluring or disheartening, filled him always with unrest and bitter thoughts. All the leisure which his school life left him was passed in the company of subversive writers whose jibes and violence of speech set up a ferment in his brain before they passed out of it into his crude writings.

The essay was for him the chief labour of his week and every Tuesday, as he marched from home to the school, he read his fate in the incidents of the way, pitting himself against some figure ahead of him and quickening his pace to outstrip it before a certain goal was reached or planting his steps scrupulously in the spaces of the patchwork of the pathway and telling himself that he would be first and not first in the weekly essay.

On a certain Tuesday the course of his triumphs was rudely broken. Mr Tate, the English master, pointed his finger at him and said bluntly:

—This fellow has heresy in his essay.

A hush fell on the class. Mr Tate did not break it but dug with his hand between his thighs while his heavily starched linen creaked about his neck and wrists. Stephen did not look up. It was a raw spring morning and his eyes were still smarting and weak. He was conscious of failure and of detection, of the squalor of his own mind and home, and felt against his neck the raw edge of his turned and jagged collar.

A short loud laugh from Mr Tate set the class more at ease.

—Perhaps you didn't know that, he said.

—Where? asked Stephen.

Mr Tate withdrew his delving hand and spread out the essay.

—Here. It's about the Creator and the soul. Rrm . . . rrm . . . rrm . . . Ah! *without a possibility of ever approaching nearer.* That's heresy.

Stephen murmured:

—I meant *without a possibility of ever reaching.*

It was a submission and Mr Tate, appeased, folded up the essay and passed it across to him, saying:

—O . . . Ah! *ever reaching.* That's another story.

But the class was not so soon appeased. Though nobody spoke to him of the affair after class he could feel about him a vague general malignant joy.

A few nights after this public chiding he was walking with a letter along the Drumcondra Road when he heard a voice cry:

—Halt!

He turned and saw three boys of his own class coming towards him in the dusk. It was Heron who had called out and, as he marched forward between his two attendants, he cleft the air before him with a thin cane in time to their steps. Boland, his friend, marched beside him, a large grin on his face, while Nash came on a few steps behind, blowing from the pace and wagging his great red head.

As soon as the boys had turned into Clonliffe Road together they began to speak about books and writers, saying what books they were reading and how many books there were in their fathers' bookcases at home. Stephen listened to them in some wonderment for Boland was the dunce and Nash the idler of the class. In fact, after some talk about their favourite writers, Nash declared for Captain Marryat who, he said, was the greatest writer.

—Fudge! said Heron. Ask Dedalus. Who is the greatest writer, Dedalus?

Stephen noted the mockery in the question and said:

—Of prose do you mean?

—Yes.

—Newman, I think.

—Is it Cardinal Newman? asked Boland.

—Yes, answered Stephen.

The grin broadened on Nash's freckled face as he turned to Stephen and said:

—And do you like Cardinal Newman, Dedalus?

—O, many say that Newman has the best prose style, Heron said to the other two in explanation, of course he's not a poet.

—And who is the best poet, Heron? asked Boland.

—Lord Tennyson, of course, answered Heron.

—O, yes, Lord Tennyson, said Nash. We have all his poetry at home in a book.

At this Stephen forgot the silent vows he had been making and burst out:

—Tennyson a poet! Why, he's only a rhymester!

—O, get out! said Heron. Everyone knows that Tennyson is the greatest poet.

—And who do you think is the greatest poet? asked Boland, nudging his neighbour.

—Byron, of course, answered Stephen.

Heron gave the lead and all three joined in a scornful laugh.

—What are you laughing at? asked Stephen.

—You, said Heron. Byron the greatest poet! He's only a poet for uneducated people.

—He must be a fine poet! said Boland.

—You may keep your mouth shut, said Stephen, turning on him boldly. All you know about poetry is what you wrote up on the slates in the yard and were going to be sent to the loft for.

Boland, in fact, was said to have written on the slates in the yard a couplet about a classmate of his who often rode home from the college on a pony:

> *As Tyson was riding into Jerusalem*
> *He fell and hurt his Alec Kafoozelum.*

This thrust put the two lieutenants to silence but Heron went on:

—In any case Byron was a heretic and immoral too.

—I don't care what he was, cried Stephen hotly.

—You don't care whether he was a heretic or not? said Nash.

—What do you know about it? shouted Stephen. You never read a line of anything in your life except a trans, or Boland either.

—I know that Byron was a bad man, said Boland.

—Here, catch hold of this heretic, Heron called out. In a moment Stephen was a prisoner.

—Tate made you buck up the other day, Heron went on, about the heresy in your essay.

—I'll tell him tomorrow, said Boland.

—Will you? said Stephen. You'd be afraid to open your lips.

—Afraid?

—Ay. Afraid of your life.

—Behave yourself! cried Heron, cutting at Stephen's legs with his cane.

It was the signal for their onset. Nash pinioned his arms behind while Boland seized a long cabbage stump which was lying in the gutter. Struggling and kicking under the cuts of the cane and the blows of the knotty stump Stephen was borne back against a barbed wire fence.

—Admit that Byron was no good.

—No.

—Admit.

—No.

—Admit.

—No. No.

At last after a fury of plunges he wrenched himself free. His tormentors set off towards Jones's Road, laughing and jeering at him, while he, half blinded with tears, stumbled on, clenching his fists madly and sobbing.

While he was still repeating the *Confiteor* amid the indulgent laughter of his hearers and while the scenes of that malignant episode were still passing sharply and swiftly before his mind he wondered why he bore no malice now to those who had tormented him. He had not forgotten a whit of their cowardice and cruelty but the memory of it called forth no anger from him. All the descriptions of fierce love and hatred which he had met in books had seemed to him therefore unreal. Even that night as he stumbled homewards along Jones's Road he had felt that some power was divesting him of that sudden-woven anger as easily as a fruit is divested of its soft ripe peel.

He remained standing with his two companions at the end of the shed listening idly to their talk or to the bursts of applause in the theatre. She was sitting there among the others perhaps waiting for him to appear. He tried to recall her appearance but could not. He could remember only that she had worn a shawl about her head like a cowl and that her dark eyes had invited and unnerved him. He wondered had he been in her thoughts as she had been in his. Then in the dark and unseen by the other two he rested the tips of the fingers of one hand upon the palm of the other hand, scarcely touching it lightly. But the pressure of her fingers had been lighter and steadier: and suddenly the memory of their touch traversed his brain and body like an invisible wave.

A boy came towards them, running along under the shed. He was excited and breathless.

—O, Dedalus, he cried, Doyle is in a great bake about you. You're to go in at once and get dressed for the play. Hurry up, you better.

—He's coming now, said Heron to the messenger with a haughty drawl, when he wants to.

The boy turned to Heron and repeated:

—But Doyle is in an awful bake.

—Will you tell Doyle with my best compliments that I damned his eyes? answered Heron.

—Well, I must go now, said Stephen, who cared little for such points of honour.

—I wouldn't, said Heron, damn me if I would. That's no way to send for one of the senior boys. In a bake, indeed! I think it's quite enough that you're taking a part in his bally old play.

This spirit of quarrelsome comradeship which he had observed lately in his rival had not seduced Stephen from his habits of quiet obedience. He mistrusted the turbulence and doubted the sincerity of such comradeship which seemed to him a sorry anticipation of manhood. The question of honour here raised was, like all such questions, trivial to him. While his mind had been pursuing its intangible phantoms and turning in irresolution from such pursuit he had heard about him the constant voices of his father and of his masters, urging him to be a gentleman above all things and urging him to be a good catholic above all things. These voices had now come to be hollow-sounding in his ears. When the gymnasium had been opened he had heard another voice urging him to be strong and manly and healthy and when the movement towards national revival had begun to be felt in the college yet another voice had bidden him be true to his country and help to raise up her language and tradition. In the profane world, as he foresaw, a worldly voice would bid him raise up his father's fallen state by his labours and, meanwhile, the voice of his school comrades urged him to be a decent fellow, to shield others from blame or to beg them off and to do his best to get free days for the school. And it was the din of all these hollow-sounding voices that made him halt irresolutely in the pursuit of phantoms. He gave them ear only for a time but he was happy only when he was far from them, beyond their call, alone or in the company of phantasmal comrades.

In the vestry a plump fresh-faced jesuit and an elderly man, in shabby blue clothes, were dabbling in a case of paints and chalks. The boys who had been painted walked about or stood still awkwardly, touching their faces in a gingerly fashion with their furtive fingertips. In the middle of the vestry a young jesuit, who was then on a visit to the college, stood rocking himself rhythmically from the tips of his toes to his heels and back again, his hands thrust well forward into his side-pockets. His small head set off with glossy red curls and his newly shaven face agreed well with the spotless decency of his soutane and with his spotless shoes.

As he watched this swaying form and tried to read for himself the legend of the priest's mocking smile there came into Stephen's memory a saying which he had heard from his father before he had been sent to Clongowes, that you could always tell a jesuit by the style of his clothes. At the same moment he thought he saw a likeness between his father's mind and that of this smiling well-dressed priest: and he was aware of some desecration of the priest's office or of the vestry itself whose silence was now routed by loud talk and joking and its air pungent with the smells of the gas-jets and the grease.

While his forehead was being wrinkled and his jaws painted black and blue by the elderly man, he listened distractedly to the voice of the plump young jesuit which bade him speak up and make his points clearly. He could hear the band playing *The Lily of Killarney* and knew that in a few moments the curtain would go up. He felt no stage fright but the thought of the part he had to play humiliated him. A remembrance of some of his lines made a sudden flush rise to his painted cheeks. He saw her serious alluring eyes watching him from among the audience and their image at once swept away his scruples, leaving his will compact. Another nature seemed to have been lent him: the infection of the excitement and youth about him entered into and transformed his moody mistrustfulness. For one rare moment he seemed to be clothed in the real apparel of boyhood: and, as he stood in the wings among the other players, he shared the common mirth amid which the drop scene was hauled upwards by two able-bodied priests with violent jerks and all awry.

A few moments after he found himself on the stage amid the garish gas and the dim scenery, acting before the innumerable faces of the void. It surprised him to see that the play which he had known at rehearsals for a disjointed lifeless thing had suddenly assumed a life of its own. It seemed now to play itself, he and his fellow actors aiding it with their parts. When the curtain fell on the last scene he heard the void filled with applause and, through a rift in a side scene, saw the simple body before which he had acted magically deformed, the void of faces breaking at all points and falling asunder into busy groups.

He left the stage quickly and rid himself of his mummery and passed out through the chapel into the college garden. Now that the play was over his nerves cried for some further adventure. He hurried onwards as if to overtake it. The doors of the theatre were all open and the audience had emptied out. On the lines which he had fancied the moorings of an ark a few lanterns swung in the night breeze, flickering cheerlessly. He mounted the steps from the garden in haste, eager that some prey should not elude him, and forced his way through the crowd in the hall and past the two jesuits who stood watching the exodus and bowing and shaking hands with the visitors. He pushed onward nervously, feigning a still greater haste and faintly conscious of the smiles and stares and nudges which his powdered head left in its wake.

When he came out on the steps he saw his family waiting for him at the first lamp. In a glance he noted that every figure of the group was familiar and ran down the steps angrily.

—I have to leave a message down in George's Street, he said to his father quickly. I'll be home after you.

Without waiting for his father's questions he ran across the road and began to walk at breakneck speed down the hill. He hardly knew where he was walking. Pride and hope and desire like crushed herbs in his heart sent up vapours of maddening incense before the eyes of his mind. He strode down the hill amid the tumult of sudden-risen vapours of wounded pride and fallen hope and baffled desire. They streamed upwards before his anguished eyes in dense and maddening fumes and passed away above him till at last the air was clear and cold again.

A film still veiled his eyes but they burned no longer. A power, akin to that which had often made anger or resentment fall from him, brought his steps to rest. He stood still and gazed up at the sombre porch of the morgue and from that to the dark cobbled laneway at its side. He saw the word LOTTS on the wall of the lane and breathed slowly the rank heavy air.

That is horse piss and rotted straw, he thought. It is a good odour to breathe. It will calm my heart. My heart is quite calm now. I will go back.

***

Stephen was once again seated beside his father in the corner of a railway carriage at Kingsbridge. He was travelling with his father by the night mail to Cork. As the train steamed out of the station he recalled his childish wonder of years before and every event of his first day at Clongowes. But he felt no wonder now. He saw the darkening lands slipping away past him, the silent telegraph-poles passing his window swiftly every four seconds, the little glimmering stations, manned by a few silent sentries, flung by the mail behind her and twinkling for a moment in the darkness like fiery grains flung backwards by a runner.

He listened without sympathy to his father's evocation of Cork and of scenes of his youth, a tale broken by sighs or draughts from his pocket flask whenever the image of some dead friend appeared in it or whenever the evoker remembered suddenly the purpose of his actual visit. Stephen heard but could feel no pity. The images of the dead were all strangers to him save that of uncle Charles, an image which had lately been fading out of memory. He knew, however, that his father's property was going to be sold by auction, and in the manner of his own dispossession he felt the world give the lie rudely to his phantasy.

At Maryborough he fell asleep. When he awoke the train had passed out of Mallow and his father was stretched asleep on the other seat. The cold light of the dawn lay over the country, over the unpeopled fields and the closed cottages. The terror of sleep fascinated his mind as he watched the silent country or heard from time to time his father's deep breath or sudden sleepy movement. The neighbourhood of unseen sleepers filled him with strange dread, as though they could harm him, and he prayed that the day might come quickly. His prayer, addressed neither to God nor saint, began with a shiver, as the chilly morning breeze crept through the chink of the carriage door to his feet, and ended in a trail of foolish words which he made to fit the insistent rhythm of the train; and silently, at intervals of four seconds, the telegraph-poles held the galloping notes of the music between punctual bars. This furious music allayed his dread and, leaning against the windowledge, he let his eyelids close again.

They drove in a jingle across Cork while it was still early morning and Stephen finished his sleep in a bedroom of the Victoria Hotel. The bright warm sunlight was streaming through the window and he could hear the din of traffic. His father was standing before the dressing-table, examining his hair and face and moustache with great care, craning his neck across the water-jug and drawing it back sideways to see the better. While he did so he sang softly to himself with quaint accent and phrasing:

> *'Tis youth and folly*
> *Makes young men marry,*
> *So here, my love, I'll*
> *No longer stay.*
> *What can't be cured, sure,*
> *Must be injured, sure,*
> *So I'll go to*
> *Amerikay.*

My love she's handsome,
My love she's bony:
She's like good whisky
When it is new;
But when 'tis old
And growing cold
It fades and dies like
The mountain dew.

The consciousness of the warm sunny city outside his window and the tender tremors with which his father's voice festooned the strange sad happy air, drove off all the mists of the night's ill humour from Stephen's brain. He got up quickly to dress and, when the song had ended, said:

—That's much prettier than any of your other *come-all-yous.*

—Do you think so? asked Mr Dedalus.

—I like it, said Stephen.

—It's a pretty old air, said Mr Dedalus, twirling the points of his moustache. Ah, but you should have heard Mick Lacy sing it! Poor Mick Lacy! He had little turns for it, grace notes that he used to put in that I haven't got. That was the boy who could sing a *come-all-you,* if you like.

Mr Dedalus had ordered drisheens for breakfast and during the meal he cross-examined the waiter for local news. For the most part they spoke at cross purposes when a name was mentioned, the waiter having in mind the present holder and Mr Dedalus his father or perhaps his grandfather.

—Well, I hope they haven't moved the Queen's College anyhow, said Mr Dedalus, for I want to show it to this youngster of mine.

Along the Mardyke the trees were in bloom. They entered the grounds of the college and were led by the garrulous porter across the quadrangle. But their progress across the gravel was brought to a halt after every dozen or so paces by some reply of the porter's.

—Ah, do you tell me so? And is poor Pottlebelly dead?

—Yes, sir. Dead, sir.

During these halts Stephen stood awkwardly behind the two men, weary of the subject and waiting restlessly for the slow march to begin again. By the time they had crossed the quadrangle his restlessness had risen to fever. He wondered how his father, whom he knew for a shrewd suspicious man, could be duped by the servile manners of the porter; and the lively southern speech which had entertained him all the morning now irritated his ears.

They passed into the anatomy theatre where Mr Dedalus, the porter aiding him, searched the desks for his initials. Stephen remained in the background, depressed more than ever by the darkness and silence of the theatre and by the air it wore of jaded and formal study. On the desk he read the word FOETUS cut several times in the dark stained wood. The sudden legend startled his blood: he seemed to feel the absent students of the college about him and to shrink from their company. A vision of their life, which his father's words had been powerless to evoke, sprang up before him out of the word cut in the desk. A broad-shouldered student with a moustache was cutting in the letters with a jack-knife, seriously. Other students stood or sat near him laughing at his handiwork. One jogged his elbow. The big student turned on him, frowning. He was dressed in loose grey clothes and had tan boots.

Stephen's name was called. He hurried down the steps of the theatre so as to be as far away from the vision as he could be and, peering closely at his father's initials, hid his flushed face.

But the word and the vision capered before his eyes as he walked back across the quadrangle and towards the college gate. It shocked him to find in the outer world a trace of what he had deemed till then a brutish and individual malady of his own mind. His monstrous reveries came thronging into his memory. They too had sprung up before him, suddenly and furiously, out of mere words. He had soon given in to them and allowed them to sweep across and abase his intellect, wondering always where they came from, from what den of monstrous images, and always weak and humble towards others, restless and sickened of himself when they had swept over him.

—Ay, bedad! And there's the Groceries sure enough! cried Mr Dedalus. You often heard me speak of the Groceries, didn't you, Stephen. Many's the time we went down there when our names had been marked, a crowd of us, Harry Peard and little Jack Mountain and Bob Dyas and Maurice Moriarty, the Frenchman, and Tom O'Grady and Mick Lacy that I told you of this morning and Joey Corbet and poor little good-hearted Johnny Keevers of the Tantiles.

The leaves of the trees along the Mardyke were astir and whispering in the sunlight. A team of cricketers passed, agile young men in flannels and blazers, one of them carrying the long green wicket-bag. In a quiet bystreet a German band of five players in faded uniforms and with battered brass instruments was playing to an audience of street arabs and leisurely messenger boys. A maid in a white cap and apron was watering a box of plants on a sill which shone like a slab of limestone in the warm glare. From another window open to the air came the sound of a piano, scale after scale rising into the treble.

Stephen walked on at his father's side, listening to stories he had heard before, hearing again the names of the scattered and dead revellers who had been the companions of his father's youth. And a faint sickness sighed in his heart. He recalled his own equivocal position in Belvedere, a free boy, a leader afraid of his own authority, proud and sensitive and suspicious, battling against the squalor of his life and against the riot of his mind. The letters cut in the stained wood of the desk stared upon him, mocking his bodily weakness and futile enthusiasms and making him loathe himself for his own mad and filthy orgies. The spittle in his throat grew bitter and foul to swallow and the faint sickness climbed to his brain so that for a moment he closed his eyes and walked on in darkness.

He could still hear his father's voice—

—When you kick out for yourself, Stephen—as I daresay you will one of these days—remember, whatever you do, to mix with gentlemen. When I was a young fellow I tell you I enjoyed myself. I mixed with fine decent fellows. Everyone of us could do something. One fellow had a good voice, another fellow was a good actor, another could sing a good comic song, another was a good oarsman or a good racket player, another could tell a good story and so on. We kept the ball rolling anyhow and enjoyed ourselves and saw a bit of life and we were none the worse of it either. But we were all gentlemen, Stephen—at least I hope we were—and bloody good honest Irishmen too. That's the kind of fellows I want you to associate with, fellows of the right kidney. I'm talking to you as a friend, Stephen. I don't believe a son should be afraid of his father. No, I treat you as your grandfather treated me when I was a young chap. We were more like brothers than father and son. I'll never forget the first day he caught me smoking. I was standing at the end of the South Terrace one day with some maneens like myself and sure we thought we were grand fellows because we had pipes stuck in the corners of our mouths. Suddenly the governor passed. He didn't say a word, or stop even. But the next day,

Sunday, we were out for a walk together and when we were coming home he took out his cigar case and said:—*By the by, Simon, I didn't know you smoked,* or something like that.—Of course I tried to carry it off as best I could.—If you want a good smoke, he said, *try one of these cigars. An American captain made me a present of them last night in Queenstown.*

Stephen heard his father's voice break into a laugh which was almost a sob.

—He was the handsomest man in Cork at that time, by God he was! The women used to stand to look after him in the street.

He heard the sob passing loudly down his father's throat and opened his eyes with a nervous impulse. The sunlight breaking suddenly on his sight turned the sky and clouds into a fantastic world of sombre masses with lakelike spaces of dark rosy light. His very brain was sick and powerless. He could scarcely interpret the letters of the signboards of the shops. By his monstrous way of life he seemed to have put himself beyond the limits of reality. Nothing moved him or spoke to him from the real world unless he heard in it an echo of the infuriated cries within him. He could respond to no earthly or human appeal, dumb and insensible to the call of summer and gladness and companionship, wearied and dejected by his father's voice. He could scarcely recognize as his own thoughts, and repeated slowly to himself:

—I am Stephen Dedalus. I am walking beside my father whose name is Simon Dedalus. We are in Cork, in Ireland. Cork is a city. Our room is in the Victoria Hotel. Victoria and Stephen and Simon. Simon and Stephen and Victoria. Names.

The memory of his childhood suddenly grew dim. He tried to call forth some of its vivid moments but could not. He recalled only names. Dante, Parnell, Clane, Clongowes. A little boy had been taught geography by an old woman who kept two brushes in her wardrobe. Then he had been sent away from home to a college, he had made his first communion and eaten slim jim out of his cricket cap and watched the firelight leaping and dancing on the wall of a little bedroom in the infirmary and dreamed of being dead, of mass being said for him by the rector in a black and gold cope, of being buried then in the little graveyard of the community off the main avenue of limes. But he had not died then. Parnell had died. There had been no mass for the dead in the chapel and no procession. He had not died but he had faded out like a film in the sun. He had been lost or had wandered out of existence for he no longer existed. How strange to think of him passing out of existence in such a way, not by death but by fading out in the sun or by being lost and forgotten somewhere in the universe! It was strange to see his small body appear again for a moment: a little boy in a grey belted suit. His hands were in his side-pockets and his trousers were tucked in at the knees by elastic bands.

On the evening of the day on which the property was sold Stephen followed his father meekly about the city from bar to bar. To the sellers in the market, to the barmen and barmaids, to the beggars who importuned him for a lob Mr Dedalus told the same tale—that he was an old Corkonian, that he had been trying for thirty years to get rid of his Cork accent up in Dublin and that Peter Pickackafax beside him was his eldest son but that he was only a Dublin jackeen.

They had set out early in the morning from Newcombe's coffee-house, where Mr Dedalus's cup had rattled noisily against its saucer, and Stephen had tried to cover that shameful sign of his father's drinking bout of the night before by moving his chair and coughing. One humiliation had succeeded another—the false smiles of the market sellers, the curvetings and oglings of the barmaids with whom his father flirted, the compliments and encouraging words of his father's friends. They had told him that he had a great look of his grandfather and Mr Dedalus had agreed that he was an ugly likeness. They had unearthed traces of a Cork accent in his speech and made him admit that the Lee was a much finer river than the Liffey. One of them, in order to put his Latin to the proof, had made him translate short passages from Dilectus and asked him whether it was correct to say: *Tempora mutantur nos et mutamur in illis* or *Tempora mutantur et nos mutamur in illis*. Another, a brisk old man, whom Mr Dedalus called Johnny Cashman, had covered him with confusion by asking him to say which were prettier, the Dublin girls or the Cork girls.

—He's not that way built, said Mr Dedalus. Leave him alone. He's a level-headed thinking boy who doesn't bother his head about that kind of nonsense.

—Then he's not his father's son, said the little old man.

—I don't know, I'm sure, said Mr Dedalus, smiling complacently.

—Your father, said the little old man to Stephen, was the boldest flirt in the City of Cork in his day. Do you know that?

Stephen looked down and studied the tiled floor of the bar into which they had drifted.

—Now don't be putting ideas into his head, said Mr Dedalus. Leave him to his Maker.

—Yerra, sure I wouldn't put any ideas into his head. I'm old enough to be his grandfather. And I am a grandfather, said the little old man to Stephen. Do you know that?

—Are you? asked Stephen.

—Bedad I am, said the little old man. I have two bouncing grandchildren out at Sunday's Well. Now, then! What age do you think I am? And I remember seeing your grandfather in his red coat riding out to hounds. That was before you were born.

—Ay, or thought of, said Mr Dedalus.

—Bedad I did, repeated the little old man. And, more than that, I can remember even your great-grandfather, old John Stephen Dedalus, and a fierce old fire-eater he was. Now, then! There's a memory for you!

—That's three generations—four generations, said another of the company. Why, Johnny Cashman, you must be nearing the century.

—Well, I'll tell you the truth, said the little old man. I'm just twenty-seven years of age.

—We're as old as we feel, Johnny, said Mr Dedalus. And just finish what you have there and we'll have another. Here, Tim or Tom or whatever your name is, give us the same again here. By God, I don't feel more than eighteen myself. There's that son of mine there not half my age and I'm a better man than he is any day of the week.

—Draw it mild now, Dedalus. I think it's time for you to take a back seat, said the gentleman who had spoken before.

—No, by God! asserted Mr Dedalus. I'll sing a tenor song against him or I'll vault a five-barred gate against him or I'll run with him after the hounds across the country as I did thirty years ago along with the Kerry Boy and the best man for it.

—But he'll beat you here, said the little old man, tapping his forehead and raising his glass to drain it.

—Well, I hope he'll be as good a man as his father. That's all I can say, said Mr Dedalus.

—If he is, he'll do, said the little old man.

—And thanks be to God, Johnny, said Mr Dedalus, that we lived so long and did so little harm.

—But did so much good, Simon, said the little old man gravely. Thanks be to God we lived so long and did so much good.

Stephen watched the three glasses being raised from the counter as his father and his two cronies drank to the memory of their past. An abyss of fortune or of temperament sundered him from them. His mind seemed older than theirs: it shone coldly on their strifes and happiness and regrets like a moon upon a younger earth. No life or youth stirred in him as it had stirred in them. He had known neither the pleasure of companionship with others nor the vigour of rude male health nor filial piety. Nothing stirred within his soul but a cold and cruel and loveless lust. His childhood was dead or lost and with it his soul capable of simple joys and he was drifting amid life like the barren shell of the moon.

> *Art thou pale for weariness*
> *Of climbing heaven and gazing on the earth,*
> *Wandering companionless . . .?*

He repeated to himself the lines of Shelley's fragment. Its alternation of sad human ineffectiveness with vast inhuman cycles of activity chilled him and he forgot his own human and ineffectual grieving.

***

Stephen's mother and his brother and one of his cousins waited at the corner of quiet Foster Place while he and his father went up the steps and along the colonnade where the Highland sentry was parading. When they had passed into the great hall and stood at the counter Stephen drew forth his orders on the governor of the bank of Ireland for thirty and three pounds; and these sums, the moneys of his exhibition and essay prize, were paid over to him rapidly by the teller in notes and in coin respectively. He bestowed them in his pockets with feigned composure and suffered the friendly teller, to whom his father chatted, to take his hand across the broad counter and wish him a brilliant career in after life. He was impatient of their voices and could not keep his feet at rest. But the teller still deferred the serving of others to say he was living in changed times and that there was nothing like giving a boy the best education that money could buy. Mr Dedalus lingered in the hall gazing about him and up at the roof and telling Stephen, who urged him to come out, that they were standing in the house of commons of the old Irish parliament.

—God help us! he said piously, to think of the men of those times, Stephen, Hely Hutchinson and Flood and Henry Grattan and Charles Kendal Bushe, and the noblemen we have now, leaders of the Irish people at home and abroad. Why, by God, they wouldn't be seen dead in a ten-acre field with them. No, Stephen, old chap, I'm sorry to say that they are only as I roved out one fine May morning in the merry month of sweet July.

A keen October wind was blowing round the bank. The three figures standing at the edge of the muddy path had pinched cheeks and watery eyes. Stephen looked at his thinly clad mother and remembered that a few days before he had seen a mantle priced at twenty guineas in the windows of Barnardo's.

—Well that's done, said Mr Dedalus.

—We had better go to dinner, said Stephen. Where?

—Dinner? said Mr Dedalus. Well, I suppose we had better, what?

—Some place that's not too dear, said Mrs Dedalus.

—Underdone's?

—Yes. Some quiet place.

—Come along, said Stephen quickly. It doesn't matter about the dearness.

He walked on before them with short nervous steps, smiling. They tried to keep up with him, smiling also at his eagerness.

—Take it easy like a good young fellow, said his father. We're not out for the half mile, are we?

For a swift season of merrymaking the money of his prizes ran through Stephen's fingers. Great parcels of groceries and delicacies and dried fruits arrived from the city. Every day he drew up a bill of fare for the family and every night led a party of three or four to the theatre to see *Ingomar* or *The Lady of Lyons*. In his coat pockets he carried squares of Vienna chocolate for his guests while his trousers' pocket bulged with masses of silver and copper coins. He bought presents for everyone, overhauled his room, wrote out resolutions, marshalled his books up and down their shelves, pored upon all kinds of price lists, drew up a form of commonwealth for the household by which every member of it held some office, opened a loan bank for his family and pressed loans on willing borrowers so that he might have the pleasure of making out receipts and reckoning the interests on the sums lent. When he could do no more he drove up and down the city in trams. Then the season of pleasure came to an end. The pot of pink enamel paint gave out and the wainscot of his bedroom remained with its unfinished and ill-plastered coat.

His household returned to its usual way of life. His mother had no further occasion to upbraid him for squandering his money. He too returned to his old life at school and all his novel enterprises fell to pieces. The commonwealth fell, the loan bank closed its coffers and its books on a sensible loss, the rules of life which he had drawn about himself fell into desuetude.

How foolish his aim had been! He had tried to build a breakwater of order and elegance against the sordid tide of life without him and to dam up, by rules of conduct and active interest and new filial relations, the powerful recurrence of the tides within him. Useless. From without as from within the waters had flowed over his barriers: their tides began once more to jostle fiercely above the crumbled mole.

He saw clearly too his own futile isolation. He had not gone one step nearer the lives he had sought to approach nor bridged the restless shame and rancour that had divided him from mother and brother and sister. He felt that he was hardly of the one blood with them but stood to them rather in the mystical kinship of fosterage, fosterchild and fosterbrother.

He turned to appease the fierce longings of his heart before which everything else was idle and alien. He cared little that he was in mortal sin, that his life had grown to be a tissue of subterfuge and falsehood. Beside the savage desire within him to realize the enormities which he brooded on nothing was sacred. He bore cynically with the shameful details of his secret riots in which he exulted to defile with patience whatever image had attracted his eyes. By day and by night he moved among distorted images of the outer world. A figure that had seemed to him by day demure and innocent came towards him by night through the winding darkness of sleep, her face transfigured by a lecherous cunning, her eyes bright with brutish joy. Only the morning pained him with its dim memory of dark orgiastic riot, its keen and humiliating sense of transgression.

He returned to his wanderings. The veiled autumnal evenings led him from street to street as they had led him years before along the quiet avenues of Blackrock. But no vision of trim front gardens or of kindly lights in the windows poured a tender influence upon him now.

Only at times, in the pauses of his desire, when the luxury that was wasting him gave room to a softer languor, the image of Mercedes traversed the background of his memory. He saw again the small white house and the garden of rose-bushes on the road that led to the mountains and he remembered the sadly proud gesture of refusal which he was to make there, standing with her in the moonlit garden after years of estrangement and adventure. At those moments the soft speeches of Claude Melnotte rose to his lips and eased his unrest. A tender premonition touched him of the tryst he had then looked forward to and, in spite of the horrible reality which lay between his hope of then and now, of the holy encounter he had then imagined at which weakness and timidity and inexperience were to fall from him.

Such moments passed and the wasting fires of lust sprang up again. The verses passed from his lips and the inarticulate cries and the unspoken brutal words rushed forth from his brain to force a passage. His blood was in revolt. He wandered up and down the dark slimy streets peering into the gloom of lanes and doorways, listening eagerly for any sound. He moaned to himself like some baffled prowling beast. He wanted to sin with another of his kind, to force another being to sin with him and to exult with her in sin. He felt some dark presence moving irresistibly upon him from the darkness, a presence subtle and murmurous as a flood filling him wholly with itself. Its murmur besieged his ears like the murmur of some multitude in sleep; its subtle streams penetrated his being. His hands clenched convulsively and his teeth set together as he suffered the agony of its penetration. He stretched out his arms in the street to hold fast the frail swooning form that eluded him and incited him: and the cry that he had strangled for so long in his throat issued from his lips. It broke from him like a wail of despair from a hell of sufferers and died in a wail of furious entreaty, a cry for an iniquitous abandonment, a cry which was but the echo of an obscene scrawl which he had read on the oozing wall of a urinal.

He had wandered into a maze of narrow and dirty streets. From the foul laneways he heard bursts of hoarse riot and wrangling and the drawling of drunken singers. He walked onward, dismayed, wondering whether he had strayed into the quarter of the Jews. Women and girls dressed in long vivid gowns traversed the street from house to house. They were leisurely and perfumed. A trembling seized him and his eyes grew dim. The yellow gas-flames arose before his troubled vision against the vapoury sky, burning as if before an altar. Before the doors and in the lighted halls groups were gathered arrayed as for some rite. He was in another world: he had awakened from a slumber of centuries.

He stood still in the middle of the roadway, his heart clamouring against his bosom in a tumult. A young woman dressed in a long pink gown laid her hand on his arm to detain him and gazed into his face. She said gaily:

—Good night, Willie dear!

Her room was warm and lightsome. A huge doll sat with her legs apart in the copious easy-chair beside the bed. He tried to bid his tongue speak that he might seem at ease, watching her as she undid her gown, noting the proud conscious movements of her perfumed head.

As he stood silent in the middle of the room she came over to him and embraced him gaily and gravely. Her round arms held him firmly to her and he, seeing her face lifted to him in serious calm and feeling the warm calm rise and fall of her breast, all but burst into hysterical weeping. Tears of joy and relief shone in his delighted eyes and his lips parted though they would not speak.

She passed her tinkling hand through his hair, calling him a little rascal.

—Give me a kiss, she said.

His lips would not bend to kiss her. He wanted to be held firmly in her arms, to be caressed slowly, slowly, slowly. In her arms he felt that he had suddenly become strong and fearless and sure of himself. But his lips would not bend to kiss her.

With a sudden movement she bowed his head and joined her lips to his and he read the meaning of her movements in her frank uplifted eyes. It was too much for him. He closed his eyes, surrendering himself to her, body and mind, conscious of nothing in the world but the dark pressure of her softly parting lips. They pressed upon his brain as upon his lips as though they were the vehicle of a vague speech; and between them he felt an unknown and timid pressure, darker than the swoon of sin, softer than sound or odour.

The swift December dusk had come tumbling clownishly after its dull day and, as he stared through the dull square of the window of the schoolroom, he felt his belly crave for its food. He hoped there would be stew for dinner, turnips and carrots and bruised potatoes and fat mutton pieces to be ladled out in thick peppered flour-fattened sauce. Stuff it into you, his belly counselled him.

It would be a gloomy secret night. After early nightfall the yellow lamps would light up, here and there, the squalid quarter of the brothels. He would follow a devious course up and down the streets, circling always nearer and nearer in a tremor of fear and joy, until his feet led him suddenly round a dark corner. The whores would be just coming out of their houses making ready for the night, yawning lazily after their sleep and settling the hairpins in their clusters of hair. He would pass by them calmly waiting for a sudden movement of his own will or a sudden call to his sin-loving soul from their soft perfumed flesh. Yet as he prowled in quest of that call, his senses, stultified only by his desire, would note keenly all that wounded or shamed them; his eyes, a ring of porter froth on a clothless table or a photograph of two soldiers standing to attention or a gaudy playbill; his ears, the drawling jargon of greeting:

—Hello, Bertie, any good in your mind?

—Is that you, pigeon?

—Number ten. Fresh Nelly is waiting on you.

—Good night, husband! Coming in to have a short time?

The equation on the page of his scribbler began to spread out a widening tail, eyed and starred like a peacock's; and, when the eyes and stars of its indices had been eliminated, began slowly to fold itself together again. The indices appearing and disappearing were eyes opening and closing; the eyes opening and closing were stars being born and being quenched. The vast cycle of starry life bore his weary mind outward to its verge and inward to its centre, a distant music accompanying him outward and inward. What music? The music came nearer and he recalled the words, the words of Shelley's fragment upon the moon wandering companionless, pale for weariness. The stars began to crumble and a cloud of fine stardust fell through space.

The dull light fell more faintly upon the page whereon another equation began to unfold itself slowly and to spread abroad its widening tail. It was his own soul going forth to experience, unfolding itself sin by sin, spreading abroad the bale-fire of its burning stars and folding back upon itself, fading slowly, quenching its own lights and fires. They were quenched: and the cold darkness filled chaos.

A cold lucid indifference reigned in his soul. At his first violent sin he had felt a wave of vitality pass out of him and had feared to find his body or his soul maimed by the excess. Instead the vital wave had carried him on its bosom out of himself and back again when it receded: and no part of body or soul had been maimed but a dark peace had been established between them. The chaos in which his ardour extinguished itself was a cold indifferent knowledge of himself. He had sinned mortally not once but many times and he knew that, while he stood in danger of eternal damnation for the first sin alone, by every succeeding sin he multiplied his guilt and his punishment. His days and works and thoughts could make no atonement for him, the fountains of sanctifying grace having ceased to refresh his soul. At most, by an alms given to a beggar whose blessing he fled from, he might hope wearily to win for himself some measure of actual grace. Devotion had gone by the board. What did it avail to pray when he knew that his soul lusted after its own destruction? A certain pride, a certain awe, withheld him from offering to God even one prayer at night, though he knew it was in God's power to take away his life while he slept and hurl his soul hellward ere he could beg for mercy. His pride in his own sin, his loveless awe of God, told him that his offence was too grievous to be atoned for in whole or in part by a false homage to the All-seeing and All-knowing.

—Well now, Ennis, I declare you have a head and so has my stick! Do you mean to say that you are not able to tell me what a surd is?

The blundering answer stirred the embers of his contempt of his fellows. Towards others he felt neither shame nor fear. On Sunday mornings as he passed the church door he glanced coldly at the worshippers who stood bareheaded, four deep, outside the church, morally present at the mass which they could neither see nor hear. Their dull piety and the sickly smell of the cheap hair-oil with which they had anointed their heads repelled him from the altar they prayed at. He stooped to the evil of hypocrisy with others, sceptical of their innocence which he could cajole so easily.

On the wall of his bedroom hung an illuminated scroll, the certificate of his prefecture in the college of the sodality of the Blessed Virgin Mary. On Saturday mornings when the sodality met in the chapel to recite the little office his place was a cushioned kneeling-desk at the right of the altar from which he led his wing of boys through the responses. The falsehood of his position did not pain him. If at moments he felt an impulse to rise from his post of honour and, confessing before them all his unworthiness, to leave the chapel, a glance at their faces restrained him. The imagery of the psalms of prophecy soothed his barren pride. The glories of Mary held his soul captive: spikenard and myrrh and frankincense, symbolizing her royal lineage, her emblems, the late-flowering plant and late-blossoming tree, symbolizing the age-long gradual growth of her cultus among men. When it fell to him to read the lesson towards the close of the office he read it in a veiled voice, lulling his conscience to its music.

Quasi cedrus exaltata sum in Libanon et quasi cupressus in monte Sion. Quasi palma exaltata sum in Gades et quasi plantatio rosae in Jericho. Quasi uliva speciosa in campis et quasi platanus exaltata sum juxta aquam in plateis. Sicut cinnamomum et balsamum aromatizans odorem dedi et quasi myrrha electa dedi suavitatem odoris.

His sin, which had covered him from the sight of God, had led him nearer to the refuge of sinners. Her eyes seemed to regard him with mild pity; her holiness, a strange light glowing faintly upon her frail flesh, did not humiliate the sinner who approached her. If ever he was impelled to cast sin from him and to repent the impulse that moved him was the wish to be her knight. If ever his soul, re-entering her dwelling shyly after the frenzy of his body's lust had spent itself, was turned towards her whose emblem is the morning star, *bright and musical, telling of heaven and infusing peace,* it was when her names were murmured softly by lips whereon there still lingered foul and shameful words, the savour itself of a lewd kiss.

That was strange. He tried to think how it could be. But the dusk, deepening in the schoolroom, covered over his thoughts. The bell rang. The master marked the sums and cuts to be done for the next lesson and went out. Heron, beside Stephen, began to hum tunelessly.

My excellent friend Bombados.

Ennis, who had gone to the yard, came back, saying:

—The boy from the house is coming up for the rector. A tall boy behind Stephen rubbed his hands and said:

—That's game ball. We can scut the whole hour. He won't be in till after half two. Then you can ask him questions on the catechism, Dedalus.

Stephen, leaning back and drawing idly on his scribbler, listened to the talk about him which Heron checked from time to time by saying:

—Shut up, will you. Don't make such a bally racket!

It was strange too that he found an arid pleasure in following up to the end the rigid lines of the doctrines of the church and penetrating into obscure silences only to hear and feel the more deeply his own condemnation. The sentence of saint James which says that he who offends against one commandment becomes guilty of all, had seemed to him first a swollen phrase until he had begun to grope in the darkness of his own state. From the evil seed of lust all other deadly sins had sprung forth: pride in himself and contempt of others, covetousness in using money for the purchase of unlawful pleasures, envy of those whose vices he could not reach to and calumnious murmuring against the pious, gluttonous enjoyment of food, the dull glowering anger amid which he brooded upon his longing, the swamp of spiritual and bodily sloth in which his whole being had sunk.

As he sat in his bench gazing calmly at the rector's shrewd harsh face, his mind wound itself in and out of the curious questions proposed to it. If a man had stolen a pound in his youth and had used that pound to amass a huge fortune how much was he obliged to give back, the pound he had stolen only or the pound together with the compound interest accruing upon it or all his huge fortune? If a layman in giving baptism pour the water before saying the words is the child baptized? Is baptism with a mineral water valid? How comes it that while the first beatitude promises the kingdom of heaven to the poor of heart the second beatitude promises also to the meek that they shall possess the land? Why was the sacrament of the eucharist instituted under the two species of bread and wine if Jesus Christ be present body and blood, soul and divinity, in the bread alone and in the wine alone? Does a tiny particle of the consecrated bread contain all the body and blood of Jesus Christ or a part only of the body and blood? If the wine change into vinegar and the host crumble into corruption after they have been consecrated, is Jesus Christ still present under their species as God and as man?

—Here he is! Here he is!

A boy from his post at the window had seen the rector come from the house. All the catechisms were opened and all heads bent upon them silently. The rector entered and took his seat on the dais. A gentle kick from the tall boy in the bench behind urged Stephen to ask a difficult question.

The rector did not ask for a catechism to hear the lesson from. He clasped his hands on the desk and said:

—The retreat will begin on Wednesday afternoon in honour of saint Francis Xavier whose feast day is Saturday. The retreat will go on from Wednesday to Friday. On Friday confession will be heard all the afternoon after beads. If any boys have special confessors perhaps it will be better for them not to change. Mass will be on Saturday morning at nine o'clock and general communion for the whole college. Saturday will be a free day. But Saturday and Sunday being free days some boys might be inclined to think that Monday is a free day also. Beware of making that mistake. I think you, Lawless, are likely to make that mistake.

—I sir? Why, sir?

A little wave of quiet mirth broke forth over the class of boys from the rector's grim smile. Stephen's heart began slowly to fold and fade with fear like a withering flower.

The rector went on gravely:

—You are all familiar with the story of the life of saint Francis Xavier, I suppose, the patron of your college. He came of an old and illustrious Spanish family and you remember that he was one of the first followers of saint Ignatius. They met in Paris where Francis Xavier was professor of philosophy at the university. This young and brilliant nobleman and man of letters entered heart and soul into the ideas of our glorious founder and you know that he, at his own desire, was sent by saint Ignatius to preach to the Indians. He is called, as you know, the apostle of the Indies. He went from country to country in the east, from Africa to India, from India to Japan, baptizing the people. He is said to have baptized as many as ten thousand idolaters in one month. It is said that his right arm had grown powerless from having been raised so often over the heads of those whom he baptized. He wished then to go to China to win still more souls for God but he died of fever on the island of Sancian. A great saint, saint Francis Xavier! A great soldier of God!

The rector paused and then, shaking his clasped hands before him, went on:

—He had the faith in him that moves mountains. Ten thousand souls won for God in a single month! That is a true conqueror, true to the motto of our order: *ad majorem Dei gloriam!* A saint who has great power in heaven, remember: power to intercede for us in our grief; power to obtain whatever we pray for if it be for the good of our souls; power above all to obtain for us the grace to repent if we be in sin. A great saint, saint Francis Xavier! A great fisher of souls!

He ceased to shake his clasped hands and, resting them against his forehead, looked right and left of them keenly at his listeners out of his dark stern eyes.

In the silence their dark fire kindled the dusk into a tawny glow. Stephen's heart had withered up like a flower of the desert that feels the simoom coming from afar.

***

—*Remember only thy last things and thou shalt not sin for ever*—words taken, my dear little brothers in Christ, from the book of Ecclesiastes, seventh chapter, fortieth verse. In the name of the Father and of the Son and of the Holy Ghost. Amen.

Stephen sat in the front bench of the chapel. Father Arnall sat at a table to the left of the altar. He wore about his shoulders a heavy cloak; his pale face was drawn and his voice broken with rheum. The figure of his old master, so strangely re-arisen, brought back to Stephen's mind his life at Clongowes: the wide playgrounds, swarming with boys; the square ditch; the little cemetery off the main avenue of limes where he had dreamed of being buried; the firelight on the wall of the infirmary where he lay sick; the sorrowful face of Brother Michael. His soul, as these memories came back to him, became again a child's soul.

—We are assembled here today, my dear little brothers in Christ, for one brief moment far away from the busy bustle of the outer world to celebrate and to honour one of the greatest of saints, the apostle of the Indies, the patron saint also of your college, saint Francis Xavier. Year after year, for much longer than any of you, my dear little boys, can remember or than I can remember, the boys of this college have met in this very chapel to make their annual retreat before the feast day of their patron saint. Time has gone on and brought with it its changes. Even in the last few years what changes can most of you not remember? Many of the boys who sat in those front benches a few years ago are perhaps now in distant lands, in the burning tropics, or immersed in professional duties or in seminaries, or voyaging over the vast expanse of the deep or, it may be, already called by the great God to another life and to the rendering up of their stewardship. And still as the years roll by, bringing with them changes for good and bad, the memory of the great saint is honoured by the boys of this college who make every year their annual retreat on the days preceding the feast day set apart by our Holy Mother the Church to transmit to all the ages the name and fame of one of the greatest sons of catholic Spain.

—Now what is the meaning of this word RETREAT and why is it allowed on all hands to be a most salutary practice for all who desire to lead before God and in the eyes of men a truly christian life? A retreat, my dear boys, signifies a withdrawal for awhile from the cares of our life, the cares of this workaday world, in order to examine the state of our conscience, to reflect on the mysteries of holy religion and to understand better why we are here in this world. During these few days I intend to put before you some thoughts concerning the four last things. They are, as you know from your catechism, death, judgement, hell, and heaven. We shall try to understand them fully during these few days so that we may derive from the understanding of them a lasting benefit to our souls. And remember, my dear boys, that we have been sent into this world for one thing and for one thing alone: to do God's holy will and to save our immortal souls. All else is worthless. One thing alone is needful, the salvation of one's soul.

What doth it profit a man to gain the whole world if he suffer the loss of his immortal soul? Ah, my dear boys, believe me there is nothing in this wretched world that can make up for such a loss.

—I will ask you, therefore, my dear boys, to put away from your minds during these few days all worldly thoughts, whether of study or pleasure or ambition, and to give all your attention to the state of your souls. I need hardly remind you that during the days of the retreat all boys are expected to preserve a quiet and pious demeanour and to shun all loud unseemly pleasure. The elder boys, of course, will see that this custom is not infringed and I look especially to the prefects and officers of the sodality of Our Blessed Lady and of the sodality of the holy angels to set a good example to their fellow-students.

—Let us try, therefore, to make this retreat in honour of saint Francis with our whole heart and our whole mind. God's blessing will then be upon all your year's studies. But, above and beyond all, let this retreat be one to which you can look back in after years when maybe you are far from this college and among very different surroundings, to which you can look back with joy and thankfulness and give thanks to God for having granted you this occasion of laying the first foundation of a pious honourable zealous christian life. And if, as may so happen, there be at this moment in these benches any poor soul who has had the unutterable misfortune to lose God's holy grace and to fall into grievous sin, I fervently trust and pray that this retreat may be the turning point in the life of that soul. I pray to God through the merits of His zealous servant Francis Xavier, that such a soul may be led to sincere repentance and that the holy communion on saint Francis's day of this year may be a lasting covenant between God and that soul. For just and unjust, for saint and sinner alike, may this retreat be a memorable one.

—Help me, my dear little brothers in Christ. Help me by your pious attention, by your own devotion, by your outward demeanour. Banish from your minds all worldly thoughts and think only of the last things, death, judgement, hell, and heaven. He who remembers these things, says Ecclesiastes, shall not sin for ever. He who remembers the last things will act and think with them always before his eyes. He will live a good life and die a good death, believing and knowing that, if he has sacrificed much in this earthly life, it will be given to him a hundredfold and a thousandfold more in the life to come, in the kingdom without end—a blessing, my dear boys, which I wish you from my heart, one and all, in the name of the Father and of the Son and of the Holy Ghost. Amen!

As he walked home with silent companions, a thick fog seemed to compass his mind. He waited in stupor of mind till it should lift and reveal what it had hidden. He ate his dinner with surly appetite and when the meal was over and the grease-strewn plates lay abandoned on the table, he rose and went to the window, clearing the thick scum from his mouth with his tongue and licking it from his lips. So he had sunk to the state of a beast that licks his chaps after meat. This was the end; and a faint glimmer of fear began to pierce the fog of his mind. He pressed his face against the pane of the window and gazed out into the darkening street. Forms passed this way and that through the dull light. And that was life. The letters of the name of Dublin lay heavily upon his mind, pushing one another surlily hither and thither with slow boorish insistence. His soul was fattening and congealing into a gross grease, plunging ever deeper in its dull fear into a sombre threatening dusk while the body that was his stood, listless and dishonoured, gazing out of darkened eyes, helpless, perturbed, and human for a bovine god to stare upon.

The next day brought death and judgement, stirring his soul slowly from its listless despair. The faint glimmer of fear became a terror of spirit as the hoarse voice of the preacher blew death into his soul. He suffered its agony. He felt the death chill touch the extremities and creep onward towards the heart, the film of death veiling the eyes, the bright centres of the brain extinguished one by one like lamps, the last sweat oozing upon the skin, the powerlessness of the dying limbs, the speech thickening and wandering and failing, the heart throbbing faintly and more faintly, all but vanquished, the breath, the poor breath, the poor helpless human spirit, sobbing and sighing, gurgling and rattling in the throat. No help! No help! He—he himself—his body to which he had yielded was dying. Into the grave with it. Nail it down into a wooden box, the corpse. Carry it out of the house on the shoulders of hirelings. Thrust it out of men's sight into a long hole in the ground, into the grave, to rot, to feed the mass of its creeping worms and to be devoured by scuttling plump-bellied rats.

And while the friends were still standing in tears by the bedside the soul of the sinner was judged. At the last moment of consciousness the whole earthly life passed before the vision of the soul and, ere it had time to reflect, the body had died and the soul stood terrified before the judgement seat. God, who had long been merciful, would then be just. He had long been patient, pleading with the sinful soul, giving it time to repent, sparing it yet awhile. But that time had gone. Time was to sin and to enjoy, time was to scoff at God and at the warnings of His holy church, time was to defy His majesty, to disobey His commands, to hoodwink one's fellow men, to commit sin after sin and to hide one's corruption from the sight of men. But that time was over. Now it was God's turn: and He was not to be hoodwinked or deceived. Every sin would then come forth from its lurking place, the most rebellious against the divine will and the most degrading to our poor corrupt nature, the tiniest imperfection and the most heinous atrocity. What did it avail then to have been a great emperor, a great general, a marvellous inventor, the most learned of the learned? All were as one before the judgement seat of God. He would reward the good and punish the wicked. One single instant was enough for the trial of a man's soul. One single instant after the body's death, the soul had been weighed in the balance. The particular judgement was over and the soul had passed to the abode of bliss or to the prison of purgatory or had been hurled howling into hell.

Nor was that all. God's justice had still to be vindicated before men: after the particular there still remained the general judgement. The last day had come. The doomsday was at hand. The stars of heaven were falling upon the earth like the figs cast by the fig-tree which the wind has shaken. The sun, the great luminary of the universe, had become as sackcloth of hair. The moon was blood-red. The firmament was as a scroll rolled away. The archangel Michael, the prince of the heavenly host, appeared glorious and terrible against the sky. With one foot on the sea and one foot on the land he blew from the arch-angelical trumpet the brazen death of time. The three blasts of the angel filled all the universe. Time is, time was, but time shall be no more. At the last blast the souls of universal humanity throng towards the valley of Jehoshaphat, rich and poor, gentle and simple, wise and foolish, good and wicked. The soul of every human being that has ever existed, the souls of all those who shall yet be born, all the sons and daughters of Adam, all are assembled on that supreme day. And lo, the supreme judge is coming! No longer the lowly Lamb of God, no longer the meek Jesus of Nazareth, no longer the Man of Sorrows, no longer the Good Shepherd, He is seen now coming upon the clouds, in great power and majesty, attended by nine choirs of angels, angels and archangels, principalities, powers and virtues, thrones and dominations, cherubim and seraphim, God Omnipotent, God Everlasting. He speaks: and His voice is heard even at the farthest limits of space, even in the bottomless abyss. Supreme Judge, from His sentence there will be and can be no appeal. He calls the just to His side, bidding them enter into the kingdom, the eternity of bliss prepared for them. The unjust He casts from Him, crying in His offended majesty: *Depart from me, ye cursed, into everlasting fire which was prepared for the devil and his angels.* O, what agony then for the miserable sinners! Friend is torn apart from friend, children are torn from their parents, husbands from their wives. The poor sinner holds out his arms to those who were dear to him in this earthly world, to those whose simple piety perhaps he made a mock of, to those who counselled him and tried to lead him on the right path, to a kind brother, to a loving sister, to the mother and father who loved him so dearly. But it is too late: the just turn away from the wretched damned souls which now appear before the eyes of all in their hideous and evil character. O you hypocrites, O, you whited sepulchres, O you who present a smooth smiling face to the world while your soul within is a foul swamp of sin, how will it fare with you in that terrible day?

And this day will come, shall come, must come: the day of death and the day of judgement. It is appointed unto man to die and after death the judgement. Death is certain. The time and manner are uncertain, whether from long disease or from some unexpected accident: the Son of God cometh at an hour when you little expect Him. Be therefore ready every moment, seeing that you may die at any moment. Death is the end of us all. Death and judgement, brought into the world by the sin of our first parents, are the dark portals that close our earthly existence, the portals that open into the unknown and the unseen, portals through which every soul must pass, alone, unaided save by its good works, without friend or brother or parent or master to help it, alone and trembling. Let that thought be ever before our minds and then we cannot sin. Death, a cause of terror to the sinner, is a blessed moment for him who has walked in the right path, fulfilling the duties of his station in life, attending to his morning and evening prayers, approaching the holy sacrament frequently and performing good and merciful works. For the pious and believing catholic, for the just man, death is no cause of terror. Was it not Addison, the great English writer, who, when on his deathbed, sent for the wicked young earl of Warwick to let him see how a christian can meet his end? He it is and he alone, the pious and believing christian, who can say in his heart:

O grave, where is thy victory?
O death, where is thy sting?

Every word of it was for him. Against his sin, foul and secret, the whole wrath of God was aimed. The preacher's knife had probed deeply into his disclosed conscience and he felt now that his soul was festering in sin. Yes, the preacher was right. God's turn had come. Like a beast in its lair his soul had lain down in its own filth but the blasts of the angel's trumpet had driven him forth from the darkness of sin into the light. The words of doom cried by the angel shattered in an instant his presumptuous peace. The wind of the last day blew through his mind, his sins, the jewel-eyed harlots of his imagination, fled before the hurricane, squeaking like mice in their terror and huddled under a mane of hair.

As he crossed the square, walking homeward, the light laughter of a girl reached his burning ear. The frail gay sound smote his heart more strongly than a trumpet blast, and, not daring to lift his eyes, he turned aside and gazed, as he walked, into the shadow of the tangled shrubs. Shame rose from his smitten heart and flooded his whole being. The image of Emma appeared before him, and under her eyes the flood of shame rushed forth anew from his heart. If she knew to what his mind had subjected her or how his brute-like lust had torn and trampled upon her innocence! Was that boyish love? Was that chivalry? Was that poetry? The sordid details of his orgies stank under his very nostrils. The soot-coated packet of pictures which he had hidden in the flue of the fireplace and in the presence of whose shameless or bashful wantonness he lay for hours sinning in thought and deed; his monstrous dreams, peopled by ape-like creatures and by harlots with gleaming jewel eyes; the foul long letters he had written in the joy of guilty confession and carried secretly for days and days only to throw them under cover of night among the grass in the corner of a field or beneath some hingeless door in some niche in the hedges where a girl might come upon them as she walked by and read them secretly. Mad! Mad! Was it possible he had done these things? A cold sweat broke out upon his forehead as the foul memories condensed within his brain.

When the agony of shame had passed from him he tried to raise his soul from its abject powerlessness. God and the Blessed Virgin were too far from him: God was too great and stern and the Blessed Virgin too pure and holy. But he imagined that he stood near Emma in a wide land and, humbly and in tears, bent and kissed the elbow of her sleeve.

In the wide land under a tender lucid evening sky, a cloud drifting westward amid a pale green sea of heaven, they stood together, children that had erred. Their error had offended deeply God's majesty though it was the error of two children; but it had not offended her whose beauty *is not like earthly beauty, dangerous to look upon, but like the morning star which is its emblem, bright and musical.* The eyes were not offended which she turned upon him nor reproachful. She placed their hands together, hand in hand, and said, speaking to their hearts:

—Take hands, Stephen and Emma. It is a beautiful evening now in heaven. You have erred but you are always my children. It is one heart that loves another heart. Take hands together, my dear children, and you will be happy together and your hearts will love each other.

The chapel was flooded by the dull scarlet light that filtered through the lowered blinds; and through the fissure between the last blind and the sash a shaft of wan light entered like a spear and touched the embossed brasses of the candlesticks upon the altar that gleamed like the battle-worn mail armour of angels.

Rain was falling on the chapel, on the garden, on the college. It would rain for ever, noiselessly. The water would rise inch by inch, covering the grass and shrubs, covering the trees and houses, covering the monuments and the mountain tops. All life would be choked off, noiselessly: birds, men, elephants, pigs, children: noiselessly floating corpses amid the litter of the wreckage of the world. Forty days and forty nights the rain would fall till the waters covered the face of the earth.

It might be. Why not?

—*Hell has enlarged its soul and opened its mouth without any limits*— words taken, my dear little brothers in Christ Jesus, from the book of Isaias, fifth chapter, fourteenth verse. In the name of the Father and of the Son and of the Holy Ghost. Amen.

The preacher took a chainless watch from a pocket within his soutane and, having considered its dial for a moment in silence, placed it silently before him on the table.

He began to speak in a quiet tone.

—Adam and Eve, my dear boys, were, as you know, our first parents, and you will remember that they were created by God in order that the seats in heaven left vacant by the fall of Lucifer and his rebellious angels might be filled again. Lucifer, we are told, was a son of the morning, a radiant and mighty angel; yet he fell: he fell and there fell with him a third part of the host of heaven: he fell and was hurled with his rebellious angels into hell. What his sin was we cannot say. Theologians consider that it was the sin of pride, the sinful thought conceived in an instant: *non serviam: I will not serve.* That instant was his ruin. He offended the majesty of God by the sinful thought of one instant and God cast him out of heaven into hell for ever.

—Adam and Eve were then created by God and placed in Eden, in the plain of Damascus, that lovely garden resplendent with sunlight and colour, teeming with luxuriant vegetation. The fruitful earth gave them her bounty: beasts and birds were their willing servants: they knew not the ills our flesh is heir to, disease and poverty and death: all that a great and generous God could do for them was done. But there was one condition imposed on them by God: obedience to His word. They were not to eat of the fruit of the forbidden tree.

—Alas, my dear little boys, they too fell. The devil, once a shining angel, a son of the morning, now a foul fiend came in the shape of a serpent, the subtlest of all the beasts of the field. He envied them. He, the fallen great one, could not bear to think that man, a being of clay, should possess the inheritance which he by his sin had forfeited for ever. He came to the woman, the weaker vessel, and poured the poison of his eloquence into her ear, promising her—O, the blasphemy of that promise!—that if she and Adam ate of the forbidden fruit they would become as gods, nay as God Himself. Eve yielded to the wiles of the archtempter. She ate the apple and gave it also to Adam who had not the moral courage to resist her. The poison tongue of Satan had done its work. They fell.

—And then the voice of God was heard in that garden, calling His creature man to account: and Michael, prince of the heavenly host, with a sword of flame in his hand, appeared before the guilty pair and drove them forth from Eden into the world, the world of sickness and striving, of cruelty and disappointment, of labour and hardship, to earn their bread in the sweat of their brow. But even then how merciful was God! He took pity on our poor degraded parents and promised that in the fullness of time He would send down from heaven One who would redeem them, make them once more children of God and heirs to the kingdom of heaven: and that One, that Redeemer of fallen man, was to be God's only begotten Son, the Second Person of the Most Blessed Trinity, the Eternal Word.

—He came. He was born of a virgin pure, Mary the virgin mother. He was born in a poor cowhouse in Judea and lived as a humble carpenter for thirty years until the hour of His mission had come. And then, filled with love for men, He went forth and called to men to hear the new gospel.

—Did they listen? Yes, they listened but would not hear. He was seized and bound like a common criminal, mocked at as a fool, set aside to give place to a public robber, scourged with five thousand lashes, crowned with a crown of thorns, hustled through the streets by the jewish rabble and the Roman soldiery, stripped of his garments and hanged upon a gibbet and His side was pierced with a lance and from the wounded body of our Lord water and blood issued continually.

—Yet even then, in that hour of supreme agony, Our Merciful Redeemer had pity for mankind. Yet even there, on the hill of Calvary, He founded the holy catholic church against which, it is promised, the gates of hell shall not prevail. He founded it upon the rock of ages, and endowed it with His grace, with sacraments and sacrifice, and promised that if men would obey the word of His church they would still enter into eternal life; but if, after all that had been done for them, they still persisted in their wickedness, there remained for them an eternity of torment: hell.

The preacher's voice sank. He paused, joined his palms for an instant, parted them. Then he resumed:

—Now let us try for a moment to realize, as far as we can, the nature of that abode of the damned which the justice of an offended God has called into existence for the eternal punishment of sinners. Hell is a strait and dark and foul-smelling prison, an abode of demons and lost souls, filled with fire and smoke. The straitness of this prison house is expressly designed by God to punish those who refused to be bound by His laws. In earthly prisons the poor captive has at least some liberty of movement, were it only within the four walls of his cell or in the gloomy yard of his prison. Not so in hell. There, by reason of the great number of the damned, the prisoners are heaped together in their awful prison, the walls of which are said to be four thousand miles thick: and the damned are so utterly bound and helpless that, as a blessed saint, saint Anselm, writes in his book on similitudes, they are not even able to remove from the eye a worm that gnaws it.

—They lie in exterior darkness. For, remember, the fire of hell gives forth no light. As, at the command of God, the fire of the Babylonian furnace lost its heat but not its light, so, at the command of God, the fire of hell, while retaining the intensity of its heat, burns eternally in darkness. It is a never ending storm of darkness, dark flames and dark smoke of burning brimstone, amid which the bodies are heaped one upon another without even a glimpse of air. Of all the plagues with which the land of the Pharaohs were smitten one plague alone, that of darkness, was called horrible. What name, then, shall we give to the darkness of hell which is to last not for three days alone but for all eternity?

—The horror of this strait and dark prison is increased by its awful stench. All the filth of the world, all the offal and scum of the world, we are told, shall run there as to a vast reeking sewer when the terrible conflagration of the last day has purged the world. The brimstone, too, which burns there in such prodigious quantity fills all hell with its intolerable stench; and the bodies of the damned themselves exhale such a pestilential odour that, as saint Bonaventure says, one of them alone would suffice to infect the whole world. The very air of this world, that pure element, becomes foul and unbreathable when it has been long enclosed. Consider then what must be the foulness of the air of hell. Imagine some foul and putrid corpse that has lain rotting and decomposing in the grave, a jelly-like mass of liquid corruption. Imagine such a corpse a prey to flames, devoured by the fire of burning brimstone and giving off dense choking fumes of nauseous loathsome decomposition. And then imagine this sickening stench, multiplied a millionfold and a millionfold again from the millions upon millions of fetid carcasses massed together in the reeking darkness, a huge and rotting human fungus. Imagine all this, and you will have some idea of the horror of the stench of hell.

—But this stench is not, horrible though it is, the greatest physical torment to which the damned are subjected. The torment of fire is the greatest torment to which the tyrant has ever subjected his fellow creatures. Place your finger for a moment in the flame of a candle and you will feel the pain of fire. But our earthly fire was created by God for the benefit of man, to maintain in him the spark of life and to help him in the useful arts, whereas the fire of hell is of another quality and was created by God to torture and punish the unrepentant sinner. Our earthly fire also consumes more or less rapidly according as the object which it attacks is more or less combustible, so that human ingenuity has even succeeded in inventing chemical preparations to check or frustrate its action. But the sulphurous brimstone which burns in hell is a substance which is specially designed to burn for ever and for ever with unspeakable fury. Moreover, our earthly fire destroys at the same time as it burns, so that the more intense it is the shorter is its duration; but the fire of hell has this property, that it preserves that which it burns, and, though it rages with incredible intensity, it rages for ever.

—Our earthly fire again, no matter how fierce or widespread it may be, is always of a limited extent; but the lake of fire in hell is boundless, shoreless and bottomless. It is on record that the devil himself, when asked the question by a certain soldier, was obliged to confess that if a whole mountain were thrown into the burning ocean of hell it would be burned up in an instant like a piece of wax. And this terrible fire will not afflict the bodies of the damned only from without, but each lost soul will be a hell unto itself, the boundless fire raging in its very vitals. O, how terrible is the lot of those wretched beings! The blood seethes and boils in the veins, the brains are boiling in the skull, the heart in the breast glowing and bursting, the bowels a red-hot mass of burning pulp, the tender eyes flaming like molten balls.

—And yet what I have said as to the strength and quality and boundlessness of this fire is as nothing when compared to its intensity, an intensity which it has as being the instrument chosen by divine design for the punishment of soul and body alike. It is a fire which proceeds directly from the ire of God, working not of its own activity but as an instrument of Divine vengeance. As the waters of baptism cleanse the soul with the body, so do the fires of punishment torture the spirit with the flesh. Every sense of the flesh is tortured and every faculty of the soul therewith: the eyes with impenetrable utter darkness, the nose with noisome odours, the ears with yells and howls and execrations, the taste with foul matter, leprous corruption, nameless suffocating filth, the touch with redhot goads and spikes, with cruel tongues of flame. And through the several torments of the senses the immortal soul is tortured eternally in its very essence amid the leagues upon leagues of glowing fires kindled in the abyss by the offended majesty of the Omnipotent God and fanned into everlasting and ever-increasing fury by the breath of the anger of the God-head.

—Consider finally that the torment of this infernal prison is increased by the company of the damned themselves. Evil company on earth is so noxious that the plants, as if by instinct, withdraw from the company of whatsoever is deadly or hurtful to them. In hell all laws are overturned—there is no thought of family or country, of ties, of relationships. The damned howl and scream at one another, their torture and rage intensified by the presence of beings tortured and raging like themselves. All sense of humanity is forgotten. The yells of the suffering sinners fill the remotest corners of the vast abyss. The mouths of the damned are full of blasphemies against God and of hatred for their fellow sufferers and of curses against those souls which were their accomplices in sin. In olden times it was the custom to punish the parricide, the man who had raised his murderous hand against his father, by casting him into the depths of the sea in a sack in which were placed a cock, a monkey, and a serpent. The intention of those law-givers who framed such a law, which seems cruel in our times, was to punish the criminal by the company of hurtful and hateful beasts. But what is the fury of those dumb beasts compared with the fury of execration which bursts from the parched lips and aching throats of the damned in hell when they behold in their companions in misery those who aided and abetted them in sin, those whose words sowed the first seeds of evil thinking and evil living in their minds, those whose immodest suggestions led them on to sin, those whose eyes tempted and allured them from the path of virtue. They turn upon those accomplices and upbraid them and curse them. But they are helpless and hopeless: it is too late now for repentance.

—Last of all consider the frightful torment to those damned souls, tempters and tempted alike, of the company of the devils. These devils will afflict the damned in two ways, by their presence and by their reproaches. We can have no idea of how horrible these devils are. Saint Catherine of Siena once saw a devil and she has written that, rather than look again for one single instant on such a frightful monster, she would prefer to walk until the end of her life along a track of red coals. These devils, who were once beautiful angels, have become as hideous and ugly as they once were beautiful. They mock and jeer at the lost souls whom they dragged down to ruin. It is they, the foul demons, who are made in hell the voices of conscience. Why did you sin? Why did you lend an ear to the temptings of friends? Why did you turn aside from your pious practices and good works? Why did you not shun the occasions of sin? Why did you not leave that evil companion? Why did you not give up that lewd habit, that impure habit? Why did you not listen to the counsels of your confessor? Why did you not, even after you had fallen the first or the second or the third or the fourth or the hundredth time, repent of your evil ways and turn to God who only waited for your repentance to absolve you of your sins? Now the time for repentance has gone by. Time is, time was, but time shall be no more! Time was to sin in secrecy, to indulge in that sloth and pride, to covet the unlawful, to yield to the promptings of your lower nature, to live like the beasts of the field, nay worse than the beasts of the field, for they, at least, are but brutes and have no reason to guide them: time was, but time shall be no more. God spoke to you by so many voices, but you would not hear. You would not crush out that pride and anger in your heart, you would not restore those ill-gotten goods, you would not obey the precepts of your holy church nor attend to your religious duties, you would not abandon those wicked companions, you would not avoid those dangerous temptations. Such is the language of those fiendish tormentors, words of taunting and of reproach, of hatred and of disgust. Of disgust, yes! For even they, the very devils, when they sinned, sinned by such a sin as alone was compatible with such angelical natures, a rebellion of the intellect: and they, even they, the foul devils must turn away, revolted and disgusted, from the contemplation of those unspeakable sins by which degraded man outrages and defiles the temple of the Holy Ghost, defiles and pollutes himself.

—O, my dear little brothers in Christ, may it never be our lot to hear that language! May it never be our lot, I say! In the last day of terrible reckoning I pray fervently to God that not a single soul of those who are in this chapel today may be found among those miserable beings whom the Great Judge shall command to depart for ever from His sight, that not one of us may ever hear ringing in his ears the awful sentence of rejection: *Depart from me, ye cursed, into everlasting fire which was prepared for the devil and his angels!*

He came down the aisle of the chapel, his legs shaking and the scalp of his head trembling as though it had been touched by ghostly fingers. He passed up the staircase and into the corridor along the walls of which the overcoats and waterproofs hung like gibbeted malefactors, headless and dripping and shapeless. And at every step he feared that he had already died, that his soul had been wrenched forth of the sheath of his body, that he was plunging headlong through space.

He could not grip the floor with his feet and sat heavily at his desk, opening one of his books at random and poring over it. Every word for him. It was true. God was almighty. God could call him now, call him as he sat at his desk, before he had time to be conscious of the summons. God had called him. Yes? What? Yes? His flesh shrank together as it felt the approach of the ravenous tongues of flames, dried up as it felt about it the swirl of stifling air. He had died. Yes. He was judged. A wave of fire swept through his body: the first. Again a wave. His brain began to glow. Another. His brain was simmering and bubbling within the cracking tenement of the skull. Flames burst forth from his skull like a corolla, shrieking like voices:

—Hell! Hell! Hell! Hell! Hell!

Voices spoke near him:

—On hell.

—I suppose he rubbed it into you well.

—You bet he did. He put us all into a blue funk.

—That's what you fellows want: and plenty of it to make you work.

He leaned back weakly in his desk. He had not died. God had spared him still. He was still in the familiar world of the school. Mr Tate and Vincent Heron stood at the window, talking, jesting, gazing out at the bleak rain, moving their heads.

—I wish it would clear up. I had arranged to go for a spin on the bike with some fellows out by Malahide. But the roads must be knee-deep.

—It might clear up, sir.

The voices that he knew so well, the common words, the quiet of the classroom when the voices paused and the silence was filled by the sound of softly browsing cattle as the other boys munched their lunches tranquilly, lulled his aching soul.

There was still time. O Mary, refuge of sinners, intercede for him! O Virgin Undefiled, save him from the gulf of death!

The English lesson began with the hearing of the history. Royal persons, favourites, intriguers, bishops, passed like mute phantoms behind their veil of names. All had died: all had been judged. What did it profit a man to gain the whole world if he lost his soul? At last he had understood: and human life lay around him, a plain of peace whereon ant-like men laboured in brotherhood, their dead sleeping under quiet mounds. The elbow of his companion touched him and his heart was touched: and when he spoke to answer a question of his master he heard his own voice full of the quietude of humility and contrition.

His soul sank back deeper into depths of contrite peace, no longer able to suffer the pain of dread, and sending forth, as he sank, a faint prayer. Ah yes, he would still be spared; he would repent in his heart and be forgiven; and then those above, those in heaven, would see what he would do to make up for the past: a whole life, every hour of life. Only wait.

—All, God! All, all!

A messenger came to the door to say that confessions were being heard in the chapel. Four boys left the room; and he heard others passing down the corridor. A tremulous chill blew round his heart, no stronger than a little wind, and yet, listening and suffering silently, he seemed to have laid an ear against the muscle of his own heart, feeling it close and quail, listening to the flutter of its ventricles.

No escape. He had to confess, to speak out in words what he had done and thought, sin after sin. How? How?

—Father, I . . .

The thought slid like a cold shining rapier into his tender flesh: confession. But not there in the chapel of the college. He would confess all, every sin of deed and thought, sincerely; but not there among his school companions. Far away from there in some dark place he would murmur out his own shame; and he besought God humbly not to be offended with him if he did not dare to confess in the college chapel and in utter abjection of spirit he craved forgiveness mutely of the boyish hearts about him.

Time passed.

He sat again in the front bench of the chapel. The daylight without was already failing and, as it fell slowly through the dull red blinds, it seemed that the sun of the last day was going down and that all souls were being gathered for the judgement.

—*I am cast away from the sight of Thine eyes:* words taken, my dear little brothers in Christ, from the Book of Psalms, thirtieth chapter, twenty-third verse. In the name of the Father and of the Son and of the Holy Ghost. Amen.

The preacher began to speak in a quiet friendly tone. His face was kind and he joined gently the fingers of each hand, forming a frail cage by the union of their tips.

—This morning we endeavoured, in our reflection upon hell, to make what our holy founder calls in his book of spiritual exercises, the composition of place. We endeavoured, that is, to imagine with the senses of the mind, in our imagination, the material character of that awful place and of the physical torments which all who are in hell endure. This evening we shall consider for a few moments the nature of the spiritual torments of hell.

—Sin, remember, is a twofold enormity. It is a base consent to the promptings of our corrupt nature to the lower instincts, to that which is gross and beast-like; and it is also a turning away from the counsel of our higher nature, from all that is pure and holy, from the Holy God Himself. For this reason mortal sin is punished in hell by two different forms of punishment, physical and spiritual.

—Now of all these spiritual pains by far the greatest is the pain of loss, so great, in fact, that in itself it is a torment greater than all the others. Saint Thomas, the greatest doctor of the church, the angelic doctor, as he is called, says that the worst damnation consists in this, that the understanding of man is totally deprived of divine light and his affection obstinately turned away from the goodness of God. God, remember, is a being infinitely good, and therefore the loss of such a being must be a loss infinitely painful. In this life we have not a very clear idea of what such a loss must be, but the damned in hell, for their greater torment, have a full understanding of that which they have lost, and understand that they have lost it through their own sins and have lost it for ever. At the very instant of death the bonds of the flesh are broken asunder and the soul at once flies towards God as towards the centre of her existence. Remember, my dear little boys, our souls long to be with God. We come from God, we live by God, we belong to God: we are His, inalienably His. God loves with a divine love every human soul, and every human soul lives in that love. How could it be otherwise? Every breath that we draw, every thought of our brain, every instant of life proceeds from God's inexhaustible goodness. And if it be pain for a mother to be parted from her child, for a man to be exiled from hearth and home, for friend to be sundered from friend, O think what pain, what anguish it must be for the poor soul to be spurned from the presence of the supremely good and loving Creator Who has called that soul into existence from nothingness and sustained it in life and loved it with an immeasurable love. This, then, to be separated for ever from its greatest good, from God, and to feel the anguish of that separation, knowing full well that it is unchangeable: this is the greatest torment which the created soul is capable of bearing, *poena damni*, the pain of loss.

—The second pain which will afflict the souls of the damned in hell is the pain of conscience. Just as in dead bodies worms are engendered by putrefaction, so in the souls of the lost there arises a perpetual remorse from the putrefaction of sin, the sting of conscience, the worm, as Pope Innocent the Third calls it, of the triple sting. The first sting inflicted by this cruel worm will be the memory of past pleasures. O what a dreadful memory will that be! In the lake of all-devouring flame the proud king will remember the pomps of his court, the wise but wicked man his libraries and instruments of research, the lover of artistic pleasures his marbles and pictures and other art treasures, he who delighted in the pleasures of the table his gorgeous feasts, his dishes prepared with such delicacy, his choice wines; the miser will remember his hoard of gold, the robber his ill-gotten wealth, the angry and revengeful and merciless murderers their deeds of blood and violence in which they revelled, the impure and adulterous the unspeakable and filthy pleasures in which they delighted. They will remember all this and loathe themselves and their sins. For how miserable will all those pleasures seem to the soul condemned to suffer in hellfire for ages and ages. How they will rage and fume to think that they have lost the bliss of heaven for the dross of earth, for a few pieces of metal, for vain honours, for bodily comforts, for a tingling of the nerves. They will repent indeed: and this is the second sting of the worm of conscience, a late and fruitless sorrow for sins committed. Divine justice insists that the understanding of those miserable wretches be fixed continually on the sins of which they were guilty, and moreover, as saint Augustine points out, God will impart to them His own knowledge of sin, so that sin will appear to them in all its hideous malice as it appears to the eyes of God Himself. They will behold their sins in all their foulness and repent but it will be too late and then they will bewail the good occasions which they neglected. This is the last and deepest and most cruel sting of the worm of conscience. The conscience will say: You had time and opportunity to repent and would not. You were brought up religiously by your parents. You had the sacraments and grace and indulgences of the church to aid you. You had the minister of God to preach to you, to call you back when you had strayed, to forgive you your sins, no matter how many, how abominable, if only you had confessed and repented. No. You would not. You flouted the ministers of holy religion, you turned your back on the confessional, you wallowed deeper and deeper in the mire of sin. God appealed to you, threatened you, entreated you to return to Him. O, what shame, what misery! The Ruler of the universe entreated you, a creature of clay, to love Him Who made you and to keep His law. No. You would not. And now, though you were to flood all hell with your tears if you could still weep, all that sea of repentance would not gain for you what a single tear of true repentance shed during your mortal life would have gained for you. You implore now a moment of earthly life wherein to repent: in vain. That time is gone: gone for ever.

—Such is the threefold sting of conscience, the viper which gnaws the very heart's core of the wretches in hell, so that filled with hellish fury they curse themselves for their folly and curse the evil companions who have brought them to such ruin and curse the devils who tempted them in life and now mock them in eternity and even revile and curse the Supreme Being Whose goodness and patience they scorned and slighted but Whose justice and power they cannot evade.

—The next spiritual pain to which the damned are subjected is the pain of extension. Man, in this earthly life, though he be capable of many evils, is not capable of them all at once, inasmuch as one evil corrects and counteracts another just as one poison frequently corrects another. In hell, on the contrary, one torment, instead of counteracting another, lends it still greater force: and, moreover, as the internal faculties are more perfect than the external senses, so are they more capable of suffering. Just as every sense is afflicted with a fitting torment, so is every spiritual faculty; the fancy with horrible images, the sensitive faculty with alternate longing and rage, the mind and understanding with an interior darkness more terrible even than the exterior darkness which reigns in that dreadful prison. The malice, impotent though it be, which possesses these demon souls is an evil of boundless extension, of limitless duration, a frightful state of wickedness which we can scarcely realize unless we bear in mind the enormity of sin and the hatred God bears to it.

—Opposed to this pain of extension and yet coexistent with it we have the pain of intensity. Hell is the centre of evils and, as you know, things are more intense at their centres than at their remotest points. There are no contraries or admixtures of any kind to temper or soften in the least the pains of hell. Nay, things which are good in themselves become evil in hell. Company, elsewhere a source of comfort to the afflicted, will be there a continual torment: knowledge, so much longed for as the chief good of the intellect, will there be hated worse than ignorance: light, so much coveted by all creatures from the lord of creation down to the humblest plant in the forest, will be loathed intensely. In this life our sorrows are either not very long or not very great because nature either overcomes them by habits or puts an end to them by sinking under their weight. But in hell the torments cannot be overcome by habit, for while they are of terrible intensity they are at the same time of continual variety, each pain, so to speak, taking fire from another and re-endowing that which has enkindled it with a still fiercer flame. Nor can nature escape from these intense and various tortures by succumbing to them for the soul is sustained and maintained in evil so that its suffering may be the greater. Boundless extension of torment, incredible intensity of suffering, unceasing variety of torture—this is what the divine majesty, so outraged by sinners, demands; this is what the holiness of heaven, slighted and set aside for the lustful and low pleasures of the corrupt flesh, requires; this is what the blood of the innocent Lamb of God, shed for the redemption of sinners, trampled upon by the vilest of the vile, insists upon.

—Last and crowning torture of all the tortures of that awful place is the eternity of hell. Eternity! O, dread and dire word. Eternity! What mind of man can understand it? And remember, it is an eternity of pain. Even though the pains of hell were not so terrible as they are, yet they would become infinite, as they are destined to last for ever. But while they are everlasting they are at the same time, as you know, intolerably intense, unbearably extensive. To bear even the sting of an insect for all eternity would be a dreadful torment. What must it be, then, to bear the manifold tortures of hell for ever? For ever! For all eternity! Not for a year or for an age but for ever. Try to imagine the awful meaning of this. You have often seen the sand on the seashore. How fine are its tiny grains! And how many of those tiny little grains go to make up the small handful which a child grasps in its play. Now imagine a mountain of that sand, a million miles high, reaching from the earth to the farthest heavens, and a million miles broad, extending to remotest space, and a million miles in thickness; and imagine such an enormous mass of countless particles of sand multiplied as often as there are leaves in the forest, drops of water in the mighty ocean, feathers on birds, scales on fish, hairs on animals, atoms in the vast expanse of the air: and imagine that at the end of every million years a little bird came to that mountain and carried away in its beak a tiny grain of that sand. How many millions upon millions of centuries would pass before that bird had carried away even a square foot of that mountain, how many eons upon eons of ages before it had carried away all? Yet at the end of that immense stretch of time not even one instant of eternity could be said to have ended. At the end of all those billions and trillions of years eternity would have scarcely begun. And if that mountain rose again after it had been all carried away, and if the bird came again and carried it all away again grain by grain, and if it so rose and sank as many times as there are stars in the sky, atoms in the air, drops of water in the sea, leaves on the trees, feathers upon birds, scales upon fish, hairs upon animals, at the end of all those innumerable risings and sinkings of that immeasurably vast mountain not one single instant of eternity could be said to have ended; even then, at the end of such a period, after that eon of time the mere thought of which makes our very brain reel dizzily, eternity would scarcely have begun.

—A holy saint (one of our own fathers I believe it was) was once vouchsafed a vision of hell. It seemed to him that he stood in the midst of a great hall, dark and silent save for the ticking of a great clock. The ticking went on unceasingly; and it seemed to this saint that the sound of the ticking was the ceaseless repetition of the words—ever, never; ever, never. Ever to be in hell, never to be in heaven; ever to be shut off from the presence of God, never to enjoy the beatific vision; ever to be eaten with flames, gnawed by vermin, goaded with burning spikes, never to be free from those pains; ever to have the conscience upbraid one, the memory enrage, the mind filled with darkness and despair, never to escape; ever to curse and revile the foul demons who gloat fiendishly over the misery of their dupes, never to behold the shining raiment of the blessed spirits; ever to cry out of the abyss of fire to God for an instant, a single instant, of respite from such awful agony, never to receive, even for an instant, God's pardon; ever to suffer, never to enjoy; ever to be damned, never to be saved; ever, never; ever, never. O, what a dreadful punishment! An eternity of endless agony, of endless bodily and spiritual torment, without one ray of hope, without one moment of cessation, of agony limitless in intensity, of torment infinitely varied, of torture that sustains eternally that which it eternally devours, of anguish that everlastingly preys upon the spirit while it racks the flesh, an eternity, every instant of which is itself an eternity of woe. Such is the terrible punishment decreed for those who die in mortal sin by an almighty and a just God.

—Yes, a just God! Men, reasoning always as men, are astonished that God should mete out an everlasting and infinite punishment in the fires of hell for a single grievous sin. They reason thus because, blinded by the gross illusion of the flesh and the darkness of human understanding, they are unable to comprehend the hideous malice of mortal sin. They reason thus because they are unable to comprehend that even venial sin is of such a foul and hideous nature that even if the omnipotent Creator could end all the evil and misery in the world, the wars, the diseases, the robberies, the crimes, the deaths, the murders, on condition that he allowed a single venial sin to pass unpunished, a single venial sin, a lie, an angry look, a moment of wilful sloth, He, the great omnipotent God could not do so because sin, be it in thought or deed, is a transgression of His law and God would not be God if He did not punish the transgressor.

—A sin, an instant of rebellious pride of the intellect, made Lucifer and a third part of the cohort of angels fall from their glory. A sin, an instant of folly and weakness, drove Adam and Eve out of Eden and brought death and suffering into the world. To retrieve the consequences of that sin the Only Begotten Son of God came down to earth, lived and suffered and died a most painful death, hanging for three hours on the cross.

—O, my dear little brethren in Christ Jesus, will we then offend that good Redeemer and provoke His anger? Will we trample again upon that torn and mangled corpse? Will we spit upon that face so full of sorrow and love? Will we too, like the cruel jews and the brutal soldiers, mock that gentle and compassionate Saviour Who trod alone for our sake the awful wine-press of sorrow? Every word of sin is a wound in His tender side. Every sinful act is a thorn piercing His head. Every impure thought, deliberately yielded to, is a keen lance transfixing that sacred and loving heart. No, no. It is impossible for any human being to do that which offends so deeply the divine majesty, that which is punished by an eternity of agony, that which crucifies again the Son of God and makes a mockery of Him.

—I pray to God that my poor words may have availed today to confirm in holiness those who are in a state of grace, to strengthen the wavering, to lead back to the state of grace the poor soul that has strayed if any such be among you. I pray to God, and do you pray with me, that we may repent of our sins. I will ask you now, all of you, to repeat after me the act of contrition, kneeling here in this humble chapel in the presence of God. He is there in the tabernacle burning with love for mankind, ready to comfort the afflicted. Be not afraid. No matter how many or how foul the sins if you only repent of them they will be forgiven you. Let no worldly shame hold you back. God is still the merciful Lord who wishes not the eternal death of the sinner but rather that he be converted and live.

—He calls you to Him. You are His. He made you out of nothing. He loved you as only a God can love. His arms are open to receive you even though you have sinned against Him. Come to Him, poor sinner, poor vain and erring sinner. Now is the acceptable time. Now is the hour.

The priest rose and, turning towards the altar, knelt upon the step before the tabernacle in the fallen gloom. He waited till all in the chapel had knelt and every least noise was still. Then, raising his head, he repeated the act of contrition, phrase by phrase, with fervour. The boys answered him phrase by phrase. Stephen, his tongue cleaving to his palate, bowed his head, praying with his heart.

—*O my God!*—
—*O my God!*—
—*I am heartily sorry*—
—*I am heartily sorry*—
—*for having offended Thee*—
—*for having offended Thee*—
—*and I detest my sins*—
—*and I detest my sins*—
—*above every other evil*—
—*above every other evil*—

—because they displease Thee, my God—
—because they displease Thee, my God—
—Who art so deserving—
—Who art so deserving—
—of all my love—
—of all my love—
—and I firmly purpose—
—and I firmly purpose—
—by Thy holy grace—
—by Thy holy grace—
—never more to offend Thee—
—never more to offend Thee—
—and to amend my life—
—and to amend my life—

***

He went up to his room after dinner in order to be alone with his soul, and at every step his soul seemed to sigh; at every step his soul mounted with his feet, sighing in the ascent, through a region of viscid gloom.

He halted on the landing before the door and then, grasping the porcelain knob, opened the door quickly. He waited in fear, his soul pining within him, praying silently that death might not touch his brow as he passed over the threshold, that the fiends that inhabit darkness might not be given power over him. He waited still at the threshold as at the entrance to some dark cave. Faces were there; eyes: they waited and watched.

—We knew perfectly well of course that though it was bound to come to the light he would find considerable difficulty in endeavouring to try to induce himself to try to endeavour to ascertain the spiritual plenipotentiary and so we knew of course perfectly well—

Murmuring faces waited and watched; murmurous voices filled the dark shell of the cave. He feared intensely in spirit and in flesh but, raising his head bravely, he strode into the room firmly. A doorway, a room, the same room, same window. He told himself calmly that those words had absolutely no sense which had seemed to rise murmurously from the dark. He told himself that it was simply his room with the door open.

He closed the door and, walking swiftly to the bed, knelt beside it and covered his face with his hands. His hands were cold and damp and his limbs ached with chill. Bodily unrest and chill and weariness beset him, routing his thoughts. Why was he kneeling there like a child saying his evening prayers? To be alone with his soul, to examine his conscience, to meet his sins face to face, to recall their times and manners and circumstances, to weep over them. He could not weep. He could not summon them to his memory. He felt only an ache of soul and body, his whole being, memory, will, understanding, flesh, benumbed and weary.

That was the work of devils, to scatter his thoughts and over-cloud his conscience, assailing him at the gates of the cowardly and sin-corrupted flesh: and, praying God timidly to forgive him his weakness, he crawled up on to the bed and, wrapping the blankets closely about him, covered his face again with his hands. He had sinned. He had sinned so deeply against heaven and before God that he was not worthy to be called God's child.

Could it be that he, Stephen Dedalus, had done those things? His conscience sighed in answer. Yes, he had done them, secretly, filthily, time after time, and, hardened in sinful impenitence, he had dared to wear the mask of holiness before the tabernacle itself while his soul within was a living mass of corruption. How came it that God had not struck him dead? The leprous company of his sins closed about him, breathing upon him, bending over him from all sides. He strove to forget them in an act of prayer, huddling his limbs closer together and binding down his eyelids: but the senses of his soul would not be bound and, though his eyes were shut fast, he saw the places where he had sinned and, though his ears were tightly covered, he heard. He desired with all his will not to hear or see. He desired till his frame shook under the strain of his desire and until the senses of his soul closed. They closed for an instant and then opened. He saw.

A field of stiff weeds and thistles and tufted nettle-bunches. Thick among the tufts of rank stiff growth lay battered canisters and clots and coils of solid excrement. A faint marshlight struggling upwards from all the ordure through the bristling grey-green weeds. An evil smell, faint and foul as the light, curled upwards sluggishly out of the canisters and from the stale crusted dung.

Creatures were in the field: one, three, six: creatures were moving in the field, hither and thither. Goatish creatures with human faces, hornybrowed, lightly bearded and grey as india-rubber. The malice of evil glittered in their hard eyes, as they moved hither and thither, trailing their long tails behind them. A rictus of cruel malignity lit up greyly their old bony faces. One was clasping about his ribs a torn flannel waistcoat, another complained monotonously as his beard stuck in the tufted weeds. Soft language issued from their spittleless lips as they swished in slow circles round and round the field, winding hither and thither through the weeds, dragging their long tails amid the rattling canisters. They moved in slow circles, circling closer and closer to enclose, to enclose, soft language issuing from their lips, their long swishing tails besmeared with stale shite, thrusting upwards their terrific faces . . .

Help!

He flung the blankets from him madly to free his face and neck. That was his hell. God had allowed him to see the hell reserved for his sins: stinking, bestial, malignant, a hell of lecherous goatish fiends. For him! For him!

He sprang from the bed, the reeking odour pouring down his throat, clogging and revolting his entrails. Air! The air of heaven! He stumbled towards the window, groaning and almost fainting with sickness. At the washstand a convulsion seized him within; and, clasping his cold forehead wildly, he vomited profusely in agony.

When the fit had spent itself he walked weakly to the window and, lifting the sash, sat in a corner of the embrasure and leaned his elbow upon the sill. The rain had drawn off; and amid the moving vapours from point to point of light the city was spinning about herself a soft cocoon of yellowish haze. Heaven was still and faintly luminous and the air sweet to breathe, as in a thicket drenched with showers; and amid peace and shimmering lights and quiet fragrance he made a covenant with his heart.

He prayed:

—He once had meant to come on earth in heavenly glory but we sinned; and then He could not safely visit us but with a shrouded majesty and a bedimmed radiance for He was God. So He came Himself in weakness not in power and He sent thee, a creature in His stead, with a creature's comeliness and lustre suited to our state. And now thy very face and form, dear mother speak to us of the Eternal not like earthly beauty, dangerous to look upon, but like the morning star which is thy emblem,

bright and musical, breathing purity, telling of heaven and infusing peace.
O harbinger of day! O light of the pilgrim! Lead us still as thou hast led.
In the dark night, across the bleak wilderness guide us on to our Lord
Jesus, guide us home.

His eyes were dimmed with tears and, looking humbly up to heaven, he wept for the innocence he had lost.

When evening had fallen he left the house, and the first touch of the damp dark air and the noise of the door as it closed behind him made ache again his conscience, lulled by prayer and tears. Confess! Confess! It was not enough to lull the conscience with a tear and a prayer. He had to kneel before the minister of the Holy Ghost and tell over his hidden sins truly and repentantly. Before he heard again the footboard of the housedoor trail over the threshold as it opened to let him in, before he saw again the table in the kitchen set for supper he would have knelt and confessed. It was quite simple.

The ache of conscience ceased and he walked onward swiftly through the dark streets. There were so many flagstones on the footpath of that street and so many streets in that city and so many cities in the world. Yet eternity had no end. He was in mortal sin. Even once was a mortal sin. It could happen in an instant. But how so quickly? By seeing or by thinking of seeing. The eyes see the thing, without having wished first to see. Then in an instant it happens. But does that part of the body understand or what? The serpent, the most subtle beast of the field. It must understand when it desires in one instant and then prolongs its own desire instant after instant, sinfully. It feels and understands and desires. What a horrible thing! Who made it to be like that, a bestial part of the body able to understand bestially and desire bestially? Was that then he or an inhuman thing moved by a lower soul? His soul sickened at the thought of a torpid snaky life feeding itself out of the tender marrow of his life and fattening upon the slime of lust. O why was that so? O why?

He cowered in the shadow of the thought, abasing himself in the awe of God Who had made all things and all men. Madness. Who could think such a thought? And, cowering in darkness and abject, he prayed mutely to his guardian angel to drive away with his sword the demon that was whispering to his brain.

The whisper ceased and he knew then clearly that his own soul had sinned in thought and word and deed wilfully through his own body. Confess! He had to confess every sin. How could he utter in words to the priest what he had done? Must, must. Or how could he explain without dying of shame? Or how could he have done such things without shame? A madman! Confess! O he would indeed to be free and sinless again! Perhaps the priest would know. O dear God!

He walked on and on through ill-lit streets, fearing to stand still for a moment lest it might seem that he held back from what awaited him, fearing to arrive at that towards which he still turned with longing. How beautiful must be a soul in the state of grace when God looked upon it with love!

Frowsy girls sat along the curbstones before their baskets. Their dank hair hung trailed over their brows. They were not beautiful to see as they crouched in the mire. But their souls were seen by God; and if their souls were in a state of grace they were radiant to see: and God loved them, seeing them.

A wasting breath of humiliation blew bleakly over his soul to think of how he had fallen, to feel that those souls were dearer to God than his. The wind blew over him and passed on to the myriads and myriads of other souls on whom God's favour shone now more and now less, stars now brighter and now dimmer sustained and failing. And the glimmering souls passed away, sustained and failing, merged in a moving breath. One soul was lost; a tiny soul: his. It flickered once and went out, forgotten, lost. The end: black, cold, void waste.

Consciousness of place came ebbing back to him slowly over a vast tract of time unlit, unfelt, unlived. The squalid scene composed itself around him; the common accents, the burning gas-jets in the shops, odours of fish and spirits and wet sawdust, moving men and women. An old woman was about to cross the street, an oilcan in her hand. He bent down and asked her was there a chapel near.

—A chapel, sir? Yes, sir. Church Street chapel.

—Church?

She shifted the can to her other hand and directed him; and, as she held out her reeking withered right hand under its fringe of shawl, he bent lower towards her, saddened and soothed by her voice.

—Thank you.

—You are quite welcome, sir.

The candles on the high altar had been extinguished but the fragrance of incense still floated down the dim nave. Bearded workmen with pious faces were guiding a canopy out through a side door, the sacristan aiding them with quiet gestures and words. A few of the faithful still lingered praying before one of the side-altars or kneeling in the benches near the confessionals. He approached timidly and knelt at the last bench in the body, thankful for the peace and silence and fragrant shadow of the church. The board on which he knelt was narrow and worn and those who knelt near him were humble followers of Jesus. Jesus too had been born in poverty and had worked in the shop of a carpenter, cutting boards and planing them, and had first spoken of the kingdom of God to poor fishermen, teaching all men to be meek and humble of heart.

He bowed his head upon his hands, bidding his heart be meek and humble that he might be like those who knelt beside him and his prayer as acceptable as theirs. He prayed beside them but it was hard. His soul was foul with sin and he dared not ask forgiveness with the simple trust of those whom Jesus, in the mysterious ways of God, had called first to His side, the carpenters, the fishermen, poor and simple people following a lowly trade, handling and shaping the wood of trees, mending their nets with patience.

A tall figure came down the aisle and the penitents stirred; and at the last moment, glancing up swiftly, he saw a long grey beard and the brown habit of a capuchin. The priest entered the box and was hidden. Two penitents rose and entered the confessional at either side. The wooden slide was drawn back and the faint murmur of a voice troubled the silence.

His blood began to murmur in his veins, murmuring like a sinful city summoned from its sleep to hear its doom. Little flakes of fire fell and powdery ashes fell softly, alighting on the houses of men. They stirred, waking from sleep, troubled by the heated air.

The slide was shot back. The penitent emerged from the side of the box. The farther side was drawn. A woman entered quietly and deftly where the first penitent had knelt. The faint murmur began again.

He could still leave the chapel. He could stand up, put one foot before the other and walk out softly and then run, run, run swiftly through the dark streets. He could still escape from the shame. Had it been any terrible crime but that one sin! Had it been murder! Little fiery flakes fell and touched him at all points, shameful thoughts, shameful words, shameful acts. Shame covered him wholly like fine glowing ashes falling continually. To say it in words! His soul, stifling and helpless, would cease to be.

The slide was shot back. A penitent emerged from the farther side of the box. The near slide was drawn. A penitent entered where the other penitent had come out. A soft whispering noise floated in vaporous cloudlets out of the box. It was the woman: soft whispering cloudlets, soft whispering vapour, whispering and vanishing.

He beat his breast with his fist humbly, secretly under cover of the wooden armrest. He would be at one with others and with God. He would love his neighbour. He would love God who had made and loved him. He would kneel and pray with others and be happy. God would look down on him and on them and would love them all.

It was easy to be good. God's yoke was sweet and light. It was better never to have sinned, to have remained always a child, for God loved little children and suffered them to come to Him. It was a terrible and a sad thing to sin. But God was merciful to poor sinners who were truly sorry. How true that was! That was indeed goodness.

The slide was shot to suddenly. The penitent came out. He was next. He stood up in terror and walked blindly into the box.

At last it had come. He knelt in the silent gloom and raised his eyes to the white crucifix suspended above him. God could see that he was sorry. He would tell all his sins. His confession would be long, long. Everybody in the chapel would know then what a sinner he had been. Let them know. It was true. But God had promised to forgive him if he was sorry. He was sorry. He clasped his hands and raised them towards the white form, praying with his darkened eyes, praying with all his trembling body, swaying his head to and fro like a lost creature, praying with whimpering lips.

—Sorry! Sorry! O sorry!

The slide clicked back and his heart bounded in his breast. The face of an old priest was at the grating, averted from him, leaning upon a hand. He made the sign of the cross and prayed of the priest to bless him for he had sinned. Then, bowing his head, he repeated the *Confiteor* in fright. At the words *my most grievous fault* he ceased, breathless.

—How long is it since your last confession, my child?

—A long time, father.

—A month, my child?

—Longer, father.

—Three months, my child?

—Longer, father.

—Six months?

—Eight months, father.

He had begun. The priest asked:

—And what do you remember since that time?

He began to confess his sins: masses missed, prayers not said, lies.

—Anything else, my child?

Sins of anger, envy of others, gluttony, vanity, disobedience.

—Anything else, my child?

—Sloth.

—Anything else, my child?

There was no help. He murmured:

—I . . . committed sins of impurity, father.

The priest did not turn his head.

—With yourself, my child?

—And . . . with others.

—With women, my child?

—Yes, father.

—Were they married women, my child?

He did not know. His sins trickled from his lips, one by one, trickled in shameful drops from his soul, festering and oozing like a sore, a squalid stream of vice. The last sins oozed forth, sluggish, filthy. There was no more to tell. He bowed his head, overcome.

The Priest was silent. Then he asked:

—How old are you, my child?

—Sixteen, father.

The priest passed his hand several times over his face. Then, resting his forehead against his hand, he leaned towards the grating and, with eyes still averted, spoke slowly. His voice was weary and old.

—You are very young, my child, he said, and let me implore of you to give up that sin. It is a terrible sin. It kills the body and it kills the soul. It is the cause of many crimes and misfortunes. Give it up, my child, for God's sake. It is dishonourable and unmanly. You cannot know where that wretched habit will lead you or where it will come against you. As long as you commit that sin, my poor child, you will never be worth one farthing to God. Pray to our mother Mary to help you. She will help you, my child. Pray to Our Blessed Lady when that sin comes into your mind. I am sure you will do that, will you not? You repent of all those sins. I am sure you do. And you will promise God now that by His holy grace you will never offend Him any more by that wicked sin. You will make that solemn promise to God, will you not?

—Yes, father.

The old and weary voice fell like sweet rain upon his quaking parching heart. How sweet and sad!

—Do so my poor child. The devil has led you astray. Drive him back to hell when he tempts you to dishonour your body in that way—the foul spirit who hates our Lord. Promise God now that you will give up that sin, that wretched wretched sin.

Blinded by his tears and by the light of God's mercifulness he bent his head and heard the grave words of absolution spoken and saw the priest's hand raised above him in token of forgiveness.

—God bless you, my child. Pray for me.

He knelt to say his penance, praying in a corner of the dark nave; and his prayers ascended to heaven from his purified heart like perfume streaming upwards from a heart of white rose.

The muddy streets were gay. He strode homeward, conscious of an invisible grace pervading and making light his limbs. In spite of all he had done it. He had confessed and God had pardoned him. His soul was made fair and holy once more, holy and happy.

It would be beautiful to die if God so willed. It was beautiful to live in grace a life of peace and virtue and forbearance with others.

He sat by the fire in the kitchen, not daring to speak for happiness. Till that moment he had not known how beautiful and peaceful life could be. The green square of paper pinned round the lamp cast down a tender shade. On the dresser was a plate of sausages and white pudding and on the shelf there were eggs. They would be for the breakfast in the morning after the communion in the college chapel. White pudding and eggs and sausages and cups of tea. How simple and beautiful was life after all! And life lay all before him.

In a dream he fell asleep. In a dream he rose and saw that it was morning. In a waking dream he went through the quiet morning towards the college.

The boys were all there, kneeling in their places. He knelt among them, happy and shy. The altar was heaped with fragrant masses of white flowers; and in the morning light the pale flames of the candles among the white flowers were clear and silent as his own soul.

He knelt before the altar with his classmates, holding the altar cloth with them over a living rail of hands. His hands were trembling and his soul trembled as he heard the priest pass with the ciborium from communicant to communicant.

—*Corpus Domini nostri.*

Could it be? He knelt there sinless and timid; and he would hold upon his tongue the host and God would enter his purified body.

—*In vitam eternam. Amen.*

Another life! A life of grace and virtue and happiness! It was true. It was not a dream from which he would wake. The past was past.

—*Corpus Domini nostri.*

The ciborium had come to him.

4

S unday was dedicated to the mystery of the Holy Trinity, Monday to the Holy Ghost, Tuesday to the Guardian Angels, Wednesday to saint Joseph, Thursday to the Most Blessed Sacrament of the Altar, Friday to the Suffering Jesus, Saturday to the Blessed Virgin Mary.

Every morning he hallowed himself anew in the presence of some holy image or mystery. His day began with an heroic offering of its every moment of thought or action for the intentions of the sovereign pontiff and with an early mass. The raw morning air whetted his resolute piety; and often as he knelt among the few worshippers at the side-altar, following with his interleaved prayer-book the murmur of the priest, he glanced up for an instant towards the vested figure standing in the gloom between the two candles, which were the old and the new testaments, and imagined that he was kneeling at mass in the catacombs.

His daily life was laid out in devotional areas. By means of ejaculations and prayers he stored up ungrudgingly for the souls in purgatory centuries of days and quarantines and years; yet the spiritual triumph which he felt in achieving with ease so many fabulous ages of canonical penances did not wholly reward his zeal of prayer, since he could never know how much temporal punishment he had remitted by way of suffrage for the agonizing souls; and fearful lest in the midst of the purgatorial fire, which differed from the infernal only in that it was not everlasting, his penance might avail no more than a drop of moisture, he drove his soul daily through an increasing circle of works of supererogation.

Every part of his day, divided by what he regarded now as the duties of his station in life, circled about its own centre of spiritual energy. His life seemed to have drawn near to eternity; every thought, word, and deed, every instance of consciousness could be made to revibrate radiantly in heaven; and at times his sense of such immediate repercussion was so lively that he seemed to feel his soul in devotion pressing like fingers the keyboard of a great cash register and to see the amount of his purchase start forth immediately in heaven, not as a number but as a frail column of incense or as a slender flower.

The rosaries, too, which he said constantly—for he carried his beads loose in his trousers' pockets that he might tell them as he walked the streets—transformed themselves into coronals of flowers of such vague unearthly texture that they seemed to him as hueless and odourless as they were nameless. He offered up each of his three daily chaplets that his soul might grow strong in each of the three theological virtues, in faith in the Father Who had created him, in hope in the Son Who had redeemed him and in love of the Holy Ghost Who had sanctified him; and this thrice triple prayer he offered to the Three Persons through Mary in the name of her joyful and sorrowful and glorious mysteries.

On each of the seven days of the week he further prayed that one of the seven gifts of the Holy Ghost might descend upon his soul and drive out of it day by day the seven deadly sins which had defiled it in the past; and he prayed for each gift on its appointed day, confident that it would descend upon him, though it seemed strange to him at times that wisdom and understanding and knowledge were so distinct in their nature that each should be prayed for apart from the others. Yet he believed that at some future stage of his spiritual progress this difficulty would be removed when his sinful soul had been raised up from its weakness and enlightened by the Third Person of the Most Blessed Trinity. He believed this all the more, and with trepidation, because of the divine gloom and silence wherein dwelt the unseen Paraclete, Whose symbols were a dove and a mighty wind, to sin against Whom was a sin beyond forgiveness, the eternal mysterious secret Being to Whom, as God, the priests offered up mass once a year, robed in the scarlet of the tongues of fire.

The imagery through which the nature and kinship of the Three Persons of the Trinity were darkly shadowed forth in the books of devotion which he read—the Father contemplating from all eternity as in a mirror His Divine Perfections and thereby begetting eternally the Eternal Son and the Holy Spirit proceeding out of Father and Son from all eternity—were easier of acceptance by his mind by reason of their august incomprehensibility than was the simple fact that God had loved his soul from all eternity, for ages before he had been born into the world, for ages before the world itself had existed.

He had heard the names of the passions of love and hate pronounced solemnly on the stage and in the pulpit, had found them set forth solemnly in books and had wondered why his soul was unable to harbour them for any time or to force his lips to utter their names with conviction. A brief anger had often invested him but he had never been able to make it an abiding passion and had always felt himself passing out of it as if his very body were being divested with ease of some outer skin or peel. He had felt a subtle, dark, and murmurous presence penetrate his being and fire him with a brief iniquitous lust: it, too, had slipped beyond his grasp leaving his mind lucid and indifferent. This, it seemed, was the only love and that the only hate his soul would harbour.

But he could no longer disbelieve in the reality of love, since God Himself had loved his individual soul with divine love from all eternity. Gradually, as his soul was enriched with spiritual knowledge, he saw the whole world forming one vast symmetrical expression of God's power and love. Life became a divine gift for every moment and sensation of which, were it even the sight of a single leaf hanging on the twig of a tree, his soul should praise and thank the Giver. The world for all its solid substance and complexity no longer existed for his soul save as a theorem of divine power and love and universality. So entire and unquestionable was this sense of the divine meaning in all nature granted to his soul that he could scarcely understand why it was in any way necessary that he should continue to live. Yet that was part of the divine purpose and he dared not question its use, he above all others who had sinned so deeply and so foully against the divine purpose. Meek and abased by this consciousness of the one eternal omnipresent perfect reality his soul took up again her burden of pieties, masses and prayers and sacraments and mortifications, and only then for the first time since he had brooded on the great mystery of love did he feel within him a warm movement like that of some newly born life or virtue of the soul itself. The attitude of rapture in sacred art, the raised and parted hands, the parted lips and eyes as of one about to swoon, became for him an image of the soul in prayer, humiliated and faint before her Creator.

But he had been forewarned of the dangers of spiritual exaltation and did not allow himself to desist from even the least or lowliest devotion, striving also by constant mortification to undo the sinful past rather than to achieve a saintliness fraught with peril. Each of his senses was brought under a rigorous discipline. In order to mortify the sense of sight he made it his rule to walk in the street with downcast eyes, glancing neither to right nor left and never behind him. His eyes shunned every encounter with the eyes of women. From time to time also he balked them by a sudden effort of the will, as by lifting them suddenly in the middle of an unfinished sentence and closing the book. To mortify his hearing he exerted no control over his voice which was then breaking, neither sang nor whistled, and made no attempt to flee from noises which caused him painful nervous irritation such as the sharpening of knives on the knife board, the gathering of cinders on the fire-shovel and the twigging of the carpet. To mortify his smell was more difficult as he found in himself no instinctive repugnance to bad odours whether they were the odours of the outdoor world, such as those of dung or tar, or the odours of his own person among which he had made many curious comparisons and experiments. He found in the end that the only odour against which his sense of smell revolted was a certain stale fishy stink like that of long-standing urine; and whenever it was possible he subjected himself to this unpleasant odour. To mortify the taste he practised strict habits at table, observed to the letter all the fasts of the church and sought by distraction to divert his mind from the savours of different foods. But it was to the mortification of touch he brought the most assiduous ingenuity of inventiveness. He never consciously changed his position in bed, sat in the most uncomfortable positions, suffered patiently every itch and pain, kept away from the fire, remained on his knees all through the mass except at the gospels, left part of his neck and face undried so that air might sting them and, whenever he was not saying his beads, carried his arms stiffly at his sides like a runner and never in his pockets or clasped behind him.

He had no temptations to sin mortally. It surprised him however to find that at the end of his course of intricate piety and self-restraint he was so easily at the mercy of childish and unworthy imperfections. His prayers and fasts availed him little for the suppression of anger at hearing his mother sneeze or at being disturbed in his devotions. It needed an immense effort of his will to master the impulse which urged him to give outlet to such irritation. Images of the outbursts of trivial anger which he had often noted among his masters, their twitching mouths, close-shut lips and flushed cheeks, recurred to his memory, discouraging him, for all his practice of humility, by the comparison. To merge his life in the common tide of other lives was harder for him than any fasting or prayer and it was his constant failure to do this to his own satisfaction which caused in his soul at last a sensation of spiritual dryness together with a growth of doubts and scruples. His soul traversed a period of desolation in which the sacraments themselves seemed to have turned into dried-up sources. His confession became a channel for the escape of scrupulous and unrepented imperfections. His actual reception of the eucharist did not bring him the same dissolving moments of virginal self-surrender as did those spiritual communions made by him sometimes at the close of some visit to the Blessed Sacrament. The book which he used for these visits was an old neglected book written by saint Alphonsus Liguori, with fading characters and sere foxpapered leaves. A faded world of fervent love and virginal responses seemed to be evoked for his soul by the reading of its pages in which the imagery of the canticles was interwoven with the communicant's prayers. An inaudible voice seemed to caress the soul, telling her names and glories, bidding her arise as for espousal and come away, bidding her look forth, a spouse, from Amana and from the mountains of the leopards; and the soul seemed to answer with the same inaudible voice, surrendering herself: *Inter ubera mea commorabitur.*

This idea of surrender had a perilous attraction for his mind now that he felt his soul beset once again by the insistent voices of the flesh which began to murmur to him again during his prayers and meditations. It gave him an intense sense of power to know that he could, by a single act of consent, in a moment of thought, undo all that he had done. He seemed to feel a flood slowly advancing towards his naked feet and to be waiting for the first faint timid noiseless wavelet to touch his fevered skin. Then, almost at the instant of that touch, almost at the verge of sinful consent, he found himself standing far away from the flood upon a dry shore, saved by a sudden act of the will or a sudden ejaculation; and, seeing the silver line of the flood far away and beginning again its slow advance towards his feet, a new thrill of power and satisfaction shook his soul to know that he had not yielded nor undone all.

When he had eluded the flood of temptation many times in this way he grew troubled and wondered whether the grace which he had refused to lose was not being filched from him little by little. The clear certitude of his own immunity grew dim and to it succeeded a vague fear that his soul had really fallen unawares. It was with difficulty that he won back his old consciousness of his state of grace by telling himself that he had prayed to God at every temptation and that the grace which he had prayed for must have been given to him inasmuch as God was obliged to give it. The very frequency and violence of temptations showed him at last the truth of what he had heard about the trials of the saints. Frequent and violent temptations were a proof that the citadel of the soul had not fallen and that the devil raged to make it fall.

Often when he had confessed his doubts and scruples—some momentary inattention at prayer, a movement of trivial anger in his soul, or a subtle wilfulness in speech or act—he was bidden by his confessor to name some sin of his past life before absolution was given him. He named it with humility and shame and repented of it once more. It humiliated and shamed him to think that he would never be freed from it wholly, however holily he might live or whatever virtues or perfections he might attain. A restless feeling of guilt would always be present with him: he would confess and repent and be absolved, confess and repent again and be absolved again, fruitlessly. Perhaps that first hasty confession wrung from him by the fear of hell had not been good? Perhaps, concerned only for his imminent doom, he had not had sincere sorrow for his sin? But the surest sign that his confession had been good and that he had had sincere sorrow for his sin was, he knew, the amendment of his life.

—I have amended my life, have I not? he asked himself.

***

The director stood in the embrasure of the window, his back to the light, leaning an elbow on the brown crossblind, and, as he spoke and smiled, slowly dangling and looping the cord of the other blind, Stephen stood before him, following for a moment with his eyes the waning of the long summer daylight above the roofs or the slow deft movements of the priestly fingers. The priest's face was in total shadow, but the waning daylight from behind him touched the deeply grooved temples and the curves of the skull. Stephen followed also with his ears the accents and intervals of the priest's voice as he spoke gravely and cordially of indifferent themes, the vacation which had just ended, the colleges of the order abroad, the transference of masters. The grave and cordial voice went on easily with its tale and in the pauses Stephen felt bound to set it on again with respectful questions. He knew that the tale was a prelude and his mind waited for the sequel. Ever since the message of summons had come for him from the director his mind had struggled to find the meaning of the message; and, during the long restless time he had sat in the college parlour waiting for the director to come in, his eyes had wandered from one sober picture to another around the walls and his mind wandered from one guess to another until the meaning of the summons had almost become clear. Then, just as he was wishing that some unforeseen cause might prevent the director from coming, he had heard the handle of the door turning and the swish of a soutane.

The director had begun to speak of the dominican and franciscan orders and of the friendship between saint Thomas and saint Bonaventure. The capuchin dress, he thought, was rather too . . .

Stephen's face gave back the priest's indulgent smile and, not being anxious to give an opinion, he made a slight dubitative movement with his lips.

—I believe, continued the director, that there is some talk now among the capuchins themselves of doing away with it and following the example of the other franciscans.

—I suppose they would retain it in the cloisters? said Stephen.

—O certainly, said the director. For the cloister it is all right but for the street I really think it would be better to do away with it, don't you?

—It must be troublesome, I imagine.

—Of course it is, of course. Just imagine when I was in Belgium I used to see them out cycling in all kinds of weather with this thing up about their knees! It was really ridiculous. *Les jupes*, they call them in Belgium.

The vowel was so modified as to be indistinct.

—What do they call them?

—*Les jupes*.

—O!

Stephen smiled again in answer to the smile which he could not see on the priest's shadowed face, its image or spectre only passing rapidly across his mind as the low discreet accent fell upon his ear. He gazed calmly before him at the waning sky, glad of the cool of the evening and of the faint yellow glow which hid the tiny flame kindling upon his cheek.

The names of articles of dress worn by women or of certain soft and delicate stuffs used in their making brought always to his mind a delicate and sinful perfume. As a boy he had imagined the reins by which horses are driven as slender silken bands and it shocked him to feel at Stradbrooke the greasy leather of harness. It had shocked him, too, when he had felt for the first time beneath his tremulous fingers the brittle texture of a woman's stocking for, retaining nothing of all he read save that which seemed to him an echo or a prophecy of his own state, it was only amid soft-worded phrases or within rose-soft stuffs that he dared to conceive of the soul or body of a woman moving with tender life.

But the phrase on the priest's lips was disingenuous for he knew that a priest should not speak lightly on that theme. The phrase had been spoken lightly with design and he felt that his face was being searched by the eyes in the shadow. Whatever he had heard or read of the craft of jesuits he had put aside frankly as not borne out by his own experience. His masters, even when they had not attracted him, had seemed to him always intelligent and serious priests, athletic and high-spirited prefects. He thought of them as men who washed their bodies briskly with cold water and wore clean cold linen. During all the years he had lived among them in Clongowes and in Belvedere he had received only two pandies and, though these had been dealt him in the wrong, he knew that he had often escaped punishment. During all those years he had never heard from any of his masters a flippant word: it was they who had taught him christian doctrine and urged him to live a good life and, when he had fallen into grievous sin, it was they who had led him back to grace. Their presence had made him diffident of himself when he was a muff in Clongowes and it had made him diffident of himself also while he had held his equivocal position in Belvedere. A constant sense of this had remained with him up to the last year of his school life. He had never once disobeyed or allowed turbulent companions to seduce him from his habit of quiet obedience; and, even when he doubted some statement of a master, he had never presumed to doubt openly. Lately some of their judgements had sounded a little childish in his ears and had made him feel a regret and pity as though he were slowly passing out of an accustomed world and were hearing its language for the last time. One day when some boys had gathered round a priest under the shed near the chapel, he had heard the priest say:

—I believe that Lord Macaulay was a man who probably never committed a mortal sin in his life, that is to say, a deliberate mortal sin.

Some of the boys had then asked the priest if Victor Hugo were not the greatest French writer. The priest had answered that Victor Hugo had never written half so well when he had turned against the church as he had written when he was a catholic.

—But there are many eminent French critics, said the priest, who consider that even Victor Hugo, great as he certainly was, had not so pure a French style as Louis Veuillot.

The tiny flame which the priest's allusion had kindled upon Stephen's cheek had sunk down again and his eyes were still fixed calmly on the colourless sky. But an unresting doubt flew hither and thither before his mind. Masked memories passed quickly before him: he recognized scenes and persons yet he was conscious that he had failed to perceive some vital circumstance in them. He saw himself walking about the grounds watching the sports in Clongowes and eating slim jim out of his cricket cap. Some jesuits were walking round the cycle-track in the company of ladies. The echoes of certain expressions used in Clongowes sounded in remote caves of his mind.

His ears were listening to these distant echoes amid the silence of the parlour when he became aware that the priest was addressing him in a different voice.

—I sent for you today, Stephen, because I wished to speak to you on a very important subject.

—Yes, sir.

—Have you ever felt that you had a vocation?

Stephen parted his lips to answer yes and then withheld the word suddenly. The priest waited for the answer and added:

—I mean, have you ever felt within yourself, in your soul, a desire to join the order? Think.

—I have sometimes thought of it, said Stephen.

The priest let the blindcord fall to one side and, uniting his hands, leaned his chin gravely upon them, communing with himself.

—In a college like this, he said at length, there is one boy or perhaps two or three boys whom God calls to the religious life. Such a boy is marked off from his companions by his piety, by the good example he shows to others. He is looked up to by them; he is chosen perhaps as prefect by his fellow sodalists. And you, Stephen, have been such a boy in this college, prefect of Our Blessed Lady's sodality. Perhaps you are the boy in this college whom God designs to call to Himself.

A strong note of pride reinforcing the gravity of the priest's voice made Stephen's heart quicken in response.

To receive that call, Stephen, said the priest, is the greatest honour that the Almighty God can bestow upon a man. No king or emperor on this earth has the power of the priest of God. No angel or archangel in heaven, no saint, not even the Blessed Virgin herself, has the power of a priest of God: the power of the keys, the power to bind and to loose from sin, the power of exorcism, the power to cast out from the creatures of God the evil spirits that have power over them; the power, the authority, to make the great God of Heaven come down upon the altar and take the form of bread and wine. What an awful power, Stephen!

A flame began to flutter again on Stephen's cheek as he heard in this proud address an echo of his own proud musings. How often had he seen himself as a priest wielding calmly and humbly the awful power of which angels and saints stood in reverence! His soul had loved to muse in secret on this desire. He had seen himself, a young and silent-mannered priest, entering a confessional swiftly, ascending the altarsteps, incensing, genuflecting, accomplishing the vague acts of the priesthood which pleased him by reason of their semblance of reality and of their distance from it. In that dim life which he had lived through in his musings he had assumed the voices and gestures which he had noted with various priests. He had bent his knee sideways like such a one, he had shaken the thurible only slightly like such a one, his chasuble had swung open like that of such another as he turned to the altar again after having blessed the people. And above all it had pleased him to fill the second place in those dim scenes of his imagining. He shrank from the dignity of celebrant because it displeased him to imagine that all the vague pomp should end in his own person or that the ritual should assign to him so clear and final an office. He longed for the minor sacred offices, to be vested with the tunicle of subdeacon at high mass, to stand aloof from the altar, forgotten by the people, his shoulders covered with a humeral veil, holding the paten within its folds or, when the sacrifice had been accomplished, to stand as deacon in a dalmatic of cloth of gold on the step below the celebrant, his hands joined and his face towards the people, and sing the chant *Ite missa est.* If ever he had seen himself celebrant it was as in the pictures of the mass in his child's massbook, in a church without worshippers, save for the angel of the sacrifice, at a bare altar, and served by an acolyte scarcely more boyish than himself. In vague sacrificial or sacramental acts alone his will seemed drawn to go forth to encounter reality; and it was partly the absence of an appointed rite which had always constrained him to inaction whether he had allowed silence to cover his anger or pride or had suffered only an embrace he longed to give.

He listened in reverent silence now to the priest's appeal and through the words he heard even more distinctly a voice bidding him approach, offering him secret knowledge and secret power. He would know then what was the sin of Simon Magus and what the sin against the Holy Ghost for which there was no forgiveness. He would know obscure things, hidden from others, from those who were conceived and born children of wrath. He would know the sins, the sinful longings and sinful thoughts and sinful acts, of others, hearing them murmured into his ears in the confessional under the shame of a darkened chapel by the lips of women and of girls; but rendered immune mysteriously at his ordination by the imposition of hands, his soul would pass again uncontaminated to the white peace of the altar. No touch of sin would linger upon the hands with which he would elevate and break the host; no touch of sin would linger on his lips in prayer to make him eat and drink damnation to himself not discerning the body of the Lord. He would hold his secret knowledge and secret power, being as sinless as the innocent, and he would be a priest for ever according to the order of Melchisedec.

—I will offer up my mass tomorrow morning, said the director, that Almighty God may reveal to you His holy will. And let you, Stephen, make a novena to your holy patron saint, the first martyr, who is very powerful with God, that God may enlighten your mind. But you must be quite sure, Stephen, that you have a vocation because it would be terrible if you found afterwards that you had none. Once a priest always a priest, remember. Your catechism tells you that the sacrament of Holy Orders is one of those which can be received only once because it imprints on the soul an indelible spiritual mark which can never be effaced. It is before you must weigh well, not after. It is a solemn question, Stephen, because on it may depend the salvation of your eternal soul. But we will pray to God together.

He held open the heavy hall door and gave his hand as if already to a companion in the spiritual life. Stephen passed out on to the wide platform above the steps and was conscious of the caress of mild evening air. Towards Findlater's church a quartet of young men were striding along with linked arms, swaying their heads and stepping to the agile melody of their leader's concertina. The music passed in an instant, as the first bars of sudden music always did, over the fantastic fabrics of his mind, dissolving them painlessly and noiselessly as a sudden wave dissolves the sand-built turrets of children. Smiling at the trivial air he raised his eyes to the priest's face and, seeing in it a mirthless reflection of the sunken day, detached his hand slowly which had acquiesced faintly in the companionship.

As he descended the steps the impression which effaced his troubled self-communion was that of a mirthless mask reflecting a sunken day from the threshold of the college. The shadow, then, of the life of the college passed gravely over his consciousness. It was a grave and ordered and passionless life that awaited him, a life without material cares. He wondered how he would pass the first night in the novitiate and with what dismay he would wake the first morning in the dormitory. The troubling odour of the long corridors of Clongowes came back to him and he heard the discreet murmur of the burning gasflames. At once from every part of his being unrest began to irradiate. A feverish quickening of his pulses followed, and a din of meaningless words drove his reasoned thoughts hither and thither confusedly. His lungs dilated and sank as if he were inhaling a warm moist unsustaining air and he smelt again the moist warm air which hung in the bath in Clongowes above the sluggish turf-coloured water.

Some instinct, waking at these memories, stronger than education or piety, quickened within him at every near approach to that life, an instinct subtle and hostile, and armed him against acquiescence. The chill and order of the life repelled him. He saw himself rising in the cold of the morning and filing down with the others to early mass and trying vainly to struggle with his prayers against the fainting sickness of his stomach. He saw himself sitting at dinner with the community of a college. What, then, had become of that deep-rooted shyness of his which had made him loth to eat or drink under a strange roof? What had come of the pride of his spirit which had always made him conceive himself as a being apart in every order?

The Reverend Stephen Dedalus, S.J.

His name in that new life leaped into characters before his eyes and to it there followed a mental sensation of an undefined face or colour of a face. The colour faded and became strong like a changing glow of pallid brick red. Was it the raw reddish glow he had so often seen on wintry mornings on the shaven gills of the priests? The face was eyeless and sour-favoured and devout, shot with pink tinges of suffocated anger. Was it not a mental spectre of the face of one of the jesuits whom some of the boys called Lantern Jaws and others Foxy Campbell?

He was passing at that moment before the jesuit house in Gardiner Street and wondered vaguely which window would be his if he ever joined the order. Then he wondered at the vagueness of his wonder, at the remoteness of his own soul from what he had hitherto imagined her sanctuary, at the frail hold which so many years of order and obedience had of him when once a definite and irrevocable act of his threatened to end for ever, in time and in eternity, his freedom. The voice of the director urging upon him the proud claims of the church and the mystery and power of the priestly office repeated itself idly in his memory. His soul was not there to hear and greet it and he knew now that the exhortation he had listened to had already fallen into an idle formal tale. He would never swing the thurible before the tabernacle as priest. His destiny was to be elusive of social or religious orders. The wisdom of the priest's appeal did not touch him to the quick. He was destined to learn his own wisdom apart from others or to learn the wisdom of others himself wandering among the snares of the world.

The snares of the world were its ways of sin. He would fall. He had not yet fallen but he would fall silently, in an instant. Not to fall was too hard, too hard; and he felt the silent lapse of his soul, as it would be at some instant to come, falling, falling, but not yet fallen, still unfallen, but about to fall.

He crossed the bridge over the stream of the Tolka and turned his eyes coldly for an instant towards the faded blue shrine of the Blessed Virgin which stood fowl-wise on a pole in the middle of a ham-shaped encampment of poor cottages. Then, bending to the left, he followed the lane which led up to his house. The faint sour stink of rotted cabbages came towards him from the kitchen gardens on the rising ground above the river. He smiled to think that it was this disorder, the misrule and confusion of his father's house and the stagnation of vegetable life, which was to win the day in his soul. Then a short laugh broke from his lips as he thought of that solitary farmhand in the kitchen gardens behind their house whom they had nicknamed the man with the hat. A second laugh, taking rise from the first after a pause, broke from him involuntarily as he thought of how the man with the hat worked, considering in turn the four points of the sky and then regretfully plunging his spade in the earth.

He pushed open the latchless door of the porch and passed through the naked hallway into the kitchen. A group of his brothers and sisters was sitting round the table. Tea was nearly over and only the last of the second watered tea remained in the bottoms of the small glass jars and jampots which did service for teacups. Discarded crusts and lumps of sugared bread, turned brown by the tea which had been poured over them, lay scattered on the table. Little wells of tea lay here and there on the board, and a knife with a broken ivory handle was stuck through the pith of a ravaged turnover.

The sad quiet grey-blue glow of the dying day came through the window and the open door, covering over and allaying quietly a sudden instinct of remorse in Stephen's heart. All that had been denied them had been freely given to him, the eldest; but the quiet glow of evening showed him in their faces no sign of rancour.

He sat near them at the table and asked where his father and mother were. One answered:

—Goneboro toboro lookboro atboro aboro houseboro.

Still another removal! A boy named Fallon in Belvedere had often asked him with a silly laugh why they moved so often. A frown of scorn darkened quickly his forehead as he heard again the silly laugh of the questioner.

He asked:

—Why are we on the move again if it's a fair question?

The same sister answered:

—Becauseboro theboro landboro lordboro willboro putboro usboro outboro.

The voice of his youngest brother from the farther side of the fireplace began to sing the air *Oft in the Stilly Night*. One by one the others took up the air until a full choir of voices was singing. They would sing so for hours, melody after melody, glee after glee, till the last pale light died down on the horizon, till the first dark night clouds came forth and night fell.

He waited for some moments, listening, before he too took up the air with them. He was listening with pain of spirit to the overtone of weariness behind their frail fresh innocent voices. Even before they set out on life's journey they seemed weary already of the way.

He heard the choir of voices in the kitchen echoed and multiplied through an endless reverberation of the choirs of endless generations of children and heard in all the echoes an echo also of the recurring note of weariness and pain. All seemed weary of life even before entering upon it. And he remembered that Newman had heard this note also in the broken lines of Virgil, *giving utterance, like the voice of Nature herself, to that pain and weariness yet hope of better things which has been the experience of her children in every time.*

***

He could wait no longer.

From the door of Byron's public-house to the gate of Clontarf Chapel, from the gate of Clontail Chapel to the door of Byron's public-house and then back again to the chapel and then back again to the public-house he had paced slowly at first, planting his steps scrupulously in the spaces of the patchwork of the footpath, then timing their fall to the fall of verses. A full hour had passed since his father had gone in with Dan Crosby, the tutor, to find out for him something about the university. For a full hour he had paced up and down, waiting: but he could wait no longer.

He set off abruptly for the Bull, walking rapidly lest his father's shrill whistle might call him back; and in a few moments he had rounded the curve at the police barrack and was safe.

Yes, his mother was hostile to the idea, as he had read from her listless silence. Yet her mistrust pricked him more keenly than his father's pride and he thought coldly how he had watched the faith which was fading down in his soul ageing and strengthening in her eyes. A dim antagonism gathered force within him and darkened his mind as a cloud against her disloyalty and when it passed, cloud-like, leaving his mind serene and dutiful towards her again, he was made aware dimly and without regret of a first noiseless sundering of their lives.

The university! So he had passed beyond the challenge of the sentries who had stood as guardians of his boyhood and had sought to keep him among them that he might be subject to them and serve their ends. Pride after satisfaction uplifted him like long slow waves. The end he had been born to serve yet did not see had led him to escape by an unseen path and now it beckoned to him once more and a new adventure was about to be opened to him. It seemed to him that he heard notes of fitful music leaping upwards a tone and downwards a diminished fourth, upwards a tone and downwards a major third, like triple-branching flames leaping fitfully, flame after flame, out of a midnight wood. It was an elfin prelude, endless and formless; and, as it grew wilder and faster, the flames leaping out of time, he seemed to hear from under the boughs and grasses wild creatures racing, their feet pattering like rain upon the leaves. Their feet passed in pattering tumult over his mind, the feet of hares and rabbits, the feet of harts and hinds and antelopes, until he heard them no more and remembered only a proud cadence from Newman: *Whose feet are as the feet of harts and underneath the everlasting arms.*

The pride of that dim image brought back to his mind the dignity of the office he had refused. All through his boyhood he had mused upon that which he had so often thought to be his destiny and when the moment had come for him to obey the call he had turned aside, obeying a wayward instinct. Now time lay between: the oils of ordination would never anoint his body. He had refused. Why?

He turned seaward from the road at Dollymount and as he passed on to the thin wooden bridge he felt the planks shaking with the tramp of heavily shod feet. A squad of christian brothers was on its way back from the Bull and had begun to pass, two by two, across the bridge. Soon the whole bridge was trembling and resounding. The uncouth faces passed him two by two, stained yellow or red or livid by the sea, and, as he strove to look at them with ease and indifference, a faint stain of personal shame and commiseration rose to his own face.

Angry with himself he tried to hide his face from their eyes by gazing down sideways into the shallow swirling water under the bridge but he still saw a reflection therein of their top-heavy silk hats and humble tape-like collars and loosely-hanging clerical clothes.

—Brother Hickey.

Brother Quaid.

Brother MacArdle.

Brother Keogh.

Their piety would be like their names, like their faces, like their clothes, and it was idle for him to tell himself that their humble and contrite hearts, it might be, paid a far richer tribute of devotion than his had ever been, a gift tenfold more acceptable than his elaborate adoration. It was idle for him to move himself to be generous towards them, to tell himself that if he ever came to their gates, stripped of his pride, beaten and in beggar's weeds, that they would be generous towards him, loving him as themselves. Idle and embittering, finally, to argue, against his own dispassionate certitude, that the commandment of love bade us not to love our neighbour as ourselves with the same amount and intensity of love but to love him as ourselves with the same kind of love.

He drew forth a phrase from his treasure and spoke it softly to himself:

—A day of dappled seaborne clouds.

The phrase and the day and the scene harmonized in a chord. Words. Was it their colours? He allowed them to glow and fade, hue after hue: sunrise gold, the russet and green of apple orchards, azure of waves, the grey-fringed fleece of clouds. No, it was not their colours: it was the poise and balance of the period itself. Did he then love the rhythmic rise and fall of words better than their associations of legend and colour? Or was it that, being as weak of sight as he was shy of mind, he drew less pleasure from the reflection of the glowing sensible world through the prism of a language many-coloured and richly storied than from the contemplation of an inner world of individual emotions mirrored perfectly in a lucid supple periodic prose?

He passed from the trembling bridge on to firm land again. At that instant, as it seemed to him, the air was chilled and, looking askance towards the water, he saw a flying squall darkening and crisping suddenly the tide. A faint click at his heart, a faint throb in his throat told him once more of how his flesh dreaded the cold infrahuman odour of the sea; yet he did not strike across the downs on his left but held straight on along the spine of rocks that pointed against the river's mouth.

A veiled sunlight lit up faintly the grey sheet of water where the river was embayed. In the distance along the course of the slow-flowing Liffey slender masts flecked the sky and, more distant still, the dim fabric of the city lay prone in haze. Like a scene on some vague arras, old as man's weariness, the image of the seventh city of christendom was visible to him across the timeless air, no older nor more weary nor less patient of subjection than in the days of the thingmote.

Disheartened, he raised his eyes towards the slow-drifting clouds, dappled and seaborne. They were voyaging across the deserts of the sky, a host of nomads on the march, voyaging high over Ireland, westward bound. The Europe they had come from lay out there beyond the Irish Sea, Europe of strange tongues and valleyed and woodbegirt and citadelled and of entrenched and marshalled races. He heard a confused music within him as of memories and names which he was almost conscious of but could not capture even for an instant; then the music seemed to recede, to recede, to recede, and from each receding trail of nebulous music there fell always one longdrawn calling note, piercing like a star the dusk of silence. Again! Again! Again! A voice from beyond the world was calling.

—Hello, Stephanos!

—Here comes The Dedalus!

—Ao! . . . Eh, give it over, Dwyer, I'm telling you, or I'll give you a stuff in the kisser for yourself . . . Ao!

—Good man, Towser! Duck him!

—Come along, Dedalus! Bous Stephanoumenos! Bous Stephaneforos!

—Duck him! Guzzle him now, Towser!

—Help! Help! . . . Ao!

He recognized their speech collectively before he distinguished their faces. The mere sight of that medley of wet nakedness chilled him to the bone. Their bodies, corpse-white or suffused with a pallid golden light or rawly tanned by the sun, gleamed with the wet of the sea. Their diving-stone, poised on its rude supports and rocking under their plunges, and the rough-hewn stones of the sloping breakwater over which they scrambled in their horseplay gleamed with cold wet lustre. The towels with which they smacked their bodies were heavy with cold seawater; and drenched with cold brine was their matted hair.

He stood still in deference to their calls and parried their banter with easy words. How characterless they looked: Shuley without his deep unbuttoned collar, Ennis without his scarlet belt with the snaky clasp, and Connolly without his Norfolk coat with the flapless side-pockets! It was a pain to see them, and a sword-like pain to see the signs of adolescence that made repellent their pitiable nakedness. Perhaps they had taken refuge in number and noise from the secret dread in their souls. But he, apart from them and in silence, remembered in what dread he stood of the mystery of his own body.

—Stephanos Dedalos! Bous Stephanoumenos! Bous Stephaneforos!

Their banter was not new to him and now it flattered his mild proud sovereignty. Now, as never before, his strange name seemed to him a prophecy. So timeless seemed the grey warm air, so fluid and impersonal his own mood, that all ages were as one to him. A moment before the ghost of the ancient kingdom of the Danes had looked forth through the vesture of the hazewrapped City. Now, at the name of the fabulous artificer, he seemed to hear the noise of dim waves and to see a winged form flying above the waves and slowly climbing the air. What did it mean? Was it a quaint device opening a page of some medieval book of prophecies and symbols, a hawk-like man flying sunward above the sea, a prophecy of the end he had been born to serve and had been following through the mists of childhood and boyhood, a symbol of the artist forging anew in his workshop out of the sluggish matter of the earth a new soaring impalpable imperishable being?

His heart trembled; his breath came faster and a wild spirit passed over his limbs as though he was soaring sunward. His heart trembled in an ecstasy of fear and his soul was in flight. His soul was soaring in an air beyond the world and the body he knew was purified in a breath and delivered of incertitude and made radiant and commingled with the element of the spirit. An ecstasy of flight made radiant his eyes and wild his breath and tremulous and wild and radiant his windswept limbs.

—One! Two! . . . Look out!
—Oh, Cripes, I'm drownded!
—One! Two! Three and away!

—Me next! Me next!

—One! . . . UK!

—Stephaneforos!

His throat ached with a desire to cry aloud, the cry of a hawk or eagle on high, to cry piercingly of his deliverance to the winds. This was the call of life to his soul not the dull gross voice of the world of duties and despair, not the inhuman voice that had called him to the pale service of the altar. An instant of wild flight had delivered him and the cry of triumph which his lips withheld cleft his brain.

—Stephaneforos!

What were they now but cerements shaken from the body of death—the fear he had walked in night and day, the incertitude that had ringed him round, the shame that had abased him within and without—cerements, the linens of the grave?

His soul had arisen from the grave of boyhood, spurning her grave-clothes. Yes! Yes! Yes! He would create proudly out of the freedom and power of his soul, as the great artificer whose name he bore, a living thing, new and soaring and beautiful, impalpable, imperishable.

He started up nervously from the stone-block for he could no longer quench the flame in his blood. He felt his cheeks aflame and his throat throbbing with song. There was a lust of wandering in his feet that burned to set out for the ends of the earth. On! On! his heart seemed to cry. Evening would deepen above the sea, night fall upon the plains, dawn glimmer before the wanderer and show him strange fields and hills and faces. Where?

He looked northward towards Howth. The sea had fallen below the line of seawrack on the shallow side of the breakwater and already the tide was running out fast along the foreshore. Already one long oval bank of sand lay warm and dry amid the wavelets. Here and there warm isles of sand gleamed above the shallow tide and about the isles and around the long bank and amid the shallow currents of the beach were lightclad figures, wading and delving.

In a few moments he was barefoot, his stockings folded in his pockets and his canvas shoes dangling by their knotted laces over his shoulders and, picking a pointed salt-eaten stick out of the jetsam among the rocks, he clambered down the slope of the breakwater.

There was a long rivulet in the strand and, as he waded slowly up its course, he wondered at the endless drift of seaweed. Emerald and black and russet and olive, it moved beneath the current, swaying and turning. The water of the rivulet was dark with endless drift and mirrored the high-drifting clouds. The clouds were drifting above him silently and silently the seatangle was drifting below him and the grey warm air was still and a new wild life was singing in his veins.

Where was his boyhood now? Where was the soul that had hung back from her destiny, to brood alone upon the shame of her wounds and in her house of squalor and subterfuge to queen it in faded cerements and in wreaths that withered at the touch? Or where was he?

He was alone. He was unheeded, happy and near to the wild heart of life. He was alone and young and wilful and wildhearted, alone amid a waste of wild air and brackish waters and the sea-harvest of shells and tangle and veiled grey sunlight and gayclad lightclad figures of children and girls and voices childish and girlish in the air.

A girl stood before him in midstream, alone and still, gazing out to sea. She seemed like one whom magic had changed into the likeness of a strange and beautiful seabird. Her long slender bare legs were delicate as a crane's and pure save where an emerald trail of seaweed had fashioned itself as a sign upon the flesh. Her thighs, fuller and soft-hued as ivory, were bared almost to the hips, where the white fringes of her drawers were like feathering of soft white down. Her slate-blue skirts were kilted boldly about her waist and dovetailed behind her. Her bosom was as a bird's, soft and slight, slight and soft as the breast of some dark-plumaged dove. But her long fair hair was girlish: and girlish, and touched with the wonder of mortal beauty, her face.

She was alone and still, gazing out to sea; and when she felt his presence and the worship of his eyes her eyes turned to him in quiet sufferance of his gaze, without shame or wantonness. Long, long she suffered his gaze and then quietly withdrew her eyes from his and bent them towards the stream, gently stirring the water with her foot hither and thither. The first faint noise of gently moving water broke the silence, low and faint and whispering, faint as the bells of sleep; hither and thither, hither and thither; and a faint flame trembled on her cheek.

—Heavenly God! cried Stephen's soul, in an outburst of profane joy.

He turned away from her suddenly and set off across the strand. His cheeks were aflame; his body was aglow; his limbs were trembling. On and on and on and on he strode, far out over the sands, singing wildly to the sea, crying to greet the advent of the life that had cried to him.

Her image had passed into his soul for ever and no word had broken the holy silence of his ecstasy. Her eyes had called him and his soul had leaped at the call. To live, to err, to fall, to triumph, to recreate life out of life! A wild angel had appeared to him, the angel of mortal youth and beauty, an envoy from the fair courts of life, to throw open before him in an instant of ecstasy the gates of all the ways of error and glory. On and on and on and on!

He halted suddenly and heard his heart in the silence. How far had he walked? What hour was it?

There was no human figure near him nor any sound borne to him over the air. But the tide was near the turn and already the day was on the wane. He turned landward and ran towards the shore and, running up the sloping beach, reckless of the sharp shingle, found a sandy nook amid a ring of tufted sandknolls and lay down there that the peace and silence of the evening might still the riot of his blood.

He felt above him the vast indifferent dome and the calm processes of the heavenly bodies; and the earth beneath him, the earth that had borne him, had taken him to her breast.

He closed his eyes in the languor of sleep. His eyelids trembled as if they felt the vast cyclic movement of the earth and her watchers, trembled as if they felt the strange light of some new world. His soul was swooning into some new world, fantastic, dim, uncertain as under sea, traversed by cloudy shapes and beings. A world, a glimmer or a flower? Glimmering and trembling, trembling and unfolding, a breaking light, an opening flower, it spread in endless succession to itself, breaking in full crimson and unfolding and fading to palest rose, leaf by leaf and wave of light by wave of light, flooding all the heavens with its soft flushes, every flush deeper than the other.

Evening had fallen when he woke and the sand and arid grasses of his bed glowed no longer. He rose slowly and, recalling the rapture of his sleep, sighed at its joy.

He climbed to the crest of the sandhill and gazed about him. Evening had fallen. A rim of the young moon cleft the pale waste of skyline, the rim of a silver hoop embedded in grey sand; and the tide was flowing in fast to the land with a low whisper of her waves, islanding a few last figures in distant pools.

5

He drained his third cup of watery tea to the dregs and set to chewing the crusts of fried bread that were scattered near him, staring into the dark pool of the jar. The yellow dripping had been scooped out like a boghole and the pool under it brought back to his memory the dark turf-coloured water of the bath in Clongowes. The box of pawn tickets at his elbow had just been rifled and he took up idly one after another in his greasy fingers the blue and white dockets, scrawled and sanded and creased and bearing the name of the pledger as Daly or MacEvoy.

I Pair Buskins.

I D. Coat.

3 Articles and White.

I Man's Pants.

Then he put them aside and gazed thoughtfully at the lid of the box, speckled with louse marks, and asked vaguely:

—How much is the clock fast now?

His mother straightened the battered alarm clock that was lying on its side in the middle of the mantelpiece until its dial showed a quarter to twelve and then laid it once more on its side.

—An hour and twenty-five minutes, she said. The right time now is twenty past ten. The dear knows you might try to be in time for your lectures.

—Fill out the place for me to wash, said Stephen.

—Katey, fill out the place for Stephen to wash.

—Boody, fill out the place for Stephen to wash.

—I can't, I'm going for blue. Fill it out, you, Maggy.

When the enamelled basin had been fitted into the well of the sink and the old washing glove flung on the side of it he allowed his mother to scrub his neck and root into the folds of his ears and into the interstices at the wings of his nose.

877

—Well, it's a poor case, she said, when a university student is so dirty that his mother has to wash him.

—But it gives you pleasure, said Stephen calmly.

An ear-splitting whistle was heard from upstairs and his mother thrust a damp overall into his hands, saying:

—Dry yourself and hurry out for the love of goodness.

A second shrill whistle, prolonged angrily, brought one of the girls to the foot of the staircase.

—Yes, father?

—Is your lazy bitch of a brother gone out yet?

—Yes, father.

—Sure?

—Yes, father.

—Hm!

The girl came back, making signs to him to be quick and go out quietly by the back. Stephen laughed and said:

—He has a curious idea of genders if he thinks a bitch is masculine.

—Ah, it's a scandalous shame for you, Stephen, said his mother, and you'll live to rue the day you set your foot in that place. I know how it has changed you.

—Good morning, everybody, said Stephen, smiling and kissing the tips of his fingers in adieu.

The lane behind the terrace was waterlogged and as he went down it slowly, choosing his steps amid heaps of wet rubbish, he heard a mad nun screeching in the nuns' madhouse beyond the wall.

—Jesus! O Jesus! Jesus!

He shook the sound out of his ears by an angry toss of his head and hurried on, stumbling through the mouldering offal, his heart already bitten by an ache of loathing and bitterness. His father's whistle, his mother's mutterings, the screech of an unseen maniac were to him now so many voices offending and threatening to humble the pride of his youth. He drove their echoes even out of his heart with an execration; but, as he walked down the avenue and felt the grey morning light falling about him through the dripping trees and smelt the strange wild smell of the wet leaves and bark, his soul was loosed of her miseries.

The rain-laden trees of the avenue evoked in him, as always, memories of the girls and women in the plays of Gerhart Hauptmann; and the memory of their pale sorrows and the fragrance falling from the wet branches mingled in a mood of quiet joy. His morning walk across the city had begun, and he foreknew that as he passed the sloblands of Fairview he would think of the cloistral silver-veined prose of Newman; that as he walked along the North Strand Road, glancing idly at the windows of the provision shops, he would recall the dark humour of Guido Cavalcanti and smile; that as he went by Baird's stonecutting works in Talbot Place the spirit of Ibsen would blow through him like a keen wind, a spirit of wayward boyish beauty; and that passing a grimy marine dealer's shop beyond the Liffey he would repeat the song by Ben Jonson which begins:

I was not wearier where I lay.

His mind when wearied of its search for the essence of beauty amid the spectral words of Aristotle or Aquinas turned often for its pleasure to the dainty songs of the Elizabethans. His mind, in the vesture of a doubting monk, stood often in shadow under the windows of that age, to hear the grave and mocking music of the lutenists or the frank laughter of waist-coateers until a laugh too low, a phrase, tarnished by time, of chambering and false honour stung his monkish pride and drove him on from his lurking-place.

The lore which he was believed to pass his days brooding upon so that it had rapt him from the companionship of youth was only a garner of slender sentences from Aristotle's poetics and psychology and a *Synopsis Philosophiae Scholasticae ad mentem divi Thomae.* His thinking was a dusk of doubt and self-mistrust, lit up at moments by the lightnings of intuition, but lightnings of so clear a splendour that in those moments the world perished about his feet as if it had been fire-consumed; and thereafter his tongue grew heavy and he met the eyes of others with unanswering eyes, for he felt that the spirit of beauty had folded him round like a mantle and that in revery at least he had been acquainted with nobility. But when this brief pride of silence upheld him no longer he was glad to find himself still in the midst of common lives, passing on his way amid the squalor and noise and sloth of the city fearlessly and with a light heart.

Near the hoardings on the canal he met the consumptive man with the doll's face and the brimless hat coming towards him down the slope of the bridge with little steps, tightly buttoned into his chocolate overcoat, and holding his furled umbrella a span or two from him like a divining rod. It must be eleven, he thought, and peered into a dairy to see the time. The clock in the dairy told him that it was five minutes to five but, as he turned away, he heard a clock somewhere near him, but unseen, beating eleven strokes in swift precision. He laughed as he heard it for it made him think of McCann, and he saw him a squat figure in a shooting jacket and breeches and with a fair goatee, standing in the wind at Hopkins' corner, and heard him say:

—Dedalus, you're an antisocial being, wrapped up in yourself. I'm not. I'm a democrat and I'll work and act for social liberty and equality among all classes and sexes in the United States of the Europe of the future.

Eleven! Then he was late for that lecture too. What day of the week was it? He stopped at a newsagent's to read the headline of a placard. Thursday. Ten to eleven, English; eleven to twelve, French; twelve to one, physics. He fancied to himself the English lecture and felt, even at that distance, restless and helpless. He saw the heads of his classmates meekly bent as they wrote in their notebooks the points they were bidden to note, nominal definitions, essential definitions and examples or dates of birth or death, chief works, a favourable and an unfavourable criticism side by side. His own head was unbent for his thoughts wandered abroad and whether he looked around the little class of students or out of the window across the desolate gardens of the green an odour assailed him of cheerless cellar-damp and decay. Another head than his, right before him in the first benches, was poised squarely above its bending fellows like the head of a priest appealing without humility to the tabernacle for the humble worshippers about him. Why was it that when he thought of Cranly he could never raise before his mind the entire image of his body but only the image of the head and face? Even now against the grey curtain of the morning he saw it before him like the phantom of a dream, the face of a severed head or death-mask, crowned on the brows by its stiff black upright hair as by an iron crown. It was a priest-like face, priest-like in its palor, in the wide winged nose, in the shadowings below the eyes and along the jaws, priest-like in the lips that were long and bloodless and faintly smiling; and Stephen, remembering swiftly how he had told Cranly of all the tumults and unrest and longings in his soul, day after day and night by night, only to be answered by his friend's listening silence, would have told himself that it was the face of a guilty priest who heard confessions

880

of those whom he had not power to absolve but that he felt again in memory the gaze of its dark womanish eyes.

Through this image he had a glimpse of a strange dark cavern of speculation but at once turned away from it, feeling that it was not yet the hour to enter it. But the nightshade of his friend's listlessness seemed to be diffusing in the air around him a tenuous and deadly exhalation and he found himself glancing from one casual word to another on his right or left in stolid wonder that they had been so silently emptied of instantaneous sense until every mean shop legend bound his mind like the words of a spell and his soul shrivelled up sighing with age as he walked on in a lane among heaps of dead language. His own consciousness of language was ebbing from his brain and trickling into the very words themselves which set to band and disband themselves in wayward rhythms:

> *The ivy whines upon the wall,*
> *And whines and twines upon the wall,*
> *The yellow ivy upon the wall,*
> *Ivy, ivy up the wall.*

Did anyone ever hear such drivel? Lord Almighty! Who ever heard of ivy whining on a wall? Yellow ivy; that was all right. Yellow ivory also. And what about ivory ivy?

The word now shone in his brain, clearer and brighter than any ivory sawn from the mottled tusks of elephants. *ivory, ivoire, avorio, ebur.* One of the first examples that he had learnt in Latin had run: *India mittit ebur;* and he recalled the shrewd northern face of the rector who had taught him to construe the Metamorphoses of Ovid in a courtly English, made whimsical by the mention of porkers and potsherds and chines of bacon. He had learnt what little he knew of the laws of Latin verse from a ragged book written by a Portuguese priest.

> *Contrahit orator, variant in carmine vates.*

The crises and victories and secessions in Roman history were handed on to him in the trite words *in tanto discrimine* and he had tried to peer into the social life of the city of cities through the words *implere ollam denariorum* which the rector had rendered sonorously as the filling of a pot with denaries. The pages of his time-worn Horace never felt cold to the touch even when his own fingers were cold; they were human pages and fifty years before they had been turned by the human fingers of John Duncan Inverarity and by his brother, William Malcolm Inverarity. Yes, those were noble names on the dusky flyleaf and, even for so poor a Latinist as he, the dusky verses were as fragrant as though they had lain all those years in myrtle and lavender and vervain; but yet it wounded him to think that he would never be but a shy guest at the feast of the world's culture and that the monkish learning, in terms of which he was striving to forge out an esthetic philosophy, was held no higher by the age he lived in than the subtle and curious jargons of heraldry and falconry.

The grey block of Trinity on his left, set heavily in the city's ignorance like a dull stone set in a cumbrous ring, pulled his mind downward and while he was striving this way and that to free his feet from the fetters of the reformed conscience he came upon the droll statue of the national poet of Ireland.

He looked at it without anger; for, though sloth of the body and of the soul crept over it like unseen vermin, over the shuffling feet and up the folds of the cloak and around the servile head, it seemed humbly conscious of its indignity. It was a Firbolg in the borrowed cloak of a Milesian; and he thought of his friend Davin, the peasant student. It was a jesting name between them, but the young peasant bore with it lightly saying:

—Go on, Stevie, I have a hard head, you tell me. Call me what you will.

The homely version of his christian name on the lips of his friend had touched Stephen pleasantly when first heard for he was as formal in speech with others as they were with him. Often, as he sat in Davin's rooms in Grantham Street, wondering at his friend's well-made boots that flanked the wall pair by pair and repeating for his friend's simple ear the verses and cadences of others which were the veils of his own longing and dejection, the rude Firbolg mind of his listener had drawn his mind towards it and flung it back again, drawing it by a quiet inbred courtesy of attention or by a quaint turn of old English speech or by the force of its delight in rude bodily skill—for Davin had sat at the feet of Michael Cusack, the Gael—repelling swiftly and suddenly by a grossness of intelligence or by a bluntness of feeling or by a dull stare of terror in the eyes, the terror of soul of a starving Irish village in which the curfew was still a nightly fear.

Side by side with his memory of the deeds of prowess of his uncle Mat Davin, the athlete, the young peasant worshipped the sorrowful legend of Ireland. The gossip of his fellow-students which strove to render the flat life of the college significant at any cost loved to think of him as a young fenian. His nurse had taught him Irish and shaped his rude imagination by the broken lights of Irish myth. He stood towards the myth upon which no individual mind had ever drawn out a line of beauty and to its unwieldy tales that divided against themselves as they moved down the cycles in the same attitude as towards the Roman catholic religion, the attitude of a dull-witted loyal serf. Whatsoever of thought or of feeling came to him from England or by way of English culture his mind stood armed against in obedience to a password; and of the world that lay beyond England he knew only the foreign legion of France in which he spoke of serving.

Coupling this ambition with the young man's humour Stephen had often called him one of the tame geese and there was even a point of irritation in the name pointed against that very reluctance of speech and deed in his friend which seemed so often to stand between Stephen's mind, eager of speculation, and the hidden ways of Irish life.

One night the young peasant, his spirit stung by the violent or luxurious language in which Stephen escaped from the cold silence of intellectual revolt, had called up before Stephen's mind a strange vision. The two were walking slowly towards Davin's rooms through the dark narrow streets of the poorer jews.

—A thing happened to myself, Stevie, last autumn, coming on winter, and I never told it to a living soul and you are the first person now I ever told it to. I disremember if it was October or November. It was October because it was before I came up here to join the matriculation class.

Stephen had turned his smiling eyes towards his friend's face, flattered by his confidence and won over to sympathy by the speaker's simple accent.

—I was away all that day from my own place over in Buttevant—I don't know if you know where that is—at a hurling match between the Croke's Own Boys and the Fearless Thurles and by God, Stevie, that was the hard fight. My first cousin, Fonsy Davin, was stripped to his buff that day minding cool for the Limericks but he was up with the forwards half the time and shouting like mad. I never will forget that day. One of the Crokes made a woeful wipe at him one time with his caman and I declare to God he was within an aim's ace of getting it at the side of his temple. Oh, honest to God, if the crook of it caught him that time he was done for.

—I am glad he escaped, Stephen had said with a laugh, but surely that's not the strange thing that happened you?

—Well, I suppose that doesn't interest you, but leastways there was such noise after the match that I missed the train home and I couldn't get any kind of a yoke to give me a lift for, as luck would have it, there was a mass meeting that same day over in Castletownroche and all the cars in the country were there. So there was nothing for it only to stay the night or to foot it out. Well, I started to walk and on I went and it was coming on night when I got into the Ballyhoura hills, that's better than ten miles from Kilmallock and there's a long lonely road after that. You wouldn't see the sign of a christian house along the road or hear a sound. It was pitch dark almost. Once or twice I stopped by the way under a bush to redden my pipe and only for the dew was thick I'd have stretched out there and slept. At last, after a bend of the road, I spied a little cottage with a light in the window. I went up and knocked at the door. A voice asked who was there and I answered I was over at the match in Buttevant and was walking back and that I'd be thankful for a glass of water. After a while a young woman opened the door and brought me out a big mug of milk. She was half undressed as if she was going to bed when I knocked and she had her hair hanging and I thought by her figure and by something in the look of her eyes that she must be carrying a child. She kept me in talk a long while at the door, and I thought it strange because her breast and her shoulders were bare. She asked me was I tired and would I like to stop the night there. She said she was all alone in the house and that her husband had gone that morning to Queenstown with his sister to see her off. And all the time she was talking, Stevie, she had her eyes fixed on my face and she stood so close to me I could hear her breathing. When I handed her back the mug at last she took my hand to draw me in over the threshold and said: *"Come in and stay the night here. You've no call to be frightened. There's no one in it but ourselves . . ."* I didn't go in, Stevie. I thanked her and went on my way again, all in a fever. At the first bend of the road I looked back and she was standing at the door.

The last words of Davin's story sang in his memory and the figure of the woman in the story stood forth reflected in other figures of the peasant women whom he had seen standing in the doorways at Clane as the college cars drove by, as a type of her race and of his own, a bat-like soul waking to the consciousness of itself in darkness and secrecy and loneliness and, through the eyes and voice and gesture of a woman without guile, calling the stranger to her bed.

A hand was laid on his arm and a young voice cried:

—Ah, gentleman, your own girl, sir! The first handsel today, gentleman. Buy that lovely bunch. Will you, gentleman?

The blue flowers which she lifted towards him and her young blue eyes seemed to him at that instant images of guilelessness, and he halted till the image had vanished and he saw only her ragged dress and damp coarse hair and hoydenish face.

—Do, gentleman! Don't forget your own girl, sir!

—I have no money, said Stephen.

—Buy them lovely ones, will you, sir? Only a penny.

—Did you hear what I said? asked Stephen, bending towards her. I told you I had no money. I tell you again now.

—Well, sure, you will some day, sir, please God, the girl answered after an instant.

—Possibly, said Stephen, but I don't think it likely.

He left her quickly, fearing that her intimacy might turn to jibing and wishing to be out of the way before she offered her ware to another, a tourist from England or a student of Trinity. Grafton Street, along which he walked, prolonged that moment of discouraged poverty. In the roadway at the head of the street a slab was set to the memory of Wolfe Tone and he remembered having been present with his father at its laying. He remembered with bitterness that scene of tawdry tribute. There were four French delegates in a brake and one, a plump smiling young man, held, wedged on a stick, a card on which were printed the words: *Vive l'Irlande!*

But the trees in Stephen's Green were fragrant of rain and the rain-sodden earth gave forth its mortal odour, a faint incense rising upward through the mould from many hearts. The soul of the gallant venal city which his elders had told him of had shrunk with time to a faint mortal odour rising from the earth and he knew that in a moment when he entered the sombre college he would be conscious of a corruption other than that of Buck Egan and Burnchapel Whaley.

It was too late to go upstairs to the French class. He crossed the hall and took the corridor to the left which led to the physics theatre. The corridor was dark and silent but not unwatchful. Why did he feel that it was not unwatchful? Was it because he had heard that in Buck Whaley's time there was a secret staircase there? Or was the jesuit house extra-territorial and was he walking among aliens? The Ireland of Tone and of Parnell seemed to have receded in space.

He opened the door of the theatre and halted in the chilly grey light that struggled through the dusty windows. A figure was crouching before the large grate and by its leanness and greyness he knew that it was the dean of studies lighting the fire. Stephen closed the door quietly and approached the fireplace.

—Good morning, sir! Can I help you?

The priest looked up quickly and said:

—One moment now, Mr Dedalus, and you will see. There is an art in lighting a fire. We have the liberal arts and we have the useful arts. This is one of the useful arts.

—I will try to learn it, said Stephen.

—Not too much coal, said the dean, working briskly at his task, that is one of the secrets.

He produced four candle-butts from the side-pockets of his soutane and placed them deftly among the coals and twisted papers. Stephen watched him in silence. Kneeling thus on the flagstone to kindle the fire and busied with the disposition of his wisps of paper and candle-butts he seemed more than ever a humble server making ready the place of sacrifice in an empty temple, a levite of the Lord. Like a levite's robe of plain linen the faded worn soutane draped the kneeling figure of one whom the canonicals or the bell-bordered ephod would irk and trouble. His very body had waxed old in lowly service of the Lord—in tending the fire upon the altar, in bearing tidings secretly, in waiting upon worldlings, in striking swiftly when bidden—and yet had remained ungraced by aught of saintly or of prelatic beauty. Nay, his very soul had waxed old in that service without growing towards light and beauty or spreading abroad a sweet odour of her sanctity—a mortified will no more responsive to the thrill of its obedience than was to the thrill of love or combat his ageing body, spare and sinewy, greyed with a silver-pointed down.

The dean rested back on his hunkers and watched the sticks catch. Stephen, to fill the silence, said:

—I am sure I could not light a fire.

—You are an artist, are you not, Mr Dedalus? said the dean, glancing up and blinking his pale eyes. The object of the artist is the creation of the beautiful. What the beautiful is is another question.

He rubbed his hands slowly and drily over the difficulty.

—Can you solve that question now? he asked.

—Aquinas, answered Stephen, says *Pulcra sunt quæ visa placent.*

—This fire before us, said the dean, will be pleasing to the eye. Will it therefore be beautiful?

—In so far as it is apprehended by the sight, which I suppose means here esthetic intellection, it will be beautiful. But Aquinas also says *Bonum est in quod tendit appetitus.* In so far as it satisfies the animal craving for warmth fire is a good. In hell, however, it is an evil.

—Quite so, said the dean, you have certainly hit the nail on the head.

He rose nimbly and went towards the door, set it ajar and said:

—A draught is said to be a help in these matters.

As he came back to the hearth, limping slightly but with a brisk step, Stephen saw the silent soul of a jesuit look out at him from the pale loveless eyes. Like Ignatius he was lame but in his eyes burned no spark of Ignatius's enthusiasm. Even the legendary craft of the company, a craft subtler and more secret than its fabled books of secret subtle wisdom, had not fired his soul with the energy of apostleship. It seemed as if he used the shifts and lore and cunning of the world, as bidden to do, for the greater glory of God, without joy in their handling or hatred of that in them which was evil but turning them, with a firm gesture of obedience back upon themselves and for all this silent service it seemed as if he loved not at all the master and little, if at all, the ends he served. *Similiter atque senis baculus,* he was, as the founder would have had him, like a staff in an old man's hand, to be leaned on in the road at nightfall or in stress of weather, to lie with a lady's nosegay on a garden seat, to be raised in menace.

The dean returned to the hearth and began to stroke his chin.

—When may we expect to have something from you on the esthetic question? he asked.

—From me! said Stephen in astonishment. I stumble on an idea once a fortnight if I am lucky.

—These questions are very profound, Mr Dedalus, said the dean. It is like looking down from the cliffs of Moher into the depths. Many go down into the depths and never come up. Only the trained diver can go down into those depths and explore them and come to the surface again.

—If you mean speculation, sir, said Stephen, I also am sure that there is no such thing as free thinking inasmuch as all thinking must be bound by its own laws.

—Ha!

—For my purpose I can work on at present by the light of one or two ideas of Aristotle and Aquinas.

—I see. I quite see your point.

—I need them only for my own use and guidance until I have done something for myself by their light. If the lamp smokes or smells I shall try to trim it. If it does not give light enough I shall sell it and buy another.

—Epictetus also had a lamp, said the dean, which was sold for a fancy price after his death. It was the lamp he wrote his philosophical dissertations by. You know Epictetus?

—An old gentleman, said Stephen coarsely, who said that the soul is very like a bucketful of water.

—He tells us in his homely way, the dean went on, that he put an iron lamp before a statue of one of the gods and that a thief stole the lamp. What did the philosopher do? He reflected that it was in the character of a thief to steal and determined to buy an earthen lamp next day instead of the iron lamp.

A smell of molten tallow came up from the dean's candle butts and fused itself in Stephen's consciousness with the jingle of the words, bucket and lamp and lamp and bucket. The priest's voice, too, had a hard jingling tone. Stephen's mind halted by instinct, checked by the strange tone and the imagery and by the priest's face which seemed like an unlit lamp or a reflector hung in a false focus. What lay behind it or within it? A dull torpor of the soul or the dullness of the thundercloud, charged with intellection and capable of the gloom of God?

—I meant a different kind of lamp, sir, said Stephen.

—Undoubtedly, said the dean.

—One difficulty, said Stephen, in esthetic discussion is to know whether words are being used according to the literary tradition or according to the tradition of the marketplace. I remember a sentence of Newman's in which he says of the Blessed Virgin that she was detained in the full company of the saints. The use of the word in the marketplace is quite different. *I hope I am not detaining you.*

—Not in the least, said the dean politely.

—No, no, said Stephen, smiling, I mean—

—Yes, yes; I see, said the dean quickly, I quite catch the point: DETAIN.

He thrust forward his under jaw and uttered a dry short cough.

—To return to the lamp, he said, the feeding of it is also a nice problem. You must choose the pure oil and you must be careful when you pour it in not to overflow it, not to pour in more than the funnel can hold.

—What funnel? asked Stephen.

—The funnel through which you pour the oil into your lamp.

—That? said Stephen. Is that called a funnel? Is it not a tundish?

—What is a tundish?

—That. The . . . funnel.

—Is that called a tundish in Ireland? asked the dean. I never heard the word in my life.

—It is called a tundish in Lower Drumcondra, said Stephen, laughing, where they speak the best English.

—A tundish, said the dean reflectively. That is a most interesting word. I must look that word up. Upon my word I must.

His courtesy of manner rang a little false and Stephen looked at the English convert with the same eyes as the elder brother in the parable may have turned on the prodigal. A humble follower in the wake of clamorous conversions, a poor Englishman in Ireland, he seemed to have entered on the stage of jesuit history when that strange play of intrigue and suffering and envy and struggle and indignity had been all but given through—a late-comer, a tardy spirit. From what had he set out? Perhaps he had been born and bred among serious dissenters, seeing salvation in Jesus only and abhorring the vain pomps of the establishment. Had he felt the need of an implicit faith amid the welter of sectarianism and the jargon of its turbulent schisms, six principle men, peculiar people, seed and snake baptists, supralapsarian dogmatists? Had he found the true church all of a sudden in winding up to the end like a reel of cotton some fine-spun line of reasoning upon insufflation on the imposition of hands or the procession of the Holy Ghost? Or had Lord Christ touched him and bidden him follow, like that disciple who had sat at the receipt of custom, as he sat by the door of some zinc-roofed chapel, yawning and telling over his church pence?

The dean repeated the word yet again.

—Tundish! Well now, that is interesting!

—The question you asked me a moment ago seems to me more interesting. What is that beauty which the artist struggles to express from lumps of earth, said Stephen coldly.

The little word seemed to have turned a rapier point of his sensitiveness against this courteous and vigilant foe. He felt with a smart of dejection that the man to whom he was speaking was a countryman of Ben Jonson. He thought:

—The language in which we are speaking is his before it is mine. How different are the words *home, Christ, ale, master,* on his lips and on mine! I cannot speak or write these words without unrest of spirit. His language, so familiar and so foreign, will always be for me an acquired speech. I have not made or accepted its words. My voice holds them at bay. My soul frets in the shadow of his language.

—And to distinguish between the beautiful and the sublime, the dean added, to distinguish between moral beauty and material beauty. And to inquire what kind of beauty is proper to each of the various arts. These are some interesting points we might take up.

Stephen, disheartened suddenly by the dean's firm, dry tone, was silent; and through the silence a distant noise of many boots and confused voices came up the staircase.

—In pursuing these speculations, said the dean conclusively, there is, however, the danger of perishing of inanition. First you must take your degree. Set that before you as your first aim. Then, little by little, you will see your way. I mean in every sense, your way in life and in thinking. It may be uphill pedalling at first. Take Mr Moonan. He was a long time before he got to the top. But he got there.

—I may not have his talent, said Stephen quietly.

—You never know, said the dean brightly. We never can say what is in us. I most certainly should not be despondent. *Per aspera ad astra.*

He left the hearth quickly and went towards the landing to oversee the arrival of the first arts' class.

Leaning against the fireplace Stephen heard him greet briskly and impartially every student of the class and could almost see the frank smiles of the coarser students. A desolating pity began to fall like dew upon his easily embittered heart for this faithful serving-man of the knightly Loyola, for this half-brother of the clergy, more venal than they in speech, more steadfast of soul than they, one whom he would never call his ghostly father; and he thought how this man and his companions had earned the name of worldlings at the hands not of the unworldly only but of the worldly also for having pleaded, during all their history, at the bar of God's justice for the souls of the lax and the lukewarm and the prudent.

The entry of the professor was signalled by a few rounds of Kentish fire from the heavy boots of those students who sat on the highest tier of the gloomy theatre under the grey cobwebbed windows. The calling of the roll began and the responses to the names were given out in all tones until the name of Peter Byrne was reached.

—Here!

A deep bass note in response came from the upper tier, followed by coughs of protest along the other benches.

The professor paused in his reading and called the next name:

—Cranly!

No answer.

—Mr Cranly!

A smile flew across Stephen's face as he thought of his friend's studies.

—Try Leopardstown! said a voice from the bench behind.

Stephen glanced up quickly but Moynihan's snoutish face, outlined on the grey light, was impassive. A formula was given out. Amid the rustling of the notebooks Stephen turned back again and said:

—Give me some paper for God's sake.

—Are you as bad as that? asked Moynihan with a broad grin.

He tore a sheet from his scribbler and passed it down, whispering:

—In case of necessity any layman or woman can do it.

The formula which he wrote obediently on the sheet of paper, the coiling and uncoiling calculations of the professor, the spectre-like symbols of force and velocity fascinated and jaded Stephen's mind. He had heard some say that the old professor was an atheist freemason. O the grey dull day! It seemed a limbo of painless patient consciousness through which souls of mathematicians might wander, projecting long slender fabrics from plane to plane of ever rarer and paler twilight, radiating swift eddies to the last verges of a universe ever vaster, farther and more impalpable.

—So we must distinguish between elliptical and ellipsoidal. Perhaps some of you gentlemen may be familiar with the works of Mr W. S. Gilbert. In one of his songs he speaks of the billiard sharp who is condemned to play:

> *On a cloth untrue*
> *With a twisted cue*
> *And elliptical billiard balls.*

—He means a ball having the form of the ellipsoid of the principal axes of which I spoke a moment ago.

Moynihan leaned down towards Stephen's ear and murmured:

—What price ellipsoidal balls! chase me, ladies, I'm in the cavalry!

His fellow student's rude humour ran like a gust through the cloister of Stephen's mind, shaking into gay life limp priestly vestments that hung upon the walls, setting them to sway and caper in a sabbath of misrule. The forms of the community emerged from the gust-blown vestments, the dean of studies, the portly florid bursar with his cap of grey hair, the president, the little priest with feathery hair who wrote devout verses, the squat peasant form of the professor of economics, the tall form of the young professor of mental science discussing on the landing a case of conscience with his class like a giraffe cropping high leafage among a herd of antelopes, the grave troubled prefect of the sodality, the plump round-headed professor of Italian with his rogue's eyes. They came ambling and stumbling, tumbling and capering, kilting their gowns for leap frog, holding one another back, shaken with deep false laughter, smacking one another behind and laughing at their rude malice, calling to one another by familiar nicknames, protesting with sudden dignity at some rough usage, whispering two and two behind their hands.

The professor had gone to the glass cases on the side wall, from a shelf of which he took down a set of coils, blew away the dust from many points and, bearing it carefully to the table, held a finger on it while he proceeded with his lecture. He explained that the wires in modern coils were of a compound called platinoid lately discovered by F. W. Martino.

He spoke clearly the initials and surname of the discoverer. Moynihan whispered from behind:

—Good old Fresh Water Martin!

—Ask him, Stephen whispered back with weary humour, if he wants a subject for electrocution. He can have me.

Moynihan, seeing the professor bend over the coils, rose in his bench and, clacking noiselessly the fingers of his right hand, began to call with the voice of a slobbering urchin:

—Please teacher! This boy is after saying a bad word, teacher.

—Platinoid, the professor said solemnly, is preferred to German silver because it has a lower coefficient of resistance by changes of temperature. The platinoid wire is insulated and the covering of silk that insulates it is wound on the ebonite bobbins just where my finger is. If it were wound single an extra current would be induced in the coils. The bobbins are saturated in hot paraffin wax . . .

A sharp Ulster voice said from the bench below Stephen:

—Are we likely to be asked questions on applied science?

The professor began to juggle gravely with the terms pure science and applied science. A heavy-built student, wearing gold spectacles, stared with some wonder at the questioner. Moynihan murmured from behind in his natural voice:

—Isn't MacAlister a devil for his pound of flesh?

Stephen looked coldly on the oblong skull beneath him overgrown with tangled twine-coloured hair. The voice, the accent, the mind of the questioner offended him and he allowed the offence to carry him towards wilful unkindness, bidding his mind think that the student's father would have done better had he sent his son to Belfast to study and have saved something on the train fare by so doing.

The oblong skull beneath did not turn to meet this shaft of thought and yet the shaft came back to its bowstring; for he saw in a moment the student's whey-pale face.

—That thought is not mine, he said to himself quickly. It came from the comic Irishman in the bench behind. Patience. Can you say with certitude by whom the soul of your race was bartered and its elect betrayed—by the questioner or by the mocker? Patience. Remember Epictetus. It is probably in his character to ask such a question at such a moment in such a tone and to pronounce the word *science* as a monosyllable.

The droning voice of the professor continued to wind itself slowly round and round the coils it spoke of, doubling, trebling, quadrupling its somnolent energy as the coil multiplied its ohms of resistance.

Moynihan's voice called from behind in echo to a distant bell:

—Closing time, gents!

The entrance hall was crowded and loud with talk. On a table near the door were two photographs in frames and between them a long roll of paper bearing an irregular tail of signatures. MacCann went briskly to and fro among the students, talking rapidly, answering rebuffs and leading one after another to the table. In the inner hall the dean of studies stood talking to a young professor, stroking his chin gravely and nodding his head.

Stephen, checked by the crowd at the door, halted irresolutely. From under the wide falling leaf of a soft hat Cranly's dark eyes were watching him.

—Have you signed? Stephen asked.

Cranly closed his long thin-lipped mouth, communed with himself an instant and answered:

—*Ego habeo.*

—What is it for?

—*Quod?*

—What is it for?

Cranly turned his pale face to Stephen and said blandly and bitterly:

—*Per pax universalis.*

Stephen pointed to the Tsar's photograph and said:

—He has the face of a besotted Christ.

The scorn and anger in his voice brought Cranly's eyes back from a calm survey of the walls of the hall.

—Are you annoyed? he asked.

—No, answered Stephen.

—Are you in bad humour?

—No.

—*Credo ut vos sanguinarius mendax estis,* said Cranly, *quia facies vostra monstrat ut vos in damno malo humore estis.*

Moynihan, on his way to the table, said in Stephen's ear:

—MacCann is in tiptop form. Ready to shed the last drop. Brand new world. No stimulants and votes for the bitches.

Stephen smiled at the manner of this confidence and, when Moynihan had passed, turned again to meet Cranly's eyes.

—Perhaps you can tell me, he said, why he pours his soul so freely into my ear. Can you?

A dull scowl appeared on Cranly's forehead. He stared at the table where Moynihan had bent to write his name on the roll, and then said flatly:

—A sugar!

—*Quis est in malo humore,* said Stephen, *ego aut vos?*

Cranly did not take up the taunt. He brooded sourly on his judgement and repeated with the same flat force:

—A flaming bloody sugar, that's what he is!

It was his epitaph for all dead friendships and Stephen wondered whether it would ever be spoken in the same tone over his memory. The heavy lumpish phrase sank slowly out of hearing like a stone through a quagmire. Stephen saw it sink as he had seen many another, feeling its heaviness depress his heart. Cranly's speech, unlike that of Davin, had neither rare phrases of Elizabethan English nor quaintly turned versions of Irish idioms. Its drawl was an echo of the quays of Dublin given back by a bleak decaying seaport, its energy an echo of the sacred eloquence of Dublin given back flatly by a Wicklow pulpit.

The heavy scowl faded from Cranly's face as MacCann marched briskly towards them from the other side of the hall.

—Here you are! said MacCann cheerily.

—Here I am! said Stephen.

—Late as usual. Can you not combine the progressive tendency with a respect for punctuality?

—That question is out of order, said Stephen. Next business.

His smiling eyes were fixed on a silver-wrapped tablet of milk chocolate which peeped out of the propagandist's breast-pocket. A little ring of listeners closed round to hear the war of wits. A lean student with olive skin and lank black hair thrust his face between the two, glancing from one to the other at each phrase and seeming to try to catch each flying phrase in his open moist mouth. Cranly took a small grey handball from his pocket and began to examine it closely, turning it over and over.

—Next business? said MacCann. Hom!

He gave a loud cough of laughter, smiled broadly and tugged twice at the straw-coloured goatee which hung from his blunt chin.

—The next business is to sign the testimonial.

—Will you pay me anything if I sign? asked Stephen.

—I thought you were an idealist, said MacCann.

The gipsy-like student looked about him and addressed the onlookers in an indistinct bleating voice.

—By hell, that's a queer notion. I consider that notion to be a mercenary notion.

His voice faded into silence. No heed was paid to his words. He turned his olive face, equine in expression, towards Stephen, inviting him to speak again.

MacCann began to speak with fluent energy of the Tsar's rescript, of Stead, of general disarmament arbitration in cases of international disputes, of the signs of the times, of the new humanity and the new gospel of life which would make it the business of the community to secure as cheaply as possible the greatest possible happiness of the greatest possible number.

The gipsy student responded to the close of the period by crying:

—Three cheers for universal brotherhood!

—Go on, Temple, said a stout ruddy student near him. I'll stand you a pint after.

—I'm a believer in universal brotherhood, said Temple, glancing about him out of his dark oval eyes. Marx is only a bloody cod.

Cranly gripped his arm tightly to check his tongue, smiling uneasily, and repeated:

—Easy, easy, easy!

Temple struggled to free his arm but continued, his mouth flecked by a thin foam:

—Socialism was founded by an Irishman and the first man in Europe who preached the freedom of thought was Collins. Two hundred years ago. He denounced priestcraft, the philosopher of Middlesex. Three cheers for John Anthony Collins!

A thin voice from the verge of the ring replied:

—Pip! pip!

Moynihan murmured beside Stephen's ear:

—And what about John Anthony's poor little sister:

> *Lottie Collins lost her drawers;*
> *Won't you kindly lend her yours?*

Stephen laughed and Moynihan, pleased with the result, murmured again:

—We'll have five bob each way on John Anthony Collins.

—I am waiting for your answer, said MacCann briefly.

—The affair doesn't interest me in the least, said Stephen wearily. You know that well. Why do you make a scene about it?

—Good! said MacCann, smacking his lips. You are a reactionary, then?

—Do you think you impress me, Stephen asked, when you flourish your wooden sword?

—Metaphors! said MacCann bluntly. Come to facts.

Stephen blushed and turned aside. MacCann stood his ground and said with hostile humour:

—Minor poets, I suppose, are above such trivial questions as the question of universal peace.

Cranly raised his head and held the handball between the two students by way of a peace-offering, saying:

—*Pax super totum sanguinarium globum.*

Stephen, moving away the bystanders, jerked his shoulder angrily in the direction of the Tsar's image, saying:

—Keep your icon. If we must have a Jesus let us have a legitimate Jesus.

—By hell, that's a good one! said the gipsy student to those about him, that's a fine expression. I like that expression immensely.

He gulped down the spittle in his throat as if he were gulping down the phrase and, fumbling at the peak of his tweed cap, turned to Stephen, saying:

—Excuse me, sir, what do you mean by that expression you uttered just now?

Feeling himself jostled by the students near him, he said to them:

—I am curious to know now what he meant by that expression.

He turned again to Stephen and said in a whisper:

—Do you believe in Jesus? I believe in man. Of course, I don't know if you believe in man. I admire you, sir. I admire the mind of man independent of all religions. Is that your opinion about the mind of Jesus?

—Go on, Temple, said the stout ruddy student, returning, as was his wont, to his first idea, that pint is waiting for you.

—He thinks I'm an imbecile, Temple explained to Stephen, because I'm a believer in the power of mind.

Cranly linked his arms into those of Stephen and his admirer and said:

—*Nos ad manum ballum jocabimus.*

Stephen, in the act of being led away, caught sight of MacCann's flushed blunt-featured face.

—My signature is of no account, he said politely. You are right to go your way. Leave me to go mine.

—Dedalus, said MacCann crisply, I believe you're a good fellow but you have yet to learn the dignity of altruism and the responsibility of the human individual.

A voice said:

—Intellectual crankery is better out of this movement than in it.

Stephen, recognizing the harsh tone of MacAlister's voice did not turn in the direction of the voice. Cranly pushed solemnly through the throng of students, linking Stephen and Temple like a celebrant attended by his ministers on his way to the altar.

Temple bent eagerly across Cranly's breast and said:

—Did you hear MacAlister what he said? That youth is jealous of you. Did you see that? I bet Cranly didn't see that. By hell, I saw that at once.

As they crossed the inner hall, the dean of studies was in the act of escaping from the student with whom he had been conversing. He stood at the foot of the staircase, a foot on the lowest step, his threadbare soutane gathered about him for the ascent with womanish care, nodding his head often and repeating:

—Not a doubt of it, Mr Hackett! Very fine! Not a doubt of it!

In the middle of the hall the prefect of the college sodality was speaking earnestly, in a soft querulous voice, with a boarder. As he spoke he wrinkled a little his freckled brow and bit, between his phrases, at a tiny bone pencil.

—I hope the matric men will all come. The first arts' men are pretty sure. Second arts, too. We must make sure of the newcomers.

Temple bent again across Cranly, as they were passing through the doorway, and said in a swift whisper:

—Do you know that he is a married man? he was a married man before they converted him. He has a wife and children somewhere. By hell, I think that's the queerest notion I ever heard! Eh?

His whisper trailed off into sly cackling laughter. The moment they were through the doorway Cranly seized him rudely by the neck and shook him, saying:

—You flaming floundering fool! I'll take my dying bible there isn't a bigger bloody ape, do you know, than you in the whole flaming bloody world!

Temple wriggled in his grip, laughing still with sly content, while Cranly repeated flatly at every rude shake:

—A flaming flaring bloody idiot!

They crossed the weedy garden together. The president, wrapped in a heavy loose cloak, was coming towards them along one of the walks, reading his office. At the end of the walk he halted before turning and raised his eyes. The students saluted, Temple fumbling as before at the peak of his cap. They walked forward in silence. As they neared the alley Stephen could hear the thuds of the players' hands and the wet smacks of the ball and Davin's voice crying out excitedly at each stroke.

The three students halted round the box on which Davin sat to follow the game. Temple, after a few moments, sidled across to Stephen and said:

—Excuse me, I wanted to ask you, do you believe that Jean-Jacques Rousseau was a sincere man?

Stephen laughed outright. Cranly, picking up the broken stave of a cask from the grass at his feet, turned swiftly and said sternly:

—Temple, I declare to the living God if you say another word, do you know, to anybody on any subject, I'll kill you *super spottum*.

—He was like you, I fancy, said Stephen, an emotional man.

—Blast him, curse him! said Cranly broadly. Don't talk to him at all. Sure, you might as well be talking, do you know, to a flaming chamber-pot as talking to Temple. Go home, Temple. For God's sake, go home.

—I don't care a damn about you, Cranly, answered Temple, moving out of reach of the uplifted stave and pointing at Stephen. He's the only man I see in this institution that has an individual mind.

—Institution! Individual! cried Cranly. Go home, blast you, for you're a hopeless bloody man.

—I'm an emotional man, said Temple. That's quite rightly expressed. And I'm proud that I'm an emotionalist.

He sidled out of the alley, smiling slyly. Cranly watched him with a blank expressionless face.

—Look at him! he said. Did you ever see such a go-by-the-wall?

His phrase was greeted by a strange laugh from a student who lounged against the wall, his peaked cap down on his eyes. The laugh, pitched in a high key and coming from a so muscular frame, seemed like the whinny of an elephant. The student's body shook all over and, to ease his mirth, he rubbed both his hands delightedly over his groins.

—Lynch is awake, said Cranly.

Lynch, for answer, straightened himself and thrust forward his chest.

—Lynch puts out his chest, said Stephen, as a criticism of life.

Lynch smote himself sonorously on the chest and said:

—Who has anything to say about my girth?

Cranly took him at the word and the two began to tussle. When their faces had flushed with the struggle they drew apart, panting. Stephen bent down towards Davin who, intent on the game, had paid no heed to the talk of the others.

—And how is my little tame goose? he asked. Did he sign, too?

Davin nodded and said:

—And you, Stevie?

Stephen shook his head.

—You're a terrible man, Stevie, said Davin, taking the short pipe from his mouth, always alone.

—Now that you have signed the petition for universal peace, said Stephen, I suppose you will burn that little copybook I saw in your room.

As Davin did not answer, Stephen began to quote:

—Long pace, fianna! Right incline, fianna! Fianna, by numbers, salute, one, two!

—That's a different question, said Davin. I'm an Irish nationalist, first and foremost. But that's you all out. You're a born sneerer, Stevie.

—When you make the next rebellion with hurleysticks, said Stephen, and want the indispensable informer, tell me. I can find you a few in this college.

—I can't understand you, said Davin. One time I hear you talk against English literature. Now you talk against the Irish informers. What with your name and your ideas—Are you Irish at all?

—Come with me now to the office of arms and I will show you the tree of my family, said Stephen.

—Then be one of us, said Davin. Why don't you learn Irish? Why did you drop out of the league class after the first lesson?

—You know one reason why, answered Stephen.

Davin tossed his head and laughed.

—Oh, come now, he said. Is it on account of that certain young lady and Father Moran? But that's all in your own mind, Stevie. They were only talking and laughing.

Stephen paused and laid a friendly hand upon Davin's shoulder.

—Do you remember, he said, when we knew each other first? The first morning we met you asked me to show you the way to the matriculation class, putting a very strong stress on the first syllable. You remember? Then you used to address the jesuits as father, you remember? I ask myself about you: *Is he as innocent as his speech?*

—I'm a simple person, said Davin. You know that. When you told me that night in Harcourt Street those things about your private life, honest to God, Stevie, I was not able to eat my dinner. I was quite bad. I was awake a long time that night. Why did you tell me those things?

—Thanks, said Stephen. You mean I am a monster.

—No, said Davin. But I wish you had not told me.

A tide began to surge beneath the calm surface of Stephen's friendliness.

—This race and this country and this life produced me, he said. I shall express myself as I am.

—Try to be one of us, repeated Davin. In heart you are an Irish man but your pride is too powerful.

—My ancestors threw off their language and took another, Stephen said. They allowed a handful of foreigners to subject them. Do you fancy I am going to pay in my own life and person debts they made? What for?

—For our freedom, said Davin.

—No honourable and sincere man, said Stephen, has given up to you his life and his youth and his affections from the days of Tone to those of Parnell, but you sold him to the enemy or failed him in need or reviled him and left him for another. And you invite me to be one of you. I'd see you damned first.

—They died for their ideals, Stevie, said Davin. Our day will come yet, believe me.

Stephen, following his own thought, was silent for an instant.

—The soul is born, he said vaguely, first in those moments I told you of. It has a slow and dark birth, more mysterious than the birth of the body. When the soul of a man is born in this country there are nets flung at it to hold it back from flight. You talk to me of nationality, language, religion. I shall try to fly by those nets.

Davin knocked the ashes from his pipe.

—Too deep for me, Stevie, he said. But a man's country comes first. Ireland first, Stevie. You can be a poet or a mystic after.

—Do you know what Ireland is? asked Stephen with cold violence. Ireland is the old sow that eats her farrow.

Davin rose from his box and went towards the players, shaking his head sadly. But in a moment his sadness left him and he was hotly disputing with Cranly and the two players who had finished their game. A match of four was arranged, Cranly insisting, however, that his ball should be used. He let it rebound twice or thrice to his hand and struck it strongly and swiftly towards the base of the alley, exclaiming in answer to its thud:

—Your soul!

Stephen stood with Lynch till the score began to rise. Then he plucked him by the sleeve to come away. Lynch obeyed, saying:

—Let us eke go, as Cranly has it.

Stephen smiled at this side-thrust. They passed back through the garden and out through the hall where the doddering porter was pinning up a hall notice in the frame. At the foot of the steps they halted and Stephen took a packet of cigarettes from his pocket and offered it to his companion.

—I know you are poor, he said.

—Damn your yellow insolence, answered Lynch.

This second proof of Lynch's culture made Stephen smile again.

—It was a great day for European culture, he said, when you made up your mind to swear in yellow.

They lit their cigarettes and turned to the right. After a pause Stephen began:

—Aristotle has not defined pity and terror. I have. I say—

Lynch halted and said bluntly:

—Stop! I won't listen! I am sick. I was out last night on a yellow drunk with Horan and Goggins.

Stephen went on:

—Pity is the feeling which arrests the mind in the presence of whatsoever is grave and constant in human sufferings and unites it with the human sufferer. Terror is the feeling which arrests the mind in the presence of whatsoever is grave and constant in human sufferings and unites it with the secret cause.

—Repeat, said Lynch.

Stephen repeated the definitions slowly.

—A girl got into a hansom a few days ago, he went on, in London. She was on her way to meet her mother whom she had not seen for many years. At the corner of a street the shaft of a lorry shivered the window of the hansom in the shape of a star. A long fine needle of the shivered glass pierced her heart. She died on the instant. The reporter called it a tragic death. It is not. It is remote from terror and pity according to the terms of my definitions.

—The tragic emotion, in fact, is a face looking two ways, towards terror and towards pity, both of which are phases of it. You see I use the word *arrest*. I mean that the tragic emotion is static. Or rather the dramatic emotion is. The feelings excited by improper art are kinetic, desire or loathing. Desire urges us to possess, to go to something; loathing urges us to abandon, to go from something. The arts which excite them, pornographical or didactic, are therefore improper arts. The esthetic emotion (I used the general term) is therefore static. The mind is arrested and raised above desire and loathing.

—You say that art must not excite desire, said Lynch. I told you that one day I wrote my name in pencil on the backside of the Venus of Praxiteles in the Museum. Was that not desire?

—I speak of normal natures, said Stephen. You also told me that when you were a boy in that charming carmelite school you ate pieces of dried cowdung.

Lynch broke again into a whinny of laughter and again rubbed both his hands over his groins but without taking them from his pockets.

—O, I did! I did! he cried.

Stephen turned towards his companion and looked at him for a moment boldly in the eyes. Lynch, recovering from his laughter, answered his look from his humbled eyes. The long slender flattened skull beneath the long pointed cap brought before Stephen's mind the image of a hooded reptile. The eyes, too, were reptile-like in glint and gaze. Yet at that instant, humbled and alert in their look, they were lit by one tiny human point, the window of a shrivelled soul, poignant and self-embittered.

—As for that, Stephen said in polite parenthesis, we are all animals. I also am an animal.

—You are, said Lynch.

—But we are just now in a mental world, Stephen continued. The desire and loathing excited by improper esthetic means are really not esthetic emotions not only because they are kinetic in character but also because they are not more than physical. Our flesh shrinks from what it dreads and responds to the stimulus of what it desires by a purely reflex action of the nervous system. Our eyelid closes before we are aware that the fly is about to enter our eye.

—Not always, said Lynch critically.

—In the same way, said Stephen, your flesh responded to the stimulus of a naked statue, but it was, I say, simply a reflex action of the nerves. Beauty expressed by the artist cannot awaken in us an emotion which is kinetic or a sensation which is purely physical. It awakens, or ought to awaken, or induces, or ought to induce, an esthetic stasis, an ideal pity or an ideal terror, a stasis called forth, prolonged, and at last dissolved by what I call the rhythm of beauty.

—What is that exactly? asked Lynch.

—Rhythm, said Stephen, is the first formal esthetic relation of part to part in any esthetic whole or of an esthetic whole to its part or parts or of any part to the esthetic whole of which it is a part.

—If that is rhythm, said Lynch, let me hear what you call beauty; and, please remember, though I did eat a cake of cowdung once, that I admire only beauty.

Stephen raised his cap as if in greeting. Then, blushing slightly, he laid his hand on Lynch's thick tweed sleeve.

—We are right, he said, and the others are wrong. To speak of these things and to try to understand their nature and, having understood it, to try slowly and humbly and constantly to express, to press out again, from the gross earth or what it brings forth, from sound and shape and colour which are the prison gates of our soul, an image of the beauty we have come to understand—that is art.

They had reached the canal bridge and, turning from their course, went on by the trees. A crude grey light, mirrored in the sluggish water and a smell of wet branches over their heads seemed to war against the course of Stephen's thought.

—But you have not answered my question, said Lynch. What is art? What is the beauty it expresses?

—That was the first definition I gave you, you sleepy-headed wretch, said Stephen, when I began to try to think out the matter for myself. Do you remember the night? Cranly lost his temper and began to talk about Wicklow bacon.

—I remember, said Lynch. He told us about them flaming fat devils of pigs.

—Art, said Stephen, is the human disposition of sensible or intelligible matter for an esthetic end. You remember the pigs and forget that. You are a distressing pair, you and Cranly.

Lynch made a grimace at the raw grey sky and said:

—If I am to listen to your esthetic philosophy give me at least another cigarette. I don't care about it. I don't even care about women. Damn you and damn everything. I want a job of five hundred a year. You can't get me one.

Stephen handed him the packet of cigarettes. Lynch took the last one that remained, saying simply:

—Proceed!

—Aquinas, said Stephen, says that is beautiful the apprehension of which pleases.

Lynch nodded.

—I remember that, he said, *Pulcra sunt quæ visa placent.*

—He uses the word *visa*, said Stephen, to cover esthetic apprehensions of all kinds, whether through sight or hearing or through any other avenue of apprehension. This word, though it is vague, is clear enough to keep away good and evil which excite desire and loathing. It means certainly a stasis and not a kinesis. How about the true? It produces also a stasis of the mind. You would not write your name in pencil across the hypotenuse of a right-angled triangle.

—No, said Lynch, give me the hypotenuse of the Venus of Praxiteles.

—Static therefore, said Stephen. Plato, I believe, said that beauty is the splendour of truth. I don't think that it has a meaning, but the true and the beautiful are akin. Truth is beheld by the intellect which is appeased by the most satisfying relations of the intelligible; beauty is beheld by the imagination which is appeased by the most satisfying relations of the sensible. The first step in the direction of truth is to understand the frame and scope of the intellect itself, to comprehend the act itself of intellection. Aristotle's entire system of philosophy rests upon his book of psychology and that, I think, rests on his statement that the same attribute cannot at the same time and in the same connexion belong to and not belong to the same subject.

The first step in the direction of beauty is to understand the frame and scope of the imagination, to comprehend the act itself of esthetic apprehension. Is that clear?

—But what is beauty? asked Lynch impatiently. Out with another definition. Something we see and like! Is that the best you and Aquinas can do?

—Let us take woman, said Stephen.

—Let us take her! said Lynch fervently.

—The Greek, the Turk, the Chinese, the Copt, the Hottentot, said Stephen, all admire a different type of female beauty. That seems to be a maze out of which we cannot escape. I see, however, two ways out. One is this hypothesis: that every physical quality admired by men in women is in direct connexion with the manifold functions of women for the propagation of the species. It may be so. The world, it seems, is drearier than even you, Lynch, imagined. For my part I dislike that way out. It leads to eugenics rather than to esthetic. It leads you out of the maze into a new gaudy lecture-room where MacCann, with one hand on *The Origin of Species* and the other hand on the new testament, tells you that you admired the great flanks of Venus because you felt that she would bear you burly offspring and admired her great breasts because you felt that she would give good milk to her children and yours.

—Then MacCann is a sulphur-yellow liar, said Lynch energetically.

—There remains another way out, said Stephen, laughing.

—To wit? said Lynch.

—This hypothesis, Stephen began.

A long dray laden with old iron came round the corner of Sir Patrick Dun's hospital covering the end of Stephen's speech with the harsh roar of jangled and rattling metal. Lynch closed his ears and gave out oath after oath till the dray had passed. Then he turned on his heel rudely. Stephen turned also and waited for a few moments till his companion's ill-humour had had its vent.

—This hypothesis, Stephen repeated, is the other way out: that, though the same object may not seem beautiful to all people, all people who admire a beautiful object find in it certain relations which satisfy and coincide with the stages themselves of all esthetic apprehension. These relations of the sensible, visible to you through one form and to me through another, must be therefore the necessary qualities of beauty. Now, we can return to our old friend saint Thomas for another pennyworth of wisdom.

Lynch laughed.

—It amuses me vastly, he said, to hear you quoting him time after time like a jolly round friar. Are you laughing in your sleeve?

—MacAlister, answered Stephen, would call my esthetic theory applied Aquinas. So far as this side of esthetic philosophy extends, Aquinas will carry me all along the line. When we come to the phenomena of artistic conception, artistic gestation, and artistic reproduction I require a new terminology and a new personal experience.

—Of course, said Lynch. After all Aquinas, in spite of his intellect, was exactly a good round friar. But you will tell me about the new personal experience and new terminology some other day. Hurry up and finish the first part.

—Who knows? said Stephen, smiling. Perhaps Aquinas would understand me better than you. He was a poet himself. He wrote a hymn for Maundy Thursday. It begins with the words *Pange lingua gloriosi*. They say it is the highest glory of the hymnal. It is an intricate and soothing hymn. I like it; but there is no hymn that can be put beside that mournful and majestic processional song, the *Vexilla Regis* of Venantius Fortunatus.

Lynch began to sing softly and solemnly in a deep bass voice:

Impleta sunt quæ concinit
David fideli carmine
Dicendo nationibus
Regnavit a ligno deus.

—That's great! he said, well pleased. Great music!

They turned into Lower Mount Street. A few steps from the corner a fat young man, wearing a silk neckcloth, saluted them and stopped.

—Did you hear the results of the exams? he asked. Griffin was plucked. Halpin and O'Flynn are through the home civil. Moonan got fifth place in the Indian. O'Shaughnessy got fourteenth. The Irish fellows in Clark's gave them a feed last night. They all ate curry.

His pallid bloated face expressed benevolent malice and, as he had advanced through his tidings of success, his small fat-encircled eyes vanished out of sight and his weak wheezing voice out of hearing.

In reply to a question of Stephen's his eyes and his voice came forth again from their lurking-places.

—Yes, MacCullagh and I, he said. He's taking pure mathematics and I'm taking constitutional history. There are twenty subjects. I'm taking botany too. You know I'm a member of the field club.

He drew back from the other two in a stately fashion and placed a plump woollen-gloved hand on his breast from which muttered wheezing laughter at once broke forth.

—Bring us a few turnips and onions the next time you go out, said Stephen drily, to make a stew.

The fat student laughed indulgently and said:

—We are all highly respectable people in the field club. Last Saturday we went out to Glenmalure, seven of us.

—With women, Donovan? said Lynch.

Donovan again laid his hand on his chest and said:

—Our end is the acquisition of knowledge.

Then he said quickly:

—I hear you are writing some essays about esthetics.

Stephen made a vague gesture of denial.

—Goethe and Lessing, said Donovan, have written a lot on that subject, the classical school and the romantic school and all that. The *Laocoon* interested me very much when I read it. Of course it is idealistic, German, ultra-profound.

Neither of the others spoke. Donovan took leave of them urbanely.

—I must go, he said softly and benevolently, I have a strong suspicion, amounting almost to a conviction, that my sister intended to make pancakes today for the dinner of the Donovan family.

—Goodbye, Stephen said in his wake. Don't forget the turnips for me and my mate.

Lynch gazed after him, his lip curling in slow scorn till his face resembled a devil's mask:

—To think that that yellow pancake-eating excrement can get a good job, he said at length, and I have to smoke cheap cigarettes!

They turned their faces towards Merrion Square and went for a little in silence.

—To finish what I was saying about beauty, said Stephen, the most satisfying relations of the sensible must therefore correspond to the necessary phases of artistic apprehension. Find these and you find the qualities of universal beauty. Aquinas says: *ad pulcritudinem tria requiruntur integritas, consonantia, claritas. I translate it so: Three things are needed for beauty, wholeness, harmony, and radiance.* Do these correspond to the phases of apprehension? Are you following?

—Of course, I am, said Lynch. If you think I have an excrementitious intelligence run after Donovan and ask him to listen to you.

Stephen pointed to a basket which a butcher's boy had slung inverted on his head.

—Look at that basket, he said.

—I see it, said Lynch.

—In order to see that basket, said Stephen, your mind first of all separates the basket from the rest of the visible universe which is not the basket. The first phase of apprehension is a bounding line drawn about the object to be apprehended. An esthetic image is presented to us either in space or in time. What is audible is presented in time, what is visible is presented in space. But, temporal or spatial, the esthetic image is first luminously apprehended as selfbounded and selfcontained upon the immeasurable background of space or time which is not it. You apprehended it as ONE thing. You see it as one whole. You apprehend its wholeness. That is *integritas.*

—Bull's eye! said Lynch, laughing. Go on.

—Then, said Stephen, you pass from point to point, led by its formal lines; you apprehend it as balanced part against part within its limits; you feel the rhythm of its structure. In other words, the synthesis of immediate perception is followed by the analysis of apprehension. Having first felt that it is *one* thing you feel now that it is a *thing*. You apprehend it as complex, multiple, divisible, separable, made up of its parts, the result of its parts and their sum, harmonious. That is *consonantia.*

—Bull's eye again! said Lynch wittily. Tell me now what is *claritas* and you win the cigar.

—The connotation of the word, Stephen said, is rather vague. Aquinas uses a term which seems to be inexact. It baffled me for a long time. It would lead you to believe that he had in mind symbolism or idealism, the supreme quality of beauty being a light from some other world, the idea of which the matter is but the shadow, the reality of which it is but the symbol. I thought he might mean that *claritas* is the artistic discovery and representation of the divine purpose in anything or a force of generalization which would make the esthetic image a universal one, make it outshine its proper conditions. But that is literary talk. I understand it so. When you have apprehended that basket as one thing and have then analysed it according to its form and apprehended it as a thing you make the only synthesis which is logically and esthetically permissible. You see that it is that thing which it is and no other thing. The radiance of which he speaks in the scholastic *quidditas,* the *whatness* of a thing. This supreme quality is felt by the artist when the esthetic image is first conceived in his imagination. The mind in that mysterious instant Shelley likened beautifully to a fading coal. The instant wherein that supreme quality of beauty, the clear radiance of the esthetic image, is apprehended luminously by the mind which has been arrested by its wholeness and fascinated by its harmony is the luminous silent stasis of esthetic pleasure, a spiritual state very like to that cardiac condition which the Italian physiologist Luigi Galvani, using a phrase almost as beautiful as Shelley's, called the enchantment of the heart.

Stephen paused and, though his companion did not speak, felt that his words had called up around them a thought-enchanted silence.

—What I have said, he began again, refers to beauty in the wider sense of the word, in the sense which the word has in the literary tradition. In the marketplace it has another sense. When we speak of beauty in the second sense of the term our judgement is influenced in the first place by the art itself and by the form of that art. The image, it is clear, must be set between the mind or senses of the artist himself and the mind or senses of others. If you bear this in memory you will see that art necessarily divides itself into three forms progressing from one to the next. These forms are: the lyrical form, the form wherein the artist presents his image in immediate relation to himself; the epical form, the form wherein he presents his image in mediate relation to himself and to others; the dramatic form, the form wherein he presents his image in immediate relation to others.

—That you told me a few nights ago, said Lynch, and we began the famous discussion.

—I have a book at home, said Stephen, in which I have written down questions which are more amusing than yours were. In finding the answers to them I found the theory of esthetic which I am trying to explain. Here are some questions I set myself: *Is a chair finely made tragic or comic? Is the portrait of Mona Lisa good if I desire to see it? If not, why not?*

—Why not, indeed? said Lynch, laughing.

—*If a man hacking in fury at a block of wood,* Stephen continued, *make there an image of a cow, is that image a work of art? If not, why not?*

—That's a lovely one, said Lynch, laughing again. That has the true scholastic stink.

—Lessing, said Stephen, should not have taken a group of statues to write of. The art, being inferior, does not present the forms I spoke of distinguished clearly one from another. Even in literature, the highest and most spiritual art, the forms are often confused. The lyrical form is in fact the simplest verbal vesture of an instant of emotion, a rhythmical cry such as ages ago cheered on the man who pulled at the oar or dragged stones up a slope. He who utters it is more conscious of the instant of emotion than of himself as feeling emotion. The simplest epical form is seen emerging out of lyrical literature when the artist prolongs and broods upon himself as the centre of an epical event and this form progresses till the centre of emotional gravity is equidistant from the artist himself and from others. The narrative is no longer purely personal. The personality of the artist passes into the narration itself, flowing round and round the persons and the action like a vital sea. This progress you will see easily in that old English ballad *Turpin Hero* which begins in the first person and ends in the third person. The dramatic form is reached when the vitality which has flowed and eddied round each person fills every person with such vital force that he or she assumes a proper and intangible esthetic life. The personality of the artist, at first a cry or a cadence or a mood and then a fluid and lambent narrative, finally refines itself out of existence, impersonalizes itself, so to speak. The esthetic image in the dramatic form is life purified in and reprojected from the human imagination. The mystery of esthetic, like that of material creation, is accomplished. The artist, like the God of creation, remains within or behind or beyond or above his handiwork, invisible, refined out of existence, indifferent, paring his fingernails.

—Trying to refine them also out of existence, said Lynch.

A fine rain began to fall from the high veiled sky and they turned into the duke's lawn to reach the national library before the shower came.

—What do you mean, Lynch asked surlily, by prating about beauty and the imagination in this miserable Godforsaken island? No wonder the artist retired within or behind his handiwork after having perpetrated this country.

The rain fell faster. When they passed through the passage beside Kildare house they found many students sheltering under the arcade of the library. Cranly, leaning against a pillar, was picking his teeth with a sharpened match, listening to some companions. Some girls stood near the entrance door. Lynch whispered to Stephen:

—Your beloved is here.

Stephen took his place silently on the step below the group of students, heedless of the rain which fell fast, turning his eyes towards her from time to time. She too stood silently among her companions. She has no priest to flirt with, he thought with conscious bitterness, remembering how he had seen her last. Lynch was right. His mind emptied of theory and courage, lapsed back into a listless peace.

He heard the students talking among themselves. They spoke of two friends who had passed the final medical examination, of the chances of getting places on ocean liners, of poor and rich practices.

—That's all a bubble. An Irish country practice is better.

—Hynes was two years in Liverpool and he says the same. A frightful hole he said it was. Nothing but midwifery cases.

—Do you mean to say it is better to have a job here in the country than in a rich city like that? I know a fellow . . .

—Hynes has no brains. He got through by stewing, pure stewing.

—Don't mind him. There's plenty of money to be made in a big commercial city.

—Depends on the practice.

—*Ego credo ut vita pauperum est simpliciter atrox, simpliciter sanguinarius atrox, in Liverpoolio.*

Their voices reached his ears as if from a distance in interrupted pulsation. She was preparing to go away with her companions.

The quick light shower had drawn off, tarrying in clusters of diamonds among the shrubs of the quadrangle where an exhalation was breathed forth by the blackened earth. Their trim boots prattled as they stood on the steps of the colonnade, talking quietly and gaily, glancing at the clouds, holding their umbrellas at cunning angles against the few last raindrops, closing them again, holding their skirts demurely.

And if he had judged her harshly? If her life were a simple rosary of hours, her life simple and strange as a bird's life, gay in the morning, restless all day, tired at sundown? Her heart simple and wilful as a bird's heart?

***

Towards dawn he awoke. O what sweet music! His soul was all dewy wet. Over his limbs in sleep pale cool waves of light had passed. He lay still, as if his soul lay amid cool waters, conscious of faint sweet music. His mind was waking slowly to a tremulous morning knowledge, a morning inspiration. A spirit filled him, pure as the purest water, sweet as dew, moving as music. But how faintly it was inbreathed, how passionlessly, as if the seraphim themselves were breathing upon him! His soul was waking slowly, fearing to awake wholly. It was that windless hour of dawn when madness wakes and strange plants open to the light and the moth flies forth silently.

An enchantment of the heart! The night had been enchanted. In a dream or vision he had known the ecstasy of seraphic life. Was it an instant of enchantment only or long hours and years and ages?

The instant of inspiration seemed now to be reflected from all sides at once from a multitude of cloudy circumstances of what had happened or of what might have happened. The instant flashed forth like a point of light and now from cloud on cloud of vague circumstance confused form was veiling softly its afterglow. O! In the virgin womb of the imagination the word was made flesh. Gabriel the seraph had come to the virgin's chamber. An afterglow deepened within his spirit, whence the white flame had passed, deepening to a rose and ardent light. That rose and ardent light was her strange wilful heart, strange that no man had known or would know, wilful from before the beginning of the world; and lured by that ardent rose-like glow the choirs of the seraphim were falling from heaven.

Are you not weary of ardent ways,
Lure of the fallen seraphim?
Tell no more of enchanted days.

The verses passed from his mind to his lips and, murmuring them over, he felt the rhythmic movement of a villanelle pass through them. The rose-like glow sent forth its rays of rhyme; ways, days, blaze, praise, raise. Its rays burned up the world, consumed the hearts of men and angels: the rays from the rose that was her wilful heart.

> *Your eyes have set man's heart ablaze*
> *And you have had your will of him.*
> *Are you not weary of ardent ways?*

And then? The rhythm died away, ceased, began again to move and beat. And then? Smoke, incense ascending from the altar of the world.

> *Above the flame the smoke of praise*
> *Goes up from ocean rim to rim*
> *Tell no more of enchanted days.*

Smoke went up from the whole earth, from the vapoury oceans, smoke of her praise. The earth was like a swinging swaying censer, a ball of incense, an ellipsoidal fall. The rhythm died out at once; the cry of his heart was broken. His lips began to murmur the first verses over and over; then went on stumbling through half verses, stammering and baffled; then stopped. The heart's cry was broken.

The veiled windless hour had passed and behind the panes of the naked window the morning light was gathering. A bell beat faintly very far away. A bird twittered; two birds, three. The bell and the bird ceased; and the dull white light spread itself east and west, covering the world, covering the roselight in his heart.

Fearing to lose all, he raised himself suddenly on his elbow to look for paper and pencil. There was neither on the table; only the soup plate he had eaten the rice from for supper and the candlestick with its tendrils of tallow and its paper socket, singed by the last flame. He stretched his arm wearily towards the foot of the bed, groping with his hand in the pockets of the coat that hung there. His fingers found a pencil and then a cigarette packet. He lay back and, tearing open the packet, placed the last cigarette on the window ledge and began to write out the stanzas of the villanelle in small neat letters on the rough cardboard surface.

Having written them out he lay back on the lumpy pillow, murmuring them again. The lumps of knotted flock under his head reminded him of the lumps of knotted horsehair in the sofa of her parlour on which he used to sit, smiling or serious, asking himself why he had come, displeased with her and with himself, confounded by the print of the Sacred Heart above the untenanted sideboard. He saw her approach him in a lull of the talk and beg him to sing one of his curious songs. Then he saw himself sitting at the old piano, striking chords softly from its speckled keys and singing, amid the talk which had risen again in the room, to her who leaned beside the mantelpiece a dainty song of the Elizabethans, a sad and sweet loth to depart, the victory chant of Agincourt, the happy air of Greensleeves. While he sang and she listened, or feigned to listen, his heart was at rest but when the quaint old songs had ended and he heard again the voices in the room he remembered his own sarcasm: the house where young men are called by their christian names a little too soon.

At certain instants her eyes seemed about to trust him but he had waited in vain. She passed now dancing lightly across his memory as she had been that night at the carnival ball, her white dress a little lifted, a white spray nodding in her hair. She danced lightly in the round. She was dancing towards him and, as she came, her eyes were a little averted and a faint glow was on her cheek. At the pause in the chain of hands her hand had lain in his an instant, a soft merchandise.

—You are a great stranger now.

—Yes. I was born to be a monk.

—I am afraid you are a heretic.

—Are you much afraid?

For answer she had danced away from him along the chain of hands, dancing lightly and discreetly, giving herself to none. The white spray nodded to her dancing and when she was in shadow the glow was deeper on her cheek.

A monk! His own image started forth a profaner of the cloister, a heretic franciscan, willing and willing not to serve, spinning like Gherardino da Borgo San Donnino, a lithe web of sophistry and whispering in her ear.

No, it was not his image. It was like the image of the young priest in whose company he had seen her last, looking at him out of dove's eyes, toying with the pages of her Irish phrase-book.

—Yes, yes, the ladies are coming round to us. I can see it every day. The ladies are with us. The best helpers the language has.

—And the church, Father Moran?

—The church too. Coming round too. The work is going ahead there too. Don't fret about the church.

Bah! he had done well to leave the room in disdain. He had done well not to salute her on the steps of the library! He had done well to

915

leave her to flirt with her priest, to toy with a church which was the scullery-maid of christendom.

Rude brutal anger routed the last lingering instant of ecstasy from his soul. It broke up violently her fair image and flung the fragments on all sides. On all sides distorted reflections of her image started from his memory: the flower girl in the ragged dress with damp coarse hair and a hoyden's face who had called herself his own girl and begged his handsel, the kitchen-girl in the next house who sang over the clatter of her plates, with the drawl of a country singer, the first bars of *By Killarney's Lakes and Fells,* a girl who had laughed gaily to see him stumble when the iron grating in the footpath near Cork Hill had caught the broken sole of his shoe, a girl he had glanced at, attracted by her small ripe mouth, as she passed out of Jacob's biscuit factory, who had cried to him over her shoulder:

—Do you like what you seen of me, straight hair and curly eyebrows?

And yet he felt that, however he might revile and mock her image, his anger was also a form of homage. He had left the classroom in disdain that was not wholly sincere, feeling that perhaps the secret of her race lay behind those dark eyes upon which her long lashes flung a quick shadow. He had told himself bitterly as he walked through the streets that she was a figure of the womanhood of her country, a bat-like soul waking to the consciousness of itself in darkness and secrecy and loneliness, tarrying awhile, loveless and sinless, with her mild lover and leaving him to whisper of innocent transgressions in the latticed ear of a priest. His anger against her found vent in coarse railing at her paramour, whose name and voice and features offended his baffled pride: a priested peasant, with a brother a policeman in Dublin and a brother a potboy in Moycullen. To him she would unveil her soul's shy nakedness, to one who was but schooled in the discharging of a formal rite rather than to him, a priest of the eternal imagination, transmuting the daily bread of experience into the radiant body of everliving life.

The radiant image of the eucharist united again in an instant his bitter and despairing thoughts, their cries arising unbroken in a hymn of thanksgiving.

Our broken cries and mournful lays
Rise in one eucharistic hymn
Are you not weary of ardent ways?

916

While sacrificing hands upraise
The chalice flowing to the brim.
Tell no more of enchanted days.

He spoke the verses aloud from the first lines till the music and rhythm suffused his mind, turning it to quiet indulgence; then copied them painfully to feel them the better by seeing them; then lay back on his bolster.

The full morning light had come. No sound was to be heard; but he knew that all around him life was about to awaken in common noises, hoarse voices, sleepy prayers. Shrinking from that life he turned towards the wall, making a cowl of the blanket and staring at the great overblown scarlet flowers of the tattered wallpaper. He tried to warm his perishing joy in their scarlet glow, imagining a roseway from where he lay upwards to heaven all strewn with scarlet flowers. Weary! Weary! He too was weary of ardent ways.

A gradual warmth, a languorous weariness passed over him descending along his spine from his closely cowled head. He felt it descend and, seeing himself as he lay, smiled. Soon he would sleep.

He had written verses for her again after ten years. Ten years before she had worn her shawl cowlwise about her head, sending sprays of her warm breath into the night air, tapping her foot upon the glassy road. It was the last tram; the lank brown horses knew it and shook their bells to the clear night in admonition. The conductor talked with the driver, both nodding often in the green light of the lamp. They stood on the steps of the tram, he on the upper, she on the lower. She came up to his step many times between their phrases and went down again and once or twice remained beside him forgetting to go down and then went down. Let be! Let be!

Ten years from that wisdom of children to his folly. If he sent her the verses? They would be read out at breakfast amid the tapping of egg-shells. Folly indeed! Her brothers would laugh and try to wrest the page from each other with their strong hard fingers. The suave priest, her uncle, seated in his arm-chair, would hold the page at arm's length, read it smiling and approve of the literary form.

No, no; that was folly. Even if he sent her the verses she would not show them to others. No, no; she could not.

He began to feel that he had wronged her. A sense of her innocence moved him almost to pity her, an innocence he had never understood till he had come to the knowledge of it through sin, an innocence which she too had not understood while she was innocent or before the strange humiliation of her nature had first come upon her. Then first her soul had begun to live as his soul had when he had first sinned, and a tender compassion filled his heart as he remembered her frail pallor and her eyes, humbled and saddened by the dark shame of womanhood.

While his soul had passed from ecstasy to languor where had she been? Might it be, in the mysterious ways of spiritual life, that her soul at those same moments had been conscious of his homage? It might be.

A glow of desire kindled again his soul and fired and fulfilled all his body. Conscious of his desire she was waking from odorous sleep, the temptress of his villanelle. Her eyes, dark and with a look of languor, were opening to his eyes. Her nakedness yielded to him, radiant, warm, odorous and lavish-limbed, enfolded him like a shining cloud, enfolded him like water with a liquid life; and like a cloud of vapour or like waters circumfluent in space the liquid letters of speech, symbols of the element of mystery, flowed forth over his brain.

> *Are you not weary of ardent ways,*
> *Lure of the fallen seraphim?*
> *Tell no more of enchanted days.*
>
> *Your eyes have set man's heart ablaze*
> *And you have had your will of him.*
> *Are you not weary of ardent ways?*
>
> *Above the flame the smoke of praise*
> *Goes up from ocean rim to rim.*
> *Tell no more of enchanted days.*
> *Our broken cries and mournful lays*
> *Rise in one eucharistic hymn.*
> *Are you not weary of ardent ways?*
>
> *While sacrificing hands upraise*
> *The chalice flowing to the brim.*
> *Tell no more of enchanted days.*

And still you hold our longing gaze
With languorous look and lavish limb!
Are you not weary of ardent ways?
Tell no more of enchanted days.

What birds were they? He stood on the steps of the library to look at them, leaning wearily on his ashplant. They flew round and round the jutting shoulder of a house in Molesworth Street. The air of the late March evening made clear their flight, their dark quivering bodies flying clearly against the sky as against a limp-hung cloth of smoky tenuous blue.

He watched their flight; bird after bird: a dark flash, a swerve, a flutter of wings. He tried to count them before all their darting quivering bodies passed: six, ten, eleven: and wondered were they odd or even in number. Twelve, thirteen: for two came wheeling down from the upper sky. They were flying high and low but ever round and round in straight and curving lines and ever flying from left to right, circling about a temple of air.

He listened to the cries: like the squeak of mice behind the wainscot: a shrill twofold note. But the notes were long and shrill and whirring, unlike the cry of vermin, falling a third or a fourth and trilled as the flying beaks clove the air. Their cry was shrill and clear and fine and falling like threads of silken light unwound from whirring spools.

The inhuman clamour soothed his ears in which his mother's sobs and reproaches murmured insistently and the dark frail quivering bodies wheeling and fluttering and swerving round an airy temple of the tenuous sky soothed his eyes which still saw the image of his mother's face.

Why was he gazing upwards from the steps of the porch, hearing their shrill twofold cry, watching their flight? For an augury of good or evil? A phrase of Cornelius Agrippa flew through his mind and then there flew hither and thither shapeless thoughts from Swedenborg on the correspondence of birds to things of the intellect and of how the creatures of the air have their knowledge and know their times and seasons because they, unlike man, are in the order of their life and have not perverted that order by reason.

And for ages men had gazed upward as he was gazing at birds in flight. The colonnade above him made him think vaguely of an ancient temple and the ashplant on which he leaned wearily of the curved stick of an augur. A sense of fear of the unknown moved in the heart of his weariness, a fear of symbols and portents, of the hawk-like man whose name he bore soaring out of his captivity on osier-woven wings, of Thoth, the god of writers, writing with a reed upon a tablet and bearing on his narrow ibis head the cusped moon.

He smiled as he thought of the god's image for it made him think of a bottle-nosed judge in a wig, putting commas into a document which he held at arm's length, and he knew that he would not have remembered the god's name but that it was like an Irish oath. It was folly. But was it for this folly that he was about to leave for ever the house of prayer and prudence into which he had been born and the order of life out of which he had come?

They came back with shrill cries over the jutting shoulder of the house, flying darkly against the fading air. What birds were they? He thought that they must be swallows who had come back from the south. Then he was to go away for they were birds ever going and coming, building ever an unlasting home under the eaves of men's houses and ever leaving the homes they had built to wander.

> *Bend down your faces, Oona and Aleel.*
> *I gaze upon them as the swallow gazes*
> *Upon the nest under the eave before*
> *He wander the loud waters.*

A soft liquid joy like the noise of many waters flowed over his memory and he felt in his heart the soft peace of silent spaces of fading tenuous sky above the waters, of oceanic silence, of swallows flying through the sea-dusk over the flowing waters.

A soft liquid joy flowed through the words where the soft long vowels hurtled noiselessly and fell away, lapping and flowing back and ever shaking the white bells of their waves in mute chime and mute peal, and soft low swooning cry; and he felt that the augury he had sought in the wheeling darting birds and in the pale space of sky above him had come forth from his heart like a bird from a turret, quietly and swiftly.

Symbol of departure or of loneliness? The verses crooned in the ear of his memory composed slowly before his remembering eyes the scene of the hall on the night of the opening of the national theatre. He was alone at the side of the balcony, looking out of jaded eyes at the culture of Dublin in the stalls and at the tawdry scene-cloths and human dolls framed by the garish lamps of the stage. A burly policeman sweated behind him and seemed at every moment about to act. The catcalls and hisses and mocking cries ran in rude gusts round the hall from his scattered fellow students.

—A libel on Ireland!

—Made in Germany.

—Blasphemy!

—We never sold our faith!

—No Irish woman ever did it!

—We want no amateur atheists.

—We want no budding buddhists.

A sudden swift hiss fell from the windows above him and he knew that the electric lamps had been switched on in the reader's room. He turned into the pillared hall, now calmly lit, went up the staircase and passed in through the clicking turnstile.

Cranly was sitting over near the dictionaries. A thick book, opened at the frontispiece, lay before him on the wooden rest. He leaned back in his chair, inclining his ear like that of a confessor to the face of the medical student who was reading to him a problem from the chess page of a journal. Stephen sat down at his right and the priest at the other side of the table closed his copy of *The Tablet* with an angry snap and stood up.

Cranly gazed after him blandly and vaguely. The medical student went on in a softer voice:

—Pawn to king's fourth.

—We had better go, Dixon, said Stephen in warning. He has gone to complain.

Dixon folded the journal and rose with dignity, saying:

—Our men retired in good order.

—With guns and cattle, added Stephen, pointing to the titlepage of Cranly's book on which was printed *Diseases of the Ox*.

As they passed through a lane of the tables Stephen said:

—Cranly, I want to speak to you.

Cranly did not answer or turn. He laid his book on the counter and passed out, his well-shod feet sounding flatly on the floor. On the staircase he paused and gazing absently at Dixon repeated:

—Pawn to king's bloody fourth.

—Put it that way if you like, Dixon said.

He had a quiet toneless voice and urbane manners and on a finger of his plump clean hand he displayed at moments a signet ring.

As they crossed the hall a man of dwarfish stature came towards them. Under the dome of his tiny hat his unshaven face began to smile with pleasure and he was heard to murmur. The eyes were melancholy as those of a monkey.

—Good evening, gentlemen, said the stubble-grown monkeyish face.

—Warm weather for March, said Cranly. They have the windows open upstairs.

Dixon smiled and turned his ring. The blackish, monkey-puckered face pursed its human mouth with gentle pleasure and its voice purred:

—Delightful weather for March. Simply delightful.

—There are two nice young ladies upstairs, captain, tired of waiting, Dixon said.

Cranly smiled and said kindly:

—The captain has only one love: sir Walter Scott. Isn't that so, captain?

—What are you reading now, captain? Dixon asked. *The Bride of Lammermoor?*

—I love old Scott, the flexible lips said, I think he writes something lovely. There is no writer can touch sir Walter Scott.

He moved a thin shrunken brown hand gently in the air in time to his praise and his thin quick eyelids beat often over his sad eyes.

Sadder to Stephen's ear was his speech: a genteel accent, low and moist, marred by errors, and, listening to it, he wondered was the story true and was the thin blood that flowed in his shrunken frame noble and come of an incestuous love?

The park trees were heavy with rain; and rain fell still and ever in the lake, lying grey like a shield. A game of swans flew there and the water and the shore beneath were fouled with their green-white slime. They embraced softly, impelled by the grey rainy light, the wet silent trees, the shield-like witnessing lake, the swans. They embraced without joy or passion, his arm about his sister's neck. A grey woollen cloak was wrapped athwart her from her shoulder to her waist and her fair head was bent in willing shame. He had loose red-brown hair and tender shapely strong freckled hands. Face? There was no face seen. The brother's face was bent upon her fair rain-fragrant hair. The hand freckled and strong and shapely and caressing was Davin's hand.

He frowned angrily upon his thought and on the shrivelled mannikin who had called it forth. His father's jibes at the Bantry gang leaped out of his memory. He held them at a distance and brooded uneasily on his own thought again. Why were they not Cranly's hands? Had Davin's simplicity and innocence stung him more secretly?

He walked on across the hall with Dixon, leaving Cranly to take leave elaborately of the dwarf.

Under the colonnade Temple was standing in the midst of a little group of students. One of them cried:

—Dixon, come over till you hear. Temple is in grand form.

Temple turned on him his dark gipsy eyes.

—You're a hypocrite, O'Keeffe, he said. And Dixon is a smiler. By hell, I think that's a good literary expression.

He laughed slyly, looking in Stephen's face, repeating:

—By hell, I'm delighted with that name. A smiler.

A stout student who stood below them on the steps said:

—Come back to the mistress, Temple. We want to hear about that.

—He had, faith, Temple said. And he was a married man too. And all the priests used to be dining there. By hell, I think they all had a touch.

—We shall call it riding a hack to spare the hunter, said Dixon.

—Tell us, Temple, O'Keeffe said, how many quarts of porter have you in you?

—All your intellectual soul is in that phrase, O'Keeffe, said Temple with open scorn.

He moved with a shambling gait round the group and spoke to Stephen.

—Did you know that the Forsters are the kings of Belgium? he asked.

Cranly came out through the door of the entrance hall, his hat thrust back on the nape of his neck and picking his teeth with care.

—And here's the wiseacre, said Temple. Do you know that about the Forsters?

He paused for an answer. Cranly dislodged a figseed from his teeth on the point of his rude toothpick and gazed at it intently.

—The Forster family, Temple said, is descended from Baldwin the First, king of Flanders. He was called the Forester. Forester and Forster are the same name. A descendant of Baldwin the First, captain

Francis Forster, settled in Ireland and married the daughter of the last chieftain of Clanbrassil. Then there are the Blake Forsters. That's a different branch.

—From Baldhead, king of Flanders, Cranly repeated, rooting again deliberately at his gleaming uncovered teeth.

—Where did you pick up all that history? O'Keeffe asked.

—I know all the history of your family, too, Temple said, turning to Stephen. Do you know what Giraldus Cambrensis says about your family?

—Is he descended from Baldwin too? asked a tall consumptive student with dark eyes.

—Baldhead, Cranly repeated, sucking at a crevice in his teeth.

—*Pernobilis et pervetusta familia,* Temple said to Stephen.

The stout student who stood below them on the steps farted briefly. Dixon turned towards him, saying in a soft voice:

—Did an angel speak?

Cranly turned also and said vehemently but without anger:

—Goggins, you're the flamingest dirty devil I ever met, do you know.

—I had it on my mind to say that, Goggins answered firmly. It did no one any harm, did it?

—We hope, Dixon said suavely, that it was not of the kind known to science as a *paulo post futurum.*

—Didn't I tell you he was a smiler? said Temple, turning right and left. Didn't I give him that name?

—You did. We're not deaf, said the tall consumptive.

Cranly still frowned at the stout student below him. Then, with a snort of disgust, he shoved him violently down the steps.

—Go away from here, he said rudely. Go away, you stinkpot. And you are a stinkpot.

Goggins skipped down on to the gravel and at once returned to his place with good humour. Temple turned back to Stephen and asked:

—Do you believe in the law of heredity?

—Are you drunk or what are you or what are you trying to say? asked Cranly, facing round on him with an expression of wonder.

—The most profound sentence ever written, Temple said with enthusiasm, is the sentence at the end of the zoology. Reproduction is the beginning of death.

He touched Stephen timidly at the elbow and said eagerly:

—Do you feel how profound that is because you are a poet?

Cranly pointed his long forefinger.

—Look at him! he said with scorn to the others. Look at Ireland's hope!

They laughed at his words and gesture. Temple turned on him bravely, saying:

—Cranly, you're always sneering at me. I can see that. But I am as good as you any day. Do you know what I think about you now as compared with myself?

—My dear man, said Cranly urbanely, you are incapable, do you know, absolutely incapable of thinking.

—But do you know, Temple went on, what I think of you and of myself compared together?

—Out with it, Temple! the stout student cried from the steps. Get it out in bits!

Temple turned right and left, making sudden feeble gestures as he spoke.

—I'm a ballocks, he said, shaking his head in despair. I am and I know I am. And I admit it that I am.

Dixon patted him lightly on the shoulder and said mildly:

—And it does you every credit, Temple.

—But he, Temple said, pointing to Cranly, he is a ballocks, too, like me. Only he doesn't know it. And that's the only difference I see.

A burst of laughter covered his words. But he turned again to Stephen and said with a sudden eagerness:

—That word is a most interesting word. That's the only English dual number. Did you know?

—Is it? Stephen said vaguely.

He was watching Cranly's firm-featured suffering face, lit up now by a smile of false patience. The gross name had passed over it like foul water poured over an old stone image, patient of injuries; and, as he watched him, he saw him raise his hat in salute and uncover the black hair that stood stiffly from his forehead like an iron crown.

She passed out from the porch of the library and bowed across Stephen in reply to Cranly's greeting. He also? Was there not a slight flush on Cranly's cheek? Or had it come forth at Temple's words? The light had waned. He could not see.

Did that explain his friend's listless silence, his harsh comments, the sudden intrusions of rude speech with which he had shattered so often Stephen's ardent wayward confessions? Stephen had forgiven freely for he had found this rudeness also in himself. And he remembered an evening when he had dismounted from a borrowed creaking bicycle to pray to God in a wood near Malahide. He had lifted up his arms and spoken in ecstasy to the sombre nave of the trees, knowing that he stood on holy ground and in a holy hour. And when two constabulary men had come into sight round a bend in the gloomy road he had broken off his prayer to whistle loudly an air from the last pantomime.

He began to beat the frayed end of his ashplant against the base of a pillar. Had Cranly not heard him? Yet he could wait. The talk about him ceased for a moment and a soft hiss fell again from a window above. But no other sound was in the air and the swallows whose flight he had followed with idle eyes were sleeping.

She had passed through the dusk. And therefore the air was silent save for one soft hiss that fell. And therefore the tongues about him had ceased their babble. Darkness was falling.

Darkness falls from the air.

A trembling joy, lambent as a faint light, played like a fairy host around him. But why? Her passage through the darkening air or the verse with its black vowels and its opening sound, rich and lutelike?

He walked away slowly towards the deeper shadows at the end of the colonnade, beating the stone softly with his stick to hide his revery from the students whom he had left: and allowed his mind to summon back to itself the age of Dowland and Byrd and Nash.

Eyes, opening from the darkness of desire, eyes that dimmed the breaking east. What was their languid grace but the softness of chambering? And what was their shimmer but the shimmer of the scum that mantled the cesspool of the court of a slobbering Stuart. And he tasted in the language of memory ambered wines, dying fallings of sweet airs, the proud pavan, and saw with the eyes of memory kind gentlewomen in Covent Garden wooing from their balconies with sucking mouths and the pox-fouled wenches of the taverns and young wives that, gaily yielding to their ravishers, clipped and clipped again.

The images he had summoned gave him no pleasure. They were secret and inflaming but her image was not entangled by them. That was not the way to think of her. It was not even the way in which he thought of her. Could his mind then not trust itself? Old phrases, sweet only with a disinterred sweetness like the figseeds Cranly rooted out of his gleaming teeth.

It was not thought nor vision though he knew vaguely that her figure was passing homeward through the city. Vaguely first and then more sharply he smelt her body. A conscious unrest seethed in his blood. Yes, it was her body he smelt, a wild and languid smell, the tepid limbs over which his music had flowed desirously and the secret soft linen upon which her flesh distilled odour and a dew.

A louse crawled over the nape of his neck and, putting his thumb and forefinger deftly beneath his loose collar, he caught it. He rolled its body, tender yet brittle as a grain of rice, between thumb and finger for an instant before he let it fall from him and wondered would it live or die. There came to his mind a curious phrase from Cornelius a Lapide which said that the lice born of human sweat were not created by God with the other animals on the sixth day. But the tickling of the skin of his neck made his mind raw and red. The life of his body, ill clad, ill fed, louse-eaten, made him close his eyelids in a sudden spasm of despair and in the darkness he saw the brittle bright bodies of lice falling from the air and turning often as they fell. Yes, and it was not darkness that fell from the air. It was brightness.

Brightness falls from the air.

He had not even remembered rightly Nash's line. All the images it had awakened were false. His mind bred vermin. His thoughts were lice born of the sweat of sloth.

He came back quickly along the colonnade towards the group of students. Well then, let her go and be damned to her! She could love some clean athlete who washed himself every morning to the waist and had black hair on his chest. Let her.

Cranly had taken another dried fig from the supply in his pocket and was eating it slowly and noisily. Temple sat on the pediment of a pillar, leaning back, his cap pulled down on his sleepy eyes. A squat young man came out of the porch, a leather portfolio tucked under his armpit. He marched towards the group, striking the flags with the heels of his boots and with the ferrule of his heavy umbrella. Then, raising the umbrella in salute, he said to all:

—Good evening, sirs.

He struck the flags again and tittered while his head trembled with a slight nervous movement. The tall consumptive student and Dixon and O'Keeffe were speaking in Irish and did not answer him. Then, turning to Cranly, he said:

—Good evening, particularly to you.

He moved the umbrella in indication and tittered again. Cranly, who was still chewing the fig, answered with loud movements of his jaws.

—Good? Yes. It is a good evening.

The squat student looked at him seriously and shook his umbrella gently and reprovingly.

—I can see, he said, that you are about to make obvious remarks.

—Um, Cranly answered, holding out what remained of the half chewed fig and jerking it towards the squat student's mouth in sign that he should eat.

The squat student did not eat it but, indulging his special humour, said gravely, still tittering and prodding his phrase with his umbrella:

—Do you intend that . . .?

He broke off, pointed bluntly to the munched pulp of the fig, and said loudly:

—I allude to that.

—Um, Cranly said as before.

—Do you intend that now, the squat student said, as *ipso facto* or, let us say, as so to speak?

Dixon turned aside from his group, saying:

—Goggins was waiting for you, Glynn. He has gone round to the Adelphi to look for you and Moynihan. What have you there? he asked, tapping the portfolio under Glynn's arm.

—Examination papers, Glynn answered. I give them monthly examinations to see that they are profiting by my tuition.

He also tapped the portfolio and coughed gently and smiled.

—Tuition! said Cranly rudely. I suppose you mean the barefooted children that are taught by a bloody ape like you. God help them!

He bit off the rest of the fig and flung away the butt.

—I suffer little children to come unto me, Glynn said amiably.

—A bloody ape, Cranly repeated with emphasis, and a blasphemous bloody ape!

Temple stood up and, pushing past Cranly, addressed Glynn:

—That phrase you said now, he said, is from the new testament about suffer the children to come to me.

—Go to sleep again, Temple, said O'Keeffe.

—Very well, then, Temple continued, still addressing Glynn, and if Jesus suffered the children to come why does the church send them all to hell if they die unbaptized? Why is that?

—Were you baptized yourself, Temple? the consumptive student asked.

—But why are they sent to hell if Jesus said they were all to come? Temple said, his eyes searching Glynn's eyes.

Glynn coughed and said gently, holding back with difficulty the nervous titter in his voice and moving his umbrella at every word:

—And, as you remark, if it is thus, I ask emphatically whence comes this thusness.

—Because the church is cruel like all old sinners, Temple said.

—Are you quite orthodox on that point, Temple? Dixon said suavely.

—Saint Augustine says that about unbaptized children going to hell, Temple answered, because he was a cruel old sinner too.

—I bow to you, Dixon said, but I had the impression that limbo existed for such cases.

—Don't argue with him, Dixon, Cranly said brutally. Don't talk to him or look at him. Lead him home with a sugan the way you'd lead a bleating goat.

—Limbo! Temple cried. That's a fine invention too. Like hell.

—But with the unpleasantness left out, Dixon said.

He turned smiling to the others and said:

—I think I am voicing the opinions of all present in saying so much.

—You are, Glynn said in a firm tone. On that point Ireland is united.

He struck the ferrule of his umbrella on the stone floor of the colonnade.

—Hell, Temple said. I can respect that invention of the grey spouse of Satan. Hell is Roman, like the walls of the Romans, strong and ugly. But what is limbo?

—Put him back into the perambulator, Cranly, O'Keeffe called out.

Cranly made a swift step towards Temple, halted, stamping his foot, crying as if to a fowl:

—Hoosh!

Temple moved away nimbly.

—Do you know what limbo is? he cried. Do you know what we call a notion like that in Roscommon?

—Hoosh! Blast you! Cranly cried, clapping his hands.

—Neither my arse nor my elbow! Temple cried out scornfully. And that's what I call limbo.

—Give us that stick here, Cranly said.

He snatched the ashplant roughly from Stephen's hand and sprang down the steps: but Temple, hearing him move in pursuit, fled through the dusk like a wild creature, nimble and fleet-footed. Cranly's heavy boots were heard loudly charging across the quadrangle and then returning heavily, foiled and spurning the gravel at each step.

His step was angry and with an angry abrupt gesture he thrust the stick back into Stephen's hand. Stephen felt that his anger had another cause but, feigning patience, touched his arm slightly and said quietly:

—Cranly, I told you I wanted to speak to you. Come away.

Cranly looked at him for a few moments and asked:

—Now?

—Yes, now, Stephen said. We can't speak here. Come away.

They crossed the quadrangle together without speaking. The bird call from *Siegfried* whistled softly followed them from the steps of the porch. Cranly turned, and Dixon, who had whistled, called out:

—Where are you fellows off to? What about that game, Cranly?

They parleyed in shouts across the still air about a game of billiards to be played in the Adelphi hotel. Stephen walked on alone and out into the quiet of Kildare Street opposite Maple's hotel he stood to wait, patient again. The name of the hotel, a colourless polished wood, and its colourless front stung him like a glance of polite disdain. He stared angrily back at the softly lit drawing-room of the hotel in which he imagined the sleek lives of the patricians of Ireland housed in calm. They thought of army commissions and land agents: peasants greeted them along the roads in the country; they knew the names of certain French dishes and gave orders to jarvies in high-pitched provincial voices which pierced through their skin-tight accents.

How could he hit their conscience or how cast his shadow over the imaginations of their daughters, before their squires begat upon them, that they might breed a race less ignoble than their own? And under the deepened dusk he felt the thoughts and desires of the race to which he belonged flitting like bats across the dark country lanes, under trees by the edges of streams and near the pool-mottled bogs. A woman had waited in the doorway as Davin had passed by at night and, offering him a cup of milk, had all but wooed him to her bed; for Davin had the mild eyes of one who could be secret. But him no woman's eyes had wooed.

His arm was taken in a strong grip and Cranly's voice said:

—Let us eke go.

They walked southward in silence. Then Cranly said:

—That blithering idiot, Temple! I swear to Moses, do you know, that I'll be the death of that fellow one time.

But his voice was no longer angry and Stephen wondered was he thinking of her greeting to him under the porch.

They turned to the left and walked on as before. When they had gone on so for some time Stephen said:

—Cranly, I had an unpleasant quarrel this evening.

—With your people? Cranly asked.

—With my mother.

—About religion?

—Yes, Stephen answered.

After a pause Cranly asked:

—What age is your mother?

—Not old, Stephen said. She wishes me to make my easter duty.

—And will you?

—I will not, Stephen said.

—Why not? Cranly said.

—I will not serve, answered Stephen.

—That remark was made before, Cranly said calmly.

—It is made behind now, said Stephen hotly.

Cranly pressed Stephen's arm, saying:

—Go easy, my dear man. You're an excitable bloody man, do you know.

He laughed nervously as he spoke and, looking up into Stephen's face with moved and friendly eyes, said:

—Do you know that you are an excitable man?

—I daresay I am, said Stephen, laughing also.

Their minds, lately estranged, seemed suddenly to have been drawn closer, one to the other.

—Do you believe in the eucharist? Cranly asked.

—I do not, Stephen said.

—Do you disbelieve then?

—I neither believe in it nor disbelieve in it, Stephen answered.

—Many persons have doubts, even religious persons, yet they overcome them or put them aside, Cranly said. Are your doubts on that point too strong?

—I do not wish to overcome them, Stephen answered.

Cranly, embarrassed for a moment, took another fig from his pocket and was about to eat it when Stephen said:

—Don't, please. You cannot discuss this question with your mouth full of chewed fig.

Cranly examined the fig by the light of a lamp under which he halted. Then he smelt it with both nostrils, bit a tiny piece, spat it out and threw the fig rudely into the gutter. Addressing it as it lay, he said:

—Depart from me, ye cursed, into everlasting fire!

Taking Stephen's arm, he went on again and said:

—Do you not fear that those words may be spoken to you on the day of Judgement?

—What is offered me on the other hand? Stephen asked. An eternity of bliss in the company of the dean of studies?

—Remember, Cranly said, that he would be glorified.

—Ay, Stephen said somewhat bitterly, bright, agile, impassible and, above all, subtle.

—It is a curious thing, do you know, Cranly said dispassionately, how your mind is supersaturated with the religion in which you say you disbelieve. Did you believe in it when you were at school? I bet you did.

—I did, Stephen answered.

—And were you happier then? Cranly asked softly, happier than you are now, for instance?

—Often happy, Stephen said, and often unhappy. I was someone else then.

—How someone else? What do you mean by that statement?

—I mean, said Stephen, that I was not myself as I am now, as I had to become.

—Not as you are now, not as you had to become, Cranly repeated. Let me ask you a question. Do you love your mother?

Stephen shook his head slowly.

—I don't know what your words mean, he said simply.

—Have you never loved anyone? Cranly asked.

—Do you mean women?

—I am not speaking of that, Cranly said in a colder tone. I ask you if you ever felt love towards anyone or anything?

Stephen walked on beside his friend, staring gloomily at the footpath.

—I tried to love God, he said at length. It seems now I failed. It is very difficult. I tried to unite my will with the will of God instant by instant. In that I did not always fail. I could perhaps do that still . . .

Cranly cut him short by asking:

—Has your mother had a happy life?

—How do I know? Stephen said.

—How many children had she?

—Nine or ten, Stephen answered. Some died.

—Was your father . . . Cranly interrupted himself for an instant, and then said: I don't want to pry into your family affairs. But was your father what is called well-to-do? I mean, when you were growing up?

—Yes, Stephen said.

—What was he? Cranly asked after a pause.

Stephen began to enumerate glibly his father's attributes.

—A medical student, an oarsman, a tenor, an amateur actor, a shouting politician, a small landlord, a small investor, a drinker, a good fellow, a story-teller, somebody's secretary, something in a distillery, a tax-gatherer, a bankrupt and at present a praiser of his own past.

Cranly laughed, tightening his grip on Stephen's arm, and said:

—The distillery is damn good.

—Is there anything else you want to know? Stephen asked.

—Are you in good circumstances at present?

—Do I look it? Stephen asked bluntly.

—So then, Cranly went on musingly, you were born in the lap of luxury.

He used the phrase broadly and loudly as he often used technical expressions, as if he wished his hearer to understand that they were used by him without conviction.

—Your mother must have gone through a good deal of suffering, he said then. Would you not try to save her from suffering more even if . . . or would you?

—If I could, Stephen said, that would cost me very little.

—Then do so, Cranly said. Do as she wishes you to do. What is it for you? You disbelieve in it. It is a form: nothing else. And you will set her mind at rest.

He ceased and, as Stephen did not reply, remained silent. Then, as if giving utterance to the process of his own thought, he said:

—Whatever else is unsure in this stinking dunghill of a world a mother's love is not. Your mother brings you into the world, carries you first in her body. What do we know about what she feels? But whatever she feels, it, at least, must be real. It must be. What are our ideas or ambitions? Play. Ideas! Why, that bloody bleating goat Temple has ideas. MacCann has ideas too. Every jackass going the roads thinks he has ideas.

Stephen, who had been listening to the unspoken speech behind the words, said with assumed carelessness:

—Pascal, if I remember rightly, would not suffer his mother to kiss him as he feared the contact of her sex.

—Pascal was a pig, said Cranly.

—Aloysius Gonzaga, I think, was of the same mind, Stephen said.

—And he was another pig then, said Cranly.

—The church calls him a saint, Stephen objected.

—I don't care a flaming damn what anyone calls him, Cranly said rudely and flatly. I call him a pig.

Stephen, preparing the words neatly in his mind, continued:

—Jesus, too, seems to have treated his mother with scant courtesy in public but Suarez, a jesuit theologian and Spanish gentleman, has apologized for him.

—Did the idea ever occur to you, Cranly asked, that Jesus was not what he pretended to be?

—The first person to whom that idea occurred, Stephen answered, was Jesus himself.

—I mean, Cranly said, hardening in his speech, did the idea ever occur to you that he was himself a conscious hypocrite, what he called the jews of his time, a whited sepulchre? Or, to put it more plainly, that he was a blackguard?

—That idea never occurred to me, Stephen answered. But I am curious to know are you trying to make a convert of me or a pervert of yourself?

He turned towards his friend's face and saw there a raw smile which some force of will strove to make finely significant.

Cranly asked suddenly in a plain sensible tone:

—Tell me the truth. Were you at all shocked by what I said?

—Somewhat, Stephen said.

—And why were you shocked, Cranly pressed on in the same tone, if you feel sure that our religion is false and that Jesus was not the son of God?

—I am not at all sure of it, Stephen said. He is more like a son of God than a son of Mary.

—And is that why you will not communicate, Cranly asked, because you are not sure of that too, because you feel that the host, too, may be the body and blood of the son of God and not a wafer of bread? And because you fear that it may be?

—Yes, Stephen said quietly, I feel that and I also fear it.

—I see, Cranly said.

Stephen, struck by his tone of closure, reopened the discussion at once by saying:

—I fear many things: dogs, horses, fire-arms, the sea, thunderstorms, machinery, the country roads at night.

—But why do you fear a bit of bread?

—I imagine, Stephen said, that there is a malevolent reality behind those things I say I fear.

—Do you fear then, Cranly asked, that the God of the Roman catholics would strike you dead and damn you if you made a sacrilegious communion?

—The God of the Roman catholics could do that now, Stephen said. I fear more than that the chemical action which would be set up in my soul by a false homage to a symbol behind which are massed twenty centuries of authority and veneration.

—Would you, Cranly asked, in extreme danger, commit that particular sacrilege? For instance, if you lived in the penal days?

—I cannot answer for the past, Stephen replied. Possibly not.

—Then, said Cranly, you do not intend to become a protestant?

—I said that I had lost the faith, Stephen answered, but not that I had lost self-respect. What kind of liberation would that be to forsake an absurdity which is logical and coherent and to embrace one which is illogical and incoherent?

They had walked on towards the township of Pembroke and now, as they went on slowly along the avenues, the trees and the scattered lights in the villas soothed their minds. The air of wealth and repose diffused about them seemed to comfort their neediness. Behind a hedge of laurel a light glimmered in the window of a kitchen and the voice of a servant was heard singing as she sharpened knives. She sang, in short broken bars: *Rosie O'Grady*.

Cranly stopped to listen, saying:

—*Mulier cantat.*

The soft beauty of the Latin word touched with an enchanting touch the dark of the evening, with a touch fainter and more persuading than the touch of music or of a woman's hand. The strife of their minds was quelled. The figure of a woman as she appears in the liturgy of the church passed silently through the darkness: a white-robed figure, small and slender as a boy, and with a falling girdle. Her voice, frail and high as a boy's, was heard intoning from a distant choir the first words of a woman which pierce the gloom and clamour of the first chanting of the passion:

—*Et tu cum Jesu Galilæo eras.*

And all hearts were touched and turned to her voice, shining like a young star, shining clearer as the voice intoned the proparoxytone and more faintly as the cadence died.

The singing ceased. They went on together, Cranly repeating in strongly stressed rhythm the end of the refrain:

> *And when we are married,*
> *O, how happy we'll be*
> *For I love sweet Rosie O'Grady*
> *And Rosie O'Grady loves me.*

—There's real poetry for you, he said. There's real love.

He glanced sideways at Stephen with a strange smile and said:

—Do you consider that poetry? Or do you know what the words mean?

—I want to see Rosie first, said Stephen.

—She's easy to find, Cranly said.

His hat had come down on his forehead. He shoved it back and in the shadow of the trees Stephen saw his pale face, framed by the dark, and his large dark eyes. Yes. His face was handsome and his body was strong and hard. He had spoken of a mother's love. He felt then the sufferings of women, the weaknesses of their bodies and souls: and would shield them with a strong and resolute arm and bow his mind to them.

Away then: it is time to go. A voice spoke softly to Stephen's lonely heart, bidding him go and telling him that his friendship was coming to an end. Yes; he would go. He could not strive against another. He knew his part.

—Probably I shall go away, he said.

—Where? Cranly asked.

—Where I can, Stephen said.

—Yes, Cranly said. It might be difficult for you to live here now. But is it that makes you go?

—I have to go, Stephen answered.

—Because, Cranly continued, you need not look upon yourself as driven away if you do not wish to go or as a heretic or an outlaw. There are many good believers who think as you do. Would that surprise you? The church is not the stone building nor even the clergy and their dogmas. It is the whole mass of those born into it. I don't know what you wish to do in life. Is it what you told me the night we were standing outside Harcourt Street station?

—Yes, Stephen said, smiling in spite of himself at Cranly's way of remembering thoughts in connexion with places. The night you spent half an hour wrangling with Doherty about the shortest way from Sallygap to Larras.

—Pothead! Cranly said with calm contempt. What does he know about the way from Sallygap to Larras? Or what does he know about anything for that matter? And the big slobbering washing-pot head of him!

He broke into a loud long laugh.

—Well? Stephen said. Do you remember the rest?

—What you said, is it? Cranly asked. Yes, I remember it. To discover the mode of life or of art whereby your spirit could express itself in unfettered freedom.

Stephen raised his hat in acknowledgement.

—Freedom! Cranly repeated. But you are not free enough yet to commit a sacrilege. Tell me would you rob?

—I would beg first, Stephen said.

—And if you got nothing, would you rob?

—You wish me to say, Stephen answered, that the rights of property are provisional, and that in certain circumstances it is not unlawful to rob. Everyone would act in that belief. So I will not make you that answer. Apply to the jesuit theologian, Juan Mariana de Talavera, who will also explain to you in what circumstances you may lawfully kill your king and whether you had better hand him his poison in a goblet or smear it for him upon his robe or his saddlebow. Ask me rather would I suffer others to rob me, or if they did, would I call down upon them what I believe is called the chastisement of the secular arm?

—And would you?

—I think, Stephen said, it would pain me as much to do so as to be robbed.

—I see, Cranly said.

He produced his match and began to clean the crevice between two teeth. Then he said carelessly:

—Tell me, for example, would you deflower a virgin?

—Excuse me, Stephen said politely, is that not the ambition of most young gentlemen?

—What then is your point of view? Cranly asked.

His last phrase, sour smelling as the smoke of charcoal and disheartening, excited Stephen's brain, over which its fumes seemed to brood.

—Look here, Cranly, he said. You have asked me what I would do and what I would not do. I will tell you what I will do and what I will not do. I will not serve that in which I no longer believe, whether it call itself my home, my fatherland, or my church: and I will try to express myself in some mode of life or art as freely as I can and as wholly as I can, using for my defence the only arms I allow myself to use—silence, exile, and cunning.

Cranly seized his arm and steered him round so as to lead him back towards Leeson Park. He laughed almost slyly and pressed Stephen's arm with an elder's affection.

—Cunning indeed! he said. Is it you? You poor poet, you!

—And you made me confess to you, Stephen said, thrilled by his touch, as I have confessed to you so many other things, have I not?

—Yes, my child, Cranly said, still gaily.

—You made me confess the fears that I have. But I will tell you also what I do not fear. I do not fear to be alone or to be spurned for another or to leave whatever I have to leave. And I am not afraid to make a mistake, even a great mistake, a lifelong mistake, and perhaps as long as eternity too.

Cranly, now grave again, slowed his pace and said:

—Alone, quite alone. You have no fear of that. And you know what that word means? Not only to be separate from all others but to have not even one friend.

—I will take the risk, said Stephen.

—And not to have any one person, Cranly said, who would be more than a friend, more even than the noblest and truest friend a man ever had.

His words seemed to have struck some deep chord in his own nature. Had he spoken of himself, of himself as he was or wished to be? Stephen watched his face for some moments in silence. A cold sadness was there. He had spoken of himself, of his own loneliness which he feared.

—Of whom are you speaking? Stephen asked at length.

Cranly did not answer.

***

March 20: Long talk with Cranly on the subject of my revolt. He had his grand manner on. I supple and suave. Attacked me on the score of love for one's mother. Tried to imagine his mother: cannot. Told me once, in a moment of thoughtlessness, his father was sixty-one when he was born. Can see him. Strong farmer type. Pepper and salt suit. Square feet. Unkempt, grizzled beard. Probably attends coursing matches. Pays his dues regularly but not plentifully to Father Dwyer of Larras. Sometimes talks to girls after nightfall. But his mother? Very young or very old? Hardly the first. If so, Cranly would not have spoken as he did. Old then. Probably, and neglected. Hence Cranly's despair of soul: the child of exhausted loins.

March 21, morning: Thought this in bed last night but was too lazy and free to add to it. Free, yes. The exhausted loins are those of Elizabeth and Zacchary. Then he is the precursor. Item: he eats chiefly belly bacon and dried figs. Read locusts and wild honey. Also, when thinking of him, saw always a stern severed head or death mask as if outlined on a grey curtain or veronica. Decollation they call it in the gold. Puzzled for the moment by saint John at the Latin gate. What do I see? A decollated percursor trying to pick the lock.

March 21, night: Free. Soul free and fancy free. Let the dead bury the dead. Ay. And let the dead marry the dead.

March 22: In company with Lynch followed a sizeable hospital nurse. Lynch's idea. Dislike it. Two lean hungry greyhounds walking after a heifer.

March 23: Have not seen her since that night. Unwell? Sits at the fire perhaps with mamma's shawl on her shoulders. But not peevish. A nice bowl of gruel? Won't you now?

March 24: Began with a discussion with my mother. Subject: B.V.M. Handicapped by my sex and youth. To escape held up relations between Jesus and Papa against those between Mary and her son. Said religion was not a lying-in hospital. Mother indulgent. Said I have a queer mind and have read too much. Not true. Have read little and understood less. Then she said I would come back to faith because I had a restless mind. This means to leave church by back door of sin and re-enter through the skylight of repentance. Cannot repent. Told her so and asked for sixpence. Got threepence.

Then went to college. Other wrangle with little round head rogue's eye Ghezzi. This time about Bruno the Nolan. Began in Italian and ended in pidgin English. He said Bruno was a terrible heretic. I said he was terribly burned. He agreed to this with some sorrow. Then gave me recipe for what he calls *risotto alla bergamasca.* When he pronounces a soft O he protrudes his full carnal lips as if he kissed the vowel. Has he? And could he repent? Yes, he could: and cry two round rogue's tears, one from each eye.

Crossing Stephen's, that is, my green, remembered that his countrymen and not mine had invented what Cranly the other night called our religion. A quartet of them, soldiers of the ninety-seventh infantry regiment, sat at the foot of the cross and tossed up dice for the overcoat of the crucified.

Went to library. Tried to read three reviews. Useless. She is not out yet. Am I alarmed? About what? That she will never be out again.

Blake wrote:

> *I wonder if William Bond will die*
> *For assuredly he is very ill.*

Alas, poor William!

I was once at a diorama in Rotunda. At the end were pictures of big nobs. Among them William Ewart Gladstone, just then dead. Orchestra played *O, Willie, we have missed you.*

A race of clodhoppers!

March 25, morning: A troubled night of dreams. Want to get them off my chest.

A long curving gallery. From the floor ascend pillars of dark vapours. It is peopled by the images of fabulous kings, set in stone. Their hands are folded upon their knees in token of weariness and their eyes are darkened for the errors of men go up before them for ever as dark vapours.

Strange figures advance as from a cave. They are not as tall as men. One does not seem to stand quite apart from another. Their faces are phosphorescent, with darker streaks. They peer at me and their eyes seem to ask me something. They do not speak.

March 30: This evening Cranly was in the porch of the library, proposing a problem to Dixon and her brother. A mother let her child fall into the Nile. Still harping on the mother. A crocodile seized the child. Mother asked it back. Crocodile said all right if she told him what he was going to do with the child, eat it or not eat it.

This mentality, Lepidus would say, is indeed bred out of your mud by the operation of your sun.

And mine? Is it not too? Then into Nile mud with it!

April 1: Disapprove of this last phrase.

April 2: Saw her drinking tea and eating cakes in Johnston's, Mooney and O'Brien's. Rather, lynx-eyed Lynch saw her as we passed. He tells me Cranly was invited there by brother. Did he bring his crocodile? Is he the shining light now? Well, I discovered him. I protest I did. Shining quietly behind a bushel of Wicklow bran.

April 3: Met Davin at the cigar shop opposite Findlater's church. He was in a black sweater and had a hurley stick. Asked me was it true I was going away and why. Told him the shortest way to Tara was VIA Holyhead. Just then my father came up. Introduction. Father polite and observant. Asked Davin if he might offer him some refreshment. Davin could not, was going to a meeting. When we came away father told me he had a good honest eye. Asked me why I did not join a rowing club. I pretended to think it over. Told me then how he broke Pennyfeather's heart. Wants me to read law. Says I was cut out for that. More mud, more crocodiles.

April 5: Wild spring. Scudding clouds. O life! Dark stream of swirling bogwater on which apple-trees have cast down their delicate flowers. Eyes of girls among the leaves. Girls demure and romping. All fair or auburn: no dark ones. They blush better. Houpla!

April 6: Certainly she remembers the past. Lynch says all women do. Then she remembers the time of her childhood—and mine, if I was ever a child. The past is consumed in the present and the present is living only because it brings forth the future. Statues of women, if Lynch be right, should always be fully draped, one hand of the woman feeling regretfully her own hinder parts.

April 6: LATER. Michael Robartes remembers forgotten beauty and, when his arms wrap her round, he presses in his arms the loveliness which has long faded from the world. Not this. Not at all. I desire to press in my arms the loveliness which has not yet come into the world.

April 10: Faintly, under the heavy night, through the silence of the city which has turned from dreams to dreamless sleep as a weary lover whom no caresses move, the sound of hoofs upon the road. Not so faintly now as they come near the bridge; and in a moment, as they pass the darkened windows, the silence is cloven by alarm as by an arrow. They are heard now far away, hoofs that shine amid the heavy night as gems, hurrying beyond the sleeping fields to what journey's end—what heart?—bearing what tidings?

April 11: Read what I wrote last night. Vague words for a vague emotion. Would she like it? I think so. Then I should have to like it also.

April 13: That tundish has been on my mind for a long time. I looked it up and find it English and good old blunt English too. Damn the dean of studies and his funnel! What did he come here for to teach us his own language or to learn it from us. Damn him one way or the other!

April 14: John Alphonsus Mulrennan has just returned from the west of Ireland. European and Asiatic papers please copy. He told us he met an old man there in a mountain cabin. Old man had red eyes and short pipe. Old man spoke Irish. Mulrennan spoke Irish. Then old man and Mulrennan spoke English. Mulrennan spoke to him about universe and stars. Old man sat, listened, smoked, spat. Then said:

—Ah, there must be terrible queer creatures at the latter end of the world.

I fear him. I fear his red-rimmed horny eyes. It is with him I must struggle all through this night till day come, till he or I lie dead, gripping him by the sinewy throat till . . . Till what? Till he yield to me? No. I mean no harm.

April 15: Met her today point blank in Grafton Street. The crowd brought us together. We both stopped. She asked me why I never came, said she had heard all sorts of stories about me. This was only to gain time. Asked me was I writing poems? About whom? I asked her. This confused her more and I felt sorry and mean. Turned off that valve at once and opened the spiritual-heroic refrigerating apparatus, invented and patented in all countries by Dante Alighieri. Talked rapidly of myself and my plans. In the midst of it unluckily I made a sudden gesture of a revolutionary nature. I must have looked like a fellow throwing a handful of peas into the air. People began to look at us. She shook hands a moment after and, in going away, said she hoped I would do what I said.

Now I call that friendly, don't you?

Yes, I liked her today. A little or much? Don't know. I liked her and it seems a new feeling to me. Then, in that case, all the rest, all that I thought I thought and all that I felt I felt, all the rest before now, in fact . . . O, give it up, old chap! Sleep it off!

April 16: Away! Away!

The spell of arms and voices: the white arms of roads, their promise of close embraces and the black arms of tall ships that stand against the moon, their tale of distant nations. They are held out to say: We are alone—come. And the voices say with them: We are your kinsmen. And the air is thick with their company as they call to me, their kinsman, making ready to go, shaking the wings of their exultant and terrible youth.

April 26: Mother is putting my new secondhand clothes in order. She prays now, she says, that I may learn in my own life and away from home and friends what the heart is and what it feels. Amen. So be it. Welcome, O life, I go to encounter for the millionth time the reality of experience and to forge in the smithy of my soul the uncreated conscience of my race.

April 27: Old father, old artificer, stand me now and ever in good stead.

Dublin, 1904
Trieste, 1914